From the Prologue:

"In very general terms and limiting drastically the diversity of readings that the text offers," declared Luis Goytisolo in an unpublished interview, "you could say that *Recounting* is the biography of a man," Raúl Ferrer Gaminde, told up to the moment when, sloughing off everything that has impeded him for years, he finally finds the adequate flow to give free rein to his vocation as a writer. "*The Greens of May Down to the Sea*," continued Goytisolo, "offers us the daily life of that same man, which he now writes, mixed with his notes, with his dreams, with his texts. *The Wrath of Achilles* is the book that is, perhaps, most disorienting right from the start, because it apparently seems to have little to do with our protagonist: the narrator is no longer Raúl, neither in first person nor in third person but rather a woman who is a girlfriend and lover of his, as well as his distant cousin, Matilde, who gives us her own image of Raúl's world and who converts Raúl into an implicit protagonist. *The Wrath of Achilles* is a work dedicated to Raúl: it's like the Earth seen from the moon. Finally, *Theory of Knowledge* is Raúl's work, a work written by Raúl" which assumes his own biographical experience, which is simply dumped into, strewn throughout, *Recounting*; his experience as writer, of which *The Greens of May Down to the Sea* offers significant glimpses, and other elements of which one has indirect notice through the testimony of Matilde.

Luis Goytisolo

ANTAGONY

Translated from the Spanish by Brendan Riley

Prologue by Ignacio Echevarría

DALKEY ARCHIVE PRESS

Dallas / Dublin

Recounting originally published in Spanish by Alianza Editorial as *Recuento* in 1973.

The Greens of May Down to the Sea originally published in Spanish as *Los verdes de mayo hasta el mar* by Seix Barral in 1976.

The Wrath of Achilles originally published in Spanish as *La colera de Aquiles* by Alianza Editorial, S.A. in 1979.

Theory of Knowledge originally published in Spanish *Teoría del conocimiento* by Alfaguara in 1983.

First Dalkey Archive edition of the complete *Antagony*, 2022.

Library of Congress Cataloging-in-Publication Data: Available.

Cover design by Jack Smyth
Interior design by Anuj Mathur

www.dalkeyarchive.com
Dallas / Dublin

Printed on permanent/durable acid-free paper

Table of Contents

PROLOGUE

I suppose that, upon opening a book such as this, a volume of such intimidating magnitude, it's best to be as direct as possible and not run the risk of encouraging the reader to plunge headlong into a journey that might become arduous, in addition to being long. So I'll start by tackling, almost by way of promotional claims, a few weighty affirmations, leaving for later the arguments capable of sustaining them.

I will say, first of all, that *Antagony* is one of the great novels of the twentieth century; comparable in its scope and achievements, and in its ambition, to such works as *A Portrait of the Artist as a Young Man* by James Joyce, *Remembrance of Things Past* by Marcel Proust, or *The Man Without Qualities* by Robert Musil. These are not random examples, but ones chosen—among other possible novels—because of the parallels that can be drawn between them and certain aspects of *Antagony*. This is, in no short measure, a novel about a writer's development; it offers a very revealing picture of a whole society, observed with extraordinary critical perspicacity; and it poses a subtle theory of knowledge based on the reminiscences awakened in the character's mind, as much by the act of writing as of reading.

Linked to this theory of knowledge, *Antagony* proposes one of the most exhaustive, rigorous, and profound explorations ever undertaken of literary creation, understood as a field in which language convokes meanings that it commonly conceals. From this investigation unfolds an implacable denunciation of the masking power of the word, and a radical concept of the novel and of the supposition from which questions can currently be raised about the exercise of this genre.

In the particular context of Spanish fiction, *Antagony*, published between 1973 and 1981, also comprises a lucid recapitulation of the historical and cultural period which was drawing to a close at that time—the era of Franco's dictatorship—and a severe challenge to every kind of rhetoric, including literary rhetorics, which prospered during the same time. At the time of its appearance, the novel signaled directions toward which, taking advantage of the path blazed until then, Spanish literature might have been able to point itself if, by those same dates, most of the newer novelists, as well as some of the veterans, had not opted for practically the opposite direction, in which many of the conventions that *Antagony* relegated to a second plane or, simply considered outmoded, gathered renewed validity.

Finally, *Antagony* splendidly illustrates, like few other novels or literary documents, the transformations of Spanish society during the decades of the sixties and seventies, delivering, in multiple passages of extraordinary incisiveness and comedy, very illuminating glimpses of the mentality, of the attitudes, of all kinds of tendencies (including ideological ones, in their broadest sense) that determined the development of Spain's much vaunted transition to democracy, and that, against all odds, have continued until the present, which gives one a lot to think about.

If the reader has reached this paragraph without having previously read the novel, the best thing would be, without continuing this prologue, for them to judge for themselves the success of the aforementioned achievements. What follows here are barely a few considerations that only serve to frame and orient one's reading enough to contribute to settling the question.

Antagony was conceived and composed over a period of almost twenty years. Luis Goytisolo has explained how "its broad outlines crystallized in a matter of a few hours one day in May of 1960." It was while he was serving time in Carabanchel prison, subjected during his weeks there to a severe regimen of solitary confinement, after being sentenced for his previous militant communism. "The structural nucleus then created, continued to develop in the form of notes and more notes, but it did not begin to acquire its own real identity until January 1, 1963." By then, Goytisolo had the general plan of the novel clearly worked out, along with many of its details. The final lines of *Antagony*, nevertheless, were not written until June 16, 1980, indeed, the very same day as the annual celebration of Bloomsday.

In 1958, at the young age of twenty-three, Luis Goytisolo had won the Premio Biblioteca Breve for *Las afueras* (The Outskirts), his first novel. After that, there was great anticipation about him, only partially satisfied by his second novel, *Las mismas palabras* (The Same Words) (1963), which he has always considered a failure, and which appeared the same year when he began to write *Antagony*, with which he sets things to rights. It's admirable that a writer still so young, and so promising, as Luis Goytisolo was in 1963, abstained from publishing anything for almost ten years, hard at work on a project as ambitious as *Antagony*. But what's certain is that, despite having the plan for the novel very clear in mind, Goytisolo did not foresee how long the novel would turn out to be. Thus his decision, at a certain point, to publish it in sections, persuaded by the need of "counting on a certain number of opportunities if he wanted to carry his journey to a good conclusion."

Thus, the novel began to be publicized long before being fully completed, which had to have important consequences on the type of reception it received, and how well it was properly understood. Although from the beginning it was made clear that *Antagony* was a tetralogy, the value of this concept turned out to be insufficient to suggest the types of connections that unite its different parts. These were largely read as stand-alone volumes, and, what's worse: given the span of several years between the publication of each one of the four volumes, many people only read one volume or another, without connecting to the others. Today one still hears talk about the different "books" that make up *Antagony* as if they were truly separate, independent novels, segregated from the greater whole of which they form a part. What doesn't get pointed out enough is that *Antagony*'s wide landscape contains a variety of different books, not just four. It's really just one novel, whose intentions are impossible to appreciate without reading the whole thing, as occurs with *Remembrance of Things Past* (nobody really considers discussing *Swann's Way* or *Time Regained* as independent novels), or as happens with *The Alexandria Quartet*, by Lawrence Durrell, another work to which *Antagony* has been insistently compared by those searching for precedents to its colossal undertaking.

The first edition of *Antagony* was brought out by the publishing house of Seix Barral, which published *Recuento* (*Recounting*) in 1973 (in Mexico, given that in Spain the book was seized by the Juzgado de Orden Público (Court of Public Order) and could not be distributed until 1975). *Los verdes de mayo hasta el mar* (*The Greens of May Down to the Sea*) appeared in 1976; *La cólera de Aquiles* (*The Wrath of Achilles*) in 1979, and *Teoría del conocimiento* (*Theory of Knowledge*) in 1981. In 1983 the novel was re-edited by Alfaguara as Number 100 in its literature collection, once again in four volumes, beautifully designed by Enric Satué. The four were published simultaneously, each individual volume bearing the general title—*Antagonía*—as well as its own. It was, in Goytisolo's own words, "the first edition, properly speaking" of Antagony. This edition—revised by the author, and the basis for this present one—was followed in 1993 by a pocket edition, from Alianza, also in four volumes, and yet another pocket edition, by Plaza and Janés, in the same year. Alfaguara even went on to republish the book yet again, in 1998, this time in two volumes on whose covers appear only the general title *Antagonía* (I and II). This began to alleviate, quite late, the general tendency to read the novel in separate sections, something that kept happening despite the fact that, since the 1983 edition, there was no longer any doubt that all four volumes comprised a single work. The best way of dealing with all that misunderstanding, nevertheless, was to publish *Antagony* in a single volume, making it inevitable that readers would have to contend with its massive whole. And that is the objective which this edition finally fulfills, more than thirty years after the novel was concluded.

Reading *Antagony* in its entirety modifies the partial readings that have happened with its separate, successive volumes. Anyone who read it over the course of several years could only, with difficulty, fully comprehend the close-knit fabric of allusions and correspondences, some of them very subtle, that are established among the different parts of the work. This is one of the reasons—beyond its unusual dimensions, daunting for many readers, and its disconcerting title—why even though *Antagony* is unanimously recognized as a major work of Spanish literature, it has, for all these years, maintained a certain dislocated position within that milieu. It occurs as if the very potent charge the novel contains slowly deflagrates, having lost the chance to go off in a single explosion.

Can we pretend that, if *Antagony* had been published from the first moment in a single volume like the one the reader currently holds in their hands, the novel's fortunes would have been different? Would it have had an impact superior to the one it obtained? Writing this, I consider the recent case of Roberto Bolaño's *2666*, a posthumous novel whose publication format—in separate books or a single volume of dimensions as intimidating as this one—remained undecided until the last minute. They finally opted for the latter possibility and there is no doubt that it was the correct choice, given the extraordinary impression that the book produced, far superior, no doubt, to the reaction each of its parts would have produced separately.

In the case of *Antagony*, what would have happened in 1981 if it had been published as it has now been brought out? Were Spanish readers, in general, prepared to appreciate such an effort? Possibly, given that it's about a novel that, as has been said, transmits like few others the pulse of Spanish society of those times; also given the fact that it proposes a passionate game of mirrors that have given it an unsurpassable place at the very forefront of a trend that has, since the early 1970s, enjoyed widespread acceptance, both in Spain and abroad: what's known as metaliterature, a genre in which the very figure of the writer and the vicissitudes of his creation claim an important role.

Considered retrospectively, however, and even with the confidence that *Antagony* would have had a much greater impact had it been published in a single volume, we can remain skeptical about the type of welcome that Spanish culture as a whole was prepared to offer a work like this one in those days. Why?

In 1975, when *Recuento* (*Recounting*), the first installment of *Antagony*, was finally published in Spain, it might have been said that a book like that, which at such an opportune time proposed an implacable "recounting" of the depressing reality that was starting to be left behind, would have been deeply important for a large number of readers who had lived through experiences similar to those of its protagonist or who could benefit from being offered a window into them. True enough, indeed, but only up to a certain point. That same year of 1975 saw the publication of *La verdad sobre el caso Savolta* (*The Truth About the Savolta Case*), by Eduardo Mendoza, and it was this novel, much more than *Recuento*, which stimulated the attention of Spanish readers, possibly those resolved to wash their hands of the recently canceled period, and enormously attracted by Mendoza's intelligent and entertaining retelling of an early twentieth-century criminal case that happened in Barcelona, (the same city, of course, which has such an important presence in *Recuento*).

In 1981, on the other hand, in the same year that, with the publication of *Teoría del conocimiento* (*Theory of Knowledge*), *Antagony* reached its conclusion, Jesús Ferrero's novel *Belver Yin* was published to great public and critical success, greeted by many as the opening salvo for what was going be known henceforth as "new Spanish fiction," a label which served to name a wildly varied multiplicity of novelistic proposals whose most recurrent traits would be a certain Adamism in relation to the genre itself, the restoration of a narrative very closely bound to old conventions, the ostentation of an often rigid cosmopolitanism and the strict refusal to have anything to do with the immediate past, as well as any hint not only of politicization but of any critical incursion into the present. Exactly the opposite of what a novel like *Antagony* involves, whose poetics insist on the significance that inevitably come into play through the act of writing—and of reading—and the relatively accessory nature of most of the elements considered to be components of a novel: argument, descriptions, characters, dialogue.

No, from the way things turned out it seems unlikely that, despite the numerous reasons that could have signaled it as a milestone destined to spread a decisive influence in the development of the fiction soon to follow, *Antagony* would have managed to exercise that influence, even published under the best of conditions. It's enough to think that, a few months before the appearance of

Theory of Knowledge, Juan Benet's other peak work, *Saúl ante Samuel* (Saul Before Samuel) (1980) appeared, yet this exceptional novel barely made an appreciable impact—despite Benet being, unlike Luis Goytisolo, an important rising writer well above a handful of writers younger than him, and quite prone to polemical interventions, not only in the literary field. In Benet's case, the strenuous effort required to read his book can explain the stupor with which it was received. Regardless, right at the start of "the high tide of the eighties" as Francisco Rico had baptized it, *Saúl ante Samuel* and *Antagony* raised Spanish fiction to a high level, to a level of quality and of challenge, exploding many of the pretensions and resources used by many of their contemporaries, especially relating to future promotions, instead embarking on a trajectory more in accord with their own spirit than with what can be understood as the culture of the Transition, which was impregnated by a new sociability with a strong degree of commercialism.

At one point, Benet complained about the "lukewarm and scattered critical reception" that *Saúl ante Samuel* received. This is not the case, far from it, with *Antagony*, which, despite everything said so far, and without supposing anything to the contrary, was the object, since the publication of its first volume, of very close readings. In fact, in retrospect, what remains astonishing is both the steady number—as well as the high level—of the reviews and commentaries that the novel received, as much from professional critics as from writers and scholars in general. Barely two years after concluding its publication, Anagrama published a volume titled *El cosmos de Antagonia* (The Cosmos of Antagony) (1983), which collected a handful of critical essays about the novel, including splendid pieces by Ricardo Gullón, Gonzalo Sobejano, and Luis Suñén, among others. As Salvador Clotas wrote in the introduction, it was an exceptional volume, in so far as it revealed "a critical capacity that is not usually, unfortunately, the most frequent in our cultural ambit." But the successive volumes of *Antagony* had already received, in a wide variety of media, very timely, sometimes very penetrating, commentaries, such as those from José Ángel Valente and Guillermo Cabrera Infante about *Recounting*; such as—specifically—those by Pere Gimferrer on *Recounting* and *The Greens of May Down to the Sea*.

Reviewing these and other commentaries makes manifest a level of critical receptivity almost unimaginable at the present time. And it makes one thing very clear: none of *Antagony*'s readers, however demanding, have failed to appreciate its value and its extraordinary merits.

Shortly after finishing the novel, Guillermo Carnero called it "one of the richest, most complex narrative undertakings in the scope of the post-Civil War

Spanish novel." A judgement that superimposes itself on the very high classification that the successive installments of the novel had been garnering as they appeared. Thus, for example, Pere Gimferrer hailed *Recounting* as "one of the four most important works of the Spanish postwar period," alongside *Tiempo de silencio* by Luis Martín-Santos, *Volverás a Región* by Juan Benet, and *Reivindicación del conde don Julián* by Juan Goytisolo. An evaluation only reaffirmed a few years later by the publication of the now completed *Antagony*, and which deserves a note: all four of those cases are single novels that are part of a very long narrative projects. (In the case of Martín Santos, his death prevented him from continuing his planned trilogy *La destrucción de la España sagrada* (The Destruction of the Sacred Spain) from which *Tiempo de destrucción* (Time of Destruction) was posthumously rescued; in Benet's case, we can understand *Saúl ante Samuel* as the culmination of the stylistic program expounded in *La inspiración y el estilo* (Inspiration and Style) and undertaken with *Volverás a Región* (Return to Región); in the case of Juan Goytisolo, *Count Julian* (*Reivindicación del conde don Julián*) is inserted into what the author himself has baptized as *Trilogy of Evil* (*Trilogía del mal*), which includes *Marks of Identity* (*Señas de identidad*) and *Juan the Landless* (*Juan sin Tierra*).

In any case, more than in any of these other novels, and the important projects they frame, *Antagony* floats above, as it were, the most recent Spanish literature, and so it is to the extent that has not ceased to question it tacitly through its own conceptions of narrative structure, according to some presuppositions that set aside, as Luis Goytisolo's words themselves put it—written, we must say, now long ago, but still valid— "all the theoretical apriorisms formulated about the novel in the last fifty years."

In this respect, if, on one hand, *Recounting*, the first book of *Antagony*, contains a severe criticism of the realist aesthetic that in such a determinant way framed Spanish novel writing in the nineteen fifties and sixties, in the successive sections of the work we see Goytisolo gradually outlining a form of novel writing that not only shelters a very powerful style but one that also proposes an ideal form through which, along with the conflicts used for scene building, the writing shows itself capable of trapping the complex and changing reality of the world.

But before continuing, it's time to explain to the reader, who still has no idea, however superficial, exactly what the "argument" of *Antagony* is. And nobody better than the author himself to do that.

"In very general terms and limiting drastically the diversity of readings that the text offers," declared Luis Goytisolo in an unpublished interview, "you could say that *Recounting* is the biography of a man," Raúl Ferrer Gaminde, told up to the moment when, sloughing off everything that has impeded him for years, he finally finds the adequate flow to give free rein to his vocation as a writer. "*The Greens of May Down to the Sea*," continued Goytisolo, "offers us the daily life of that same man, which he now writes, mixed with his notes, with his dreams, with his texts. *The Wrath of Achilles* is the book that is, perhaps, most disorienting right from the start, because it apparently seems to have little to do with our protagonist: the narrator is no longer Raúl, neither in first person nor in third person but rather a woman who is a girlfriend and lover of his, as well as his distant cousin, Matilde, who gives us her own image of Raúl's world and who converts Raúl into an implicit protagonist. *The Wrath of Achilles* is a work dedicated to Raúl: it's like the Earth seen from the moon. Finally, *Theory of Knowledge* is Raúl's work, a work written by Raúl" which assumes his own biographical experience, which is simply dumped into, strewn throughout, *Recounting*; his experience as writer, of which *The Greens of May Down to the Sea* offers significant glimpses, and other elements of which one has indirect notice through the testimony of Matilde.

One passage in *Theory of Knowledge* offers an inverted version of this hasty synthesis. There we read how Ricardo Echave, whose notes occupy the center of that novel (the novel written by Raúl, remember), cherishes the project of writing "a work composed of various books articulated according to the following scheme: starting with Story A, which presents itself to the reader as a finished whole, explore the real boundaries of Story B, the author of Story A, considering it exclusively from without, as a character seen by other characters: next, get closer to the origins of Story A, to the process of the work's gestation, the notes taken, the previous writings, if possible in the context in which they were written—daily reality, dreams, etcetera—in order to conclude, finally, with a reconstruction of the life of Story B. Meaning: include the author in the work and, with the author, the time, the time that the work's development gives back to the author."

Regarding *Recounting*, Pere Gimferrer rightly said that its style was "an art of time and of structure." There is no better way of synthesizing the proceeding of *Antagony* in its whole, animated as it is by the proposal "To include the context in the text, the author no less present among the characters than the reader, and like them involved, one and the other, in the plot."

For his part, Juan Goytisolo has pointed out that "the literary art of *Antagony*—the centrifugal unfolding of a text whose language expands through a group of association, similes and metaphors of probably Proustian origin—could be collated to a certain point with that of the author of *Remembrance of Things Past*, to the degree that both include the author in the work, and along with him, the time that the material gestation of the novel takes; but a Proust who would have inserted into that work not only *Jean Senteuil* but also the first babbling version of the Mass."

The entire artifice of *Antagony* is designed so that when the reader finally begins to read *Theory of Knowledge*—the novel by Raúl Ferrer Gaminde, the text that crowns and transcends *Antagony*'s radical undertaking, the one that opens the novel itself to directions even newer and more unexplored—they find themselves in possession of the fabric of references to which the greater part of the elements present in this book refer, in conditions of appreciating how the elements of reality are transformed into writing, and of capturing the resonances that his work gathers in the mind of the author, as well as in his own mind.

To achieve this, Luis Goytisolo not only conceived of the basic mechanism which has just been sketched out very succinctly: he also made use of, like a submerged correlative, a very ample mesh of recurring motifs that run throughout the whole novel, that establish among their distinct parts connections sometimes barely perceptible, that act almost subliminally, and that contribute to equip it with the convenient density (density of time, of accumulated experience). Within the same novel we find allusions to the form in which these motives operate in the text through a process of prefiguration and post-figuration of those things which—as it advances—are revealed as its central themes. In general, it's about the highly charged metaphorical images that are repeated in different places in the novel—how, at the start and the end of the same, the image of that officer mounted on a white horse—but also about situations, scenes, characters who appear and reappear sometimes under different situations, under different disguises.

On another level we can locate motives—similarly recurring—that act as reflections of the novel itself, illustrating it in a certain way. Thus, for example, that map of the Ideal City (tacitly counterpoised to the very real city of Barcelona) whose design reveals the structure of *Antagony*. Or the references to the paintings of Velazquez (*Las meninas, Las hilanderas, Las lanzas*), that provide a graphic correlative to the way in which that structure is dramatized. Or the mentions of Dante and his *Divine Comedy*, which fulfill a similar function. And then there are, acting surreptitiously but very significantly, devices, like the subtle organization of the work around the number 9, "the only number whose multiples, reduced to an inferior figure through successive sums of the elements that compose them, always give as a result the number 9 itself. Thus: 9 x 3 = 27 = 2 + 7 = 9."

"It's a question of weight," Luis Goytisolo has stated with respect to

Antagony's sophisticated scheme, "of space, of balance, that counts no less than the composition of a painting or a symphony, two kinds of works with which, in a certain way, *Antagony* could be compared, and in which that structural preoccupation has always been made most evident. So that then the structure is not visible, so that it seems to have been retracted, as one takes down a scaffold once the building is complete, there's nothing special about it; that is their function, that of being assimilated by the reader without being perceived. Nor do readers usually count the number of syllables or verses of the poem they're reading."

Of all attempts to describe the complex narrative plot of *Antagony*, the naturalness with which it is articulated is inevitably abstracted, how agreeably it unfolds, always in the service, as it must be, of a dazzling reflection about the nature of the creative act and about the type of knowledge it leads to. It does not make much sense to try to gloss the achievements of that reflection, because it's about something that can be picked out to a very slight degree throughout the course of the whole novel, and which finds unsurpassable formulations in passages, sometimes very explicit, about the same, like the aforementioned notes of Ricardo Echave in *Theory of Knowledge*, in which many of the glimpses scattered throughout the whole text are largely recapitulated.

The critic of *Antagony* usually feels a certain sensation of redundancy, given that they're reflecting on a novel—because that's what it deals with— that says everything about itself. Very summarily, and succumbing almost inevitably to the temptation of stitching together one quotation after another, we can point out that the nucleus around which the whole novel unfolds is the intense experience that "the author, by projecting himself into his work, creates himself even as he is creating his work." Creative writing, whatever be the form it adopts, will come to constitute the "objectified expression of the consciousness and, above all, the unconsciousness of the author." As such, meaning, as far as "objectified expression," is set up in the design field not only the obsessions and the conflicts of the author, but also of the reader, given that "the phenomenon of reading is the shadow, the negative of the phenomenon of the writing." Thus, the ultimate meaning of a work of fiction need not be sought "in the text, nor in its author, nor in the reader, but in the relationship that links the work with one and another, a relationship through which the work comes to life, is made vivid, at the same time that it illuminates the figure of the author as well as the figure of the reader."

All of *Antagony*, to say it again, arises from the untangling of that "golden moment" when—finally, while locked in prison—Raúl, the novel's protagonist, discovers his own vocation as a writer, feeling seized by "the sensation that by means of the written word, not only creating something autonomous, alive by itself, but that in the course of this process of objectification by writing, he managed at the same time to understand the world through himself and to know himself through the world."

The emphasis placed on the written word as unleashing that "process of objectification" that *Antagony* tries to construct analogically—constituting itself in the novel about a novel—obtains all its reach and its relief in pronounced contrast with the very overwhelming criticism which, in the novel, is made from the "assignative power of the word, its faculty of stereotyping daily life, of interposing itself between one and things, between one and other people, between one and oneself." While yet trying to find his path as a writer, Raúl is aware, and again and again, perplexed, of the natural tendency of language to become sclerotized, to conceal reality. And throughout *Antagony*, but very especially in *Recounting*, an imposing arsenal of resources unfolds to show how it occurs this way.

Considering the first book of *Antagony*, José Ángel Valente offered this spot-on assessment: "The identity of the future narrator, whose existence is announced by the final sections of *Recounting*, is established, really, against the ideological crystallization of language, against what in any of the aspects of the ideological occupation would constitute, with one sign and another, a totalitarian or paralyzing language."

For his part, Pere Gimferrer singled out—also regarding *Recounting*—the weight that what he very playfully dubbed "the deadpan parody" has in this book, understood as such to mean "parody based not on the deformation or characterization of the facts of the case, but on their extremely faithful and succinct but decontextualized transcription, in such a way that, upon isolating it from its habitual context and comparing it to others, it becomes an example of irrational discourse, despite its appearance or, rather, pretension, of maximum rationality."

"This process"—continues Gimferrer—requires, on one hand, a singular capacity for observation, for recreating spoken language," something for which, as Gimferrer himself observes, Luis Goytisolo finds himself to be exceptionally gifted, along with a good part of the writers of his same generational swath, educated in the practice of behaviorism. And it requires, as well, a formidable "aptitude for pastiche, be it of an existing literary genre or of the linguistic convention of a specific social group."

Goytisolo is an unsurpassed master of both things, and as a consequence, all of *Antagony*, and not only *Recounting*, contains an ample repertory of every type of verbal behavior which is put on display, generally with extraordinary comic effects, the language contributing in a great variety of ways to the stupidification of the subject, to their unconscious alignment within a previous stereotype. In this sense, Gimferrer (whose perspicacious criticism forged, during the same period in which *Antagony* was published, some of the most unerring reviews that have ever been written in the Spanish language) long ago indicated how "Luis Goytisolo possesses, perhaps like no other contemporary peninsular writer [circa 1973] the gift of transcribing stupidity, ridiculousness or wild bizarreness, empty convention, or incoherence"; a gift that he has always maintained, and which, without subtracting one iota of the profundity of his approaches, imbues the reading of his books—*Antagony* included—with priceless cackles of laughter.

Goytisolo's keen ear for capturing idiotic, ridiculous, vicious, or directly aberrant verbal behavior recalls that of Karl Kraus in the Vienna of the first third of the twentieth century. Through "deadpan parody," Goytisolo records, one after another, what Elias Canetti—a disciple of Kraus—denominated as "acoustic masks," a name with which he baptized the particular use that people usually make of the language, and which is characteristic of the limits that they impose on their relationship with reality.

Canetti never ceased to be astonished by the "rotundity," by the "firm blindness and obstinacy" with which these "acoustic masks" exclude how much remains to be said about the world ("the majority of it, everything"); again and again he was scandalized by the fact that, instead of being open to that richness, human beings prefer to cling to a few words, reserving for themselves "one single attribute: having to repeat and repeat themselves incessantly." Well: all of *Antagony*, as has been mentioned, is shot through with minute and infallible recordings of this type of linguistic behavior. In this aspect it also matches *Auto-da-Fé*, Canetti's one and only, and portentous, novel. Suffice to mention here, very succinctly, the pathetic image of Raúl's father, now old, obsessed with disguising his own failure with "a history remodeled over time." "He was speaking—we're told—like one who uses a tape recorder to try out different variations of the same speech"; "he deployed his verbal artillery against that undesirable who had fallen in with him, who had happened to be his brother-in-law, the bohemian, the disaster, the shameless one, the ignominy of his in-laws, etcetera, in order to end up invariably in that business of 'if only your poor mother could see you,' etcetera, etcetera, elements of a fixed and ordered sequence, by force of repetition, in a kind of litany."

The "deadpan parody," on the other hand, is displayed to decidedly savage effect, especially in *Recounting*, in four ideological discourses that frame Raúl's education: one on the falangism more or less similar to the triumphant

Francoism, one on the communist resistance, and others covering Spanish and Catalan nationalisms. The tempestuous tirades corresponding to these last two resound with alarming familiarity in the ears of today's reader. The same does not happen with falangist rhetoric, now completely obsolete. Regarding the speech of the communist resistance—which Goytisolo knew very closely—his "incredibly faithful transcription" documents something more than what might seem to many an ideological relic: it allows any reader today to understand retrospectively some of the reasons why the important capital, no less political than moral, which the Communist Party enjoyed under the Franco dictatorship came to be squandered in barely a decade.

The progressive hypertrophy and mutual overlapping of these discourses—according to a process of mutual interaction that goes far beyond that employed by Joyce in *A Portrait of the Artist as a Young Man*; which is, in fact, based on an ability to mimic, parody, and superimpose speech mannerisms and styles that recall *Ulysses*—produce the phenomenal joyous racket of Recounting, which precipitates the growing awareness, on Raúl's part, of the redemptive power of writing. In the rest of *Antagony*, with Raúl now committed to his destiny as a writer, Luis Goytisolo's parodic art is dedicated to recording, in a less overwhelming but equally incisive way, the latent discourses in the Spanish society of the late Francoist period, raised up since the nineteen-sixties to a certain prosperity and to a slight opening thanks to the boom in tourism.

Starting with *The Greens of May Down to the Sea*, Goytisolo's gaze centers, above all—but not uniquely—on the attitudes of a new and emerging affluent bourgeoisie, ideologically evolved, sexually liberated, and progressively engaged in a consumerist lifestyle. Goytisolo's accurate portrait of this sector of society offers special interest in so far as it corresponds, in broad measure, to the sector that led the Spanish transition toward democracy, as much from the political point of view as the cultural, and that ended up lighting the way to a new plutocracy. It deals with a sector legitimized by its militancy in the anti-Franco resistance, from which it opportunely wriggled away, and which permitted it to wash its hands, at the right moment, of its progressivist ideology, or rather: to promote neoliberal politics from an imperturbable sentiment of representing the left. Reading *Antagony* now, after thirty years, turns out to be highly instructive, showing how well Goytisolo's portrait of this social sector hold up, a very eloquent index of both its persistence and its inertia. No less instructive are the perspectives that the novel traces about the influence that nationalist ideologies have had upon this sector.

The gradual irruption, during the development of *Recounting*, of "the deadpan parody," runs simultaneous to that of another stylistic recourse which, even more so, ends up being the most characteristic of *Antagony*. I refer here to Goytisolo's use of broad comparisons whose terms, very disparate among themselves, are juxtaposed with such a prolixity of details that the reader's attention tends to be distracted from the supposed nexus that would have to justify the comparison, in order to remain absorbed in the interest of each one of the terms by itself.

Gonzalo Sobejano has made an excellent analysis of this stylistic resource, emphasizing how it constitutes "a way of exemplifying the spectacle of reality configured by the writing through a fabric of latent correlatives." A procedure aligned—underscores Sobejano—with the conviction, expressed by the narrator of *The Greens of May Down to the Sea*, that "alongside one thing there is always another, and another counterposed to another collateral and another anterior which contradicts and denies it, which alters and confuses it to the point of obliging us to reconsider the initial hypothesis, the question about whether the structure is really an instant of the process or the process merely one line of the structure. The supra-tale and the infra-tale, the two authentic levels of a work, in relation to which the tale in itself functions as a simple vehicle."

Regarding the progressive enormity with which this stylistic resource is deployed, Sobejano has referred to Luis Goytisolo's style as "an emanative style," alluding thus to the form in which "the emanation of similitudes through the assembly of comparative frames set one within the other ("así como" [just as; as well as]; "así también" [as well as]; "de modo semejante" [in a similar way]) reaches a point where, among so many associations, the comparison is lost to sight."

Both Sobejano and Gimferrer, among others, have pointed out the Proustian sign of these comparative series, which Sobejano contrasts with those of Juan Benet's style. Gimferrer, for his part, hastens to emphasize how, in Goytisolo's case, the comparisons have an inverse sign to the Proustian ones, given that, "instead of fulfilling a function of synthesis, of *raccourci*, as in *Remembrance of Things Past*, they are translated into amplification and insistences, and in the last place into rhythmic delays."

Once more, the best characterization of this practice is found in *Antagony* itself. Referring to "the diary of Carlos junior," which occupies the first part of *Theory of Knowledge*, the aforementioned Ricardo Echave observes how, when it comes to style, "it's not difficult to discover the influence of Luis Goytisolo: those long series of sentences, for example, those comparisons that begin with a Homeric "Just as," in order to conclude by connecting with some "so," in a similar way, not without first inserting new extended metaphors, secondary metaphors that, more than centering and sharpening the initial comparison, expand it and even invert its terms, not without first laying the foundation for new subordinate associations, not without first establishing new conceptual relationships not only similar to one another, and new associations with the same colloidal appearance as the mercury and brimstone that alchemists mix together."

The passage is indicative of the self-referentiality—replete with mistakes—that, in its own unfolding, *Antagony* assumes; from the way that the novel constitutes all by itself a system of autonomous references in which reality appears subjected to different levels of fictionalization, including the author himself, Luis Goytisolo.

In this point, the "Family reading of *Antagony*" that Juan Goytisolo made in his day and which led to an unusual exchange of articles between the two brothers remains of particular interest. Unusual because of the improbability of the fact that two narrators, both very notable, tackle the same family scene, the one—Juan, in *Coto vedado*—in an openly autobiographical tale, and the other—Luis, previously, in *Antagony*—in a novel whose protagonist presents abundant traces that invite the reader to take it as a likeness of the author himself. The "confrontation" between the two memories facing off against each other constitutes a passionate document that illuminates Antagony's deep treatment of memory as the way toward knowledge; a way, that is, replete with traps, voids, and false appropriations.

"The paths of memory" one reads toward the end of *Recounting*. "Something similar to visiting one of those cathedrals built atop an older one, constructed in its turn from the remains of pagan temples, stones belonging to that other city excavated beneath the present-day city, subterranean ruins that one can visit contemplating what were streets and houses and necropolises and protective walls, pieced together almost always from the remains of earlier cities. A tour, however, that one usually finds not only in the base of one's self-knowledge, but also in the full realization of all creative impulse."

It's been said above that *Antagony* "floats above" the course of Spanish fiction. This has continued to circulate in recent decades along many of the ways opened up by that fact. One of these ways is, precisely, what has been called from then until now *autofiction*, a term whose proper understanding contributes magnificently to this novel—as farther on, expanding its important glimpses in this field plagued by misunderstanding, *Estatua con palomas* (1992), by the very same Luis Goytisolo.

We might propose a reading of *Antagony* superimposed upon the development of Spanish fiction in the thirty years that have passed since its publication. In doing so, one would notice how the novel lucidly explores and integrates narrative uses that have since become relatively common, such as the tendency toward digression, toward fragmentation, toward branching or fractal structures, toward autobiographical impostures, overlapping planes of fiction and reality, mixtures of essay and novel. Not to mention Luis Goytisolo's so very uninhibited and explicit treatment of sex. Or the register of a hybrid tongue—the Castilian Spanish spoken in Catalonia—at the margin of all normative orthodoxy.

As a result of the conception of narrative writing that moves through *Antagony*, the novel itself radically questions conventions of every sort, beginning with those related to typographical markings such as italics, quotation marks, hyphens and dashes, with the evident intention of underlining the indistinct nature of what happens to integrate the material of the text. Previously, the treatment that can be given to descriptions, argument, characters, dialogues, to the very figure of the narrator had been redefined little by little, elements that are subordinated to the fact that the real value of the writing is found at deeper levels—deeper than those that serve as a background.

Antagony itself speaks of "Novels that in no way seek to imitate reality, that are in no way mimetic, nor offer any insubstantial rejection of all reality, as they so vainly pretend at times; no, none of that: novels that are a metaphor for reality, meaning, that proceed by analogy, the only way of approaching the proposed goal, a goal that, as in the case of the thinker, is more about the journey than the destination, or rather an objective whose goal is precisely the journey itself, a creative impulse that, at the same time as it reflects itself in the works that it generates, may be the analogous reflection *par excellence* of the creative process."

Antagony proposes itself as one of those very novels. Like all great works of art, it invents its own form. A form in which the reader participates as an active element in the plot. A plot that traps it in an adventure of knowledge destined to move deeply the relationship that it maintains with language, with the world, with itself.

Thirty years after its conclusion, *Antagony* not only preserves intact its literary payload but also its capacity to question the entire system of fiction writing in the Spanish language, driving it to a reconsideration of its own premises.

Beyond the legend that has been woven around it all this time, and beyond the misunderstandings of every type which it has caused (or precisely because of that), *Antagony* continues offering itself to the present moment with all the novelty that it supposed in its day. Thus this edition, the first that finally presents the entire text in a single volume, imposing without disguising its compact unity and its imposing stature, must be hailed as an important event, as the recognition of a work about which there still remains much to discover, to learn, and to come to terms with.

Ignacio Echevarría
Barcelona, November 2011

Translated from the Spanish by Brendan Riley

BOOK I: RECOUNTING

For María Antonia

I

The rolling thunder of the detonations came booming back down the valley, and above the hills, amid the smoke that seemed to be rising from the woods, you could just glimpse the flash of cannon blasts. Two motorcycles and several dun-colored trucks came advancing slowly along the highway, and at the crossroads, a group of soldiers was maneuvering an artillery piece. There was also an officer mounted on a white horse, prancing, galloping back and forth with his saber unsheathed; an officer mounted on a white horse.

Ramona wound up the gramophone and put on a record, but Aunt Paquita immediately removed it, making the needle screech. Once set in motion, the gramophone couldn't be stopped and the turntable kept on spinning until the spring wound down. They were all there in the front part of the house, in the drawing room, with the shutters half-closed. Whispering. Kyrie eleison. Christe eleison. The dining room, by contrast, gave onto the back porch, where there was plenty of light. La Quilda was with her family, downstairs on the first floor, and Felipe said that they had used their mattresses to cover the windows.

The rumor is the Committee members have left town, they said.

When they went outside they could still hear some cannons firing in the distance, some random shots. They'd opened the windows wide, laughing and crying, embracing one another, and out in the street they shouted and sang and everybody raised their arms, ran, pushing and shoving, running after the soldiers toward the plaza. The soldiers were tall and they walked very quickly, with blanket rolls, soft rope-soled shoes, and cooking gear hanging from straps, a flood of rifles, and the slow, measured rocking of their elbows. La Quilda caught Ramona in her arms and Ramona began to cry, too, but no one paid her any mind. There were tons of things scattered everywhere, old clothes, books, crockery shards, and the school building was deserted with straw strewn about the floor. Nor was there anyone to be found in the militia headquarters, where Felipe and Padritus scrounged up some tins of sardines and condensed milk, and in an abandoned car in the yard they found a pair of binoculars. At the fork in the road, a column of brown trucks followed the highway, leaving the town behind. *Mira los moritos*, they said. There go the Moros.

Felipe was also marching. And Padritus. Really quite well, said Papa. They were drilling on the soccer field, with wooden rifles, and at last they all marched in red berets and blue shirts. Behind the soccer field was a line of bare gray poplars without leaves. Really quite well. The chubby sergeant was barking orders at them, and Papa went to see him in the mornings and they chatted sitting out in the sun, in the yard outside the militia headquarters. The garden was spacious and damp, labyrinthine, and the branches of the shrubbery formed a sort of shady cote over the dark smooth ground.

This hand grenade is a bomb.

Pere Pecats was killed by a bomb. There had been many deaths. There were stories, a little boy twisting up a fuse or playing with some ammunition or pointing a pistol at another one or fiddling with a grenade, etcetera. The hiding place was underneath the steps in the orchard where there were two bayonets, a rifle without a bolt, a Russian cap, a helmet with a bullet hole, a gas mask, gleaming artillery shells, and especially, bullets, bullets for pistols, for rifles, for machine guns. The town children also had their own and they'd had to dig trenches. People said they went hunting toads, they'd fill them with gunpowder and blow them up. Felipe had learned to remove the powder from the rifle shells. Blowing up fuses in the Valley of the Riders of the Purple Sage was more fun than picking cabbages and beets for Pere Pecats.

A lot more fun. But raw beets tasted very good, eaten in bites, a little prickly, very juicy. They pulled them up from alongside the road at the edge of the field, fat and pale like bacon, and waving them over their heads, Felipe calling: Pere Pecats! Pere Pecats! Or he ran ahead through the winding rows of cabbages, mature and densely whorled, all of them calling Pere Pecats. And Pere Pecats came out shouting and swearing, but he was twisted and hunched over and couldn't run. In other gardens you had to post a lookout; Padritus and Felipe climbed the trees, and Ramona gathered pears and apples in her skirt. Chestnuts could be carried in hand baskets, but you had to hide them underneath mushrooms picked in the woods. La Pilate and Nieves would thread the strawberries on really fine blades of grass so that when they ate a whole string of them together they tasted more delicious. The water at the falls shone in the sun and Pilate took off her shoes and waded along the bank. Felipe fished for crabs with a butterfly net. Nieves wasn't there. The stones were slippery, and in the quiet pool the water floated still over a bottom carpeted thick with brownish leaves. At dusk those still pools were frightening, the water opaque. Pilate was going to the militia dance.

Pilate whistled furtively to Padritus, and to Nieves and Felipe and Lalo. At night.

The light bulb glowed dimly, reflected in the window glass, isolated and radiant beneath its opalescent platter. El Mon had brought two squirrels and a skinned rabbit; he was a large, red-haired man, with a goiter. La Quilda bent over the hearth, black and big-nosed as a witch. Papa said that was no rabbit. It's a fox, he said. He traded some soap for a hen from a woman who came with La Quilda. The woman haggled, saying the soap was not very foamy. She pulled the hen out of a basket, by its feet, but it had a fine-looking head; she laid it on her forearm caressing it, all puffed up like a feather duster, furled crest, furious eye. The kitchen gave onto the porch and the fields were covered in snow. La Quilda sank her shears into the hen's body, she singed the feathers, laughing; she felt around in the entrails until pulling out a yellow, nubbly, clustered, botryoidal lump of flesh. There was also the decapitated duck staggering round the kitchen, silhouetted against the reddish black of the hearth.

La Quilda came upstairs to help Nieves when she had to butcher some animal. She lived downstairs, on the ground floor. She came heavily dressed, and when a package of food arrived she ate the thickest slab of ham. El Mon was her sweetheart, el Mon-Jamón; he had a rifle and a balaclava.

Snow. They walked obstinately, small and red, with chilblains, their necks retracted, shoulders stiffly squeezed together, hands in pockets, scarves hanging down their backs, socks slipping loose down their calves. The schoolhouse was alongside the road, and Felipe had to pass by the house of Señor Daunis. Señor Daunis was really skinny and he wore a long overcoat, cinched tight, with the lapels turned up. He was tubercular and you had to keep away from him. From Pere Pecats, too; Padritus said that Pere Pecats threw a stone at him, in the plaza. He often went to the bar. He cursed at the children and threatened them with his fist. He talked to himself and limped, and everybody teased him.

Señor Daunis stayed hidden and he managed to avoid being seen by the Committee members. Like the priest who lived above the tobacco shop and the two nuns from Can Vidal. Papa said that in Barcelona they wanted to shoot him because he attended Mass and he owned a factory. He had many kids of his own that nobody wanted to play with, because they had tuberculosis, and they were often very hungry. He was a widower. They said that the river had frozen over.

The divine Mozart, said Aunt Paquita.

And Ramona put on a record. She was seated on the wicker sofa, next to the gramophone, swaying her legs. Aunt Paquita wondered what that pain could be. She came over at night, to listen to the radio, sometimes accompanied by

Miss Lourdes, blonde and thin, with plucked, painted-on eyebrows. They were studying a Michelin road map, tracing along with their fingers, taking off their eyeglasses, hunched over the map. They were chatting: the Reds, checkpoints, avenues, the jail, in disguise, devoutly Catholic, words spoken in undertones. A table lamp topped by a shade with amber flecks. Let your cousin sit in the rocking chair, she said.

Grandfather wasn't listening to the radio. He was still at the table eating, methodically, indifferent as a cactus, as a lichen-furred stone. Grandmother, on the other hand, was moving about, helping; she was wearing a flowered dress, black and white. They got off the bus, in the plaza, and they walked together slowly, arm in arm: Grandfather came out of his room in his pajamas, his face creased by the pillow, his eyes squinting, his hair white and tousled, clearing his throat. For dessert there was watermelon, enormous slices of red watermelon, and grandfather spat the black seeds out onto his plate, one by one. The dining room was fresh, luxuriant with plants, the shadows of the leaves quivering on the ceiling. Ramona danced in the parlor and everyone applauded. She wound up the gramophone, put on a record and danced. Dance with Ramona, they said.

My lovely darling, said Papa.

The parlor window opened onto the street; the sunlight came in only during the morning. The furniture was dark, wicker, and the records had to be stacked atop the console, neatly ordered. There were many: Ramona, Matonkiki, the *Jupiter Symphony*, etcetera. The record sleeves were mostly alike; gray paper, with a dark blue drawing of a Negro band playing for several couples.

Does Ramona belong to Ramona?

The Valley of the Riders of the Purple Sage was very green, with rows of poplar trees running down the hillside. Beyond, the gully was choked with brambles and bushes. You crossed over the creek on a footbridge of logs thick with dark moss. Padritus was unbuttoning his fly; he had to drop his pants. Ramona took off her underpants, she lay down in the grass. Look how it gets big and hard, she said. They examined Ramona's little hole, compared themselves and all that. They took turns masturbating. Lalo, going last.

Following the creek led to the river. There the meadows widened out, smoothly extended, and there were piles of wet logs stripped of their bark. Downstream the river flowed swollen and foamy, and you had to shout over the sound. Pilate was there; she hiked up her skirts and stepped in to wet her feet in the shallows. Cold, cascading waters, of melted snow. The slow quiet stretches lay further down. The water sounded throughout the valley and the sun shone resplendently on the dew, oh my dew. The slopes were covered with beech trees, and higher up, above the shadowy fern-covered slopes, on the talus scree slopes, the mountain peaks stood out, sharp, naked. Crabs eat the dead.

Pilate was ironing on an ironing board set up in the kitchen, in Aunt Paquita's house. She was singing absentmindedly to herself, sometimes answering, wondering aloud. *Soñar dientes, muerte de parientes*, she said. *Soñar muelas, muerte de abuela.* Teeth gnashing, cousins passing. Molars grinding, grandma dying. She brushed on rouge, singing softly to herself, she curled her hair, daubed on eye shadow, lipstick, the butterfly blossomed from the chrysalis. She danced in the militia men's house. Nieves had a sweetheart and didn't go. The music could be heard from out in the street, but to see them you had to go into the dark garden, lie in wait in the hedges, crawl through; the iron gate was open. They were dancing in a brightly lit room, with crystal chandeliers, and some couples were leaning over the railing, shouting and laughing, jostling one another. Thinking about your desires I'm going to lose my mind; it takes my breath away. Ramona stumbled, dazzled by the windows.

Felipe spoke with one of them. The day was cold with a white sky. The militia men had kindled a small fire in front of the fence and they were eating sitting on the ground, around a blackened pot.

Are you hungry? he said.

And also: these are lentils; take them if you want them, if not, leave them.

He was unshaved, with his cap tilted to one side and his cape over his shoulders. Another was scratching inside his boot with a bayonet.

More arrived. They camped next to the road, among the chestnut trees, and the smoke from their fires drifted about like a fog, level with the bare branches. There were also refugees, dark and bundled up. And a file of prisoners. As they passed by they looked toward the parlor window, they gestured to show they were hungry. One of them got jabbed with the butt of a rifle. Downstairs, in Quilda's house, they were lodging a woman and a little boy who had one eye bigger than the other. She said they were from Málaga.

And make sure you don't wander off, said Papa.

They said that the Reds had shot down a plane, a fighter, that it had been going to crash right on the railway line, shot down in flames. And the kids in town found a dead soldier, floating in a quiet bend of the river, all tangled up in the brambles under the water; he was half-rotted away and there was no way of telling if he was a Red or a Nationalist, an infiltrator. Or a deserter. Or a Russian. Barely sunk in the quiet shallows, the water like a clearer air upon the bottom like marmalade; the crabs. Padritus said that he had seen him and Aunt Paquita slapped his face for telling lies. They were whispering, their ears glued to the radio, and in the parlor Ramona was dancing about aimlessly. Felipe was not going to school; he came in chewing on a beet, excited. Yes, the bunch of them from the Valley of the Riders of the Purple Sage. And there were others, from *la colonia*, the summer houses, from the town.

The boys from Puig Sec caught Padritus and said that if they caught him again they were going to hang him from a tree, over a bonfire. Besides, it was a question of spying on Señor Daunis. The garden was fenced in and from there, at nightfall, it was easy to make it to the verandah; then you had to spy through the window standing up, everyone silent, waiting in vain for it to happen again. The one time that, peeking through the window, they saw Señor Daunis crouching on the bed, naked, shaking his left hand very fast, between his thighs, his right hand behind, the crooked fingers twisting back and forth, his thumb sunk into his ass. They could hear a muted boom and people said that was the sound of cannon blasts.

A completely clear day, with the sun softening the brown fields, the sharp snowy mountain peaks. In the dining room the windowpanes were shaking and through the trees' naked branches you could clearly make out the cannon flashes, smoke rising from the hills. And the motorcycles, the brown trucks, the cannons; they were motorcycles with sidecars. And the officer on the white horse galloping with his saber unsheathed. They found Pere Pecats under some thickets, blown apart by a hand grenade. They said it was an accident, that he'd been drinking and it went off on him, or that the Moros had done it, that the Moros hadn't understood what he was shouting.

He slept in the room next to the parlor: he was in his uniform, with glasses and red beret. I'm the chaplain, he said. *El páter*. Nieves drew a bath for him. He spoke with a hand on Felipe's shoulder, and the others laughed, seated around the table. He brought out a glass jar with little white pears in syrup. There was everything, bananas, preserves, and at the town hall they were handing out small loaves of bread.

A Mass was celebrated in the plaza, facing the sun, the rose of epiphany. Many people wore red berets and blue shirts; chatting in groups, intoning couplets, serenades, and *el Carrasclás*, the Nationalists' favorite song. They sang, faces to the sun, forming little choirs, celebrating. *La victoria fue tuya porque así lo esperaba cuando muerta de pena, a la virgen rezaba tu novia morena. ¡Tu novia morena! ¡Tu novia morena!* The victory was yours because, dead from sorrow, you longed for it so, your brown-haired girl prayed to the Virgin, your brown-haired girl! Your brown-haired girl!

Señor Daunis hugged Papa, and Miss Lourdes told again the story of her father, who died in Africa when he was about to be promoted to commander. Father Pascual's soutane stood out on the steps of the church. Swordsmen presenting arms, shining bayonets, golden braids, glory, incense and victory.

Uncle Pedro arrived with gifts. They're some views of Genova. And I've got some records with all the hymns. He also had a uniform, a green beret and a kind of cape. They were gathered talking in the garden of a villa, out on the sunny lawn. There were wicker chairs and a gramophone playing. There was a woman who was smoking.

Is Barcelona the biggest city in Spain?

Does it really have a harbor and a park and trolley cars and subway trains and buses and cinemas?

Are the Reds still in Vallfosca?

Are there animals in Vallfosca?

Miss Lourdes gave classes in embroidery and German, and Aunt Paquita offered to teach singing to the summer girls from the colonia. They came back from their hike, feeling somewhat hot, sweaters knotted around their waists, and they passed by under the window singing, young and healthy, walking slowly hand in hand, the song about the five roses. It was a splendid day, springtime. Rosebuds and blossoms, flowers and fruits like fresh hot coals.

The troops passed by, tight columns of trucks bristling with rifles, armored cars, artillery pieces, and only the chubby little sergeant remained. Pilate had already gone and Aunt Paquita was searching for another girl. They cut Pilate's hair very short, a crew cut, because she was a Red. Aunt Paquita managed to get them to let her go, on the condition that she leave town. They said that when she got on the bus she was crying, her head covered with a scarf. Nieves told us.

There was a picnic. Grandma was there, and Uncle Pedro brought lambs. Grandma got busy preparing things, hunched over, the white bun in her hair coming undone. Don't vex me, she said. Nieves and Quilda were helping her, and Aunt Paquita was coming and going and telling her not to worry, that it was more than alright, Doña Gloria. There were many guests. And Ramona was dancing in the front room and everyone was applauding, etcetera.

II

They prayed the rosary in the chapel throughout the whole month. The rosary, and then came the *Memorare* and the theme for reflection. The prayers, mortifications, offerings, and sacrifices carried out in the course of the day were recorded in the columns of a small folder, everyone kneeling down, leaning on the back of the pew ahead; there was always someone who'd forgotten their pencil. For each good work you put in a grain of wheat and they said that with the flour ground from those they'd make wheaten hosts. The little children were the last ones to enter, but they sat in the first pews of the left nave, dedicated to the Virgin. They processed forward along the center aisle, genuflected before the altar and turned toward the left, slowly, with a flower in their hands, *rosas d'abril*. They sang, encouraged by a priest. *Venid y vamos todos con flores a porfía, con flores a María, que madre nuestra es*. Come forth and we will all go together with flowers in abundance, with flowers for Mary, she who is our mother. The organ played up in the loft and the setting sun filtered through the narrow windows, mysteriously coloring the gloom. They also filed out two by two, blessing themselves with the holy water in an endless succession. Father Palazón was praying, motionless between the two extended lines, impassive as a Roman before the wild wind that fluttered his soutane. Nevertheless, when their eyes met, it made him glance away.

The altar of the Virgin was adorned with wreathes of white flowers. The following month they decorated the altar of the Sacred Heart with red flowers, in the right nave, but exams were upon them and—it was said—one individual visit sufficed during recess, a simple Credo and some short prayers in the secluded light of the shrine.

I'm very devoted to the Virgin of Montserrat, said Gomis.

Well, I'm for Saint George.

A priest had been listening to them, and smiled. They hung up their classroom smocks, put on their jackets, picked up their pencil cases, books and notebooks, satchels. Gomis was a day pupil and in the afternoon he went home with the boys who took the bus. He wasn't leaving, he was going to wait for his grandmother. They got off in silence, in orderly fashion, and did not break ranks until reaching the caretaker's lodge in the park. Felipe was finishing later on.

He explained it all to her, occasionally asking her opinion, assuring himself that she was listening to him. They bought comic books at the kiosk, in front of the trolley stop, and they started reading them on the street, absorbed, sucking on mint popsicles, not stopping sucking on them except to exchange some comments. They didn't have much time at midday but in the afternoon they had a soda at La Granja, sipping it directly from the bottle with a straw. One day, Felipe and his friends spotted them and invited themselves, pulling up a chair. They stopped going to La Granja; they started going to a bar, although the bar stools didn't spin round. He carried her satchel and she carried the bag with the snack in it.

Nieves prepared them breakfast and grandma stood in line to buy bread. She also took charge of the rationing and kept the ration books in the upper drawer of her dresser inside of a brick-colored folder. She counted the coupons, naming off items: sugar, oil, meat . . . *No me amoines*, she said. Don't bother me. Nieves bought the rest in the market except when the delivery boy came from Vallfosca. The basket! The basket! he shouted from the gate, and everyone crowded out into the garden. They pulled out the sack tied with a cord to the mouth of the basket. Look, Raúl, look at this chard! Look at this escarole!

He ate breakfast in the dining room, with Felipe, and then they went out together. For morning recess he took half a baguette with olive oil and sugar, and for afternoon recess, the other half and a tablet of household chocolate. Gomis brought a green thermos with hot chocolate and a cold veal sandwich; the bread, white, from the black market. He began to eat during class; he raised the lid of his desk as if he was looking for something and snuck a bite. Do you know what "fetus" means? he said.

On Thursdays, by contrast, there was communion and Nieves prepared him an omelet sandwich and a hydrogen peroxide bottle refilled with milk with coffee syrup and a lot of saccharine. The bottle had a rubber washer fitted snugly round the porcelain top and it sealed tightly thanks to a wire clamp. He didn't eat breakfast until after Mass, during a brief recess, and amid everything an hour sped by like no time at all. With the prayer book open between his hands he contemplated those lines of imitation stone, the arches and columns painted as if they were cut marble, the stucco capitals, the golden reliefs. He always tried to be able to sit next to the middle aisle and did what he could to be one of the first ones to receive communion. There were two priests distributing the hosts, moving back and forth, now converging, now moving apart along the length of the communion rail. His priest was moving faster, barely leaning forward between the altar boys, the Ciborium against his chest, his glasses refulgent with light. All for nothing: he rubbed his upper lip with his fingers wet with saliva. He returned to his place and knelt down, palms against his face, his fingers slightly parted to see. They were still filing up along the central aisle, two by two, toward the chancel, the congregants with their sky-blue sashes, crowding round the steps, making way for those who were standing up from the communion rail, taking their places, getting back up in their turn, and returning along the side aisles with their hands joined and their eyes lowered, their knees dusty. He squinted his eyes and the rays of light from the candles intensified and grew until blocking out everything else; he could see nothing else. *Ser apóstol o mártir, acaso, mis banderas me enseñan a ser*, they sang. To be an apostle or martyr, perhaps, my flags show me what to be.

For confession on Wednesdays he went to a different priest each time and confessed the same thing. Then, kneeling in his place, he dragged it out as long as possible, as if the penance given was very heavy, and before returning to class he took a long turn round the deserted park, at most a visit, someone's relatives wandering along beneath the plane trees on the avenue. He strolled the quiet paths, a careful open labyrinth between close-growing plants, and as he walked along the blackbirds fluttered around with their flutelike trills, then flew away. In front of the building was a great rectangular esplanade, bare. The sound of singing, voices in chorus, and from the kitchens floated gusts of the pleasant aroma of roasted coffee beans.

Others did the same, a lively, swarthy boy with vaguely Asiatic features. But he stayed in the church with his group, whispering, laughing quietly in undertones, and on their way back they ran pushing and shoving and chasing one another. His last name was also suggestive: Vélez de Guillén. He looked at him furtively and during games he liked to be on the same team with him. One morning they happened to reach the front door of the school, on the way to the patio, at the same time. He was able to catch up with him, and matched his stride, commenting as naturally as possible on some fact which concerned them both, some common problem, most likely some type of ironic observation about their classes or teachers, something that would establish between them both a certain climate of solidarity. It was getting late and they were huffing. Vélez de Guillén glanced quickly at him, he considered his jacket too long, his golfing trousers too long and too wide. So young and already wearing hand-me-downs? he said to him.

Felipe was on the roller hockey team and he went to practice on Sundays; he kept his gear and uniform in his closet, locked away, and his whole bedroom smelled like a locker room. On the walls he had stuck up pictures cut out from magazines, photos of cars, movie actresses. In the afternoons, coming out of school he played ping-pong in the back room of a bar. Sometimes he brought his friends; their voices could be heard joking and talking, shut up in his room. They horsed around in the garden without listening to his grandmother, paying her no mind, trampling the lilies. Then they waited until grandma went into the little WC underneath the archway of the stairs, and at a signal from Felipe, they pulled the chain from upstairs, by opening the little hatch that gave directly onto the water tank. They also set out bait for her, some hard crust of bread on the little vestibule underneath the wall lamp. Grandma walked by shaking her head, and when her eyes fell on the bread crust, she would pick it up.

What does "bait" mean?

On Thursdays, between Mass and manners class, after recess, the morning passed by quickly. In the Assembly Room, Father Palazón spoke to them about how they must behave themselves in each circumstance in life, at the table, when visiting, and how and when they must practice their personal hygiene and change clothes, how to go to bed and to get up in the morning, for example, how to get undressed, and in what order, so as not to be, in any single moment, completely naked. First the shirt and the undershirt, so as to immediately put on the pajama jacket and, only then, to begin to undress from your waist downward, shoes, socks, pants, underpants; and so, the same for getting dressed, but in reverse order.

They had the afternoon off. And he went out with his grandmother; they didn't say anything in the house, but they were going to the cinema. Like on Sundays, when they said that they were going to the movie at the school, but they went instead to the one in Sarriá, the one that the week before had advertised a better selection of movies. Grandma forgot the money and they had to go back to look for it and they missed the beginning. Don't grumble anymore, please, she said. I just forgot. And after supper, when he was already in bed, he started to cry. What do you want? That I kneel down and beg your forgiveness? Well look, there it is. And she knelt down by the side of the bed with her arms outstretched and he pulled on one of her hands so she would stand up. Papa came in. Come on, enough games, he shouted. Go to sleep.

When they had guests the kids ate by themselves, in the small living room; almost always macaroni and roast beef. There they could re-read comics and talk about them. It seems almost impossible that they managed to escape from the steel men, she said.

The most exciting thing is when they almost discover them. Thanks to Zarkov.

I know I wouldn't have been able to stand it, not likely. I get nervous just looking at them.

She talked to him about when she was a little girl, about the games she played, her baby brother, the other little brother who died, about the vacation house in San Gervasio that they had torn down to make way for an apartment building, about a dog she rode like a horse, about a swing; she explained how they went riding in a phaeton, that her Aunt Marta published poems under a pseudonym, that her father, for Lent, bought them cream puffs. She stored the bread crusts in her dresser, a black piece of furniture, overstuffed, with brass handles and fastenings that smelled slightly of bread. The drawers were deep, difficult to open and close, and they were full of bundles of letters and postcards, folders, little boxes, holy cards and scapulars, lockets, medicines, a sewing kit, her missal and mantilla, some purple garters, keys for who knows where. On the marble top stood family portraits in oval frames, two slender vases, and a candelabra, and above, hanging from the wall, an engraving of Moses and the burning bush.

She was searching for the ration booklets, pulling out ribbons and funeral cards, papers, expired ration vouchers. One afternoon she forgot the money and they couldn't buy popsicles; she emptied out her worn-out coin purse. Forgive me, child, she said. I must have left it at home. On the way back he made her carry his schoolbag and he rang several bells in a row. She caught up with him when she rounded the corner, without daring to turn her head, hunching over, more than ever, in order to go faster, quite worried. They'll yell at us, they'll be furious. She was searching through the drawers, muttering, unable to find her pills. After eating she used her napkin to cover a piece of bread, a fruit peel, and while they were getting up from the table, she hid it in the cuff of her sleeve. Felipe arched his eyebrows, smiled. Then she went out into the garden to shake out the tablecloth, whistling; the sparrows knew her whistle and flew down to peck at the crumbs. Felipe elbowed him. Come on, let's go trap her, he said. They barged into her room.

Here's some food, he said.

Food? asked grandma.

Yes, we brought you a little bread.

Ah, thanks.

They spied her half undressed, flaccid and shapeless, with her petticoats raised, adjusting a garter, and she covered her breasts. There were little bouquets of acacia blossoms in the vases on her dresser, the four candles in the candelabra burning, lighting up the engraving, the burning bush. Felipe was hiding in the hallway; a voice was heard.

Gloria! Gloria!

Grandmother opened the door, squinting. Francesc? she said. Francesc? Who's asking? She moved as far as the vestibule, hiding the banana peel.

Nieves took charge of picking up the food rations and kept the ration booklets in the kitchen table drawer. But sometimes later on she still went, without ration vouchers, to pick up what had already been picked up, standing in the bread line. One day they telephoned, with a warning. Papa shouted. As if we didn't have enough headaches already! he said. She didn't come to pick him up at the school door either and he came running home, ringing doorbells. Now he didn't cry like the first time, when she mistook the hour and he found himself alone when the lines of children all dispersed at the school gate. They had given him a smock with a number embroidered in red above the pocket—1017—and they lined up on the patio, in front of the building; a large smock, somewhat stiff, not like the one Vélez de Guillén had, that fit him like it was tailor-made. Many of them already knew each other and they chatted until the priest made them be quiet; it was a gray day and the ceiling globes were illuminated. They sat him near the back and then they passed out the school supplies. His desk partner put his books in order, and his folders; he had a leather case with colored pencils. My brother knows how to light up his farts, he said after a little while. And also: the Americans shoot bales of cotton over here in shells, like that, *pzzztt*, right over the ocean. My father buys whole batches of it.

Gomis was a tiresome boy, with a thick nose and sleepy eyelids, who sort of smelled like butter. They also got together at recess, and during lineups. They talked about all the movies; Gomis had seen almost all of them. Another thing was that the caretaker's boy from their building had a lot of comic books and they traded with each other. He was a boy who was a little older, but not any bigger, brown-haired and angular, with a wolfish air about him. He made deliveries for a pharmacy and used his tip money to buy second-hand comics that he later resold or traded, two for one. The pharmacy was next to the school gate, and Manolo, in a moment, took out his comics, and spread them out on the sidewalk. Grandma was poking around in her coin purse, then paid. And on Thursday afternoons she accompanied him to the cinema. They came back hand in hand, reciting the list of his classmates in alphabetical order.

Farré
Farré
Fernández
Fernández

Ferrer Gaminde
Ferrer Gaminde
Fisas
Fisas
Folch
Folch
Fuster
Fuster

Not anymore now. She disappeared, and Papa called on the phone. Let's go, we've got to track her down, said Felipe. They found her—they said—standing in line in front of the back door of a convent, with all the beggars waiting for the free soup. She was shuffling along singing, how happy we are the two of us living in our little paper house. She was with several people, with her heavy stockings half-fallen, drooping pleats above her gray felt slippers.

Papa and Uncle Raimón were closed in the study talking and Papa raised his voice. Uncle Raimón quieted down and, when he came out, patted them very quickly on the back, kissed grandma on both cheeks, all in a hurry; straightened his overcoat, with a tic in his chin, put on a hat with the brim turned down and hiding his flexible hands in his pockets, left through the garden sort of swaying back and forth, with a long adhesive stride, as if he feared to fall down or make too much noise. Papa was shouting. Is it my fault that he pissed away all his inheritance when he was young? Is it my fault he decided to pursue music? I would've liked to have been a bohemian, too! Aunt Dolores was a horror, and our cousins a bunch of kids with black circles under their eyes who stank like piss. There were secret family meetings and grandma said: I'm half-crazy, Raul. You're all very attentive to me, but you're making me crazy with so many questions. The notary came by today.

They accompanied her to the taxi, a taxi with a gasifier; they loaded her suitcase and a bundle of clothes tied with several straps. She wore an overcoat and a black hat festooned with artificial flowers, and she limped a little, surely owing to the fact that she had bunions and her shoes pinched her feet; Papa also got in the taxi. Don't cry, they said. She'll come back soon. They cleaned out her chest of drawers and put everything in order. They pulled out the moldy crusts of bread, the scraps of rotten fruit, and some macaroni wrapped in newspaper.

The fact is, he's a blood relative, said Papa. And I'm nothing more than collateral.

Felipe was parting his hair in front of the mirror, tilting his head; he daubed it with green gel. Aunt Dolores has had another boy, he said. You know what she called him? *El Pitoletas*. The little weenie. He seemed very relaxed. He bought cigarettes and on the way out from the school he was going to wait for the girls from Sacred Heart. Do you say *jodear* or *joder*? Fucker or fuck?

They were also attending a Catholic school. They went in through the back part of the garden, which gave on to a stream, and you had to slip through a spiny hedge and past a dry palm branch. That was as thick as a real forest, and then there were paths bordered by toadstools and ponds and a hanging bridge and an enormous grotto with stalactites. Hidden among the laurels and the cedars and the pittosporums they spied on the little girls who were playing in a small plaza, around a small tiled pond with a spraying fountain, its sliding shadows rippling in the sun, now low, which was filtering through the hedges, yellow beams among the leaves and a large butterfly fluttering above. They watched them running and shrieking and chasing each other and hiding behind the columns of the huge porticoed hypogeum which led into the grotto with the stalactites, under the domes where everything echoed like in an empty room. And then, when the nun's handclaps signaled the end of recess, they saw them pass over their heads across the hanging bridge which swayed and oscillated mischievously, flooded with that parade of pink legs that disappeared up into the depths of their skirts.

Look, look, said Manolo.

But you can't see anything.

Damn. Even their panties.

So what? Panties cover everything.

More exciting, much more, was to make it to the orchard, at the far end of the garden, and steal something, even if it were a persimmon, without the gardener seeing them. They said that he had a shotgun that fired rock salt. He also had a German shepherd, which he kept in a chicken coop, and he only let it out at night.

It was the Month of Mary and the chapel was hung with white garlands. They prayed, some of them a complete mystery with their arms outstretched, the rosary hanging between their fingers. Then they informed him that Father Palazón wanted to see him and he stepped out of the line. Father Palazón was waiting for him in his office with many windows, standing next to the table. He stared at him for intolerable long seconds before speaking, serene, peaceful, his clear features, his short smooth hair combed forward. Are you sure that you're making honest confessions? Are you sure that you're not holding something back, that you're not hiding something you're ashamed of? Why, Raúl, why are you so stubborn, if God also knows it? He continued smiling, barely, static, he seemed like Julius Caesar, and he avoided his gaze in fear, as if blinded. How,

how was it possible. And the priest was saying to him that there was still time, and that besides he also now had a great responsibility, that his father needed him, that the most important thing was to conserve his purity, his modesty. Your brother isn't bad, but he gets caught up in bad company. You're wiser and you shouldn't imitate him because he can't give you anything more than a bad example. The corridor was long and it was empty, with after-dinner odors. The side passages led off to the classrooms, voices, the reflections in the glass, the Latin declensions.

On the patios were burly plane trees, like stone, forming ample naves, domes of boughs. It was forbidden not to play, to just stand around, so that if you wanted to chat you had to take advantage of coincidences, like getting a drink of water or stopping in front of the lavatories at the same time. The priests walked back and forth on the terraces, along the balustrades, and there was always someone accompanying them. The walls were high and they scaled them by following the slope, crowned by a small roof of glazed tiles, but in spite of everything the ball got away and then they opened the side gate, made of black iron, and they went out, looking at the steep street, the few passersby. When recess was over they lined up in a hurry and after the second bell everything went silent. The gym teacher appeared at the balustrade flanked by priests. *¡Por el Imperio hacia Dios!* he shouted. For the Empire toward God! And over the tightly formed lines, all of them with their arms uplifted, was raised an immense cry of *¡Arriba España!*

When they all stood in line, he didn't like to have Gomis behind him, who would put his hand on his shoulder when they told them to salute; he didn't like it and he shook him off since when, on one occasion, as he was raising the top on his desk, Gomis wiped a fat sticky booger on the edge on his side. Gomis was always touching himself, and then he would sniff his fingers. He got poor grades and didn't even know how to copy by hand. Everybody shunned him, quarreled with him. He's a girl, they said. The priests punished him and when they meted out punishments with the ruler he was always one of those who got smacked. They ended up moving him to a separate desk, where he kept a cardboard box with caterpillars, silkworms. He spent classes with his head resting on his crossed arms, indifferent and listless. He didn't have anything to do with Manolo either, he said that his father had forbidden him to. And Manolo said: wait till I get my hands on him.

They went out together every Sunday. Manolo knew the cinemas where they showed the best movies, some of them all the way across town, buildings more like garages, the facades covered with gaudy posters resembled some shattered decoration. The atmosphere was murky, almost fermented, and the crowd shouted at the hazy screen and shook the rows of seats. Guys who looked like soldiers who'd just crawled out of the trenches. After the show, back out in the street, they discussed the convenience of learning Morse code. And they never missed a single neighborhood festival, the stalls and booths for the fair set up, according to the season, in various streets and plazas. Manolo led the way and he tried to not let him out of his sight when they all poured onto the streetcar together, separated by jackets and overcoats, with some woman's purse crushed into his face. And a tit that she tried in vain to protect with the lappet of her overcoat; underneath she wore a red sweater and a fine necklace, a very tight sweater, pleasantly perfumed. The light was ashen and the street was wide and monotonous, the neighborhood with its dirty houses, interminable walls, sharp corrugated uralite roofs, telephone poles and wires.

They also went to the cinemas in Sarriá. And when they came out they pretended to shadow someone suspiciously, each one on either side of the street, and at a distance as if they didn't know each other. Above all, when they followed the newspaper deliveryman, named Papitu, who they said touched little boys. And then, at home, during dinner, he acted reserved, as if embittered, and he swilled down his milk, as if he were getting drunk. And the next day, during recess, at the school that they called the cage, he talked about the teachers in a low voice, as if they were the warders in a prison and they were planning to start a riot. He carried a pistol tucked into his waistband, and when they were trading picture cards, he handed them over like a spy. And Vallfosca was India or the Wild West, and he was preparing his traveling gear.

Manolo didn't like reading novels. Not even the ones about the Coyote. He said there were too many words. And they could never agree about comic books. He preferred *The Phantom* over *Flash Gordon*, and *Juan Centella* over *Jorge y Fernando*. And just like Felipe, he liked *Tarzan* better than *Merlin the Magician*. And they traded punches. In Sarriá. While they were buying comic books and anise cigarettes at the newsstand, watched over by the old woman across the counter, they leaned forward far enough that, when they chose to, they could cram something into their waistband, under their sweater.

For Holy Thursday they visited several churches in Sarriá and Bonanova, they compared monuments, the altars framed by cascades of flowers, with tall, slender palm fronds, upright, lightly tousled. No cars on the streets and the families strolled along leisurely, enjoying themselves, united and at rest; greeting one another, smiling. Many uniforms in sight and women all dolled up with their black mantillas and ornamental shell-shaped combs, loose folds of lace. They shunned acquaintances, including Father Palazón, who was coming out of a convent accompanied by another priest. The church smelled strongly of incense, of wax, and the people knelt before the purple banners, listening to the prayers of the nuns that floated in from the cloistered choir. But Gomis saw them in the atrium, they saw each other; he was with his family and his eyes shone and he, suddenly, malign and satisfied. Manolo didn't say a word either; they continued thus a while more, as if without the desire to talk, and they said goodbye right away, the two of them very pissed off and dejected.

In order to see the procession, the slow pass of the hooded figures and penitents, they went to Las Ramblas. Manolo said that in his house there had been a big blowup with his older sister. She goes out with a lot of guys and my mother finally ended up just having a look at her and discovered that she already had it open. Had what open? Her pussy, stupid! Sometimes you really seem totally stupid.

He also spent Easter in Vallfosca, with Papa and his aunt and uncle, and then they visited the churches in two or three different towns, in a horse-drawn trap. They heard the *De Profundis*, they attended the Tenebrae. El Polit and La Merè came out to greet them, and their dogs recognized him right away. But the field was cold and naked, silent, and even the smoke from the farmhouses seemed lifeless. It wasn't like in summertime, and walking on the mountain with shoes and socks, with his city clothes, made him feel uncomfortable, out of place in those woods, pallidly sunny, without birds. The farmers went about heavily dressed, with sheepskin coats and hunting jackets, and the women covered with scarves, their faces red with cold. Also, El Mallolet served as an altar boy, dressed in red and white, and he went around with the *caramellers* in their processions, in such a way that they hardly had a chance to see each other. He went with them from house to house, and when they finished singing, it was he who passed the hat and collected the money people threw to them. He asked him if Rosalía was still his girlfriend, Rosalía, slender and silent, all eyes, always following him around. Rosalía? said Mallolet. I couldn't care less about her! He didn't know what to say, what to do; the days were short, the time flew by. The same as when, at Christmas time, El Polit showed up in Barcelona with two chickens and sat down in the little sitting room, corpulent and ruddy-cheeked, stiffly formal, with his black beret tightly on his head, with his overcoat open, unbuttoned, owing perhaps to it being too tight for him. He clapped his gnarled hands, big-knuckled, with scratches. Well, Raúl, he said. *¿Qué fotem?* How the hell are we doing?

On Easter Sunday *la mona* that Gregorius had ordered for Felipe arrived. A little house of almond croccante with chocolate eggs around it and candied egg yolk spun on top. Or a fruit basket made of almond croccante with chocolate eggs and candied fruit. Or a chocolate hen inside an almond croccante basket.

Raul didn't get a *mona*; his godfather was Uncle Raimón. On the other hand, for Palm Sunday, Aunt Paquita gave him a decorative palm frond, *un palmón*, with a big silk bow and hanging decorations, little sugar figurines. They went to the parish church, and along the way, each one was looking at what the others were carrying and, once in the church, they had to compare heights, to see who had the tallest one, and at a specific moment, always unannounced, to strike the floor with the stem until it splayed, to see who made a better broom. Then they hung it with taut wires from the balcony railings, light, ivory-colored, ruffled dismay.

Manolo whistled from the street and he came out; they went to the nuns' garden, to the cinema, to kick the ball and mess around. Every time he talked to him about Vallfosca, Manolo fell into a bad mood. He said that his grandfather also had a country house, in Aragón, a big stone house, with a patio and a coat of arms above the door. It seemed like it bothered him that Raúl had gone away. When they went on a spiritual retreat in Manresa, he had gone with him to buy adventure novels and real cigarettes and a bottle of moscatel wine, some things that would help to offset, in the solitude of the cell, the effect of the sermons, death, condemnation, hell, a botched confession, and a sacrilegious communion. But going to Manresa meant an excursion and a few days less of class. But that's pretty wild, man, I'm not sure that's such a good idea, said Manolo. I'd be really careful. Some of those priests are real vampires. When they opened the tombs in the convents, they found a lot of children's skeletons.

Sometimes he got mad for no particular reason. Manolo raised his voice, almost shouting, as if he wanted people to hear him, and he said things that made no sense. Goddamn it! Well if you don't like it, that's too bad, you idiot. So there. They went their separate ways. It was All Saints' Day and they went through a cemetery as if being carried along with the flood of all the other visitors. They followed the dusty paths, between white blocks of burial niches, with crowns, with flower vases, with portraits and burning candles, with marble plaques, with iron rings; they read the inscriptions. There were loudspeakers broadcasting Gregorian chants and the cypresses stood out black and dry against the whitewashed walls, against the chaotically confused pantheons, cupolas and crosses, iron railings, stone statues. They stumbled upon a funeral and, lost in the respectful crowd, they could see a little, startled, the lid being raised for the last time, a black coffin, with sparkling incrustations. The harsh sunlight made the mourning clothes seem more intense, and the hot wilted flowers, stems drooping, smashed chrysanthemums, gave off a poisonous smell. And the next day—or the day after—Gomis said to him: Manolo's gone. They arrested them for being thieves. They were in the middle of a lesson and he didn't finish telling him until later on. Each night Manolo's father went into the pharmacy and stole a few pesetas from the register; the pharmacist wound up discovering him, he spoke with the owner of the building and they forced him to move out before midday. My father says that they've even been too good to them, he said. He explained it all in an affected manner, his eyelids heavy with delectation.

Alright, so what do you have to tell me?

He went back there, and on one of his meandering walks he was able to see the new caretaker carrying out the trash cans. He also wore a striped shirt but he was younger and didn't have a sickly face. He observed him for a while from the corner pretending that he was waiting, bored, just as if he had agreed to meet someone.

He went alone into the nuns' garden. He crept along, pushing his way through the foliage, spying, fighting and conquering, destroying the plants with blows from his fists, rushing forward in sudden charges or strides, branches, enemy weapons. And he explored the grotto: it was the Cave of Sesame from the story of Ali Baba and the Forty Thieves.

Coming out from school he bought packets of picture trading cards at the kiosk, movie trading cards, from *The Thousand and One Nights*. They all had their own collection, and he bought them not so much to fill up an album as for having a chance to trade his doubles with the others. It was forbidden and you had to do it underhandedly, in the schoolyard. The one he especially liked was that card showing María Montes dancing, arching backward, showing her tits. Gomis said that Virginia Mayo was better built, that he'd seen a naked photo of her. Liar, they told him. Vélez de Guillén preferred Ivón de Carlo.

Vélez de Guillén shared a desk with him and they helped each other. His mother was young and elegant, and his father walked with him on his arm, like a friend. He saw the three of them strolling by with the rector, during recess. Afterward the boys in the gang gathered round to slap him on the back, to tell him that he was sure well-protected, and he pushed them away, with a smile. They got together at every recess and when school got out for the day they took the same streetcar. They had their own private jokes, allusions that only they understood. But one day he also invited him over, he invited him to his saint's day party that they were going to celebrate on Sunday afternoon. He answered that he couldn't make it, that he already had a date, something to do with his cousins.

Before dinner, chores finished, he followed Eloísa around the kitchen, peevish, excited. And the Carthaginians came and wiped out the Greeks and the Romans wiped out the Carthaginians and the Visigoths wiped out the

Romans and then the Moors came along and wiped out the Visigoths. Beat it, go on, get out of here, said Eloísa.

It was raining and it was still too early to go to the cinema. From the study he stared out into the dark rainfall, a May thunderstorm that came sparkling down wildly over the garden, over the lilies thrashing about. Windows fogged up from his breath, a pale gray vanishing in which it was so much fun to draw something. He searched around curiously a while in the wardrobe, checking the jackets to see if he could find some forgotten coin in the pockets. Then he went back into the study. He took down a large edition of the Bible and, seated on the floor, below the window, he looked through the engraved illustrations, Joseph and his brothers, Moses and the Pharaoh's daughter, the Parting of the Red Sea, the Death of Moses on the peak of Mount Nebo, and especially, the chaste Susana. He sang to himself softly and with the nail on his index finger he enlarged an already open hole in the plaster of the baseboard.

The house had two stories and a terraced roof, and balconies whose iron railings interlaced in the form of tiny bouquets, like along the gate, with a gray dried palm frond like the one in his room. The rust had run down and stained the house's yellow facade, the flowered friezes, the festoons. The staircase was short and two large ceramic planters, with gray cacti, stood guard at the pilasters at the gate. There were two planted rows of three acacia trees; the tree grating was made of four quarter-sections, half raised, and weeds sprouted up through the sparse gravel. Besides lilies there were old woody lilacs, some volunteer pittosporum, and in the backyard, a plum tree. The greater part of the neighboring houses—Villa Gloria, Villa Hortensia, Villa Josefa—also had their own small gardens, their hedgerows overgrown with wisteria or honeysuckle, a neighborhood of quiet streets, badly paved. Nearby there were enormous tracts of open, fallow land, gullies, clearings scarred by paths, barren fields, trodden down with footprints, which, in good weather, resounded with the shouts of small children.

III

Uncle Gregorio had gotten to the house before them. El Polit told him that at the station, when they got into the trap, and of course, like any other afternoon of any other summer, they found Gregorio in the garden, seated next to the table, with his coffee already cold, his newspapers, and his pouch of shag tobacco. He never gave any warning, just made up his mind abruptly, and sometimes that's what happened, they would find him waiting there for them; everything depended on what the weather was like in Barcelona, on the withering heat, and, in this latest instance, for example, on a simple desire to enjoy the long beautiful evenings. Usually, however, they were the first ones to arrive. Later Aunt Paquita came up, and the cousins, around the beginning of July, and Aunt Paquita stayed there until September, although Ramona and Pedro stayed at the beach all through August, just like when Uncle Pedro was still alive. Uncle Gregorio would also be leaving early and not returning until early September, when the grapes started coming in; he always went to the same place, a spa where the weather was cool. By contrast, Montserrat and Juanito came up in August, and on the fifteenth Montserrat threw a party. There were many guests, and around tea time more people began to arrive, groups of summer vacationers, some of them practically strangers. Montserrat brought her little girl, but she almost always left her in the care of Aunt Paquita, who was family. Both Ramona and Pedro, along with Felipe, all went out with the boys and girls from the summer colony.

In the trap, as they drove alongside the creek, Polit brought them up to date. He talked about the drought, explained that Jaumet was no longer working at the house, that Chispa had died of distemper, and that Estrella had thrown a litter of fourteen puppies. They asked him for news, and he summarized the year's most important events. He gave them the gossip from the neighboring houses, from the town, and he complained about the crops. He caught up the reins softly and, now and again, shooed away the horseflies with his switch. He answered reticently, smiling, squinting his scanty blond eyelashes while Raúl, seated alongside him, watched the softly variegated hills, the vineyards, the cherry trees loaded with red fruit, bent over, near bursting. So many cherries! said Eloísa. Behind, coming more slowly, progressively falling behind, the trap with the luggage was following them with a boy riding atop—Ramón or Jaumet or Mario—a horse-drawn cart loaded with trunks and suitcases, everything necessary for spending the summer there. Soon the reeds would be so high, bending close over the road, they would brush the cart's canopy. Then the road turned up and away from the creek, and right there, for a moment, you could see just a flashing glimpse of the house's rooftop, just before heading into the woods. There the branches were all a tangle and the roof didn't appear again until just at the end, right before they reached the garden. Uncle Gregorio stood up and, a few yards away, two showy hoopoes took flight, fluttering their wings like fans. His shirt was stained with coffee and he was wearing some slightly baggy, blue-and-white striped pants, his belt loose, his fly buttoned halfway. He swatted him with his folded newspaper, then took him by the shoulder, explaining to him, for example, that that morning he'd witnessed an amazing fight between a lizard and a snake. They entered the house together, chatting. Soon it was time to go exploring, to inspect his dominions, the very quiet bedroom which smelled uninhabited, the warm porch, the attic, the dark corners of the garden.

He would meet with Mallolet in the evening, when he came back from the field. They generally met up at Polit's house, and sat together in the driveway, among the farmhands awaiting their dinner. Polit busied himself taking care of the animals and he didn't return until just before dinner was ready; he appeared in the doorway, barefoot and bare-chested, his belly sticking out, moving slowly. If he was in a good mood he started picking on someone, whomever was talking at that moment. Sometimes he kept quiet; he drank a long thin stream of wine from the *porrón*, and then rolled a cigarette. The mosquitoes were out, and they only turned on the outside light to push together several mismatched tables, set out the plates, the bread, the wine, and the bowls of salad. They sat down at the table and then Mallolet left, but Raúl stayed chatting until they called him home for supper. Can Mallol was further up the road, on a steep slope above the valley. They also met there when it was cool, on the threshing ground, but the older brothers were there, too, and they never left them in peace. They gave Mallolet a hard time, but made fun of Raúl, too. Wait till the Russians come, you'll see how they make you snap to, you lazy ass, that's the only thing you do well, lazing around. The crickets chirping sounded like a faint bell ringing and, as the day cooled into evening, the tawny owl would begin hooting, a sign, they said, of the coming autumn. La Mallola repeated that they were waiting for Emilio. She said it in a letter, oh, yes, he was arriving the day after tomorrow. She was sorry for not being a very good cook, worried that his parents might think she didn't take good care of him. At mid-morning he ate a thick slice of bread smeared with tomato, and a plain omelet, and she scolded him because he was reading a novel at the same time. He swallowed, hardly chewing, his arms resting on the table, encircling his plate, his gaze descending the page fixedly, from line to line. At these hours the women were alone in the house, Mallolet's mother and sister-in-law, and Raúl listened to them waiting for Emilio, assuring them each day that he'd already had breakfast. So much studying, they complained, so many books. Emilio stood up suddenly. Dammit, he said, my revolver jammed. And Mallola, possibly half asleep as she knitted, started, told him he was a little bit kooky. Emilio left his novel on the sideboard, the pages dog-eared, and got his shotgun. He was taller and skinnier than Raúl and never really got tan; he wore a dress shirt with the sleeves cut off for the summer, and for a belt he wore a dark, thick enviable leather cord. They went hunting all morning, through the woods, along the creeks, shooting at blackbirds, crows, magpies, the way they had once gone out with their air rifles. There was a game warden with a gun and they didn't dare to go hunting in the fields and vineyards, the lower mountain, the field with hot stones and brambles, aromatic, where they could always end up flushing out some bunch of partridges. Mallolet went with them on Sundays; Raúl lent him a shotgun on the sly and the three of them went out together. Mallolet shot randomly, seemingly not aiming, and then went searching uselessly among the bases of the trees, among the shrubs. Emilio, however, shot at least as well as Raúl. They went into the woods separately, without making noise, listening, watching the branches for a sudden flutter or whirl among the leaves. They would definitely shoot something.

They said that Uncle Pedro's shotgun was the best one. An old Holland, with double triggers, but better than the newer ones. Uncle Pedro hunted by stalking his prey, along the creek, around midday when the pigeons went to water at the millpond. Aunt Paquita insisted on accompanying him and she returned delighted, explaining how she'd managed to frighten them all. Uncle Pedro feigned that he was only pretending to scold her, as if in protest, but he was a poor actor, and you could see that he really was irritated after all. He made some sweet, funny face and then started using the ramrod, squinting and frowning down the gun barrel. Aunt Paquita sighed, reclining on a bench in the gazebo, fanning herself. So what I don't understand, then, Uncle Gregorio told her, is why you spend the whole day spraying that Flit up and down, everywhere. Why spare pigeons but not mosquitoes if they're God's creatures too?

He laughed with his belly, his eyes malicious, squinting through the glasses he wore for his myopia, his hair gray and uncombed, like a pelt. And he explained how he'd pissed straight into the mouth of an anthill until the damned ants abandoned it completely, in a mad rush. Aunt Paquita ended up getting mad. For the love of God, Gregorio, don't be such an ass, she said. She stood up and left and when she came back out it was to dust off and clean the glass on an oval picture frame, medium sized, a tacky, garish picture of the Assumption. Uncle Gregorio had found it: Mercè prayed before a reproduction of *La Gioconda*, the Mona Lisa—some calendar page, surely—that she had framed in the dining room. It was a Sunday, after coming back from Mass. There was no room in the trap and Raúl came back walking, with Uncle Gregorio, and they sat in the shade of the plane trees, in front of Polit's house. Mercè also came back walking, with Eloísa, but they stayed behind chatting on the porch of the church and arrived later. By the shortcut you could go quicker and they were already there when the cart passed by in the distance at a good trot and slipped into the lush overgrowth of the garden. They waved. Polit was coming back from the field, his feet covered with mud, his pants rolled up, his faded t-shirt some uncertain color; some boy was with him. Mercè showed them the picture, the heavenly Virgin in celestial blue, the choir of angels, and she stroked the smooth frame; she said that it was beautiful, better than the other. They appeared circumspect. *Prou*, said Polit, enough. They chatted under the plane trees while the dogs went sniffing around and licking themselves, playful, sleepy, in a state of semi-erection.

A luminous morning, with a clean, dry wind. Mercè gathered in the clothes from the line, the white crackling of the dry bedsheets, the wide pants stretched out even wider, full of patches, stiff like pasteboard, just like the shirts.

Mallolet and Emilio appeared with their air rifles and also sat down on the stone bench, against the wall, looking listless. The house—*la masía*—was built of stone, and it seemed—with its doors and windows framed in brick—more like an industrial building or a small train station from the turn of the century than the large old farmhouse it was. The outbuildings were built perpendicular to the sides of the main house: the cowshed, a long aisle with seven or eight cows all lined up along one side; the pigsties, a succession of low enclosures, the majority unoccupied, empty and airy, gray with dust; the horse stalls with soft floors, warm and dark; the grape presses and wine cellars, the roofs made of corrugated asbestos panels, the excessively large storerooms containing old, outdated incubators, complicated artifacts, of some uncertain use, all in a jumble alongside the grain hoppers and the sacks of nitrate. As a whole, the buildings bordered a rectangular patio enclosed on three sides from which, there below the plane trees, the visibility was poor. You could barely make out the wide fields at the end of the valley, the stubble, and beyond, the hills and woods, the vineyards, the dark dusty green of August.

They followed the creek bed a while and then they went up into the woods, fanning out in silent advances, from thicket to thicket, creeping along until reaching that rock, sometimes signaling with the rifle barrel to stay alert, a gesture of intelligence, the same as when the hero moves and a German soldier sneaks up on him, or a Japanese sniper pops up from his hiding place, and in the moment when they draw a bead on him a shot is heard, and the hero turns just in time to see the Japanese soldier keel over and, from behind another rock, a companion waves at him silently, smiling, raising his rifle. Some Sunday, on the way back, they swam in a pool, first making good and sure that there was no snake on the bottom. They smoked a cigarette lying out in the sun and they whiled away the time naming the colors they could see with their eyes closed, as they squeezed their eyelids shut. Red, yellow, purple, black.

They soon grew tired of the creeks. Above their heads, the foliage was still, slack in the sun, the birds seemed to have disappeared. They climbed up a slope, through the thickets, and came out into a vineyard with young, well-pruned vines. They ate warm, sour grapes, still a bit green; they parted the leaves, picking the fattest grapes from each bunch, from each vine. Then they set their air rifles to one side and rambled about for a while. Emilio had made some bolas and they argued about the best way to throw them for greatest accuracy, and they tried unsuccessfully to get them to wrap around the trunk of a tree. It got late. Dammit, man, said Emilio. His parents had come to spend the weekend and they were waiting for him to have lunch, and he had to be with them. In the late afternoon, nevertheless, they let him go with Mallolet to the dance in the town. But then the one who couldn't go was Raúl. They had guests, people from the summer colony, and he had to stay home. Or he had to return a visit or accompany Felipe and his cousins to a children's tea party, by bicycle. Emilio and Mallolet came back after it was already dark, when it was time for supper, the two of them acting very rowdy and, as it were, in cahoots. They said that Rosalía had let all the boys feel her up.

Summer people. They were joking, wandering about the garden, through the house, leaning on their elbows on the porch railing. In the gazebo there were trays of canapés, pan con tomate y jamón, pitchers of lemonade and horchata and, for the adults, sangría. The adults gathered there mostly, and on the croquet pitch, from which they could hear dry thock of the mallets. They also strolled out as far as the reservoir, to the most hidden spot, a small stream which flowed across the transparent water, grown thick with shadowy algae.

The paths crossed at irregular intervals, with the odd stepping stone here or there, and in the little clearings there were concrete benches, hefty, made to look like split trunks. The ivy covered the flower beds, spread out like a lawn; it climbed up the tree trunks, hanging from the boughs. The wooded area was thick and dark, lime trees, cedars, yews, cypresses, dwarf palms, pines, the boughs grown close together, pressing tight against the barely visible house, enveloping it like some tangled nest. It was a three-story house, imposing, salmon-hued, and the roof, very steeply pitched, was of glossy blue ceramic tiles. The chapel lay to one side of the house, with its own entrance, although there was also an interior passage which communicated with the vestibule. Now it was no longer used, but when his aunts and uncles were little they had a priest-in-residence all summer long, and there was Mass every day. The last time it had been used was for Papa's wedding.

Beyond the vestibule, the staircase rose in a tight turn, naked, with gray balusters, illuminated by a skylight. Upstairs there were opalescent glass windows and the shadowy rooms were still dormant, darkened by the thin blinds rolled down, sliced by thin strips of light. The floor was paved with small tiles bearing a concentric geometric pattern in muted tonalities. The walls and ceilings were whitewashed, and the lime masked the moulding, the stucco edgings, making the highlights that had once been a different color nearly imperceptible. In the sitting room, symmetrically arranged around a small table of pink marble, there was a sofa and two ample armchairs with cretonne slipcovers. There were also small, triangular corner tables, Isabelline chairs, wicker armchairs, a piano, a rocking chair, and, on the console table, in front of the mirror, a crystal bell with a bouquet of dried thistle, pieces of nacre and everlastings. Two deformed silhouettes stood out behind the frosted glass, their laughter audible. Raúl continued examining the house, going upstairs, up to the dormer windows in the attic. The interior rooms were dark, with built-in shelves and wardrobes, and the water trickled in the uralite tanks. Below the inclined plane of the roof, a narrow passageway, with tiny floor-level windows, ran along the outer walls, opening right onto the canopy of the trees. The western side was warm, the dusty floor littered with dead, dried-out flies and butterflies. There were a few odds and ends, some furniture, trunks, and, forgotten in the corner, Uncle Raúl's terrifying wheelchair, a reclining chair with bicycle-type wheels, all covered in cobwebs. By means of a very steep, narrow wooden staircase you could climb up as high as the lookout, a small tower with four windows through which it was possible to go out onto the roof and, clutching the guy wires for the lightning rod, reach the slippery, translucent skylights. Below, you could glimpse the hidden corners of the garden, and beyond, ensconced among the plane trees, Polit's house; then, the folded slopes behind the stubble field, the compact pine groves, the cork oaks. On the croquet pitch an argument was unfolding, with the players all gathered around a wicket, leaning on their mallets.

The most important party happened on Montserrat's birthday, on August 15th. That's also when we celebrate the Ascension of Montserrat, she said. It was Montserrat who had the chairs in the garden painted white, as well as the iron parts on the pedestal tables, and bought lawn chairs with striped canvas and cushions in bright colors. They chatted in the gazebo, and Juanito talked about a friend that had even seen a party of Maquis just a hundred meters from the spa, strolling about quite casually with their machine guns. He complained about the government's ineptitude, about everything. He used to dress for the city, a linen suit, perfectly ironed, generally navy blue or white, and his shoes were white and black, with a basket weave pattern. He sat with his knees very close together and the tips of his feet touching one another; occasionally he threw one leg over the other and then took the opportunity to pull up his sock, to smooth out the ankles. With Uncle Gregorio, when the time for coffee came, the conversation came alive and he talked about lots of different things in a very general way. It usually lasted until around mid-afternoon, when Uncle Gregorio stirred them up once more before leaving to take a stroll. Raúl called the dogs and accompanied him. They left the others all in a heated wrangle, Juanito very insistent, attacking the Regime, explaining the rude remark by Duchess Somebody to Franco's wife, highlighting the betrayed ideals of the Renovación Española, agreeing with Uncle Pedro, both of them monarchists first and foremost. But what the fuck are you all complaining about? they heard Montserrat shouting. If you'd spent the war like I did, in hospital after hospital, then you might have something to say. But the only ones who really have the right to complain are those who gave their life for the cause, like our brother. She spoke in a lofty voice, pushing back her chestnut-colored hair, brusquely, her face contorted by bellowing, and surely Uncle Pedro had to reemphasize the vitally important idea that someone remain in the rear guard for the purpose of organizing. My darling niece, please, let's not be so simplistic. People took sides, established alliances; if they'd let the Russians and Japan, if the Americans weren't so stupid, if instead of obliterating Germany, Germany, Germany. Uncle Pedro's words filled his mouth, and he savored them like a spoonful of honey or jam. Juanito was an Anglophile and he disagreed. He turned back to Raúl.

Alright, kid. So how are those studies coming? he said. Are you already learning Greek?

He didn't listen to Raúl's answer. Pensive, looking away, he hummed a few bars, shook his right foot resting on his left leg. When he smiled he showed very clean teeth. He arose late and spent half the morning in the bathroom; Uncle Gregorio was sure he dyed his hair. He went about impeccably shaven, but the oddest thing was his being so tanned without ever sunbathing. His only breakfast was a cup of coffee under the lime trees. Good morning everyone, he said, waving his hand slightly. He always pronounced his words with a certain difficulty, concentrating to avoid making mistakes. Papa and Uncle Gregorio were discussing the possibilities of trying out some reasonable way of making money by selling off the property.

Look, Jorge, said Uncle Gregorio. It's one thing to do the math for the milkmaid and it's something else to start a dairy, a model farm or whatever you like. If you're not planning on living here all year round to manage the business directly, then you'd better stop dreaming.

Dreaming? said Papa. Do you think Papa was dreaming when he built all this? You know as well as I do that he did it, precisely, with a view to creating a model community farm. And now it turns out that was just a fantasy?

Juanito cleared his throat, said that the important thing was to keep in mind the profitability of the investment; he fidgeted with the corner of the handkerchief poking up from his blazer's breast pocket. By the way, he added, where do the farmers sell their products?

After eating dinner, if the night was nice, he went out to the garden with Uncle Gregorio, far from the bright lights of the house, and they lay down in some small clearing, free of trees, to gaze at the sky. They watched the stars, the constellations, and how they turned and shifted as the summer passed. Sometimes Montserrat also came out and sang very softly, to herself, her arms crossed behind her neck making a pillow. Papa would come out but then quickly go back inside again, saying it was cold. And Raúl positioned himself to stare straight up at the zenith, without any nearby reference, and ended up getting vertigo from the sky. The earth was fresh and from the deep hollows came the sound of water running between the trees, and the hooting of the owls, the song of the nightingales, and the chirping of the crickets, which sounded like falling stars.

Later, after Montserrat and Juanito had left, they criticized them. Papa more critical of Juanito, and Aunt Paquita more critical of Montserrat, or Monsina, as she called her: her habits, that she went out around there with soldiers and big shots. Besides, she's got quite a vocabulary. She uses some words and expressions totally inappropriate for a woman. The fact that her marriage failed justifies nothing. How can she raise her daughter with the way she's acting lately? What's she going to learn, the poor little thing, besides barracks talk? Apart from her fling with the German, which has been a disaster, you could see that coming a mile away. He was just an adventurer, a player, a Don Nobody. It was obvious he was going to disappear all of a sudden the same way he showed up, just as easy as you please. They were in the dining room, seated around the table, and Uncle Gregorio was serving himself some salad.

Montserrat's like me in that way, he said, concentrating carefully on choosing the best leaves of lettuce. She likes what's fresh, green, and tasty.

Well, all I can tell you is that, if the little girl turns out to be a woman like God commands, it won't be for the example and the late nights of her mother.

What about him? Papa said. How's he going to have authority over his sister with the gluttonous life he leads, every night at the cabaret and all that, chasing floozies? Excessive behavior only leads to moral, financial, and even physical ruin. Sexual abuse ruins a man more than anything else; some men go crazy from doing it so much.

I don't think that in Juanito's case these effects are appreciable, said Uncle Gregorio, cheerful as a mischievous gargoyle. In the end, it's only natural for a man. It would be worse if he went the other way.

Papa smiled, incredulous.

The other way? I saw one of those years ago, on a streetcar. He spoke, and even moved, just like a woman.

He said that instead of expending energy, what one had to do was accumulate it, that that was why Juanito was so lazy, a person without willpower. Grooming himself, having fun, and not working a lick the whole damn day . . . the best way to live. Sure.

If that's supposed to be some passing reference to me, Jorge, you're wasting your time, said Uncle Gregorio. Your opinions roll right off me. When you talk about doing things the way I have, what you really mean is that I've not accomplished a thing; by my age you'd be much richer.

Inevitably, someone dredged up the theme of the old mansion on Calle Mallorca. The millions it would be worth now if it hadn't been sold and knocked down to build an apartment house. Aunt Paquita still lived in one of the flats. The millions the land would now be worth. The responsibility carried by Raúl, Uncle Raúl, the father of Monsina and Juanito, as the oldest brother. His crazy blunder.

They went out for a walk, with the dogs, and Uncle Gregorio gave him some background information. Doc, Chisa, Estrella, c'mon, c'mon, shouted Raúl. Even the annoying Balet came along, who was always following at his heels, a yellow dog, an Irish setter mix, with a regal profile, a rosy snout, and a faggot's yellow eyes. The other two trotted along on their own, sniffing around. And he told him the secret, the story of when Juanito almost lost his inheritance, about how one day some kind of chorus girl just showed up at Uncle Raúl's house saying she was pregnant, and how Juanito, although he swore he had nothing to do with it, ended up having to pay. By then Uncle Raúl was already a paralytic, but he was wise to everything going on; he said that Juanito would never receive any inheritance from him as long as he was in a state of mortal sin, and he sent him packing off to Montserrat, for spiritual exercises. Uncle Gregorio had some binoculars slung across his chest bandolier-style and a staff of peeled acacia wood for a walking stick. Generally they went along the creek and then they followed a fern-shaded path to reach some freshwater spring. The pipe was iron and the water poured out onto a circular font, sunk down level with the earth, partially covered over by the thick fallen leaves. There were rough stone benches, curving round following the sinuous slope, and they sat down at the foot of the tall plane trees, contemplating the trembling boughs. The trunks were covered with hikers' carvings, and there were remains of bonfires, ashes, blackened stones, a crumpled rusty can. Uncle Gregorio brought out some bread and chocolate, the tablets a little bit softened inside the silver paper.

America, he said.

He encouraged him to leave, to emigrate like his grandfather, but not to Cuba, not even to Argentina, where everything had already been done and practically no opportunities remained, but to Venezuela or Brazil, a country with a real future. In the interior the climate is good, and you can raise cattle. What are you going to do in Spain? If I were young again . . . They talked about Mato Grosso or Los Llanos like a shared memory, a landscape familiar to them both. None of that, by contrast, seemed to interest either Emilio or Mallolet; they barely glanced at the maps, and the idea of the three of them emigrating together attracted them no more than any other theme of conversation. And Raúl buried himself in his atlas, with its tracts on cattle farming. When they finished their snack of bread and chocolate, Uncle Gregorio drank a little fresh water from the spring and then he rolled two cigarettes.

What about Africa? asked Raúl.

The mill was a bit further down, in a hollow. He went there alone, following a little-used cart track, with the wheel tracks nearly hidden in the grass. The mill was in ruins, roofless, mostly a collapsed mess of fallen stones, and through the wall grew a tangled copse of holm oak. Nevertheless, a section of it had been rebuilt, and you simply had to untie a slender cord to open the heavy wooden door. Inside, the floor was covered with a thick bed of dry, fragrant grass, a bare room, with iron rings set into the walls. The window looked out onto the creek, to a spongy mass of ferns over which butterflies flew and the light poured through green, filtered; an ideal spot. He shut the door.

Once he brought Mallolet and Emilio along and, hiding his excitement, he proposed that they make the place their general headquarters. It's also the perfect place for casting out bad spirits, said Emilio. Mallolet was the least interested; any place is good enough for me, man. Raúl immediately regretted bringing them there but, fortunately, they seemed to have forgotten it and he stopped insisting. Emilio paid them no mind; he talked to himself, shouting, as if he were performing some comedy, rattling off classifications from botany class. Mallolet finally told him to shut the hell up. Sometimes you act crazy, he told him. And Emilio let out a wild cackle. His mother had come to visit for a few days and every afternoon she made him study. She sewed on a sewing machine in the living room, with Mallola, and they talked nonstop for hours. Mallola watered the floor in a zigzag, emptying the water jar, and then sat down to thread a needle, the clothes on her knees. They sewed sitting very close together, with their glasses pushed on tightly, taking long pauses to laugh heartily, while the daughter-in-law, sitting apart from them, simply smiled. Then the sewing machine whirred again. The shutters were closed tight against the sun and the flies.

The boy's going through a growth spurt, said Emilio's mother. And he'll be just as hairy as my husband. If you saw him . . .

She spoke slowly, concentrating on her work. Mallola spoke about her daughter, who would now be the same age as Emilio. Lately, they were just saying, there was a cure for tuberculosis. Quiet, woman, hush up, said Emilio's mother. They'd known each other since they were young, since Mallola was in Barcelona, working as a maid. They were reminiscing, and when at last the two of them toppled over, struggling friskily, as if they were tickling each other, the others just stared at them. Mallolet and his brothers worked for Polit on the thresher and they all went out together, with the dogs. They were winnowing on the threshing ground, enveloped in a whirl of rough sunny bright chaff, and a hand from Valencia who kept the horses walking round on the hay spread out on the ground was singing jotas. Raúl and Emilio accompanied the ones who were going out to the field, to bring in the sheaves. Someone stupidly tried to frighten them with stories of scorpions hidden among the haystacks. At mid-afternoon they rested a little and the porrón of wine made the rounds from hand to hand. The roof of the house stood out in the distance, above the green mass of the garden, shining in the sun. And while Mallolet amused himself by masturbating his dog, Raúl questioned Polit. Polit contracted the fissure of his lips. A sad affair, he said. The Mallols, he said, have suffered a lot. During the war, when the oldest son departed, Polit promised to celebrate his return with a dinner, a really fine dinner. It took him a few years to return, to return from the concentration camps, pale as a ghost, and he was only back a short time before he died, and he pulled his sister right along behind him because she contracted tuberculosis from him; and they didn't celebrate anything. They'd been harassed a lot and, even now, none of the family had a license for guns. They've suffered a whole lot, he repeated. Mallolet wasn't really named Mallolet, nor his father Mallol. But because they lived at Can Mallol, they also called the old man like that, and the old lady was la Mallola, and the youngest one, Mallolet, even though his name was Quim.

They continued bringing in the hay, and it was almost night now when Polit stood up straight and, with his arms akimbo, said it was time to pack it in. Let's go, boys, he said. They drove back in the cart along the shadowy roads, leaning against the sheaves, contemplating the sky turning every moment more colorless. Later, seated on the stone bench, against the wall, the stories and ramblings continued. That very night, probably, Polit recounted the circumstances of his imprisonment, after the Nationalists arrived, the diverse anecdotes about his being held in the town school until he was paroled, thanks as much to the deliberate intervention of Aunt Paquita and the sergeant as his own ability to mount his own defense, having argued that even if he could be held partly responsible for the fact that the church had been turned into a warehouse, it was certainly the lesser of two evils, in fact because if nothing else, the structure itself had been spared from almost surely being burned to the ground. They called Montserrat the sergeant, a nickname that dated, said Polit, from the time she went about wearing the Red Cross chief's uniform. Even now she always came over to talk a little while, to hash things out with Polit face to face, and Polit followed her lead, they knew how to understand one another. Now and then she got the urge for making jam and then they saw her arrive out of breath, loaded down with fruit. She dropped the basket and sat down with her legs extended, her hair loose, her face dripping with sweat.

You, you don't say a word, you're too restrained, said Polit.

Shit, what about you? said Montserrat. If you had a little more self-restraint you wouldn't have such a gut on you.

Raúl stayed with them while they ate dinner, until they shouted for him from his house. On the other hand, Juanito, like Ramona and Pedro and even like Felipe, sometimes left without even having come over to say hello. Besides, more and more they all came less frequently to Vallfosca, and for less time;

Juanito, at the most, came for a few days around the Feast of the Assumption. Ramona and Pedro preferred the beach, and Aunt Paquita lamented her loneliness, but she continued to allow them to spend long stretches in Palamós, with Uncle Pedro's family. Felipe did the same, barely staying at all; he went to Puigcerdà, to a friend's house, and Papa said that he had a semi-serious girlfriend there.

A girl from the Roura family, wealthy, well-connected people. He started chasing her and, from the looks of it, she hasn't discouraged him.

What do you expect, said Aunt Paquita. They're spring chickens now. It's natural at their age they get interested in each other.

Spring chickens? said Uncle Gregorio.

I'm not saying this because he's my son, but Felipe really is a very good boy. Well, and Raúl, too, of course. Just you wait, wait and you'll see how he also starts to step out. Isn't that right, Raúl?

Felipe refused to give explanations. He shut his bedroom door and wrote letters. He transformed his room, he traded his bed for a cot, and the nightstand for a three-legged stool, then removed the mirror, leaving the walls blank without any photos or clippings. When he was at home he hardly left his room; and if he did it was just to take a stroll in the garden. One afternoon he came into Raúl's room. Go on, go on, he told him, and Raúl tried to resume his reading—a study about the adaptation of diverse European beef cattle breeds to tropical climates—under Felipe's watchful gaze. Felipe had stretched himself on the bed and was smoking a cigarette. After a bit, however, he asked him if he wouldn't like to play tennis. At your age you'd learn right away. I've got extra rackets and we could go together. It feels really good, y'know? And, look, you also get to talk with people besides, and all that. He also asked him what he was planning on studying when he finished high school.

I don't know, Raúl said, shutting his book. Maybe Law.

Of course, man. Law is really good, said Felipe. It's a career with a lot of options.

Then he proposed to go to town by bicycle, to take a look around. He helped him straighten the part in his hair, made him put on a clean shirt. But, man, take off that fishing hat, it's ugly as hell.

It took them a while to find the other kids, gathered under the pine trees at an apartment house, on the outskirts of town. They were planning a nighttime exploration of the cemetery and the girls were shrieking. What we've got to do is plan another day at the beach, said one of the girls. They talked about their last outing; the sea wasn't far, you could glimpse it once you crested the hill, but it was very steep and you had to pedal really hard. Someone recalled when Celia fell.

And they all got a prizewinning view.

You're all so fresh, you've really got a lot of nerve.

The same thing happened every September. They were all a little fed up with outings, with hiking to picnic at one spring or another, always the same ones, lately, and having to pedal more than two hours to get to the beach, and the parties, and afternoon teas which every family gave, occasions on which Javi Solans would inevitably end up singing those green eyes, most beautiful poppy, it's impossible, my life, to live so far apart. Looking at Celia as he spread his arms wide, at the most meaningful moments. They grew tired of the mid-afternoon walks, of the jokes and even of the grudges and gossip that had been growing throughout the summer, and the conversations grew ever more boring and rambling. And then September arrived and although they still had a whole month ahead of them, it was as if the summer had already come to an end. The ones who'd flunked some class had to cram and, in some cases, leave early for Barcelona, to take private classes. The thing is I'm flunking math, I'm sinking, said an older boy, almost as old as Javi Solans. And they talked about movies that had just opened or the ones advertised in the papers, yet to premiere. And in spite of the fact that everything pointed to the start of a new school year, the urge to depart, to be already in Barcelona, to see other friends, classmates, to go to the cinema or shopping, to get outfitted for the autumn, was practically contagious. The same process as in June, when everybody was arriving, but in reverse.

Only Raúl seemed to like September, now that he need not accompany Felipe to a town that was emptying of summer vacationers, now that Emilio had left and Mallolet was busy helping with the grape harvest. Going out walking alone he discovered that the spots which years earlier had seemed mythically distant, which when he went with his cousins required a whole day for the outing, with backpacks, picnic baskets, bakelite dishes, folding cutlery, and thermoses, he could now reach them with an autonomy and speed that not even Mercè herself could believe when she saw him return before lunch, back already.

Faker, you're just a faker.

They served more drinks, horchata, beer. In the background, Raúl listened without loosening his grip on his glass. Suddenly he crossed eyes with Felipe and guessed that he was going to be mentioned. This guy is a real Don Juan, he heard him say. He's got a whole girls' school in love with him. Everyone looked at him. He tried to meet their expectant gazes, smiles of sympathy and encouragement; he drank quickly. None of it was true. Perhaps, if he ran into a group of schoolgirls, they laughed and made a fuss, or rather, if he ran into one alone, he saw her walk by very stiff, tense in her uniform, upright, head held high, staring straight ahead; but nothing more. And he didn't even really like them, nothing in them attracted his attention, their too-chubby legs, flat chests, and big bottoms, but not tight and pretty, only large and, in any case, shapeless, their faces undefined, looking self-conscious, with some irritating little pimple, the result of the very changes of the age, as well as an unrestrained passion for eating pastries. No, they were unconvincing despite their attempts to approach him and walk on by, hieratic in appearance, but uptight, ears eagerly wide open: useless, completely useless. The one he really did like was Celia, nicely tanned by the sun, with her hair mussed up and her mouth thickly painted with lipstick. She wore a long yellow bodice with Japanese sleeves and when she raised her arm it revealed the soft hair in her armpit, the gentle swelling of her tit. She, evidently, had noticed it herself, and frequently repeated the gesture: she leaned back, hooked her hands behind her neck and laughed.

He also observed her during Mass, on Sundays. Celia always sat in the last pews, among her friends, wearing her cardigan and mantilla. Sometimes she picked up her missal and pretended to read, but the most attractive thing was the expression on her face when she returned from taking communion, her full lower lip slightly moist, her eyelids half closed. Raúl stayed with the other boys, standing against the back wall. Papa and Aunt Paquita, however, invariably occupied the front pew on the left. They drove in the trap, arriving early so that, as Aunt Paquita wished, there would be no need to whip the horse. Raúl preferred to walk, taking the shortcut. He left later but arrived first, in time to witness—one of so many among the onlookers—the sudden arrival of the cart in the church plaza, Aunt Paquita seated up front, black and erect, covered in veils like a saint, facing the driver. The boy jumped to the ground and helped them get down, while some acquaintance, some older lady, approached and greeted them cordially. The horse stamped, agitated by the crowd surrounding them, by the cars that kept appearing, and the boy had to dash forward and grab its bridle. The summer people huddled together in groups, exchanging greetings, and the townspeople, standing slightly apart, commented on them, observing their clothes. Then they heard the bells ring again and they began to enter the church. Raúl stayed behind in the background, remaining at the entrance to the atrium, and as soon as some straggler came in, he took advantage of how slowly the door closed to slip out. He lit a cigarette and, dazzled by the sun, went into a bar, on the other side of the main street. He took a seat next to a large window from where he could watch the whole plaza. The main room was long and deep—with echoes and fluid transparencies, like an aquarium. Beyond the back of the room a small door opened onto the patio, onto a violent cascade of blue bellflowers. There were rows of small tables and, facing the marble counter, two men were talking, their voices intermingling. Closer, with a vermouth on the table, Uncle Gregorio was staring at him silently, from above his open newspaper. *Caramba*, Raúl, he said. He invited him to join him, to order a vermouth for himself; Raúl felt uneasy and couldn't quite relax.

Really hot, isn't it?

Yes, said Raúl. But it's nice here.

They smiled after a while and Uncle Gregorio patted him on the back, delighted.

Look, the truth is I haven't moved from this spot. What color harnesses were the priests wearing today?

Green, I think.

They watched the sparrows in masterful possession of the whole deserted street, in broad shadow, and their conversation developed pleasantly until people began to filter out of the church. Then Uncle Gregorio paid and they let themselves be seen in the plaza. The people emerged slowly, looking for one another, planning for later, the ladies from the summer colony closing their purses and folding their mantillas, gathering under the shade of the plane trees, florid and ostentatious, while some began to wander off, reanimating the side streets of the old town through which, on other Sundays, Raúl went walking before Mass was quite finished. He wandered through the quiet town, among deep doorways and tiny windows, lichen-colored walls, corner patches with sunflowers, hanging geraniums, radiant climbing plants. All that warm quietude was like a siesta that would inevitably be destroyed when the soft trilling and cooing from the chicken coops and dovecotes was drowned out by the sudden hubbub rising from the plaza, and Raúl had to go back and rejoin the crowd.

In Barcelona there was no problem, and when he sometimes accompanied Mireya to eleven o'clock Mass, at the Pedralbes monastery, he joked implacably in a muted voice, making scathing observations for her benefit. She said that, more than anything, she went there for the marvelous beauty of the place, for the organ music, and then, as they strolled around the outskirts she let him feel her up. In the afternoons he would take her to a bar with reserved tables and dim lighting and background music. He bought himself a lighter and sunglasses and helped himself to a gold-plated cigarette case which Felipe never used. He usually smoked black tobacco, but when he went out with Mireya he bought loose blonde cigarettes and refilled the case. Now in the bar, he opened the case to offer her a cigarette and, as he'd seen in a film, lit his at the same time as she lit hers, from the same flame. He blew out a slow and penetrating mouthful of smoke, and then put his arm around her shoulders.

During the week they could hardly see each other; Mireya had classical dance classes in the late afternoon and her father had forbidden her from dallying afterward or to arrive home any later than nine o'clock sharp. She was really fine and wore her hair in a long, thick braid, and she seemed older than her years. She talked about the box seats at the Liceo, about other boys, about an old engineer. I really like you because you look so young, she said. And one afternoon, upon leaving school, Raúl took a chance, slipped into Madame Rita's, where—people said—no one asked your age. He hung around outside until some man went in and then, slipping into the salon, sat down by his side to make it look as if they were together. He sat there a while, sunk down in the worn velvet sofa with mushy springs, examining the whores one by one. Especially attentive to the right way to disappear with them, how you had to act, in the manners and customs of the place, in the words and gestures. The whores chatted and laughed, they caressed each other, they fanned the sweaty naked parts that showed through beneath their nylon folds, approaching him now and then, repeating snatches of some song. Too late. It was the time for exams, he was finishing the year, and Mireya was holding out, resisting his advances, proving to be obstinate and distant; she said she was fed up with dark bars, mezzanine tables, and private rooms, of always hearing the same records, all that business of let's go for a stroll and maybe we'll see each other later. He saw her riding on the back of a moped, softly clutching the guy driving, and he managed to not let her see him when they came to a stop a few meters ahead, waiting for the light to change. The afternoon was waning and Raúl kept walking round the streets submerged in Sunday quiet, sticking his head into the bars with the most activity, stopping in front of the entrances to the cabarets and the whorehouses, trying to get a look inside. He made up his mind sitting in his threadbare velvet corner: a very dark woman, with thick eyebrows and puffy eyelids, her lips almost blue with the shadow of a mustache at the corner of her mouth. They went upstairs to the next floor; the hallways, very old and silent, slightly illuminated by gray globes, smelled like warm laundry. Raúl struck up the conversation with some random phrase, doubtless premeditatedly cynical, meant to facilitate the preliminaries, the problem of whether he should undress or undress her or both things at the same time and in which order and starting where, thus advancing all questions about how to proceed, as if this wasn't his first time at all. But she didn't ask anything. She climbed on top of him, on all fours, offering him her ass, wrapping her arms around his thighs, warm, slippery, sticky, wet, her hanging breasts tinted by the dim red gloom.

I'll do something that you'll like, she said.

He told Mallolet about it the first chance he got, and Mallolet, with sly eyebrows, said he'd done the same. He explained what the brothels were like in the country towns and they got into the details, of how often, how many times, and for how long. I do it my way, quick, said Mallolet. He called his brothers and they kept talking with total freedom, as if among friends. They were on the wall around the threshing ground and the brothers related their experiences. Anecdotes of when they were in the military service, principally, until Mallola called them in for supper. And when Emilio arrived a few days later they received him with great excitement, tossing him allusions, discriminating hints, holding back as long as possible from telling him exactly what they were getting at. Emilio protested, he assured them that he'd done it, too, yes, already, and that everything went smoothly, alright, although, just afterward, he'd felt some pain. But his story wasn't quite coherent, and they all ganged up on him. The quarrel left them tired and conciliatory, and they changed the subject. There was only one more year to finish high school and it was pleasant to make plans, to map out the future, in which everything was reduced to knowing how to endure nine more months. Nine months and there would be no more lining up or Mass or smocks or sneaking cigarettes sitting on the toilet or Sundays spent doing equations, and—the most important, including outside of school—nothing that smacked of still being a schoolboy. For Emilio, however, those considerations seemed to matter very little; what worried him was his college career, his studies, his future, and they talked seriously. He'd arrived for the summer very changed, taller, and of course now he shaved every day. People said his father was earning a lot of money, that he'd been lucky, that being an electrician included the possibility of turning his work into a full-fledged business installing electrical systems. But Emilio insisted that his real ambition was to study medicine. Yeah, yeah, bullshit, said Mallolet. He was leafing through comic books without paying much attention to what they said, getting impatient. And they went for walks, the same as other summers. There were still some cherries hanging on the picked-over branches and from the fig tree in the vineyard hung large young unripe figs—pale, insipid fruit, not like the figs in September, sweet and oozing, with soft skin white as curds, bursting at the touch, with red fissures, among the dark, rough leaves. They argued about the annual town fiestas; the feast of San Ireneo fell on Friday, but Mallolet was sure that the best time was always Saturday night. They agreed to meet for a walk, to check out the dance.

In the gazebo, Uncle Gregorio was balancing in his chair, leaning back with his feet resting on another chair, pensive, the thick gray hair tufting out of his half-open shirt. Was he, perhaps, watching the clouds, distant as he seemed from the conversation? Upon the table, his eyeglasses folded, the newspaper, his pouch of shag tobacco, an empty cup, with golden-yellow coffee stains.

He eschewed the noise of the evening street parties. Or fled the humid heat of Barcelona. Or from Leonor, scolding, bossy, and grouchy, always upbraiding him for being absent-minded, for not washing or changing his clothes enough, for his love of making a mess in the kitchen, for his bad habits. She's always got to be complaining about something, he said. Such a good woman that she's unbearable. It was better in Vallfosca.

Fiestas? he said. That's for people who work.

He complained about the heat in Barcelona, the nighttime fiestas, the bright glow from the bonfires and the fireworks, the music and the explosions that didn't let him sleep a wink all night. I've come running back here. What I wasn't counting on is the mosquitoes being so bad up here this year. Aunt Paquita was also there, tired from the trip, increasingly strict, fulfilling her devotions, a practice—the precise one—for every occasion: the Holy Hour, the five Saturdays of the Immaculate Virgin, the five Sundays in honor of the five wounds of Saint Francis, the six Sundays of Saint Luis Gonzaga, the seven Sundays of Saint Joseph, the nine first Fridays of the months, the fifteen Tuesdays of Saint Anthony . . . Fulfilling, accumulating indulgences, speaking of the particular protection enjoyed by those who wear the scapular as well as those who carry a simple rosary in their pocket, always ready, discreetly put away, recounting still the horrific death of Voltaire or the irremissible condemnation of Isabella of England. Her rosary beads were olive pits from an olive tree in Gethsemane, and she slipped them between her fingers. Then she would play the piano, a tall black piano with sconces for candles, more out of tune every year, the keys worn and broken from being hammered on one summer after another. Her waxen fingers, like slender bamboo shoots, would play Liszt, Chopin, and Beethoven, and Papa would inevitably say that Paquita played with great feeling.

On the feast of Saint Irenaeus it was the first Friday of the month. Aunt Paquita and Papa drove the trap into town to take communion. It was probably then, when the Mass was concluded, when the rumor began to spread that Rosalía had aborted her baby. Emilio told Raúl, very excited. Later, at night, at Polit's house, they learned more details; that she'd been three months pregnant, that the hemorrhage had been stopped, that the hemorrhage had continued, that she had done it with a knitting needle, that she'd done it with a stem of rue, with an ivy leaf, that the doctor made his diagnosis by slicing open a frog and examining its entrails, that just like in the case of Toni, and unlike the case of Mariona, etcetera.

Well, of course, said the Aragonese. Who in the hell could you hold responsible if the girl, starting with her brother on down, has whored it out more than a mother hen?

Yes, playing, always playing, and now look, said Mercè.

She was carrying in the plates, the silverware. They had switched the lights on, and Polit, sitting on the stone bench, yawned hollowly, with his arms tensed. Raúl listened to the frogs, the croaking like a broken gurgle that reached them from the pond. And I was counting on her for the dance tomorrow, said Mallolet. He was touching it through his pocket.

They had a good time at the town's annual festival, *la fiesta mayor*. They saw Polit with his daughter and his son-in-law, who lived on the coast; he was wearing a new beret and a white shirt, his belt cinched low beneath his paunch. He called them over, invited them to have a cognac; the outside tables were packed and they had to drink it standing at the bar. There were people from all over the region, summer vacationers, groups arrived from other towns who filed along in tight lines past the fair's booths and stands. By contrast, the area under the awning was still fairly lifeless: rows and rows of empty seats and the orchestra playing for a few couples. Two or three little girls from the summer colony drew near and waved to Raúl, mischievous and shy at the same time, while Emilio and Mallolet watched and waited to see. They adopted a casual air, apparently impertinent, but it showed that they were bored, that they wanted to invite themselves over. Then they kept on bumping into them, too many times to be accidental, and Raúl finally pretended not to see them. They returned to the shooting gallery and won more cigarettes and a little bottle of some horrible alcoholic concoction. They drank beer and ate clams, and in another bar they invited them to have some wine; Mallolet said that he liked the clam best of all. It was hot, they were sweating. Now at night, under the dazzling bright awning, Mallolet danced with a girl from the town dressed in pink, but it didn't take long before they saw him coming back, pushing through the crowd, laughing like crazy, infecting them with his laughter. They laughed and pushed each other, and Raúl felt invincible. On the way back they ran into Polit driving the wagon—the land yacht, they called it—and he let them load their bicycles in the back and climb in. Dammit will you listen to me! shouted Emilio from the back, turning his back on them, with his legs hanging outside bumping along. Polit knew some *habaneras* and they ended up singing, all four of them, saluting in chorus the passing cars that lit up the shadowy turns of the highway. It was like the summer before, when the mountainsides caught fire and everybody worked together to put out the fire; Polit had a small barrel of wine with a bamboo reed spigot and they drank and came back singing, too, and Raúl didn't notice how much fun they'd had until it was all over.

On Sunday it was even hotter, a hazy, muggy morning, clouded over, with a quiet dry glare, like ashes. Raúl lent them the shotguns and they went out, he was carrying Uncle Pedro's gun. They talked about the night before, about Rosalía. And they managed to shoot something: Raúl got an old rook that he ended up shooting to pieces among the cork trees with their gray branches. They met up at the edge of the woods. Just ahead, in some spot among the dark, undulating vineyard, the partridges were singing. It was a few feet away, hardly past where the hill began to slope down, when they heard a voice cry Halt, immediately followed by a shot, brief and cutting. The game warden was coming after them, also coming down the hill, trampling the vine shoots, the barrel of his rifle smoking lightly.

Halt! he repeated.

They looked at each other. The game warden, said Emilio. He saw him running off, to the side, dodging the grape vines, escaping. Another shot sounded and Raúl looked back, jumping sideways, plunging between the twisted vine stumps. Mallolet hadn't moved, he stayed frozen in the same spot, in front of the warden, with his arms raised. He heard the ground crunch and a rustling of leaves, and he saw Emilio crawling toward him from a little ways further down. He caught him, he heard him say. They heard a third shot and the guard's voice shouting at them to put down their guns and stand up. C'mon, up! Raúl noted the taste of dry earth between his teeth. They stood up, maybe with their hands raised. The other two approached, slowly, Mallolet in front, pale, his mouth hanging half-open, his face slack, as if he didn't see them. The game warden, a short ways behind, came toward them with his rifle level, aiming from the waist. He was breathing heavily, hunched and sweating beneath his discolored flat cap. From Vallfosca, eh? he said. He picked up the shotguns and they set out marching, the three of them ahead of him, silent.

They found Papa in the garden, under the shade of the lime trees. Uncle Gregorio came out immediately, putting on his glasses, and also Aunt Paquita, still wearing her mantilla. Papa began to apologize, to say that he'd already warned Raúl. He promised that they would not do it again. He talked with the game warden about the town mayor, about the parish priest, about a prefect who was a friend of his, he offered him a drink, some refreshment. The warden shook his head no; he said that, apart from the fact that none of the three boys had a hunting license, hunting at that time of year was a crime, in the middle of the closed season, when the animals were still with their babies. Eloísa, her eyes wide, frightened, followed the scene from a respectful distance in the background. Then Uncle Gregorio intervened, he took the fellow aside. C'mon, fella, let's talk, that's how people understand one another, he said. They talked a while. Then they saw Uncle Gregorio reach for his wallet.

They went toward Polit's house.

Idiot, said Raúl. He wouldn't have dared to shoot us.

Chicken, said Emilio. Faggot.

They all met up later. What happened? asked Mercè. The hands, just in from the fields, resting, a few shaving by the water tank. And Polit, sweaty and potbellied, barefoot, his pants rolled up, in a t-shirt.

This guy sure is a sissy.

Suddenly Mallolet pulled away, ran to hide in some empty stall in the barn. They chased after him, and in the sudden gloom they could barely see him against the back wall, kneeling in the bed of straw, crying. Polit appeared behind them, on the threshold, surrounded by yellow light, arms akimbo and a straw between his teeth.

Let's go, he said. You two, scram.

IV

Coming down to Las Ramblas meant not only a change of streets but also, and above all, a different state of mind. You noticed it the moment you left Plaza Catalunya, for example, starting to take those first steps under the fluid river of plane trees, strolling, falling into step with the crowd, slow and tight, in full play of searching gazes, advances, grazing you, brushing up against you. A leisurely atmosphere of gentle warmth that only thickened when, further on down, the street narrowed between the flower stalls and the calm air of the long afternoon smelled faintly like lilies. The people emerged from their places of business and there was something like drunkenness or fever in all that coming and going, light clothing, perspiring skin, in that ebb and flow without any fixed direction which could just as well sweep them along to the porticoes of the Plaza Real as to the taverns along Escudillers, on the right-hand side, map-wise, north of Las Ramblas, while, imperceptibly, the first street lamps and the first flashing signs flickered to life. Or else toward the left, southward, taking Conde del Asalto or Arco del Teatro, toward Calle San Ramón, San Rafael, San Olegario, Tapias, Robadors, confusing alleys and side streets with their little dives which stank of hashish, alleys where, as it grew dark, the shining lights isolated the ground floor businesses, the red doorways, the worn, narrow pavement, the filthy paving stones, high-heeled shoes, bulging hips, necklines, long manes of hair, painted eyes, a succession of bars, of turf marked off and intensified by cigarette smoke. From Calle Tapias you could emerge onto the Paralelo Boulevard, wide and luminous, plastered with handbills, dreary, but the boulevard didn't get lively until later, when the shows started, and they decided to head back through El Raval, still barhopping, drinking cold wine, slightly sour. Now fewer people were on the street; they began to hear songs sung in chorus and there were characters hanging around on the corners, waiting for something. Only Las Ramblas was still as lively as before, as at any hour of any day. A salty breeze, smelling like the port, wafted among the plane trees, phantasmal in the neon light, thick with birds perched quietly among the leaves. And there, on the patio outside some bar, closing time caught them as if by surprise. They were cleaning up, and the roaring of the cars cranking up their motors right along the sidewalk, and the rolling metal shutters clattering down, was deafening. The side streets had gone dark and unidentifiable groups invaded the sidewalk mixing with the dense trickle of cars and motorbikes and their fitful procession heading up Las Ramblas.

They were tireless. Later, walking along the bland, quiet streets of the Ensanche, they kept on talking and arguing. Sometimes Leo got a kick out of adopting suspicious attitudes to startle the sleepy night watchmen. They laughed. They talked and expounded. First they all walked Federico home, and then Leo accompanied Raúl or Raúl accompanied Leo, and they ended up taking a streetcar, clear and empty. As Raúl entered the house, the light in Papa's room switched on, and when he passed by the door, slightly ajar, he heard a cough, the agitated stirring of a spoon against a glass. But not until he returned from the bathroom did he hear him call: Raúl, he said. Yes, said Raúl. It's very late, son. Where have you been? He looked at him sitting up in bed, wearing a faded shirt with cuffs unbuttoned, clutching a glass of milk. At Federico's house, Papa, said Raúl. And Papa would say: the Quintana boy? He would say that he'd met old man Quintana, a true personage, that the Quintana family were people of great wealth and social standing.

Federico preferred gin and then it didn't take long for his tongue to loosen up, for him to get involved in conversations. He insisted on stopping by Los Maños or the blind men's bar, la Gran Bodega, where small-time pickpockets, thieves, thugs, and con men gathered around the ash-gray wine barrels fashionably turned into tall tables and porróns of *vino verde*. *¡Viva la policía!* he shouted. And the gray-haired man, who was explaining that he came from Melilla, turned around with a bitter look on his face. What d'ya mean, you? The ones nearest them stopped talking and there was a sudden tension of bodies, of pale hands, of heads close together, of shabby berets, of skulls with dark spots showing through scanty hair. Leo intervened. He said, *Viva la policía*. Why? asked the gray head. Because they keep order, said Leo. Fine, said the gray head. But let's hear it in a different tone of voice. I didn't like how that sounded. We understand each other, right? He turned back to his friends. Don't let those little pipsqueaks fool you. Out in the street Federico started singing and Leo said again that the truth is always subversive. He was the one who guided them through the night, who knew all the obscure joints to visit, who decided what they were going to do; Federico didn't know how to find his way anywhere. Let them put me in chains, he said. I want them to arrest me and clap me in irons. Los Maños was a vast smoky space, with a flimsy door and a counter with burners and stews in casseroles. A worker from the slaughterhouse came in and sold the owner a heavy package of cow entrails, which he brought wrapped in pink, dripping newspapers. Afterward they ran into an old man who was gathering up papers and stashing them in a sack; he stood bolt upright on a corner and, as if bursting out of his wide winter jacket, stared at them sweetly, with large, crazed eyes.

A direct experience of reality, immediate, tangible, epidermic, life on the jagged edge, raw naked life inside a whorehouse, a brawl on Saturday night, a roundup of whores, two or three night watchmen or *guardia civil* clubbing some drunkard, an argument between a whore and her pimp, sordid bars, each one with its regular customers, a pack of blind men selling lottery tickets, for example, or pickpockets and petty thieves, or dope dealers, or whores, or just simple jerk-offs, or queens, more whores, more drunks, the foggy assurances of some man who fought along the Ebro, or so he said, the eyes of a whore kissing a marine while she counted the money right behind his blond neck, things you could never learn in a family setting, nor in residential neighborhoods, nor at university, unique experiences, in the face of which all the habits and principles of their own class were just a charade.

The twenty-first of June, Leo had not accompanied them, perhaps still studying for some exam. In the upper part of the city they heard isolated explosions and, occasionally, the trail of a rocket sparkled across the golden afternoon. A neighborhood procession wound through the streets around Los Maños, people playing music and various characters dressed up in peasant clothing, with oversized wooden spoons and suckling pigs and lambs carried over their shoulders. From each bar people came out to present them with bottles, and two or three boys passed around the traditional red Catalan cap—*la barretina*. After another band—now one in uniform—following the chairman, following the large candles and banners, with the priest, came a double file of young boys, and then, preceding the dress uniforms which closed the parade, isolated, haughty, enveloped in veils and redolent of crushed broom, displaying the emblems of virginity and martyrdom, the Saint—an adolescent girl, her chewing gum the only flaw in her performance. They were enraptured by the sylvan scent of those yellow handfuls of broom that people threw before her, as if they were pieces of gold; several whores fell to their knees. What this saint is doing is called unfair competition, said Federico. They followed along the streets draped from side to side with undulating streamers, and now near Las Ramblas, in a quiet and sophisticated bar, with soft music, dimly illuminated by colored light bulbs, they met up with Adolfo Cuadras. He was with a friend and he made room for them at the bar. Alright boys, he said, have something to drink. To his right there was a swirl of loose straight hair and a pair of eyes gazed at him from over a shoulder, above a shoulder strap.

I already know this guy. Don't you remember?

No, said Raúl.

At Adolfo's house, silly. This last winter.

This autumn, said Adolfo Cuadras. This is Nuria Rivas. Then she had only just started at university, she'd had her hair in braids and hadn't said a word.

He introduced them to at least a few other fellows and to a girl whose name was Luisa or María Luisa and who said that she was celebrating her saint's day. She's the saint, said Federico, but the others didn't understand his jest, and he blushed. They were joking, and Nuria, with her back to the bar, sitting astride the stool, closed and parted her knees beneath her mini-skirt. She nodded to Federico. And this one? she said. Is he one of those quiet types? She talked freely, dropping the occasional swear word, loose tongue and casual manners. It was fun; they were in another bar, surely somewhere around Calle Escudillers, and everyone insisted that they not leave. It's Luisa's turn to pay tonight, they shouted. And Luisa laughed and repeated: look you're all going to end up drunk. Nuria was hanging on Adolfo Cuadras's arm.

What I don't understand is why you all have to drink so much, she said. One drink does it for me.

Well, each to his own, said Adolfo Cuadras.

They ate something in some kind of grocery with mountains of sandwiches displayed on the counter and legs of ham hanging from the beams, lean, dark, like mahogany. Federico had ordered another gin, and Raúl noticed that Nuria's shoulders were lightly freckled.

I can't forgive you for not even remembering me, she said. You look like you're wondering, did I go to bed with her?

Well, really, that's the first thing to get straight, said Raúl.

And Federico said: so you were a virgin then? They ended up at Nuria's house, in the living room with the doors closed and the windows open. They talked about families, parents. She sat facing him, perched on the arm of a chair, with one thigh resting on the other and her elbow against the backrest, next to Adolfo Cuadras's head. She stretched a strand of hair toward her mouth, without even looking once at Raúl, then suddenly she stood up to change the record. Adolfo Cuadras barely joined in the conversation; he was smoking a pipe, listening, his neck against the headrest. On the sofa, Federico was explaining that it was a solemn moment, because it would take another three hundred and sixty-five days before the sun would once more precisely intersect the Tropic of Cancer. He tried to play the piano and dance with Luisa, but in the end he started wandering around. The apartment seemed spacious; there was a predominance of wood and, in the corner with the fireplace, there were bookshelves and copper knickknacks. Come back again whenever you feel like it, said Nuria. Just pick up the phone.

For the evening festivities the three of them went out. On the eve of the feast of San Juan the city was lit up by the splendid glow of bonfires, by the volleys of fireworks, disintegrating in partial and discontinuous images, fleeting, chaotic, angular, beneath the explosion of the rockets and the rain of sparks and the fizzling star castles and the brilliant flaring sparklers and the zipping eruption of a brick of firecrackers, a chain of explosions, zigzagging through those compact blocks deafeningly loud, shooting through like intermittent hot coals in the blackness. Breathing in the clouds of gunpowder, little by little, the low sky going quiet in a soft smoky cardinal red blur. It was muggy and the streets shone brightly, thronged with boisterous turbulent revelers, tangled up in the shredded streamers and splashed confetti. Along the sidewalks, the bars were illumined by the deep hues of Chinese lanterns, vibrant fringed streamers, and little paper flags. They found a spot in the corner of the bar, next to the fan. The owner was wearing a red cardboard fez and his wife a cap of pink silk paper that went very well with her whorish face, whose reflection in the metal butane canisters looked far more beautiful than the real thing. The music played louder than usual.

What are we doing here? said Francisco. We'll just run into boring old Count Adolfo. This place is his personal fiefdom.

Adolfo Cuadras? said Leo. What've you got against him?

He's a spoiled little prick, said Federico.

Well, he doesn't seem like a bad guy to me, said Leo. All things considered, he's one of the best guys at the university.

No way, said Federico. He's an asshole. Besides, he smokes a pipe.

In the Plaza del Teatro someone gave them a more-or-less-phallic-shaped mauve balloon. There were booths selling flat cakes—*cocas*—brightly lit by candle lanterns, stands selling hats, cane flutes, scarecrows, party hooters called *espantasuegras*—designed, as the name implied, to frighten anyone's mother-in-law—fake mustaches, and shrill toy trumpets. Revelers converged on the spot from every direction. It felt like there might be a big brawl, and then some drunken guy tried to get everybody together, to make them listen. Well, here we are, in the navel of the world, said Leo. And he proposed that at dawn they go to the open-air cafés in Barceloneta, then watch the sunrise on the beach, among families and couples and sticky used rubbers tossed onto the sand.

They asked about Teresa. Federico said she was clever and very good-looking. Why don't you go out with her?

What about you? said Leo. Why don't you take her out, instead of sitting there all quiet in the corner?

She's only got eyes for you, said Federico. And she'll end up chasing you. One of these days she'll jump you in the fitting room, and then you'll have to marry her.

Raúl had run into her that evening when, in the fading afternoon, he went to pick up Leo. Entering the building's vestibule he heard her calling him and turned to see her running across the street, a hanger in her hand. She was wearing a light-colored housecoat, sleeveless, buttoned in the back, and some light sandals loose at the heel. Hey you, she said, let's see if you tell Leo to let me come out with you guys. She preceded him through the damp shadows, up the steep stairs, and on each landing the gray clarity of a small open arch at floor level highlighted her too-chunky calves. They were all in the loft; their father was cutting, piecing sections together in shirtsleeves, with his glasses on, and her sister was at the sewing machine. The canary was twittering in its cage to one side of the window, and Raúl could glimpse a still sunlit terrace roof where poor boys and girls were hanging small Chinese lanterns and paper streamers, and testing their record player. Federico arrived and, with shy, elusive eyes, sat down next to Leo and lit a cigarette. The brother-in-law also showed up, smelling of lotion, his bluish cheeks freshly shaven, his already gray-streaked hair perfectly wavy; he listened in silence. Then he reappeared in shirtsleeves, hairy and taciturn, and the first explosions could be heard outside in the streets. Teresa and her sister sat apart whispering together, Teresa leaning her elbow on the machine, sewing the seat of a pair of pants. Her father paused and, looking over the top of his glasses, suggested something cold to drink. Are you hot? he said. And then they said yes, and started to laugh. We're very hot, said Teresa. She touched her forehead, and the other pretended to cover her sister's mouth.

Alright, alright, said their father. Instead of talking, go get a few beers. What are you doing with your arms crossed?

They drank beer, the sister drank soda pop, and they explained to them that they were planning to go and eat *cocas* on Montjuich, all of them, including the children. Teresa said: maybe it'll bring me good luck and I'll get a boyfriend and, then, we'll get engaged. They laughed again. C'mon, you, that's enough already, said her sister. Watch out or you'll turn into an animal. The worktable was a dining room table and there were disordered patterns lying underneath heavy pairs of scissors. The radio was in the corner by the sofa bed, between worn-out chairs, atop a small table covered with a runner that hung over the sides like a shawl, slack and faded, with a fringe of yellow beads. And the father was saying:

Listen, Ferrer, I want you to understand me: first and foremost, I'm a humanist. And what that means is that I'm for the human being. I believe in progress, and that the world, sooner or later, will take a leap forward, the same way that water, when it reaches the boiling point, turns into steam. And after this leap forward—call it revolution or whatever—a new era will begin, a society without classes will be born where each person will be provided for according to their needs. That's where the world is going, toward socialism, and you people, the educated ones, the technicians, the scientists, are the men of tomorrow. Not us, we already tried once and we failed, precisely because we weren't prepared. You see, I'm the first to say it, and I've fought, and I've done time in jail. And my son-in-law, he was very young then, but he had his ideals and he was always on the front lines, he'll tell you the same thing. We didn't serve for nothing, and we can only show you, with what we did, the things you shouldn't repeat.

Don't worry, what's got to be done the next time is perfectly clear, said the brother-in-law. And that'll sure be a good fiesta. A really big one, I mean.

He spoke brusquely, contentious, and if they asked him some question he looked at them with suspicion. The father waited, letting him finish, and afterward, as if closing a parenthesis, moved to conclude the sentence where he'd been interrupted. Their memories contrasted, and the conversation concluded by drifting toward anecdotes about the Civil War: the assault on the Atarazanas barracks, the disorder in the Republican camp, Teruel, the fall of Alicante, the retreat, the jails, the firing squads. And at last when Leo stood up, the father stood up, too, his voice uncertain, his eyes feverish, searching. Excuse me, he said. Forgive me if I waste your time with my stories. I'm not someone who's had a lot of schooling. I can't measure up to you either in studies or in culture, but all these things I'm talking to you about are things that I can pass on because I've lived them. And I believe that you, who are the men of tomorrow, need to know them.

It was a season of fires. Not a day went by without hearing, at some moment, the fire engines' sirens fading into the distance. The newspaper covered the string of fires, reporting how in such and such a warehouse, or industrial plant, at such and such a number on this or that street, in spite of or thanks to the opportune and effective intervention by the firemen, etcetera. Raúl read in the shade of the plum tree, in the back part of the garden. He arose late and, while he ate breakfast, Eloísa gathered up the fallen plums. She said that they were the best and she complained about the birds that, even before dawn, flew down to eat them. When she felt like chatting she sat on the steps, with the plums hammocked in her apron, and after some innocuous question she made him put aside his reading and they talked a while. She told him that when she went to the market no one could believe that her hair was natural, that thick braid rolled up like a crown with which now she fiddled around tenderly, chubby and satisfied. Raúl made her some joke about men and she assured him that however much they flirted and teased her she didn't even bother to look at them. Men! she said. They were questions and responses already well-known, commentaries already commented, a chat that always observed the proper tone. How old must she have been? Fifty-something, beneath that appearance at once both infantile and coquettish? Thursday and Sunday afternoons she went out, mysteriously. To see some relatives, she said.

Once in a while a new plum fell and if Raúl was alone it didn't take long for him to hear the stirring of the birds among the leaves. Then he took a stroll, going up through the neighborhood to where the streets ended, cut short by the slopes of dry grass; then he climbed the sinuous paths and from some steep slope along the barren hills he contemplated the immense city, sunken in its lowering haze, shot through with sun, with the moraceous bulk of Montjuich rising up in the distance.

Around mid-afternoon he usually met with Federico. Leo was out of town since the feast of San Pedro, even since before, spending some days in the village. And one night Federico invited him to his house; he asked him over the phone, sounding quite casual. They put on records, lazily slumped in padded leather armchairs, and a maid served them whiskey on the rocks. It was a quiet, impeccable room, and the adjoining dining room, just a step or two slightly higher, also gave the sensation of hardly ever being used. They dined facing each other in the middle of a long oval table, and the chandelier above their heads seemed to be a cascading spider of shimmering tears. Federico explained to him that his family had left for summer vacation; he spoke little and smiled as if concealing some joke, as if mulling over some hidden complicity. Afterward they went out, but without Leo the usual bars didn't feel the same; they didn't know how to get involved in conversations, how to provoke the most unthinkable situation with a single phrase. They felt flat, extinguished, out of place, and now returning home, sleepy, they agreed that they had to discover some new place to go.

And it ended up happening on its own. A woman with a very affected voice answered the phone, and Nuria took awhile to pick up. Oh, yes, come over right away, she said. I've been having the worst afternoon; I read the same paragraph three times and I still don't even get what it says. They'd had quite a lot to drink and Federico got carried away. Nuria greeted them at the door in blue jeans and a black shirt, her eyes bright, like a sprite; the vestibule smelled of blonde tobacco and, further inside, they heard the sound of heels, on the parquet floor, walking away. They went up to the attic on the top floor by an interior staircase. Nuria running, her light, straight hair sweeping her shoulders. Here, we'll be by ourselves, she said. It was a large, comfortable room, with the bed set into a set of shelves, with oaken doors and, facing the terrace window, a spacious desk covered with books and papers. Outside on the terrace there were two or three canvas chairs and a portable record player, and the view from the edge, at the railing, was dominated by a compact panorama of rooftops and terraces. They drank gin, and Nuria pulled out a lighter that felt heavy in her shirt pocket and spoiled the line of her bosom.

I like your shirt, said Raúl.

It's my brother's, said Nuria. Since he's getting taller, his things fit me really well now, so I wear them.

They smoked sitting on the floor, hugging their knees. Federico looked through the records by himself, as if to kill the time. Leo Ferrer, he murmured. You like Leo Ferrer. And suddenly he asked: if you smoke why don't you drink? And she said: are you stupid or do you just say stupid things? Federico started laughing. Look how mean she treats me, he said, and pouring himself some more gin he listened to them talk, his face flushed, with smiling heavy eyelids. What did they talk about? Nuria was cracking jokes, abruptly, aggressive, and Raúl followed the game. As it grew dark they turned on the light, under the awning of brown heather, and Nuria stroked her Siamese cat, a keen, inscrutable cat. Someone mentioned Adolfo Cuadras. I love him very much, said Nuria. I've known him since I was a little girl, from the summertime, and he seemed so much older to me. She said it now in the doorway, when they were leaving. And then Señor Rivas arrived, cordial and expansive, from playing tennis a while or, at least, with the look of having done so; he held open the elevator door meanwhile he stretched out his hand to them like a friend. A youthful man, his hair beautifully white in contrast with his tanned skin, his eyes the same as Nuria's, and from the threshold he still smiled at them, with one hand resting on the nape of her neck.

Immediately, Federico said:

You liked her, tell the truth.

What about you?

Nope, you first: tell the truth, admit it.

Well the thing is she's not bad at all. She's got something that makes me pretty horny.

Well I prefer Santa Luisa, she gets me much hornier. This one is a cautious, sober girl: a little bourgeois Catalana, modern, with her cats, her record albums, and her little intellectual dabbling. No doubt she's a disciple of Count Adolfo. Santa Luisa is a lot more funny, she's more real, more feminine. Why don't we go out with her?

The next time he went back to her house alone, also around mid-afternoon, and he suggested that they take a walk. They went to the Plaza Real and had something to drink under the arches, contemplating the short wheeling flight of the pigeons whose shadows flowed across the yellow facades in the setting sun, as if tossed up suddenly into the air. They generally met there to talk, seated on any terrace under the arches, and afterward they strolled Calle Escudillers for a while, stopping here and there for tapas. They also walked around the south side of Las Ramblas, toward Calle Robadors, past whores who gazed after them and characters who stopped to look at her, make comments, softly sing suggestive snatches of song as they walked by. They stepped into a bar, and in the reddish glare, the people opened a small space to let them in. Raúl smoked a bit mechanically, barely hearing the observations she was sharing with him, covering her from behind with his arm reaching to the bar. Hey kid, he heard them saying. Man enough to handle that all by yourself? Nuria, however, was absolutely at ease, hanging on his arm, laughing, sticking out her tongue, thumbing her nose at them. She pulled away and paused at length in front of a display case of condoms. Let them say what they want, she said. They didn't go to Los Maños, let alone La Gran Bodega. With Nuria, Raúl preferred to visit the sophisticated bars near Las Ramblas, the jazz caverns, the flamenco venues. They talked about sexual prejudices, about inhibitions causing frigidity, homosexuality, and religion. Nuria admitted to believing vaguely, although she didn't practice; neither did her father, and she still remembered her mother's recent attempts to take them to twelve o'clock Mass as if to a social gathering. Why does the world have to have a creative principle distinct from itself? said Raúl. Why does God not need a creator but the world does? Nuria thought about it. Adolfo thinks the same as you, she said. He says the same thing about almost everything. One of those afternoons the three of them went out together. Nuria's mother had started the summer vacation with the little ones; Nuria stayed in Barcelona with her father and a housemaid. At most, her father might appear around lunchtime, and that afternoon, when they had already decided to stay in the house, quietly, to listen to records, Adolfo Cuadras showed up. He showed no surprise nor did he ask anything, no more reticent than on other occasions. Sitting loosely, he talked with Raúl about exams, etcetera. Nuria reappeared in a change of clothes. Let's go out, alright? she said, and they went out. Adolfo

Cuadras asked about Federico, and Leo.

Leo who? said Nuria. Leopoldo?

Just Leo, said Raúl. He was born in August and they named him Leo. But officially his name is Leonardo. He's one of those babies who were baptized after the war.

Do you all study the same thing?

Not Federico; he studies mathematics.

And I'm the old man in the class, said Adolfo Cuadras.

They occupied exactly the same seats as before, with Nuria between the two of them, with her back to the bar. In the mirror facing them, behind the bar, above the lines of bottles and the commemorative photos, her light hair was highlighted by the cloudy penumbra of subtle colors. Their conversation was dry, sticking with safe, general questions, the merits of some work by Sartre, or Pavese, the moral and intellectual asphyxia of the times they lived in, the lack of unrest demonstrated by students at the university, the mediocrity of everything. Nuria said that things were even worse in the School of Philosophy and Letters, that one single class had been enough to leave her feeling fed up with that parochial environment of priests and monks, of exhausted, pale-faced young men, of girls studying simply to find a fiancé or because they were in despair of finding one. They wandered aimlessly, walking in circles, and the winding streets turned gray in the long afternoon. But Adolfo Cuadras took them to La Venta. There were two flamenco dancers with red heels and, in a corner, a guitarist who wasn't playing, and a man selling peanuts, strips of dried codfish, and hard-boiled eggs. The guitarist was a gypsy—fat, serious, gray-haired, with hands like small toads. There were also customers, leaning against the bar, drawing the sluttish waitresses with their witty conversation. And one of the drag queens passed by in front of their table, haughty, twitching her tight black pear-shaped ass, looking at them rudely as she broke out in a hoarse verse of fandango. It smelled like a urinal, like a basement. There was a false parapet and a false window with iron grillwork, with paper flowers, and the walls were covered by a latticework frame of green lath, simulating an outdoor patio, all of it quite shabby, in the low light of dim bulbs.

It's too early, said Adolfo Cuadras. This place gets lively at night, very late, when the bars close.

We can come back another day. Any other night we're out around here.

Yes, we'll have to come back.

They were sitting on the terrace, in the shade of the heather-covered trellis. Nuria played one record after another; she said that the maid's room was right below them, that she knew for a fact the maid sat by her open window to eavesdrop on them.

I love him very much, she said. But sometimes he exasperates me. He stares and stares at me, and his eyes get big like a sheep's. Poor Adolfo.

She explained that he'd been in love with her forever, almost since she was a little girl, when they spent their summers in the same town. And he had never dared to tell her explicitly nor tried to touch her. He was fairly attractive with his shadowy, angular face, and there had been a time during which, if he'd been more daring, he might've gotten her to pay attention to him. He'd been very ill for quite some time, with tuberculosis, and she thought he'd get over her. But no, with the illness he only missed a year of his studies. He lent her books and wrote poems.

And who hasn't written some at one age or another? said Raúl.

Well, the thing is that his were really good. If he studies law it's only to justify himself in his family's eyes, to do something, anything, because being a writer is something you can't just declare ahead of time. But now he writes stories, and I'm sure that sooner or later, he'll decide to dedicate himself entirely to writing.

She turned to face him, hesitant, disturbed. And I'd like to do the same, she added. And from the edge of her chair, her elbows on her knees together, she revealed to him all her plans, all her doubts. She'd forgotten her cigarette in the ashtray and she uttered her words hastily, nervously. Drop out of the university? Work as a secretary for her father? Open a bookstore specializing in art books? Her father had proposed to finance the venture. Go to England to study languages, and so have more time there to write? They talked it out. Raúl made her see that working as a secretary for her father would always be a phantom job, and that books, from the point of view of the bookseller, were, definitively, units of merchandise like any other. If I could go to England, he said, I wouldn't think twice. To England or anywhere. And he confessed that he didn't have the least interest in pursuing a career in law, that he was only studying it because he wanted to be a diplomat.

I hear that's a tremendous career, said Nuria. Travel, see other countries.

And above all, it leaves you time to write, study, or do whatever you feel like. By the way, let's see if you'll show me what you write.

Oh, no, laughed Nuria. I don't plan on doing that until I've got something that's really worth the trouble.

They realized that it was late. A light, refreshing breeze was blowing. Nuria, seated next to him, opened her arms across the backrest, as if stretching. It's fine to talk that way, about these things, once in a while, she said. The day had been hot and, after lunch, Raúl walked up to the bone-dry hillsides, while the sun went down, distorted by the dusty haze. He arrived all sweaty, and Nuria asked him if he didn't want to shower. He heard her singing lightly and then she passed him a bath towel through the door that was slightly ajar. Raúl had given her a trinket he'd bought at a booth on the street, a tiny cardboard elephant, pink and squat, with a vaguely obscene nakedness. They sat on the terrace, side by side, and he made quite sure to not touch her.

Intrigued, they tried to get him to spill the beans. But Raúl wouldn't let himself be caught off guard.

How's it going with the little lady? asked Leo.

What little lady?

Well, I already know who it is: one of Count Adolfo's disciples.

They argued again. Raúl said that Adolfo Cuadras wasn't such a bad guy, that he was smart and worth knowing.

And if this coming year we want to do something in the university, of course we'll have to include him. If there were only more like him.

He's a metaphysic and a dandy, said Federico. Come on, he's a hollow stiff, a bore. You only have to take one look at him, dammit. A dandy.

And you think you look like a worker. Well, it's not enough to just remove your tie to stop looking like a rich boy.

They heard a siren, coming closer, penetrating, and the traffic was interrupted by whistle blasts. Two or three onlookers emerged from the cafeteria, and a few customers on the patio stood up to watch the red fire trucks flashing past along the suddenly empty avenue. When it was over, Leo drew their attention to a clutch of old men at a neighboring table who were listening wearily to their conversation. It was in the Nebraska or the Arkansas or some similar joint, next to Federico's house.

It's our lot to live in a somber time, Leo began.

He pretended to sound pensive even as they furtively exchanged malicious glances.

Bad times, yes. One might say that we're on the threshold of a new Middle Ages. For the last several years, the West has been doing nothing but going from surrender to surrender: first the Asians, then the Africans, and even the Papuans. In the end, you'll see, it'll be those people who will end up sticking their noses right in our own business here at home.

Well, the fact is, from that point of view, the decadence of the West, thanks to its loss of position and influence, is not even worth discussing. I was referring to its own internal decomposition, to the social upheavals that are corroding it like a cancer.

Right. To the triumph of the masses, to that society of robots toward which we're moving slowly but surely.

Exactly. One way or the other, come hell or high water, that's where we're headed. A world of equality where there won't be any room for private enterprise, a world without stimulating benefits or incentives of any kind.

Neither spirituality nor religion serves to impede human instincts, to slow even the most basic passions.

A vulgar and materialistic world.

And it's logical. What else can you expect when the upper classes disappear and the lower classes end up in power? Especially when they're people without culture, without ideals, without any notion of a fatherland or any other interests than their pitiful wages.

It was pleasant to be able to understand one another with a simple glance, with half-uttered words or, even, with no words at all. Leo had come back quite tanned, fortified, with even greater vitality. One of these mornings they were going to Barceloneta to take a swim, or maybe late in the day, when the beach emptied of families and the whores started showing up. The sand was a little bit powdery, and where the swells broke there was almost always a scummy line of people's trash. But they dove in and swam a long ways out, to the clean blue waters. Then they stripped off, splashed around, and let themselves drift with bathing trunks in hand. They sunbathed and entertained themselves contemplating the well-toned athletes who strutted in public, arrogant, muscles tense, their tight bulging bikini briefs well-packed, with a packet of blonde tobacco sticking halfway out of the waistband just above the thigh, and a small gold medallion between their hairy pectorals. And at the pool, the exhibitionists on the diving board and the creepy faggots waiting to pounce. Afterward they drank a beer in the bar, under the shade of the thatched awning. One Sunday, Floreal accompanied them and they asked him once again about the general strike in '51, the streetcar boycott, the cars burned, the direct action, the mass demonstrations, the cars set on fire. There was a climate of true exasperation and we managed to create a pre-revolutionary situation. He explained his job at the bank, the employees' empty consciences, so out of touch, earning the same as a laborer they thought themselves better than simply for wearing a necktie. They talked about the shop assistants and grocers' boys, the worst of them all.

When I was young, I had sketched out a plan for robbing my father's bank, said Federico. He's been a big shot for so long you can't even imagine how much I'm uninterested in finance. But of course I tell him I am. For my part, the revolution would be worthwhile if it were only to see how he'd take refuge in any boat docked in the harbor flying a foreign flag, just to see him hobble up the gangway disguised as a whore.

They made the trip back uptown on the streetcars, squeezed in among hot, sweaty passengers, wet canvas bags, encrusted with coarse sand. The line was long and Raúl had suggested taking a taxi but Floreal said it wasn't worth the trouble. Leo didn't seem to care either; he laughed and joked, separated from them by the crush of passengers, imitating the girls. Every morning he took a sandwich and he ate it in the bar, washed it down with a beer. That's what Raúl preferred, the everyday calm, when the beach wasn't excessively crowded and the bar never lacked an open table. And there were two girls sipping Coca-Cola from a straw and Leo began to act silly and say things to them, and Raúl the same, and they ended up picking them up. Federico kept quiet, remaining on the outside, and had to wait for them. Leo came out smiling. Raúl's girl, however, while they were changing in a double-sized changing room, only let him touch her and, when they kissed, some residual food, perhaps some meat fiber or strands of orange pith, slipped from her mouth into his. Her breath smelled bad.

He spoke with Nuria on the phone and they agreed to meet up as always. When he arrived, she opened the door for him herself, in one swift pull, and she looked at him significantly. Come up, come up, Adolfo's here, she said. On the terrace, Adolfo Cuadras was listening to some poem from *Les Fleurs du Mal* sung by Ferré. He smiled pleasantly.

I thought I'd come by in case you two felt like taking a walk, he said.

Whatever you like, said Nuria. You two go out. I prefer to stay home.

She complained that nothing had gone exactly right for her all day, one of those days when everything goes backward. She listed the advantages of being a woman, an object so respected that she couldn't permit herself any of the liberties the come so free and easy to men. She expressed herself mockingly, mixing in here and there the requisite shits and fucks and goddammits with the greatest aplomb. Raúl asked Adolfo about some book, and they exchanged impressions about their classmates, about the monotonous and languid university life. Nuria drew herself apart, dragged a large cushion to the railing, and sat sideways against the balusters, in silence, almost turning her back on them. She was wearing a light, pastel dress, and it made Raúl think she was going without a bra. I think I'll end up hating Baudelaire, they heard her say after a little while, without turning around, dejectedly laying her face on the railing. They put on another record, and it was then when Raúl noticed that she was looking at him over Adolfo Cuadras. The conversation started stretching out, with increasingly longer pauses between one sentence and the next. Raúl responded with vagaries; he had to make an effort to say something, and even more to pay attention to what was being said. It began to grow dark, but nobody got up to turn on the light. Then Adolfo Cuadras gathered up his tobacco, his lighter.

Well, he said. I'll leave you two alone.

Nuria didn't move.

Ciao, Adolfo, she said. I won't see you out, alright?

Nevertheless, she stood up immediately and moved the cushion over by the record player. She took a drink of gin, lit a cigarette. He's such a bore sometimes, the poor guy, she said. She had sat at his feet, and thanks to the plunging neckline Raúl confirmed that she actually wasn't wearing a bra. They were almost there in the dark and there was a silence. Then, Raúl slid down to the floor. I feel sorry for him, he said. They kissed, deeply, she clinging to his neck, intertwined, twisted around, and between his hands appeared her breasts, very white in the faint light. They found themselves inside, atop the bed, and everything happened in a way that was, perhaps, rushed. It was in the second half of July, a Thursday, possibly a Sunday, and they were alone in the house, the maid had gone out. He stayed lying down in bed, naked, and she returned wrapped in a bath towel and said: looks to me like you got what you were after, Raúl. That night, of course, they spoke again on the phone. A long conversation.

Sometimes they forgot the record player and then Nuria had to get up and go out to the terrace in a rush, barely covered, to load it up again with LPs. They joked, they played, they experimented, and the time went quickly by, experimenting, testing the effects of lifting up a leg until folding it over her tits, or of lifting up both of them, stretching them out, or of sitting face to face, rocking back and forth in an embrace, or of doing it from behind, on all fours, hooked together like dogs, problems of angulation, of inclination, of twisted desires, a demonstrated taste for difficult positions. Those games and those experiments which suddenly turned into something different, that sudden seriousness which swallowed their laughter as in a mute struggle, that tickling sensation and the rolling over to a squeezing and tremulous embrace while, with the record player stopped again, from outside came voices and cries, the sounds of little children. A sudden bias, the brusque change of tone when he was inside her and, as if in spite of herself, all sarcasm abandoned, her poise was broken and, with a pained expression, her head rolled upon her tousled hair, closing her eyes as her breathing came faster, tighter, then grunting and gasping madly, her rising spasm proudly achieved. Afterward they smoked, lying very close, and she exposed her worries to him. She leaned up on her bent elbow.

What do you think, Pipo?

That you're wrong, *hombrecilla*.

Don't call me "little man." And tell me, why am I wrong?

What about you, why do you call me Pipo?

And she: because I feel like it, dammit.

And then she turned over, and he held her down, immobile, and they recommenced the game, warmly sweaty. But the hours were always short and they had to get dressed all in a hurry. Nuria fixed her hair, masked her flushed face with powder. She also remade the bed and washed the towel, and put it out to dry on the terrace. She said she didn't trust the maid, that little young woman who, when she opened the door for Raúl, smiled like an accomplice and moved so silently.

They'll end up catching us, she said.

She spoke about her family relations, about her father, a man of an extraordinarily youthful and open character, of good instinctive taste, capable of juggling the paper factory and tennis, and tennis with a true passion for art and books, gallery shows, concerts. The night before they had gone out together, she said, her father took her to have dinner and then to an open-air cabaret, happy—she assured Raúl—as a twenty-year-old boy. My mother is different, she said.

Señor Rivas seemed to feel sympathy for Raúl and never asked what they had done. He received them cordially, without formalities, when they arrived at the house, and he drew Nuria to him, hugging her against him, saying that his Nuri was the most lovely and intelligent woman in the world. They chatted about hunting, and Señor Rivas showed him some photos of the spaniels that he had at their country house, for duck hunting. Raúl had to promise him that next winter they would go hunting together some weekend.

By then they knew that they were going to be apart for two weeks, the first half of August; that her father was taking some vacation and Nuria had to accompany him. Now they hardly went out to the bars, and they even seemed tired of the Plaza Real. They didn't go out much at all, at most to have a drink in some café in the upper part of the city. One day he took her home to his house, the day she gave him the tiny turtle, and they went to set it loose in the garden. They sat for a while on the steps, contemplating the turtle's cautious exploration. They discussed which sex it might be, agreeing that it was most likely a male. Nuria proposed that they call him *Camarlengo*, meaning Chamberlain. But given that it was a turtle and, above all, for the splendidly designed shield that was his shell, they agreed to call him Achilles. Eloísa had received them with suspicion, seemingly stunned, and disappeared immediately; but, when they went back out, Raúl perceived the delicate click of the slats of a Persian blind and, like an almost physical sensation, the weight of her gaze which followed them out onto the street.

The evening before she left it was he who gave her a new present: a big ugly bird. All his money was spent and he had to sell more books, dusty leather-bound volumes which a secondhand bookshop bought from him: *Ascent of Mount Carmel*, *The Sinner's Guide*, *The Mansions*, an illustrated edition of *Paradise Lost*, etcetera. But the ugly bird seduced him the moment he saw it, as he passed by the shop window, a ceramic piece in dark, gloomy tones, an amalgam of friar and hookbill bird, something a schizophrenic might design.

I hope it doesn't bring bad luck, said Nuria. Depending how you hold it, it looks sort of like a crow.

No. It's a beneficent being. Ugly, but good.

It was not an afternoon like the others. She seemed somewhat withdrawn, lying on her side staring at the ceiling. All of a sudden she rolled over onto Raúl and he caressed her back, her small hard buttocks.

But do you love me? said Nuria.

Of course, silly, said Raúl.

She looked at him, her pupils inscrutable from so close; then he felt her slide off, hugging him. They got dressed sooner than usual and, seated on the terrace, they listened to some song, *le rouge pour naître à Barcelone, le noir pour mourir à Paris*.

Maybe I could just not go to England, said Nuria. Maybe I can learn languages from here.

But why? Seems absurd to me. If I could go, I wouldn't think twice.

Nuria didn't respond. She smoked, the Siamese cat asleep on her knees. In the street outside, the open windows of summertime were alive, illuminated with voices and people. They said goodbye, and then she put a sealed envelope into his hand and squeezed his fingers. Don't read it until tomorrow, she said. Promise me. And she closed the door without waiting for him to step into the elevator.

He read it standing against a streetlamp, all in a rush, and walked back home, a song in his heart. There he read it again, and only the next day did he try to decide if it was better to answer right away or better to wait, if his response should be brief, or if he should write at length. He'd planned to go out with Leo, but beforehand he shut himself in his room and wrote his letter over and over again, until he managed to get the right tone all the way through.

They were having an argument, and the canary's pecking at the fine wires of the cage was getting quite annoying. The revolution has got to be peaceful, her father repeated to make himself heard. And the sister ended up joining in, from where she was ironing, leaning over the white swirls of steam. Let's see if you can't talk quieter, my goodness, the whole neighborhood is going to hear you.

Then her father took the opportunity to insist that violence doesn't achieve anything, proved perfectly by the Civil War. Back then, they stood up to power empty-handed.

But you've got to look for some way to get people fired up, goddammit! shouted the brother-in-law. Or do you think the same thing didn't happen before? And how were the strikes broken? With guns! With bombs! You've got to wake people up. Now they don't think about anything besides soccer. You've got to give them a good shock to wake them the hell up.

The others just listened from the sidelines. Leo, Federico, and Floreal all appeared to be amused. Teresa listened and kept quiet. Raúl had seated himself on the sofa and, inevitably, his eyes wandered to the big color picture in front of him, a reproduction of some academic painting, no doubt, which showed Nero stroking a lyre and watching Rome burn to the ground. Her father talked about how it was necessary to educate people, about people being prepared, and the brother-in-law interrupted him again, saying that the true revolutionary was the one who lived like a dog, that you shouldn't trust anyone else. When the worm turns, then we'll settle the scores, he said.

There was a moment of tension, and her father looked at Raúl and at Federico over the top of his glasses, as if embarrassed. But the brother-in-law continued his harangue, saying that not even the workers were organizing, not even when they really had nothing to lose, just their miserable salaries or a ticket to the soccer match. He shook his index finger, struck the table with his fist. If not, come to the factory and you'll see. I'm an optical technician, and I've seen how people change when they reach my level.

Before leaving they looked into the little windowless inner bedroom, where, under the bed, in a suitcase, her father kept the remains of his library, works by Marx and Engels, Lenin, Bakunin, in old editions from before the war. These days, this is a treasure, said his father. And Leo let them borrow another book. Floreal went out with them.

I like your brother-in-law, said Federico.

He's a good guy, said Leo. But he talks too much.

And Floreal: all bark and no bite.

He said he still had the mentality of the same people who'd caused the war, that he was still an anarchist at heart. He doesn't understand that the basis of everything lies in mass action, and that the only possible tactic is to attract the petite bourgeoisie, and even the non-monopolistic bourgeoisie oppressed by the oligarchy. There's your true enemy, right there: capital, in the hands of the big feudal landowners. He left them at the Metro entrance, cocking his chin at them, heading down the steps with a cigarette stuck to his lips, hands in his pockets.

Well, said Federico. But this Floreal, is he a communist or is he not a communist? I mean, if he's a member of the party.

Of course, you idiot, said Raúl. You just figured that out?

Leo started laughing. A Kremlin agent, he said. Thick as a brick, this was the bad part about him; too dogmatic and simplistic, maybe because they'd sent his father to the firing squad. And he had grown up in an atmosphere of such politicization that he went around as if his ideology were the most natural thing in the world, something that the people, oppressed by a powerful few, should necessarily share, without any qualms or doubts whatsoever. In this way he allows himself to be alienated, the same as my father or my brother-in-law. Otherwise, he's the only one in my family you can talk to. And he used to like going out, having some fun. If I know the Barrio Chino from one end to the other, it's thanks to him. Not anymore, now he's married and his wife won't let him, she's a kind of puritan leftist. And when they do go out around there it's to go to the movies or to take their little boy for a walk. That's all, he only goes to soccer matches.

Federico had become meditative. He said that his interest in Marxism was purely philosophical, lacking any sentimentality. Workers, individually, don't concern me. What interests me is their historical role, the fact that, for being the only ones with nothing to lose, they are destined to herald the revolution.

It's just that if you try to solve their personal problems then you're talking about charity.

Right. In reality, what it's all about is class solutions, not individual solutions.

And, of course, the worst are le petite bourgeoisie.

Exactly. Their historical role is always objectively reactionary. In a certain way, one could almost say that monopoly capital is more revolutionary.

They argued about whether the revolution was really a historical necessity, as Leo said, or whether it was not and, precisely for that reason, had to occur. That was Federico's theory. They agreed that the goal was to liberate mankind from all types of alienation; not simply to improve the living conditions of the working class, whose objective situation converted them into a potential subject of the revolution: de-alienation.

They wandered, and they found their rapport, their unity of ideas, their camaraderie of shared concerns to be stimulating. The complicity created by their conversations was exciting, the discovery of a secret world of relationships and activities, clandestine, underlying, imperceptible in appearance, as if camouflaged by the life of the city, by the most quotidian realities. The first contacts, the first meetings with Marsal, with Escala, the first meetings of the cell in nondescript outdoor locations.

They went back to their usual haunts. They offered them joints of marijuana for five pesetas, and there was a whore who strolled back and forth along the bar, more stoned than drunk, shouting *eso, eso, a lo loco*—yes, that's right, get crazy—and she yawned and shook out her hair and fanned herself with a magazine and flirted her skirt and roared with laughter. She looked at them; I'm dying for something to refresh my mouth, she said. Neither Raúl nor Leo had any money and they invited themselves to a drink on Federico. Federico always had a little extra, but he didn't usually buy drinks and he paid for his share almost furtively, as if he was embarrassed. He asked Raúl about his girl. He seemed to be in a good mood and he told them they were playing with fire.

And your little sweetheart?

Just fine, thanks.

And Teresa? he asked Leo. I don't understand why you all don't go out together. The four of you. Raúl with his little baby doll, and you with Teresa. Are you biased because she works for your father? If not, why don't you go out with her?

Why don't you take her out? I already told you I'd let you have her.

I prefer Santa Luisa; she's more prissy. The three of us could get married together: Raúl with his girl, you with Teresa, and me with Santa Luisa. Why don't we do it? You've got to play with fire.

They rambled on about women, about marriage. Leo said they thought too much about it, that he preferred a wide playing field, a broad landscape. Women only interest me on Saturday night. They all agreed that the important thing was to not get married.

A country landscape? said Federico. I've never been out in the country. Well, just driving, seeing it that way, on a trip.

He was noticeably distracted from their conversation, chatting at the same time with one of the bar girls, attentive to her coming and going as the customers flagged her down. They were in a bar that had recently reopened, now transformed into a café. Federico drank several glasses of gin and ended up agreeing to meet the girl at closing time. Looks like this is my Saturday night, he said. And there was a guy with the face of an overripe sodomite with oily jet-black hair forming a big wave across his forehead, another guy with mustaches and long curly sideburns, nicotine teeth and Moorish eyes, a black shirt and tight denim jeans, very low in the waist, with his stomach and ass showing as he walked across the room to feed money into the jukebox, walking with his bowed legs, and with each step, above his shoes, sharp as rooster spurs, his red socks flashing out like fire, dominant, euphoric. With his elbows resting on the bar, he leaned over toward Federico.

Go find yourself something a little fresher, kid, he said, expertly, with an aguardiente voice. That slut's already screwed every guy around here.

Exactly, said Federico. That's why I like her.

He stuck around, and Leo kept Raúl company a while. They talked about the countryside, about Vallfosca, about Leo's town. When they split up, Raúl kept walking, back uptown, considering if maybe the time hadn't come for breaking up with Nuria, to get some distance from each other, little by little.

But one afternoon, as he walked through the half-empty city, he felt that he missed her, and he resolved to stay with her at least for a while longer. It was a complex mood, a mixture of placidity and nostalgia. The calm heat wave had something enchanting about it, above all on Sundays, when his neighborhood was almost totally deserted with only some isolated passerby and some car, some motorbike, unexpected, out of place. They went for a walk, and then he heard again only the breath of air among the plane trees with their fibrous leaves, their rustling drier by the day.

He wandered about indolently, overcome by the sensation that the street belonged to him, that he could walk anywhere he felt like, sit down on the curb or against the trunk of a tree and savor that amplitude and that silence. In the bowling alley on Paseo de la Bonanova, some youngsters, just a few, were trying to kill time and compensate for their loneliness by making as much noise as possible. The patios outside the bars were mostly empty, at most some loyal customer sitting reading the newspaper, looking for company, to have a conversation. Only Las Ramblas remained as lively as ever.

There was one particularly agreeable day, very likely the same fifteenth of August. Public transit was barely running and the buses and streetcars circulated like ghosts past the leisurely city dwellers. The metal shutters in front of the shop windows were rolled down, with their signs saying closed for, closed until, etcetera, and the doormen brought chairs out onto the sidewalks, and gathered to gossip. The windows remained sealed shut and in the street one glimpsed, at most, a maid in white walking the dog, some solitary man in mourning, sweating and morbid, boys swarming about on bicycles, and on La Avenida Diagonal, some anxious drag queen, some miserable whore. It was then when Raúl remembered Nuria, when he thought about her imminent return.

Then, the weekend was over, everything changed again, and toward mid-afternoon the streetcars passed by packed full, there were no taxis to be had, and the sidewalks were an interminable procession of sunburned, sand-encrusted beachgoers, in bathing suits, with floppy canvas bags, a torrent of overheated young people, families, little kids. And the main access roads turned into a chaos of automobiles loaded with items for the beach, motorcyclists with their wives riding behind, family-sized sidecars with bundles, paellas, fishing rods, all passing by, overtaking each other, zigzagging in and out, insulting, splitting off, rushing headlong in a sudden invasion.

And the rash of fires continued; many of them forest fires. One morning, Raúl noticed a great billowing cascade of smoke blotting out the flanks of Tibidabo, and the next day he could see the track of the fire blackening a still smoking valley floor, as if it had been burned on the grill. He went walking and skirted those hillsides and when he got back home put on records in the sitting room, at top volume, and with the window open he listened to them from the garden, under the plum tree. He talked with Papa, who brought news from Vallfosca, about Aunt Paquita, and Ramona. Ramona was engaged, she'd found an excellent match, a fellow quite a bit older than her, twelve or fourteen years older, one Jacinto Bonet, very involved in the business world, with a promising future. Apart from his personal fortune, he had studied in Madrid, was very well connected, and moved among influential people. Poor Paquita, however, had the whole family worried. Her migraines, her constant pains, perhaps only worries, but the truth is she had certainly hit a real slump. Besides, she had now devoted herself to the task of securing the beatification of a prematurely dead seminarist, a young man from a good family, skinny and big-eared, with oligophrenic characteristics, judging by his face in the pictures; and, beyond that, to founding a new religious order, too. Look, maybe deep down it does her good. It takes her mind off things.

Raúl had not seen her since the previous summer, the few days that he spent in Vallfosca, the minimum amount of time possible. It was when Estrella had a litter of pups and nobody knew where she'd hidden them. She was exhausted and flighty, coming and going every which way, slithering around like an otter. But she guided him through the woods, with a hurried pace, turning her head—almost smiling—as if to make sure he was following her, and so she led him to a small hollow formed by some rocks, and went inside to lie down by her puppies that scrambled around in search of her rosy pink dugs, on a bed of moss and clawed-up soil, while she looked at him from within, her luminous, topaz-colored eyes shining green in the gloom. He and Polit brought the puppies up to the hayloft, although there, she still wouldn't let anyone else come near, drawing up her lips to bare her teeth, growling.

The family was gathered on the verandah, around Aunt Paquita's chaise longue, and they discussed Felipe's unexpected vocation for the priesthood, his sudden enrollment in a seminary of the Opus Dei order. They repeated ad infinitum that, as Felipe was the oldest son, it was sad for the father, but that if he felt a true calling, etcetera. Uncle Gregorio opined that it was already going well with Felipe, and Papa said that while it was a shock that didn't stop it being a consolation, too, having brought a pastor of souls into the world. It's a sacrifice, no doubt about it, but if God calls him, what greater honor for a father than to offer God his first fruits. Everyone nodded, highlighting the fact that it could not be considered some whim or heedless decision, given that Felipe already knew the world, he was a professional man, a lawyer, and he'd also done his military service. With all that experience, he'll surely be ordained right away. That's one way the Jesuits haven't changed; they still want people who are prepared. There was some disagreement about the real characteristics of Opus Dei; someone said that being a normal, everyday parish priest, in continuous contact with the parishioners, with the problems of modern life, was most meritorious. For Aunt Paquita, going to Vallfosca was now nothing more than swapping one chaise longue for another, one verandah for another, that porch behind her house was just suffocating, the way it heated up like a greenhouse in the afternoon sun.

They talked in Papa's room, Papa lying atop his bed, dressed, his hands folded behind his neck, his little suitcase like an old-fashioned doctor's kit bag on the chair and his overcoat folded across the backrest. He said that he was tired of Barcelona, that he was going to return to Vallfosca as soon as he could; he'd only come back to town to take care of a few business obligations. The Company, his retirement, human ingratitude, the usual. When I left, I did it with my head held very high: healthy assets and fresh possibilities. And now they go and deny me my retirement, as if the founder and manager of a company had fewer rights than a typist. And I was stupid selling my stocks before taking up this matter. That was my big mistake. Now they have the control and they'll do what they want. But, look, I was feeling old and tired, and they abused my trust. Then they were all smiles. I don't know; nowadays people have lost all sense of morality, and now I'm the first to point out to you that if you want to avoid big headaches, don't get mixed up in the business world. He said that earlier, including during the years of the Republic, a man could trust in his friends and relatives. By contrast, in recent years, a whole breed of nouveau riche had appeared, people with fortunes made after the war, a bunch of Don Nobodies, those kinds of guys who, with powerful patrons, lots of financial backing, linked to the big banks and finding protection in the public powers, commit all kinds of outrages.

There's no more morality, son, no morality or confidence, and the only law people respect is the law of the jungle. And look, the Company was a business that I started with all my hopes and dreams, for you all, so that someday you could all succeed me. But with your legal studies, what you should do is specialize in something. Maritime Law, for example. Have you thought about that? Maritime Law is a nice specialized field that still has a lot of open possibilities.

Yes, of course. But I think I'd rather be a diplomat.

That's not bad either. Nowadays, everything that's about getting connected, everything related to the State, that's a secure life. And if that's your vocation, follow it. You already know that I've never wanted to encroach on your desires.

He was wearing a well-cut alpaca suit; but seen close-up it was full of wrinkles and stains. And beneath, a yellow shirt, cheap fabric, and sandals with socks on his feet. He asked Raúl when he was going to go up to Vallfosca.

Maybe in September, when Uncle Gregorio is there. He just sent me a postcard from the spa asking me to specify some dates.

I'd prefer that you come with me. I feel a little lonely, you know.

He became fond of the garden, watering the parched plants, stimulated in a certain way by Eloísa's example, who had planted geraniums, daisies, and marigolds. At first it was just a simple distraction, dig, prune, water, but he ended up taking a real interest in it. He pulled out some acacia saplings and pittosporum that had grown outside the beds, in the thin gravel, and he replanted the flowerpots. The wind rang light and clear among the acacias, shaking the dry seedpods. In the back part of the garden was a great creeping vine, stretching out along the ground, luxuriant with sickly leaves and wild grapes that never ripened, small blackish beads. He repainted the garden chairs green, and in the morning sat down to read in the shade of the plum tree where the sun was like a blinking gash among the leaves. He chatted with Eloísa, while she, talkative and frisky, moved around the garden, showing him the new sprouts and buds. She even seemed to have accepted Achilles' presence, and she entertained herself pampering him, praising his graces. *¡Animalito!* she cried. Atop the walls of the neighboring gardens crept rosebush feelers, long and limp, and explosive boughs of red oleander with a mellifluous odor. Jasmine floated on the air.

Nuria returned at the end of August. Her hair was even lighter, and her eyelashes; her skin, brown and freckled, almost rough. She opened the door for him herself and she seemed to him shy and awkward, as if they were two strangers. Then it passed, in bed, as they made love like crazy, and everything returned to the way it was before. The Siamese cat had slipped into the room and playfully tried to join in; they had to throw it out. He stared at her stretched out on the bed, her slender thighs and pointy breasts, her mouth determined and stubborn, her golden eyes, eyebrows darker than her hair. See how the ugly bird didn't bring us bad luck? he told her. And just like before, they listened to songs by Leo Ferré on the terrace.

Nuria asked him about his previous erotic experiences. Raúl became mysterious. Santa Luisa, said Nuria, as if annoyed. Evasive, Raúl refused to say either yes or no. He did say that what he'd never liked was visiting whores, not only because as an institution it struck him as degrading, but also because it humiliated him to have to pay to make love. But that wasn't what bothered Nuria. If sometime you like some other girl more than me, you have to tell me, she said. Promise?

One afternoon they were walking back to Raúl's house, strolling along without any hurry. Nuria with her camera. They were planning some getaway for around the end of summer, without their families knowing, a few days in some town on the Costa Brava, Rosas, for example, or some other. In the neighborhood, from Paseo de la Bonanova heading downhill toward the city center, every time you looked there were more new buildings, half-constructed lots, tall cranes, gray structures, and more than one old villa had been replaced by heavy blocks of flats. And they criticized the ugliness of the new buildings, peering through the fences into the shadowy old gardens. Raúl stopped before the outer wall of a convent, a sunny wall, eroded, with cracks and weeds, crowned with glittering shards of broken glass; a few steps away, spying through the cracks in the wall, a motionless boy, aiming his air rifle.

I also used to come this way, to this wall, he said. To hunt lizards.

Poor things, said Nuria. Only a really bad person does that.

Don't worry, I'm increasingly tenderhearted about stuff like that. Lately, I'm even starting to feel sorry for rabbits.

Work had stopped at the construction sites and the streets stretched out, peaceful, lonely. They walked along, hip to hip, their arms around each other, and the afternoon was lovely. A clear western sky, rainbow hues in the distance.

Later that Sunday, when they went out at night to hit their regular bars, they ran into Floreal and Leo. Raúl greeted them without introducing Nuria, as if they were on the move, and they observed her with amused eyes. And your wife? he asked Floreal then, and Floreal answered him with a wink. They had a drink at the Plaza Real, under the arches, still lit by the sunset, and they also went barhopping along Escudillers, now lively and bright in the nighttime. They crossed over Las Ramblas into the streets on the south side: Conde del Asalto, San Ramón, San Rafael, San Olegario, Tapias, on toward Paralelo. From there the mass of Montjuich was visible, looming near, as if surging up out of the blocks of houses, on fire, volcanic. From the bars came songs sung in chorus and there were characters hanging out on the corners, looking for action. It was then they ran into them and Raúl told them that she was Swedish, a fresh pickup.

How do you understand each other?

Really lousy; in English. But that's the least important thing.

She wanted to know who they were, and Raúl said that, along with Federico, they were his best friends. Federico was out of town at the moment, he said, in Sitges, with his family.

I like these guys better, said Nuria. Federico is, I don't know, a little strange.

Strange? Why?

I don't know. Just strange.

They ran into them again in the next bar, and in the next. And also out in the street, always going in the opposite direction. They must have gone on ahead of them and gone all the way round the block, running, and when they crossed paths again they greeted them by bowing their heads gravely. They retraced their steps, along Arco del Teatro, and at a newsstand on Las Ramblas they bought a Swedish newspaper. The air was still and the plane trees seemed peppered with sparrows, as if petrified. They went back along Escudillers. At last, in La Venta, they struck up a conversation.

What's happening in Sweden? they asked.

Nuria folded the newspaper and, to maintain the charade, answered them in English.

What do you want?

He is a friend of mine and this is your cousin.

Oh, they are very nice.

Leo looked back and forth at them.

So, this is the famous little lady? he said.

And she turned right around and laid into him.

What do you mean little lady? My name's Nuria, hotshot.

They joked, Raúl a little uncomfortable, but the others only stayed a short while, long enough to have one more drink; they said it was late, tomorrow was Monday. Raúl felt relieved, more relaxed now. Seated in their corner, they ordered another half carafe of dry sherry. The bar had filled up with some well-known queens and the frowsy flamenco dancers and singers stamped their heels and clapped their hands and sang a chorus of obscene songs.

You're gonna turn me into a little drunkard, Pipo, said Nuria, leaning her head back. But I feel really good, like I'm floating.

After closing time they found their way to a bakery and ate some fresh *ensaimadas*, hot out of the oven, to pick themselves up. The bakery was long and deep inside, red and black like a forge, full of the late-night crowd. As they went up Las Ramblas, the halos of the street lamps were growing faint in the dawn. An auction of carnations was in progress right in the middle of the paseo, and they were able to have coffee at a newly opened bar inside La Boquería. Then they kept on walking back uptown, with their heads together. The streetcars running were overcrowded and in the alleys and side streets the tricycle carts and delivery vans were making their rounds. All the lighted signs and advertisements and neon were switched off, and the long cross-streets stretching into the distance suddenly bespoke misery, the filthy paving stones and the gray dilapidated facades. The narrow sidewalks were crowded with workers and laborers trudging off to their jobs, and dowdy women loaded with baskets, all of them silent and withdrawn. And up above, over the cornices and rooftops, over the whole city, a mauve-colored halo.

And when, the same day, after a few hours of sleep, they went up to the top of Tibidabo, they visited the deliciously outdated rides and attractions, and Nuria clutched his arm, the two of them standing before the metal railing, thrashed by the wind, taking in the view of the whole city at their feet, temptress, open, generous, inviting, stretching out until lost in a misty horizon, *omnia tibi dabo*. In the distance, starting at the port, one could make out the Gothic belfries of the old city, intricate and crowded, and encircling it, the grid of the Ensanche with the spiky towers of the Sagrada Familia in its heart, the Ensanche narrowing uptown, reaching into the residential neighborhoods, San Gervasio, Bonanova, Sarriá, Pedralbes, now on the dry flanks of the hills, and on either side of the city blocked in by the working class townships and districts, Barceloneta, Pueblo Nuevo, San Adrián, San Martín, La Sagrera, Santa Coloma, El Clot, San Andrés, Horta, Collblanch, Sants, Hostafranchs, Hospitalet, El Port, Casa Antúnez, blue-collar districts surrounded by the red belt of swirling industrial fumes. Nuria took photographs of the city, her hair flying on the wind, a squat, ugly city, quadrangular, compartmentalized, juxtaposed, superimposed, anarchic, unstructured, immense, submerged in a low sun-soaked sea mist, extending to the foot of the hills, Turó de la Peira, Montaña Pelada, Mount Carmel, naked hills running in a line, like spurs jutting from Tibidabo toward the Besós River on the left, and to the right, Vallvidrera, San Pedro Mártir, hills descending toward the plain of the Llobregat River, and directly facing them, standing out above the port, rising above the shining saline fog, Montjuich, butting into the city like a sheer rugged cape. Montjuich with its Morrot, with its peaks and yawning fissures, there, the hill of the Jews, with its quarries and slabs, moats and fosses, its parks and open spaces, its tin shanties and ersatz palaces, a mountain now silhouetted flat against the sun, thrust forth like a bruised black snout.

V

Loosen the guy lines some more, man, my rainfly is starting to soak through.

Well, go fuck off. I don't feel like it.

But you're closer to the door, you cunt.

Sure. Tomorrow you can shave me.

You can do it no problem, asshole.

And so what the fuck? This week it's Ferracollons's turn.

Hell, he's on leave.

Ah, well, loosen them yourself. It's not leaking on me.

This Ferracollons is a cheapskate. He didn't sweep up, didn't fill the water jug, nothing. So much for a guy whose name means "balls of iron."

We've gotta do something to fuck with him good.

Right, man, but if someone doesn't adjust those ropes quick, we're gonna get more water in here than the other night.

I don't care, man, let it leak. I'll wrap myself in plastic and go to sleep.

They all raised their heads and looked at the tent pole in silence, the dull brown canvas darkened by the moisture. Around the base of the pole, in the gun rack, there were rifles standing vertically. There was also a water jug and a broom and, halfway up, tied with wire, two extinguished candles. They remained motionless on their worn-out sleeping mats, atop their flimsy cots, in their thin, ineffective jackets, wrapped in dirty blankets. Raúl closed his eyes again; he smoked sitting up, sideways, resting his muddy boots on the neighboring mat.

What's a real pain is that the rifles will get all fucked up. Whoever's gotta go on parade tomorrow can do something about it.

Goddamn, man, the thing is the weather on this mountain is worse than monkey shit.

Fuck, this is the asshole of the world, fucking dead-end street to nowhere. It can be raining here and down at the beach maybe they're lying in the sun. And when it doesn't rain, the wind blows you away, or the sun peels the skin off your nose. And the fog, man. I've never seen the way it is with the fog here, that everything is dry except under the trees, the exact opposite of what happens with the rain.

But, why do you think they chose this spot? The camps are always in places like this.

And now, since there's firing practice tomorrow, you'll see how the weather's nice. Here it only rains on Sundays.

There's just no fucking place to go, man. There's no room in the canteen, and outside the tent you get soaking wet.

Aw, fuck, inside the tent, too.

You can't even go from one place to the other, man. Why don't they let us have umbrellas. They just want us to get wet.

And why did you have to spend your money in the canteen, dammit? Could've eaten in the tent. For half the money you eat much better. Me and these other two prepared a fucking good meal. Right, man?

Well, you know what I'm telling you? The best thing to do on Sundays is to eat chow in the mess hall. There's almost nobody there and you can eat almost like in the canteen.

No way, man. I'll take anything before having to go stand in line. The best thing is eating in the canteen, which is the closest thing to actually eating like a real person, you know, quit talking shit.

The best thing is to go find some whores in Tarragona, man, and get a really good blowjob.

There was a wave of laughter. Now, insistent, there was a dripping sound, increasingly watery, perhaps against the bottom of a small jar or pot.

Well, for me these passes to go on leave are worth less and less every time, you know what I mean. Between traveling and everything, you end up with less than twenty-four hours, and then, when you find yourself back up here, it's even worse.

Yeah, man, it's true. The only pass worth getting is the pledge of allegiance pass.

That's why everyone without a pass was Catalan.

Well if you don't like going on leave, you can all let me have your pass. I would've been in the whorehouse, I would've been on the beach, found some place with good romesco sauce, and right now I'd be headed for the dance, dressed like a normal person.

Oh, man, but with the pledge pass, it makes sense that they give preference to the Aragonese. Some of them live way far away, and weekend passes don't do them any good.

No, fuck, no. They do them the same good as they do us, that theoretically for the same reason we can't go to Barcelona. What happens is that the Aragonese have got it made. All the connections are for them, quartermaster, postmaster, everything.

Oh, man, do they ever. But it's not that they get preference because they're Aragonese, it's that they fucking hate us because we're Catalan.

Yes, sir, now you're talking. This is what it is, we Catalans don't like the army and they know it and so they fucking hate us.

On the other hand, most of the officers have gone through the military academy in Zaragoza, and all the Aragonese get recommended to them. Whichever way you slice it, in Zaragoza everybody knows someone in the army.

Swell guys these Aragonese, man. Lucky that there's none in this tent. Do you know any of them who shower? I've never seen guys who are filthier or cause more trouble.

When I think about that bastard who five minutes before the bell for formation goes and asks me to borrow my rifle and on parade they give him an extended pass because I had the thing so clean, man, and when I tell him I deserve the pass, he answers me, yeah, in a pig's ass. That's exactly what he said, man. That's it, I'm not lending it to anybody for a long time. Fuck.

That's what happens for being too nice. I swear he wouldn't do that to me.

No, man, really, the guy's got no right. We're always working, sweating it out, way overloaded, and they're always slacking off, ducking out of work all day long. But in the end, no worries, no Aragonese gets in trouble. And if one of them makes colonel it's only because I'm not exaggerating.

And always stirring up shit. Saying Catalan is just a dialect and all that. Them, they're all veterinarians, think they've got a right to mouth their opinions, man. Calling the language of Ramón Llull a dialect, the language of Ausias March, Joanot Martorell, Verdaguer, and Maragall, a dialect!

Joanot Martorell? Well I don't know who that is either, man. Joanot? That's a fucking joke of a name.

No, man, the one who wrote *Tirant lo Blanch*.

Ah, right, of course. You had me confused there, man.

You think they'll ever not be respected? A language is a language when it has a dictionary, a grammar, and a literary tradition, dammit, and Catalan has all three.

Well, if you want to piss them off, tell them that Agustina de Aragón was Catalan, man, which is the truth. She was the daughter of Fulleda and she was married to Commander Roca, another Catalan, doomed to die in Zaragoza.

And Jaime Primero ended the Reconquest before Castile, and Catalonia was one of the principal powers of the Mediterranean. And the Almogávars conquered Italy and North Africa and half of Turkey, and they were Catalans, man, the Aragonese did nothing. And when the Castilians tried to take Barcelona they had to besiege it for eleven years, and we gave the French more shit than anybody. It's just the truth, for fuck's sake. We don't like the army, but when it's time to fight we've got more balls than anybody. They saw that in the Civil War, man; the Montserrat Third Regiment was the best there was, and all of them volunteers. The thing is we like to work better than lie around, and that's why they've got it in for us.

Sí señor. Before the army, or anything else, man, better to break rocks. Being a soldier is spending your life in the shit, working nonstop. Pure bureaucracy, goddammit, and that's a no go for us Catalans. But then, when they let us be, there's nobody'll beat us. Not in sports or anything, man. And right here, it's the fucking truth; the Catalans always get the highest marks in company. They don't like to acknowledge it, but it's true, man, no one's got bigger balls.

Well, that seems pretty fucking stupid to me, man. The best thing is to go unnoticed. If you stand out for being good, you look like a volunteer and then you never stop working. And if you stand out as a slacker or for being a good little ass-kisser, you're fucked. Look at Pluto Farreras; he ended up without an extended pass, without even leave for today, and I'll bet you what you like, just for the failing grades he's received, they'll kick him out. But with me, I sleep through theory class, I copy on the tests, I don't even try hard, but I'll pass. You have to be as invisible as possible, man. The captain doesn't even know me.

But the lieutenant does, and he says that you're a lazy ass.

So what, man? He's even lazier. If you meant the second lieutenant, fine. But the lieutenant's a joke.

The one guy who's not bad is Captain Mauriño. Really, man. He's not here to fuck around and he's a little bit stiff, really, but he's incapable of fucking you over. And I prefer a guy like that over one like Cantillo, from la Primera, who jokes around a lot, but later on he fucks you. And another one I like is Sánchez Clavijo; he'll never ask you to do something he's not capable of doing himself.

Strict? I'd say he's oligophrenic.

And what the hell does *oligophrenic* mean?

Well the second lieutenant is worse, he's also a son of a bitch, and doesn't even crack a joke. That's something I can't fucking understand. A guy who went to university like us and has also been a cadet and a sergeant and that, during the months of training, has been a bigger bastard than the guys who are career officers. I swear that I'd like to run into him someday when the two of us are discharged, in the street, man to man. I swear.

What the fuck for? What good would it do? When I make second lieutenant I'll also put all the little lambs to work, make them eat shit. When you're a fucking cadet they all screw you over, right? Good, well wait until I'm second lieutenant and you'll see how I'll be the one who'll give all the other ones hell. Around here, man, the only law is fuck with 'em first before they fuck with you. And that's all there is to it, man.

Goddamn, poor regimentals. Now that's a shitty time. At least with us, they don't smack us around or cut our hair short and we don't have to clean latrines, man.

Well, that's really fucked. At least regimentals are good for something.

Alright, that's enough, eh? That's enough. How many times do I have to tell you I don't want anybody sitting on my mat?

He waited by the door and the one who was on his mat stood up. Shut up. Fuck, they told him, you sound like a broken record. Why don't you start by being a little more polite, dammit, he said. He removed his cap, and from underneath his rain poncho produced a compact package. He shook out the folds of the blankets and knelt on the seat. Turning his back on them, he began to stow the contents of the package in his suitcase. You guys have mixed up all my stuff. Who used my little stove? He looked again at the other guy who, now seated again, went on eating cookies, quietly, as if minding his own business.

It was Fofo. He also swiped himself something to eat.

Cookies?

Fuck, what a stupid ass you are, man. Yeah, we used the stove to make some food for ourselves, but we used our own canned heat.

Well, gosh, at least ask permission. I've already told you all that I don't want anybody touching anything in my suitcase.

Don't be stingy, you dickhead. Did you get a visitor? Hey, what are these novels? Lend me one, man.

No, fuck it. I'll do whatever I feel like with my own things. And I'm sick of sleeping near the entrance, and how you all sit on my stuff. Which I suppose you did just to piss me off.

Well, fuck, of course.

Man, looks like it's stopping.

Come on, lend me that Wild West one. You're not gonna read both at the same time.

No, dammit, I already told you no.

Yeah, man, it's stopping. I'm gonna take the opportunity to take a dump.

Raúl also stood up; he put on his heavy cape, his cap. He pulled out the letter from between the pages of a book, the envelope stuck slightly to a page by the postage stamp moistened maybe too much, and he tucked it into a pocket of his military jacket. He buttoned his cape. From all the nearby tents soldiers were looking out, crowding around, shouting to each other back and forth.

Lemme have it, dammit.

Go fuck a duck.

An immense fluid flotilla of dirty clouds loomed very low, and the camp appeared isolated in the countryside, only that multitude of brown cones sticking up above the small bare scrubby trees, fences, and boundary lines of whitewashed stones wavering away across the undulating terrain, among more tents, more trees. They were pines with round tops, now glazed, glistening sharply with rain, the needles still dripping quietly, and a few soldiers playing at getting wet with raindrops by means of shaking the most flexible trunks, ramming into and chasing each other with the impetuous vitality of young bulls. The company had become populated with voices, soldiers sprinting, and in a few moments a tumult formed around the fountain spouts, bodies gathered with water jugs, aluminum pots. Raúl discovered Federico waiting for him at the edge of the next company; he wasn't wearing his Sunday best but coveralls instead, with a machete hanging from his equipment belt. He was smiling, his thumbs hooked in his belt, and one foot resting on the white track of aligned stones.

What's up? he asked.

Nothing, man, pretty fucked, said Raúl. I think I'm gonna head over to the post office again in case there's a telegram. Why don't you come?

Fuck no, I'm on barracks duty and it pisses me off to ask permission from the bastard of the week.

He'll never fucking notice. Just put your poncho on and tell any guy to stand in for you.

Nope, follow through, you've got to follow through. Discipline before all else. You've got to follow through to the very end.

Well, the end comes sooner or later, no matter what.

All the more reason, all the more. What you could do is pass by the Co-op and bring me a bottle of gin.

I don't know, man. I'm suspicious that Nuria hasn't come, and we don't even have more news.

Maybe she's had some problems. But, hey, don't forget about the gin.

I won't forget, dammit, don't be a drag. The most logical thing, really, is that nothing has happened to her. They'd catch us first.

Do you think so, man? If they catch us we won't get out of the castle for the rest of our fucking life. Together till death do us part.

Leo won't say anything. Besides, the logical thing would be that any arrest comes through Floreal, and Floreal hasn't been bothered . . . Alright, dammit, I don't want to think more about it. The best thing is to wait until Fortuny tells us what's happening. It could just be something unimportant, some little scare.

Or maybe it's something so important that even poor Fortuny's already been nabbed.

They read the telegram over again, the gray letters grouped in strips, between bluish creases: *León grave primo bien Nuria*: León serious cousin fine Nuria. Sure, said Raúl, if she means Floreal it's to make us understand that, although he's fine, that's the path they'll follow to us. A soft drop fell on the paper and brightened the blue.

Or that Floreal is the only one who hasn't been nabbed, said Federico. Listen, that's good, about the castle. The prisoners of the little Castle of If.

Drizzling, not drizzling, and the mud meandering away in brown streams. Raúl moved along the row of latrines; one by one, he inspected the small compartments lined up facing the wall, some occupied by squatting soldiers, clutching the doorway, their coveralls wadded up between their knees. It smelled bad and the flies covered the brick walls, the clogged drains deliquescent. On the extreme opposite side of the row appeared a prissy gentleman cadet in his Sunday best. Taking a stand, he began to unbutton his belt with a moronic smile. Fuck, sounds and smells like a livestock auction, he said, and there were several audible grunts, most likely from annoyance.

He opted out. He had to skirt the last companies, penetrate the woods for a few hundred yards, into deep shadows. The pine trees grew tall, thick, and black, in intricate patterns; then the forest opened out, as the ground gave way to a shallow depression, a flat, spongy terrain with a mossy oozing humus. The declivity was slight, brusquely interrupted by a low precipice, forming a natural barrier that isolated the spot from the noise from the army camp. There, in the shelter of the rocks, one could glimpse the residue of other visits, soggy papers, dissolved by the rain. He chose a new spot, fresh and clean, without flies, facing the empty space invaded by the fog, and distracted himself contemplating the bare track of his footsteps. The river churned somewhere down below, surging more forcefully into the ravine, and occasionally some dark crow glided silently out of sight. A few steps further on was a flat spot between the rocky crags, above the sudden cliff, a perfect spot to read peacefully during free hours or, simply, to reflect, something just as important as showering or shaving every day. He was facing north, above a landscape now only sensed, a quiet landscape, inhabited, enclosed in the distance by that bulky mountainous massif that stretched across the sky like a horizon unto itself. Flat, mesa-like, sparsely vegetated, a massive mountain wall, which occasionally seemed suddenly to loom over him, always startling him with equal intensity, as if he were seeing it for the first time.

Walking back, the camp offered a vast and surreal panorama, one saturated with imprecise sounds, like sonorous anthills, just barely emerging from among the camouflage of those rough scraggly boughs, like a forest on the march. They were in the magazine tent, playing poker, seated in a circle around a folding cot, covered with a blanket; the canvas flap was drawn closed across the doorway, and the halo from the candle enlarged their oscillating shadows, blending into the tightly wrapped boxes and bundles. In the background, someone was tuning the strings of a guitar. They raised their heads, and Pluto, taking a carbine down from the gun rack, pointed at him in challenge.

Who goes there! he shouted.

¡España!

¡Santiago!

White Horse!

Yeah, boy, wish I had a bottle of that. Have you eaten in the canteen?

They were talking about Captain Cantillo's latest dirty trick, yesterday, in the first company, when he ordered a surprise weapons inspection, and one of the guys who was already set to go on leave had to stay behind because they had swiped the rear sights from his rifle and he had no time to go and borrow some from another company. They said that the poor guy was in the cantina totally shitfaced drunk. But, can we say that this guy is really having a fucking bad time? asked Pluto. Because, here, what matters most is that you have a shitty time, a really shitty time.

The others called his attention, and Raúl studied Pluto's hand. The only saint that interests me is Saint George, said Pluto, as he studied the discard. Hunt dragons, that's what they all must have done. He poured himself some more cognac; they drank from a motley assortment of plastic cups stolen from the canteen. The bottle with the candle, the cigarettes, the piles of coins, the cards face up; he'd lost. Raúl asked how it was going.

Fucking great, man. If only they hadn't swindled me out of my pass, right now I'd be with my girlfriend in Sitges; or with the English girl in Tossa. But forget it, I'm here and they're cheating on me with any old son of a bitch. This is what you call plucked and fucked; I'm beaten and she's cheatin'. Goddamn it to hell. And all because of one lousy button, fuck.

He paid out carelessly, like one stubbing out a cigarette. This happened to you for letting yourself get caught by a cliché at the beginning, they told him. When the captain said to him, Farreras, what do you think, you're in an Ursuline girls' school here? And he said yes.

It's the captain, he's such a nitpicker. What's wrong with an Ursuline girls' school?

Cut it and shut it, dammit.

You cut it, man, instead of yanking it, 'cause it's showing. Fuck, this place is full of ascetic jack-offs having fun with Miss Rosy Palm. What are you all laughing at? Well, next Sunday you can all have some fun giving yourselves a good one thinking about how I've got my girder in good hands, meaning not my own, because I'm outta here whether I have a pass or not, I swear.

He spoke and swore at the same time, ceaselessly, replying, quarreling with someone who was starting to tell about how, the last time he was on leave, with some skinny little chick, etcetera. Sure, man, you got lucky. They saw you together, and everybody was saying how you had a plan and then you fucked her and all that. Alright already, we know. He was betting borrowed money and said he'd lost more than three hundred. Fuck, it's just that I'm nervous. Today was my day for carnal exercises and they screwed it up for me. And after I've been stuffing myself all week . . . What's the matter with you all? Haven't you ever heard of the path toward perfection? You're all a bunch of illiterates. Above all things, love, that's what it says in the Bible. Not divine love or human love, no sir; feminine love. That's what nobody understands. Not Kempis, not anybody. My bedside reading is the Kama Sutra, or the Pinchatwattie or the Pentateuch or the Brahmapudenda or whatever you call it. It's the book that describes the 69 elementary positions. Of course some of them are pure bullshit. Besides you'd need to be hung like a horse. The others were getting flustered, there was laughter, protests, and that medical student ended up getting really pissed off.

C'mon, c'mon, no need to be an animal. Show a little respect, for Christ's sake.

What's the matter? Have you read it? Then don't talk. I almost joined the Jesuits, and I know what I'm talking about. What do you think you learn in the Seminary?

You wanna shut up already? Seems to me that although you don't believe, the least you can do is not offend other people's feelings with your bestiality.

Fuck, who's offending whom? Did anyone this morning consider asking me if going to Mass might offend my feelings?

They argued with increasing anger, their sweaty foreheads shining brightly in the candlelight, and at some point two or three miserable fucking cadets came in, also very heated up. They were talking about getting a jam session going in their tent and they needed the guy with the guitar to come. You come, too, Gaminde. And fucking Pluto Farreras. They said they had bottles to spare, they were going to have more fun than playing cards but except for Pluto, the others from the card game weren't sure. The one with the harmonica patted Pluto on the neck. Come on, Pluto, shit. Pluto looked at him over his five cards.

Man, I don't give a shit.

He'd lost again. He threw his cards onto the cot and stood up violently; he shouted that he was going out to piss, but that the game was still on and if anyone quit he'd knock him out with his rifle. He was sweating, and everyone went quiet. C'mon, Raúl, he said. He turned around, moving away, pulled back the tent flap to reveal the bleak, cloudy brightness, and let Raúl exit first while inside behind him arose, with growing clamor, a booing, woah, woah, easy, man, slow down, that'll make one less. They walked toward the latrines, heads down and hands in pockets, skirting puddles.

If you don't put on a bit of a show these sons of bitches will never take you seriously, said Pluto. But now I'm going to skin them all. I plan to leave them broke. It's not exactly a trick, y'know; it can backfire on you. Of course then I don't pay them. That's why I always play with borrowed money. Shit, I mean in this fucking place, you can't ever tell who you're really dealing with, not even the guys who aren't out to get you, even though you can keep your eyes on them, can't be trusted. Besides, I plan on swiping some rubbers and ramrods from them. Have something in store for emergencies. Fuck, so many thieves. I'm so pissed off . . . I think I'm going to lay low for a few days. But it won't make up for losing my pass.

He emerged from the latrines buttoning his pants. At the fountain they had a drink of water. They talked about Leo.

I was waiting for a telegram, said Raúl. Now I don't think it'll come.

Poor guy. Do you think they've made him squeal?

Fuck, I know about as much as you do. I suppose Fortuny will bring some news.

If you need me for anything at all, you already know where to find me. I'll be playing cards with these assholes all afternoon.

That was a fantastic avenue, running past the fountain and the latrines, a fantastic avenue that, rising gradually toward the Parade Ground—*la Plaza de Armas*—divided the camp into two, a large open area, laid out on the terrain as if on a blueprint, on a one-to-one scale, with its boundaries of whitewashed stones, with its symmetrical crossings, laid out perpendicularly—also of whitewashed stones—and its ornamental motifs, some truncated arc, some isolated column, of brick, and the officers' little huts, diminutive, almost like models, and the partitions of more latrines, of more shower stalls, and the shelves of more fountains, and the tips of the tents among the pines and the tall posts and the spectral cables, of phantom urbanization. A city traced in lines and squares on the gentle flat plain of rickety trees, a quadrangle of companies, of avenues counterposed to transversal streets which led to the service areas, Mess Halls, First Aid and Sick Bay Stations, Co-op, Infirmary, Post Office, etcetera, while the three avenues, the main one in the center, el Paseo de Gracia, as they called it, opened out into the vast parade ground, seat of the officers' headquarters, and public buildings, the Major's headquarters, the church, Central Command, etcetera and, as if to give it a happy air, off to one side, the canteen.

The men from artillery lined up in front, four by four, at ease, nervous, those who had permission for leave particularly nervous, with their gear all packed and ready to go, adjusting their caps, checking every minute the smallest details of their uniforms. Companies kept arriving and falling into formation behind them, as soon as each sergeant delivered his report to the lieutenant, each lieutenant to the captain, and each captain to the Week Commander's assistant. The Commander was from the artillery division, and he began the inspection with his own battalion. His voice rose sharply—Battaaaaaaalion! Attennnn-nn-shun!—the lines tightened up crisply and stood facing the sun, as if nailed into place, while up there, at the head of the avenue, a sharp-edged silhouette was outlined against the sky above the Parade Ground. Another figure was visible, too, surely the assistant captain, and he ran to meet the commander, to give him the report. The commander was sickly-looking, short of stature, and he wore smoked glasses. Clamped under his arm was a baton of heather wood. Flanked by scrutinizing officers, he noiselessly passed through row after row, between restrained breathing and fixed eyes staring straight ahead as if blind. Hardly had he passed by when Raúl could already glimpse, out of the very corner of his eye, the expressions of joyful pleasure among the formation, although the baton had already pointed at Pluto's jacket, signaling, with a solemn pause, the poorly disguised flaw, the broken symmetry, the empty buttonhole, an irrefutable sign of the missing golden button. They moved on, and Lieutenant Noguero, on noticing, said between clenched teeth, *esta vez te va a caer el pelo, Farreras,*—this time your hair is going to fall out—smiling, perhaps amused by the man's bad luck, by the fact that the previously pardoned punishment for the negligent loss of his rifle sights, granted by Captain Mauriño at his request, had turned out to be so much in vain,, in the same way that his previous sworn prediction—the one about how they are going to skin you alive, Farreras, meaning that, from his perspective, Pluto was destined to end up without a pass—was fatefully fulfilled when, upon rehearsing the very same exercises, the commander singled out Pluto in front of the entire battalion, asking him which company he belonged to, telling him, very possibly without even listening to the response, well you're putting your captain in a perfectly outstanding situation, *muchachito*, really outstanding, you know. That lieutenant from the theory classes under the pines, if the captain was absent, made Pluto go to the chalkboard, for everyone's amusement, and stand before him, when, for example, he discovered him urinating on a bush and called him with his deep voice, let go of that thing and come over here, Farreras, indolent, well-built, and ruddy, always appearing to be sleepy, good for spending time with, for killing time, getting caught up in one of those arguments that made the morning more entertaining, wherein Pluto knew so well how to loosen his tongue and respond with agility and precise indolence, skirting the very limits of what was publicly tolerable.

The start of class was delayed and Captain Mauriño, behind his field table, silently contemplated them all growing more restless by the moment. Captain Mauriño, his pauses, his empty silences, taking refuge behind his black glasses, his inhospitable eyes, feigning a forceful furrowing of the brow, on the point of remembering, of seizing the thread, of specifying what he meant to say, and especially, what he meant it was supposed to mean. Lieutenant Noguero chewed out the one responsible for not assigning someone to bring the chalkboard. So what's the colonel supposed to do, graze on the grass? he said. And Captain Mauriño made a vague gesture, the gentle valley, the quiet pines limned with splendid radiance, in the direction of the camp. C'mon, move, go and bring it. Go that way, through the fog.

Captain Mauriño spoke about logistics, and Lieutenant Noguero went to pester Pluto, furtively. He approached him during formation; that morning, when, after reveille, happy and Spanish, he appeared with his sleepy cat face, and they marched in step, maneuvering toward the mess tents, crossing the central avenue and the Artillery groups, in search of the obligatory Sunday morning breakfast, with the queues forming up before any one of the three boilers ready to ladle out the steaming slops. Pluto went ahead of Raúl, his head down, dejected, clinking his tin cup, and Lieutenant Noguero, puffed up like a big cunt, said to him, pretty little view, eh, Farreras? And Pluto answered, sure, splendid. The mess tents were lined up perpendicular to the cliff, a sheer precipice that plunged straight down to the terraced skirts of the sun-soaked barrens. From there one could see clear out over the dark plain below, stretching out into the distance, and, beyond, the sea, the sea and the clouds that, like an explosive crater, enclosed first the sun, the endless sea, an endless bronzed smoothness, with metallic reflections, auric, steely, stained with gloomy continents, with terraqueous globes, submerged, an endless surface finished in low saline flashes, in caverns of light, covered with stratified clouds, piled high in the shape of a lofty city, like a mountain, an embattled city, with high walls, with towers and cupolas and celestial banners, a city with its own radiant light and its own cloudy marine horizon, generator of suns and planets, of days and nights, rotations, periodic cycles. Past the mess tents, also backed up to the cliff, there remained the quartermaster's warehouse and the commissary and, on the other side of the parade ground, the first-aid hut and the infirmary, and, on the corner of the parade ground, the post office barracks.

He asked the soldier at the counter, a distracted regimental officer, who sat reading a Wild West novel under the spotlight of a desk lamp. Back outside again, he dropped the letter into the mailbox; he barely glimpsed the sentry at the motor pool passing by in the fog, rifle shouldered, bayonet sharpened, sparkling, and also like an angel, another crow appeared, gliding languidly by. At the head of the road, as if hanging above the void, the outlines of the first-aid hut and the infirmary, the path of lazy cunning devils and humiliated men which, as it led straight to the abyss below, served as a definitive warning. There from the parapet, on clear days, the panoramic view was splendid, now that the late dawn coincided with reveille, joyful and Spanish, the aura of the aurora refreshing the face, pleasant smells of pine woods and dew. He squatted down, and while he waited in the door of the first-aid tent, out of the wind, he saw the companies dispersing from the parade ground, marching in-step, singing. They moaned their complaints, shrunken, huddling, curled up, convincing themselves of their own misery, and Raúl leaned his elbows on the parapet. The sun turned the fields and the flatlands rosy pink, the tender stands of pine, the violet-colored gorges, the dewy steaming grass of the valleys, thin mists belonging more to the coming equinoctial September. Then the mist began to dissipate and little by little one could clearly see the populated plain, the flat beaches from which the white sails of the conqueror of Mallorca had departed, and the sea widened and widened in lucid blue. Closer, above towns and cultivated fields, rose the first foothills of the sunny lands, a stepped mountain of successive planes and spurs perpendicular to the plain and parallel to one another, steep craggy precipices, masses of overwhelming presence, difficult to climb, a jagged wasteland of a mountain of ancient abandoned terraces, of knolls overgrown with brambles, rising to the flat summit, without any animals, possibly some overflying crow, rotating in flight, on the lookout for garbage heaps. And facing away from the parapet, above the camp, inland, more terraces, heights even higher and further back, flat-topped pillars of rock, a brittle progression of notched heights broken by steep narrow canyons and deep forests, more flat peaks, rising higher and higher, from which one might see, standing out sharp, clear, and unmistakable, Montsant, Scala Dei, rocky and stepped, to the west, perpendicular to the Ebro Valley. It was a clear morning, and the cold harsh wastrel wind out of the southwest raised whirling dust devils across the Parade Ground. Then the orderly came out, with his insecticide halo, reporting that the captain doctor had said that they either shut up immediately or he was sending them all back to their respective companies. He knew him from before, from when he'd been in the infirmary several days—how many?—at the start of the summer, and the orderly ran errands in exchange for tips and he rented out gunfighter novels. That infirmary where you were admitted with a broken leg and discharged with colitis, or you went in with the flu and came out with furuncles. That hot, whitewashed room, with white beds in a row, and that toilet where you had to throw the paper in a wastepaper basket, and the prodigious bitter pill as the single remedy for every malady, and the insecticide smell, and the convalescents' conversations, hours and hours chatting about any old thing, planning ways to fool the captain doctor. They put him between some softly-worn and still-warm sheets, and the guy in the next bed whom he started to get to know pretty well as his fever came down was Fortuny. Federico came by with Pluto and they brought him cigarettes and his mail, letters from Nuria and a postcard from Papa with a painting by Velázquez on the other side, a Venus with a sinuous derriere that caused a sensation. Nuria informed him that she had definitively decided to abandon her studies, and instead of taking a vacation, she was starting immediately to work for her father, as a secretary. Nuria? The perfect tachymechanostenomagnodactylotyphonographic secretary, cliclick, cliclick, click? *Pajarraco*. Slyboots. Big ugly bird.

The Parade Ground spread out like a marsh, miry and exhaling, evaporating, and the fog seemed to burn off and different shapes took shape successively in depth and detail, the mass of the water tower, square and heavy, crenellated, stone by stone like a fortress, with its gargoyles in the form of tiny cannons and the ramrod flagpole which clashed so much with the clock that was better-suited to a parish belfry, tiny little castle that might . . . Yes, it was clearing up, the mist vanishing from the parade ground, its wide expanse now visible, the whole face of the camp clearer and clearer, a rectangular plaza, enclosed on three sides, with the water tower and the officers' barracks dominating the first stretch of the longest side, before reaching the central avenue that, branching off from there, symmetrically divided the base, facing—also symmetrically—the main guard house, on the opposite side, open to the countryside, to the highway; and past the avenue, now in the second stretch, the chapel and the command post, and toward the back, directly opposite the post office, face to face, the porches of the cantina, the sharp rooftops of the grocery, the tobacco shop, the barbershop, and the savings bank. A harsh, unpleasant place, yes, and the fucking brown slimy mud sticking to your boots, weighing them down, thicker and lumpier with every step. He heard a few undefined rhythms on a harmonica, and to one side of the water tower he spotted a couple kissing, she wrapped tightly inside the soldier's poncho, the pair suddenly revealed by the thin, lifting fog, a fog just like in the morning, not dense enough to skip outdoor Mass celebrated in the presence of the three battalions in formation there, between trumpet calls, all standing at attention, immobile before the brightly-colored chasuble visible even from the back rows, green for the umpteenth Sunday after Pentecost. They had the second lieutenant behind them, but toward the end, when the ite misa est was pronounced, Pluto could whisper to Raúl, that's one less, man.

The canteen was still packed, overflowing with families stuffed full with Sunday paella, drinking coffee, tables covered with dirty plates, with bits of rice and chicken bones sucked clean, fathers in a good mood, satisfied to see their sons healthier and more manly, remembering their own youth, better times, times past, and one mother, perhaps a widow, who tried to win over an easy, affable sergeant major in the name of common acquaintances, recommending to the embarrassed young fellow, a fucking cadet with a technician's lanyard, to get him some preferential treatment, some privilege. Behind, on the smoothly sloping meadow, prudently close to the cantina's protective eaves, more visitors, relatives, fiancées, small groups here and there on the grass, with their scotch plaid blankets, their thermoses and their baskets of food, as if on a picnic. Raúl ran into the day patrol, three or four miserable fucking cadets following the lieutenant on a boring round, and now outside of the enclosure, he looked for a rock beyond the families, past the armory clearing. The time Nuria came up to visit him, they had gone as far away as possible, and in a bright clearing she laid out the contents of her basket, the most traditional sort of wicker basket. She behaved as if the situation were still so very amusing, but she no longer had the natural ease as when she'd jumped out of the car, radiant, dressed with those lizard colors which looked so good against her complexion and her sunny hair, and she kissed him in front of everybody, not even when they left the cantina behind, she holding his arm, her hand resting upon the stiff sleeve of his army jacket. Raúl made an effort to ask questions, and as she seemed to relax, as if she'd caught his mood, he put his arm round her waist. They even had to make an effort to make love and, afterward, to laugh at what a disaster it had all been. He wrote her the same day, almost immediately after she left, and they agreed that she should not come up to visit again. When he had a weekend pass things were different, quick lustful trips to Sitges or to Tarragona, out of uniform: on

Saturday night and on Sunday morning everything went well but, after midday, the two of them started to fall quiet once again.

The big rock was flat-topped, with bright, spongy moss; it was wet and slippery, and he had to sit down, spreading out the folds of his cape. The armory, sunk into the terrain, appeared to have become a quagmire, and the artillery pieces, wrapped in tarps, looked monstrous in the pale puddles as if drinking from them. To his left was the camp and to his right, toward the west, the black gloomy forests, the gorges, the heights covered by the fog that had lifted, stony, castle-like, crowned by Montsant, of the which, on a clear day, from that rock, you could, at most, discern its smooth peak, distant and diaphanous, a rough mountain elongated like a ruined wall running toward the Valley of the Ebro. In the parking lot, below the canteen, there was a lot of movement, and two or three cars drove slowly along the barely visible stretch of the muddy, rutted road. On the parade ground, at the main sentry post, there was a changing of the guards. That was a bad spot, too close, with officers passing by constantly and you had to salute and count their stars and announce, Guards, attention! Then he reached the cover of the shale rocks, for example, or the arsenal, which was even further away, and he could smoke in peace. Before the pledge to the flag, the only ones to stand guard were the regimentals, and they, gentlemen cadets, not sworn soldiers, were on alert, kept watch, drilled, had four straight hours of instruction, practiced, and during free time, scaled the rocks on the perimeter, to water the wheat sown along the fence line by the tents so that it would sprout as couch grass, to inspire their decorative motivation, any frivolous gaudy doo-dad with an inscription, with a touch of spicy humor, borderline naughty, demonstrating, to the eyes of future family visitors, their youthful spirit and virile joy. They worked the whole afternoon, first each company on its own, executing the same movements over and over again, timed by the whistle blast, Captain Mauriño screaming himself hoarse, Pre-seeeeeeeent . . . Arms! Rest . . . Arms! And they opened ranks and spread out, making a tight formation, all the companies of the battalion now joined, facing the commander, wrapped in a cloud of brown dust, literally scared shitless by the chance of turning to the left instead of the right, or skipping a beat, or falling out of step, a misstep that would cost them their extended leave pass, of that ceremony so many times rehearsed before the battalions finally paraded one after another past the colonel along the length of the parade ground. A perfect parade, memorable parade, the parade which culminated with the brilliant display, the parade ground—la Plaza de Armas—adorned, shining, awash in flammiferous reflections, the air aglow, the sun floating in a golden halo that twenty-fifth of July, the day of Santiago, Saint James, the knight on his white charger, savior of the

Christian *Patria Hispana*, the Spanish Fatherland, when the horse cadets, in the presence of a large public, were solemnly made soldiers, deacon militants of the war. They waved the flags in an explosion of red and yellow, and the band played military marches uninterrupted, on swearing to the flag I kissed it and my kiss was a prayer, *madre mía, madre mía*, the kiss that I would give you with my heart. And the brief but emotive allocution, not of an orator but rather of a soldier, sounding distant and indistinct on the esplanade of petrified formations, Spain, glorious warrior nation, sacrosanct fatherland, our longing and our pride is your greatness, that you be noble and strong, and by seeing you feared and honored your children will go happy to their death. And also, from the presidential viewing stand, the homily of the august cardinal in purple or red, the same difference, his invocations to God and to Caesar, today the feast day of Santiago, lord of the armies, the proto-apostle proto-patron of the proto-patria, lightning bolt of the war that has so often intervened providentially, saving Spain from the international enemy, from conspiracies, intrigues, and hatreds of the which traditionally, gentlemen cadets, our fatherland, and its interests has been the victim, or better, exhortations about how the earthly peace of the fatherland must be called a celestial peace; saying how the social peace is tranquility through order, a harmonic disposition of similar things or similar people, each one in their proper place; saying how when the earthly city disturbs the peace, the children of the City of God resort to war, a just war because its objective is peace, the restoration of the destroyed order, and then it is God who conquers through his children, who gives them victory; saying how this is the way of human history, how while the earthly City endures there will be children of the saber and rifle. And, to conclude, a final call, here above, near to the bright stars, on this mountain of battle-hardened ruggedness, propitious to meditation and repentance, to firm resolutions, wrathful domain of thunder and lightning.

A little boy was exploring the muddy arsenal ground, wandering in zigzags between the artillery pieces sheathed in canvas, stopping here and there to look, head held high, eyes raised, the menacing inclination of the cannons, at the ready below their covers as if for some forgotten salvo. Hardly any visiting families remained, and the first fine drops of rain hastened their dispersal in a few seconds. All voices gone, the invisible river was audible again, far below, plunging down through the gorge, the white cascade wildly pouring onto the calm water, a dark quiet pool, with small fine bubbles, and eerie semicircles spreading out, diminishing. The rain came, slanting down, running through the woods like a chilly shiver, and in the opposite direction, toward the west, the fog seemed to descend again, to invade the ravines of raw rock, light and soft, ghostly. The last cars drove out in procession, very close together, and now departed, coursing the tight curves, moving ahead with caution, wheels almost to the gutter, to allow an old passenger bus that was arriving to slip by, doubtless bringing back the first ones returning from leave. Raúl buried his face between the upturned flaps of his poncho and made a skittering run to the parking lot behind the canteen. No more than half a dozen got down out of the bus, all of them miserable fucking cadets, with their backpacks, and they ran off quickly, splashing in the mud, splattered by the rain. In their place the few visitors that still remained climbed aboard, and only one couple lingered before the open bus door, still embracing, the girl pressing up against his poncho. Hands waved in the small windows and one heard words of farewell, messages, orders, errands, advice, *adiós, adiós, mi lindo marinero*, my handsome sailor. Raúl went back up the hill of the canteen with his face to the diminishing rain, a passing spell of weather, now reduced to brown drizzle. The atmosphere inside the canteen had changed, the airy porch now half empty, the benches and tables spattered by the rain all along the railing, below the dripping uralite eaves, limpid, vitreous shining drops falling rhythmically from one end to the other, now no one there from outside the camp, only sergeants and miserable fucking cadets and a small group of officers midway along the bar. They served him a hot cognac. Someone was arguing about whether soccer was spectacle or sport, and separated by a dribbling leak from the roof, several sergeants were listening, doubled over with laughter, man, and he said, hut orderly? he said, fuck that's the first time I see a sergeant being a hut orderly, just like that, man. They doubled over, clutching each other by the shoulders in a rowdy chorus. Goddammit, man, that was shocking. And before he told him, and this gentleman, what does this mean? And the captain had had it, man. And two sergeants were arguing, each insisting on paying, alongside the officers, don't fuck with me, dammit. The officers were also in the mood for screwing around, Lieutenant Noguero and Captain Cantillo and the captain-major and the sub-captains, more than one ass-licking second lieutenant who, taking advantage of the momentary suspension of all hierarchy, laughed along with them sympathetically, as if among his regular drinking buddies. And the captain-major ended up going round to the other side of the bar and started serving them personally, filling glasses, making fun of the colonel, oh, I was saying, aw shit. But the one who had the singing voice was Captain Cantillo, with his voice like burnt silk and his dramatic, heated, slightly crazed gestures, red-faced, his heavily-veined neck, like a boxer, and the others joining in the chorus, all of them singing gleefully together, a real laugh riot. And then the Aragonese joined in, *I really love the wineatippletipsy, so tip the bota high*, and Captain

Cantillo talked about the female soldiers when there was the war, not just girls but real good time broads, that the only thing they were looking for was good treatment with the ramrod, that's right, syphilis guaranteed, the secret weapon that the Reds never hit on using because Durruti didn't have half a brain; he let everyone surrender to us instead of shooting them. Or all that business with the whore from Tetouan, with her little shoobedoobedomedaddy, Captain Cantillo, with a fleck of grape on his tongue, big drinker, stiffer than a rifle or a 133 caliber mortar, with bigger balls than a bull. Well, you shouldn't dip your wick in any old shit in Africa, either. Fuck, you can't tell, catch the clap and anything else. Fuck. Fuuuck. Hah. You can't tell. Worthless shit the ones from Africa. That's right, they suck it harder than a kif pipe. Fuuuck. Hah. And the worthless whores there, begging till I agree and I tell her, strip it all off right now or you can fuck off. And she climbs on the table and takes her clothes off, the fucking whore, when she's bare ass, she squats down and starts pissing. And I tell her, I am gonna stick it up your ass, girl, and she tells me, let's see if you really mean it. Fuuuck. Fuuuck. Hah. What're you drinking, goddammit. Raúl ordered another cognac.

The canteen barmaid. She croons in a lilting voice.

La, la, la-la, la-la, la, la
La, la, la-la, la-la, la, la
La, la, la-la, la, la
La, la, la-la, la, la

The beer-barrel polka. Captain Cantillo.

He breakfasted on churros and thick, hot chocolate while the loudspeakers blared out popular paso dobles from scratched records and, like at a religious festival, visitors continued flowing in, a crowd of families and fiancées, and seemed to celebrate the fiesta, the brash carnivalesque joy, right up to the time before the approaching official ceremony; he ate breakfast sitting there, in the cantina, hung all around with rippling flags and banners, next to his chaste, brown-skinned spouse, chaste and in mourning, busty and chaste, her hair in a bun, *olé, olé*, you're the envy of the flowers, María Dolores, Spanish wife, both of them silent, him, covered with shining golden decorations, proud warrior, victorious crusader, blue divisional commander Captain Cantillo, with grizzled mustache and vacant gaze, distant eyes that seemed to contemplate the growing pandemonium of the dust clouds, spiraling rebelliously above the parade ground as if a white horse had just gone galloping across it, meditating perhaps on the promotion ladder or perhaps, simply, enjoying the leisure of being there, killing time, while in the wink of an eye, with a Major's commission the bonus pay for July doubled almost automatically, with its credits and meals, in memory of the glorious victory. Or even, for example, Captain Cantillo in the city, in conversation, a conversation with comrades in arms accompanied by their respective spouses, all in civilian dress, with their sober and well-cared-for Sunday suits, gathered together surely in some room at the Casino Militar or in some formerly renowned locale, now with neon where there were once chandeliers, the seats reupholstered in plastic, an old *cervecería*, yes, but still socially acceptable and, what's even more important, with moderate prices. They chatted, they conversed using the most stale Spanish courtesy and liberality of sentiments, manliness, courtesy, stately deportment, with elegance and authentic wit and bonhomie, and their respective wives corresponded with cunning modesty, nodding their heads, studying one another, their lacquered permanents, their tight Astrakhan cuffs and necks, fake pearls, smiling, jealously hiding their most intimate thoughts; nice tranquil evenings out. And, suddenly, once again in a field uniform, now departed in the train amid crammed goodbyes—*sag mir wo die Blumen sind*—now in the camp, with a company under his command, a company of miserable fucking cadets in coveralls, and with their hair cropped short, provisioned now with folding cots and straw for their mattresses, with marmite, tin cup, water cooler, and blankets, everything necessary, once there, far from the world of daily life, on that mountain of flat peaks, abruptly terraced, stepping up and up like the promotion ladder itself, when with the first formations, as if starting from zero, he began a new life, the brusque transformation; damn it!, you can go now, like a bat out of hell, get your cap, for fuck's sake. And Lieutenant Noguero asked him, how's it going, Gaminde. He turned to the others, this one's turned into a lazy hooligan, too, but he's a silent killer. Captain Cantillo fixed his eyes on him, very black and penetrating beneath his hairy eyebrows, with a penetration that immediately seemed to dissipate, as if clouding over, perhaps from incapacity for persistence, perhaps for lack of interest toward such an accidental reality. Well, fuck, let Gaminde's son have a drink, he said, and the captain major served him, solicitous. For you, boy. Lieutenant Noguero asked him again how things were going and Raúl started to say they were alright, but no one was listening to him, everybody attentive to Captain Cantillo, who was talking about how things used to be, except for exceptions, the recruit, the soldier, the little lamb, the young replacement, the common soldier, the small fry, with neither spirit nor heroism nor balls enough, country bumpkins, uncivilized yokels not worth wasting time trying to train, or inculcate in them feelings they didn't have, or treat them humanely, in any other way that wasn't at the point of a rifle, or a good clean slap across the face. And the second lieutenant, a malicious affected little dandy from Andalusia, with smoked glasses, listened smiling, entertained himself twirling the little chain of his whistle, coiling and uncoiling it round his index finger. And in the war, all that stuff about having to be at the front of the troop is just stories. Behind, at the rear, and with the pistol, and for the one who tries to retreat you just give me a clear aim at him and you avoid getting shot in the back, fuck, I've been in Russia, said Captain Cantillo, methods probably not shared by Captain Sánchez Clavijo, who arrived too late to participate in the Civil War, in the Eastern Campaign, and in the fight against the Maquis; he, who in the academy—he recalled again and again—had his hands turn bloody from handling the rifle so long when the cry came—Attention!, conscious of the formative character of that oh-so-apparently mechanical training, first phase of the road leading to the long awaited battlefield. Fuck, man, Clavijo, come over here, they said. Really good to see you, goddammit. C'mon, man, don't fuck with me. Whose idea is it to get started at this hour? They offered him a glass and Captain Sánchez didn't say no, barely resisting, corpulent, with a guileless face, with his red cheeks, and his mustache like a tin soldier, clumsy and astonished until he'd had a few drinks and then he proved to be one of those shy guys that let loose and turn out to be funny as hell. Mauriño, Mauriño, *no tengas morriña*, don't you start yawning, he suddenly shouted on seeing Captain Mauriño in the back, all by himself. Watch out, you'll turn Gallego, all their wordiños endiño in iño. They shouted to be understood above the vociferous choruses, above the verses sung monotonously within the shelter of the bar, rhyming virile consonance, *coño y moño; cojones y purgaciones*—fucked but outta luck; balls, balls, the clap calls—vulgarities repeated over and over again, from one soldier to another, from class to class, year after year applauded in the canteen, on Sunday afternoons, like a drug that summons memories or evasions appropriate to one who, like Captain Cantillo, knows that he'll never rise above lieutenant colonel.

The air blew in chilly and gray from the parade ground, the parade ground framed between the brick pillars and the still dripping eaves, vast, swampy, the puddles shining like blind pupils. Another captain came along and, for a moment, the group broke apart into two or three small knots, a good moment to bid farewell to Lieutenant Noguero with some witty, impudent remark which he tried in vain to summon up, offering instead a brief explanation about the fact that it was getting time to rejoin his company, or his plan to buy a bottle in the co-op, saying goodbye to take advantage of the moment to get out of the way, to be forgotten, to transform into one more of the cloaked forms wandering about the parade ground, where, little by little, the canteen bar, elbows and glasses and caps and cigarettes would be getting mixed up as in a vague struggle, the songs and noises increasingly dampened, and Lieutenant Noguero's see if you save a slug for me.

Not like Captain Cantillo, nor like Captain Mauriño, serious, yes, but already very worn out, with a lesion, the consequence of an old wound, which incapacitated him, in fact, from greater responsibilities than commanding a company. No, Captain Sánchez Clavijo had neither Cantillo's voice nor his manners, nor, above all, his vision of the military life, which showed rather plainly when Captain Mauriño had the flu and Captain Sánchez Clavijo, without abandoning his company, took charge, as well, of the instruction and theory classes for the Third Company. He supervised Lieutenant Noguero's work and, at times, took command directly. He spoke to them about the war, and everyone, seated in a loose semicircle under the pines, made themselves comfortable, placidly disposed to listen, and even those who were reading westerns on the sly put them aside. But instead of sharing with them some anecdotes or life experiences, he unreeled disquisitions about war as a natural and, simultaneously, social phenomenon, and soon nobody was listening, beginning with Lieutenant Noguero himself, who was leaning against a tree trunk, chewing on a stalk of oregano, whispering under his breath to Pluto; they started reading again, they studied the movements of the insects among the grass, they half closed their eyes, sleepy from the sun and the aroma of warm sap. To live is to fight and life is combat. War is the normal stuff of daily life; peace is an illusion, abnormal. The war between peoples, as history so well demonstrates, will always endure, and the word peace is nothing but a cover which nations like to use and abuse to cover up their will to dominate. His concluding words turned out to be embarrassing, a sudden and tense pause which seemed to make them wake up while he looked at them in silence from his folding table, heavy and taciturn, embittered—people said—because his wife had cheated on him and they'd had to separate. Only during drill did he fly off the handle, screaming himself hoarse—one, two—when at last, as the afternoon drew to a close, they paraded before the colonel across this vast and swampy parade ground, clotted with puddled footprints. He looked at the sky, the low dome of cruelly flattened clouds, the barracks' rooftops made thin, sharp, and steely, burnished by the fallen rain, and, as he approached the stony bulk of the water tower there sounded again, now with greater clarity, the sad harmonica rhythms. It was then, more or less, when he observed the presence of a small group of trumpets and drums gathered before the water tower, belfry or scaffolding, now too late to turn and run and, turning to the left, to take refuge in the co-op before, outside, the weather seemed to stop and everyone froze, as if paralyzed, while the consecutive drum and bugle calls for flag and prayer lasted, a ceremony repeated day after day, an ancient summons resounding when, each afternoon, the companies lined up on the parade ground, first facing the east while they lowered the flag, and then, facing about, toward the west, standing at attention until the last long trumpet call ceased, their gaze fixed on the low dying sun, white and tenuous as a sacred host, veiled by a fluid, yellow mist, the landscape populated by barely visible hills, calm pine stands, and rough, rocky crags, evocative of the approaching equinox, of the summer in the throes of vanishing, the same as those increasingly early sunsets. He stood stock-still, therefore, among other scattered figures equally immobilized wherever they had been surprised by the bugle call, in that hour of nostalgia and recollection, suited to contemplating the visits received, those beloved absent beings and their daily life down there, while there at the camp, above the clock upon the embattled tower, the enormous flagpole stood naked, erect, out of service. And at the same time, mingled with such sentiments and longings, a comforting expectation based on the irreversible character of the passing of time, on the evidence that one day more was one day less, that with the approaching autumn there also approached the moment in which, like the veterans who would graduate in July, they would retrace, one by one, but in reverse, the various stages of their arrival. They rolled by packed into trucks, everything now fulfilled and purged, singing, shouting, waving with their caps, enveloped in the violent liberated dust, little Spanish soldier, brave little soldier, the pride of the sun is to kiss your forehead. They sang, they shouted, *adiós, muchachos, adiós cantina, adiós* retreats and all the goddamned silly imaginary things, all the mechanical jobs completed, cleaning latrines and scrubbing pots. For them there would be no more corporals nor thrashings, nor crewcuts, and there would be others than them, equally unknown and close-cropped, the ones who now would be wandering around the companies of the miserable fucking cadets in search of some leftovers or scrounging a tip, offering to shine boots, clean rifles, wash clothes. There would be others in their place because they would no longer have to go scurrying along carrying their bundles, furtive like spirits or malefactors, stinking, slinking, scheming, snooping, swiping; for them, that was all over now.

But he would keep on as always, following a route opposite the sun's direction, opposite the company's at the canteen, in a northwest direction, his face to the shadowy gorges, to the forests, and the cliffs and escarpments of that mountain range which, like a staircase, ascended in a brusque succession of buttresses and mesas, spurs, precipices, above whose heights stood out, far away, the smooth peak of Montsant and the Carthusian monastery of Scala Dei, toward the Ebro Valley, and then, crossing the parade ground, from the canteen to the co-op in a southwest direction, as if threading the parapet of the camp, the steep pitch of the sunny spot tumbling in craggy masses toward the flat plain of subtly shaded farms and fields, with the high sea in the distance, in order to return at last to the point of departure through the clustered artillery, in a north-south direction, the shadow lying ahead, twisted toward the right, tiny, flattened. Only occasionally, with some concrete purpose, looking into the post office, for example, would he take a north-south-west roundabout path to reach the canteen and from there, now returning, retrace his steps, crossing again the parade ground and, now facing the post office, turn to the left and after making any purchase in the co-op, fruit, a quarter pound of ham, a bottle of gin, waiting patiently in line, like in some small-town grocery, then walking through the artillery cluster once more, toward the central avenue, his company's road. And the next day, at the firing range, down below, on a steep slope of the desolate sunny ground. They descended along a rough, rocky trail loaded with their full field equipment, one by one, an interminable trail, and from the fellow ahead, owing as much to an excessive abundance of legumes in the daily diet as to the uneven ground, a continuous ether of stinking fluted sonorities burped from the depths of his trousers. I don't understand how you still have the desire to climb a mountain, said Pluto. The only thing you'll see from up there is other mountains. And after work, when they were resting in the shadow of an outcropping, he still insisted. I don't give a shit about the mountains. Everything in view but nothing at hand. Fortuny was there, too, and Federico didn't take long to find them. They talked about the first thing they would do when they got back to Barcelona, when they were all done. Well, this whole experience out here in the country, here at the camp, seems to me an interesting one, said Federico. Look, just like a spa treatment where they bathe you, make you swallow purgative waters or depuratives or whatever you call them, and you come out fresh as new. Well, here, it's the same. Living together with other people, discipline, brutal treatment, giving them the most hellish time possible. And all to end up naming you an officer, linking you to the hierarchy, turning you into one of them. And Pluto: fuck, just like vampires.

More than a spa, it makes me think of jail, said Fortuny.

What the fuck do you mean a jail? A girls' convent. I already told the captain. The only difference is that here people cuss.

Well, tell me what difference you see between a prison and an army camp. At least there you're in for something you've done. Here, however, just because you're a certain age and you're more or less normal. And lemme tell you, for sure, for the same amount of time, I'd prefer prison. At least in jail you know that once you're there they can't do anything more to you.

Fuck, don't be so dramatic. This place is a school, nothing more. Where else could you learn about playing war if not here? Playing war at our age, fuck, a bunch of adults playing war.

He turned to Raúl. Why don't you write something about this, since you like novels? And Federico: this is a job for Count Adolfo, our official chronicler. He'd take the job more seriously, like Hemingway, bitter people, hard drinkers, and the protagonist has to desert and all that.

With eyes half-closed they contemplated, at the feet of those steep flats topped with a dry crust, the fields on the plain, olive groves, locust tree groves, vineyards, symmetrical hazelnut groves, the toasted fields in the colorless midday quiet, the wide open towns, the chalky vapor, from the sea and the sky, the beaches from which the conquistadors' victorious ships had set sail, the blessed standards which they planted like a wildfire on the sweet island in the serene sea. They had set up tents and, upon going to fill the water cooler, they discovered a long, blood-chilling, verdigris snake, resting between the clear pebbles in the spring. It turned and reared up at them, hissing, fork-tongued, then slithered out of sight, disappearing in an almost imperceptible way. Or instead of the firing range, guard duty; it was his turn in the main guardhouse and Captain Cantillo was the one reviewing parade. Hope nothing goes wrong for you, they told him. But he managed to get out of it by complaining he wasn't feeling well, and while the others marched, he remained in the tent, pacing back and forth like a tiger until it was time to present himself in the infirmary. He awaited his turn leaning on the window sill, from where he could still make out the last columns descending, torturous files of soldiers and mules disappearing from sight in the imprecise panorama of little groves, rosy pink flats, violet-colored gorges, vast valleys seemingly forged even as the fog burned off, and when they called for him he complained it was colitis, a sham formality, sufficient for them to dose him with medicine and send him back to his company. Then he prepared himself calmly, his uniform, boots, buckles, belts, rifle, machete, and, without any mishap, managed to survive that parade inspection in which Captain Cantillo managed to punish almost all of them, not by checking how they held their rifles but by checking to see if there was any dust in the joint groove of their machetes. The rest of the time, it was even agreeable to stand guard; in front of the slate-roofed shed, for example, thoughtfully smoking, the lonely hours spent in those pine groves softened by the breeze, silky green, as if water-streaked, sounds on the air, like an organ playing lightly. And the magazine on a blazing hot afternoon, there, so isolated and dominating, within the shelter of the sentry house, the hazy plain, the waxy mountains, the pocked and whitewashed plain, and the mountain seeming to flatten itself from peak to peak, tumbling down step by step, and the quiet canyons of stratified rock in curved depressions, and the muted brightness of the rocky crags and outcroppings, and the few trees, blackened lattice, just as if they'd been burnt to a crisp upon the airless sunny barrens, and that light droning of cicadas arising from the lower mountain, below a sky of hot steel. And even the guardhouse graffiti, inside that dumpy little cavern of reverie, the detailed drawings as inside a urinal, the declarations: In this place, your father solemnly whacked himself off in celebration of his final guard duty, an encouraging inscription, perfect to awaken the imagination, to think about what his daily life would be when all that had concluded. And the other scribblings, more reflective, inciting one to ponder the ephemeral character of such dreams, the miserable reality of their real situation: Dear Fucking Cadet, don't you dare celebrate your last guard duty without first thinking that you still have another summer to go. A summer wearing sergeant's stripes, but definitely another summer, a passing stay, limited time, but not, for that reason, wasting a single minute, time no less real and irremissible for one who, no mere visitor, does his time up there and endures it. The same mornings spent in theory classes, the same afternoons drilling, and above all the same imperfect variation in formation which so exasperated Captain Mauriño; in response, Lieutenant Noguero organized a quintet in which each man had to follow the nightly rotation, to present himself a certain number of times, in the course of the night, now with full field gear, now in his Sunday suit, now in workout clothes. And, especially, after the flag pledge, exercises in open order, the so-called tactics, the marches, and the maneuvers. And at the end of the day, the return, the songs, the hymns along the road, long columns flowing in triumphantly from all parts, streaming onto the parade ground to the martial rhythm of the drums and the ta-ta-ta of the trumpets, singing, tired but proud, yes, fired up deep down inside, virile machos, their shirtsleeves rolled up and the hair on their chests puffed out gallantly, singing to Lily, the phenomenal blonde, or perhaps to the dark-haired Madelón, not too bad-looking either; singing to Margarita Rodríguez Garcés, a bing-bang girl, a solid .50 caliber; singing to Sole, Sole, Soledad, *oirí, oirá, oirí, oirá a la española una y nada más*; singing and carrying the rifle the same as all the others; and the three battalions all congregating, the showy ceremony of striking the colors from the crenellated water tower, a true little castle, steadfast in formation, facing the east, and turning round, facing west, absolutely motionless while the ancient trumpet notes hung in the air, and then, in a tremendous final procession, again singing thunderously, company after company, the descent along the fantastic avenue toward their respective barracks.

He took a shortcut, on the diagonal, through a battery of sergeants, between the tents, and there witnessed a fight. Songs drifting out from under some dark tent, songs sung in chorus, accompanied by guitars and ukuleles, in some sad and lonely tent, boys from the student music group perhaps, students nostalgic for another time and place, for bygone university days, no longer able to be nostalgic for that naughty and unworried—namely sane—university life about which old settled men only remember the good bad times they went through, young love with many girlfriends, whoring with the whores, and the books they pawned, etcetera. And two men emerged to fight, slipping in the mud, beating the living shit out of each other, egged on by the onlookers they attracted, until the day watch arrived, and the lieutenant cut through the crowd and stopped the fight. Come on, with machetes, goddammit! You can fight with machetes, like in the Foreign Legion. What? Now you don't feel like it? Idiots! Well with the report I'll write on you you'll be under guard for at least a week. And what are the rest of you all looking at, goddammit? Who else wants a boot up his ass? There was an uproarious general dispersal, hasty flights, tumult, shouting. Among the tenebrous tree trunks, the rigid pines, without relief, the camp appeared populated by shadows, by faint radiances, forms in movement, peals of laughter, songs. The tents looked morbid, pale puffy canvas, with deep folds like the mouth of a furnace, smoking, aflame.

Inside, the candles wired to the tent pole dripped thick grease upon the edge of the gun rack. We've made one hell of a dinner, man, they told him. A real fancy spread. They ate dinner seated on their cots, face to face while, on a little stove, the water for coffee heated up, calmly debating the fact or fiction of the rumor that the next day on the firing range there might be hand grenade practice. They chatted easily, enjoying themselves, and as they watched him cut a slice of stale bread to make himself a ham sandwich they asked him if it was good. However, they started picking on Fofo when he speared an olive from the salad; they'd had work detail and Fofo came in to fetch his silverware.

Listen, you ugly bastard, you mind telling me who invited you?

Fuck, man, Fofo is one of those guys who never misses a meal.

Aw, fuck, he can go fuck himself, for fuck's sake.

Raúl went to look for Federico in the neighboring company. He was drinking with some others, by the door of the tent, and they invited him to come in.

Come in, come in, a man with a bottle is always welcome.

I'll pay you for it tomorrow, man, my money order's supposed to arrive, Federico said. Today I'm broke.

Spent all the money you never had, man, said Raúl.

Huh? Federico grunted. Ah, right. What's in store for us? Twenty years? They'll lock us up together, in a castle. And Raúl: quit talking bullshit. They spoke apart. Federico with his eyes smiling and lazy, as if thinking about something else. Nothing, nothing, the Castle of If is what I meant. And he asked him if he knew how to compile an inventory. Outside, someone called barracks corporal! barracks corporal! inspection! and then everyone in the tent started shouting, that corporal, c'mon, that corporal, he's turned into a mean bastard. Federico put on his cap in a hurry. Fuck, the inventory, he said. I have to go to the major's post. Then he reappeared in the armory tent in search of a second-year cadet who, once located, explained to him, in detail and with paternal seniority, the proper way to write up an inventory. And the one shuffling the deck said: damn it, man, this thing's a mess. And Federico: yeah, man, I'm fucking it all up. They argued about whether, to become a second lieutenant, it helped at all to learn how to compile an inventory, and Pluto said yes, that it was fundamental, and expounded his theory of the inventory as the prime mover or breath of life in the army. In the beginning there was the inventory. And the inventory didn't add up. And the inventory had to add up, and then there was the army. He was winning a lot of money, around five hundred pesetas, and in a certain moment he winked his eye at Raúl and slyly showed him a set of rear sights from a rifle in the palm of his hand. The other three, however, seemed to be in a bad mood. C'mon, play, and quit screwing around, said the medical student. And Pluto: yeah, man, I don't mind taking you guys to the cleaners. The cognac was finished, and between games, they passed the bota from hand to hand, a thick, bitter wine, a tense black stream which, the throat pulsing and gulping it down, stained the seams of the lips, the chin. And a heavy guy came in with his uniform covered in mud, as if he had slipped and fallen, and he said that in the canteen there was a scary fucking sight and that the officers were making toasts and giving the communist salute, raising their fists in the air. Shit, man, I'm so loaded, he repeated, laughing, and he let himself fall onto the canvas that covered the supplies, getting it all muddy. Listen, you oughta hit the sack, they told him. They talked still about how different everything was going to be when they were second lieutenants, how they would treat the troops. You'll say that, well, of course, there's a difference, said Pluto. A huge difference. Like when someone gets hit by a car; it's better to be the driver than the guy who gets hit. The uproar from the jam session in the other tent became deafening, harmonicas, guitars, and a drum set made of tin pots, so loud that the only way they knew the bugle call for curfew had been sounded was because someone stuck his head outside to pass the word with a shout. They went out relaxed, unhurriedly, until the rumor started that the second lieutenant was making the rounds and then they stepped it up noisily, jostling one another, piling up at the end of the formation, clinging to the one ahead to avoid being pushed still further back, to the last positions. But it wasn't the second lieutenant's voice, it was Lieutenant Noguero's, deeper, which they heard while the sergeant focused the flashlight on them, to be rewarded with the come on, let's go, that line. I'm going to take names on the last six men, screamed the sergeant, and in the white light, after one final spasm, the lines finally stabilized.

Hey, Ferreras, how's that going, said the lieutenant, his face seemingly haloed by the shine of the flashlight. How'd the poker game go?

Nothin' special, Lieutenant, sir, said Pluto. I only won a thousand pesetas.

There was some naughty laughter, which turned into wild shrieks when the lieutenant said, you see, man, how much fun you would have missed if you hadn't stayed here. They were still moving, covering ground, furtively, and in other companies they were already counting off. Ten, eleven, twelve, shouted from various points, like an echo, four, five, like an echo repeated from different distances, resounding deeply across the now quiet camp. Well, enough joking around, said the lieutenant. And when it turned out that the numbers didn't square, the sergeant made them reform the lines and began to recount them by threes to see if they were out of formation, the lieutenant said that was alright already, that each time it would come out worse, and he signed the tally. Then, supplied with light by the barracks corporal, the sergeant read the report and the list of guards and of reserve guards and, on breaking ranks, there was a violent ovation which bit by bit decayed into a hullabaloo, as they dispersed into the darkness, everyone repeating that the lieutenant was one hell of a great guy.

He'd pulled second reserve guard. They walked in a group, straggling along, as if groping along, blinded by those walking ahead of them, agitated forms, confusedly standing out against the faint light from the tents.

Did you hear? said Pluto. They're saying tomorrow we're practicing with live grenades. If it's not just some rumor, of course I'm getting out of it. They scare the shit out of me, fuck it.

No, it's not a rumor. They heard them telling that prick captain about it.

Well, it's dangerous, man. There's some guys might kill four or five. Imagine that Ferracollons throwing grenades, for example. I'm sure one'll slip out of his hand when he throws it, and it'll land right on our heads.

Fuck, he's the least of your worries, said Pluto. What happens is with the noise I end up deaf for a few days. It's a question of having balls.

Balls? What the fuck, balls! Cock! What you've got to have is a big cock. And the bigger the better.

Later, now alone, he tried to get news about Leo. Nothing new? he asked. Look, it's just that I've thought that we might have to do something, man. These people are animals, and they might just beat the shit out of the poor guy and, if you don't do something, they'll give him twenty years on top of it, y'know. My father knows some retired colonel, but he was a military judge or

I don't know what and he has quite a lot of influence. He's a guy who owes him favors and stuff and, if my dad asks him for it, he'll do what he can. He also knows a police commissioner. What do you think if I write to him so he can talk to them? Do you think it'll do any good? And, at the fountain, two or three miserable fucking cadets from some neighboring company were holding up some slack body, shining a light on the spewing mouth, eyes closed, mouth hanging sloppily half-open. C'mon, you stinking carcass, they were saying, and another stood by waiting, cleaning his eyeglasses on his sleeve, timid and serious, blinking. There was a sudden rush toward the latrines with their off-white walls, a coming and going as if on a carousel, boots sounding adhesive, sticky, on the muddy pavement of the corridors. They followed one another in silence, occupied the shadowy compartments, and, without talking deeply, exchanged lazy words, humming between their teeth, more or less absorbed in their own difficulties of urinating, as the feeble sputtering stream did little more than splash and spatter upon soggy papers, upon stagnant backed-up waters, until, with a brusque pull of trouser bottom, they laboriously stuffed their pricks back into their pants and vacated the stalls. Micromacromundi, that panorama of drifting green-black ordures, floating collard greens, sulfurous brussels sprouts, viscous heads of garlic, broccoli trunks, phosphoric onions, explosive radishes, powder dry mushrooms, dark eggs and gelatinous toadstools, mucilaginous seas, densities, abyssal liquids with reflected firmaments, close quiescent constellations, swampy stars, vaporous moons, snorting extrusions from convulsive craters, streams of stars, revolting evacuations, burning, a profound series of warm infernal dumpings, cataclysms and transmutations, cosmogenic semblances and images.

Soon the last ones would arrive to close the canteen, a quick drink before they closed, or perhaps, at the grocery, a yogurt to settle the stomach, and in the tents everyone would begin to open their cots, to prepare their mattress, the sleeping bag, disputing whether this, that, or the other thing left no room for the rest, about whose turn it was to do the cleaning and fill the water cooler that week, commenting on the day's most outstanding events, the scuttlebutt, the shitty luck, still singing, drinking the last swallow, arguing, commenting, retelling, swilling, disputing, a diffuse rowdy clamor of voices that would only stop when, after the bell for silence, the night watch began its round.

He ran into Emilio and they said hello briefly, as if in a hurry. He'd thought that he'd glimpsed him during the first days in the camp, in the canteen, with sunglasses and a mustache, and then, one Sunday, he definitely recognized him strolling by, accompanied by his parents, also greatly changed. And even on leave, in Tarragona, also around the beginning of summer, one Saturday when he was out with Nuria, he spied Emilio in the middle of a group, all of them sporting their uniforms, walking behind some girls. But they didn't speak until a different night, some days later, when coming out from the latrines Raúl lit a cigarette and then, a few centimeters away, appeared that smiling face, of diffuse outlines, the tiny tongue of fire shining brightly in his pupils, highlighting the fuzz around his trumpet mouth, that of a spoiled, unweaned crybaby. Don't salute, man, he said, and it was the same voice. Don't salute. He asked him what he was studying and if that girl was his girlfriend; he said that he was studying medicine and that everything was going well, and it turned out that he was in the same company as Federico. What? he said. Do you still remember how to throw the bolas? And inevitably he ended up mentioning the death of Mallolet. Tuberculosis. For us, specific bilateral transmission with hematological origin. They had done one of the first marches of the season and the company was on the verge of getting lost in the fog. They camped out in some fallow fields, next to the small village, a tiny hamlet of abandoned orchards, abandoned streets, abandoned houses, a lovely ruin where, judging by the bed of straw and flattened cow pies covering the floor of one room, cattle sometimes sheltered. After eating he searched through the intricate and narrow interiors with Pluto and Fortuny, the floor barely paved with rough stones, worn by the centuries, a labyrinth of dark stairs, blackened ovens, nooks like grottoes, rotted, worm-eaten beams, gaping gray walls, open to the fog, and that odor of manure, of burnt stone. They entered the bare church, with its echoing vaults, and outside someone from another group rang the bell in the tower by throwing stones at it. Behind, in the little cemetery choked with nettles, they examined the niches with their illegible inscriptions, the iron crosses nailed into the earth, twisted, rusted; the graves marked by a border of pebbles, and only after a few minutes did they notice that the spongy ground, among the damp weeds, was sown with bones, orange vertebrae, shards of skull, jawbones with teeth, spindly ribs. And further on, to the northeast, on the other side of that mountainous massif which stretched out like a horizon, flat, plateau, stark, barren, a mountainous massif now only sensed, swallowed up by the fog, on the other side, within the shelter of the wooded gloom, at the foot of the steep slopes of pine stands, the monastery of Poblet dominating the clear open hills of la Conca, a sober isolated compound, with its towers and high walls, dark sepulchers, a calm golden ruin, Gothic naves, cold and resonant, damp flagstones, recumbent statues, bas-reliefs, lost slag heap of conquests, of glories and victories, splendid epitaph of trophies, Mallorca, Valencia, Murcia, Sardinia, Sicily, Tunis, Algiers, Athens, Constantinople. And the walk one could make, solitary, through the half-collapsed Romanesque cloister, and through the Gothic cloister, with its serene fountain, and the cypresses and laurels, and the rose bushes, and a delirium of swallows in headlong flight.

He found the first reserve guard, his tent. He was sitting on his duffel already packed while his companions, as if in a chaotic dance, got theirs ready stooping, asses in the air, or squatting down, or undressing in a hurry, hopping about on one foot in floating shirttails, hairy legs in socks, in worn-out underwear, meaty buttocks, some going to sleep in their coveralls, joking, the candle flames fluttering from their stirring about, capering shadows on the canvas. And when Raúl offered to take his place as reserve guard, the other one glared at him angrily, raising his voice as if to attract attention.

Right, smart ass! Then I do the second shift, eh? No way, wise guy.

Fuck, I wasn't talking about switching, said Raúl. I'm just saying, if you want, I'll do your shift, too.

La, la, la-la, la-la, la, la.

He packed his duffel bag, he opened his cot, the thin mattress, the sleeping bag, blankets; he removed his suit and put on clean coveralls. There was the same racket as in the other tent and, as he crossed off one more day on the calendar traced in chalk on the canvas, the raucous shout in unison: one day less, one day less, one day less of being here. And, while they undressed in a no less chaotic and extravagant dance, they talked about the joking that went down in the canteen, whether or not it was a rumor about the grenades, about the ones who'd died during maneuvers the year before, of the inferiority complex and the rancor because of them, because of the miserable fucking cadets, inside they felt grateful for the commissioned captains who'd been promoted from the ranks, thanks to the fact of them being career soldiers with superior training, as compared to the ones who in six short months were promoted to be officers; about whether Captain Cantillo would have at least made commander if they hadn't found out about a little side business he was running out of the quartermaster corps; about how fucked a soldier's life really was, to spend your whole life as they were doing now, always working your ass off; about what a terrible fucking climate there was in this place they'd chosen for the camp; about how little all of this would matter to them in the coming weeks, faced with the tantalizing perspective of the imminent end of their sorrowful stay; of what they would do first upon getting back to Barcelona; of the hazings they'd inflict the next summer, when they were sergeants, on the new batch of miserable fucking cadets; about how no way in hell would they ever again spend a week as fucked as the first one from this summer, in a stupor all day long, without understanding anything, forever running at the ringing of the bells; about who was in charge of the cleanup and filling the water cooler that week; about what a bunch of animals the Aragonese were; about the evident superiority of Catalonia above all other lands, etcetera. The candles consumed, reduced to short dripping stubs, hardly shedding any light on anything but the conical peak of the tent, they argued about whose turn it was to replace them and each one ended up lighting one of his own atop his duffle bag; they passed round the bota and picked on el Fofo, who was busy examining his hemorrhoids with the help of a little mirror and a flashlight. C'mon, finish, fuck, this would turn anybody on. They considered the dirty tricks they could play on the ones who were on leave.

Sew their sleeping bags shut, man.

No, fuck, then they'll wake us all up.

Leave Fortuny a note saying he's pulled guard duty.

Exactly, man, 'cuz tomorrow he's on parade.

Or dissolve some laxative in their water cooler.

Yeah, man, Ferracollons has got colitis.

That's doing them a favor, man. Then they'll be out sick and won't have to do target practice.

Right, a good purging.

Fuck no, man.

Raúl searched for his machete and flashlight; he buttoned up his cape. Federico wasn't around and, when he asked where he was, the other guys in the tent, now all in bed, began shrieking in women's voices. Oh! A man! He's from another company! Come in, come right in, and we'll fuck you, I'm a Virgo, really crazy, and he had to step out, and wait outside. Federico appeared with his shaving kit and a towel draped round his neck.

Monte Cristo! he said. The condemned count.

Quit talking shit, dumbass. You know well enough the only one who'll get caught is Leo.

Au contraire. I think we're all screwed. Except Count Adolfo, he's one of those guys who always comes through without a scratch.

Well, yeah. What I wanted to tell you is that I'm doing the first two reserve watches, which means I can talk with Fortuny the moment he arrives.

That's good: solidarity, moral support, symbolic expiation, that's really good.

Fuck, Federico, you're such a pain in the ass. Would you please quit fucking around? If there's any news, I'll wake you up.

Right, wake me up. I want you to wake me every hour. You can give me the news.

Every fifteen minutes, if you want.

Even better, every fifteen. But please just admit that we're screwed. Admit it.

Alright, fine. We're screwed.

And the bell for quiet rang, when every solider's mother is praying for him. Quiet! they were saying in the neighboring companies, and the reserve guards tapping on the canvas, tense strokes, flashing flashlights. Fuck, these lights. The patrol will be coming around. Coughs, laughter, complaints, quarrels, interrupted songs, left hanging as if in suspense, on a clear night, of white stars, my lover's sweet complaints, my sorrows. Raúl sat down next to the tent, against a tree trunk, sunk down within his poncho; a trunk almost too slender, a bit uncomfortable. The wind gusted, spluttering their words, voices like echoes in the ominous forest, the empty, sterile wind, the dark sound of branches, and the oppressive premonitory passing of the dense, heavy clouds, opaque, moving away in closed masses.

Give me that photo, man. Let's see if I still have time to jerk off.

Turn off the light and let me sleep, for fuck's sake.

Fuck, here he goes with his cough again.

You're fucking screwed, you're tubercular.

It's the humidity, man; what do want me to do?

Well, hold it in.

The first one who snores, I slice his dick off.

Shut the fuck up all of you.

Go scratch your balls.

And you, go suck your schlong.

Really wish I could, man.

Did you loosen the guy lines?

Don't be a jerk.

I don't give a shit, man, I'm wrapped in plastic . . .

I hope it does rain and we don't have to go to target practice.

Shut up, faggot.

You shut up, the way you snore.

Go fuck yourself.

In your dreams.

Voices separating little by little, quieting down, falling off, and then only the wind, emptiness, nocturnal abysms, dark night, serene and starless night, calm, clear, quiet, a night transfigured, burning, opaque, pitch-black, placid, dark, black night black as a crow's wing hovering overhead, menacing, and so, clamor of complaints or perhaps wild laughter, and so, and so, so falling and rising and fading away, and so, and so, in slow inquisitive semicircles. So?

VI

Clouds, brilliances, transparencies, neither red nor topaz nor celestial, an unstable sunset. It was dazzling, this way, looking at it straight on, at the end of the street, above the perspective of two rows of foliage shrinking, vanishing in confluence.

Down below, no. Gazes, flashes, reflections in the windshield, in car windows, in streetcars, in the mirrors of shop windows, in the glass of front doors, superimposed images, fragmentary, in motion, the too-slow march of the passersby, hindering, exasperating. He slapped his sunglasses back on.

They walked along very close together, arm in arm, perhaps too quickly. There was a newsstand or, at least, people standing around a newspaper seller, and the stand was selling roasted chestnuts. Also there were people standing outside an appliance store window, watching television. And further on, in front of the trolley stop, all waiting in expectation, crowded together in undecided assault toward the step not yet come to a stop, already too many of them while the screeching grew louder and the glass became filled with flashes of light. He noticed that Aurora was looking over her shoulder.

The fuzz, he heard her saying.

They were on the broad chamfered corner, the snub nose of a patrol car sticking out past the parked cars, and the machine guns were clearly visible, carbine barrels, peaked caps tipped down, boots, hands gathering up the leaflets scattered on the sidewalk upon which, suddenly, a space had opened out among the pedestrians. Don't turn around, Raúl said. They weren't far from the corner, two or three doorways. He quickened the pace, squeezed the sheaf of leaflets against his thighs, in the pocket of his overcoat. They turned the corner to the right, the facade of the Sagrada Familia rising up sharply across the street, a hollow structure expanding broadly in the empty air. There, the traffic was much lighter than on Calle Mallorca and the sidewalks stretched out, bordered by straight walls of brick, under the auspices of the dazzling, rapid sunset, peaceful, only a few people looking upward.

Federico's car was half a block away, across from the entrance to the church construction site, the motor running, not so much parked as already pulling away from the curb, softly shifting into gear to head off up the street, accelerating, until turning to the left, at the first cross street. But what's this imbecile doing, said Raúl. Look, said Aurora, and it was as if in obedience to her cocking her chin that the pair of cops appeared coming down the middle of the sidewalk toward them, their slow uniform stride, their stiff guns standing out in parallel fashion. Wait, said Raúl. He put his arm around Aurora's shoulder and kissed her on the cheek, his left hand sunk in his pocket, against the leaflets, as if gathering in his overcoat. They crossed with their heads together toward the entrance to the enclosure around the Sagrada Familia, a small hut open in the wall which, functioning as a vestibule, plastered with postcards, brochures, pennants, and bulletins, gave access to the interior of the lot, to the staircase leading up to the temple. From the first steps it was now possible to take in the whole street in all its width and breadth, from over the wall, and they could watch the police patrol, slow, vigilant.

On the stairs and landings there was a certain number of visitors, couples, families, tourists taking pictures of themselves before the portico, people seated on the parapets. They contemplated the high, bristling towers, the smaller cupolas, and the porticoes of the facade, a rough triptych gouged out from the beveled wall at the doors; the Facade of the Nativity, of the east, of the dawn, destined to express the mysterious pleasures which surround the coming of the Redeemer, the beginnings of his life. The Door of Charity, for example, in the center, limned by great arboreal columns with their bases carved as tortoises and open capitals in the manner of palms, boughs of welcome, trumpets of angels announcing the good news, a door divided by a wooden interarch linked to the earth by a coiled serpent, tree of paradise lost, remote cause of all that, of that classic Nativity Scene situated at the base of the tympanum, with the ox and the mule standing out beneath the empty frame of the stained-glass window and the great rose window, the Child adored by Joseph and Mary, and, from the beveled cantilevers and reliefs in the walls, by kings and shepherds, gray flocks gathered, roosters, capons, Christmas turkeys, and, higher up, the archivolt of the portico, magnificent curvature which, from on high, vainly invited one to cross the threshold, to penetrate it, a growing avalanche of lobed, dripping, frond-like forms, like secretions and adherences of flower or bivalve, like ice floes and flower petals, stars configuring the zodiacal plane of the sky in that dark night of Bethlehem, of messianic destiny, Gaudian delight, a pleasure that so soon disappears and once gone gives pain, for no rose grows without thorns. And higher yet, the archangelic scene of the Annunciation, crowned in the apex of the archivolt by a great cupola, root of the finialed gable piñon which, sharply erect, rising, now between the four towers, takes the form of a bushy ceramic cypress, eucharistic canticles, Sanctus, Sanctus, Hosanna, Alleluia, a heart bleeding love, bread loaves, an amphora, the pelican, delight, country of wonders. And on each side, symmetrically flanking that conglomeration, two other doors of smaller proportions, and the not-yet-visible Portico of the Rosary, with its Virgin wreathed by a rosary of pink roses, rose of epiphany, a large vaulted doorway to the nonexistent cloister which, by means of amniotic isolation, should envelop the temple, isolate it from the daily roar of the city. Thus, to the left, the Portico of Hope, with its floral corbels and its friezes in the bevels, the massacre of the innocents, the flight into Egypt, providential detours along the path of Redemption, and scenes of Nazareth on the tympanum, the tender baby reappearing, with saws, hooks, chisels, and hammers sculpted on the lintel, the protean archivolt curling as if in eruption, up to the cupola crowned with a grotto, from whence, among rocky crags, emerges the saving ship piloted by Saint Joseph and the dove, tongue of fire, crowded pyramidal crags on the pinnacle, abrupt crests, harp-shaped summits of Montserrat, crown of rocks, stone scepter rising high with mystic emphasis, dominant. And to the right, the Portico of Faith, enraptured altarpiece centered on the presentation of Jesus in the temple, with an outline of images now solemn and impassive, now violent, like the one of John the Baptist preaching in the desert, foretelling the coming of the Messiah, all that upon an embroidered background of wretchedness and suffering, of an interwoven framework of thorns and flowers, buds, corollas, thalamus, sepals, petals, stigmata, honeybees drawn to pollen, and superimposed on the bramble-crag crenellations, the lantern, a three-peaked oil lamp, eternal triangle, base of the Immaculate Conception, dogmatic effigy rising in ecstasy, like an ejaculatory prayer from within a large cascade of sprigs and grape clusters, all those details one can spot carefully from any one of the points of the belfry towers, as you climb the airy spiral staircases, from the doorways, from the enclosed balconies sinuously integrated on the projections of the architraves and cornices of the frontispiece, balconies with bulbous wrought iron railings, small contorted galleries, catwalks, small steps, intestinal cavities, twisted corridors of irregular relief, passages conjoined in a coming and going from the belfries to the facade, four intercommunicating bell towers, harmonically erect, which, if near their bases appear rather strangely compounded with the parameters of the porticoes, as they separate, each acquiring its own shape, they become curving vertical parabolic cones, the two outer pairs equal in height, the two center towers taller. The ascent can begin with the one situated furthest south, on the extreme left-hand side of the facade. There one confirms that the two plinths which serve as the starting point for the archivolts are quadrangular sections evolving toward the circle. This cylindrical part, with apertures that spiral upward, is followed in each bell tower by another form of parabolic silhouette, developed in twelve perpendicular striations which, higher up, become reduced to six, resulting in a prismatic volume of triangular section and polyhedric facets concluding in a finial in the shape of a mitre, a ring, and a crozier all fitted together, four bud-like crests, mosaics, shining, of Ferruginous qualities, carbonaceous, vitreous, porcelain, polychromatic in carmine, incarnadine, pontifical gold and white, bottle green, mauve, crepuscular rose. Passing from one bell tower to another, negotiating a series of narrow catwalks, hyperbolic arches, cramped twisting galleries, small steps, irregular corridors, intestinal cavities, passageways stinking of urine scrawled over with inscriptions and drawings, the large window openings formed by overlapping spirals, enable contemplation of both the foreshortened reliefs of the facade, its cupolas, canopies, vaulted niches, groups of sculpted figures, and the ruinous amphitheater of the empty interior curving toward the north by the vertebral sweep of the temple's central apse, from which we see, as the towers rise, the city spreading out in ever-greater breadth. An exuberant locale, in the heart of the Ensanche's grid, that neighborhood dominated by the spiny shell of the apse, an airy skeleton with specters of empty frames awaiting their stained-glass windows, open to the air and undulating molded waterspouts, gargoyles imprinted on snails, reptiles, lizards, braided serpents, sylvan crenellations of finialed gables and brambly pinnacles, a frenzy of tight rosebuds, of sprigs and thorns, bunches of grapes, rose corolas, of pure lily, wild leaves, virgins, violent deflowering, stems, calyxes, petals, stigmata of passion or pleasure, fossilized faunal flora, curling tension, sprouting stonework sheltering the desolate central esplanade, with its numbered ashlars among weeds leveled by the dust, stones cut from Montjuich, laborious work, an anthill of laborers, wheelbarrows and pulleys, planking, wooden platforms and scaffolds, hammer blows, all done very much according to traditional handicraft, as churches are forever built, stone upon stone. There was the sound of a whistle and the workers called it quits. They turned toward the barracks, gathered around a spigot, scrubbed themselves clean, combed their hair, changed their clothes. Meanwhile, high above, the stonework structure appeared carved from brilliant flashes, doorways opened onto thin air, entrances which led to nowhere, bright flashes rising higher and higher from that splendid sunset, the sun sinking down to the west of the city, heavenly corolla, carmines, purples, garnets, ambers, corals, vermilions, tonalities of flame perhaps degraded, perhaps somewhat altered by the dark lenses of his sunglasses.

Why don't we just drop them all from up here? said Aurora.

That would be spectacular, right? said Raúl. A kind of socialist miracle.

They took all the leaflets out of the bag and the pockets of his overcoat, and Raúl made them disappear, dropping them into the dark round mouth encircled by a wooden handrail, which opened in the center of the slender rotunda, the base of the final section of the belfry, a well blinded with debris, rubble, plaster fragments. The rotunda stank of urine and, above their heads, the tower rose in a tensile hollow, striated with lights and resonances. Exclamations could be heard at varying distances, disjointed commentaries, calls of imprecise origin while down the stairs, a fading echo of heels. I'll keep the map, said Raúl. What harm is there in a map? He opened the map in successive folds, and with his ballpoint pen started randomly adding new marks, notations relative to the city's parks and museums, underlinings, improvised indicators, monuments marked out with a traced circle, a line like those already drawn around the Obelisk of Victory at the intersection of Avenida Diagonal and Paseo de Gracia with its black inscription stone with the eagle clutching a yoke and arrows in its talons, or around the Columbus monument at the Puerta de la Paz, overlooking the port, a stepped circular base with lions guarding the raised bronze column crowned by an observation deck in the form of a terraqueous globe, a golden pedestal for the statue of Columbus discovering America with his index finger, a lordly gesture unfolding against that sky of flashing leaflets fluttering down in soft flight, falling slowly upon the traffic below, in the vast plaza open to the dockside, crossroads of governmental buildings, Customs, Military Headquarters, Naval Administration, the Royal Shipyards Museum, with enough time to take the elevator back down and exit through the underground passage before the employees notice what happened and, blending in with the crowd, to watch the arrival of the police minutes later, pushing through the crowd, cordoning off the area, watching them from the sidewalk like killers who return to the scene of the crime. There were also other marks more difficult to conceal, all in the northeast sector of the city, through the slums of San Martín, San Andrés y Horta, locations of the principal industries, Hispano Olivetti, Enasa, Fabra y Coats, La Maquinista, etcetera, working class neighborhoods, housing projects like Verdún, La Prosperidad, La Trinidad or el Buen Pastor, including the bridge of Santa Coloma along the banks of the Besós River, now outside the city limits.

A city with its back to the sea? Not entirely, not always. Not the old city. The medieval town stretched from watchful Montjuich to the seaside district of Barceloneta, with its moorings and its small anchorage, without sea walls or docks or wharves, right up tight against the sandy flats, a Barcelona centered around the Mons Taber, built outward around the slight grade of its lower slopes, a prominence now buried, almost imperceptible beneath this crowded nucleus of broken alleys delimited by Las Rondas, surrounding avenues laid out along the perimeter of the demolished walls, a polygon crossed perpendicularly by Las Ramblas, starting from the Columbus monument at the wharves, a protonaut in the attitude of discovering America, still decked out a few days earlier in flags and pennants, floral anniversary offerings, a river of plane trees flowing with gentle undulations, as along a fertile plain, prematurely withered and faded by the persistent storms of September, shining tobacco-colored in the subtle atmosphere of October, dividing the Barrio Chino on the left from the Barrio Gótico on the right, the backbone of an enclave so full of enchanting romantic spots like la Plaza Real or la Plaza Medinaceli, peaceful patios like the former Hospital de la Santa Cruz or el patio de los Naranjos, cloisters, bell towers, here Romanesque like San Pablo del Campo, there Gothic like Santa María del Mar or Plaza del Pino, San Justo y Pastor, Baroque facades, Belén, San Severo, San Felipe Neri, La Merced, temples and palaces, the Neoclassical restraint of el Palacio de la Virreina or La Lonja, the medieval commodities exchange, regal buildings, public edifices, el Ayuntamiento, previously el Consell de Cent, opposite la Diputación, the former seat of the Generalitat, the two of them facing off, the space between them forming la Plaza de San Jaime, of Santiago, of Saint James, white knight, defender of the Spanish fatherland, and el Palacio Episcopal and the Civic Government, the old Customs House, and the Military Government and Headquarters, construction executed upon what was the central office of the Mercedarian Order, and the Comandancia de Marina, strategic points like the Telefonica office or the Post Office, at the foot of Vía Layetana, a street choking with traffic which splits the old quarter wide open, a defile of offices and agencies, shipping companies, insurance companies, delegations of governmental organizations, the sinister Superior Police Headquarters, a fosse of overwhelming rectangularity barbarously drawn with a ruling pen amid that glowering mass of towers and dark corners from other times, smoke-darkened stone beneath industrial city vapors which turn the jumbled declining streets gray, mansions converted into flophouses, shops, taverns, hooker bars. The belt of Las Rondas, laid out around the perimeter of the walls demolished in the nineteenth century to allow expansion beyond the confines of the old city, linking a series of important urban junctions like Plaza Urquinaona or Plaza de la Universidad and, above all, at the top of Las Ramblas, Plaza de Cataluña, a hideous commercial epicenter formed by God's perversity between the arched portals of banks and hulking department stores, dislocated masses, discordant compositions, lumpy buildings from which, shortly before closing time, the scattered leaflets fluttered down, white like doves of freedom winging out in a loose whirlwind upon the gawkers clustered together before the shop windows, those bustling avenues tracing the circuit of Las Rondas in the form of an irregular hexagon, with one of its longest sides perpendicular to the line of the sea, a polygon forming the borders of the old city and bounded by all the rest of the city, an outline whose eastern side offers proud nineteenth-century perspectives, delimited by the Ciudadela Park and its Modern Art Museum, which so ephemerally housed the Parliament of Catalunya, while the western side borders the Paralelo Boulevard and its faded accents of the roaring twenties, its gunmen and cabaret singers, striking cartoon facades, footlights, nocturnal lights, la Calle del Marqués del Duero today a mere scarecrow of its former self, a hard bleak chugging artery of heavy traffic, the main axis of the Pueblo Seco district and its slums, now within the limits of Montjuich Park. Enveloping the old city and on an inclined plane toward the amphitheater of surrounding hills, the Ensanche, the work of Ildefonso Cerdà, prophet in the desert cast out from his own land, a monotonous close-knit grid of perpendicular and transversal streets laid out in modules of chamfered intersections, like at Avenida José Antonio, previously la Calle Cortes or, simply, Gran Vía, and el Paseo de Gracia, before reaching los Campos Eliseos, luminous commercial focal point and stock exchange with its ostentatious shop windows and its cafés, hotels, concert halls, splendid flowing rivers of tobacco-colored plane trees, an oasis in that endless succession of straight streets, exactly identical, those parallel to the sea: Aragón, Valencia, Mallorca, Provenza, Rosellón, Córcega; those perpendicular: Nápoles, Calabria, Sicilia, Cerdeña, a whole well-archived empire, a clairvoyant plan of realization, systematically pre-destroyed, uglified, adulterated, Phoenician greed, mean poverty, blind bourgeois incapacity, a snub-nosed grid crucified on a crooked cross, radially, from the point of intersection of the Plaza de las Glorias Catalanas, an unfulfilled center of activity for greater Barcelona, along Avenida Meridiana, city axis running north-south, and along the Avenida del Generalísimo Franco, once called—and still—before the fourtheenth of April, Avenida Alfonso XIII—vulgarly dubbed La Diagonal—running east-west. El Ensanche, a district whose name means expansion, an already narrowed expansion, latticework fenced off in turn by new ramparts of towns once peripheral, old towns annexed by the expansive inertia, populated areas difficult to assimilate, still characterized by their old, small-town atmosphere, working-class districts like Gracia, and Las Corts with its immense stadium el Camp Nou, more leaflets fluttering down upon bleachers and grandstands, before one hundred and fifty thousand spectators, residential neighborhoods like San Gervasio and Bonanova, of graceful and subtly variegated villas, harmonies of times gone by, Sarrià, Tres Torres, Pedralbes, sunny gardens, peaceful roads cut into the gentle slopes rising up to the foot of the mountainous neighborhood, again with a view looking out to sea, over the city, and the working class suburbs to the south and west, the gypsy neighborhood of Casa Antúnez butting up against the Montjuich Cemetery, El Port, Hostafranchs, Sants, Collblanch, La Torrassa, Hospitalet, and now along the banks of the Llobregat River, San Feliu, Esplugas, Cornellà, and to the east and north, the poor industrial districts of Pueblo Nuevo, San Martín, El Clot, La Sagrera, Campo del Arpa, Horta, San Andrés, and on the far side of the Besós River, toward Badalona, Santa Coloma, San Adrián, chemical factories, iron and steel foundries, textile mills, streets and streets caked in soot, smoking chimneys, flames from furnaces, cement-colored walls, gray warehouses, rust, square housing projects like blocks of funeral niches, between vacant lots and garbage dumps and a stalled conglomeration of basic brick buildings, a chaotic development of muddy sidewalks, streets broken by erosion and neglect, of undulating pavement, with puddles, places without automobile traffic, appropriate for driving at top speed. Federico at the wheel and Aurora and Raúl in the backseat, tossing out leaflets in a white trail, at dusk, before the patrol cars on duty doubled in number, when people were coming out of work, throngs and throngs on their dark march.

They ran out of gas on a side street in San Andrés, a few hundred meters from the Buen Pastor neighborhood, and they were stuck. They had to go and look for the nearest service station and they had to ask to borrow a watering can to carry the gas back to the car. Can you imagine how absurd this would be if this had happened to us five minutes earlier, right in the middle of scattering these things about? said Federico. They also went out at daybreak, and the workers gathered on the sidewalks, before the heavy doors of the factories, picked up the leaflets, naked arms, naked proletarian hands, Catalan or not, immigrants from elsewhere in Spain called charnegos, workers from the south, Murcians, Andalusians, emigrants from the countryside, people with bodies bent and curved like sickles, from reaping and harvesting olives, labor lured to the big city, reserve army of capitalism, lumpenproletariat, now workers like the rest, like those who had always been, like the workers who were sons of workers and grandsons of workers, each one united to the others by common class interests, and during the rest break at noon they argued collectively and, now by night, under the kitchen lamp, around the pinewood table, drinks and black tobacco, ideals, a dawning of consciences, of notions and grievances, catchwords shared, the seed of clandestine organization, cells and committees, picket lines, Red October, leaves withering away and cold in emergent crisis, naked arms, fists raised, pumping, pupils like ruffling cedars, wrathful, stand up! famished legion of workers! sons of the people, on your feet, to the barricades!

Look, Daniel, said Escala. What distinguishes us from any other political party, apart from the structural differences of apparatus and organization, is the fact that we possess a totally scientific method of analyzing reality. Which means that we are capable of appreciating reality just as it is, with its laws and its dialectic, without letting ourselves get disoriented by phenomena, by appearances and veils which can obscure it, by its partial or static aspects which don't let you see the forest for the trees. Evidently there is room for errors of interpretation or application but, the same as in any other scientific terrain, subjective errors, it's the person not the method which fails; the method is sound, as objective as reality itself. So, why tell you all this? Well, because, before an action like the one we've got planned, we're obligated more than ever to study reality like an equation or a theorem, without letting ourselves be swayed by ideals, mysticism, or metaphysics, which can lead us to opportunistic or adventurous attitudes. So, yes, if we calmly examine the present situation, what typical traits do we find in the foreground? How do we formulate them and apply them correctly within the frame of our political line? Overall, the unquestionable reality is that the first part of the battle is won. Three short weeks after the start of the academic year we have succeeded in making the strike triumph in every school and department and have effectively shut down the university. The initial phase of our agitation campaign culminated when the police, in order to suppress our attempt to demonstrate, and in an attempt to avoid repeating the events of last February, invaded the university campus and environs and arrested dozens of students. We presented them with the alternative of either trampling their own laws underfoot once more or respecting them, and once more they made a mockery of them. The student committee's response was to plant an explosive device on the Obelisk of Victory, an act which, fortunately, caused no real damage and which, not being claimed by the party, did not compromise our political line either. Although, let's say it directly, it could have had grave consequences. It was an action only partly justified by the student committee's confused state following the arrests and, to a greater extent—the paradox is justified—by its proven inefficiency, but, and this is perfectly clear, under no circumstances should such an action be repeated. Because what we now intend is that the action not stop here, that it continue, elevating it to a level that is quantitatively and qualitatively distinct. From the university we have moved to the street, and we hope that our appeals to the citizenry's opinion and, primarily, to the working class, uniting with other economic demands of a purely political character, that they might crystallize next Thursday in a general strike and a boycott of public transportation. Our comrades in the metalworking industries, textile workers, construction workers, militants in all cells, are all working in the same direction, but for basic security reasons our activities must not be interfered with. Besides, given the situation, it is precisely we, with our departments closed and our students arrested, who should act as a kind of spur to provoke an outburst comprising a series of chain reactions which, as experience shows, if they triumph in Barcelona are likely to spread to the other industrial centers of the region. With only five days to go, the prospects, quite frankly, are good, exceeding all our predictions, permitting us to be optimistic even supposing we fail in our attempt to extend the strike, given that, when a struggle for demands is not in decline but rather in full development, as in our case, any frustrated attempt is not a step backward, but one forward, a simple phase of the process which leads to subsequent actions with positive outcomes. And if from the examination of the current situation and its possibilities we move to a much broader, all-encompassing examination, if we examine the present moment integrating it into the general process of the struggle against the dictatorship, if we compare it, for example, with the situation as it existed in February, what differences can we notice? What conclusions can we reach? For us, the most appreciable change in the objective conditions resides in the evidence of a growing collective awareness, in the distance that goes from a more or less irrational outbreak of rebellion to a massive, rigorously planned action, one charged with political implications previously non-existent, likely to develop into a social context with an increasingly broad base. I refer to the new qualitative fact that our ideology, the communist ideology, can take hold, as it has in various levels of bourgeois society, through their own children, the youth, the Spain of tomorrow, a phenomenon which is obviously the fruit, the evidence of the level of decadence to which the Regime has fallen, and of the now insoluble conflict which exists between the forces of production and the oligarchical regime controlling production. And I also mean the prospects which this new fact opens up to us, in agreement with the postulates and objectives of our political line, and, more concretely, the possibility of finally uniting the diverse parties and opposition political parties, representatives of all the social classes, including the non-monopolist bourgeois and the working class and, why not, certain factions of the clergy and even of the army itself, against their common antithesis and the fascist forms of the government. Which means, the same line of alliance with all classes and social levels who are victims of the oligarchy, which is showing such good results all across Europe, now adapted to Spain's particular situation. The October Revolution, the great Chinese Revolution, were the product of some very concrete circumstances, of a situation assisted by the

European war on one hand, and by the World War on the other, circumstances, although not unrepeatable, it's true, at least imponderable, facts that don't have to be counted on, because none of them have to do with the present Spanish political situation. It's for this reason, Daniel, precisely because the objective now in the foreground is unity, for which reason we cannot permit ourselves the slightest false step, nothing which deviates from our aim of national reconciliation and peaceful overthrow of the dictatorship, now that, as was so well demonstrated during the time of the Maquis resistance, the country is fed up with violence, and any type of direct action would be exploited by the enemy in order to separate us from our possible allies. This, alongside deeper theoretical considerations, such as to what point, in the current circumstances, the recourse to violence does not presuppose a certain lack of confidence in mass actions and in the combative capacity of the working class. So let's put aside all those dreams of sabotage and assault against radio stations until the objective conditions are different.

They moved on to the study of practical methods, how to distribute the work, the writing and printing of leaflets, distribution on foot and by car, dividing up the city according to the official map, marking key points, streets, plazas, buildings, heavily visited spots, hubs of communication, metro stations. They also decided to agree with the remaining university opposition groups to, in a single night, emblazon the walls of the city with calls for the strike, and finally, they discussed the security measures to be taken in case statements made by arrested students gave the police any clues.

Escala: his predilection for museums as the perfect place to speak quietly and furtively. Thus, the Romanesque galleries in the National Art Museum of Catalonia, on Montjuich; or the Royal Shipyards factory museum with its Gothic naves, the present headquarters of the Maritime Museum; or the Museum of Modern Art in Ciudadela Park, inside the old armory which had seen so many different uses before it became the museum, inhabited successively as a royal residence and the ephemeral Parliament of Catalonia; or the Diocesan Museum, installed in the old Seminary, set ablaze in 1936, or the Marés Museum, located within the main building of the Grand Royal Palace, or the City History Museum in the former Casa Padellás, always changing locations, of course, without insisting on anything other than caution. The most important thing: to always have more imagination than the enemy.

It seems like all that business about torture and giving prisoners electric shocks is pure mythomania, said Federico. They've beaten others much less than Leo and almost all of them have spilled the little information they knew.

But it's not the same thing either, said Raúl. Leo had a responsibility that these guys don't have. After all, they're just a few poor bastards picked up randomly.

It's nothing, nothing at all, a slap on the wrist.

There were rumors of new arrests, in which a student wound up dead, that the Falangists were making a blacklist, rumors of searches, of people followed, their telephones bugged. And before they visited Leo's family they'd called on the phone, to see if Floreal was there, and he didn't think it was safe to meet them. Floreal was there, but, more than wanting to leave he seemed desirous of exchanging impressions.

They'd not seen him since before summer vacation, at the end of the spring, when he set up an interview for them with Cayetano, a middle-aged textile worker who'd fallen in with Marsal, the same as Leo, and he brought them regards and encouragement from Leo. A man who'd spent seven months in jail, until the court martial, and as he'd neither said nor admitted anything, he was released, acquitted. The mythic Cayetano, who in the course of the interrogations was black and blue from the blows, and they shocked him with electrical currents right in front of his wife, dislocating one of his kidneys and almost ripping off his scalp, while he was hanging from a heating pipe, with several ribs broken and his feet so swollen they wouldn't fit into his shoes. And he stayed that way for around three weeks, and several more in the hospital, constantly under guard, but neither he nor she had talked, and they were acquitted. Floreal received them happy and excited, showing off a little, saying that Leo was a great kid, that he'd earned the sympathy of them all. Six years? He'll be out again and back in the breach in less than three, dammit. And he told them about Maruja, a connection that had turned out the same as him because she also kept her mouth shut. She's a woman, but I swear to you she's got more balls than most men. And that matters more than the teeth she got knocked out in the police headquarters. She didn't say anything about Marsal, although, he said, you've got to keep in mind that she was tortured for almost a whole month and she's still got no feeling in her thumbs from the days she spent hanging from some handcuffs. And he told them about the comrade who was on the point of committing suicide by making a kind of noose with his handkerchief. About Leo he said that he wasn't having an especially hard time, a few truncheon blows and several hours handcuffed squatting down, until his wrists swelled up like clubs. He was lucky; he was one of the last ones to be caught, and the police were already tired and by then they'd learned enough.

And Floreal: I think it's going to be a success, he said. The working classes are with us. At the bank it's the only thing they talk about and I understand that in the factories there's a tremendous desire to resist. The very use of force and provocation by the police does nothing more than backfire against them and popularize the strike. And it's just that the people won't put up with more, they're not willing to tolerate the dictatorship any longer, starvation wages, and unemployment. Everywhere there's nothing but business failures and bankruptcies, suspension of pay, unpaid bills; and the discontent which the government's political economy awakens is so great that the non-monopolizing bourgeoisie has definitively turned its back on the dictatorship. There are even industrialists who are willing to help, to back the strike. They're for the workers, for a minimum living wage with a sliding scale, for the right to strike, and for democratic liberties.

Let them help, let them help, said Leo's brother-in-law. Then later we can work things out with them.

Floreal smiled, sure, superior, without taking him seriously. There'll be no need, man. Let their own contradictions destroy them. The politics of communism is no trick, simply this: let things run their course. In the very heart of the monopolist oligarchy lie ever greater contradictions, contradictions natural to the imperial phase of capitalism, and this economic crisis has no solution of any kind. Because you've got to keep in mind that there are two kinds of contradictions: the antagonistic ones, meaning those of Spain, and the non-antagonistic ones, meaning the ones from the socialist camp, and peace-loving countries. These are surmountable problems, sibling rivalries, as it were; the others are overwhelming. And the petite bourgeoisie and the middle class are beginning to understand it and to realize that the only solution is socialism. And, listen, man, what I'm telling you, they'll end up accepting it voluntarily.

Voluntarily? The only way is with a pistol pointed at their heart . . . I don't know about theories or about the cosmopolitan bourgeoisie, but I do know how you achieve power, because that's not a question of theories, it's about having balls. I was there when things were going seriously and I know that the one who convinces others and calls the shots is the one who's got the upper hand.

Leo's father intervened, smoothing ruffled feathers. There was something, he said, that he'd seen with his own eyes: Mane, Tecel, Fares, hurriedly scrawled in chalk by some impetuous graffitist along the corridors of the Metro, in the Plaza de Cataluña, on the ad posters. The thing is, it's all just like the grand feast of Belshazzar, like the last days of Pompeii. Capitalism knows that its days are numbered and, while the people suffer, it indulges itself in all kinds of debauchery. He tacked the cloth together as he talked, his glasses slipped down to the tip of his nose, and Teresa listened from the ironing table, serious and working carefully at the same time. The canary in the cage, the dining room table strewn with patterns, the sofa bed and worn-out chairs, the sideboard, the vividly colorful picture of Rome burning, the radio atop a side table covered by a shawl with a fringe of yellow beads. He commented that on Sunday they'd gone to see *Don Juan Tenorio*, the immortal play by the great Zorrilla. A work which, although inspired by religion, never stops being a denunciation against the mentality of the powerful and privileged. What pride! What contempt for their fellow human beings! And the thing is that Zorrilla, a man of the people as he was, could not stop criticizing those who believed that their wealth and position entitled them to have everything, that their life need be nothing more than a succession of wasteful carousing. For wherever I went, I trampled reason, I scoffed at virtue, and mocked justice, and I sold women. He looked at them from above his glasses.

That's the idea! said Juan. And why? Well, because he's got the strength, and whoever has strength can only be conquered by force.

And Leo's father: one way or another, socialism will triumph, that's inevitable. But we all have to do what's possible for the change to be peaceful, because it's the people who suffer the most from violence. Faced with the despotism and outrages of the repressive forces, our peaceful position makes it possible for socialism to garner the sympathies and respect of all, Catholics or agnostics, democrats or bourgeoisie. Bit by bit, each one will be won over to the cause of socialism.

No, sir! No, sir! If one day you convince the bourgeoisie and the priests, it will be because you'll have stopped being a revolutionary. We live in a military theocracy and all the evils of Spain come from the clergy. And that's it.

Now this is another topic. The only religious thinker who has been, at the same time, a humanist was Confucius. And there's no doubt that Christ, as a man, was a great man, but the Catholic Church, however, has always been against progress and liberties, oppressing the true forms of Spanish life, which come from the people, in society. Long before the Romans, the Arevaci, and I don't remember which other early inhabitants of the peninsula, already had a kind of communism. And, if you go looking, throughout the course of all history you'll see how the people have been rebelling, rebelling, here with the peasants purchasing redemption charters, there with the *comuneros*, the men of the Castilian townships who rose up against Charles I, the Revolt of the Brotherhoods in Valencia and Mallorca, and on the other side the Catalan Reapers' War and the viticulturists' revolt and, more recently, the revolutionary impulse of the Catalan and Basque working classes, of the Asturian miners, and the Andalusian farmworkers. It's taken many inquisitions and exactions to subdue these natural impulses of the people, many, mind you. And there lies your role, that of the intellectual humanists: to give culture back its true popular character.

The brother-in-law said that he, too, was for the people's culture, but that of a people in power, exercising revolutionary vigilance. Culture without power only serves to carry you before the rabble, like with Ferrer Guardia. For the people, there can be no culture without power. Of course, then, once their liberties are crushed, yes, then, yes, you might then talk about the spread of culture, spiritual as well as physical. The conversation moved toward the heart of scientific truth contained in popular knowledge and natural medicine, so despised by the bourgeoisie, a class of people who live on the backs of nature, so slandered by the selfish interests of doctors. They spoke about the benefits of a more natural life, one opposed to clerical obscurantism, of rational nutrition, of physical exercise. The father nodded: *mens sana in corpore sano*, he said. And he began to talk about a curandero, a faith healer, who'd relieved his pain when, after having visited who knows how many expensive doctors . . . But the other one didn't let him continue: he explained the necessity of doing away with the family, and liberating sex, the healthy effects of nudism, of exposing the genitals to the sun and the air, that part of the body most usually hidden when it is precisely the one most in need of natural conditions. Sex must be liberated and the family done away with, he repeated.

Lucky that Antonia can't hear you, said Floreal. And I'd like to see you if she decided, I mean, c'mon, to strip it off, and start liberating sex.

But that's got nothing to do with it! It's that nudity is not a vice! Nudism is in no way indecent. It's a serious and scientific thing. Very simply, what's natural.

Floreal smiled, but one noted a certain embarrassment, and he conspicuously insisted on changing the subject; he folded his hands together between his parted knees, looking at the floor, and, now and then, at Raúl and Federico, as if nervous. They talked about Leo. They explained to them again the last visit they'd paid him, in Burgos, and how Teresa was able to see him by passing herself off as his sister. Teresa said that when they saw him, his morale was outstanding and that, apparently, all his companions in jail respected him greatly. Even the guards, said his father. There was one who approached me and asked me if I was his father. I told him, yes sir, and mighty proud, too. And he told me, well you've got yourself a smart one there, you can sure count on him, you can be satisfied. Teresa said: he's got prestige everywhere. And she told how everyone in the neighborhood asked about Leo, how was Leo doing, when was Leo getting out, even people who barely knew him. That was an outrage, that one, said his father. When they came to take him away, if you'd seen them. They behaved in such a way, turning the place upside down, threatening, saying they might just haul us all downtown, that we Reds didn't even have a right to live. And their faces, the hatred. He stopped talking and there was a silence. Then he pointed to the color illustration of Rome burning, under the watchful gaze of Nero, in the foreground, strumming a lyre. We're like the early Christians who suffered as many as ten persecutions, he said. They spoke about Leo's future when the Regime would fall and how he'd have all the doors open to him, about the possibility that he might be pardoned, as they'd been told by a general's chauffeur, and be released in September. If the Regime lasts until then, they said. The people, they said, weren't willing to suffer the consequences of the crisis, hunger, unemployment, and would not tolerate again what they'd already been through after the war, that terror and that humiliation, some in living conditions more appropriate to the Middle Ages.

Each morning, in the marketplace there is a real protest about the high cost of living. All the women complain. Fact is, they can't make it, the money doesn't pay for their groceries.

It's just that after the war people put up with rationing, smuggled goods, abuses, everything, they put up with everything, because their morale was defeated. Now, however, people are filled with the spirit of victory.

I remember eating that rationed chocolate, said Raúl. It was pure carob.

Well, if that's how it was for you, imagine what it must have been like for the worker, said the brother-in-law.

At home we had everything, said Federico.

On leaving, in the car, they talked about how those visits were beginning to feel painful.

Poor Leo, if he could hear them, said Raúl. But, how can you contradict them? Even Floreal himself seems a bit out of touch.

The thing with Floreal, he's just like that, y'know, the guy's a few cards short of a full deck.

Stupid? No way, man. Floreal's a good guy. But he's so engrossed in his discussions and political readings that he's losing sight of reality. He sees everything so clear that if you told him that things are not so easy as all that, that the Regime might still last for quite a while, that it might just take a few years for it to fall, he'd think that you were the one who'd lost sight of reality. And it's for this reason, because he must only talk to people who think just like him; and if someone disagrees with him, he won't even listen to them.

With Adolfo Cuadras it was different, with Fortuny himself, so moderate, no love for passing judgment, for talking too much. With them you could argue, really get into things, they shared many common assumptions, although there might be differences, like when Adolfo Cuadras questioned whether the actions set for Thursday would be successful.

In '51 and including last year, too, the strikes and the boycott of the trolley cars started in the street. Which means, from the ground up, and not the other way around, like now. Then there was no need for appeals or leaflets. At least, I don't remember seeing any.

Because you weren't involved in the matter, said Raúl. But behind things like the strike in '51 there's always some organization. I remember perfectly how the word strike was written everywhere, in chalk, or with whatever was at hand.

That's what I mean, that in every case the initiative started with the masses, it was something in the air. But not now.

Well, then, what good is political activity? If there are no favorable, existing conditions, then someone has to make them.

Excuse me, the ones possible to create get created, although it seems a trite thing to say.

Fine, if the workers don't answer the call it's because they're sons of bitches and they deserve everything that happens to them, said Federico.

Besides, if there were strikes last year in the textile industry, impromptu shutdowns on the factory line, trolley car boycotts, and all that, why not have them now, when the economic crisis is so much worse?

They were in the bar of some big hotel, relaxed and comfortable, with its light odor of blonde tobacco, Chez Adolfo, as they said on the phone to arrange a meeting. Aurora said, look, she's going to lose her slip, and their eyes all swiveled to follow a showy jeweled woman, tinkling, resplendent. They laughed, and Aurora looked at them meekly, quiet, as if waiting to participate. But she also started laughing when nobody was laughing, while they chatted about any old thing, without any specific comic intention. She laughed unexpectedly, inopportunely--by now nobody bothered asking her why--tittering over any random word, repeating it with her light initial stuttering, suppressing herself all the while. Then she went back to her gentle silences, her hand on her cheek, her eyes looking down, focused on the floor. She stayed on the edge of the conversation, and if they asked her opinion, she just said it was fine, or she came out with some marginal observations, questions about the details expressed in a deep voice, barely audible, leaving her sentences unfinished, hanging in the air, seeming to say something more out of courtesy than for being interested in the subject. She was quiet, somewhat withdrawn, and only sometimes, when they'd most forgotten her, did she then raise her eyes, and Raúl felt her gaze, almost sensing her, furtive, penetrating. He looked at her, too, and then she turned her eyes away, looked back again at the floor. When did that start? And when did she stop avoiding his gaze and, like joining one's reflection in the mirror, finally meet the challenge in his eyes and hold his gaze? Not many days had passed since the moment when, the strike in full swing and them planning to spread the protest from the Law School patio to all the university departments, Federico appeared at the meeting accompanied by Aurora, smiling and silent, limiting himself to introducing her as their connection to the Faculty of Medicine. Afterward they gave her a lift to her house and Raúl asked her if she also studied medicine so she could dedicate herself to helping children. Aurora said no, that she didn't like children, that she was majoring in medicine because it was what a cousin of hers was studying, and well, look. Now he's got a fiancée and he's going to get married, she said. She spoke with that deep voice, without turning around, seated next to Federico, but her serious face was reflected in the rearview mirror, her lips very carefully painted, her black eyes looking straight ahead, her hair short and very black. They dropped her off across from the street door, on the sidewalk opposite, and she crossed the street running.

Hey, where did you find her? asked Raúl.

It's a mystery, said Federico.

You brought her along because you like her. C'mon, because if not, I don't get what she's doing here.

The medical students. The medical students have picked her as their liaison. It's their deal.

Fine, but you like her.

Why do I have to like her? She looks like a drag queen. You're the one who likes her. C'mon, I noticed it right away. You like her, tell the truth. She looks like Nefertiti.

She's not bad, man.

Better than Nuria? Who do you like better, for example, Nuria or this one?

What kind of question is that? They're not a bit alike.

Nuria suits you better. She's the right kind of girl, more active, more independent, with her own life and job; y'know, what you might call a partner, a female partner. Look, she'll become an interpreter at the UN. The two of you could work at the UN together. Like that, together, but you each do your own thing. When does she come back?

Well, in June, I suppose. Maybe she'll come for Christmas. Or for Easter. And if she doesn't come, we'll meet up in Paris.

And then you'll get married? In secret? You could choose someone important from the party to be the godfather. Mr. H himself. Mr. H would be fine.

And who's telling you we're planning to get married?

Then, what? You'll be one of these model progressive couples? The ones who don't get married, but it's like they were married and they try not to cheat on each other and everything?

But what the fuck are you saying about cheating and all this bullshit? I couldn't care less about cheating.

Ah, so you don't care if Nuria sleeps with other guys?

Of course not. Y'know, I mean it's a question we've never even brought up. If she's got to spend two years in England and I'm here, it seems like the logical thing to me.

That's good. You're mature people, evolved, that's very good. So then, what you've got to do is sleep with Aurora. I knew that you'd like her, I was sure.

A pale and fragile girl, seeming to lack vitality and yet, so subtly variable, that pale nakedness of full, clean, burnished breasts and tight, lean midriff, the delicate outlines of her lithe, flexible body, the points of her breasts, dark like her lips, like her sex that opened below the soft trim arrowhead of hair, Aurora, now walking ahead, leading him along a series of steps and narrow footbridges, winding along within the forms and projections of the facade, interlinked with the inner hollows, twisted corridors, small rotundas stinking of piss, the contents of bulging bladders aerated upon the columnar bases. She answered him that she wasn't tired. You're agile, said Raúl. And Aurora: well, it's because I have a classical dance class every day. They stopped in some hidden corner and examined the graffiti, names, dates, initials. Nice spot for poor lovers, said Raúl. Through the sinuous aperture one could make out the expanse of the city spreading out toward the setting sun, crepuscular, sonorous as a seashell, the Ensanche extended toward the west in mechanical repetition of the now aging grid of streets, a formula planned more than one hundred years before, Cerdà's plan, an enterprise born under the most auspicious auguries of the oh-so-energetic and driven nineteenth-century bourgeoisie in those years of grace and disgrace, of good fortune and misfortune, of pain and pleasure, of revolutions and restorations, of barricades, repressions, assaults, and communes, when a phantom ran through Europe, an enterprise destined to transfigure the city, predestined, an expansion still being carried out, only now a bit meaner and cheaper, square as an inventory, only on the map, atherosclerotic grid, without parks interspersed nor open blocks with tidy central gardens, but instead blocks closed in around garages, warehouses, small workshops, tight edifications mechanically repeated, windows facing windows, balconies facing balconies, terraces facing terraces, with an ample panorama of more terraces, balconies, and windows, plus some highly coveted attics and penthouses, all facade, artificial stone, dwelling places now no longer homes nor containing the highly-prized symbolic hearth, now simply points of family concentration, mechanically conventional with respect to some forms of life too quickly fluctuating, flats now lacking the spacious nineteenth-century comfort, no proper parlor, the dining room and bedrooms rigidly planned, without dark vestibules or sunny galleries, a sitting room and nothing more, and a stingy profusion of dividing walls, interior patios, flimsy partition walls, calculated inventories of interior height, square footage, cubic footage, palms, handspans, narrownesses, ruinous streets crossed by a degraded extension of a network once previously projected as liberating, cellular excrescence, gray railings, bars, grates and grillwork, the phantasmal outline of those verticalities, four towers like prongs rising up in the dusk. The Sagrada Familia, unfinished temple of rare perspectives, four belfries, an apse and a facade of exuberant imagery, stars, blood, children, flocks of sheep and kings, sculptural groups, ecstatic altarpieces, a precursor or prophet of burning word made flesh incarnate in rapturous effigy, colorations of the sunset, unfinished work, simple anticipation of the promised future, prophetic structure of presumptuous forms, elegant, mere initial phase of what someday was going to be an ambitious shape, the form of a great enterprise realized and raised upon the sacrifices of generations, dogmatic protoplasmic form raised upon what was once only a shadowy wasteland of spectral profiles. Superhuman project, that temple of ardent mystic outer body, the interior wrought like a celestial Jerusalem of leafy branching cedars, a city bound for destruction, that future factory with its unfinished porticoes of the Nativity, Passion uninitiated, Glory unfulfilled, rosary of mysteries in the respective facades east, west, and south, where the sun is born and then vanishes after touching the zenith, with its mass of towers, a serrated mountain of towering summits, craggy thorn stalactite bell towers, Christ's conical ciborium swelling higher than all else, flanked by four evangelical obeliskoid peaks, eagle and child, lion and ox, of the twelve apostolic bell towers, the immaculate cupola of the apse, the dome of the ciborium, the four ovals of the sacristies, slender cusps, pinnacles, pompous pinnacles, lofty aggregate shaped by the dark valley of a cloister, expiatory temple, burning redemption, haughty iron sconce of purification, sharp flames, crested, spiked, and thrusting, shaping a sonorous organ or radiant beacon, all light and harmony, prodigal precursor of most highly purified forms, discoverers in radial forms, ascendant, ovoid arrangements, angular, sloping, waves of undulating lines, vibrant, brambled, elliptical figures, parabolic, hyperboloid, fan-shaped, serrated, sagittal, bulbous, gravid volumes, potbellied, stones set with drafty chinks, chaotic masonry, finials with vertical limits, hypertrophic forms, protean, eruptive, delirious, frothy, rough vegetable luxuriance, bone-dry mosaic, madrepore, crustacean, fruit. Strange edifice, structured from fragmentary elements, indistinct, joining them in a shifting whole, evolving, full of contradictions and coherences, of asymmetrical symmetries, contrasts, resonances, repetitions, gyres and ellipses, allusions and elisions, meticulous concretions, abstractions, forms derived and derivative, in fugue, like a helix which ascends and turns, vanishing in the void. Above the city, the clouds lost their pink tints and turned pale, limp roses of autumn, and the bells rang mildly, like an angelus announcing midday, sonorous city, stretched out toward the west.

Beautiful russet sunset contemplated from that vantage, from the south slope of Montjuich, its back to the city, from the cemetery on the southwest flank, when the glittering sun slid down from the highest part of the columbaria, sunk behind the lowlands around the Llobregat River, fading distances, skies oozing mother-of-pearl slowly losing color, fading to gray. Serene clarity, before a distant terminus of mountains, one glimpsed quiescent shorelines and plains, the incipient intermittencies of the airport, hazy mudflats, smokestacks, and chimneys, quiet smoke unfurling from the industrial outskirts, and closer, almost confused with the cemetery, cubic forms of whitewashed shanties, and further, now along the edge of the waterfront, the Campsa company oil and gas tanks, silvery masses planted around the foot of the Morrot, the promontory of Montjuich brusquely plunging into the sea, blocking the port, leaving only long wharves sticking out, the lines of the breakwaters and counterdikes, the faint beams spinning from the lighthouse. At its arrival, the sun dyed the dusty dividing hedges yellow, low, beneath the swollen foliage of the avenue among the long lines of trees. They left the car and walked on foot up the streets and tilting pavements flanked by Monk's Pepper, gnarled lobed cypresses, clouds of sparrows blowing away, multiplying. The initial nucleus, developed in a gentle slope from the wide avenues, stood out ostentatiously with its solemn mausoleums, human vanities, privileged zone of pantheons crammed together among the luxuriant foliage, cupolas, towers, needles, obelisks, a silent succession of clasped wrought iron gates, locks, grilles, wrought iron, bordered in chains, wrought iron gates spun around pavilions and chapels, Neo-Romanesque structures, Neo-Gothic, Neo-Plateresque, Neoclassic, Neo-Mudejar, Neo-pharaonic, sculpted cyclopean slabs, truncated columns, tombs, crosses, some hieratic bust, an adolescent boy with a wilting stalk, a little girl with tousled curls, wings and drooping bugles, flaming swords, fallen pageboys and sleeping beauties, epitaphs, crowns, pale withered flowers and black ribbons, dry nosegays of everlastings. Further up, as the slope grows steeper, surrounding the sector of pantheons, a wide area of hypogea set into the earth, one avenue atop another, a varied network of facades of modernist flavor, a series of successive doorways, airily curved corbels, dark stained-glass windows, mosaics, floral overlays, wrought iron garlands and grape clusters, an open iron gate, the echoing voices of washerwomen, the stink of bleach. And the sound of hammer blows, a cortege of cars swiftly rounding the turn. And still further up, more visible every moment, between increasingly steep slopes and longer stretches of stairways, the first blocks of niches monotonously repeated, a grid of columbaria and trapezia rising up like skyscrapers, glass gleaming in the sun, reflections interweaving, blocks increasingly bare and vertical, sepulchers now not even whitewashed near the flat crest of the hill, designed like a hypocritical application of the evangelical principle, in a way that while the privileged classes were buried in the lowest areas of the cemetery, the humble people were raised up, the inverse of earthly life, even to the most high, a purely utilitarian, bureaucratic arrangement, final dwelling place or passport, the final number, outskirts with ashen scullery women preparing and cleaning, borrowing the ladder to climb to the top, cleaning the earthenware flower urns and the opaline vases, pouring in water, bouquets, plastic flowers, dusting off portraits and relics, brightening up the inscriptions for their own eyes already set on the soon-to-come All Souls' Day, when along the paths, among the sepulchers, a mournful multitude in a line like ants would heed their call: Barcelonans, in memory of those who fought to give us a more dignified life, in memory of those for whom you fought to provide them with a more dignified life, Barcelonans! . . . They'd set a date to meet at Chez Federico, a nondescript bar-bodega near his house, and Raúl was the only one to arrive on time. The radio was broadcasting the twelve chimes of midday and a brief prayer in Latin. The bells announcing the angelus, the good news which would be fructified in the joyous nativity nine months hence. Before long, the place filled up with construction workers, mostly *charnegos*—non-Catalans—Andalusians, dingy, threadbare, road-weary. They talked, loudly and excited, how the new trolley cars were so badly inspected, about a soccer pool with thirteen correct guesses on the card, about a woman standing outside the construction site. Women can go fuck off, goddammit. Here, smoke a real man's cigarette, dammit. *Ideales*? Sure, fella, they don't kill anybody. This time I got a good pack. Sí, señor, these are the good ones, this batch got properly inspected, they've got the right amount of tobacco in them. I bought them yesterday, no, the day before, when I got off work. And the moment I walked out, I see it's a good pack, I go back in and buy another pack. I get home and I say, goddamn, for once finally, and yesterday, yeah, yesterday, I go back and buy myself thirty. Yeah, you can tell they've been properly inspected. Good, but what the hell do you mean inspected? Look at this gal, look at those pants. Psst, psst, hey baby. I'd give you such a fucking. Hey baby, right here, baby, let's see you loosen that tight ass and shake it more. Baby, baby. She'd come sniffing right around my zipper . . . In short, the typical lumpen conversation, *charnegos* from the countryside without class consciousness or the spirit of making demands for themselves, monotonous chatter about their monotonous work and the monotonous holiday distractions, using leisure time with the leftover fruits of their labor, soccer and cinema, dancing, the bars, whores, girlfriends, wives and children, family meals, Sunday strolls along the streets filled with people out walking, like everybody else, consequences of a life made of empty spaces filled in with too immediate necessities. Joyfully getting comfortable in the new apartment finally granted to them, for example, any old flat on any old block of workers' apartments, feeling pleasantly at home among those four walls after so many years of moving from one crowded house to the next, of sublets, of shanties, now the whole family reunited, a joy identical to that of knowing how to read comics and censored, government-approved publications, or of being able to listen to whatever the radio was broadcasting, or watching, in the bar, the television programs, until, perhaps a word or phrase from some companion, maybe a brief conversation or even reading a leaflet, would unleash in them the unalterable process of becoming aware, the conviction that they'd left their hometown behind for something more than a plate of lentils, no longer the necessity of a greater salary, but rather of a different social structure, other ways of living.

When Aurora came in, the *charnegos* in the doorway stopped whistling and there was an uncomfortable silence while she advanced toward Raúl between smiles and muttered comments. Federico made them wait a little while more and didn't even sit down, leaning toward them, his hands tensely clutching the edge of the table. We'll have to leave the thing with the cemetery for the evening, he said. He explained that there was danger of new searches and arrests, that he'd had to change the location of the Gestetner machine, move it to another, safer place. He had it outside, in the car.

But, what's going on?

Nothing really, I suppose, collective panic. The only sure thing is that those guys have squealed themselves hoarse. But it's in case they end up saying something they don't even really know but it turns out to be correct.

Fortuny watched them from the backseat, covering the cyclostyle with a folded overcoat. We've thought about Pluto's studio, they said. It was a clear morning, transparent, of limpid autumnal clarities.

Goddammit! shouted Pluto. I was afraid of some shitty luck like this. What, don't you have any better place than my pad? Just let you print all your papers here, man, like it's nothing. You guys are crazy! Crazy!

I warn you that if they catch us you're going to be in trouble, said Federico. The owner of the house always catches the worst of it.

Ah, well, I'm warning you guys that I'll sing, alright? Come the first shakedown, I'm spilling all the beans. Besides, you guys aren't serious about anything. To start with, why do all four of you need to be here, like some committee meeting? Wasn't it enough for the one guy to come who had to take care of this piece of junk? That's what I think, at least. And now, there'll be guys trooping in and out. The lady at the front door is going to think I've turned queer.

Pluto's studio was on the terrace roof, with a view down into the center of the block. It consisted of a single room with a large loft, barely furnished, a bed with oversize pillows like a sofa, an electric heater, glasses and bottles, a record player on the floor, set on a colorful striped blanket, the walls with clippings, most of them reproductions of nudes. On the roof, the door of the toilet banged now and then, flimsy. Pluto watched, seemingly astonished, as they placed the cyclostyle in the center of the room. At other times he would be relaxing on the sofa, spinning his brilliant disquisitions, for example, about the need to officially resurrect the phallic cult, starting with the basic idea that all human beings naturally tend to seek maximum pleasure, now physical, now spiritual, also called mystical, only achievable by the overcoming of the individual ego, only achievable through the complete physical union with another being or mutual understanding, a pleasure which no one achieves by themselves alone, since no one can be united with themself, also demonstrating the always frustrated character of the pretended self-unions or masturbatory practices, owing to the impossibility of being, at the same time and in the same sense, each one of the two parts or determinate objects of the union. Therefore, the pleasure results from the performance or penetration of one exterior agent in action, in the same way that the kinetic energy of active heat, which is the fire, causes the log, which is potential heat, to become kinetic energy as well, and thus modifies it. Just as a cane doesn't move if it is not moved by the hand which clutches it, it is therefore essential to make reference to the said modifying agent, the penetrating subject or phallus, necessarily adequate to the task, the efficient cause or creative act par excellence, and to accept the cult, now unofficial, its function almost furtively described as being consubstantial with human nature, converting it, consequently, into the official cult of humanity. And he offered an examination of the singularly rich vocabulary that popular language uses in naming the aforementioned phallus, generally allusive expressions, owing perhaps to its external apparatus, perhaps to its driving power, expressions of every kind, feminine, ambiguous, neutral, epicene, exploring the attributes of omnipotence and omnipresence which have always been traditionally applied to such a venerated tool. But now he was in no mood for jokes.

At least take it up to the loft, he said.

The others, however, as if suddenly exalted, rushed back down the stairwell in a whirlwind, pushing, reckless, a staircase with kitchen odors, voices, radio music, echoes gathered from floor to floor, beneath the dim central skylight, and now in the doorway, they laughed uncontrollably when Aurora, straggling behind them down the last flight, asked them to explain the precise meaning of the word carajo. Splendid noonday, yes, all in the full sun and a lovely feathering of cumulus clouds. And in the car they started arguing again about whether the time had come for direct action. Federico said that, the risk being more or less the same, they might as well do things seriously.

I find it absurd that they'd shoot you simply for planting a purely symbolic explosive, he said. This is playing Prometheus.

Well, but the explosive's already gone off, alright? said Raúl. Even if the police picked us up now, it's not like they're catching us red-handed, so I don't see why they have to know that we set it.

Oh sure, like they're just some thumb-sucking idiots. They'll know perfectly well it has to be the same people who were dropping the leaflets. What's funny is that Pluto thought he was just joking when he said they'd beat us black and blue if they caught us. He thought he was teasing me. But the police don't sit around sucking their thumbs. They wouldn't treat us like the ones they caught at the university.

Alright, alright, don't get on my case, a small explosive is one thing, a real bomb is another, said Fortuny.

I know that. Except for the police it's the same. That's why I say it's ridiculous, man. We might as well plant bombs. Why don't we? Why was Mr. H chewing your ass?

No señor, no, because then you'll change the subject away from the peaceful tactic of mass action, said Raúl, which is the only thing possible right now. Look at what happened with the guerillas. Apart from the fact that Escala does nothing more than toe the party line, which is exactly what we've got to do.

Not to mention how much it costs just to get a simple strike going, said Fortuny. Well, let's be a little reasonable, dammit. Who's likely to follow us if we use violence?

We've got to get them to follow us, that's irrefutable, said Raúl. Revolutions have never been carried out with peaceful means. But first we've to go manage to create some objective conditions of a pre-revolutionary system.

Mr. H. dixit, said Federico. The boss has convinced you. The boss is the boss and you've let yourselves be handled.

Boss, my ass, said Fortuny. It's just the way it is, man. Violence is always the last resort.

The other way around, the last resort is what we've got right here and now, something symbolic. They're willing to shoot us and we're contenting ourselves with symbols like the Obelisk. If there's no real direct action it's because we're incapable of carrying it out and then we console ourselves by saying that a peaceful strike is more effective. Is that why we learned to throw bombs? See, they're more realistic in the army.

C'mon, c'mon, don't say stupid things, Escala's totally right, said Fortuny. What do you think, a few bombs are going to topple the Regime? Arguing about this is like continuing to worry about Budapest when our situation is precisely the opposite. Just nonsense.

And, in any case, Escala doesn't say so because he's Escala, but because you've got to think that Escala knows the objective conditions better than we do. He has a broader vision, less partial, in fact, and knows things we don't know which serve as a basis for the analysis that the leadership is making. We always move in the same circles. Besides, if we belong to the party it's not to make war on our own account. By ourselves, we're not going anywhere.

That's perfectly clear. And think of the repression that would follow any real bombing.

Better. That way things will really heat up. Everyone knows that. The weird thing would be if there were no repression, seems to me.

C'mon, c'mon, don't talk like an irresponsible fool, dammit, said Fortuny.

He seemed annoyed, and Federico insisted on pestering them with his descriptions of arrests and torture. They'll accuse us of setting every bomb in recent years, he said. And Raúl just joined up. And then, the firing squad. Accomplices like Pluto will get thirty years. Firing squad? said Federico. If we survive that long. After the electric shocks, after they rip out your fingernails, after they cook your feet over a brazier. Can you imagine? And Aurora said *qué horror*, the same as when she said *qué susto*—what a fright—without intonation, without emotion, more as if she would like to feel the horror than as if she really felt it. They dropped her off in front of her house, on the opposite side, and she crossed the street at a run. So long, Epaminondas, said Federico. Upon entering the doorway, Aurora turned briefly and waved. Raúl had moved up to take her seat, in the front.

And to you, Pelopidas, said Federico. I'm going to call the two of you Pelopidas and Epaminondas.

What's that supposed to mean? said Fortuny.

But Federico didn't answer, his eyes amused, deliberately fixed on the steering wheel, with the same expression of days before, when he asked Raúl what was going on with Aurora. Are you lovers? he'd said. At that moment they'd also been in the car, except without Fortuny. What nonsense. Why do we have to be? Raúl had said. And Federico had said: because, that's why, because you look at each other, the expected observation, expected since, a few days earlier, sitting in a creamery, Raúl noticed that Federico had noticed the looks he'd exchanged with Aurora. Just the looks but nothing more, not that contact beneath the table, the foot sought out, the foot not withdrawn, in mid-discussion, when he said, it seems very good to me, and she said, me, too. And Fortuny said, the what? Chez Fortuny, a neighborhood creamery, and of course Adolfo Cuadras was absent. They talked about Adolfo Cuadras and his opinions about the convenience of balancing political action with—if not subordinating it to—professional training. I don't mean to be nosy with Count Adolfo, said Federico. It seems fine to me that he devotes himself to his novels and all that. I also switched from Pure Math and now I study Economics, which is what interests me. The only thing I have to say is that, objectively, political activity is more important. Now alone together, Federico tried to get him to talk as he drove him home. When they got there, he shut off the motor and they kept chatting for a while.

You're sleeping together, he said. I know it for sure. C'mon, it was obvious right away. And it's fine, totally fine. Perfect revolutionaries. Clandestine behavior must be organized just so, by couples. Then there would always be this thing of emulation, of trying to look good in front of each other, I mean. Like the Sacred Band of Thebes.

The university now closed down, as they were leaving the meeting where it had been decided to take the demonstration to the street, it was Aurora, the liaison to the Medical School, who offered to help them. If you want, I can help you, she told them. Federico made fun of the precautions they were taking, of the meetings on the patio in front of the Central Library, at Chez Adolfo or Chez Raúl, of their sunglasses and synchronized watches. Seems like we're just playing at being spies, he said. But when the time came, his hands and forehead were sweating. When in the translucent, colorless dawn, the city streets, el Paseo de Gracia, frozen, inert, Raúl walked with Aurora toward the steps around the Obelisk of Victory, arms around their waists, and he passed her a cigarette, the fuse sticking out of her open purse, she said I don't know how to smoke, blowing in an attempt to fan the cigarette tip that didn't ignite the fuse, and because of the delay, Federico drove by to pick them up at the exact time without them having finished, his face frozen in the frame of the car window, the motor in first gear, while Raúl was still busy placing the explosive at the foot of the black plaque with the imperial eagle. They pulled away, driving up Avenida del Generalísimo Franco, the three of them in silence, until, a few blocks further on, the liberating explosion sounded from behind them, their emotions running no higher, really, than when simply scattering leaflets, the same wait, the same slow series of dizzying seconds of vacillation, as if desiring to suddenly pull back from the now-arrived present moment, the leaflets dropped from atop the Columbus Monument, from a rooftop, from any random street corner, in the magnificent sunset. And then the handoffs in cars, at twilight. Did they really think a mishap was possible? They were seized with an excited euphoria or delight, and even the little blunders made them laugh, when they ran out of gas after just finishing that drop-off, for example, after visiting the Montjuich Cemetery, through the industrial neighborhoods, which shortly thereafter, now at night, would be a glowering no man's land, with their strings of street lamps and spotlights illuminating empty streets, of extended uncertainty, boxed in between endless walls, squat masses, silhouetted chimneys, whitenesses like skylights.

Shining city, there below, windows, shop windows, symmetrical streetlights, weak like early morning stars, and the sky, the clouds dissipated, not wild, but smooth, neither carmine nor purple, nor scarlet, nor vermillion, nor flame-colored, nor pink, now only mauve, lilac, distant blues, livid distances, vast finale to the sunset, empty skies, finally pacified, pearly paleness increasingly higher or further away, crystallized, forged from cold stars. A broad expanse overflowing from sea to mountain and from river to river, open on the west to the flats of the Llobregat and on the east to the Besós and Maresme, a city without rivers, between rivers, of shining arteries traced upon the boulevards, built upon the now buried sandy loam, alluvion deposited in the shadow of Montjuich, great hulk tumbling down above the sea like a cape or promontory, solitary, quarried, with its pergolas and lookouts, shanties and palaces, museums, its Pueblo Español, and its cemetery, its prison and its amusement park, Tierra Negra, dark as a wolf's ass, where the whores gathered, its park, its autumnal avenues, woodsy avenues scoured by the crisp October wind, boughs stripped bare, and at the end, at the far opposite end of the city, the outline of the chain of hills, San Pedro Mártir rising before Puig de l'Ossa, Vallvidrera, Tibidabo formerly called the Sierra de Collcerola, with its funicular and its rides and attractions crowned by the Church of the Sacred Heart, expiatory temple, new

Acropolis from which, on a clear day, it was possible to glimpse, standing out far in the distance, the massif of Montserrat, ogival rocks, a monumental group like an arrangement of miters or scepters, Tibidabo and its foothills, Carmel, Güell Park hosting elegant waltzes, subtle wit, art of ingenuity, lucid Gaudian delight, el Turó de la Peira, nicknamed la Pelada—bald mountain—a relief of hills closing in like a fortress wall, opacities rising higher as one descended, almost gropingly to the dim window apertures formed of overlapping helixes, reflections from the streets snuffed out the dark foundational stones. They had discovered Federico's car parked in the same spot as before, in front of the building, illuminated by a street lamp. At the foot of the bell tower, in the interior esplanade, two or three figures were moving beneath the dim glow of a few light bulbs, and someone said to them in French that they'd need to leave by the other gate, on the Calle Cerdeña, where someday they were going to erect the Facade of the Passion, to cross that desolate spot surrounded by dimensions magnified by the gloom. Sacred institution, enterprise born beneath the best auguries of the oh-so-influential nineteenth-century bourgeoisie in those years of the Lord, of disgrace or delight, of revolutions and restorations, or barricades, shrapnel, repressions, attacks, uprisings, pronouncements, revolts, communes, when a phantom ran through Europe, flower of the east, temple raised like an immense spiky flower, amazed at having sprouted up there in this restless, turbulent city, among mischievous, violent, and incendiary people, an enterprise destined to transfigure the city, predestined, Gaudian proto-project, prophet in the desert, superhuman work, temple of hopes and certainty, of glory and passion, of resurrection and death, of redemption and fall, an eminence of towers and towers like summits gathered in a ring, sum of obelisks, Sardana of giants, Corpus Christi, flowering broom, striated sierra, streaked red and yellow like the Catalan flag—la senyera, mountain of the brown-skinned Virgin, pointy, like scepters or miters, crown of thorns, Catalan rose of flowering April, angelic organ, mosaic, tall and slender, immense expiatory iron sconce of sharp flames, monumental future. But now, now along Calle Mallorca, where someday they would raise the Facade of Glory, only a brick wall which barely permitted one to see the rough, incongruous back side of the four bell towers and the curve of the apse, the empty inner area, all facade, the Facade of the Nativity, appreciable in all its details as one turned the corner on Calle Marina, altarpiece dedicated to the rosy epiphany, to the joyful coming of the beloved bonny baby boy, offspring of non-parents perplexed and joyous, not conceived, hosanna, alleluia, come to the world to fulfill his historic role so many times prophesied, to suffer, redeem, and be glorified, Star of Nazareth, of Mount Zion, Jerusalem of branching cedars, celestial city, chosen people, captive people, liberated, led, and driven to a new homeland by that messianic pre-messiah born of the waters, visionary who, by the favor of the powerful ones among whom he had been raised, preferred the cause of the oppressed and fought for them, although in spite of them and of their own weaknesses, knowing that he would never set foot in the promised land. Unfulfilled destiny, ruin or mountain or rose of four holy thorns, four traces of blood upon a background of gold, lost colors, neither crepuscular gold nor blood, starry sky, bright lights and sparkles from the street.

Sagrado Aborto—Holy Abortion—a work which merely seems something wherein the Barcelona bourgeoisie might have wanted to see its own reflection, but, above all, to perpetuate, project, and give itself permanence, to embody its future in stone, like in an open book situating the family at the center of all social organization, a family that if, on one hand, reproduces the scheme of the most Holy Trinity or the unity of the three—three persons in one single nature—on the other it is conceived in the image and likeness of its own family ideal, with a father that is more, much more than the man equal to any other who pretends to be, a father who is really the creator, the founder, the generative force par excellence, and a mother of immaculate purity and, above all, a beloved son who, satisfying the expectations placed on him, after overcoming, one after another, the trials life holds in store for him, will definitively consolidate the paternal enterprise, converting it into a true empire. Except that this enterprise might very well not flow along the expected channels. It might well be overwhelmed or crushed by an enterprise no longer distinct from it but even opposed to it, and it fit that that Dies Irae, Dies Illa was not the long-awaited one, and while that empire fell, a new one was constructed from its ruins, in its place, a temple sporting distinct facades, the Facade of the Popular Uprising, with its stony reliefs of the masses taking the streets and barricades with weapons like raised fists and explosions and fires, fire at will, a people on the march against the repressive charges and discharges, advancing, overwhelming, crushing, with a red deployment of flags, a final flourish, proclaiming their triumph. And the Facade of the Revolution, depicting the construction of socialism per se, where hammers and sickles would cease to be weapons in order to become tools, where the machine would not be used to contend against muscular strength but would augment it, in that singular representation of a construction which constructs itself, soberly but harmonically, in the light, with the strength of intelligence, like a sun soaring high in the sky. And in the center, flanked by the other two, the Facade of the New Society, for some reason, like the *Divine Comedy*, more abstract, more difficult to express or perhaps, to imagine. An enterprise not metaphysical but materialistic, not mechanical but dialectical, critical of criticism. What sense would any other task, or any other problem, have in the face of this one, the most intimate reasons for living, writing, setting down, like a line of ants, one word after another, one paragraph after another? What importance could the rest have? What might be comparable? Gaudeamus! Gaudeamus igitur!

Did they think it possible? Any mishap? They chatted on happily, without any excess emotion, Raúl leaning on the back of the front seat, his head between Aurora and Federico, and Federico, attentive to the traffic, talking about what happened. Then it's turned out well, he said. Young people willing and with initiative. It's turned out very well. And he told them he'd gotten rid of the remaining leaflets, tossing them out at several intersections, over near Horta. I didn't see any cops around there. They must have all been around here, trailing us. He spoke to Raúl, looking at him at intervals in the rearview mirror, his eyes bright, smiling. I thought they were coming for me. Suddenly I had the feeling that I was driving the only red Renault in Barcelona. And I thought, now they're going to shoot and they'd shoot holes through the cans of paint. Can you imagine if they shot up the trunk and I started leaving a trail behind like Tom Thumb and they ended up catching me? Man, no matter how fast I drove, I'd be leaving a trail and they'd nab me. I'd have no way out. Just like some wounded rat, like common vermin. And they talked about that night, when the police caught them painting slogans and, now at police headquarters, they started to ask them about the names of those who, in the other sectors of the city, would be also emblazoning the walls with a call to strike. Now Aurora was quiet, still, looking straight ahead. Hasta luego, Epaminondas, said Federico on dropping her off, and she crossed the street and waved. Raúl took her seat, wondering, without saying it, whether or not now was the time to sever ties. They agreed that Federico would come by to pick him up at a quarter to twelve on the dot. The car stopped in front of the shadowy garden wall. Federico cut the engine and leaned on the steering wheel, turned partly sideways. They'll stick us in there together, he said. In the same cell.

The family was gathered in the study, Papa, Felipe, Uncle Gregorio, and Felipe would lead them in praying a rosary. The litanies echoed darkly. What are they doing, he asked Eloísa. Well, they're praying the rosary, said Eloísa in a low voice. She told him about Uncle Gregorio and about Leonor, how every day, shopping, she came up to her to share her frustration about Uncle Gregorio. It seems the poor man is a mess. He forgets everything, loses everything, his overcoat, his hat, everything. If it weren't for Leonor, he might well have walked out naked into the street. And she's desperate. She always tells me that if this happens, that if that . . . such a talker. And ugly. She's got a face like a lumberjack.

But look, it seems she takes good care of him. Since she's been with him so many years. Besides, each to his own. And people talk so much that I don't listen to anyone anymore. She turned back to her pots and pans, evasive, seemingly eager to change the subject.

Felipe: the sense of strangeness which increasingly, inevitably, his brother's aspect aroused in him, perhaps because of how infrequently they now saw each other, that soutane fitted to the waist and, then below, open in well-cut pleats which he gathered as he sat down, those skirts which, when he walked, offered quick glimpses of his light shoes, his hands, white and nervous, searching in his pockets, and his seemingly weightless fluttering black cape. An attire which, as if by contrast, seemed to alter his figure, and even his physiognomy, more than the passing of the years, his cheeks seemingly dislocated, his curly eyelashes around his close-set eyes, with soft dark bags under them, and his mouth affable and slack, and his slight prognathism; his whole aspect, in short, suggesting something of Velazquez's young monarch.

Uncle Gregorio leafed through magazines from a jumbled pile next to the lamp, reading them very close to his face with one eye open, the other covered with the palm of his hand. The lamp glowed like a distant planet and sat in a corner of the table, that table with legs carved like a beast's claws, with its escritoire and table cover, its bronze paperweights, and the tall glassed-in mahogany bookcase to one side, and the cubistic armchairs crowding the too-small room. They chatted about the strike, and the closing of the university.

This is what they call nowadays hooliganism, said Papa. In my time the same thing happened with the business about Maura yes, Maura no.

Well, from the looks of it, the students who were arrested have been beaten terribly, said Raúl. They're saying, too, that they've been tortured with electrical shocks.

Just gossip, said Papa. In this country, anything that will make the authorities look bad is sure to get plenty of attention.

He said that what young people needed to do was study more and protest less, that with these things you only played right into the hands of politicians and troublemakers. Look at Ramona's husband, this Bonet boy. And Pedro himself. They sure know what they're doing. How are you going to compare a Jacinto Bonet, an Arcadio Catarineu, responsible, organized, well-educated people with good reputations with this bunch of sinister characters who talk about fixing the world, who promise the world and heaven to come after a revolution when we all know already how it will turn out? How can you conceive of a world without lawyers, notaries, property records, administrative agencies, protocols, registries, and all those things which are the reality of everyday life, the things that make the country run? Very nice all this thinking that everything belongs to everyone. But theory is one thing and the realities of a practical society are something quite different. The magazines slipped off of Uncle Gregorio's seat. He'd stood up and they accompanied him to the door.

Eh, let them protest, he said. They're young. I'd protest, too. Never a lack of motives, never will be.

C'mon, Gregorio, don't talk gibberish. My son studies, he does well, he pays his expenses doing some translation work he found, and that's what counts. At our age, for pensioners like us, the main thing is peace and quiet. And may God keep it that way.

Felipe said grace and Raúl, sitting across from him, had to pretend to cough in order to not join in on the Amen at the end. Papa took their hands, Felipe's left, Raúl's right. Tonight my happiness is complete, he said. The two of you here, with me. One son a priest, dedicated to God, and the other who will succeed me in the business of this world, Raúl, who is already like a consolation, a support in my old age. He'll get married and he'll be a great lawyer. What more can a father ask of God? Felipe in turn squeezed his hand and made some joke, he said that, besides, with soups like the ones Eloísa makes the happiness was even greater. He spoke excitedly and with a certain haste, anecdotes from his life in Jerez, of the mentality of Andalusian women, so distinct from Catalan women, always thinking about parties and balls, bullfights and hunting parties, charming women and well-meaning at heart, yes, but predisposed, by the upbringing they received and what they might say, to persist in their anachronistic customs of pomp and ostentation, and of the enormous work that could be performed from the confessional correcting, inexorably, their weaknesses, awakening a sense of charity deeper than mere holiday fundraising, stimulating their moral responsibilities to help those in need, the masses of people without work and without any true spiritual formation. He didn't want coffee with dessert but he asked Raúl for a cigarette. Now he said that given that Raúl surely saw social problems from a different angle, someday the two of them had to talk at length, with complete frankness. And he was concerned about the poor priests, generally older men, who didn't give social questions the importance they deserved, who kept spending all their good intentions fighting against modern dance styles and women's fashions, as if there existed nothing more than the Sixth Commandment. Prudish sanctimony. I find it absurd that those priests want to invent problems when there are so many real, urgent ones. What's the problem with this rock music or whatever they call it? It's physical exercise like any other. They were alone in the small sitting room, in the armchairs of the three-piece sofa, and Felipe looked at him smiling, those pleats hanging over his pointed shoes; a stranger, a stranger evocative of distant memories, no more familiar to Raúl than when, still a seminarian, during some Christmas vacation, he spoke to him of his sudden vocation upon reading *The Way*, his journey to Damascus. The Way is Jesus Christ and to find our way is to find Christ. It was after dinner, before Felipe retired to his room, and there was a silence. Then he'd said, you must think, oh man, everybody knows I've got a brother studying to be a priest, and he laughed sitting across from him, in the other armchair by the three-piece sofa, next to the record player with the built-in radio. It was that same night, later on, when Raúl discovered a forgotten hair shirt in the bathroom, next to the sink.

He closed the door and put a record on the turntable, at low volume, one selected at random. The seat Felipe had occupied was still warm and he moved to the other one. He glanced at the northeast sector of the map, the city unfolding toward the east in successive creases, from left to right, toward the Besós, toward San Andrés and the ancient town of San Martín. Folded up again, he left the map on the small Moroccan table. He looked again at his watch. Footsteps sounded upstairs, the rattling cascade of a toilet flushing, and in some nearby street, rhythmically moving away, the sound of the night watchman's staff. He settled down in the armchair, sideways, his legs hanging over one side. The sitting room was to the left of the vestibule, opposite the office, and it communicated with the dining room through a glass door that always stood open. Dining room in what style? By the light of the sitting room it was possible to make out, among four chairs, the square table, thick spindle-shaped legs, ringed, symmetrically striated, the chairs studded, with initials in repoussé on the black leather backrest and, in the shadows behind them, the solid dimensions of the sideboard and trencher, with its small brass shields and its gray marbles. The sitting room offered a more homogeneous aspect, the haughty Imperial table pushed up against the wall with its non-functioning bronzed clock, an allegorical cluster of agricultural figures and tools, and its alabaster lamp, the wood carved like palm trees and opaline globes, the small glass table with tubular framework, the Dutch vase, the glass cabinet with porcelains and silver, crystal, cups for drinking chocolate, ivories, Chinese knickknacks, tiny baskets of zinc flowers, presents from Papa's wedding or perhaps from Grandpa Jorge's or Grandpa Francisco's, and the photo of Mama in Port de la Selva, and the painting, that garden scene in a golden frame with a rose bed in the foreground. The three-piece suite had no specific style, simply overstuffed, upholstered in caramel-colored plush, slightly worn, the sofa sunken down at one end, next to the floor lamp, the whole set centered around the Moroccan table, which had come from the old chalet on Calle Mallorca, a small marquetry table with arabesques, geometric patterns, heavy and low, with closed horseshoe arches, very inviting for a child, easy for them to imagine that it was a castle or a fortress.

VII

They're not going to let you eat in peace, Eloísa said. All your food's going to get cold.

Who was it? Papa asked.

Uncle Gregorio, said Raúl, he's coming over for coffee.

Above all don't forget about Arcadio Catarineu, Papa said. You should thank him for the interest he's shown: good manners cost nothing. He's a wonderful person and I'm sure that he must've moved heaven and earth. He's a very close friend of mine.

When I get back from school, Papa, said Raúl. Right now I've got a pounding headache.

You should rest a bit, Papa said. Why don't you take a little nap?

You're going to go to school today, too? Eloísa said.

Of course, said Raúl. Just like every day.

Right, just like every day, Eloísa said.

She smiled again through her tears, her face in shambles, her features momentarily smudged. She stayed standing, behind Papa's chair.

And Achilles? Raúl asked. How's he doing?

Achilles? Eloísa said. Oh, he's doing really well . He still hasn't gone and hidden away. Since the weather's been nice this morning, really nice, he came out and took a walk in the sun.

She tucked her handkerchief inside her sweater cuff, now composed, though her voice was still rough from sobbing.

He's a smart turtle.

Sheesh, it seems unbelievable how smart that lil' creature is, Eloísa said. Everything, he understands everything. The same as a person.

More, said Raúl. More than many people.

More, more, said Eloísa. Can it be possible, so small? But have some more cauliflower, help yourself. It's no good cold. Here, eat, eat.

She wanted to know if it tasted good, with so many delays she was worried that it might have turned out bad, that she might've overcooked it. She couldn't keep an eye on the oven like that, with the telephone ringing all morning. Really, hasn't it gone all mushy? she said. Ah, and also that girl with the man's voice called, twice. And that young lady who sounds like a foreigner. And that tall, handsome boy, the one dressed in brown. Well, he didn't say who it was, really, but I figure it was him. He said that he'd call back. And well . . . She lowered her eyes, as if embarrassed, as if embarrassed with satisfaction.

Well, yes, yes, Papa said. Everybody has shown maximum interest in you. And it's those moments when you find out who are your real friends and who aren't. They've all offered to help me, unconditionally.

All of them, really, you hear? Eloísa said. The telephone hasn't stopped ringing all morning. How was it possible these bandits weren't going to release you right away? Look how they wanted to keep you prisoner.

She cleared away the dirty plates, put the dish of cauliflower in the oven.

Well, as you've seen, they haven't been able to, Raúl said.

Right, that's it, they haven't been able to, they heard Eloísa saying from the hallway.

But, damn it, son, you've given us such a scare, Papa said. Such a scare.

He explained that when they gave them the news, Eloísa almost had a nervous breakdown. And he began making calls immediately, to seek out influential people, Jacinto Bonet, a Jesuit father, Arcadio Catarineu, Montserrat. Montserrat has performed magnificently, he said. And that morning when the inspector showed up to request information, Eloísa looked at him as if she was going to claw out his eyes. I served him some coffee and told him, come on now, this is all absurd, the fact that you ended up locked inside the university didn't mean that you were one of the troublemakers, after all, you're a good student and a good son. And this perfect animal goes and says to me that they're not so concerned with all that as with what's behind it all, because it's always the communists who are behind these things. Can you imagine! He was the typical sort, the very lowest kind. And then I explained to him, see, what our family stands for, that we've always been Catholics, right-wing, and I'd belonged to the Maurist Youth, what we endured in the war, how persecuted we were, how your cousin died and the posthumous medal they conferred on him for his heroism. And Eloísa, when she served him coffee, looked and looked at him in that way, and didn't even seem to hear me. I was finally able to send her out to go shopping and then he asked me if she was nuts, or I don't know what kind of rude thing he said. A real beast, what you call an animal. Only when we were done, as he was leaving, did it occur to him to tell me that it really wasn't a very important matter, just a pure formality; after the whole time having me on the edge of my seat. A real animal.

Eloísa served Papa a ground chicken breast patty and Raúl a sirloin steak with green peppers. Papa added a few spoonfuls of his preserves to the ground meat and then licked the spoon. Eloísa had returned to her spot behind Papa's chair, watching Raúl eat. Raúl raised his eyes, their glances met, and once again she scrunched up her features around her eyes.

That man, she said.

But you see now, they acted ridiculous, Raúl said.

My boy, my boy, Papa said. Thank God it was no more than a scare, but you've put us through a real trial. Why didn't it occur to you to get out of there in time? To have to tolerate questions about you from a man like that, especially about what you do and what you don't do, the same as if you were a criminal. And the way he asked, so irritable and aggressive. I told him that you weren't mixed up in politics: your father, your studies, and nothing else. That when one is young there's always the danger of bad friends, of falling in with the wrong crowd that takes advantage of your good disposition, like this Leo, whom I've never liked. But I told him that you hadn't let yourself be fooled.

You talked to him about Leo? Raúl said.

Yes, of course, but I told him that he was already in jail, Papa said. He asked me all kinds of questions, about your friends, what you read, if you attend Mass on Sundays, if you play some sport, and God knows how many other things. And by the way, this fellow Quintana. They've caught him, too? Goodness, my boy, look what fools you're all turning into; to let yourselves get caught in this trap . . . Then the communists come along and take advantage of it to make propaganda. Such an awful situation, my boy.

The telephone rang and Raúl stood up again. Leave it, I'll get it, he said to Eloísa. It was Aurora's voice. Hola, he heard her saying, her deep Hola, followed by a pregnant pause filled with expectation, with meaning, her voice exasperatingly unalterable, the way she said Raúl stretching it out, softly accentuating both vowels, as caressingly as ever, as if nothing had happened. Would it be possible to go back, to recover what was lost with the same naturalness that he had always managed to maintain, without explanations or any type of scenes, to turn into a mere passing accident how much had happened since he began to notice the glances Aurora and Adolfo Cuadras exchanged, the soft, gentle eyes suddenly raised, staring silent and steadily while the others talked, feet touching underneath the table and brusquely separated when, at last, midway through dinner, Raúl bent down to pick up the napkin that he'd previously let slide off his lap? They met alone one afternoon, before he stopped calling her, save for questions strictly about political activity, and they kissed. Tongues sliding back and forth, twisting, just like at first, when they took advantage of any pretext to lag behind, to embrace with violence or fury and then rejoin the others in the most imperceptible way. Good fellow, Adolfo Cuadras, right? he'd said. Since he's like that, rather cold and reserved, at first he's sort of inconspicuous. But the more you know him, the more you appreciate him. And she said: I find him fascinating. He walked with his arm around her shoulder a little longer. They'd met on the way out from classes and they went walking casually along the curving unkempt streets of Vallcarca, among stepped gardens, gallant noucentist towers, peaceful atmosphere of yellow facades, as if the sap lost by the leaves as they withered, dried, crackling, curling inward, colored the very calm air, perfumed by the smoke of autumnal bonfires. Then Raúl said that deep down inside he didn't care for anything or anyone, not even his own skin. Only to destroy, to contribute however possible to the disappearance of the society they lived in, of himself, if it were necessary, to put an end, once and for all, and at any price, to this monstrous farce.

Sometimes I'd like to be a bomb, he said.

And he scrutinized that light, those transparencies, losing himself inside her pupils, eyes tranquil, elusive, shifting gaze. Thinking what? Wanting what? The sensation that he had just admired a landscape that was not only impossible to embrace but one whose beauty was impossible to evoke.

Everything is so strange, Aurora said.

They seemed to be searching for the stairs which linked the cross streets in brusque openings, offering unexpected views. From the top, leaning against the hard iron railings, Aurora contemplated the city, and Raúl, giving her a light, also lit his own cigarette, two glowing coals from the same flame. Now returning, Aurora stopped halfway across the viaduct. Down below, framed by the populated striations of El Putxet and Mount Carmel, their confluence in the foreground, they glimpsed the buildings at the port, cranes, metallic towers, ships anchored and tied up alongside the most distant wharves, the line of the seawall and, as if surging from the hazy horizon, the trail from a jet plane cutting through the sky above, drifting, in a light arc. It's like one of those illustrations in a children's book, Raúl said. He watched her look, raise her glance, her face like a projection of her neck, as if emerging from the loose straight hair, gleams of light from jet and black patent leather, nocturnal suns, mercurial reflections, raising her glance and slowly dropping it, as she continued, features slanted, marbled lines and something like the shadow of a wing upon her face, impenetrable augury. He walked her home and at the door kissed her lightly, hardly brushing her with his lips; he crossed the street without turning around. Ciao, he'd said, and smiled, and she followed him with her eyes while he walked away or perhaps not, or perhaps she was on the verge of calling him or she called him perhaps too late, uncertainties imagined beforehand, as he tried to imagine her attitude, and now recalled, now that he wouldn't go to meet her when he finished teaching classes for the day. He contemplated them, given over to a giddy excitement increasingly less dissimulated, unsettled, audacious, playful, affectedly naughty, turning with insolence toward their companion, the hypocritical countenance, crafty movements, the eye lively and greedy. He rapped his knuckles on the table, and as the calm spread among deliberate shhh-shhhs and the final comments of the slowest ones, the final winks of pleasant guiltiness, noise of chairs and impudent coughs, the conjugation *yo fui, tú fuiste, él fue* became more and more pronounced, chanted in a chorus in the class downstairs. The classroom was spacious, surely an old dormitory superficially remodeled: the balcony, open to the canopies of the trees, centered between tall wainscoting of painted in green latex; and a row of coat hooks hung with small jackets, and a chalkboard which at these hours always gleamed and made it necessary to turn on the florescent lights, and the distorting, emery-polished glass door, and the pattern on the floor turned gray by the scrapes and scratches made by the legs of the tables and chairs. They were arranged by order of height on the staircase in the entryway, very straight and tidy, very close together, in their new suits, short pants or golf trousers, neckties straightened, hair impeccably combed, slick with pomade, affable, goofy expressions, lightly squinting against the light, smiles, mouths slightly open, some eyelid half closed in brutish stupefaction, in vacant gaze; in the first rows, the freckled face of Ángel Gómez, the dead naughty boy, who knows if unconfessed, run over by a streetcar coming back from the beach, in Barceloneta.

You can consult the book. It doesn't help you at all either if you copy from your neighbor because I'll notice it right away. The theme I am going to set you is general, it does not correspond to any specific question. I'll not be satisfied with names, dates, and battles. What I am interested in is the concept.

The concept? He looked over those rows of crossed arms upon the table, in candid, astonished attitudes. Was it possible there might not be anything more behind those faces, apart from the habitual solitary double life, smug secrets shared by all, that there might not be anybody with even some imprecise discomfort, some incipient unease, or a need to rebel, though not manifest, or exteriorized, something that might emerge instead of the conventional mischief and pranks, someone with an indocility more insane than mischievous, more horrific than applauded by his elders? Not five nor three nor even one? The class downstairs had fallen silent, and now, from the balcony, came the dry rattling of the foliage, the golden brown plane trees pattering like the rain. Behind and above, the fan-shaped fronds of a tensely slender palm tree opened to the sun, a pompous projection from the dark scanty garden, without plants, crushed by all the footsteps, with a delicate filigree of iron fence over which the boys climbed wearily during recess. He had the luck, just upon leaving, of spotting a taxi coming slowly down the street, solitary, and now in Via Laietana, as they drove past the main police headquarters—la Jefatura Superior de Policía—while the taxi driver spun out his ideas to resolve the increasingly urgent traffic problem, he stared meditatively at the balconies' thick iron bars, the police standing guard on the sidewalks. He got out at Plaza Ramón Berenguer, a bronze equestrian statue of the gallant count standing tall before the fosse of green grassy spaces which extended to the foot of the old Roman wall, cornered blocks of stone crowned by the bell tower and the buttresses of Santa Agata's chapel and, rising behind, King Martin's Watchtower, with its rounded arches, the towers and spires of the cathedral, a strict composition of ogival heights and arrogances. On the lawn were old stones, cippi, head-stones, columns, Roman remains, carefully arranged, and black ivy crawling up the walls, and some cypress airily elegantly erect, rough, with gnarled burls. There were still a few minutes remaining and he felt the serenity of walking into those streets from other times, without cars, without the din of traffic, vertical narrows and reliefs, towers, cornices, sober facings, sliced buttresses, gargoyles, reliefs animated by the wingbeats of pigeons, stained-glass windows, long windows, blazoned arches, a deep portal open to a patio with porticoes, with flights of steps, a tranquility made almost oppressive as one plunged into the subterranean passages of the City History Museum, upon descending to the level of the Roman and Visigoth buildings excavated from the subsoil of the Gothic Quarter, either from the entry in the Casa Padellás, in the Plaza del Rey, or more probably entering from the area around the ancient Palau Reial Major on Calle de los Condes de Barcelona. He wandered through the vast rooms of coffered ceilings, like clear skies, low and white with the dull buzzing of the air extractors and the insect-like squalling from some sputtering fluorescent light, women's heels striking the wooden floor, walkways edged with cord stretching along between foundations of bulwarks and ruined walls, disinterred remains, dolios, pools, drains, sewer culverts, fragments of mosaic floors, columns, mutilated sculptures, funeral amphorae and tombstones engraved with epitaphs, display cases holding ceramics, oil lamps, earthenware vessels, domestic utensils, a wheel rim, and almost exactly at five o'clock, without any more delay than the time needed to arrive at their meeting, he saw him appear from the opposite direction, approaching casually, eyeglasses sparkling, satchel hanging perpendicular, barely swinging. Now walking together, they continued visiting the museum, following the outlines of the ruins spread out in the quiet light, terreous walls, hollows, fragmentary pavements, pausing before the display cases, sarcophaguses, models, marble busts, talking without looking at one another, looking without seeing those neatly labeled objects.

The analysis of what we might be able to call momentary logistical factors, by the light of a panorama characterized, on one side, by the undoubtedly generalized development of the protest movement and, on the other, by the progressive isolation and increasingly evident weakness of the inner circle wedded to power, offers us a somewhat paradoxical balance of appearances. But the paradox, Daniel, is nothing more than a problem superficially raised or resolved, in such a way that, if we probe a bit deeper into reality, the apparent dissonances will begin harmonizing until they finally coalesce through distinct phases of an absolutely logical process. For example, there's nothing casual about us seeing ourselves bound to a situation in which, with respect to the preceding phase, the relationship between forces and possibilities is, in fact, found to be inverted. While the leaders of the principal labor sectors were ruined as a consequence of the arrests caused by the repressive spread of the dictatorship, and from that point on it proved impossible to push the masses of people toward a general strike, currently, the party apparatus is not only being reconstructed cell by cell but also the number of new militants—the vast majority of them young people—has multiplied exponentially, giving us a much wider foundation than any other postwar movement. Furthermore, as the economy is presently in crisis, with no long-term stability, and the emigration of manual labor abroad serves to conjure up the ghost of unemployment, the opportunities for action in the industrial centers are much more favorable, now that the workers don't feel threatened as before with massive reprisals, when there was the constant risk hanging over their heads of being fired from the company and going on to swell the ranks of the army of reserve labor. However more stable the situation of the proletariat, however higher its standard of living, the greater is its ideological maturity and, consequently greater, too, is its willingness to confront and combat both economic grievances and, no less aggressively, political ones. That's why, precisely, they should be the Asturian miners, and the Catalan and Basque working classes—not the lumpen Andalusians—the most traditional and dependable redoubts of all truly revolutionary action, those workers capable of moving beyond blind, sporadic violence, albeit the recent awakening of the southern farm workers denotes a degree of political awareness heretofore unseen and very worthy of being considered in the future, especially because all reports we've received seem to confirm that their movement is somehow related to our own. The situation in the university, however, is found to be characterized, perhaps, by some less positive traits, the fruit, nevertheless, of the considerable degree of development we have achieved. The active opposition minorities are notoriously more numerous than in years past and are more politicized, their organization better aligned with the diverse interests that they represent; but due precisely to this process of radicalization, they are similarly and on the whole more disconnected from the collective student mass and, at this time, can boast of fewer possibilities of converting the university into a true spur of genuine political uprising. It's appropriate to elucidate this point to the maximum, not in order to resign ourselves to the possible failure of the strikes and student demonstrations in solidarity with the Asturian miners we are planning to develop starting Friday but rather in order to take the opportune measures leading to reducing the negative potential of this situation and, in any case, to face realities, in order to comprehend that the simple labor of agitation which we have deployed in summoning people to these demonstrations, distributing pamphlets, gathering signatures and, above all, the fact that the university departments have joined the debate, and one of them, the Faculty of Economics, has approved a motion of support for the striking miners and against police repression, is now, in itself, a giant step forward in the current objective conditions. Moreover, the fact that for the first time the students have let their voice be heard, no longer solely in clandestine newspapers but directly, through their university departments, is such clear proof of the fertility of our tactic of making use of the legal possibilities that I almost dare to say that the role of the remaining anticipated actions, demonstrations, and strikes, need be no other than that of further enhancing and amplifying the political triumph already achieved. Which does not prevent—quite the contrary, it's one more argument in its favor—considering the matter of Friday as vitally important whether we frame it within the actual university protest itself—a fire which must be kept burning at all costs—or if we situate it within the entirety of our politics of national reconciliation against the dictatorship, with its demands for constant, growing, aggressive challenges at all levels and in all areas, in light of the fact that what matters least is whether we meet those demands or not, that the final objective is different, so much more so when the capitalist system, torn by its inherent contradictions, is naturally incapable of satisfying them in any real and definitive way, of applying another politics—not stopgap solutions, not hot compresses. Our fight progresses in a field where, strictly speaking, it is not fitting to speak of isolated successes and failures without referring continually to the political context considered in its internal dialectic, to the general sense of the work undertaken. And at the present time, given the gap which exists not only between one local sector and another, but also between the different environments of each local sector, our line of strategy is that of stimulating all the partial actions possible, however small they be, as an inevitable prelude to vaster actions that will end up culminating in the anticipated strike on a national scale—precisely, the national political strike—and the subsequent outcome, the overthrow of the dictatorship. For this reason, our primary foreground objective before actions like what's coming on Friday, an objective which must not be confused with our principal objective, is no other than that of preventing the pre-existing rift between politicized minorities and the student movement from becoming dangerously accentuated. It's essential to not lose this contact with the mass of students although it might be a momentary lessening of the political level of the actions already begun; we have the obligation to establish closer ties with the student masses, making their challenges our own, joining with them in mutual understanding, galvanizing them with an aggressive program of protest capable of helping to precipitate the surrounding potential energies. As a vanguard organization, our role consists of this, to be attentive and to know how to put into play all the elements capable of consolidating people's willpower and to widen the operative base, so that our final objectives will appear framed in a more general panorama of demands, such as those specific to the university and, above all, those proceeding from the specific history of Catalonia. This is the direction our work must take. Meaning, aside from the fact that in university circles we find ourselves avoiding an impasse, perhaps the one which precedes the final assault, our principal effort in this phase of consolidation and reorganization—of biding our time in winter quarters, as it were—must be to move toward emphasizing more than ever problems such as Catalan nationalism and the Catalan people's politico-cultural aspirations for national independence. In other words, from this point on, to raise the most appropriate challenges so they take root and develop in the present, and in the future, to unify, around our axioms, the overwhelming majority of this youth of bourgeois extraction which fills the lecture halls of the University of Barcelona. It's about a question already present, in the street, not created by us, but now our duty, if we want to prevent the forces of the bourgeoisie and the anti-Francoist petite bourgeoisie from distorting our traditional position in this regard, the position of a working-class party, from raising our flag as their own, as some exclusive standard of bourgeois nationalism. If we wish to avoid this, our duty is to assume the vanguard of legitimate popular aspirations and channel them, and give them a correct and revolutionary solution according to the Marxist-Leninist postulates of the national problem. Let's recap.

Escala, a fascinating personality, all logic and realism, rigor and method, implacable and precise like a machine in both his theoretical analyses and his expositions expressed in dialectical terms--above and beyond operations only formally true--as well as in the practical verification of such analyses, in their modifying application of an objective reality of whose examination they were, at the same time, a product. A man of action, equally fast and reflective in decisions, serious, inflexible, meticulous, resolute, cautious to the maximum, with his notes hidden in the false bottom of a matchbox, in his packets of cigarette papers, on a candy wrapper, his codes, his security methods for attending meetings, his system of making the telephone numbers which he made unrecognizable by removing from them some previously determined digit, his habit of not leaving behind even a single cigarette butt.

What should reality be called? said Fortuny.

They were wondering if he might live in secrecy like other members of the leadership or if, as seemed most likely, he concealed his true activities under a completely legal situation. In that case, given his education and abilities, how could he not be some well-known person, at least in intellectual circles, especially because nothing in that world, probably, followed any of Escala's deliberate intentions, of avoiding public life, of being completely devoted to the revolutionary fight, a complete dedication full of stimuli and suggestions, an impassioned perspective indicated by the clarity of his conduct and his objectives, by his necessary withdrawals, an enterprise which made any other task, by comparison, diminished, contingent, ephemeral, and absurdly marginal. And they considered the attractions and risks that, in contrast to the monotonous and insignificant exercise of practicing the law, could offer them this double life, an anodyne exterior hiding a pseudonym popularized through clandestine writings, a subversive action quite dangerous enough to keep all the police in the country in a state of anxiety, a political responsibility which grew in secret and, in the decisive moment, to appear at the front of the revolutionary forces which like a phantom army would sprout up in the street, raised against the established powers, in an uncertain fight. Fortuny insisted, however, on the convenience of creating for himself a solid academic position, not now as a personal future but rather, above all, as a political platform for the future; a professorship, for example, he said. With Federico, however, it wasn't possible to talk seriously about these things, always with his little smiles and reservations when he found out that they'd attended some committee meeting. What, what does this boss of yours matter, he'd say, or simply, what does Mr. H. matter, with reticence and sarcasm ringing in his voice directed especially at Fortuny, and Fortuny, catching his drift, accepting the game, patiently began to defend the theoretical principles or practical details called into question, while Raúl rarely joined in. But when he did, as if, in Federico's presence, he couldn't resist pestering Fortuny, he contradicted him and recanted himself to take Federico's side, in order to back him up with some obvious sophism or joke.

Saint Lucas is right, said Federico. If we manage to raise enough hell for them to close the university, now that will be accomplishing a lot. We've dedicated so much just to play at conspirators, to organize committees, liaison committees, and committees of committees, that we're no longer capable of organizing anything else. And this business of taking advantage of the legal opportunities seems to me a Machiavellian folly. Why make demands through channels that we never tire of denouncing as antidemocratic? What kind of revolution is this that makes use of the same legality it claims it wants to destroy? What you'd have to do, instead of wasting time infiltrating it, is to create a new and parallel power, a real power, which will turn the official legality into fiction. This is playing their game and Saint Lucas says that he's fed up with games, and he's right.

Alright, alright, let's not kid around, said Fortuny. I respect Cuadras as much as you do and I consider him to be a valuable person, he writes very good material. Or put it this way, as a friend and as a writer, he's very good, but when it comes to politics, forget it, man, he understands nothing. And not because what he says isn't true, but rather because, although it's true, he's politically incorrect. Those are two very distinct points of view, and Cuadras, for however much he does, will never know how to see reality in terms of a political perspective.

They let Federico drive them to Miramar, to stretch their legs, he said, to get a bit of fresh air, and the car sat parked underneath a streetlamp's cone of light, and they wandered along the deserted sidewalk, stopping here and there, leaning on the parapet. Below them the glassy reflections of the port looked deeper and deeper. Speak: also like a reflection in the water, not yet like a footprint in the sand, still looking at the present and not the past, formulating oneself while formulating what one believes, explaining to yourself in the act of explaining it, meaning, creating what you believe or wish to believe or what you wish would seem that you believe. They'd spent the afternoon at Adolfo's house, arguing the whole time. Adolfo hadn't intervened, nor Aurora, seated at his feet, next to the record player, taking no notice as if she were part of some group of sculptures, the record spinning round and round, tiny inexorable singers, hybrid tendernesses again and again, infinitely, barbarous ire or delirium, exalted triumph of death. And Adolfo ended up interrupting them with his listening, this is the best thing in the world, directed at Raúl, as if they hadn't heard it enough already, and turning up the volume on the record player he made them be quiet, whether they were listening or not, quantus tremor est futurus, the choirs interrupting, uninterrupted torrent of madness, cries, bugles, liber scriptus proferetur, and then we will see in the lower part, underground, the black fire and the claws, naked, contorted, clawed open and burnt, the serpent sent to strike at a friar's sinful sex, condemnation into which the reprobates are hurled, right and left, from the tombs broke open by the tumult, chaos of those abducted and stolen away, angels and demons, reptilian bats, dragons, Capricorns, celestial wings, and there above, in glory, above meeknesses of beatitudes, a rupturing of roaring vermillion, rent asunder in a full cataclysm of blues, the Incarnate, the Born, the Suffered, the Dead, the Entombed, the Resurrected, with his arms extended as a discoverer or navigator now come to demand accounts, open wounds on his hands, descending at the vanguard of a whirling headlong rush of exterminators just as implacably just as justly implacable, final judgment, a grandiose miniature belonging to the so-called Missal of Santa Eulalia, on display in the Chapterhouse Room of the Cathedral, masterpiece of the master Destorrents, the very image, at the same time, of the cathedral which serves it as refuge, this cathedral of lugubrious sepulchers and cryptical darknesses, stone beneath stone beneath the which there is nothing more but necrosis and folded layers of ash, and on high, the glorious light, stained-glass and rose windows projecting themselves in a circumference one could easily imagine eternally crossed by reflections, by polychromatic incidences refracted upon the gold of the altarpieces. Raúl drank in silence, careful not to look at Aurora, seemingly lost in thought and meditative, feigning not listening more than to be polite, or at least trying his best to look like what he was pretending, as if, at heart, disinterested, as if for the sake of pure respect and deference toward Adolfo, as if especially so many personal questions could separate them, noble, decently.

It was the night before, at most the night before the night before. Federico came by to pick him up after dinner, and they had coffee together. Raúl talked to him about Aurora, said that he was beginning to question her sincerity. Federico asked him about what, in what way.

I don't know, in everything. Politically, for example.

Of course. What did you think? C'mon, man, it's obvious that Nefertiti doesn't, as they say, give a flying fuck about politics. Ana María, yes, she does, you see. Ana María is sincere. Besides, the fact that her face looks exactly like a squid puts her in an objective situation comparable to that of the proletariat: she's got nothing to lose.

But the thing is, Nefertiti's case is very curious. She's the daughter of exiles and it seems that her father was one of those men who wouldn't listen to any talk about coming back to Spain as long as Franco was in power. I mean, she grew up in the most politicized environment possible.

That's why, that's why she's already immune. She's a communist because she fell in with our group. She could just as well have hooked up with some Carlist bunch, and now she'd be a Carlist.

Sitting by the windows, either careless or sleepy, he rambled on between yawns about the advantages of having received the most reactionary kind of upbringing imaginable, despite however much conditioning that might imply, because being raised in such a way awoke, in those capable of overcoming it, an inevitable predisposition for radicalism and intolerance. In that way I'm an old-fashioned kind of man, he said. The best saying is that one about spare the rod and spoil the child. It's what normally allows a sour-tempered person to become most broadly developed. And there's nothing that makes one quite so stupid as these modern pedagogical methods, with classes designed to seem like games, just inane, without any challenges. Old-fashioned, I'm an old-fashioned man. He looked at him cheerfully, and as the conversation drifted toward the dangerous waters of raising the child to be a sociable being, in conformity with contemporary society, Raúl had to redirect the focus to Nefertiti.

Well, of course, in the case of Nefertiti you can't talk about intolerance. On the contrary, she's one of the freest people I know. And I warn you that this, too, has its advantages. Our relationship, for example, has been totally open, without the exclusiveness or fidelity that all women demand. In that way, at least, she's like me, very independent. She's always done just what she feels like, and I do the same, and it's never occurred to either one of us to ask the other one what they're doing or to make scenes or anything. We've never really felt tied to each other, not ever. This has got nothing to do with politics, of course, but what I mean is that meeting a woman like Aurora is a nice break. When it runs its course, we can go our separate ways and still be friends. At least she's got this going for her: she knows how to behave herself.

She was among the first ones caught, under the porticoes swept by the water cannons, among the students who had remained on the periphery of the crushing crowd throttled by the narrow doors and interior staircases, a stumbling staggering avalanche toward the garden and the patios that had happened when, as the explosives were set off, the police charged, a compact mass bristling with billy clubs that poured in through the vestibule over the broken glass and fallen sopping placards, and Raúl saw a policeman point him out with his finger, then he felt a strong blow on his arm, next to his neck, while he stood there as if blocked, against a military jacket with metal buttons, and they pinned his arms behind his back, lifting up on them, pulling him along doubled over, shoving him, into the lecture hall, and they locked him in with others, a few of them all soaking wet and everyone battered and bruised to one degree or another. And then they made them come out one by one, at gunpoint, and started putting them into vans, the plaza completely cordoned off, full of cops on foot and horseback who chased away groups of onlookers, rerouted traffic. As he looked around vainly trying to spot Aurora he saw two or three policemen bring Federico out, almost dragging him, handcuffed, struggling in his jacket, and at police headquarters he caught a glimpse of him again from the peephole in the underground cells, after they'd booked and fingerprinted him they searched his pockets, tamquam reus, a cell where there was already some stranger who asked him what he knew about it all, with whom he had nothing in common, and the cell started filling up, all of them looking at the stranger, all somewhat disoriented, some stranger who didn't look like a student, and so many detainees kept arriving that they had to move the whores somewhere else to make room, or maybe the drag queens, or at least this is what they understood the guard was giving orders about, let's see, move the girls, and in one cell they started to sing *Gaudeamus Igitur* but they made them shut up immediately before anybody else got the urge to join them, and as the first names were called to make their statements the place started to go quiet, and when he saw Federico through the peephole he asked the guard to open the door and tried to meet him at the urinal, and Federico said, Daniel in the lions' den, and they immediately separated them, move it, move it, Federico toward a cell further away from the stairs, and he ended up reappearing partially visible in his field of vision, below the peephole, when they called him to make a statement without him coming back down after a short while, like the others, who came back downstairs saying that they'd heard shouts, saying that the police had discovered a mimeograph machine, saying that somebody had squealed, saying that they were beating the shit out of some student from Sciences, that they were searching everybody's house, that they'd made a film of the demonstration, talking about it, more and more frightened, and he stayed there glued to the peephole and then he heard his name, Raúl Ferrer. Badly lit stairs, iron bars, the guardroom, more stairs, blind corridors, doors, skylights, inner offices, interconnected offices, cold throughout the whole way, his hands in his pockets, preceded and followed by two sad-faced cops, and the inspector invited him to have a seat. There was a calendar with a color picture of an alpine landscape, and the inspector made small talk; he wanted to know if he was there because of what happened at the university and he talked about how when he was a student, too, before the war, and about his admiration for Ortega and the poetry of Juan Ramón, and when the voices that reached them through the skylight increased in violence and those inarticulate sounds became clearly defined as a kind of cry or whining he smiled at him, his eyes luminous, before, naturally, they took him into the adjoining office, which had a window with translucent panes and that neon light so annoying, buzzing and chirping like an insect, and he entertained himself contemplating how the glass turned clear in the light of dawn until a man dressed all in black appeared who shouted at him to stand up. Are you tired? Well, look kid, I'm even more so, just look how things stand. Two or three others had come in, staring at him in silence, and when they removed the Coca-Cola-style wall calendar, showing a picture of a girl with long blond hair and big showy tits, in the little window frame he caught a quick glimpse of some shining pupils. They left him alone again and, after a short while, in the office where they took down his statement, the cop in black offered him a cigarette as the interrogation started, questions and routine answers which he dictated laboriously to the typist, questions intoned with sarcasm and a certain lack of enthusiasm, assuming the answer to be yes, no doubt, no reply necessary, he'd learned about the demonstration by reading a handbill, if he didn't know, of course it's clear, who were the ones responsible for destroying the portraits of Franco, and for setting off the explosives, if he didn't maintain relations or contact with some clandestine organization, if he hadn't incited his friends to cause a disturbance, if he hadn't shouted subversive slogans, if he didn't know one Francisco Guillén, student of economics and, once the statement was signed, personal questions, if he was happy, for example, or what were his political ideas and his religious feelings, questions offered an equally concise and negative response: I'm not a strong supporter of Franco, I'm not interested in politics, I have no religious beliefs, etcetera but not, for that reason, accepted with any less friendliness. We don't persecute anyone for ideas, out there each person is free to believe what they think, they said. What we do persecute is when those ideas are demonstrated with subversive motives. And they took him out into the hallway, and he saw that Federico was sitting a little further down the hall, his expression alert and expectant, and as soon as the cop in black stuck his head out a door and shouted, Jenaro, get these guys out of here, another one of the cops who was there said to Federico, alright, and tell your family that next time there's no need to move heaven and earth, it's not the end of the world. Nothing happens to the guy who's done nothing wrong. And here you've seen we're not cannibals eating human flesh. The same inspector who'd accused him of being Federico Quintana, the one who'd destroyed the portraits of Franco, and who had given him three minutes to talk if he didn't want them to tune him up, because he wasn't saying a word, like a communist, three minutes which Federico watched closely on the clock until it ran out, and then he said, time's up, and the policeman knocked him down with the first backhand, this one's a cocky stuck-up little son of a bitch.

But they didn't touch me again.

They must have noticed you're a masochist.

No way, the flesh must be tamed, subdued, disciplined. This is what's called an experience. Getting arrested, I mean. Mr. H. will help you see its positive aspects right away. It's a forge, a school, etcetera.

They ate breakfast on a café patio, euphoric and haggard, their faces seemingly illuminated by the early morning sun reflected off the sidewalks. They'd gone inside to the telephone in the back, on the right, through the sordid interior sown with wet sawdust, to call their respective houses, Federico saying, it's always back and to the right, and Raúl, this reminds me of the police headquarters, and on the way they cleaned up in the men's room, lightly, hurriedly, without stopping their chatter, exchanging conjectures, reconstructing the events. They suddenly changed their behavior, said Federico. It must have been when my parents started using their influence. It seems that they showed up at the Headquarters and, since they wouldn't let them see me, they got the governor to intervene or I don't know what. Like a gentleman, I've come out like a gentleman. From the looks of it, going into my house, the police shit their pants. And Raúl: my father also just told me that he got in touch with I don't know how many people. And Federico: it's the police who started all the trouble with their searches. The only thing that pisses me off is that they haven't returned my address book. Did the guy with the mustache question you, too? And Raúl: with the mustache? Yes, but not your guy. That one dressed all in black. Listen, and Nefertiti? Do you know if they released her? And Federico: Nefertiti? Of course. She was wonderful. And Federico explained how he'd been in the next room when they questioned her and he'd listened to it through the skylight. She stammered a lot, and I heard them saying: this girl is an idiot, he said. They released her right away. I think they let all the girls go. They asked what she was doing in the very front line and she said that she'd wanted to get out of there, right away, but that, when she saw so many billy clubs in front of her, it scared her. A truly great performance. They'd ordered another café con leche and more ensaimadas and, as the waiter brought their coffee and was clearing away the other cups, they sat back in their chairs, as if lost in their thoughts.

Then Raúl said: the one who I'm sure I didn't see, not even a hair, is Adolfo Cuadras.

He leaned on the table again and watched the coffee-soaked sugar lump on his spoon slowly dissolve, without raising his eyes, but Federico's sarcastic tone as he said that guy, that guy, made it easy to imagine him shaking his head like one who wants to feign annoyance, laughing with his eyes.

That guy, that guy. He's our evangelist but he lets himself miss an episode like this one. Bad, very bad for a writer. I always tell him that, as a writer, he's got to try everything, seek new experiences. Everything, you've got to try everything.

Go on, keep cracking jokes, one day you'll find yourself in the shit without knowing how it happened.

They talked about Guillén. Federico said that the one who'd squealed was Puigbó, that they'd found him with a packet of propaganda and then the guy spilled the beans. I don't think they caught Guillén. He must be hiding out. What's going on is that Puigbó must have said that he was the one who passed him the propaganda, and now they'll charge him for the explosives and the pictures of Franco. He'll have to run up to France. And Raúl: and García Moll? Nothing, said Federico. If his name hasn't come up yet, that means it won't. They also talked about the advisability that some comrades should hide out for a few days no matter what, and they studied the precautions they should take for themselves, starting with the supposition, more than probable, that they were going to be followed and that they would have to be very careful using the telephone, how to reorganize themselves as soon as possible, of re-contacting Fortuny, Fortuny, who, at these hours, would be out walking with Escala around the sunny cloisters of the cathedral, spacious corridors, their floors worn smooth, with sepulchral stones interlaid among the flagstones, inscriptions, emblems seemingly filed down, barely decipherable, around the patio enclosed by iron gates, framed by the spare, meticulous openwork of the transept arches, the patio, the quiet mass of palms and magnolias, the Well of the Geese, the shrine of the lavatorium, cold stone, fountain of clear bubbles and oozing mossy excrescences, with the sparkling spout which seems to center the attention on the keystone of the shadowy vault, in its high, jutting relief, Saint George battling the dragon, brambly vertigo, the flight of feints and claw strokes which precedes the decisive blow, the final victory, triumph and transmutation, Saint George, rival of Perseus and Siegfried, rescuer of captive princesses, destroyer of chimeras, of the mythic griffin which, once dead, becomes a rosebush or a maiden no longer spellbound, Riquilda, mystic rose of April. He'd entered through the portico of Saint Ivo, stepping directly in from Calle Condes de Barcelona, one more visitor among those wandering beneath the lofty naves, like leafy palms or cedars, lightly visible above, vaults deepened by the tenebrous transparency of the stained-glass windows, enhanced by their Gothic ribs, ribs which, as they meet in tight knots, at the bottom of the column, turn shadowy and join together, rising black heights, uncertain emptiness, a penumbra in which irradiations and golds took shape bit by bit, the thorny darkness of the choir stalls emerging in the center, penumbra gradually populated by concrete presences, columns with bases worn smooth by passing hands, shiny contours, pews worn thin from use, golden images, patinas, fulgencies, smokes, odor of wax, forms of worshippers facing the iron bars of the side chapels, gazing upon inspirational effigies of special devotion, arrayed before the polychromatic altar of the Virgin of the Rosary, for example, or before that of Saint Severus, facing the altarpiece of the Transfiguration, before the soberly sculpted sarcophagus of San Raimundo of Penyafort, or, above all, in the Chapel of the Holy Sacrament, kneeling before the Christ of Lepanto, Corpus Christi, brown and contorted, defender of the faith, protector of poor shameful men and whores, Ecce Homo of dusty carnal blackness elevated above the flickering altar lamp, ephemeral flames one puff away from extinction, undulating in a single tension or fusion, waxen ex-votos, humility and decorum, genuflections, mantillas, figures kneeling, seated, kerchiefs poorly placed over long curly manes, hands clasped on laps, hats resting on knees, reverent bald heads, canes or crutches, deformities, a child wailing, mourning clothes, grilles and confessionals, mutterings, sacramental discretion. Like one visitor more among those that were praying, contemplating the polychromatic carvings, the gilded curling crests, lingering before the ambulatory side chapels, forming the apse in the sad light of the stained-glass windows, toward the coming and going in and out through the cloister doorway, the cloister obfuscated by the palm trees' crowns, of the magnolia leaves lustrous from the rain, the spacious corridors, with their flagstones worn smooth, viscous stone, gargoyles spouting cascades, deliquescent colors of the leaded stained-glass windows.

A coffee bar rebel. That's what Lucas is. He takes himself for a writer and it disgusts him to collaborate on such anonymous tasks as writing for *Realidad*, just a simple underground university newspaper. He must think it's beneath him, he must think that it's a lot to ask of a professional like him, that it's a job for some nobody, anybody, you, me: that it means nothing to him. A typical reaction from a pure intellectual. No, your observation doesn't surprise me at all. After all, you mustn't forget, his father is one of those lawyers who works as a bloodhound for financial groups, one of those people who came up after the war, taking advantage of their condition as ex-combatants, a rich little dandy from a family fallen on hard times who, if not for the war, would never have been anything more than some no-name shyster, the most immoral kind of individual, with a sweetheart who knows everyone in Barcelona. And that's how the son turned out. Like in the case of Esteva, he's a product of his family's connections, and don't start defending Esteva simply because he's a friend of yours. Judge his attitude dispassionately, put aside the appreciation you might have for him and other subjective motivations, separate them from the strict consideration of Esteva as one militant more. Judge him impartially and you'll find no more than a slight degree of difference between his attitude and Lucas's, and then only outwardly, not any deep internal difference. No, Daniel, let's be serious; Esteva is a very similar case, just as their respective family circles are similar, although to tell you the truth, the comparison will put Lucas in a bad light because his father is a paid defense attorney for the interests of the monopolist oligarchy, meanwhile Esteva's father, as far as being a bank director and, above all, as a member of a dynasty of financiers, is fully integrated into that oligarchy, something always preferable, now that his position has at least greater solidity, more sociological coherence. And there's only one thing worse than the capitalists themselves: their lackeys. But, don't fool yourself, Esteva's joining the party is, more than anything, the product of a temporary crisis of conscience, including the well-known reaction against family and social circles. Meaning, the search for a solution to personal problems, not to objective problems. A defect, unfortunately, very typical of the pure intellectual. Of course, there are exceptions, like you, like Ferrán, but, lamentably, the intellectual who plays at being a revolutionary is frequently moved to do so by hidden anger, by idealized arguments, often concealing a hypercritical and antisocial personality, one that is most definitely ill. Those are not the sane, healthy principles of the proletariat, class interests, factors based on economics—all nonexistent in the case before us. No, such individuals do not make firm and steadfast companions, nor can they, because their roots are neither firm nor sure. We're not talking here about true, devoted comrades; in these kinds of people there is almost always some artifice which, if they don't make a great effort to overcome, always, unfailingly, ends up creating complications for us. So, the best thing to do is think it over calmly and consider it carefully, from the beginning, the elements in question, accepting how much good they can do for our struggle, without allowing yourself to be deceived. It's the only way to avoid future disillusionment and fatal consequences. And when their class conditioning ends up dominating them and they turn out to be the creatures of their class that they really are, so much the worse for them. The history of revolutionary movements is full of these inevitable desertions that, as we already know, usually lead to the individual's total frustration, to his ruin, not only moral, but also professional, and I would almost dare to say physical. It is they, not the party, who come out on the losing end. Fortunately, for the revolution, there is no one who is irreplaceable. Let Lucas continue, let him go on with his stories which, on the other hand, apparently don't get censored, which could already be an explanation, a manifestation of unconfessed impotence. If not, why not take advantage of the legal possibilities that censorship offers, however thin they might be, and thus be able to reach the people, making censorship, in consequence, a useless instrument? Is it that the people, the Spanish people precisely, are too deaf to hear what truly interests them? Does he think that people can't understand him, which would be bad enough, or rather that they have no interest in what he might be able to tell them, which would be worse, although perhaps more accurate? Be that as it may, however, doesn't there exist here an evident aristocratic attitude, an indubitable undervaluation of the popular taste, of the taste and the interests which should ultimately constitute the touchstone of the true, legitimate intellectual revolutionary? Let Lucas continue with his stories and Esteva with his professional doubts. Also these indecisions, Esteva hesitating between mathematics and economics, Lucas between law and his fondness for the pen, ultimately demonstrate that they are hardly serious. The thing is, with this type of people there's always something of the spoiled boy lurking in the background. Well fine, first let them grow up and then we'll see. A writer . . . Who's he writing for, then, if he doesn't publish what he writes and then shirks his duties when it comes to collaborating on *Realidad* and some other underground publications? It's clear as far as I can see: he doesn't write for anybody. His contempt for praxis is one of the chief characteristics of the pure intellectual. Given over to his subjective speculations, the pure intellectual frequently seems to forget that we, the truly intellectual revolutionaries, unlike bourgeois thinkers, may not limit ourselves to theorizing about reality, we must transform it. We don't pretend that the truth and exemplification of our arguments are manifest only in books, but rather also in praxis, a praxis which even as it sanctions those arguments, also creates, by virtue of its own dialect, a new analysis. And what are the regime's recent and various concessions made in response to, if not to the latest urgent demands of the working class, an application in the field of praxis of the theoretical analyses of the objective reality carried out first and foremost by the vanguard of the proletariat, the communist party? Let Lucas write his stories. That won't alter in any way, shape, or form the fact that the true history is written by the masses.

The smashing rain shredded the patio gray, thrashed the pond and the black ivy, the ever-fluttering geese, shattered into turbulent mercury stars, poured off the long shadowy leaves, spattered the stone, and everything became a great cascade from gargoyles and shimmering liquid cornices, slippery viscous stained-glass windows in that cloister of sharp arches and worn flagstones, framed by the parameters of the cathedral and the Romanesque chapel of Santa Lucía and, in its outer wings, along the Calle del Obispo and the Calle de la Piedad, an exterior of severe reliefs, the sharp-edged prismatic buttresses, the symmetrical facade and its enormous windows, austere iron grilles, rows of finials, water-spitting figures spouting down from high above, fantastic knights, riders with extravagant mounts, hounds, serpents, unicorns, gryphons and Tarasques with gaping empty mouths standing out in this crowded group of naked horizontal masses of stone, with the bell towers, steeples, and spires striking the note of verticality, dominant cathedral, raised on the summit of Mount Taber, above the city, above the town stretched out before the sea, a domineering town, haughty, airy arrogances all across the area from the northeast flank of Monjuí, Montjuich, with a knight dallying with a lady in the foreground, at the foot of a tree, and, now on the luxuriant verdure of the rolling plain, a variegated composition of orchards and gardens, a farmer plowing with four oxen outside the city walls, before the Almerian walls, a double ring of fortifications encircling the city, the belfries, the clustered high-rises, and beyond, a fertile distance of hills and cultivated fields populated by small towns and, along the coastline, between promontories and shoals, the port, the shipyards, the suitable and sandy beach, perfect for tourneys and jousts, and a full arcing rainbow touching down in the east, over the coast, in a meticulously feathered sky, exalting the fallen rain, the merry laughing sea and the jocund earth, the long and spacious sea, more full than the lagoons of Ruidera. There were argosies, galleys strung with pennants and streamers waving and fluttering in the wind, and they swept the placid waters, and from within sounded bugles, trumpets, and oboes with soft bellicose accents, while in the city, upon lovely horses and to the sound of many oboes and kettledrums and the noise of hawk bells, out rode an endless train of knights bedecked in dazzling livery, and all the people seemed infused with sudden delight, the joy of San Juan, radiant solstices of summer, and from the galleys the soldiers fired their guns into the wind in festive salvos and those atop the city's walls and ramparts responded in kind, and with a dreadful thunder the heavy artillery broke the air, turbid with intoxicating clouds of gunpowder. A great expanse of sky and, like every summer, a pattering burst of trilling swallows grazing the towers, vertigo, flight reiterated, enthralling phoenix, the city transfigured, rebuilt upon its own ruins, reconstructed, superimposed, juxtaposed, implicated, interlined, expanded, raised up, enclosed, locked away, compartmentalized, fragmented, cornered, bees bottled up in cork hives, deconstructed, demolished, buried, resuscitated from its own ashes, cryptic dilapidated landscape, ruins, roofless walls beneath cloudless, transparent skies, quiet light and the smell of dead earth, coppery necropolis, historic mausoleum of splendors, glories, and apogees, an entire past petrified, simple earthy vestiges, roughness and crudity of those that once were, oh the pain, the sorrow, delicacies and urbanities, harmonious symmetries, classic severities of the Roman metropolis, suffocated panorama, its length and breadth spanned by the creaking rope footbridges, beneath the humming air extractors and locust-shrill neon radiance, vast rooms of coffered ceilings, a white succession of low planes suspended over an itinerary of sliced-up, sectioned buildings, fragments of wall, shards of mosaics, remains of pavement, baths and cisterns, drains, sewers, truncated columns, funerary amphorae, sarcophaguses, pedestals, torsos and heads, busts, mutilated statues. The visitor will now have to undo and retrace the route he has followed, passing by the ticket counter at the entryway, and he shall discover in Hall D, and at his feet, some Roman silos or dolia, and some plinths placed back in the same spot where they were discovered. In Hall E, dedicated to the sculptures found in the excavations, the visitor will be able to admire: a mutilated statue of Diana, along with the torso of a young man and various marble heads, awaiting identification. By contrast, some outstanding pieces, the heads of the Empress Agrippina and the Emperor Antoninus Pius.

A bust, supposedly of the Empress Faustina, daughter of the former and the wife of Marcus Aurelius.

A model of the Temple of Augustus.

A relief sculpture with a lithe dancer, worked from Montjuich stone.

A bronze statuette known as The Venus of Barcelona.

Because, if it is indeed true that we defend the unquestionable political and cultural personality of Catalonia, we do so as communists, meaning, as the vanguard of the Catalan working classes, for them and representing them and without, on the other hand, prejudice against the interests of our fellow workers in the other towns and cities of Spain. We reject the old Catalanism, the traditional bourgeois nationalism, which foundered during the Civil War, more bourgeois than truly national, and its selfish class interests camouflaged in folklore and sentimentalism. And if before the Civil War, the upper-crust Catalan bourgeoisie, already driven by its fear of the proletariat on the march, was the first to betray its own cause when, with Cambó and company, it abandoned the ship of nationalism and its crew of petite bourgeoisie and middling hands, upon repeating, with the help of Primo de Rivera, the Paviada—the coup d'etat led by General Manuel Pavía y Rodríguez de Alburquerque—which so effectively helped put an end to the First Republic, since then, in the postwar period, it has done nothing more than ratify its betrayal by completely and definitively joining the Spanish monopolist oligarchy, thus bringing its expansionist interests into a phase of sharp conflict not only with the interests of working-class factions but also with those of their old separatist allies. But in the same way that it failed in its role as the leading class, in the same way that it failed in its political management, it will fail, it is already failing, in its economic management, and now it is the turn of the Catalan working classes who, raising their old flags charged with revolutionary tradition, must build, alongside their remaining brothers in Spain, Euskadi, and Galicia, a community of socialist nations. Meanwhile, our party, the Catalan communist party, though rather well and intimately integrated with the Spanish communist party of Spain, still remains an outside organization, and this reality already, not coincidentally, constitutes in itself the badge of complete political authenticity. The fact that a significant portion of the Catalan proletariat, the greater part, I would venture to say, is comprised of non-Catalan workers—a result of Andalusian and Castilian emigration—is important merely from a systematic and economic point of view, given that Catalonia's assimilative capacity is a fact well-known to all. It was finely demonstrated in the Civil War, when the Murcians, so-called at that time, acted in defense of their class rights, in solidarity with their own Catalan companions, meaning, as a Catalan working class, without any evidence of competing interests. Their class rights, not the interests and privileges of the Catalan bourgeoisie camouflaged as national rights, this middle class which, after failing in its attempts to enrich itself with the political monopoly of Spanish capitalism in its incipient imperialist stage, ventured forth on the roads of separatism in order to then utilize the rebirth of the old national dreams as an element of negotiation with the central power, with whose most reactionary sectors it eventually allied itself.

Glimpses of display cases, vestiges of the primitive settlements of the Barcelona plain, corroded wagon-wheel rims, pottery shards, Campanian, Iberian, Greek ceramics, remains of the diverse pre-Roman cultures who settled within the geographical region of the present-day city. A display case on the mezzanine floor of the Casa Padellás, at the patio level, between the steps leading down to the excavations and the staircase to the upper floors, a historic itinerary commencing on the underground level of the ancient Palacio Real Mayor, from the ruins in the Roman forum, a progression of subterranean spaces, a series of enclosed ceilings above a panorama of columns and pedestals, mosaic floors, pilasters, columns and capitals, bases of equestrian statues, sculptures, togaed torsos, marble hands, reliefs, votive stones, altar stones and vaulted niches, epigraphs, funerary inscriptions, archeological pieces belonging to the opulent city of the Augustan age, the majority of them unearthed in the course of excavations carried out along the foundations of the city's outer wall, Barcino's protective belt rebuilt in the third century with the rubble of Augustan Barcino, razed by the first barbarian invasions, defensive works to whose construction the new city consecrated—literally, you might say—all its resources, perhaps in expiation of its impious past, its paganism, its dissolute customs, the Christianizing city of the Early Roman Empire, with such a thoroughly monumental wall, its imposing presence completely enclosing a poor and diminished urban nucleus, without any luxury whatsoever nor any trace of earlier splendors, to judge by the visible remains in Rooms G and H, the latter excavated right underneath the Casa Padellás itself, the museum's central location, as a way of extending the underground hall from the Plaza del Rey, the wall's inner face dominating an area of ruinous rooms and masonry walls, outlines of streets and sewers, drains, cisterns, modest constructions with all their domestic elements, fornax, silos, millstones, useful objects, utensils now displayed in glass cases, glasses and glass jars, loom weights, lamps, punches and pins, personal effects labeled, all that situated at a lower level than what the Visigoth necropolis occupied, centuries later, now all covered over with earth, buried beneath the sepulchers of tiles and urns now set out next to the foundations of the wall, a stony perimeter embedded in earlier constructions, digested by the city in its development, residue of residue, prevailing wall upon which so many others were built, to serve as protection for the new medieval towns, outlying suburbs developed successively beyond the walls, la Ribera, el Arrabal, San Pedro de las Puellas, expansions tightly enclosed by the new fortified Gothic walls of Jaume the Conqueror and Pedro the Ceremonious, expansions slowly erected and fortified, modernized until well into the eighteenth century and finally, with romantic impetus, demolished by need of expansion, for the sake of the urban demands of the age, the city's limits and buffer zones now surpassed by the Ensanche, the nineteenth-century quadrangle staked out and developed along the entire width of the so-called Barcelona plain, absorbing the ancient towns, invading the fields planted long ago, extending to the shadow of stout, delicately curved walls, Gothic crenellations, watchful battlements, gates and portcullises, escarpments, postern gates, bridges reflected in moats, in the virtual oscillating skies, fascinating image, sublimated, evaporated, vanished, forms prefigured and survived by these others, so long buried and blended into the earth and, at last, flourishing anew, period to period, from the entrails of the old quarter, its outline excavated, cleared, patiently rediscovered by the municipal pickaxe, progressively cleaned and free from adherences, residual traces of the concealing edifices now demolished, panels of tiles, floral wallpapers, plaster moldings, vanished staircases, black chimney stains. The Roman wall, irregular nine-sided polygon with a current measurement of just over one kilometer around the perimeter, according to the plan on display on the ground floor of the Casa Padellás, Room Number One, at the terminus of the route through the museum's subterranean section, a wall not hard to imagine defying the air with its seventy towers and seventy-times-seven battlements enclosing Barcino, a populace of urban structures still recognizable today, centered around the current Plaça de San Jaume, situated at the approximate location of the ancient forum, the intersection of the Cardus Maximus with the Decumanus, meaning, the current intersection of Calle Fernando and Calle Jaime I, crossing the current intersection of Calle Obispo and Calle de la Ciudad, the city of Mons Taber, a colony established by the legions of the Republic on an isolated promontory, surrounded by marshlands that safeguard it from the pre-existing nearby towns, Barkeno, or Laye of the Iberians, a people probably Etruscanized, a nuclei preceded in turn by earlier elements in the region, as it seems, from the expansion of diverse peoples, Celtic, Illyrian or Pre-Celtic, Almerian or Proto-Iberian, etcetera, invasions crossing over a more ancient background, amalgam of vestiges of cultures by then already completely extinguished, Pyrenean culture, cave culture, dolmenic culture, beaker culture, etcetera, migrations and meanderings which, doubtless, knew the nearby surroundings of that promontory jutting out at the sea's edge like a natural fortress, shelter of sailors and colonizers, beaches where Heracles or Hercules, as his ninth ship arrived, the others scattered by the storm, must have founded Barcanona, a city, in this case, of maritime origin, though its roots could just as well be Punic, a small factory of Carthaginian making founded by Hamilcar or by Hannibal, from whose common patronymic, Barca or Barcino, that in both cases means a flash of light, would thus proceed the city's denomination, which could therefore, on another hand, also be called, in memory of its namesake of Cyrenaica, or as a derivation of Barschem, a Hittite or Phoenician name for the planet Saturn, a possibility that must not be discarded and that, precisely in this case, one might suppose, without a doubt, that Barcino was a colony of Tyre, a theory seemingly confirmed by the discovery of clues that would prove the existence of a local cult devoted to Astarte—the moon—and to Tanit, a manifestation of the starry heavens, as well as the sun, Baal, the latter identifiable, even, in the opinion of Don Salvador Sampere i Miquel, with the Egyptian Amon, although there are also those who insist on attributing Greek origins to the city, without managing to trace them back to Heracles, who offer hypotheses no less conclusive in favor of the presumed existence of a colony under the command of either Pelasgians and Tyrrhenians, or of Carians who came from Bargylia, a place near Mileto, or better yet, as in the case of Empúries, of a Phocian colony radiating from Marsilia (Marseilles), Greeks from the diaspora established, why not, at what must have been the head of a natural bridge, attractive to the maritime power on duty, a point destined to pass from the control of one group to another, from the hands of the descendants of Dido—extreme beyond controversy—to the hands of the descendants of Aeneas and, more concretely, from the hosts of Gnaeus Cornelius Scipio, who might have added the cognomen of Favencia to his conquest, just as Caesar would, perhaps, add that of Julia, and Augustus himself that of Augusta, upon officially proclaiming a Roman colony the delightful Punic seat of government known until then generally as Barcino, despite the fact that in ancient times there was no shortage of other names for the city: Barcenone, Barcinona, Barcilo, Barcelona, Barcelona la Pía, Paterna, or Patricia, noble titles, epigraphs established over the years, petrified epithets, now as epitaphs from that city whose full and complete name probably was Colonia Favenica Julia Augusta Paterna Barcino, parvus oppidus, the small town, dominating the whole area between the rivers Betulón and Rubricatus and between the massif of Collserola and the peninsula of Mons Jovis or Jupiter, that lofty lord of lightning and thunder. Small port of Hispania Citerior, subsequently called Provincia Tarraconense, a great city whose expansion was cut short by the first barbarian attacks and which resurged afterward boasting perhaps the most solid walls in the Empire, the Pax Romana uncertain, cornered, subverted, rich in popular martyrs, like Santa Eulalia or San Severo, victims of persecutions and repressions, bloody centuries, palm fronds and crosses, daggers, poisons, assassinations, betrayals, conspiracies, vile deeds, daily disasters in Arian Barchinona or Barcino of Ataulf, ephemeral capital of the Visigoth monarchy in those times of conversions, of dark metamorphosis, a city under full medieval shadows would appear transformed into Saracen, or more precisely, Mozarabic, Barschaluna, temporarily infidel, unfaithfully lost and recovered, now allied with the enemy, now an enemy of the ally, scabrous terrain, of frank uncertainty, preponderant center of Afranc, no man's land, the frontier overrun indistinctly by Franks, by Arabs, by Normans, land of incursions, exoduses, blights, sackings, pillaging, atrocities, a land where, between rapine and forays, there began to form the cloudy embryo of a homeland, among the mists, at the intersection of the Pyrenees and the Mediterranean, from the rude mountain refuges of Otgar de Cataló and his nine famous barons, Otgar or Otger Catalón, Kathasolt, Gazlantes, Gotlantes, or Gotlán, strong fortunate man, enterprising forerunner of the celebrated Catalonia or Catalonya, land of castles, conquests financed by Vifredo I el Velloso, also known as Wilfred I the Hairy, although there was, perhaps, an earlier Vifredo, in which case he would be the second one, Vifredo or Seniofre, Wilfred, Guifred, Gifré, Xifré, Jofre or Guifré, better known as Almondir, that is, El Bravo, by the Muslims, first virtual sovereign of the County of Barcelona, although, according to the feudal hierarchy, known as Marquis of Gothia or

Marca Hispánica, belonging still to the Dukedom of Septimania of the Kingdom of Aquitaine, vassal of the Carolingian Empire, a prince with whose blood Carlos the Bald personally traced the four bars across the shield of gold, which became from that moment forth the very blazon of the city which still remained to be overrun by Almanzor and reconquered for the Cross by Christian arms, with Saint George leading the knights, brandishing a bolt of lightning, the dead and resurrected head of an incipient state, fatherland of fratricides and excommunicants, merchants and crusaders, troubadours and navigators, Catalunya, crown on horseback of the Pyrenees, its authority extended to Provence under the scepter of Ramón Berenguer el Grande, bi-member state, Crown of Aragón, monarchy of poly-member development impelled by James the Conqueror, man of deeds, cofounder, along with Saint Pedro Nolasco and Saint Raimundo de Penyafort, de la Merced, Order of White Knights, redeemers of captives and capturers of infidels, re-conqueror of Valencia, as well as Mallorca, *dolça illa daurada*, the sweet golden isle, the most esteemed of his conquests, the neighing of horses and sound of arms, a trail of sails and flashing steel covering the sea in white, the island running red, and the Donjuanesque Don Jaume shouting, an asp on the crest of his helmet, a bat unfolded, wings spread to frighten, terrifying, sending men to their grave, shouting Victoria soldats! Victory, soldiers, victory, victory and glory imposed by the forceful blow of swords, *¡desperta ferro!* swords awaken! *mors stupebit et natura*, death and nature will be astounded, a Mediterranean confederation in expansive apogee, Sicily, Corsica, Sardinia, Naples, Calabria, Malta, Jerba, Morea, Gallipoli, Athens, and Neopatria, trophies secured after great difficulty by the Almogavars and their valiant swordsmen, saviors of empires, usurpers and destroyers, rampagers, vengeful Catalans, mercenaries, soldiers of fortune earned in countless combats with Moors and Turks, Greeks and Bulgarians, French and Genoese, when not even a single fish could swim across the seas without the emblem of the four bars and the Parthenon was called the Seo de Santamaría, empire on horseback of the Mediterranean, from island to island, from peninsula to peninsula, golden isles on the horizon, scattered crown, poured out, spilled, blood, bars of gold, greed, and evil uses, land of farmers and highwaymen, warriors and artisans, mystics and cartographers, lords and servants, redeemers and redeemed, revolts, repressions, uncivil and revolutionary society of the fifteenth century, aborted Humanism, Renaissance of adversities, with its bitter repertoire of misfortunes, plagues and famine, crisis, calamities, time of decline, implacable perigee with antagonisms instead of harmony and dreams instead of realities, the Cataluña of Ferran or Fernando forging Catalan national unity almost without realizing it, a monarch too ambitious for a people too self-absorbed, unconscious of the fact that upon enmeshing itself with a flourishing Castile, strengthened and enterprising, it had agreed to form part, the lesser part, of a superior entity, the Spain where Isabel counts for as much as Fernando and even more, the Catholic Kings in the act of welcoming Columbus upon his triumphant return from the Indies, the beginning of a grandiose colonizing labor, of the creation or destruction of an empire, a question of perspective or rather of color, of the color of the skin with which one watches, royal offering in any case, a new world at their feet, as if served up on a platter, a world already become village, discoveries and gifts of all kinds, birds, fruits, precious stones, plumed redskins alongside pages and heralds, prelates, men-at-arms, cuirasses, mantles, red damasks, ermine pelts, feathers, pennants, pikes, trumpets, miters, and scepters gathered presumably in the Saló del Tinell, below those arches like palm trees spread wide, vast throne room of the Palacio Real Mayor, with a view, from the adjoining antechamber, constructed atop the Roman wall, of the plaza of Ramón Berenguer the Great, favorite son-in-law of El Mío Cid, the old warrior on his bronze horse, helmet heightened by the beating wings of a dove alighting on it, fine sprightly warrior seeming to direct the traffic along the Vía Layetana, a trench brutally plowed across the width of the Old City, directing or simply witnessing, his back turned away from the rear windows of the Palacio Real Mayor and the rear facades of the adjoining edifices, the Chapel of Santa Agata, also constructed upon the towers of the wall, the royal chapel and, later, over the course of the years, school, warehouse holding decorations from the Gran Teatro del Liceo, printing house and workshop, presently restored, after so many vicissitudes, with its polychrome coffered ceiling intact and its altarpieces of the Epiphany and Pentecost, Calvary and the Resurrection, single inner pointed nave which communicates thus with the antechamber of the Saló del Tinell as with the upper floors of the Casa Padellás, conjoined edifices, all encircling the Plaza del Rey, intercommunicating spaces which, along with the network of subterranean excavations, form the current City History Museum, a grouping of zones and enclosures with its central headquarters in the Casa Padellás, a Gothic construction organized around a patio with corridors where an open staircase leads, in a single flight, up to the main floor, a palace vacated, due to urban necessities, from its earlier site and moved here, rebuilt stone by stone the way churches are, like the Temple of Mount Zion, for example, now on the Rambla de Cataluña, or Santa María de Junqueras, now the Parish of La Concepción, on the corner of Calle Aragón and Roger de Llúria.

Which means, said Escala. In three quarters of an hour, at six. On the patio in the Faculty of Humanities. A gathering of students from all the university departments with the goal of compensating for the individual defections they expect from each department. To form a protest line intended to prevent from entering those who, by belonging to departments situated in la Ciudad Universitaria, might lack the excuse for showing up at the university's main campus downtown, la Universidad Central. The motion approved by the Economics Committee in support of the Asturian miners and against the repression in Asturias will be read aloud, and all present will be invited to join in solidarity, also gathering as many professional and political demands as emerge from the masses gathered together. Banners will be unfurled and displayed, the portraits of Franco will be thrown down on the patio, and, taking advantage of the fact that at that hour the streets are filled with people coming home from work, we'll try to march out in demonstration toward the Civil Government following the planned route, Gran Vía, Plaza de Cataluña, Las Ramblas, and the Paseo Colón. We've got to use any means necessary to get the authorities to close the main campus. That accomplished, we call for a strike in protest of the holdout university departments refusing to join us, and make sure that there is a general suspension of classes throughout all the university campuses in the district. That way, the Catalanistas' light explosives can have some positive effect: to force the authorities to intervene, precipitating the events; in a word, to catalyze the situation. Although such acts deviate from our political line, perhaps it's not a bad idea, under the present circumstances, that they be carried out by others. The socialists promise they'll do the same, but it's surely just one of their characteristic bluffs. Your role consists of resolving, along the way, however many questions that come up, always keeping in mind that you must remain embedded in and identified with the mass of student protestors. Make the opportune decisions without it seeming like you are the ones who make them. Centralize the picket line activity. Order the unfurling of the banners. Channel the demonstration toward the bishopric, just as the Catholics wish, instead of toward the civil government, if that seems to be the predominant opinion. Counteract the police's dispersive actions. Avoid clashes, except when the police try to make arrests. Let me emphasize that those of you in positions of responsibility must not draw attention to yourselves, at no time should you stand out from the mass of students. It would be a grave mistake for the organization to reveal the one secretly responsible instead of the one who appears to be the real leader. That's what people like Ros, Martinell, and Guillén are for. As for Ferrán, it doesn't seem prudent to risk exposing him to the investigations he'd arouse, were he arrested, being as he is the son of an old, well-documented militant. He shouldn't even get close to the fray, especially because no one has recognized him yet, and by staying on the sidelines he's the perfect person to maintain the security connection. If you run into some delay or feel that you were being watched, he can go in your place to the meeting. Tomorrow at eleven, in the cloisters. The only thing necessary is that he not receive your call, that you don't call him tonight from a pay phone saying you want to go to the movies or something. And then he'll show up. Cover your asses and cover me. Be especially careful with telephones. And get rid of any compromising papers. No notes.

Keep in mind what the last ones who got arrested went through, the new surveillance techniques used by the police. When they follow someone, various agents do it at the same time, relieving each other continually to avoid attracting attention, communicating with each other by radio. They use cars and motorcycles. As a rule, you should mistrust men wearing typical, dull, everyday uniforms, soldiers, tram drivers, street sweepers, etcetera. Don't forget either that women also participate in surveillance operations. Take every kind of precaution. Catch the Metro at the second to last station on the line, for example, where it's easy to spot if you're being followed. In case you notice anything out of the ordinary at the meeting place, take out your handkerchief to blow your nose. You always meet by crossing paths, planning each person's route ahead of time. You appear to run into each other by accident and then each person goes their own way. One goes toward the exit at the Plaza del Rey and the other toward the exit for Calle de los Condes de Barcelona. Or rather, whoever enters via Plaza del Rey must leave by way of Calle de los Condes de Barcelona. Or rather, at the Cathedral, entering by Calle San Ivo, also called Calle Inquisición, and coming out on Calle Piedad or Santa Eulalia, both at the cloisters. Or entering through the Chapel of Santa Lucía, a Romanesque structure integrated into the structure of the cathedral, and leaving from any other door, onto Calle de la Piedad, Calle del Obispo, right at the front steps, leave and get lost in the convoluted violet side streets of the Old City, take Calle Puertaferrisa or Calle Canuda toward Las Ramblas, Calle Pelayo and Plaza de la Universidad or, crossing Avenida de la Catedral, take Calle dels Arcs toward Puerta del Ángel, Plaza de Cataluña, Las Rondas, and Plaza de la Universidad, wide plazas and streets, thick with traffic, the city's shopping district, monotonous alignments, grandiose buildings with ground-floor windows, banks, cafés, enormous department stores, leaving behind that nucleus of rancid narrow streets and damp stone, wafting odors, belonging to the streets surrounding the cathedral, businesses and crafts developed within the shelter of the Church, an always-attractive temple for the sale of goods, fleeting effluvia, wax, crammed antiques, books passed through umpteen hands, rough matting and wrought iron, odors successively diffused upon a more general background of choking industrial vapors, contrasting morning atmosphere of yellow light penetrating the shadows, transversal and turbid, metalized sunlight, as if infused with metal filings, revealing the eroded palaces now become neighborhood houses, corroded facades, gray rough cast, disfigured by touch-ups, bricked-in doorways, poky windows clumsily open in the thick stone walls, balconies sporting potted plants, clothes hanging between Romanesque, Gothic, Renaissance, Baroque, Neoclassical, and Isabeline architectural elements, gargoyles and cornices, *ajimez* windows, large doorways and staircases with little boys, tourists photographing arches no longer triumphant, battered doorways for horse and carriage, now bodega or antique shop, grocery store, herbalist, tobacco shop, secondhand bookshops selling souvenirs and postcards, the workshop of, the warehouse of, etcetera. Or even on any block of the Ensanche, a quadrangle repeated to labyrinthine extremes, on the block formed, for example, by the following streets: Diputación, Sicilia, Consejo de Ciento, and Cerdeña, turning circles counterclockwise or vice versa, until you run into Escala or, on occasions, directly with Obregón, each time on a different block, apart from the meetings, also with Obregón, at Park Güell, in the mornings, Obregón with another outfit and dark glasses, contacts so much more precious because so less frequent, notified previously by Escala in the course of a meeting conducted on some block: Córcega-Nápoles-Rosellón-Roger de Flor, for example, turning clockwise, or again at the City History Museum, entering through the ancient Palacio Real Mayor, which later became the very seat of the Inquisition, the shield of the blazing cross above the portico visible even today, on Calle de los Condes de Barcelona, and leaving through the Casa Padellás, in the Plaza del Rey, after having met, perhaps, in the basement passages, perhaps at any point of the itinerary which, including the Salón del Tinell and Santa Agata's Chapel, both places approximately at the second-story level, leads toward the upper rooms of the Casa Padellás, on the third floor, rooms decorated in the styles of successive centuries, with corresponding relics, histories and events set in stone, sculptures, carvings, portraits, shields, weapons, flags and standards, cannonballs, furniture, glass cases with ceramics and fabrics, antiques and reproductions, models, explanatory charts and maps, classical resemblances, typically gorgeous eighteenth-century pieces, illuminated illustrations, cavalry marching away, the horses' prominent hindquarters, modernist flourishes, dioramas, illustrations of sieges and expositions, receptions and revolts, fiestas and solstices, trophies and disappointments, days of ire and delight, images of war and peace in Barcelona, an engraving in simple colors, of aged yellows, the city seen from Montjuïc or Montjuich or Monycich or Montjony or Montjoin, etcetera, fortified and guarded seawall previously called

Mons Jovis or Mons Judeorum, Barcelona of the sixteenth century, mirror, lamppost, star and north of the knights errant, school of hidalgos and archive of courtesies, Barcelona the rich, fertile, and plentiful that made the young Carlos say I prefer to be Count of Barcelona more than Emperor of the Romans, Carlos I of Spain or Carlos V, Emperor of Austria, heir of kingdoms and principalities, dukedoms, counties, scepters and crowns, the Crown of Aragón and its stele of Mediterranean domains, the German states and Castile, Burgundy and Granada, Luxembourg and Navarre, Flanders, Artois, Brabant, Holland, Zealand, etcetera, plus the North African possessions and the growing Viceroys of the Indies, the inheritance of four grandfathers all grouped together, extended throughout the four cardinal points radiating out from Barcelona, temporary Imperial court thanks to his telling preference for its optimal residential qualities, appropriate, on the other hand, to a progressively provincial city, one given over to the petty consolations of a marginal, vegetative life, the simple capital of an exhausted and decadent principate, too impotent to prevail, striving too hard to be eclipsed, *aurea mediocritas* of a noble city, all facade, lovely crenellated walls, polygonal towers, gates and moats, portcullises and escarpments, battlements, roofs, belfries, patios and gardens, a select orchard of pomegranate trees, lemons, oranges, palms, pines, grape vines grown close to the walls, palaces, churches, belfries floating on high, the cathedral where the emperor convoked the Conclave of the Knights of the Order of the Golden Fleece, amid incense and purple, brocade, velvet, angelic songs, emblems unfolded, stepping forward to receive the collar, under the emblazoned Lion of Spain, Cristerno of Denmark and Segismundo of Poland, arrogant kings, dreamers, heading the list of knights, their names detailed minutely *et in saecula saeculorum* in the choir stalls, neither gold nor purple in this oil sketch painted from behind at the radiant high altar, shadowy chiaroscuro of stained-glass windows and luminaria, organ pipes, sconces, skylights, and ogival windows like an echo of songs, no more crimson mantles nor entourages, no moments of splendor, only past glories, venerated victories, el Cristo Negro, the Black Christ, ensign of Lepanto, champion of Christianity and defender of the Faith, the bolt of the Sublime Door, fourth quarter of the Half Moon, unprecedented confrontation of argosies and galleys, apocalyptic butchery with its all-too-famous consequence of scars and mutilations, hands lost for the plume and for the sword. Decisive battle, apogee or zenith of an empire where the sun never managed to set, galloping across three oceans and five continents, from Sicily to Chile, from Florida to Oran, from the Philippines to Flanders, unfolded omnipotence of the eagle, black wings, black legends, penitential robes, sentences hung from the defendant's neck, bonfires and gibbets, *rex tremenda majestatis*,

Philip II in his isolated Escorial, pantheon and cradle, first and last residence of so many monarchs, king of kings, lord of the armies until then undefeated in all kinds of fights, regiments and armadas ultimately vincible, sunset of Flanders, lances so long raised erect now broken and folded, turned against themselves, internal wars of a decaying empire, hegemony called into question, absolutism relativized, uprisings, separatist and centrifugal movements, as on a sinking ship, fleeing from the shipwreck, Netherlands, Portugal, Italy, Catalonia, land or terroir on the political periphery because it is neither economic nor spiritual, with its industrious towns and its cultivated fields, wrought with brute strength from the naturally rough and wild landscape, hermitic mountains, apt for the contemplation of the supernatural, shelter of ascetics and destination of pilgrims and palmers, crags afire with broom. The Black Virgin of Montserrat, to whom Saint James offered his sword, Montserrat, sanctuary of retreats and meditations, inspirations, visions, determinations, heart of a principality weary with costly but effective discriminatory favoritisms, raised against the bureaucracy with its affected elegance and purity of style, developed in the shadow of the royal sclerosis, true dynastic decadence, a despotic void of power throughout the whole government, capital problem of a country where life is a dream, court of miracles, country of monks and Don Juans, of court jesters and maids of honor, rogues, adventurers, ruined hidalgos, the empty purse of Don Dinero, powerful knight, unpaid soldiers' salaries dispatched only to quell unrest, the cause of sackings and anarchy, rioting by the soldiery, the cause of revolts against the soldiery, a vicious circle enclosing the turbulent Barcelona of the seventeenth century, true threat to the Spanish monarchy, virtually felt to be strange and foreign by a city jealous of its privileges and customs, exasperated by the subjugation of its traditions, capable of both begging to God and asking for help from the very devil himself, a rebellious land, insurgent, sickles, black veils, and severed Castilian heads in the Bloody Corpus riot: reapers turned butchers, a people up in arms, a city of fearless defenders, a city assaulted by sea and land, as much by the Spanish as by their occasional allies, French, English, Germans, by the Marqués de los Vélez, or by the Duke of Vendôme, or by the Duke of Anjou, or by the Admiral Lord Peterborough or by the Duke of Berwick, images of siege from a bird's eye view, with a description of the positions and camps of the besieging forces and of the disposition of the blockading ships, as well as the fortifications and defenses of the plaza, bastions and batteries, the shield of the city in a corner of the engraving, escutcheon in four quarters, as can also be appreciated in the various reproductions displayed in the vestibule, war themes, patriotic motives, causa belli, a shield with the cross of Saint George in the first and fourth quarters upon a silver field, and four bars en gules in the second and third upon a field of gold, gold and blood of an outlaw nation, rich in bandits, popular heroes, defenders of lost causes, successions and secessions, Catalonia with its castles shattered and razed, like a battered warrior with broken ribs, cast out from Castile, muted by having its tongue cut out, minimized, reduced by force, centralized, meaning isolated from all central power, distanced from its own destinies, dispossessed of privileges and autonomies, its university moved away and traditional laws suppressed by royal decree, *la Nueva Planta*, unwelcome weed of a land still fertile in spite of all, lush and flourishing, precisely, in proportion to its distance from imperial life, stripped of its avatars, consequent grandeurs and subsequent decadences, a land soon flourishing anew in the frame of a Spain drained of blood that did not cease to decline, a region soon adapted to hard reality, times of capitulation and recapitulation, times of integration and work, of enlightened progress, lights of the century, eighteenth-century allegories, just counterpart of an integration that, if it closed some doors, opened others, those of America, to the new full-fledged Spaniards, commerce delayed but no less decisive for the Principality, and which, together with its inhabitants' natural virtues of industry and good common sense, would create an incipient process of capitalization, a base of industrialization developed without pause from then on, notwithstanding the mishaps of time, wars and guerrilla fighters, invasions, independence defended, hardly in any unanimous way, by all the peoples of the peninsula, all indisputably tied together against their common oppressor or liberator, the Catalan people confronting Napoleon as they had once long before confronted Hannibal, Caesar, or Almanzor, crusading spirit enveloped in wrath, war proclaimed by the priest, a call to arms from altars and pulpits, plebiscite tribunes, together declaiming themselves against the Revolution or the Empire, uncertain cut-throat struggle, executions by firing squad, by impaling, Goyaesque horrors of war forever engraved, their hybrid seed perhaps also forever rooted, hybrid, prolific, fecund nursery of fervors equally apostolic and liberal, revolutionary or absolutist, the hundred thousand sons of San Luis marching openly, watering the land with blood, unconstitutional paths, holy alliances, secret societies, terrorism, military uprisings, declarations, rebellions and restorations, monarchists, Isabelines and Carlists, bands opposed, irreducible, warlike, passing the time exterminating one another, a Spanish crossword puzzle, Iberian circle of asses, witches, and apes gathered in an orgiastic dance, ferocious nineteenth-century witches' sabbath of that renascent Principate, impeller of progress and democracy alongside a lawless traditionalism, impeller of republican, federalist, cantonalist, anarchist movements, all the while reformist, protectionist, colonialist, imperialist, festering acrimonious contradictions of a Catalonia both working-class and bourgeois, antagonies spreading at the same time as the rising smoke of its industrial centers, between riotous turbid revolts and punishing cannonades, Barcelona under falling bombs, explosions of violence and unrest, the riot on Las Ramblas, for example, when the rioters assaulted the Governor's Palace and murdered General Bassa, a romantic scene of workers, farmers, and intellectuals joined in brotherhood, and who knows if not students, too, frock coats and striped blouses, dark top hats and red caps as if they were Phrygian caps, sabers and pistols, rifles bristling around some defenestrated body, broken, burned in a bonfire kindled with the papers thrown from the balconies of the Police Delegation, fluttering down upon the exultant mobs, fists thrust on high, wrath, a dog sniffing at the debris, recriminations, choleric expressions, physiognomies altered by wrath, strange factions, irreconcilable positions, class warfare, anarchist furor, attacks, lethal exterminating explosions, Orsini bombs hurled at the audience in the Gran Teatro del Liceo opera house, one of them, which did not explode, exhibited alongside the pictures showing the fear which filled that tragic November night, while Rossini's *William Tell* was being performed, people fainting and weeping in the lounge, the big wheel spinning, and an agitated image of the streets with carriage horses rearing, kicking, whinnying, shouts, running, livid flashing of eyes, the anarchic flip-side of the coin of a society in full expansion at a tremendous rate, a Catalonia of an increasingly greater weight in the public life of the Spanish nation, presence incarnate, without going further, through General Prim, kingmaker, persons with redeeming frailties and whims, rapidly rising career, from Reus to Castillejos, from Castillejos to Barcelona, from Barcelona to Madrid, from Madrid to heaven through the sublime Puerta del Turco, amid the stench of a regicide, transported by a carriage possibly similar to the one he had used in Barcelona in order to make his entrance in the Plaza San Jaime or the Plaza de la Constitución, at his victorious return from the Moroccan campaign, a tremendous reception offered by the city to the man whose meteoric ascension seemed but a prefiguration and omen of a collective providential destiny, victories, triumphal arches, flags and pennants, streamers, red and yellow striped flags fluttering in the wind. Also in this room of the Casa Padellás, a model of the equestrian statue of President Prim, a horseman of haughty presence and military bearing, who presides over the elegant eighteenth-century perspectives of the Ciudadela Park, a monument erected by a Barcelonan society that converted into gardens what had been a fortress executed by Vauban, with its parade ground, its dungeons and its gallows, the impetuous steamroller of a society on the move, forms of life in transformation impelled by a bourgeoisie that was going to outstrip the limits of the past with its new initiatives, to smash down walls, to project a new city in its own image and likeness, the effort of visionary clairvoyance or, more simply, a question of vision, with a good nose and refined calculation, the Barcelona whose expansion only appeared eccentric, its plans only partially extemporaneous, a city of colossal enterprises, of modernist extravagances, the Barcelona of the Universal Exposition, romantic and delirious expansions of grandiosity, days of euphoria and jubilation, not even dampened or overshadowed by the miseries of 1898, the gradual degeneration of a Spain at the heart of which, and in the name of a reality, Barcelona now reclaimed the power or the authority, with so much nineteenth-century bourgeois Catalan impetus, and without beating about the bush; the renaissance of a Catalonia equally traditional and innovative, capable of initiating the monumental work of the Expiatory Temple of the Holy Family and, simultaneously, restoring the facade of the cathedral, that Gothic museum of past splendors, petrified histories and legends, resonant naves, murky penumbra, the organ and the choir, the crypt, spectral forms, incense-bearing angels, recumbent images, sepulchers, Santa Eulalia's for example, or the sepulcher of San Raimundo de Penyafort, and by the door that communicates with the cloister, the sarcophagi of Ramón Berenguer the Old and his wife Almodis, founders of the cathedral which predated the present one, the vanished Romanesque cathedral, built, in turn, upon the ruins of an even older one, the early paleo-Christian basilica of uncertain fate, re-consecrated after having been a Muslim mosque and, previously, in a no-less-episodic manner, the seat of an Arian episcopal see, a temple whose foundation is attributed to Saint James, all that in the immediate area where stood the pagan temple dedicated to Augustus, superimposed constructions of which now only remain vestiges in the subsoil of the current stonework.

An interior pierced by sunlight, a relief vault aureoled by the early morning lights, iridescent beams from the stained-glass windows, oblique transparencies coloring the ribs of the columns, ashlars, flagstones, chromatic stains increasingly lower down, increasingly conspicuous in the depths of the transept, grave symmetries, gloom thickened by the sheen of old gold, yellowishness from days gone by, carvings, Baroque sculptures, altarpieces, paintings veiled by a bright reflection, veiled and unveiled according to how one advanced under the radiance of the multicolored corollas of the apse, toward the dazzling opening and closing of the door that offered flashing glimpses outside, the cloister, a corner of serenity and even traditional solace, pointing to the oil painting painted from that very same angle, an eighteenth-century family in the foreground, next to the shrine of the spout, the father with walking stick and top hat, the mother in the attitude of turning to her little boy who appears stuck to her skirts, as if she was telling him something, who knows if something about the dancing egg, *l'ou com balla*, or about Saint George and the Dragon, an enchanting traditional image with the patio's vegetation in the background, flowerbeds, young trees, just barely flowering, all framed by archways without bars, arches repeated, the geometry of their fretwork projecting itself oblately on the flagstone pavement, progressively diminished by the perspective, luminosity similar to that of today, no less today in spite of the vegetation's growth, the patio's gated thickness, tall palms with their hearts like pollen, great magnolias splashed with iridescences, solar sparkles, and the honking of the geese, and the mossy bubbling of the waterspout, ivies, shady stone, odor and light of undergrowth in the corridors of that enclosure open to Calle de la Piedad through the door of the same name, and to Calle del Obispo through Santa Eulalia's door, facing the monument to the martyrs of Bonapartist tyranny expressed on the exterior adornments of the Church of San Severo, a sculptural group flanked by panels of tiles with explanatory texts and illustrations about the event, an expressive vocation of the diverse events befallen which followed from the horrifying scene, or rather, following the execution of five patriots on the glacis of the Citadel, when meanwhile the sentence was carried out against the five Heroes, three more valiant men of Barcelona, namely Don Ramón Mas, Don Julián Portet, and Don Pedro Lastortras, who sounded the alarm bells in the cathedral tower to call together the People and liberate their brothers. The Napoleonic troops raced there and, locking the church, mounted the most careful search. Desperate after not finding them, they offered to pardon them, shouting it so at such frequent intervals that the three aforementioned men finally emerged from beneath the organ bellows after having gone more than seventy-two hours without eating or drinking anything. They managed to reanimate them with generous draughts of wine, thus fanning the promise to pardon them, the same soldiers who then, breaking their word, pressed for their death, which sentence was executed the twenty-seventh day of that same month of June in which they died gloriously, the remarkable composure and exemplary bravery of some men who, for faithful devotion to their cause, for loyalty and abnegation, for requisite nobleness, for solidarity with their comrades, risked and lost their own lives in the attempt to sound the alarm with a useless outburst, all for nothing, Barcelonans with their ears shut tight, for whom the bells toll, for whom they toll and toll again from these towers, preeminent cathedral, rising high, surrounded by churches and palaces, raised up like a raised projection of what was once Mount Taber upon a sinuous contour of edifices from other times, mixed styles, superimposed elements, all set at different levels. Thus, without going further, taking a simple turn around the outside of the cathedral, starting from the portico of Santa Eulalia, for example, on the northwest slope of this prominence of intercrossing side streets, and turning always in a clockwise direction, we will find, at the foot of Calle del Obispo, the Episcopal Palace, of Romanesque origin, and turning the corner, along Calle Santa Lucía, La Casa del Arcediano, a building of plateresque design jammed against a residual section of the Roman wall, a compact building that, next to la Casa de la Pia Almoina, erected in the fifteenth century with remains of earlier buildings, frames la Plaza de la Catedral or la Plaza de Cristo Rey, spread out between both buildings, the steps that enhance the facade's nineteenth-century pastiche, and turning again to the right, skirting a ring of visitors listening to their jabbering tour guide, we head into Calle de los Condes de Barcelona, where we happen upon the worn stones of the ancient Palacio Real Mayor and the Archive of the Crown of Aragón, previously el Palacio del Lugarteniente, and after turning again to the right, along Calle de la Piedad, torturously clinging to the line of the apse and to a wing of the cloister, las Casas Canonicales, a group of buildings lovingly restored which runs as far as Calle del Obispo in its confluence with Calle de la Piedad, before the Gothic side of the old Consejo de Ciento, a bifurcation that, turning right, will lead us back again to our starting point, and to the left, following Calle del Obispo in its downward slope toward the southeast, all along the Gothic side of the old Consejo de Ciento, currently called la Diputación, leads to Plaza de San Jaime, formerly Plaza de la Constitución and, also periodically, Plaza de la República, the city's administrative center, location of both the City Hall and the Catalan Diputación or Provincial Council, the two facades with their rigorous lines facing off; San Jaime, Jacobo, or Santiago, patron saint of Spain and battering ram of Christianity, captain of the armies, champion of battles, son of the thunder, knight on his white charger, who, reaching Barcino, ascended to the summit of Mons Taber and, after contemplating the city, founded the cathedral there on high, core chthonic cornerstone, touchstone, like a transformative philosopher's stone, like a talisman or enchantment, transubstantiation of the Acropolis, consecration of the temple, prevalent tabernacle, exalted, Mont Taber or Mont Miracle, Mountain of the Disappearance, neither Moses nor Elijah nor shining lights, mountain transfigured, flattened by the very growth of the city, buried, up in smoke forever et in saecula saeculorum, centuries of history contemplating, phantasmagoric vision, spectral procession of empires and dominations, a city condemned to relive, to survive itself, Rome engendered by lost Troy, vertex of a fatherland built bit by bit over the course of the years, with the passing of the states and sovereignties, a rhetorical train of titles, exiled names, flatus vous, Aquitania, Septimania, Occitania, Marca Hispánica, the Crown of Aragón, poly-member monarchy, Mediterranean empire on horseback, vapor trail of golden islands of an archaic empire, meaning, precocious and, in every case, outdated, short-lived, an empire soon dismembered, unhorsed, riderless steed, wagon enmired, a kink in the rope, a litany of misfortunes, banners flagging, lowered, dreams of greatness dissipated, agonic delirium of an inconclusive destiny, aborted, failed, the rose of April topped, crown of thorns, crown of flowers, its sole court the crenellated complex of Poblet, slag heap of triumphs and splendors, buried conquests, remote relaxing isolated retreat, monastery of gilded stones, with its towers inhabited by soft solitary owls and the sluggish swallows flitting round the cloisters, while in the high vaults the shadows deepen ever more absolute, alabaster monarchs in repose, empty pupils, one last look, self-absorbed center bitten the dust, returned to dust, and blown away, anonymous earth, mixed, crucible and crossroads of the old world, classic route of invasions, occupied country, fatherland unrepentant, thirsty for freedom, famished for independence, hunger and epidemics, endemic ills, ill-fated days, of displeasure and disgrace, of discouragement, Dantesque times, of fury and cholera, of plague, of oppression, of racial abysses, moats and declivities, rotund walls, a fortified city, enclosed and surrounded, city of Numantian sieges, assaulted, conquered, re-conquered, conqueror, impeller of expeditions and occupations, city of traded fortunes, liberator and captive, subdued and reborn, recalcitrant and fractious, uncivil, city of rebellions and restorations, of uprisings, riots, attacks, bombs, barricades, massacres, lynchings, charges, discharges, machine guns, bombs, festive bonfires, city of flaming bright colors, yellow, red, yellow, red, yellow, red, yellow, red, yellow broom flowers, pure smokeless flame, inextinguishable fire, phoenix of April, re-flowering on the wind, flag praised in song and hoisted high, *la senyera*, dominant, singular flag, the red and yellow Catalan flag, golden shield with bars of blood and, upon a silver field, the white cross of Saint George, chivalrous patron saint, providential and decisive rider, savior and martyr, slayer of spiders, oh fable of time, city of nonexistent patron saints, ubiquitous Virgin of Mercy, Eulalia flayed, despised maiden, her breasts hacked off, neither virgin nor martyr of Barcelona, rather, pious splitting of her namesake from Mérida, a phenomenon similar in its development to that of San Severo, whose feast day is celebrated today, the sixth of November, Severo de Rávena, bishop and martyr, fallen in the course of some persecution and later brought here with his life and miracles, including the one with the fava beans, mysteries of history, *aucas, aleluyas*, funny faces, jocular mouths, shocking giant heads, the king and queen of golden coins, as depicted on *la baraja*, the Spanish deck of cards, spinning on their tiny feet, their features ecstatic, gestures modest, Catholic kings of cardboard and cloth, ceremoniously lording over the street, retinues, popular festivities, flags unfurled and streamers fluttering in the sun, pennants, tremulous oriflammes, tall standards flowing gracefully, ecclesiastical standards, banners, damask and purple, draperies, tapestries, bands of musicians, cornets, drums, kettledrums, horns, cymbals shimmering like suns, wind and brass in rhythm, riders, white horses, glittering plumed helmets, dress uniforms, the Guardia Civil, waists girded in red sashes, Catalan caps, shimmering confetti, streets threaded with streamers, a procession emerging from the cathedral, large, calm, moving deliberately, hieratic steps, guards, canopies presided over by prelates and dignitaries, gregarious swaying procession, multitudes on the march toward Calle de los Arcos, Puerta del Ángel, and Plaza Cataluña, sidewalks crowded, streets cordoned off, congregated masses, concentrated in Plaza de San Jaime, given over to the most beautiful dance, the pulsating Sardana, circles forming and breaking apart, carpets of flowers, sketches of petals, broom, carnations, the ground colored red for Corpus Christi, cardboard heads, carnivalesque masks, carnal assaults, Bacchic promiscuity, generalized debauchery, grape vines and laurels, palm fronds of welcome, religious feast day celebrations, joyous carefree city, smiling, foppish, handy, Barcelona good and malevolent, with its New Year's Eves and its ancient celebrations of Midsummer's Eve, summer saturnalias, cakes and champagne, paper fringe, foil paper, sequins, lanterns, fireworks displays, nighttime bonfires, fires deliberately set, convents burned down, smoke of gunpowder and gasoline, *civitas diaboli*, rude, crude, and cowardly Barcelona, always quick to break its word, to besmirch all that is human, all that is divine, whore disguised as nun, nun disguised as whore, humiliated countess, princess sans principles, queen of drag queens, *res publica*, archive of courtesans, second Rome, traitorous Barcelona, quick to applaud and acclaim, to offer an ovation, to receive warlords and drag bodies drawn and quartered along Las Ramblas, to celebrate downfalls and liberations, dominations and thrones, dethronements and executions, disjointed conjunctures, tortures, dislocations, inquisitorial judgments, rigorous sentences, exemplary punishments, torture turned fiesta, duels become norm, anniversary become commemorative exaltation, divergent perspectives, different aspects belonging to one place, simultaneously the cradle of honored citizens and bandits, capital of a coarse, untamed land, fields sown and fertilized with violence, a coastal region raised upon one accomplishment after another, from century to century, turbulent, rebellious serfs and freemen, *cadells* and *nyerros*—sixteenth-century civil-military factions defending landed interests—puppies and piglets, head-hunting reapers, using sickles to cut off Castilian heads, bandits and indentured grape growers, repressive squads, *mossos d'esquadra*, mobs, conflicting parties of soldiers, emphatic interferences, wounds inflicted thanks to ancestral rivalries, a situation prolonged over the course of centuries, tolerably passable, passably unsustainable, forever knee-deep in adversity, wading in it, evading it, falling into it, unlucky land of castles destroyed and counties condemned, Count Arnau, unrepentant lord of abuses, extorter of servants and violator of abbesses, condemned soul with tenebrous retinue, nighttime rides like steel scorpions, sparks, galloping echoes, a country accursed, land of blasphemies and sacrileges, of ransacked sanctuaries, Friar Garí or Garin, outrageous violator and murderer of Riquilda, daughter of Wilfred the Hairy, maiden returned to life fresh as a rose when, seven years later, perhaps nine, the despised hermit, changed into an unrecognizable wild beast, was captured on the crags of Montserrat by a group of hunters and taken back to Barcelona in a cage. There, all hair and nails, he confessed his crime to the astonished court, a carving by an unknown artist placed in a landing of the staircase, exposed to the people's curiosity, people disposed to render tribute and acclaim, to praise even upon the scaffold, unhappy star of Juan Sala, alias Serrallonga, native son of Viladrau, prototype of the good thief, knight-errant to the poor, to the needy, cunning knave of the Guilleries mountains, like Robin Hood, bandit immortalized like Tallaferro y Trucafort, like Perot lo Lladre, meaning, the Quixotic Pere Rocaguinarda, better known as Roque Guinart, popular heroes, gunslingers of the people, race of illustrious libertarian inclinations, Ferrer Guardia, victim of injustice, the Sugar Boy—*El Noi de Sucre*—Quico Sabater, laureled martyrs, done to death, start all over again, reset accounts, a race of iconoclasts and image makers, saints and criminals, mystics and forerunners, transporters and navigators, saviors, poets, visionaries, fratricides, conquistadors, Phoenicians, Philistines, merchants, a bastard history of transactions and conspiracies, activities secularly centered in Barcelona, prostituted city, city of leisure pursuits and occupations, of political ambitions and courtesan hopes, prisons and gallows, lost glories and abandoned empresses, miracles and revolts, perverse and versatile city, twisted, malicious, pharisaical, Manichaean, sweet-talking, dissimulating, keen, dissolute, insolvent, anarchic, separatist, fundamentalist, reactionary, plutocratic, rich loafing laborious city, libidinous, lascivious, insane, profaner of sepulchers, incendiary, blood-streaked city, caked in blood, underworld of hoodlums and crooked cops, bullies and bombers, employer of bodyguards and syndicate gunmen, terrorists and shock troops, assault experts, policemen, civilians, Civil Guards, esprit de corps cloaked in wrath, organizations polarized just as the *cadells* and *nyerros* once were long ago, a beam sought in another's eye, eye for an eye, tooth for a tooth, a cocktail of violence, a mixture of explosive Chicago and camorrista Naples, a chronicle fundamentally marked off by black events and bloody days, tragicomic weeks in a city accustomed to settling questions in public, to liquidating them around the corner or along the streets stretching away into the distance, if not in the no-less-expeditious revolts of Montjuich or La Rabassada casino, the gutter become law, law of the loophole, a people oppressed, a people persecuted, a people held captive, a messianic people, always in exodus toward itself, quicksand promised land, city built on sand, below Las Ramblas, from mountain to sea, from river to river, soil born from the waters, terrain sprouted from the receding salt marshes, sprung up between alluvium and sandbank, islands and peninsulas gradually enlarged and extended until forming one single misty bubbling plain of sedimentary clay, of algae and fungi, drifting viscosities settled gradually into a pasty green germination, accumulated herbaceous vegetation, woody entanglements, gigantic branches, roots securing the earth, climbing stems enveloping it in tangled hangings, reverting to earth, decomposing, fermenting in slow vital cycles, laying down the bases of the fertile plain, of future Barcelonas, a fleeting succession of flowerings and desolations, phoenix deceased and revived, reborn from its prostrate ashen wingspan, a city today unfolded within the arms of the encircling mountainous amphitheater, from Tibidabo to the port, from the Llobregat to the Besós, boundaries overflowed each day by the Mediterranean's greatest human concentration, peripheries woven from posts and cables, chimneys, iron interwoven beneath low-hanging layers of industrial vapors, factories upon factories, railways, arteries of ingress, labyrinthine slums, suburbs more and more dense around the city center proper, pleasant seat as much with very lively centers of activity as well as outlying residential zones, calm and quiet beneath other skies, lighter airs, tremulous foliage along peaceful avenues and boulevards, delightful quiet flowering orchard, cultivated land of poetry contests and spiritual exercises, a city traditionally open to progress, preserver and restorer, archiver of past splendors, words and gestures made myth, fantasies in stone, a profitable archeological past unearthed by the city government for the benefit of all, stimulating, ennobling, valuable profundities, fecund excavations, arches and aqueducts, truncated columns, facings cleared, left open to view, urbanized ruins, recomposed perspectives, limpid green lawns sprouting long thin lampposts, ivy-crowned heights, classic cypresses, myrtles, fructified stone, and triumphal laurels, Barcelona, city of trade fairs and conventions, as that great sign planted in the green grass proclaimed, before the old city walls, perchance since the equinoctial festivals last September of La Mercè, the Virgin of Mercy, before the walls of the exterior circuit of this involuted labyrinth of back alleys and side streets, crossed slantwise by the declining afternoon sun, populated by anonymous footsteps, little children's clamor heard amid a natural rumor from the unexpected small plazas and open spaces, winding turns and hidden corners, patios, staircases, gates and porches of run-down houses, overshadowed by the dark gray edges of the cornices, by the iron rust run down the wall to the low graffiti, large old doorways standing open to dark interior workshops, small businesses, antique shops, artisans, image makers, ornate establishments crammed with goods, narrow shop windows, second-hand bookshop, bodega, souvenir and costume jewelry shop, postcards on display outside, diverse views of the cathedral and its surroundings, Plaza San Jaime, Plaza del Rey photographed from the Casa Padellás, Plaza Ramón Berenguer el Grande seen from above, at dusk, against the acid yellow of the dusk and the nitid crosswise cirrus clouds, views from Calle Obispo, from Calle de los Condes de Barcelona, from Calle de la Piedad, following the outline of the cathedral apse, detailed views of the cloisters, the medallion of San Jorge, for example, in the keystone of the temple, carved stone, archivolts and capitals, the door of Santa Eulalia, the door of San Ivo, the portico, and more standard architectural compositions, the facade in the background, and a projecting section of the Roman wall in the foreground, the entire cathedral head on, the nucleus of what was once Mons Taber taken in its entirety, a structure of rooftops, of ochre reliefs with interspersed green spaces, aerial panoramas from the commercial center, from the wharves, from the Ensanche, a partial view of the city from Tibidabo, with the amusement park rides at the very top of the mountain hanging out over the void, or from Montjuich, the castle parapets silhouetted before distances tightly packed with buildings and in the hazy distance a terminus of hills like clouds, partial views, sunsets and backlit western skies, glowing nocturnal blues, typical images of Barcelona, the Columbus monument streaming with pennants, Columbus against the heavens, the terraqueous globe like a pedestal, Columbus in the spotlights, pointing to the darkness, Columbus hanging on the rigging of the caravel Santa María anchored in the port, as if mounting the heavens on his terraqueous globe, the Arco de Triunfo, triumphal arch, the Obelisk of Victory, the Sagrada Familia spectrally illuminated, the stadium in Las Corts filled to capacity with spectators, the fountains of the 1929 Exposition, the Ciudadela Park thick with amazing lucent April yellows, Park Güell and its quiet paths, perfect for morning trysts, petrified paths and passages, trees of rock, rough and writhing, Park Güell and its oblique columns, its airy serpent of multicolored mosaic, flowers formed from fragments of flowered tiles, snapshots of the streets, bustling drudgery and pleasures of daily life, Las Ramblas, polled plane trees with naked boughs, with spring shoots, dry leaves, tobacco-colored, hanging on edge above the passersby, a variegated coming and going between kiosks selling books and magazines, pictures and postcards of the city, among flower stands, bouquets and plants and freshness like dew, chrysanthemums, nosegays of everlasting, stiff wreaths of golden Butcher's Broom, funeral offerings, sad Novembrists in memory of those who shall nevermore, of those who no longer come and go nor even stop nor will stop before the kiosks on Las Ramblas, before the flower stands, in anonymous coincidence, the instant fixed forever, in a corner of the postcard, from behind, a painter before his easel colorful with sketches, everything picturesque, local color, movement, Las Ramblas and El Liceo, La Plaza de Cataluña seen from Las Ramblas, Plaza Cataluña overflown by pigeons, La Plaza de la Universidad spinning with traffic, various currents turning and branching, trams, family cars, taxis, buses, a plaza congested, presided over by a facade of sober symmetries, twenty minutes to six on the clock tower when he entered the building through the main gate with determined step, after confirming the presence of police detachments stationed at all the surrounding side streets, jeeps, horses, police forces prepared to intervene at the first symptom of agitation, to cordon off the plaza, redirect traffic, break up the groups of spectators, keep the pedestrians back while the water-wagons moved into action, while they blasted the porticoes of the entrance hall, clearing the way for the police on foot, opening a path for them through the broken glass and the fallen sopping banners. At first, except for the very small number of students gathered, fewer than even the most pessimistic predictions projected, everything proceeded according to plan, even too closely for the final result to proceed according to plan, for it to create an inflammatory climate of confrontation capable of liberating energies, of empowering and spreading, of spontaneously unchaining a process of sweeping, uncontainable galvanizing actions. But the morally decisive factor in the later march of events, more than a mere question of number, was, perhaps, the crude confirmation of the unquestionable inefficacy, by circumstances not so imponderable as mysterious, of all their appeals to the conscience of the university, an immediate and manifest cause, in the long run, of the situation they now found themselves in. They were few, the usual suspects as they say, those directly responsible, the committed few, and their fervent activity proved insufficient to compensate for the absence of the masses summoned, insufficient even to silence an increasingly less precise conviction of having embarked on an enterprise headed straight for disaster. Two hundred, perhaps? At least one hundred eighty? Some spoke out from atop the patio benches, encouraging their companions, but next when they read, without even a breath of improvisation, their declaration of solidarity with the Asturian strikers, it all came out rushed and confused, almost unintelligible. The signs and banners also appeared too suddenly, without seeming very natural, unexpectedly small and isolated, and the shouts sounded almost furtive, like asides, a feeble chorus. They burned a few newspapers that had published the official reports on the strikes in Asturias, and the portraits of Franco and José Antonio, tumultuously pulled down from the lecture halls, were soon lying shattered on the ground, and their voices seemed lost in the rounded strophes of the *Gaudeamus Igitur*. The movement toward the street started with certain indecision, without it being completely clear to everyone where they were headed, which route to take, along which streets they planned to carry out their demonstration, maybe because no one really believed that they could make it past the front doors, the doors where they usually congregated, unsure, confused, confronted by the police phalanxes, by the water wagons spraying, now shouting *Libertad! Libertad!* while struggling against the pounding water until, when the explosions went off, one after another, too powerful, the police responded, charging them in a tight formation of boots and billy clubs and steel helmets. It must have been just after six in the afternoon.

I went because I was curious, to see what was happening.

Curiosity, nothing, said Montserrat. You can drop your stories with me, I'm not the police. You went because you had to do it.

Well, but out of solidarity with my friends, I mean. Nowadays all you do is ask for freedom and they instantly call you a communist.

Now? They'd even call José Antonio a communist.

Eloísa cleared the table and, from the sitting room, through the open glass door of the cabinet, they saw her run with her plates toward the kitchen, her face suddenly contorted, clouded with tears, just as when Raúl had arrived home and Papa hugged him and she heard him saying to him my son, my son. Montserrat interrogated him with her glance. They were alone. Papa had left the room, probably gone to the toilet, moments before Montserrat appeared, who stopped just in the doorway, emphatic and triumphant, and without answering his greeting, she was upon him throwing her arms wide to squeeze him tight between repeated kisses, pulling him, her purse and gloves against the back of his neck, holding him at arm's length to see him better, holding him by his shoulders while she kept repeating *machote*, *machote*, you're such a big boy now. Raúl refilled the coffee cups, poured more cognac in Montserrat's; his own, however, remained untasted, not very appetizing as tired as he was and, especially, so amazed, tension resulting from the unusual events of the last hours, of the condensation of events, of the absorbing character of the accumulated emotions leaving him dry and rough, as if hungover, his head thick with somnolence, soft haze, deforming his perception, words sounding against open spaces, echoing against incoherencies, the binding thread of the phrase, questions difficult to formulate and even more difficult to answer. An even greater difficulty given that Montserrat's conversation was now in itself rather incoherent, scattered ideas, fleeting, expressed with exaltation and haste, changing themes too brusquely, José Antonio's personality, young people of an earlier generation, ideals. The real José Antonio: a sublime character, irreducible, the poetical and manly qualities of his style, and his speech. She had met him in a meeting, during the days of the Republic, when Jaime was one of the Falangist leaders of the university. People with an immeasurable capacity for sacrifice, contagious, people totally and passionately devoted to the cause, above and beyond selfish interests, devoid of all pettiness. The unforgettable magnetism of an era, of a way of being, men who mattered, who knew how to shake things up, real men, like José Ramón and José Pedro, like Florentino, like Vittorio, like Ernst himself, who, at least in this aspect, regarding manliness and bravery, had no reason to envy anyone else. A generation of heroes, something unimaginable to those who had not lived through it, that attitude of bravery and sacrifice, of disregard for life, always betting against death, living as if for a brief moment, squeezing out every last minute of their short leave from guard duty, just as happy as naughty boys. Such temerity! Bold features and bold gestures! Arrests, disdain, fierceness, arrogances, contempt, exploits . . . Impossible to express what that time was. The best died and, now, the others, the deserters who never fired a shot, string us along like we don't matter. Because we didn't fight a war for these leeches, for that gang of the Opus Dei, for today's Falangists, for those who run the show and take their cut first, and look out for their own interests while they talk about stability. Their money, that's what they want to keep stable. Do you think anyone would have given, let alone risked, their life for the pretty faces of these black marketeers, the insiders, the nouveau riche, for these bankers and financiers who've taken control of the country's economy? *Tocinaires*, as we called them back then, pork butchers, scoundrels, scumbags who didn't even have anywhere to lie down and die before the war and then made a killing on the black market. They sure helped themselves. In the worst way. Even disappearing while there was danger. If only José Antonio could rise from the dead! There are so few remaining, the faithful, those dedicated to the true cause. But it's a consolation knowing that you can count on them for whatever you need, that they'll answer you unconditionally, that they'll move heaven and earth if necessary. When I heard about your situation, I only had to call Madrid, to speak with Florentino, a dear friend, the one who recommended you when you were an ensign. Montserrat, he told me, I'm going to put in a good word for the lad as if he were my own son. That he was misinformed; wrong about the facts. Or at least he had some distorted idea of things. But, for God's sake, Florentino, don't you realize that with the way things are now an honest young man these days can't possibly adopt a different attitude? Or that his attitude, deep down, and even though perhaps not even he himself knows it, is that of a truly committed person, given his basic, fundamental loyalty, if not to the letter then definitely to the spirit of the same principles which inspired us? Have you forgotten about when we were his age? Do you think, confronted with a situation like the one nowadays, we would've behaved any differently? And I've made him see that for us you even represent an obligation to encourage, support, and direct, as we can, as many of you as we can, in these times of confusion and sinking values, you all appear morally healthy, with concerns and courage, with ideals, with altruism. And Florentino told me that, well, of course he was going to show the same interest as if you were his own son. He's a perfect gentleman, completely true and proper, incorruptible. She was quiet for a moment, shaking her head, arching the faint outline of her plucked eyebrows, nostalgic. There were moments when her face seemed a mask, that slightly swollen smoothness of features in a cluster of folds pasty with makeup, her face powdered and white, her hair clear and stiff, straightened, and her bulging eyes in the middle of her face; it seemed to make her lean forward in her seat, her elbows on her knees, as if on the attack, and then leaning back against the chair, her legs stretched out, her glass of cognac resting on her bulging belly. She asked him about his life and his projects, about Nuria, about his studies.

And your girlfriend? Is she still in England?

Nuria? Yes, in England. But she's not my girlfriend.

Girlfriend or whatever you want to call her, you understand me, we're not going to start beating around the bush, you and I. Did you let her get away?

Well, the truth is we've never really been a steady couple. And now not even that.

Ah, well, you see my question was completely innocent, I didn't know anything. You know I'm not one to try to rub you the wrong way. That's for everybody to figure out on their own. But if you want me to tell you the truth, I think you did the right thing. I'm sure that you're a ladies' man, and the last thing you want is to get married. Well and good. You're still very young to be forming serious attachments. For that matter, I'll tell you the truth, if I were a man, I'd certainly never get married. And I don't say so for the sake of the freedom that you'd surely sacrifice, but rather for the lack of trade-off, for the disappointments that you have to bear, for jokes and misunderstandings. Believe me, there's no more thankless responsibility than marriage. And how it weighs everything down. I don't know exactly what you plan to do with your life, but I'd bet my neck that it won't be something ordinary, but rather, the opposite, something very unconventional, that demands independence and personality. Writing, for example; because I don't know exactly what it is you write, but I'm sure you do write, you can't fool me, I've got a sixth sense for these things. Well, imagine that now, what a problem. Monsina, because she's a girl, and for a girl things are different, because a girl always has everything to lose and you've got to be careful, but I swear to you that if I'd had a boy instead of a girl . . . Especially, forget about falling in love, above all. You do what you want, but don't fall in love, I'd say. Set things up so that you don't make a mess of things and, if you do, fix things so they don't drag you down. And if someday you really feel like getting married, get married, but don't fall in love, because then you're lost . . . Of course, the girls today aren't the best ones to inspire lofty sentiments. The girls, and the boys who are really no better. These arrogant little pups, they seem like they were raised in a nursery. From the looks of it, it's a worldwide problem. You've traveled so you'll know if it's true. What I can assure you is that, at least here, these little stillborn puppies these days, the ones who come by the house when Monsina throws a party, are really the last straw. At least I can't figure them out. It's like they have chocolate milk in their veins instead of blood, no passions and, at the same time, no principles, no problems, no remorse, no struggles, neither here nor there, I don't know, they're just insipid. I'm sure you must think differently, but for me it's essential to have religion, to have principles. You must have other convictions, but at least you have this, convictions, and don't think, I've also been down in the dumps and faced doubt. But the truth is that I wouldn't know how to live with myself or get along without Sunday Mass, for example. Without Mass, Sunday would be for me a kind of crippled day. The thing is, I believe it brings me luck. On the other hand, not for them, you don't see any contention in them, no compunctions, no convictions. It's as if they had nothing inside them, nothing to contain. On one side, they know it all; but on the other, nothing interests them. And if I, who am almost an old woman, feel young compared to them! But them, nothing, they've got no ideals, no worries, they're just indifferent to everything, they only talk about nonsense . . . You don't see them with something, what you call character, mettle. I don't even think they're interested in girls. They only talk about clothes, just like girls. Anything that's not their clothes, their records, their guitars . . . Does that strike you as normal? Only a few years ago, four, five at the most, this didn't happen. You, for example, at their age, you were different. And the thing is, kids like you, although you didn't experience the war, you remember it, you're part of a different generation, no doubt about it. And it shows. At the same age, you all had more nerve, more drive, you were always searching, you chased girls, all perfectly normal, of course. It was more like in my day, the way it's always been. And I think it's for that reason, because of the war; you saw it, even though you were kids, you touched it, you grew up within the struggle, and so you know that the reality of life is just that, struggle and fight, no feather bed. On the other hand, talking about our war to these youngsters coming up now is like talking to them about the Stone Age.

He held Montserrat's gaze, but without looking straight into her eyes, without establishing a reciprocal relationship and, as if inert, he let himself drift through that stare, nodding. It was like stubbornly continuing to read when distracted by something, getting only partial intuitions of the sense of the text, isolated flashes that instantly vanish, forcing yourself to make connections between them, to reconstruct their continuity. So then he heard her say: recollections, contrasts, contrapositions, evidences. Then: volunteers dead at seventeen, sixteen, even fifteen; Jaime, at twenty-two. He watched her search through her purse, root around in her purse while she talked, and carefully pull out the photo that she finally handed him, a face with very pronounced features, a full warm youthful smile, hazy and retouched around the edges, as if haloed, cardboard with dirty, worn edges, smelling old and handled, like a wallet. Now, however, now: where will it end? Boys increasingly effeminate, girls ever less female. Toward a complete confusion of the sexes? She asked him again about his projects. Would he try to earn a teaching position via competitive examination? Sociology? That's what we need, teachers, leaders, brains. People to look out for society. Competent, well-trained people, with vision, with authority. People who govern, not for the benefit of a few, but for all. With social sensibility. Who expend no energy on private interests or granting favors. The common good. Inflexibly. A difficult road, full of misfortune and bitterness, so many people failing, giving up. Sad, a recent disappointment suffered with someone who was a very close friend. I considered him true and uncorrupted but he turned out to be what we call here in Catalonia *un torracollons*, someone who stabs you in the back and roasts your balls over the fire. Believe me when I say I admire you. But I couldn't, by now I've forever lost my confidence in other people, I've taken too many blows in life. She had finished her cognac and now refilled their glasses, ignoring Raul's negatory gesture, his hand trying to cover his glass. Too many, she said. And then right away: c'mon, let's get smashed. She dipped her fingers into a packet of blonde cigarettes and rummaged around distractedly, without success, and ended up crushing the empty pack over an ashtray. She silently accepted a cigarette of black tobacco, and Raúl, as he gave her a light, noticed that she was looking above him, toward the door, and he saw her stand up, releasing a mouthful of smoke, smoothing her skirt. Uncle Jorge, darling. Stubbornly reading and re-reading, words superimposed, simultaneous sensations, impressions unfolding, turning the pages again, searching the newspaper unsuccessfully for some reference to the incidents at the university. Look, thank God, just a scare. Maybe it taught him a lesson at least. Folding the paper, gulping down his coffee, checking the time, the cup on the small table, the newspaper folded on the chair, to his side, images reiterated; going to school, teaching class, catching a taxi, the appointment with Escala or Santiago or with some connection, or a strategic planning committee meeting, or a meeting with Fortuny and Federico, at Adolfo's house, theoretically to discuss some practical questions, if it was the right time to approach Marius Cots and ask him directly about joining the party, to see if he still harbored any residual feelings of his earlier petit bourgeois *Catalanismo*. And when there were no practical questions to discuss, they met anyway and, in fact, went over the same themes again, rehashing perpetual problems, theoretical disquisitions, the circumstances that fostered Stalinism, Budapest, socialist countries and proletarian internationalism, the possibility, probability, or certainty that the Spanish communist party, accepting the parliamentary gambit just like so many fellow parties, would end up becoming institutionalized in perpetual opposition, problems and distinctions which, impelled by Federico's designs, drifted easily toward personal territory, here, in Catalonia, communism has always belonged to the petite bourgeoisie, Cots will become fast friends with Fortuny, I told him that if Catalonia is not an independent nation there must be some reason, etcetera, going round in circles, fluctuations of tone and even arguments around an unalterable nucleus, the attitude or, if you prefer, each person's role, personal positions dressed in variable and derivative concepts, as words, for example, lead the singer in a patriotic hymn, with all their residual debris, as they develop into specific ideological expositions or some story of apologetic nature, with its hypotheses and interpretations so frequently articulated by rhetoric, an exegesis likely to become lost in the course of a sentence, in the roundabout language and commentary of the period, conclusions seemingly created by the very dynamic of the oration, by the magnetic attraction that some words seem to exercise with respect to others, independently of what is appropriate to their application, in agreement with a fundamental development not so much in the objective data to which one believes it to refer as in the words employed, words, words, who knows if with a certain awareness of what the only thing that remains certain in the end might be. Montserrat said, you can be proud of him, and the telephone began to ring, and Papa looked at her with suspicious eyes, and Raúl said I'll get it, and he went ahead of Eloísa, and Fortuny, surely calling from some pay phone, said that no one was seriously ill, that everyone was recovering, that he'd not lost the ignition key, diaphanous codewords, due to the telephone being bugged, explanations almost more incriminating than if spoken in a normal way even as Papa was saying Oh, c'mon, c'mon, the authorities thoroughly bungled the situation, what more proof do you want than that they had to release him, and Raúl asked if he knew whether there had been any classes held at the university, if anything else had happened, and Fortuny said no, that classes had taken place as usual, that he would be calling him, but that afternoon he could not meet in the usual place. But no one can say I've been negligent raising my children! said Papa. Meeting at Adolfo's house, arguing, digressing, playing records, drinking gin, simultaneous images, reiterated. Adolfo with Aurora at his feet, as it were, Aurora listening or seeming to listen, fascinating sentences, some cataclysm repeated perhaps until daybreak, irreparable drunkenness, *dies irae, dies illa, illa daurada*, lost golden isle, vanished intonations, abortive youthful Mozartian madnesses, requiem for youth and life, Teste David cum Sybilla, dolorous awakening, Michelangelo beauty, reclining and naked, enigmatic, marble Aurora. And Adolfo, serene, *pensieroso*, the left hand grasping the smoking pipe between his teeth, for as long as he didn't topple from the pedestal, as long as the myth didn't crumble to pieces; for that long. Why respected? Why fascinating? Fascinating for whom? Fascinating for all? Respected by all? By all. Including Federico, and perhaps respected by everyone just as long as he remained respected by Federico, respected to the point that not even Pluto would dare to crack jokes at his expense. Or well respected because everyone agreed that he was a very intelligent guy although, in truth, since he hardly ever said a word, there was hardly any way of knowing if he really was intelligent or not. Or because everyone said that he was writing a great novel, a great work which, on the other hand, no one had seen, except for fragments, and which, consequently, might just as well turn out to be a disaster, in the safe supposition, just like with everything else bound to happen, that he'd manage to finish it someday. And so much more respected because, who knows if for a priori reasons or as a result of their own collective attitude, all of them, Raúl first, implicitly granted him a certain measure of authority or acquiescence, quieting down as soon as Adolfo asked them, ending up in discussions from which Adolfo refrained, letting him impose his voice when, having listened to anyone else besides Adolfo, they wouldn't have managed to even hear him. They all clammed up, Raúl first, and they drank their gin without listening to the music or listening to it in spite of themselves, acknowledging, one by one, what Adolfo might have said, not so much because they agreed as because, on the verge of agreeing or disagreeing, they discarded beforehand the opportunity to cast doubt on him, in accordance with a kind of deference imposed by the mood, a mood most certainly established by themselves. Where might they locate the root of such deference, of such respect? Or rather: what quality did Adolfo have that no one else had, neither Federico nor himself nor any other person no less intelligent, no less sharp or brilliant? Fascination? What was the exact sense Aurora imparted to the word? Something definitive, of total value, absolute, coming before anything else? He tasted his cognac.

Quite frankly, what I don't understand is how you can listen to Juanito, man. Don't you see that Juanito is what's called, speaking realistically and calling a spade a spade, a real shithead?

Because I'm a lawyer and I know what "apathy" means. And what he's accusing me of is gross negligence.

But don't you see that he's the one who really doesn't know what apathy means? If he knew the meaning of what he's saying, then he'd instantly cease to be Juanito.

Man, oh, man, for the love of God. Look what he's saying, that I, who've got a son who's nothing less than a priest, that I've been a negligent father, precisely when the family environment they've been raised in couldn't be more Christian, when I've given all my loving care for them to attend the best religious schools, and I've never hesitated to make any sacrifice regarding their education. What fault is it of mine about what my sons do later, if I've done everything I could? Besides, this thing with Raúl is nothing more than a mistake of which he's been a victim, just the same as could have happened to anyone else. The proof is they had to release him. It's these people working for the police who want to find fault with the very same people who pay for their dinner, no matter what. He was attending classes, like any other day, and he got caught up in all this craziness. That's his big crime.

You can be proud of Raúl, that's all I have to say. He's made of the same stuff as Jaime. None of his other cousins is good enough to shine his shoes.

Well, for heaven's sake, let your brother mind what he's saying a little. You can't criticize people that way, without rhyme or reason, without having sufficient evidence for judgment. And without it, c'mon, because things are not as simple as they seem. Judge not and you won't be judged, much less launch an attack that way, like hurling a stone. When you don't know what you're talking about, the best thing is to keep quiet. What does Raúl have in common with your poor brother dying like a hero, fighting against the Reds? Because he was a hero.

What do you mean "poor"? The only poor fellow here is Juanito. Poor for lacking spirit. Jaime was anything but poor-spirited, he was the personification of courage and generosity, he was greatness itself. Neither in his life nor his death is there anything that deserves to be called poor. God help us from wishing some misfortune on Juanito, but God always takes away the best. I promise you that's true.

Well, you see what he's going around saying. That he wants nothing to do with the people who killed his brother. That's exactly how he said it. To Gregorio, just this morning.

Two of a kind. Gregorio has also turned into a big gossip. I'm sure he wasted no time coming to tell you about it. Now, regarding Juanito, why do we need to talk? Lots of badges and so much of his highness up and his highness down, but in the hour of need, he wouldn't be capable of risking even one of his dyed hairs for Don Juan, not one. And, apart from this, don't pull him away from his Equestrian Circle, from the ultraviolet lights, and from his little whores at the Bolero, that's where all his ideals crawled away to die. Ah, and from the Association of Friends of Model Railroading, where they've named him spokesman or something like that.

That's what I'm complaining about. That someone like him, who's suffered no wear and tear, who doesn't even know what it means to work, who's always been dedicated to chasing the good life, now dares to criticize me, who, apart from being his father's brother, from the respect he owes me, I'm a man who's fought, a man who's given himself to his work, who's consecrated all his efforts to give his children a Christian education. After being destroyed by life, after the grief of losing Eulalia, I suddenly found myself with two sons in the world and no wife, eh, and hounded by the Reds, and that in spite of everything I've managed to give them a steady, healthy upbringing. No, nobody knows the things I've had to suffer.

For God's sake, uncle, of course I know it all too well. But Gregorius also made a mistake telling you something that, coming from whom it comes, has no importance. He's an incorrigible gossip, now and forever, for the rest of his life.

I wish you could hear him. You'd see how I've not invented anything.

But for God's sake, uncle.

I'd just like you to hear him. He should be here right now. He was with me this morning, in the garden. And he said that he'd come right back after lunch. I don't understand how he takes so long. He knows I always take a little nap afterward.

He must have forgotten. He'd forget his head if it wasn't attached. He forgets everything, he falls asleep everywhere.

I think it's because he takes too many pills. All that crap for insomnia leaves you wrecked. But if you have a healthy routine, then you're ready to go. And besides they're really expensive, a real drain on finances. He also says that he's got anxiety. I think he's full of manias. Sometimes he seems, I don't know, kind of crazy.

He must be crazy with love.

Well, the thing is no one would say so, but I'm six years older. And Paquita herself, half-disabled and everything, the way she is, the poor thing is eleven years older, and her head is much clearer. Gregorio is senile, he's not in his right mind, honestly.

It's what I'm telling you, love. You only have to see him out on the town, with Leonor. They walk arm in arm like two young people in love, like a couple little turtledoves. I ran into them one day, months ago.

It must have been when he was going through that depression. Poor Leonor, well, she's a good woman. She's like Eloísa, she's been so many years in the house. He's lucky to have her, that he's not so worn out yet. I don't know what he'd do otherwise. He's like a little boy, he needs them looking after him all day long.

You can be sure I'm not criticizing them. On the contrary. The idea that she's a nursemaid doesn't count for me. As if she were the queen of England. Gregorius is perfectly free to get involved with whomever he wants. The thing is that she's not precisely what you'd call a paragon of charm. That's the only problem I see with his Leonor.

Montserrat, Montserrat, you know I don't like you talking so freely. You say things in jest, but someone who doesn't know you can take them seriously and, well, it creates a bad impression. And then things get repeated, people are terrible. You mustn't make rash judgments, Montserrat. You're quite the one to make them and it's not right. At least not in front of me. And I'm telling you seriously, honestly.

But uncle, you know well enough I don't say it against him. I don't mean to criticize him. I love Gregorius very much, with his strange qualities and everything, and I know perfectly well that he'd be lost without her. He's completely absentminded. It's enough to tell you that some years ago, when Monsina was nine or ten, I had to forbid him from taking her to the park. You know that Gregorius is crazy about Monsina, well, about all kids, perhaps more about Monsina, and that children always love him, who knows why, but Gregorius is a kind of institution for the children. Well, then, I had to tell him that I wouldn't let them go alone to the park anymore, that if they didn't go with Leonor or some responsible person, then no. And the thing is, you know how crazy he is, playing with her, seems they were struggling, he was lifting up her skirts, that he was playing that he was going to paddle her, and so one day a circle of people gathered around, and a policeman even appeared and started to ask him questions. A real spectacle. And he was lucky that there were some people there who knew him from other times. They must have taken him for one of those crazy perverts who chase after children. Why am I telling you all this? Ah, yes, well nothing, because the little girl is all grown up now, a young woman, he keeps on with the same jokes. And, of course, people who don't know how he really is will just think that he's just some dirty old man. But he doesn't even realize that he makes Monsina miserable; she blushes red as a tomato and one time she started crying and everything. And I said, but, for God's sake, Gregorius, don't you realize that you can't touch a fifteen-year-old girl on the ass?

Of course, Gregorio is really the last straw. And what do you think about that time they stole his overcoat in the park? He says some young fellow asked him what time it was and before he knew it, his overcoat had disappeared off the backrest on the bench. I think he must have fallen asleep.

Nothing surprises me. He falls asleep, he forgets things, and then he thinks that he's been robbed. He even falls asleep in the cinema. Seems that one time he scared the hell out of the ushers, they thought that everyone had left the theater, and there he was in his seat like a dead man.

Right, right. He acts like someone deranged. I think he's out in the sun too much, and the sun cooks his brain and leaves him stupefied. So much sun can't be good. He falls asleep like a dormouse and then, of course, at night he's wide awake and can't get to sleep and so he takes sleeping pills. That's just a vicious circle and he doesn't know how to break out of it. Paquita's head is much more clear, I tell you.

Aunt Paquita? What do you want me to tell you? I think that if she were in her right mind she would never have swallowed all these stories about the ancient history of the Ferrers and the family crest that these genealogy swindlers use to rip her off. Of course it's Juanito's fault, he's such an idiot, and he filled her head with all these ideas; but only a few years ago, she would've paid him no mind. We've all got our own little manias; she's got hers, like praying to saints, and religious observances. Well, as I recall, I'd never before heard her talk about family histories and coats of arms. And now she sounds like a broken record, she only talks about how in 1963 or whenever it's the family's thousand-year anniversary and if for some reason she's not around anymore, we mustn't forget to celebrate it. Poor thing. Imagine, how are these disgraceful heraldic investigation people going to know things about our family that we don't know? But they stir up people's vanity with noble coats of arms and family trees that they simply invent, and they actually make a living from it. The only one who takes them seriously is Juanito, who ordered a seal for his ring and goes around bragging about it, telling everyone that the first Ferrers were lords of the Ampurdán who went south to establish themselves in I don't know what lands in Tarragona province. And I tell him, don't you see, you stupid idiot, that Ferrer is one of the most common names anywhere?

Look, everybody has their little manias. It's perfectly harmless.

It does no harm, but it makes him look ridiculous. His monarchist friends must be the first ones to joke about him the second he's out of earshot. Of course they don't have much reason to be proud either, newly minted titles for most of them, awards for civic virtues and good business, no real glorious origin stories there. Everybody knows that in Catalonia there have never been nobles in the conventional sense. Nor have we ever needed them, by the way. There have been counts, that's true, and the rest were lords and that's all. And where did all these marquesses come from now? But if any of these pseudo-titles now looks so ridiculous alongside the Duke of Alba or Medinaceli, you can be double sure how foolish Juanito looks pretending to have noble blood.

So what, woman, so what. Besides, who knows if there isn't some truth at the bottom of all this.

For goodness' sake, uncle, honestly, we never heard such nonsense at home until Juanito ran into these swindlers. What's happening is that, you know perfectly well they've got Aunt Paquita hooked on that ancient history business, and that's where we're at.

Poor Paquita, she's also got quite a cross to bear with her bad health. Life hasn't given her much more than difficulties and misfortunes. She's got it like me, that apart from seeing her children well set up . . . First she loses her oldest child, then her husband, and now she's sick, slowly eating away at her for years and years. And so many other beloved people just disappearing, your parents, the two of them in full health, eh, in the prime of life. You might say God wanted to put us to the test. For my part, I've always accepted it all with resignation, but sometimes I think why, my God, why. Eulalia's death was a terrible blow to me, you can't imagine, I don't know what kept me from losing my mind. Without faith, without religion, I believe I would've done something drastic. Lucky also to have my children, who obliged me to react, to keep fighting to make a life for them. Apart from them, I had no other dreams, I'd lost my desire to fight, completely. And I'd barely recovered, the war, the persecutions, and once again starting all over, one blow after another. But losing Eulalia marked the start of my misfortunes, it was the true tragedy of my life. If I'd had her by my side, I would've never retired from the company the way I did, tired of life and everything. But without her I felt old before my time, without strength, and once my kids were on their way, one of them a priest and the other completing his studies, I lacked incentives to stay on as the head of the company. Of course a man of frugal habits like myself, who has no needs, lives with nothing, and our income covers all the household expenses, thank God. But it's not the money, not the desire for money, no. It's the moral aspect. I had skills and drive, and I could've managed to become, let me tell you, a man like Jacinto Bonet, a real somebody in the business world.

Jacinto? Well the truth is that I don't know what you see in him, apart from him being filthy rich. To me he seems like nothing special. I don't know, pretty ordinary, I'd say.

Jacinto? Ordinary? For the love of God, Montserrat, don't tell me that. Jacinto is a good fellow, everyone knows it. At his age, the connections he has, and the position he's made for himself. I, for one, think he's amazing. He's a man who's had, well, great success. What more do you want?

He's just one more out of so many who suck on the public tit. And that way they can have fancy cars and servants and always be traveling around from here to there. Besides, a man who goes to America by ship and to Madrid by car because he's afraid to fly, excuse me, but he's not my type.

But look, woman, you've got to see beyond those things, they don't mean anything. Ask whomever you like in Barcelona about Jacinto Bonet, go ahead, and if it's someone in the know, someone who's really involved in the business world, they'll tell you to show some respect. Jacinto Bonet is a man of recognized worth. So he's got enemies? Like any important person. In this world it's all envy and slander, that's well known. But the ones who criticize him are the people who help themselves to what's really yours. And they sure help themselves, alright. The bottom line is, the secret in the business world is this: knowing how to make the most of situations. If people had no desire to make money there would be no economic activity. As long as you don't infringe upon the laws . . . And this Regime might have many defects, but the Stabilization Plan was a necessary measure. I'm speaking to you as a businessman. A medicine that had to be administered to the country, and the Regime has done it and, believe me, time will show that it was the correct response, although right now it might be hard for everyone to swallow. As people already know, you've got to take the good times with the bad. And even with all the defects this Regime might have, anything is better than returning to the past. That insecurity, always on the edge of our seats, expecting to be shot down in any ditch, that they'd kill you for no other reason than being someone of standing or because you'd voted for the right wing. Or simply because they caught you wearing a scapular. Those criminal bands on the loose, riffraff unleashed, secret police, raids. They stole our jewels, silver, everything they could. There's not even a proper name for everything they did. And now we're going to complain about stabilization? Come on, come on. As if stability wasn't what was precisely needed, stability and more stability. The thing is that we Spanish are never content. Do you want any greater misfortune than a revolution, social and economic chaos, reprisals, the loss of so many loved ones?

So tell me then, uncle. And this is what I'm complaining about, that Jaime didn't die for what we have now. This all might be a lesser evil, but he didn't die for this.

Yes, look, things never turn out the way we want them to. Poor kid, he was a hero, a true idealist. In these matters the just men always pay the price for the sinners. And precisely him, so young, so full of life and energy. He had such bad luck. Certainly, and you, for your part. It seems that destiny wanted to fatten us up for the kill. Deaths, infirmities, wars, economic disasters, every kind of calamity. Misfortunes never come just one at a time. Who was going to tell your father, for example, when we were young and we were playing in the big house on Calle Mallorca, that he was going to be the first? Of course he was the oldest brother, but at his age, in the prime of life, it seemed impossible. Now, the oldest is Paquita. And then, me. Do you remember the big house on Calle Mallorca?

But, how could I remember, uncle? I think I wasn't even born then. I'm old, but not that old.

Well, it was something worth seeing. One of the best little palaces of its time. Now it would be worth millions. And it was sold, I don't know, for some ridiculous price, for a song.

That's how we all are now, the crippled leading the blind. None of us has any real chance of buying Vallfosca from the rest of the family. It's still an indivisible property. Save Jacinto, of course, who'll end up owning the whole thing.

Ah, no. I've already told Gregorio, no. From a legal point of view, there's nothing to prevent him from doing it, but as the oldest sibling and with the moral force that gives me, I'm roundly opposed. I've already told him.

So what do you want to do? One by one we're leaving it behind, and that house is more and more abandoned. And now I don't know what's going to happen. Poor Polit, what with everything, even though he's a shameless scoundrel, you can't deny he's managed it well. But the fact is that a country house that belongs to many different people can never be kept up in good shape. And at this rate, in the next generation, it will have fifty different proprietors. But Gregorius will sell his share and, in the long run, it'll be the Bonets and their children who'll end up enjoying it. By the way, it seems that Ramona is expecting again.

No, really, I promise you otherwise. I've spoken with Gregorius and I'm confident that I've been able to get him to forget the idea. That place is like the family manor of the Ferrer Gaminde family and it must stay that way. I've not tired of repeating it to him. But isn't Gregorius something. To side with them now. Who would imagine it?

Excuse me, uncle, but it makes sense up to a certain point. If you're the first one to declare Jacinto some kind of prodigy, as the pride of the family, and Jacinto goes and says to him that he'll buy his share from him, and Gregorius agrees and it seems like a good price to him, well, then it all makes sense.

Not true, not true. It was Gregorius who made the offer to Jacinto, not the other way around; it was Gregorius. And Jacinto accepted, naturally, because he's got vision and knows that in the future, that place is going to be worth a fortune. And this is what Gregorius doesn't see. But it's all his fault for offering it to him. I've told him a thousand times. Don't be a blockhead, it's crazy, really crazy. Who would think of making such a proposal to Jacinto? Don't you understand that Vallfosca is, has been, and must continue to be the Ferrer Gaminde family heritage?

Oh brother, what do you have to tell me about inheritances and entailed estates. To start with, if we'd applied it in our case, by now we wouldn't be arguing because neither you nor I would have our share. Everything would have passed on to Raúl's children, to Juanito, more precisely.

If you don't want to understand me, then don't understand me. It's not for the material interest, it's because of what it represents for the family. That place is linked to our family name, it's our family estate, not just any old property.

His hat was tilted over his nose and he looked at Uncle Gregorio from the shadow of the drooping brim, stretching his neck in a haughty show of bulging Adam's apple, protruding chin, hooked nose, and eyes staring from behind. Inquisitive and still like an old bird. And Uncle Gregorio, seated sideways in his chair, almost with his back turned to him, protected himself from the sunlight flaring round the plum tree with a folded newspaper. Eloísa listened from the steps, pretending to be shelling peas.

But what're you telling me? I've got no descendants. And I don't know what good I'd be doing my nephews leaving it to them when I die if the state will just seize almost everything. Besides, Ramona is just as much my niece as any of the others. They'll settle things between themselves then, don't you worry. And meanwhile, well, I'll make a few pesetas. That's the problem. What good is it for me to keep my share? What do I want it for? On the other hand, if I invest its worth in stocks, in paper, it produces something for me, brings me income.

You're unbelievable, Gregorio, stubborn as only you can be. When you talk like this, I don't know what to do with you, you drive me insane. You're a perfect idiot. Isn't there any way to make you understand that the property you're now willing to sell for peanuts will someday be worth a small fortune? Now that everybody is starting to own their own car, if you subdivide it for development, people will line up to take the lots off your hands. And figure how many houses that could fit there. The only thing needed is to promote it.

Sure, exactly right there. They've got all Catalonia to choose from, but they'll drive their nice little cars right straight up to Vallfosca. Or maybe the rest of Catalonia will end up selling itself off by the centimeter, too?

And why not? It's happening everywhere. With cars, people will now all want to have their own chalet, and it's such a lovely place. The beaches will become impossible. You only need to see the photos in the magazines, the hordes of people. They're so full that sooner or later people will start to return to the countryside. They look like canned sardines, the way they're packed so tightly together. Besides, with a car, that property will be, as they say, just steps away from Barcelona. And it's got millions and millions of centimeters.

Look, Jorge, don't make me laugh. By then, we'll all be bald old men.

Gregorio, you don't know what you're saying, you're just raving. Don't you see that the only thing needed is to promote it, find some capital to set things in motion? There are so many places that don't have all the good qualities of Vallfosca, and yet they're already in fashion. For God's sake, don't be shortsighted.

Well, let's see if you find the money. For my part, I'm delighted. Now, if it's such a good deal as you say, what I don't understand is why you don't just buy out my share among the lot of you. I'll sell it to you really cheap and then everybody's happy.

I don't know what's the matter with you, Gregorio. It makes me so angry to hear you talk that way, I'd like to box your ears. You seem like a cold ingrate. So little attachment to your family name, your house, your own people? Because you know perfectly well, at the moment, none of us is in any condition to do that, to buy out your share.

Of course I know. I'm just talking. But really I don't know what you want me to do. Life is ever more expensive but income stays the same. That's why it seemed the best thing to do was to sell my share to Jacinto.

Well, it was a lousy idea, honestly. It's like selling your inheritance for a plate of beans. Jacinto might promote that for his own benefit, as an interested party, but he can never be the titleholder of our family inheritance. That place is the future of our family.

Well, I can't tell what difference you see between me selling my part to my niece's husband and selling off parcels to strangers.

Well, it was just a lousy idea.

El Polit, sucking in one of his cheeks, clucked his tongue, said that it was all ready. During the war, then, back then. And afterward, when there was rationing, when the people came from the city and bought potatoes and greens at any price, eggs, flour, fresh meat. And the hands worked for low wages and they kept the farm as tidy as a garden. Now, no; now, just me, one single worker, doing everything was too much, I could barely keep it weeded. And when you take your potatoes to market, now they don't give you anything. Not for wheat either, or corn, even less for vegetables, tomatoes, fava beans, peas, green beans. And grapes aren't even worth harvesting. Ever since they started farming down south in Almería, and it seems they harvest sooner. Seems they grow vegetables all year round. And here you go to market and what you take for sale isn't worth anything now. And on top of it, before the harvest, they still import from abroad and they lower the prices on you. Seems like they only want to give farmers a hard time. Now, nothing but the trees, poplars, plane trees, everybody's switched to planting trees. And, at least, after a few years, and without worries, it's easy money. I told his lordship Jacinto myself: trees. He raised his head and turned it slowly, as if taking in the luminous afternoon sky and hills, the golden stubble field, barren expanses, fallow fields, overgrown cabbages among the weeds. A light now without swallows, of autumn, in the quietude the stark arcing flight of the wood pigeons. El Polit. Neither on the stone bench nor in the bulrush chair: seated on a wicker chair, swollen, purplish, with some dark glasses planted before his eyes. He said that those who came afterward would eat the figs without even knowing that it had been he who planted the fig trees. In the Hospital de San Pablo he also came out to the vestibule in the pavilion and sat on the stairs. He contemplated the poor withered garden, the clouds flowing over the buildings. He smiled as if self-conscious. A stroke, you see. He asked him for a cigarette, said they'd taken away his tobacco since he became ill, but that the nun on duty in the morning didn't say anything, she was alright. And now they wanted to give him a job as a doorman, here in Barcelona. It was surely his wife's doing, his wife who'd asked Señorita Ramona. Or Señorita Montserrat. She can't fool me with her little stories. He turned to the nurse. Well, ma'am. When do I get to go home? His peasant coloring contrasted with the paleness of the other patients, and his large knuckly feet, gnarled like wood, shod in sandals soled with tire scraps. And upon returning to Vallfosca, no sooner than getting out of the taxi, the first thing he did was sit down there, under the plane trees by the threshing ground, facing the fields, at the foot of woods and hills. In his house there were no armchairs and they had to bring him one down from their house. He sat rigid, elbows stuck to the creaking wicker armrests. Calella, they would go to Calella with their daughter. They said there was a lot of activity there, all along the coast, foreigners, meaning tourists. There would always be something to do there, and it wasn't like the city. Mercè had always enjoyed the city, but, in this case, he preferred Calella. His gaze followed a flock of wood pigeons, his eyelids squinting behind the dark lenses. He'd already sold the animals, he said. The chickens, ducks, rabbits, cows, pigs; and tomorrow they were coming for the horse. He still had the dogs. And the cats. No matter where he ended up, he couldn't take them with him. The scratching, sniffing, howling dogs, the whole pack gamboling playfully, growling, snapping their teeth, tails wagging, flirting. They seemed restless, watchful, or perhaps unaccustomed to the silence of the corrals and stables, to the calm yards not yet pecked over by the hens, unscratched, unexamined, roosters crested and cackling, pecking at the tomatoes, chicks, egg layers, hens in motion, startled eyes, staring, necks cocked to one side, suddenly running, escaping, flapping wings giving bursts of speed, heads pointing forward, taking big steps, the feet covered in loose yellow skin shooting out like springs. No chickens, no ducks, no rabbits, no cows, no pigs, no horse.

He took a taxi to reach Llinás, right from the station, and along the way he arranged with the driver to come back for him first thing in the morning. Outside of the house, in the transparent shade of the autumnal plane trees, a small multitude of neighbors and relatives had already gathered, serious and expectant people, dark, silent farmers making way for him with circumspection when the car departed. Inside the house the women held sway and it was hot, stuffy rather, from lack of air, and the sweaty expressions of affliction and mourning were heavy, overwhelming, cries of grief accentuated to a fever pitch as the coffin was carried out. The procession followed a lengthy route, and the widow and daughter followed the cortege in a trap, squeezed in among other women, almost unidentifiable beneath their black veils. The greater part of the attendants bid farewell in the town, upon leaving the church; only a few chose to make the climb up to the cemetery. The road flowed, twisting and slanting through the vineyards, steepening, ruined and rutted, and the priest climbing up into the cab of the black and golden hearse, alongside the driver, awkwardly silhouetted against the afternoon skies, heights still frequented by flashing pigeons. It was a difficult slope and, besides, the hearse left behind a redolent stench, perhaps from the grease caked around the axles. Raúl had walked in the company of the son-in-law and they explained to him some family mess, one of Polit's sisters with whom they didn't get along and who had now shown up, full of reproaches, daring to bring up some old differences with Mercè. He walked among the poor crosses of the tombs, between funeral niches grouped together, along the sandy paths bordered by cypresses, past unpleasant hedges with birds taking shelter; hammer blows rang in the air.

On the way back, the people began to split off into small groups, as their paths took them, and some farmers loosened their collars along the way, after a while, removing their jackets and even their shoes, while they chatted between yawns, loquacious and unrestrained, once again familiar, with the relief produced by returning to the world of daily life. Isolated in the calm, soft as dissipating smoke, their voices drifted away from the diminishing clarity, shortcuts, evasive paths of that landscape so well trodden, solitary, filled with wildlife, so thickly sown with rocks and pebbles, with movement, muted, grapevines and stubble, interwoven boughs, and only the soft sound of the wind through the pines after the gunshot, the pigeon fallen like a fluttering angel, in a feathery tumult, the same hills now opaque, now that the turning of the sun is lower each day and the dawn of the night that comes earlier, the lights cut off, the valley growing dark, reliefs vanishing, fields almost extinguishing themselves in the austere nocturnal emptiness. The trap had driven on ahead of them and, when they arrived, the women were already working away in the kitchen, not letting Mercè do anything. Her daughter, however, was cleaning greens, to keep her mind off things. Mercè, by contrast, said nothing, staring into the fire, and suddenly she began to pout again. A sigh, and they all continued their tasks in silence, cousins, sisters-in-law, relatives come from other towns. The men talking in the dining room, killing time, vague phrases, at odd intervals, general sorts of observations; they passed round the porrón, tobacco. They ate dinner together there, taciturn, Mercè wanted nothing to eat and ended up scrubbing her plate, far removed from the talk, anguished. The dogs prowled about infuriatingly, startling them with their sudden howls, all rushing out together, and the son-in-law had to go out and tie them up. One remained, curled up next to Raúl's chair, awake and sniffing about, its eye edged with fright. The doorway suddenly bright, the fresco of the threshing grounds, the road to the house, a smooth curved slope penetrating the threatening bough-thick, storm-clouded sky, the garden strewn with leaves, toward the building as if sheltering against the sky, the blind windows, the dark eaves. And then, inside, the sitting room, the portraits of the grandparents, and of the great-grandfather, an oil portrait painted, by all appearances, from a photograph and, very possibly, after his death, in reverent memory. And the framed photographs lining the hallway, hard, yellowed cardboard, Cuba, the uncle's factories and their products, his house, his lands, his sugar harvest, his livestock, his blacks, estates and heirs, children, daughters-in-law, sons-in-law, distant relatives, anonymous family faces, ocher poses, astounded, an instant frozen in time, backgrounds showing balustrades, gardens, parlors with portraits and mirrors, belonging, perhaps, to the chalet on Calle Mallorca, in this dimly lit hallway, gloom, exemplary shades, funeral memories. Muted night, of unease, of insomnia and imaginary figures, until the white dawn lit up the sky, opaline. And the black birds fluting and flittering about.

Ancient faces. He faced her, haloed by bouffant hair, re-dyed blonde, alcoholic breath, burning, firewater, her words more and more fiery. Quit telling stories; for me, the Ferrers begin with our great-grandfather. I wouldn't search any farther on, I always tell Juanito, maybe you'll find one who was a church canon. That's why, when I talk about our ancestors, I refer exclusively to our great-grandfather's generation and those that follow. Namely: great-grandfather Jorge and his brother Jaime, who appears to have participated in the African campaign with General Prim. He's included in the Gallery of Illustrious Catalans, and it seems he participated in the Battle of Tetouan or the Battle of Castillejos, a feat immortalized by Fortuny in a grandiose tableau visible everyday from 10:00 am to 2:00 pm, holidays included, in the Museum of Modern Art in the Ciudadela Park. There is a very interesting letter which makes reference to the embarkation of volunteers in the port of Barcelona, la Ciudad Condal, a true historical document. There is also a mention of a Ferrer who fought as a lieutenant under Cabrera in the Carlist factions; but of all this, in relation to the family, nothing is certain. And the same can be said of another Ferrer who figures in the chronicle of the anti-Napoleonic wars in Tarragona province. We know from great-grandfather Jorge, however, that he emigrated to Cuba in his youth, to Matanzas, and that in only a few years' time he amassed an immense fortune. He married María Ignacia Gaminde, of pure Basque stock, belonging to an old Guipuzcoan family, from Rentería, a family name that stands out among the lords who gathered around the tree of Guernica. It's also known that great-grandfather Jorge, although the uncles and aunts don't like it to be mentioned or recalled, sowed the island full with mulatto bastards. Well, he was what you call a *machote*, a vigorous man. With him, with him begins the history of the family that, like the history of nations, has its periods of ascendence and its periods of decadence. Grandfather Raúl, for example, a perfect gentleman; he installed himself in Barcelona shortly before the loss of Cuba, built the chalet on Calle Mallorca, and invested his money, which was a lot, in stocks and some other properties. It was he who added his mother's family name, Gaminde, to the Ferrer family name, intending to prevent it from disappearing, at least within our family, now that, from the looks of it, he had no male descendants. That's where the name Ferrer Gaminde comes from, properly speaking. It seems that Raúl's grandfather was a very pious person. They even managed to offer him a Pontifical title in return for his charitable works but he refused it, because he wasn't seeking any social compensation, nor is nobleness a mere question of a title. What we were saying before, authentic nobility, the genuine kind, is something different; nothing one merely inherits: a person is either noble or they're not. For this reason I prefer to speak of the nobility instead of the aristocracy, because not every aristocrat is, strictly speaking, noble. And even less so here in Catalonia, where, like in the Basque Country, the lords have always been simply lords. A more legitimate conception and, above all, a higher one, not dependent on a title: nobility not of blood, but of spirit, something that people nowadays call coming from a good family, having a good name, really nothing more than rich bourgeoisie, people who will never have power, with their cowardice and mean characteristics, enclosed in a narrow world, without greatness. A proud style, a broad outlook, a gallant attitude, this is what distinguishes the wellborn. And grandfather Raúl, even without having his father's ambition, was such a person. The grandmother's family was something else, liberal bourgeoisie from here, a dynasty of lawyers and notaries, like your mother's family. What I call Calle Fernando people. People with everything, completely respectable, but without the personality of the Ferrers, of the grandfather, without that special something, that *je ne sais quoi* which grandfather possessed. And his siblings: Felipe, who with the loss of Cuba moved to North America, and Cecilia, married one Andechaga, of Basque origin, in Santiago, where there are still descendants today, the Andechagas of Santiago, who continue feeling very Spanish. Juanito still corresponds with them occasionally, as well as with the Ferrers in North America, who, I believe, live in California and are also extremely proud of their Spanish and—more concretely—Catalan ancestry. And their children, Cecilia—who died when she was a little girl—Papa, Aunt Paquita, Uncle Jorge, Gregorius. Gregorius has always been something special, but the others, in their youth, hobnobbed with the best of Barcelona. And it's not for nothing, but it seems that Papa was really a person endowed with superb mettle and intelligence. And don't think that it's just a matter of my personal memories which, naturally, have little value for third parties, but rather of the testimony of so many people that had the opportunity to know him, that still truly adore him. For some reason he was named after grandfather. Just like you were, by the way. And both your father as well as Aunt Paquita herself, here where you see them, it seems that they were some real pampered angels, their whole life laid out nicely before them. Now they're well along in years with all the typical quirks of the Ferrers, because, you've got to admit, we Ferrers are an odd bunch. But your father, well, it seems that he was a very fine fellow. It was after the Republic, more or less, when we started having a real hard time, when all kinds of misfortunes began to rain down on us, like blows in the darkness. After Papa died, and Mama, Aunt Eulalia, who was so close to Mama, Jaime, all of them gone, one after the other, in such a short time, with hardly any time between them. I think that only a general tragedy like the war, a massacre like that, could distract us, as much as possible, from our own family tragedy. The war and then this inflation and the constant devaluation of everything, which has ruined the country while a handful of well-connected people got filthy rich from the black market, just like now with the Stabilization. It's the whole big-fish-eats-little-fish double standard. Because Gregorius always says that if Uncle Jorge had had a sweetheart instead of going into business, he wouldn't have lost so much money. Of course, that's easy for someone like him to say, he's spent his whole life living off a fixed income. But I'll say this, and in defense of your father, I've had to fight to make my own way to get ahead in the cardboard manufacturing business, which keeps my daughter alive. I guarantee you, life has gotten very difficult, and nowadays it's almost impossible to stay afloat this way, surrounded by big hungry sharks. Besides, let me tell you, Gregorius has always played it safe, and if he hasn't lost money it's because he's never risked any, but he's also starting to think twice before spending a single peseta. And it's not that it makes me happy, but it's good for him. Inflation spares no one, much less people like him or Juanito, who think that only idiots like us actually work. In their hearts that's what they really believe. And the thing with Gregorius, with all his talk about how if he were young again he'd go to America and do God knows what, you can be sure that in reality he'd still turn out to be exactly the same, that he'd never go off to America or anything and that, now that your father's not around, he'd end up marrying that skinny bitch, which is how he'll end up, for sure, in time. You'll see. He isn't the typical sort who, because he always goes his own way, taking the easy way, never manages to get anywhere. And look, I love him very much, but the truth, the real truth, is that Gregorius is a loafer, and selfish as only he can be. And among us cousins, as you see, there's not too much good hardwood, as we say. It's not for the sake of flattering you, but really the only one in the family I see who has pride, real pride, is you, the way Jaime was, who was cut from the same cloth as great-grandfather. Even physically he couldn't have turned out to be more of a Ferrer. Give him a mustache and beard and tell me if he doesn't remind you of our great-grandfather. Because what all the others are is soft, soft and lazy. Ramona married this man, who must have made a huge fortune and everything else, but I consider him to be basically dishonest, and

I'm smart enough to be able to affirm it. Pedro, rather unsubstantial, small potatoes; Juanito. That's it, period. Well, and me, I'm the worst off of all, since I'm no longer good for anything. Ah, and Felipe, who by the way is increasingly worthless. He hasn't always been that way; he used to be, I don't know, a pretty normal fellow. Seems it's this stuff with the Opus, busybodies can't leave well enough alone. The last time he goes and comes out with this nonsense about how he doesn't want to sit next to me in the car. He must have been scared that people would think he was driving around with some floozy or I don't know what, and so there I am in the front with him in the back seat and me driving him around like I was his chauffeur. Does that seem normal to you? I just can't understand people nowadays. Some turned into posh snobs, others are prudes, and we're all in a real mess. When I compare young people today with the ones from my time. None now like Jaime, who was just exceptional, one of a kind, you had to see him in the months before the uprising, in the meetings, serene and proud, gallant, undaunted, the very picture of fierceness, calmly facing the hordes of people that had it in for him. Not with Jaime but with anyone else. Someone like Florentino, like Abelardo, fellows who, without being anything out of this world, had this manliness, this decisiveness of those days, things that seem to have been swallowed up by the earth, characteristics, qualities almost extinguished, practically withdrawn from civilization. Or maybe it was my lot to live in a privileged time, a generation of heroes who blossom young, and what happens is that I'm just spoiled for the world now. But for someone who lived through it, it's something that marks you, something unforgettable. You'd have to have lived through it to understand what it really was. The Montserrat Regiment—el Tercio de Montserrat—la crème de la crème of Catalonia, young men in the prime of life who risked everything for the sake of everything in order to be able to slip across the border into France and take up their duties for all of Spain and there continue risking everything for the sake of everything. And the provisional ensigns enlisted in the shock troops, in the Legion, in the Regulars, in the anti-tank troops, like Jaime. And the captains of the warships, and the pilots like José Ramón, a flying ace, who flew one hundred battles and received a special award, he died so absurdly, during an aerial exhibition of acrobatic flying. That's the way things go. Perhaps if he'd survived, I might have married him instead of Ernst, and my life would have taken a very different turn. But that's what life is, a roll of the dice. I met Ernst and look; we had a three-week relationship, what they call a war marriage. The typical story of those days; I was his wartime godmother, and we wrote to each other and I mailed him packages, until one day I met him in person, when he was on leave, in San Sebastián, and it was the craziest kind of love affair. With Vittorio I had a relationship in the hospital while he was recovering from an injury. What a man. One of the few truly manly Italians I've met, not a bit cowardly or effeminate. I mean that he wasn't like one of those men from Guadalajara, one of those little gents who seemed more like ladies, and even wore hairnets. No, Vittorio wasn't one of them, I assure you. He seemed Spanish, well, like the Spanish men of earlier times. I'd like to know what must have become of him. He must have died, those kind of men never last. And the truth is that Ernst was also a man of irresistible courage and attraction. That's what dazzled me; while I was passionately in love with him I was blind to everything else. And naive as I am, because that's what I am and what I'll be my whole life, a naive fool and a dummy, I only realized that he was a social climber after it was too late. He started to get really deep into business and he ended up, inevitably, a crook, embezzling money and running off to South America with that nasty whore. Oh, the things I've suffered thanks to that almighty son of a bitch. And like this one, so many other unhappy disappointments. They say that only scoundrels prosper, stooges, wise guys, cynics, smooth operators, deserters, the ones who've never fired a shot and take advantage of the time when others are doing the fighting to usurp their places, to help themselves to key positions and get rich at our expense and then, on top of it, leave crumbs for everyone else. If at that moment some prophet had foretold for all of us pure-hearted men and women that everything was going to end up the way it did, we would have taken him for an agent provocateur, for a Red propagandist. It would have seemed inconceivable to us. It was the climate of those days, the enthusiasm. Imbeciles, that's what we were, that's what I think now. And, nevertheless, other times I think that I'd sign up again, that despite the disappointments, that's always preferable to the inertia of young people nowadays. There was a richness of experiences, an intensity of emotions, of feelings, I don't know, such an elevated vital tone. Life had a different sense, more strength, with death like a sword always hanging over your head. And the risk, the spirit of sacrifice, the companionship, the same form of loving, of commitment. And those moments of apotheosis, of brotherhood, of entering a newly liberated town, for example, something indescribable. Things that have disappeared, that have been lost, that seem unbelievable to people nowadays when you try to explain them. And, what's worse, young people nowadays are not even interested in them. And the younger they are the more indifferent they become, the more unbearably stupid they get. And I see it each day in these spoiled little brats who follow Monsina home and who aren't interested in anything but silly things. Real good-for-nothings, not only are they pansies, spiritually they're hollow as jugs. You only have to listen to the way they talk, the vocabulary they use, which is revoltingly poor.

Four vulgar expressions, pablum, and a handful of adjectives that they use for everything. Things are either shitty or awesome, and they use the word "excellent" to substitute for the thousand different shadings in our language that distinguish one word from another, beautiful, sublime, pleasant, handsome, attractive, comfortable, harmonious, and hundreds of other words that I can't even think of now. For me, the most symptomatic thing, given that such a loss of expressive richness is only the reflection of a general loss of values. Monsina, no, Monsina is different. And don't just take my words for a mother's doting, because if she were an idiot or a prissy I'd tell you just the same. But really she's a delightful girl, and very chic, a real doll; she seems like a little German girl. And her temper, sometimes she's got such a temper and says the wildest things; of course you know where she gets it. After all she'll be, she already is, tremendously successful. But I'm not going to let it go to her head, and I try to raise her according to some very strict moral principles, because apart from the fact that it's my duty, as a good Catholic, which is what I consider myself to be, a good Catholic, that's right, without prejudices, apart from that, I'm a thinking person, although it seems old-fashioned to say it, that religion always provides a check. I know some people here in Barcelona—it's just a tenement house of a city—they skin me alive, say I neglect my daughter's upbringing, that I do nothing more than set a bad example for her, that I'm an irresponsible mother, etcetera. People were also saying, I know, that I had a banker friend who took care of me. Oh, wouldn't I like that, poor me, nothing less than a banker. But precisely because I know how people are and what life is, I've devoted myself so much to Monsina's upbringing, because she's a girl and not a boy and, in our society, don't kid yourself, an honest woman, of good faith, a woman honest enough to trust in her own natural impulses, well, she's bought and sold already. I can assure you because this is what happened to me, and it's what I don't want to happen to her. Because, and please pardon the pun, I'll tell you that they've screwed me too many times without letting me enjoy it, I've had too many bad times and none of the good. So I'll do the impossible so that Monsina can go out into the world prudently and not have to go through the same, so that she's got some common sense and discretion. I prefer that she knows what's what right from the start, that she's not going to be fooled. Like one of my godsons, you must know I've got many godchildren, his parents were going to send him to a boarding school run by monks, and I tell him right away: watch out, they'll try to grab your pecker. And Maruja: but for God's sake, Montse, what a thing to say to the poor kid. Me: really? Well, keep your eyes open and you'll see. And well, we take him to the school and, no sooner do we arrive, than a monk comes flouncing out to greet us with such a sashay in his step, I thought, sure enough, here he comes. And sure enough, not long after, the great big scandal, that when a boy got sick the monk in the infirmary gave him abdominal massages and all that. You tell me. As if I don't know anything about monks and nuns. And it's better to warn him, so the little fellow knows what to watch out for and you avoid him having a nasty shock. And with Monsina I do the same. I don't want to lead her astray, but at the same time I don't want her to be a prude. She needs to know how things are, simply to look out for herself and, for the rest, be a normal modern girl, so she's not a fool or one of these girls with problems. And above all, that she not marry for love, which is the most foolish mistake you can make. Let her marry some rich man, and later she can do whatever she feels like. If she were a boy and not a girl, I don't say that I would've raised her the same. But she's a girl and that fact, in our society, changes everything. A man can flirt and have affairs as he likes and nothing bad happens, but a woman, on the other hand, she's stuck dealing with her big bulging belly. Just a slight difference. Apart from that, I'll tell you that I'm almost happy that she's a woman because that means she won't get into politics. Really, at least not like men do, who are the ones who have to put their balls on the table when it all comes down to it, when the shooting starts, because that's the truth, however much you want to say that women are equal to men and all this drivel, the result has already been seen that they gave the Reds their famous female militia, those big broads that they themselves had to end up shooting, and the truth is, what cannot be cannot be, however much one tries, and, with the nonstop idiocy they keep repeating to us, we're not going anywhere. War is a man's business and that's all there is to it. And that's why I tell you that although I really do admire your rebellious spirit, really very much, I don't dare say that, as a mother, if I had a son, I'd urge him to follow your example. I've already seen too much blood and too many dead. And I've had to bear too many disappointments, too many blows. People's ephemeral memories and the ephemeral nature of friendship, so many times, in the moment of truth, they just leave you to fend for yourself as best you can. Time is a sieve, and if among all those who call themselves your friends you end up holding on to a handful of faithful ones, you can be satisfied with that. When I have occasion to meet with some of these few friends who've stayed true, with Claudio—el Claudillo, as we call him—or with Florentino, who's surely been the minister with the shortest tenure in his post, because he could neither grant favors nor could they allow him to not grant favors, because this is the truth of what happened, because we always end up gripped with sadness when we remember those times, our frustrated dreams, how our ideals were betrayed. Besides, there are fewer of us all the time. Except for Abelardo, who, as long as he was an honest man, couldn't fail, and like him so many others. And, above all, the ones who have left us, Carlitos Martí, Xènius, José Pedro, who died there, confined in the VI Region, as General Captain, when in all honesty, it was his right to be Minister of the Army. But, in spite of everything, for the few of us who remain, we've got more than enough young spirit left in us to have a good time if we go out on the town there, making the rounds in Madrid. Because, don't think any of us have lost our fire over the years, and, thank God, we're all still simple people, happy and honest, and what we really like, well, is that, good spicy tapas and Valdepeñas wine. I've enjoyed myself sometimes, life doesn't have to be all thorns and, truth be told, sometimes I've enjoyed myself, and now I only regret that it wasn't more often, that I've not done more as I pleased, which is what I would've done if not for Monsina, with my responsibility as mother. Our circle, when we were all together, was exceptional, that's the truth, select people, elite, and everyone got along so well, thick as thieves. I think I've never laughed so hard as that time we were all in the Atheneum, listening to Xènius, who was giving a lecture, the great Xènius, a great person and a great friend, and Xènius, when he saw us in the crowd, a bit tipsy, by the way, he goes and starts reciting, almost at random, that satirical romance in honor of that silly twerp the Duke of Windsor when he abdicated his throne, a romance that, truly, is so little known that I think it remains unpublished. Well, it made you want to piss yourself, the whole slate of monarchists right there, totally nonplussed. I think I've never laughed so much in my life. And Xènius wasn't just a first-rate mind, maybe the best brain Spain has seen in this century, Xènius was, besides, an extraordinarily human person and a dear friend. And each one in his own terrain, all the people in the group, people of clear competence and authority, intellectuals, politicians, military officers, financiers. And true friends all of them, the kind who show you their friendship through their deeds, the kind of people capable of moving heaven and earth for you. Always, whenever I've needed help, whenever I've had some problem with my little cardboard factory or with anything, they've known what to do, they've helped me. You'll see, you've got to live, you've got to defend yourself. And I'm a single woman with a daughter to feed, and if you don't have a deft touch and, especially, good connections, then you might as well throw in the towel. When you see so much immorality everywhere, you can sure enough conclude that you'd have to be a sucker not to make use of your friends' influence. In the long run they're purely disinterested favors, pure exercise of friendship, and in this sense, something completely natural, that if there's one thing in life that you deserve, something worth the trouble to save, that's friendship. Besides, their women are their women, but in terms of the group, the fact is that I'm the only woman, and of course, the men adore me, and there's nothing on earth they can deny me, just as there's nothing that I, with my limited possibilities, could refuse them. In a certain way, I am, as we might say, a bit like their little sister, and there's neither pain nor joy which they don't share with me, nor any problem I don't share. Claudio, for example, never fails to call me when he comes to Barcelona, to find some time to share, no matter how busy he is, like the good Catalan he is, Catalan of pure stock, Catalan like Jaime, like our great-grandfather, like his brother Jaime, he has the same name as my brother, the other Jaime Ferrer, good Catalan men precisely just as they are good Spaniards, insofar as they belong to a key part of the Spanish whole, to a whole of which, secularly, they've been forerunners and proclaimers, men of military lineage, enterprising men, true conquerors. True Catalan men who, like always, traditionally hold themselves higher than petty personal interests, proven defenders of Spanish integrity, willing to invigorate the cause of national unity and of its supreme interests with their own blood so often necessary and, wherever it has been necessary, whether in Cuba or in Morocco, and in Catalonia itself, so often in the trenches and on the front lines of the motherland; Catalans of the kind by which Catalonia would perish if its personality must only be seen as an impediment to the Spanish personality; Catalans, in short, who've aligned their greatest yearnings with the task of building forever, outside any distinction of creeds and colors, a Spain for all, an enterprise of which, with all their being and all their vehemence, they are the safety and surety.

A noble people, a patrician land, rich in art and commerce alike, in pleasures as well as industries, panoply of feats and reputations, of honors and of triumphs, to the envy of the world and of the stars. Persistent homeland beyond vicissitudes, recovered under adversities, Principality or Crown, province or county, viceroyalty or Generalitat, republican experiment or libertarian hypothesis, fatherland in exodus, fatherland of exiles and incarcerations when not their sepulcher, common grave of natives and strangers, a never-completed extermination, a land of laws and atrocities, of silences and screams, reborn like the broom covering its land, inextinguishable flame of April, omnipresent from mountain to sea, from peak to peak, angelic golden mountains. A long history of splendors haloing the exploits and adventures of Barcelona, city of rancid traditions and modernist extravagances, a city charged with resonance, echoes of choirs, of scheduled dances and sonorous choral societies, eulogistic scene of festivities and popular spectacles, explosions of collective jubilation, of violence, insurrections, popular uprisings and purported low blows, blind furor, charges and discharges, fire, gunshots, shrapnel, sickles and knives, clashing broadswords, city of factions, bipartisan, consumed by internal struggles when not by conquest in the name of expansion, bifid effigy, a winged asp cresting the helmet, the very image of great deeds, champion Barcelona, a place frequented by knights, from Santiago to Don Quixote, passing through Saint George and the Knight of the White Moon, the real emulation of the no-less-white nor less-real White Knight Tirant lo Blanc, and who knows if even through Roland himself; the Barcilona of Don Remont, prisoner of Myo Cid de Vivar, errant bandits, wrongdoers, propitious place for the creation of fantastic fabulations, histories of a people, a land, and a language, the word so often made blood by the conjugation of diverse factors, always somewhere between dream and reality, between common sense and castles made of sand, between death and resurrection, city of delights and disappointments, disenchantments, desolations, disappearances, city of death throes and resurrections, uncertain trances, yearnings, raptures, annihilations, city buried and unburied, sepulchral, mummified, petrified, a city transfigured like heavenly Jerusalem *qua resurget ex favilla*, phoenix reincarnated from its own ashes, the heart of a people of contradictory impulses, of strengths discovered and eventually lost, the useless efforts of a homeland seated on a border, on the frontier between Catalonia and what is not Catalonia, apparitions and disappearances of an identity centered around Barcelona, ancient hegemonic county of an expanding Mediterranean empire, today simply an honorific escutcheon on the family tree of its Don Juan condemned, a count languishing in the golden exile of Estoril, a virtual title in the same way that, once royal, when being Count of Barcelona meant being King of Aragon, of Mallorca, of Valencia, of Naples, of Sicily, etcetera, so, too, and no less virtual were the titles of King of Hungary, or Lord of Dalmatia, of Croatia, of Serbia, of Bulgaria, just like the Duke of Athens and Neopatria or the King of Jerusalem. Unfortunate civitas. What was its unlucky star in the deep firmament? Or was it perhaps the divine enemy, violent impious nemesis? Or was its insensate lightness alone the cause of so many sorrows, of so many perditions and blows redoubled? Neither republic, nor principate, nor county, nor kingdom, nor any glimmer of a chariot of fire, dominions dismembered, sovereignty dethroned, a crown of thorns and a scepter of reeds after the four blood-red bars of the emblem, passion lampooned, time's vandalizing deterioration, history's disgrace, an intricate history, full of rough roads and mysterious difficulties, sinister dalliances, narrow ways, frequently unholy solutions, denouement of intrigue, complex city, a once-magnificent amphitheater, today mere stage machinery and footlights, unhappy scene of farces and comedies, parodic trickeries and superstitions, a lamentable relic populated by pedestals and effigies, figurations, dead kings, and supplanted myths, histrionic mausoleum, now ashes, now loneliness, no less than legendary Italica or fallen

Troy, of ruined Athens, or Rome lost but not found in Rome, homeland of gods and kings. Past splendors, lights eclipsed, bloody gilded islands vanished in the distance like a shimmering sunset, inner fire, faded yearning, mere ideal lost in thought, taken refuge in the hermetic folds of Montserrat, arid heart of this poor, sad, and luckless homeland, unyielding castellated temple in its merlons of rocks and crags resonant with chants, swan song, slow substitution of one tongue for another, from above and below, from within and without, bifurcated fatherland, slowly drawn away from its primogenial image, Catallunyàna, rocky land of songs and disenchantments, land of castles, sandcastles, castles built of playing cards, châteaux in Espagne, land of holy mountains, a landscape more classically supernatural than natural, a mountain dedicated by the ancients to Venus, more sensible of the sensual, venereal nature than the ascetic implications of its reliefs, the Roman Extorcil, indecorous décor in excess for its future scatological functions, crags like hermits or phantoms, a pleasant, welcome land for pilgrim patrons and knights-errant, apostolic missions, predilections, dissipated hoaxes, processes unraveled, unknown quantities clarified, a noble land without nobility, county sans count, principality without a prince, estate without land and land without estate, decapitated capital, headless homeland, bound hand and foot once again at the feet of Spain, delivered to its mercy, the Black Spain reanimated, reanimated but not resuscitated for it never was dead, reanimated and perhaps eternal as they say, penetrating across the Ebro, flooding it all like a rising river, land captured, uncivilly conquered by Francoism, a reconquest from the past, a plot reversal, end of the adventure, the occupation and consequent unhappy ballad of penuries and heavy griefs without even the manners of other times, no longer a pleasant reaction, no longer retrograde scholastic criteria: a purely troglodytic clawing. Historic personality of characteristics not respected by fate, discontinuous errant destiny, drifting away from events, from the whims of destiny, the separatist Barcelona of 1934, the anarchist Barcelona of 1936, the communist Barcelona of 1937, the fascist Barcelona of 1939, cheering, triumphal, overlorded, symptomatic versatility, ominous spectacle, ignominy extolled in the memory to the point of volatilization, a presumed nocturnal nightmare if not a carefully mounted Potemkinesque mise en scène. The history of a people more rewritten than written, adapted to the historic necessities of the people, linked to their rebirth, a grandiose epic, epic incarnate, made reality in the ambit of the fantastic. Vicissitudes, experiences, hopes and expectations of a more-than-battered cause, Catalunya, romantic bourgeois sublimation of an erroneous collective behavior, disheartened independence without vigor or without spirit, political incapacity taken for individualism, unfortunate bloody-mindedness confused with Numantian resistance, clumsy rapacities transformed into virtuous laboriousness, obstinate meanness transmuted into common sense, avaricious poverty recounted as austere gesture, ancestral characteristics, images greatly magnified in the mirror of time, peculiarities reclaimed so much more the more outdated if not nonexistent, residues of the past converted into an excuse for present-day impotence, into dreamy contemplations of the future, after-dinner longings around the table, speculative conversations, being from here, one of the few important things that one can be in life, destiny amid the universal, best thing in the world, gift of God, messianic quality, promised entity, mythic Mediterranean motherland now made reality in decorative maps for the parlor, territories and borders, regions and frontiers in a golden frame, Catalan Countries—els Països Catalans—more than forty, extending from Alicante to Rousillon, not to mention from Murcia to Provence, materialization of Catalan spiritual identity, poly-member entelechy, pompous rapture, the smug flush of erudition, lyrical utopia of merchants or Philistines, fortunate island, a truly ideal country, peonized by *charnegos*, the shifty nightcrawling southern immigrants, and financed by tourism and foreign investments, better than civilized, urbanized, for sale by the centimeter, simultaneously loom and hostel, landscape dulled neither by the spindle, nor manufacturing activity, nor enterprising spirit, nor private initiative, both an idyllic corner of nature and an agile, efficient organization, eminently practical and simultaneously sublime, vision or dream of the epigones of some hypothetical Mediterranean Netherlands, of what might well have been a Belgium or a Holland, a Portugal even, empire still on horseback of four continents, in spite of the fact that nobody pays it too much attention, or possibly and above all, a kind of sunny Switzerland, traditional haven of peace and foreign currency, a spot of oil in a puddle of blood, privileged land and people of the Iberian arena, where the dogs were leashed with spicy pork sausages, dreams that someday, and why not, they would no longer be dreams, they would be realities, only a little bit late and not in the way foreseen, less heroic, less decisive and showy, when, at least in this part of the world, the national problem being that, more than anything, a question of calculations, convictions, and conveniences, more an affair of the pocketbook than the heart. Polemical dreams, conflicting theories, conceptions, separatisms, centralisms, Spain as sorrow, Spain as a problem, Spain without a problem, Spain, Europe, Catalonia, entities with their own personalities no longer historical, cultural, or geopolitical, but rather substantial, ontological, the Mediterranean and the Meseta, the Meseta and the Periphery, centrifugal movements and centripetal movements, decadences, renaissances, grandiloquences, pompous words, conjectures, precisely symmetrical and reiterated mechanisms, pieces of attractive but inexact dialectic and even stupid, pretty little nothings not, like everything, unfeasible or non-demonstrable, unethical theses about transcendental preeminences, the Iberian and the Roman, the Arabic and the Germanic, dilemmas, elucidations, Mediterranean or Atlantic vocation, American or African, folklore and *costumbrismo*, typical subject matter, lamentable cause as well as the effect of topics made flesh by force of being believed and repeated, made alibis, profitable reflection, justifiable mental restriction, lying by simply not speaking or naming, a language not simply sclerotic: cadaverous. Rejection of Spain, proclamation of Catalonia, forgery of a recently dead dream, of a lost empire, supplanted by the memory of another now reverted to dust, that of the Catalonia that would be if it were or if it had ever been.

The Reality, here and now: an industrious Spanish region where labor is massively non-Catalan and, in short, the capital interest, the benefits of integration, always the preferable lesser evil. The slow reduction of an ideal, gradual materialistic penetration to even the most recondite places, a visceral anguish and intimate rending produced by the dissociation of ideals with respect to the material base upon which they rest, the inevitable corruption of an always obsolete, out-of-touch enterprise, either because of a lack of driving force in the opportune moment, or for lack of sufficient elements susceptible to being set in motion by the driving force, either, in this case, pure formal residue, hypostatic fable, or rapture. Like a gem crystallizing too slowly or a floral geometry killed by frost, an annunciation without epiphany, gestation without childbirth, promise or prophecy unfulfilled and inconclusive, for so many other people, in the conjuncture, in the romantic age of the *risorgimenti* and its irrevocable affirmations, when, having overcome the latest convulsions resulting from Catalonia's status as despised stepdaughter, now one among equals, an indiscriminate participant in the peaceful exploitation of colonial possessions, of the colonization of the possessions, of the pacification of the diminished but not negligible exploitations, Catalonia even tried to Catalanize Spain, to infuse it with a different spirit, to renovate it. Not then, but rather when the hard times arrived, the final colonies worth considering were lost, the good times were over, a problem presented doubtless as a political alternative to colonial politics, a market problem, of imported goods and foodstuffs, a domestic question, the talk in the street, spreading like wildfire capable of igniting social intercourse, of igniting the language, of fanning the flames of the past, of raising standards, of unfurling flags. Not in the opportune moment nor with due decision, vacillating always between remaking Spain in its image and likeness, with Prim and the First Republic, who gambled and lost the game, or marching for the sake of the habitually steeper path of independence, the uphill ascent of direct action, movement without fights, without true national uprisings, without heroes, a cause that, if it had not had its Petöfi, was not going to have its mayor of Cork; a cause, in fact, sincerely undesired by the local governing classes, something like that woman who, with her daring attire worn to high-society gatherings, with her attitude and her words, can well make her admirers believe they'll have no trouble seducing her or becoming her lover, and only after the disappointment do they understand that her true intention was not to cuckold her husband but, by offering him the solicitations obtained, to increase her value in his eyes, more an element of negotiation than an instrument of separation and liberty, namely, like Manuel del Palacio's sonnet "*El Enano de la Venta*", more of a verbal threat than anything, a wildcard to play according to the circumstances, in response to socioeconomic vicissitudes. Catalonia apostolic and liberal, land of bourgeois protectionists and anarchist workers, the whole repertory cast, active players one and all in the spectacle, eagerly devoted to the historical mishap of the Spanish farce, a romantic comedy of comic opera personalities, grotesque unloved monarchs and grim, funereal warlords, simian characters, of atavistic reactions and totemic spirituality, lamentable pullulation of witches and asses, of Figaros and strolling cigarette vendresses, with a bloodstained danse macabre for a backdrop, impossible to be further removed, completely deafening mob and excremental excrescence, decrepitude of an empire that was, on horseback across four continents, perhaps the greatest power that ever existed, from Cathay to El Dorado, with its oriental specie and its occidental mines, prized precious metal, Age of Gold slipped away like sand in an hourglass, and the metropolis like a crumbling arena, its ancient image, a prefiguration of John Bull or Uncle Sam, reduced now to a picturesque field of exploration for curious travelers arriving from other latitudes, from higher levels, a land held up boldly at gunpoint, attractive only as an anachronism, rather like Garibaldian Italy, pleasant local flavor and pugnacious operatics, but with a touch of the cruelty and mystery of the Sublime Ottoman Porte, intolerances, brutalities, circus tent and boxing ring of savage pugilism, the circle squared, nineteenth-century Spain coming apart at the seams, canton by canton, junta by junta, interchangeable constitutions, minor military uprisings, pronouncements, the scourge of violence spreading through decorative institutions, characteristic images: the Spaniard and his honor, the Spanish woman smoldering behind her wrought iron lattice, Torquemada and El Cid, Don Quijote and Don Juan, bullfighters and priests, gypsies and guerrillas, soldiers, shameless thieves, hands outstretched to plunge the dagger or beg an offering, heads or tails, the right-hand side and the other side, one single history lived out in diverse ways, differences derived from two degrees of development, adjusted to the distance that measures between one degree and another, bourgeois vulgarity of a lofty-sounding and moirological Catalonia, land of grasping idiot magnates, predatory men, locked and loaded, ready to shoot, Phoenicians among Phoenicians, men of the world by dint of being polished by roughness and, notwithstanding, always close to the earth, with the persistent vices of one who knows the ground he walks on, peasant crudeness and coarse manners, abrupt manifestations under a certain appearance of provincial cosmopolitanism, clumsy commerce and hypocritical self-restraint on one hand, self-contradictions of an industrial society, and on another, coexisting alongside, all that is properly Spanish, meaning, Castilian, and especially, characteristically, from Madrid, the convoluted quintessence of Castile, of its fields sown thick with garbanzos, stubby mesas taken for superiority and stepped isolation understood as dignity, generic traits softened in the court by their peculiar festive animation, aberrant virtues of an existence carried like a reliquary, frugal drynesses or big-bellied silhouettes, a sad figure, Old or New Castile, plain, flat, encumbered or not, no less the one from up north or the one from down south, the high clergy, the military classes, feudal lords, idle landowners moved directly from the habitual immobility found in all absolute monarchies and consequent hierarchical rigor barely tempered by corruption, to corporations, to the councils of administration, people not given to compromise and dialogue and, much less, criticism, people with a propensity for levying coups, for maximalist solutions, for favoritism and agreements between gentlemen and only between gentlemen, colloidal pride and abysms of class, a situation maintained by direct and indirect procedures, by the one who strikes first, a practice, on the other hand, also familiar in the rest of the peninsula, in general a propitious land for retrograde movements, preemptive uprisings struck down as if by a saber blow, preemptive and curative, deep cuts, life-saving amputations, barbaric reactions, elemental, committed with shocking naturalness, rammed through with almost relaxed good humor, like slap-happy old friends playing around, and the compensatory logic of all that, progressive miseries, anarchist actions realized with rough imprecision, without rhyme or reason, and vain attempts to give them a certain coherence, to inform them with a poor dialectic, refried ideologies, abstractions brought from other meridians, simplified to the point of foolishness by the reduction implied by all transport and, in the absence of a revolutionary mentality capable of infusing them with some new originality other than their heroic impotence, reverentially sustained against wind and shrapnel and, even more painful, against all lucidity, by moderately intelligent mediocrities, progressively idiotic, a prolonged saga of mutual affronts, of bitter confrontations, of a civil war that gestated for years on end, an organ created by the very exercise of its function, a fabulous spectacle, the sleep of reason, cortege of monsters, diabolical caprices, the black and red once again, tonalities of explosion, a circumstance barely adequate to sustain now-marginalized questions about the central nucleus of the conflict due to the very dialectic of the events, hardly able to safeguard ephemeral autonomies and other fictions proclaimed by the political representatives of the local petite bourgeoisie, Sunday fishermen on a river too wild, incidences of an enterprise fatally whirled away on the fly, swallowed up in the course of the fight between centralist bourgeoisie and revolutionary proletariat, destined to lose no matter who loses, to be unrealized, at least the way it was dreamed, a motherland—which one—undiscoverable, only its ruins as unique evidence, as it crumbles and falls away from an implacably objective analysis of the events, its rubble. A distressing awakening.

A Barcelona stretching from sea to mountain peak and from river to river, yes, but not according to what was imagined, so much less Catalan the bigger, the more massive it gets, populated with immigrants, converted into El Dorado for *el charnego*, the immigrant from southern Spain, Mecca for the lumpen, reduced now to a shadow of its former self, surrounded by its suburbs, progressively assimilated, all within a superior and distinct unity, officious infiltration, often overlapping, neighborhoods frequently nonexistent on the map, of casual etymology and nomadic toponymy, Somorrostro, Casa Valero, Casa Antúnez, Torre Baró, Campo de la Bota, etcetera, multiplying slums and shantytowns, tidy whitenesses, thin whitewashed walls and flimsy roofs, warp of tin and tar mixed with sand, earthy suburbs, ashen, breezeless, sun-beaten, out-of-the-way places, rich in folkloric scenes, in impressionist colors, naturalist blights sooner or later resolved one way or the other, homes and hearths eventually well-established into compact constructions, extending as far as the eye can see, from the Besós River to the Llobregat, from Tibidabo to Montjuich, a human agglomeration, an explosive environment naturally predisposed, like a germinating seed, to soak up communist ideology, as tinder accepts the spark, as sails the wind, a reserve army no longer quite so capitalistic as socialistic, productive forces in development, a forest of spreading, climbing, frenetic industries on the move, formations of gray blocks closely surrounding the city, interwoven antennas, sparkling windows, sunny fluttering rags, as if advancing, looming over, closing in around the city, so splendidly planned by the nineteenth-century bourgeoisie, the quadrangle of the Ensanche, the perimeter of Las Rondas, the Old City divided by Las Ramblas, Mount Taber to the right, in the heart of the Gothic Quarter, museum of past glories, of petrified triumphs, the Gothic Quarter composed of stately streets and plazas, Plaza de San Jaime, Plaza del Rey presided over by King Martin's Tower, Plaza del Rey with its

Salón del Tinell and its Chapel of Santa Agata, the Archive of the Crown of Aragon, its Casa Padellás, principal seat of the City History Museum, the womb of that recomposed complex of Roman city walls, of Romanesque arches, of Gothic spires, of churches and palaces, an age marked by belfries, from angelus to angelus, resonant spaces, hieratic austerities, the cathedral towers above all, prevalent, overflown every summer, by identical iterations of swifts and swallows. Triumphal ruins! Royal grandeur! Magnificence magnified! Fructified residue. Perdurance of the metamorphosis, of the ruined glory in rubble, of the stone become temple, stone by stone, discoveries disinterred, images brown and venerated, museum become vainglory, cemetery become victory, permanence of vertigo, fugacity of stone! And now? The denouement, the final phase of the process, the synthesis of contraries or negation of the negation, meaning, affirmation, resolution, dissolution of the diverse contradictions developed over the course of history of this small town, a minor people resurged from the spoils of the Romano-Visigothic slave-owning society, in the High Middle Ages, a people of precocious Mediterranean expansion and also of precocious social conflicts in the metropolis, conflicts as much between the farming class and the feudal structure of the age, its servitudes and evil misuses, as between aforesaid structure and the incipient bourgeois classes of artisans and merchants that emerged under the guise of the gradual enlargement of the empire, political forces in ascension thanks, frequently, to the support of the monarchy and, in symbiotic correspondence, its absolute disinterest, utilized by the monarchy to finance royal power, the crown ceaselessly reaffirmed and enlarged until the dawn of the Renaissance, when in the full period of economic and demographic decadence and reemergent social agitation, coinciding with the general tendency of the age toward the formation of nation-states, driven toward the doubtful proposition of forming a nation, almost in spite of itself, by virtue of its union with Castile, as a cornerstone of the modern Spain, a new State constructed not only at the expense of the fact that Catalonia—the weak partner in the marriage—might fatally relinquish its ancient Mediterranean hegemony, but rather also because, even in the same peninsula, its area of influence would be seen to be reduced to its current regional limits, disconnected from those who were brother countries, converted by the law of the jungle into the tail of a lion, a simple provincial principality separated from all colonizing enterprise and facing a frequent crisis of survival with the reigning absolutism and its local representation, the viceroy sent by the court, a principate encrusted in Spain more than integrated, wound round the imperial crown just as much as Flanders or Portugal or the Kingdom of Naples could possibly be, no more Spanish in practice nor with more rights nor weaknesses nor more official function nor benefit, without that being an obstacle, rather quite the contrary, for the progressive lack of involvement of the so-called flat state and of Catalan economic life in general, spared from complete insolvency by the same ostracism to which it had been subjected, development consolidated when the suppression of the restrictions that impeded commerce with America, upon opening new markets in optimum competitive conditions, permitted the incipient industrialization to be built upon sound material foundations, the basis of prosperity and the rising prosperity of the nineteenth-century Catalan bourgeoisie, in contrast to a Castile that was now eroded by decadence, in the heart of a Spain more than anachronistic, regressive, barbarously enraged, and at war with itself, a contrast that did nothing but clarify the ascensional movement of this Catalan bourgeoisie gradually identified with the ruling classes of the rest of the nation, a bourgeoisie increasingly more elevated, more and more Spanish, day after day, of patriotic sentiments grown in direct proportion to the amplitude of the new markets, Spanish to the end, to the point of attempting, and in a certain way of achieving, to make peace with the central power, of molding Spain to its image and likeness, meaning, of fomenting and realizing the bourgeois revolution in Spain, attempts reiterated and, as if the reiteration, more than riveting, caused a loss of impulse, progressively timid, the more timid the more identified, as a class in ascension, with that power, how much more unnecessary when the goals were made not undesirable, more a process of osmosis than assault, an impulse ultimately scuttled, braked, by the phantasm of social agitation, a weakness of attack or arrest that would later become widespread in proportion to the very meaning of its corresponding historic role in the imperialist phase of capitalism, always insufficiently decisive, always grave, always mortgaged by its own scarcity, grandiloquence and pompous words to cover up its lying probity, its frightened prosperity, its tendency to promulgate favorable laws and to violate unfavorable ones, its mastery in bribery and speculation, its custom of receiving a granted baker's dozen, of remaining middle of the road in all matters, the mediocrity of an attitude simultaneously attributable to the weakness of the economic structure which served as its support, namely greenhouse production and winter tourism, manufacture and commerce appropriate to a land poor in natural resources, of scanty attractiveness, in principle, for other sources of capital than the resultant accumulated labor of its inhabitants and, in consequence, more given to industrial dispersion than industrial concentration, and similarly, attributable in no lesser degree to the ambiguous character of its relations with the rest of Spain, simultaneous bureaucratic corset and market stimulant, contradictions apparently written into the fate of this regional bourgeoisie which, when it seemed launched upon the enterprise of redeeming Spain from its historical hemophilia, of establishing new constitutional formulas which would wipe the slate clean of all the monstrous inherited landowners, was pulled brusquely backward, you might say that it was frightened by the turn of events, by the consequence of the exercise of the liberty so long demanded and finally achieved, contributing to the dismantling of the First Republic in the same way it had contributed to building it, enclosing in parentheses what came to pass, unleashing the monarchical Restoration, events that, as they introduced the upper Catalan bourgeoisie to the ebb and flow of Spanish political life, severed this one from the middle classes of its own land, where the primitive federalist regionalism of some intellectual nuclei was exchanged for separatist nationalism, in accord with a phenomenon of radicalization which, somewhere between courageous and reticent, was ceaselessly promoted by the political representatives of the upper bourgeoisie, not as a real aspiration but as an instrument of negotiation with Madrid, as blackmail or as a straw man, thus twisting an ideal previously and seamlessly interconnected into an exclusive benefit for the interests that they represented, trafficking with the popular sentiment, selling it and selling themselves, the deceptive realities of politics that could only end up depoliticizing the only social class totally removed from the interests at stake, the working class, the working masses of Catalonia objectively forced toward anarchism and libertarian maladjustment, toward all manner of violence, of direct action as a response to public order, a singular dialectic whose crescendo could only unchain once more the hard line of an authoritarian regime which might deserve the confidence of the ruling classes, a reaction or coup in which the upper Catalan—and more concretely, Barcelona—bourgeoisie now acted in a shamelessly self-promotional capacity constructed to defend its positions from the sudden blows of history when this totalitarian scaffolding would inevitably collapse, and driven by the fear of the newly liberated popular forces, set in motion in the course of the Second Republic, wasted no time in resurrecting once more democratic legality from the archives of Francoism, in frank, open civil war with its own people, as well as with the remaining peoples of Spain, a betrayal made complete once the interests of this upper Catalan bourgeoisie became definitively integrated with those of the Spanish monopolist oligarchy, with the which it was going to be identified to the extent of being converted anew, no longer an accomplice but an objectively responsible party, following the polarization of positions and the modification of alignments resulting from the Civil War, from the political oppression of the Catalan reality in particular, as well as the economic exploitation or, rather, the plundering of the Spanish people in general, an unprecedented situation, qualitatively new, given that, upon adding to the fundamental contradiction between monopolist bourgeoisie and Catalan national bourgeoisie, contains the seed or implication of not only the logical alliance between proletariat and non-monopolist bourgeoisie, but also the surmounting of the historical antithesis between Castile and Catalonia and, in the final analysis, the fusion of such diverse social, political, economic, and national elements in a revolutionary synthesis, a true qualitative leap which foregrounds the antagonism existing between Franco and his party, on the one hand, and the Spanish people as a whole, on the other. Catalonia and Castile, two peoples called to complement one another once redeemed, rescued from so many differences imposed from without, from above, that have managed to separate them, to join together in fraternal unity with Galicia and Euskadi, countries of equally problematic existence, united in the task of building a different Spain as a voluntary unified socialist entity, a unity without uniformity, a unity in diversity, decentralization compatible with democratic centralism, revolutionary nationalism understood as opposition, as unanimous support for the politics of the Soviet Union and other countries within the socialist landscape, an enterprise in which such an important role is reserved for this Barcelona of immense working-class suburbs charged with revolutionary ferment, the first industrial center of Spain, the capital of a land traditionally shaken by liberation movements, libertarian Catalonia, Catalonia of the Generalitat, of Red October, of July 19th, reddened by fire and conquered by Franco and his mercenary legions, his Moors, his battalions of Moroccan Regulars, flags of blood and gold, thunderous troops; Catalonia treated unjustly, subjugated, Catalonia fallen and risen again, back on its feet, now in another direction, with a different designation, now decidedly on the move after the communist party, vanguard of the proletariat and final and decisive political force, appeared in the fight, root, stock, and cornerstone of a society on the verge of being newly forged, of a new fatherland, an illustrious future where there had been a mistaken past, sweeping progress, fasces of hammers, triumphal drum rolls, wings and bugles, final battle, judgment failed, now resolved by history. No Spanish Empire much less a Catalan Empire, no more specters from the past: instead, *la Unión de Repúblicas Ibéricas Socialistas*: URIS––the reality before which, Daniel, all the rest will be only a dream within a dream.

VIII

Sadder, yes, if possible, sadder, but not with the tender sadness that satisfies one deep inside nor with any selfish sentiment, not sunk in solitary daydreams, no, but rather with the depressed spirit of one who contemplates the victorious arrival of enemy armies and, in contrast to the movement and the surrounding acclamations, does not perceive his body as anything more than a grave presence, a stone irreparably fallen. Low, lower in spirit than others during those same days of nefarious pre-Christmas atmosphere, when the season's greetings of good cheer pile up in the vestibule and the shop windows are decked out in stars and the streets are garlanded with lights and tinsel and in front of the cathedral one finds the tangled alleys of the Christmas bazaar, la Feria de Santa Lucía, selling nativity scenes and yuletide boughs, mistletoe, moss, holly, flowerpots with shrubs glazed in rainwater, shining and green in direct contrast to the sadness and choking pressure and fury accumulated throughout the year. And especially greater today, thanks not only to the progress of events, or even the omens, or at least not only them but also, no doubt, thanks to the grim looming clouds and coming rain. Like the spring, like the rain. What relationship exists between the low tonalities of the soul, the depressive levels, the inner fog, the inert emptiness, and the rain? What causes of physical order, what actuation of atmospheric factors, what influx of certain fluids upon the organism? Or of symbolic order? Such as when the shoots break out and push forward, and the buds burst open and the rosy stems and the vine tendrils stretch forth, and what at first happens one by one soon multiplies uncontrollably, extends, recovers, gains thickness, and gazing upon the fresh fronds one feels as if they, too, had roots, not for transmitting any impulse but for an infusion of strength, of dynamic breath, to become fixed in the earth, to mineralize it, to be conquered like a pagoda overgrown and swallowed up by the luxuriant jungle growth, immutability in the change, impotence in the action, appearance preserved. So too, this rain that might seem to let up, momentarily, as if by magic, although not enough to make the umbrellas and overcoats disappear from the street, the shimmering plastics, the moist air somehow soothing, the translucent heights of December, middays like evenings, the whole day between two lights, the anodyne clarity of the neon and the worthless frippery of the Christmastime trappings against the black glare of the expanding clouds, the shifting glimmering light above the plaza, where, as if awaiting the cataclysm, the earth opened in the center of it, and the sepulchers traded places with the flowerpots, *Dis Manibus Flaviae Theodote heres ex testamento*.

The peculiar sound of footsteps treading a pavement more sticky than wet, along the blind reflection, along various streets, Canuda, Vertrallans, Santa Ana, and, crossing Puerta del Ángel, along Condal, to Number 20, headquarters of the Municipal Court Number 4. Dead dull asphalt, softened by dissolved pollutants, streets of a somber tone, the city's violet-gray which, like the red of London, the black of Paris, or the golden glow of Rome, characterizes Barcelona, the color of slag or a tumor which, in the Gothic Quarter, joined to the general degradation of the facades, acquires a particular relief, however much that fact, possibly, escapes the notice of the Barcelonans, in the same way that, beyond a certain degree and by virtue of the cityscape's familiarity, its startlingly convoluted corrugations and drynesses makes people forget how old it all is. A comparison so fateful as to be exact! The baneful exterior of Municipal Court Number 4, for example, the severe patio suggesting a prison, the sinister staircases, the gloomy interiors; everything there exudes disgrace and shelters corruption and bribery. Everything, even the most common objects and implements give off a certain oppressive sensation which quickly imposes itself on the visitor, the furniture of the successive offices and departments, the desk equally ignoble and indestructible found in the most sordid offices, the chairs, the filing cabinets, the abominable small stove, the lamps that barely shed enough light to orient the citizens who wander about or wait, men and women whose expressions configure the feigned rancor, atrocious servility, or abject avidity appropriate to those who, like the inmates of an asylum, know that their situation gives them no more right than what it graciously wants to grant them. For their part, the functionaries, from the ancient female typist to the chief secretary, carefully allow their attitude to make clear, as much through what they say as what they remain silent about, that it is indeed so, that once inside those hostile domains, nobody can rightfully hope for anything more. In that way, limiting ourselves in our considerations to the functionaries in charge of the Civil Registry, if the despotic conduct of one of them can give the reasonable impression that the whole place is rather more of a police station, the taciturn cynicism of the other, who with a twitch of his snout indicates that he's already noticed Raúl's presence and is considering it, makes one suppose himself in the presence of one of those men who survive in their job despite the vicissitudes of every different political and social regime, Monarchy and Republic, Catalan Generalitat and Francoism. A place, then, that a writer like Balzac would have not hesitated to qualify as *rongé, crevasse, execrable, puant, étouffant, nauséabond, lugubre, affreux*, and not without first satisfying the curiosity *du passant, du voyageur*, revealing that the building in question had once been the property and residence of the Ollet family, for instance, until the ruined family had it sold at public auction for the ridiculously cheap price of eight thousand seven hundred reals, and might have ended up pointing that out in order to show how a formerly noble mansion is now reduced to such a state, *il faudrait en faire une description qui retarderait trop l'intérêt de cette histoire et que les gens presses ne perdonneraient pas.*

I'll be right with you, said the clerk who had responded to Raúl's greeting. Catalan, peevish, efficient. The other, not Catalan: self-important, evasive, volatile, and, in consequence, more capable of softening up despite his initially tyrannical manner, of having a humanitarian expression, of being not only a bureaucrat, but also, and above all, of being human. Very human, almost paternal, as he pockets his tips. Of saying thanks, son, and pressing his elbow with an intimate gesture, in an expression of inexpressible sentiments. The Catalan clerk, by contrast, more efficient, expeditious, including when he picks up his cigar or the twenty-five pesetas left on the desk, half opening the drawer with his left hand and sweeping the coins in with his right, cleanly, as if to better highlight the proverbial, though voluntary, character of the compensation, discreet but significantly evoked by the golden ring of the Havana cigar that stuck up from the breast pocket of his suit jacket. Imperturbable, resistant to effusiveness, without even the impertinences of his colleague, verbal aggressivencss always capable, in the end, of offering a certain degree of belligerence, of giving way to dialogue; more unfriendly, more myopic, more manic, his pencils and ballpoint pens and fountain pens and nibs and stamps and ink pads and paperclips, all systematically arranged, between one tic and the next, automatic gestures. A sly old cat, his craft distilled through experience, wisely skeptical, implacably closed thus to both public protests and gratitude, insensible and deaf to the complaints of the never-ending supply of impatient waiting clients who, possibly because of a singularly irascible temperament or some inferiority complex, cannot suppress their disgust on seeing themselves passed over in favor of the managers and other professionals who gather there in the habitual performance of their duties, people naturally pushier and better connected, disgust, contrariness, and reprobation often translated into imprecations muttered in an undertone, evidently meant to extend their personal ill humor to all the others waiting, making them feel individually and collectively despised, fathers of newborns too proud to let themselves be dragged down by bitterness, widows with too many hours of experience to try to force the fatality of waiting in lines, old men too shrunken, adolescents already too habituated to their adult roles, all imperturbable to the greater resentment of the troublemaker, also Catalan, a functionary with the look of a bricklayer become building contractor, simultaneously pissed off and melancholy, the unmistakable victim of the headaches inherent to his social ascension—children, wives, bills—the type with heavy eyelids, stocky, hairy, dark, reeking of tobacco, with the rough tattered voice of a man whose throat is ravaged by cancer, mouth ruined by cognac, and chapped from constantly licking his lips. Insensible and deaf, as well, to the gratitude expressed in the form of promises or future projects that the obtaining of solicited permits and certifications usually elicits from some people, promises fully sincere when uttered, impelled as they are by the joy of the moment, leading to a quasi-superstitious feeling of gratitude toward the authorizing bureaucrat, the material incarnation of the task resolved as well as of the advantageous consequences that can result from all that, a gratitude no less ephemeral than sincere when a few minutes, not hours, later they will have completely forgotten that grave and prudent man for whom they just felt so much spontaneous appreciation, that anonymous and unselfish being who spends his life serving the public, enormous forgetfulness, clearly, considering the firm resolution recently adopted while dealing with him at the edge of the bureaucratic barriers that separate or bring together those administrating and those administrated, to create a relationship of true friendship, always useful on the other hand, to return another day and have a drink on the way home from the office or even go out to have dinner some Saturday with their respective wives, and while the ladies chat about their silly ideas, during the after-dinner conversation, each man with a good cigar, one tells his friend his opinions about life, his problems, thus inviting the other to share his own. All that in the supposition that once back out in the city streets, barely reintegrated into his typical daily drudgery, he won't start to recapitulate, to build up little by little, each time more the farther away from the Municipal Court, a mental summary of all the little servilities committed and humiliations borne, and transform his meek cooperation into rancor toward a few fellows who, because they work as pen pushers in some shitty municipal court, think themselves something they're not, and it seems that they do you a favor attending to you when it's nothing more than their obligation, that's why they collect from the taxpayer, directly from oneself, if you take a look, with the goal of getting the bad taste out of your mouth and overcoming the irritating memory, in a healthy exercise of mental hygiene, he'll make long-term plans, for the day when he's somebody, a well-known and respected personality in some field, with influence, and then drop in here some morning and take pleasure in seeing this whole string of faggots all lined up to lick his ass, because in life you pay for everything and where they give they take, etcetera, interior monologue developed according to a scheme all-too-familiar, no doubt, to the Catalan bureaucrat, conclusions more than well-known in order to consider any of those initial effusions with any other attitude than reserved indifference. Sensitive, however, perspicaciously attentive and receptive when it's a question not of an occasional, informal contact but an ongoing professional one, the manager, the attorney, the lawyer, the true client, assiduous and able, confident and experienced who, as is customary, knows how to proffer a tip properly couched in phrases simultaneously witty and conventional, the deal closed between subtle shadings upon the basis of a tacit understanding, with the touch of a seducer who in each bed accommodates the rules of the erotic ritual to the particular longings of their lover, as intuition dictates, according to an experience that in the long run always turns out to be preferable. Bird in the hand, neither fathers of large families, nor disconsolate sons and other family members, nor cuckolds in the trance of separation, nor passive widows, nor stupefied servants, nor philosophical old men, nor uncultured idiots who surely know how to make money, but not how to utilize it opportunely, nor drama queens who insist on suggesting that they've already suffered enough in this life so why wait for the next life to come, factions of tricksters and troublemakers, charlatans, disgraced men, cheaters, gamblers, card sharps, crooks, blunderers, show-offs, and adulterers, an Andalusian laborer ready to work, mute and submissive, asking, almost affirming, whether or not he will also need a certificate from the parish, possibly with the goal of showing his good disposition, unlike others, in the face of administrative requirements, an unconditional adhesion that leads him to comply in full with the rigorous pertinent requisites, completing them and perfecting them with new proofs and additional documentation, an attitude fatally destined to arouse the mistrust of the Catalan bureaucrat, for being unusually removed from the normal and reasonable antagonism that tends to manifest itself among those who need to show any kind of certification and those who are in charge of authorizing it, and who in fact does grant it, but not without a tug of war equally conflictive and fruitful; mistrust and censure exteriorized through a glance over the top of his eyeglasses, an interrogative repetition of some parochial term and a leafing through his papers muttering something, some formulation or judgment which, by the twisted dilations of his mouth, might well be some beastly comment, some beastly comment or something similar. Mistrust and censure only certain to intensify in direct proportion to the humble worker's greater efforts to neutralize or at least mollify the bad impression obviously produced from the start, and more insistent his determined effort to show that he was nothing if not precisely that, a lowly worker, a laborer as ignorant as willing and eager to please and, surely, in need of guidance, and what's more, with the moral right to demand assistance, to have the opportunity of making patent his obedience, he, the docile one, the laborer with neither ideas nor learning, which for that reason I'm asking, simply on the off-chance, and pardon the question, I asked it because I don't understand those things, I understand that you people here must be fed up with everyone asking you foolish questions, but you understand these things, which I've asked in order to facilitate your work maybe, for simply on the off-chance, an obstinate and useless and even counterproductive remark when addressed to the Catalan bureaucrat, hiding behind his mutterings in a savage game of stamping papers, he would end up turning instead, as one might suppose, to the non-Catalan bureaucrat, more vulnerable to the purely deferential compensations of character and truly disposed toward confraternity, even managing, obviously flattered by the allusion to the complexity and responsibility of his job, to resolve matters with a stimulating and comforting bit of don't mention it, my good man, that's what we're here for. Thus, one could establish a correlation or equivalence between the willing worker and the non-Catalan bureaucrat, the former, as a member of the public, a replica of the latter, as a bureaucrat, in the same way that the troublemaker with the face of a bricklayer-become-building-contractor could be considered the Catalan bureaucrat's doppelgänger, all that resulting in a new and illustrative antagonistic relationship, more about the behavior of the elements considered than their different functions, a divergence or polarization not of horizontal but vertical lines, a contraposition between what might be properly considered a reverence for mere appearance and formality in the first case and, in the second, an instinctive animosity toward rules, precepts, and other strange circumlocutions when they do not run counter to what is strictly practical.

A fanatic's pupil behind his Coke-bottle lenses, the Catalan bureaucrat stood up and, with angry but stubborn step, walked decisively to the balcony as if to check on something happening outside, or some information pending confirmation, although quite possibly he simply needed to rip some unstoppable fart whose sound would be masked by the traffic noises out in the street, not a perfectly improbable explanation, especially in light of how rigidly immobile he remained as he executed the maneuver, destined by all evidence to avoid the logical loss of prestige that not exiting would have caused him in the eyes of the waiting public, faces of a quiet variety, slack expressions reflecting, as a breeze-riffled puddle, passing curiosity about the others in the room, flights of insubstantial ideas, almost on the edge of sleep, a proximity that perhaps favored the tepid closeness of that angry atmosphere made noxious by the damp clothes and shoes which, with the warm humidity, caused the body to emanate its most intimate effluvia, postures momentarily slack and distracted then suddenly again upright and intent, as if corresponding to someone in the midst of requesting something, patiently awaiting their turn, a passivity that in no case excludes their attentive observation, the search for some partiality, the struggle to get ahead of the other people, to accelerate the necessary paperwork and shorten the waiting periods by any means possible, exceptions granted, obviously, for those who come here to register a birth if, on one hand, the very nature of its management means they are exempted from coming back another day, the euphoric state that such happy events usually bring, on the other, it makes their waiting more bearable, so that they frequently reach the point where they consider themselves the center of the event, forgetting that the true protagonist of the inscription is someone else, the real newcomer to a circus where the only easy thing is getting a ticket to the main event. Like forgetting, one Sunday at noon, what it must be like to go out in the afternoon, the passersby with their heavy digestions, the lines outside the cinemas, the full stomachs, the harsh sunset; or like ignoring, once again, the no-lesser abomination of the days that follow this time period of bubbling Christmas, when all the twinkling glitter comes down, and the bustling streets outside the cathedral, particularly lively today with the excited groups of seamstresses celebrating the feast of Santa Lucía, December 13th, Tuesday, the Spanish day of bad luck, a date quite expressive enough to resume the black streak of recent days, the string of misfortunes, the repeated setbacks, events not foreseen or at least not foreseen as a problem capable of affecting him, the business about Pluto's girlfriend and the death of Aunt Paquita and Nuria's father's accident and the loss of his overcoat and the doors of the subway train pulling away right under his nose, small mishaps no less exasperating than the big ones, a chain of events whose examination, in an attempt to reconsider its origin, to precisely identify the starting point, would force him to accept the conclusion that Achilles's death was, without a doubt, the first bad news.

Could Raúl have ever imagined telling Florencio Rivas Fernández, when they saw each other for the last time, precisely at Aunt Paquita's burial, that only a few days later he would be holding Florencio's death certificate in his own hands, who could have imagined it, a man like Florencio, so full of life, with so little experience of the irreparable, etcetera, meditations appropriate to the difficulty of accepting the fact, that in the case of Francisca Ferrer Gaminde, widow of Giral, death had brusquely, brutally, irrevocably, and unceremoniously snatched her away. An uncontrolled tumor, no one sure exactly when it began, when her perpetual complaints and pains and her fears and her migraines all began to roll into one, to form part of the process, nor when the family learned the truth, nor if she suspects it, if her capacity for deception permits her to keep on believing it nothing more than just an accumulation of small complaints, not major ones, just complications from sciatica, rheumatism, cramping, intestinal infections, as a way to explain the progressive prostration of a body officially, supposedly, affected by a mild case of hepatitis, even though from a certain point it becomes barely believable that the truth has not dawned on her completely and that, in fact, she's doing nothing more than pretending to believe her relatives in order to spare them the necessary behavior of family members who know that she knows it, who knows the nearness of the end and the name of her illness, that thing that it now seems they're on the verge of curing or, at least, of identifying, of discovering, which is saying a lot, and whoever does, well, it's that you've got to build them a monument, and the most curious thing is that it seems that it's not, properly speaking, some illness, not an illness like other illnesses, I mean, not just a microbe or something that comes from outside, but rather something that she carries inside, something that the body itself produces which ends up destroying the organism that produced it, a kind of disordered development of the cells which acquires powers from the ordered structure from which it proceeds and then kills it off, without it really being known why, nor what unleashes that random, unconstrained growth, the only thing known is that it's not contagious, luckily not that, some people get it, others don't, and if it gets you then you're finished, bad luck, and if not, well, no one escapes death either, and, if you're going to go, well look, it's so much the same, that thing as any other. How are you, aunt, said Raúl. And she said, very well, Raúl. He nodded his head at her comments about the bother of such an unpleasant illness like hepatitis and its truly alarming spread or frequency nowadays, although it's also possible that he didn't really pay her any attention and only nodded from habit. She looked at Raúl and asked him about Nuria, when they were getting married, and about his studies, obliging him to assume the air of a young beau confused by his elders' questions or, more precisely, of a nephew who feigns feigning a certain embarrassment, given that the questions formulated usually follow a well-recognized pattern of interest in the one interrogated, whose merits demand open declaration, to effect their future familial consecration. Well, look, said Aunt Paquita, earlier, to be precise, I had a dream about you. Well, in all of them, you were also there. We were in Vallfosca, in the garden, and there was a kind of picnic going on, and they were handing each of you a glass. She rubbed the back of one hand with the other, aching from the intravenous hookups, small burst blood vessels, black and blue and yellow, not much more immobile between the sheets than in her chaise longue in Vallfosca, nor more weightless than upon the discolored cretonne cushions, her voice no less distant than when she called them from in between sun and shade, in the corner thick with hydrangeas, vivacious irradiations, green sounds, the early smell of the streams and rivulets, sour grapes, warm straw, wasp nests between the ceramic roof tiles, the porrón that the young men carried with them out to the fields, the magpies at dawn embroidering the sky. It must have been quite a few years since he'd seen her, and when they said that she'd slipped into a coma he went to see her, more than anything so that Papa would stop reminding him each night that he should go. Why go back? What inertia or force made him say that he would return again next week, against all expectation in the moment of saying it, and indeed return, and again say that he would come back and then return again, however much each week he supposed that by then she would be dead? Was it some subjective unscientific understanding, based merely on the conviction or desire that the situation cannot worsen, but the opposite proves true, that it can indeed worsen, and what was merely a question of hours ends up being one of days and weeks, a condition between life and death showing that her prior composure and much-commented-on serenity now mean nothing more than if they described the behavior of a mushroom or a larva?

The decline that starts the moment when the discussion of the patient's suffering is invalidated by a surprising recovery of their faculties, all the nervous worry expressed by family members and close friends changes tenor, the calls, visits, explanations, and the embarrassing fact of having to clarify for all involved that it was only a false alarm, and so much the better, although, of course, in reality she's weaker every day, the poor thing, she's like a flame slowly dying out, I warn you that sometimes it happens that in their final hours they seem to respond to treatment and it looks like they're going to get better and everything, but it only seems that way, of course, and you see her head's completely clear, a true miracle, the doctor no longer dares offer an opinion, the important thing is that she doesn't suffer, go on in if you all like, better not to overwhelm her now, she's resting easy, that's why, perhaps she could sleep, words in a low voice in the next room, and inside, the odor of Sterilair, the excessively bright lights, the way Aunt Paquita likes them, the way she scrutinized him when she discovered him alongside her bed, perhaps seeing that Raúl's pupils already reflected death, and the doctor took her pulse and said there was nothing wrong, a reckoning always awaited with a certain anxiety, such as a verdict or the exam results read aloud at the end-of-term party, for all present to hear, even those least informed about a disease's particular details, unlike the family members surrounding the patient who becomes intimately acquainted with its progress, their progressively shifting interest, initially centered on the patient's personality, toward the details that characterize the evolution of the illness from a more technical point of view, more properly clinical, the more definitive the prognosis the more unnecessary, the consultations following new complications, the difficulty of effecting compromised micturition, the impossibility of ingesting solid foods, tests, medicines, injections, punctures, sedatives, open sores, etcetera, the phenomenon of movement or passage, or better yet of supplanting what, in the end, only leads to the certain and gradual reduction of the person to an elemental organism consisting of one single large tube, simultaneously mouth and anus. The cat seemed to be everywhere, rubbing itself noiselessly, relaxing, staring, eyes reduced to slits, the clear green iris, like crystallized moss, in the vestibule, in the parlor, in the small adjacent sitting room, although it's also possible that there were various cats instead of only one, and that they were exactly identical. Murmurs, heads together, exposition of similarities, exchange of impressions, if she's recognized Pedro, if now only Ramona can understand her, if it doesn't seem that she's suffering, but it appears that she's experiencing something like hallucinations, that's from the sedatives, yes, the effect of the sedatives, they go right to the poor thing's head, look, it seems that Ramona asked her if she wanted the guaiac, and she said I don't understand, it's just that the poor thing isn't aware, I think that sometimes she doesn't even know where she is, nor whether she's still here or if she's already in heaven, because with the devotion she shows to this relic, I'll put it here for you, Mama, on top of the bottle of saline solution, and the picture of Pope Pius and the scapular of the Virgin of Mount Carmel and the small medallion of the Immaculate Conception she received when she made her First Communion, and the one from Fatima and the one of Saint Francis of Assisi, and the framed benediction from Leo XIII from when Grandpa Raúl took her on a pilgrimage to Rome, and the photo of Gemma Galgani, and the rosary made of olive pits from Gethsemane, objects for which she professed a special fervor and which, linked with specific practices, orations and short prayers, signified a substantial wellspring of indulgences, one hundred, three hundred, five hundred days rescued from Purgatory, an estimable quantity, very much on the human scale, given that an immeasurable remission, fifty, one hundred thousand years, might be counterproductive, disheartening more than encouraging to the person in grace, the only possible subject of the blessing, doubtless inhibiting ahead of time any attempt at maneuvering in a realm where the operative quantities are of a similar magnitude, an uncertainty covered in every case by the plenary or total exemption resulting from exercising such practices as observing the nine First Fridays, the cycle of nine months fulfilled time and again by Aunt Paquita, in uninterrupted succession throughout her whole life, a fact that might explain her now apparent disinterest for piousness, devout exercises for those who only seemed to surrender, when their condition allowed it, suggested by those trying to comfort her this way, the Creed, the Hail Mary, the Confiteor, some mystery of the rosary, some litany, the Viaticum, including extreme unction, even though, in this respect, the most probable thing is that, in that moment, her awareness of receiving a sacrament from the living was practically null, Latin phrases muttered, as if yawning, by a poor, miserable parish priest, with habitual abbreviated celerity, the superficial application of the holy oils, the forehead, the hands, the mouth, in invocation, *per istam sanctam untionem*, of the most merciful compassion of God. We can stick our heads in a minute, if you all want to; she'll be excited to see you, said Ramona. Maybe she's resting a bit. She had such a bad night, the poor thing. Better not, better not, actually. I'll tell her that you've been here. You should certainly rest a while, you must be wiped out. She's the one who carries all the weight and if she doesn't take care of herself she'll end up getting sick. It just seems that with the poor thing you have to help her with everything, and like Ramona she's the only one who understands her. Such tension. Ramona's a girl with a lot of spirit. She and Elvira, they're so lucky to have Elvira. She's been in the house for so many years it's as if she were one of the family, one of those people you don't find anymore, not like the ones nowadays, it's that they don't know anything about anything and they're always thinking about something else and everything seems to matter very little to them, with that talk of how people abroad earn so much and how much, I don't know what we're coming to, our maid drives me insane, she threatens to quit for any little thing and then starts looking through the want ads and calling up her friends and the days go by and, then, after all, she doesn't leave, but one day this will come to an end, because I'll take her at her word and I'll tell her, very well, you've said that you want to leave, it's true, well go then, let's go, what are you waiting for, let's see if you find another house like this one, and I'll just kick her out, and then you'll see how she backs down and asks me if she can stay, but by then I'll already have found someone else and I'll tell her no, that in this world no one is indispensable, and it'll be her loss, because besides she's grown really fond of the kids, which is lucky, they grow really fond of the kids and then it's hard for them to leave, so if she hadn't already walked out on me when I least expected it, with the guests all seated at the table, and look she's a good girl, that when she wants to she knows how to do things, but it's just that this can't go on and can't go on, with her blackmail she really gets on my nerves, and all because you treat them with too much consideration and then they abuse it, they take you for a fool, you've got to treat them like maids, because that's what they are and it's the only language they understand, being talked to like maids, maids who live in a world of maids, their friends, they're like a gang, the boyfriend, the dates, the telephone, family relations, the foolish things they say, the gossip, the affairs, the tantrums. Not Elvira, no. And it's not because she's not a grumbler or doesn't have a temper; when she's in a really bad mood she's capable of tongue-lashing the morning star. A tremendous Navarran, one of those who's a real force to be reckoned with. You see, those Navarrans, splendid people, folks, I don't know, sort of whole, sort of real. Look, they liberated Barcelona. The Navarran brigades from Solchaga. As if I'm going to forget, that emotion, that enthusiasm. I remember, in Calle Cortés. The Navarrans. Praise for the Navarran: a real man, from head to toe, loyal and brave, hard-working, of sound constitution, big heart, noble sentiments and virile religiosity; traditionally traditionalist and jealous of his customs; at the same time, he's a very hospitable host, a friend of the good table and, of course, likes to booze it up a bit, but in no way corrupt or womanizing, prone rather to healthy recreation, fighting rams, betting, and other pastimes he shares with the Basques, the brethren of his race, those whom he resembles so much thanks to what they have in common, only without separatisms or social problems. Nevertheless, Jacinto expresses the classic Catalan pessimism, appropriate to one who's already seen too many things in life, which, nevertheless, will of course break down, he hopes that the Basque Country is going to be industrialized and you'll see how they break down. Navarra already is an industrial region these days, it's changed a lot and more change is coming, and then all that will be lost and Navarra will stop being what it is, body and soul of tradition, stronghold of pugnacity, people who rise to the occasion without a second thought and deliver themselves to the cause hand and foot and defend it tooth and nail, capable of having their throats slit for God and country and, in the end, and in virtue of what we represent, by ourselves, those here gathered to the sad awaiting of the last breath, fainting, dead breath, omega of life. Go in, go in. Won't she be tired? If she's not resting, we'll just stick our heads in for a moment. Come in, come in, for Heaven's sake, the poor thing doesn't rest for more than five minutes at a time. Just a quick minute: come in and then out you go. Listen, listen, although I don't know if she'll recognize you, come close, this bright light is unpleasant, but she asked for it, maybe when she could no longer see more than silhouettes and colors and movement, faces suddenly up close, though not, like the voices that arose and faded out, any less disconcerting. The tall stand with the hanging bottles of saline solution at the foot of the bed, a small table with the instruments for curing her, gauze, syringes, ointments, cotton, cologne, adhesive tape, and the nun with the fisherman's face muttered something to him in such a low voice that Raúl responded to her with a prudently affirmative cough, as if absorbed, his attention focused on those eyes that did not seem to see anything specific, watery, with an increasingly superficial shine, her tresses like those of a little girl who braided them herself, an ashen contrast to the puffy whiteness of the bed. The adjacent room appeared illuminated by the television screen, clarity without sound, and as if silhouetted on the horizon against the dawn sky, the whispering figures, the teacups, the teapot, the ladyfingers. There were quite a few people in the room, and the talking was inevitably too loud. Ramona moved from one group to another, attending them with mundane aplomb and responding to their shows of interest and moral support, and a maid was offering drinks. The balcony doors were halfway open and, like a tulle fog, the light animated by the cigarette smoke escaped toward the darkness outside. Discreet conversation, without stridencies, branches of the old trunk distanced one from another by unequal luck or fortune, relatives and relatives' relatives who only now meet up on solemn occasions, obligatory appearances, weddings or funerals, and they fulfill their obligations, expressing interest, offering polite responses to courteous questions exchanged again and again, your health, your mother, the little ones, how things are going, the latest problems, housemaids, financial difficulties, some imminent ministerial reassignment, how everything is getting to be so screwed up, problems without solution, always expressed with that mix of indignant surprise and fateful certainty, points of view, generalizations, sharp positions reiterated more than anything as a character trait or affirmation of personality, family anecdotes, Gregorius, who's a disaster; Merceditas, who is expecting again; Pedro, who's become a ne'er-do-well crackpot; Montserrat, who is a daring, carefree woman; Jacinto and his obtuse Francoism; Juanito and his ideas, everything treated with an exquisite respect by the family lines that over time have stereotyped each other's social images, with tact, affability, and tolerance, in a tacit search for what harmonizes and unites, including when the conversation ends up focusing on the hottest controversy, on what all Barcelona's buzzing about, what invariably interests us all because it refers to our own environs, by what it implies for everyone in terms of indirect retaliation, either exemplary retribution or identification with the triumph, some transparent gold digger in an obvious marriage for money, for example, or, better yet, an especially scandalous separation, here discussed while carefully avoiding all delicate or scabrous detail, saving for a more opportune moment, with more intimate friends, the retelling of a conjugal crisis that began with a civilized agreement between both spouses to live and let live, and ended with judicial summons, private detectives, public notaries, compromising photographs, witnesses, disappearances, abandonment of family, and the argument that she was the first one to actually take a lover, notoriously consented, and the counter-argument asking why wouldn't she since he could only reach orgasm by means of a warm enema administered by four naked women wearing masks.

From any balcony in the Ensanche, the city offers the stranger—always more attentive to general impressions than details—a view approximately identical to any other view from any other balcony, from any balcony around this busy intersection on the corner of Calle Mallorca and Pau Claris, for example, on the monotonous facade of the six-story building erected on the lot after the grandfather died, a property that until then had been occupied by the Ferrer Gaminde family's chalet, according to the now classic Barcelona custom of demolishing old buildings with the greatest possible frequency in order to replace them with new, and invariably uglier ones, a practice that, for whatever speculative benefits it might bring, might also be considered consubstantial of all bourgeoisie, and in this specific case, of Barcelona only tacking its vulgarity, bad taste, and aberrant modesty onto its frustration over what was a grandiose nineteenth-century project. Of the excitement and geniality that once attended it, there now only remain adulterated glimpses, sufficient, nevertheless, to give an idea that such a vision could be realized with such a high degree of mediocrity, a sign of the vast distance between one generalization and those that follow it, an extensive mediocrity seen throughout the very same early embellishments and grotesque dreams of an upper-class bourgeoisie converted into an aristocracy by force of imagination, by the power of pontifical titles and provincial cosmopolitanism, a mimetic fascination for the Castilian nobility, for its virtues and its shortcomings, a collective attitude that, in the economic field, perhaps explains the development of a marked, heartfelt proclivity for absentee land ownership and speculation, stock exchange, insurance policies, finance companies, real estate, land, concessions for public services, namely, legitimate business, and the same for the situation of privilege, for exclusivity and protectionism, just like its allergic reaction against any frugal, coupon-clipping concept of industry, seeing it instead as an enterprise to be directed and, consequently, its distaste for the rest of the Catalan bourgeoisie, those industrialists and merchants with whom a good family must only relate as a last resort, if the hard mandate of necessity demands it, through canonical connections, people who, for having reinvested their fortunes, generally of identical overseas origin, into industrial activities, and for having inculcated in their descendancy a strict identification with family name, product, family tradition, and factory continuity for the sake of a constant competitive growth and improvement, turn out to be perpetually assimilated into the social image of the nouveau riche, the newly moneyed businessman, a being easy to identify by his undisguisable lack of class, lineage, and nobility, his eagerness to insinuate himself and make social relationships, his disgusting manners, his strong Catalan accent, his strident laugh, there's nothing about them undeserving of scorn, both his splendid love of showing off as well as his spectacular flukes of luck, the same for the money earned in circumstances which, thanks to their immediacy, necessarily turn out to be murky, and his shameful ruin, frequently as sudden and rapid as his accumulation of wealth and assets, suspension of payments, fraudulent bankruptcies, foreclosures, what doubt can there be about the unapologetic reprobation of those who, in the worst cases, by selling their luxurious properties, are able to spread out their general decline over the course of several generations, their pronunciation ever more snuffling and nasal, their presence evermore pompous and affected, their minds evermore cretinous, evermore hare-brained, block-headed, thick-lipped, and lisping, following the natural course of such things that come, the declining arc from the ancestral heights to the current levels of mental retardation. Forms of decadence which their haughtiest and most quick-witted prolongers acclaim before denying, converting them into their opposite, distancing and distinguishing them from those who now hold economic power, converting them into conjectures about how different everything would be if things had gone differently—unassailable in their nostalgia over what never came to pass, in their capitulations and recapitulations, lamenting only that the ancient feudal lords of Catalonia, perhaps from excessive confidence in the rights and merits of their own lineage or from a hierarchical itch that could only inhibit all exuberant noble dignity where the highest aristocratic rank was a mere count, but in any case with an unspeakable lack of foresight, without a precise awareness that family names come and go while dignity remains—they might not have worried about giving objective immanence and validity to their concrete prerogatives, about sanctioning and qualifying their generic lordly status with the usual hereditary titles, or about arranging and articulating those titles in a formally immutable body, thus arranging how many had to succeed them as the leaders of Catalan society, to the natural aristocracy of future centuries, languishing in a state of notorious and lamentable inferiority relative to the nobility of the rest of Spain and Europe, trying to justify it, submitting it to prolix and vexing explanations, particularly in those times when nobody has too much time, condemning them to the recourse, humiliating at bottom because of the messy quality and consolation they imply, of sporting a fin-de-siècle title, if not something even more recent or pontifical, the only means of overcoming the pedestrian, and highly uncertain, notion of a mere good name; or lamenting that, perhaps owing to the polymember development of the Crown and its precocious apogee, prior to any conception of the city more civil than military, what could be a continued enrichment of the Barcelona court and harmonic accumulation resulted in a vast dispersion of efforts, always insufficient achievements: Palma, Valencia, Zaragoza, achieved at the cost of the monumental density of Barcelona, a city devoid of the tradition of street as art or the small plazas characteristic of so many small Italian towns of incomparably minor significance and rank. We are not speaking now of a Campidoglio, of a Lido, of a Piazza del Duomo, altars where before the eyes of the whole world a city is consecrated and the privileged inhabitants of such a splendorous past are ennobled, an aristocracy for which the problem of remaining in their ancestral residences is, mostly, a problem of taxes, unlike in our own palaces, whose primitive sobriety and poor magnificence excuse to a certain point Barcelonans' general disengagement with respect to their good luck, the consideration that it's the business of the municipal government to rescue from abandonment and demolition some mansions that they have just turned into *conventillos*, tenement houses, insofar as they are incapable of compensating with prestige the lack of comfort common to all medieval construction; or lamenting the fact that Felipe V's indiscriminate rancor against Catalonia—however just his intention to punish those who opposed his installation of the Bourbon dynasty—impelled him to no less a retribution than ordering the destruction of all the castles of the Principality, almost half of those extant in Spain, reducing to now-eroded ruins what would today be the glory and splendor of the landscape, the scenery and symbol of social elevation; or lamenting that the exclusion of their ancestors, for whatever reasons, from all participation in the conquest of America during close to three hundred years had deprived Catalonia of the importance and influence that other Spanish regions had indelibly inscribed in the history of the new continent, great feats and discoveries, foundations, honors, fortunes, vice-royalties, as well as the logical reflux of riches toward the metropolis, which instead, unfortunately, shows an almost complete dearth of Baroque sumptuousness; or lamenting the fact that some people in Catalonia, with incomprehensible stubbornness, still insisted on expressing themselves in Catalan, thus establishing, in relation to the rest of Spain, a wall of misunderstanding, suspicion, and automatic antipathy that forces those of us who express ourselves in Castilian Spanish, a tongue whose turns and accents unmistakably indicate its origin, to firmly remember that, thanks to the grace of God, not everyone in Catalonia is automatically reduced and relegated to be traveling salesmen and textile manufacturers, and above all, that it's one thing to be Catalan and another, but very distinct, to be a Catalan nationalist, a minority individual whose small, narrow-minded mentality we are the first to denounce and scorn, now that all the nations in the world are speaking about joining together, they come out with these separatist notions, you've got to look up higher, see beyond the simple provincial image of the little house with its tiny toolshed and garden plot promoted by such figures as Maciá and Companys, seek objectives less minimal and narrow, ideals worth defending with something more than the Virolai and the Sardana; or lamenting the Catalan's political incapacity, understanding as such his ineptitude for reaching the peak of power, as well as the less-vaunted and even frequently ignored economic incapacity, understanding as such not his lack of skill in making money, but rather his instinctive rejection of how much is required to combine efforts and to fuse capital resources, no longer capable of creating true industrial complexes, in accord with the gigantism that is nowadays a question of survival, but rather including, unlike the Basques, some major bank that, by backing projects of a certain importance, would contribute at least to the remodeling of an economic landscape characterized by industrial smallholdings and de-capitalization, all that fruit of our radical individualism and long-term suicide. The fact is, that's how we are and we have no remedy, being individualists among the individualists, and in the same way that what was here during the communist era was not communism but anarchism, so too in businesses and in everything, so that that might not work against us but rather in our favor, we're too gentlemanly, too lordly, too lacking in honorable mercantile qualities that distinguish us from so much new money and so many vulgar, grasping, bloodsucking parvenus, that exonerate and purify us of all confusion with the surrounding and so grossly adulterated atmosphere, capable as we would be, like Samson, of pulling down the Temple upon our heads and perishing before compromising—in the matter of principles—with the times and the upstarts, criteria and considerations that if in a general way propitiate skepticism and desperation, the idea that history, for example, does not seem to make coherent sense and perhaps does not have to, much less provide an obligatory happy ending, they also propitiate a unified disdain toward innovation, in the bitter confrontation about what's being lost, in the form of closing ranks against what's transcendent, here and now, everyone, like always when the bells toll for someone's death and everyone else comes and gathers round, a comfort in time of pain, consolation for affliction, united, joined together, unanimous, marching along one after another conscious of the support that represents, not only for the relatives, but also for each one of those of us who march, made fervent by the way in which those present mutually empower one another and by the depth that the circumstances confer upon the act of clutching and pressing a hand, signing the book of condolences or placing yourself entirely at their disposition, sincerely moved, no doubt sincerely moved, as we offer ourselves to the relatives of the deceased, a great lady with whose disappearance disappears for all a little bit of our own past, of what we usually understand to be our times. Around two in the morning, in the sitting room there now only remained men, relatives of varying degree, friendships particularly attached to the family or especially trustworthy gentlemen, and Pedro, as if to correspond to what was doubtless expected of him, became the focus of the attention of some of those present with his anecdotes about whores, skirting, through precise, ingenious circumlocutions, every crude or scathing word, a deference ostensibly directed either at the maid who brought more coffee and emptied the ashtrays, or at Ramona, who sometimes drew near to light a cigarette in his company. But, do they do it for pleasure or for money? asked Ramona, snug against the arm of the sofa, while not even the naturalness of the tone employed nor the simultaneously serene and objective and confident gesture were sufficient to prevent even a stranger, or a person unfamiliar with the economic power that Jacinto Bonet represented in Barcelona, from understanding everything immediately, his wedding, his impossible desires, the reasons for that impossibility, and under any appearance of mere curious interest, would not guess the fascination that was evidently produced by everything relating to the matter and, more concretely, the key to the erotic mechanism, the mystery of a forceful penetration; amorous affections. They also told political jokes, not without criticizing that oh-so-very Spanish custom of always criticizing the one who governs, inverse to how the English consider it incorrect to simply raise the subject of politics during gatherings, and they talked about the superiority of the Anglo-Saxon educational system, of our team's chances for the Davis Cup, about the striptease shows one can see in London, more outrageous than the shows at Crazy Horse, various topics, adequate for a situation in which the night is still young and it's better to chat about entertaining things in order to ward off the tension produced by the presence of a body lying in some adjacent room, the waxen gloom of the burial mound. When Raúl said goodnight they were talking about the terrorist sentenced to death, coinciding besides, in essence, with the criterion that had prevailed in Leo's house in what's referred to as the causal act for the sentence, the work of a madman, now dramatically reassessed due to the news of the sentence having appeared in the afternoon paper, even though here the assessment of madness was based on the conviction that only a madman could attempt to effect change and bring about the progressive economic development of the country with bombs at the very moment when the fruits of Stabilization were beginning to reach the most humble classes. Meanwhile, at Leo's house, a similar recourse to some methods already mentioned in "*The Bakuninists at Work*", almost one hundred years before, had been rejected as counterproductive, only . . . it could be considered as one more example of the exasperation of the popular masses, without the negative and even provocative aspects of the action being an obstacle, nevertheless, so that all the pronouncements of solidarity with the victims of repression were formulated and, more concretely, the victims of police brutality, whatever their political creed might be, the same as in cases like those of Marsal or Obregón, in the case of this poor boy, surely so full of generosity as to be misguided, that if he'd not already been executed by firing squad, after an even more hasty, summary trial, the reason was, without a doubt, because his physical condition had prevented him from testifying before the court-martial with greater urgency; extreme theses, or conjectures, too far removed from the daily life of those gathered at Aunt Paquita's wake—raised as they were by some unsuspecting spirit and with little sense of the situation—for basic sensitivity or etiquette to have prevented them from expressing support for the idea that, for admonitory purposes, the execution be carried out in the public plaza, as with Juan Sala, alias Serrallonga, or any other villain of old. Serrallonga, who on the eighth of January, 1634, according to the chronicles, was lashed, had his ears cut off, was paraded about on a wagon, his flesh pierced with red hot pincers, then drawn and quartered, and his severed head displayed on one of the towers of the Gate of San Antonio of the present city. *Anima eius requiescat in pace*. Amen.

When will the martyrology end! said Leo's father, and like in a picture from the Baroque era where the supernatural plane is imposed triumphantly upon the overwhelmed witnesses to an apparition, thus, in the meditative pause that followed his words, such an implicit and respectful homage of silence, the image of Obregón hung by his arms from a water pipe became almost palpable, his wrists bloody and raw, his feet crushed, his skin marked by cigar burns, or the image of Marsal handcuffed to an iron bed frame transformed by electric shocks into a screaming abyss, or Leo himself, felled by a round of blows, scenes always with something unreal about them, perhaps due to the sordid familiarity of the surrounding circumstances: offices that could belong to a notary public, fellows that could be insurance agents, all quite vulgar, devoid of the plasticity and mythical weight of a Sebastian pierced with arrows or a Savonarola on the pyre, but not for that reason any less realistic and immediate, something like what happened to Obregón could have become reality for Floreal if he'd not hidden in time, something that no one stopped imagining was already really happening to Escala when the rumor circulated about his arrest, in the same way that the sheer luck of having beaten the police to the flat where the fellows from the student committee kept the mimeograph machine had prevented it from becoming a reality as well for Raúl and Federico. This is like the last days of Pompeii, said Leo's father. The volcano will soon erupt. Already, back in the days of Hegel, the great German philosopher whose thoughts, although he was an idealist, served as a basis, perhaps, for those of Marx, Barcelona was already then a world-class city that counted among its history more fights at the barricades than any other, and now the final battle draws near. On one side will be the powerful people, with their luxuries, their vices, their profligacy; on the other, the people with their hunger and misery. While the rich are increasingly rich, the poor grow ever more poor, and the millionaires and plutocrats see their enormous profits and their personal dividends constantly grow larger, and at the expense of workers' salaries. That's why the revolution is the worker's task. The worker is the only one who has nothing to lose, except his chains. But it's foreseen that the same progression of events goes on demonstrating its truth and then, in their fight, the working class will receive the support of other classes and social levels, democratic students, progressive intellectuals, small liberal bourgeoisie and non-monopolistic bourgeoisie, as well as ample sectors of the clergy and even the army, meaning, from all the people of goodwill who, before the disaster of capitalism and the perspectives that socialism offers to resolve the problem in Spain, are beginning to see things clearly. We believe that the land belongs to those who work it, and for that reason the farmer, as he makes this principle his own, is converted into the natural ally of the working class. This does not mean, however, that we need to be against private property, just the opposite, we even defend it from those who would attempt to monopolize it to the detriment of the community. The proof is that, in socialist countries, even nowadays various kinds of private property continue to exist. And with the question of the Church, the same thing happens, that we've got nothing against the fact that the good and faithful Catholic practices his religion. Here Teresa intervened: it seems that in Poland, for example, she said, the people attend Mass much more than in Spain. And Leo: besides, he said, in reality now it's not about making a revolution, but about restoring parliamentary democracy to Spain, a transitional regime in which all democratic forces and tendencies in the country are represented. And I can assure you all that, when the moment arrives, not only the soldiers recruited in the heart of the town, but the very members of the repressive forces—armed police and civil guard, as well as a great number of sub-officials and heads of the army and even some public officials and bosses—will all join the peaceful national strike. You cannot fathom the discontent voiced in the flag halls, about the ridiculous salaries that Francoist agents collect for doing a job that disgusts them, about how shabby the prison workers' uniforms get. I was talking quite a bit with one fellow from my building, and I assure you all that we can count on many of them not only when it comes to overthrowing the dictatorship but also in the transitional phase toward socialism. And the same with the Church, said Leo's father; the lower clergy, who see the workers' problems up close, will end up playing their part and pulling their weight, and the hierarchy will have no other choice than to do the same. The first thing that priests would have to do is go with women, said Juan. Now, with them having to do it secretly, they all turn into faggots. The Development Plan will fail, said Leo. Only recently they nailed one there up on Montjuich, in the Tierra Negra, said Juan. And that stuff about the parish priest from Pueblo Seco, who fondled the little boys in the parish, if the police hadn't intervened they would've lynched him. The only thing the Development Plan will do is create contradictions, said Leo. There are too many rifts and too many antagonizing interests and forces in conflict for it to make progress. Inflation, unemployment, depression, a deficit in the balance of payments, when it's not one thing it's another. And that's owing, apart from the fact that the country is on full sit-down strike, as that one guy says, since the Civil War ended and that's why production is so low, a real boycott on a national scale, that's owing to the fact that the Regime has already decayed to such a degree that now the same groups and factions that make up the Francoist party are the first ones to jam a spoke in the wheels. From what it seems, even Franco's inner circle itself is willing to support your national peaceful strike against the dictatorship, Federico said as he was leaving. And Raúl: maybe, Leo could tell you. Well it's a bad affair, said Juan. If they have so many allies, it must be for some reason. Here the same thing happens like with that business about winning the war before making a revolution. For what and for whom? Well, the same thing happens here. Talking about overthrowing the regime alongside the bourgeoisie is deceiving the people. If it took a world war to bring down Hitler and Mussolini, what the fuck do you think you'll achieve with peaceful strikes? And they know it all too well. That's why they shot that poor kid who set off the bombs. Arming the people is what's needed, arming the people. And Leo: the fact that they shot him is one more proof of the Regime's weakness, he said; the cat turns dangerous when it's cornered.

Obligatory question: can a fellow like Leo turn stupid, meaning, behave as if he were, or was it more about an appearance appropriate to the state of disorientation that he doubtless experienced upon coming out of prison after everything he had experienced in there for more than three years, or perhaps he was already an idiot before and they had simply never noticed? But this was not the only change in his behavior they observed: a certain instability, too, like uneasiness or apprehension, nervous manners, his laugh a bit strained, or coming too soon or too late, after a sort of stupefied reaction, symptomatic, perhaps, of a relative absence or alienation from what he was saying. The impatience that showed plainly through his silence while the father was saying, no, it's because we are men, Fortuny, and it's human that for a father the first thing is his son, but Leo has already paid his debt, and what he has to do now is to dedicate himself to his own business and wait, be reserved, keep things to himself, look how well he served his time and these people are judging him. Finish his studies, earn a living, get married, start a family; and although he didn't mention Teresa at all, it was as if Teresa began to grow like an inner tube being pumped up, how it swells out and stiffens and takes shape, getting larger until it becomes noticeable even for one not watching it, in the same way that, although it might have fallen outside of our visual field, a spark becomes perceptible to us. Impatient, uncomfortable, self-conscious, as if controlling himself so as to avoid letting fly some inconvenient remark or uttering some incongruous phrase, with the exasperated impotence of the one who only keeps quiet because any word he pronounces will only become redundant in the thorough explanation of a theme whose mere mention he would have preferred to avoid, so that it were better to feign absent-mindedness, as if Leo did not seem affected or as if at least Raúl did not notice that he seemed that way, forcing the conversation, unfolding it, for example, with any phrase directed at Leo when the father was asking Fortuny, isn't that right, Raimon? and Fortuny said yes, it was, that an attorney now plays an important political role simply by pursuing his career, limiting himself strictly to taking advantage of the legal possibilities, at the margin of all clandestine activity, and Federico was saying, well it's true, to defend the humble man from the abuses of the powerful one. And then Raúl asked Leo and they talked about sleeping pills, or about some specific tranquilizer, a surefire maneuver to change the subject, one of the few topics about which they could extend themselves without tension or reticence, once they'd mutually identified themselves as people who took pills, meaning—without it having to be said—that they each presented, although distinctly characterized, a neurotic portrait, more properly depressive in Leo, more nervous anxiety or anguish in Raúl, with insomnia in both cases, and to compare reactions experienced and secondary effects of the medication, always disregarding, as if by tacit agreement, all reference to motivations, to the cause of their need to take pills, always a very personal theme and, at bottom, no less removed from the realms of consciousness than the realms of willpower, regardless that in any given moment, for perfectly obvious reasons, it might sharpen the need. Obregón's arrest, for example, in Leo's case, and more concretely the responsibility, just as involuntary as effective, that doubtless corresponded to him for the fact of having contributed to swelling Obregón's police record, the charges which Obregón now had to answer, thanks to his declaration from three years ago, when Marsal was arrested, when he, Leo, knowing that Obregón was safe, hoping to limit the interrogations as much as possible, had admitted belonging to the communist party and maintaining contacts with Obregón, and later with Marsal trying, so far unsuccessfully, to create a university committee, a statement not only coherent and credible, given that there was no other student's telephone number in the coded notes found in Marsal's possession, but possibly even clever, in the supposition that Leo would have been quite sure that Obregón would never fall into the hands of the police, a more than questionable presumption, as the events had just demonstrated with abundant emphasis, for it had been, precisely, Obregón, and, among the sectors affected, precisely the university, so that it would not be risky to suppose, regarding Leo, that where they had to seek the immediate conflictive nucleus was in the mental reconstruction of his own arrest, more than Obregón's arrest, in the same way that it could not be said that for Leo the problem was properly one of fear when he sent Raúl the final order from Escala, received via Floreal only hours before he would also, in turn, disappear from circulation, as if to better underscore the gravity and urgency of the events, of an arrest that deeply affected the metalworking industry, university students and administrators, sectors that, apparently, between people arrested and in hiding, had led to a total collapse, without organic contacts of any kind, a situation, more than uncertain, more alarming by the moment, a chain-reaction breakdown to which someone had to react, in some way, however possible, to prevent it from becoming a true catastrophe. With no time to lose, he had to remove any compromising papers from the apartment where the student committee printed its propaganda and, if possible, save the mimeograph, get everything out of there before the police arrived, if they had not already, a risk that had to be undertaken that very night, as soon as they closed the building's main entrance, load it all in Federico's car, you and him, the two of you will be more than enough, it would be counterproductive for me to come along with you, they're surely following me, the Social Investigation Brigade all know me, considerations taken not exactly out of fear, not, at least, from fear of a new arrest, or not only that, from the fear of a new and more painful interrogation, of the physical pain, of more years in jail, the fear that he might end up talking if apprehended again, like his fear, above all, about what he might have ended up saying if the interrogation had lasted a bit longer, if the detective, overcoming his carelessness or his fatigue or his routine, had insisted a little more, the eyelid contracted so as to better dominate his twitching pupil as he looked at Raúl, his lips pressed tightly together as if to say if you haven't been through it don't talk, if you haven't been through it you can't even imagine what it's like, his attitude thus referring to an experience that he seemed to consider nontransferable, very mistakenly, no doubt, given the fact that Raúl's reaction, like that of the apprehensive man who, thanks to his own familiarity with disaster, ends up being capable of facing it serenely, it could be well determined, for having already imagined it too many times and, including lately, almost desiring it, arriving at the flat to find the police there, for example, the interruption to his current situation it would have meant, to his problems, who knows, perhaps even to himself, and so, in passing, teach a lesson to Nuria, who was so good at repeating, when something needed to be done, well, then you just do it, the only thing you need is balls, equally clear and determined in her judgments as Teresa and much more free in her expressions, a lexicon that to Teresa, in all certainty, must seem just as inconvenient in a woman as improper to a self-restrained revolutionary, strikes, scattering leaflets, police repression, demonstrations, tortures, acts of heroism, phrases that on Teresa's lips had the potency of an incantation, the gift of summoning the heroism of the people more than just simply witnessing it, when, examined closely, she would do better speaking less, that after all, Escala said, Leo's conduct has not been precisely that of a Dimitrov. That's the most that can be said in his favor: that he behaved with weakness. Raised in a semi-proletarian environment, Serra has been able to study, however, thanks to his parents's effort, like any other child of the bourgeoisie, permitting himself as well, also like any child of the bourgeoisie, to be a lousy student when the prestige of his political activity demands the exact opposite, that the communist student must also be a good student. Neither an intellectual nor a worker, Daniel, Serra has those defects that have remained in him halfway along, without the ideological rigor of a Ferran, for example, nor the characteristic solidity of our militant workers. An ambiguity that perforce had to be made clear in an extreme situation, which is exactly what an arrest is. Of course in an arrest the comrade responsible crumbles, just as Marsal crumbled, the demoralization is usually contagious to the other ones who've been picked up, and that's precisely what happened then; but that doesn't erase the objective fact that Serra's comportment was incorrect. Nobody was arrested on his account, that's true, but his comportment as a good militant communist leaves much to be desired. If he wasn't expelled from the party, like Marsal, it was only because he didn't bear the same responsibility to the party as Marsal did. After all, what did Marsal do? Turn into a traitor, into a police informer, deliver the organization he was responsible for into the hands of the police? Of course not. He gave an address: the one where he was living. And there were notes there, telephone numbers. And one of the numbers was repeated: in code, like the others, but also not coded. And with that the police decipher the rest, foil all of Marsal's contacts with the different party cells, arrest the connections who've not had time to get to safety. Serra among them. One of those connections, the textile worker, caves in and tells the police what he knows and part of what he doesn't know. The result? Almost fifty arrests and the need to rebuild the organization from top to bottom. And Serra? What does Serra do? Turn us all in, his university pals? Not that either. Serra is alone, he's the only student arrested so far and knows that he has to stay the only one. But he doesn't feel strong enough to take the bull by the horns, so he looks the police right in the eye, to tell them, in effect, gentlemen, I belong to the communist party, for which reason, it is my pleasure to tell you that you're not going to get a single word out of me, the statutes of my organization prohibit me from revealing anything to you. That way, face to face. He doesn't feel strong enough and instead is opting to try to fool them, to make the police believe that he's giving in, that he's ready to squeal. He talks about Obregón, about how he met him in Paris, through a Spanish student, the son of exiles; about the contacts that he later maintained here with Obregón to study a plan to infiltrate the university; about how Obregón introduced him to Marsal before leaving again. An ingenious declaration; talk but without telling the police anything useful, even shortcutting the police's guesses with respect to the university by confessing himself the only one responsible for the party activities in that sector. But what's ingenious is not the same as what's correct. There is a question of principle, an attitude when facing the police, that was not, shall we say, what Serra displayed. But there's even more. Does Serra really believe that he didn't tell the police anything useful to them, that he didn't compromise anyone with his statement? Does he imagine the police don't remember? That they won't use his signed statement against Obregón, if someday they manage to catch him? Reflections that, at this stage, everyone, except Teresa, now seems to have made, as if she'd ignored or might have forgotten all the details relating to Leo's arrest when she added her voice to Nuria's, both of them emulating each other with impetuous fervor in declaring their militant integrity, a political fidelity in which, perhaps, given its inappropriate insistence, they saw the depersonalized symbol of a desirable nuptial fidelity, with which Nuria and Teresa identified completely, however much separately they did not waste a chance to criticize each other, to create some distance, Teresa presumably lamenting that Nuria had ended up trapping Raúl, in the same way that Nuria lamented that Leo, who's really handsome, had ended up falling into Teresa's net; Leo deserved something better than this girl who's been waiting three years to get him into bed when he got out of jail, to really sink her claws into him and marry him and get him away from his friends as soon as possible, which is what she's trying to do by whatever means possible. An insidious campaign by Nuria, a contagious phenomenon or a coincidental reaction, the hostile climate Teresa experienced among their friends since they released Leo was something nobody could pretend to overlook, especially Leo, sensitized to the very smallest allusion, the smallest sign, getting lost in his own thoughts, drifting in the clouds, not antagonistic contradictions, but certainly aspects of the daily usury that in some way could contribute to his psychic stability, a stability put abundantly to the test recently by the transit supposed in moving from ideological discussions about the Spanish reality, in prison, to direct contact with that reality, or rather, with its appearance, so irritatingly plagued by oblique particularities, scattered incidents, disorienting exceptions, and parasitic excrescences, that the mere effort of keeping his ideas clear, to keep perceiving within such a tangle the key aspects of the true reality, was something that had its price, that was paid in some way, a sudden sensation of tiredness or somnolence, for example, a downy muffling of the intellect, manifestations of prostration that Raúl was capable of recognizing insofar as they fit his own experience, although, regarding what concerned him, unlike what could be presumed about Leo, every attempt to define the cause, the active principle of that kind of discomfort, of isolating the concrete fact, the word, the thought it had provoked, ended up leading him, more than to a shock from the depressing personal circumstances in which it was debated, generators not so much of a slack tension as of petrification, not so much a sensation as a state, more than to that, to a run-of-the-mill ideological discussion, to the debate about the praxis of some theoretical principle, to the abstract formulation, argumentations which, in the way a toxin infiltrates the bloodstream and infiltrates all the body's members one by one, seemed to spread out inside him, and like a fever, distanced him from what was being said, marginalized him from the conversation, isolated him, a progressive absence that with much difficulty he managed to assume as a thoughtful silence, sometimes with the impression of already having experienced that moment, of knowing exactly what was going to happen and then, the trembling of the feathers against the wires, the old man with a kerchief knotted around his head moved across the landscape of empty rooftop terraces, what Federico said upon breaking contact and turning halfway around, leaning on the steering wheel, Aurora bringing ice, the sidewalks of any block in the Ensanche, the terrace of a bar, pigeons fluttering their wings, suddenly meeting Escala, two friends running into each other in the street and walking together a while, the most normal thing in the world, self-criticism, Daniel, the need for self-criticism, errors derived from an overly penetrating analysis, of overestimating the enemy's intelligence, their danger, because the fact that the Stabilization Plan has not been a complete disaster does not mean, not by a long shot, that the Development Plan must necessarily constitute a success; we're not going to be the kind of people who surrender our plans to the enemy beforehand. The reality is that the precise conditions necessary for the triumph of a peaceful national strike do exist. But even if the conditions were not optimal we weren't going to play into the enemy's hands by proclaiming it out loud, nor simply cross our arms waiting for better times. There are occasions when a certain dose of subjectivity is not only healthy, but also absolutely indispensable. What would have become of the party if the comrades in charge of it had not let themselves be guided by that healthy subjectivity when, at the end of the Civil War, they found that it was necessary to start again, almost from the very beginning, if they hadn't believed that the hour of revenge was near, if they'd known it was going to take so long, and that at this point, more than twenty years later, they were still going to be in the underground opposition? Wouldn't they have been defeated by discouragement, by compromising and defeatist attitudes? How can you doubt the fact that without the constant and enthusiastic action of that subjectivity on Spanish political reality it would not have been possible to cover, as has been covered, the distance between the situation then and the way things are now, between the installation of the Franco dictatorship and its overthrow by means of a peaceful national strike in which all the anti-oligarchical forces will convene without exception, conscious of the fact that their political future depends on them demonstrating in the street? That's right, we must stimulate the formation of various groups: Catholics, socialists, pro-Catalan factions, or simply democratic groups, help them to become aware of the interests they represent, of the historical role awaiting them as spokesmen for the different social classes and strata, make them know our democratic alternative. The democratic alternative: topple the dictatorship; the immediate formation of a provisional government without institutional trappings and with communist participation that organizes free and democratic elections, the party's role in the new resultant regime, a transitional regime characterized by the party's acceptance of the parliamentary game, the triumph of socialism by a peaceful path; the flash of those lenses, more substantial, you might say, than adjectival, as if the glasses' true function was not to sharpen his vision as much as to hide, behind the reflections, his look, his thoughts, his personal secret. It seems that when he was a student he created the first postwar communist cell in the university, right during the time of the Maquis, said Fortuny. Don't mention it to Federico. Seems that it didn't take root, someone was arrested, but nothing happened to him personally. By contrast, during the general strike in '51, when he was already a lawyer, someone squealed and he was fully implicated and he had to flee his house over the terraces and rooftops; he was the person responsible for propaganda and they'd even managed to set up a little print shop in a basement. Ever since then he's been underground. He knows almost all the socialist countries. The People's Republic of China, the most wonderful country after the Soviet Union. I'll tell you Daniel, personally, despite my unlimited admiration for the Soviet Union, I've always thought that everything would have been easier if, as Marx expected, communism had not been born in Russia but in Germany. More rigor, without a doubt. Notwithstanding, although on the global level dogmatism indisputably represents a great danger, revisionism continues to be the greatest danger on the national level. And in Catalonia, especially, Titoism, because of how it flatters the spirit of petit bourgeois nationalism. And Trotskyism or leftist deviationism. Regarding Cuba, Castroism is only a passing phenomenon; Castro is to Cuba what Kerensky was to the USSR. As a spectacle, perhaps impressive to someone like Lucas or a crazy fool like Esteve. And Federico: or rather, an adventurer, a romantic. And Floreal: the very same; the proof is that when he wants to do something serious he's got to turn to the party cadres. And Juan: well, if you ask me, the guy's a fascist. And Leo: a positive phenomenon that will be overcome by the very dialectic of the revolution. And Federico, at Adolfo's house, or perhaps in the car: Abstractions! Madness! Have you noticed? This shows just how dangerous the police are. If when they nab guys like Obregón or Zorro they're capable of beating them to death it's because they're just as crazy as them. Mass actions in which you only see cops and a vanguard of the proletariat but upon closer inspection it seems to be formed mostly of students, children of the bourgeoisie, spoiled brats like you and me. And Juan: isn't that the truth? Shitty little brats, yes, sir. And the father: let's not generalize. Just like everywhere, there's a bit of everything. But I find that the worker tends to be best understood precisely by the student. And why? Well, because the student is a cultured person. The thing is that the lessons of culture, which until now have been the privilege of a few, need to be channeled to all people. Give the people culture, that's what needs to be done. That's why we've made sacrifices, so that Leo can study. And the sister: Leo is different. Leo is, how shall we say, a worker. And Juan: you be quiet. Don't talk about what you don't know. Do you think that workers nowadays are like ones before? I'd let the workers nowadays have it myself. Now, if their salary isn't enough, they take overtime and sit around talking about soccer. But wait until the Republic returns and you'll see how then, it'll be legal to go on strike, and then they'll go on strike for any damn thing. I'd let these sissies nowadays have it with the machine gun right in the face. And Floreal: and what's so wrong with young people liking sports? I'm sure young people in '31 liked sports, too, and who would have said, a week before April 14th, that there would be a Republic? The thing is that you're stuck on the war years and you think everything's got to be handled through violence. But the world has changed in many ways, and even Lenin himself, if he were alive now, would be on the side of peaceful protest. And Juan: the one who really brought about the Russian revolution was Magnus, and then Lenin had him killed. And Leo: the problem is not that the intellectual cannot be a revolutionary. The problem is that, though he be a revolutionary, he doesn't truly know the working class. He's not in contact with the masses, not integrated with the people, and his vision is partial, theoretical, only seeing the working class from outside. He doesn't know the true reality. And Floreal: the intellectual revolutionary, thanks to his greater preparation, currently has before him a great task to carry out in lecture halls, discussion circles, social groups, and associations of a cultural character, choral societies, sports clubs, parish centers, etcetera. And the father: Leo cannot get mixed up in trouble. He's really worn out and they've got it in for him. And Floreal: that's how we'll all be soon enough, the word will be that we've managed to convince them all, but we'll be eating our words a few days later, like in an empty cell, sarcastic echoes for whomever succeeds in remembering them, for although no one gave much importance to the first news, to the first signs of an arrest, a comrade's arrest, an administrative employee of a pharmaceutical laboratory, not necessarily proof of anything, one swallow not making a summer, one tumbling rock doesn't automatically make an avalanche, in the same way that nobody worries about the porter's ironic smile as they leave the building, although one does start to get uneasy if they run into the same look wherever they go; from the typists in the office, the waiter at some café, passengers in the metro, staff in your section at work or in the notary's office, students in your department at the university, mourners at a burial, how everyone started to get uneasy while the alarming information proliferated and occurred at such a rhythm that, for a moment, they began to fear that Marsal's arrest had only been like a rehearsal for the one now, whose true dimensions were concentric circles spreading out from the starting point, the presence of the police in the home of the person arrested, the search, the agent boasting about how the detainee had been tailed for quite some time, that they'd caught him red-handed with one of the big shots, with a member of the communist party leadership, the confirmation that said big shot was Obregón, rumors of more arrests, in the metalworking sector, among office workers and bank employees, that, through a comrade from the savings bank who studied economics on his own, the arrest had spread to take in the whole university group, tales of tortures, of a suicide attempt, searching houses to nab the ones who had to hide out, the news that Fortuny wouldn't return from Paris until the situation became more clear, Escala's disappearance, at first thought to be an arrest, Floreal's flight only a few hours before the police showed up to look for him, his last instructions, waiting in Federico's car watching the door of the building, going up to the apartment with two empty suitcases, the moment it took to open them, getting the typewriters and filling the suitcases with all the writings and stencils they could find, now without even thinking that the police, like a spider on its web, could be there waiting inside, waiting for them, for Federico, for Raúl, could also be waiting for them outside, in the street, to catch us with our hands in the cookie jar, carrying all kinds of stupid shit, look, look, pamphlets and handwritten drafts, copies of *Realidad* and personal letters, little love letters, look, Dear Mireya, I'll bet she's really ugly, little love letters between comrades, a nest of love and revolution, imbeciles, thanks to the fault of these imbeciles they're going to catch us as if we were communists. Or do you think that you're still one? What're we doing here? Why've we come? For love of Leo? For moral support? Excessive sweat, characteristic of a physical effort greater than carrying all that, eyes spinning like a whirlwind of frightened pigeons, the same irrepressible laugh from when he found out about Pluto's girlfriend, a contagious laugh, product, probably, not so much from the desire to annoy that Fortuny might attribute to him, as much as an exaggerated sense of the ridiculous, joined with the habit, not precisely new, of situating himself in the center of the imagined situation, converted into an object of general derision, making Raúl out to be some common criminal, for example, a militant communist finally jailed for his complicity in an aborted attempt, don't you see that Pluto, just by making a joke, is capable of spilling the beans until they bust you all? It'd be funny to end up in jail, not with the politicians but with the thugs. And he added: in any case, I'm sure it's better with them than with the politicians, a sure guess, absolutely, as if Fortuny weren't waiting in Paris for the smoke to clear, but rather with them, in Adolfo's house, with Nuria and Aurora and Pluto and Mariconcha talking about going out for a stroll on Las Ramblas, just like months before, when Leo got out of prison, before he started going out with Teresa and, if he got a little drunk, he still got euphoric, too, almost like the old days, mingling with people, loquacious and incisive, although with a painful tendency, perhaps not completely new, perhaps for that very reason necessarily painful, to offer a political interpretation to what could just be a mere alcoholic manifestation, of teasing, for example, some poor tacky person without class consciousness or fraternizing to excess with some presumed proletarian in search of a scapegoat, following any astute suggestion, possibly as insincere as intuitive, the affirmation that he didn't kiss anybody's ass, or some similar sign of politicization, a natural attitude, despite everything he'd been through, just like the old Leo, not cowed, not inhibited, without hardly drinking, like on the increasingly less frequent occasions when he'd still accompanied them since he started going out with Teresa, his circumspection increasing the growing distance between his old life and his new one, between his old friends and his new relationship with Teresa, conscious of that distance, just as they were equally conscious, and for the same reason, with all evidence, closer and closer to Fortuny, now that they'd almost stopped seeing him too, without which Raúl's progress toward the intellectual cell and the fact that Fortuny had become the organizational secretary for the student committee were sufficient to explain by themselves the change, the close relationship created between Fortuny and Leo, the growing distance of both from the group, a reticent posture to which, no doubt, certain observations by Escala were not irrelevant where, under the explicit references to Federico and Adolfo, any wise person could discover a clear warning directed at Raúl. The working class is not one worker, Daniel, but rather the proletariat considered as a whole, a whole that is different from the sum of its parts, and therefore not simply theoretical data, but, similarly, eminently operative in the terrain of praxis. The working class is not one of those workers whom you can just happen to run into some Saturday night in any bar in thc Barrio Chino, the working class is something more than that, and if there is an ideal symbol for it, it's that worker who works his eight, ten, twelve, and even fourteen hours in factories and construction sites, who goes from his house to the job and from the job to his house on mass transit, metro, streetcars, buses, from point to point in the city, a trajectory frequently more tiring than the job itself, that worker who lives in apartment buildings like beehives, if not in shacks and slums with fathers, children, brothers, sisters, and sister-in-law and brothers-in-law all crowded promiscuously together; that worker with a wife who, like a true companion, does housework and errands, extra hours, whatever it takes, because they've got to help their kids get ahead and the daily wage just doesn't cut it, this, this is the working class, Daniel, hardship amid opulence and not the personal and atypical image that Esteve or Lucas might have formed as a consequence of their nighttime incursions as rebellious little rich boys, especially Lucas; to judge from what he writes, one would say that the workers's job means sitting in the bar, in any old bar that he might slide into on one of his nights out, exploring life in the gutter, his encounters with drugs and alcohol, homosexuality and delinquency, prostitution and the lumpen—all examples, in short, of what a worker is not, of what has got nothing to do with the rigid morals and fine political instincts that characterize the worker—the only kind of people you can find in the company of Adolfo and Federico, on a Saturday night, for example, with Aurora, with Nuria, with Pluto, with Mariconcha, with Manolo Moragas, on an insane hunt for the filth necessary to justify filth itself, the lasciviousness to justify lasciviousness itself, the inebriation to justify inebriation itself, meeting up once more at any old altar of their ritual pilgrimage, before a bar swabbed off with a wet rag and some glasses not even dried off, and who knows if they were even washed, again running into the two oddball regulars, the two proletarians given over to wild Saturday night revelry, the two of them a little more drunk than the last time, the *charnego* from the south clapping his hands and striking his heels, goofing, reveling in his dark suit, his necktie flashy though loosened, his pointy shoes, and the other guy, the Catalan—possibly a mechanic, judging by the lustrous grime underneath his fingernails—now still singing his companion's praises, repeating his most amusing expressions, urging him to show off even more, apparently resigned to his role as a sidekick, accompanying and inciting him, now seemingly absent or absorbed, as if sunk in his thoughts, perhaps really admiring the guy—an Andalusian, or a Murcian, or an Extremaduran—and envying his nice dark suit, with its flashy tie and his pointy shoes, in humiliating contrast to his checkered flannel shirt and duffel coat clashing with his pants, surely rescued from some old suit, also envying the other one's diabolical talent for making friends with people, of amusing everyone with his witticisms, of seducing women with just a few silly words, remarks that would never occur to him, not even when drinking, other words and, above all, another way of saying them, not in a rush or furiously, like when he drinks and he blurts out everything like a machine gun and nobody can shut him up and then the women end up sending him out to take a walk when the guys get pissed off with him and he ends up getting in an argument with anyone, frustrated, misunderstood, maybe from his incapacity to express himself, maybe for the lack of an audience to whom he could be funny speaking in Catalan, more sardonic, more rural and down to earth, based, for example, on the interlocutor's exaggerated praise, counterpoised to an equally exaggerated minimization of oneself, a humor that in order to be completely effective requires the listeners to know who is one and who is the other, in a way that the respective situations of the one and the other in the community become objective and unanswerable support for the irony, but where nobody knows anybody and when it's not even sure that they understand what one is saying, it becomes just as impossible as imitating the other one successfully, the Andalusian, who's graced with a more parodic sense of humor, founded in metaphor or burlesque classification, essentially formal and descriptive, a kind of humor for which the Catalan simply lacks the language, the accent, the sarcastic edge and, above all, the facility, coarse, low approximations which, far from fooling anybody, are evidence of the joker's clumsiness and evil shadow, marginalizing him, at the level of a personal relationship, in any circumstance requiring a vital display of wit, rejected as a valid partner in the conversation, excluded from the dominant mood as long as the mood of the language dominates, limited to his improbably appreciated jokes in Catalan, returning to his exaggerated praise for the other fellow and to his self-vituperation, a contrast that, upon not being duly understood and celebrated, neither by his antagonist nor by the people gathered there, can make him seem a touch menacing, even to force a more explicit inversion of terms, making the conversation swerve toward dangerous extremes, put up your dukes, out in the street, man to man. And it's then when the Extremaduran has got to intervene and make peace and clear things up and put the matter to rest by buying everyone a round, the Extremaduran once more the polarizing force of the general attention, with the disdainful security of the potter who, as if deaf to the exclamatory astonishment of the onlookers, strives more and more in the portentous conjugation of rotative movement and digital sorcery that turns the clay into perfect forms, lording over the situation without more authority than the emanation of his natural elegance, complying perhaps not without reservations nor rancor for the Catalan, but compliant, one of those Catalans whom he admires for always knowing where they're going and, especially, that they go, stubborn, tenacious, always capable of distinguishing what's essential from the merely accessory and of going after something and messing it up completely in the end out of the pure cussedness that they have, a people who don't know how to drink nor have facility with words nor any grace, with that ability to start laughing by themselves, in excess and ahead of the punchline when they make a joke no one finds funny, and that because they're always thinking, because their head is always somewhere else, about what they have to do and to stop doing, not in the fact that today is Saturday, but that the day after tomorrow is Monday. But today is Saturday and there is no reason at all to be thinking about Monday morning, not even about getting home at dawn, nodding off on the first metro if—as is most likely—he's not got enough left in his pocket for a taxi, nor his wife who's waiting for him in a bad mood, nor his children, nor how they're going to manage to pay next month's rent, nor the excuses he'll make to the landlady when she comes to ask for the back rent they still owe, nor when his brother starts reproaching him about how he hasn't tried hard enough, what face to put on so he won't make any reproaches, that at this rate he won't be able to get married nor ever have his own flat, about how many back in the village dream of it, and when they bring the mother, and if when he gets married, and when his wife says she should never have married him, and his mother will ask why did God ever have to punish her by making her bear such a cross of a son, and the little children will cry, and the people in the shack in the lot next door will scream for them to be quiet, and the people in the flat downstairs will bang on the ceiling, so you might as well order another Cuba Libre and forget that you can't continue that way, without saving, without a flat, without getting married, living in a sublet and going out on Saturday nights, spending like people who really have some money, he, who has nothing, who is nobody, who is a disgrace, with a selfless woman he doesn't deserve, with some beautiful children he doesn't deserve, with a beloved mother he doesn't deserve, who is old and worn, who will surely die without the peace of mind of seeing him well-settled, because time passes by and he's not getting ahead, and he can't get ahead as long as he doesn't change his way of living, as long as he lives from day to day, trudging on until he's no longer any good for anything, that is if he doesn't have an accident first and end up totally disabled, living this way is no life, what you've got to do is forget, not think, think that you've got to forget, that life is a tango, a puff of air, a roulette wheel, failing and failing, don't gamble again, not with your heart, I'll tell you, not with your soul in your hand, not that way for the world, you're one of those people who would give it all away and so then they take advantage of you, the world is full of false friends, of bad friends, of sons of bitches, your brother, your sister, your wife, your brother-in-law, your girlfriend, your mother, all of them bitches and bastards, all except your friend, and you've got to tell him to let him know, put your arm round his shoulder, sing for him alone, so that he knows, that's a real friend, one and only, and all the rest are just sons of bitches, all except that one, a true friend, there, that Catalan, a person with a heart so big, despite him being a bit abrupt on the outside and the natural differences in character, a man who doesn't laugh so easily, less voluble and communicative, usually rather frowning, with the look of a person who thinks, who turns things over, a guy with ideas, with ambitions, who knows where he's going and what he's after, this gal, that motorcycle, I'll be damned if I don't have one before the year's out even if it's secondhand, man, she's gonna sleep with me no matter what, they don't know how good they've got it, if I was a woman fucking hell, drinking all day, night classes, correspondence classes, a tool maker, some kind of technician, specialist, and then they rip you off, and you, yes you, you say, not you, you pussy, I'm going to this company that pays me more, and if they don't pay me more I'm going to Germany, fuck you, you already know, man, that's life, like in the army, man, and then everybody respects you and you're somebody and then all the neighbors can fuck off, goddamn, he's got a motorcycle, shit, he's screwing all the girls, fucking hell, he's buying an apartment and getting married, and you move out of the building and they can all fuck off, they all smile politely and come around to butter you up, but they can all get fucked, and you man, drink that down, drink and drink and drink, and they can all fuck off, they'll all see then, when they see you've got rooms of your own, that you're getting ahead, married and with your own home and watch your wife just as you would your neighbor, the one who doesn't keep his eyes open better that he gives up, man, in this you've got to have your ideas clear, it's the asphalt jungle, man, and the guy who doesn't get wise will never be more than a tacky, low-class charnego disgrace, and people will just piss on him, meditations, without doubt, of a distinctly different content than the Murcian's, but of very similar value from an ideological point of view, probably because of his churlish manners, his passion only tempered by the mistrust of the fact that he's not sure of the ground he walks on, the colors of his complexion, including, they pointed out that it couldn't be any other way, the same as his companion, a classic example of domestic migration, of south-to-north movement, of country-to-city exodus, the farmhand absorbed into the industrial workforce, into the reserve army that the capitalist economy demands for its development, cheap manual labor, to the extent that, for his very misery and rootlessness, devoid of class consciousness—he also came from the country, from some backward part of Catalonia, some interior district mired in economic depression, in such a way that, although being Catalan and finding himself in Barcelona, his belonging to a proletarian flood composed almost exclusively of Spanish-speaking people places him in the uncomfortable and ambiguous situation of being a stranger in his own land, a case just as sad—if not more so—than that of the typical emigrant, the one from southern Spain, and of course no less conflictive, a circumstance that results in his lack of integration, despite being Catalan and a worker, into the Barcelona working class, a traditionally revolutionary proletariat, born from the decomposition of the last guild-based structures, the residues of the hierarchizing and negotiating spirit of other times put early to the test by the industrial revolution and its compulsory suburban decoration, cobblestones and smoke, distress and shifty rascals, overcrowding, tuberculosis, hungry legions aware early on of exactly what kind of progress the steam engine meant for them, ready to take justice in their own hands, which the bourgeoisie did not delay in proclaiming an ominous international hand, dangerously skillful in handling pistols and bombs, a reincarnation of the Anti-Spain, secular enemy of Spain and of the secular values that Spain represents, something that comes in from outside like a microbe and which, like a microbe, must be treated or, even better, prevented, with the traditional reactions, with a strong right hook, for example, the hard right of the right wing, thus verifying itself as a phenomenon, more than of approximation, of identification between the great Catalan bourgeoisie and the Spanish oligarchy and its healthy antidotal and therapeutic values, a parallel phenomenon of inverse logic to proletarian internationalism, a reality, as a matter of fact, more dialectical than real, except for what might result from refusing to get involved with the Catalan national problem, relegated over time between one group and another, like the ground-floor seats at the Liceo, for exclusive use of the middle classes, a meaningful indication of the elevated political level of a proletariat that, thanks not so much to its economic development as to its demanding combativeness, has managed to reach a fairly free and unencumbered, if not brazen, position, of a proletariat that not for finding itself, owing to its high technical qualifications and the fact of having been replaced by the southern immigrant in the very hardest jobs, on the very fringes of the working class, where the worker becomes a technician, and must renounce his sensitized class consciousness, relative prosperity which, doubtless, does nothing but accentuate, by contrast, our mechanic's bitter thoughts, the lumpen Catalan, the oddball regular, pushing him to seek the compensations that the capitalist system offers the people, cheap vice, the saturnine Saturday night rounds of cognac and whores, anxiously on the lookout from one bar to the next, propping up the bar, given over to the operation of selecting the right piece of meat, of adding her, even if only mentally, to his delirium of colliding bodies, of rearing ejaculations, a pursuit capable, although independently of the final result, of making him forget for even a few hours the reality of his situation, Catalan and poor, or better yet, an unprosperous Catalan, with a bad temper completely similar to the bad temper which is to a certain point inherent in the condition of the prosperous Catalan, but without any of the satisfactions that for the prosperous Catalan undoubtedly derive from a greater respectability, the logical sour temper of a Catalan who has had to emigrate to Barcelona, like some southern Spanish charnego, and to live in Barcelona among charnegos, without help, without relations, without significant figures close by, some family member, some person from the same town who has been successful and will now offer a hand to his fellow countrymen who followed in his footsteps, or something like that, nothing, everyone in a situation similar to his own, leaving the town behind like him, with one hand stretched out forward and another behind him, a town of unfortunate people offering misfortune to anyone unfortunate enough to be born there, a town without lands worth the trouble to cultivate nor sufficient natural pastures, nor industry nor tourism, nobody went there and if anyone did they drove him away with stones or nearly so, bumfuck nowhere, some mountain town, that's right, very healthy, mountain air, mountain water, mountain cooking, long-lived people, good complexions and thick blood, ardors that light the eyes with passion and make your eyes misty and fire the veins bursting with desire, your member swollen to extreme sizes with unbelievable frequency, just like that, from the slightest stimulation whatsoever, his cock like a fencepost, totally stiff, just like that, looking at those girls, especially the one with all the long hair, if they knew it, if they knew what he was capable of doing, how they came round to jump in bed with him, the way he slams it home, bang her and bang her and bang her, he drove them wild, if he had the chance with one of those girls with rooms of her own, like the one with the big hair, one of those rich dolls, and if she couldn't forget him, and if she took him with her to see the world, in her car; give me the world and I'll raise it up with my cock. The pause that refreshes. Maestro, two more Cuba Libres. A generous gesture from the other oddball regular, from the charnego, trying hard once more to light his incombustible Farias cigar with a certain lassitude, as if sleeping momentarily on his well-earned laurels, the glittering fixedness of his stare, his mouth slack after such a flight of merry chatter, a touch of triumph and a dash of scorn in his expression, scorn for all those who could not share his triumph, the triumph of being from a land that even though he had to leave it behind to make a living and which, like all those who had emigrated, like all those who would have to emigrate, a place he wouldn't return to for the whole world, but it was, doubtless, a unique land, boy, flamenco, manzanilla, the deep-fried gobies they call *chanquetes*, bulls, smooth clams, the impervious randiness of the women, the grace and flair of the people, truly unique, truly true, the astonishment of foreigners, the attraction of tourists from all parts of the world, something grand, boy, the white towns, the sun, boy, something the whole world envies, and he was from there, boy, he, fortunate among the fortunate, Andalusian, receptacle of that joyous beatitude only comparable, in terms of self-contemplation, to what another Andalusian might harbor, whether landowner or peasant, whether laborer or the owner of a large estate, uniquely separated from one another, definitively, by a few thousand hectares, the farmhouse and the Baroque palace, but each one possessed of the same conviction of existential privilege and the same rakishly goodnatured and elemental ignorance with respect to all that is not Andalusia, affinities cemented upon a singular coincidence of tastes and identity of interests, whose enjoyment, for the large estate owner, will be understood as the natural wonder of a harmonic universe, the spontaneous gift of a domain where each thing is in its place, while for the laborer, it can only signify something much more immaterial, a state of being more than anything else, a state which you can always inhabit again, similar to that weightless repose attainable through the practice of various yoga exercises, the exact location almost doesn't matter when one comes from there, all that's needed is a favorable disposition of the spirit and a little company and a little singing and a few small drinks, even if they're just Cuba Libres, within arm's reach, as they say, saying there I go and, as if conjuring up the atmosphere in the room, rhythmically fluttering a palm atop the bar, suddenly reactivated, eh, boy, *Viva Málaga*, back downtown once again, he was also looking at Nuria, doubtless provoked by the way she shook out her hair, for a moment his exultant eyes insistent, willful, as if saying to her, don't pretend, little girl, I know for a fact that you like it when they eat out your pussy. The call of the *taconeo*—the stamping heel—hands clapping with redoubled intensity, now impossible to pay attention to anything else, propitiating the precise unction and reverence in order to step out now for fandangos or cachondeos, the lively Malagueño, a night of making the rounds and carousing, *un tangáy del caráy, ay que me mu con el guirigay, que al Uruguay no me voy, guay guay, con el marabú, con el ay, sal y pimienta y guindilla y aguardiente, la que se arma*, ululations one might interpret to mean, *a crazy goddamned mess, I'm struck dumb by all the chaos, but I won't run away, won't fly to Uruguay with the stork, oh woe, oh woe is me, won't flee that hungry plague of ants, just give me salt, black pepper, spicy chile, and firewater, or whatever you've got on hand.* But the other guy, Mr. Stickhisdickinit, Mr. Tittieslurper, was in no mood for stories, waiting there with his arms crossed for the lively Malagueño to conclude, like someone agonizing over his florid coplas, and on seeing that those three whores were getting up with their johns, he immediately began, his eyes like burning coals, as the saying goes, and his nervous hands in his pockets, to scan the remaining females present, to size them up, to consider the possibilities, firm in his brutal resolution of fucking, of getting his hands on some girl, and finishing off his wild Saturday night in bed, both of them naked, going at it, tongue and groove, unwilling as yet to accept the end of each week, or the habitual conclusion of his desire in some unhappy transaction, with hookers, on Calle Tapias, one of those women with a macabre mouth, belly scrawled with stretch marks, sphincter broken in, used, and yielding, without giving up his hope yet, with the dogged perseverance with which a mentally handicapped person with homosexual propensities—fierce longings, if not impossible, indiscernible—guarding his stubborn intention of someday sodomizing the admirable citizen on the corner, whom he glimpses in the mornings from his balcony. Without renouncing the possibility of fucking some girl, too, of prying her open and slipping her the handle, of laying her, banging her, shagging her, humping her, screwing her. Without renouncing anything, the night is young, life takes many twists and turns, and it's a small world, as is demonstrated, without going further, by the fact that our two irregular oddball regulars cross paths with them again, now in the final phase of the habitual Saturday night Stations of the Cross, as Pluto would say, attending one of the last stations, a dive bar with flamenco and wild women, Mr. Stickhisdickinit or Mr. Tittieslurper working like the devil to get under the barmaid's dress, the Lively Malagueño screaming himself hoarse for a person with the look of a foreman or manager and his coterie of guests, seated around half a dozen bottles of manzanilla, a kind of petty Ottoman despot, severe and sarcastic, the typical Andalusian with a silhouette like a cracked and damaged tree, spongy, sallow, with a pudgy snout and lisping speech, hyposexual, without any room for doubt. They went to the Jamboree and the Venta, at that slightly lugubrious hour when the bars start closing up, the waiters winding down, turning off the lamps, the metal shutters rattling down, while the people regroup, frustrated, hesitant, as if disoriented, taking something like two hours to find some other bar with music, dancing, cabaret, some cavernous locale with flamenco. They walked in behind the albino, just in time to make sure that it was him and to walk back out again, just as the haggard faggot at the door finished rudely hawking his invitations to come in, all hope lost. At the Jamboree they hadn't done anything more than step in for a moment then leave in a hurry, as soon as their eyes adjusted to the gloom and the smoke, too many familiar faces for it to be attractive to stay there, unless of course their purpose had been to gather in a free assembly and move to approve some moral revolutionary manifesto in erotically charged solidarity to the blues of Gloria Steward. It was then that they saw the albino, walking just ahead of them, the memorable albino, apparently, from the first or one of the first nights that Leo went out with them, after getting out of prison, a purblind albino, so very drunk that, with the elevated lightness of the music lover, singing tangoes in that bar ennobled with horns and banderillas and autographed photos of supposed bullfighters, and the barman said to him, listen señor, show some taste. And the albino: listen, I haven't insulted anybody. And the barman: well, you tell me, if you think it's correct to come and get sloshed in my place, I'll have to put it to you another way. Wounded dignity. The albino tried to stand up and gather himself together, clutching the bar for support, with the rigor of one who might well be an authority, a person of influence, an important functionary whose services we might need someday and who, as an enemy, can cost us dearly: listen you, you don't know who you're talking to, you. And the barman: with who? well, with an albino, for fuck's sake. Ignominious expulsion, an incident that must have tested Leo's peculiar sense of humor: to celebrate the triumph of superior wit over the ridiculous presence of the exploiter, roles, in this case, difficult to precisely identify, to somehow connect with historical reason. In reality, that's all quite sad, said Leo, the night now hopeless, the disappointment and dejection ineluctable, no matter if they left one bar and immediately started arguing about what would be the next place, as if the happiness of their night out depended so much on whether they went to one place or another, as if the effort itself of trying to make things turn out like the old days wouldn't sharpen in them the awareness of how time had passed them by, Pluto's jokes, for example, useless, extemporaneous, if not counterproductive, like when he said that if he'd never gotten into the party it was only because he'd never smeared its reputation, and Federico's laugh became so hysterical that it could only end up provoking, in both Pluto as well as Leo, an unease similar to that which a misunderstood joke usually creates at any worldly gathering, as it forces a certain faction of those present to recognize that its laughter obeys different and even opposing motives than those of the others present, a muggy sensation of being hoisted by your own petard, a sense of fractured time, the introduction in their friendship of an element of uncertainty that could only infuse them all with an acerbic memory, as it betrays Pluto's attitude, now that with the business about Mariconcha they started to see each other again with a certain frequency, her anguished determination to make herself seem conventional at any cost, his nervous bewilderment as he kept trying too hard to top his own jokes, fluid, euphoric, absurd, the stuff of the Pluto of old, and that, evidently, not because the self-parody pleased him nor because he still believed that it was going to please anybody, but rather, more than anything, for fear of the void that might well be opened between them if, although only for an instant, he flagged in his attempt to maintain the tone at any price, of not giving a margin to the discontinuity under any circumstances, even at the risk of enraging Mariconcha or perhaps with the deliberate purpose of exciting her wrath, of exploiting the value of the spectacle that usually surrounds all scenes between a couple, an effect likely to result from any obscene or simply impudent expression, as you all well know, her lack of mental brilliance is more than made up for by her sexual prowess, her scintillating orgasms. And she: you want to shut up now, you clown? And he: the fact is that, at least in bed, we thrash as wild as a couple of crocodiles, right Mariquim? And she: that's enough, alright? lowering her voice, with the blushing restraint of one who really means to say: what are your friends going to think of me? And if she doesn't say so it's only for fear of ridicule. And he: that's why we screwed up and got knocked up, because of our excessive love of pleasure, interrupting the coitus interruptus, also known as *el salto del payés*, literally the farmer's trick, the peasant's geyser, a home remedy which some have dubbed splitting before the eucharist, not because it's abominably disgusting or bad for the nervous system, but because it's sanctioned by tradition. By having attended to what's prescribed, we wouldn't be talking about this, dammit. Meaning, if we'd rhymed our method with the rhythm method, if we'd followed her period, period, without trying to force it. But our problem is what we might call over-zealous rutting, just like dogs. Saint Augustine said let the member be vigorous, and, well, you see what we get for listening to him. This one, I mean Mariclam's clapper, or Marifluke's flapper, or Maripain's pussy, is no jaded player, it still gets a thrill from each new performance, ending up in ecstasy. Maripain hurled a retort he could easily dodge, with a roguish annoyance, as if amused at heart, that barely concealed her real irritation, the ease with which her laughter could dissolve into tears. Really, I think your friend Pluto's name suits him perfectly, said Manolo Moragas. He's just like a big friendly yokel. A guitarist and four crazy flamenco musicians, two fat women with birthmarks, and some kind of old woman, a queer midget stamping his heels center stage, thump, thud, a horrendous blockhead, from Mount Porón, then out came a little Nordic amateur, straight hair and starry-eyed, the tails of her shirt knotted below her tits, and the lesbians urged her on, tossing money to the guitarist so he wouldn't stop, shrieking like a redskin, her nails sharp, the indignation with which the house dancer finished up, stalking off stage, furious, scorned. And there was a sailor stiff as wood, lizard eyes, offering Federico a drink, looking to hook up. They talked about Santa Luisa. Santa Luisa? Luisa Valls, do you all remember her? Well, seems she's a lesbian. And Carbonell, that guy from the Sindicato Español Universitario, el SEU, who turned out to be queer. Like me? said Federico. And Nuria: nothing would surprise me less. What I don't understand is that there's any woman who's not a lesbian, said Adolfo. Or any man who's not a queer, said Federico, evidently for Nuria's benefit. See, you're not a man, you're a shemale, said Pluto, but Nuria paid him no attention; following the direction of her gaze, Raúl glimpsed Marislit or Marislut or Maributch or Maricunt at a corner table, alone, holding her face in her hands. I'm sick of this hysterical hyrax, he heard Pluto say. Nuria was partially crouched down next to Maripain's chair and was talking to her, and Maripain shook her head without taking her hands from her face. And the Nordic woman seemed to be tied to the post, naked, hair disheveled, wide-eyed, the lesbians dancing all around her. I don't want you to cheer me up, said Marifuck. I don't want to cheer you up, Nuria said: what I want is that your mascara doesn't go running down your face: look at yourself. She pulled a little mirror out of her purse and, taking her by the chin, forced her to stare at her reflection, her eyes blurry, horrified. Marigrief pointed at Raúl. And him? Is he a good person? This guy? said Nuria. This guy is a prick. Well, get lost, said Mariache. Make him go away. I don't want to see him. Not you either. Not anybody, I want them to get rid of it. What I want is for them to take it out of me. She covered her face with her hands again. It's not even four more days, said Raúl. Well, I just can't wait anymore, said Maripang. I can feel it growing. It's like a tumor that eats away at you from inside. I'm not gonna be able to stand it until then. And Nuria: yes, you can, you'll see. And Raúl: she better not drink any more, don't you think? And Nuria: why? Better she sleep. Did she get a little dizzy? asked one of the witches with the birthmarks. She died, said Nuria. Raúl helped her take Maripiss to the ladies' room; Marithrob's hands were wet from sweat, appropriate to a person tormented by anguish, to the nymphomaniac or politician. Raúl was in the men's room, half done pissing, and a guy stumbled in, puking, barely giving him enough time to avoid being splashed. Back in the barroom a fight was about to break out, chairs knocked over, and the hunchback selling peanuts—simply a tottering cripple, perhaps—was complaining about people's lack of charity, that someone had spat on him. Everything, the cackling of the women, Adolfo's unusual loquacity, the ingenious displays of Manolo Moragas, the sticky shine of Aurora's eyes, Federico's euphoria, Pluto's collapse, green, mute, everything pointed to the end, the definitive close, their final gathering in the Plaza del Teatro, under the watchful eyes of the monument to Pitarra, a Saturnian culmination; ritual apogee, the last date, the last opportunity to hook up, to find there among those gathered together a fraternal breast or a complimentary sex, in that blind bend along Las Ramblas, in that tenebrous sphincter of the dark before dawn, eyes, smiles, approaches, anxious observation beneath that stony excrescence seemingly humid and erectile, seemingly lingual or clitoral, a point of confluence for the swirling nocturnal crowds, habitual noctambulists or Saturday night owls, congregating from all points, flowing en masse through the shadowy streets, in a turbulent procession, with the progressive indiscrimination which is established along the course of a mass pilgrimage and that ends up triumphing as the diverse groups of pilgrims come arriving at the sanctuary, the different forces present slowly intermingled, while they advanced in showy deployment from their diverse departure points, from the Avenida Paralelo, Calle Tapias, and Calle Robadors, for example, on the left side of Las Ramblas, along Arco del Teatro, Conde del Asalto, Calle Unión, and Calle San

Pablo, the filthy dregs of prostitution along with the dykes in the singing cafés, the dope peddlers and thugs, as well as other addicts to the many different kinds of dildos available for sale; on the right-hand, north-side of Las Ramblas, along Calle Escudillers, from Calle Códols, Calle Serra, Calle Nueva de San Francisco and Plaza Real, the whores there relatively expensive and, in general, the streets of town with a more sophisticated tone, more bourgeois in terms of clientele, less popular, invested in exploiting both sexes, jazz aficionados, progressive-leaning students, daughters of families who are theoretically spending the weekend in the country invited by a friend; along the lower part of Las Ramblas, from the upper part of the city, like lazy outdated types with an aversion to working, the well-moneyed homosexuals, attracted by the tug of war with the zipper, when the prices go down, like in all markets, with the change brought on by a sale; and the rich boys and girls at the Liceo, also along the lower Ramblas, barely risking to show off their etiquette beyond the avenue's central promenade, sufficiently stimulated, on the other hand, in their viscous erotic progression, by the simple intuition of sin; and, who knows from where, the crippled beggars, the retards, the frightening oddballs, all of them coming out, like tributaries, to increase the river's flow, the multitudes already gathered around the stone monument, where, in the way of fanatical worshippers of some obscene deity, apart from the curious passersby and the inevitable presence of the fuzz, they came together, seeking some kind of satisfaction, the active representatives of all kinds of vices and deviance, wastrels, fags, drug addicts, sadomasochists, alcoholics, coprophagists, viragoes, hermaphrodites, a tumultuous concentration that a superficial observer or a person unfamiliar with the city's customs might well take for a demonstration or a public meeting.

We should try to make an effort to go out less, said Nuria. I used to handle it better, but now, the next day, I feel like shit. And Raúl: you're the one who always ends up suggesting we go out for a stroll. And Nuria: naturally. Or do you think I'm amused by your plan of going to Adolfo's house, we get drunk talking about stupid stuff, always the same gossip and the same lame jokes. What I don't understand is the need to see people every night. Is it so difficult that just you and I go out around there alone, peacefully? And Raúl: you know well enough that's worse. What you could do is not get so drunk and the next day you wouldn't feel like shit. And Nuria: and how do you want me to stand it then? Besides, the worst thing isn't the alcohol, it's the tobacco. Drinking, you smoke twice as much, and I think that's what gets me the most wasted. But without a glass of something and a cigarette, I can't stand it for even five minutes; it's almost a problem of expression, of what face to put on while you're getting fed up hearing the same thing every day, Federico's little jokes, those witty little boasts from that idiot Moragas, how Aurora puts on such airs. I don't know how you stand her. And, above all, that habit of criticizing people who aren't there, which is what makes me most uneasy. Oh, Jesus, all night talking about Maripain, the poor thing is so stupid, it's a provocative stupidity, as Federico would say, similar to those people in the movie theater who do nothing but talk to their friend next to them, but what's happening now? Is she cheating on him? And it drives us to the point of physical aggression. Or talking about Pluto, about how fucked up he was, or all about Leo again, about Fortuny, or who knows, maybe about themselves too, when they weren't present, in the same way that they started making cracks about Moragas, he'd just barely left, that night when he'd assured Federico that the king was gauche. At any rate, said Adolfo, better a bourgeois snob than a bourgeois who's not a snob. Don't let Moragas hear you, said Nuria: I've practically memorized his whole spiel about the difference between the bourgeoisie and the aristocracy. The one who's really odd is Ana Moragas, said Federico; she's one of those people who seem really fun at first and then it turns out that what they are is really stupid. Aurora challenged Federico: and that girl you're going out with? Why don't you bring her along some night? That's what you'd like, said Federico. Besides, she's a completely different case. Less stupid than Mariconcha, but much prissier. And Aurora: almost perfect, right? She spoke with aplomb, almost with indifference, hardly looking at her interlocutor, as if she were directing her words to someone else. I wouldn't call it aplomb, Nuria was saying on her way out. The only thing she's got is that unction of an already well-settled woman, a little bourgeois who's going to get married and who's closing ranks, her Adolfo, her penthouse apartment all decorated, a conversation piece. Just because they're living together without being married is nothing more than a front for them trying to be hip, it's got nothing to do with the other thing. If it weren't because in reality she might perfectly well be a lesbian, I'd consider her incapable of all those wild stories she tells about Adolfo and her. Considering how boring she is, you tell me. But it only took Aurora's presence, to see her moving through the living room, to hear her rather infrequent remarks, for all the conjectures and presumptions spoken in her absence to vanish as if before some evidence to the contrary, neither could Aurora's almost insolent serenity be confused with the placid satisfaction of the socially well-positioned woman, nor did her relationship with Adolfo have anything in common with a wife's contented renunciation of an independent life in exchange for the material security and morality implied in marriage, but rather with something much more mortifying; the natural dependence on love with respect to the beloved one, the unconscious tendency to be at every moment attentive to their desires, the conscious desire of carrying, as much as possible, such servitude beyond the limit of their own strength. Equally impossible to try to remember her in less fortunate moments, to revive her image from the past summer, for example, when her broken ankle coincided with some kind of condition which produced sores in her mouth, and she followed them everywhere with her foot encased in plaster, unable to go swimming, pale, clumsy, excluded; he was able to remember the facts, the events, but not her image, the way she looked now, superimposed, was stronger, her beauty implacably reaffirmed by the changes in her way of dressing and fixing herself up, progressively introduced by Adolfo, she seemed thoroughly more complete and also more sophisticated, with a decadent touch so suggestive as to have been heretofore unsuspected. Except for the terrace, where Aurora cared for her plants as if they were puppies, the entire top floor also showed Adolfo's influence, that quality of an apartment as yet uninhabited, almost finished, white, nude, without any kind of personalized details, the built-in stucco shelves and benches in the sitting room, the cushions, fitted carpet, the curtains, the enormous bed that would look abandoned in an empty room, facing a mirror, the worktable completely clear, like brand new, pipe and books arrayed as if to add verisimilitude to the setting, including the music, Italian compositions from the Baroque, operas by Mozart, cantatas by Bach. And the *Requiem*? asked Raúl. Don't you play it anymore? I save it for when I'm working, said Adolfo.

Federico went out with them. In the car they talked about Adolfo's novel. Do you think it will win the Nadal? said Federico. I'd be happy for him, said Nuria. But, even though I've only read bits and pieces, I think Raúl's right, you can't write about reality without compromising yourself, without being fully committed to your party, without having put it all on the line. And Raúl: well, I don't mean political commitment: what I mean is that nobody can write a novel about us, which is, in fact, what his novel is, a *roman à clef*, limiting himself to give testimony to a partial version of our acts, without going deeper, without at least giving things some meaning—whatever that might be—that make it literarily valid. Lacking all that, the tale is pale, darling. The simple objective transcription of our comportment, of our drunken sprees, of our affairs, no matter how well written it is, couldn't possibly interest anybody who knows us. And Nuria: besides, it seems to me, I don't know, sort of immoral, to submit an unfinished novel to be judged for a prize. And Federico: but if the judges decide it's good. I agree, said Nuria. But isn't that, like Raúl says, sort of an excuse? Isn't it more about how he doesn't know how to finish it? No, no, it's not that, said Raúl. And Federico: the thing is, it would be a lot to expect, don't you think? And Nuria: apart from whether or not the protagonist's rebellion consists in going to live in a penthouse apartment with Aurora, it's a great idea. Why, instead of rebelling against society doesn't he seriously try to change it? Moving into a penthouse with Aurora, it's practically a joke! And Federico: fuck, that's real bad luck. And only then Nuria seemed to understand the game, as she noticed Federico's amused smile. Indignant, and too aggressively, she pointed out that she did not like pretending; that if she had something to say about someone, that person would be the first to know it, that she didn't say anything about someone that she wouldn't say to their face, and Raúl stopped talking, somewhere between irritated and worn out or sleepy. Once back at home the telephone would ring and Nuria would carry on talking about the same topic, she'd repeat from beginning to end exactly what she was saying now, blaming everything on Federico, and he'd let her talk and then tell her that Federico had only made an observation about her way of talking about people, about her verbal violence, about her expressive crudity, and that, substantially, Federico was right, that you can't talk trash about everybody to everybody without everybody ending up finding out, and she would protest, the thing is that I'm not a hypocrite and I don't know how to be nice to people who, the moment you turn your back, start flaying you alive, which is exactly what they do; and he, having a sense of humor doesn't mean flaying anybody alive; and she, well, then I don't have a sense of humor; and he, and I don't feel like arguing about nonsense at this hour, and he'd hang up, and she'd immediately call back, mollified, Raúl, please, let's not fight; we're just going through a bad time, but let's not make things worse, and who's the one who's making things worse? I am, I know, it's just that I'm really nervous, don't get angry with me, Raúl, and the next morning, if not that same night, her first call would be, doubtless, to Nuria Oller, and she'd unload, telling her everything for an hour, Federico's meanness, Aurora's feebleness, Adolfo's equivocation and, above all, how cruelly, even worse, how brutally Raúl treated her. Verbal violence and expressive crudity that, undoubtedly, were not far from the sort of provocative talk people usually expected from her in bars and public places in general, nor from the fact that most taxi drivers ended up making her propositions when she caught a cab by herself, a kind of talk that Raúl had at first considered part of her passionate, uninhibited charm, but that now—for some reason that he would do well to specify with greater exactitude: adolescent vivacity transmuted into bitter aggression, perhaps—seemed to constitute a personality trait that was not only unflattering, but also downright unpleasant. And that was increased by the depressing situation in which she now found herself, her father's death, the sordid circumstances surrounding it, the new presence that her mother's relationship with Amadeo had acquired within the family; more depressing even than the chaotic economic situation created by the sudden death of Señor Rivas, the suspension of payments that threatened to become bankruptcy, that seizure of assets and freezing of accounts that ruins one only momentarily but ruins nonetheless, actual poverty, a less traumatic factor than the accident itself and the sudden solution of continuity created with respect to the past, but no less capable of eroding morale with its persistent presence, not so much for the change of plans this might mean for Nuria in the future, an obligatory renunciation of certain projects, the need to work, to deal with things, being the older sister, her family responsibilities, as much as for the limitation it would impose on her present life, a constant reminder, like placing a ring on a different finger than the habitual one, of the disgrace befallen her, the limitation of having to make a budget, of having to calculate, of suddenly having to be conscious, for example, of the fact that taxis cost more than the metro, or that a glass of gin is ten times cheaper than a glass of whiskey, of seeing herself in need of pawning her watches and jewelry not just to get some spending money but from the need to pay for daily expenses, a particularly hard situation for a person like her, for whom it had previously been almost impossible to go out in the city without buying something: books, records, some article of clothing, half a pound of marrón glace, doubtless not from some zeal for collecting or accumulating, since she hardly ever tried the candy, forgot about the books, never got around to listening to the records, and gave away the clothes she bought before she even wore them, but rather more for an unexpressed tendency to maintain as much as possible the external circumstances that had informed her childhood. So much pride, so many luxuries, and now look, said Eloísa, serious, almost serene, not exactly with delight, of course, but yes, in a certain way, with the relief of one who witnesses, once again, the final triumph of justice in the world, the implacable oscillation of a colossal scale, its two sides seeking the point of balance. Seated on the edge of an armchair, hands in her lap, she watched him eat breakfast, everything, the shady sitting room, the sun barely touching the middle wall of the garden, the newspaper open to the light of the lamp, the headlines whose contents she tried in vain to make out, everything exactly the same as days before, as if it was the same conversation or as if the similitude of formal elements might propitiate or prefigure the similitude of thematic elements, when meekly overwhelmed, shocked, Eloísa had brought him up to date on the death of Achilles. Look, Raúl. Do you know what's happened? Achilles. Achilles? Yes, Achilles. The garden at nightfall, the pile of dry leaves, the bonfire and, that morning, gathering up the ashes, the turtle's blackened body, stiff, cold, burnt to a crisp, poor little animal, the little animal must have suffered so much, details and reflexions that she might have well omitted, however much that not even by omitting would have spared Raúl the recurrence of his own reflexions and details, nor changed the basic fact of them being a dreadful omen. Yes, a dreadful omen, introduced into the panorama of his oh-so-obstinately rejected, but no longer concealable, private superstitions and maniacal rituals, flowering like an inexorable spring in the most diverse environments of his daily life, a panorama of obligatory gestures and systematic repetitions, directed to neutralize, as much as possible, the ominous signal, the adverse prophecy: the rigorous succession of acts that constituted his morning toilet or proceeded his nighttime repose, for example; the complexity of operations apparently as simple as washing hands or brushing teeth, the need to rinse exactly seven times, taking into account that in the not-entirely-infrequent case, of losing count, the surest thing was to begin the count again, including for the purpose of computing, the indeterminate number of previous rinses in the first of the rectifying series, and breaking down the last into seven more, with the goal of making sure to not end up on the number thirteen; or rather, the convenience of clearing the three garden steps in a single leap and with his feet together, or of picking up the mail on the way out of the house, never when returning home; or of centering the mat outside the front door of every flat he was about to enter and only then to ring the bell; or of always choosing, from a series of identical objects, the one in the center, and in the case of there being only two, always the one on the right-hand side; or use his pipes or shirts in a series of inflexible rotations; or to lay out his books and papers on his work table in a pattern no less rigorous than that of the crockery on the breakfast tray, disciplines only observable, it's clear, thanks to the implicit knowledge and even complicity of Eloísa, an assistance both invaluable and discreet in the work of counteracting the threat derived not so much from the fateful value of an objective fact or of a subjective projection—no less valid in practice—as, more properly, from the failure to comply—forced or voluntary—with the rituals necessary to avert them ahead of time, an operation destined to infuse his conscience with the moral strength proper to one who attends to his duties and obligations, an instrument more precisely defensive than expiatory, just as with the other weapons in his panoply, like the mediation of propitiatory elements, people, or things, an article of clothing, for example, or his recourse to invocative formulas, humming some specific song to himself, capable, occasionally, of firing the spirit's protective mechanisms, of provoking a change of mood, of making us soar, like some wondrous liquor, of annihilation, into that anguished post-coital state, when something in the heart seems to have burst and overflowed at the same instant as his sperm. All useless, nevertheless, when like now, after a night of sleepless agitation, a sweaty and shrunken subject of nightmares impossible to reconstruct, one mishap after another, slipping in the shower, spilling his *café con leche* at breakfast, breaking the worn-out mouthpiece on the current pipe in his rotation, nothing in the mail but a few odd bills and some hateful advertising circulars, heading out just when it started raining again, missing the bus by a matter of seconds, on the next bus buying a ticket whose number was only five digits past being a palindrome, also missing the metro, unmistakable warnings that today, December 13th, Tuesday, Santa Lucía's Day, the day of the blind, of Catalan literature and the modistes, everything was going to turn out ineffective if not counterproductive, the sterile emptinesses argued in the sociology seminar, the impossibility—one would say—of ever finding someone at home when you called them, the fruitless attempt to get a fresh advance on future translations, his request foreseeably denied, although the literary director at the publishing house didn't know that he'd not yet even started the last translation he'd been paid for, as foreseeable at least as the uselessness of his appointment with Curial in the Atheneum library, thus what stood out as the morning's only positive outcome, as the only significant success, was obtaining a death certificate on the spot, so it seemed better to just return home and not move until tomorrow instead of walking around there with his hands in the empty pockets of his overcoat, the same shapeless blue overcoat he'd worn in his last years at school, rescued from the mothballs by Eloísa with embarrassing alterations done by Señor Vericat, as a substitute for the one he'd lost weeks before, forgotten in the taxi or perhaps in the brothel itself, right as the cold weather set in, a substitution which if, from the start, was a little embarrassing, would not be long in proving to be, besides regressive, literally regressive, in terms of experience, returning after several years to Señor Vericat's house, a prestigious tailor solidly rooted in the family circle, the best tailor in Barcelona, people said, the most classic, even though, curiously enough, outside the family, his name didn't seem to ring a bell with anyone, a fact that Raúl perhaps would have never reconsidered if he'd not seen himself, forced by necessity, in the situation of having to enter once more that silent and shadowy apartment, where in any moment he might expect to see the apparition of a grandfather between the curtains, to face once again, only with another attitude, produced by distance, more critical, Señor Vericat's jovial surprise upon recognizing him, his mechanical way of speaking, absorbed, like that of a teacher become childlike from dealing with children, his trembling fingers, the stench of torturous digestions that emanated from his half-opened mouth while he took his measurements and the models and figurines from the deserted waiting room, indications that, more than classic, the more proper expression for all that was that he was out of fashion, the setting proper to a person who, peacefully settled into the immobility of the postwar years, has rejected as ephemeral the latest mutations in fashion, hoping that things will go back to what they always were, and who continues waiting, and only the identification of criteria and chance, joined with a relative stability in price, is capable of explaining the loyalty of those, doubtless few, who continue to be his customers; and regressive, besides, as a symbol, a compromise that doubtless failed to fool anybody, but that even independent of whether it was noticed or not, made him feel himself, in certain circumstances, like the soldier known to have launched an attack without the necessary artillery support, diminished beforehand and with his morale undermined, such as at the burial of Nuria's father, before the appraising eyes, like a jeweler's, of so many manufacturers from Terrassa, before the watchful eyes of so many present who only waited for the last floral wreath to be laid down to become a pack of creditors, people who would not fail to notice the detail and, what's more, with increased sarcasm, the fact that in the first interviews he had with them he was still wearing the same shabby overcoat, just as neither the notary nor his classmates failed to notice it, in the sociology seminar, however much he carried it under his arm as much as possible, or even just for that reason, alerted by his incriminatingly self-conscious manner, and even less invisible, at school, to the rapacious penetrating gaze of his students, the satisfaction it must have given them to see him arrive, hasty and crazy, completely distracted, seating himself in front of them as if in front of a jury, with the happy row of their small, plush coats as a backdrop, an embarrassing and disturbing situation not so much for how keenly aware the children might be of the contrast as for them identifying his own awareness of the fact that he'd also come in wearing his own school overcoat, only ten years later, the sensation of a lack of progress implied, that in reality, nothing had really changed so much, uncomfortable mistakes and parodic impersonations, Papa asking him if he could pay for the gas or the pharmacy, for example, more than for a true lack of resources, doubtless, although the cost of living goes up so much, son, and we have less income than before our big setback, and now the company's booming, I should never have left it, but losing Eulalia left me disillusioned, son, not so much for that reason as, obviously, for the moral satisfaction of being able to depend on a son who's already bringing money home, who writes translations or I don't know what, who teaches, who's a lawyer, who's training to be a professor, so it turned out to be preferable to take the bill and pay it although it came at the cost of selling some books or an old suit or borrowing the money from Federico until he could collect another advance, all that before breaking it to Papa that he had no intention of becoming a professor or, much less, of practicing the law, nor did he intend to explain to Federico what Federico, like Adolfo, could only think was some stock phrase, that his own case wasn't like theirs when they said pay for my coffee, man, I don't even have five pesetas, and they bought just fifty pesetas' worth of gasoline at a time and they didn't mind eating any old thing at any cheap dive bar, something that for them could almost qualify as exciting, for the impression it gives them of connecting with reality, but which does not correspond in any way with his actual situation, although it might be difficult to pinpoint that subtle difference, for the same reason that now in the high school it was difficult for the rich kid to notice the difference that separates him from one who only appears to be, economic straits too little dramatic to get anybody excited but keen enough to make one fed up even more so on days like today, now, once again beneath the street's brilliant lascivious shine, without knowing exactly where he was directing his steps, without feeling like doing anything or seeing anybody, in that state of mind capable of making any interlocutor into the typical gypsy woman trying hard to cast some good luck on a young fellow, picked out from among all the passersby due to his innate shyness, and to the one who will fatefully end up imposing herself thanks to her ability to catch people off guard, so that the unhappy young man will pay her whatever it takes to get her to cease with the show, now only anxious to escape, to get away, to evade the matter, flee up into the air carried by a pigeon, toward the gloomy ridges of the wet cornices overflown by the pigeons, the air an exaggeration of dimnesses and scattered metallic glimpses. He retraced his steps, toward Puerta del Ángel, not without first having discretely dribbled a bit of saliva into his handkerchief, as he did each time leaving Aunt Paquita's house or, in a more general way, from stuffy places, with cloying atmosphere, metro stations, cinemas, buses, etcetera, heading toward Puerta del Ángel, and from there, as if carried by the minor effort required to head down instead of up the gently sloping street, toward Calle dels Arcs and Avenida de la Catedral, the weight of inertia, the weight of money in inverse relation to its value, in the same way that nothing lighter nor more stimulating, including from an erotic point of view, than feeling against one's breast the pressure of an encouraging hand, the check waiting to be cashed palpitating inside his wallet, especially for that one who, trapped between adversity and his own despondency, sees himself impelled—his capacity for action, as well as for decision, blocked—toward the burnout of repetitions and recurrences, toward the maneuvers of compensation, a self-imposed behavior in order to be obliged, one might say, to not do what one should do, his libido inhibited like his creative faculties, no more brilliant when staring at the target of the blank white page than in the target of the white bed, yesterday, with Nuria, nor in fact in any other terrain, from thence his lapses, his forgetfulness, and, above all, his apparent unpremeditated renunciation of punctuality, his propensity for arriving late everywhere, indicative, with all obviousness, that his desires to go anywhere or start doing anything were really null. And his insomnia? The difficulty of getting to sleep provoked by a systematic recounting, the moment the light was out, of how many problems there might be capable of keeping him awake. And why not avoid thinking about them? Because it's really a question of not sleeping. Why? Well, to delay as much as possible the start of another day like the one before, that confronts him again with the problems keeping him awake, slow arousals drifting between what reappears oppressive and the falling weight from what is reconfigured, a sensation that from then on would not stop driving him all day long as if between two dreams, finding himself suddenly walking along Calle dels Arcs like some defeated Balzac, not piercing reality like Jupiter's bolt, not dominating it, but rather, at its mercy, injured and vexed and harassed like one of those adulterers from past centuries, exposed to the general merriment atop the back of an ass driven through the whole city, naked, sins confessed, surrounded by anonymous cackles of laughter and sudden anonymous blows, subjected to the cruelty of a multitude of every kind of vile, unhappy persons, redeemed of their frustrations by the simple opportunity of projecting their own vileness and misfortune onto someone else, of materializing them, of incarnating them in someone to sacrifice and through his torment be saved, externalizing then the jubilee and celebrating the fact through the streets, sauntering through them like the modistes saunter through them up and down in rowdy groups, perhaps making fun of his overcoat, hubbub and lights and pre-Christmas sparkling brightness, the chorus of the carols returning funereally from the loudspeakers installed who knows where, ashen December, somber solstice of Capricorn, the season of Advent, the announcement of Christmas and the augury of Epiphany, the inexorable course of Adolfo's good star that on the eve of the coming of the Three Magi was going to help him win the Premio Nadal, gold, frankincense, and myrrh for his novel *Los Ángeles*, a work with enough attractive qualities, no doubt, to impress the jury, youthful rebelliousness and objective technique, formal correlation and thematic rawness, ingredients turned into epithets, epithets made slogans, not promise, revelation, not revelation, consecration, and while Raúl persisted in his immobility, the kind of insensitive prostration that far exceeds what any stone experiences, a tombstone, for example, upon which the rain falls and which feels it falling and which feels the unstoppable erosion, incapable of saying no longer to Fortuny, nor to Federico either, nor to anybody, not that what he was writing was better than however much Adolfo had written or was able to write, but incapable as well of insisting on the simple fact that he too was writing, Federico's attitude was too skeptical for him to insist or offer some kind of proof in support of his pretensions, not to let Aurora claim he was writing in reaction, out of jealousy or spite, in the same way that Nuria's firm confidence in his creative powers, without any other basis for judgment than his personal antagony with Aurora, the reduction of a problem of competition to a competition in bed, neither could it serve as comfort for his undeniably sensitized self-love, to his distrustful defenses not exempt from wise prophylaxis nor the superstitious habit of not speaking about things not yet done, unassailable in his isolation. Better not to tell anyone and one day surprise the world, unexpectedly, with a masterwork, and suddenly leap to the highest rank, the inverse of Adolfo, everybody talking about him as a writer, but one whom nobody's really read beyond a few short stories or fragments of that novel that he never ended up finishing, his self-confidence particularly grown since he got up the courage to read Adolfo's manuscript, conquering his fear that, given their experiences and friendships in common, Adolfo's work, impacting his own, would have beaten him to it, a trial by fire from which he emerged nothing but fortified, not only because contrary to however much he was able to suppose based on the commentaries and observations of those friends who had read the unfinished manuscript of *Los Ángeles*, the relationship between what the one and the other were capable of writing was barely more than anecdotal, but above all for the resulting conclusion, his personal conviction about the superiority of his projects over Adolfo's accomplishments, the certainty that *Los Ángeles* was nothing more than a sublimated mimesis of Adolfo's personal circumstances lacking true talent, a world more like what he would want it to be than what it really is, more intelligent, more free, almost like dolled-up pedagogical intentions or, perhaps, as if describing it in that way, the author might find in the work of doing it the satisfactions denied him by reality, a work which if Raúl felt compelled to praise, it was only, putting aside the problem of Aurora, so that he would be thought envious of the writing when in fact he was envious of Adolfo's luck, not so much the fame or the money, for example, but the implications of the prize itself and the implications of the implications, the circumstance of being somehow protected from arbitrary police despotism, the Premio Nadal would be awarded to Adolfo Cuadras—consider it a fait accompli—for his novel *Los Ángeles*, in the ballroom of the Ritz Hotel, in the longer term, but with no less exactitude than the fact that tonight, in the inner sanctums of the Hotel Colón, they would be announcing the awards in Catalan literature, justly here, in a spot facing the cathedral, when all those stalls selling nativity scenes and Christmas wreathes would be closed up and, the sidewalks, calm and quiet in the light of the street lamps, from the fixed reflections of the cars lined up, without gregarious joy or Christmas carols, without those modistes dancing in a circle, hand in hand, around an astonished solitary passerby, those groups of modistes at large in the city on the hunt for the obese, the mourners, terror of vicious men and exhibitionists, cruel forays from the Cathedral to the Ciudadela Park, from Canaletas on down Las Ramblas to the Port, when boarding the little pleasure boats that go around the harbor, the assault on the breakwater, defying the city from the boisterous decks, proclaiming the vigor of the construction cranes, the dead weight of the overladen ships at anchor, the panorama gaining amplitude with the distance, as the wake they carved opened and closed upon the oily water, the Puerta de la Paz and its pigeons, the monument to Columbus perched there with his imperious finger thrust out at the turbulent clouds, as if calling the city's maritime facade to order, high ranking officers, Naval Administration, Military Government, Harbor Command, Post Office, Civil Governorship, buildings taking form seemingly conjured up by Columbus's energetic gesture, and the caravel Santa María and the fortified shape of vigilant Montjuich and, within its scope, the extended sands, perfect for tournaments and racing horses, triumphant Knight of the White Moon, champion of legend, personification of myth, proclamation of the reality of the imaginary, consecration of superstition, Troy lost and reincarnated, Rome in Rome renewed, transubstantiated into Rome, like a new god laid down atop a dead god, under other species, with the same nooses, the permanence of metamorphosis.

Awakenings like dreams or fantasies. The abysses that open in the mind of a traffic guard when, in the course of one of those bottlenecks that thicken the central locations in a city at peak hours, he discovers himself blowing his whistle until he nearly chokes, and not precisely with the spirit of reestablishing the fluidity of the traffic but rather, quite the contrary, joining his whistle to the clamor of the car horns, with a sudden, violent desire to become captain of the chaos, to put himself at the head of the din, inciting with his showy gesticulations the simultaneous massive surge forward in every direction, beyond lights and signals and traffic laws; or, rather, the abysms of one's own awareness when the guardian that rules it also ends up challenging the traffic cop. Thus, with the insecurity or lack of direction that characterizes the behavior of that astonished man, perhaps not so much for the magnitude of the events as for the inner vertigo, he turned to the right, from Calle dels Arcs, and headed down Calle de la Paja into the neighborhood, pausing before the secondhand bookshop windows and antique dealers, without any other apparent motivation than preferring that street to the agitated movement of the Avenida de la Catedral, the peaceful winding streets of the Gothic Quarter, the medieval city, a tightly pressed warren built stone by stone, laboriously, tenaciously, with neither refinement nor ostentation, the sobriety of a people faithful to its austere peasant traditions, defined more by its tenacious hard work than its natural riches, no friend of pomp and uncompensated squandering, a generalized propensity that can also be understood, as Dante called it, *l'avara povertá di Catalogna*—Catalonia's miserly poverty—and in the same way that an unexpected fortune—inheritance, speculation, the black market—facilitates in families an adventurous and prodigal or destructively wasteful attitude, which usually leads to a disaster no less expected and rapid, or, at most, to the ephemeral splendor of a few generations, meanwhile some constant investments, be they modest or growing, serve to stimulate the economies and, thanks to their transcendence in other orders of life, are even more important, causing a marked tendency toward calculation which endures across generations. Thus, Barcelona is the result of a patient collective savings, a city that owes its survival more to its own obstinacy than to any geopolitical element, a city which, if it cannot boast of Rome's golden halo or the absolute geometrical monarchy of Paris or the accumulated capital of an empire like London, can boast, at least, of a positive quality: solidity. A common characteristic, in effect, as much in the Gothic Quarter, image and likeness of Barcelona's medieval society, as in modern Barcelona, the nineteenth-century Ensanche and the new urbanized areas, whose spirit of frustration is a reflection of its citizenry's frustration, of its prudish prejudices, bourgeois rectitude, demure appearance, all facade, steady indicators, after all, as much in the Gothic palaces as in the nineteenth-century mansions or in the residential villas of the postwar era, of the fact that the rich people here were always less rich than the rich from other places, however much the myth that the passage of time—yellowed photos, family anecdotes, social histories, paintings of the age—arises and flows from this alone, making possible in the young generations, as the years turn round, the illusory identification of the provincial and underprivileged world of their ancestors with something similar like the world of Guermantes, which does not exactly mean that the world of Guermantes was not underprivileged and provincial as much as, perhaps, that modernist Barcelona never discovered its Marcel Proust, with no greater luck than in previous eras, a city without mention and news of better travelers than Festo Avieno and Cosimo de Medici, without other literary references than the purely anecdotal and circumstantial ones of a Cervantes or, in the wider scheme, of a Genet, without more living literature than at the level of *aucas* and *aleluyas*, a neighborhood genre, as they say, apt, in its way, for local application or consumption. Yet, all things considered, solid: prototypical fruit of an essentially well-organized bourgeoisie, each thing in its own time and each time in its place, take the wife to the Liceo, the lover to the Excelsior, and out with friends to El Dorado or the Eden Concert music hall, more vulgar and loutish, and by way of spiritual compensation from so much devotional social exhibition, from material support, from economic power, undertakings like the Sagrada Familia, expiatory temple erected in the heart of the Ensanche, that urban expansion laid out in a vast grid for the purpose of providing a better—and, above all, more prosperous—life, without its development there never would have been an obstacle to thinking as well about the other life, in that other ensanche extending uphill, along the slopes of Montjuich, the New Cemetery—el Cementerio Nuevo—destined to immortalize this passing life, to magnify there above the transit to the great beyond, to another world in the image and likeness of this one, posthumous luxury of mausoleums, tombs and obelisks and other showy monuments which, along with good advice on fiscal questions and timely testamentary arrangements, contribute so much to calm the fatigued conscience in its confrontation with the cruel questions, pantheons constructed one by one, garishly, their structure reflecting that tormented conscience: a neo-Gothic exterior, for example, something like a miniature cathedral, with its spires, its gargoyles, its reliefs, its stained-glass windows, its portico leading to the small chapel, and inside, in the center, the foot of the altar, and the dusty golden glow of the everlasting flowers, under the tilting marble slab, the opening to the damp green ladder which, between niches with dates and initials, descends to the bottom, on whose floor, as a kind of milestone between history and prehistory, a final slab of alabaster, smaller, square, separates us from the ossuary. The Sphinx comes for us all, Eloísa said. You can have millions, it comes just the same. What a fortune Ramona must have spent to save her, between doctors and medicines. But Jacinto's millions are good for nothing when the Sphinx says time's up, not even if he had a hundred times as much. That's life: some live on and others pass away and some are called up to heaven and others dragged down below. And the one who's down today can be up tomorrow. Look at Leonor, and I'm not about to start calling her Doña Leonor now, look how well everything has turned around for her, and with all the right gadgets, washing machine, blender, central heating. She wants for nothing. By contrast, everything's going downhill in this house: a cheap oven that doesn't draw well because the chimney is crumbling, the heating that doesn't start up because replacing the plumbing means tearing up all the floors, the drains clog, the light bulbs burn out, the dampness, the vents, the switches, nothing works here, everything's old, everything's broken. The best thing to do with this house would be to tear it down and build a new one in its place, completely modern. Ah, but there's got to be the means to pay for it, and as there looks to be none, I'm the one who pays for it, who deals with all the extra fuss. Like a slave in olden times, without a washing machine, with a prewar clothes iron, with an icebox the junkman wouldn't even haul away, not even if repaired, with the oven that starts smoking depending on which way the wind blows, with a stove that can't handle all the pots of food the old man wants me to cook, he thinks that fifty pesetas is enough for all the shopping, he doesn't realize that fifty pesetas nowadays doesn't buy what it used to, he thinks two hundred pesetas is a normal salary, I'd like to know who he thinks he could find to work for three hundred, anyone would be horrified just seeing the house. Like a slave in the olden days, that's how I am; and everything's going downhill around here. But I don't really care; if I end up in the charity home, well, that's the end of it. Raúl asked her about her wrist; talking about her wrist put her in a good mood. Eloísa showed him the swath of little-red-riding-hood-colored knitting hanging from her needles. Look, see, it's almost done. I only need to finish the cap. Everything else is done, the skirt, the blouse, the socks. I'll skip the bloomers. Of course if it's wintertime, poor girl. You'll catch a cold, eh, girl, won't you catch cold? She fluffed up the skirts: lovely, beautiful, who loves you. And Leonor tells me, you seem crazy, she tells me. If I don't like the cinema or even understand it, so what. And so I prefer to make little clothes for dolls instead of for the little girl, it makes me happier. And the neighbor who lives above my relatives, well, above my nephew, well it seems to be true, well at least they're saying it's true. She makes little bracelets and she says she'll make one for her, right, my little queen? She's my nephew's neighbor. And I might even ask her to do a little pearl necklace. Let the little girl's mother make her clothes; if not, why get married. And Leonor tells me, you really are strange. And you know it's true that I am, even though I don't look it. I don't care if I go out of the house with brown shoes and a black purse. I'm really odd that way. I don't care if I go out looking that way. I go on Fridays. Not Sundays. The house where I go, my nephew's, right, they were already waiting for me, right, but I realize that it's the day when they go to the afternoon movie and I don't want to be a pest. I prefer to be here, with my things. On the other hand, on Thursdays we meet in the backroom of the shop and, look, we watch TV and that's how we spend the afternoon. Because they have a television, and nowadays people are really rich or poor. Their little girl already knows all the programs. Don't you think she'll really love the doll? It's her present for Epiphany. She kept on knitting the skirt, her head tilted a bit to the side. She'd begun to dress the doll around mid-October, just before the bad spell began, the way an early cold snap, along with the fallen leaves, increases the obituaries. And she'd not yet finished: the slips, the scarf, a tailored suit, a fine blouse, another little overcoat; the possibilities of enriching the trousseau, of completing the wardrobe, were limitless. And on Sunday, devastated, she realized that the doll had no nightgown or négligée. Look, Raúl, what am I going to do now? Raúl had returned relatively early. In the little sitting room, the only lights the radio dial and the pale blue butane flame, an aria from an opera was playing, *Le Nozze di Figaro*, probably. Eloísa was listening from the kitchen, with the door open, busy removing the lace from an old salmon-pink petticoat. I don't understand how he can fall asleep next to the radio, she said. The music grew quieter. Is that you, Raúl? Papa called. He'd turned on the lamp and was waiting in his armchair, sitting very stiffly. It's *Le Nozze di Figaro*, from The Liceo. I thought that maybe you were there. I've been with some friends, said Raúl. And Papa: who are those friends who have a box there? The Moragases? I used to know a Moragas, a doctor. But they never had a private box, not in my time anyway. I went a lot when I was young. Before I got married, especially. That's where I saw Eulalia for the first time, and I wouldn't stop until I got up the nerve to introduce myself. After that we got to sit in the best boxes. Poor Paquita and me, I mean, the older ones. The divine Mozart. Raúl went up to his room. The window offered him a shadowy reflection of his bright room, not the night outside, the back part of the garden, the ashes of the dead, raked-up leaves like the dark body of an immense bird struck down from the sky. What sex was Achilles?

The problem presented by Uncle Gregorio, how to give him the news, how to avoid telling him, given his current state of health, turned out to be, in fact, precisely because of his condition, a rather simple solution. All it took was for Leonor to remove the obituaries page from that day's newspaper. And just like the child whose mother dies when he is too young to even understand the meaning of the word death, and will only understand that she has left him, without managing, however, to comprehend the brutal motivation for such behavior, thus he will erect the same defenses against that original injustice, those which will color his progressive comprehension of the event with indifference and even disinterest, the same as old people, for the greater convenience of everyone, usually get used to, without too many questions, the disappearance of those who have formed part of their world, turning the gradual gaps in their world into comfort at being alive, while at the same time sparing their nearest relatives the unbearable daily contact with that awareness, present but unexpressed, of death at hand. The important thing, for the moment, was to spare him not only the last image of Aunt Paquita, the tomb, the four funeral candles, the gaunt sunken arms of the crucifix, the black veil, of stiff, heavy folds, snuffing out the waxen glow of the casket and that body beneath the glass, its probable banana-skin quality, limp and empty, and the smell of Sterilair not even masked by so many flowers, but similarly, let's be practical, the hard trial of a funeral sung aloud, that windy morning when the purples of Advent were swapped for black, the black wind and the golden drifting leaves outside, borne aloft, like in the songs, upon leaving the Church of la Concepción, where, in the miserly light of the shortening days, he would have had to dismiss the mourners from his chair, alongside his brother Jorge, his nephew Pedro, his step-nephew, confronting each one of those faces, both mournful and stiff with cold, filing past in endless succession, offering their respects one after another, while the most intimate friends—or those most desirous of fulfilling their duties—regrouped buttoned up against the cold and climbed into the cars, waiting to depart in an impossible cortege toward the cemetery at Montjuich and, once there, retrace the route already followed when they had to bury poor Pedro, alongside whom Paquita was now going to rest permanently, a pantheon not like that of the Ferrer Gaminde family, centrally located and of imposing presence, but situated rather higher up, further away, and if it had a rather excellent view of the mouth of the harbor, it was much simpler, a simple slab covering the opening to the crypt, flush with the ground, at the foot of an angel with a finger to its lips, as if demanding silence: the stone guest. To get there they had to follow a path between the gnarled cypresses and the dark shapes of the funerary structures, a peaceful panorama that, along with the silence, broken only by the hammers tapping ever closer, along with the hieratic marble figures and reliefs, seemed to invite an attitude of reflection, respect, and meditation, of resigned solace, *vanitas vanitatis, sic transit gloria mundi*. There is, however, on such occasions, a general tendency among people, to try to hasten things along, to consider settled matters still being settled, and so, even before reaching the cemetery, inside each comfortable car the first symptoms of change can already be observed, talking about other things, returning to the mundane, to life's small compensations, so violently interrupted by the reality of the cadaver and only gradually reestablished in full with the complicity and the relief of those who only expect someone to open fire, pressed, perhaps, by the terrible justice of the sentence, let the dead bury the dead. So, an ordinary comment about the departed person, it's curious that by the end she couldn't stand the light, for example, that she only repeated turn off the light, shut the door, although the light was out and the door was closed, a comment like that, stumbles, generally, against a sterilizing climate of emptiness, that usually makes its propagation impossible. Ramona herself, unfailingly serene and measured, was the first to set the standard, as much for her presence of mind as, in a show of class, thanks to her own attire, neither mantilla nor veil, but a stylish hat, no dolefully dyed clothes, but black furs, somber elegance in her garments and tact in her manners that made them presume and applaud a resolute decision to immediately overcome the misfortune, to return to daily life without further delay, to reestablish habitual rhythms, fully aware of breaking loose from the sudden quarantine, far removed from old-fashioned mourning, incompatible with the modern world, rigors imposed by society as a preventive measure, moreover, defensive, and not understood, evidently, as affliction and desolation, as a precaution toward debts more than as a posthumous distinction for the deceased, not so much an emblem of faithful memory as an easy distinction or external sign of betrayal; a guarantee for the community of the limitation of the interrogations that unlock the blackness in daily life, with the grave risk of altering its normal course, of interfering in one's neighbor's affairs, a sure way to distinguish and frighten away the sad and mournful, the gloom, the silent, the jinxed person, especially in those places and occasions of a necessary relaxation. It wasn't strange, therefore, that the atmosphere in the cemetery was, from the start, not very oppressive, nor that, as if contagious, as the mourners began to gather again, the mood became light and even artificial, in the way that everyone made an effort to not let the tone decay and, the brief prayer recited, the peak moment of the ceremony—the lowering of the casket—happened as discretely as possible. They were talking about a town in the mountains that someone had discovered on one of those weekends, a lovely place, unchanged since the Middle Ages, intact, with pigs and chickens and a restaurant for having lunch, like that, in the rustic style, ribs and rabbit and sausage all grilled over hot coals, everything delicious, and so cheap it was almost a joke, so look, there were six of us, and the food, the wine, the flan for dessert and eight, no, nine coffees, how much would you say? Passionate expectation, everyone awaiting the answer, under that spell that causes rich people to save money, the satisfaction they experience buying something cheap, their love for discounts, sales, bargains, not simply the fruit of avarice nor mere compensation for their obsessive idea—not entirely unfounded—that everywhere they go people raise the prices on them because they guess that they're wealthy, but something at the same time more subtle and with greater substance, the tangibility of money saved, meaning, personally earned from the seller, in a way that's totally direct and immediate, a money of much greater reality, less abstract, than that produced by the mechanism of negotiation, in accord with a psychic process similar to what makes the soldier's sadistic instincts find an infinitely more intense satisfaction from running his enemy through the guts with a bayonet than annihilating an entire city from the air. Near Rupit? Don't tell us, it'll get ruined right away, and the way everyone has a car nowadays, it's impossible to go anywhere on the weekend. No, nonsense, near la Bisbal, really close to the Costa Brava. Imagine: people will start buying houses and remodeling them, and then it will lose all its charm. You sure have a beautiful piece of property, Vallfosca. Papa nodded. He seemed to pay little attention to those words intended to take his mind off things, refusing as much as possible the conversation offered by those faces which, as if obeying a systematic plan of relays, stood out one after the other among those present, uninterruptedly, from among that crowd busy exchanging greetings and talking with one another; neither the fluidity of movement nor the changing arrangement of the groups, constantly shifting between forming and dispersing, was an obstacle, nevertheless, as far as an attentive observer could determine, with barely any margin for error, the relationship that, in broad terms, could be established between the members of each group, or classified by their belonging or affinity to such and such a branch of the family, or in agreement with the motivations for their attendance at the funeral. The Giral family, for example, the uncomfortable ambiguity of their position, at once hosts, the center of the ceremony, as proprietors of the pantheon, as well as an excluded presence, relegated to a secondary role due to their merely collateral and political connection to the deceased, at the same time praised for the quality of the gathering, for their social and economic weight, and bitterly conscious of the fact that the actual prestige of their family name was not precisely the object of such a turnout, the true reason why people had gathered together, and also, aware that Aunt Paquita's passing also meant the dissolution of their most direct link with that part of the family, and the distance now separating them from their cousins was becoming unbridgeable, more concretely their distance from Jacinto Bonet and from how much Jacinto Bonet represented, completely aware, with the lucid pessimism of those cut out of the will, with the clairvoyance and even the relief with which a ruined human contemplates how topsy-turvy the world is in order to thus dissimulate and even justify their own ruin, given that, like that poor wretch after whose catastrophic conception of the universe, from which he can divine no other way out than self-immolation, hides nothing more than his own misfortune—professional disasters, conjugal quarrels, bounced checks—mere personal unhappiness that, through force majeure, he would like to see dissolved in a catastrophe of universal proportions, thus the imperious pessimism in families that, in one way or another, are no longer what they once were; even if, in spite of his condition as priest, Father Giral, of the Sacred Hearts, as he spoke of Aunt Paquita already watching them from heaven, with the same contrived naturalness with which a materialistic spirit speaks about death, or with which a faggot talks to another faggot when they get old together. How to not guess that for the Girals in their tormented reserve, any detail, cousin Ramona's new Astrakhans, any chance observation, any comment caught on the fly, the excellent location of cousin Pedro's office, on the corner of Gran Vía and Pau Claris, felt like a recitation of their own death warrant? For example, the feeling of inadequacy they also seemed to experience in the presence of the Ferrer Gamindes, who knows if because of Vallfosca or, more simply, as a consequence of the vertical perspective of a plunge to the lowest depths, usually the result of the very dynamic of demoralization. Papa, distant, taciturn; Raúl, now a lawyer and, as was generally accepted in the family, future professor of sociology; Montserrat, with her allusions to the Ferrer Gaminde pantheon, with her magnification of the grandfather, confused in her memory, one might say, with the image of one of those old irascible men in the movies, some retired colonel, for example, implacable conqueror of the weakness of the youth of today, authoritarian, sarcastic, and a bit mythomaniacal, what's known as a real character; Juanito himself, who even now, and with being that nullity of man who, in the emptiness of his adolescence, from some courteous and casual consideration made by some friend of the family as a deliberate compliment to his washed-up personality, seems to be English, for example, channels and settles his physical appearance, his garb, his knowledge, and his manners, with such sense, converting the jealous maintenance of that appearance into his purpose in life, even so, Juanito did not, for that reason, cease to inspire respect from those who knew him even superficially. How could the Girals see the Ferrer Gaminde family in their decadence any other way? Only the figure of Uncle Raimón, the reasons for whose presence nobody had been able to quite explain, clashed with those gathered, shy and fearful, intimidated, as if wanting to negate with his attentive and respectful attitude, betrayed only by the details, his denigrating condition as an insurance broker, the sickly sweet loquacity that comes with the job, the sonorous rumblings of his guts, the result of a difficult, high-pressure life, as difficult as his impossibly alleged honorability; nevertheless, the disgust with which Papa received his presence and the reticent distance that he maintained toward him was fully evident, in every point, as if denying him any and all right to represent the part of the Morets, a family name which, in terms of social class and recognition, was in no way less worthy, save in the case of that undesirable man, than the name of Ferrer Gaminde. It became undeniable, however, that the greater part of those gathered there were present by virtue of their connection to Jacinto Bonet, an economic power with sufficient weight in the life of the citizenry to bring together at the same time around his person—as Raúl would have to discover weeks later—both Nuria's father and Amadeo García Fornells, or spontaneously bring together busy people visiting Barcelona on business, like that friend from Madrid, such a Madrileño, with that admiration for everything that's happening in Catalonia only comparable to the enthusiasm of the Catalan for everything that manages to get done outside of Catalonia, all meaty and full-throated, duly provided with the typical little mustache and burgeoning double chin, that, in general, distinguish the members of the Madrid monopolistic oligarchy. The rest of the people there belonged to that class of people whose cultural orbit was harder to define, distant relatives or relatives of relatives, or family friends or relatives of friends of the family, cordial and respectful gentlemen, subjected to a pitiless process of going bald and getting paunchy, people hard to place, the same as the señoras, a tad uniform due to their common bourgeois pomp and their precocious resemblance to the Sun King, even though only formally and at first glance, without the halo, with a touch of Louis XIV, in effect, but more reserved in their impertinent and foolish self-assurance, more stuffed-full, with that invertebrate and definitive inert quality of the calamari which, along with some other features, characterizes them, the sphincter-like mouth, prudishly pursed between flaccid hungry jowls, eyes only dully alive, eminently stingy, and those powdery little wrinkles formed from smiling so much at young ones, and the rigid blond hair teased into a solemn tower, and the small pearl earring set discretely in each earlobe, and above all, when smiling, the teeth, now almost like those of a skull; and then, the questions from that gentleman we don't recognize, but who recognizes us, you're Jorge's son, more assertive than informative, all wisdom and sharp perspicacity between his contracted saurian folds, with his singular knowledge of the human soul which, apart from an old man, only an attorney can have, thanks to his daily contact with the reality of life and death, of bequests and inheritances, ins and outs and hidden snags. And so what do you do for a living, he asked. Montserrat was talking about Gregorius's wedding, the trip to Teruel, Leonor's family from Aragon, they're splendid people and quite well-positioned, from the country, but people of position, with land, and as they are so many—the siblings even have grandchildren—and all of them determined to flatter us with gifts, and what with Teruel being the land of *jamón serrano* and since I more or less represented the groom's family, I've never seen people eat so much, the least of it was the wedding reception itself, which was outrageous, but it was just one big party after another, and with the wine from that area, it hits you like a hammer, like wine from Cariñena, and on top of it all, after the wedding, one of the brothers-in-law, who lives in Vinarós and he owns a shipping agency, who insists on inviting us to Vinarós, to eat prawns, exactly what Gregorius needed, considering how much he loves prawns. I left them there, I wasn't going to act like some chaperone on a honeymoon, and it looks like they made it all the way to Valencia;

I'm not saying that business about the infection he got from the injection didn't contribute to causing his collapse, but what I can assure you is that all the big dinner parties those days were enough to raise the cholesterol of a whole army regiment. Look, the lucky thing is that it was no more than a scare. And, above all, Leonor de Aragón's luck, she's a really good woman, with her character, with her spirit, like everybody, but with a heart this big. It's her luck, she couldn't have found a better companion. She bathes him, tidies him up, helps him get dressed and looking smart, she looks after him, she takes him out for a walk, and when the weather's bad, she takes him to shows, to the big department stores, to the Corte Inglés, once I think she even took him to the grand opening of a new metro station, she arranges everything to entertain him any way possible and, look, she looks out for him and she's got the patience of a saint, considering how peculiar and careless Gregorius is, and how he was hooked on barbiturates, there was a moment when he was fit to be tied, when I thought he wasn't going to come out of it, that's how things would be for us, and look how I, unfortunately, have experience in seeing how things can go belly up. What would a disastrous bachelor like him have done, who would have taken care of him like she has, however much we all love him, if they'd not gotten married? The truth is, I like seeing them walking arm in arm through the park, like two lovebirds. I call them the lovers of Teruel. Scabrous point, right at the limit of what can be aired in public, there where the slight non-antagonistic conflict, considered outside the heart of the family, could become an antagony, where the raw enunciation of the facts—he married his housemaid—deprived of the heat of their context, could not help but make the Ferrer Gaminde family close ranks, now that, at last, with the exception of Juanito—he's intolerant, I don't understand—it was the general position to consider such an outcome as a lesser evil, and now he's got better company, and besides, he had to straighten out his life some way. Papa, after the shock, had even stopped blaming Gregorius for selling his share of Vallfosca to Jacinto Bonet, almost as if he regretted having accused him previously, what do you want, if he was interested in selling his share, the only person in the family who could have bought it was Jacinto Bonet. Better him than some stranger. Of course. I think he's done well; what he needs is a steady income. Why does he want to hang onto property that generates no income if he's neither got nor going to have any children? So that the State can just take more than half of it when he dies? I wouldn't be surprised if Leonor pushed him into doing it, that between leaving something to her nieces and nephews or Gregorius's, she must certainly prefer to bequeath something to her own family, something that can be easily liquidated, something easier to hand out than a portion of an undivided bequest.

Well, I think that, more than anything, he's done this because it must have been embarrassing for him to go there with her, playing the role of his wife. Don't think, in fact for years he's barely made ends meet, and the truth is that lately he's not been so buoyant either, economically I mean, the same amount that used to let you live like a prince is now barely enough to survive on. I'll let you know we also go up there very infrequently; Pedro goes the most, some weekend now and again, with his bunch, half a dozen cars. The only one who really keeps going there is Uncle Jorge. I don't know, it seems a shame to me, especially since Polit died, he was a scoundrel, a sly fox, a smooth operator, you name it, but, look, he had a big heart; in Vallfosca he was practically an institution. Now, look, with those Andalusians who don't take care of anything, that what's happening, I think, is that they've not made things clear with each other, I mean, they're not *payeses*, not real farmers, not from there. No, it's not that, the problem is that the land just doesn't produce anymore. And, besides all that, there aren't any more real peasants, no real farmers like years ago. Exactly, because now the land doesn't produce. And where it does produce they buy a tractor and they work it themselves; what they don't want to do is work for someone else. Oh, that business of sharecropping is history now; nowadays, if you find a husband and wife from Andalusia who want to care for your property a little, charging only whatever occurs to them to ask you for, you can consider yourself satisfied. Let me tell you that some of them are very fussy and tidy in their work. Unfortunately, that's not the case with the one taking care of Vallfosca. Paco, Pepe, or whatever his name is, I never remember, just one rough Extremaduran like him. Well, with things the way they are, it's almost better that Gregorius doesn't even go near the place, now that everything is so abandoned. Gregorius? The last time he was there Polit was still alive. Abandoned, yes, that was the word, abandoned more than untended, the crops, the terraced fields, the grape vines overgrown with grass, the forest growing in around the clearings, paths lost, roads that no longer lead anywhere, rutted, eroded, what were cart tracks now turned into dry washes, the garden choked with brambles, the ivy spreading, the weeds and undergrowth hardly cleared back from the house. As far as the inside of the house, only a superficial impression could make you suppose that it was kept up the same, not smelling, not noticing the deterioration that comes from use just as much as from disuse, from the lack of life-giving contact for objects, which means using them, inhabiting them. The vestibule, the stairs, the dining room, the parlor, the verandah, the bedrooms, especially the bedrooms, progressively emptied of furniture, untouched, as if tied to the destiny of their titular occupants, assigned to them for life. Gregorius's room, for example, with less disorder than Papa's room, but in far worse shape, almost stripped of personal elements, as if it really belonged to a pension in town, with that aroma like a crushed-out cigar that impregnated it instead of that drugstore smell that dominated Papa's room, without the chaotic accumulation of Papa's room, without his leftover medications, nor his collections of insects, nor his books of botany filled with dried, pressed leaves, nor his law textbooks from when he was a student, nor his walking sticks, nor his binoculars, nor the collection of materials for his little inventions that always made it impossible to close the bureau. And between both of them, Aunt Paquita's room, closed, but intact, exactly the same in appearance as the last summer that she spent there—ten? twelve years ago?—so much exactly the same that, doubtless, it must turn out to be surprising to not see the gloom, her pupils looking up from the pillow, her soft eyelids, her sickly sweet breath, the bed warmed by her intimate emanations. Everything so identical, but only in appearance. Because just as in nations, so it goes in the patriarchal home—*la casa pairal*; like in those nations subject to the inevitable phases of splendor, decadence, and rebirth, like in that nation that after a period of dissolution and absentee landownership, of abnegation of all responsibility toward public concerns, of general surrender to the corruption of private enterprise, there arises a patent need for someone to put an end to the dissolution and laxity and, with a firm hand, take the reins of power and wield them in an absolute and totalitarian way, like in that nation, in *las casas pairales*, following a whole period of undivided atomization and necrosis of the family ties, families also end up imposing the condition that the property in the end reverts to a sole responsible proprietor.

Let's see: Raúl Ferrer Gaminde i Moret, son of Jorge and Eulalia. That's right, his name was Jorge. I knew your father, just as good as he was crazy. Is he still alive? Drawn up February 6, 1960. So you're a lawyer too, eh? Or rather, you represent the widow Rivas, according to the powers that Doña Dulce authorized in my presence last December, general powers in favor of, indirectly, Señor Bellido and yourself.

Why do lawyers' offices always have that vague resemblance to police headquarters or, more certainly, the atmosphere of a grandfather's apartment? Perhaps owing to their dark, heavy decorative elements? That's right, with a placidity and prosperity not frequently seen in mere offices, public and private alike, for however long and uncomfortable the wait in the anteroom might be, in the reception area, in the hallways and even among the stacks of files and the typewriters, alongside the desk of a graying official—superior in knowledge, doubtless, as well as in dedication, to the lawyer himself—where even the words of his dictation and the secretary typing, far from bewildering, produce in the client a rather more soothing and invigorating effect, the way the spring rain does to the farmer, words that are heard the way one inside the house hears the rain pattering outside, comfortably, the encouraging mystery of the juridical formulas, the ritual rigor of the terminology employed, sounding almost like a prayer, psychologically supporting the confidence the client places in the mechanism of the profession, in its incorruptible probity, a secular defender of the individual's interest in the face of the Administration and, more specifically, when facing the Treasury, according to tradition—especially in Catalonia—of singular antiquity and deep roots, *et propter enmendacionem ipsius culpe per hanc scripturam donations nostre damus vobis ipsum Castrum quod dicunt Portus quod est in territorio barchinonensi a parte occidentali predicte urbis ad calcem montis cuiusadam qui vocatur iudaicus in marinis litoribus*. All that, joined to the character, more desired than merely voluntary, of the agreements normally contracted in lawyers' offices, as well as the habitual happy ending of the events, contributes to the fact that inner peace shines through the features of so many who otherwise remain self-absorbed there, who, standing at the ticket window in a station, so parsimoniously gather their change after buying their ticket, conscious that they, unlike most of the people waiting impatiently behind them, will take the next train without racing to catch it; and that the chatting from more garrulous clients with any one of those aged amanuenses has that tone somewhere between conciliatory and viciously crafty belonging to the general ideas that tend, in such cases, to be imposed as a conversational theme, the advantages created by the State granting concessions to private capital for Telefonica or railroads, for example, how rapidly the result would be achieved, how quickly service would be improved, because the State can't, not if there's no stimulus, not if there's no initiative, because stealing from the State is no sin, it's for the good of the individual, because taking your complaints to the bureaucracy is a waste of time, because the bureaucracy is just a crooked free-for-all, blame the blacks, blame the Chinese, because with a half-dozen atom bombs, because Chinese cooking, let's be honest, I think we understand each other, Chinese cooking can't hold a candle to a good plate of *butifarra con judías*. Thence the animation and good humor and that man's crafty eyes, undoubtedly a minor industrialist, who invited the graying official to have a smoke while he took a final glance at the key clauses of some document awaiting a signature, enriching the contractual aridity with vivid commentaries about the development of the negotiations whose culmination and synthesis were the present contract, without ceasing to point with his winks toward the waiting room, where, it seems, the other party was waiting, the buyer, a foreign investor, a German, representative, from the looks of it, of a firm interested in the industrial sites for sale, interested and it's not risky to suppose—given that he bought them—even satisfied with the conditions of acquisition, conditions that he probably judged advantageous, without ever suspecting that the minor industrialist Bertrán judged them to be even more advantageous for himself, Bertrán, as he called himself, or Beltrán, happy liquidator of an industry amortized a hundred times, of equipment never renovated so as to not lessen the benefits, everything always ready for when the moment arrives—as it had doubtless arrived—in which prospects seem to worsen, and he could then convert, without further ado, his company into a ruined enterprise, resort to filing an official statement of financial difficulties and shake off the death with maximum celerity and neatness; and then, money in hand, on to something new, public works contracts, plastics, suburban developments, what most represents what is called an occasion, an opportunity, what turns out the best, the same as a soldier of fortune goes wherever they pay the best, just like his glorious medieval ancestors, the Almogavars, who trooped to Sicily, Tunisia, Greece, Turkey. Yes, like the Almogavars, like them that Bertrán or Beltrán and so many like him, small-time and middling businessmen, who constitute the vanguard of the Catalan industrial collective; and as with the Almogavars, the first impression you can have of them being rather negative or unfavorable, due to their mere presence, only serves to facilitate the later inversion of that first pejorative image in favor of one of admiration and astonishment when faced with their innate fighting mettle, speed, and fearlessness. People with clear ideas, who laugh at those who don't know how important it is to laugh first, to get off to a good start, and to get the last word. Woe betide the one who underestimates their reactions and resourcefulness or downplays their mobility and business sense, their killer instinct, true Almogavars of our time, hardened, pugnacious men skilled in schemes and stratagems, as Josep Sol i Padrís, the great poet of Valencian Romanticism, sang of their resolution, especially when their swords shone anew as they cried *Desperta, ferro!*—Iron, Awake!—yes, that's how jealously they defend their enterprises. Let's not despise, then, the small Catalan industrialists nor underestimate their positive attributes in the name of abstract principles, nor let us ignore their capacity for maneuvering because of, for example, their assumed individualism or a presumed absence of associative mentality which impedes them from joining with others in the task of creating the true industrial empire, the gigantic enterprise demanded by the economy of today; nothing more deceitful than letting yourself be carried away by theoretical schemes or by prejudices relating to ancillary matters, their gross tastes, their ostentations, their delusions of tycoon grandeur, their heavy-handed manners, characteristics explainable in the long run by virtue of the mimetic relationship that tends to become established between the man and his business, in such a way that, as it isn't difficult to suss out in the herdsman attitudes and even traits of his livestock, similarly there exists an evident correlation between a mechanism's repetitious function and the social comportment of a representative of small-time and mid-level industries. To our understanding, there is only one single proper and pertinent yardstick to measure the worth of those small and mid-level businessmen of that industrial collective: their undeniable, better yet, their extraordinary talent for making money; any other basis of judgment would not be more adequate; for example, estimating the Almogavars not for their excellent fighting skills but for their rough aspect or their rudimentary arms. It was precisely this error, and none other, that cost Gulaterio de Brionne and his French horsemen their lives, when they saw that ragged infantry, without understanding that the troops' lack of a shield was its best shield, that its light tunic was its best mount, that its predilection for stones among all weapons fired, flung, or hurled was its best source of arming itself and, above all, that that miserable appearance was, precisely, its great secret weapon: the surprise factor. The ermine's counterpart: the dog that hunts it; the same for the collective industrial enterprise, perfectly knowledgeable that, like the French cavalry, there are few things more vulnerable than an industry *comme il faut*, where, in general, its Achilles heel is usually nothing more than its own prestige.

Trompas, tabors, senheras e penos et entresenhs e chavals blanc e niers veirem en brieu.

E no pot enser remasut, contra cel no volen tronzo, e que cendat e cisclato e samit no.i sian romput, cordas, tendas, bechas, paisso e trap e pavilho tendut.

Adoncs veirem aur et argen despendre, peirieiras far destrapar e destendre, murs esfondrar, tors baissar e deissandre e.ls enemics enchadenar e prendre.

Tan grans colps los ferrem nos drut.
Lo perdr'er grans e.l grazanhs er sobriers.
Anz sera tics qui tobra volontiers.

Trumpets, drums, banners and pennants,
ensigns and horses, white and black,
we'll see them all go flashing past.
And no strength will stop
the splendid glittering lances
as they fly through the sky
nothing prevent the vestments
of sendal, golden cloth
and richly embroidered silks
being shredded, rent to tatters,

nor the ropes, tents, stakes,
canvas cloth and lofty pavilions
from being wrenched and torn asunder.
Then we'll see gold and silver squandered,
catapults winding up, taut, hurling,
walls collapsing, towers broken, torn down,
enemy ranks captured and clapped in irons.
And we'll punish them with such blunt and brutal blows.
Great will be the loss, but much greater the gain.
Or rather, rich will be the man who plunders as he pleases.

Charlatans and braggarts to a certain extent, perhaps, but it would simply be suicide to mistake their vehemence for bluster or to consider the activity they develop to be anti-economical. Quite the contrary: generally gathered around big industry, the industry we could call structural, those mid-level and small-time businessmen, the collective industrialists, are truly the very tip of the lance and, simultaneously, the rearguard of all industrial development; lighter, more fluid and dynamic forces, but in some way useless, negligible, and to a far lesser degree, condemned to disappear, as some disgusted materialist might prematurely conclude, now that, far from being the small fish destined to be swallowed up by the big fish, they more closely resemble those delicate little birds that clean and sharpen the crocodile's teeth in a tacit symbiotic relationship and, thus, the strategist would be mistaken, thanks to overconfidence in the penetrating and demolishing efficacy of his armor-plated divisions, forgetting in his logical plans the decisive role played by the infantry that advance behind the wagons, scouring the terrain, making it entirely their own; equally mistaken would be the economic planner who discards the role that the mid-level and small-time businessmen play in every process of development, and the efficacy and other practical virtues of those men with whom we are concerned.

In contrast to the collective industrial activity we can now typify the figure of the structural industrialist or major industrialist, attending preferably not to his belonging to this or that sector of industry, but to his company's volume of production, as well as its longevity—centuries, frequently—factors which, on the other hand, given the kind of life they are obliged to lead, usually affect the individual's personality, vigorously differentiating him from the other members of the upper bourgeoisie, components of Barcelona's mercantile, financial, or professional bourgeoisie, against whom, even currently, one might say, the structural industrialist, for motives equally futile and sophisticated, enjoys less consideration and audience, socially speaking. Flagrant injustice, it need not be repeated, not only toward one of the firmest bulwarks of Catalan progress, but also toward the same human quality of the representatives of a preeminent social class, of a designated social class, according to the most faithful interpretations most authorized by the very members of that class, meaning, closer to the criteria with which a family tree is reconstructed, more sensitive to the magnifying sentiments that are appropriate to attribute to all clients of a genealogical research bureau, described, as mentioned, in archetypal terms, like captains or conquistadors, men fundamentally sound in both body and soul, conscious of the advantages, both in the moral order as well as in the energetic one, of a prudent excess of weight, the hard, innocent eyes of the one most purely convinced of the rectitude and universality of his principles, his concept of the economic benefit not only as a right or privilege as much as an obligation, his militant social paternalism—or rather, patriarchalism, his inflexible righteous will to cheat taxes, his scant appetite for outside signs—more than for purely fiscal motives, for his intimate belief that only a peseta saved is really a peseta earned. In short, a life drawn in the image and likeness of a Sunday newspaper, morning copulation, and Mass, a sunny stroll with the kids, and the long, slow conversation after the midday meal, the visit to the grandparents, a little television, a frugal supper, the theater, an exemplary image that, by banner blazon and licit behavior, in the way that a book of etiquette must serve not only for the young generations to match their steps to their elders' steps but, especially, to offer a model to the titleholders of the new fortunes, riding the crest of the rising and falling tide of history, of its choppy waters, its tumultuous and episodic fortunes, that will only settle and solidify if their economic consolidation matches their moral integration along the way. Meaning: a mentality whose most adequate historical antecedent we could find precisely in the Catalan expansion throughout the Mediterranean, an expansion of eminently familiar and patrimonial character, conquests made to acquire lands for one's offspring, as property or wedding gift, fortunes that will perhaps be dissipated with the parents' deaths, if the heirs turn out to be prodigal or inept, meaning, something that no longer has anything in common with the traditional concept of Empire but rather, simply, with that of the modern State, a fact that although it cannot contain any moral judgment, neither favorable nor adverse, according to the mentality of the age, still shapes the character of a people who, thanks to the avatars of history, never surpassed such a state, nor have known the successive phases of development and decadence common to the other peoples of western Europe. All things considered, and having excluded from our exposition any suspicious element of partiality, any notion that the members of the elite Catalan industrial bourgeoisie show a propensity for encomium more than objectivity, in order to present as a collective enterprise and public utility what is, overall, a business for personal profit, to convert the industrialist's family name into a myth, to involve it in cultivating the arts and sciences by means of petty patronage and rapacious collecting, to understand social coexistence like a social game, all, perhaps, excessively sublimated for the reticent contemporary retina, in the same way that, gazing upon the portraits arranged in the Gallery of Illustrious Catalans, a critical-minded spectator will probably relate those venerable hoary beards not so much with Captain Ahab as with the protagonist of *Don Mendo's Revenge*. Thus we are conscious, in all things, of the limitations of the essentially literary image sketched by us, of its defects, from a scientific point of view, of the provisional character of our conclusions, valid, at the most, there being no more definitive and satisfactory interpretation established, an interpretation not idealistic but rather materialistic, not metaphysical but rather dialectical, meaning, an interpretation which, unlike the present one, must be the fruit of something more than simple intuitions and anecdotal observations, superficial and insufficient, however much they might be based on facts that are just as certain as they are, on the other hand, truly shocking. Thus, Florencio Rivas Fernández: a self-made man, alert, dynamic, insightful, a born winner, and, notwithstanding, barely integrated into Barcelona's upper-class bourgeoisie, his natural social environment. And this not due to any lack of economic heft, nor less so for his particular lifestyle, almost exaggeratedly high, nor again for his rather attractive personal conditions, his friendliness, his natural elegance, and—if not natural, adopted with extraordinary aptitude—his apparent good taste and, as far as it goes, even his relatively cultivated spirit. Or better yet: not for economic, professional, or personal motives but surely for something in some way related—especially formal—with all that, in how it relates to the antagonic, the way in which any sagacious interlocutor glimpsed in him, against all expectations of an industrial impresario who had come as far as he had, his ultimate indifference to money, the gambler's special indifference, for whose passion money is only a means while the game remains the true goal, or the way in which, even without ostentatious bad taste, his carefree refusal to link professional reputation and private life was evident, or to not consider, not even for the sake of protocol, private life as an extension or complement to professional reputation. Obviously, a man like that could never be fully integrated, especially given his own resistance to being integrated, not least because, in principle, the non-integration was lacking—or must have been lacking—repercussions in the normal development of his activities, in the mechanics of the business world and its laws of credit and solvency. Least important were his origins, or better yet, his record, his career: from failed publisher of popular editions of the classics to manager and majority shareholder of one of the most important graphic design companies in the city, meaning, in the whole country, altogether something obscure, during the obscure years of the forties; really the least important thing. What was important was the other thing, well-demonstrated by the commentaries raised by the circumstances of his death: something that in any other case, in relation to any other person, might not have been considered so much an accident as something casual and fortuitous, was here generally judged to be the inevitable consequence of a moral attitude, of a line of conduct; temerity, contempt for form, scandal. It had to end that way: early one morning, crashing into a lamppost, doubtless drunk, in company not remotely dubious. What would be most difficult to precisely determine is if, just as when a man joins his life to a woman who's had a great deal of experience, the aloof and impartial observer won't know how to say with exactitude if she was the one who chose, if she preferred that man to her lovers up to that point or, on the contrary, if he was the first in the series to be honest enough to cope with her, to make up the difference, i.e., the final victim of the catch; thus in the case of Florencio Rivas Fernández, the doubt—essentially sterile—resided in knowing if his way of life, especially in recent times, was what drove him to that fatal accident, or if the accident was the a posteriori cause of his later lifestyle becoming public domain, a lifestyle that if it hadn't ended in tragedy could have gone on indefinitely.

The telephone. One Saturday night. They'd gone out with Federico, Moragas, and the Adolfos, and upon dropping off Nuria, in front of the entrance to her building, they'd argued with that irritability that alcohol sometimes causes, but when he got home he found out that she'd already called, telling him to wait for her, that she'd swing by to pick him up. Papa scrutinized him with his eyes wide open, somewhere between suspicious and apprehensive. Looks like her father has had some kind of an accident, Raúl said. In the taxi Nuria told him that the maids had met her at the door in tears, saying that they'd called from the clinic; her mother and brothers and sisters had gone to spend the weekend in the country. The nurse in the emergency room said, yes, a car accident; are you family members? And Nuria: but how is he? And the nurse: hold on, woman, I first need to find out where he is. And he consulted a directory and appeared to write down a telephone number, and taking advantage of Nuria's distraction as she lit a cigarette, showed the paper discretely to Raúl: dead. And he said, come this way, you'll speak with the doctor. It was the same nurse who later said to Nuria, do you want me to remove it? Remove what? His ring; with a little soap it'll slide right off. Rigor mortis.

Nevertheless, despite the telephone ringing, the telegrams piling up, and the succession of visitors offering their condolences, there was an upheaval of time as well as of space in the Rivases' invaded house, where one quickly observed, along with everything else, a certain improper undercurrent in the climate which usually develops around a death in the family. Beneath the familiar expressions of grief, and the exaltations of the departed, and the vacuous topics relating to the dangers of driving, everyone recalling cases, telling about careless close calls, horrors, everyone a little like that widow fishing around in others' lives to see if she can discover some drama in the other person and can thus establish a nexus of affinity and mutual comprehension based on their respective misfortunes, beneath all that, one could intuit more and more the tenebrous theme of conjectures and suspicions, it was enough to take into consideration the same absence of questions about the circumstances of the accident and, above all, the disquieting silence that followed one of so many anodyne utterances: you see, nowadays, just getting in the car is suicide itself. The well-intentioned but useless remark from the joker on hand: pretty soon you won't even be able to have an accident in peace. Raúl slipped away to hide out in the bathroom, to smoke a cigarette; the enamel on the edges of the toilet bowl was cracked in two places, one almost in the middle and the other on the outside, residual signs that, although carefully cleaned, indicated the habit of one or several family members to squat above the bowl, perhaps one of the boys or Señor Rivas himself. Señor Rivas's house occupied the top floor and penthouse of a relatively recent, multi-story addition constructed atop a modernist building on the Rambla de Cataluña, a building with a horribly mutilated exterior, with the cupola lopped off and the group of sculptures above the portal torn down, no doubt to disguise, in a flush of rationalism—and profitability—that horrid blob of artificial stone, very 1950's, placed atop a facade of erstwhile asymmetrical harmony.

If the generalized presumption of a suicide was the first notice of the reigning atmosphere, a rumor probably founded on the fact that Señor Rivas had taken out a very valuable life insurance policy, completely out of character for a man in his position, who logically needed to trust more in the good progress of his business than in the benefits of his death, when it came to thinking about the children, it was Bellido, stunned, nearly whimpering, to whom the very development of the events, by virtue of his position as family attorney, became a fledgling herald of catastrophe: the firm's most delicate economic situation, the banks' more-than-reticent attitude, the household employees' possible infidelity, and the intransigence of the creditors, monolithic, maximalist, orchestrated, perhaps, by the same brain that had provoked the banks' negative reaction to Señor Rivas's death as well as the defection of those personnel until then considered discreet and trustworthy; in short, the need of enacting an immediate suspension of payments that might gloss over, for the moment, what might well end in real bankruptcy. And with the same anxiety and anguish with which, as during an earthquake, a nation's government, legally constituted or simply installed into power, receives the initial and confusing news of something more than a mere riot turning out to be a coup d'etat: a statement from the military academy, support for activating garrisons both on the border and abroad, as well as several bodies of special forces, ambiguous conduct from the air force and the police themselves, the radio stations and presidential palace fallen into the hands of rebel factions, the radio broadcasting problems, press communiqués, contradictory news relating to supposed petitions for political asylum, arrests, summary judgments, executions, H-Hour in which everything is surreal to the degree that it remains uncertain, although not so much, of course, to make it impossible not to conclude that something grave and even irremediable is unfolding. Thus, the Rivas family saw the events happening quickly, with the fatalistic impotence with which those developing or, frankly, under-developed, national governments contemplate the violent finale of their mandate, far, very far, from the serene and solemn ritual succession that, as in the death of Aunt Paquita, is foreseen by the constitutions of Western-style democracies, whether the naming of the head of state be elective or hereditary, following the death of the queen of some Nordic country, for example. And then, treachery, the low blow, the evidence that only one person who in theory enjoyed sufficient confidence with Señor Rivas as to have direct access to his desk in his office could have placed in circulation that sheaf of photographs found in a drawer—so they said—while organizing files, those photos whose existence, on the abstract plane of vicious rumor, finally took shape when deposited, with hypocritical solicitude, in Bellido's law firm, confronting him, no doubt with all premeditation, with what a man like Bellido, like the rope around the neck of a condemned man, felt incapable of confronting: scandal. Not least because the identity of that beady-eyed little slut joyously posing in various fornicating positions—on all fours, head on, with her tits hanging down like goat's udders, on all fours from behind, her head cocked round facing the camera, smiling, on all fours from the side, raised up on one elbow in bed, her backside attractively displayed, etcetera—was quickly determined, and her relations with Señor Rivas were revealed like an open secret among the household staff: Mary, the very same woman, no doubt, appearing up close and personal in the photographs, recognizable by her anatomical details despite the closeness of the lens and the arrangement of the photographic elements, a mouth, that mouth, in the throes of slurping two erect male members, one of them darker, one of them apparently a negro's; a woman—her hair covering her eyes—engaged in the same operation but sucking only one cock while being penetrated by the other; or what is more striking and curious, the woman, the same woman, apparently being penetrated by a man, and penetrated at the same time, unmistakably, by another male member, the dark one. Mary and the black man. But who snapped the photos? All things considered, more significant than the personality of the members of the trio was the clarification of the personality of who now was moving the threads of how much was happening and of the motivations that they had for moving them, to create such a dramatic situation for the Rivas family: a name, Plans, the paper manufacturer, a fact quite concrete enough to give footing not to heated conjectures but to hopeless conclusions. And then another clarification: the kind of relationship existing between Señor Rivas and his wife, beyond suspicion for those people closest to them due to their very proximity, in the same way that frequently the most immediate family members of a homosexual man are the last ones to realize his habits; unsuspected more than unsuspicious, in fact, something very simple, the classic conjugal arrangement for when it's too late and, although better late than never, turns out to be obvious, for however little lucidity one has, that it's no longer possible to remake nor straighten anything out, to save yourself in the end from the abject matrimonial gratification, from their merciless fulfillment, from their licenses that are increasingly sordid with the passing of time as bodies grow creakier, hair turns gray, wrinkles, loose teeth and loose sphincters, varicose veins, hernias, hemorrhoids, but, above all, mutual hatred and repugnance and aggression that one tries to bury, as much as possible with this kind of arrangement. And the blow, the low blow, consists of the simple fact of that private arrangement becoming public news, and that not only Bellido but also Doña Dulce and Nuria, not to mention the little ones, found out about it: that it had become news, with all the charm of a historical record. How dare they talk about it? said Nuria. What do they know about my father much less my mother and what do they care what kind of relations they had? These men, cuckolds frequenting the whorehouse, how dare they cast the first stone? My father did what he wanted and he did well. My mother also had a lover: Amadeo García Fornells, everyone in Barcelona knew it, my father was the first to know. Everything was clear between my parents, without hypocrisy, without bullshit. And that's all they're interested in? What do they know about him, about what he was like, about his capacity to love? The efficacy of the low blow, mission accomplished: undermine the morale of the Rivas family, destroy their security, make them focus their attention on the problem of maintaining a good reputation with the goal of distracting them from the root problem, doubtless essentially economic, and more than seeking the root of this problem and its possible solutions, to ensure that the family worry about the surrounding reactions, that they feel wounded and exasperated, for example, by all the inconsistencies of people's rumors, on the one hand, that the accident seemed to be a suicide and, on the other, that Señor Rivas, when the accident happened, was accompanied by unmentionable acquaintances, whose presence had been hushed up. Raúl guessed it the same day as the burial: for one of those present, all that was nothing more than an interval, the pause that precedes the gesture of turning the cards face up; let them finish burying the dead, that's why they had come. And, if he wasn't just guessing, the widow Rivas must certainly have had some sense of foreboding during the ceremony, serene and weeping, sincere and insincere, unharmed and despondent, with the confusion and distress that can result as much from the deepest sorrow as from that type of stunned guilt—features clouded, flaccid—that usually succeeds in the wife, dilatorily, after several hours of intense carnal pleasure, confusion, dumbfounded, in her role as widow, more than pallid, almost translucent among her black veils, with sufficient residual intuition, notwithstanding, to sense something, even though, like the spendthrift overwhelmed by his bills, letters, expiring contracts, payments coming due, still strives to find a better explanation for his lack of money—a mistake, misplaced funds, some swindle, bad luck—resisting accepting the naked fact that he's spent more than he could afford, with the same innocence Doña Dulce failed to guess correctly to be able to explain to herself the basis of that presentiment. Impossible to really specify anything with her, neither then nor in the following days, as events unfolded, too vacant to offer any more ideas or clarifications, let alone an opinion, about Bellido's catastrophic predictions. Bellido was a competent attorney, perhaps, for routine matters and paperwork but not for facing up to a situation like the present one, characterized by the celerity and forcefulness with which the events unfold in these cases: the banks blocking all kinds of credit and discount following the death of Señor Rivas by using the firm's eminently personal character as a pretext; the declaration of a suspension of payments; the disappearance or, at least, inability to locate important documents along with the evasive role, almost a bald-faced boycott, assumed by more than one high-ranking household employee; the report of bankruptcy, that the company's debts were greater than its assets, the announcement of meetings and assemblies intended to create a council of creditors; the involvement of Plans, the paper manufacturer, behind all that, his evident determination, in his condition as minority shareholder and principal creditor, to acquire the company for a song and build it back up once he had it under his absolute control. And Bellido, knowing himself outclassed, also knew, doubtless beforehand, like the sergeant who in the thick of battle loses all his commanding officers, who could expect no outside help, that her babbling and clumsy suggestion—too dramatic to be natural—of resorting to Amadeo for help, as if somehow deprived of good sense, that suggestion pregnant with so much significant expectation of being accepted, as if desperate that it should turn out that way, that it be grasped differently than it was grasped, with Doña Dulce's silence and Nuria's complete refusal. Nobody there seemed capable of proposing any intermediate solution between the halting negotiation and the heroic, last-ditch struggle that, by adjusting itself to the terrain chosen by the paper manufacturer Plans, meant, by any reckoning, playing the game according to his rules.

The facility with which the businessman, throughout the course of a fierce argument, can become a gangster or policeman, especially when there are various people participating in the verbal harassment and the attacks from the opposing side grow stronger, a morose debtor, for example, or a casual creditor or any other person which the nature of the commercial relationship places in a lesser role, in a way that only the lack of the proper channel or legal support—due to negligence or scruples from the legislator—prevents them, working together, from moving directly to applying the third degree; yes, for poor Bellido, the first skirmishes with Plans's people must have been a tough test. However, when Raúl began to accompany him to the meetings with the creditors' legal team, more for moral support than from really considering himself useful, the tone of these meetings no longer had the character that, if he could believe Bellido, they'd had initially, when he found himself inside those same offices, among a series of individuals gathered together with the tough determination one usually feels from part of the crowd exiting a boxing match, like hired thugs on the way to teach someone a lesson, spurring each other on with brutal sarcasm. Either because they must have made quite an impression on Bellido, or because they considered that time was on their side and they judged their own position to be increasingly strong, what's true is that now they seemed to be in agreement about adopting the relieved attitude and affable calm of the man who knows himself to be in possession of the exact key needed to close the deal and, in consequence, exempted, if he so please, from keeping up appearances, of being friendly, free to be a gentleman or a swine. In the process, on the other hand, Bellido's true measure was even more on display, his scant qualification for such confrontations; the sort who prefers to wait for a taxi on a lonely corner than fight it out with others waiting for one at the intersection of two major avenues, so Bellido seemed to prefer to deal with the creditors' proposals—better yet, conditions—as if they formed part of a normal although not entirely favorable business deal, than to have to consider it like a suicide maneuver, as—pure and simply—a filthy rotten mess, something that obliged him to behave in a way unnatural to him, he, Bellido, a meticulous and well-ordered person, very hard working, known and commonly appreciated in the national Treasury office, the courts, civil registry, notaries, and public offices in general, but always among the ushers, secretaries, interns, the type of person least likely to be measured against predatory men like those working for Plans, habituated to act according not to the idea of who strikes the first blow but rather who strikes the last. Raúl, in his turn, so brusquely turned into a practicing attorney, felt no more secure than a construction worker who, returning home, crosses through a residential neighborhood in the city, feeling disturbed, or what's more, overwhelmed, by that sumptuous and relaxed atmosphere and, especially, by the elastic and confident stride of some women who seemed to neither expect nor fear the obscene expressions that he, in any case, would not have dared direct at them. Thus, despite all his experience, not judicial but intellectual, Raúl felt inept among such people. His overcoat was only one more element, a detail—a quick fix—that could not have escaped the notice of any of those present. Had it dawned on him in time, Raúl could have shown up without an overcoat and simply made some passing allusion to his supposedly capricious hatred for overcoats, even though, to avoid being even more conspicuous, he should have also prepared some excuse—nearby errands to run, a visit, another meeting—so that when the meeting was over they wouldn't have caught him off guard, asking him the way they did, where, given the harsh weather, he'd parked his car, obliging him to admit that he didn't own a car, that he was going to catch a taxi, thereby giving Plans's people an opening to triumphantly offer him a ride home. But that wasn't really the most important thing, rather something much more general, his lack of conviction about his role in that whole affair, his scant confidence in the efficacy of his performance and even in the mere impression he might make on Plans's people during each meeting, each time, as they wrapped things up, with the nervousness of a person who, when relating some incident, conversation, or argument, becomes self-conscious of his own words, and doesn't recount what he really said as much as, in retrospect, with everything said and done, meditated and reconstructed, the thing unsaid which would have been better to say, some quick retort, expressed with measured transparency, the brilliant response that the situation required which he never managed to utter. And nevertheless it would almost be possible to guarantee that, in the long run, Raúl's interventions, if they had some significance, were more positive than negative, by reason of the surprise, confusion, and even uneasiness, that they produced in Plans's people, due to how unusual they appeared to be in the kinds of deals so familiar to these men: his courtesy, for example, in a certain way improper given the circumstances, or his tendency to ask questions, the answers to which, in reality, really didn't interest him, more appropriate to a train compartment than a business meeting, the result, no doubt, of being a natural stranger to such business, of an unformulated rejection of the problem that made him delay actually starting the discussion as much as possible, not so much from cowardice as from repugnance or embarrassment, not like the criminal in chapel who avoids thinking about the blue gleam of the rifles but rather more like that man who suppresses the memory of a steamy sexual experience; hence the reaction of Plans's men, impatient—the impatience that the conduct of the young man who shadows her time and time again without talking about more than the cinema or novels can provoke in a young woman—at the same time mistrustful, the same type of mistrust aroused by the sangfroid of the unknown gambler as he coolly accepts his first round of losses at a gaming table, the fear of the others upon finding themselves in the presence of a professional who after stringing them along, completely fleeces them all, a reaction that very possibly contributed decisively to hastening events. It was as if, from inconvenience more than haste, they had decided that the matter was already ripe enough so that it was necessary to continue interweaving proposals and counterproposals, that they had reached the most delicate point of the entire negotiation, the moment of specifically defining and revising, of properly dealing with the thing once and for all when, apart from what's being said or no longer being said, each party knows already what to be attentive to with respect to the other party, there's no other solution, handsome, it's not true that they've made you another offer and you know that I know, and the other guy knows it and only hopes that his opponent doesn't also know that, although being some tougher conditions than the ones he initially believed he would manage to get, he would sign even though they were even less favorable on the condition that they be done with it once and for all, of finally breaking the tension produced by what's about to fall out; and with everything, even knowing what's coming—the same as when, in trench warfare, to move beyond the impasse of the stabilized lines, a sudden concentration of fire announces the imminence of the bayonet charge—fearing the decisive instant, of the slump, the mouth half-open, eyes staring, guessing by the other's apparently indifferent expression what he was going to say even before he said it, what he would pronounce: the ultimatum. The fair amount, meaning, just enough, given the circumstances, for it to be accepted, now that, however much is lost, more would be lost by not accepting and, in every case, no need to say, you, as legal advisor, and you, young man, as intermediary, representative, or whatever you are, you will also have your piece of the pie, no need to worry about that, that in the end this is about a sale and when there is a sale there is a commission. That's right, we're interested in knowing your response before next Tuesday, Señor Rodriguez (wasn't he the bad guy before?) has managed to get Señor Vilá (wasn't he the good guy before?) to convince Señor Plans to wait until then; it seems that Señor Plans is increasingly less interested in dealing with a matter like this one, so messy, we might say, so uncongenial, but Señor Vilá has been able to convince him that it won't take more than a week, although Señor Plans says that he would prefer to invest in a different venture that's become available to him, a real opportunity apparently, and let the bankruptcy run its legal course, given that Señor Plans has already wasted quite enough time and money on this matter with Gráficas Rivas. Well, hell's bells, that's it. Accept the terms, like it or not. Just like in Goya's capricho, *Trágala, perro: Swallow it, dog*, depicting some raving monks with a giant syringe about to forcibly administer an enema to a trembling man in the presence of his veiled wife. And Bellido, attempting to gain more time, to justify, at least formally, the fact of not formally rejecting a proposal that was, according to its minimum requirements, thoroughly unpalatable, to grease the business with a little bit of vaseline, so, we'll look it over, Señora Rivas, well, the Widow Rivas—a touch of melodrama—has the final word, and in her situation, a widow; and the others, Plans's men, of course, of course—more vaseline—but you realize of course, a bird in the hand is worth two in the bush, you know, no amount of vaseline will make this any easier. The double error committed by Plans's men: on one side, their haste, tightening the screws too tight and too soon, like kidnappers who, once they've collected the ransom, come back smiling toward the little body of their victim, bound and gagged and roped to a chair, saying, now, let's do him! without having previously made sure that their hideout isn't surrounded by the police; on the other side, lack of resolution or perhaps of calculation, not striking in the heat of the moment once their game was discovered, giving a week's time to consider instead of just twenty-four hours, not thinking that the opposing side could use that time to start playing a different game of their own; in a word, dozing off, falling asleep like the seducer who promises his young victim a life of happiness in his company and, having stolen her virtue, while she trembles in his embrace, smokes a cigarette thinking about the most expeditious way of ending the already tiresome story, still far from imagining that the most likely conclusion to that story will be a wedding. Thus even Bellido himself would dare to insist again on the need to see about resorting to other weapons and even Nuria herself would accept the advisability of consulting Amadeo, of bringing him up to date on the situation.

The meeting was short and polite, almost formal, given that if something now seemed evident it was that Amadeo didn't really need to be brought up to date on anything, however much he listened to Bellido's explanations and more than once asked Raúl's opinion about some detail; but the ambiguity lay especially with the person not named: Doña Dulce. And also, perchance, in the not quite sufficiently concealed curiosity with which Amadeo seemed to be weighing Raúl, a curiosity logical enough to a certain point, as Raúl was his lover's eldest daughter's lover, and perhaps increased by the red communist halo that the Rivas family must have seen floating over Raúl's head; in fact it was to him and not Bellido to whom he spoke when he said: call me tomorrow. I'm one of those people who never make a decision without sleeping on it first; the best kind of divination, believe me. More intellectually, and even physically agile, than Raúl had imagined; younger, more alert, more cynical as well. It only took one interview like that one to understand that Bellido's efforts were not misguided, that if anyone could yet save the Rivas family from ruin, that someone was precisely Amadeo García Fornells; however, only later, once he was out in the street, thanks to the change of mood brought on by all feelings of relief, he could begin to be amused by the idea that he was starting to make inroads into the domains of monopolistic oligarchy in a real way and not from a purely theoretical and speculative plane. On the phone, Amadeo's voice was, if possible, even more convincing: I've been weighing the various aspects of the problem, he said. And if we're looking for some professional capable of handling the matter with the highest guarantee of responsibility, I think it's worthwhile to choose the best specialist in the field, Espada, to my understanding, a superb attorney, besides being an excellent person and a great friend, an ace negotiator, a master swordsman, if you will, a real ace of spades. So I've taken the liberty of arranging for you a meeting for tomorrow. Operation Counterstrike: make initial contact with Ace of Spades, offer a fresh summary of the situation, whether or not Ace of Spades even worries about trying to disguise to what degree he was already informed, too busy, doubtless, to beat around the bush. Ace of Spades agrees to take on the case or, rather, doesn't conceal what he had accepted beforehand—Señor García Fornells need only ask me. Raúl and Bellido arrange new meetings with Ace of Spades, not so much because their direct collaboration is needed as much as to be up to date on the progress of the anti-Plans plan, the beleaguered Bellido increasingly less beleaguered, again feeling at home in his secondary role, in his modest position of auxiliary or conscientious manager. Working hypothesis: Plans has undermined the banks' confidence in the future of Gráficas Rivas, S.A., in order to provoke suspension of payments and to take over the company's assets and liabilities at bargain basement rates. Ace of Spades' strategy: act in a parallel manner and move quickly, without allowing time for matters to reach the judicial level, making the board of creditors abort their efforts before they officially partner up. Method: first, get the banks to grant a new line of credit to Gráficas Ricas, S.A.; if necessary, by means of an increase in capital which, I'm convinced, we'd have no trouble covering; next, simultaneously—I've done my research about this—make Plans see that the situation with his paper company is not entirely without complications if it's found, for his part, that the banks limit his discount, not to mention credit restrictions, as long as, of course, we all believe it advisable. So, all in all: we want Plans to understand that he's in no position to take over anything. A stratagem truly worthy of an ace negotiator, although admitting that his strength lay not so much in his own skill as in the tutelary shadow of Amadeo, without whose backing all skill would have been for nought. However: for Raúl, all that could not fail to leave him somewhat rattled; despite his ideological foundation, despite his perfect comprehension of the fact that Amadeo's probable triumph over Plans represented once again, in the most basic scheme, a highly illustrative example of the triumph of the oligarchy over the non-monopolistic bourgeoisie, it was inevitable that Raúl would become aware that, similar to the floating, displaced image of his high-school overcoat in a cloakroom, was the fact that someone might have to deal with cases like the present one with no other prior experience than having studied historic examples and test cases at University, in the same way that the housemaid who decides to turn to prostitution, however unfamiliar she might be with the legendary qualities of a dowsing wand or with the different ways of getting a male member to stand up straight, becomes familiar, not without awkwardness, with the slang of her fellow water witches and the demands of their clientele—beatings, whippings, rear penetration—by virtue, above all, of the time it takes to adjust to the new codes and revelations, to the apparent reality in which, until then, her life has unfolded, the environment to which she was accustomed, the house where she served, the owners, the friends who frequently visited, whose habits and behavior acquire a totally new significance in light of her own current experiences.

At the cemetery, after the prayer for the dead, before concluding the ceremony, the priest wished to direct some words to those gathered, an old clergyman, friend of the family who, as he stammered to explain, in a strong Catalan accent, had baptized Florencio with the same hands with which he now blessed his coffin, and he spoke of the Enemy, the crusade against Satan, that Tempter, who, due to the fall of our first parents, managed to plunge humankind into sin, expose them to the threat of eternal punishment, to the true death, the death of the soul, compared to which the death of the body was only a pallid reflection, this that has so violently struck the body but not the soul of God's servant Señor Florencio Rivas Fernández, dear friend and exemplary Christian, the same as if, from spite, the Demon must have been pleased to make him die on the eve, as it were, of the birth of the Baby Jesus and of his glorious Epiphany, depriving him of the joy of the feast days with which all humanity celebrates and commemorates the appearance of that small star in the heavens above Bethlehem which shone to proclaim man's Redemption. That old clergyman was also responsible, with two other no-less-ancient priests—days later—for saying the solemn funeral mass, officiating that endless ceremony, pronounced by some deacon through a microphone, hands extended, bodies curved forward, eyes fixed on heaven, their lips kiss the altar, Christ's bed, a kiss of adoration; etymologically, adore means to raise to the mouth something that is venerated and, in Greek, to venerate—*proskunien*—is to kiss while bowing down. Various people took communion, Papa among them, and Raúl remained seated on the pew the same as when, in high school, he had to let pass by those who stood up to receive or who were returning with their eyes half-closed and their hands together, the same odor as then, like paper money, the smell of the kneelers, of the prayer books, of the boarders' little prayer rugs, while he thought, I've got seventeen masses left to go, ten masses left, seven left. You shall receive communion with your eyes lowered, your hands folded together or crossed over your breast, with devotion and modesty, making acts of faith, of sorrow, of hope, etcetera. When receiving communion keep your head straight and, the tip of your tongue upon your lower lip, you will receive the Holy Form with modesty and devotion, you will try to swallow it as soon as possible. Finally, return to your place, kneel down, think, meditate, reflect, what you have done, Whom you have received, how you can thank Him for such a great boon. Regarding eucharistic fasting, the rule is three hours for solid nourishment and one hour for liquids. Water does not break the fast, but it is preferable to abstain from it as well. And Gomis, with hypocritical perfectionism and a spoiled boy's hunger for attention, perfect for one who, more than interested in the strict enforcement of the rules, wants to make everyone aware of his pious conduct, raised his hand and asked: What about saliva? Is it alright to swallow that?

He returned home with Papa, by bus; he'd not taken the bus in some time, far longer—years—since he'd ridden it with his father. The breeze was blowing, black, fearsome. Why do you want a taxi? asked Papa. The bus is more convenient. He counted his change parsimoniously, perfectly poised on the raised platform at the rear of the bus, in spite of the relative roughness of the ride; before sitting down, and removing his hat, he said hello to the wife of an acquaintance. Seated just ahead of him was another one of those acquaintances, vaguely neighbors, people who for years had taken the bus at approximately the same time and gotten off at the same stop; during the ride, Papa and the other man, half-turned toward one another, spoke about that, about the years spent riding the same line, first the streetcar and now the bus, before the city was so built up, when the neighborhood was only individual houses and the passengers who rode to the final stops knew each other by sight, there was no pushing and people were more polite, although, despite everything, the bus was still the best way to go, without the problems and worries of a car, with so much traffic, and dangers, always getting worse, exactly, you see, we're just coming back from burying a close friend who was killed in a car accident. A new neighborhood had been growing from the Paseo de la Bonanova downhill toward the sea, densely built up, all in tune with that enterprising and optimistic air of the young couples living there, and what had once been an open landscape of fields and empty lots, was now simply a classic middle-class composition, as decorous as it was monotonous, smooth wide sidewalks, small businesses, utility vehicles, maids doing the shopping, mothers with their little ones and strollers and bulging pregnant bellies; the streets above Bonanova hadn't been saved either from a progressive transformation, even while conserving its garden-like ambience amid reforms and demolitions, renovated villas turned into clinics, high schools, kindergartens, remodeled houses, enlarged in area and height to the very limit authorized by the municipal ordinances, compartmentalized, subdivided into apartments, but this is a mistake, it's better to hold on until they change the municipal ordinances—sooner or later they have to change—and you'll be able to build on the entire property, and then, with no problems from tenants, think about it; I won't live to see it but you will, and although we don't have much garden around the house, the lot is just about eleven hundred square meters with fifteen meters of facade, figure that they'll pay you a little over five thousand pesetas per square meter and, look, that's a tidy sum of money. The rusty creaking iron gate, the anarchically overgrown garden, all a mess, the few flowers all intermixed, like in a slum, the faded blinds, the delicate wrought ironwork of the balconies, its rust stains running down the facade, coming loose from the airy moldings of the cornices, from the garlands and festoons and floral copings, almost down to the base of the facade, swollen and breaking off from the damp. Papa waited by the gate while Raúl pulled it closed and then followed him through the garden, lagging behind a bit. A man in full possession of his faculties, he said. Poor Paquita, on the other hand; for her it was almost a liberation. She was the oldest child. Now I am. As if isolated in the opaque, overcast sky, the hammer blows from some nearby construction reached their ears. He carefully wiped his shoes clean on the doormat. It seems that his company had financial difficulties and now everybody's going after the poor widow. Human ingratitude; I know it all too well since the disaster with the firm. The static repetition of his shoes scuffing the mat, the molten amber of his eyes that seemed to be interrogating him, stunned, innocent, resigned, with the fatalism, for example, with which the customer receives, once again, the sorrowful confirmation that he is only worth any respect before paying, when, purchase completed, he turns to the salesman, till that moment entirely at his disposal and now devoted to some other customer, wanting to ask some final question about his purchase, in order to only run up against cool replies and sardonic manners, whose meaning, as implicit as ostensible, is nothing more than to say: if you want more courtesy make another purchase.

Evidently, the Rivases' economic situation worried Papa not only because of the family itself, for the affection and sympathy that he might have had for Nuria, but rather, above all, for Raúl, now that, since he had never asked questions about the nature of Raúl and Nuria's relationship, perhaps because, although still unannounced, their engagement seemed obvious and, by consequence, for more than reasons of tact, he judged it preferable to not bring up the matter, it was clear he couldn't help worrying about Raúl's future with a woman who, contrary to expectations, would perhaps not be able to bring anything to the marriage. But he seemed unaware of the other circumstances surrounding the death of Señor Rivas, very probably because, like with a child who must be kept in the dark about certain things, nobody would have dared to involve him in the current gossip. So, how are things looking? he asked Nuria on Sunday, during lunch. And Raúl: what do you expect? deliberately, as if Ace of Spades' plan had not already been set in motion, or at least established, the night before. He was in a sour mood, and had been since waking up, with a hangover, feeling bad, and neither the turn of fortune that the Gráficas Rivas, S.A. affair had taken the previous afternoon, with the simple exposition of Ace of Spades' anti-Plans plan, a turn by whose light the decisive meeting set for next Tuesday with the people from the paper company seemed like something very different from what the other party must be imagining, which only intensified the satisfaction of flatly rejecting, with measured indifference, not only their ultimatum but also the need to prolong the conversations, leaving them perplexed, incredulous, incapable of reacting, possibly, to what could only seem to them the result of the other side's madness, if not their own; neither that turnabout nor the subsequent night out on the town with Adolfo and Aurora and Federico and Pluto and Marichone, their euphoric ramble through the Barrio Chino until dawn, nor then, the time—how much?—he spent with Nuria, given over completely to their erotic distillation, to the liquifying pleasure, none of that now seemed to him sufficient motive for feeling, not necessarily content with himself but simply content, futile facts and even out of place before the dark panorama of the day, lunch with Papa and Nuria, the visit to Leo's house, the somber desolation of a Sunday afternoon and above all and in a more general way, before the cruel entity of the unquestionable: he was more and more bound to a woman whom he didn't love, he was a lawyer and disgusted by being one, he wanted to write and he couldn't write, and he had no money, and he couldn't talk about any of that with anybody, not with Nuria, or Federico, or Aurora, or Adolfo, or Leo, or Fortuny, he couldn't, or better yet, he didn't want to, he was tired of them all, they bored and depressed him and he had nothing to say to them. But as with Papa, his worry about the Rivas family's economic future and its possible consequences in no way affected how warmly he treated Nuria or, if it did affect it in some way, the result was nothing more than an increase in attention for her, but with Eloísa, on the contrary, as if in the spate of adversity that had fallen upon the Rivas family she had found a kind of official sanction for hostility against Nuria, the events of recent weeks had accentuated, if possible, her irrepressible recourse to slights, goads, and rude remarks. After lunch, while Papa went to take his siesta, Nuria, in one of her repeated attempts to gain Eloísa's goodwill, counterproductive to the degree that they instead stimulated in her the awareness of power of the one who knows themself solicited, went to have a chat with her, to ask about how she was coming along with the clothes for the doll she was making for her nephew's daughter, etcetera, and Eloísa, with radiant malice, had to show her, knowing perfectly well that Nuria could not at all have failed to notice that, on the contrary, the doll that she had so uselessly given to Eloísa some time before, was still perfectly intact in its box, exactly where Nuria had left it, atop a small console in the sitting room. What? Raúl heard. Bad weather? Well, the sun was out bright and early this morning. People who sleep in late miss everything, you know. Eloísa, tyrannical, triumphant over things as simple as pretending to not understand someone else's words and make them repeat themselves, thus scuttling, implacably, their spontaneity, or rather forcing them to specifically explain the meanings of obvious expressions, or even, ultimately, adopting a purely negative position, slamming the door on however many assertions the other made, however indisputable they might be. And all that, according to a reaction which it would be very mistaken to interpret as simply a desire to wound, given that it was fundamentally about clearly establishing a position of primacy, similar to how in a child, the act of tipping over an ashtray a second time, for example, must be understood, not so much as an act of defiance, a purely contrary spirit, or swinish stubbornness, as much as, in a more abstract manner, a manifestation of clarifying whether the adults' punitive response is strictly in answer to the act of spilling the ashtray or if it's the result of a more sporadic and arbitrary nature.

Supposing that Nuria's obstinacy toward Eloísa was simply an attempt to improve her position, by dint of perseverance, among the people who in one way or another formed part of Raúl's life, her already established habit of paying a visit now and then to Leo's house responded, however, more probably, to an effort—although one more modest but no less useful—to strengthen, to secure her past, to remain loyal to the people, places, and customs from the times when she and Raúl first met, to keep alive as many elements as possible that might represent a nexus of union between the both of them, of turning them into allies, even at the cost of denying the damage and artificiality of some visits identical to themselves, like going to Sunday Mass and, like this, painful in their recurrence. Leo and his girlfriend and his sister and the old man with his soliloquy and Juan with his outbursts, interruptions which, as a form of counterpoint, the old man seemed to incorporate throughout his monologue, absorbed in the exposition of his concepts about that man who although slogging through life—family, business, competition, thoroughly harried—sometimes glimpses something great in the world, in the sky that cleared up over the city after the rain, for example, or in an eighteenth-century Dutch seascape, or in a book that he doesn't understand, but which doubtless contains some magnificent idea, something great that he would like to express and in fact tries to express, to express to his friends all that he glimpses, to his clients, to his colleagues and his workers, words that elude him, conceptual clarities that become cloudy in the very moment of trying to grasp them, stammers, gesticulations, emphatic hoarseness that—with eyes popping out, mouth gasping—little by little, irreparably come to define him, in the increasingly wider circles of his world, like the classic bore you've got to flee from at any cost, the drip, the drag, the pest, the nag. But if Nuria was right in saying that, all in all, Leo's father had always essentially been known for being a tedious talker, pigeonholed as such by everyone, it was still unacceptable, however, to have to keep tolerating the cumulative effect of his oppressively concentric digressions, ever more reduced as the years went by, like a sauce thickened by endless stirring. And, still more objectionable, the utility of putting to the test in such unfavorable circumstances her uncomfortable relationship with Leo, of updating each time his increasing distance, much greater—and of different significance—than when he was still an inmate at the Modelo prison, before the trial, and Raúl and Nuria went to visit him once a week, going in, preceded by the guards, through that succession of hallways and doors that shut behind them, everything smelling like the inside of a high school, like a cafeteria, like a refrigerator, and in the visiting room, on the other side of the double grating, Leo would appear, and they talked almost without knowing what they were saying, self-conscious like on the platform at a train station; an ever-greater distance between them, as if it had to come up each time, since he was released from prison in Burgos, when, out of touch due to the time he'd been away or perhaps not yet adapted to being free, they could talk, however, almost the same way they'd talked before, nobody afraid of being misunderstood, like that morning when, precisely, he talked to them about his father, a little congested from drinking vermouth, the sun shining on the terrace outside the bar, I don't know what's the matter with him, he's become unbearable, I come home and I find him slumped in an armchair, and he says so many times that he's tired that it starts rubbing off on me. He makes me sick, he only talks about retiring, that he's now old enough to retire, that a son's first duty is to his father, that he sees me just as little as when I was in jail, that he feels lonely, that now that he's old he finds himself without a happy home. And before prison he wanted to get me a clerk's job in the firm of some fourth-rate lawyer friend of his, a sort of crook, some lifelong communist who—as he says—has been forced by life's circumstances to abandon the struggle; now he's talking to me about some other friend of his who owns a mussel farm. I suppose he'd like me to work with him, that I marry some industrious wife, have children. Me, not my sister; my sister's kids don't have his family name, and besides he says that my sister looks like my mother and I look like him. I think that's why he never paid her much attention, because she must remind him of my mother, and he never paid any attention to my mother. And I never see my sister's kids more than a few times a year, and he doesn't want my sister to come and clean or tidy up during the week, he says Teresa does a better job. And it's not really that, she doesn't do a better job, she does everything; my father takes the customers's measurements and then he goes and sits in his chair, and she's the one who cuts, sews, and irons the clothes, and makes the deliveries, while he talks and talks about the revolution, about socialism. You understand what I mean, Ferrer? And the socialists get treated the same as the Arabs, people think they were savages but in reality they had more culture than us. The Almogavars, the Almohads, the Beni-Merins, they all left us immortal monuments that attest to their culture. The real savages were the Christians who, with the obscurantism of the Inquisition, persecuted wise humanists like Fray Luis de León, who said that God had made the world for all, but that kings subjugated people. The same as today, the way capitalism treats men of good will, like the Rosenbergs, a crime of lèse majesté. But hell or high water, everything comes together, it all turns out the same, the world rushes ever faster toward socialism. And the thing is, as long as there's no exploitation, the human being feels more responsible and surrenders more and puts socialism before everything else. You can see this even in the Olympics, where socialist athletes continuously break their own records. And man will conquer space in the same way, and explore the depths of the oceans, descend to the center of the earth. With the help of socialism there's nothing that man cannot achieve. You see, in the socialist world everything has a different meaning, work, sports, human relations, and this is because human exploitation has evolved into the administration of things. And all that this is, we might say, is only the prelude. Because as socialist society becomes communist society all man's problems must necessarily disappear, except, obviously, the ones that are natural phenomena, like death, earthquakes, etcetera. Then there will be no need for armies, or police, or jails, because if someone's against it, it means that they're crazy, because only a madman can be against it, and this is a matter for doctors, who are the ones who have to cure them. And everyone will have time to devote themselves to culture, we'll all be poets and musicians, we'll all paint, and art and literature will be things made by everyone. Churches, for example, could be converted into true temples of culture. Without prohibiting worship, of course, as long as there continue to be religious people; but, outside the hours for worship, they are places that already exist, we've already got them and should use them to bring culture to the people, to give them ideals and save the young generation from this wave of sexuality and pornography that's corrupting capitalist countries. Because although I'm personally agnostic, I think that we must respect the beliefs of Catholics of good faith, who are in many cases the first people to be scandalized by the fact that the Church, contrary to the teachings of Jesus Christ, has put itself at the service of the rich. We saw *Fabiola* the other day. Now that's a moral film, and although it's about early Christians, it's perfectly applicable to socialists nowadays. And the audience understands that what Fabiola presents about the Christians then is still true of us today. And the thing is, Christ was not God, but he was a great man and a great revolutionary. The same with Confucius. What happened is that, over time, the Church stopped worrying about the poor, and it preached one thing and then did the opposite of what it preached. But there are still Catholics of good faith, and priests of good faith too, even today. Well, then they should do something and not sit idly by, said Juan. With workers you've got to take the bad with the good. And, winking an eye at Raúl, mimed jabbing his elbow. He seemed cheerful; upon sitting down he slapped Leo on the knee, as if to strike away the somber look on the other's face. Teresa brought out some pastries and, while she prepared more coffee, insisted they pour themselves some more brandy, more anise. And Leo's sister said that they just might be moving to Germany, to work in an optical plant in some city or other, where they'd heard from some people who were already there that a good technician like Juan could earn a fortune. Juan interrupted, as if annoyed by the way she'd announced the news, or as if he feared that her explanations might be misinterpreted, without the proper political context; he pointed out that they hadn't really decided yet, but the current situation was unbearable and nobody was making a move or doing anything; and the bad thing is that this is precisely what the capitalists want, that the worker who thinks for himself a little gets tired and leaves the country. I warn you that it's a double-edged sword, said Leo; it's been shown that workers who emigrate come home more politicized than before. And with money in the bank, said Raúl. That's right, said Leo's sister. A lot of them save everything they can and when they come home they open a business, said Raúl. And the sister, Antonia: that's what I tell Juan: start something, a business, something. I know some folks who opened an electrical shop and now they've got an appliance store and a company that installs electrical systems. Others start with a restaurant. Or with a bar. And Raúl: whatever it is, the important thing is to have some foresight. He caught a flashing glimpse of the wrathful look Nuria shot him, eyes bristling and flaring like the mane of a wild rearing horse, and Leo's more ambiguous face, somewhere between disoriented, almost pained, and critically composed, like the face of one who finds themselves caught in a lie, more or less guilty, while, with forced humor, toying with some related idea that, of course, it might well happen that they return home transformed into some greedy capitalists or something like that. And, now that the old man had taken him aside to speak one on one, it was likely that Raúl's eyes would also give him away, as the old man was saying, because I accept what's natural, hot and cold weather, earthquakes, what I don't accept are the things men are guilty of, what's natural can't be bad; it's simply natural, but men, perhaps, divorced from nature, are the ones who do evil, look, Ferrer, I believe, and while he said it and expounded his thoughts it was likely, it wouldn't be at all unusual, that the others present—except the old man—saw equally in Raúl's eyes his desire to get out of there, to tell Leo' father, I don't give a flying fuck what you believe, and beat it the hell out of there.

If the old man's endless spiels didn't seem to drive Nuria as crazy as they did Raúl—his unflappable oratory, his uncomfortable tendency to identify himself with whomever he was talking to, to talk about religion, for example, as if Raúl were some young vicar with social concerns, offering concessions, criticizing himself, considering the problems of the church almost as if from within, finding only a few formal problems to argue against, celibacy, money squandered on liturgies, and a few other damned little things, provided that, being fair and reasonable, his goodwill also be taken for granted, so that, all misunderstanding cleared up, they might both, the old socialist and the young ecclesiastic, agree to a common base of understanding, as well as goals, which, as they talked and talked, seemed to become something not only feasible but also real. If Nuria didn't get exasperated, or at least not as much as Raúl, perhaps it was because, infected by the atmosphere of sincerity and conciliation reigning in the house, she herself, when offering an opinion, frequently spoke in a similar manner, when, as if to slip away from the small circle of the women, she firmly reclaimed the general attention toward her remarks, contentious issues that might have some value discussed in a family setting, for example, as an affirmation of one's own independence from parents, but which in the present context turned out at least extemporaneous, subjects like the immorality of canonical marriage being annulled as a cover for rich people being granted divorces, an undeniable immorality even from a Catholic point of view; tiresome, out-of-place questions from a real bore, even considering Nuria's mental instability, that oscillation, for weeks now, between oppressive anxiety and irritated excitement, nerves like lit fuses sputtering toward an explosion that never happened, a truly propitious state for any neurotic reaction, to the exhaustive review of as much traumatic information as she could possibly gather, her father's death, her critical relationships with her mother and with Amadeo, her difficulties with Raúl, financial problems and more, with a marked tendency to seek a common denominator, a general cause, a single person responsible for all that, some elusive subject in whose absence Nuria's accumulated rancor and vengeful—and contagious—wrath were usually discharged on someone else, usually Raúl. I don't see what's funny joking about these poor people by being cynical like Federico. Honestly, I don't see what's so funny. You seem like Delacroix's Liberty leading the people with her tits pointing them the way to freedom. See? That's exactly like something Federico would say. I wouldn't be surprised if you two were lovers; I don't know what you'd do without each other. We wouldn't know how to survive. As far as Federico goes, I'm telling you it wouldn't surprise me one bit. He's more of a mental faggot than most I've seen. And he's the one responsible, with his mean jokes, for you growing apart from Leo, from politics and everything. I think he must be jealous. If not, then I can't understand why he just rips into these people who'll never be intellectuals or geniuses or anything like that, but at least they're good people, which is saying a lot, and a very close family and no one's got the right to go after them. And you think you're such a communist and all that; well you don't seem to me to act like a communist, not you or any of your friends. And that's why, with Leo, who's the only sincere one among you, you're all trying to get under his skin. Well, no señor, I'm not kidding about this, and Leo's right. Art that's not accessible to everyone, art that's not meant for the people, I've got no use for it. The problem with you all is that you've got all the typical intellectual deformities, but workers aren't intellectuals. Unfortunately. Look, in England I also met some communists and I can promise you they weren't like you guys; there they're the real thing. And Raúl: apart from you, I don't think that anybody in the world is worried about what English communists are like or not like.

Louis. Nuria's little pal, her London adventure. A childlike figure, an affectionate presence, uninhibited, available, a presence that, like in the case of that fiery revolutionary in residence at university, whose abstract radical demands usually reveal, however, the viscous imperiousness of his more crude desires—that they rub it, that they take it out, that they do whatever he says to make him orgasm—thus, with Louis, in a similar way, the exterior appearance offered no obstacle, doubtless, to his inner self harboring the most sordidly camouflaged designs, appropriate to the behavior of one who, accustomed to the lethargic sex of the Anglo-Saxons, feels simultaneously attracted to and daunted by Nuria's spontaneity, so that, incapable of seducing her directly, or simply taking her to bed, acts cunningly, disguising his intentions with oblique propositions, political or moral arguments. The erotic Chinese pillow book, for example, that Nuria had brought back from England. A gift from Louis, surely. A program of common experiences? An attempt to use this kind of reading material to compensate for his instinctive capabilities, undoubtedly scarce, well proven by the fact that, after all, it was not him but Raúl whom Nuria latched onto?

They kept on walking without talking, without any determined destination, although, like with the inert force of a tropism, they unconsciously drifted toward Las Ramblas, to have a drink in some bar, withdrawn, hateful, diminished, without anything else to do or anywhere to go, without money and, as a consequence, without any desire to do anything or go anywhere, with all the oppressive feelings that the people out strolling in the streets on a Sunday afternoon can exercise on the spirit, the crowds, the patient lines outside the cinemas, under the misty drizzle with the reflections of neon signs and the lights of the traffic, and especially, that hasty atmosphere of young people rushing to get to their planned destination—a party, a dance, into bed—groups, couples, cars passing by honking merrily, and which, like the contrast between certain lively avenues and their deserted cross streets, or, for example, the even greater gloominess in someone already numb from anxiety, typically aroused by the contrast between themself and the contemptuous displays of vitality from the male whores strolling the avenue, which could only increase the sordidness of their own inane wandering. Or the annoyance of having to adjust your stride to the steps of others until finding an opening and being able to zigzag ahead threading your way through various ranks of pedestrians, controlling the irresistible impulse to push people aside and run them down and open a path by any means possible, leaving behind once and for all the vast example of that whole family, or the pained faces of that young married couple, their small, frugal steps, the wife in an ostentatiously interesting condition, trapezoidal and grave—her water predestined, you might say, to break on Christmas Eve—the husband holding her firmly by the arm, possessive, defiant, holding his head up high against any possible affront, to the least sign of someone noticing his ignominy, that he was clearly and notoriously caught; especially as they passed the Church of Our Lady of Bethlehem, where, due to the narrow sidewalks, they reduced their pace to a particularly slow, careful walk, and it was also particularly disheartening to walk beneath the triumphal arches of light bulbs strung across the street between the naked boughs of the plane trees and the luminous hanging street lamps, and the loudspeakers with their enervating Christmas carols, proclaiming the apotheosis of the hopeful expectation, the imminent Nativity and the Epiphany, the adoration of the Child in Bethlehem, a Catalan sort of town, with its large old stone farmhouses not far from the famous stable, and its meadows and its small bridge over the stream and—if we overlook the exotic touch added by the Three Wise Men and their caravan of camels—the delicious images of the farmers and the sheep and the pigs and poultry and the hunter with his shotgun and the parish priest with his umbrella and—the most suspicious of all for being so incomparably more popular—the crèche figure of the *caganer* squatting down to shit behind a bush. And the sharp needles of the fir tree glowing with raindrops and the moss and the mistletoe.

O vos omnes qui transitis per viam atendite et videte si est dolor sicut dolor meus. Waning moon spirit, sun slipping away, time of waiting. For what? Killing time, walking along with hands in empty pockets, as if he'd never done any other thing, just as indifferent to sorrow as to beauty, the shake of a gorgeous mane of hair, for example, that young woman coming out of one of so many different antique stores, shaking out her hair as she adjusted her coat, her profile barely glimpsed before she turned away and with a firm step gained some distance on him, leaving him behind, further away with every step, no less deaf to the splendid cascade of that golden hair than to the ringing of the bells still sounding as he shut the door, the beauty of that hair disappearing among the people on the street just as useless as her naked body gracing the bedsheets, indifferent, indifferent, Calle de la Paja just up ahead, shiny cobblestones, polished smooth by the slippery water, dim, almost a mere reflection, obsessive as the certainty of what awaited him that afternoon, Tuesday, December 13, the decisive meeting with the men from the paper company, more distasteful the closer it came, despite all the sweetness of revenge, given the inevitable hardness of the meeting, while approximately at the same time, around five o'clock, the midwife was preparing Maripain for the second and last time, now on the eve of the abortion, of the unwelcome visit they would pay her when everything was over, now in Adolfo's house, without the completely unlikely prospect of having to handle afterward a hysterical crying jag worse than the one yesterday. The recollection of not having been and the pain of continuing to not be it, with the rootlessness of one who not only feels distant, but also without any desire whatsoever of being close, lifelessly, absently, scrutinizing the engravings and books displayed in the windows, beyond the blind reflection, forcing himself to assimilate the meaning of what he was contemplating, trying to feel interested, fascinating windows certainly, even lacking sufficient morale or money to buy anything, or the self-confidence to go in and browse around and end up saying that he'd return soon, even though, in the last place, it wasn't so much the effort of going in and returning the bookseller's greeting and saying clearly that he was only there to have a look around, without other explanations or justifications of any kind, almost aggressive, and stay there looking around until closing time, barely half an hour, without the bookseller having any reason to object, on the contrary, there's always something new, you know, make yourself at home, tacitly offering, no room for doubt—like on the screen, eyes closed, nostrils dilated, she parts her lips slightly—the access to his inner sanctum, the small backroom where, with the seductive power of prohibition, the books kept out of immediate view display their titles, mostly old editions from the years of the Spanish Republic or newer translations printed in Argentina or Mexico, a relief from all kinds of anxieties, given their thematic variety, from *Das Kapital* to the *Kama Sutra*, by way of *The Treasures of Magda*, Lenin's *Two Tactics*, and Engel's *Anti-Dühring*, appropriate materials for students interested in pursuing such thinking, as well as people interested in sex, as is normal when the male sex juts out like a challenge, in those schoolboys desirous of knowing what sex holds in store for them, or to try to figure out, when it goes soft later, what might have awaited them, but really did not nor will not await them, with the typical defects of everyone close to old age, people who, if not comforted, will find ample ground for some fantasies when they learn that the women of Maharashtra enjoy practicing the seventy-four arts of pleasure, speaking words in a low voice during intercourse and desiring the men to speak to them in the same tone, or that the women of Pataliputra are of a similar temperament, but only express their desires in secret, or that the women of Uda suffer an interminable tickling in their Yoni that can only be satisfied by a rock-solid Lingam, or that the Punjabi woman is driven wild by Auparishtaka or cunnilingus, the sort of clientele easily identifiable the moment they enter the shop, with the tense naturalness of the couple that slips into a private room. The simplest thing to do being not to accept the implicit invitation, Raúl went back to leafing through items closer to hand, folios of prints and lithographs, without the bookseller paying him further attention, more interested, obviously, in the interrupted chatter, a conversation initiated between two customers, under his auspices, one might say, insofar as they did not know each other personally, while the bookseller, on the contrary, as if deliberately, seemed to know enough about them both, their refined or complimentary features, in the manner of an equally experienced and disinterested procuress, without other options or proposals than that of establishing contact, thanks to their good service, between two people who would thank him for doing it, although if only for the pleasure procured by that improvised conversation, although the conversation had no regular continuation, nor did it grow progressively into a kind of milestone or institution, like the milestones of other times in Barcelona's cultural life, nor would this moment establish henceforth some permanent bond of friendship, under the bookseller's somber tutelage, respectfully withdrawn now to a secondary position, silent and contemplative, essentially like a beneficent gargoyle, similar to that individual—obstetrician, staff member of the Civil Registry—whose ogreish appearance conceals the spirit of a refined thinker or sensitive poet, woefully unacknowledged. What else could have generated the spark between the noted sculptor smoking a Peterson's pipe filled with mellow, fine-cut tobacco, interested in any kind of print bearing a viticultural theme, and the bibliophile with the crazy glittering eyeglasses and bald pate beaded with sweat, a collector of books about gastronomy and the proprietor and the owner of a restaurant serving typical regional fare, specializing in cuisine from Tarragona? How, between these two strangers, without the bookseller's propitiation? However, as much as the match must be rubbed across the striker for the head to burst into flame, it's no less necessary that the quality of the striking surface be adequate to the quality of the match head, meaning, apart from the bookseller's mediation, the two conversationalists shared a common idiosyncrasy, a common desire not so much for discussing as for corresponding, cultured people with whom one can speak, predisposed to understanding, to offer mutual support and agreement, people who know that their own tastes are shared by the other, who each see their own reflection mirrored in the other. And what's more important: an intelligence based on a material more subtle than the match's flame, which is the tongue, in this case the Catalan tongue, intelligence established from some phonetic, syntactic, or morphological nuance present in the first words the bookseller invites them to exchange, starting with the correct meaning of some expression or word, in contrast to the degraded Castilianisms that have slowly infiltrated colloquial Barcelona speech, centering on the linguistic terrain, by way of countersign, the basis of approximation and, even more so, of identification, between the two conversationalists, in the same way that a certain adhesive quality in the look or a laugh loosed in excess or a simple impertinent intonation are always present in the beginning of the adventure which, in the loneliness of walking the street, drags homosexuals down toward the lower reaches of the Ramblas after nightfall. Thus, in a similar way, must have occurred the conversationalists' mutual recognition, thanks to a fluid interchange equally rich in suppositions as in prospects, terrain which is a gift to survey and which, as usually happens in great moments, the morning of the wedding in the bride's house, for example, when they give the final touches to her dress and resolve then and there the little mishaps that always arise, and the people come and go and wait in an atmosphere of high tension and joy, of bewilderment and efficiency, tending to create a general atmosphere not only of trust and mutual understanding but also of exaltation and euphoria, the relief of having been found, the anxiety of exploring, of explaining oneself to each other, of externalizing their desire for understanding, the firmness of their convictions, and not only on a theoretical level, everyone mobilizing, sympathetic and solicitous, when the taxi driver burst in, a thickset Catalan man, of pachydermic pleasures, not missing from his calm sardonic haste, and requested a copy of the *Calendario del Payés*—the farmers' almanac—for the coming year, I buy it every year he said, his car parked right outside the bookshop door with the motor running, and everyone took charge of the situation—traffic cop!—and while the bookseller hurriedly took care of him, and the noted sculptor stepped outside to keep an eye out, the gastronome offered him oral moral support voicing his scorn for traffic tickets, taxes, and bureaucracy, until the taxi driver sped off victorious, not even hastened by a honking horn, everything executed perfectly like a sleight of hand, and the conversationalists, overcome with happiness resulting from fulfilling one's duty, met again in the peace of the bookshop, even more at home if possible, complicit, twinned, the bookseller, the gastronome, and the noted sculptor, and even that young man with an educated look, Catalan probably or, at least, someone who enjoyed the bookseller's confidence, and if he didn't join in the conversation, it was for youthful shyness or for commendable respect for his elders, he seemed at least an aficionado of prints and lithographs, considering the youth of today that says a lot, *Le Cap de Quierz, Plan de la Ville de Roses en Catalogne asiegée le 2 d'Avril par les Armées du Roy très Chrès Commandées par le Marêchal du Pléis, and A General View of Barcelona from Montjuich*, and *Interior of the Cathedral of Barcelona,* view from the choir, with the high altar highlighted against the clear light from the dome, stained-glass windows, and rose windows projecting into the depths of a world one could well imagine flooded with color, radiances, and polychromatic incidences scattered about by the gold of the altarpieces.

Like the cook who does not begin his work until having gathered all the ingredients required by the recipe, so, only after the first exploratory sallies to delineate positions and define themes, the conversationalists applied themselves to the manipulation itself of the elements under consideration, a job of alternately glossing and breaking down the material in question, with the goal of configuring, like a sculptor, their clay, the desired image, ready to receive the breath of life: Catalonia: the Catalan character, its most distinctive traits: realism, laboriousness, sensuality, individualism, an indissoluble individualism united with a strong sense of fraternity, an ironical spirit, civilized, wisely skeptical, almost pagan, sensitive to natural beauty, to the pleasures of the senses, devoted to his traditions, gifted with instinctive mercantile attitudes, inclined, in case of dilemma, to the most reasonable solution, to the transaction, removed from all unshakeable dogma, from all fanatical furor, traits quite expressive enough to define the reasons for Catalonia's superiority, in the most diverse fields, about how many different peoples surround it, economy and art, sports and culture, landscape, even, a landscape that is the fruit of the perfect conjunction of nature and human labor, a superiority that is, in the final estimation, that of a richer, livelier, more open way of life, if we might permit ourselves the redundancy, because on the one hand, through work and tenacity, the Catalan has been able to make prosperous a land scarce in rich resources, he lacks neither vitality nor joy, and on the other hand, when it comes to celebrating that effort, in order to surrender himself to the feast of the senses and, especially, to the most exciting of pleasures, the flesh, spectacularly successful even in that, far from the funereal repressions or alcoholic intoxication of other peoples, a total superiority that explains so much the impotent animosity that the central power has always manifested toward Catalonia, like the attraction that it exercises upon the inhabitants of other less-gifted lands on the Iberian peninsula, upon the emigrant, the now so-called *charnego*, assimilated today as well as yesterday, at the turn of a generation, through the vigor of Catalan society, in a manner similar to how, in the past, Catalonia roundly imposed its own personality upon the heart of the Confederation, always ahead of Aragonese, Majorcans, Valencians, and Neapolitans, James the Fornicator, Peter the Glans, the rapacious ferocity of the Almogavars, the phallic aggression of a naturally peaceful people, but who, when consumed with wrath, are terrible; I understand that currently, in Greece, Bulgaria, and Turkey, they still remember the Catalan vengeance, like a raging hard-on whose historical resonance, thanks to the general ignorance of nations and to the administrative silence with which Spanish centralism traditionally misplaces the glories of the peoples it oppresses, can end up reduced, in the eyes of the younger generations, to little more than the boastings of a sexagenarian who recalls chasing skirts when he was young or the fantasies of one who permits himself the liberty of bragging about sexual exploits, despite his shrill voice, his bean-fattened paunch, and his presumably ridiculous little shriveled pecker. Empty your mind, play dumb, a premeditated centralist attitude taken to such extremes as forgetting that Agustina de Aragón was really Catalan, born in Fulleda, married to Corporal Roca, also Catalan, accidentally identified as a Zaragozan, not to mention the most scandalous mix-up of them all, Christopher Columbus, Cristóbal Colón or Colom, about whom the experts, Porter, in fact, offer evidence, increasingly more conclusive, that he was neither Genovese nor Mallorcan but rather Catalan, possibly of Sephardic origin. Castilian antipathy, the envy that all things Catalan have always inspired. An envy founded, typically, on fear. Fear of Catalonia. Logical, to a degree, considering all that Catalonia could have become! What it might still become, if the old virtues weren't lost and replaced by new ones, if different peoples could coexist, the old temperament, characterized by savagery, like today's smug potbellied pomposity, a product no doubt of industrialization, of the sedentary habit that in the long run supposes using machines, especially when run by foreign operators; what it would be: lucubrations, astonishment, lamentations and, above any other consideration, the zeal to set itself apart from the brutal Iberian peninsula to which it is historically and geographically anchored, from its grim and fitful development, equally distant from French splendors and Italian harmonies, a peninsula where even the art might be called more nomadic than settled, Romanesque here, Gothic there, Baroque and Neoclassical over there, but always separated, exclusionary, as if cultivating the one demanded the confinement, if not the demolition, of the others, a problematic distinction, on the other hand, if in order to excel at something one must first elucidate one's own boundaries without really knowing what ours are, since who knows where this Troy upon Troy begins and ends, this buried land, whose presence, however, we still sense, the way pigs sniff out buried truffles, a perfume that sprouts from the earth making a fading impression, a rhythm to which we try to match our own and which gets away from us, perhaps for being too accelerated, not like the Barcelona of times past, with its rhythm of life like a Swiss or Bavarian city, one of those populations structured by the centuries, inhabited by hardworking citizens, meticulous, patient, punctual, unhurried, precise, of equally elevated financial and technical levels, one of those cities of old stones and stout bellies, cities where craftsmanship is an art, where progress is perseverance, where perfectionism is the only objective and high quality the reward, virtues that were, and which could continue being, our own, if only the city were not becoming so virtueless, if only it were not growing so fast until it is no longer our own, centralism, immigration from the south, basic urban expansion, distances that demand ever greater velocity to cover and, what's most dangerous, the inner velocity that inevitably ends up possessing the inhabitant of a large city, destroying all moderation and moral hierarchy, disquieting symptoms already evident in the streets and for which, perhaps, like a cancer, the only treatment is the diagnosis itself, a clinical picture before which only remains to us lucid withdrawal and the pleasures of nostalgia. *O trist de mi! Quin fet pot ser aquet? De cuant en ça esta axi Barselona? ¡Catalunya la vella! La yaya! La tieta! Oh, woe is me! What can this be? How long has Barcelona been this way? Old Catalonia! Our nana! Our aunt!*

Catalonia of old, Barcelona of days gone by, its festivals, its markets, its bacchanals, its religious ceremonies, its wonders, the Holy Christ of Lepanto in the cathedral, who grants one of the three solicited graces, the sanctuary of Santa Rita on Calle del Carmen, she who resolves impossibilities, San Nicolás on Pasaje de los Campos Elíseos, who offers help to all who come seeking it, who, with all due modesty, touch his knees, all three centers of attraction only comparable, although in a different way, to those who, then as now, in so many spots in the lower part of the city, gathered each night, according to the erotic specialty of the establishment, a true multitude, joined in fervent fraternity for the gunslinger and the loose cannon, for the lumpen and the bohemian, a city with cultural anxieties no less intense than its mercantile or social concerns, a city of intellectual conversations, of artistic movements, the Barcelona of Els Quatre Gats, of Rusiñol's *L'Auca del Senyor Esteve*, the days when any Barcelonan could recite from memory the most obscene rhymes of Pitarra, the Barcelona of El Patufet and Pere Fi along with, simultaneously, *El Be Negre* and *L'Esquella de la Torratxa*, magazines coveted by collectors just like everything that is now only a memory, like these *aucas* and *aleluyas*, the most faithful chronicles of Barcelona's customs and traditions, a permanent calendar of how much that is endearing is lost and forgotten, institutions like the Nativity Scene and el Rei de la Fava, belonging to the Feast of the Epiphany; the blessing of the sea on the feast day of San Raimundo de Penyafort, patron of sailors first before he became the patron of lawyers; the processions on horseback of Els Tres Tombs on the feast day of San Antonio Abad; the pig sale on the Paseo de San Juan followed by the slaughter right in the middle of the street with the help of an expert butcher, in front of each house, a good excuse for a family party and some enjoyment with neighbors and passersby; and, on the feast of Saint Agatha of Sicily, the traditional distribution of candles called La Candelaria, as well as special loaves of bread, which had the power to keep a woman free from any ailments in her breasts for the whole year; the carnal license of Carnival, Carnestolendas, or Carnestoltes, and its immediate expiation, Lent, allegorically represented by a fishwife with seven feet sticking out from under her skirt, the very number of weeks of mandatory abstinence; parades and religious processions for the Feast of San Medín, in memory of miraculous fava beans which saved San Severo; the pilgrimage of Santa Madrona, martyred in Thessaloniki, in proper observance of the saint's unspoken will that her mortal remains, carried to Barcelona by a tempest, remain in Barcelona; the dessert called Crema Catalana served in celebration of the feast of Saint Joseph, whose carpenter's plane, preserved in the cathedral, was drawn across the chest of young women who wanted their breasts to grow bigger; the feast of palmas and paletones, sweets to be blessed on Palm Sunday, and the Seven Churches Visitation on Holy Thursday, and the devotional Caramellas sung in choir on Holy Saturday, and the roast lamb and special pastries on Easter Sunday, the folk processions and dancing of sardanas on Easter Monday, the jousting tournaments on the Feast of Saint George, replaced over the years by the Festival of Lovers, with books and roses for sale in the streets around the present site of the Barcelona Provisional Council, and Arbor Day on May 1; the blessing of the whole municipality of Barcelona from atop the cathedral roof, in commemoration of the Invention of the Holy Cross; the Fair of Sant Ponç with its open-air market along Calle Hospital featuring candied fruits and herbs and homemade liqueurs, the Corpus Christi procession upon carpets of flowers, with its trumpets and drums, enormous papier-mâché figures: the dragon, the eagle, both symbols of St. John the Evangelist and the herald of Barcelona itself, the giant king, a Goliath who came to represent Charlemagne, founder of the historical county of Barcelona, the giant queen, angels, demons, the grotesque *cabezudos*—human figures with enormous heads—and the scenes mounted under the direction of the ancient guilds, farcical interludes and floats depicting the Creation of the World, Hell, Adam and Eve, Moses and Aaron, the Prophet Daniel, the Three Wise Kings, the Phoenix, the Martyrdom of Santa Eulalia, Saint George on Horseback, the Maiden of Saint George and her parents the King and Queen Mother, all in slow procession with their retinue, following a predetermined route along the streets and through the plazas, and the wondrous sight of *l'ou com balla*, an egg dancing and spinning in perfect equilibrium atop the spurting fountain jet in the cathedral cloisters; the summer solstice, celebrations on the eves of the Feasts of Saint John and Saint Peter, bonfires, fireworks, all of it beguiling people into drunkenness and lechery; the melon market of Saint James, in the eponymous Plaza San Jaime, the saint who procures a husband for many single women, James, Jaime, Iago, or Santiago, the white knight who converted the Barcelonans with his preaching from atop Mount Taber, the traditional clay and ceramics fair in Puerta del Ángel, based on the old custom of inaugurating new clay water jugs with the blessed healing water of Saint Dominic, in memory of his stay in Barcelona, where he introduced the cult of the Blessed Rosary; the sweltering feast days of the Ascension of the Virgin in mid-August and the rainy feast days of La Mercè—Our Lady of Mercy—around the autumnal equinox; and the marzipan *panellets* on All Saints' Day and the flower markets set up at cemetery entrances on All Souls' Day; and the students' petitional processions on December 6 celebrating the Feast of Saint Nicholas Bari, their patron saint before he was supplanted by Saint Thomas Aquinas; and Saint Lucy, patroness of the blind and of seamstresses, who today, December 13, as in days gone by, throng and mill about in front of the cathedral, which encloses the chapel dedicated to their cult of worship; and the festivals of Saint Thomas, on the 21st, coinciding with the winter solstice, the little booths that sprang up along the city sidewalks, grouped together according to the kinds of products they sold, butter and lard, garments, dish cloths, and tea towels in the Boquería, silk, embroidery, and lacework in Calle del Call, pastries and confections in Calle Petrixol, jewelry in Calle Argentería, ceramics in Plaza San Jaime, blocks of hard nougat candy—*turrones*—in Plaza Real, second-hand books on Las Ramblas, and so on in so many other places, but the three big fairs that remain only preserve a trace of that old spirit, the toy fair on Gran Vía, the poultry fair on La Rambla de Cataluña, and the advent fair of Santa Lucía in front of the cathedral, with its crèches and wreaths and greenery, as always a prelude to the Nativity, with its ritual of the hollow Christmas log filled with presents, and its gastronomical apotheosis, followed by the Feast of Saint Stephen to finish the feasting, and the Feast of the Holy Innocents so that we might have some good cheer as we approach the witches' coven of New Year's Eve, the single step that separates one year from the next, a step that the Barcelonan of times past—unlike today—tried to start off on a good foot, convinced that the first day of the new year would be a reflection or a prefiguration of the whole year awaiting him.

A moment to take stock, to make a reckoning of the past year: of what the new year might hold in store for us; what will be Catalonia's destiny, based on what we are, in the months to come; what luck awaits us based on the past months and years, and centuries. Because, for example, as in modern-day Italy, where the passing of millennia of radiant culture—the optimum breeding ground for natural good taste—along with, no doubt, the secular exercise of political, economic, and moral chicanery—established now and forever—as an inevitably human complement to the gilded stones of empire, weighs upon the daily habits of the Roman people and their descendants; so too and no less, the sediments of the past weigh heavily upon modern Catalonia, traits like the Catalan's tenacious application of the concrete and tangible and his instinctive mistrust of any superior organization, however more abstract or more broad, that could not be glimpsed from any of his mountains, as they say; a logical reaction, to a certain degree, in the inhabitants of a land that, passageway and causeway par excellence, has seen the rise and fall and even extinction of the political structures of the many different peoples who have invaded it. A frontier land, a natural route for invasions, overrun time and again from the four points of the compass, its comportment is not, in effect, less conditioned by the past than is the behavior of that man who, as a boy, was a frequent eyewitness to his mother's infidelities, and who will show himself powerless to lead a stable erotic life, incapable of preventing, every time, his every love affair from sliding into disaster, disappointments that will inevitably be blamed on some incompatibility in the lover, without ever realizing, perhaps, that his deep, unconfessed, unformulated desire was, precisely, that the affair would collapse; meaning: a personality prone to oft-repeated incriminating slips and failures, desires and aspirations developed on an oneiric and frequently nightmarish plane, by virtue of his own unconscious repressions. In other words: a clear example of historical hysteria, of collective neurosis, with periodic crises that tend to be repeated, to suppress the initial trauma each time that similar circumstances reoccur, the impossibility of assuming one's own personality and acting accordingly, of renouncing their consubstantial masochism, humiliated, beaten down, stepped on, like one of those women forever complaining about the cruelty and mistreatment they suffer at the hands of their lover, too often complaining to not eventually conclude that the mistreatment and cruelty are her only ties to her lover: departure. Stretching the terms, in the same way that, on a metaphysical plane, if God were Spanish, Satan would be Catalan, in the same way, moving from neurosis to psychosis, we could even come to categorize the two terms of the Catalonia-Spain counterpoint as entities with schizophrenic and paranoid traits, respectively; Catalonia, sunk in auto-libidinous sentiments that lead it to bitterly contemplate the destruction of the beloved, meaning, of itself; the other, Spain, completely given over, without any kind of limitations, to its mythomania, its delusions of grandeur, its persecution complex; traits which, in both cases, do nothing except, possibly, conceal, like a mask, a latent homosexuality. In consequence, as if in some way we had to qualify the historical attitude of the one as well as the other, we would have to conclude that Spain's role is typically sadistic, while Catalonia's is essentially masochistic; a type of personality that, if it were possible to cast a whole people's horoscope just as one casts an individual's, the only possible conclusion would be to consider, in light of its historical profile, that it was born under the masochistic and self-destructive sign of Scorpio, with the bi-member sign Gemini in the ascendant, at its most unformed or immature, and clearly subject to the nefarious influence of the planet Saturn. Thus, for example, a succinct examination of traditional Catalan cuisine, in its most characteristic features, defines it for us as imprinted with a marked infantilism, by reason of its nature, at once elemental and spontaneous, rough and robust; a style of cooking that knows few spices, far from elaborate, vegetables raw or parboiled, meats barely grilled, lamb ribs, chicken, rabbit, all the meat somewhere between bloody and burnt to a crisp; the Catalan's love for applying his own condiments directly to his favorite dishes, as well as for gathering or capturing mussels, limpets, urchins, all kinds of shellfish eaten raw, wild mushrooms, snails, small game; his marked preference for those foods which he considers especially vitalizing, frugal, and flatulent, all those nasty popular inside jokes about the properties of beans, take, for example, the idea about their special nutritive and energetic power, derived from the sponginess and fermentation that their consumption produces within the digestive system, followed by compression of the diaphragm and subsequent expansion of gases, that is, the fart, tacitly considered, in diverse social milieu, as a manifestation of dynamism, vitality, and being good with people; their worship of foodstuffs with phallic or excremental shapes, *botifarra*, *bisbe*, and other typical sausages, fava beans, turnips, peppers and eggplants, garlic, onions; his obsession that the wine be fresh and unchilled, a strong variety, drunk from a bota, from the countryside, the kind that makes a man get good and hard, and spring water, with recognized therapeutic and revitalizing qualities; his tendency to celebrate with such foodstuffs, out in the open air, taking advantage of holidays, long weekends, and vacations, as many banquets as possible, by the streams and meadows of the forest, a propensity for which one need not be Sigmund Freud to make the connection with ritual practices of sexual initiation, individual or collective. Generally possessed of an excellent stomach, the Catalan man is capable of assimilating, as Catalan society absorbs southern immigrants, the most undigestible foods, and of defending Catalan gastronomy with a total conviction in the universal value of its appetites, in the same way that the greedy man who exposes or relates his savings operations attributes to his listeners a pleasure similar to what he experiences as he contemplates accumulative phenomena. Good proof of that is the Christmastime tradition of the Tió, not Santa Claus nor Papá Noel, not even the green Christmas tree itself, but rather, more elementally, an old, dry, hollow log charged with providing each family with the adequate holiday sweets when conjured by a chorus of the children in the house loudly singing the "Our Father of the Trunk"—*¡Caga Tió, caga turrons i pixa vi bo!*—"Oh, Christmas log, shit nougat candy and piss white wine!"—as the log is beaten with a stick, blow after blow delivered as punishment, a luckless scapegoat that purges beforehand, with its coveted droppings, the brutally shocking indigestion that comes with the day, apart from emphasizing the symbolic aspect of the obscure excremental origins of the most sweetly savored things and, on a more conceptual plane, of the dialectical relationship existing between the natural processes of ingestion and defecation, a fact so much more interesting and revealing when considering that, in Catalonia, food at Christmastime is the very finest, the best food of the year, a ceremonial culmination that opens and concludes the gastronomic year with its grueling menu: chicken soup, stew, crudités, stuffed golden capon, melon and pineapple and pearly bunches of grapes in a decorative arrangement, and nougat candy and rolled wafer cookies, all of it accompanied by generous quantities of table wine, champagne, malmsey, and spirits, the bottles in the background, a plastic composition, a still life, always appearing in holiday pictures, as well as, suggestively haloed, on old-fashioned Christmas greeting cards dropped in the mailbox by the neighborhood watchman or garbage collector, to brighten things up for the holidays, inscribed on the back with some bland stock verse praising their services rendered, thus justifying their expected tip, and offering wishes for a prosperous new year, elements evocative of the joyous popular climate and the impatient excitement surrounding these holidays, a matter somehow far removed, on the other hand, from those poets writing the best vernacular verse, who have traditionally found Christmas to be an endless source of inspiration. The reason being, apart from gastronomy, poetry is the other last bastion of Catalan culture. A poetry that notwithstanding the unfavorable initial impression that the phonetic contact with the tongue in which it's written might produce in the curious traveler, a crudely onomatopoeic language apt for composing puns and tongue twisters like *setze metges mengen* *jutges*, which declares that "sixteen doctors devour the judges"—or something like that, and that one about *en Pinxo va dir a en Panxo vols que et punxi amb un punxo?*—"Pincho asked Pancho: want me to puncture you with a punch?"—and so on, a language that's been capable of reaching the highest heights of contemporary poetic orography, works like *Els Carquinyolis de Sarriá*, its timeless verses of pure everyday speech, classic by reason of their exact human measure, universal by their Mediterranean concretion; or the lucid desolation of *El Triomf del Minotaure*; or the magical realism of *Me la va desfer Monna Lisa*. A living, up-to-date, poetry, which this very night, in the tutelary shadow of Santa Lucía, will see its storied past enriched with one title more, which, along with the titles of the other award-winning works, belongs to several other literary genres, making it absolutely clear once more that poetry is really nothing less than the only living form of expression in Catalan literature, and that Catalan literature is not the only integral element of Catalan culture, and that Catalan culture and its material support, the Catalan language, are not the only foundational elements of the authentic entity of the Catalan Countries. A literary lottery awarded in the grand rooms of the Hotel Colón, at No. 7 Avenida de la Catedral, by means of a patient alternating or rotating mechanism, not so much—as one might judge lightly and with bad intentions—so that the jurors and various prizewinners are announced in as judicious a manner as possible, as because materially the result can be no different, by reason of the very abundance and variety of prizes for a limited number of cultivators of a language enjoying a numerically modest public, modest to the point that any of its mandarins—author, reader, jury, prize, prologue writer, anthologist—upon confirming the watchful attendance each year of the secret police, proud, at bottom, of the relative restlessness that such events seemed to inspire in the authorities, and especially proud of the unanimous and reiterated fortitude, as well as of the punctual regularity with which, each year, the attendees of the event offered a measured challenge to those authorities, proud, almost happy, one could say: if a bomb exploded now, that's the end of Catalonia, a somewhat disgraceful utterance for whomever might understand it without any lofty thoughts, ignorant of the true reach of the problem, ignorant of its character, or what's worse, indifferent to the losses that the inexorable human condition, meaning death, infringes upon those assiduous faithful in so many of their spiritual leaders, fewer and fewer every year, although we still have figures like Uirpse, known to the world as Salvador Espiru, and Quart de Pere or Pere Quart, not to mention less-well-known but no-less-estimable figures, Moll, Coll i Alentorn, Aramon, and the somewhat compensatory uncertain appearance of promising young writers, though their almost complete lack of reputation doesn't prevent them from bringing new sap to the old trunk nor of counteracting with their presence the implacable annihilation that takes pleasure in attacking, perhaps, those enterprises most targeted by misfortune, the only explication of the perseverant circumstances that have always shadowed our culture since the origins of the development of Catalan literature. Because it's true, yes, that its appearance on the landscape of the literatures of the Romance languages came rather late, due to a purely oral existence, in stiff competition with Provençal and Latin, until then exclusively written, and which, having barely consolidated their independence, including before, including while, their different and defining features were taking shape, it already had a parallel process of dialectalization and fragmentation, according to the particularisms of the various reigns of the Crown of Aragon, unhappily being the Principality of Catalonia, least wondrous in achievements among them all; and it's also true that after the first flowering of Catalan literature, whose merits are still, on the other hand, insufficiently recognized, perhaps because its diffusion and influence were of a more moderate character, perhaps because it had premeditatively tried to marginalize them and even ignore them or silence them, a phase of the eclipse begins, an interval of almost four centuries during which Catalan literature ceases to be, literarily and literally speaking, for reasons that at first glance can seem mysterious, especially to the naive reader's blinking eyes, merits not in reality difficult to figure out through a correct analysis of the very structures of Catalan society during that period; a lacuna or void that lasts until well into the nineteenth century, when the resurrection of Catalan literature begins with the appearance of the poem in the vernacular—though written in Madrid—"La Patria"—a progressively accelerated reflowering, as if propelled, you might say, by a steam engine, a progress inevitably linked to the political, social, and, especially, economic avatars of the age, progress that must necessarily culminate with the scientific re-elaboration of that progress, codifying the language's grammar, in 1913, concretely, when everything seemed to indicate that the economic structure of that homeland in revival and its much desired political superstructure, were going to find their most natural flowering in poetry, cultivated, as in times past, preferably, by scholars and clergymen. Yes, all that is true, yes, *la Renaixença*—the Catalan cultural revival and its historical disaster; and was that disaster due to excessive confidence in the language, and a prudent fear of resorting to other kinds of weapons, equally certain and tangible as the last splendors of that poetry, which surface, like the fortune that comes to one's hands when they are too old to enjoy it, or how bodies tormented by agony usually look more beautiful after death, or to put it more crudely, like the swan's song? But it's no less certain either that everything might have been different, that the weight of the literature would have been able to reach far enough to set history aright, that even politics would have had to bow down before some literary events of greater significance, if the history of Catalan literature had been different, if from its origins it had experienced an archaic but definitive development, the equivalent, let's say, of the Provençal lyric, or if at the right moment its own Dante had appeared, capable of making the language coalesce around his work, or with a normative Renaissance like the one in France, or something like Elizabethan drama, or with a Baroque Counterreformation like the Castilian one, or from a wider perspective, if Catalan literature, although discontinuous, might have had at least, in the course of its history, just one single figure of indisputable universal worth. Therefore: isn't its late arrival proof of the cosmopolitan and elevated degree of culture of a people who wrote in Latin and composed verses in Provençal while speaking in Catalan? And is its ready dialectical modulation not a demonstration of expressive richness and subtle nuance? And isn't its rebirth after almost four centuries of silence proof of its vigor? Of producing a poetry like its contemporary forms, whose surreal omegas have no reason to envy the best poetry written in Spanish or in any other language in this century? Is it nothing more than the product of a sick and wasted culture? No! Ridiculous! Is there any doubt that such a literature cannot die, that like in olden times, as always, Catalan literature will know how to overcome the unfavorable circumstances in which it is currently unfolding: its reduced human base, the increasing difficulty of absorbing some largely non-Catalan popular classes, the lack of support and collaboration—if not disrespectful misunderstanding—in the heart of the properly-called Catalan society, on the part of its ruling classes, of its driving leaders, of its most representative personalities, politically mortgaged to the central power, diverse kinds of human agents who mutually empower one another in a sickly vicious circle, agents who if they socially circumscribe the use of that literature to the field of bourgeois media, from an internal, strictly literary point of view, seem to slowly move toward the alternative—in its dramatic struggle at a level of linguistic survival, with the consumption of energy that the defense of a problematic existence supposes—of choosing between triviality and localism, something in every case minor or quotidian, things marginal, if not alien, to the interests of any person not directly implicated in the problem, situated beyond its diminished limits; what room for doubt that in spite of so many obstacles, such as the centralist administrative obstacles which victimize us, obstacles that our enemies, gaily celebrating their habitual ill will and malicious spirit, will not hesitate to classify as excuses? What doubt that Catalan literature will endure, that it has seen and has survived worse times?

What doubt can there be, what personal convictions, of inner sanctum or chancel, difficult to hold onto out in the city streets, where the atmospheric element, demoralizingly de-Catalanized, capable of dissolving the firmest resolution, makes its clumsy embarrassing defense, that lack of popular support, that indifference so much worse than the violent enemy, that fear of feeling, that lack of necessary lung power, extemporaneous, ridiculously outlandish, in a city that is ours, in our Barcelona, a city whose most traditional features seem to be disassembled day by day? But, and from a Marxist point of view, in light of historical materialism, what future can await a literature initially written with apostolic ends, pious babble masquerading as homilies and sermons, with the goal of making them accessible to the public, to reach the people who, over the centuries, had ceased to understand Latin, a language more and more removed from its own rough formative language, when now, with equally apostolic ends in mind, to reach the proletariat, with the great pain and sadness and despair of Fortuny, one must abandon writing all political propaganda in Catalan, if one plans to have the people in the working-class neighborhoods manage to understand the significance of the pamphlets distributed? What future, considering that if the birth of Catalan letters must be attributed to the inadequate character of Latin and Provençal and the new realities of the age? Must you not then consequently recognize the ineluctable character of the progressive inadequacy of Catalan letters to address the new realities of Catalonia? And another new fact: the appearance of writers born in Catalonia who write in Spanish, an occurrence at least as new or unusual as the fact that one hundred years earlier, for the first time in four centuries, it was simply that writers appeared, a phenomenon which, contemplated from a Marxist perspective, seeking some material, structural, or economic reason, could be attributed to the conversion of Barcelona, immediately after the war, into the primary center of the Spanish publishing industry; or considering for ourselves other criteria, entertaining other perspectives, a kind of sociological analysis, for example, the advantages those writers had for having been born, as a rule, in the heart of bourgeois Barcelona, meaning, in a city, Barcelona, particularly open, restless, and reformist, among all the cities in Spain, and into a social class, the middle class, objectively more progressive than the sclerotic Castilian feudalism; or attributed to the decline of Spain, or to the decline of Catalonia, none of that discovering any great explanation at the heart of the matter, nor, on the other hand, the explanation, any explanation, being too interesting, not even our purpose in examining it. In short, taking good note and drawing the attention of the sociologist, or the scholar, or the simple aficionado, to a fact that, for being common to the greater part of that new generation of writers, can facilitate the description of the phenomenon, not only its interpretation: they are not ours, they are not integrated into Catalan life proper nor do they cooperate in its maintenance, generally foreign to the privileged classes, belonging to those families which, although Barcelonan by name and birth, are culturally Castilian, or for their foreign ties, or for a question of principle, meaning, for what the national unity of Spain, firmly safeguarded by the armed forces, represents for them as a guarantee of stability and order, families who are unconditional supporters of Francoism who, after the turn of only a single generation, are thus purged of their browbeaten renunciation of Catalanism, their cowardly and corrupt defection from the Catalan cause, with some children whose uneasiness—not only literary—seems to lead them to no longer renounce only Catalonia but Spain as well, their fatherland, their religion, their ilk, their class, their blood, adding apostasy to their treachery and political subversion to moral terrorism, communists, nihilist anarchists, a reaction equally unforeseeable and widespread, unfortunate in that we are all, to a certain extent, responsible, we who fought and won a war for them, for them and for the political, moral, and territorial integrity of Spain, a Spain that we wanted to hand over to them exactly the same as we had received it, or if possible, even more pure, even more purged, more identical to itself, and nevertheless, given that it's not conceivable to speak of just punishment in relation to a cause both just and victorious, we committed some error, some mistake whose nature we have not yet fully understood, so that spurious throng nests in our own guts, that new and negative generation of writers who by their conduct make all purely literary sanity secondary and accessory, given that their personal circumstance, just like any other element from the rest of the peninsula, frequently rubs shoulders with common crime, depraved drug addicts, alcoholics, homosexuals, and, who knows, maybe even parricides. Ineradicable moral cancers! Lear, oh Lear, old and blind and crazy and abandoned! What would the men of Barcelona from the turn of the twentieth century say? Men like Don Eusebio, Don Manuel, Don Juan, Don Antonio, Don José, Don Augusto, Don Francisco, what would they say now if they could rise from their graves? The loss of values, the dissolution of customs, and what's worse: the extent of evil, of which the reprehensible creations of a handful of writers and artists are only one of so many symptoms, the simple material of an intellectual conversation for people with common obsessions. A classic generational conflict brought up when one is young, and forgotten and resurrected again, only on the inverse of the equation, with roles reversed, when one is old? Is it all a result of Barcelona's social structure when, even though it's got nothing in particular that is manifested in the son of the southern immigrant who lives on the city's industrial periphery, according to his class interests, an attitude of defiance and rebellion, the same as in the world of people like the Tarrés family, of technicians and specialists, self-employed workers and administrators, and even, with the irritation and bitterness that defeat usually brings, in certain sectors of the Catalan petite bourgeoisie, the big victim, along with the proletariat, of the Civil War, cases like those of Aurora's family and the Fortuny family, for example, the argument is not quite so satisfactory and turns out to be more than incomplete, when such an attitude can occur in homes like those of a person like Rivas Fernández, typical representative, no less than the paper manufacturer Plans, of the non-monopolistic bourgeoisie, or in family names like Ferrer Gaminde, not for being families in decline, after various generations of absenteeism, completely deprived of social consideration, or in the heart of families like the financier Quintana, a relevant figure of the Castilian aristocracy, linked by marriage to the upper-class Barcelona bourgeoisie, or the attorney Cuadras, an eminent member of that bourgeoisie, an attitude that would doubtless be exaggerated to consider as genuinely revolutionary, but which, although if only for its true disinterest in class interests, in his class, seems to us frankly atypical, a product of something deeper than a logic and a passing antagonism between parents and children, because what's certain is that before, or more exactly, until now, all this, what's going on now, never happened? Jacinto Bonet, incidentally, a relatively young man although he doesn't quite look it, however, barely forty years old, oligarch par excellence, no mere technocrat in the service of the oligarchy like Amadeo García Fornells, but an oligarch in the strictest sense, an involvement that Jacinto Bonet, father, simple lucky black-marketeer, member of the postwar nouveau riche, with everything and having amassed a solid fortune, would never have dreamed of, inhibited perhaps by his somewhat clumsy or primitive manners, or perhaps for the Catalan businessman's instinctive reserve—founded in reasons essentially fiscal—regarding all excessive gravitation toward the upper circles of administration; a spirit forged in the happy postwar years, on the other hand, our oligarch has not had experiences different from those of so many other young people of his time and of his class who, like him, have known how to respond to their upbringing and education, a greater show of richness perhaps, stronger family ties, a more optimistic vision of the opportunities that life offers, a mentality nowadays in short supply, constrained to disguise its nostalgia for those times and mold itself to the present moment, obliged to feel sincere desires to forget the origins of all that, the last blood and the first gold, to cast earth and even mud over the memory of such mythic times, over the so-poorly-understood ostentation of the nouveau riche, a Thomist need to touch in order to believe, to see in order to experience the miracle of transubstantiation of bread into gold, of the tin into gold, of the quotas of anything into gold, of living to see the incredible reality of money, a technicolor life like in those contemporary American films, high-rises with swimming pools, big luxury cars, beloved wives and darling children and beloved beloveds, and more than anything, the wild, giddy sensation of impunity that comes, in a system of generalized corruption and coercion, of economic power unleashed, without conflicts, neither labor-related, nor fiscal, nor social, nor even domestic, with the most absolute liberty of abusing everything, of knowing that there is a way to fix absolutely everything; a nostalgia just as comprehensible, unfortunately, just as inadmissible, a sad necessity, a sadness sadly sad from denying not only any relationship with all that but also of convincing themselves of the convenience of leaving all that behind, just a caprice of history, the versatility of time, which makes young people starting out now, unlike those who started in the hard-but-fascinating forties, and who, shaped by the positive principles that informed Spanish life of those times, are now responsible men, unlike them, the young people now, whose loving upbringing and the family harmony and social peace in which their lives developed from earliest infancy, contained the expectation of maximum integration into the environment, everything seems to turn out less clear for them—life, the world—more imprecise, if not contradictory and even crazy—everything rolls along in such confusion! Moral metastasis. The inconsistency and lack of consideration from today's young people is simply inconceivable; their pastimes, pleasures, and habits so different from those of our days, going to the Liceo, flirting in the boxes, and Sunday mornings, on Avenida Diagonal, strolling the sunny sidewalks, up and down the street until reaching Plaza Calvo Sotelo, up and down, with the ebb and flow of the crowd, and the festivals and booths along the street, and those old time dances, slow-dancing, cheek to cheek, mouth to ear, things that meant so much then and nothing now, as if nothing from those days means anything to young people now, and not for lack of desire—although at the same time you can't discard a possible loss of vigor in the generation as a whole—as much as for considering it little more than a waste of time, something puerile or too formal or insufficiently exciting, at the same time exceeding the norm, the detours and evasions that years before regulated the relations between boys and girls, and the exception, the veteran pride of some girls, heroic fornicators of the forties, their secret passions, their licentious memories, scandalizing them, worse, decanting them, cornering them, with how easy everything has now become, the hard-earned privileges, from house to house, family by family, almost without the parents themselves managing to understand how, their parties, their meetings, their amusements about which so little is known and so much is rumored, that elusive and famous dolce vita that so obsesses people who are no longer quite so young, questions—what do they do, where do they do it, who's doing it—which everyone—which everyone supports with their own private erotic frustrations, orgies that a feverish mind might well situate, for example, in an apartment like Adolfo's, or even right in the family house, the Cuadrases' place on the weekend and the house in the hands of Adolfo and all his friends, everyone looking for costumes, petticoats, and formal dinner jackets, top hats, suspenders, garters, liveries and corsets, furs, liturgical ornaments from the family chapel, albs and chasubles, cinctures, the dusty smell of the lace dominated by the camphor smell of the cloth, no less fatally destined, in spite of the loving care with which the parents conserve the grandparents' clothes up in the wardrobe, to the solace of the grandchildren, to give some spicy flavor and hot temperature to the new generations' parties, and adequate environment—as the poet says—to their impossible propensities, in their progressive search for times gone by, in their journey through the past, from garment to garment, until the final culmination, everyone with their original, old-time outfit, the pure and simple, collective and promiscuous nudity, in the half-light, music playing softly, glasses half-full, cigarettes—maybe marijuana, who knows—scenes to which the aforementioned feverish imagination might well add a Sistine jumble of intertwined bodies. Seems there's girls getting it on together and everything else, whatever you like, said Nuria. People always exaggerate, said Raúl. Has anything ever happened right in front of us? Nothing has happened and nothing ever will happen because Aurora knows I've got more guts than her and she's afraid of me. She knows I'm capable of going way farther than her in everything. And as for her, if she's not the center of attention, she's not interested. Well, you know the one I can't imagine in the middle of these things is that wimp Adolfo. Adolfo? I can assure you that if she gets into such things it's only for his sake, because she knows that's the way to keep him hooked, only for that, to please him. Considering what a phony manipulative little bitch she is, she'll do anything, whether she likes it or not, just to keep her claws in him. Well it seems fine to me; I've got nothing against a good, old-fashioned orgy. Me neither. What's happening is that in Spain people are too uncivilized for these things; here everybody just goes their own way, and with things that way, it just can't happen.

Uncivilized? Was that supposed to mean that England was civilized? A place where it was possible to practice all thirty fornicatory positions envisioned by the sexual rituals of Taoist eroticism, including Autumn Dog? The same stupid discussion, the same stupid conjectures and suspicions that in the morning, in that bar on Plaza San Jaime, after going to pay the gas and electricity bills and after she pawned her jewelry, not yesterday, yes, yesterday, Monday, but not the morning, in the afternoon, after accompanying the Plutos to their appointment with the midwife, everybody in Adolfo's car, while they waited in a bar, and Adolfo looked for a parking spot and the assistant must already be ushering the Plutos into that cold white echoing room softened by shadows, where they would soon hear the midwife's husband's ringing voice, a sudden fright not attributable to the discord between the timbre of his voice and the loving words she would doubtless use to receive Maripain, nor to how easily he spoke while getting ready, as if instead of proceeding to dilate her cervix he was doing her nails, but rather to something at the same time more superficial and disquieting, by virtue of its very unreality, the sensation that might provoke in us, for example, the apparition of a peasant farmer with bulging cheeks, his mouth painted with bright-red lipstick; an argument brought up again in this case, by way of recourse, as a means of distraction, some polemical thing that would console them or put them at ease even if only for a few moments, the time they had to wait, at a table disagreeably close to the opening and closing door, for Adolfo to pick them up and, in his company, wait for the Plutos to return, in a kind of dress rehearsal for what had to happen the day after tomorrow, everyone awaiting the joyful advent of what must not be born, a malign algebra made flesh incognito, neither X nor Y, definitively dismissed, an epiphanic abortion. This chick, just a touch of her big dyke fingers and you'd be seeing stars. She's a lesbian, see, and she was crazy about you, didn't you notice, Maricunt? asked Pluto. And Maricunt: well, kiddo, must be that I don't like dykes. And Pluto: I always said you were a prude. And Maricunt: I hope the doctor's got better hands and that it's true they use anesthesia, though I swear, in the long run, the pain is the least of it, I swear, Nuria. Just figure it's going to be awful for a little while and then you go through it and that's it, she was saying, then it's all over, more cheerfully, of course, and also more relaxed than Nuria, a Nuria totally incapable of lending her the moral support which, in principle, one might suppose was appropriate to her role in all that, strained, gloomy, almost lugubrious, slumped down out of sight in the back of the car, as if exhausted by their brief run in the pouring rain, from the door of the bar, or even confused by the furious drumming of the rain on the useless umbrella, or feeling swamped already by the redundant voice of the windshield wipers sweeping back and forth the whole way, clearing away the gray with their endlessly repeated no, no, no, more dejected than in the morning, when Raúl arrived in such a hurry as if late to the meeting place, a bar in Plaza de la Villa de Madrid, to find that she hadn't arrived either, and he, for not having stopped along the way after leaving home, had no cigarettes, and was still hesitating whether to buy a pack at the bar, where he knew they wouldn't have his brand, or walk to the tobacco shop, always a better solution, because even if his brand didn't automatically bring him good luck, it wouldn't bring him bad luck either, and that was something, and besides the tobacconist was just a few steps away and nobody, absolutely nobody, could have foreseen the horrible bother of a housewife buying Christmas gifts, her tardy thoroughness, her drivel, her coin purses, her fat cheeks, her blather, her stories, her repugnant calculations, her silly nonsense, her pasty unction of a sexually experienced and socially respectable woman, placidly taking her time choosing every single item, displaying her tastes, explaining why, not so much, evidently, for the impression that her personality might make on the tobacconist, as on the impromptu public audience that her sluggish shopping was causing to grow larger by the second, and finally, for the pure and simple pleasure of stating her personal opinions and tastes out loud, no, nobody could foresee such a waste of time, so that, when he got back to the bar, Nuria was already waiting for him, still with that glazed looking of someone just awakened, it's a good thing, I thought I was late, she said. Well, you are late, said Raúl. Well, chico, you got here later than me. Don't I have time for a coffee? And Raúl: no, there's no time, and refusing any explanations, he took her by the arm and, almost running, led her along Calle Canuda toward Puerta del Ángel, letting her go breathless telling him that Mariconcha and Aurora had telephoned her, that's why she'd been late, that they had set a time to meet about the midwife, that Aurora had been strangely sympathetic, that she'd said why didn't she go to her house while the others accompanied the Plutos, I told her if it was for Mariconcha's sake, but look if your little Aurora really is a dyke and what she wants is to throw herself at me, if not, I don't understand it, frankly, she's got to know I don't really have much regard for her, wait, wait, I can't go any faster. They entered the Catalan Gas and Electric building, Puerta del Ángel 20-22, at three o'clock sharp, precisely when the porter was closing the enormous iron gate separating the cashiers' windows from the main offices, leaving barely enough room for Raúl and Nuria to slip inside, unlike the two women coming behind them, two friends or cousins or neighbors, in short, two women who after hearing the lock snap shut, clinging to the iron bars like prisoners, immediately began to complain, to beg the porter to let them through, simultaneously displaying various fairly pathetic arguments, they lived far away, their lights were going to be turned off, he'd just let that young couple through, etcetera, at the same time that the porter, doubtless a man of rigorous standards, calmly withdrew his key from the lock. It was open then and now it's closed, he said, unable to disguise the pleasure of feeling, although only for a few brief moments, the long arm of an implacable power, whether he grants or denies, his features waxy and swollen, fleetingly reanimated by a despotic spark, rules are rules, with the delectation that certain spirits find—dark revenge for all the injuries life inflicts—in the fact of being able to personally give bad news to the interested parties, to the closest friends or relatives of the victim of some accident or misfortune, that kind of pleasure experienced by one—there always is a one, an agent of authority, eyewitness, or spontaneous messenger—who fulfills the painful duty of participating—at first without daring to look at the anguished face of the message's recipient—the sad, tragic news, a fatal accident, for example, his glassy scrutiny, later, upon accurately clarifying: burned to a crisp, something horrifying, his sure observation of the cathartic reaction, that for once the other externalizes the pain that he carries, emotional discharge frequently of such force that he even ends up contaminating another, for making someone sob, meaning, our messenger, venting his emotions in a flood of tears, looking for relief, inner peace, feeling firm desires for remaking his life, for improving, behavior which, in turn, usually does nothing else but increase the intensity of the emotional response of the others present, contributing to the general despair and stupefaction and paroxysm, a phenomenon whose origin is doubtless similar to the greater public's love for TV series and soap operas, crying about what one has done when they cry about what happens on the show, to expiate one's own fault through the propitiatory expiation represented, sins that, in general, attack the family ties, an adultery of unfortunate and exemplary repercussions, the premeditated exclusion of the parents by the child who has prospered and is now ashamed of them, the cowardly abortion undertaken because of what people will say, etcetera, etcetera, questions of mental hygiene to those who were probably not strangers to the case which concerns us, as seems proven by the fact that when Raúl and Nuria left, the porter, always behind the bars of the gate, and who only opened it to allow those few remaining inside to go out, even continued chatting with the two women there, attentive to their problems, in the attitude of one who tries to put himself in the other's position, to adopt their points of view about life, no doubt giving them some good advice, some surefire direction for the future.

An itinerary very similar to today's schedule, with the small variations that happen in any artisanal motivation repeated to the point of obsession, because in the same way that from the Plaza de la Villa de Madrid they had reached Puerta del Ángel by way of Carrer Canuda and not by Vertrallans and Santa Ana, so, when they got to Avenida de la Catedral, at the spot known as Plaza Nueva, from Carrer dels Arcs and Puerta del Ángel, unlike today, they had continued along Calle del Obispo and Plaza San Jaime, to Number 6 Calle Jaime I, a small door leading to the section of pledges or deposits for the Caja de Ahorros y

Monte de Piedad savings bank, whose central headquarters has its entrance at Calle de la Ciudad 1. Other differences: the Christmas fair selling crèches and wreaths in front of the cathedral was perhaps not yet properly inaugurated, and instead of rain, in the way of those truces that have no other objective than to undermine the enemy's morale, the air was damp and hazy, the light like a lemon-juice-colored halo that seemed to soften everything, the sounds, traffic dampened, isolated facades, spectral lamp posts, people hurrying along silently, almost feeling threatened you might say, cold and sweating at the same time, streets and plazas that, unlike the streets and squares of Dickens's London or Balzac's Paris or even, at a stretch, the Madrid of Perez Galdós, had not found and perhaps would never find a faithful chronicler for their grandeur and their misery, of their anonymous daily dramas, a Balzac who would have so thoroughly enjoyed himself witnessing the spectacle in the waiting room at the Monte de Piedad, seeing the possibility of appreciating the thousand shades that distinguish the people who come there for their appointments, from the most humble people, whatever their origin, or those fallen on hard times, but in every case people of honorable poverty and laudable honesty, self-sacrificing mothers, exemplary wives, loving daughters, to the most varied gamut of figures with a whole range of criminal faces, ruffians, pimps, swindlers, prostitutes, homosexuals, usurers, card sharks, as well as thieves in general, every kind with every speciality, each one with their own problems, each problem a complicated web, conflictive situations that, given their own individual matter, could only possibly define us in a rigorous way by resorting to the subtleties of juridical terminology, the fine distinctions which, thanks to such language, we can establish between the complex elements concurrent in a woman who goes to pawn her jewels, some mistress, for example, doubtless caught up in an emphyteutic relationship with someone who maintains her: the difference existing between ownership (in this case, her own body), possession (of the woman by emphyteusis), and dominion (the pimp's right), for whose benefit and by any reckoning she pawned her jewels, thus redefining her relationship with this man through a renewed emphyteusis, only now inverse to the first arrangement, the money obtained in the pimp's possession and her services to him consequently demanded, only under her control; lives, in short, that lend themselves to infinite conjectures and unfathomable opinions, thus gathered before the penetrating eye of the creative genius, of that climate of longings and anxieties, in that truculent atmosphere, populated by narrowness, passivity, debts, struggles, calculations, disappointments, pledges, achievements, depreciations, interest, a bank vault of misery atop a mountain of sleaze. An environment propitious, on the other hand, for dialogue as much as for confidence and even for indiscretion, according to the ties of solidarity that tend to develop between those companions who share both expectations and sorrows, such mistrust and distance resulting from jealousy or embarrassment, that of the scolding nunlike old maid, to cite one example, the old woman who while managing to avoid all contact with the woman sharing her bench—a ruined, whored-out forty-something showing the desperate degradation of a deeply beleaguered fornicatrix with the broken face of one who'll settle for being roughly stitched up—even as she huddled deeper into her dandruff-dusted overcoat, at the same time, alert, defensive, watching each and every one of those present, her features, closed tight as a clamshell, making it easy to guess at her nostalgia for a Barcelona now fallen, like herself, on hard times, the Barcelona of her youth, the good old Barcelona of streets like Calle Fernando, and Calle Petrixol, and Calle Puertaferrisa, of Calle Ancha, streets where people could and did live, and life followed a rhythm that was both as friendly and meticulous as in a haberdashery, the opposite of Barcelona today, full of strangers and inconsiderate people, full of dangers: cars, shameless people, the crush of the metro, thieves, slips, falls, gypsies, drunkards, and worst of all, the exhibitionist, that man with a satanic hard-on who stalks the lonely streets at nightfall; considerations from which, in the mind of that damned little old woman—one of those hybrid bodies, shriveled from virtue, which one always tends to consider an individual due more to periodic secretions of humors than, as when she was younger, because of her menstruation or periods as they are called—Nuria and Raúl would surely not escape, doubtless judged even more severely, if possible, by the appraiser, whose way of looking at Nuria through his blonde eyelashes, ironic, condescending, in the confessional-like intimacy of the pledge booth, evinced his conviction that the operation of pawning a handful of jewelry from a rich girl—lockets, bracelets, earrings, her watch—was nothing but the fatal invoice of evaporated extravagance and nocturnal pleasures, an impression that Nuria uselessly strove to dissipate with her chatter, from an excitement so excessive and unjustified that it could even make the appraiser presume that the girl standing in front of him found herself on the verge of prostitution, occasional prostitution, who knows if impelled by her silent companion, her boyfriend, her gigolo, surely. A wounding prefiguration and a cruel replica of the image that, soon thereafter, in the café on Plaza San Jaime, they themselves, Raúl and Nuria, might have conjured up about the infirm old couple sitting at a nearby table: she, a woman with her hair so lacquered as to appear synthetic fiber, who looked hard and affluent, a characteristic of the moral dominion that economic superiority instills in nations as well as people; he, equally mature and no less conscious than she about what the role of money means, including, in the terrain of erotic relationships, the inferiority that comes from not having it, a lucid comprehension that transpires not only from its tidy presence—that obligatory pulchritude of one who no longer has any presentable clothes to wear—but rather, above all, of the somewhat strained deference of its treatment—the numbness of the offended dignity—as well as his outdated manners, the emphasis with which he removed his sunglasses, for example, or the smirk, more smirk than smile, of his mouth, bitter tics and a correctness maintained beyond all humiliation, beyond all suffering; the desolate correctness of the man who knows how to fit in or, more simply, of the silly idiot.

They had walked into the café as if buoyed by the euphoria and comfort implied by finding themselves suddenly liberated from the most immediate economic urgencies, under that impulse of wanting to go out somewhere right away, to recap, before that very recapitulation begins to overshadow the initial and hurried bewilderment of the celebration, before an approximate reckoning of their small debts against the four thousand pesetas they had just been paid made them see that, in fact, once they'd paid back all the loans, their situation wouldn't be much more liberated than before pawning Nuria's jewels, that they'd have enough left over, so to speak, to just barely pay for the coffee they were drinking, slowly quieting down and hostile again, in sharp contrast to the lively movement of the café, its customers, in general, working in the nearby office buildings, a constant turnover and renewal of clientele, dynamic, efficient, people habituated to a different rhythm of life, to a measured and organized schedule, constantly working to accomplish real tasks; people whose mere presence usually accentuates the stifling sensation of marginalization and abnormality of one's life, uncertain, almost parasitic, although the ease and fluency of their comportment remains rooted, for any reflective spirit, in the senseless and irresponsible confidence of those who go through the world ignoring the fact that man is not a rational being composed of body and soul. How to not feel it somehow wrong—a disordered life, secrecy, problematic love affairs, economic difficulties, unrealized creative anxieties, sordid legal activities, abortions, pawning one's goods—to a certain point, or rather, in a certain way, when facing the physical and moral health of a person, let's take, for example, a woman like this one, a woman around thirty years old, Catalan beyond the shadow of a doubt, who drinks her quick cup of coffee with a friend or an office coworker at the next table; wrong and minimized when faced with the multiplicity of plans with which, fully confident, someone else is capable of simultaneously coping? A woman with the luxuriant vivacity and serene aplomb that are the fruit of an organism in perfect working order: a perfectly regular menstrual cycle, as well as in the various phases of the digestive process, impeccable neuro-vegetative nervous system, complete psychic equilibrium; a woman of vigorous complexion and athletic aspect, tanned, with the healthy bronze skin that comes from skiing, agile gestures and a harmonious laugh, lesbian lips, an equally efficient personal secretary of some company division head, probably, as she is a housewife and helpful mother of her family at home and a punctual adulteress in her private life, without any of all that getting in the way for her—coffee finished, leaning back in her seat, enveloped in the smoke of her cigarette—to also resort on more than one occasion to the studied and lilting laugh of a woman who knows herself ogled by a libertine. Because it was on her, undoubtedly, that the crapulous man was focusing his attention, his staring eyes encircled by deep purple bags, full of libidinous designs, on her and not her friend at the table, against what one might think at first, in spite of being the friend of one of those women—not necessarily mature—who, whether it be due to a certain lassitude in her features, or her facial hue, with shades of mauve and brown, or especially, perhaps the deep shadows of her pupils, tend to suggest to us, or better, to incite us, to practice with them all kinds of perversions; with her, the Catalan woman, and not with her friend of uncertain origin and lascivious appearance, on the Catalan woman—family mother and some business manager's secretary—because at first glance you might well think the crapulous man was ogling the other woman, trying to establish between them both a fluent affinity, an understanding of depravity, it would be not only hasty but totally erroneous to exclude the possibility that it was justly her, the Catalan woman, the secretary and mother, who constituted his true objective, precisely for the reason of her fresh naturalness, of her juicy constitution, a choice that did credit to the young libertine, on the other hand, at the same time, who, as a man of discerning taste, as a penetrating connoisseur of the profundities of the feminine soul as well as their bodies, knows well what a woman like the Catalan secretary can manage to give of herself, the sweet, select words she's capable of uttering, the inspired expressions warmed by her cloying accent, the passionate phrases of love she manages to employ and that nobody imagines, neither in her family environment nor in her work relations; her fervent, feverish form of surrendering herself; the rough sketch of her sex with its full powerful lips. And nevertheless, our secretary and family mother would also be fooling herself if she were to believe that she was the only object of the libertine's desires, of his obsessive, wide-eyed stare; she, yes, it's true, but also and equally the ham sandwich she devoured before her *café corto* and half-smoked cigarette; what's more, it might even be affirmed, for its symbolic value, the most important thing for him in these moments was the ham sandwich, the most fully realized expression of the uncertain thoughts and feelings which seized him, of his most imperious appetites, to eat, drink, smoke, and fuck that woman with his eyes, all at the same time, dominating everything, devouring everything all at once, his mind flying a thousand miles a second, his calculations intermingled with lustful images and insatiable designs, the typical stamp of the person who is a prisoner of the cannibalistic reaction usually triggered by obtaining some unexpected or highly anticipated income, the product of bribery, inheritance, speculation, or mendacity, a reaction on the other hand that extended to his two companions, to their ravenous ferocity: not eating but clutching the sandwich, sinking their teeth into it, swallowing it, wolfing it down in the blink of an eye, before you could say Jesus-Christ-on-a-bicycle, just as the big fish swallows the little fish, absorbing it with all its projections and emblematic values, just as in primitive tribes the hunters devoured their prisoner's hearts, while they commented on the favorable impression—to judge by their voracity—of the interview that they just completed in some office in the City Hall or in the Administrative Council, or in the Savings Bank, an impression that, for being true, might well constitute the departure point for an excellent business deal from which everyone would benefit, gaining their percentage, their commission, the avid young libertine, his associate, the intermediary and even the one most conspicuously absent, the personality that just received them, the one bestowing the favor, all with the thought already filling their mouths, ready, willing, and able to seize their part just as they now clutch their sandwich, as if it were really two handfuls of ass, even though the projects differed according to each one's personal case, more ambitious, no doubt, in the young libertine, like in the player who wants to take advantage of the run of luck or the strategy that exploits with uninterrupted pressures the victory obtained, more ambitious and also more imaginative, illuminated by the flashes of the color polaroids that they show to one for whom money opens all doors, even more seductive women, luxury hotels, ferocious pleasures, while their associate, an older man and, especially, more broken by life, with all the look of bearing, more than anything, along with his knowledge of bureaucratic mechanisms, the experience of repeated disasters, gave himself over to obviously more modest or realistic calculations, made difficult by the effort of pretending to listen with reverent interest to the story that the third man in the group was telling, the relational element, the intermediary, for whom all that formed part of his daily routine, as very probably the same story that he was telling, about some woman, whom he almost seduced last weekend, something scarcely believable in a man his age, but that the other, the associate, the poor devil, pretended to follow as if awaiting the outcome, taking refuge in polite deference—compensating for the manifest lack of attention from their young, vicious associate—the expression of a man somewhere between amused and admiring, almost incredulous, only betrayed in his calculations by the evident vacuity or absence that veiled his gaze, considerations relating to the bills he might be able to pay and to the diverse debts no longer possible to refinance that he might be able to liquidate with the happy ending of all that, the gravy train that was at last about to come his way, under the auspices of the comfortable atmosphere of a coffee shop and the fair tone of the conversation, now centered on the singular beauty of a certain landscape, the object of the business deal in question, possibly, with that peculiar satisfaction that usually comes from the possibility of allying business and beauty, propitious for the revelation of an impetuous lyricism and of some elevated sentiments, unsuspected, even, by the very person who formulates them, the industrialist who decides to personally baptize a product ready to be launched, for example, a new shampoo, for example, that might well be called Sunbreeze, a name both poetic and catchy. Then, the conventional dispute about picking up the tab, the gestures of pulling out the wallet as if it were a revolver and, as if it really were a revolver, to silence anyone else, to beat them to it, even the youngest man, faster and more confident or with better reflexes, the eager one, the libertine, still cleaning his gums with his tongue, as he pulled out a wad of green bills in a silver money clip and peeled one off, making it crackle between his fingers and setting it on the table, sanctioning his valor with a swipe of his hand, with the characteristic imperiousness, impatience, and inclement hardness of the new generations that act so aggressively, less interested in respecting the rules of the game—for them pure formality or farcical ritual—than in hunting for their opportunity, always more combative, more contentious, more implacable, climbing the ladder no matter who topples off, surprised only by the fact that the powerful person whom they intend to supplicate in order to prosper in their shadow or overleap their corpse, perhaps for having been softened before hardened by the years of fighting, perhaps for having enjoyed the relaxation and dissipation his fortune permits him, seems to have scruples, however much of a shark he might be, about making others feel, with maximum tangibility, the true weight of his power, something incomprehensible for those who harbor some hidden aggressive feelings similar to those of that erudite young man who, upon demarcating his area of research, manages to specialize in some minor question of secondary importance, important enough to bring him a certain notoriety, but not enough to make any of his professors nervous, thus assuring himself the surprise factor when the moment arrives for him to suddenly attack one of those teachers' positions, conquering them one by one and—the luck of the dispossessed in his hands—permit himself the pleasure of personally delivering the coup de grace; some methods and a disposition which, nowadays, for being widespread, seem to flatly deny the alarmist lamentations and doomsday prophecies of so many people who blame today's youth for indulging in dissolute and hedonistic behavior even while spouting excessive idealism, forgetting that similar judgments are usually repeated in each generation when they begin to see their successors popping up on the horizon, however much, in practice, the facts are quick to demonstrate the contrary. What other image, for example, should Plans's men have formed of Raúl? What role could they attribute to him, other than the well-connected young lawyer with aptitude and ambitions, involved with fast deals and speculative insurance policies (patently exclusive, for construction, licenses, and public works projects), those types of deals in which everything is a question of perspective, determination, and helpful godfathers?

The power of words to assign, their faculty of stereotyping daily life, of interposing themselves between one and others, between one and oneself; like the shy man who, in his dealings with the man on the street, in order to mask his difficulty with communication, resorts to jokes he's heard others use on similar occasions, but when voiced by him, possibly for lack of aplomb or knack or graceful touch, perhaps for some defect of exposition or nuance, run the risk of being misinterpreted and even of gravely offending their interlocutor, thus Raúl felt inhibited and uncomfortable when he saw himself obliged to respond, even though only externally, to whichever one of the roles he might have to play as the circumstances demanded. At university, for example, the professor of some subject that did not interest him in the least, carefully watching as examinations progressed, moving kindly and silently through the lecture hall, exchanging comments in a low voice—obvious remarks—with the department chair, to give a minimum of verisimilitude to all that; bumping into his colleagues, in the hallways, on the patios, in the vestibule, the need to adopt a decisive step, without him showing any sign that he's already seen them coming toward him from an opposite direction, while preparing to offer some greeting at once original and conventional, adequate for the type of relationship uniting them, and then, almost as if he'd just noticed them, a flickering look of surprise, a smile of intelligence, his words ready all in a hurry. Or when, all at once, when Señor Rivas died, he suddenly became Nuria's fiancé, and the people who came to pay their respects at the widow's house always found the moment to ask him, between introductions and condolences and words about what a terrible thing it was, if they had been engaged for very long, and he, as if urged on by some immediate problem that required his attention, said excuse me a moment, and in the next room sidled up to any group too focused on the conversation in progress to notice his presence, or he cut short any specific question by saying something to one of the servants, or he simply locked himself in the bathroom to smoke a cigarette. The same sensation of strangeness, or better yet, of being wrong, that with no less intensity he had experienced when he still belonged to the university committee and Escala had taken him to a meeting of the labor committee, introducing him as the comrade responsible for the university sector, who's going to explain to you all in a few words some details about the struggle underway and its political prospects. What could he tell the comrades on the labor committee, not about the struggle and its prospects, but about the university itself? What could he tell them? That he had studied law only to please his father? That, from among every career, the law was the one he most detested and that this was precisely the reason why he'd chosen it, to distance himself to the maximum from university life, properly speaking? That extra-curricular activities occurring in this sector, meaning political activities, were far from what Raúl had imagined when he joined the party? That the prospects for the kind of fight like the one that was unfolding were rather poor, and the possibilities for improvement within the current policy were scarce. What could he tell them without avoiding saying what was expected of him to say and, at the same time, without leaving out the truth, without either disconcerting or confounding those difficult and attentive expressions that contemplated him like something exotic, at once mistrustful—with the instinctual mistrust of any collective toward some outsider—and comforted, under the spell of the moral support which the confirmation that its principles and norms of conduct are in force, even beyond its own confines, usually gives to the members of one of those collectives? How to explain to them, in a few words and in these circumstances, the ideological conflicts under consideration in the heart of the university sector, to specify for them the doctrinal differences that split the students into diverse factions, to make them see that, with everything and against what it might seem at first glance, that situation represented progress in contrast to the university of some years ago, the university that he was still getting to know, a university defined by the uncultivated professors and the students' inane stagnation, an environment that by virtue of its total and crystal clear vacuity about the quite-obvious necessity of political compromise, of taking action, of integrating with the only organization that, precisely to the degree to which it was considered a negation of all currently active values, was revealed as the only way out, namely, the Communist Party, the Communist Party, period, without further distinctions or subtleties, something, doubtless, much more clear, more natural, more sane, from the point of view of what his audience expected to hear? The university of years past: not attending to the education of the student body; keeping it in line. Not education; blatant taming. No vocational community between teachers and those they teach; hostility, confrontation, the law of force-feeding, swallow it, dog, only the strong survive. No guidance; spare the rod, spoil the child. No exercising of faculties; police detection of the weak spot, of the tender foot, of the Achilles tendon. No willingness to encourage; despotic imposition of farragoes selected for their capacity to inhibit, to stultify, to exhaust. No, nothing in it that could evoke the serene climate of invitation to the study of a prototypical Central European university, for example, no point of contact, either, with Anglo-Saxon education, directed not only toward the assimilation of knowledge and understanding but also, as already mentioned, forging useful members of society, and more particularly, to the United Kingdom; no, nothing in common with all that in the postwar Spanish university, expeditionary center of academic titles which students attend not so much for vocation or their own desire as because their parents' social status requires it, and where the only thing that mattered in their university career was getting the degree, especially a law degree, because, as everyone knows, the law is the career with the most opportunities for success, the one that most enables you to defend yourself, to get to know what life is like, trust, emphyteusis, usufruct, usury, a pact in any case, my son, legal concept or legal fiction. A degree that, ultimately, guarantees the gradual familiarization of one who aspires to obtain it, throughout the course of studies, with the jargon of the discipline, almost equal to how one becomes familiar with the habits inherited from the traditional student picaresque, between classes, from the patio to the bar, and some healthily roguish rigamarole, someone at the lake, for example, an old porter or some real posh snob or some real country bumpkin, and the initiation into bar crawling, learning drinking songs, books pawned for drink money, etcetera, and the episodic visits to brothels, and the always more accessible recourse to jerking off, and the timid attempts at rape on some specific female classmate, or simply a girl that I know is good for a bit of fun and whom you can be sure to get into bed, attempts generally resulting in the sacrament of matrimony, according to the most canonical rites, in the end, youthful matters, phases they must pass through that come and go, giving way to a growing sense of responsibility, of the which the formalization of the courtship is only one of its symptoms, one of so many facets of desire that our young man experiences from settling down once and for all, of getting on the right track, of forgetting the madnesses he's committed or that he was on the verge of committing, and that's how his anxieties begin to be reflected in his relationship with the reality of life, in the sudden interest he displays for the distinction existent between matrimonial property assets and extra-dotal property, or in the difference existing between legal action and court ruling, or between claim and accusation, or in the determination of concepts such as corruption or formal flaws, and even a certain sense of nostalgia—almost improper for his age—toward institutions such as censuses and rights of agnation and pre-nuptial agreements, today on the verge of disappearing, for the sake of what's practical and to the detriment of what, for its long-standing, deserves to form part of our historic patrimony, a nostalgia which, abounding in the diverse opposite extremes, confirms the continued habituation to a language, the progressive command of a cryptic and esoteric lexicon, imputable, like that of oracles, to the need to duly appraise his future emoluments. Do you remember? Fortuny asked. So different from the university these days. And what still needs to change. Imagine, when in Spain there are even only formal freedoms like in Italy or in France, imagine what prestige for the party when you're the Sociology Department chair and I'm the chair of Labor Law, for example, examples and reflections—while Raúl wondered what sociology really was—of a suspected parallelism or, more precisely, coincidence, regarding Escala's allusions about the role of the true revolutionary intellectual, approximately around the same dates when Raúl moved from the university committee to the intellectual cell, meaning, from being a leader of the former to a low man in the latter, and Escala accompanied him to the first meeting of the cell, and in his statement—without any apparent justification, with the irritated aggression with which the forty-something man usually receives young initiates, whatever their background, directly proportional, in general, to the degree of weakness belonging to the sex—criticized the posture of those who considered militancy something similar to the military, a moral obligation which one fulfills for a determined period of time and then leaves in the hands of younger followers, as if political activity and the risks it brings had something to do with age, or as if its mission would be concluded when the dictatorship was defeated, as if in a transitional regime to a parliamentary democracy—ideal conditions for the struggle, according to Lenin—there might no longer be any reason to keep fighting, as if precisely when they came to power they weren't more necessary than ever, as much for the effort that the construction of socialism represents because it would be very naive to suppose that the enemy will give up, that it won't still be there, watching, waiting to take revenge, and you'll have to remain vigilant and our ranks will demand, more than in any other moment, leaders willing to occupy their positions of maximum responsibility, political leaders borne not by personal ambitions, like bourgeois politicians, but by the legitimate aspiration to contribute to the socialist cause according to each person's exact capacity. Previously, while walking to the meeting place, rather, he had touched on some practical considerations: the convenience of Raúl changing his current code name—Daniel—for some other—Luis?—in order to sever any organic ties between university students and intellectuals, to erase all tracks that might establish connections to the past, so that the police might never be able to relate the former Daniel to the present Luis, the Luis who was going to form part of the propaganda arm of the intellectual committee, in direct connection with Blanch, secretary of the cell and the comrade responsible for the committee's propaganda. There was no drawback, however, to the fact that the cell members utilized among themselves their own names, because there's nothing less suspicious than what's natural, and nothing more natural than a doctor, a lawyer, and a graduate student of philosophy being friends and getting together for some conversation now and then. But for any other member of the various cells composing the intellectual committee, for any other kind of contact, stick to the new name, forget the old one, and do not involve under any circumstances any of his old university comrades in his current activities and, much less, guys like Lucas, Esteve, all those who, luckily, have been getting off the bus, so that none of these pseudo-intellectuals would even imagine that you're now part of the secretariat of propaganda of the intellectuals' committee of Barcelona, where there really are some serious leaders, scientists, researchers, economists, professionals, artists, prestigious people recognized in their respective fields, whose membership in the party is only kept secret for basic reasons of security. Of your companions in the cell, Ruiz is perhaps the one with the most penetrating analytical powers, but Blanch has a greater capacity for synthesis.

They met at Blanch's apartment on Saturday afternoons and his wife served them sherry and pastries. They had agreed to first dispatch with the practical problems: to reorganize the system of courier-houses in anticipation of receiving suitcases with false-bottoms containing printed matter; buying a typewriter that would be used exclusively to bang out the clichés for the mimeograph; to assign to each cell in the group a specific number of names and addresses of the people to whom to send propaganda through the mail, with the goal of diversifying as much as possible the characteristics of the envelopes to be used and—still more important—the mailboxes and the hours of distribution; the darkroom materials necessary to be able to send to Paris the negatives of the photocopied reports and documents in place of the originals; quotas and economic support from sympathizers, etcetera. Later, time permitting, a period of ideological discussion, starting with the party's latest publications or some classic text: Raúl proposed *The Holy Family*, but Blanch said the *Manifesto* was preferable because, in fact, it had it all. Ruiz said very little, at times distracted, perhaps, choosing some pastry from the tray, that he ended up choosing almost furtively; also, his hands were sweating, and he was skinny, keen, myopic, with a miserly smirk on his face like a witch. In general, however, when they finished with the practical questions, they limited themselves to discussing current national or international politics, and Blanch complained loudly about how poorly the Spanish National Welfare Institute organized medical care throughout the country. Look, these people are starting to have a lot of nerve, he was saying, and he stroked his mustache. He pulled out a copy of *Paris-Match* with a report about Spain. I keep it for the pictures and graphics, quite good, frankly; but the writing is so reactionary that it seems subsidized by the Ministry of Information and Tourism. They don't see—or they don't want to see—typical Spanish culture beyond what's folkloric; it's unbelievable. And the struggle of the Spanish people, what about that? What Marxism is lacking is a metaphysics, said Rois, then blushed. Tirant stroked his mustache. It's interesting, he said. He talked about his seventeen years of militancy in various places in Spain, and the eleven manhunts he'd escaped before settling in Barcelona, always escaping in the nick of time; he spoke slowly, his gaze turned inward, with a sort of contagious somnolence. A single careless mistake can expose and ruin the work of several years. And then, back to square one. That's why I consider that all the precautions we take are really, after all, very little work; you've got to know how to protect yourself so that, when Franco does fall, the party's future will depend on the militants who are free and operating, not the ones in jail. The fellow from Corella nodded, or maybe he'd only just swallowed a too-hastily chewed pastry. In any case, with all evidence, the objective of that exchange of opinions about political reality was really nothing more than a search for examples or theoretical proofs, to reaffirm one's own convictions, to hear each other reaffirming them and—Cheer up!—all taking heart together, without raising doubts, without quibbles or posing possible discrepancies with respect to the interpretations of the facts obviously intuited as ideologically correct and, in such a concept, approved beforehand in a climate where the critical insistence remained tacitly out of place, for reasons similar to those whereby, in a community of neighbors, for example, social harmony would become impossible if each person did not respect the privacy of others, if they did not courteously greet one another when passing in the building vestibule, each one pretending to ignore everything he knows about the other, controlling as much as possible, depending on the case in question, the permissible experience of commiseration or joy, an implicit pact of good neighborliness, which, if not observed, would make the simple fact of living together unbearable, for having to share the same staircase, the same elevator with the other tenants of a building where everyone ends up knowing everything, everybody's shady secrets, the solutions and arrangements that life demands, that circumstances impose, the time that passes, things like Señor Sancho, at his age and with his ailments, he still overcomes them to keep the proprietress of a haberdashery happy, or how much the Valls family on the fifth floor, apartment number two, owe to the fact that she knew how to carry on an affair with the office manager at her husband's place of employment, or that Pepito, the porter lady's son, had been gang-raped, and all the way from the patio you could hear his parents wailing when they discovered the hemorrhage, matters which no one mentions in the presence of the people directly affected and which, in the supposition that, in some exceptional fit of rage or hysterical aggression, someone would dare to violate the unspoken rule, such an indiscretion would be relentlessly, unanimously, and harshly criticized by the neighbors. And just as the psychopath with a persecution complex finds that current events alone usually offer him an especially wide base for his obsession, so Tirant and Curial found that a daily reading of the newspaper proffered sufficient proofs about the decline of capitalism in the face of the great triumphs of socialism, whose setbacks, unlike those experienced by the capitalist world, only constituted the requisite tactical rough patches along the road toward victory, in the same way that all orthographic depression is an inevitable prelude before reaching some new height, some new peak, in a way that, by extension, the internal contradictions and conflicts of the socialist camp appeared barely a fabulation or phantasmagoria unworthy of consideration. But the fact that, even in a wider cultural context, the relationship of forces was equally favorable: Pavlov, the Curies, Yuri Gagarin, and, in the novel, Gorky, Sholokhov, Asturias, and, above all, Howard Fast; and Balzac himself, although personally reactionary, his professional honor—as well observed by Marx—made him faithfully reflect the contradictions belonging to the society of his era; and poets like Neruda and Nicolás Guillén and Aragon and Miguel Hernández and Nazim Hikmet and Blas and the voice of Paul Robeson, social and good, a kind of father figure, or the vigorous popular strength of the Soviet choirs, or the songs of Atahualpa Yupanqui, with more spirit, especially apt, in the university environments, to propitiate one's erotic maneuvers when trying to get closer to some female comrade, after all there's nothing bad about free love between comrades, on the contrary, it's almost a moral obligation, one more way of combating bourgeois conventions, although these aspects might be out of place here for both Tirant, prudent father and family man, and Curial, due to his motives for precision, in this case, evidently as laborious as unnecessary. And was this last extreme a consequence of both men's common extraction, of their undeniable membership in the petite bourgeoisie, that social class which if it has some predominant character trait, it's decency, a trait that remains imprinted even, or more strongly, especially, when one becomes a communist, either from family tradition, like with Tirant, or as a reaction to an opposite reaction, like with Curial, ex-seminarian before earning his master's degree in philosophy, a professor of French and Latin and a party militant? A consequence of that but not the only cause, by itself insufficient to explain any further the subconscious's complex mechanisms, let alone the subject's mere comportment amid life's stimuli, given that, like the young man's ostentatiously conservative attitudes, not really a reflection of any political position, both because the respect for formulas such a position supposes and an unwritten but customary code of behavior safeguard the distance from people that his shy and fearful nature needs, thus in Tirant and Curial their militancy was not only a hereditary question nor one of family or social environment but also, and above all, a self-defense against the snares and wiles of the surrounding world. Of course, the same dynamic of their choice, of the compromise acquired, frequently led them to situations rather unlike their temperaments, and like that adolescent whose static narcissism, craftily fostered by some pederast's vulpine wiles, is seen irremediably destined to move from disquisitions on friendship, love, and beauty, on Plato and Gide, to the actual events. Thus, similarly, Tirant and Curial occasionally found themselves confronting the need to realize, in the terrain of praxis, the result of their theoretical conclusions, to participate in some pro-amnesty demonstration, for example, or at least some attempt at a public demonstration, a case which seemed to promise solidarity, that the whole thing was finally going to be something more than parading in the sanctioned zone indicated in the official announcement, in uneasy search, more than for familiar faces, for people looking like students or workers, waiting for the moment when the cohesive nucleus of shouts and movement would coalesce. But, even on the verge of such extreme situations, there were moments when the tough demands of the clandestine struggle made Tirant and Curial feel, if not fully spent then, at least definitely, overwhelmed by the responsibility of the task, activities such as gathering signatures for a document protesting academic sanctions, a document that had to be set in motion and circulated through the various intellectual circles with maximum urgency, in order that its publication serve as a sounding board for the new actions predicted by the university committee, which had to be concluded by the coming December 21, taking advantage of the traditional public laxity with which students celebrate the feast day of their patron saint, Thomas Aquinas. I'm afraid they'll have to make some decision, said Tirant. And suddenly, with Curial's complicit silence, he turned to face Raúl: Luis, would you be able to take charge of preparing the document's outline, and of writing it? I understand that you've had some practice.

One of Escala's typical initiatives was to take full advantage of the public actions organized to coincide with the Feast of Thomas Aquinas. To this end he'd given Tirant specific instructions during a meeting also attended by a comrade from the university committee leadership; from what Raúl could deduce this comrade was Fortuny. He also guessed something more: the significance of his own absence from a meeting to which, in his former role as student committee director and current member of the group of intellectuals, he would normally be invited, especially because as a professor he remained connected to the university. The fact that he'd had to learn about the plan secondhand—as well as previous events: Obregón's arrest followed by a whole string of subsequent arrests, and Escala's and Fortuny's disappearance along with most of the university militants—all thanks to a momentary lapse by Tirant, a Tirant possessed by despair. Also, the way Escala admonished Raúl when the latter was transferred to the intellectual committee, so strongly highlighted by the fact that they'd had no contact since then, and Escala's insistence that Raúl sever all ties—organic and even non-organic links—with his old companions acquired new shades of meaning, along with the fact that Fortuny had replaced him on the university committee without any forewarning: all symptoms, in short, that now seemed like déjà vu, like something already observed in other times, in relation to other people, an experience that permitted him to have similarly perfect awareness that the elements perceived by him constituted only a disconnected, fragmentary, and partial image of an average incident, which always turns out much worse if it is related by one of the individuals directly implicated than if it is related by some third party, an objectively-positioned spectator who contemplates it in its fullness and, above all, from outside the situation. The same process as with Federico, as with Adolfo, this repetition doubtless played an important role of developing proofs in the charges brought against Raúl, whose involvement in the present situation pointed to a previous involvement, along with the additional, and aggravating basic fact of the friendly relationship that the three had maintained between them; as in the case of Esteve and the case of Lucas, by now it probably took no more than some higher-level leader, Escala perhaps, making an incidental comment to some member of the university group, one of the worst of them is Daniel, for the censure to begin circulating, illustrating with an accumulation of different characteristic elements, less political than moral, the people he dealt with, his friends, Nuria, their various relationships, their nocturnal outings, really any fact equivalent to what, at that time, could demonstrate passion for playing games, for what the poker games, with elevated bets, revealed in Federico, or Adolfo's pet name for Aurora, his concubine, as he called her—an expression of anonymous origin which immediately, and somewhat surprisingly, caught on, based on the fact that she and Adolfo had lived together. Something like that, with full confidence, must have been enough for Garrido to begin phoning him less frequently, and the Corberó girl stopped looking for him on the patio in the School of Humanities, and it didn't take long for what Iglesias had said to reach him, and what Terrades had said, too, opinions and testimonies all the more decisive for being all the more vague and conceptual, how much the better they characterize the disaster of personality that cannot stop accompanying a chosen political position that is subjective and erroneous, a position that for whomever maintains it becomes the cause of their progressive distance from the correct line of thinking, producing at the same time around him, in the heart of the cell to which he belongs and like a corresponding logic, a climate of emptiness, which the individual's involuntary or premeditated lack of initiative and enthusiasm only accentuates and extends, meetings celebrated without his presence, in part because he doesn't ask, because he doesn't try to stay informed, in part because he is not advised, absences which, when he does finally attend, make him feel not only marginalized and estranged from the topic being discussed, but also useless and extraneous, in his ignorance of the precise new details for which his appraisals deserve to be considered, inadequate to face up to his previous responsibilities, gradually replaced by some other rising star, someone named Ferrán, for example. The first indication that the shock wave had already reached the upper levels: his final, disastrous trip to Paris, shortly before summer—his rendezvous with Nuria, his wish that she had not come to meet him, that she leave him in peace for once, and the climate of tension, of reticent reserve, of poorly contained verbal violence, and the erotic frustration, and the rain and the cold, unseasonal, and the goddamned proliferation of the springtime, and the tulips in the Tuileries punished by the downpour, and the tender and slippery fallen leaves, and the appearance of Pírez, the typical jinxed idiot, a Canary Islander from the Cité Universitaire who came recommended by Guillén and who wanted to return to Spain, to Barcelona, to foment the true revolution, and needed them to find him a job, as a laborer, of course—when he went to the scheduled meeting at the specified address, and reaching the same house from the other times, near Bastille, he ran into Escala and some unknown comrade, some guy who looked halfway between a junior member and a Russian violinist, and despite showing himself attentive and even vigilant to the meeting's progress, Raúl almost didn't open his lips, a trip he needn't have packed for—even the coffee they offered them seemed, this time, made of old, used coffee grounds. Paperwork hassles were quickly dispatched, almost by way of preamble or a courteous, preliminary sounding-out of what it was clearly all about, about the real reason for his presence there: to proceed to what had brought them there: a vigorous ideological cleansing. Everyone incapable of perceiving the real verification of our ideology in praxis, who does not perceive it or who puts it in doubt, is so because his class conditioning prevents it. Because our ideology's criterion for rationality is determined by the individual's concrete place in society, by his class conditioning. Thus a displacement, however small, of that conditioning, a simple change in his way of life, necessarily impacts his appreciation of our political praxis, to end in the long run, fatally, by opening cracks in the ideological plane, because the dialectical relationship between theory and praxis is of such a nature that all deviation from a certain aspect of the party line, for example, always ends up calling into question the very essence of Marxist ideology. These are the well-known positions of so-called non-communist Marxists, of the communists without a party, of the communists creating another communist party, of those who think the time has come to go beyond Marx, or to revise him, or to update him, or to attend more to the letter than to the spirit of his texts, or to separate him from Lenin's ideas, his historical consequences; of those who invoke the pre-marxist Marx, of the renegades, of the defects, of the revisionists, and also of the mechanistic and dogmatic thinkers. They want to divide the indivisible, what constitutes a whole and which must be taken as such, hypercritical positions generally belonging to intellectuals who consider themselves disappointed or disillusioned for not having found in the party what they could not find: lingering traces of bourgeois idealism. And the thing is, even treating of objective realities, these things always contain, at bottom, some preexisting bias, almost a question of faith, of believing or not believing, so that for a mind that might not be dialectical and materialistic, for a mind that is metaphysical and speculative, socialist constructions will refute the practical results of our ideology, the palpable proofs that it offers the whole world, and even contradict any idea those minds had formed about the realization of communist theory. Due to their incapacity of seeing what is evident they are truly sick minds, but history shows us that such sick people can turn out to become even more dangerous elements for the party than the avowed anti-communists, given that, availing themselves of skillfully manipulated pseudo-Marxist arguments, they can sow confusion and even division within our ranks, undermine the confidence of the militants in the political line, in the leadership that has fashioned that political line of thinking, in the party's role as the vanguard of the working class and even in the role of the working class itself and, finally, in our capacity to transform the world and create the new society, the new man; all considerations in some way personal though not animated by any particular animosity against Raúl, but rather, the expression of an opinion little less than unanimous in the party base, the faithful image of what a thinker like Floreal's or Leo's father might have formulated thereon, of having relied on the ideological baggage and a command of terminology like Escala's, in line with a vision of the militant, of the party and the general march forward of the world, whose most adequate plastic representation would be one of those American musical comedies from the forties, one of those scenes in which a certain couple steps out to dance in some nondescript place, a banquet hall, the street, an ocean liner, and then another couple steps out and another, and little by little everyone present follows their lead and they all join in the dance, until stepping together in a single choreographically perfect body, similar in a way to how, according to that vision or conception of the world, they go on overcoming contradictions and harmonizing the interests of the popular forces, thus slowly but surely establishing the bases not only of the new society and the new man but also the true beginning of history.

Aristocratism? Adventurism? Petit bourgeois leftism? Well I think they're right; in fact, it's the truth. Look how I, unconsciously, instinctively, chose a field name that couldn't be more petit bourgeois: Esteve. And you chose a prophet's name, and Adolfo chose an evangelist's. On the other hand, the one that's really good is the one Penyafort picked: Ferrán, the name of a Catholic king. And Escala's is the most graphic: it suits him much better than any nickname you might hang on him, like when we called him Mr. H, or Zorro or just Z, like they call him now. What we should really do is all get psychoanalyzed, like the friars from Cuernavaca. Clarify the compulsion that drove each one to join the party. To talk about a guilty conscience is pure lyricism, and about awareness or about rational conclusions, you tell me. But it was he himself who said it when Fortuny was still sometimes coming over to Adolfo's house, and perhaps for that very reason, because Raimundo Fortuny de Penyafort was present and he without any doubt wrote down the things he said, even though only part of it, too calculated an effect to believe that it wasn't Federico's intention that they also reach Escala's ears, that bit about offering Escala concrete examples with which to illustrate his prophecies, his judgments, to be accused, for example, of having said this and that, at first as if in jest, a character soon dispensed with, not only because of what he was really saying, but even by the way of saying it, by the very rigor of the argumentation, exposed according to an almost Ciceronian scheme of articulation, that might be summed up in the following propositions: Western communist parties, conscious of the fact that their numbers alone are insufficient to foment the revolution, accept the so-called democratic alternative, namely, the parliamentary game that comes with a bourgeois democracy; upon accepting the rules of the game of a bourgeois democracy, Western communist parties can only defend the interests of the working class by setting up, through labor unions, an efficient mechanism of protest; the working class, certain economic demands satisfied, tends to be assimilated by the system, within whose boundaries the worker hopes to achieve individual emancipation, to rise above his working-class condition; in consequence, the wider the spread of demands satisfied thanks to union action, the lesser the real interest of the working class to subvert the established order through violent revolution, respecting which, as happens in countries with a higher standard of living, the workers can end up becoming the strongest opponents of communism. That, more or less, was what Federico said or meant to say, almost without stammering or loosing a laugh, calmly, although not without anguish in his shining eyes, like a horse in full fury, and probably for that reason, for the unusual brilliance of his exposition more than for any originality of concept, the sense of sacrilege that had doubtless been planted in everyone's spirit grew stronger, a sacrilege that might be called collective to the degree that an evasive silence, of guilty neutrality, was the collective reaction of those present, while Fortuny, incredulous, about to erupt, unable to detect the sophistry, if in fact there was any, and for lack of the clamorous and scandalized refutation he seemed to expect, searched with his eyes for help at least from Raúl, saying, as if to gain some time, awaiting reinforcements that were not coming, Raúl's ideological support, of some intervention that never came, saying, alright, alright, from a Marxist point of view it's not like that, and Federico, but from a non-Marxist perspective, yes, and Fortuny, well, this is all subject to debate, a Fortuny beside himself and confused like one who thought he was going for a round of golf and, with his clubs on his back, finds himself on a deer hunt, confused and perhaps also intimately humiliated, sensible of the lack of prestige represented by the fact that a lawyer and a political leader like himself did not manage to overturn Federico's argument, of someone who, objectively considered, was nothing more than a guy who had left the party just the same as if he had hung up his career and who, nevertheless, had known how to drag him into a kind of controversy—not from within, granted—not from some commonly accepted bases, but from without, questioning precisely the validity of these bases for which he was not prepared, a situation finally resolved by Pluto, saying that what's more than doubtful is that stuff about how the proletariat make better lovers, a literary topic best represented by Lady Chatterley's love affair with her gardener. At that point, however, they still didn't really know who Zorro was. It was a bit later, near summer's end, when Federico made his discovery. He'd recognized his photo in one of those promotional shots, with gilt edging, that one of the lawyers who worked with his father had hanging in his office. Younger, but the same man; his name was Salvador Puig and now, some years after finishing his studies, he was working in the advertising business. Can you imagine? That's where he must have learned his craft because it seems that nobody knows anything about his political activities either at university or underground. He must be one of those old foxes who always escape just in time; a true savior always starts with himself. At the end of the summer, yes; the start of autumn at the latest. Louis had already left and Adolfo had decided to apply for the award, and more or less around that time they began to have dealings with Moragas; better to say: Moragas became a regular visitor at Adolfo's house. *Los Ángeles*: a novel intended to ratify Escala, in case he were ever really ostracized, in all his criticisms and predictions, by providing him with the most conclusive documented proof—clearly an autobiographical tale, almost a confession—of the scant confidence that he deserves in general, insofar as political solidarity is concerned, that sector of bourgeois youth that today, in open—and ideologically incoherent—conflict with their social environment, make the rounds in a dissipate nighttime life with revolutionary pretensions, whose marked radicalism only conceals, in most cases, the search for solutions to their personal problems, when not seeking to satisfy unconfessed desires or selfish ambitions, an essential duplicity not avoided, but rather, masochistically highlighted, by the work's very own narrative structure, built from a confluence of diverse thematic threads which, developed through objective technique from different points of view, contrast the insincerity and the self-deception not only in each one of the characters, but even of the novel itself as a literary form. In fact, said Moragas, it turns the reader into another character, into something like a special witness to the falsity of all involved, the characters, the author, of oneself as a reader, *tout le monde triche et tout c'est une grande tricherie*. He wrote quickly in his notebook and turned to look at Adolfo: listen, why don't we focus seriously on the possibility of a film adaptation? Cinema interests me as much as, or more than, the novel, said Adolfo. The same words, the same gestures, and even the same people as before, when they first talked about the manuscript of *Los Ángeles*, literary digressions from which Raúl, irremediably connecting them to his own work, felt completely distant, without any intention of creating an interesting argument, nor of deeply exploring the characters' psychology, nor of being a faithful reflection of society, and what seemed even more serious: without any formal apriorisms nor any kind of pretensions to technical experimentation, all questions which, apart from meaning nothing to him, were disagreeable due to the aggression implied in the no-less-painful fact that they couldn't discuss his work instead, a work which, not being finished, it made no sense to keep writing, and about which the others, in consequence, barely knew anything, an ignorance which, on the other hand, strengthened him and became his principal defense, a field of his own personal reveries, telling himself that not even one of those passersby he encountered, for example, or those regular customers at a secondhand bookshop, had the least suspicion that they were standing next to a future great writer, whose works would perhaps someday be the critical object of their spontaneous intellectual discussions. Henry James? said Moragas while he wrote down the name. I thought, I don't know why, that he was the author of books like *Gone with the Wind*. Federico looked impatient. *Io mi voglio divertir. Io mi voglio divertir. Io mi voglio divertir.* They had to go to the Liceo, to Moragases' private box, except the Plutos, who said they weren't in the mood, but they agreed to meet back up later at the theater entrance, to pop around to a few of the regular spots, surely until closing time. What was the most important element among so many that influenced Moragases' sudden intrusion into Adolfo and Aurora's life or, better yet, into the dependent situation in which he had placed himself in his relationship with them, apart from the availability and free time a man of wealth and leisure like himself enjoyed, calling them or seeing them every day, inviting them everywhere, invariably accompanying them on their nighttime outings? A sincere interest on Adolfo's part? The snobbish satisfaction belonging to a man in his position and with artistic anxieties about dealing with a writer? The suggestion that he could exercise over him a way of life deliberately in conflict with the ruling principles of the social class to which they belonged? Something like all that, no doubt, but in the first place, probably, the attraction that for some people—among which, he, Manolo Moragas, found himself—seemed to irradiate Adolfo's personality, an attraction based not so much on what Adolfo did or said as much as what he didn't do or what he left unsaid, what he kept quiet about, his well-chosen silences, a kind of attraction similar to what drives the majority of women to prefer the indecisive or ambiguous man over the typical macho, to the degree to which he thus removes himself from the obligatory sexual response conventionally attributed to him, to which she has the intimate conviction of not measuring up, and to play along, to pretend that she does, requires too much effort, to try to fit into her assigned role of wild female, of manipulable object, of shock absorber or wind-up toy, not so much from a secret aversion to the other sex or instinctive repugnance, as much as for simple fatigue, so that her awareness of the fact that the accepted man can be found no less inhibited than she is when facing the image of satisfactory behavior officially demanded of him, and this only serves to make things much easier.

Zorro is the real Don Giovanni, said Federico. I, personally, identify with

Donna Elvira. And you're Donna Anna, and Leo is Zerlina, and Fortuny is Leporello. From the bar in the lounge they contemplated the splendorous movement of the crowd up the staircases and through the hallways, spurred by the announcement that the second act was about to begin. The people, I tell you, are the true spectacle, said Manolo Moragas. You see every kind of tacky fool; the other day, even our dairyman's oldest son. But take a good look at them: the men look like waiters and the women like dolled-up fishbones. Or theater extras playing a crowd of mingling bystanders, said Adolfo. Exactly, man, excellent observation. It would be fun to rile them up somehow, I don't know, appear in the box in blue coveralls or something. I promise you, there was a time, the life of the common people in the cheap seats, assholes and all, had its attractions. What's happening now is merely symbolic: the rise of one class and the fall of another. You think so? said Federico. People come to the opera now who never came before and most of the people who used to come don't come anymore. But that's because the Liceo is no longer an important social gathering spot. People meet in other places now, and in other ways, and the distance between the upper bourgeoisie and this bourgeoisie that's storming the Liceo is not stable, it's growing. Fine, I'm speaking as a Marxist: excuse me, excuse me. Zorro would congratulate me, but I think it's the truth. This is, precisely, the drama of the whole bumpkin bourgeoisie, of those people so eager to show off their prêt-à-porter tuxedoes and their bargain-basement gowns, the dress that by this time of the season has lost its first luster, from being starched, still carrying the fragrance of its first outings, when, newly touched up by some domestic dressmaker, it could still turn a few heads; anxious to be seen with that outfit and, above all, anxious to be seen here, in this sanctifying temple of prosperity itself, in this picture window that only displays triumphal artifacts, with the zeal of squeezing out, of ratcheting experience up to the maximum, of reducing, as much as possible, the price of a seat, the price of a private box, zeal expressed with applause, not only extemporaneous, but even excessive, not so much because the performance was to their liking or not as for the simple fact that nobody likes to be a sucker and, as with any other deal, the value of the show must correspond to the ticket price. A drama that, with tragic fatality, seems only to increase in direct proportion to the money one possesses: when the tuxedo isn't mass-produced but hand-cut by the priciest tailor in Barcelona, and the evening gown is only one of the many exclusive designs selected at the start of the season, meaning, when it's a question of the nouveau riche who are truly rich, unequivocal in their gauche trappings and in their disconcerted discouragement, particularly sensitized to the bitter reality that, as if in parallel fashion to their economic and social ascent, the good family names withdraw as they get closer, the same as in a nightmare where one walks and walks but never advances, and so too, now that they find themselves in a situation of providing for their children, relatively well-groomed thanks to an easy and comfortable upbringing, quite different from their own, the polished touch and the archetypal manners of the moneyed youth of their generation, that natural distinction from those days that they never could nor ever will reach, now that they find themselves in a situation to which at least their children will have access, into which they can at least elbow their way, now, now it turns out that kind of distinction consists of being up to date with the latest extravagance, lamentably imprecise, incomprehensibly within reach of all, at the margin of all criteria of value, as if the category had been stripped of all quality. As if, once seated on the train, they could shift the engine into reverse and retrace the route not yet traveled! And it's the same way that a bar or a dance or a prostitute becomes fashionable among young people, and with them those things mature, get old, and fade away, the same with the Liceo, born at the same time as a specific society, as some tremendously bourgeois forms of life, their own identity now lost and become something else, just as those ways of life die out so, too, that society into which they were born. Now that we believe that history repeats itself, said Federico, if someday they revive *William Tell* we've got to get seats in the thirteenth row of the orchestra section.

But, besides that, who is Manolo Moragas? A rejuvenated posh snob, a dandified little boy from the forties who now, when he's almost twice as old as he was then, seems to have found, through Adolfo's circle, a second lease on youth, incentives he'd missed the first time around, and like in one of those cases of latent homosexuality, even a satisfactory explanation of himself, of his way of being and even of his incapacity of being anything different, similar in a way to how a precocious bibliophile, wounded by his love for belles-lettres, usually reacts, a poet, for example, more astute than gifted, preempting all possible criticism, pretending that the banality and clumsiness of his youthful works of poetry are deliberate, premeditative, and even innovative, as if with banality and clumsiness he might fashion something not banal or clumsy, as if any attempt in this sense would not irremediably end with the work in question being assimilated into the genre of banal and clumsy works, and especially, as if banality and clumsiness did not constitute the essential, and irrepressible characteristics of that young poet, so, in much the same way, ran the defensive arguments of Manolo Moragas, his compensations, transforming his ignorance into a capricious disdain of all cultural information that was not essential to Adolfo's circle, and into frank scorn for the appreciation of the cultural values traditionally belonging to his milieu, with the cynical nonchalance that a high-society woman displays among her friends when one of them starts talking about how boring it is to have a husband. In fact, a past susceptible to acquiring, in light of his current attitude, a certain entity and even a certain interest, almost legendary, doubtless propitiated by that attitude of challenging conventional ideas and his social position, his fortune, his wife, his wife's fortune, the delicacy that distinguished the relationship between them both, overall too excessive to express the fact that, for both of them, everything was reduced to that, to keeping up appearances; a challenge, on the other hand, that in no way altered, naturally, the habits appropriate to their social position, from the sunny outdoor luncheons at the Real Club de Golf or the heavy all-night poker games lasting until dawn at the Círculo Ecuestre, passing through a summary inspection, though much less unconcerned than could be believed at first glance, of the progress of his business deals, activities in which his jokes, his misogynist boasts, his peevish, scathing comments, his remarks like: the only thing wrong with New York is that it's so terribly provincial, or: I only sleep with a married woman when her husband gives his full approval, or: the only way of avoiding sentimental complications is to have women fall in love with your money, not with you, etcetera; all of this conferring on him, among the people of his social sphere, a halo of originality and brilliance, of a person indispensable for any kind of get-together, for the same reasons, although considered from the opposite angle, for which his behavior could become suggestively unusual in such a circle as that of Adolfo Cuadras. And then, his anecdotes, his recollections, his bygone summers, I don't know if you've all heard about them, if you remember them, but the thing is that until after the Civil War, summer vacations continued being almost like early in the century, when Barcelona high society added, to the old family house in the country, a villa in a fashionable summer colony, with shady gardens and terraces with a view, seeking a cool place to escape the heat, the obsession of the time, fruit not only of the country's climate but also of an excess of fats and carbohydrates in the diet and, especially, of an excessive fidelity to the London or Parisian style of dressing, stubbornly ignoring the simple fact that August in Sitges or Caldetas has more in common with Alexandria than Dauville and, in consequence, a salakót would better serve the circumstances than a bow tie. Things that one could now consider not only with a certain perspective but also with longing and nostalgia to the degree that, in spite of the liberation from the customs prevalent in the twenties, blatantly strengthened at the start of the thirties, something of that world had endured in Spain, where, after the interval of the Civil War, everything seemed to be fixed and even going backward; in that Spain that was like an island in time, a paradisiacal island where, at the height of World War II and in full demoralization of the previous years of revolt, everything continued as always, a rhythm of life and a world that wouldn't have to disappear entirely until well into the fifties, those pleasantly uninterrupted three months of summer, now passed into history in the reiterated identity of their gentle course, like so many other things of the past that nostalgia and longing allowed to be sublimated due to their distance in time, the Liceo of an earlier time, horse-drawn carriages, the first automobiles, the cabaret singers' derrieres, gambling, scandals, wasteful luxury, gardens like the ones Rusiñol painted, top hats, straw boaters, frock coats, bustles, fur muffs, veiled hats, fans, the kind of elegance found in the jottings of Casas, narcissistic sublimations so much more intense than in an age like the current one, surpassed and forgotten in the good families whose origins have some philistine aspect, the constituent phase of their patrimony, the great-grandparents' obscene calculations and cogitations, in a time like the present one, with so many recent booming fortunes, the more that some nouveau riche is perfectly identified and, on some occasions—painful ones—even hunted down, money no longer suffices to distinguish distances and differences, and the weight of the presence of one's ancestors in the common social repertoire becomes a measure of caste and class distinction, just as, to a certain point, it is also the problem of those young people today, of their inability to adapt to social conventions, of those fallen angels that appear—you might say with preference—even in the best families, a peculiarity that comes to add one more element of tribulation to the good family names of Barcelona, already so punished by the most traditional problem of frequent mental retardation, the dismal offspring of their heinous fornications. An upper-crust bourgeoisie truly more regressive than progressive, lacking the creative spirit of its great-grandparents, of whose virtues it only preserves, perhaps, their stinginess; a high-class bourgeoisie with its wagon hitched more than ever to its own snobbism, about cinema and art and essays and vanguardist drama, organic architecture, serial music, informal painting and, above all, an elusive dolce vita—always next time or somewhere else—that generally doesn't go beyond ordinary adulterous misbehavior; an upper-crust bourgeoisie that, nonetheless and thanks to its snobbism and the patina conferred by the passage of time, can permit itself all kinds of transfigurations and projections, starting with the most elevated vulgarity, the sad luck of Antoñito Canals, who killed himself so absurdly, or poor Totem, a darling little girl, who married and was so disgraced and who fled and ended up so badly, etcetera, we have a good example of that in Manolo Moragas, with his remembrances and reflections, with the magnified profiles of his memory, when he talks about Alicia and Sunche, when he talks about Grandma Magdalena as if she were the Duchess of Guermantes and as if

Grandpa Augusto were the duke, and Doña America were Madame Verdurin, and that crazy Tito Coll a sort of Charlus, while he, Manolo Moragas, the narrative I, an apathetic Marcel, too skeptical to take the trouble to write anything, the only reason for him not having already withdrawn into his cork-lined cell, to become a chronicler of Barcelonan society, the literary transcription of whose avatars, for any reader not directly implicated in that world, would awaken the same interest, probably, as that generated by one of those prose stylists who write for the Sunday edition of a provincial newspaper, who achieve a certain local notoriety by the agreeable character of their collaborations, stylists who philosophize like sheep chewing their cud before the ruins of the Parthenon, not in service to the validity of the ideas developed, but rather, to please their bumpkin readrship vis-a-vis their original viewpoint and graceful exposition, and like that writer's stylized prose, so runs his interest in the specific problems of that world, in the characters capable of inhabiting it, and he goes grazing and watering among the ruins of the culture, with the grace and subtlety and elegance of a horned head that, like a Narcissus, gazes at its own reflection in a puddle. They headed down Las Ramblas, penetrating the saturnine Saturday night atmosphere of tenebrous lights and anonymous movement, long endless hours making the rounds to the usual places, as if awaiting some small event, within the scant margin of variation, a phenomenon of perception both heightened and fleeting, growing to enormous proportions, conferring personality on the night, a drunken albino, the parallel pilgrimage of two workers working hard to have a good time, or any other spectacle that might offer an occasion for exercising one's own ingenuity to celebrate it, running into some acquaintance, joining up with some other group of pub crawlers, trading some rather sardonic jokes, laughter lubricated and faces lit up by alcohol. Like pulsing accordions: the memory of having been and the pain of already not being.

Ah, when he felt like he was cut in half, especially after drinking, with a hangover, all the next day, half-man, half-goat, the thick tuft of hair where the pastern joins the hoof with the low hanging belly as a support or a throne for the imperious serpent poised to strike, quivering with electricity, possessed of his fury, impelled by his energy, like a hunter plunging through the thick woodland after his wounded quarry. Not like now, behaving rather like a dog skittering here and there pissing along the trail, not like now, entering almost just because in the secondhand bookshop, helpless against any lovely head of hair, with the stabbing pain of memory: of not having become. Is this early and perhaps irremediable decline in his progress a transitional state or rather the price of excessive precociousness? No, yes, no, yes, no, no? Was this the cursed fruit of autumn, after a rough summer, full of tensions and long, drawn-out quarrels, hangovers, erotic gluttony, from the moment Nuria returned from London and phoned him to tell him that she wanted to see him, just to have a nice peaceful chat for a while, and he agreed, despite their definitive breakup, last spring, when they met in Paris, when she told him about Louis, and he said for quite some time now he hadn't seen any reason for them to consider themselves tied to one another, and why not let things take their course, she could do what she liked, and he could too, and she said no, she wasn't breaking up, that her fling with Louis was finished, and the one she loved was him, only him, and he, however, said no? While they ate dinner, Raúl was polite but cold, almost hard in his implacable distance despite all Nuria's maneuvers to get close to him, efforts that, like the rules of urbanity, have not so much the goal of facilitating relations between people belonging to the same privileged class as of easily distinguishing people who do not belong to that class and immediately establishing a separation from them, thus, Nuria's efforts to reactivate the old codes of their intimacy were directed, more than to stimulate an immediate change in Raúl's attitude, to make it possible to discuss, between parentheses, how much might have happened to each one of them on their own. They went back to their old hangouts, and even the accordion music was the same, the tango that pulls and rumples and falters, as if it had not stopped playing since then, or better yet, as if they had never left the place. I know it's all finished, said Nuria. But the thing is, I want you. You'll never be able to avoid it; me neither, even if I wanted. They were a little drunk and in the taxi she leaned back against his shoulder, while she slowly caressed one of his thighs. Why don't you come up? My family's out of town for the weekend. They kissed almost without pause starting in the vestibule, and in the elevator she unbuttoned her blouse, or maybe he did it, the fact is that she was unbuttoned, and on the landing they stayed there in the darkness and she fished around in her purse without finding the keys while he, with his other hand, felt around under her light summer clothes according to the principle of progressive reiteration, going deeper, with the satisfaction with which a water diviner sees his spring begin to flow, toward the areas of deliquescence, and she, against the door, felt like her legs would give way, and they opened the door and went inside, she almost naked, and they stopped in the living room, exploring each other with their hands, lips, tongues, warm clothing slipping off suddenly, her soft hair below, centered around her flush rosy harmonies, Raúl hunched over her breasts, over her thighs raised high, gripping his torso, over her belly, twitching, thrusting, when, hair flying and eyes rolling, the growing rhythmic violence converging even as the burning fusion recedes, converging and receding—for a very long time—the bubbling rush that, like the enormous relief that comes from releasing an enema or like some calcium pill that neutralizes burning stomach acids, would liquefy their bodies, calming them, after such a frenzy, after that absorbed sighing silence only disturbed by the creak of the springs and the suspicion, bright as magnesium flares, that one of the servants might be moving about the house and, especially, the exasperating tapping of the back of the sofa against the wall, which he tried to stop, placing his foot firmly on the parquet floor, like shifting gears on a motorcycle, to move the sofa, to separate it from the wall, without interrupting his principal activity, until abandoning his effort and his conscience, he plunged into the convulsive knot of their bodies. Coming back to themselves, they noticed that the sofa had carried them almost to the center of the room.

There were still a few embers in the fireplace. Raúl blew some life into them and added several logs. Nuria clicked off the lamp, and by the firelight, naked upon the thick carpet, they drank whiskey straight from the bottle. From fucking we come, keep fucking we must, said Raúl, ashes to ashes, and dust to dust. Sooner than you think, said Nuria. And, in fact, went right back to it, vigorously, on the carpet, on the sofa, on the carpet, using their time well, his cock in her hand, grasping it like a dagger, up and down, up and down, a dagger she plunged into herself or whose sweet thrust she accepted, sweetly up and down then starting again right away, before it got too late for them to couple again, in the heat of passion, without letting each other fall asleep, awake, active, efficient, up and down doing it over again and better every time, growing hot again and stoking their passion anew, and if necessary showing off her best sword-swallowing skills, I like it so much, I love you so much, I couldn't live without you, Pipo. Yes: recovered. He went out onto the terrace and contemplated the city in the glowing clarity of the dawn, the silence of the accumulated apartment houses, chaotic conglomeration of facades and rooftops and skylights and antennas and cables and sooty cement, a panorama of volumes and spaces that will soon begin to discharge, just as that plump gray pigeon flew away in a flash, an opaque mist of trepidation and traffic. It was already full daylight as he walked back toward his house and it took him a while to find a taxi; and as he went along, as if dazzled, by the pleasantly deserted streets, those mixed feelings of discouragement, disgust, and even revulsion gradually disappeared, the same as in other times, after other amorous adventures, they'd not taken long to flit away, thanks to the propitious oblivion one usually encounters when we're bothered by the memory of our frailties committed, of the confessions made at the insistence of others, affirmations, if not completely false, certainly, at the least, exaggerated, sentiments pretentiously experienced for some time now, or rather brusque but irresistibly raised, unequivocally fictitious asseverations, for however much in that instant one would like them to be not only real but also definitive, and that under the insistent antagonic stinger, and could even come to believe they are, desires exposed as facts, facts adapted to the circumstances, love, love, word and talisman and breath of life; an overreach of which one only becomes completely conscious in the very moment after orgasm, just a few seconds after, but already too late, confused awakening like on an unlucky or sorrowful day that one knows they must confront, the death of a loved one, an accident, something already irreparable like the fact of having said something you've said, repeated outbursts, one after another, affirmations that although they might be reduced to a simple yes, leave us, in any case, when all has passed, with the impression of having talked too much, an impression, notwithstanding, like being subjected to auto-inoculation therapy or to the physical principle according to which every action generates an equal and opposite reaction, soon giving way, as one walks home, to a healthy reaction of cynicism, inducing one to recreate the pleasant aspects of the affair, desires satisfied, to feel the intimate pride of having been able to demonstrate one's own competence in matters erotic, in a certain way now with thoughts fixed already on the next time, at the end of the day it didn't matter if they continued to see one another this way now and then, always provided that the situation remained well clear, the kind of relationship that from now on was going to be established between them both, if Nuria accepted his conditions, absolute freedom for each one to do what they felt like, without any sort of interference whatsoever, not even the smallest right to call the other to account for anything, conditions that although unconditionally accepted—I'll do anything just to be able to keep seeing you—were no serious obstacle to prevent Nuria, after only a few weeks, from asking him, quite casually, if he'd had many adventures during all that time, and with whom, and what they had done and if they'd done it well, as if with amused curiosity, playing the mysterious one, with the assurance of the one who knows something the other doesn't know, and then Raúl would ask her in turn if there had been others besides Louis, and Nuria would tell him no, though not very convincingly, and Raúl would ask her for details about her fling with Louis, and Nuria would ask about his affairs with other girls, and as if all that excited them both, they would end up, with reconcentrated application, making love again, or rather, depending on the day, getting furious with each other, having a violent argument, seeking offense, verbal aggression, and also making love, yes, but more like a married couple already worn down by the convenience of it, a man and woman still young returning home after a night out with other couples whom one always tends to consider luckier, friends from other times, men and women about whom each married couple can imagine that things might have been different with them, not like now, the evening spent, when, in the silent apartment, they give themselves over to lovemaking, possessing one another with cruel, suicidal fury, each one in a fierce battle with their own ruin, with their rancors, their frustrations, enclosed, like boxers in the ring, in the lugubrious matrimonial landscape. Because just as with the sprightly statue of Count Ramón Berenguer atop his horse, doubtless concealing under his dashing warlike image the trembling spirit of a lady, only comparable to the spirit of the Lady of Orléans in his vehement desire to conquer by giving his all, to possess by being possessed, thus the essential sadomasochistic ambiguity of Raúl and Nuria's relationship.

Nuria Oller's appearance, with her London memories, first of all, calling to mind his own orgasmic adventures with Nuria Rivas, their talk of mutual friends, the mishaps of her wedding to Peter and more, everyone well-informed of Nuria's fling with Louis, and, then, the arrival of Louis himself, doubtless introduced, on the other hand, new shades of meaning into the development of those relationships. It was one thing to imagine Louis from afar, his presence in Nuria Oller's photographs, where he appeared alongside Peter and the two Nurias and the other members of the group, a group whose members, as Nuria Oller pointed out significantly, shared everything right down to the last penny, but another thing was his physical appearance, his very real presence in Barcelona. It must have been around the first days of September when Nuria told him that Louis had written to her from Madrid, and that he was coming to Barcelona, and could they try to find him a room for a few days. That's all the letter said; they were in a bar and Raúl could confirm it by taking advantage of the fact that Nuria went to the bathroom for a minute, taking the letter from her purse and reading it before she returned. However: might she not have left that letter right there on purpose, maybe even dictated it herself, sticking out of her purse so that he would read it—just as he had read it—and, more trusting, accept that her story made sense, right in line with the image of the nice young fellow who likes jazz and plays the clarinet, of that hairless beardless fellow, one of those sneaky consolers of lonely women, whose leftist flirtations perhaps only serve to mask their sexual misery, their stupid fascination with the more-than-dubious myth of the hot-blooded Spanish woman, the seducer's oft-celebrated *mille tre* conquests? Another clue: the fact that when Louis finally arrived, Nuria slipped up and called him Pipo, and that, when she realized that Raúl had not failed to notice her lapse, Louis thought he should explain that Nuria called everyone whom she loved Pipo, an explanation that if on the one hand no one had asked for, on the other it was unexpected and not very reassuring, especially given the husband's typical disadvantage compared to the lover who, like a gambler, considers the wild card of adventure to always trump the sure-bet card of convenience, meaning transience over permanence, so, Louis or any other of those beloved people found themselves, in that respect, in a frankly privileged situation, a privilege whose weight could be decisive in the serene and thoughtful examination of how many arguments could be counterpoised—in the supposition that someone would spend time pondering the matter—about what Nuria's behavior might be in a similar situation: the apparently sincere fondness that Nuria seemed to feel for Raúl in all situations, careful to avoid, for fear of losing him, making a false step, given women's characteristically infinite capacity for deception, the tranquility, for example, with which she could say goodbye to him from the terrace, while Louis, already naked in bed, watched her. Nuria Oller had also come out to receive Louis on his arrival and at night ate dinner with them and then they all went to the Jamboree. I feel like I'm back in London, she said. Too bad Peter's not here. Your clarinet? asked Raúl. You haven't brought it with you? Louis shook his head. It's a shame; the hotels don't let them in. He danced a song with Nuria, and when they returned, Raúl said that he was leaving, that tomorrow he had to get up early. Do you mind seeing her back home? He patted him on the back and kissed Nuria lightly on the lips. And another day when the three of them had a date, Raúl called at the last minute and said that he just couldn't make it, that he had a meeting he couldn't miss; and one afternoon, at Nuria's house, he said that he had to go and, from the street below he looked up and saw her waving him goodbye from the terrace. Because how could he ever be sure? Had that beardless Armstrong really arrived the day he said and not two days earlier, during which time Raúl had barely seen Nuria? Had the two of them really spent the morning looking at the Romanesque galleries in the Museo de Montjuich or had they just stopped in there for a moment, because Mr. Strongarm, Mr. Flop Cock, had an idea that they buy an art catalog and some postcards as proof? Why, if they had really gone there, instead of getting a room in a brothel, did they talk so much about the details, the David and Goliath by the Master of Taüll, and the Pantocrator and the Host? Why did they change the subject when he came back from the restroom? How could he know if Nuria was really going to stay at home all night, in spite of when he phoned asking for her with an English accent, they told him just a moment, and she came on the line, hello, hello, click? How could he know if Mr. Flop Cock, or Mr. Prickloose, or however they said it in English, wasn't there with her, since the one place he definitely was not was his hotel, or at least that's what they told him? Didn't Nuria rely on the servant's complicity, on the maid, surely the one who stayed in the flat when the rest of the family was away on the weekend?

And why did Nuria play the prude and, as if embarrassed, pull away, let me go, hands off, people are going to see, when after she danced with Louis Prickloose, Raúl started caressing her hair while discretely starting to feel her up, as if in a feverish rush, exploring her in search of telltale wetness and dilation? And wasn't it possible that when he arrived at Nuria's house to find that Prickloose was already there, wasn't it just possible that he'd not really just arrived like he said, or that, in fact, where he'd just come from, and she, too, was the bedroom, after helping her to smooth the sheets and change the bathroom towels thinking that Raúl just might show up to snoop around? Couldn't they have also done it without a diaphragm, given that, as he had occasion to confirm, her diaphragm was in its case, like always, in her vanity, couldn't they have done it like that, maybe because she might have lied to Louis about her period saying she didn't need to use it that day, maybe because they decided to skip the diaphragm, however unpleasant it is to have to practice coitus interruptus and pull out at the last second, so that Raúl, when he spent that night with her, taking advantage of her family being away, wouldn't be suspicious that she was already wearing it, and only the complicit maid, the procuress, was capable of appreciating from her room, with equal parts derision and discretion, the different sound of the footsteps on the stairway to the upper attic? The least of it was the image of Nuria wrapped in another's arms, her orgasms in another's embrace, her somewhat sorrowful expression that Raúl knew so well, the light—more precisely than the gaze—from her eyes. Thus in cases of sudden or violent death, emotional crises of greater intensity are experienced by those who were more intimately linked to the deceased, those who usually go on living with the small details which, once the first external displays of sorrow are past, after the burial, continue bearing witness to their unbelievable absence, the pack of cigarettes hardly smoked, the suit they bring back from the dry cleaner's, correspondence that keeps arriving, details about whose common afflictive value it would be wrong to give any other explanation than the irreparable rawness itself by which what no longer exists is manifested, thus, it would be no less mistaken to consider equivalent the lacerating lashes that a simple gesture, phrase, or specific posture of the faithless beloved can provoke in the person who is or who believes themself victim of an infidelity, even long after the events, when everything seems back to normal, or even more, the recurrent vision of that woman giving herself to the other, the imaginary reconstruction of her erotic behavior, to consider, in other words, that all those fluid representations in the memory are hardly more than the external expression of something much more abstract: betrayal in itself, the bare fact that infidelity has been possible. And more concretely yet: not so much the betrayal itself—especially when in reality one does not love that woman, when one is fed up and what they're trying to do is break things off, to get rid of her—as its verbal formation, meaning, the lie, which during the time she was consummating her infidelity, she was capable of writing, of repeating, of continuing to say, I can't live without you, you're the only person in the world I can love, just as that very night, the same as so many others, Nuria—although especially sated, Raúl being certain of his theory that when he arrived she had just been screwing Louis—surely had to say it. Why don't you ever tell me you love me, even just once in a while? said Nuria. Because you know perfectly well that I'd be lying, said Raúl. She pushed away from him, turning toward the other side of the bed. You don't understand anything, not a thing. She would cry a little, each time more softly, as if waiting, as if she knew that he was going to embrace her from behind, body against body, caressing her, holding her, penetrating her. And then she would say: you do love me even if it's only a little bit. And he would say: yeah, just a little.

Nevertheless, by then, the general deterioration of their relationship also affected, possibly, the erotic aspect, altering, depending on the day, his or her or both their libidos, diminishing it, annulling it, and it would be very difficult to determine if the posterior events—all the stuff with Achilles, Aunt Paquita, the overcoat, Señor Rivas, the Plutos, etcetera—were the final drops that caused the glass to overflow, or rather the excuse, the justification for dejection and lack of enthusiasm that possessed them, the not now, Raúl please, I'm too nervous, if not the I know what's wrong, you just don't feel like it anymore. Why did they stay together? From the inertia that keeps miserable people together or, more simply, by a phenomenon similar to the empty stubbornness with which a brain blocked by neurosis passes the time playing with a word, a proper name, Paitubí, for example, perhaps jarring, perhaps not, Paytuby, Paytobe, Paytobuy, Buytopay, Tobepay, Tobebuy, or with a Latin declension, or with an irregular English verb, forget, forgot, forgotten, a reflection of who knows what sort of startling spells, what lugubrious associations? And, apart from how many factors might have intervened in the decline of their relationship, to what other elements and to what level of awareness might it be possible to attribute the fact that, like the solitary person obsessed by the idea that drowning himself will garner not an unequivocal response but rather a sentence, like in that song about the lost keys—*Dónde están las llaves, materile, materile, en el fondo del mar, materile, materile—Where are the keys, la la li, la la li, at the bottom of the sea, la la li, la la li*—sung in chorus by some children on the street, which then becomes a sinister ritornello in his mind, thus in a similar way, the most fortuitous and insignificant event in his daily life could represent for Raúl the most mocking reply of his fallen state of mind? What doubt, in any case, that the person going through a phase of anguish, or perhaps of lucidity, as his self-confidence fails him, his confidence in his intellectual and moral conditioning, in his own sexual vigor, what doubt that in that individual a defense mechanism of ritual and compensatory character will start up, where the preventative and not rudely hygienic meaning of the ablutions he practices before going to bed or upon rising, for example, will come to be defined by the same implacable order and systematic rigor with which he practices them, a tendency that will only grow sharper to the degree to which the somber tone of his thoughts that assault him is accentuated, questions, interrogations, I'll go back and walk down this street that I've never walked down before, which of those old relatives only seen at burials will I never see again, to what point will the end of others no longer form part of our own end, when was its beginning, when does it begin to end? There are cases, there are people, there are moments, unforeseeable of course, in which the same threatening stormy horizon seems to induce one, more than to escape, to seek refuge in another body, to integrate, to penetrate the body, to be materialized in the other, to be the other, losing oneself until disappearing in some lips, in some breasts, in some buttocks, in the roses that unfurl within the smooth nether hair, as if on each one of those parts they might be able to encounter the whole, the hidden secret, the Cave of Sesame, a process no less disintegrating, though apparently the inverse, than the bureaucratization of love, the love that over the years, between old lovers, ends up being finished off as if it were no more than some administrative file, and just as regulatory processes, by their very nature, engender prevarication and bribery, so the continuity and habit of the sexual life engender and announce betrayal, the attraction to adventure, of projecting the same desires onto another body, of repeating upon it an identical erotic ritual, the lascivious unction in the mouth, on the breasts, on the buttocks, on the sex, attributing, in general, to that other body appetites complementary to one's own appetites, given how many general ideas circulate about it, his own eyewitness experience helping spread the myth, *auparishtaka*, for example, women's fondness for taking a man's sperm in their mouth, a belief based, more than on a true confirmation, case by case, on the simple fact that they currently practice it, perfectly knowledgeable of their efficiency, of the hot manifestations of recognition that its execution usually costs her; and based, especially, on the desire that they like what men like. And the counterpart to *auparishtaka*: kissing the yoni, according to the anthropomorphic concept of the fundamental feminine nymphomania, the idea that nothing drives a woman so wild as prolonged oral stimulation of her sex, something that they never forget, that forever subjects them to whomever has got them to achieve such intense pleasure in this way, a very common idea based on the concept of the *madanashastri* or clitoris as the equivalent of the penis or lingam, and, consequently—how sad and denigrating for the woman that a guileless mind could think them the same—on the indisputable superiority of the clitoral orgasm over the vaginal, a superiority defended as much by those women sincerely addicted to it, in defense of their unequivocally lesbian and onanistic appetites, as by those women who don't wish to stop seeming so, without daring to reveal, believing them abnormally insane, their vaginal preferences, be it for purely psychic motives—narcissistic women, in general, sublimated through transcendence, appreciating the pleasure their body is capable of generating, reaching orgasm together, etcetera—be it for being associated with a certain physical reality, deductions and deep suspicions that in the man, according to a process similar and no less tendentious, usually increase in direct proportion to the lack of fulfillment of his desires, not being infrequent so that, habituating himself to repression, that man ends up finding greater satisfaction in imagining in detail the sexual act in all its phases and variations, than in the sexual act itself, in exercising it, a satisfaction that has the advantage of permitting him, on the other hand, to attribute to the woman, with full liberty, freely, without any possibility of being contradicted, an exact replica of his desires, with the tendency to forget that although in her those desires are diffuse, as diffuse as her body's eroticism, they are for her no less concrete. Less studied, however, as an aspect of male eroticism, is the recondite appeal that a woman's buttocks and their mesial depths hold for a man, his compulsive propensity to want to explore them, to penetrate them, a far more widespread fixation than usually believed thanks to a general resistance to discuss the subject, desires that men don't discuss among themselves nor boast nor brag about, not so much perhaps from the fear that as a clumsy analogy, through a rough and mechanical transposition, they be interpreted as symptomatic of some unconfessed homosexuality—a hypothesis, however, somewhat disposable, as is the previous and larger problem they raise: the obscure meaning such desires represent for an individual, the esoteric substrate that vivifies them, less easy to explain, for example, including for an analytical spirit, than the application with which the young man, from his first sexual experience and in a totally unconscious way, sucks on his partner's breasts; more difficult and, above all, more surprising, by virtue of the charge of profanation that the act comprises, in maximum violation of the intimacy of the person who is the object of our desires, more so, of their individuality, the will to transcend supposed by that desire to enter—not always easy—the most reserved part of the other body, of fusion, of total communion with the other organism by means of direct access to its true center, to the point of confluence or outlet of all its assimilative systems, something rather like the royal throne room. Desires, it's clear, one only gets used to putting into practice—except when one resorts to the brutal example of force—from a proven erotic understanding, from a progressive coupling of rhythms, from a mutual physical concession, inserting its realization, when not substituting it for the habitual final penetration, at any moment of the ritual: caresses, kisses, sucking, ears, neck, breasts, buttocks, belly, the slow, gradual descent centered on the new world that opens up merely by spreading the legs.

The purpose and final end of the sexual act is conception. Do you all remember? said Pluto. To hell with conception and engendering: Orgasms! Orgasms! All the rest is just the desire to impregnate. That only happens to idiots like me who for years and years have believed in that stuff about the blessed fruit of your womb Jesus Amen, and then they go and knock up some idiot like that fool Marihole. They were getting drunk and Mariconcha or Maripain or Marihole started crying again. Aurora paid her no attention and Nuria didn't seem to hear, absorbed and a bit withdrawn, fed up, you might say, by the mere fact of being there, like a mother with her little children on Sunday afternoon, stupefied, saturnine thanks to them, on the verge of dementia, dancing as if bewitched to the sound of their pooping and their crying and their baths and their games and their squabbling tantrums and their baby food. She'd not said a word since they arrived, while they established their definitive plan: Mariconcha or Mariwhatever would tell her family that she was going to spend two or three days at a friend's house, La Molina, for example, to see the snow; at nine o'clock sharp the day after tomorrow, Wednesday, the fourteenth, she and Pluto would be at the midwife's house and Adolfo would be waiting for them at the same bar as today and would bring them here and here they would wait until she was in a good condition to return home, not precisely tanned from the high mountain climate, but rather somewhat diminished, the bad weather and, especially, the misfortune of an especially pesky period, the periodic bleeding that would come from those shapeless swellings and magmatic palpitations, happy and rapid conclusion to the arrangements begun on the ninth, the day after Mariconcha's saint's day, the Immaculate Conception, when Raúl went to see the midwife, I don't know if you remember me, you helped my wife it must be about four years ago, and the midwife remembered, so she received the Plutos, and they made an appointment for the twelfth, today, she would prepare her, and the intervention would be the fourteenth. Correct, said Pluto: a question to resolve between conception and Nativity. And the doctor? said Adolfo. What guarantee do we have that he knows what to do? You tell me, said

Pluto. The kind of guarantee you get from a big son of a bitch. We still haven't seen hide nor hair of him. That very white hair and his big white mustache, in contrast to his sixty-something tanned complexion, almost like a photographic negative; he would appear, he appeared, at just the right moment, when everything was all ready and she was in the correct position, well open and raised up, and he'd peer through some glasses as he sat down before her to examine her, indelicate and cynical like that leisurely passerby who stops to contemplate the fruitless maneuvers of some clumsy new driver trying to parallel park their car, contributing nothing more with his bold stare than to roil the development of their repeated attempts and to intensify the beginner's feeling of haste and embarrassment, not simply for a lack of tact, doubtless, but rather, also, premeditatedly, with insidious delectation, perfectly aware that, after bumping repeatedly into the cars ahead and behind, his victim would finally give up and drive off in a hurry, feverish and muddled. Thus, the doctor, while the midwife prepared the anesthetic, would calmly slip on his gloves and conduct a rough vaginal examination, as if he enjoyed the situation or considered, perhaps, its effects to be cathartic for the patient, completely indifferent to the shame and horror she might be experiencing, sinister in his manners and his aspect, more a dungeon master inflicting torment than a surgeon, a sordid impression, a product, of course, more of the circumstances than his physique, a face, a presence, which in another context would perhaps have nothing especially disagreeable about them, like that Nazi officer in the movies who interrogates the members of the resistance, blonde and gray, snakelike, cruel, but who in another role, in another guise, might pass for a friendly queer. Then when she woke up, he would say, he said, look, it was a little girl.

They walked with the Plutos until they found a taxi. You two take it, Nuria said; Mariconcha doesn't feel well. The worst that can happen to her is that she aborts, Pluto said. Raúl and Nuria stood there, waiting for another taxi to come along. We could also walk a little further and take the Metro, Raúl said. No, said Nuria; pawning my jewelry will at least pay for a taxi. She turned to face Raúl: do you have anything you need to do in the morning? Nothing: an appointment with some idiot at eleven, in the Atheneum; and then pop round to the Registry Office. Then, why don't you spend the night? My brothers are at my grandparents' house. And your mother? Who cares? Maybe she's with Amadeo. Alright, I'll come over, but only for a while. Why not spend the night? Because of my dad, you know perfectly well. If they wake up and I'm not there, they'll think I've been arrested again or something, I don't know. In the taxi, they sat without talking, and when they reached Nuria's flat they went straight up to her room. When Raúl came out of the bathroom he found her stretched across the bed, still wearing her overcoat, and shoes, squeezing the strap of her purse, looking at the ceiling. We should have started living together before it was too late, she said. If someday has to be too late, it's not worth the trouble to start, said Raúl. But the surest way for it to be too late is to make things slow down. And the quickest way, not slow them down. Nuria lit a cigarette. Really, I don't understand how your affair with Aurora didn't last longer. You two are so much alike; what people call soul mates. You're a much better match for her than Adolfo. And Raúl: what would be better for me is some gorgeous girl with no brains. If Adolfo wants to deal with Aurora, that's his business. I'll keep looking for the brainless beauty. And Nuria: you mean I've got to hang around with you waiting until you find some idiot to dump me for? And Raúl: no; I can also take off right now. I'm already nervous enough myself without having to handle someone else's worries. Nuria took his hand. Forgive me, she said: I'm the idiot. Raúl removed his hand to light another cigarette. Why has everything gone to hell? said Nuria. We should have decided to move in together when all that was happening. That screwed everything up and hurt us both. You know I don't blame you for anything; I was a complete coward. And Raúl: don't worry, that didn't change anything; I loved you, but I wasn't in love with you. And Nuria: but what does being in love mean for you? And Raúl: something else. And Nuria: Why? Why? I've loved you so much since the beginning. She took Raúl's hand again; the way his pupils changed, like the colors of an aquarium with gaping fish staring through the glass. Sorry. I'm an idiot. I'm sorry. So many things all at once in such a short time. But that's not the problem, Raúl said. And she: I know, I know, shaking her head, as if refusing to listen, extraordinarily similar to her mother in her moments of sorrow, days before, when, shattered and exhausted, her face almost erasing the familiar Doña Dulce of always, resolved and self-sufficient, a sort of woman whom, although unaware of it, Raúl had never met before, her relationship with Amadeo, it wasn't difficult to see in her the determination and sangfroid typical of that housewife who, discovering her husband's adultery, makes the first likely-looking taxi driver she can find drop her off at a brothel, and there gives herself over to every kind of sexual activity, offering the incredulous man all the pleasures she's been denying her husband since their wedding night.

He stroked her hair, kissed away her tears, and she, as if sensing that their saltiness would excite him, let him caress her, motionless but every moment more tense, more docile, as if under the effect of a relaxing massage, until suddenly, tears still wetting her cheeks, but now without holding back her crying, she began to return his kisses, almost brutally, ravenous, as if she'd foreseen that frantic undressing between more kisses and more caresses and more sucking, following their ritual, lips, ears, neck, breasts, belly, ass, sex, etcetera, besides, of course, any other variant introduced along the way, any other spontaneous initiative, things that appear in one of those pornographic pulp novels sold in secondhand bookshops described in this way: and he used his powerful penis to kiss her breasts, applying it to them like a blowtorch, and as if it were a blowtorch, she got hotter and hotter while he continued using it to caress her neck, her ears, her throat, and then she, trembling with pleasure, grabbed it, kneading it furiously with both hands, her left hand around his testicles, her right hand squeezing the base of the gland, caressing it with her silky blonde hair before starting to suck it deep, smooth, and eagerly, etcetera, or with a similar tone and diction; or expressed not quite so graphically, more conceptual, resorting to the various procedures, sanctioned by her own experience, by which one manages to give variety and prolong the sexual act to the maximum, given how much more easily the man reaches orgasm than the woman (Kinsey, Stekel, Tong-Hiuan-Tsen), not so much a question of erotic self-gratification—quite the contrary on occasions—as an elemental norm of masculinity, a question of prestige, as well as a progressive deference to the satisfaction of the feminine libido, satisfaction understood as a woman's inalienable right, discarding, of course, the case of greater strength, the case in which one is seen specifically obliged to delay orgasm as long as possible, whether for not being in the right mood or not having a good body or whatever, and it takes him time to get in the right frame of mind, and the effort of forcing oneself to do so ends up leading one to a rapid and undesired conclusion, even without having achieved the standard required conditions of size and consistency, in the same way that without the warmup exercises, cold, no athlete would reach their desired goals; or put more poetically by Tong-Hiuan-Tsen, being especially mindful when the woman takes the man's jade stalk or lingam, while he caresses the woman's jade gate, also called her yoni. Thus, the man will also experience the influence of the Yin, and his precious stalk will be elevated with vigor, erect as a mountain peak pointing toward the Milky Way. For her part, the woman will experience the influence of the Yang, and her cinnabar cleft will become moist with rich secretions. Next, the man will place his jade stalk near the entrance to the vagina—the yoni—that bushy region that seems a tiny pine forest surrounding a deep grotto. When the cinnabar cleft pours out its rich secretions, the lance—the lingam—penetrates the vagina, spilling secretions that mix with those of the woman to water the sacred field, above, and below, the shadowy valley. Tong-Hiuan-Tsen said: the jade stalk then plunges into the cinnabar cleft up to the Yang terrace; that jade stalk then seems a thick rocky crag that blocks a deep valley. Meaning: the way that a general cuts a swath through the enemy field or the wild horse plunges across a deep river or the seagulls play above the waves or a rock sinks into the sea or the serpent slowly slithers into his den to hibernate or the falcon swoops down upon the flitting hare or the brave boat sails into the teeth of the storm, that is the way until the woman begs for grace; thus. Tong-Hiuan-Tsen said: and when a man feels that he is about to come to orgasm he must wait for the woman to also climax so they might both enjoy the pleasure together; so then, the man will give light taps between the cords of the lyre and the grain of rice, and the taps must seem like the movements of a baby nursing. And then, let the man close his eyes, concentrate his thoughts, press his tongue against the back of his palate, curve his back, stretch out his neck, dilate his nostrils, contract his shoulders, close his mouth and hold his breath. In this way, his sperm, the Kama-salila, will move backward by itself. Or it will not go back and everything will have been for nothing. Something that can also happen, like the general or the seagulls playing above the waves or a rock plunging into the jade sea, before he has penetrated the cinnabar cleft; before: when the woman, turning her head and shaking her hair, as if in a surge of ecstasy, as if attacking or taking shelter, abruptly resolves matters, directly and deeply, and then the vision of the man tends to vanish, taking as a vanishing point the image of that hair that falls in a swirl, over her face, upon the juicy precipitant rhythm, that cozy suction cup pulsing like a hot gusting wind. Or even without *auparishtaka* or simple fellatio, or complemented with its inverse practice, meaning, a sixty-nine; even without that, even under the simple but persistent caress of a blonde mane. And even before the virile member had acquired its habitual proportions in such circumstances. Mistakes that can be avoided or at least mitigated, more than following the lessons prescribed by Tong-Hiaun-Tsen for such situations, more than realizing the acts advised by him, simply trying to remember them in the right order, although the key to success might very possibly reside in the mere mnemonic exercise and its material execution, might only be a skillful diversionary maneuver. Or rather, more simply, thinking about whatever might be, the most depressing thing possible, Aunt Paquita's death, for example, or the death of Señor Rivas, according to the principle of mental concentration as an inhibitor of the libido when its function is not specifically stimulating, in an attempt to distract oneself through memory, of centering the attention on something anodyne if not unwelcome or worrisome, seeking thoughts capable of interfering with the rising bubbling sensation, avoiding thinking that it's coming, thinking distract yourself, forget what you're doing, don't go on like that, don't think about that, tell her to stop, don't stoke that burning fusion, don't think, think about something else, about people, in banal expressions, the memory of having been, and Manolo Moragas who said the truth is all that sex business is just a drag, and Federico who said that Escala does everything he can for the sake of seeming what he is, and Leo who said that one cannot lose contact with the masses, and whoever fails to participate regularly in political discussions and the life of the party ends up losing it, and whoever loses it is, to the party, like a priest who hangs up his habit is to the church, worse than the one who never had faith to begin with, and Federico: Like Stalin and like Pluto? And Leo's father: Tertullian was a great man and if he were alive today he would be a communist, communism has always been pro-culture, Lenin enjoyed Mozart's music and Marx liked Balzac, and Federico, the best way of assisting the workers' petit bourgeois aspirations is to label as petit bourgeois whomever does not share them because they don't share the aspirations of the majority of the working class and for that reason they are petit bourgeois, and Floreal, the true realities are the subsistence wages and the accidents on the job and the misery and torture, this is the reality that must serve as an inspiration to writers and artists, and Leo, the party is always right and only one position can be right, and Floreal, I'd almost say that sometimes it's more important to keep the party strong than drive ourselves crazy thinking about the revolution, and Leo's father, humility is the most difficult of all the virtues, and Federico, what Leo's saying will happen but in reverse: the proletariat will ally itself with the petite and middle-class bourgeoisie, with the upper class bourgeoisie and even with the monopolist oligarchy. A popular front, only backward. And tomorrow, the meeting with Curial at eleven o'clock, at the Atheneum, and then to the Registry Office. Tirant and Curial and Rocaguinarda and Rocafort and Entenza and Roca Guinart and Serrallonga and his men, Pixafort and Cagaferro[1], or something like that, gentlemen and bandits or gentlemen bandits or bandit gentlemen. The meeting with Curial and the Registry Office. And in the afternoon, see the Plutos, to see if everything's going well, to cheer them up, and the meeting with Plans's men, the Rodriguezes, the Vilás, the monstrous offspring of that oh-so-characteristically Barcelonan bourgeoisie, not very different, however, from any other solidly established bourgeoisie in any other European city. Another conjecture: that the intended conflict with Plans, which Amadeo seems to have so satisfactorily and skillfully resolved, has been, after all, something much less Machiavellian than the mental reconstruction of the events, fruit of a widow's mistrust, an attorney's ineptitude, and a general climate of neurotic imagination that had settled over them. Simply: the maneuver—not conspiracy—of a living person, Plans, to get the most out of the situation, undoubtedly difficult, in which Gráficas Rivas found itself; or more

[1] Translator's note: i.e. Cockstrong and Ironshitter, respectively.

simple still, to not get your fingers caught in the trap, to cover up any possible rupture. And, in this sense, Amadeo's intervention might well have softened the consequences for Plans as well as for the others. And his lost overcoat? And the ashes of the fallen leaves like the dark body of a bird struck down from the sky? Vertigo and whirlwind, names, things, people, occurrences, happening one after another, transforming, metamorphosing, that fantastic vortex, with the desire, in the center of the depths, of stopping and thinking, stopping and looking around and forward and, above all, behind, recounting it all, stopping anywhere, looking from anywhere, around, within, to the very bottom, above, up to where the summit ends, stop there and look around. And so like a man who exerts himself in response to the amorous stimulations of his partner and, carried by that impulse, only tempered by breathlessness, fatigue, and absence, does not delay in intuiting that he's gone too far too fast, the adequate form too forcedly acquired under that wild head of hair haloing his sex, or rather, by the time he'd penetrated the woman with that awareness of disaster, trying desperately to avoid the inevitable void, holding back sudden ejaculation, reestablishing the necessary rhythm, resisting the tensions that herald the final comfortable peace, the damp warm repose of one body atop another, united by the slippery, still-oozing, dilating rose, counteracting this end even when it comes on time, resorting to any old thing, mnemonic concentration, Chinese procedures, thinking don't think a thing, thinking don't be ashamed of the end result beforehand, don't accelerate the unavoidable abandon, lost morale and dejection and disenchantment that surrenders itself to the rising ardor, to this finish so brusquely ended.

IX

The worst thing in life: that it turns out exactly as we feared. A Purgatory where we are punished not specifically for offenses committed, but rather for our a priori assignment to this or that sentence, to this or that sector or field reserved beforehand for a certain kind of punishment. The rest, Paradise, Inferno, are only the two endpoints, interchangeable incidentally, of a metaphor that alludes to certain extreme or, for being analogous to everything one would like to find that is not found upon the mountain's arid heights, apparently imaginary situations; opposite perspectives from the same topographical accident. Why did Dante come to rest on the description of the tenth heaven, beyond the nine moving heavens and even the nine angelic choirs? Why did he lack the strength of his elevated fantasy to give us an image of the culmination of the Empyrean? Why is the word feeble itself too feeble a word to explain to us what he saw in the center of the light, the nature of the fire in the Third Circle, the reflection of an iris reflected in an iris? Why could he say no more than *un fante che bagni ancor la lingua alla mammella*? Because in the center of this fire he discovered the eye of the Inferno, and he understood that this last circle of Paradise was simultaneously the ninth circle of Hell or, if you prefer, the point of union between both; that, center against center, were in fact one and the same thing, like facing a mirror where you really don't know which side you're on, where the nearest thing touches the nearest thing. Meaning, what he'd long feared: having reached the vertex of the Inferno, contrary to what he could expect from his exceptional powers of observation placed at the service of a sadistic delectation, Dante announces his resistance to writing what he saw up there, higher than the deepest depth, given that however much he said about it would be too little, too feeble. Something that, well considered, was already obvious to the attentive reader of Canto 34, the end of the *Inferno*, that canto which like a wasteful excess, the same as the tenth heaven, seems to break or contradict the poem's symmetry and ternary structure, 3 times 33. How is it that no scholar or critic has yet fallen into the necessity of investigating more deeply the meaning of that extra canto, that added canto, that canto that gives the *Inferno* just one more than the *Purgatorio* or the *Paradiso* and which perhaps, to offer a more precise correspondence, should bear the number 100, as the nexus or bridge between Paradise and Hell, as it closes and brings the poem full circle?

The process, the linking of events and, even more, the immediate motive that had led him there, to that situation, to that forced attitude, solid as a rock or a militant or a sentinel with a sharp bayonet, was in a certain way a question without importance; like a nocturnal Count Arnau with no need of the sparks from his fiery horse, of those hooves that ring like chains, to know himself condemned, or like the rapist Fra Garí in his errant bloodsucking life among the crags of Montserrat, a product not of his guilty conscience, as could be naively deduced, but of a roundly objective sanction, or like an impious Serrallonga in his surplice, so Raúl knew that one day or another, it was fated to happen, just like an Al Capone, finally brought down by perjury or tax evasion, the one just as lethal as the other. Nor, in the long run, would the predominant role which certain conflictive personality traits of his could have played in all that carry greater interest—the virtues or pietas of an Aeneas, his capacity for dedication to an impersonal goal, to a collective enterprise, exercised with the shrewdness and calculation of a Ulysses or, quite possibly, to the inverse—without managing to explain to us previously the why and the wherefore of that conflictive personality; no, no greater interest than that of highlighting, for example, the decisive role that Modesto Pírez played in his arrest, the baneful Modesto, just the sort of stool pigeon who must have helped bring down Al Capone, one of the first things he saw at Police Headquarters, Modesto Pírez sitting in a chair, tied to it with a belt, and the look on his face of an adult caught red-handed masturbating, the supplication for understanding contained in his desolate eyes, the acceptance of his guilt, the hope that everything would end happily. Some occurrence had to pull him out of that quotidian life that was the image and likeness of Purgatory, an image of which institutions like school or the military are, in their turn, images, forever awaiting the degree, the diploma, the final redemption, and then everything will be different. Granted, too, that the lover's natural element is the prison of his love, as for a mystic it's the prison of the body, which supports his trances. Thus, vivifying fire can become the real prison for the condemned man, to the point that, like for the mystic or the lover, if that prison does not exist, they invent it.

Motionless, standing at attention before the open door of his cell, like a Farinata standing upright in his burning tomb. But unlike Farinata, and although equally stung by curiosity or tedium, not by self-will, but—conveniently confronted—obliged to attend, like it or not, the ceremony that, marked by cornet blasts, is celebrated upon the circular platform of the prison's Central Tower, the very navel of those vast confines, somewhere between cathedral nave and ship's bridge; to look without seeing the distant purple flashes and the ritual of the movements, no less rigorous in their execution than his own, realized throughout the course of the day, crossing his cell diagonally, for example, counting his steps—seven in this one, four in the previous one, three in the first—stepping always on the same tiles, turning always to the same side—the right—bumping his elbows against the angled walls each time he turns, and starting again, one, two, three, four, five, six, seven. Or when he rinsed seven times after washing. Or when he ate his grub—lentils, beans, lentils, garbanzos, lentils, beans, lentils, garbanzos, lentils—in exactly seventy spoonfuls, always capable, however, of being adjusted. Or with each recounting, counting to twenty, thirty, forty, depending—although finely adjusted, risking more each time, however fast he counted—before taking his place at attention before the doorway, in the interval he measured between the arrival of the block boss passing by, opening the cells, and the incoming or outgoing officer who recounts and his entourage, the interval calculated according to the distance, each time variable, separating the boss's passing from the others as they checked the cells opposite and, especially, when they reached the end, the last cell on the other side and passed by on this side, according to their voices, 237 one, 236 one, 235 one, louder as they approached his cell, until the moment they appeared, 234 one, to find Raúl, cutting it closer each time, just in front of the cell door, standing at attention, as if whisked there more by fright than simply leaping into place, his expression tense and a current of air at his back, cowed by the silent expectation of the prisoners on the opposite side of the gallery, where the block boss, running his key the length of the balustrade, now went from cell to cell, inspecting or simply meting out punishments, according to the situation. Or in his obsessive arrangement of his belongings behind the headboard, his toiletries, his t-shirts, underpants, socks, toilet paper, tobacco, pen, matches. Or the strict order he followed for dressing and undressing. Or the regularity with which he smoked a cigarette every half-hour without the need to check the clock; miscalculating by three minutes more or less was a bad sign. Like an error in the order of putting on or taking off his various garments, or in arranging his things; or losing track when counting. And how, in general, also, the weather was bad, the cloudy skies, the rain. Clearly neurotic interpretive tendencies and rituals, of course; but not especially heightened by the circumstances. In the same way that now, without his medicine, without his sleeping pills, without his tranquilizers, without his stimulants, he slept no worse than before nor did he feel more tired or depressed. On the contrary. Although, of course, if he had his pills he'd go right back to taking them. Not only from fear of the insomnia, fatigue, and depression that might assault him, but also from the bad luck he could bring on himself by not taking them. An insomnia, however, you might almost call induced—despite the care with which he took to spread his overcoat over the bedstead of the bunk overhead, to block out the light bulb, a light bulb mounted on the wall, above the door, that stayed lit all night long—voluntarily provoked thanks to a methodical inspection, at bedtime, of his mind, his thoughts, his memory, his imagination. Insomnia: eyes, circles, owls.

Not only a manic ritual. No. A way, too, of marking time, a personal system superimposed upon the order of the penitentiary regimen, upon its rhythms of meals and head counts, subjecting the sequence of hours to a rhythm previously unexperienced, according to which the days passed quickly and the hours slowly and, even more slowly, the minutes. Thus, one would say that the minutes expired before the present instant had gone by more slowly, nine and nine, if his watch kept good time, than the whole week gone by since last Sunday at this same time, a Sunday that prefigured, no doubt, what this Sunday was going to be; repetitions that as they prolong the instant also warp—vertigo or immobility, acceleration or pause—the passing of time. Pauses which after brusquely breaking the course of his reflections, like an alarm clock that forces us from sleep, made him return to them with renewed penetration, with renewed distance, as if in the interval the key he'd previously sensed had come to him of its own accord, precipitating the mechanisms of conscience, enriching them, the same as other pauses into which all men drift who are subjected to isolation: exchanging the greatest number of words with the loutish men dishing out the grub; with the always more than cordial block boss, one Barquero or Botero; reading the latest issue of *Redención* from the first word to the last, the sole echo of the sublunary world; sing aloud songs that feed the spirit or bring good luck; hunt down the dust mice that floated through the cells (like landladies) on the air currents; look out the window, from the top bunk, when the prisoners went out into the yard; or, attentive to the noises from the gallery, to the footsteps, the voices, guards knocking on prisoners' doors, the voice of the cellblock boss asking their number, numble? cornet blasts and crazy laughter, the loudspeakers, keeping your eye glued to the stool pigeon like on a microscope eyepiece, trying to decipher the peculiar rhythms of daily life in prison; and the dialogues from cell to cell through the wall, with his neighbor, number 233; trying, also, to follow as much as possible the message of la Merche, confusedly repeated over the loudspeakers, words about the coming Easter—*la Pascua*—a commemoration of the passion and glory of the Lord, Pascua meaning crossing, passing over, and celebrated in ancient times to commemorate the crossing of the Red Sea, but, and what is a man's life but a crossing, a transit toward his eternal salvation or punishment? Retracing the shapes already discovered in the puddles on the flagstones; following the sunlight crossing the floor of the cell, following the course of its mutations from it first entering like a tiny crack and then growing and taking on geometric shapes, oblique polygons, irregular quadrilaterals, rhombuses, rectangles soon deformed, rhombuses, in the opposite direction from the first one, growing thinner until disappearing as if through a slot, geometries resulting from the projection of the bars upon the floor, a reticule of shadows superimposed on the sunny grid of the flagstones like the public bus and streetcar lines are superimposed on a city map, laid out in a grid like the Ensanche, that Ensanche which is home to the Cárcel Modelo—the Model Prison—in the space delimited by four different streets: Rosellón, Provenza, Entenza, and Nicaragua.

How many times had he not dreamed of this recently? A detective was about to arrest him on Paseo de la Bonanova, or in the garden at Vallfosca, or—also in Vallfosca—a truck full of police with rifles and steel helmets, like German soldiers, suddenly came round a small bend in the road, or several plainclothes policemen chased him through the Galerías Astoria department store, situated in the same location where the Almacenes El Siglo had been located, destroyed by a fire a few years before he was born, on the eve of the Feast of the Magi or some similar date of equal importance. And he had to flee or hide and, as he fired, the pistol jammed, or at least the bullets didn't shoot. Or rather, in an office, various detectives asked him about something, something always difficult to remember once awake; and he lied, invented alibis. The same when he really was arrested, while he was interrogated for real, not only in the symbolic sense of the word, not by police who really act like repressive agents of the superego. A dream that had stopped recurring the moment his arrest became reality. Just as he had not dreamed again, conscious that he did not know how to drive, that he was driving a car at high speed and, although he handled the controls at random, managed not to crash and burn. A rather exciting sensation, somewhat similar to when, as a boy, he rode the bumper cars with Manolo at the neighborhood carnival; a sensation he'd not experienced again in his dreams from the moment when he started practicing to get his driver's license, even before he'd passed the preliminary written exam without any trouble, that cold January morning on Montjuich, when nervous about something deeper than the simple extreme jitters accompanying an exam, perhaps the situation itself, childish and regressive because of what it had in common with other such previously experienced situations, like in school or military service. Like a presentiment that he was already being followed. Because that's how it must have been, given that the police themselves had made a detailed report of his comings and goings on the feast day of San Raimundo de Penyafort, the 23rd of January, the day before the exam. And everything seemed to indicate that it was precisely that day when they began to follow him, the feast of San Raimundo de Penyafort, illustrious jurist, transporter *super undas* and patron saint of lawyers; the reason for the mock trial held in the patio of the School of Humanities against a student dressed up as a policeman, when he spotted Modesto Pírez among the spectators and decided to get his attention, not only for the mix of irritation and unease that the Canary Islander's personality, and even mere physical presence, caused him, but rather because he'd come to confirm the apprehensions that Leo had expressed to him about Pírez only a few days before. One night when they went out to eat together, his worry about the confidence that Floreal seemed to have placed in a phony like that guy, whose behavior only seemed to increase his danger, moving as he moved, showing up at all of Guillén's friends' houses, friends, names, and addresses that Guillén could only have given him in a moment of Parisian drunkenness, or irresponsible nostalgia. He drew him aside—no doubt observed not by a student dressed as a police officer but by a policeman dressed as a student—to let him know there were secret police there, that his presence could draw attention for more than just having come with a university friend, especially if they took the trouble to find out that he wasn't a university student, that he'd recently arrived from France and was working construction. Don't worry, friend, before I talk I'll hang myself with my own belt if necessary, said the Canary Islander. A brief conversation, but one the police could not miss or the police who were already following Pírez and who from then on, probably, began following him, too. Until February 12, Santa Eulalia's Day, when, shortly after arriving home from a night out, during which time, fortunately, he'd not had too much to drink, the doorbell rang.

Because it might not have ended relatively early or relatively peacefully. One of those times, for example, which, the next morning, in the shower, with a hangover, made him promise himself not to give in anymore, to not agree anymore from pure habit, because until then he'd always said yes, to their proposal of going out for a walk at night, when around mid-afternoon Nuria, Federico, Fortuny, Pluto, the Adolfos telephoned him, evening excursions that didn't appeal to him, that bored him, the places, the people, his friends, everyone, he himself in the first place, adjusting to certain kinds of jokes, to their habitual role, a parody of themselves and of other times, scenes fraught with a terrifying reiterative quality, of a degraded attempt to go back or—almost worse—of carrying on the same way. The least of it was that only on rare occasions did they go down to Las Ramblas, whether for being naturally tired of that part of the city, whether for the comfort and quality of the alcohol that, along with the prices and the type of people, characterize the nightlife in the upper part of the city. Different locales, different crowds, but the same buffoonery. And if the simple phone call, the proposal accepted with such little conviction, was enough to spoil his work for the rest of the evening, when he was drinking as well, when despite his intention to not drink too much, things got messy and, in a given moment, after a certain point, he forgot his good intentions and what time it was, and suddenly realized that the sun was already rising and that he was drunk, and so then he lost the whole next day and, sometimes, even the next one, too, fog in his head and acid in his guts and—the most persistent thing—the oppressive exhaustion produced by everything unfinished, which only vanishes by getting back to the work abandoned because of the fateful telephone call. What might have happened if he'd been arrested coming back from one of those sprees, not around New Year's Eve? But, let's take for example, the night they stumbled into Montserrat at Las Vegas, accompanied by Monsina and some tongue-tied young fellow in a navy blue jacket with silver buttons? Raúl, hey big guy! The best of the Ferrer Gamindes: you're fucking great! She made them all sit down, almost had to force them, and ordered another bottle of whiskey. Me? Well, just as fucked as usual; in the worst sense of the word, unfortunately. She turned toward the next table, in the shadows. Claudio, goddamn, Claudio, look what a fucking great cousin I've got! Mama is an angel, said Monsina. She stepped out to dance with the fellow in the navy blue jacket with silver buttons and Montserrat grabbed Adolfo. C'mon, you, I don't want to commit a mortal sin with my first cousin. She hung on Adolfo's neck, falling down drunk, and they came back to the table right away, Montserrat tripping her way through a sort of involuntary tango. She slipped down between the chair and the table, dragging some glasses with her as she fell. Hitting the floor with a thump seemed to clear her wits, although she kept turning back and forth in her chair with a self-conscious smile, her gaze too fixed and staring. Goddamn, Raúl, when the hell are we gonna go out and have a few drinks, just you and me. By the time they finally managed to shake her, Raúl had swallowed four or five whiskeys, and didn't mind to keep going and, once every place was shuttered, end up at the flat of any old more-or-less-familiar good-time Charlie picking up stragglers along the way.

The night of his arrest, however, February 12, he was feeling too shitty from the start for drinking to make any difference. A listless Federico, who could only get more dull and lifeless. A certain M. M. more of a pain in the ass than ever. And the women being real bitches, shooting to kill, and Mariconcha trying to make everybody listen to her, the problem with servants, and Pluto cutting her off. The bad thing is the filthy cooks. They spit right in the soup before serving it. They stick their fingers up their ass when they're making meatballs. When they're on the rag, they mix it right into the tomato sauce. It's very well known. Like the bakers who fuck the dough while they're kneading it. And Marihole: you're the filthy pig, you swine, worse than swine, you've always got to say something to fuck it all up. And Nuria Oller repeating: why don't we go up to Mount Carmel? C'mon, man, c'mon, let's go up to Carmelo. Trying to catch Raúl's eye, looking for some significant spark of understanding, insistently trying to remind him of that other night, around the end of October, when Federico proposed that they go up to Carmelo and, split up into three cars, they chased each other around the choppy curves up high as close to the summit as possible, and then, amid slamming doors, through the quiet darkness, they continued on foot, hand in hand, feeling their way along, dazzled by the splendid brilliance that haloed the peak, and once there, against the crest, sheltered from the north wind, as if isolated in space, as if halfway between the frigid sky and the city that, like a mirror, seemed to reflect the glimmerings and blacknesses up there, shouting, they recited fragments of St. John of the Cross and Góngora and Quevedo and of the *Moral Epistle to Fabian*. But it was while they were looking at the constellations when Raúl felt Nuria's hair caressing his cheek, a light touch that if he at first considered accidental, its very persistence, along with the innocuous comments about the stars whispered into his ear, as if kissing him, left no doubt in his mind. To feel her breasts, too, while she, right behind him, right up against him, pointed upward asking some question, was almost unnecessary.

Although unanticipated, the circumstances in which his arrest took place could hardly have been more conventional. To what point could Federico picking up Raúl in his car have distracted the police so much that they, afraid that he might slip through their grasp, decided to drop the bomb once and for all? It must not have been even one o'clock when Federico said he was going to sleep, and Raúl seconded him, and Nuria ended up agreeing, rather reluctantly. They dropped off Nuria first and then swung by Raúl's house. Federico parked and killed the engine right in front of the entranceway and leaned against the steering wheel but they only stopped to talk a little, neither with much enthusiasm. It was about twenty minutes later—already in pajamas and with his sleeping pill swallowed—when the doorbell rang. He put his overcoat on over his pajamas and opened the door himself: three detectives. The driver and a policeman were outside, pacing in front of the doorway. The night was very cold. While he dressed they casually searched the room, superficially, glancing at his papers. He thought they took something he'd written. Papa came out in his bathrobe. Eloísa watched them from the end of the hallway, a white shawl over a long white nightgown in the darkness. Don't worry, just a routine inquiry. And Raúl: be sure to tell Nuria everything's alright. Before leaving they let him take a piss and go back to his room to get his cigarettes, but without letting him out of their sight. They put him in the backseat of the car, between two detectives. If you want to come out on Paseo de la Bonanova, take the next street, he told the driver. This one's a dead-end. Yes, we already know you know your way around the city very well, said the detective who'd sat in the front seat, turning halfway around; you've got to stay on your toes to follow this guy. One of the men beside him patted him on the thigh. But what really interests us, more than how well you know your way around, is your knowledge of the party. And Raúl: what party? And the man sitting next to him patted him on the thigh again: you know much better than I do that there's only one party. And Raúl: I'm sorry, but I don't understand what you're talking about or what I'm doing here. And the man next to him: of course. Anybody would start off denying it, right? What were they going to think in Moscow? A deliberately unpleasant smile, a smile that placed between parentheses, sincerely and without a doubt, the part of sincerity that could have been on Raúl's side, the reality of his perplexity, the meaning of an arrest occurring when he found himself practically marginalized from all party life, how his mind raced with questions, much faster than the car carrying them, questions that he only began to orient correctly when, as he crossed through the offices of the police headquarters, he came face to face with Modesto Pírez, sitting in a chair, tied with a belt. The specific concern of the statement immediately taken from him by a polite, almost shy, policeman brought the question into focus, clarifying who was working against him. Name? Age? Status? Profession? Did he know Modesto Pírez, alias Salvador, member of the Communist Party? The declarant says he does not, the officer repeated out loud as he transcribed the answer; he typed with a beginner's slowness and made no objection at all to the answers he was receiving. University professor, he said as an aside. It must be fascinating to dedicate your life to teaching. He set the original and the copies in front of Raúl and asked him to sign them. Now if you'd please be so kind as to wait here, professor; now, let's see if they like it, he said, and gave him a wink. He left him alone in the room, a small inner office, with skylights that allowed him to see the florescent lights in the adjacent rooms. He heard voices and laughter coming from different directions. At one point, a thickset, red-faced man, thoracic like a Negro, stepped in to look him over; he went out, looking at Raúl all the while, the way a collector admires his latest acquisition before sleep. In turn, Raúl stuck his head out into the hallway and asked an officer walking by if he could make a phone call home to reassure his family. I'll go and ask, the other man said to him, and Raúl went back to sit down and await the answer, important not only as an indication of the mood in the station, but also, in case they allowed him to, what that would mean for both Papa and Eloísa as well as for his friends, and after the phone call that Papa must have made to Nuria when they took him from the house, they would have already sounded the alarm, especially Leo, but also Fortuny and even Federico and Adolfo, given the confused origin of all that. Papa, who lately, as if he sensed something, while Raúl was working, opened slightly the door of his room and looked in for a moment before closing it again, without saying a word, as if to make sure he was there, or perhaps, just like when at night, on hearing him arrive, he rattled a teaspoon in his glass of tea, making the sound to make it clear that it was he, not Raúl, but he, who was home.

I am a man who, in a continuous fight against adverse circumstances, has given himself over body and soul to the fulfillment of his Christian obligations. I have done God's will. I have fulfilled my duties as a husband and the father of my family. I have honored my neighbor, working for the country's industrial and economic progress. And I've taken so many hard knocks already in this life that I think I've pretty well eluded whatever place in Purgatory might have been reserved for me thanks to what I've already suffered in this world. First, losing Jorgito, my firstborn. Then, losing Eulalia, like a hammer blow. Then, the time of the Reds, always on edge, living like a refugee there in a town, with two children to feed and no resources. Then, my company collapsing. And now, in my old age, I won't mention my economic difficulties, but I do have to count every last cent. And with all the money I used to manage! He spoke slumped down in an armchair in the sitting room, as if overwhelmed by the ignominy of having tried to play the Philistine but failed. And Eloísa listened to him from the hallway, seated next to the door, knitting stockings. Ay, Señor, she said. Once in a while she went into the kitchen, to check on the broth for dinner. And Papa talked about the company, failing to mention not only the accusation about his supposed incompetence as head of the corporation—his disorderly management, his administrative carelessness, his whimsical projections and schemes—accusations that had provided management with a basic consensus for removing him from his position, but also omitting the fact that such a usurpation had taken place, taking for granted the official excuse of retirement, a retirement, that's right, to his understanding completely unnecessary even though he might have been of retirement age. It's human ingratitude, that's what it is. To me, the founder and majority shareholder, the man who got the company up and running, when they start to see me old and sick, without the energy I had when I was young or the support and encouragement when I had Eulalia at my side, but still in full possession of my faculties, dammit, and they go and force me to retire, as if I was no longer good for anything, the way you throw away some piece of trash, abandoned and forgotten by everyone, without any of them even being good enough to wish me well on my saint's day. That's how they thanked me for what I did for the company. My mistake was having sold my shares. I think now they're paying better dividends than ever. Of course it's almost better to never see how others reap what you've sown with your hard work, with your contacts, with your initiative, with your legal advice. And Eloísa: don't worry, their time to retire will come, too. And what good will what they've done or stopped doing serve them when the Sphinx turns its eyes upon them? And Papa: at least my conscience is clear. And what God has taken from me on one side he's given me back on the other. This house, for example, when I got married everybody was saying how far out of town it was. I bought it for a song and now it's worth a fortune. And I expect that the municipal authorities will authorize, that they'll eventually authorize it, adding floors above, like on Paseo de la Bonanova. Imagine it then: worth millions. Remember what I'm telling you: this house has got to be the nest egg for my children. He fell silent, as if absorbed in his mental calculations. And the country house, Eloísa chimed in: what that must be worth. Imagine. The amount of land there, and nowadays, when they're selling it by the centimeter; however much you like. Such a stupid mistake Gregorius made, selling his share. The poor man was no longer in his right mind. And, look, seems they put this idea in his head. The shame is about the poplars, no one grows them anymore, they don't bring any money. Oh, and the potatoes from there were so good; and the vegetables, and those chickens Polit used to raise. Do you remember every week when the basket came? You think I'd forget. That was good, fresh, natural food; not like nowadays, everything chemical. There was a silence. Raúl, can you see, son? Your eyes'll fall out. Why don't you turn on the light? Quiet, I can't even see my knitting needles. It's not the end of the world? Put on the radio, señor, this house scares me. Well, it's foggy out, woman. Can't you hear the sirens from the port? It's all so dark. Well, the autumn's been really bad so far: fog, rain, cold. I don't know, señor, but this is like the twelve plagues. Egypt! That's right: I wouldn't like to die without first seeing Egypt.

He spoke like a person in front of a microphone rehearsing different versions of the same speech. And Eloísa, like that aging spectator who never stops going to see *Don Juan Tenorio* each November, and who knows whole speeches by heart, listened attentively, nodding, surprised, now you see, now you see. Less flexible than Papa in her judgments, when it was sunny, for example, and Papa sat in the garden and folded his paper. At any rate, Eloísa, it's our lot to live in a great period in history. In a few years we'll travel to the moon the same as we go to Vallfosca now. And man will travel through the solar system and learn the origin of life. The prospects have never been so exciting. And Eloísa: and what does the moon and the solar system matter to us or anybody, we can hardly handle a toothache. All this talk about the moon and science is like television, if you want to watch, then watch, but however much you distract yourself with it nobody can change the fact that you're here and not there, and your problems are what you've got here, and nothing else. Less versatile, yes, her mood less variable, except when Nuria came over, and then, no matter what they did, she closed up tight, leathery, incorruptible. These are not the times for spending money on flowers, she'd say if Nuria brought flowers when she came to have lunch. And if she brought bonbons and Eloísa couldn't resist the temptation: I'm not particular. I'm not one of these people who go around saying, I like this, I don't like that. I eat everything. And when Nuria brought the photograph showing them both together in the garden: I don't like photos. We should live the time allotted to us. You're young and, before you know it, you're already old. And she then complained about guests, meaning Nuria, as if I didn't have enough to do already with everyone in this house, the day they thought of buying dinner ahead of time, in addition to the dessert from the buttery, a stuffed capon, she left them all sitting there in the kitchen. Fine. Then I can go lie down and rest. I can tell when I'm not needed. For me, so much the better. If you can feed yourselves so well without me, well then, when I go to the retirement home, everyone will be happy. If it was a holiday or her day off, she left the house without saying goodbye, with her overcoat and her purse and her babushka knotted under her chin. She would still be angry when she got home, while she prepared dinner without a word, banging the pots and pans, and sometimes all the next day. And Papa's attempts to soothe her nerves only produced the opposite effect, due to an instinct similar to what spurs the boxer to hit harder when he sees blood welling up in the cuts on his opponent's brow. But Eloísa, guapa, my dear, don't you see they did this with the best intention, to save you some work? Come on, woman, for God's sake, don't be like this. Work? snapped Eloísa. Is she the one who washes the clothes without a washing machine and has to manage in a kitchen that's just an embarrassment, and do the cleaning without any appliances and prepare your little concoctions?

And would she stick up for you when the pharmacy assistant or whoever delivers something here and you don't give a tip or when they come to collect some bill and you have me tell them to come back another day just because, to delay paying a few pesetas, and I don't even know what to say or how to look them in the eye, when you just as easily sign a check for those crooked door-to-door encyclopedia salesmen, and you pay whatever subscription price the first one who shows up asks for? It's fine, then, just fine that the Russians have the atomic bomb. That way we'll be finished and done with all this nonsense once and for all. With all the trouble it takes to live. Better we all fly to the moon. And Papa: But Eloísa, Eloísa, don't get so angry, they did this for you. For me? Would she do it for the wages I earn? Don't you know there are some who get paid more than twice what I'm getting? Imagine that, what a crazy idea. The world has gone completely crazy. People nowadays are almost afraid to go out in the street. Well, between not going out, and ending up in the charity home, then that's the end of it. To be here, preparing those concoctions you're always taking. And then you're always running to the bathroom. Because I'm sick, woman. Sick? How could you not be sick with all those concoctions that are killing you? And from the kitchen, while Papa initiated a prudent retreat to the sitting room, she continued exclaiming, expounding her idea of good health, of what's nourishing, of what's beneficial, of what's good for the body, according to a scheme whose main points, established by comparison, would be the following: above all, whatever is good and hearty. Meaning: what's substantial over what's not. Spiced and spicy dishes over ones with no spice. Salty food over bland. Fatty and tasty cooking over unsavory, fat-free recipes. Sweet over dry. Rich, thick food over thin, weak food. Astringent, cleansing foods over laxative ones.

She came in quietly, wrapped in cold, with her overcoat, her big purse, her babushka. No grumbling or ranting. She sat in a chair in the kitchen, waiting for the vegetables to cook, as if she'd forgotten her rude remarks to Nuria, how she slammed the door that afternoon on going out. Look, Raúl, my nephew's mother-in-law has cancer. It's malignant. She doesn't know it. They've told her it's rheumatism and that's why they're giving her shock treatments. It seems that for some time now, at night, she could hear that tumor inside her, hear it and everything, it's that big, eating away at her from inside; but she never said anything. And now it seems they're telling her, no, it's rheumatism making her bones creak and crunch. But it's cancer. She sighed. And she spoke about her nephew's grief and her own grief for the two of them, for the poor woman and her nephew, still completely unaware that just as Raúl knew that her name really wasn't Eloísa, but Eulalia—she had changed her name because Papa had asked her to when she came to work at their house—he also knew equally well that her nephew was not really her nephew but her son. All the rest, the circumstances of the case, were unknown even to that son of hers. Seduction? Rape? Statutory rape? And the father? The priest in whose house she first worked as a maid? Some rich kid like in the soap operas? A family man? That riot policeman she spoke about sometimes? Something only she must know with exactitude, the subterranean part of her secret. A secret that only weeks later she discovered was not really a secret from Raúl, and essentially hadn't been for years; although Raúl was the youngest, although he wasn't the man of the house like Papa nor a priest like Felipe. It was a result of José—Pepe—raising the question of Eloísa going to live with them. Probably, a question related to the mother-in-law's declining condition, and to the problem of when she left them—as he put it—of who was going to mind the children while the parents ran the bar; very probably, yes, although none of this was mentioned, of course. He'd called one Sunday afternoon asking for Raúl, surely taking advantage of the fact that Eloísa was minding the children, to talk personally, he said, about a confidential matter. The bar was located in the Santa Catalina Marketplace, and Pepe—José—told him that he wasn't making a fortune from it, but he did have a steady clientele, sufficient to save some money every month. Raúl hadn't seen him for some time; he hadn't been stopping by the house lately, not since he got married, more or less. He was changed. He was approximately the same age as Felipe, but he might have passed for his father, heavy—still eschewing an apron—and almost bald. They'd like his mother to come to live with them, he explained: she was getting old, and there she could help them without getting too tired out. When my wife's mother's bedroom is empty, he said. It's not really very large, but once we repaint it, it'll look real nice. Raúl told him of course they'd agree to whatever she decided; but it was he, her son, who had to speak to her. He did so at the first opportunity, the following Thursday. Eloísa returned home earlier than usual, quite out of sorts and furious, who knows if from the terms of the proposal, or from, probably, the abrupt way he explained it to her, from José's probably somewhat infelicitous words, or, more likely still, from the sudden revelation that Raúl, the youngest, also knew about her so-called secret. She said that she'd be leaving, that she was going to the charity home, that she didn't want to be a bother to anyone. And Papa followed her through the house, Wait, woman! Hold on there, woman! Her indignation only began to abate when she believed that it had not been their idea but rather her son's, José's, Pepe's. He's a stupid fool. Stupid, I've always said so. Stupid. I'll really let him have it. I'll teach him a lesson. She was still wearing her babushka, her overcoat half-open, only unbuttoned, revealing her heavy round heaving bust, her whole person smothered, her wrath, the heat of the kitchen. I'm better off here, with the people in this house. And Papa, but of course Eloísa, my dear, for God's sake, of course this is your home, you're like one of the family.

Papa urinating in the garden, his sex like a root between his hands. He turned as he heard Raúl's footsteps on the thin gravel. It's very good for the plants, he said; organic matter. Each day I pee on a different one. He buttoned up distractedly, shaking his head. Poor Eloísa. She's really upset about all this business with that blasted Pepe. Luckily she's got her head screwed on right. With a tragedy like hers or like mine one can only save themselves by keeping a level head. It's so easy to let yourself fly off the rails. Look at Gregorius. As if I didn't have temptations, too. But I knew how to resist them. It's not that I want to complain about poor Leonor, I mean that, and in every other way she's a good woman and, in a certain way, it's lucky that it was her and not a different one. But she's not the right person for him, for a man of his class, of his culture. The fact is, Gregorius has always been a disaster, a loafer, selfish, someone who only thinks about himself. He's never struggled like I have, he hasn't suffered. Now you compare: a completely different case. Completely. I still almost can't believe the day they came for lunch. It still makes me angry. Poor Leonor completely ill-at-ease sitting at our table, trying to help Eloísa, to not call attention to herself, and he, on the other hand, so cool and collected, worried about nothing but his food. It made me furious to look at him. He never took his eyes off her while she served herself. He sat there stiff, peevish, censorious, just lashing her with his eyes. But when it was his turn, he just took any old thing from the platter, myopic and indifferent. I like it fresh and I like it spicy, he said.

Leonor opened the door for him and he found Gregorius seated in the entrance hall, in a t-shirt, his gaze abstracted, staring at the bright ceiling globe. Hearing voices, he seemed astonished at the sight of Raúl, with a disbelief and an effusion that could only be explained by the fact that he had confused him with some relative or friend from his own childhood, long dead. He embraced him repeatedly, pushing aside Leonor, who was saying they should move into the living room. Enough, let me be, woman, it's nicer in here. His breath smelled bad. When Leonor heard that Raúl had come to invite them over for lunch, partially from her astonishment and partially because it really was true, she hastened to let him know that although Gregorius was quite recovered, he was still not the same as before. And as if to prove her right, while she talked, Gregorius's gaze swam back to the globe above. Look, there's just no way I can get him to put on his shirt. And this is because he sees that it's sunny and so he says that he's hot. But if he sees that it's cloudy, even though it's summertime, he insists on going out with an overcoat. And he takes pills secretly, when I'm not looking, he eats and drinks and smokes and does everything the doctor's forbidden him, and there's no way to control him, he always manages to outsmart me. I've even caught him smoking sitting on the toilet. During the week, I take him out to the Corte Inglés or Sears or to some museum, and that's how we spend the afternoon. Or to the Barraquer Clinic, to the waiting room, and he sits there and reads the magazines. But Sundays, after Mass, where can I take him except the park? Sometimes, now that the weather's good, I'll take him to sit on the terrace at some bar, but then he orders a vermouth or a coffee with Anís del Mono, and if I say no, he gets furious and really throws a fit, until everyone is staring at us and he ends up getting his way. I can't leave him alone. I still don't know how he manages to buy cigarettes and sausages. And when he goes into the bathroom to sneak a cigarette he's crafty enough to open the windows to get rid of the smoke. Quiet, said Gregorius. He took Raúl by the arm, subjecting him again to his penetrating halitosis. Hey, are you planning to go to Vallfosca this summer? I'm really ready to go. It's much cooler there. And if we go together it's more fun. You let Polit know to wait for us at the station in his cart.

Early November, all saints departed. They arrived after dark. They were riding with Federico and Nuria Oller was following, in the Adolfos' car. As they got closer to the house, along the final turns up the hill, the headlights pierced the darkness, cork oaks with white limbs, years of deadfall, ghosts. An impression only heightened there inside the car in the resonant quiet, hostile, you might say, to those voices, to their laughter, their footsteps, that came to disturb the silence of memories, the flitting images that animated it like shadows of a movement, apparitions, or better yet, disappearances. Like the landscape. The low fogs of morning, clinging to the hollows, coating and insulating the hills like a balsam, the same as years before when he went out hunting after it cleared. And the same smells of autumn, shifting, nuanced, pervasive seeping emanations from the damp yellow fall, from the sickly carpet of leaves, soft under foot. While the others slept he took a walk around the property, the old plantings, the flatlands alongside the fields sown with young black poplars, slender graynesses stripped of their leaves. Heading back he saw the caretaker's kids around Polit's house, a welter of children watching him from different places. Only the recessed doorway and the window frames were whitewashed, and these touch-ups, which seemed to hollow out the deteriorated facade, and the flowerpots, gave the house the look of a skull with makeup. At the far end of the threshing ground there was now a rose tree that dropped its flowers here and there upon the empty pigsties, their gates hanging open, deep pink flowers so often growing through the fences surrounding the small gardens that town switchmen and stationmasters often plant next to railroad tracks. He returned along the winding paths through the yard, abandoned now to the weeds, invaded by creeping reptilian ivy, crouching brambles, dry creaking claws.

If the weather was inclement, the house was uncomfortable, a circumstance that perhaps influenced the general tension and bad mood. The night before, when they arrived, after having stared up at the cold sky from the porch, the moon now like wintertime, with its violet medusa halo, and those stars like ancient ice, then finding themselves in the toasty warm front room sitting before the fire, they all felt an unusual joy rising inside, an almost physical euphoria, quickly heightened by alcohol. They explored the house, and Nuria Rivas proposed getting naked atop the altar in the chapel and celebrating a black mass, provided they warmed the place up with enough candles. They ended up playing strip poker by the firelight, and whether because they were starting to come down from the booze, whether for how the game played out, whether for the women's jealousy when facing one another—their feints, trying to gain the upper hand, settling scores—what's certain is that the tone of the party grew increasingly tense and gloomy by the moment. And if, on the one hand, the estrangement that had for some time begun to reappear between Adolfo and Federico became official that night, according to a dialectic that was rather unclear for anyone who'd not watched it develop up close, on the other, the mutual antipathy between the two Nurias—Señorita Rivas and Señorita Oller—for the first time erupted into open hostility. Later, in the icy bedroom, Nuria Rivas insisted on making love beneath that mountain of blankets, perfectly aware, no doubt, that Nuria Oller, in the next room, alone in her chilly bed, could hear her intense cries of pleasure loud and clear.

In fact, Nuria Oller, with her poorly disguised behavior, was the first to make Nuria Rivas suspicious: the silent libidinous relationship that she tended to establish with Raúl in front of others, as if the others were not capable of noticing it, or perhaps calculating, correctly, that they would notice it this way. Her emphatic messages that evinced, in the context of the gathering, a tacit understanding between them both, like one of those code words or gestures adopted by the participants in a conspiracy, too clumsy to not be decoded in time by the security agents. Raúl, why don't you put on some record by Brel? she said. Meaning: not just any record, the record. The specific record that they had heard together on such and such an occasion. Their record. A record she now wanted to hear continuously, the way one hears a marriage processional or a victory march. In only one detail, possibly, was Nuria Rivas off-track: to wonder how something that could happen was, in fact, happening. The date. The taxi. The brothel. The smooth skill with which Nuria Oller's fingers slipped into his fly, the arching feline movement with which she, both of them half-dressed, slid toward the foot of the bed, as if in haste to contemplate her work, her half-open mouth already watering like a communicant about to receive the sacrament. Her obvious knowledge of masculine eroticism, although, one could suppose, not so much from natural intuition as from experience, almost hurrying rather than going at a steady pace, almost with a desire to show off, with too much movement and accelerated rhythm that might even become annoying, although as things progressed she proved to be unquestionably effective and there was no room for such considerations, or any others, while they were hot at it, the thread of conversation lost amid their writhing, reversing position, bodies intertwining, almost suffocating between each others' legs and asses. Afterward she fell asleep. One night shortly before dawn. Their agitated awakening indicated the degree to which their erotic action came to be a continuation of that feverish state, between sleeping and dreaming, amid desires like realities, penetrating penises, brandished naked balanus, hood flush and spread wide, glans ramming forward like suckling piglets, and the fascinating scrotum, like some strange edible sea creature, cousin to both kelp and urchin, its viscous vegetable mobility pregnant with ejaculations, as if perpetually retracting, breathing, as if peristaltically displacing itself, and the erect haughty tropism of the penis that she knows so well how to arouse and put to thoroughly good use, she, hardening haughty penises, rearing back, taking stiff drinks from their stiffened lengths, manipulating, obtaining spectacular erections, nice warm hard-ons, tense, bodies hotly wedged and dovetailed together, Raúl's lance all to herself. Nuria Oller saying I don't know what's up with me but I really love you, and Raúl saying me, too, and Nuria Oller saying maybe I'm just one more girl, but you have to promise me that if you ever get tired of me you'll tell me right away, and Raúl saying you're not just one more and I see no reason why I've got to get tired of you, and Nuria Oller saying I'm so happy with you, and Raúl saying me, too, and Nuria Oller, everything is so strange and complicated but I think I love you, and Raúl, me, too. And how do you know you love me? (Oller). Tautology (Raúl). I'm happy with you. You make me feel peaceful. But you'll soon get over it (Oller). I don't know why (Raúl). You're the first one to say that no love can last (Oller). It's just a saying (Raúl). Saying, telling, kissing, sucking, licking, embracing.

They stared at their naked bodies reflected in the mirror, atop the twisted, wrinkled sheets. And I thought I could never love anyone. And I think that everybody has always loved me too much. Starting with my husband. And it's not that I don't like that they love me, of course. But I wish they weren't so stuck on me, that they didn't act as stupid as sheep. And look, Peter has a nice mustache and we get along really well in every way. But it's something different. I'm not sure you understand what I'm trying to say. I wish they were like you. Everything is so different with you. For me, everybody loves me too much. My father, my brothers and sisters, I've always been the family favorite, their little pet. And then on the other hand, every woman hates me sooner or later. And usually sooner rather than later, almost just by seeing me. I don't know why but right from the start they seem to assume that I'm only looking to steal their men. And I can promise you sometimes I feel like proving them right. They start things with me, one woman almost attacked me in public, scratching me and everything. And the truth is I haven't had so many affairs as all that. In any case, it's the guys who want to fuck me. Before you notice a thing they're suddenly trying to cop a feel, groping you. You can't imagine: they drop off their wife and five minutes later they're trying to rape you right there in the car. And when I was a girl it was always flashers: on the street, in the cinema, in doorways. Really disgusting. I figure I'll end up a whore, fucking them all just to see if they get sick of me. Sometimes I'm really just about to have a nervous breakdown. I can't stand them touching me that way. They almost make me feel frigid. And you know I'm hardly like that. She was talking to him from the bathroom, while Raúl lay on the bed smoking, still naked, exchanging confidences perhaps not entirely appropriate to share, given their heightened state of excitement, while possessed by that characteristic post-coital mood, when, inert and empty like the castaway who, reaching dry land, doesn't even feel capable of confirming whether or not that beach is more than just a desert island, as if struck down by fatigue, without strength to move, or to locate his clothing, confronted by the most radical questions and reproaches, what are you doing here, why do you always have to end up saying the foolish things you've said. An annoyance that would quickly increase his impatience with the incalculable and detailed routine that Nuria Oller called getting ready, showering, doing her hair, makeup, a process perhaps similar in its mechanics to that herbicidal obsession of some elderly people, who systematically dedicate their leisure time to the task of weeding their yard, purging it of weeds, raking it smooth, an obsession only interpretable in terms of being a symbolic and compensatory act.

You think I don't see she's after you? said Nuria Rivas. It's enough to see how she sits down; with her legs as wide as possible. We know each other very well. In England all she did was try to fuck every one of her friends' boyfriends. And I can promise you that Peter is an alright guy, for a while. But maybe it's better for him; that way he'll get so sick of her cheating on him so much he'll finally shake her off for good. Like me this afternoon: I hung up on her. I've already got enough going on with the Plutos to have to deal with her on top of it. She was irritable, in a bad mood; she said fuck going to see the Plutos, the Plutos were depressing, that she didn't see why they were obliged to automatically go out with them just because. And at the café, while they were waiting, she argued violently with Federico. Because if Adolfo is the Count, then you must be the Countess (Nuria). Right. And I don't like the count. A conjugal problem (the Countess). Well I don't understand why. I don't find him so bad (Nuria). But I do. The ideal thing is the hermaphrodite in the Louvre. And the Count might have enough cock but he seems to be lacking tits. The opposite of your case (the Countess). Ambiguities turn out painful for me; what you should do is define yourself once and for all, accept the reality of what you are (Nuria). The thing is reality is always ambiguous. For example, I only started to be aware of being a transvestite when I found out that my mother, when I was a little boy, dressed me up as a little girl.

They'd not started out talking about Adolfo but about M. M. Stands for *memo*: neither cretin nor idiot nor imbecile nor dummy nor stupid: *memo*, a fucking vegetable, said Federico. But M. M. wasn't really the problem. Like a transvestite of a certain age who over the years has gone about acquiring the knowledge about things in life appropriate to an old maid, the slightly pessimistic prudence of one who has already seen many things and withdraws; thus, the exact personality of M. M., his shrewd wit, his nostalgic memories, inevitably had to end up getting on everyone's nerves. The problem was Adolfo: Nuria's suspicion, or perhaps her desire—a pretext for venting her anxiety and pent-up belligerence—that Federico's attacks on M. M. were, in fact, directed at Adolfo, indirect shots against the one who had made M. M.'s presence at their meetings possible. And Federico's intention—previous or provoked throughout by the same attitude from Nuria—that it be understood that way, his unequivocal desire to make Nuria upset. Speculations, relative to his appetite for mundane life, signified, for example, in Adolfo's case, by his continued dealings with M. M.—not so serious, after all, however suspicious a person of supposed creative intelligence and moral liberty dealing with a rich *memo* and with the people from his world might be—if not by his disguised collaboration on a vague film project, a project which, in its turn, very possibly disguised nothing more than his increasingly undisguised literary sterility, his still-unfinished novel, his fear of finishing it, that its publication would put an end to a myth based on the small support generated by a few heavily promoted short stories. Arguments beyond the reach of the Plutos, the sort of people who were also unaware that the internal motivations for the argument lacked any sense at all. Especially people like Marihole, whom they had already seen in her element, overcome by motherhood, plugging up her baby with bottles and suppositories, a peepeecaca yowler of a baby, a redolent fartburper of rebellious screams and projectile vomiting.

But also for Pluto, an expansive and witty Pluto, yes, although more of a role imposed on him than his habitual comportment. A role—it would be no surprise—reserved exclusively for them, in order that everything between them all continue the same as always. And even so, like that shy fellow in love who insinuates himself only a little in hopes of the first sign of reciprocity, on certain occasions, when things were going well, allowed a glimpse of reality: how the world of business is so truly fucked, getting up at seven o'clock, slaving away for real, climbing the ladder without allowing himself a single misstep, rising at the expense of others so they don't rise at yours. Putting out feelers, to see if they caught his drift, if the others had followed his own transformation and all that was needed was for someone to be the first one to break the ice. A transformation that had possibly begun shortly before his wedding, startled by the bounced check and the volley of bills, a matter resolved by his future father-in-law in his own way and, no doubt, according to his conditions. The rest, his jokes, his stories, his way of exasperating Marihole, was rather more like telling some army camp anecdote, a kind of toll he paid when they all got together. My father-in-law is a beautiful person, he said. A man with a big heart, and a big cock. He married into such a fortune that he just pisses money and thankfully, even we can live off it. But you must tread carefully with him. If you don't do what he likes, he zips up his fly. Marihole's protests, Pluto's retort, etcetera. And nevertheless, something went wrong. Raúl tried to laugh like he meant it. But Federico had started chatting up a rent boy at the bar. And Nuria: it's weird that it doesn't bother you to talk just as if you were still in the army. Federico, very tipsy, came over with the rent boy and made the introductions, Raúl, Nuria, the Plutos, my friend Whosie-whatsit. And you, what's your name? asked the rent boy. And Federico: the Countess. They're about to close up here. Why don't we go to Castelldefels? They don't close up there (the rent boy). I don't even have money for gasoline; but we could go turn some tricks on Las Ramblas to scrape up some money. You on one side of the street, me on the other (the Countess). Alright (the rentboy). Just what the Plutos needed: that those two went off and disappeared by themselves. And they didn't take long to slip away themselves, as if they feared to be seen mixed up in something seedy. Or, more possibly, as if Pluto feared that Marihole's behavior might not rise to the occasion. A sort of reaction that a person like Leo would have never had, although it would later cost him hours of explaining things to Teresa. And it's true that just like when love comes to an end, it ends definitively, and then what's repeated is the whole scheme of amorous behavior, the same passions, the same tests, only with a different person. By contrast, all friendships created in the first flush of youth, regardless of distances and even fallings out, tend to be maintained throughout life at a level of understanding unreachable for any friendship established later on, with Pluto, for example, with Fortuny, perhaps because, in fact, one loses the capacity for making new friends and thus leaves young adulthood behind.

It was as if Leo had been rehabilitated, as if he had recovered not only his self-confidence but also his lucidity and even his sense of humor. He could crack jokes and, beyond any kind of reservation, talk frankly, almost like in earlier times. A sort of relationship which only months earlier would have seemed impossible to be reestablished someday. To tell him, for example, that his rehabilitation was a shameless case of nepotism, influenced by Floreal—a Floreal whose spectacular political career in exile, during his forced sojourn in France, so different from Fortuny's disappointing experience—was not at all safe from his ironic conjectures. Obregón's arrest kickstarted Fortuny's career, and then he had literally managed to escape the clutches of the police and reach Paris, given that without such antecedents, in another situation, he might possibly have never had occasion to deal with the leadership, to show his thoroughly discreet character, and become so perfectly well integrated with them, to secretly return to Barcelona, now become one of the key pieces in the machine, just as casually as the poet who, toying with a rhyme, hits upon a profound idea. Floreal—Federico concluded—is no small-town fellow but a man from the tough slums; some such remark like one of those local football hooligans who, from the grandstands, orchestrate scandalous mayhem, serving to whip up the home team and demoralize the visiting one, one of those goons who for his generally grotesque appearance, be it for his rather outlandish attire, or for his simian antics, seems to exercise over the spectators the magnetism of a tribal witch doctor. His loyalty is, precisely, beyond reproach. In fact, in both his case as in Fortuny's, his leaders have shown a most penetrating psychological awareness.

And Leo? As far as Leo goes, he's like that lifelong bachelor who if he's never married it's perhaps only because he can't share a bathroom with a woman, more a question of shyness than the selfishness commonly attributed to him; so, it would be equally mistaken to classify his current position with respect to the party as simple opportunism even if he himself would define it in similar terms. Because, like the person in possession of his horoscope—which he considers not only flatteringly accurate but also beneficially stimulating—he contributes what he can, from then on, so that the heavenly designs might be fulfilled and he finds in everything proofs of how much everything that happens is neither more nor less than what was foretold. Thus, in a similar way, not only

Leo or Floreal himself but all militants in general tend to make every effort so that the image they offer their hierarchical superiors of the country's reality coincides as much as possible with the theoretical suppositions of the political line established by them.

The actual extent of his responsibilities—about which Leo showed himself quite reserved, although it proved no risk to link them to the neighborhood commissions, and who knows if also to the Barcelona committee—was indicated, as usual, by the details. By the fact that it was he who informed him, confidentially—and rather cheerfully—that Fortuny had fallen into disgrace, before, surely, Fortuny himself was informed—certainly coming as no surprise to him—that, now that he was back in Barcelona, it would be convenient that he abstain from all political activity until further orders. They say—and who but Escala could have said?—they've realized that his intelligence is no greater than his resolution, said Leo. A crisis whose gestation had occurred in Paris, a result of the leadership's suspicions being confirmed when they dealt with him more closely, or what he guessed about them, or both things at once, or what he began to tell or comment, or what they found out he was saying and commenting. And if personal matters, when gossiped about, are capable of destroying a marriage, can't they certainly dissolve a political relationship? Not unlike that young newly married middle-class woman's astonished intuition of some different reality beyond her household, which usually coincides with her first explosive exposure to foul language and low-class gutter exclamations unleashed in her husband by the news of some business setback, is the similar, customary, almost incredulous reaction to the first clashing ideas voiced by the neophyte militant within the inner circles of his political organization. Doubtless, it costs him a lot of effort to get used to that dimension inherent to every kind of teamwork, objectively setting aside personal conflicts, hidden rivalries, and preeminences less related to protocol than to an effective control of power, to organizational management. It's difficult to accept that, similar to the amusing discretion with which the little local literary world circulates those anonymous letters written in the form of burlesque rhymes loaded with specific allusions to this or that writer, the work of any old gazetteer of regressive ideals and frustrated aspirations, of some slug grown rich in the solitary exercise of sleaze and defamation, wholesome brazen relief from the daily labor of newspaper reporting, universal announcement of how many universal values exist and, especially, have existed, a case of mental hygiene or, perhaps, a case of mental weakness, whose political equivalent can sometimes shorten the internal life of an organization. It's also difficult to learn to support without reservation a position according to the official political line when those muffled tensions surface, reaching his corresponding level in the organizational structure, and are resolved in a purifying disciplinary sanction, depriving the element or elements whose attitude was in error—provided they are sanctioned—of the proper number of responsibilities, leading to their expulsion if necessary, if the gravity of the case warrants it, charges that can stretch back very far, imputations that suddenly encompass his entire history or histories of militancy and which suddenly become the motive for a verbal report—if not an official declaration—about the faction's deviation, repeatedly and unanimously approved from one meeting to the next, from cell to cell, from each sector directly implicated by their former, now culpable, comrade's fall from grace, a sector where, logically, his erroneous position might have been able to spread and branch out, accusations exposed with the same nervous agitation and bitter fury with which an old man in a convalescent home shouts into the ear of his moribund roommate: Failure! You've been nothing but a failure! With that kind of rancor that comes from having to stifle too long what one was bursting to express. It's difficult—why deny it—to do all that, but no less necessary than in a marriage, dealing with all the trivial vulgarities involved in living together, without which the essential goal and proper functioning of the institution would be little less than impossible.

However, there are cases in which, according to one's experience of party life and the opportunities they've had to exercise their political tact, everything learned can be forgotten, as if from the effects of some trauma or, what's worse, turn out to be useless. A very common subjective reaction, especially when the disgraced comrade is oneself. And then they stop seeing things from the inside, which is how they must be seen, as is generally admitted, and start seeing them from outside. This makes it necessary to assess with opportune deliberation every unilateral version of the events, the judgments each person uses to defend or attack, frequently dictated by passion, a product of the subjective, observed reaction. Thus, Fortuny's stupor, not unlike the wife or husband who, after an intense extramarital erotic life, suddenly learns—inconceivable!—that their partner is fucking someone else. I assure you all that the intellectual level of a good part of the leadership couldn't be lower. The only thing that worries them now is the Chinese problem. And although it almost seems incredible, many of those leadership committee members don't know a single word of Marxism. And Federico: I assure you that this is rather an advantage. Although it must do them little good in a situation like the current one, without any objective conditions that propitiate the formation of a revolutionary vanguard capable of propitiating the objective conditions. What a tragedy for someone like Z! To be born with a vocation to be a revolutionary hero in a time without revolutionary heroism must be almost as bitter as not knowing how to be heroic in a revolutionary situation. And Fortuny: but try and imagine Floreal just all of a sudden asking you: have you seen the sonsofbitches these Chinese are? And you ask him why. And he says: fuck, they're just a bunch of mean dirty bastards, and then he gets hysterical, and says that the Chinese are imperialists and racists and fascists, that you can't expect anything good from them, that they're like the blacks, that when they manage to produce someone good, like Lumumba, they're the first ones to kill him. In those very words. For the love of God, do you all think that this language is worthy of a Marxist? And look, even by temperament I'm not really very suspicious of pro-Chinese attitudes, personally I believe first and foremost in the struggle of union labor. But if you just ask what's going on because you want to stay up to date on things, that's all it takes for them to consider you actively pro-Chinese, especially if they find out you've got anything to do with Guillén, who's been expelled for being pro-Chinese, but despite his radicalism he's one of the few people there with whom you can actually talk. Poor Guillén, he's so fucked. Comment from Federico: well, I don't know what he's complaining about. Expelled from the party and unable to enter Spain: the ideal situation. And Fortuny: and the stuff about Cayetano. It also occurred to me to ask about him and they told me he was crazy, that the tension of the struggle had ended up disturbing his mind. And then Guillén told me what'd happened. Alright, do you all remember Cayetano? That textile factory manager who also had to escape when they nailed Obregón. This was a guy who belonged to the Communist Youth Union during the Republic, who fought in the Civil War, who joined the Maquis in France, who returned with the guerrillas, who was captured and tortured and condemned to death, who had his sentence commuted at the eleventh hour and then marched out to demonstrate along with the others who'd been pardoned, and when Marsal went down they arrested him again and when they got Obregón he had to go into exile. Well, because it seems that in Paris they went after him with the same stories about the Chinese, and he said no, that they didn't make him think that the Chinese were either imperialists or fascists, and he told them all flatly that it's one thing to be a communist and another to be a Russian, and that he wasn't a Russian but a communist. And it seems they had to almost push him out of there. And he asked me: how much do you wanna bet that if the Chinese said what the Russians say and the Russians said what the Chinese say, the Russians would be the ones who would continue to be right? He was ready to climb the walls. That must be why they're saying he went crazy. Thirty years of militancy and now he's crazy. Crazy. He looked at them almost in disbelief, as if instead of seeing them he were contemplating a Gothic diptych, whose unusual story was, for example, San Cayetano martyred by his fellow martyrs followed by San Cayetano rushing into hell. New comment from Federico: sovietism, the senile sickness of communism. And Fortuny: and the worst, Z. The same thing that the Floreales repeated later on, only with more formal rigor. You can already imagine it for yourselves.

And, really, it took as little to imagine Z in action as to imagine Fortuny seeing himself as one of those movie heroes, bounced from a party—generally for having tried to flirt with a girl far above his social condition—walking off alone into the night, mortified not so much by the humiliation of having been tossed out onto the street, by the ugly scene, by the door slamming loudly behind him, as much as for imagining what must be happening inside the mansion, not only the father shrugging his shoulders, but all the servants smoothing their ruffled livery, the conversations resuming, the party continuing. The fulmination of thrashing about incoherently. The triumph of dialectical reason. And Z saying, those far left-wing mouthpieces, those extremists of yesterday and today, Maoists, Trotskyites, anarchists, sick paranoid minds, little splinter groups, disconnected from the masses, deeply entrenched in their own impotence, have no other option than blind, sterile violence, forgetting that during the Civil War it was not exactly them, but us, with the generous and fraternal Soviet assistance, who fought against Francoism and its Italian and German allies, a fight from which we might have emerged victorious instead of having been victims, besides, of an international conspiracy, of the betrayal by our supposed Western friends, of the puppets and marionettes of imperialism. So let me ask you now, aren't these revolutionaries who want to revolutionize the revolution also true counterrevolutionaries, objective allies, puppets, and marionettes of imperialism? Purported Spanish Marxists, as ignorant of Marxism as of their own country's history while they overlook the fact that it's only possible to correctly interpret the Spanish Civil War by inserting it into the general course of the Spanish people's struggle for liberty, whichever battle you're talking about, whether the Ebro or the Jarama or Bailén or the battles of Bruch, and so many other heroic struggles of our people, the people who invented guerrilla warfare—the revolutionary struggle par excellence—against the Napoleonic invader. And keeping in mind Franco's use of Moorish mercenaries, it would then make sense to extend the line of continuity back to the time of the Reconquest, with the eight centuries of continuous resistance that the Spanish people sustained against Arab expansionism, Roncesvalles and Las Navas de Tolosa, Mallorca and Seville, Valencia and Granada, milestones of our history which Spain's eternal enemies—those devious anti-Spanish pawns—prefer to overlook. In other words, our historic achievement can and should be situated along the line of other great national achievements, of those singular enterprises whose symbols are El Cid, Isabella the Catholic, Don Quixote, Cortés, Pizarro and so many other heroes whose exploits have been celebrated by our people for hundreds and hundreds of years and which, whether through historical chronicles or through oral tradition, have passed down from generation to generation, and also, from generation to generation, the people have kept alive our glorious Crusade for Liberation with new contributions of their own blood, the most recent in no way inferior to those of olden times, great feats like the siege of the Alcázar in Toledo, or the Battle of the Ebro, feats which, thanks to their literally miraculous characteristics, could have well been propitiated by the direct intervention of Saint James the apostle—Santiago. Because it's not a vain notion to believe that the History of Spain begins where Sacred History ends. A Spain already chosen by Christ when he called Santiago to become a fisher of men, assigned to the future Spaniards the mission of saving Christianity from Islam as well as from the Reformation, from any kind of reform and revolution, from any kind of subversion, the chosen people, a nation chosen since the beginning, since even before it existed as such, entity or entelechy genetically informed by a universal spirit and role, predestined to discover new worlds and Christianize them, destined to extend its blood and its values to heights and extremes that no other empire reached nor ever would reach, a history that has got to conclude with the triumph of our truth throughout the world through the final confrontation between Spain, on one side, and freemasonry and international Judaism, on the other. Sword of Rome and Bastion of the West, Defender of the Faith, whatever that might be, provided it express, in an orthodox fashion, dogmatic affirmations not very distinct, on another hand, from any other people given over to megalomaniac or simply narcissistic deliriums, like in the case of Catalonia, without going further, the fact of being Catalan, classified as a gift from God by the poet, inspired perhaps like a Tiresias, there being no evidence, with the divine gift of prophecy.

I agree, said Leo. Soviet society is currently about as revolutionary as its foreign policy. And, as far as we're concerned, the party does not follow a true revolutionary line and even if it did follow it, within current national and international circumstances, we would have only the most minimal possibility of bringing the revolution to pass. In that case: propose me an alternative. Are we going to be the first to declare that there is none? Are we going to renounce all activity and voluntarily dissolve ourselves like merchants liquidating a business? And another thing: what do you want me to do? I'm not like Fortuny. I am, or at least I think I am, a person with the party flowing in my veins. Apart from politics, and concretely from the party's politics, there's nothing that interests me. What could I do outside the party? *Quand on n'a pas ce qu'on aime on doit aimer ce qu'on a.* Think whatever you deem best, but also think about what lies behind an attitude like Fortuny's. His belated guess that the party wasn't going to offer him the political career he was expecting. A career that his relaxed social democratic temperament must have imagined would be complemented by his legal practice and, above all, by the famous Chair of Labour Law. Also, when they nailed Obregón, he barely dodged the proverbial bullet, and this must have made him reconsider. It would be an enormous coincidence, it would go against every probability, if I were equally lucky the next time. And, finally, think what you like, but keep in mind that, in every case, I continue running risks that for him no longer exist.

They'd agreed to meet in the early evening. But Raúl had stayed longer than he anticipated at Uncle Gregorio's house and he arrived late. And, once they started talking, they decided to eat dinner in some place and keep chatting. Leo called Teresa and told her laconically that he wouldn't be home for dinner, as if to demonstrate that, unlike Pluto, he didn't need to offer his wife explanations. Raúl called his house, and Nuria and, curiously, it was Nuria who started being a pain: who was he with, and why couldn't she join them and, finally, he hung up saying he was going to Adolfo's house. Better that way. They felt comfortable and talkative, in a mood to discuss personal matters, possessed of that impunity that alcohol brings and permits you to talk about party problems right at a table in some bar. In the restaurant they went to take a piss, and Leo, as if he felt a little flushed, splashed his face in the sink and dried it with his handkerchief, looking at himself afterward in the mirror with that expression one only puts on in front of the mirror, more how one wishes they looked than how they really look.

What objection? How to reduce to a single word something which transcends words like sincerity or cynicism, lucidity or nonsense? The fear of the quotidian, of one's own daily life, of that dimension that one intuits they are missing, which they pretend to find in others, outside of oneself, to fulfill or replace that suspected absence by entering the seminary or becoming the member of some sporting club or getting married or joining a political party. Something like that. The important thing is escaping from this quotidian life that is only comparable, due to the tedium it can end up producing, to the reading of one of those poems that speak of astonishment and wonder, of doubt between the perhaps and the maybe, slender distinctions between silly trifles or simply of the minor personal experience, so small that it demands consideration of the author's dry mind, the value of his oh-so-doltishly handled language, the multifaceted emptiness of his verse, his vegetative metropolitan idiocy; thus, like just such a poem, the habits, the tics, the rhyming detritus of daily life. That's why the priest with his apostolic labor first saves himself. The soccer fan sheltered by the colors of his team. The militant engrafted with the hysterical mysteries of his ideology and its postulations. The husband and wife ensconced in matrimony, consoled, comforted, fortified, accommodated, sitting back with their feet up, safe from all the tricks and traps the world has to offer. All of them so similar to that soldier who, dispatched to a frontier fort—where he'll be stationed until retirement—is prepared to take maximum possible advantage of the situation, absolute ruler of his little kingdom, local despotic deity, with only one single idea in his head, just like Satan upon taking possession of his shadowy dominions inspects the troops who pay him honor: converting the isolation into power and confinement into strength; fortifying himself. A tendency to withdraw that only grows with the years, under the usury of time. Nothing more depressing, for example, than that married couple who stay the course, each one supporting the other half until death do them part, defeat after defeat, failure after failure, beyond impotences and frigidities, beneath downfalls and surrenders, two cadavers in one single sarcophagus.

Who is it? he heard Gregorius bellowing. I'm giving him a bath, you see, said Leonor. What's going on, what's the matter, shouted Gregorius. He found him in the bathtub, without his glasses, naked, his withered peter peeking out from the bubbles. Bring him a chair, he said. And Leonor: come on, slide down a little more. Don't you see you're showing him everything? She left them alone a little while, but as she came and went around the apartment she kept predicting the topics of conversation. Now he'll tell you about Mallorca. Now he'll talk about America. Now he'll talk about Vallfosca. She returned with a ratty bathrobe and some slippers. Good, now close your mouth, you're going to get soap in it. She knelt down next to the tub and, with a rough sponge, began scrubbing the old man from his head to his toes. If he had his way, he'd never bathe in his whole life, she was saying. And the more you scold him, the more he ignores you. He pretends not to hear and starts whistling like that cuckoo that pops out of the clock every hour, as if it really was a bird. I can't deal with him, I simply cannot. And one of these days he's going to cause a scandal with his mania for cuddling little children. The people who know him from the park still put up with him. But, someone who doesn't know him, seeing him looking the way he does, they might think anything. Doesn't change his clothes, doesn't wash, doesn't shave; he'd be happy to go around looking like a homeless beggar. Just the other day I had to finally throw away all his old clothes and shoes, they were the only things he wanted to wear.

From beneath Leonor's energetic arms, Gregorius stuck up his soapy head and, at the edge of the tub, gave Raúl a sly smile, before sinking back down, while Leonor ranted on, with the anger of that country doctor who, when examining the patient's virile member, discovers that the supposed venereal disease is nothing more than simple local irritation resulting from a lack of hygiene, relentless anger increased by the way that filthy bumpkin tolerates the doctor's shower of invective, his phlegmatic scorn, his lack of haste. In fact that very invective, Leonor's complaints, which forcefully dominated the visit, more than his chatting with Gregorius, were the reason why he arrived late at his meeting with Leo. The last one. And, as if he'd had a premonition, it was precisely that night when Leo told him about how he was worried about the confidence that Floreal seemed to have placed in Modesto Pírez, putting him in a position where, in case he were nabbed, he could implicate many people. As if he could guess what was going to happen on February 12, the holy day of Santa Eulalia of Sarriá, virgin and martyr, victim of the cruel repression decreed by the Proconsul Daciano against the Christians for their subversive activities, flogged, breasts torn off, arms and legs twisted from their sockets, her body quartered and burned in pieces before the crowd gathered in order to not miss the spectacle of torture that took place on what is now the street called la Bajada de Santa Eulalia, although perhaps the martyred maiden was not from Sarriá and none of that happened in Barcelona, but in Mérida, then called Emerita Augusta. It was all so many years ago . . .

You, what are you doing here? a detective asked him. It was nine o'clock and he seemed to have just come in, active and lively, charged up with that morning energy which office managers of a dynamic temperament use to start their working day. He elbowed him, as if in complicity. You must have dragged some poor girl out into an empty lot, right?

He soon returned and, without a word, gestured for Raúl to follow him. He led him to a nearby office, more or less the same as the previous one. Stay here, he said. From different directions came the sound of conversations mixed with the clicking of typewriters. Then, some more distinct voices stood out above all the other racket. As much for their special resonance as because they kept coming closer, the chatter seemed to come from a hallway. The tone was like some friendly conversation, with jokes, laughter, one voice almost like a woman's. They were discussing the convenience of applying a fresh coat of paint. That's right, the canary sings so sweetly.

A finger pointing at him from the doorway. I'll be damned: El Pipa!

Three or four more men followed him in. Yes, it's him. You're darned right it is. Communist: you can tell right away. El Pipa! El Pipa! We've finally got him! It was me who arrested him; me. I've had to follow you around as if you were Marilyn Monroe, you little faggot. That woman's laugh. Tell us something about Alsina. Alsina? A box on the ear, almost the brain; the one with the crazy laugh. And you don't know Matías, either? Or Salvador? More blows to the ear, to his ears, from both sides, from behind. And Leonardo Tarrés? Yes? Well, that's something. And Floreal Conesa? And Modesto Pírez? Not Pírez? Another blow. Wait, don't ask, let him talk, let's see if we like what he's got to say. Nonsense; we'll clear this all up right now, you'll see. Or maybe you know Tarrés and Conesa, but you don't know Matías or Alsina? A hard punch right in the stomach and, as he doubled over, stamping on his feet. They held him up so he wouldn't fall over. What's the matter?

A bald guy with glasses was staring at him. The others made room for him. This son of a bitch wants to play the tough guy. Don't be stupid, kid. Here, everybody sings. If your bosses are the top guys, you don't want to take the fall for them. Don't you see your friend from the Canaries has sung for us, just like a canary himself? Don't worry, I'll sing just like in the opera. That's exactly what he said. And without having to lay a finger on him, I swear.

Cackles of laughter. You don't know Pírez, eh? You never gave him any of those pamphlets you shitty little rich college boys write? They shoved him around from one to the other, all asking him questions at the same time. What can you tell us about Floreal Conesa, alias Matías? What can you tell us about your friend Tarrés, alias Alsina? That's right, man, Alsina; you all used to call him Serra. You think we don't know everything? You think they haven't sung for us? You think you're not going to sing? You didn't know the local committee's mimeograph machine was in Pírez's flat? And that's where they ran off the pamphlets you wrote?

A knee to the groin he was able to dodge slightly, tipping him off balance. Someone stepped in through the pushing and shoving arms waving a photo. Look, I've got the proof right here! Your picture! It was Raúl's photo ID card.

What do you mean what proof? A hard fist to the stomach. Then another. He saw a pistol appear. Now they struggled with the man with pistol, and subdued him. I'll kill him! I'm telling you I'll kill him! Get him out of my sight or I'll kill him!

The bald man with glasses. Alright, leave him alone for later. And you, watch it, no sudden moves. Stand up, on your own two feet, no leaning on anything. Someone stay with him.

He glanced at his watch: it read ten minutes past ten, but the minute hand wasn't working. The stem or something was broken. So, you're El Pipa, eh?

said the man guarding him, seated on the other side of a desk. The famous El Pipa. He spoke as if to say something, to kill time.

They moved him to another office, adjacent to the room where the bald man with glasses was, possibly his office. The man took a few steps out, just to keep an eye on the hallway. Raúl saw three detectives arrive: in a hurry, with the brusque movements of a bad mood. The birds have flown, he heard them say. What birds? Tarrés and his chick. When we couldn't reestablish contact, we decided to go in. Just what we were afraid of: they've been gone since last night. He heard a door slam. Very muffled, curses and insults, shouts sounding like a furious scolding.

Everything quieted down. Lunchtime, possibly. Still soaked with sweat, his clothes stuck to his body. Perhaps that explained why he didn't especially need to piss. But he wanted something to drink. And, especially, a cigarette.

Come over here, comrade, a gray-haired man said to him. Another move to another room. A little bit tired, right? Well if I see you move an inch, it's gonna get a whole lot worse. In Russia you're all tough, but you'll see here we know how to be tough, too. He brought a transistor radio: he sat down next to the door and turned it on. Soccer. The announcer's excited voice, the shouts, surprises, the reversals, the cheering crowd.

It was already dark by the time the detective who'd taken his statement when he'd arrived reappeared; the windows in the corridor caught reflections from the streetlights outside. You see, Raúl? If you'd been honest from the start, you would have spared yourself all that. He told the man with the radio to leave them alone. He had them bring Raúl a glass of water, and offered him a cigarette. Look, here you've got to tell the truth. You're a lawyer and you should know that, when facing the examining magistrate, the report we make about the arrestee's character has almost as much importance as your statement itself. But the thing is, apart from this, the person who doesn't adopt a reasonable attitude can have a very bad time of it. You'll see, all kinds of men work here. One maybe because it suits his temper, because he's got a passion for it, another because the Reds shot his father, or who knows, because he's got the urge, for devotion to the trade or whatever, he just gets involved and it never ends. He shoots. And then it's hard to stop him. He goes crazy and from then on the other one is just his darling, his delicate prey. Listen to what I'm telling you, believe me. There's every kind of big ape here. I don't know, they almost seem to enjoy it.

No? Raúl stood only halfway up to set the glass on the table. The heavy fist sunk him back down on the chair. They looked at each other almost in bewilderment. The glass must have rolled off the table and now he heard it shatter on the floor. Alright, you all, get in here! shouted the other man. They all piled in at once. He still wants to play the tough guy, said the other man. Arturo, you're Arturo. Well, let's get slaphappy with Arturo. They stood him up. They formed a circle around him. Right, time to torture Arturo. No, wait, Arturo's another guy, but it doesn't matter. Both of them are Reds. Laughter. Hands grabbing and shaking him hard. You've really been busting our balls. Now we're gonna bust yours. More laughter. Hands pushing and shoving him. Why don't we play seven, fourteen, twenty-one? I was starting to feel like I needed to loosen up a bit. Do you like to dance?

The questions started again, and the punches. In his stomach and his liver, especially. That's right, Armando. Let him have it.

Armando's always the first to get lively.

What'll your bosses say when they find out we nailed you? What'll Nikita say?

All yours, Armando!

They incited each other to hit him, while Raúl, for his part, tried to keep his composure, responding calmly, though haltingly, without showing signs of hatred, fear, or anger, as if interrogator and interrogated were, equally, agents of some higher power driving them against one another, protagonists of a situation that, for being out of their respective control, demands a measured response; where one sees crime, the other sees error, both points of view to the same degree fatally antagonistic. All that in the belief that if he managed it, if he could manage to modulate his reactions according to that tenor, looking at them and speaking to them with all the serenity he was capable of mustering, he'd won the match. A hypothesis of greater moral than scientific value, it's true, of inverse probability to the importance the interrogator places on getting answers, but not for that reason—even when the theory crumbles in practice—lacking in all reason. The idea that, pretending to accept the situation imposed by them, made them accept, in reality, the relationship created by him. With the certainty that even the most basic resources available to the police, floodlights in the face, etcetera, are not intended so much—perhaps without even the interrogators knowing it, only from experience but without knowing the reason why—to dazzle the suspect, making him wince and grimace, as to protect themselves from his gaze, in the same way that dark glasses, for those who wear them, more than offering a constant appearance of impassivity, serve to permit them to perform any kind of violence without having to try to make the expression accompany the act or even to acquire the proper conviction. To create an atmosphere no longer unusual but surreal. And, insofar as being surreal, capable of breaking any course of action, of turning the person being interrogated into a barely human object, of transforming him into a terrorized being, into a despicable cornered critter, abject, weeping, suppliant, crazed; or, according to his nature, enrage him, drive him to insolence, make him lose his cool, shouting insults and offenses that authority has no choice but to repel or punish; or even, manage to unleash his hatred and pique his pride, get him to declare himself a communist, threatening them with the people's justice that will come for them sooner or later, and then they, now properly hating him, give that Red his just desserts, settling the score now that he's in their hands, almost as if in self-defense, give him a proper beating, kick him, twist him, dislocate his joints, give him electric shocks, pushing the button just like on the telex machine. Meaning: promoting within themselves a state of exasperation uniquely comparable to what a mother can feel who is especially frazzled by her baby who won't allow her any peace and when it finally does, when it finally calms down, it's she who shakes and smacks it so that it starts crying again and gives her a fair motive to keep on loathing it. Because in the same way that a pedagogical system rich in punishments and discipline reveals on the part of the educator, whether they be a family member or teacher, not only repressed sadomasochistic and, eventually, homosexual tendencies—and when involving relatives, incestuous ones—but, above all, a phenomenon of transference onto the child of their own impotences and frustrations, which tend to be more overwhelming given the intensity of the punishment applied; thus, when a policeman beats a suspect, he does so, normally, blinded by the terrors of his own conscience.

What to do then when the police beat someone until they're swollen black and blue? Not like one of those soccer or rugby players who, after falling like they've been shot and making a show of writhing around on the field, finally stand up and, after limping painfully for a few steps, take off running like greyhounds.

Because the praxis affirms the theory, because the others found themselves getting tired, and it's certain that their blows were not as virulent as the ones they'd landed in the morning, neither the hardness nor the duration of the session were like the first time. They watched him, also out of breath. This guy's not like the opera singer. This one's cold. They're the worst. What he needs is electric shocks. Don't you see he sweats cold? We've got to make it hot for him. Laughter. Yes, a little electricity will make him feel good. That's right: it's cold in Russia; a little electricity will do the trick.

The one who had taken his statement upon arrival stepped away from the others and passed the red-hot tip of his cigarette before Raúl's eyes. We're gonna crush you; you've been asking for it. He went back to the others. Take him down to the cells and tonight we'll bring him back up. This was just a dress rehearsal.

The jail cells, in the lowest basement. An iron door with a peephole or a vent. A bare light bulb set into the wall near the ceiling. A cement bench with a wicker mat. He couldn't sleep or he wasn't sleepy. And, nevertheless, when they brought him upstairs, it was like he was dreaming. It was cold; his legs were trembling with the cold. The corridors, the offices. So much light all of a sudden was blinding. An open door here or there: Floreal. Floreal? He was sitting on a wooden armchair, barefoot, his head lolling on his breast. They pulled his head up by the hair so Raúl could see his face. His features looked Chinese. And his hands swollen, like a boxer's. And at least on one wrist, the only one visible, an encircling welt or wound between yellow and black. Do you know him? Leo's cousin? We already knew that, handsome. He thought he saw Floreal give him a wink, although it was difficult to be sure.

They took him back downstairs. The air thick and heavy: whiffs of private odors, a stench like a urinal. Once more, he did not sleep. In the guardroom they'd taken away his belt, necktie, shoelaces, wristwatch, ballpoint pen, and matches. To smoke he had to ask the guards for a light. Like when he had to piss: he shouted his cell number, 18, and the guard opened the door and followed behind without taking his eyes off him. Through the peephole he saw a body slide by, dragged along by two guards, toward the cells at the far end. He called the guard to ask for a light. He was a guy of a certain age, rather taciturn. Floreal Conesa? No, son, this one's a tram driver. Another session like this one and they'll send him to heaven. Floreal Conesa? There's nobody here by that name. I'd remember a name like Floreal.

They served him a hot liquid, dark, in a grimy, dented bowl; he drank it. Later they handed him a package in the guardroom. The guard that brought him up there, a Galician, had not made it clear why he was being summoned upstairs, as if enjoying making him think that it was going to be another interrogation. Walk ahead, he had told him, like someone fulfilling a painful obligation. They opened the package in front of him and carefully examined its contents. Cigarettes. Chocolate. Cookies. Condensed milk. They made him sign a receipt.

He didn't think he had fallen asleep, but it was obvious he'd been awakened by the racket the guards made serving the meal. Afterward he began tracing and retracing, in a diagonal line, the space between the door and the cement bench. Four paces, or rather, footsteps, then turning around, touching the corner of the door with his elbows on each turn. Once in a while he ate some chocolate. The order to go upstairs coincided with the dinner ration service.

From the beginning it became evident that something had changed in the attitude of the police, the climate, their manners, not unlike the change that comes over the erotic relationships of the libertine when he employs that sudden, skillful disinterest in the pleasure he's already enjoyed. And not simply—or in spite of it—because the detective invited him to sit down before his desk, not because he offered him a cigarette. It was rather—it was in the air—as if the police were bored with the whole matter, as if they wished to be done with it once and for all the way one dispatches something grown tiresome and annoying. Look, kid, he said. We've got some undeniable facts here: you're acquainted with a member of the central committee and a deputy of the political bureau of the communist party. You also know a member of the Barcelona committee, up to his neck in matters involving the neighborhood committees. You say you don't know Folías, but we found a book of Marx in his apartment with your name in it, in your handwriting.

He tossed the book onto the table. *La Sagrada Familia. The Holy Family*. Had you forgotten that one? It often happens when people lend books. But it's yours. You wrote your name in it like in so many others you have in your house. Only this wasn't in your house, it was in Modesto Pírez's house. Besides, we followed you two. We've seen the two of you together. On the patio at the university, specifically. I'm sure you remember. And we know that you two met in Paris: through Guillén, another communist, as you know perfectly well; and although he's exiled right now, you were still classmates together. So, you must understand that all those things can't remain unanswered. That you've got to give us a coherent explanation about all that.

He listened to Raúl with a certain impatience, as if he knew beforehand what he was going to say, although what he was thinking in that moment was: alright, now this is something different. Alright. Before, they accused you of other things, of more things. And in the same flat belonging to Folías we've not found anything in your handwriting or anything from your typewriter. And before they were accusing you of writing the publications for the neighborhood committees. So what? Whether they accuse you of one thing or another is the least of it. What you've got to do is give a coherent explanation about some concrete, irrefutable facts. As a lawyer, you must know that what counts, apart from proof to the contrary, is what you say or declare. Or rather, let's see: you admit to knowing Modesto Pírez, isn't that right? Very good. But that relationship between a university professor and a person like Folías, what was that based on, what was his objective? Find a job in Barcelona for the friend of a friend. Okay. But that common friend turns out to be a communist. You can't expect me to believe that you two didn't discuss politics. And that's it, you discussed politics. And you never talked about, or he never suggested to you sometime that you get actively involved? Only theoretical problems. But Marxist ones, of course.

The bald fellow with glasses listened to them without talking, sitting on the corner of a different desk. He slapped his thigh. Alright, enough for today. Tomorrow you can start again from the beginning, make sure it all gets typed up and that he signs it. And make sure he talks about Conesa and Tarrés. He turned to Raúl. Don't you want a glass of milk? It'll do you good.

From that moment until the day when they transferred him to the prison in the kangaroo—a blind metal cage without windows or ventilation—he spent almost as much time in the offices as in his jail cell. In the jail he slept, although neither deeply nor steadily. Perhaps that was why time passed more slowly in the offices. And although his statement was brief, there were many interruptions, and always some policeman coming by who felt like having a chat, as if from curiosity, or perhaps because he had nothing better to do, and, one might even dare say, to improve the impression that they might have made on him. Especially after he signed his statement.

When asked if he is affiliated with or belongs to the communist party, he answers no. Asked if he knows Floreal Conesa under the assumed name of Matías or some other nickname, he answers no. Asked how he came to know the aforementioned Floreal Conesa, he says from frequenting the home of his friend and former classmate Leonardo Tarrés, first cousin of Floreal Conesa. When asked if such meetings were of a political nature, he answers no, although sometimes they might have discussed politics.

An old man stuck his head in the doorway. What, has the kid started talking? he said. Also, the bald man with the glasses came over and reread the sheets. Alright, alright, but just make sure he doesn't come off sounding only like a sympathizer and nothing more. This has to include information about his complicity or, at least, of concealment. The last thing we need is for the judge to think we're a pack of idiots.

If all that is true, if you're not trying to fool us again, you don't know the trouble you've saved yourself from, said another policeman, pointing his pen at Raúl. You don't know the communists very well. And if you believed in God, because you don't look like a believer, you should give him thanks that we arrested you in time. Look, just to give you one example, the case we had a few days ago. A tram driver. A good man, at heart. But he got into trouble, let himself be fooled. And it seems now, as he realized what he'd done, he got so desperate he started ramming his head against the wall. He looked like bleeding agonizing Christ. Lucky that the guard downstairs overheard him and stopped him before he killed himself.

One of the cops who'd arrested him came in, the one who seemed to have a singer's voice. Well, you won't complain about how we treated you, right? You can see we're not a bunch of savages here. Man, I won't lie and say sometimes we don't get a little carried away, like with this Conesa; he could try anybody's patience. But, more than anything, it's just our reputation. And don't think it bothers us. That way people get frightened and talk without us having to touch a hair on their heads.

And the cop with the pen: that's right, yeah, here everybody talks. At first, they always say they don't know a thing or the really cocky ones who brag that they'll never talk. But that's just a bunch of hot air. In the end they talk.

And if sometimes we're a little hard it's because we've got no other choice. Police are the same everywhere. How do you think they act in France, or in England, or the United States?

And the cop with the pen: What about Russia? How do you think they'd treat me if they caught me there someday on an assignment?

Another cop chimed in, very young, almost like a recruit. Raúl identified him as the one who'd given him a karate chop. What about the Chinese?

Even worse. Russians aren't bad, they're good-hearted men, like us Spaniards. But the Chinese hate whites. Chinese are cruel. Chinese tortures are famous the world over.

But what do they do?

The cop who had taken Raúl's final statement patted the other man on the shoulder. You don't want to know. If I told you even a few things you wouldn't be able to sleep.

He wasn't like the others, the younger policemen of the present generation who didn't look like police exactly but more like rookies and amateur athletes, like players on the neighborhood soccer club. No, he wasn't one of them. He was one of the veterans, from older times, as Raúl remembered them or as one tends to imagine them, even without having been arrested years before; the salt and pepper mustache, the bitter face, the thin receding hairline, nicotine breath, and the unhealthy complexion of that fifty-something man who accelerates his physical and moral decline playing dice at the coffee shop bar, who has no problem with gambling or alcohol or tobacco, let alone women, but simply by spending time at the coffee shop bar.

Again the bald cop with glasses. Alright, let's get to work. What're you all doing here? He's signed it already, right? Well, let's do something else. And you, when you get out, tell your people it's not such a big deal. And that it doesn't do you any good for someone to make such a fuss over you. Of course that's the last thing they care to hear. What they want are excuses for kicking up a fuss. Intellectuals, professors, lawyers, priests, even priests from Opus Dei. La Acción Católica, the priests, there always has to be someone sticking their nose into it. Just wait till they lift the ban on celibacy for priests and you'll see how quick we sort things out. Like these four fucking monarchists. We maintain order so they can enjoy life with all its benefits, and they still protest. They want us to do what we do, but they don't want to know how it's done. They forget about the Civil War, that they'd end up being the first victims, all over again. Way before us, I can promise you that. And you? What d'you think you'd be doing in Russia? We, on the other hand, are needed everywhere. We've got colleagues who were cops during the Republic, and they still are cops, and if the Regime were to change, they'd go right on being cops. What do you expect? Don't kid yourself.

Within the darkness of the cage inside the police van, at the start of the trip that would only end when they reached the inside of the prison, where all the pilgrims find themselves surrounded by deep moats and high walls in no way surpassed by those of the city of Dis, the atmosphere of mistrust and mutual scrutiny was pervasive, all of them with something in common in both attitude and aspect. Next to Raúl, one fellow enveloped in a miasma of putrid gases he seemed unable to contain, especially with the van bumping and rattling, effluvia no less deadly for being silent as it spread persistently, as if adhering to the folds of his clothes, filthy and terrified, with the perfect mug of a petty thief, though it would not be very correct, nor very elegant, to dismiss out of hand the possibility of him being a political prisoner. Then, among those seated at the back, two or three of them started muttering about the brutal treatment they'd received, how the cops had gotten enraged with them, how they'd all had to appear before the examining magistrate. Someone leaned toward Raúl. And you, why're you here? Well, I still don't know why, said Raúl. Facing him, silent, as if stupefied, as if it took a great effort to understand what was being said, he thought he recognized the tram driver. Does the examining magistrate beat you? he heard him ask at last, just as they were arriving.

Name?

Raúl Ferrer Gaminde Moret.

Son of?

Jorge and Eulalia.

Any other name or nickname? Distinguishing marks or characteristics?

The same questions, more or less, as when they registered him at the police headquarters. The photograph, fingerprints. And, in a certain way, even the same sort of person. Specifically, the one who took his fingerprints; except that here—not so lucky—the man wore the brown uniform of a prisoner serving his sentence. If I had my way, with the Reds, I'd string 'em all up by the balls, he said, as he inked Raúl's fingers somewhat violently. He spoke while twirling the classic little gray mustache of the combat veteran, that product of the Civil War who, from his position as victor, considered in the spirit of the letter, in the absolute sense, has plunged headlong, or without the proper wits and skill, along the paths of corruption and bribery, at every available opportunity—black market, importation licenses, real estate speculation—until ending up, with increasing frequency, cooling his heels in prison, where his old friends, relations, and merits can no longer help him secure anything more than a certain situation of privilege, sufficient, notwithstanding, so that, just as when free, he always found himself among the hardline party faithful when it was time to participate in commemorative rallies, demonstrations of support, or official receptions; nor in captivity did he waste the opportunity to show his combative spirit—like that poor student in a religious academy who, enormously mistaken, believes he can make up for his habitual bad grades through his pious conduct—by keeping his distance from those who, imprisoned just the same, cannot brag about their past—the majority of the prisoners—and, with greater motivation, with respect to those doing time for political reasons, in order to be identified as much as possible with the established powers both inside and outside the prison, to be able to justify his own disgrace, attributing to the enemy all the evils that, like the mother country, beset him.

The frisking, however, also conducted by several prisoners under the supervision of an official, was much more rigorous. They let him keep his pen and his belt, his matches and shoelaces, but they made him strip naked and searched the seams of his clothing, with a scrupulousness similar to when he was arrested—which, although perhaps according to regulations, might well be interpreted as excessive zeal—and they examined his rectum and testicles. They opened up a few cigarettes and his can of condensed milk, and they gave him back his pillow, torn open with half the stuffing missing. His chocolate and tobacco had vanished, small thefts practiced by some low-level prisoners who for not failing to perform various internal prison functions cease to be what, with an obvious sentiment of predetermination, is usually called fresh meat, instead they are that small-time crook who steals in prison and who, by continuing to do so once released is soon back inside, perhaps the same day of their release, neither more nor less—you might say—than if the police were waiting for him or if he had gone to his meeting, recalcitrant as that sodomite who, now on his knees before the executioner, upon noticing the thick bulging underneath those purple leotards, as tight as possible to allow one to clearly see the main veins of his member, asks with humility, as a final favor, permission to administer a blowjob. The men in charge of the prison peculium charged him two-hundred-fifty pesetas of the money he had on him for services. For the rest they gave him a receipt. They also confiscated all the papers and cards in his wallet that bore hand-written words and numbers. And a snapshot of Nuria on the beach, in a bathing suit, from when they went to Rosas. A ceremonial rupture with respect to the outside world similar to, in its preparatory significance, the state of mind students are made to experience as they initiate a period of spiritual exercises when they enter the residence where the retreat will take place. One of those retreats such as were developed in Manresa and which usually end with a visit to the cave of St. Ignatius of Loyola.

An impression redoubled in Raúl's case, now walking from his cell along a series of bare, seemingly deserted, corridors and galleries but full of echoes, thanks to a detail as ridiculous as his allowance of chocolate, cookies, and condensed milk, what a schoolboy carries with him when he goes on a spiritual retreat—apart from alcohol, tobacco, and banned books. A cell, on the other hand, not very different in essence—solitude and reflection—from the ones in a retreat house. Including the crude drawings and writings on the walls, despite how different their content—P. P. was here 120 days for smoking hash; I was here for smoking weed—they both responded to the same sense of expiation and purification as the professions of faith and intentions to reform that could be read on the inside of the box of the plain deal table, in the cell at Manresa. Before returning to the world, I want to write, in my own blood: I promise to never sin again.

First that lugubrious place, underground, which, despite everything, was better than the jail cells at police headquarters. Six paces instead of four. It was ruled over by an individual whose somber medieval presence lacked only a hood. His manner, however, was comforting, and he spoke almost as if excusing himself. These cells are for punishment. But you're not here to be punished but to be kept incommunicado. It seems that there was no space upstairs. And they've told me that they're already preparing a whole floor of the sixth wing for you all. You'll be better off up there. The cells there are not so damp.

A cell that would be number 243, on the third floor of the sixth wing. And one in which he would grow accustomed to the liturgy of life in the penitentiary, to its rhythms, its echoes, forever awaiting the examining magistrate. And after making his declaration, what's called the period, meaning another five or six days of isolation, maybe not even that long, in Pedro Botero's opinion, bearing in mind the ones they'd already taken away. And then, freedom within the prison. An examining magistrate who each day was going to come tomorrow.

Invaluable, the assistance offered him by Pedro Botero, the chief of the third floor, and, in his condition as both prisoner and jailer, a true incarnation of the system's ambiguity, a system in which what matters, much more than making sure the established rules are followed, is—like in all societies, on the other hand—making sure people believe they are being followed. A poor devil? An abject and subaltern demon? A Belial? Possibly, but not for that reason were his powers any less efficient and far reaching. In fact, one of those servile beings who know how to charge for their services. One of those people who keep you informed, who protect you against thieves—here you don't trust anybody, or what they say about anybody—even as they're cleaning out your wallet. Hardened people, and at the same time sincerely human. And, something in them that always remains a failing, with a certain weakness for those people whose ignorance of the system, almost bordering on stupidity, is accompanied, as in Raúl's case, by an intuition and sense of opportunity—their proper largesse with tips, for example—so it doesn't take long for them to be seen worthy of everyone else's respect and esteem. A good disposition, formerly ephemeral and superficial, dominated by that unquestionable realism of the old sinner converted into the owner of some typical restaurant along the coast, who, questioned by the police for transporting the bodies of two accident victims in his car, recognizes them as the amorous pair who ate that day in his establishment and, witnessing those fresh corpses, cannot help thinking: what a waste of lobster.

Another admirable trait: discretion. Ask no questions and, obviously, unlike the majority of the regular prisoners, show no desire to be questioned either. Given that, like the solitary boy who interposes an adult behavior between his persona and that of his terrified companions, like the declining woman who finds the exact justification in the sicknesses she invents, like the old man who proclaims himself a victim of adversity, like the adult clinging to a childhood that protects him from his responsibilities, so, in jail, with the same helplessness, everyone tends to tell their story, everyone is sure of having done their part, except, precisely, the crime for which they're serving time or for which they must be judged. A childish reaction, at any rate, to the degree to which it ignores the fact that what the adult punishes is not some specific act by the child, but the child itself. But also, as in certain bars frequented by gay people, it's not strange to see them give themselves over to patently childish group songs and games, when the atmosphere is good and they find themselves feeling relaxed, that old *voulez voux planter de choux* sung out in a happy chorus, verses that without a doubt take them back to the key age of their personal conflict—the simple fact of having witnessed similar scenes, assuming their having frequented such bars, could now well turn out to be an index of such conflict—thus the prisoner's mere condition, so similar to those of the student and the soldier, usually provokes a marked regression toward typically infantile attitudes and habits. A phenomenon doubtless exacerbated by the very structure of the penal system, thanks to its essential formalism, similar to school or the military, where the basic element of all classification resides in such facts as age or height or alphabetical order of family names, and so, in prison, although each prisoner is there as a result of something they've done, for the specific crime committed or presumed to have been committed, in practice, the prisoners are classified and distributed or grouped according to previous categories, independent of all consideration unrelated to the penal system itself, purely according to the prisoners' objective membership in any of the categories by which, in a deductive manner, the system is structured. Hence their being segregated into different sections: whites, homosexuals, political prisoners, sodomites, jailbreakers, etcetera. A division that responds to a conception not merely idealistic but also artificial, because just as sovereignty does not exclude lechery, belonging to a specific prison classification does not preclude the existence of sufficient motives for belonging to any of the others.

Raúl knocked on the door.

Number?

243.

There on the threshold, quick as a cork from a cava bottle, appeared Pedro Botero, with his tidbits of news, his tips, his guidance, his services. He kept him up to date not only on the action in his section, but also about life in general throughout the prison. About those choruses of Pardon Me Lord, or God, My God, for example, he could hear sung somewhere far away. It's the men in the fifth ward, he said. Spiritual exercises. They always sing those at the end. Here, in the sixth, the session begins on Monday. It's not required, but many attend in order to be on good terms with the Mercedarian father. The thing is, after the warden, the priest is the person with the most influence here. Much more influence, naturally, than the chief of services and the doctor. We call him Mother Mercedes or, because he's from Madrid, La Merche. He's not a bad person. The little girls all love him.

Sometimes his advice was spontaneous. When Raúl asked the commissary chief to beef up or change the monotonous rotating menu, lentils, beans, garbanzos, lentils. Steak or a couple fried eggs, Botero said, like some maître d' who takes the liberty of recommending the house speciality; that's the simplest. He brought him wine, his own ration, according to him, since the solitaries were excluded from having a share. And there was no doubt that under a less severe regimen, once his solitary confinement was lifted, it was he, Pedro Botero, who presented the clearest path toward getting hold of stronger, better quality alcohol, and even marijuana. He brought him copies of *Redención*, a kind of Sunday supplement, the only publication authorized for prisoners, as well as one of those detective novels smuggled inside that get passed from cell to cell until, in order to keep things looking normal during an inspection, they are confiscated, along with things like can openers, a hand-drawn deck of cards, and an alcohol stove fashioned out of a Nescafé can. He also provided him with an ink cartridge and toilet paper, because writing paper, unlike the fountain pen, was forbidden to prisoners in solitary confinement. A kind of assistance which, along with his self-imposed ritual discipline and the arhythmic rhythms of the system itself, had contributed, without any doubt, to his getting quickly accustomed to his cell. Sometimes it took the announcement of a headcount or the echo of some unusual movement in the passageway to remind him that he was in a cell in the Cárcel Modelo, and not in his bedroom, working, let alone in his room in Vallfosca, where, as a boy, he closed the door to think.

The prisoner in 242 liked to sing tangos. Especially "Confesión." Unlike the man in 244, withdrawn and silent, who sometimes communicated with Raúl through the wall. Naturally, it was also Pedro Botero who informed him of his name: almost like you: Farré, Ferrer, Farrés or something like that. Politician; they say he's a big fish. And Botero was almost sure that, having gotten Raúl interested, if Raúl had enough trust, not only in Pedro Botero, but also the guy in 242, he offered to transmit messages. But from every point of view it seemed preferable to continue with those necessarily brief conversations, however difficult and uncomfortable, that 242 had first initiated. Like a telephone. Tapping was the call signal. To talk, you had to cup your hands around the exact spots where the tapping had been. To listen, flatten your ear right up against the same spot on the wall. You like tangos? Yes. That's good; I even dance them. And you? You don't sing? Only inside. It's better to sing aloud. And dance. Things going badly for you? I don't think so. And you? Man, for a few years, I suppose so.

Not until the previous Sunday did he get the chance to find out what he looked like, when they brought them out onto the gallery, each one in front of his cell and with a guard behind him, to attend the Mass being celebrated in prison's Central Tower. He was about middle-aged, although his hair was already white, and he seemed quick-witted and cheerful. He glanced at the altar with a look of admiring astonishment, nodding his head in approval. Raúl did not remember having seen him before. Of course Felipe, when he came to visit, at first didn't seem to recognize Raúl either. And he himself, after nightfall, climbing up to the upper bunk to look at himself reflected in the window, also had a hard time recognizing himself. Long hair, bags under his eyes, swollen and puffy: Monte Cristo.

The visit took place after Mass, shortly before mealtime. I swear, it's just like when we visited Leo, except on the other side of the bars. How are you? Are they treating you alright? You look like you just crawled out of the catacombs. He spoke excitedly. He'd had to move heaven and earth and then some to obtain permission to be able to visit him before he appeared in front of the examining magistrate. But everybody had done everything possible. Papa is gathering signatures. And Montserrat says she's ready to disown any of her friends who try to ignore the situation. But the most effective move has been made by your girlfriend's family's lawyer, this García Fornells, who seems to have a lot of influence. Seems that Jacinto Bonet, however, has refused to talk about it. But things are looking really good. Your arrest has unleashed a real flood of protests, students, faculty, lawyers, all demanding your release. And the most important thing is that even in the factories the workers know that there's an intellectual, a university professor, imprisoned alongside their comrades. Your case has become both a denunciation and an example to follow. A denouncement of social injustice and an example of solidarity. Not words. An example.

He watched Raúl with that dazzlingly calm professional authority, not very different, in the end, from any other young clergyman's affect, more traditional in his proselytizing, when he asks his parishioners: why must you always hurry? Why is everyone in such a hurry? I never am. Why must one be? A question meant to signify: this is the inner peace of those of us who have learned to choose eternal life. However, the sermon concluded, for any attentive observer, his lightly tense smile as he withdraws, the slightly forced lightness of his steps, the volatility of his manners and gestures, seem rather to contradict the firmness of his implied principles, gravely compromising the value of a confidence more superficial than profound, allowing one to glimpse the mere mouth of what might well be an abyss of questions and uncertainties.

And with the same ineffable humor: I have to let you know that I've also got more problems with the reactionary sector of Opus Dei, from the old fogies. And concealing his laughter with his hand: when you get out, you might find they've put me out on the street, too. With that sense of humor, with that euphoric exaltation with which some people respond to an accumulation of obstacles. Another delay? Magnificent! One more problem we'll overcome. In a theological way, too. No, God's not dead, he might say, for example. He's simply drunk, sleeping it off like old Noah.

Before saying goodbye they exchanged wristwatches. The band on Felipe's watch smelled of priest.

In the afternoon, a providential storm broke up that atmosphere that felt like a small-town casino or a bullfighting club that had taken over the patios and galleries, prisoners strolling in their dress uniforms, some even wearing a hat and smoking a cigar, tipsy with the more-or-less free beer from the commissary and the paso dobles playing over and over through the loudspeakers, depressing verses from *In a Persian Market* as the only variation to that background music that set the festive mood with which the prisoners talked in small circles and played Spoof and exchanged bets on the handball games, all magically coming to a silent halt when the radio broadcast was interrupted to announce the results of the professional league soccer matches. If the storm didn't stop the revelry, it at least served to clear the patios; and seated on the upper bunk, face against the window, one could almost ignore the buzzing from the gallery. Thunder and lightning in the darkened skies, even before the rain came slashing down from the turbulent clouds, and the sensation that in a few moments, whole years went flashing by, in which time ran backward and the images floated one atop the other, as if he were not in his cell, but in Vallfosca, and different music was vibrating the glass where he rested his forehead, contemplating the landscape all blurry beneath one of those late-August or early-September thunderstorms, instead of those twisting skies above the prison's rectilinear architecture, the clouds convoluted like a mass of straining muscles in titanic combat, herculean onslaughts, centaurs with matted, tangled manes galloping away amid flashes and detonations, leaving behind them broken tensions, lightened spaces, renewed clarities, until on the western horizon there opened a crater of white sunlight, celestial glories revealing, as the rain lessened, a panorama of growing magnitude, cumulus castles, temples rising, cathedrals on the march with their violent towers, sharp naves, and labyrinthine crypts like ruined cities, violaceous shapes fading and dissolving where the Sierra Collcerola is no more than a shadowy black silhouette against the now extinguished western sky. Barcelona's violet hue, a tonality more in its light than in the city itself or in the colors of its stones and structures, like a vapor shifting from mauve to purple that emanates from its streets, from its buildings, a product of who knows what, possibly the proximity of the sea, the sombre reverberation of the encircling mountains, the trapped, stagnant humidity and the industrial atmosphere, polluted airs filtering the transparency of the elusive twilight sky—it's hard to say—of a day coming to an end.

And that liturgical purple? A Lenten color, proper to the time, but especially the circumstances. A penitent color, of tormented flesh, of cardinals, bruises, burns, and bumps, resulting from the right combination of fire red and iron blue, characteristic attributes of condemnation and damnation. The purple Mass, the Novitiate Mass, a Mass compared to which the vulgar Masses, the other Masses are only a dramatization that disguises a spectacle of much greater importance. Because, what other conclusion could an analytical spirit reach about that celebration of holy sacrifice held on the highest floor of the prison's Central Tower, above the guards' command post itself, a circular glassed-in office whose basement is the place where capital punishment is usually delivered, by garrote, to those prisoners sentenced to death? What could be the significance of its being celebrated precisely there, ostensibly for maximum visibility, except for the grandiose purpose, worthy of a delirious creativity, of giving the ritual more exemplary and authentic character, of exalting the commemorative symbolism, renewing, upon the intangible presence of so many who had really been executed there, the death of the Redeemer between the two thieves on the heights of Golgotha? Yes, right there, in the geometric center, not only the center of that series of exterior walls and moats, but also the very center of that radial layout, the confluence of the various prison wings that form the prison's internal structure. And similarly, in ceremonial terms, the axis or nerve center of daily life in the prison, in the same way that communion is the essence and synthesis of the holy sacrifice of the Mass, and the Mass, the essence and synthesis of the entire liturgical year. Concentric wings, and in each one of them, no doubt, the inmates similarly distributed. So, in the sixth ward, along the ground floor, the old and infirm in the first rows, closest to the altar and with the right to a pew because of their age and condition. Behind, already standing, the rest of the repeat offenders. And conveniently separated, the little girls, the queer prisoners, dressed up and made up in accordance with the importance of the event, their weekly opportunity of showing off in front of the other prisoners. And above, along the third-floor railing, those in solitary confinement, motionless before the doors of their respective cells, each with a guard at his back.

And while the celebrant read the gospel to himself, the loudspeakers broadcast, beloved brothers, the words of La Madre Mercedes, only a few words, most cherished and beloved sons, to remind you that the prisons of men are not the true prisons, just as the death of the body is neither the true death. Only the death of the soul is death and only eternal damnation is prison. And man's judgments, his sentences, are not what must matter to us. For what do human judgments count for in the face of God's? Faced with that Final Judgment which must inexorably precede the definitive establishment of the City of God, when the final trumpets sound, announcing the end of the world, of a world sunk down into the slavery of sin, and the tombs are opened and the flesh is revived and legions of angels elevate the blessed ones into the presence of the Most High and hordes of demons drive the reprobates headlong into the eternal fire? What will you hide from his terrible gaze, how will you escape from his fearsome voice when He summons you to his presence and, all simultaneously and at the same time each one individually, asking you: what have you done with my ships? Where is my fleet? How will you then stand a question which is in itself a condemnation? Because you have sinned and for that you are here. Because you have ignored Saint Paul in not obeying the law. Because you have ignored Saint John when he told you to love the world. Because you have failed to keep all the commandments and have trampled upon all the rules. Because you have sinned against Heaven and against Me. You, faggots and heretics, obstinate lawbreakers and fugitives from justice, communists, suicides, adulterers, fortune-tellers, terrorists, traitors. Like Fra Garí you gave in to the Tempter, to the Fallen Angel, and like him you have been condemned. Like Fra Garí or Garín, the holy hermit who defiled Montserrat, that expiatory temple that nature itself has raised up in the heart of Catalonia, by committing rape and murder there on the holy mountain: the holy blasphemer become wandering beggar of those rocky peaks, those rigid royal effigies. Damned like the whore Riquilda, that little slut, that Lolita. And like her father, Jofre or Wilfredo, first Count of Catalonia, blinded, like King Lear, for his incestuous love. And like Santa Eulalia, guilty of the original lie. And like Saint George, who invented a dragon. And Saint James the Apostle, the imposter. And like Tirant lo Blanch, a coward's projection. And like Don Quixote, the creation of a sick and twisted mind. And like Cide Hamete el Campeador. And here we are, all of us, in the vaginal depths of Persephone, in the penetrating realms of Hades, where wisdom and mental retardation, weakness and strength, are all confused in the dark ambiguity of the elemental. All of them, Prometheus the pyromaniac, Sisyphus the incompetent, Vulcan the cuckold, Saturn the castrato, and together with them the thuggish Hercules and the wrathful Achilles, and Orpheus and Ajax and Odysseus and Laertes and Anchises and Aeneas and Virgil and Dante and Milton and La Merche. And I, from the center of every circle, I address my thoughts to you all, and especially to my closest companions, those who have sinned with their intelligence as well as with their sex, the enemies of God, of the Fatherland, of their governors and benefactors, to you I speak and particularly to you Raúl Ferrer Gaminde i Moret. To you and to all, princes, potentates, warriors, splendor of the heaven in which you dwelled and which you have now lost. Is it possible that such stupor can overpower your spirit? You, who in another time destroyed those giants masquerading as windmills? Is this now possible? The spirit carries its own dwelling within itself and can by itself make a heaven of hell and a hell of heaven. How many times has it not pleased the Almighty himself to reign among thick black clouds without obscuring his glory, to surround his throne with the majesty of the darkness from which burst forth the resounding thunderbolts of concentrated fury, to the point when the heavens then resemble hell? What do we fear, then? There is no longer any depth that can contain within its abysms our immortal life. Here, at least, we are free. Let us live, therefore, in this vast retreat for ourselves, free, without having to account for our actions to anyone, preferring a hard liberty to the light yoke of a pompous bootlicker. Because what is the world except a prison of darkness? What is the world but sterile land, rocky ground, a green field crawling with serpents? In which you will see, as Fray Luis de Granada said, how much this world has in common with hell. And what other name is there for paradise—if indeed it once existed—which reduced us to our current state? Wake up then, pick yourselves up, or remain forever fallen. We will build here our own paradise.

No longer the writhing multitude, the intermingling floods of passersby, colored masks and trumpets, party hats and onanistic zambombas all in their promiscuous dance, going and coming, plunging in and pulling out and spinning around, between the streamers and the confetti, between the sparkling glowing streets, wandering over the squashed grapes like blissful souls, fed up with contemplation, they might have resolved to exchange it—led on by the Almighty himself in the form of a statue of Frederic Soler, better known as Serafí Pitarra, suddenly come to life, his involuted pedestal in la Plaza del Teatro turned into an entertainer's podium—for more substantial emotions and pleasures, no longer all that, but rather, more concretely, the same horrendous scarecrow of La Venta, the same overblown waxed and painted faggot, stamping his heels and singing and clapping his hands, swaying his loose, sagging hips, almost an old man, surely, more frightening than obscene with his depressing residual synthesis of the romantic balladeer and mystic poet, his hoarse, braying rhymes, *Españia, mi vida, cariñio, mi ser, amores, primores, morir, mi existir, olvido, perdido, entrañias, volver*—which might be rendered thus—Españya, my life, my darlingah, my soul, loves, marvelous treasures, die, my existence, my oblivion, my abandon, my bowelsah, come back. And the lesbians' demonic laughter and the guitarist's big drunken-buddha eyes. The same one and the same ones, the Adolfos and Nuria Rivas and Nuria Oller and Pluto and Federico and even Fortuny and even that pain in the ass M. M. Everyone, maybe from the inertia of the routine, how each year they all made a date over the phone, maybe for just the opposite reason, as if they all somehow knew that, given their fraying relationships, that New Year's was going to be the definitive one, the last New Year's they would ever celebrate together.

Pluto showed up alone. Marihole had stayed home with their little boy. I think I'm gonna keep her pregnant the rest of her life. Pregnancy already takes up nine months and between bedrest and all the other stuff, it's a whole year. She's delighted and so am I. The great advantage with Marihole is that she's really stupid. Today, for example, I told her that I had a business dinner, and she thought it was perfectly natural. Look, it's well known that in Spain there are three forms of payment: pay, don't pay, and pay with an IOU. And Marihole is like an IOU.

Fortuny, already several drinks ahead of everyone, laughed stupidly. It shows you're what they call a man of letters. And Pluto: see? A guy like you would've been just right for Marihole, like that, sensible, just a little bit too careful. I've got to find some way for Marihole to cheat on me with you as soon as possible. That way she'll leave me in peace night and day. What this guy is proposing me to do is another one of his crackpot schemes! (Fortuny) You didn't understand me, pal (Pluto). Just an endorsement pure and simple. And with a promissory note if you like.

Federico was also pretty lit. Nuria Rivas called him Federica, a certain libidinous touch in her provocation, but he paid her no mind. As was normal when he drank, his conversation kept coming back to politics. He cornered Raúl. Why don't you just leave the party? It's absurd to let things just fizzle out by themselves. These situations have always gotta be clearly resolved, like when you get divorced. I want Leo to arrange me a meeting with Escala to request the official release. And tell him the proletariat is a kind of Frankenstein monster, a patchwork creature cobbled together from the trash of every social class.

Outrage Escala, give him a nervous breakdown, biliary colic, a coronary. The fact of the matter being, with the enraged amazement of the faithful wife who after years of marriage accidentally discovers, thanks to her girlfriends' gossip, that the frequency with which her husband performs the coital act with her is barely worthy of a eunuch and, after an initial phase in which she manages to hide her shame, so, too, the seminarian who on the eve of ordination decides to hang up his cassock, but only upon finding himself out in the wide world does he recognize the lie he has been living, and then gives himself over to all kinds of excess, so the defrauded wife, once she's been replaced, falls easily into nymphomania, and so Federico, unlinked from all political activity, seems to enjoy adopting, although only on a verbal level, the most provocative attitudes of all the orders. What's painful, he said, is thinking that humanity has had to wait so many thousands of years for its true History to begin. Oh, the poor people whose lot it was to live in a feudal, or theocratic, or capitalist society. What a tragedy, for example, to have been born a Hittite!

In fact, just like always when something occurred that seemed to lend the night a touch of the unusual, they were all rather on the same wavelength. No doubt things started to get heated with that guy from the other bar. A guy who went back and forth through the bar, sometimes stopping right in front of them. He gave them a look somewhere between friendly and defiant, with an oscillating smile. When he made sure he'd gotten their attention, his opened his shirt, now with a scorpion's triumphant gaze, showing them his chest splattered with scars seemingly from shrapnel, bare patches of red flesh amid the fine gray hair. He lit a match and, with a conjuror's flamboyant pauses began to scorch his chest hair with the small flame, meticulously scouring any areas missed at first, lighting one match from another, his belly trembling with silent laughter. Neither the bartender nor anyone else seemed to notice him. They all invited him to have a drink. When I was in the war, you all were just babies, he said. The Iron Ring of Bilbao. The Ebro. They asked him which side he'd fought on. Which side! He laughed and laughed. He pulled out a dark, worn wallet, giving them a peek inside, like someone flashing a deck of cards, the papers stuffed inside, money, identification. He ran out to the street and right in front of the bar door, threw his wallet straight into the mouth of the sewer. And then he did the same with everything he had in his pockets, loose change, a key ring, cigarettes, handkerchief, matches. He laughed, and seeing that he'd acquired a certain audience, he strolled slowly back inside, looking at them the whole while. They invited him to have another drink. He also asked them for a Celta, delightedly filling his lungs with the smoke. They couldn't convince him to stick around with them. He turned crafty, pretending to be too clever to let them connive him. But by then they were all pretty well drunk.

¡Vivan las revoluciones! Federico shouted. He'd showed up with an Argentine couple, the woman was his first cousin or close relative, or at least that's what Federico said. The husband, or whatever he was, was dressed up as an Englishman; a big talker, stocky as a ram with a ram's bludgeon forehead. The cousin wasn't too bad-looking, but a real bore once she opened her mouth, too fond of trying to deliver momentous remarks. She apologized for bringing along another friend they'd run into. Not at all, it's much more fun with two women; just so long as she's got a little sprinkle of dyke in her (Federico). The friend appeared a little more spirited or at least more in the mood for a good time, making sure to let her dress straps keep slipping off her shoulder, and then readjusting them as conspicuously as possible, expansively blowing kisses to the Buddha with the guitar.

Pluto had his eyes on her. A little prissy but definitely good for a gallop (Pluto). The cousin, however, looks exactly like a suppository. Difficult to remove once inserted.

And there was another girl, some sort of little whore, who'd also come with Federico. A model, as she explained. The cousin seemed tense with her companion, or maybe irritated with Federico, and was making eyes at Adolfo. And Adolfo, whether from morbid curiosity, or to dodge Nuria Rivas's insinuations, followed her lead.

At the Jamboree, Raúl sat apart with Aurora. How long since we talked? (Raúl). I don't know, a long time (Aurora). She leaned back on Raúl's shoulder, closing her eyes. I think it's a shame it all went to hell; I wouldn't dare tell you if I wasn't a little drunk (Aurora). Well, let's finish getting drunk (Raúl). Oh, Raúl, I do so many stupid things. But I can't take any more. I'm sick of him, of his head trips, how he likes to surround himself with a bunch of idiots, and the idiotic life we've got. Some days I think that if he's not really such an idiot then he can only shine when he's got bigger idiots around him. And if we're living this life it's not for weakness of character but because he feels incapable of doing any really creative work, and he just uses this life we're leading as an excuse. But I can't stand it. And then I do stupid things. Like how I slept with Federico just to piss him off (Aurora). Don't worry, you're not the only one. You tell me what I'm doing sleeping with Nuria Oller (Raúl). They kissed in the hallway outside the bathrooms. Then they slipped inside one together. Aurora unzipped his fly and knelt down in front of him. Come on, come on, she said next, pulling down her clothes, offering him her naked croup, propping her elbows on the toilet seat cover, the two of them spurred on faster by the door handle rattling when someone tried to come in.

Had La Rivas seen them or noticed something? In every case, it was really Aurora with whom she'd been drinking that night and not La Oller. Perhaps only because La Oller, who could not attribute Raúl's sudden coldness with her to more than an exciting cynicism, to a desire to guard the privacy of their shared secret—their tryst that afternoon in Pedralbes—was trying, with complicit dissimulation, to first make eyes at M. M. And it must also have been obvious for La Rivas that Adolfo was ignoring her, simply from being in a bad mood.

That evil bitch, with her enigmatic airs, she really gets on my nerves (La Rivas). And your nerves. You think they don't bother anybody? (Raúl). Defend her, defend her. You two would be so good together. You with Aurora and me with Adolfo (La Rivas). And you slept with him once, right? No skin off my nose. (Raúl). Well, look who's talking, the man with the golden prick. Let me tell you, it's no big deal for me either to pick up any guy at all. If I didn't have my period, I was gonna go with one (La Rivas). Do it anyway. You can always do something (Raúl). La Rivas turned away. Touché. Raúl's defenses, his capacity to be bluntly unpleasant, of replying acerbically to her hysterias and her stories, as roundly as that policeman who, the interrogation barely begun, cuts right to the chase with a few sharp blows upside the head.

Not unlike the Argentine gal with the shoulder straps. Except that the alcohol provoked a more violent response in La Rivas. She stepped out to dance with someone, pulling him close, as tightly as possible, her tits almost falling out of her dress. And later, the scene, her compulsive need to end up starting a fight. Some greasy groper, or some wayward hand on her ass, or something like that. Go grope your mother! she screamed or she would scream. They moved aside as she barged between the tables. What do they think? They think women are like mules? She sat down unsteadily. Nerves, anxiety, a drowned, sinking, pissing wreck.

Pushy in her outbursts no less than in her chatter, capable in both cases of being exacerbating to the limit, like everything that gets repeated and repeated. When, voluble and passionate, she started chattering, or better, arguing with a taxi driver, with the waiter, with whomever, to explain her position to them about any problem, themes which she had generally seen them develop with proselytic purposes in other times, when they first met, the injustice of charity, better working conditions outside Spain, the need for political liberty, etcetera, a depressing regression directly proportional to the frequency of the chosen subject, like that hit record from years ago, years that hold nothing for us but painful memories.

On one hand, her tendency for sexual adventure was evident. Maybe to escape from Raúl, maybe for just the opposite reason, to prevent Raúl escaping from her. Preferably some happy little fling, necessarily brief as the circumstances required. Over and done with and each one back to their commitments, with the vivid memory left by all short-lived love affairs, cut short before the mutual misunderstanding of the coupling dissipates, not so much being on the same wavelength as simply a chance for each one to strip naked before the other's eyes, projecting themself onto the other like standing before a mirror, contemplating themself in the other, wrapping themself around them. Before finally discovering that the other person was someone different, a stranger with whom they had nothing in common.

On the other hand, her unfulfilled temptations. Her loss of velocity, some days barely idling along. As if now mistrustful of the vitality that formerly sustained her, of the power of her impulses; as if she had become afraid of life.

The sensation of flying along the highway, about to smash straight into a wall at any moment. As if the repressive attitudes with which she'd been raised and educated suddenly became valid, no matter how much they'd been effectively exploded by her own family reality: inexorable punishment, the classic example of the family madwoman, of her fateful example, that remotely familiar aunt or cousin they talk about, one of the first to smoke in public and to go out alone with men, beautiful and uninhibited then, and now aged and impoverished and, above all, alone, one of those people who at first can be a lot of fun and entertaining when recounting their adventures, but whom everybody eventually shakes off because nobody's attracted to ruination and unhappy endings.

A slow process of inhibition, whose occasional rupture some night, fueled by alcohol, only grew worse later, upon waking up with a hangover, facing another day. A process which her relationship with Raúl, increasingly difficult, failed to explain sufficiently. Not united like a shaft of light through two windows into the same room, or like the water in a streaming current in the sea, or like the rain falling upon a river or a fountain, not even like two candles joined so closely that although being two, the flame seems one. Like water and oil.

In some way, simply the result of normal daily problems or of a specific conflictive situation, it were as if Nuria Rivas felt canceled out by something less specific, as if something were impelling and shaping her own behavior, perhaps her mother's personality. As if her childhood memories about the relationship between Doña Dulce and Amadeo, whose character she had taken a long time to understand, far from having served her as an example to follow, as a norm of conduct, they had, over time, dulled her daring and self-confidence; when they summered in Lloret de Mar and in the afternoons Doña Dulce had brought her along with her to Amadeo's house and left her playing in the garden with the chauffeur's daughter. An obvious co-dependency, even physically. Not because Doña Dulce was well preserved; because they could almost be mistaken for sisters. The difference lay, above all, in their attitude, in their bearing. Wise and mature, grave and mature fullness, impeccable presence and splendid features, like one of those mares with brushwood and bullwhips in her eyes.

Not yet Nuria. Amadeo's own mother, perfectly in keeping with her own legendary amorous past. A widow, too, authoritarian, lucid, stingy, dressed with adamantine sobriety, still personally overseeing the management of her business affairs, with the poise and class of one who moves through life as if the world were nothing more than one vast Ritz Hotel. Her powdered face, taut from cosmetic surgery. Her hair gathered under a silk turban, her eyes behind dark glasses. The interior of her black car finished in wood paneling and quilted leather, and she, giving the chauffeur orders, barely looking outside through the half-drawn curtains, imperturbable and solitary like a general or like death. What were Nuria Rivas or Nuria Oller going to learn from a woman like her or a woman like Doña Dulce, daughters of a time made difficult for being anodyne and amorphous, a time of transition, like that street thief who has neither the professional precision of the old-time gangster, nor the natural ease of the addict who sallies forth to score his daily ration of injectables? Was a behavior similar to Nuria's conceivable in them, in the widows, in their good times? Might it have once been? Even if only for reasons of social standing?

The strange loneliness of marriage, the feeling that any ordinary expression uttered by one's spouse can suddenly create, despite the havoc of cohabitation. The discomfort of a glance, even a loving one, the disbelief with which one wonders who is she, who is he, and, especially, what the fuck are they doing together. An episodic transubstantiation of the familiar fully as unforeseen as inevitable, the same as when the screen flashes the full moon behind some clouds and the tormented wolf man is powerless to stop the deadly transformation once triggered. In the same way, in one of those parentheses of unreality peculiar to married life, Nuria Oller spread her legs for Raúl in Pedralbes, on the last afternoon of the year.

Perhaps Raúl was starting to get tired. Perhaps he was starting to search for defects in her: the discordant rise and fall of her laughter, a tone of voice perfect for roosters, her too-hungry eyes, expressive of that perpetual state of agitation that characterized her, eager with desire, as if always walking on hot coals. And her habit of laughing with her hand covering her lips, a holdover, no doubt, from when they fixed her mouth when she was younger and she wore a bridge.

But none of all that would have been enough. The decisive turn was Nuria Oller's transformation into Nuria Hyde. When after weeks, months, years, of speaking nicely about Peter, attractive, enchanting, a good companion, one of those people whom you know you can always count on, everything suddenly changed. Peter was filthy. Peter was clumsy. He didn't know how to make love. He snored. And she had her own plans, everything figured out down to the last detail. And she divulged them, not with the simple perverse calculation of the Lolita who, out hitchhiking along the road, gets picked up by three taciturn forty-somethings, and then, once inside the car, asks suggestively, You're not all going to rape me, are you? No, not with that kind of calculation, but with something really despicable in the malign victory of her smile: divorce and, as she had managed it well, the surety of obtaining, according to English laws, a nice alimony. She held all the trump cards. She contemplated her nakedness in the mirrors, radiant like a vengeful goddess, without noticing that it really seemed, at least in Raúl's mind, like that afternoon was truly their last. Not unlike the boy who hears the ladies of the house discussing the news of the sudden death of some gloomy neighbor, commenting how the man said that he'd like another piece of gâteau, and as they were serving it to him he began to slide right off his chair, so that for the boy, for many years, the word gâteau inevitably carried the horrendous connotations of a curse whose spell he would do everything possible to not say aloud, and so for Raúl, Nuria Oller had certain accents, certain attitudes, no less traumatically dark, of which he really only became aware that afternoon.

Perhaps he had never really thought deeply about Barcelona's middle-class women. Not the current young crop, free and attractive, who'd learned to overcome so much conventionalism by themselves. Not the girls of today, or at least not them especially, but rather their mothers, their grandmothers, those women whom the young ladies today often judge rather severely for simply failing to understand their youthful behavior. What do they know about the difficulties of former times? Keeping up appearances, following protocol, appearing modest, the obstacles involved in simply finding a place to carry out an adulterous encounter. And in another area, the family, their excellent organizational qualities, their administrative gifts, their perfect control of the wardrobe and the pantry, their keys. And their awareness of the value of money, in no way inferior to that of the working woman, because if the latter will manage to get the best deal possible for what she needs to fill her shopping basket, our keen wife of a wealthy businessman will prove herself just as resourceful, relatively speaking, in playing her part, to get the discounts at shops where she is valued for being a good customer, of finding real bargains in the antique shops by paying cash, of obtaining the maximum rent on both the summer house and the furnished apartments for which she providently holds the deed in her name during the months when she doesn't use them.

Of course in a world in perpetual motion—and today's world more than ever—there are always some families who flourish while others decline. And it's in the heart of these families, the ones whose economic descent eventually shows in their social relations, where that aptitude and that competitive edge, contrary to what one might suppose, begin to be blunted. Now it's no longer the wife but the whole family that, from a lack of adequate material support, begins to lose footing, and along with the rhythm of activity, the notion of prices, finds itself trapped in a vicious circle that only turns into an ever more dizzying downward spiral. That's when that family finds the tables turning, becoming victim to antique dealers, speculators, unpaid bills, mortgages. Just like the crazed husband who arrives home denouncing today's youth—Nothing but faggots!—with the idea of psychologically preparing his wife, of better emphasizing the fortune that awaits her depending on how willingly she submits to his clumsy carnal embrace, so, too, families in decline: their progressive withdrawal and isolation is usually accompanied by some disrespectful theorizing about how impossible the world is becoming, a judgment which, more generally, is also usually the favorite theme of all people when they grow old. Thus that gentleman who, well on in years, retired from business some time ago, goes each morning to the bank to exchange, more than anything else, a few words with the assistant manager or, if the assistant manager is very busy, with the financial manager, or with the cashier, or with the porter, about his obsession, that neither his stocks nor his income are now what they once were, about being known and respected, about reaffirming his respectability, or mentioning his friendships and personal relations, of proclaiming yet again his conservative ideas, in both political and economic matters, how bad everything is, how lucky we are to have Franco, etcetera, and in passing—banks have big ears—of disregarding the fact that his son is in jail, it's what happens with students, everyone knows, it was the same when I was young.

Speculations, artifices. In the same way that an old joke ends up turning into a real anecdote and, over time, to enhance the effect, is repeated by everyone, like something that happened to a friend or even, as incredible as it might seem, to themself, in the sincere belief that it really happened that way and that only a lapse in memory makes it difficult for one to specify the circumstances, so, too, function family histories, in their development from the past to the present. The blood ties, inheriting a personality but not a fortune. The tendency to consecrate some secret family code in the face of any less genetic explanation. An explanation that might, for example, exclude any consideration of blood relationship from the reason why Aunt Paquita's death could affect Raúl much more than anyone could have foreseen. Instead, let's imagine that the reason might be the fact that for Raúl, along with Paquita died a whole nexus of relations between the conscious past and the remembered one from their summer stays in Vallfosca, and that other more forgotten but no-less-intensely-shimmering time at Montseny during the Civil War.

In fact, that old upper-middle-class Barcelona society, now in decline, and the new large middle class share only one thing: their common uprooting, save in economic matters, from the places and lands where they were born. In one case, through devotion to a tradition that permits them to keep believing that they are still what they once were. In another, through the convergence of their interests with those of the central power, in whose shadow they have thrived, in the heart of that monopolistic oligarchy to which they belong. And as much in the one case as in the other, although in a remote and unformulated way, their common feeling of lost identity, one of those national destinies aborted the way coitus interruptus aborts an orgasm.

The destiny of a people who, with its expeditions to the Orient, with its warlike Almogavars, unemployed reconquerors, technically on the dole, must prefigure the conquest of a new world for the West, in which it would not be permitted to participate. A people who, with its mariners, navigational charts, and, even, money, was going to establish the bases of that discovery, of that enterprise from which it would remain excluded. A people who, from its union with Castile, forged by its leaders, was only going to manage to be marginalized from any true center of power. Or what amounts to the same: by taking the side of the Archduke Carlos in his fight against the Prince of Viana, by embracing the cause that cannot triumph before then choosing the contrary, they end up losing just the same. And thus, at least, conserving the letter of the myth, of the unfinished enterprise. Just as the sociological pretension which holds that social context both explains and shapes a man in equal measure only begs the question, because, quite the contrary, it's man's relationship with different social contexts amid which he has developed since childhood, and his behavior in each circumstance, which must lead us to the understanding of what the subject was already essentially, including before his first memories, an understanding which in turn leads us to clarify what man is generally when removed from all specific contexts, as the component of a civilization itself, and this clarification returns us to any point in Catalonia's history. For example, its revealing identification with the prince of Viana—a poor devil, the classic born loser—will infallibly conjure up the various facets of each disaster, one after another, and we now find—in this point as in any other—how many elements configure and embody the luck of the cause itself, of Catalonia's final destiny.

Well, if not, then what explains, for example, the fact of having adopted Saint George as its patron saint? Or having taken as an emblem the knight's victorious battle against the dragon? How to interpret that, if not as the projection of some internal problem, as the symbolic expression of a desire, of Catalonia's anxiety to resolve through a chimerical combat, the real combat with itself that it keeps avoiding? A struggle, of much more uncertain outcome, which postulates the triumph of order and formal rigor, the dominion of reason and the sovereignty of wisdom, over the sordid ruins of a shadowy collective unconscious. A similar impulse, in the end, to what leads a people to construct cathedrals or expiatory and votive temples.

Dragons, princesses, images very much on the level of the middle class and *le petite bourgeoisie*, the most solid nucleus of that conflictive personality called Catalonia. Because, like that young typist emotionally shaped by radio serials and soap operas, so, in Catalonia, the drippy, professional-mourner mentality of its middle classes. And what other material can we point to if we discard an immigrant proletariat and an upper middle class that has renounced its historical role as the leading class, from the point of view of Catalan nationality?

The myth, the literary topic, the proparoxytonic rhetoric. Barcelona, a city proclaimed to be mirror, lantern, star, and destination of all knight-errantry, epithets accepted without even a trace of irony, insofar as they're applied to an exultant city, in the full solstice of its fiestas, which a few lines later will receive such an illustrious guest by slipping a stalk of furze under the tail of his mount and laugh behind his back after hanging a sanbenito upon him, or mocking paper dolls called *llufas* inscribed with ridicule, dirty slander, and buffoonery that could only go over the head of some idiot reader or some babbling councilman who, reader of hearsay, resorts once more to the cliché, in the course of any plenary meeting, reception, tribute, or municipal blowout party. An archive of swindles and whoring, a city that enjoys, like an open-air street party on the eve of a saint's day, the spectacle that might be offered by the unseated horseman, the fallen rider, the shipwrecked castaway on its beaches, destruction or end, form or purpose of being amused, of killing time like one kills a bandit, how he's quartered and decapitated on a scaffold. A city that injures and spits on the fallen, spits, flattens him, butchers and kills him, a killing, a bloody scalping, and the public celebrates it with 21-gun salutes and fireworks and bonfires, school of courtesans, sepulcher of strangers, and exile of messengers, the capital of a people who perhaps confronted the armies of history's greatest generals, Hannibal and Caesar, Almanzor and Napoleon, perhaps all of them, and lost. History repeated throughout time like the story of a damsel in distress repeatedly raped by successive saviors, each time between passionate promises of eternal love.

This city that can so well contemplate itself in its vastness from the heights of Mount Carmel, black weeds in the foreground, against the scintillating embers of everything far down below, and the immense sea beyond the city, and the gray vessels of the Sixth Fleet anchored in the port, and the factory smokestacks, and the flags and pennants fluttering in the sun, and the soldiers marching in file with enormous palm fronds on their shoulders, commemorating the joyful advent of the Epiphany, the reestablishment of calm, the end of the burnings, of the churches in flames, as if the heavens might have granted the bishops' prayers, heeded their Petendam Pluviam, and a saving rain would have wiped out the city from the Llobregat to the Besós, from Montjuich to Tibidabo, turning it into a plain of faint reflections, earthy water, germinative loam, a swamp surely not very different in appearance from the original, when

Montjuich was a rough cape jutting into the sea, a colossal Alcides from whose side Barcelona must be born, and like Moses, emerged from the waters, born and reborn like Ilium or Troy or Hissarlik.

On the slopes of Mount Carmel we find the Gaudian Park Güell, and at the bottom of its foothills, a short distance away, in fact, although already well into the Ensanche proper, the visitor will be able to appreciate the no-less Gaudian spires of the Sagrada Familia, reaching up, one might say, like jagged crags of a sacred mountain. A work that if it were ever terminated someday would probably have very little in common, like all slow-built cathedrals, with the original design, the same thing that usually happens with a city's urban plan, always surmounted in its development by newer realities neither foreseen nor foreseeable. One of these pre-unfinished enterprises—at least according to the image its founders had made of it—to the degree to which the burden of its realization usually falls to, or is left in charge of, future generations. Sacralization of the means, the mediatization of the objective. Dominant temples, standing out in general—perhaps for their location, perhaps for their height alone—from the collective cityscape, as if so that from their summits, in the rather most exceptional case when it is not a traveler who is inspired to climb to the top of the high towers, the citizen will obtain an unprecedented panorama of their city, to which, according to their taste, they might add the dose of future they prefer.

A red city, for example, as if burning in the fires of the West. Paralyzed by a general strike of greater significance than the one in '51. A general strike that, by means of a qualitative leap forward, will lead to a true revolutionary situation. A brief notice, a small sidebar in Le Monde, that will suddenly dominate newspaper headlines the world over.

Revolutionary November in Barcelona. Barcelona, 9 Nov. The general strike has triumphed. Following industries, public transportation, as well as banks and businesses, have closed their doors. Demonstrations are growing throughout the whole city. More than 50,000 workers and students marched in demonstration along Vía Layetana singing "The Internationale." Army troops have been confined to barracks and public buildings appear to be protected by barbed wire and heavy police forces. After mid-afternoon, the city has remained in darkness due to the flow of electrical power suddenly being cut off. Unconfirmed rumors affirm that curfew has been imposed. At press time isolated gunfire can be heard in the streets. The situation is very grave.

Barcelona, 10 Nov. The revolutionary strike initiated yesterday in Barcelona seems to have displayed especial strength in the city's industrial sector. Eyewitnesses there affirm that various police stations and barracks have been attacked. There are rumors of hundreds of victims ranging from dead to wounded. In a poignant radio address broadcast early this morning, the Civil Governor of the province has called for an immediate cease-fire, at the same time explicitly offering his resignation, if that will help to calm the mood in the city.

14h. The Cabinet, meeting in Madrid in special session, after denying reports about the civil governor of Barcelona's resignation, announced the declaration of martial law in the four Catalan provinces. Reliable sources affirm that, in Barcelona, the people have taken control of the central headquarters of Telefonica, the Postal and Telegraph Office, and various local radio stations.

19h. The masses have taken barracks and official centers by storm. Among others mentioned are the City Hall and the Regional Council. Still holding out are the Civil Government, the Military Headquarters, and Police Headquarters. On the contrary, it's been affirmed that, in the barracks, soldiers are siding with the people. Radio stations are broadcasting nonstop revolutionary proclamations and exhortations.

21h. According to the latest bulletins, the Government has now proceeded to dispatch forces by air to Catalonia.

Revolution in Spain. Madrid, 11 Nov. The revolutionary strike begun two days ago in Barcelona has now spread to various parts of the nation, Asturias, Guipúzcoa, Bilbao, Valencia, Seville, and the capital itself. The actions of the masses seem to have acquired especial violence in Asturias and the Basque Country.

Official sources affirm that the Government is poised to declare a state of war in the entire national territory.

Although news reports reaching Barcelona are quite unclear, it seems that hospitals are taxed beyond their limits and the streets are littered with bodies. The situation of the last centers of resistance is classified as desperate.

21h. Madrid, urgent. Unconfirmed rumors insist that units of the Sixth Fleet are sailing at top speed toward Barcelona.

And then? A holocaust, possibly. But also the beginning of war, not just a civil war but a full-blown insurrection, the long march entailed by the development of the European Revolution.

The trip to Madrid that November, the frustrated attempts to establish between the two local organizations more direct and agile methods of contact than the habitual party mechanisms, with the goal of coordinating the projected mass actions with maximum efficiency. The premonition of disaster that assaulted him as the plane descended over Barajas airport, at twilight, that surprising urban proliferation rising in the eroded dryness of the dusk, in the center of an arid, empty horizon of mackerel terrain, made the flowering of such an immense illuminated panorama seem truly wondrous, neon lights and skyscrapers sheltering the same old Madrid as always, hardships and dire straits, moral and economic retardation, the same propensities for barhopping as the chosen form for human relationships and as the verbal solution for all kinds of repression, black humor and basic business, simultaneously farrago and quintessence, at once crucible of Spain, of plain and simple purisms, bald-faced snubs and good-natured generosity, a smiling showplace of affected sesquipedalian raciness.

The meeting with the comrades in charge of making contact. Minds lovingly carrying the weight of eighteen ninety-eight impoverished by other ideological residue remotely translated, a mentality prone to intellectual constipation in its exhausting search for topical authenticity, more populists than scientific socialists, more provincial than puritan, more beatific than dogmatic, although also dogmatic, and puritans and scientific socialists, with the shrewdness of the meseta in its ideas as well as the fecundity of the wasteland. Living incarnation--despite his position at the university--of that positive hero of social realism, of that militant example, of that worker normally called Juan or José or Pedro, simple names like the people themselves, an honest and self-sacrificing man in the factory, among his fellow workers, as well as in the neighborhood, within the vicinity, always willing to lend help to whomever needs it, whether with his strength or his counsel, to show by his example what is the correct line. The positive sort, some fellow capable of sacrificing a whole Sunday of well-deserved rest and family life, scouring half the city so as to deliver to its intended destination a package accidentally found on the street, a route that serves as inspiration for the novel that offers a true panorama of the various environments our hero feels obliged to experience, maintaining at all times an unimpeachable conduct. The sort of man who can soothe people's spirits, rightfully rebellious, like the neighbors of a property condemned by City Hall, thus preventing the municipal employees from suffering indignity or some ill because, in the end, those agents are not the ones truly responsible, but simply salaried employees like them. A fellow, in short, whose humanity leads him to mediate between striking workers and police, in order to avoid unnecessary violence, and who ends up accidentally run over by the ambulance he himself had called to take care of a little boy struck by a stray bullet. And then his companion Antonio, the individualist, the worker of anarchic temperament, practically dissolute, has an epiphany and joins the party.

And like someone who one day reflects that his devotion to a landscape, to a people, to a smell, to a wine, has got nothing to do with the word motherland, however much others would like to make him believe the opposite; in fact, they are greatly mistaken, and more real than patriotism is his being a loyal fan of this or that sports team, the result, at least, of a voluntary choice; thus Raúl's indifference, if not his impatient displeasure with the series of questions brought up at those meetings, not for any conceptual reason but for the way they were raised.

Suddenly, absolute disenchantment, that disenchantment which is confused with physical fatigue, a consequence of all activity developed around a misunderstanding. Realizing that just as he had overestimated the party's capacity to mobilize the masses in Madrid, his comrades in Madrid took for granted that in Barcelona, unlike with events in Madrid, it was simply enough for the party to give the signal for the masses to take to the streets. How could he even try to make them understand that, like an old man waking up from his siesta, his return to reality in full feverish drowsiness, his awareness of the impossibility of going farther with that flaccid semi-erection, destined to disappear not only from the least physical exertion inherent to the sexual act but also from the simple fact of abandoning the warmth of his recliner, so, too, in practice, the revolutionary impulses of the Barcelonan masses seemed to vanish into thin air? Because, who doubts that in the same way that desires are based in reality, realities are based on desires? More than being about ideas, aren't ideologies about the exclusion of ideas? More than reasons, aren't ideological principles acts of will, if not of faith?

The final struggle, the transitional phase, and then, the pre-established harmonies of the new society, principles induced or deduced from the course of History, revealed on one occasion and since then hammered soundly into place on a daily basis. But if apart from that confidence in the future, it turns out that one's son has married a good girl who also works and also has socialist notions, and between the two of them they gather what's needed, and if it happens that the family's property out in a small country town, thanks to tourism, is now worth money, and the world generally seems to be on the right track, and one can finally retire with peace of mind, what more can you expect from life? This leads to a decline in one's clarity of mind, as lately evidenced by Leo's father, because just as a long stay in bed tends to aggravate an older person's condition, a bout of excessive happiness can end up affecting their normal thought patterns.

Like that old customer who drives a specific make of car, who has remained faithful to the company from the start, purchasing each new model, as far as his finances will allow, turning casual choice into habit, a habit based on principle, the principle into a proud personality trait, and that trait becomes a reason for solidarity with other drivers of the same brand; and now, after so many years, upon receiving some honorary reward for his loyalty, one of those distinctions established for publicity purposes, a medallion, for example, or a scale miniature of the first model ever produced, cast in some precious metal, the emotion overwhelms him as it's presented to him, the culmination of a dialectical process, in as much as it objectifies the dual relationship between existing reality and the sublimation of that reality, between magnification of the object possessed and jealous custody of the object magnified, a ceremony for the which, like on a Christmas holiday celebrated by the family, the tears that blur his vision seem to facilitate the dizzy series of images, the lights, the candles, the songs, the gifts, wife, children, little grandchildren, all those present and missing, the dead, the winters, the evenings, old age, a whole life of devotion and fidelity now almost concluded, while the effusions of which he is the object only serve to deepen his sweet sadness and his thoughts about the goodness of everything; thus had Raúl found Leo's father to be the very picture of such a man.

Wait, he said. And without further explanation spread out a street map of Moscow on his old cutting table, stepping back immediately, studying Raúl's reaction with a smile. The son-in-law of an old friend just brought it, a young Spanish-Soviet engineer who'd gone to spend Christmas with his Soviet family there. The old friend had played a very significant role during the Civil War. Now he had a very comfortable position and was retired from politics, but that didn't mean he was not among the ideological forefront as usual. Twelve years ago he put in a brand-new dining room. It's still untouched. You can be sure he's finally going to use it one of these days. And he arched his eyebrows in complicity.

He showed him the map. This is the Neva River. Red Square and the Kremlin. The Mausoleum. The Opera. Seems that up there the bakeries are real bread factories. The University, a kind of skyscraper. Gorky Park. A lot of people there really enjoy ice-skating. Children smile and eat shortbread.

And so, suddenly, the world. The New Society: its historical necessity like destiny, like the fruit of the divine will revealed (Moses, Christ, Mohammed), like, in its origin, any of History's other grand constructs, Rome, Byzantium, Islam, the Holy Roman Empire, Imperial Spain. And this, against any human effort to impede it, against any apparently insurmountable obstacle. The revolutionary character of the revolution will always triumph over the harsh and brutal repression of the brutal dictatorship. And the New Society will be installed. A happy age and happy centuries which our children will call golden and not because gold, so esteemed in our steel age, will be easily obtainable in that happy venture, but because those who will live in those times will not know the words "yours" and "mine."

The Milestone. And its consequence, or perhaps its cause: the New Man.

A vision that Leo's father, who struggled to express himself, had to represent in an eminently physical form, like some memorial project, from one of those allegorical group sculptures, like now, just in the moment of consecration, facing a panorama of kneeling inmates, heightened in their solemnity by the motionless concentric silence of the prison galleries, something, too, of allegorical monument in that precise instant of the ceremony celebrated upon the platform in the prison's Central Tower, which the elevated host in turn converted into its center.

A monument of monolithic composition, graduated in depth and height. A huge, vigorous work, a creation of power and fury, of love and piety, a titanic undertaking, of leaders emerged from the masses, here a young man with an angry face like a stone, there the arrogant torsion of an old man showing the lapidary law of the people, both standing out against a background in relief, a mass of muscles in ferocious battle, all of that dominated by the figure of the dialectical sybil that announces the imminence of a society void of class or contradiction, a synthesis of contraries, apotheosis or final judgment, which from on high, in the accurate unwavering scales of justice, appeared resolved, in an attitude of a pensive peace, by the image of the New Man, equally distant from extremists and wild youth, symbolized by the lewd adolescent naked feminine body, and of the crepuscular and decadent residues of the past, represented by an old man decrepit right down to the tip of his withered pecker; a New Man who with his serene calm, now rising above all conflict, seemed to preside as if from a throne, as a finishing touch, to the monumental group of sculptures.

Meaning: the culminating moment or qualitative leap, the moment of transubstantiation, when God descends and becomes the Sacred Form. The definitive consecration of the consolidation of the installation, once and for all, definitively consecrated following the decisive final battle, consolidation of the installation of the definitive conquest, once and for all, finally established, as a decisive culminating conquest, as a final consecration of the definitively installed culmination, as an installation of the consecration once and for all, a royal presence that commemorates the mystery of the incarnation, of the God who became man, and who was garroted.

The consecration. Indispensable requisite of communion, the very essence of the holy sacrifice of the Mass, a communion whose way was prepared the night before by the general confession that had brought to a close the cycle of spiritual exercises carried out over the preceding days. Confession or penance, a sacrament whose importance La Merche had emphasized so much in his talks, so appropriate to the expiatory weeks of Lent, the time between

Epiphany and the Passion. He spoke, one might say, not through the prison's loudspeakers, but rather though a microphone, exclusively for the inmates of the sixth wing doubtless gathered on the ground floor, from an improvised pulpit, in the abstract glow of the gallery, its symmetrical architecture almost like a Masonic temple. At four o'clock sharp, during silent time, he began testing the microphone. Hello, hello, this is La Merche speaking to you all. From his cell, even though Raúl had his ear glued to the peephole, it was hard to hear. He was talking about man's principal business, his salvation.

Today I'm going to invite you all, my dearly beloved sons, and ask that you come with me and ascend Mount Carmel, ask that you follow me without falling nor toppling from the summit. So, carefully, hand in hand. Let the youngest be a support to the oldest.

Let us consider. What is offered from here to your eyes in the nocturnal splendors, what extends from here to our feet? A city. A city built around what was once Mons Taber, the ancient acropolis, a prominent spot to which the travelers of old, like the Apostle Saint James, must have come in their anxious excitement to contemplate the city.Yes: that mountain no longer visible. Mons Taber. Neither Horeb nor Nebo nor Tabor. Simply Taber. But isn't that enough, now that it's converted into a cathedral? And before it, in the distance, as if pointing to the sea, Montjuich, the mountain of Jupiter, or the Jews, Mount Sinai of the law, an eye for an eye, a tooth for a tooth, a death for a death, God's mountain in every case. And behind us, at our back? That prominence of the Sierra Collcerola nowadays called Tibidabo. Tibidabo or the Devil's Mountain. That mountain to which the Tempter transported Christ and told him: all that you see shall be yours. This is, my dearly beloved sons, a mountain from whose peak one can see not only the whole city and its sins, but also catch sight of, farther away, and higher, Montserrat. From there, a ring of crags clustered together like the towers of a temple, Gothic spires, pipes of an organ played by angels, like figures frozen in movement, starting to sway back and forth, now to the left, now to the right, as in a dance, in a beautiful ring which forms and dissolves. A mountain carved by the angels themselves, pure geological eroticism, with its nests of phantoms and its golden cascades of broom and its clusters of vampires, reliefs and erections like elephants' trunks and scrotum and buttocks, in colossal copulation, a place where the deflowered virgins blossom anew like wild roses, a mountain born of the waters or by parthenogenesis, the same way a virgin is born of her rape, or a pre-Crusoe, a pre-Andrenio or any castaway reborn from the waters, who makes a sanctuary of their catastrophe.

What better watchtower for the soul, then, children of my womb? What better vantage point for Jaime the Conqueror when from there he planned to seize Mallorca, perfectly visible to his penetrating vision, more than to his sight? What better throne from which to contemplate his dominions, no longer the nearby Tibidabo, beneath whose sheltering bulwark extends Barcelona, but also, equally, Montsant, Montsech, and Montseny, with the white Pyrenees beyond, below that stimulating landscape of esoteric peaks and phallic protuberances? What better abode or cell, after all, than this spot which so well fosters contemplation, meditation, and inspiration? A place of retreat for conquerors and prophets and saints and founders and discoverers and navigators, a sanctuary that preserves their swords, their victories, their flags, their discoveries, Lepanto and Mallorca, the Society of Jesus and America, Montserrat, primacy of a New World, as a symbolic prefiguration of the City of God. For that reason I call on you now, my beloved children, for you all to make your journey to Damascus, to ride with me like this masculine saint who after a libertine adolescence in which he gave himself over to gambling and petty theft and to concupiscent thoughts and acts, including unnatural ones, rubbing elbows with bad company, stealing to go play soccer or billiards or go to gymnasiums or attend dances or visit bathhouses or whorehouses, later committing armed robbery with malice aforethought under cover of darkness, in a gang, attacking man or woman, becoming perverted and perverter, without any kind of faith, a sacrilegious diabolical blasphemer. And then, behind bars for his great waywardness and many vices, in the solitude of his cell, precisely in that isolated room, far from the noise of the world and its sins, isolated like a hermit, there, as a result of a divine call, there, after an internal struggle with himself, right there, overcame all his wickedness, and renounced the world, the devil, and the flesh, drunkenness and dishonesty, and recognizing his previous miseries, took up the banner of Christ, surrendering himself to him like a wife to her husband, crying out, fallen from his steed, Forgive me, oh my God, have mercy and forgiveness, crying out, yes, crying out, Augustín, Pablo, Saulo, Saúl, or Raúl, or whatever the hell your name is. The world! The true prison, as the philosopher said! And what are its shadows if not the blindness in which the wicked dwell? What chains are these that imprison them if not the strength of the devotion with which their hearts cling to the things they so inordinately love? And what hunger is this they suffer, if not the insatiable appetite they have for infinite things they cannot reach? And they, these captives, are the ones who have built the prison where you find yourself, which, as a negation of denial, is an affirmation, a place of salvation and freedom. The cell! An abode of greatness which the benign Jupiter, who calms the heavens with his lightning, surrounded by a thousand virtues, has created for you. For you are only in prison because the Lord wants your indignity to bring you understanding, so that you might know the weakness from which you suffer. And having come to know the truth, you might lead as many fellow inmates as you wish to also loathe that weakness, so that they might not be lost and instead reach paradise. It is not so much your crimes as God's mercy that brings you all here. So that in this way, those of you traveling the wrong path will be able to redeem and save yourselves. And now repeat after me: oh, Lord, do you never tire of granting me mercy? Then together we will sing *Perdón, oh Dios mío*.

Outside, to judge by the sunlight pouring in through the window, forming a slanted square on the flagstones, the morning must have been splendid. One of those mornings with a strong wind, a wind that sweeps clean the stagnant city atmosphere and dissipates the traffic noises, permitting the sun to shine brilliantly through the clean air. It gives one the desire to unbutton their overcoat and feel the already warming sun. A day that makes them forget the harsh winter weather that must naturally return, a prefiguration of the springtime that already evokes the summer. And while he remained there, motionless before the open cell door, witnessing the ceremony unfolding, everything in the street must have been movement and light. That sunny wind mussing up people's soft hair and light skirts, sudden mischievous gusts that draw from people's faces expressions like supplication or supreme pleasure, warm rushing breezes that suddenly accelerate the cycle of the seasons, the rotation of the roots, the swelling of the shoots and buds, luxurious abundance reactivated and ready to burst forth.

Like that morning when he drank a Campari in the sun with Aurora, on the terrace of a bar in the Ensanche facing the late morning sun, not far from the university. You won't leave Nuria, Aurora had told him. And Raúl: it's just that there's nothing there to break up. We've had some time together, without ever talking about the future. And that time is over. And Aurora: this is what makes things more difficult for you; having refused to talk about the future. And Raúl: I don't see why. Right now she's in England and I'm here, with you. And Aurora: and this summer? And Raúl: well, I don't know. I suppose we'll see each other. We're still friends. And after summer vacation, she'll go back to England. And Aurora: do what you like. I don't know if you're alright with me, but I am with you and, on the other hand, you don't seem to me to be alright with Nuria. I mean that, with her you should be how you really are.

She was wrong: he wasn't alright with Aurora either—what she was implicitly insinuating—and he didn't have the least intention that their relationship outlive the summer. However, throughout that summer, when he began to perceive the Adolfo-Aurora convergence, far from feeling the relief he'd believed he would experience upon seeing himself liberated from a connection he was beginning to grow weary of and which, in every case, he was planning to sever, the reality of the facts made him feel more like the victim of treachery. A treachery that, without a doubt, at least for his part, made him hasten the breakup, as much to push the events forward as to prevent his observation of this growing convergence from becoming something verging on obsession.

The road that leads to these notes written upon the smooth face of rough sheets of toilet paper. A long and winding route, sometimes seemingly blocked, as if cut off; sometimes getting lost as one gets lost on mountain paths that lead nowhere. And, nevertheless, he received the first tangible result of that vague intuition early one morning, while he was standing guard next to the magazine, east of the camp. An intuition or perhaps a recovery of forgotten intuitions, precisely of that which, when he was a little boy, in his school essays, he tried not so much to reveal as to conceal, writing not what he would have liked to write but rather what he supposed he was expected to write. In the same way that perhaps that turn of standing guard by the magazine was not the decisive one. Nor that dawn. There were other hours of guard duty before and after that, and other dawns.

His first worthwhile experiments, or at least satisfactory ones, different from how much he might have written up until then. And he poured himself into them, possessed by that demented sensation of reality experienced by an explosives expert who believes he's invented a bomb that cannot be disarmed, which will always be capable of exploding at any moment, and he consumes his nights assembling it with great care. Because like the little boy with a windup toy that gets jammed, who opts to completely destroy it, so the childish sadisms or an early passion for hunting or a later vocation as a terrorist usually end up sublimated into any specific activity, always given that in such an activity the individual finds an adequate channel to give satisfactory expression to his destructive feelings that lie at the source of everything; meanwhile, on the other hand, when the individual in question does not find the ideal channel to give vent to the sentiments engendered within him, the accumulated destructiveness then turns against him and his more immediate world, giving way to the creation, both in his personal relationships as well as those with his neighbors and coworkers, of his small personal hells.

It was indisputable, however, that the army camp had acted as a catalyst in awakening those vague notions, until then dormant or undisturbed, latent in some previous phase of his mutations. That their appearance, the last stage of his metamorphosis, had been propitiated by the prevailing atmosphere there. As a reaction to a type of life that could be characterized, in general, by mental haze and moral brutalization. A world rotating around two poles—hard work and sloth—which for being simultaneously antagonistic and complementary, tended to neutralize one another in praxis, to be synthesized in a wise formula of compromise, lauded by tradition, according to which the important thing is that everyone without exception strictly complies with their duty to cover up appearances, like a present time applied by extension to the most minimal details of the system, to the most obviously impossible demands of conciliation. A world whose most prototypical fruit was perhaps the neighbor in the infirmary who just happened to be next to him, when upon emerging from a feverish delirium—produced by the flu or some other viral condition, they never informed him of the diagnosis, if indeed the doctor in charge ever established it—he found himself occupying the second-to-last bed in the row, between Fortuny and that stingy bastard who pretended to be sicker than he was so he could stay there as long as possible, in such a sordid atmosphere, reading comic books, and having lost his light gloss of middle-class scion and future doctor or lawyer or engineer, he offered instead the aspect of an enormous and stupefied child, a halfwit somewhere between jocose and incontinent, stinking of stale piss and putrid discharges, his hands sticky, bright red cheeks like a clown, while between cyclopean yammerings he masturbated with all his might.

It was after his stay in the infirmary. Standing guard outside the magazine. Or, more precisely, that Sunday when, back from a weekend leave, it was his turn to stand the fourth watch, in the middle of the night. It was surely then. When they woke him up it was still completely dark, but the sunrise was not long in coming, the quiet clarity lightly green until the clouds began to catch light.

Upon returning from one more of so many leaves, in the end all blending into one single weekend pass. The arrival in Reus, accompanied by Nuria, after a day at the beach: *ingemisco tamquam reus*. Their last walks together, now uncomfortable, under the porticoes of the Plaza Prim, saying hello to their acquaintances who kept on showing up in those corners, awaiting the hour. The last drink shared on the patio of some bar, as a way of saying goodbye completely to civilian life. The load out, between goodbyes to girlfriends and relatives, in a dark bus driven by some fierce-looking guy, some degraded Virgil, turned into Charon's assistant oarsman, totally incapable of guiding anybody anywhere except the far shore of Acheron.

And the nocturnal sea of fog in which they disappeared little by little, making their way back up the castled crenellated mountain, along a road through that harsh, uninviting landscape, where those without a weekend pass wandered about, making the most of their last gasps of Sunday indulgence, to the strains of the "Beer Barrel Polka" that would soon be silenced by the first rounds of the night watch. And disembarking in the darkness, passing before a sentinel with a glittering bayonet, the moment of jumping down from the truck, carrying their duffel bags, and, nostalgic and sad, dispersing in silence toward their respective companies, tripping over the taut guy-ropes, pushing aside the cords and canvas flaps stiffened by the fallen rain, undressing by candlelight amid the curses and complaints from fellow soldiers awakened, as well as their own, provoked by the absence of sufficient space to open up their cots, folding his heavy army jacket carefully to avoid staining it with mud, melancholically contemplating one more date crossed out on the calendar drawn on the canvas, meaning, one less date, one day less of being here, finally stepping out to piss, now in pajamas, covered with his cloak, finding his way with a flashlight, the earth sticky, the damp tree trunks shining, until reaching the latrine and, flicking off the light, looking about drowsily, as the wet papers hissed beneath his stream of piss, staring at the opaque overcast sky, searching vainly to see the stars.

Leo had been arrested, and now he and Federico could expect the same at any time. A waiting almost like ecstasy or madness. The clear ambiguity of a flame. The isolated flame of a candle that barely reveals the vague movement of its outer edges. Casting just as much shadow as light, primarily revealing the person who carries it. That black night black as a crow's wing, what, what, that enfolds and circles overhead, standing out softly against the deep blue sky, a wing that threatens and circles overhead and disappears as if scattering as it descends and blending into the black green hillsides in its descending circles, as if becoming crag and pine and low mountain in motion, only that what, what, omen or invocation or prophecy, what, what, uncertain circles, interrogations, what. What? Destruction? Creation? Immolation? Immolation and creation and destruction.

He had seen him several times in the small knots of students on the patio of the School of Humanities, entering or exiting a lecture hall, in the bar. And he had caught his attention not only for his mordant comments but also for his easy, uninhibited attitude and presence.

He came up alongside him outside the lecture hall doors and, in the tumult of students entering, commented that they were all treated like cattle or something expressed in similar terms, in the same type of acid humor the other used. And Leo said: obviously. The last thing they're interested in is people learning how to think. Raúl sat next to him, and throughout the whole class he analyzed the two extremes of that proposition that had made such an impact on him: the generic but concrete interest that someone, that nameless they, that third person plural, had in themselves, and the fact that their interest consisted, precisely, in preventing them from thinking for themselves.

We really look like a bunch of sheep, he said as they were leaving. And Leo: what do you expect? That's what a middle-class education is designed for. Workers have at least this one advantage: they haven't been educated and they know instinctively what interests them.

They had a beer in the bar. You would need a well-trained minority, said Raúl. And Leo: if that minority isn't the vanguard for the majority, it won't do much good. And Raúl: right. A new coup. It wasn't a question of standing apart from the majority as he had, without much interest in the problem, supposed until then—perhaps for simply shifting from literary terrain to the political—but, just the opposite, of leading them.

Federico had spoken little but astutely: he mocked his family, the stupidity of pretty girls from nice families, talked about the worker's awareness of reality, much more developed than any middle-class person, and the same with their sexual vigor. He'd become friends with Leo before Raúl had, but for Raúl it was evident that he and Leo enjoyed a certain rapport that simply did not exist between Federico and Leo.

They talked for hours and hours. Long afternoons in rambling conversation, sharing their ideas, finding out how much they agreed on. The obvious impossibility of being a true intellectual these days without being a Marxist. Dialectical materialism as key to the necessary identification or synthesis of form and matter. To make freedom and commitment compatible; even better, to discover the freedom within commitment, etcetera. The revelation that he was not alone in his dissatisfaction with the world. That his dissatisfaction responded to an objective reality and that objective reality had its ideological interpretation. That that ideology was not limited to interpreting the world; that its true end was to transform it.

They headed down Las Ramblas. The contact with reality, the feeling Raúl experienced of having touched it, derived from finding, in any old bar in the Barrio Chino, some guy whose expressions—lively and ironical or bitter and destructive—and tacit allusions, and even his laugh and his movements, revealed him unequivocally, as does a slogan or a password, as the owner of a political conscience, the exegetical key for those underworld factions organized around robbery, prostitution, alcohol, and dope, things that were so distant from the family life of the Ferrer Gaminde family as to be thought practically mythical, guilty ignorance which the middle class uses to proscribe and make exotic the inevitable result of its own existence, the face on the flip side of the coin, misery and degradation always susceptible to be transformed into precious revolutionary material in a given moment—the riffraff, the splendid and explosive riffraff, following a collective realization, in whose crystallization the voices of guys like this one, converted into leaders by the very masses from which they had emerged, were destined to serve as clarions, clarions as well as fuses. Theoretical appreciations doubtless irrefutable although frequently, at the hour of realizing them, owing to young people's natural lack of experience or to a certain hasty and arbitrary judgment, also part and parcel of youth as they tend to confuse what a thing is with what one would like it to be, easily based on some mistake; take, for example, for the sake of class conscience, the remembrances of a mythomaniac or any disgraced individual who's a bit drunk and now doesn't remember very well that time when, incidentally, he had been seen to be implicated in some way in the Republican cause; that man who fought in Teruel or in the Ebro or in Belchite, and met, to name a few, Tito, Lister, the Campesino, Clement Attlee, he's not very sure, who congratulated him. Or what's nothing more than some whore's palaver, trying to sweet-talk those three young fellows who look like students so they might buy her a drink, a maneuver whose ingenuity and calculated foresight is only betrayed by her sly flirting, the sign of someone who still doesn't know how things work. And even if that were true, said Federico, she'd be within her rights.

On the other hand, Adolfo did not make a positive impression on Leo, much less on Federico whose reservations about Adolfo were personal while, in Leo's case, it was more a question of ideological motivations. Raúl had started getting to know him early in the semester and since then they'd gotten together occasionally and Adolfo chatted about Baudelaire, and Sartre, and the American novel. But Leo's arguments—Who in our society is free without money? And if you don't write for the people, isn't that just being complicit with the goals of the reactionary forces?—seemed to interest him insofar as they served to put a dent in his sarcasm, biting, almost disdainful, as if Leo was especially irritated by Adolfo's apparently critical and hedonistic position. Because, contrary to that petit bourgeois rudeness, particularly rooted in Catalonia, those tacky jokes and gags told for courtesy's sake, to make the other person feel comfortable, at ease, to foster a climate of cordiality and understanding, Adolfo's polite but reserved attitude seemed rather to point to a climate of separation and even antipathy, his secret formula, perhaps, for the aura of respect and prestige that seemed to automatically surround both his person as well as his opinions and even his literary projects, while the facts failed to demonstrate the contrary.

A posture that verged on punctilious courtesy, a conciliatory character which certain people display the day after getting so drunk that they remember almost nothing of the night before. But which, from Leo's point of view, might well be interpreted in classist terms.

Nuria Rivas's case was different. She got along well with people and was accepted without reticence. What happened is that, for reasons difficult to pinpoint and in spite of her frame of mind that saw all her own political, religious, economic, social, and sexual theories as valid, or perhaps precisely for that very reason, she was not taken very seriously. At least not on her own, not apart from Raúl.

And Raúl? How could he have not discovered before, against all class conditioning, such a total conception of the world? How could he have managed without knowing it? An image of everything so real that the deeper he delved into it the greater was the feeling that he was only discovering traces, revealing to himself what he had always known deep down inside, in short, to be reading reality itself transcribed into words. An obvious consequence: ask to join the party, a party which, however clear its historical role, its actual practical functions remained unknown, an organization of mysterious and exciting character both for its members' double personalities as well as the subterranean ubiquity of its presence.

A decision that, apart from representing the logical consequence of his feelings of disgust and hostility regarding the state of the world, liberated him from all objective responsibility in relation to the true victims of the present society, workers and farmers, from the moment in which he began to form part of its political vanguard, the communist party. And, at the same time, it freed him from all the moral principles of the world in which he'd been raised that he could not attack nor, in fact, had ever attacked except on the outside. And from all the hateful schemes for resolving life's personal situations that the middle class offers its children—college education, marriage, career, blind goals, if not complicit and aberrant ones, in the face of a task like the one he'd set himself, facing the enterprise in whose development he was going to take part: the violent transformation of the world.

That feeling of coming into contact with a hidden power like the one that can be experienced in a session of spiritualism, when the medium begins to speak. There was no need for Leo to tell him he was that man. He walked ahead of them, uphill, along a deserted path in Park Güell, slowly, reading the newspaper; no doubt he'd already been there a while, surveying the terrain. And as they caught up to him he said, Hello, Daniel, without waiting, as Raúl expected—doubtless conditioned by middle-class formalities—for Leo to make any introductions. And for anyone who might have seen them from a distance, Escala seemed to be saying simply, Hey, fellas, what are you two doing here?

And the first results of his activities, the first protests at the university, the first police charges into the crowd that they watched rubbing their eyes, so to speak, more than their hands, almost incredulous that everything they were seeing was the fruit of their work to foment agitation which they had developed according to a correct interpretation of the party's political line.

The accolade: represent the Communist Party in a meeting with the representative from the Socialist Party of Barcelona. The meeting was proposed by the socialists, in order to establish a modus operandi, as his contact said, with an eye toward a boycott of public transit that was being prepared and, eventually, a general strike.

The contact took place in a *chocolatería*. The socialist was there, having hot chocolate topped with fresh whipped cream and ensaimadas for breakfast. A middle-aged fellow, on the mature side. He seemed surprised at Raúl's youth and appearance until—it showed in his eyes—he matched him with the right stereotype: the typical little communist rich boy. This discovery must have contributed to him regaining his self-confidence.

To the point, he said: the waiter can be trusted. But he started to ramble. He talked about the Civil War, about the French resistance, about alcohol and women, all that joined to fervent expressions about worker solidarity. He knew the communists well, he said. But he wasn't willing to be some Kerenski; that's why, during the war, he never let go of his pistol, not even when he went to sleep.

Maybe back then he didn't have such a paunch. And one thing that was certain: he wasn't carrying a pistol these days. And that stuff about the shock troops, his young socialist commandoes he spoke of mobilizing, was pure fantasy. And the character that he pretended to give to the interview, like that of gangsters dividing up the city's sectors between themselves, lacked all verisimilitude, despite the chocolatería's certain ambience—no doubt selected in order to give the impression that everything had been calculated with the goal of not arousing suspicions—despite that clientele of voracious old ladies and flabby, delighted, milk-fattened, whispering little girls. On the wall, a photo mural of a Pyrenean panorama formed of whipped cream and marmalade, the living stamp of a Catalonia as sweet-toothed and chaste as the very customers in the chocolatería, like the idyllic and socially-democratic Europe that dreaming windbag was blathering on about.

Because, like Spain, Europe also feared the true revolution. And in fact, for them, the norms of clandestine life, the precautions they took in Barcelona with respect to their meetings, continued to be the rule in Paris. Paris, that city that came to be for him so familiar that, each time he found himself walking through the Gare d'Austerlitz, he had the impression of returning home after a trip, an impression that leads one to consider as parenthetical everything that happened since their departure. And nevertheless, dissipating the initial mistake required his time. Because, as on the Costa Brava, for example, the natives, the people from the towns, also took years even to figure out that the first tourists to come to their beaches were not necessarily any powerful or important people, unlike what they might have assumed from a first glance, but rather, frequently, storekeepers, and even laborers, thus Raúl, in his first trips north, tended to see in all of France the complicity of a leftist militant. A mistake similar to the one he made with Obregón after several meetings, when he realized that the peaceful alternative, renunciation of an armed struggle, according to the party's political line, was not responding so much to a stratagem as to a real imposition of the circumstances.

Paris, friends male and female. And the freedom of speaking out loud on the terraces of the bars along the Boulevard Saint-Germain. And of buying the books he desired in Le Globe. Almost an obligation, like attending a certain number of sessions at the cinemathèque, after the Pantheon, completely at ease between that public of young people who looked unambiguously leftist, with a touch of the guerrilla and at the same time of the intellectual, too, from his presence and even the way he treated his female friends. To see a film by Eisenstein was like attending a religious ceremony. Eisenstein and Soviet cinema in general. Thus, that film they watched in a cinema near the Boulevard Montmartre, a film set during the war and while he's fighting at the front she's cheating on him back home, and when she learns that he's died, she goes to the station and hands out his flowers to all the returning soldiers, like a socialist Ophelia only saved from madness by joining the masses. And as the lights came up afterward he had to blink to clear his vision and he had to clear his throat and think about something else and make a show of lighting a cigarette, then pretend that the smoke was getting in his eyes, and walk out of the cinema saying the film wasn't too bad, without further commentary, without insisting unnecessarily, the identity of the situations was already eloquent enough, the struggle and its rupture, the problem of soldiers' wives being unfaithful, the sacrifice, the inexorability of everything.

Sessions of lovemaking carried out in sordid hotels, with crooked parquet floors, upon swaybacked beds, with stained coverlets and washed-out curtains, shoving aside the bolster pillow that kept rolling onto them, sweating and naked, in the early morning, just back from Place de la Contrescarpe or from some very interesting invasion of Montparnasse, he and she, after leaving the others absorbed in abstract discussions. The excitement of the foreplay: exploring each other, pressing, delicately testing each other out, undressing with delicate feline nicety, perfect white tits, the dark thatch of her sex, the bare cheeks of her ass. Even with Nuria it was better in Paris than in Barcelona, perhaps because of its quality of being a passing encounter, because Raúl knew that afterward they would each go their own way. The same reason, surely, that it was good for them in Rosas, when he did his second-lieutenant training in Figueres and, taking advantage of any long weekend, she came down from England and he sorted out his guard duties and waited for her at the station and they went to Rosas. It was in the springtime and, when sunny, it was already nice to swim.

Not like at first, of course, like the first times, when everything seemed to come together and harmonize so that even his relations with Nuria went marching right along perfectly and the general exaltation that possessed them was reflected equally in the erotic terrain. That night, for example, when they'd drunk quite a lot and Adolfo was insisting that they go out to see *Yerma*, and Nuria gave Raúl a blowjob during the first act, under the shelter of his overcoat folded over her head.

Like that person who after a whole night of lovemaking and, especially if it's been well done, and far from being sated with it, quite the contrary, rather stimulated, sleeplessly contemplates the city from atop a mountain and the very splendor of the morning seems only to heighten his cravings for more activity, his impatience to accelerate the triumph of the revolution, to finally abandon for good his paltry legal studies and give himself over entirely to the work of contributing to the formation—beyond simple theories, and now in the area of praxis—of a true popular army of liberation, and when the moment comes, have a good laugh at the terror-stricken stupor of the middle class, lawyers, financiers, property agents, notaries, registrars, businessmen, speculators, people who in their closed-minded routines had believed themselves busy with important things and who, suddenly, saw the earth crack, gaping wide beneath their feet, the crust of a world they had taken to be real and which was suddenly revealed to be a mere game of hypocritical appearances; thus did Raúl, facing a similar panorama of synchronous harmonizations and answers, feel at that time. Thus: like a wandering horseman or a sailor or a founder or a prophet, with that characteristic willpower of transcending oneself, of transforming oneself by transforming, only comparable to the demented lucidity with which a scientist proposes to himself to destroy the world, telling his conscience that the madness lies not within himself but within the world around him.

And just as Don Juan never feels remorse or guilt for seducing women, nor does he care about what luck might befall his victims because, like the terrorist or the thief, he's not unaware of his inevitable final damnation, so Raúl felt equally predestined to play out the role that had been imposed upon him to its final consequences. Predestined, almost like a chosen one, like that being born from the waters or from the slime or from the fruit of a tree or from the copulation of archangels or gods or, like the inverse of what happens in Ovid, from the metamorphosis of a cactus or a hawthorn tree into a boy. And then, after an obscure childhood, now grown into a man, one fine day he conceives—or it's revealed to him—a certain idea of the world, of life, of himself, a future that he designs and fills with images like one who contemplates a western sky or the heavens at dawn, the cumulus clouds shaped like castled, crenellated cities, with temples and great walls and skyscrapers reflected in the celestial seas.

What importance could all the rest hold? Everything was easier from this perspective of surrender and letting go. Including financial problems. Living a hand-to-mouth existence, without falling into a calculating, middle-class mindset. Enough to get by on, and that's all. How? By doing any old thing at all, working at whatever was available, doing enough, to keep going. The translations he wrote with Leo, for example; badly paid, of course. So what? It was no use complaining about this, this wasn't, precisely, the kind of exploitation he was worried about. Nor did they rack their brains to find just the right shade of meaning if it took them long to do it. The money was enough to help them get around and that was what mattered. And translating didn't have that childish or frivolous character common to the only solutions Raúl had found so far, the result of systematically scouring the want ads in *La Vanguardia*, how to earn money easily in his free time, etcetera, growing mushrooms, lead soldiers, taxidermy, car insurance. Or buying at a real bargain price some of the various get-rich-quick formulas sold by that crazy old man in El Clot to whomever wanted to buy them, living in a sad kitchen that smelled like gasoline and rancid bacon, while some kind of a witch gutted and sliced blue fish—barat or jureles, surely.

There were minor problems. How he felt uncomfortable with Nuria, for example. Not alone with her, but when in the presence of their friends she showed her undisguisable middle class touches, her ideological incoherence. An annoying lack of tact similar to that of the boy who, intuiting his parents' suspicion that he's running with a bad crowd, dares at last, in order to deny it as much as possible, to bring a friend home and with anxious embarrassment, incapable of reacting, becomes a witness to how his friend, with a surprising lack of awareness for situations, perhaps a result of his juvenile boasting, only confirms all the family's worst fears, for the which, quiet and watchful, their expressions and even their mere disposition are nothing but conclusive proofs of how their young offspring is addicted to wicked practices.

Problems perhaps subjective, perhaps imaginary. But just as in the geophysical world, the straight line and the flat surface are only an illusion of the senses, an excessively close and immediate appreciation of what in reality is curved and spherical. In the same way, it would be equally superficial to explain Raúl's amorous behavior, his short-lived enthusiasms, his sudden tendency at distancing if not abandoning entirely—excluding on principle all hypotheses that such behavior might seem to rule out by itself an exaggerated misogynistic aversion, for example, or a predominant homosexual component—in light of the kind of women with whom he'd had relationships, without then wondering why precisely he'd had relations with such women; or arguing that the important thing for Raúl was to safeguard his freedom, without then wondering what kind of liberty it was that made him dismiss out of hand any possibility of voluntarily continuing the relationship; or blame it on his belief, so often expressed, that there is no love which does not end, and the ends are rarely happy, without finally wondering how it could turn out otherwise when he was the first to set about hastening that end.

In fact, the idea of marriage had always disgusted him. Even more: the verb itself, *casarse*—to get married; literally, to build a house together—filled him with a sensation like shame. The same as when as a boy, without yet knowing the precise amount of sexual attraction implied by certain words, he was irritated by Felipe's jokes, about whether or not he had a girlfriend, *la niña rubita*—the little blonde girl—a girl whom he passed every morning on the way to school. And the adults talked about engagements and weddings. It seems he's proposed to her, he heard Aunt Paquita say.

No longer the uncertain and embarrassing question: do you want to marry me? Simply: I love you. Words that he could never bring himself to pronounce.

In every case, just like in a station, seated next to a little window, the soft arrival of a train on the adjacent track can produce the impression that we are the ones starting to pull out of the station, thus, in these moments it was already difficult to see clearly if Raúl's amorous relationships were dominated by a certain fatality or if it was he, with his behavior, who determined the fatal character of those relationships. Because just as the young man from a family fallen on hard times is always a potential revolutionary, not only for the desire to see his particular domestic experience of progressive reduction and progressive straits repeated, in all the families belonging to his social class, meaning, from rancor and resentment, but also from the necessity of finding an explanation or justification of objective value and general application for the cyclical phenomenon of the splendor and decadence of human things, so Raúl seemed predisposed toward a certain type of woman or, at least, to a certain type of relationship with women. But in the same way that years must pass in order for the seducer of a middle-aged married woman to come to understand that the key to adultery does not reside within himself, in his virile attributes and in his skill at fornicating, nor in a supposed inferiority of the husband who gives rise to a coherent rationale of his own triumph, but in her and only in her, in the one presumedly seduced, in the dank well of conjugal life, in her desire to redress, in her anxieties of seeing reflected in another the unsatisfied love for herself, so that nearly the least thing is the erotic entrapment of that other, given that for her the outcome of the affair, especially if it's a short one, must be necessarily happy; so it was inevitable that Raúl should have lived so long without thinking of any question relating to the nature of love.

Neither conjectures nor interrogations: concrete plans, directed toward resolving the problem in the least traumatic way possible. According to what was possible, to the degree in which, in a young man, intuitions at once clear and imprecise are confusedly intermixed with feelings and ideas. To be with Nuria one more time and then let her fly away; let things calm down bit by bit and they could simply remain good friends. Thence the annoyance that she, as if she sensed it coming, asked him so often if he loved her. Especially when the situation began to stretch out, without any end in sight, and Raúl discovered that in front of others she called him my boyfriend and that, as a girlfriend, she hung on his arm on days when he had a leave from the camp, no sooner did she get off the bus in La Plaza de Prim in Reus, evidently proud—although she wouldn't admit it, full of that atavistic pride women usually feel when in the company of a man in uniform—of having a boyfriend of her own. Your girlfriend and mine came on the same train, Ferracollons told him.

And then, the abortion. The complication that resulted from all that, the necessity of continuing with her still once more. And the relief, the prospects for a definitive solution later supposed by her idea of leaving to study in England, who knows if with the hope—mistaken—that a temporary separation would favorably influence the course of her relationship with Raúl.

The normal thing, in principle, was that everything would turn out like in those language-learning methods, one of those courses where, through the lessons, one develops a simple theme, which serves to introduce the student to both the knowledge of the language as well as the customs and way of life of the country in question. He or she arrives. It's their first visit, but some family friends of their parents are already waiting in the station and will host them during their stay in the country. So, what better way of getting to know the country than through its people?

Sometimes, the person visiting arrives accompanied by their parents and, if it happens to be a young woman, the local couple generally has a son, also young; and vice-versa. The couple is usually grumpy, stingy, easily fatigued. The women, more active and irritating, show a profound sexual frustration. And, in any case, the final lessons usually coincide with the young couple getting engaged. Except that, in reality, things don't have to turn out like they do in the language course lessons. The girl's father, for example, can turn out to be a fearful sodomite who buggers his young foreign guest. Or the driver of the car who picks up our young friend as she walks along the road, a highway killer. And the loving couple who invite her to spend a weekend in the country, a couple of sadists who submit her, in the impunity of the cellar, to every kind of torture, outrage, and cruelty from the one hundred nights. So that perhaps the lesser evil and the fastest way of learning the language is for Nuria, of her own free will, to go to bed with anyone, and wind up forgetting, with time and distance, everything before that. Because, what better way of getting to know the people from a different country than by copulating with them?

What else could happen when something similar had already occurred, when the time and distance that separated them then were much less? With Adolfo, while Raúl was in the army camp. We were really drunk, Pipo. We'd gone out around there and I don't even know how it happened. What I can assure you is that it was a complete disaster.

She told him that story years later, during one of their trysts in Paris. The final day, in the bar at the Gare d'Austerlitz. One of those trips he made in a second-class couchette, carrying a suitcase with a false bottom. And, once over the border, in the morning, he thought that, coming from a woman with whom he had nothing in common, it was not very important. From the window, like always, the sharp young women from Montseny announced that the station at Llinás was coming up, his station, so close to Vallfosca, the pines and the vineyards, the familiar landscapes, ancient lands, of eroded contours. Some peaks that, in fact, separated his childhood from his earliest infancy.

Aunt Margarita. His mother's younger sister. She died shortly after the war. A faceless figure, in a bathrobe, eating breakfast on the verandah at Vallfosca, surely during one of those days she must have spent with them in summertime. A face he could reconstruct with the help of the few surviving photographs of her. And the room she stayed in, that room he'd entered suddenly, without knocking, surprising her as she was dressing, her breasts naked, and she told him to come in and shut the door. A room where there had once been a sink which, for some reason, was later removed. But the shoddily patched opening to the drain remained visible, a small mouth with a tiny hole plugged up with cement.

He checked out all the whorehouses, repeatedly, the same way that the lone terrorist studies the chosen target ahead of time, searching for the best spot to plant the bomb. In the end he found himself in a bed, gripped and grasping, in the act, attentive to what he was doing, like in a circle of children where any mistake in the game meant you were disqualified. Or like obeying the instructions of a gym teacher who, after warning us that he is older and stronger than us, might however, while we were performing the rhythms and movements of the exercise to the letter, add that we've got nothing to worry about. Or like that person who dreams repeatedly of being a galley slave only to be awakened by the crack of the whip next to his ear.

Only one single inhibition: dancing. Because of its inherently competitive element? Because of his repugnance for forming part of a spectacle in which, for the mere fact of knowing himself observed by those not dancing, he was going to find himself suffering by comparison to those who know how to dance and who enjoy it? A rejection, at any rate, of an operative terrain—erotically marginal—as an appropriated terrain, insofar as being synthetic and symbolic, to settle questions that were not at all symbolic or synthetic. In short, to turn the fact of not knowing how to dance into something positive, similar to that runner who leads the race but overcome by his fear of seeing himself passed up on the homestretch pretends to stumble and fall. It would be, by contrast, rash to trace that inhibition, at least wholly, back to the time when he liked Celia, for example; to the fact of seeing her dance, knowing that, given their difference in age, she could not seriously believe that a boy would dare to ask her to dance.

They were below the plane trees in the plaza, sitting along the benches, chatting, and their bicycles were resting against a wall, next to the fountain. The plaza regulars, the old men, as if displaced, had all gathered together on only two or three of the benches, and even in front of the church, sitting on the steps. They were suddenly interrupted by a little pack of excited dogs, tails quivering, ears stiff and flattened, snouts wrinkled, eyes glittering and teeth shining, running in a circle, growling and whining, all grouping up, yelping wildly, and in the middle of their circle, a bitch called Bullseye, being mounted and humped at a weird angle by an ugly mutt with big ears, both dogs looking cowed in that tense climate of barely contained violence. What a picture, said one of the old men. And one of the girls asked the typical question about why didn't they separate them. And they all pretended they hadn't heard her, obstinately talking away. An old woman stuck her head out of a doorway and faces—crafty, sullen, and lascivious—began to appear in the windows and a bucketful of water came pouring down, which, more than dispersing the pack, scattered it toward the church, leaving one poor long-haired dog a tangled mess. The old men laughed, and the people in the doorways, and from window to window. And one of the boys said: but isn't she your dog? No, said Felipe. And someone said, these dogs. And then Celia seemed to decide to stop trying to hold back her laughter, her self-absorbed expression melting all at once, a contagious laugh, which spread with the help of someone's saucy comment about how those two dogs should go get a room somewhere. And at last, the fearsome observation: look how much Lalo is blushing.

They organized an outing to the cold spring called Font Freda, a hike of a little over two hours. They packed a knapsack and took turns carrying it. They and their cousins headed out from Vallfosca and the others from the town and they met up halfway there. They talked about the cinema, the films that were already being announced for the next season. Someone commented with a severe good sense inappropriate for his age, an echo no doubt of some judgment heard at home, that they were already starting to get sick of these psychological movies where it always turns out, in the end, that what is going on is that, unconsciously, the boy is in love with his mother and although he despises his father deep down he really loves him and who knows what other stories. The conversation had that carefree tone one hears from repressed people talking about sex, as if it was something amusing and unimportant, surreal, endured, something no one could take more seriously than a joke; as if in their sweaty vigils the presence of sex were for them nothing more than some grasping octopus from which there is no escape. Had Celia noticed that Raúl hadn't taken his eyes off her for a single moment? Her laugh, her ironic look, her movements not quite so provocative as already lascivious.

An unusual case, to be sure, given the girls in those years. Because in the way that a certain anxiety in the eyes reveals a nymphomaniac even before discovering, in bed, her prolapsed flesh, her bruised vulva, her distended, misused, labia, so, in a similar way, even in her unmistakable external appearance—the good girl of those times, unlike now—she was ostensibly distinct from any other young woman of her age but of a different social level or condition.

The pretty little rich girl of those times, her modesty, her chronic display of an essentially moral upbringing, a natural product of that Barcelona middle class of the postwar era, installed in her own city as if on summer vacation, as a way of prolonging, or better yet, making last forever, the truncated summer of

'36. Those youthful times of the postwar era, the posh snobs of the forties, maintained, thanks to the historical circumstances themselves, in absolute isolation from the surrounding world, the past close and remote, and the future possible, and what's worse: the present time of the adult world. An optimal situation for selfishness: once the established moral foundations were firmly inculcated, the last and most necessary principle might be assimilated by themselves without any unnecessary explanations: maintain one's own immorality in completely enclosed compartments, like any other business venture, like some additional aspect of professional life, something that occurs outside the home, away from family, social life, and summer vacations, those months of peaceful leisure in which the people of his class debut the fresh new white clothes in their wardrobe, white as innocence itself, a pleasing contrast to the dark tonalities of the poor peasants garbed in black, gray, and blue who hid crouched down in their vineyards like redskins, with the exclusive goal, perhaps, of spotting one distracted passerby reaching out to taste their grapes, and then falling on them in a rage, howling atrocious blasphemies, wrinkled, toothless, furtive, deformed, rapacious, looking especially rancorous when their wagons were overtaken by young summer vacationers on bicycles. And those more familiar with the life of the summer colony were no less hostile than the workers from the city, those ragged beings one glimpsed while crossing the fields of Barcelona or, in the residential neighborhoods, around the buildings under construction, their faces inconceivably brutish and ugly, almost as if alienated or mentally deficient, with their habit of eating like savages around some embers, of singing, of getting grossly drunk, of sleeping obscene siestas lying right on the sidewalk, and then, gregariously, with their lunch boxes, with their old, faded, foul-smelling clothes, clumsy, talkative, gesticulating, simian, returning to their fields, where everything is ugliness and degraded cohabitation.

The rabble that killed, set fire, looted. Why so much sacrilege? They were riding to church in the horse-drawn cart and Polit was driving, the reins soft in his hands. And Polit, as if feeling obliged to justify watching some church burn, said that, in one of these, as he approached to see what was happening, he came upon a crucifix thrown to the ground, and as it pained him to see it that way, thrown away like a piece of junk, he preferred to push it into the bonfire. Raúl stationed himself carefully, standing against a column from which he could observe Celia with equal amounts of discretion and privilege.

When did he start to lose interest in horseback riding, sword fighting, lancing shrubs and brambles, creeping and crawling along with his compressed air rifle? When did the rocks cease to be high crags above defiles perfect for ambushes, and the woods jungles teeming with tigers, forests with hidden natives in the underbrush? When did he begin to appreciate not only Celia's attractiveness, but also that of the landscape, that complex knot of hills, and the vineyards, the lines of poplar trees stretching away into the distance, the clean tidy architecture of the planted stands of pine trees?

One morning when the weather was bad, at Easter. And he was on the verandah playing records, a little tired of having to crank the gramophone, and he was going to listen to the *Jupiter Symphony* when he felt, first, as if he had already experienced it, the sensation of watching the cloudy roiling sky from a window, and then, that sensation of feeling himself a part of what he was watching, of the quiet skies in motion and the mountain turned gray and, at the same time, of something distant and clear, with a resonance that, like that word we feel on the tip of our tongue but which doesn't come out, becomes difficult to locate. And Papa asked what are you thinking about, Lalo, and he said, I think I'm going to go for a walk before lunch, and he walked among the oak trees with peaceful euphoria, without feeling like playing ambushes or anything, eluding the thought that school would start again in nine days.

Or perhaps before, the first time when, arriving in Vallfosca, he became conscious of the house's peculiar smell, the front hallway, the verandah, the sitting room, his bedroom, rooms in which, just by entering, unchanged since then and now when he would drop by there with his friends, he was assaulted by such an accumulation of simultaneous sensations. That smell old houses have, impossible to get rid of even when renovating and repainting them from top to bottom, only managing in the end to add one more layer to that well of lives upon lives, formed by the passing of the generations, the deterioration and the misfortune.

The house, surrounding the garden like in a cloister. A garden of peaceful thickets, softly, subtly shadowed at dusk. Then, the nocturnal emptiness, the owls, the frogs croaking, the sound of the water falling into the cisterns, much more clearly than during the day. Uncle Gregorio said that there would be a shower of shooting stars that night, and after dinner they all went out to the gazebo. And the stars rained down and they were pointing them out to each other with great excitement, each one of those shooting stars falling in silence. Look at this constellation, Raúl, said Uncle Gregorio. It's the Dragon. The hardest one.

In September the nights were already too chilly and the sky was not so clear. And from the garden one sensed the soft steps of the foxes and the snuffling of the wild boars and the cunning badgers and nearby, like a ghost, the shriek of the tawny owl.

He liked to go for walks on hot mornings, without clouds, with sunflowers in the sky. He followed the muddy paths along the creek, oozing, flowing with freshness, between the thin bamboo stalks enclosing the creek bed on both sides, along the sandy wheel tracks, continuously eroding, that centered the darkened trail of soft prints and the warm horse droppings. And with his ears alert, his air rifle ready, he penetrated the forest, opening a path between the ferns, through the gloomy mottled shade. Or maybe along the streams, poplars straight and crisp in the green clarity, reflected in the quiet, leaf-strewn water. And at midday, he went out to the parched stubble field, the sky now like zinc, colorless, hot, like a seamlessly welded iron plate above our bodies. And then, the drowsiness and heat of the afternoons, when, after lunch, the house went silent and, during the siesta, it was just right for a languid session of masturbation.

The beginning of vacations: three full months awaiting. June, with its soft greens and the warm trill of the blackbirds, trembling in the thickets, spinning through the brambles. And the storms. You could feel rain in the tense quietude of the air and the tenseness of the birds between the bristling leaves; and that horizon of moving clouds that sounded, perhaps, like a distant sea or a seashell pressed against your ear.

In general they were short rainstorms, devious fizzing cloudbursts, soon dispersed by the warm wind, by gashes of jubilant blue, by the rainbow arcing over the fruit trees full to bursting and clean in the early evening, with the last cries of the swallows and the first calls of the night birds.

Before school let out he already felt the excitement over the preparations for the trip—better yet, the expedition—to Vallfosca. Steamer trunks, provisions, clothes, suitcases, his own suitcase, his books, his weapons, everything indispensable, everything, basically, that he was going to use during the next three months. And finally, closing tight the Persian blinds and shutters and turning off the gas and water mains, by the front door and the gate, everything now loaded into the taxi, getting in and saying goodbye, not without a touch of sadness, to the trees, to the houses, the ice cream vendor who didn't even see them go by, to everything that would remain the same during his absence, reflections made while they crossed through the city riding along its most central streets, the drive to the station, where he would take the Orient Express, starting out on a long route through Central Europe, the Balkans, Asia Minor, Turkey; days and nights and more days on the train, Persia, Afghanistan and, finally, India, where there awaited him a cavalry detachment, native lancers that, among rough landscapes, were my body guards and escorted me to my unit, of which I had to take command.

One of the first things he did was to go over to Mallolet's house and let them know he'd returned. A large old country house with warm white puppies smelling of pee, with round swollen bellies, suckling away, and raucous ducks which, in a wedge formation, cut a path of clear water through the green scum atop the pond, and haylofts with wasps' nests under the roof tiles, and a horse with patient eyes in the paddock. And that dense smell of freshly-watered garden, tomatoes, peppers, eggplants, watermelons, melons, zucchini.

A note about Polit. Why did he have that premonitory intuition when they told him: Polit got stung by a scorpion just above the heart when he was picking up a hay bale? And another question: why did they call Polit "El Polit" when his name was really Josep?

Easter meant that there remained only one trimester of school. And in Vallfosca it was barely noticeable that it was Easter, apart from the Sacred Heart from the chapel that Aunt Paquita shrouded in purple, as one shrouds or covers the body of a garroted man. Raúl came back from religious services and at home said that when it came to visiting monuments he preferred to do it alone, by bicycle, through the towns of the region. There were many people from the summer colony and although the holy days came earlier, that in itself was already a harbinger of summer. April's tendernesses, marvelous exploding yellows, resurgent waters, tones, cascades of softness opening to the sun. The pathways alongside the stream appeared fluted with long reflections. He contemplated from above the poplars' serpentine undulation, the bushy tangle of flowering boughs like a pink mist. When the blackbirds stopped singing he could hear the grass breathe.

It wasn't simply that the geography and history lent him, like the cinema, creative material for his games. In his fascination with geography and history he had to seek deeper motivations until they surrendered themselves to him like absolute and unappealable realities, places that existed although he would never come to know them, totally independent from the course of his life, events unmodifiable for having already occurred, facts perhaps incredible but true and equally autonomous and unappealable, susceptible, with their mythical and miraculous elements, with their arbitrariness and incoherencies, with their essential irrevocable tragedy, of unleashing, in the spirit of the student with imaginative or neurotic predispositions, the most radical questions.

Perhaps it was the counterpart to his religious coldness. That irreligiousness appropriate to a child whose father possessed none of the typical fatherly attributes, a man defeated, his illness real or imaginary, more needful of help than capable of lending it. Surely, at times, in the school chapel, touched by a certain exultant note on the harmonium or by the oblique colorations of the stained-glass windows, he fell prey to trembling and terror, and for an instant ineffable heavens opened beneath his feet, around his irredeemably perverse reality, destined for damnation. The devil's reality, so far superior to that of the gods.

Short-lived spasms but sufficient ones, alright. Like upon returning home, when in the gloom of the hallway he practiced the exciting game of making himself panic by pulling strange faces in front of the mirror, rather more terrifying than a coconut, for example, with thick bristling hairs all around the eyes.

But something persisted, there was some constant in those crazy fits. The grief with which they marked him, as if exposing him to public compassion, for example, when his grandmother died. The shame, the rage, and the rancor toward all those watching him, their faces somewhere between intimidated and withdrawn, at school and on the street, with his everyday clothes frighteningly dyed black, humiliatingly calling attention to him, no less conspicuous than the macabre stench of the dye. Or the first day of school, when he left home accompanied by his grandmother, his valise strapped to his shoulders like a backpack, and his fountain pens rattling inside, and the folds of his school smock sticking out.

Coming out of the cinema, on Thursdays or Sundays, he was grateful for the cover of darkness, shocked as he was by the immoral baseness that every adolescent usually discovers in themself with much greater clarity at the movies than in church, as they contrast the chaste physical contact and elevated sentiments the protagonists show in their amorous encounters with the dark indecency of their own thoughts and desires.

If it was some detective thriller, afterward he pretended to be a gangster or spy, hiding in the doorways to make sure he wasn't being followed. And Manolo signaled to him from across the street, furtively. Or together they would shadow any suspicious-looking character, perhaps a double agent.

Calle Mayor de Sarriá, the big street that served as his Ramblas in those days, ground zero for all the children in the surrounding residential neighborhoods: Bonanova, Tres Torres, Pedralbes. Axis of that nucleus of narrow russet lanes, complicated cross streets, more like a country town than an urban neighborhood, and on the outskirts quiet convents and ricocheting sparrows, garden walls overgrown with languid vines, ivy and wisteria and Virginia creeper, thick with pines, plane trees, Peruvian pepper trees, and palms, nineteenth-century touches in their townhouses and flowering almonds in their gardens.

The center of the neighborhood almost as much like a country town as always, thanks, no doubt, to the very narrowness of its streets, still redolent of bakeries, grocery stores, and dark doorways. The dairy store or the candy shop, where he bought popsicles, now closed, with lace curtains covering the plate glass windows, the door still painted the same blue, but without the sign above the lintel. Would that bell still tinkle if he walked in? And the fabric shop where his grandmother, while selecting buttons, bought him a little tin windup car that would rattle off a short distance, laboriously, like a rickety jalopy. And the cinema, the films now advertised on printed posters, not on a chalkboard; during the intermission they gathered at the bar to drink whiskey or rum depending on whether the movie was a gangster or cowboy picture, or one about pirates. And the magazine shop where he bought comic books and anise cigarettes. The shop lady, the previous owner's daughter, was sitting under the dusty light bulb without a shade, exactly in the same spot and in the same wicker chair her mother used to occupy. Now she, too, had white hair and as she informed him that they no longer made anise cigarettes, she looked at him over the top of her glasses, just as her mother used to do, without recognizing him. That was then. Nowadays people go to the tobacco shop and buy real cigarettes.

He went back walking along the newly laid-out streets, a grid of large blocks spreading over the fields and gardens that once marked Sarriá as a separate town, back when he used to say he was going downtown, saying I'm going to Barcelona. New buildings whose implacable geometry rose up like a fortress wall above the patchwork of old roofs, tall mercury streetlights recently switched on instead of the old gas lamps converted to electricity, heavy traffic and lively sidewalks, bars with terraces and endless glittering shop windows.

Grandmother and Manolo and Emilio and Mallolet. But he got used to playing alone. Better. He preferred it. That way there was no interference and everything turned out the way it was supposed to turn out. Playing with others was like going to see a movie that everyone had already been talking about at school and which, upon seeing it, proves disappointing; the things we heard about happen but not the way we'd imagined them. And in the way that a spy or a secret agent moves in closer, he infiltrated the world of adults. That's why, when Papa took him visiting and there were also children in the house, he tended to hang around the adults until he was inevitably shooed away. Raúl, would you please go and play with the other kids?

It was as if then he already intuited the whole process, the moment when a boy, patiently shaped by a positive upbringing, appreciates for the first time the substantial sense of some key words when he thinks about getting married and having children, and begins to see himself within a historical perspective, and he begins to be seduced by the idea of someday telling his own kids how he got to climb aboard the steam locomotive or how with only a hundred pesetas they did so many different things, and furthermore the idea that someday when his kids have kids of their own they tell them all about him, and that they would even enjoy selecting their own personal future anecdotes and character traits—he was such a character!—by which he might be characterized, and so, instead of feeling blinded by his vision of the sordid circles of this limited but infinite world, as if complying until the end with that first appropriation of the adult world, now coming full circle, everyone now bald and hairless, heads, bellies, and buttocks, to end up talking about Peter Pan, about when he was a boy, about his mischief, about the nostalgia he felt for his memories of that time.

Nothing more hateful, nothing more loathsome, than the figure of Peter Pan, the self-pitying sublimations he implies, his transmutation of childhood oppressions into refuge and paradise, his refusal to enter the world as soon as possible, becoming the keys that, like a talisman, will permit us to confront the dragon.

Grandfather: an old mossy log; random musical creaks, crackles, and squeaks sounding inside his body. Raúl and Felipe spied on him from the hallway. Look, said Felipe: he's a Quaker.

The end of lunch infallibly produced a loose string of torturous intestinal gurgling and rumbling poorly masked by a dry cough, while he moved the chair he'd been sitting in, pushing it back under the table, feints or ploys not always effective or executed at the right moment, although, to judge by the unruffled reaction of those present, everything contributed to make him believe that he'd carried it off.

Felipe and their cousins and the whole bunch of them mocked his grandfather the same way they would later mock his grandmother, just the way children make fun of old people, about their sudden emptiness, their iguana-like faces and skin, mocking them if not treating them tyrannically, once having glimpsed their vulnerability and expendability.

Classification and denomination of their farts according to their sound quality, duration, and stench: cannon, blowgun, cornet, canary, longboat, and depth charge. Felipe proposed more names: skunk, theodolite, noogie, and pun. The theodolite was like a kind of camera Uncle Pedro and his coworkers were always standing next to in photos from some dam project or another. And pun was a word Aunt Paquita was always using. Like noogie. Do you like puns? she asked them. What are you all laughing about, if I might know. You sound like retards. What if I start giving out some noogies. And they all ran away laughing. And the fava bean, said Felipe, you can also call that one the executioner.

Grandfather's death came just after the liberation, they had hardly returned to Barcelona; perhaps even before the war was over. Grandmother came to live with them; she probably died years later than Aunt Margarita. But it was like it had happened before, because she'd been a long time in the convalescent home. And Uncle Raimón showed up at the house to take care of that sad, gloomy bedroom and the belongings grandma had left behind: a somewhat ratty fur collar, an overcoat dyed black, some print dresses, her muff and mittens, her purses mildewed from disuse, a box with papers and photographs, her dentures.

It was a holiday and he and Felipe went to visit her, accompanied by Nieves. They took her an afternoon snack, some pastries. Look what a pretty garden, said Nieves. A nun, young and smiling, opened the garden gate for them. Look, how nice, Doña Gloria, you've got some visitors. They went in with her—the nun taking her by the arm—along the gravel paths, between laurel trees, acanthuses, and pines. Such lovely grandsons, you must be very proud, Doña Gloria. They sat and ate the pastries on a stone bench, and they said what Nieves told them to say. She didn't pay them much attention, as if she saw them every day and their stories didn't interest her, or as if she were busy, with other things on her mind, and they'd interrupted her. Isn't this chocolate delicious? the nun said. They went back, slowly, by the opposite path, making a circle. Well now, say goodbye to them Doña Gloria. And Nieves: come on and give your granny a kiss. And Grandma said goodbye, goodbye, looking at them for a fleeting instant. Once the gate was closed she immediately turned away, and the nun had to run after to catch her. They watched the two of them move off, Grandma with her wrinkled stockings and her felt slippers, speaking docilely about some matter that seemed to worry her, moving ahead, in the darkening late afternoon garden, of dark greens and golds. To get there you had to take a train.

Meaning: I am that sun in the leaves, I am that metal sky, I am those wheel ruts in the sand; and I am the noise of rushing water in the night and I am the snowy peaks of Montseny. And the peculiar shine of the earth when the sun strikes the garden paths, an almost blinding light, surely owing to the mica flakes in that old soil of decomposed granite. And, especially, the verandah, the attics, the wine cellar. I.

Fixed images. Impossible to think about Papa or Gregorius or Eloísa looking any different than the way they do now. And the figures from his childhood, Ramona then, Padritus, even Felipe himself, were only that, figures. Faceless figures, like the people that have disappeared or died long ago, Grandma, Grandpa, Nieves, Pilate, Quilda, Uncle Pedro. Except for Polit, maybe. Because Polit had always been the same. Or was this identity also illusory?

Because in the same way that a confidence that serves not so much to expose a motive as to disguise it, so do certain memories, and the mechanisms of memory. His initial preference for specific things about Vallfosca, the shadowy woods, the flatlands with poplars, and, almost like an obsession, the points from which you could glimpse the distant and craggy summits of Montseny. Meaning: the aspects of the landscape bearing the greatest similarity to the panoramas of Montseny itself which were the luminous setting for his first memories, liable to function as a bridge or nexus, as an intermediary scene between one epoch and another. And to the degree in which these, those nearest, affirm and establish, those others, their antecedents, tend to lose importance until they disappear, to be concealed anew by a second representation, whose attraction for us might well end up seeming to us unmotivated, arbitrary, and capricious, a question of taste.

A storybook landscape: a dark forest, with ferns and mossy green stones and cavernous tree trunks and rough boughs covered with lichen, and ragged drapes of moss, craggy dry logs, and further up, hollow layers of leaves, shadowy frondosities. And the violets between the grass and the bitter fragrance of the wild strawberries. Everything perfect for stories of enchanted princesses as well as bandits. And then, returning years later, that forest turns out to be, simply, a forest. In fact, the deeply shaded clefts of Montseny, upon whose sunny expanses lay Vallfosca.

Thus the pull that the most recondite and humid aspects of Vallfosca exercised upon him, the ones most similar to those on the other side of that massif that, as between the north and the south, stood between one period of his childhood and another. And in the same way that from Vallfosca he searched for the silhouette of Montseny, its uncertain summits frequently thrust up into the fog, from here, beyond these peaks, at the very foot of Matagalls, from Viladrau, far away, the snowy peaks of the Pyrenees could be glimpsed, almost like clouds in the afternoon sun.

Montseny. Mountain of reason and common sense. A mountainous massif separating not only two landscapes, but also two epochs, two worlds. And the distance between the two points, which then seemed so far from one another that the trip to either place from Barcelona meant taking a different railway line, could now be accomplished by car along mountain highways in less than two hours. Going to spend a weekend in Vallfosca, for example, passing through Viladrau.

Of course, just as when we return to the scenes of our first childhood we invariably discover for ourselves that everything is lesser, smaller, more reduced than what we remember, the adult similarly tends to minimize, to subtract importance from, and consider trivial and negligible the problems that tormented him most during his childhood. But in this latter fact he is completely mistaken, because, just as, in relation to the child he was, the objects that surrounded him were enormous and continue to be so in his memory, those problems were really no less enormous, nor the importance his impressions of those times held for him and continue to hold.

He had returned. And he saw everything accordingly, as if on a reduced scale, the sizes, the distances. But the crossroads at the highway which he could see from the house was still, in any case, quite far. How was it possible then that he could have perceived with such precision the movements of the troops at that crossroads, with the detail with which one can appreciate the people one encounters less than a stone's throw away?

The tricks and traps of memory, its empty spaces, its disguises, its appropriations. Like with Nieves. La Pilate touched Padritus, and Nieves touched Felipe and him. She laughed a lot, when she put him to bed, to see him get hard in the dim light that hung down from the fixture inside the shade. The same as that other time when Quilda was also there and some other woman from the town, all of them leaning over his bed, laughing like conspirators as they put a bit of oil on his bottom, just as if they were there to pluck a chicken, with that kind of delight that arises, when various friends are together, from the sight of the village idiot masturbating in the church plaza, and his huge, mammoth ejaculations.

For the rest, how to be sure he wasn't superimposing images? The memory of what Padritus told them: that Pilate had sucked him off. Something that Raúl then talked about at school, making it sound as if it was something that had happened to him.

And Pilate and her army boyfriends, men with a railroad look about them. And what they saw when they looked out the windows. Were they things they'd seen personally or that the others talked about seeing or having seen? The victory and its commemorations. The parade that they witnessed from the balcony of Uncle Pedro's study, all the cousins gathered together watching the steady march of the cavalry, captained, one might say, by Santiago himself, Santiago or Jaime or Jacobo or Yago or James or Santiago or Sanseacabó, meaning eternal and everlasting, patron saint of Spain, with his hosts of Moors and his legionnaires, and then the tanks and the artillery pieces and the gray companies of the military police and the Guardia Civil, armies of land, sea, and air, flags and military bands, marches sounding while on they come, on they come, the sappers to the front, those troops who appeared to have keys bristling from their shoulders, between arms raised on high and children in arms, songs and cheering, a steel orgy of sharpened blades, theirs was the victory and the full dress glory of red and golden yellow, the photo of Franco, the young Caudillo saluting the tight formations passing before his platform, on the front page of *La Vanguardia*, a full-page photo, against a sky flowering with impeccable squadrons, the picture of that happy early shining spring repeated year after year.

Because there is only one type of comprehensible war: civil war. The war that permits the individual to project the scars of his sick personality onto society. The war where one can concretize and put into practice the abstractions of their adopted ideology, for whatever the motivations might be, without having to step outside their small quotidian world, and apply them to their most immediate vicinity. That's why civil wars might be the only ones capable of exciting the people's passions, and why other wars, foreign ones, might only be felt to the degree that they suppose the prolongation or consolidation of some of the elements at play in previous civil wars: the expansion of a religious belief, an ideology, a way of life, of any common trait of the citizenry which they desire to impose on neighboring peoples. Or the inverse: the defense enacted by a people united by traits that give them cohesion the same as blood ties or a common language, their fight to remain independent from any expansions that endanger them, by safeguarding these principles which, following a phase of savage internal strife, ended up not being imposed upon the people but accepted by a citizenry persuaded of their rightness. Also because when those circumstances do not occur, it's necessary to summon the image of chains and imprisonment, as in the ancient armies of slaves, and cultivate antimilitarism anew, and pacifism, and the reason for desertion, the general lack of understanding for a cause whose motives, for being too technical and alien to the individual, are incapable of striking a spark among the people.

Not so in the case of civil war. When a phenomenon of double liberation takes place, understood not as the annihilating victory of one of the battling bands, as the end of horror, blood, and vengeance, but, quite to the contrary, as its unleashing. Better than horror: terror. Not the kind that the worker sent to the firing squad can experience, before falling, shot for nothing more than what the thick callouses on his hands testify about his condition; not for a man for whom the evil of war is nothing especially new when compared to his previous life, hunger and exhaustion and rags and unemployment, and his daughter's prostituting herself to help feed the family, and the strike or boycott or sabotage as a collective solution, with their inevitable consequences, police precincts and soldiers' barracks, mounted police charging on horseback, machine guns, gunfire, shots to the gut, and the employers' thugs awaiting him. Not that kind of terror, not at all. But the terror that makes a prisoner of a good and honest man, of the middle-class citizen, of the aristocrat, of honorable, well-educated people with money, with principles, terror, on the verge of hallucination, of those kinds of people facing the coup de grâce, no longer delivered for being a hard boss or a shrewd landowner, but now simply for attending Mass or taking a summer vacation, not to mention for simple cordiality and bonhomie. Apparent arbitrariness become the norm. Crime become spectacle, buildings on fire and dead bodies on the pavement become urban planning and landscape. Summary executions as a daily habit, madness as logic as one crumbles into the black suns of the gutter.

And that is when such a double liberation occurs: an active liberation for the executioner, a passive one for the victim. The liberation that for one and another represents everything related to the aberrant character of our relationships with our neighbor and the stickiness of things and the mummifying effects of our institutions.

A frustrated liberation, a goal never reached. And like the castaway, the one who lacks strength to reach the coast and his spent energies leave him at the mercy of the drifting tide, so too a society emerged from a civil war, like from an intense emotional explosion, whose only remaining strength seems to be inertia, whose only weight seems to be prostration, without the capacity to react, with the meekness of one who ends up half imbecile but has saved their skin, and the punitive violence of the weak victor against the still weaker loser. An extenuation even of desires, similar to the experience of one who has made love too many times in a single night, so that, upon dressing, the last thing they want is to start fucking again.

An idiotic life. More meek and placid than really peaceful. High school, college, army, girlfriend, diploma, marriage, profession, children, and then back to square one. Like a nightmare, when one dreams they're back in high school and that the teacher, although he's wearing a soutane, is the captain from his army camp.

So that, in these conditions of repressed aggression, one might well show an early love for hunting. For shooting one animal after another. Including even before the proper age. Something as clandestine as Raúl's fascination with fire, when he created marvelous lamps by burning alcohol in jars or tried turning his desk drawers into ovens.

Insufficient trials. Anguished and uncertain, Raúl's conscience was the exact inverse of that inner peace felt by the rural landowner in November, when all the crops are harvested and stored away and the new cycle of sowing begins, and who knows that the only way a year of bad weather could affect him would be increased compensation thanks to higher prices for his crop, so lacking in bad produce. The same as in adolescence, without knowing very well why, one thinks that in life everything ends in failure and that nothing is worth the trouble, and so feels proud even of his own lucidity, satisfied with his perspicacity. Until everything begins to fail and nothing really is worth the trouble. The reality of the game.

This sensation of attending a ritual performance, for example. One of those shows somewhere between carnivalesque and liturgical, with its profusion of images like fireworks, in which Moors and Christians face off each year in various festivals along the Levantine coast, mock battles in the course of which the whole town usually participates, without anybody, on the other hand, knowing with absolute certainty the heroic deeds being commemorated. A parody that doesn't even know itself to be a parody, objectified, sacralized, converted into a ceremony. A kind of consubstantial performance by some actors who stubbornly insist on repeating it again and again, even without an audience, within the ruins of an amphitheater. Or in these long straight galleries where since 19 July 1936, so many lists have been recited, so many names, so many ranks of prisoners dispatched to the firing squad, rebels, fascists, anarchists, Trotskyites, communists, years and years of life awaiting execution; fascists dead before having to helplessly witness how the dissolution against which they had fought undermined the foundations of victory in their very homes, how that dissolution was incarnated in their own children, how it was illusory to use weapons to recover time now past; anarchists dead in time to not have to get to know the workers of a consumerist society; Trotskyites dead in time to not have to see the revolution grinding to a halt in nation after nation, due to the national interest of each people more than class interests; communists dead in time to not have to fight, to save the revolution, against the proletariat itself, against the very vanguard of that proletariat, against the very direction of that vanguard, against themselves. But as if the amphitheater were not in ruins, as if the public's applause still echoed there, the actors continued their performance, some as if they were still able or still wanted to foment revolution, others as if they were preventing it from coming, as if the dissolution of values they claimed to contain were there, enclosed in that jail, and not installed in their own homes. And only the fatigue of the years that pass would prevent them from sending prisoners to the firing squad like in days gone by, in the same way that habitual duelists, once they've complied with all the requirements of the regulations, end up firing their pistols into the air.

As in a sacramental act interpreted according to the Stanislavsky method, with the verism that is derived from identification, a sacramental act in which the actors persist to the point of staying in character even after the play is finished, beginning with the Author himself and, once offstage, continue adjusting their behavior to their respective characters, the paranoid King, the schizophrenic Peasant. And especially the Author, a demented fool who believes he continues to be the garroted prisoner, with his heavy beard and his tunic or smock, now become his shroud, still sitting against the post, a cross between his stiff hands, oblique as an erect, ejaculating member.

Number?

Just as Dante, in the exposition of his journey through the darkest zones of his conscience—under the guidance of the genial pederast, whose personality is sublimated, as they wend their way upward, until being transformed into the unreachable purity of a dead little girl—does nothing but project his own repressions and venereal or sadistic perversion, and articulate them in a system, to immortalize his rancors and frustrations with his characteristic delectation, with the same vengeful spirit that permits him to judge and condemn not only the world in general, but, above all, his most immediate society, in the same way that whoever tolerates seclusion and solitude can draw from them the greatest conceivable liberty and clairvoyance.

And just as the heaven-hell relationship is one of coincident inversion, like the image of a hand against a mirror, the one a continuation of the other, but inverted, thus the relationship between God and Demon can only be understood as one of an essentially dialectical nature, insofar as, the one representing the harmonic order and the other transgression, when after various failed revolts the uprising triumphs, and with it the chaos that, as it settles down and takes hold, always makes way for a new and definitive order, the roles are exchanged: the Demon, the victorious rebel, occupies the place of God and, even as he installs a new definitive harmonic order, engenders his opposite, a new principle of dissolution, a new Demon, that ancient all-powerful overthrown one, an indomitable force conquered which, from its present Tartaric summits, will attempt again and again, disaster after disaster, the reconquest of the Olympian heights, the reestablishment of the lost Golden Age, once again the Demon against God, Saturn against Jupiter, the promised goodnesses of the new order converted with time into tyrannical arbitrariness and into a horror of the good, while the subversions of that order—transgression, evil, terror—acquire the value of liberating acts, and the Tempter's deceits become great deeds, and his agents' nature becomes archangelic, as the one who has descended to the deepest depths well knows, not like some curious traveler, like Ulysses and Aeneas and Dante, but rather like Prometheus who descended into the inferno in search of his Eurydice, who had proposed to give men freedom by eating of the forbidden fruit.

Because the diversity of the names of the Creator, the ambiguity of his origins, his confusing parental ties, Jupiter, Jehovah, Ormuz, Elohim, Saturn, Ahriman, He. Meaning, he who has no name, the unnameable. He that is the one true self and its opposite.

This Great Narcissus with a taste for games who, as if to make a show of his power, upon giving himself over to one of those acts of onanism of the sort from which a world sprouts, seems to take pleasure in mutilating man, amputating a certain number of his components, so that, according to a demoniac calculation of probabilities, it might be just as mathematically impossible for him to find his perfect soulmate in love as to find freedom in cosmic equilibrium. His lapidary laws that made Moses ascend the heights of Mount Sinai and cry to the cloudy sky: speak, Dog!

Because in the same way that it becomes difficult to discern if it's more terrifying to consider, for example, the conditioning implied by events so remote in time and space, such as the founding of Rome, the formation of Barcino in the heart of the future Roman Empire, its conversion to Christianity following the arrival of Saint James, its reconquest by Wilfred the Hairy, the reception for which the city charged Columbus upon his return from his voyage of discovery, the departure toward that America of one Ferrer who there made a fortune and married a Gaminde, one branch of the family's return to the Iberian peninsula, settling the grandfather in Barcelona, the wedding of his son Jorge with Eulalia Moret, the birth of Raúl, the Civil War, school, the military, the party, Leo and Federico, the Sagrada Familia, Nuria and Aurora, the cathedral, Modesto Pírez, the Model Prison, I here in this instant, or on the contrary, the idea that such a chain does not exist, that the alternative of a contingent fact cannot be anything else but another contingent fact, the absolute dominion of the arbitrary.

And no less radical and traumatic than clarifying the dilemma is deciding to break one fine day, for example, with the daily grind, with its ties and servitude, with family members whom we don't even want to see, acquaintances whose behavior we can no longer stand, women whom we don't love but whom we haven't left yet, the past, in short, that we have been carrying along on our backs, a spiderweb that entangles and gets dusty and moldy, relationships which, however, generally persist and endure for life, not so much for fear of the fact itself of breaking them off as of the solitude and helplessness that come in their wake, fear of the freedom, in the same way that what frightens us is not so much suddenly conceiving of progress as a constellation, a drawing obtained by tracing an imaginary line that links stars picked out on a whim, figures, in the end, projected by ourselves. What really frightens us are the consequences that come from this idea about the conception of the world.

Because, just as with the lover, her infidelity confirmed, the problem is knowing if her tears correspond to her shame at having been found out or her rage for the mess that such a discovery means for her continued plans, so, in a similar way, it becomes problematic to know, in the diverse phases of life, if it's not more appropriate to consider what we call maturity as the end of childhood, or inversely, generalizing, if what we believe to be the start of a new epoch isn't really the end, the death throes of the preceding period.

The great difference that stands between guilt and punishment. The case of the unlucky one, for example, who when young had a brilliant idea, and while articulating it and developing it the years went passing by until he grew old, more than ever and forever down in the trenches with his handful of ridiculous ideas, a sociologist or a psychiatrist or a linguist or whatever, ever more enclosed within his personal prison, with the disastrous support of his wife and four unconditionally faithful friends. And it's then when life manifests itself with full clarity like a mountain of piety and penitence, of redemption, that we must climb up step by step. What else, if not, do those stepped pyramids, the Buddhist temples, stand for? And the cupolas on the mosques, the towers of the cathedrals, the same predilection that the gods have always shown for the mountains? A world like a mountain whose summit we must reach, given that, like on the heights of Purgatory, one still finds there the earthly paradise, from which we are only separated by the crystalline flow of the River Lethe, the river of oblivion, whose poisonous waters one must needs drink. So that, when one has served out his sentence, he dies. And heaven will be the non-existence of hell and hell the non-existence of heaven.

On the other hand, just as for our cuckolded lover, the discovery of the betrayal can be the cause, especially if his personality is prone to this, of a true neurotic crisis, with repercussions even in one's own sexual equilibrium, so for Raúl, the insecurity derived from ceasing to contemplate the world vis-à-vis a specific ideology in which every question has its response, in which everything gets explained, had momentarily affected, no doubt, not only his psychic and sexual stability but, what's worse, also his creative capacity, plunging him into uncertainty, indecision, and impotence, as if—just as the lover's infidelity can provide a splendid resolution for ending some relationships already well past their prime, one of those occasions that rarely reoccur, emancipating himself from that ideology, liberating himself from a perspective accepted not without effort—it were not capable, analogously, of widening his field of vision before reducing it.

And this all the more true given that, if on one side he couldn't say that he fully trusted the validity of those points of view he defended, no less anesthetic now than they had been during his now-past ideological crisis, nor could he trust, on the other hand, with respect to the sharpness of his mental faculties, the effects of his devotion to his practice of the accepted ideology. Because just as a good middle-class citizen compensates for his erotic dissatisfaction by collecting one thing or another or endlessly remodeling his house, or that old rural landowner who overcomes all his personal frustrations—what he might have been had he acted in time, what he might have experienced, what he might have seen, whom he might have loved, if he'd not stayed in that goddamned tiny out-of-the-way place—thinking about his properties and, especially, those not his own, those he still needs in order to finish that noose he's wrapping around the town's neck, so with Raúl, in the long run, the routine of some political activities in whose worth he didn't believe, the exercise of a militancy for militancy's sake had supplanted the development of his creative impulses, suffocating them, inhibiting them, in exchange for the protection of a moral justification that supported him in the meantime. An alternative that had not arisen at first, when it seemed that everything was unified: action and creative strength and liberty and compromise and love. Meaning: before he ended up feeling like that knight-errant who, after fulfilling all requirements, passing all required tests, and following the strictest rituals that the rules and regulations demand of one who wishes to join the order, and now knighted, goes riding and riding without ever encountering any giant or dragon, nor being able to participate in any tournament nor trade boasts with a foe nor rescue kingdoms nor princesses nor, much less, find the lost Holy Grail.

In the same way that for a person whose father played almost no role in his early childhood, due to his being weak and sick and depressed and worn-out, the last person capable of inspiring admiration and fear in a boy, in the same way that that person will always be, most likely, possessed of enormously fragile religious sentiments, so Raúl, in his childhood when he felt more moved by his fear of the Demon than by his love of God, due to the much greater tangibility of the maleficent powers in the world and, above all, of his feeling of condemnation, convinced as he was of his total incapacity to fulfill the necessary precepts to earn his way into heaven, given the dark feelings of destruction and vengeance he sensed inside himself, he began trying to conjure up as much as possible that irremediable sentence, or at least distance himself from it as much as possible, by means of ritual bets—reaching the corner of Paseo de la Bonanova before the streetcar arrived, finishing counting seven times to seventy at the precise moment of stepping through the school gates, etcetera—and, in a more general way, with his daily behavior, among whose traits his tendency to create strict obligations and responsibilities in relation to certain people, to specific tasks, and the reparative self-sacrifice in certain situations was not the least outstanding, insofar as it compensated for the regrets he failed to feel.

However: how was it possible not to relate that profound irreligiousness in a specific phase of a person's life with his previous age, not so much a lack of revolutionary conviction, as insincerity about socialism? Given that like in Dante, the Christian mysticism he shows off turns out to be obviously insincere and, in the *Divine Comedy*, scholasticism is a superimposed ideology, so too, in Raúl, the Marxist interpretation of the world as a key to reality had, from the beginning, been based—although voluntarily—less on rational evidence than a desire for liberation and even for terror, far removed from any constructive purpose.

Or his patriotic indifference, which although formulated late, was, nevertheless, already present during his years at school, manifesting itself with a sentiment like annoyance when, immersed in the universal history, it collided with Spain, with the encomiastic image which the texts ascribed to its singular role. Annoyance if not repugnance. No greater, on the other hand, no more intense than what a Frenchman might experience, or a Russian or an American, with a certain critical sense with respect to their own country. Something similar to what eventually leads one to feel respect for his own city when he lives in it, by reason of its very immediacy, the environs containing all the burdens that weigh upon one's life. And if, being far away, one can remember Barcelona almost even with a longing, being there in the city itself, one is frequently assaulted with the desire to live in any part of it as long as it be north of the Besós and south of the Llobregat.

Breaking with habits. No longer pretending to accept what one really doesn't accept. Fighting petrification with stimuli, liberating creative impulses. Because sometimes there is something unexpected inside of oneself, that has its own precise time, like a birth, like death, like a time bomb, and then erupting like volcanic lava or orgasmic sperm. And that is the only way we become truly aware of the development of a woodland that's familiar to us, or of a garden, a street, a forest, by staring at a photo taken years earlier and making comparisons, confirming specifically the things that have obviously changed, by seizing upon their previous dimensions, and so Raúl, only after examining the development of such impulses from the beginning, could establish the degree to which they had ended up imposing themselves on his imaginative activity, his creative willpower.

The fact is that, unlike what adults seem to think when they turn to the child telling him: that will teach you, an announcement that is usually the prelude to the application of a severe corporal punishment, the things we forget are no less important than the things we remember. This forest that lies before us at the start of our life, and of any other life we might find in the future, will only be a faint shadowy echo.

The paths of memory. Something similar to visiting one of those cathedrals built atop an older one, constructed in its turn from the remains of pagan temples, stones belonging to that other city excavated beneath the present-day city, subterranean ruins that one can visit contemplating what were streets and houses and necropolises and protective walls, pieced together almost always from the remains of earlier cities.

A tour, however, that one usually finds not only in the base of one's self-knowledge, but also in the full realization of all creative impulse. In these notes. Because just as Hercules founded Barcelona after being shipwrecked, and Aeneas founded Rome after the destruction of Troy, so Raúl confronted not so much his past as his future as he wrote his notes on those pieces of toilet paper, with the application and the vigor of a Robinson in recovering the notion of time or of a Monte Cristo in drilling slowly through the rock. And what he wrote there was not like what he wrote before, when instead of imposing himself on the words, the words imposed themselves on him as objective material, according to, doubtless, the repressive role of the language upon personality, to the degree to which any relationship between names and the things they designate is simultaneously an expression and a reflection of a specific external reality. And through those linguistic relationships, the prevailing relationships in the external world take shape in the child's mind. And in this way, while a specific system of relationships between names and things is established in earliest childhood, from that point on, any other kind of system of relationships is excluded.

Such a possibility, however, exists; we can intuit it during a certain number of years, sniff it, ever closer, pinpoint it. Only that its realization, meaning its birth, is not simple, nor must it necessarily be auspicious. And it almost seems necessary that some shipwreck or destruction or punishment occur as a catalyst for this phenomenon.

A surprising result. For the first time, as he stared at the words in his notes, he had the feeling of creating something and not—like that actor who one fine night discovers the tedium of repeating his role for the umpteenth time and wonders what he's doing there on stage if he was never truly interested in the theater in the first place and if, in reality, he might devote himself to something else less monotonous and repetitive—the impression of playing a game for the sake of playing it, not because it really interests him. The feeling, in other words, of creating a new reality instead of telling a story more or less in the way you would tell any other, the triumph of a strike that is, at the same time, the triumph of a growing awareness, or the moral emptiness of those who lead a dissolute life at the margin of all compromise with society and other things that are written, descriptions, dialogues, tales, internal monologues, counterarguments and clarifications such as "what's up, said Juan," or "he lit a cigarette," or "she burst out laughing," etcetera, just as boring to read as to write, including when it's all for the sake of some productive way to earn a living.

Is there any difference between a flamenco dancer who, interviewed on TV, speaks with complete self-assurance about her art, and the author rescued from obscurity by his writing and the grace of some literary prize; a national master or some small-town municipal secretary, myopic and frog-faced when he talks about the personal character of his writing or his social ideas, but later, when he gives a reading of one of his pieces, the amazed spectator discovers that beneath the ferocious appearance of that Bête who keeps the princess prisoner there beats a heart filled with love and that, behind that frog face, lives a man who loves and apostrophizes, who speaks of balconies bloody with geraniums or how the people's sovereignty fills him with vigorous inspiration? No, it's nothing remotely like that. On the contrary, one has the sensation of configuring, with nothing more than words, a reality far more intense than the reality which all that literature pretends to witness or replicate.

Even more: it was as if the words, once written, turned out to be more precise than his previous purpose and even clarified for him what, beforehand, he'd only had a vague notion of what he was going to write. A book that could be, not a reference to reality, but, like reality, an object of possible references, an autonomous world about which, theoretically, a reader with creative impulses might write, in their turn, a novel or a poem, free of themes and of forms, a creation of creations.

One might say that just as a fertilized human egg already contains the germ of everything the person is going to be, and whose development will culminate with their birth, there are, equally, moments in a man's life which, for their metaphorical strength, come to be a summary or compendium of all his conscious and unconscious perceptions, the concentration, one within another, of all implicit experience, instant and duration, a time vastly superior, in its elasticity and amplitude, to chronological time. And to secure that instant, that duration, requires a centrifugal development, successively dilating circles, spreading out like waves that grow ever larger around the spot where the stone plunged into the still water or the way that one metaphor nested within another makes a tale.

The golden moment, the sensation that by means of the written word he was not only creating something autonomous, brought to life by his own hand, but that in the course of this process of objectivization through writing, he would at the same time manage to understand the world through himself and know himself through the world.

Beyond, then, the words, beyond his simple principle. Something that does not reside in them but within ourselves, although, in their turn, they are what gives us reality. The supreme union. The communicants processing to the prison's Central Tower. First the queers—the little girls—like mannequins that come walking along the catwalk. Next, only some pious being, shrunken, guilty. And a handful of invalids and hypochondriacs, or some old man shuffling his feet quickly along, as if afraid to be left behind, of not arriving in time. And some crook desirous of ingratiating himself, of getting in good with La Merche. And the queers, with their hands together and their eyes lowered, kneel before the executioner's hood, purple as a bruise, and then the executioner raises the host. And La Merche starts muttering, let the little girls enter into me, do this in memory of me, only say the word. And the little girls, Lord, take this cup from my lips. Eating the true flesh and drinking the true blood of a Garroted man.

No one is alone, each one said to himself, under his breath. Between ourselves we keep each other company.

Just as in the course of a long journey by train, the kind of passengers who board and disembark change as slowly as the landscape outside, so that the trajectory of the trip ends up being the only point of contact between the points of departure and arrival, thus, with the passing of the years, almost everything ends up by being linked with death and very few things with life.

Nevertheless, just as birds continue gleaning without being frightened at the start of a solar eclipse, their quick chirping and peeping betraying no worry about the day's sudden unusual brevity, so goes the passing of time during youth, the innocent conviction that throughout life one more year is only one year more. But the same way that the misty glaze of our respiration begins to disappear the instant we move our face away from the glass, so just like our breath, our life dwindles and fades, as long as what we are watching remains there, on the other side of the window, outside, just as the things we tried to dominate in our lives will remain there, including those things we believed we had overcome.

Allegorical drama: life is but a dream. Except, perhaps, for the one dreaming, who will then be the only one to make it out alive. *Ite missa est.*

Then the final prayers and benedictions, the final gospel, the final miserere nobis. And then the national anthem, and to its rhythm, the recession of the prisoners, gallery after gallery, past the platform in the Central Tower—now converted into something like the presidential grandstand in Red Square, where the various prison authorities sit in a hierarchical arrangement around the warden—the political prisoners coming last, without matching the rhythm, although by then, in order to avoid any unnecessary conflict, the warden had already turned away, ignoring them, alerted to their arrival by the preceding group, the little queens, who, on the contrary, attired and made up in the most exaggerated fashion possible for that great moment, approached, strutting provocatively, their formation no less tight and martial than the chorus girls in a musical revue.

Next, while the prisoners from solitary were locked away, each one in his own cell, for the others, the free time on the patios, the movie, the little queens following behind everything, apart, according to the sexual structure of the penitentiary organization, so much less arbitrary the deeper we go into the psychic darkness of its artifices. And the paella with olives and a sardine instead of the normal daily rations. And the afternoon, the Sunday binge, the betting, the loudspeakers, the scores from the official league soccer matches, *In a Persian Market*. Later, another week, another Sunday, the declaration before the examining magistrate who, despite the news from Pedro Botero, would finally arrive, only a few days behind schedule, due to the traffic jams and bottlenecks on the way. And the daily routine of Raúl's life as a political prisoner until the court-martial, after which, absolved or sentenced to a symbolic sentence, which in fact he had already served, he would be immediately released.

Motionless before the door, he turned his gaze back into the empty cell, the sun on the flagstones reticulated by the oblique projection of the bars. He was sleepy. Wouldn't he let himself be conquered by an invincible drowsiness when he found himself back inside? Or perhaps overcoming the invincible drowsiness, feeling a little bit drugged, he would take his pen and set himself to writing on the smooth side of one of his squares of toilet paper? Rambling notes, written according to some still very vague plan. Nothing in common, however, with his unconfessed poems of adolescence. Nor with the heroic prose of his time in the military. Nor with his previous frustrated attempts and, for some unexplained motive, always thematically unhappy, suicides, ill-fated love affairs, processes of deterioration. One question: When did he begin to write? Another question: Why?

Or, without any desire to write, wouldn't he, in that state of wakeful vigilance, allow his mind to wander, to think about when he might be released, his return home? The chaotic overgrown garden, his original design of flower beds and acacias now completely wrecked, a mess of morning glories and geraniums and mallows and nameless flowers and volunteer dwarf fruit trees and strange creepers with pumpkin-shaped fruit and reptilian ivy and the honeysuckle invading everything, introducing its willful shoots between the iron bars, along the slats of the Persian blinds, disquieting, entwining. Very healthy, Papa would say. It's like living right out in the wild. And taking advantage of the few open spaces in that degenerative overflowing, he'd planted thyme and oregano and southern wormwood and rosemary and rue, aromatic plants, a vegetable proliferation whose overgrown cluster scumbled even the outlines of the house. And each of the damp shadowy spaces inside the house, no less present than the intangible odors, occupied its own corresponding place in his memory. The light stink of gas in the entrance hall, next to the gas meters, especially noticeable, the same as that moldy smell, enclosed, upon entering the first floor, making your way through it, the vestibule, the small sitting room, the dining room, and, upstairs, almost to the top floor, when they returned from Vallfosca, at the end of summer. And the closet in his room, which smelled like a rifle, and the sideboard in the hallway like medicines, and the pantry like dried, peeled chestnuts. And his grandparents' room, and Felipe's room, the dampest ones, smelled like emptiness. And the attic, filled with the dusty piles of disassembled furniture from the conjugal bedroom Papa once shared with Mama, smelled like old clothes and stale silk. And Papa's own bedroom that smelled like medicinal herbs and a drugstore exactly the same as in Vallfosca; and his desk, an accumulation of failed projects and unrealized inventions, of useless patents, of the swindles of which he'd been a victim. And the large cracked floor tiles and buckling molding along the walls with soft chipped coats of plaster, and the pipes flecked with solder and the burned-out light bulbs of so many lamps, not replaced, and the carefully conserved ruin of the kitchen pots and utensils. Overall, it's good enough for two people, said Eloísa. Her old patched bathrobes, her ratty aprons, her broken eyeglass frame fixed with a Band-Aid, her slippers with the seams cut open on both sides so as to not squeeze her bunions. And Papa equally disastrous: covered with stains, clothes falling apart at the seams, as if stuck inside the same old rags, and his oldest pair of shoes. It was as if during Raúl's absence they'd let themselves go, and by virtue of his very absence, made the extent of their abandon all the more clear to him. Why buy myself anything, son? At my age that's just throwing money away. And the small problems, the complaints, would come. His father's mania for ventilating every part of the house, of throwing doors and windows wide open. I don't know how we haven't caught pneumonia yet, Eloísa would say. But he'll end up killing us all. Eloísa's eyeglasses; now it didn't seem to bother her to wear them all day, and not only for sewing.

Or would he take up his pen, as if hallucinating, only to set it down again, sleeping from the geometrical splendor of those bright slanted squares that the sun projected on the flagstones, finally overcome by sleep, by a dream, one of those little catnaps that, suddenly interrupted, do nothing more than leave us with our spirit shrinking and our head heavy for the whole day, like waking from a nightmare which, for the moment, we perhaps do not even remember having dreamed, dreams that are not dreams, that in the memory end up even imposing themselves on reality, however disagreeable this might be, fixed with greater precision in the memory?

A state similar to the one which, after waking, must have possessed him years later, one morning, Vallfosca, Papa's room, the early morning sun gleaming on the tiles, Papa, evidently dead—why evidently?—coming in with this wide-brimmed hat, his overcoat folded over his shoulder, without paying him attention, as if worried or lost in thought, and Raúl sitting up in bed as if he had just woken up, shouting or as if he were shouting, but what're you doing here, how did you come back, and Papa without looking at him, looking through the things piled up on his desk, as if browsing in a shop, well look, everybody's got their own things, distracted and distant, looking for something, you might say, and Raúl, wracked with palpitations, stay here, stay here again, as if the fact that Papa had died so few days before might allow for a solution, that it was only a question of goodwill or determination, only four days before the boy would turn one year old and only a few days after Raúl's own birthday, an event that everyone thought about but which only Eloísa dared mention, the same morning of the burial, coming back, when she saw the little boy crawling around in the garden and she picked him up in her arms, and just as the boy was not astonished by the adult but rather the adult by the boy, so, then she said, poor little thing, what does he know about death and age, four days before, a relationship between dates that had the virtue of diverting her attention, of making her forget for the moment the time transpired between the first manifestations of the process of illness and the last ones, with their details, the prescriptions, the injections, oxygen, and above all, the sentences, the words, his words, his worries about Eloísa's sorrow when she still spent part of her time sitting in the armchair, poor Eloísa, with her rheumatism and this problem with her leg that must be sciatica, she would need to have a doctor check it, then, when they were still receiving their periodic visits from Uncle Gregorio and Leonor, and he and Uncle Gregorio talked unfailingly about the friends of their youth and Uncle Gregorio asked him every time about Arcadio Catarineu, you remember,

I haven't seen him for a while, and Eloísa and Leonor tried to get them to change the subject, because Papa didn't know either that Arcadio Catarineu had died only recently, Eloísa had spirited away the obituary page from the newspaper, and Papa said you're looking skinny, son, you should try to make yourself eat, and he asked him when he would finish his doctoral thesis, and asked him about work and told him he was a very lucky guy to have Nuria, that she was a girl with a very good heart, and he looked at the little boy's toys in the center of the carpet until one day he himself was the first to say that it was better they didn't bring him to visit anymore for the moment, that a sick man's house was no place for a little boy, and when he got worse and Felipe showed up again and said that they were reassigning him to Barcelona, he said that he was very happy, pretending he believed it, and from that moment when he could no longer get out of bed he said he didn't want any more visits from the doctor, that they should take care of him, the one person whom I would have liked to see is Gregorio, but a sick man always shocks people, and with his state of health, I don't think it would do him good, while, very possibly, Uncle Gregorio didn't even find out about this change in his habits, at most, someday, proposing suddenly to pay Jorge a visit, and then forgetting about it right away, and Eloísa said poor man as they left the doctor's office after each visit, seeing that Papa accepted without any kind of objection all those explanations relative to the fastidious complications that were presented, as if he were more relaxed seeing that they saw him at ease. Only at the end, when he began to need oxygen, taking advantage of a moment in which he found himself alone with Nuria, he told her, help me to take off my rings now. Later it's worse.

It was as if since he got out of prison the rhythm of time had accelerated, events, and not only for him—his wedding, the job that Amadeo procured for him, his son—but as if the phenomenon were obeying some general law, Amadeo's own wedding with Doña Dulce, and Monsina's slightly more hasty wedding, prompted—like his own wedding with Nuria—by a pregnancy, although the motives for keeping the baby were not the same in either case—in Monsina's case the demand and agreement of the respective families—and the birth of Monsina's baby boy shortly before Nuria's, followed by Monsina's immediate separation, no less hasty than her wedding, like a premonition, also, of Raúl's inevitable separation from Nuria, not because they quarreled as before, or for any tension or violence in their relationship, but rather the result of a mutual indifference, correct and even respectful, although if only the result of fatigue, but strong enough to make them understand the lack of sense in continuing to live together that way, in a furnished flat in the upper streets of the city which never felt like anything more than a way station, once they resolved the best possible way of dealing with the problem of their little boy. A conviction which, curiously, seemed to crystallize in both of them from the moment they found themselves married.

How to explain the process? Was it as if for Raúl, like for so many men, the helplessness of freedom had made him turn back momentarily to the fold? No, nothing so simple and concrete, nothing capable of being reduced to a single clause. Rather more as if the simple return to family locations had charged him anew with the problems of daily life, questions that he had to resolve and which, without him hardly noticing, had ended up enveloping him once more, one after another, like a chain reaction, Papa and Eloísa, his duties to them, the need to work, Amadeo's favorable disposition in that regard, his debt to Nuria, etcetera. As if only after three years he might have been able to react, recuperate, emerge from his stupor, to say, definitely, enough is enough. And get back to writing his book. And, for the moment, take a few days off to go to Rosas. And quit smoking a pipe.

His notes from prison, those notes written on squares of toilet paper, which upon his release, with the sudden rush of events and the vertigo of time, came to seem to him like those notes one takes upon waking up in the middle of the night, because the ideas seem to be extraordinarily important, but which in the morning, if they seem to make any sense at all, never usually mean what they did before. It was as if, in order to recover their meaning, it were necessary that from the many personal elements which had served as a basis for the literary material collected there, that from the many points of reference to reality he might have used, he didn't really need to keep absolutely anything, everything reduced to just that: words: as if all that he'd destroyed in his notes also had to be destroyed in reality so that his notes might acquire autonomy, become their own entity. And only then, that chaotic recording of reflections, plot nuclei, descriptions, evocations, dialogues, etcetera, might recover its cohesion and meaning and, above all, as if suddenly, the central idea would be revealed to him: a book like one of those paintings, *Las Meninas*, for example, where the key to the composition is found, in fact, outside the frame.

The idea of spending a few days in Rosas obeyed the writer's occasional need to exam anew some setting from his work. But, at the same time, the notes he'd selected to take with him, that he had to use in writing the first chapter of his book, a book still lacking a title and without any proper names for the characters, given the chosen location and the current state of his relationship with Nuria, took on an almost prefigurative character, now that he was returning precisely to Rosas and precisely with Nuria. A man fresh out of prison. His psychic state is unstable and his relationship with his lover, in a critical condition. In a final attempt to salvage the unsalvageable, they decide to spend a few days in Rosas, as in previous times, returning to the starting point. That's how he opened the book.

The visit they paid to Eloísa the day before their departure, seemed, doubtless, like an attempt to cast a spell. Not in the evening but in the morning, without taking the little boy along, as if to avoid—uselessly—what had happened the last time, on their dismal trip to Ibiza—nothing but rain the whole time—when the afternoon before they left, they went by the house so Papa could see the boy, but only after they returned from the island, upon learning that he was sick, they also found out that just before the trip, although he'd told them nothing, he'd gone to the doctor, and only then did Raúl start to make connections, realizing that the symptoms that had been showing up, the first perhaps only a few months earlier, not yet married to Nuria, the night when, arriving home, he'd found Papa vomiting into a urinal, doubled up and frail upon the bed like an eaglet in its nest. It's the antibiotics, son, they've upset my stomach. And I've had to take so many because of these damned boils. Then, as now, they'd left the little boy with his grandmother, with Doña Dulce. Now Felipe was living at home so as not to leave Eloísa alone, although she almost never stopped doing things. And Eloísa fell asleep listening to her transistor radio. They'd bought her a television set, but she said it made her eyes tired, made her dizzy, that she preferred the radio. She was most interested in the news and one day, she told them, she'd even called the radio station to see if they'd yet found poor Antoñito, the little boy who'd disappeared. It was almost unbelievable that she didn't associate, didn't relate, one thing with another: her rheumatism, her sciatica, her liver, her circulation. She listened to the diagnoses they invented without paying attention to their meaning, almost pleased, perhaps, almost proud, of the attention the doctors focused on her, of the instruments they used to examine her, of the vocabulary they used, mysterious, almost, like a prayer in Latin. The operation won't do any good, the specialist had told them. The cancer has spread everywhere. She's probably got three months at the most. But at her age you never know. She might live a few more years. He and Felipe agreed for the moment to say nothing to her son José, known as Pepe.

The other time, the trip to Ibiza had been in January, seeking—as it turns out—a bit of good weather; not like now, already springtime, after Easter. They walked without any hurry along the quiet street, and there was a boy hunting lizards with an air rifle in front of a sunny wall. Do you remember? Nuria said. And Raúl, I don't know why, but I knew that's exactly what you were going to say. It's as if we've already lived this moment. Outside the cave, of course.

Papa was organizing photos, writing on the back who was who. He showed them a family portrait taken in the living room of the chalet on Calle Mallorca: the parents, the wet-nurses and the children all arranged like in an advertisement, Jorge in the foreground sitting on a cardboard rocking horse. This is Paquita and this, Gregorio and this one, poor Raulito and, here, poor Cecilia; behind them, leaded stained-glass windows, crowded with palm fronds, the foot of a staircase. I'm writing their names, he said, because it's the only way in a few years to know who they were.

He took the child and, assisted by Raúl, held him up in front of the mirror, while the astonished little boy contemplated the double image of his two servants, at once in front and on each side, signaling to and pointing from, the cynically grotesque character of the third person who appeared there, only in front of him, perhaps the solution to the mystery.

He came out to the garden to say goodbye to them. He said that, at the least, he would come to see the child each day. Don't worry, they'll bring him over to you in the mornings. Good, he said, so then I'll come over in the afternoons. He said goodbye to them from the gate, warts clustered around his eyes, under his white eyebrows, his eyes themselves brimming with nightfall, each pupil piercing the horizon toward infinity, with lichens and ruins, far away.

Hammer blows. From some building under construction.

THE BAY. Like two fish that swim in opposite directions. A way of being more than a sign of the zodiac. Explication of the ambivalence of our getaway. With her: more separated than ever. To Rosas: a town that is gradually no longer what it once was.

We went to the same hotel as always. Now enlarged, ruined by tacky renovations. The owner embraced us both and although she didn't say anything, by the way she did it and her liquid eyes and trembling chin it was clear she knew about my prison stint. I cut the conversation short. That's not what I came here looking for.

Her husband didn't say anything either, but as if to offset his secondary role in everything, he made sure to fulfill his obligation of speaking out against the Regime. Uncomfortable on the other hand. The fisherman's problem, a lifelong anarchist who ends up finding himself the owner of a prosperous hotel on the coast.

THE TRANSPARENCY OF THE TRAMONTANA. To go swimming, we preferred to not follow the coast along the bay, to the right of the town, the low continuous shoreline, dunes, weeds, sand ribbed by the wind rimmed at length by the line of clinging scudded sea foam, short choppy waves obscured by the remains of rotting vegetable residue, drifting seaweed.

We took the path toward the lighthouse, to the left. As we rounded the promontory, the town was lost to sight, and the bay seemed no more like a lake as we moved toward the open sea. From there, the coast turned rough, eroded rocks, crashing surf, shattered reefs, pure geological demolition, with sharp cliffs and basaltic coves.

The sea also changed color. Without the softness of tones seen on the bay. Much more accentuated and dense, and deep.

We swam in one of those coves. She lay on the sand bathing in the sun and I explored the rocks on both sides right at the water's edge, sunny flora flecked with foam, with something like sex, like lager beer. The water was good for swimming a few strokes and then getting out, but too cold for calmly swimming underwater.

Quiet, quiet cove. Mineral. Hardly another soul. Only one other couple: tourists, almost always. Better. Hope they speak Dutch, Norwegian.

Sheltered from the Tramontana the breaking waves are neutralized. And looking seaward it almost seems that the water is flowing away from the land, as in an estuary. A breeze, a *Briseus*, light at first, gusting from the brilliant shore, grows stronger as it moves away, unfolding and fanning out, free, accelerated, metallic glazes moving like a bird's flight, like the shadow of its flight, far away, every moment farther, toward the white madness of the horizons, one after another, like snow flurries and manes and whirling saline mists.

The clarity of the atmosphere with the Tramontana. From the hotel room, the Pyrenees are perfectly visible beyond the bay, almost nearby, snowy peaks, splendid as icicles.

À QUOI RECHERCHER LE TEMPS RETROUVE? A coastal town in the off-season, agreeably empty.

In the afternoon we went for walks, climbing up the rough paths. Between slate walls and stunted thickets, flanked by the open slopes of the lower mountain, beyond the gullies with brambles and cursed twisted fig trees.

The springtime came sooner than other years. Green and green the mountain. And the coral outcropping of the poppies in the fields. And the thistles along the edges, mauve asteroids, celestial bodies. And the solar splendor of the broom.

Our walks. We would depart the town walking between whitewashed walls, the wisteria along the patios growing sparser. And further on, the white, narrow, curbed roads. A landscape of vineyards and olive trees and serpentine walls of slate. And the green slopes of the lower mountain. In the distance, upon a promontory, dominating the entrance to the bay, the ruins of Trinidad castle, little more than an eroded crag, perfectly integrated into the orthographic stone of that promontory, the whole thing crumbling apart. One more alluring spot for the new urbanized surfaces.

The inner town remained almost intact. We meandered, snooping along the white windswept streets, smelling of tar and then just as strongly, salted fish; and the same cats grooming themselves in the doorways. And the swallows. Their golden descent upon the church plaza, winging sharply, plummeting straight down, cheeping pitilessly. Their flashing disappearance into the vespertine limpidity, as if sucked into a vortex and shot out by a centrifugal force, after spinning and spinning like gusts of wind around the church.

We walked along the breakwater, roaming the seafront of the town from point to point, like tourists in search of local color. The setting sun an immense pupil upon the bay. Fluid gleams, crucibles, multihued agates, from purple to turquoise, crepuscular tonalities, a sunset of tattered skies like a furnace or an eruption, eyelids squinting as tightly as possible. The same chromatic expansion that must accompany the sun wherever else, in the same instant, it was dawning, even as it sank down here. A dawn that is a sunset.

We walked as far as the dock, ambling along the wharf, almost lifeless this time of year. Some man fishing with a pole, some tourist taking advantage of the fading light to snap their photo of that flaming horizon on the white synthesis of the transit, blue waters burning yellow, red skies burning blue, pinkish greens, orange-hued violets and lilacs and indigos and mauves, an iridescent sunflower of oily spots in the calm opaline bay, still warmed by the fading colors, now translucent rainbows, now colorless translucence, now gray, now heavy, now lead.

We visited the ruins of the citadel or, on the opposite end of town, Trinidad castle. We went into town, we followed the paths that lead to the mountain. We walked along the breakwater. To the dock. The church plaza. The swallows.

Now dark, we returned. It was as if with each walk we sought a new proof of the failure of our relationship.

I couldn't fall asleep until daybreak. She slept peacefully, and this always makes the one who can't sleep more anxious. I finally went out to the terrace wrapped in a blanket. Perhaps I needed to see the dawn. Hoping that another parenthesis would open, and banish my insomnia. Inverting the terms of the metaphor.

A plain of glittering phosphorescences, with flakes of light, bit by bit transformed into cloudy hazy blues. Still water, and the wake of a boat like a vanishing point, opening up the quiet sparkles of spreading rings, circles more and more colored in those first lights of dawn like mercury, more and more amber, the decreasing vibration of the motor marking the silence. And in the emptiness the coppery mountain slopes began to take shape, polished, glowing in the first rays of dawn.

Only then did I sleep. Until midday.

THE SUPREMACY OF THE LANDSCAPE. Now dark, we returned. Smoothness of steel in the distance and a descent of nocturnal forms, saline hills, quartz trees, stark branches, the moon spinning fantasies.

Blue night sky. And the taut crackling firmament, crystalline pinpricks.

Or the moon. The moon flowering above the stony shoots, glowing pink like a jellyfish. And, in the town, a proliferation of windows in the massing shapes, illuminated windowpanes, interlocking shadows and whitenesses.

The description must predominate at the start. To give the sensation of serenity, of something peaceful and relaxing. What he wants to find. In contrast to the newspapers he doesn't buy, the radios he flees from, the television, a motive for walking out of a bar when they turn it on.

Avoid local color: fishing boats arriving, the fish auction, etcetera.

However, now in the course of the first chapter, the descriptions must shed their objective almost enunciative character. They will become subjective, surreal, in a certain way. Like the landscapes one images when contemplating the clouds from an airplane. Contradictory repetitions.

In the following chapters, the same as with the dialogues, they will slowly disappear.

THE CAPE. Going to Cabo Creus by boat, from Rosas, is a problem. Not a technical one; simply finding a person who's willing to take us. But the hotel owner found us a fisherman, an old man willing to take us if the weather that day was good.

It's not that I don't feel like it, just the opposite, she said. But it's three or four hours if the sea is calm. And that many more to come back. And I: but you can only get to the cape by boat. And she: what I don't understand is what you hope to see from there. And I: the other side. And she: we've already seen that:

France, the Gulf of Lyon. Let's rent a car and we'll see it all in one morning. And I: but not like we'll see it from the cape.

PENTECOST. In the morning we made love, with the sun shining on the bed. It was bad.

A splendid day, almost like summer. Cerulean atmosphere, igneous in the zenith, burning bramble, and the moving incandescence of the distances.

Ideal for the town to seem like summer holidays, too, invaded by cars, travelers, mostly day trippers from Barcelona, and also French from the Midi-Pyrenees. It took us a while to find a free table on the bar's terrace.

It was time for their aperitif in the sun. Catalan petite bourgeoisie, avid and porcine, showing off the family style, obscenely prosperous, with the respectability of appearances of those who want to make their social ascension absolutely clear, their right to be accepted by those who are already wealthy, and along with them close ranks against those who still aren't, the respectability of those who meet all the requirements, wife, children, stroller, little parcel of land, all manifestations, just like a certain excess weight, of the country's general economic development, but above all, of their own personal triumph, external signs for those who are willing to pay, if necessary, even more taxes!

But not only Sunday drivers. Sunday is usually also the best day to formalize certain kinds of business negotiations. Speculators, promoters, salesmen, contractors. Talking about real estate properties the way others talk about slaughtering a pig: you get him with the hook, you tie him up really nice and tight, you cut him to pieces, and then, sausage for everyone.

At the next table, French couples, young married couples surely. Mon petit trésor, said one of the group as if suddenly effusive, drawing close, smooching, like suction cups, applying his lips to her rough cut scallop of a mouth, to her defiant contempt, a contrasting attitude of the two elements of copulation, derived, no doubt, from what was for her an unsatisfactory ending of the habitual amorous exercise, unyielding, in consequence, to the heat of such transports, incapable of sharing any allusive gesture to such non-reciprocal pleasures, only worthwhile for him, for him hidden in that stubborn little body and only for him, his particular practices, his intimate manipulations, *ces petites cochonneries*. Anal erotic.

And the charnegos all dressed up in their Sunday best. And the pairs of hikers, lively and garrulous under their backpacks. It seemed that more than the commemoration of the descent of the Holy Spirit in the form of a tongue of flame, it might have been ultimately the meaning that the holy day held for the

Jews, commemorating Moses's going up the mountain. And once atop, each one disappearing to shit behind a shrub.

Bird-beaked old people, frightened away by all that activity. Too many years old now to not lose out, to follow the rhythm of the changes experienced by the town in recent times. What they have seen, what they have heard, what the television says, what's being built, the millions the land is worth, the millions of tourists who show up, their children's habits, their grandchildren's, the external appearance they've acquired, they almost seem like tourists too, confirmations that they've been reaching until losing all capacity for surprise, for discerning the possible from the impossible, accepting as such the impossible without other disruption than a greater propensity for paranoia and megalomania. But the euphoria past, if, in fact, it happens at all, the eyes increasingly wide open and demented in their nests of tiny wrinkles, so much transformation ends up shrinking them, by making them feel, each summer that passes, that the world is ever stranger, that they are ever stranger. And it's then when they become bird-like; the facial skin almost transparent; the scarecrow body twisted and limping, doubled over at the kidneys; their hands made to grasp hoes and pull nets, almost already molded to their shape; their voices made to speak in shouts, in the field, out at sea, at home, shouting at his old lady, at the kids, at the dogs, a voice which, from shouting so, is reduced to little more than a hoarse crackling, stridencies that go twisting around the few slobbering teeth they show us when they smile, unsure whether they've greeted us or not. So, in full season, they only venture out to the fish auction, doing everything possible, as if they intuited their role, to seem typical. Old people are birds already.

That afternoon I went out walking alone. Watching the clouds that were forming: bright perfect stratocumulus alternating with clear patches of sky, forming orographical vastnesses, shaping islands and oceans, peninsulas, mountains or valleys like craters, crests, more crests, islands, peninsulas, shorelines, plains, rivers, isthmuses, capes, bays, and below, cloudy skies and, above all, between the cracks, a yawning terrain, like the ocean floor when one goes diving down.

NOCTURNAL BROUHAHA. They only saw the end of it. Others told them about the rest. They'd had quite a lot to drink and took a while to catch on. It was cold to be sitting at the tables outside.

El Roc was drunk. The town bohemian: half-fisherman, half-alcoholic, with sufficient artistic gifts to paint oil paintings, copied from postcards, which he sold to tourists. He'd drunk his fill in some other bar around there and that night he started to kick up a scandalous row. Then the policeman on night watch showed up. The barman said nothing was wrong, that he'd sort things out with El Roc. But the cop had already made up his mind because El Roc, when he drank, started trouble with every mother's son and the gods they worshipped, and wished long life to communism. At other times he'd had problems with the Guardia Civil, but they'd always preferred to let him off, and take no notice of him. What happens in small towns: everybody knows each other. One night in the jail and that's it.

And El Roc, they said, seeing that the cop was raising his billy club, wrenched it out of his hand and threw it out into the street, and the cop's peaked cap fell off. Strong fellow, El Roc, stout. And then the cop fired two shots into the ceiling and told him to get out of there, to go stand and face the front of the building, with his back to him. He smacked him in one of his knees with his club, from the side, and when he saw him double over, gave it to him in the other one. El Roc grabbed hold of the iron bars outside a window, his legs limp as dishrags. And then the cop smacked one hand, and then the other, and dislodged him. And once he had him laid out on the street, he kept working him over, kicking him.

They arrived at that very moment, just in time to see the final blows to El Roc stretched out on the ground, and a couple of Guardia Civil arrived, and as they dragged him away he was spitting out his loose teeth. The people looked on in silence. A silence that became hostile when they heard them say: that's right, let him cool his heels in the cell. A good taming is what he needs. A fat Andalusian smoking with a cigarette holder.

We returned to our bar, to our table. I realized that she was leaning against me, crying, her face buried in my shoulder. I can't stand to watch them beat a man like that. That monster, just because he's got a pistol and a uniform, beating a man like that. I can't stand it. I can't stand it. I can't stand it. She went running to the bathroom.

Develop the scene stripping away all kinds of atmospheric elements. Principal features of the prose that must be included in this first chapter: density, tension, intensity. A syntactic stretch. A semantic entwining.

METAPHOR. How to contemplate the landscape from the lighthouse, the rocks beaten by the breaking waves barely visible above the sea foam, dripping with anemones and mollusks and black urchins, overflown by the seagulls, savagely beaten, rearing up in white. And beyond the crumbled promontory, beyond the ruins blending back into the stony slopes, the bay dissolved and calm below the saline sky, and the bright jellyfish floating and drifting, carried by the clear western breeze. And the town, between the ruins of the castle and the fortress. And the port, the boats anchored in the shelter of the dock, the piers, the wooden gangways perpendicular to the wharf, and the rigging and the radar antennas and the woven texture of all the gear bordering the footbridges, curtains of nets and of brown corks and the rough rope along the gangways, and the smell from the gangways like piss and tar and fresh paint, and the muted splashing under the gangways, against the ships' hulls, against the stones of the jetty. And the town, the whitewashed walls and the vertebrae of the lizard-hued roofs; and farther on, the long dirty beach, dry seaweed, sinuously accumulated, and driftwood and branches like bones and organic flotsam and indestructible plastics and footprints leading nowhere, footprints erased by the swirling sand, undermined by the deliquescence.

The rocks discolored in the midday sun, below the waxen zenith, the coast like saltpeter or gunpowder. And a front of clouds advancing menacingly, like flocks or dust clouds or the white eyebrows that sharpen the sight of a madman scrutinizing, scrutinizing like a lighthouse in the night, again and again, again and again like a lighthouse lamp turning, an obsessive gaze that encompasses 360 degrees, not so much to be seen from the sea intermittently as to scrutinize, to watch over it as it watches the wild windswept coasts, coasts that turn the way a sardana turns or the way the whole bullring revolves around a slain bull, stones tumultuously set, protean masses which, to a penetrating eye, quickly show themselves to contain, perfectly identifiable, petrified battles, cavalry charges, city walls besieged, ships foundering, everything immobilized by the centuries of an eternal instant, like Pompeii or Machu Picchu, everything turned to stone as in a grotto the dripping water turns to stone, phantasmal forests of stalactites, chaotic rocks like a madman's brain, aeolian demolition and eroded ruin below those wrathful skies and the violent crashing waves, a bay roused to fury by the storm, devastated directly by the east wind, that tense line which on clear days like today, the weather calm, cloudless, and bright, rising in the far distance, clearly, sharply visible, the ruins of Empúries, Iberian, Greek, and Roman stones, towns swept clean by the wind-driven sand, buried by the beckoning sea, that wind and that sea which brought here the battles and the shipwrecks like those ships that smash and founder, horsemen and horsemen galloping, besiegers of walls upon walls, these waters and this air that are barely an image of the impulse which brought them here, of the gales, of the seas they carried inside, the ultimate key to the landscape. And the diaphanous sapphire of the cierzo wind blowing cold and hard from the north and the arid zenith high above the protean relief of the coast, rocky excrescences, stony disintegrations. And the dirty ashen sky and the black sparkling water, hidden rocks, reefs, boulders hurtling down and smashing to pieces upon the defenseless plain, upon the short, storm-chopped waves, implacable foam and roaring air. And the gray hangover, that current that detaches a person from terra firma, pulling him out into the gray sea, into his brain.

FIGURES ON THE BEACH. I don't like sunbathing lying still on the beach. I don't even like the sand. I prefer the rocks.

She was talking to me while lying on her stomach facedown, her bikini straps loose. She said that they hadn't been able to locate the house from the years when they used to summer there, after the war. She only remembered that it was a fisherman's house, on one of those streets parallel to the sea inside the town. Then we started going to Lloret. Papa had more money and he thought it was more elegant. But I've always had better memories of Rosas.

It's as if with everything there had to be something that came between us, I said. Why? she said. Well, because I had spent a summer just around the other side of the cape, in Port de la Selva. Before the war. I don't remember anything, of course. But there's a photo of me there. I must have been just a little more than a year old.

A pebble beach, with boats. And I'm on a boat, and she's holding me. You can barely notice but, given the season, she must have been quite pregnant. It might be the last photo of her. She's looking at the camera, smiling more with her eyes than her lips.

Translated from the Spanish by Brendan Riley.
August 2016

BOOK II: THE GREENS OF MAY DOWN TO THE SEA

Contents

V

VI

I

THE OLD MAN.

The slopes were smooth, the terrain only slightly uneven. A vast abandoned garden whose principal relief was shaped by the ruins scattered across the landscape. Similar to the vision that some traveler who has never actually visited Athens can nonetheless call to mind: the Parthenon rising in the distance, its ancient stones visible among the cypresses and pines and pepper plants, the fallen capitals, the truncated columns, the laurel boughs some climber might grasp to help them conquer the markedly steep slope. Save for the fact that, beneath the threatening storm clouds of the gloomy dusk, under a sky whose darkness made it necessary to light the oil lamps as if night had already fallen, it all resembled, more than any serene acropolis, a freshly destroyed city, the air still thick with smoke, dust, and ash. So much more because other elements of the landscape—the geometry of the chain-link fences, the hollow emptiness of the sentry boxes, the blackness of the barracks—contributed to reinforce the sense of catastrophe. Even worse: the men wandering about with their gray manes of hair and hostile faces; they'd worn their clothes away to shapeless, nondescript rags. By the shadowy red glow of a fire, they prodded and stirred with their poles a thick, pasty mass that rose to the edge of a gaping trench, brimful and yawning wide as a bomb crater in a terrain blasted and leveled flat, the quicklime bubbling where various solid masses floated and spun, the way drifting logs float and spin. The flames burned a moon-bright alabaster. He approached an altar: the marble of the bas-reliefs broken and shattered as if smashed with a hammer, along with the columns supporting the altar and the naked corbels offering the white headless image of the virgin, the finishing touch on the shrine's white facade. He opened the doors of the shrine: inside, yellow bones, almost orange. From higher up on the mountain he could hear voices, coming closer every moment, and he began to flee between the wire fences. The ground ran mostly flat through the woods, and the large trees were far enough apart so the intricate foliage of each canopy stretched out as far as possible. The voices seemed to be calling from different spots, moving and ricocheting between the tree trunks. He spotted the man as he was crossing a clearing, just as the other one emerged from the woods. One of those beggars, perhaps, from a Buñuel film, ragged, greedy, their deliberate degradation converted into strength, their misery and their years become a reason for terror. He advanced toward him slowly, smiling. And he waited until he was close enough and then flung a sack over his head and knocked him down, and squatting down on his chest he bludgeoned him through the cloth with a heavy stone, striking him again and again in the skull and the face, grasping the stone with both hands, feeling teeth and cartilage, jawbones, eyebrow ridges shatter and collapse beneath the cloth, shouting, howling, difficult to know if he or the other one or both at the same time.

DOWSER? DOWSERS?

A vine shoot split down the middle into a Y shape. A hazel switch would also work, they said. You had to grasp it by the two ends of the fork, one in each hand, softly, the same way you hold a set of reins, and start walking slowly, taking care to keep the main stem parallel to the ground, as loosely as possible, without exerting any pressure. On passing over the elusive, much sought-after spring of water, the tip of the shoot will begin to stiffen by itself, to rise, more and more the shallower the spring and the greater the flow of water. The man wore a gray, collarless, white-striped shirt, and after having located in the hidden torrent the optimal spot for digging a well, he made a demonstration in the garden itself, not far from the house, in one of the small squares formed by the intersection of the stepped paths, an arbor shaded by the tree's luxuriant foliage, darkened by the surrounding ivy: there's water here, he said. And Uncle Rodrigo: you must have found the sprinkler line.

With a grimace Papa resigned himself to the test, much more headstrong than Grandpa. What do you want me to tell you, fella, I don't feel a thing. Of course, if you really put your mind to it and try your best, I'm sure it'll rise. And Papa: And then what do I do? And the kids? And Vernis? So, after all, it's really nothing more than the power of suggestion? He'd spent days crossing and recrossing the arbor, before breakfast, after siesta, considering as many favorable points as possible, thoroughly reconfirming the positive results of his experiment, contemplating, perhaps, the idea of hiring men to do another survey, studying the whole thing again, and sinking a second well, even if only to show on which side lay the truth. Something like that, at least, must have been in his head the day when Vernis showed up to talk about stripping the cork from the oak trees.

This man looks like a Roman centurion, Papa said, patting his shoulder. And, the truth was, his strong, well-proportioned features suggested more than a touch of the classic bust, his tight blond curls brusquely cropped to the contours of his skull, and even his serene presence and forbearing manners boldly suggested a sculptural solemnity. He dressed just like any one of his workers, a shirt of coarse knit blue cloth and dark corduroy pants, and he seemed no less skilled than they in handling an axe. But he didn't stay out in the woods for the duration of a job the way they did, sleeping under their leantos built of branches, with their blankets, their straw mattresses, their provisions, their jugs, their little wineskins with a straw spout that they passed from hand to hand while eating, all sitting around the campfire's glowing coals. Vernis coursed the mountain roads on his motorcycle, from forest to town, from town to forest, supervising the cutting performed by each one of his crews, watching them weigh the loads of cork and wood, making sure the work at the sawmill proceeded smoothly. But perhaps his aforementioned similarity to a Roman centurion, more than his undeniable diligence, was the underlying reason why Papa, in everything relating to the woods, preferred to deal with him before any other contract laborer in the district. No matter how much people said that with Vernis, when the job was done, the loads of wood never really squared with the official tally, his resemblance to a Roman centurion and his sagacious attitude, a mixture of deference and distance, made dealing with him seem more personal, more deliberately favorable than simply businesslike, made his visits to the house seem downright friendly. And Papa, carried away by that surging happiness the summer resident experiences from anyone just dropping by, those welcome, unexpected arrivals that break the monotony of country life, didn't miss the chance to tell Grandpa again, as if it were some sort of hobby, go on, show them how the dowsing works. Come on, Don Eduardo, come over here, see if you have any better luck. It worked perfectly for Vernis.

He'd nabbed him in the exact moment he was leaving the garden, trying to escape—the newspaper finally secured, tucked under his arm—to the corner with the hydrangea, both shaded and exposed to the full heat of the setting sun. He made him set down the newspaper, grasp the two sides of the supple dowsing fork, and start crossing the arbor in every direction, turning and turning again, slowly, the vine shoot dangling before him, while Papa, standing next to Vernis, from the first step of the terraced path, commented aloud on his movements, sarcastic, with the confident impunity that always comes from sharing company with a Roman centurion, alongside that man who listened to him in attentive silence, smiling inscrutably, perhaps understanding, perhaps not, perhaps feeling uncomfortable and inhibited, perhaps persuaded that, in any case, the best thing was to simply surrender to the moment. Come on, Don Eduardo! Vernis found it on the first try! And Grandpa went back and forth, no longer trying to find the spring nor claiming any success nor, much less, fussing nor trying to get out of it, possessed by the frightened resignation of one who only expects that, sooner or later, the stifling exhibition whose protagonist he's become, thanks to some bad luck, will cease. Seems that it doesn't work with women, Papa said. You've got to be a real man for it to work right.

Another reason for confidence: the fact of being on his own land, in the family home, *la casa pairal* bearing the family name which, in his status as the firstborn, it was his honor to represent, a large country property (*La Noguera*—the walnut tree? Some kind of name that suggested luxuriant foliage, the perfect name for a fresh, secluded spot), which although undivided and of lasting economic significance for the old family fortune, was still at least that—the family patrimony, of his family, a situation of moral dominion evident even in Eugenia, her habitual rude remarks and sharp comments notably more restrained here than in Barcelona. Definitely in Eugenia's case, despite her declaration—repeated every summer—that this was the last year she'd let herself be fooled, definitely in her case, that of a woman from the city, there was no doubt whatsoever that spending three months in the country offered some compensations, not least among them the preeminent position that her energetic temperament had helped establish for her among the other women who worked on the property. Consequently, Grandpa was the only real victim, drawn out of his own world, out of his daily rhythms, fatally sacrificed to the children's need for fresh air and open space, their need for a change of atmosphere, to escape from the vicious city environment. At least during summer vacation. And, in terms of country land, there was nothing like the farm itself, of course, impossible to find any place healthier, and without all the expenses involved in staying at a summer colony, which you've necessarily got to take into account. Perhaps, on the other hand, the fact that Papa was on his own family's land and thus contributed as much as possible, even if it was only through the money they saved, to the household expenses, stabilized in equal measure his relations with Grandpa, a circumstance which the old man, being its most immediate beneficiary, did not fail to notice. It was as if, on the contrary, the ongoing situation in Barcelona—where the chalet was in the children's name (yes, but thanks to Grandpa's largesse) and where Grandpa's increasing economic contribution to the family budget provided a remedy which, from year to year, had no other effect than exacerbating and maximizing Papa's harsh, embittered treatment of his father-in-law; as if he were no longer mortified by the unfavorable effect which a son-in-law's economic dependence on his wife's father could produce in third parties as much as, above all, the misapprehension, the objective confusion that might arise from what was, beyond all superficial appearances, nothing more than the result of two different views of life: the contrast between a pugnacious and creative attitude, full of risks, of audacious initiatives that might have, the same way major setbacks might have, propelled him to triumphant success, and, variously, a passive, conservative attitude, lacking in imagination, inclined to invest in reputedly secure stocks, though not, for that reason, in any clearheaded analysis, any less doomed to fail, given the worldwide scale of growing inflation, to become increasingly less profitable, consigning their owner to the slow death of reducing his own expenses as the buying power of his income decreases. Two attitudes, yes: the one generous even in adversity; the other stingy, as well as blind, confronting his destiny, no less inexorable no matter how slow in coming. And this was the bad thing, precisely: that he and not Grandpa was the person most affected by the problems of monetary liquidity, inherent to all times of crisis and socioeconomic convulsions like the one we're currently going through.

What's more, in Barcelona their confrontation was contained, quiet, direct, without the presence of an Uncle Rodrigo, whose contradictory spirit spurred on Papa's verbal brazenness or, simply, by denying him total priority, unleashed a dicey race each midday, when the newspaper arrived from town, to see who would be first to snag it, a contest that Papa did not usually let slip through his fingers, even if it meant going out to meet Dionís the moment his wagon appeared in the distance. Then, returning to the garden, and once comfortably settled in his chair, he would be able to start announcing the latest, most outstanding local or international stories, letting no details diminish the pleasure of his scoop: Trini Pàmies is dead! or American troops land in Korea! Uncle Rodrigo stood up and walked off whistling, as if he'd heard nothing, the same as he might have done years later, when his deafness suddenly got worse, apparently not feigned, which made it necessary to speak right into his ear with the help of a rolled-up magazine for an ear trumpet; later, this process now useless, and reluctant as he was about using any of those hearing aids, which he called deafening devices, there was no other way to converse with him than by jotting questions and answers on paper. Phenomena of parallel development: Uncle Rodrigo's increasing deafness, Papa's increasingly complete economic dependence on Grandpa, the courtship and wedding of the oldest of his children, and the fact that the youngest one had barely stopped by the house since he'd matriculated at university, always out on the town with his pals and with that girl, as Eugenia called Rosa. Phenomena all closely linked, too, to Papa's unilateral rancor toward Grandpa. His revenges, his punishments, the satisfaction with which he emphasized, thanks to his privilege of reading the newspaper first, the most catastrophic aspects of the international situation, the inevitable decisions he would have to confront, selling everything and emigrating, going to live in America or, at least, to the Canary Islands, as far as possible from the scene of a third world war, from its epicenter, Europe, Spain, Barcelona: the crater of a volcano. And when Grandpa stubbornly insisted otherwise, that he wasn't about to move away: But what do you think? That you'll do any good staying here? That you'll defend your values, your properties, this house? You think I wouldn't stay here if I knew I'd be able to defend my part of the farm, a part which, in the long run, would've ended up being worth quite a lot more by itself than everything you have? What do you think the Russians will do with you when they see you? They'll shoot you! Right away, right out here, in the garden, they'll stand you up against the lemon tree and shoot you! Grandpa stood up shaking his head, his chin trembling, his step uncertain. Well, I'm not leaving! I'm staying right here with my things! Papa followed him to his room: Stay here! Stay here! The Russians will finish you off! What I wouldn't like more than to never see you again! And, as if to better illustrate his desires, he slammed the door from outside with the emphasis of the guard or jailer who locks a cell, with the violent twist of wrist of an executioner tightening a garrote.

He had bought himself a yellow, short-sleeved, safari jacket and some electric blue pants.

How do you like it, son? he asked while looking at himself in the mirror, almost in profile, tilting his head, his eyes half-closed. It's the latest fashion. I bought it at the summer sales. Don't you think I look Japanese? The arrival of summer was a breath of fresh air for everyone. In Papa's case because he went for three months to Santa Cecilia (a better name than *La Noguera*). For Grandpa, for the same reason: Papa was away for three months. Eugenia, because she said she was no longer good for those quick trips, that she did better to stay here, in the garden, that it was like being in the countryside, and everyone was more relaxed.

Papa's return, however, like that of a jealous husband, was anticipated with no less fear than resignation, given that it would inevitably constitute one of the most critical moments of the year: Papa's suspicions, his skeptical questions about how much had happened during his absence, his mistrust about the peaceful harmony of Grandpa's daily life all those weeks; the man's easy, blameless relations with others which he had the nerve to conduct; the fact, for example, that his eldest son and his wife and their little boy would drop in to visit him on their way through Barcelona; or that the reckless Rodrigo, deaf as a post and everything, who now barely showed his face around Santa Cecilia, had dared to keep visiting, as if he couldn't care less that he, Papa, his older brother, was at home or not, however much everyone knew that his visits were nothing more than an excuse to satisfy his desire to read the newspaper in the garden, the same way a person visits a public park; or how Rosa's deference for him, under whose good auspices they might have celebrated Rodrigo's birthday—normally ignored—even taking into account Eugenia's reticent attitude regarding Rosa, that girl who's going out with the youngest son, could only have worked against the day turning out happily. Thus, from the very first day, like that officer who, striking while the iron's hot, takes advantage of the opportunity offered him by his first speech to the troops to announce the measures which sanction his firm purpose to restore the exemplary discipline so much lost or relaxed under his predecessor's command, like that boss or official in the act of taking charge, so Papa once again strode brusquely into Grandpa's room, almost as if he were expecting to catch him engaged in some shameful act, and throwing the creased, wrinkled, and reread newspaper onto the bed: Grandpa: your paper. Then he withdrew slowly, never taking his eyes off him, while Grandpa: Oh, thanks very much, moved to pick it up the way a hen zips about to gobble up the freshly strewn grain; never taking his eyes off him while he was closing the door, and then, no less brusquely than he'd opened it, closed it; he'd enjoyed too much liberty already not to clap it shut again the way one locks away some unpleasant memory, especially if the memory refers to oneself, if one appears therein as the principal protagonist.

It was Grandpa's saint's day and Rosa had brought a box of chocolates. After lunch, while she was chatting with Eugenia as she helped her wash the dishes, vainly trying to get on the woman's good side, Papa burst into the sitting room, eyes popping crazily out of his head, as nimble and jumpy as a witch doctor in the throes of casting a spell. He just called me a ninny-hammer! he shouted, followed by Grandpa, the box of chocolates trembling in his hand just as his voice trembled as he addressed himself to Rosa and Eugenia, the way one might address a jury, announcing that Papa had squashed the sweets, and little by little it became clear what had happened, between Grandpa's babbling and Papa's furious punctuating interruptions, each one coming, however, after longer pauses, the same as if in a certain way he took pleasure from the old man's faltering narrative about how Papa had seized the box, what do you suppose they've got inside them, Don Eduardo, let's see, chocolate's very bad for the liver, let me see, and one by one he'd squashed the bonbons, let's see what's inside this one, Don Eduardo, liqueur! pure poison! one by one until Grandpa managed to wrest the box from him, with the few remaining intact chocolates, the projection of an inner smile on Papa's face now as the old man reached this point in the story, although not without the shadow of a worry he would only express that night, after dinner, in the seclusion of the sitting room: Where the devil did he ever come up with that word, ninnyhammer?

Each man accused the other one of eating the grapes from the vine in autumn, before they even ripened, and the loquats in springtime, with the express purpose of getting under each other's skin. Papa always started it, and it was Eugenia who had to provide a third-party defense of Grandpa: well, señor, please be so kind as to leave poor Don Eduardo in peace once and for all, there are no secrets in any household, and the one who always goes dashing off to the toilet is you, not Don Eduardo, and you tell me what causes such a rumbling in the guts if it's not from eating green fruit. And then Papa, already somewhat defensive, mentioned his broken health, his tragic life, the battering blows of misfortune. And the thing is, he knew the rawness with which Eugenia tackled a subject, her surefire capacity to hit the target once she fired, sí señor, you're always quarreling with poor Don Eduardo and complaining about everything, but tell me where you'd be without him, and where would we all be if not for him? After all, he's the one who pays. Because there's no question about it: in this house the one who pays is Grandpa. And then Papa initiated a tactical retreat, an opportune withdrawal, aware, no doubt, that her defense of Grandpa was merely the start of a fearsome frontal attack on his own positions, full of harsh details and cruel punctuations, a crushing verbal display that would end in lamentation, in bitter reflection, the unhappiness of having ended up in that house where, eventually, it was she and she alone who paid for the broken plates, she who stuck up for the others, yes, that's right, run away, hide so you don't have to hear me, that way you'll avoid me with the hot-flashes I get when the kid from the grocery store or the pharmacy comes by and you tip them twenty centavos, which is worse than giving them nothing at all; so, I prefer to go there instead and carry everything home myself even though my legs can't take it anymore. And when a bill collector comes by? Ah, then you do remember poor Don Eduardo. But without twisting his arm, of course, acting like you don't owe him anything. You think I don't notice? You go into his room just like you were going to belt him and you unload on him: Grandpa, they're here for you to pay this bill. As if you had nothing to do with the cost, as if he wasn't paying for everything! As if poor Don Eduardo isn't paying all the expenses in the house already. And on top of it, you've got this crazy idea that the bill collectors are stealing flowers from the garden while they wait. Not likely, not with what I've managed to coax the best I can from those four cuttings I transplanted, not even if they were orchids! And what happens is, you're upset because they come to collect the bills that you can't pay, and it has to be poor Don Eduardo who takes care of them. That's what happens. The same as with Uncle Rodrigo when you complain about how on the farm he uses up what you've bought, the sugar, the oil, everything, and I'm sure it's the other way round, that it's you who uses his things, because there's no one there to pay for you, because there's no grandfather to look after the family. And now you're doing just fine, alright, keeping poor Don Eduardo locked up here as if he were some prisoner, and the day he's gone, without his money, I don't know what'll become of you, I don't know what's to become of all of us. You'd best look after him like a golden treasure.

Eugenia's taking a position which invariably favored Grandpa, comprehended not only the compassion one could feel for him—a naturally affable and peaceful man, always concerned with causing the least bother, trying to be as unobtrusive as possible—but also, and especially, the simple fact that it really was he, the owner of the house, and not Papa, who paid. A position which did not cease to be a reflection of, a contagion of the climate which Papa himself had created in the house upon turning Grandpa into a symbol of his own economic disasters, into a personification of his life's tragedy, something, in short, shameful, unpresentable, something to be kept out of sight, the less seen by people the better. A gradual isolation, and not only of Grandpa but also of himself and of Eugenia, which the three of them had made for themselves, discovering, even, its advantages, a state almost like placidity and absorbed recollection that Papa was the first to break upon overstepping his bounds with Grandpa, upon externalizing that spitefulness comparable only to the cruelties which the repressed homosexual is capable of inflicting upon the one who is openly gay, thus providing a foothold for Eugenia's replies, for her scenes, for the judgments and pronouncements through which she exercised her right to punish the transgressor of an order, of a balance, of which he was, at the same time, the author. Visits? said Eugenia, her legs stretched out in the sun, resting atop the other chair. I'd prefer nobody come. They do nothing more than bring problems, complicating people's lives, etcetera, affirmations too conceptually ambiguous while at the same time too confident about the cause-effect relation for it not to become evident that the general plan was becoming personal, and, more concretely, that the object of her declared aversion to visitors could be perfectly reduced to a single person. Rosa, that girl whom Grandpa, on the contrary, by competing with Papa in the displays of friendship they lavished on her, received with such affection, a girl who brought gifts of bonbons and pastries, and about whom, surely, he barely knew anything besides her name, not even if she was the grandson's girlfriend, or whether they were perhaps married and had not told him, or perhaps they had told him, and he'd attended their wedding and everything but had forgotten all about it.

Grandpa would always be the first one in the house to rise in the morning, up even before Eugenia; Papa claimed that it was he, intensely insomniac, who always woke up first, but that he preferred to stay in bed a while longer even if it were only to wait until the bathroom was free. Eugenia served Grandpa breakfast in the kitchen, always a more substantial breakfast than the yogurt and four pieces of toast Papa ate alone in his bedroom. But, before that, Papa came out to get a breath of fresh air; in truth, to pick up the newspaper first. Once read and reread, without any hurry, he went into Grandpa's room and tossed it onto the old man's bed: Grandpa: the paper. At that hour, the sun—if there were any—was already sufficiently strong, and Papa, while Eugenia went out to do the day's shopping, went into the garden, to check on things, as he said, and Grandpa, with his newspaper, went up to the terrace on the roof. I don't understand how he can stand so much sun, Papa said during lunch; hours and hours sitting there stuck right up against the wall like a lizard, with the sun straight overhead, cooking his brain. They sat eating together at the same table, but not the same meal, Papa sticking fast to his routine, according to the strict diet which the doctor had once prescribed him due to his delicate health, not because of his now-reduced appetite. After eating, he had first dibs on the toilet, because, also on the doctor's orders, he had to withdraw to rest a while, a few hours of siesta amid the daily strife, moments of calm Grandpa took advantage of to enjoy the garden in the splendid afternoon. At dusk, Grandpa returned to his room; or perhaps, when Papa was out because he had to meet someone or attend to some obligation, he might relax in the small sitting room, listening to the radio with Eugenia for company. When Papa didn't go out, it was he who ensconced himself in the small sitting room and listened to the radio, chatting, perhaps arguing, about life with Eugenia, while she came and went, busy preparing dinner. Papa ate dinner in his room, sitting on his bed, and Grandpa ate in the dining room and, in general, although he sat a little while longer in the sitting room, he and Papa wouldn't see each other again until the next day. In summertime, Papa could only think of getting out of town and going up to Santa Cecilia, and getting Grandpa to stop spending so much time up on the terrace.

Grandpa: his maladies, his remedies. He wore a thin cord tied around his right wrist. Look, he said: I notice how it really helps me. In winter he sat in the center of his room, under the single light bulb: he claimed it was warmer there. And then the summers, when he enjoyed the garden as much as possible, a garden which he'd almost grown to form a part of, blending into a wicker chair like just one more object, friend of the birds and lizards, he always seemed to be waiting, between sleep and mealtime, between meal and toilet, between toilet and armchair, raising his eyes, barely, just a brushstroke, as soon as he heard the call to come eat again, looking around sort of like a snail peeking out of its shell. The fact is, he's an introvert, said Papa. That's what Rodrigo told me when he was still sane, when his mind was still clear: and he told it to me as a doctor: an introvert. An egotistical creature who only thinks of himself, who takes no interest in what other people might be going through. It seems that when he was a student his friends already saw that he was an odd duck, they even thought it was strange when he got married and had children. For poor Grandma, their marriage must have been a real cross to bear. And he, by contrast, just look at him: his wife dies on him, his two daughters die on him, and yet there you have him, cool as can be. And me, just losing my wife, I was right on the verge of coming unglued! But he's always just gone his own way, always there alone all by himself, all blessed day. I'd like to know what he must do and not do up on the terrace for so many hours, with the sun boiling his brains. I don't even know how he stands it: any normal man would have already become deeply disturbed by now. But he handles it all, he's got an iron constitution. And it seems that's how introverts are, they can stand everything. They don't suffer. Nothing touches them. You only have to compare him with Rodrigo: Rodrigo is a confirmed bachelor and a loafer and selfish and he's always been a bit crazy. But at least he's normal.

One sunny day, probably a Sunday; a day when Rosa had come over for lunch and they discovered that Eugenia hadn't set a place for her, as if she'd forgotten, and then, defiant, she came out to say there was no coffee; a spring day, the garden almost feverish, with scents, with flies and wasps, blackbirds trilling. Or maybe it was a cloudy day, with the wind sounding almost like rain among the dry leaves. He'd spent the day with Rosa and, on returning to the house, now dark, he ran into Papa and Eugenia—it must have been after Grandpa died—talking about hell, that place where they were never going to end up, said Papa, because they'd already suffered enough in this life. In fact, take me, for example, if I'd not had faith, I would have committed suicide. And she: well, then, you would've gone to hell. And he: not at all, woman. If a person commits suicide it's because they've lost their mind, and someone who loses their mind, in a fit of madness, is not responsible for their actions. And she: yes, they do go to hell, yes: whoever does something evil goes to hell. And Papa:

that depends, woman, that depends. A friend of mine, well, an acquaintance, committed suicide after having been ruined by a woman; but, even so, who are we to judge anybody? How can we know what their final thoughts were, if they died repentant or not? And Eugenia: do you see? Miserable the man who falls into the hands of one of those women. Miserable. And Papa: judge not and you shall not be judged, Eugenia. Forgive and you shall be forgiven.

It was not only a loss of aggressiveness; it was also as if Papa found himself feeling more tired, and that slump in his physical condition would have repercussions on his morale and his attitude toward life. Like Uncle Rodrigo's deafness: perhaps from too many antibiotics, that was the doctor's theory; perhaps from refusing, once and for all, to listen to the world at large, and to his old servant in particular, the final link in his personal relationship with the world. In addition to avoiding his bad breath, his ever-dwindling number of visitors found it easier to communicate with him through writing, jotting their questions and answers on any one of those sheets of paper that piled up on his sitting room table, intermixed, juxtaposed with other affirmations and interrogations which, read in retrospect, while the people filed past his coffin and offered condolences to the old servant, the person, in short, closest to him in terms of cohabitation, not relation, and everybody remarked on the noticeable similarity of that body to Papa's, the family resemblance lost since childhood and recovered by both in rigor mortis, with such scant difference of time, besides, etcetera, a blahblahblah that sounded like the ambient music of those sentences written in distinct moments and by different people, pronouncements which, read in such circumstances, would acquire, more than a supernatural significance—like messages arrived from the beyond—an anticipatory and more appropriate meaning, thanks to their internal logic; comparable only to what the Tarot generates, from the ambiguous values of prediction: The planet Venus, Santa Cecilia? I'm also leaving, It's worth a fortune, The well.

Papa contemplated, with a calculating stare, a pile of cork stripped from an oak, ready to be carted away. The strips, especially if they came from a cork oak peeled for the first time, were wrinkly and gray like the skin shed by a snake, and there was something sinful in the pallid nakedness of the trunks stripped of their bark. It began to grow dark; they went back toward the house, making their way up the steep garden paths, without any hurry, in time to see Grandpa come in, attracted perhaps by the merriment from the kitchen, the windows brightly lit, the jokes exchanged by the women, the clatter of the pots and pans, a signal that dinner was on the way. Papa shook his head, as if agreeing. Life, he said. I, who married a beautiful woman, now find myself condemned to deal with a sullen old man!

Digging on the well in the arbor was abandoned when they hit solid rock before going down even thirty feet. Nevertheless, given its proximity to the house, the work was not a complete loss, because, blocked up or whatever the old cesspit was, it was judged preferable—before getting into unquestionably bothersome repairs with potentially unpredictable results—to appoint the newly-dug well for that purpose, its characteristics so perfectly suited to the task that it seemed to have been made to order.

APHRODITE DIALOGUE.

They've shared some secrets with you, he told her. She smiled; it showed on her face that they had indeed shared some secrets with her and that she really wanted to spill the beans. And he: Who? Aurea? The German? Your dyke friend? Someone from the yacht? Carlos? Carlos? Carlos, she said. And he: at the Nautic? And she: of course. He dropped by, sure he'd find me, he knows perfectly well that if it's sunny out, at that time of day, I'm always there on the terrace. He made a face like he was surprised, what a coincidence, and since I was reading, he insisted he didn't want to bother me, that he was headed for a different table; well, you know how he plays the gallant masochist when he's hungover. But the moment I told him to stop being a pest, that he should pull up a chair for god's sake, that it was my turn to buy him a drink, he started talking all at once, like some introvert who suddenly discovers his tongue. You can imagine the scene: Carlos seated to my left, glass in hand, talking to me staring out at the bay. He said he wanted to apologize, that he doesn't remember it too well but he thinks that yesterday he was a bit rude to me. Of course he was talking about when he started arguing with Aurea and me because we were sitting apart talking by ourselves, and he called us a couple of gossiping whores. I told him he needn't apologize, that I hadn't felt offended by anything he'd said. I realized what he really wanted: to share some secrets; that bit about apologizing was just an excuse, a way of breaking the ice. What he was really interested in was discussing his relationship with Aurea. But, well, you know him, his tricks, his odd little complications, how he beats around the bush, like any real Capricorn, and so before all that he had to go back and start talking about his grandpa: the story of the grouper; seems he'd already forgotten he'd told it to us just yesterday. That one about when the grandfather went to see them in Barcelona and told them that in the morning, before catching the train, he'd almost caught the biggest grouper he'd ever seen in his life, and he spent the day saying that Barcelona made him feel ill, that he didn't understand how they could live there, breathing such filthy polluted air. And the next morning he told them that he'd dreamed that he caught the grouper and he went back to Rosas on the first train and there he caught the grouper in the very spot he'd dreamed about catching it. Anyway, his mania for always starting at the beginning, of going back to explain how everything started: his grandfather, his mother, his father, his brother, Aurea, and finally, but in the center, himself, Carlos, the ultimate cause of his stories. That's why I noticed right away that he was going to start telling me that he'd had an unhappy childhood. That his father, with a son dead in the war, and the other, Carlos, little more than a boy, and him, the father, fresh out of jail or the concentration camp or whatever it was, and without any steady employment, only some occasional repair job as a plumber, electrician, or mechanic, nothing more, he, the father, felt overwhelmed by the circumstances, incapable of reacting, of even getting a certificate stating he'd been cleared of charges and doing something to find a real, steady job, tired of fighting, inert. And that it was she, the mother, who saved the house by doing odd jobs, killing herself as a cleaning lady from dawn till dark. And that this situation of incapacity and dependence could only aggravate the father's depressive state, the parasitic sense of his existence, or rather, subsistence, undermined, too, by an old pulmonary lesion flaring up, phthisis now instead of tuberculosis: somber, silent, submerged more and more each day in the darkness of his bed. The only thing he wanted to see before he died, he said, was a body hanging from every single lamppost along the Diagonal, a priest and a soldier, and a priest and a soldier, and so on. Carlos, with an elementary school education, plus the cultural baggage he'd picked up by himself along the way—that typical autodidact education, reading in the public library, where they've got the widest variety of French authors, why so many I don't know, Sue and Descartes, Dumas and Rousseau, Hugo and Renan and Zola, all so woefully translated, works that our young autodidact usually reads, always with the same goal: to learn as fast as possible, to grow up as quickly as possible, to escape as soon as possible—he began to work as a pen pusher in an office at age fourteen. He changed companies several times, leathery, indifferent to the workplace relationships his friends seemed to dutifully accept; more than the work and even the salary, he was interested, very much so, in the possibilities of continuing to read, to keep preparing himself for the adventure for which he thought himself destined; to read and read wherever he might, on the streetcar, in the metro, at home, at the office, hiding his book among the papers on his desk. The only exception, his only distraction was Aurea, who worked as a typist in the same department. The only woman for him—possibly the first—given their general similarities: the same aversion to the environment in which they were growing up, the same secret ambitions and hidden projects, mutually revealed in the course of a long, cautious process of identification. By that time his father had already died; he never learned that his oldest son was alive, that he was in Argentina and that things were going well for him. When they received the news it was as if the sun began to spin backward; but there was no room for doubt: a handwritten letter brought directly by a traveler who'd previously found out the family's current address from their old neighbors. That was like the signal Carlos and Aurea were awaiting, and when they told his mother that they were going to Buenos Aires, that they'd be sending money until they could write to her to join them, that she mustn't worry, that everything would turn out just fine, she said yes, that they must go, that she would follow along later; it's your chance, she said. I've never found out if she already knew then that she was gravely ill, that she would never see us again nor, of course, meet up with us in Argentina. In her letters she never told us anything and the first news that things were going to turn out exactly like that, that we'd never see her again, came to us in a letter from Grandpa, when she was too ill and could no longer write. Sometimes I think, deep down, I also knew it, and that I simply didn't want to acknowledge it. The impulse to flee, to run like hell away from that horrid office, from that world full of imbeciles and maniacs and sons of bitches, was too strong an impulse, I think. And the weight of everything I'd never had, which others had and have always had.

Carlos lit another Romeo y Julieta with a strip of the cedar wrapper, slowly, burning the tip equally all the way round before taking his first puff. He watched them study the photo, several children and women posing for the camera in a neighborhood that suggested a still from some Italian neorealist film, the close-cropped heads, the sandals, the droopy socks, the striped bathrobes, runny noses and—spontaneously converted into the center of the composition, almost as if it were surrounded by a halo—that face with a smiling mouth and anguished eyes, belonging to the one who tries to dissemble however possible, to seem normal and even content, one more among those other children who, facing the event implied by the presence of the staring camera lens, reacted by searching for an expression both dead serious and benumbed, or audacious and arrogant, or stupidly kind. A boy like all the rest. Not one of those boys who, affecting a docile attitude and hypocritical meekness before his elders, which frequently garners him praise so that he's even held up as a model of good behavior before other more fully, openly rebellious boys, conceals sentiments and ideas whose knowledge would leave his closest relatives stupefied; little haters with a copious history of cruelty and destructive actions, pyromaniacal tendencies, anonymous evils: that fire rapidly snuffed out, nobody knows how it started, those scraps of chopped-up fruit bat, that poor neighbor who lives on the mezzanine floor who's got to stop trying to grow flowers in the four little pots on her windowsill, who must renounce her pointless care of a few plants regularly destroyed by some heartless soul. And the worst thing of all: our little hater would love to rain down his horrors upon that person who so affectionately caresses his hair. Later, now a big boy, his solitary sexual experiments, always somewhat frenetic, as if he deliberately wanted to go blind, to crush those obsessive images that agitated him. The repugnance he felt for whores, however much they sometimes excited him, and the subsequent disaster—kept secret—of each attempt, always realized through some friend's initiative, the oft-mentioned Ignacio, for example, or some fellow from work whom he might despise and to whom, precisely by virtue of such contempt, he cannot allow himself to show any weakness in the face of the obligatory acts of initiation characteristic of seventeen-year-olds. Disasters which, perhaps, he would not manage to conquer until he entered into some intimate relationship with a girl from the office, a relationship which, begun by way of adventure, as a first seduction or conquest, will surely end up becoming something much more long-lasting than initially foreseen. Other outstanding facts: his proposals, or rather his frustrated attempts, to be an aviator or a sailor (fly, sail, escape) counterposed to the pragmatism of the projects which his mother—something more than a servant?—expounded on at dinnertime, plans relating to the most lucrative short-term work for a youth of fourteen without other resources, sixteen, eighteen years old, a job in the future and which, at the same time, might bring some money home. Overcoming each such maternal project thanks to the undeniable effort of our solitary young hater, thanks to his hard-won self-education, thanks to his readings directed toward acquiring a general cultural knowledge before any specialized concrete knowledge; meaning: the anteposition of his anxious desire to know about the daily necessities of subsistence. His mother's calls to face reality against his deep passion for reading. The success that being able to start working as a pen pusher in his first sinister office surely signified for him. His search for other jobs and ways out, his search for the long-awaited opportunity in the newspaper advertisements, his systematic preparation for the great adventure. The expected signal, the arrival of that opportunity, the possibility of beginning, with his brother's support, a new life in Argentina. And everything in order to finally land here, said Carlos. He looked around him: the Bay of Rosas, deep black under that starry sky, the reflections especially intense along the shoreline, the chiaroscuro of the town, distant music from a discotheque, the motel garden, the pebble beds discretely illuminated, the porch, chaise longue, glasses, bottles, the

Siamese cat, the insects accumulated inside the streetlight, the Moorish gecko motionless by the lamppost, the thermometer and barometer hanging from one of the porch columns, the panoramic view of the Ideal City hanging inside, opposite the window, a drawing in Chinese ink, colored in pencil, the work of an anonymous artist, very likely a madman.

Coming back to what I was talking about yesterday, he said, now in that moment in which the same mental stammering—of which verbal stammering is simply a reflection—makes one forget their intention to stop drinking for a while and pour oneself a tall whiskey, because what really matters is being in a good mood, loquacious, on the verge of brilliance, nearly dominating the situation, practically dominating the world. Meaning: the moment of interrogative perplexity now past, the void vanquished, the stray transitory thread recovered, the point at which the subject came to a rest, a theme developed night after night with exceptional conversationalists, friends unimaginable to the Carlos of yesteryear, now participating in a conversation he himself initiated and, what's more, a conversation which he managed to focus on himself, impelled not so much by the intellectual level of those friends or by their capacity of understanding and the consequent pleasure of displaying it before people of a similar level as by the possibility that, upon doing so, he himself might manage to clarify the ideas in question. A fleeting theme, difficult not only to delimit but even to raise, its very complexity, his shyness, the fear of expressing himself badly, of becoming irksome, even of seeming stupid, the very alcohol drunk to conquer that shyness, obstacles which each night postponed for yet another night the possibility of reaching any conclusion. The theme: can a concept as rational as the concept of class explain the incoherencies not simply of behavior but, even, of personality? Or rather: what then is the cause that makes me how I am? Or rather: What's happening to me?

The thing we might least imagine: my brother, the dead hero, defending his Marxist ideology, not only had he not died but he wasn't exactly a hero either. His conduct on the front left much to be desired—isn't that the way it's usually phrased?—especially at the end, when he collapsed before reaching the front itself, and executed an opportune desertion which perhaps saved him from the firing squad. Was he also a traitor, as some of his old friends said, or simply a coward? Neither one, I think. These kinds of dilemmas are merely stupidities. There are always earlier questions, problems of conviction, indirect reactions. In fact—and this is the only certainty—as soon as he arrived in South America he completely disavowed both his ideology and his friends. Was this a consequence of his previous desertion? Responses to the cause itself, to the reasons why he deserted them? The fact is that, once in Argentina, he dedicated himself exclusively to making money. And quite successfully. We ourselves, without his help, would not have enjoyed the luck we had. Or, at least, the early days in Buenos Aires would have been much more difficult. To get used to the way those people live is, all by itself, a trauma. But the worst thing was the other Spaniards: the exiles, with their stories and their bitter grudges, some fellows who didn't deal with my brother nor, luckily, with us either. And the others, the emigrants themselves, pure scumbags and riffraff, Gallegos who thought of nothing but saving money so they could sail back home as soon as possible. The same as us, on the other hand. But only in appearance: for us, on leaving Barcelona, the truly fundamental thing was to get away however possible, to escape from the environment in which we'd been raised. And they, on the other hand, continued living like in Spain, without thinking about anything but Spain, about when they would return to their dear little fatherland with their savings, about the business they were going to start in the town to the admiration and envy of their fellow countrymen. Frightening people. They were right to say in Argentina that we were worse than the Jews, incomprehensible, unassimilable. And the Argentines, well, they're Argentines, tacky, prissy, and affected, smarmy, unbearably pretentious. For that matter, I got along better with the Yankees, business executives, executives from other companies who were friends of the firm's executives, embassy employees, CIA agents, in short, the American colony. At work everything was clear with them and, at least, on the weekends they also needed to get drunk. Perhaps they did it as a matter of social standing, or for public relations, or so they could be more productive come Monday, or for whatever reason, but the fact of the matter is that they were preferable. Aurea also preferred them. Right? She had an affair with one of them that lasted quite a while, some guy named Bob. One of these guys from Nebraska or thereabouts, tall, handsome, healthy, blunt, and even less stupid than what you might think at first glance. It's even within the realm of possibility that he wasn't a horrible lover. That's what I think, at least; of course in this matter, it's Aurea who has the last word. Very sweet and affectionate in any case, one of those guys who always pays proper attention to women. Exactly as you're imagining him, I'm sure: the typical American stuffed full of principles, a little naive for non-Americans, a complete idiot, I mean. Sort of a tennis jock, let's say. But women really enjoy these sorts of idiots once in a while. Anyway, that was Aurea's most significant romantic adventure in Buenos Aires. As far as I know, of course. Nothing else like Bob the Boob. They got together while I was in Barcelona making arrangements for the return trip, apartment-hunting and all that stuff, and she, in Buenos Aires, closing down our house there, using up all the supplies and groceries right down to the last minute. Very discreetly, that's for sure. I don't even think my brother ever found out. And he must've known Bob, who was a friend of friends. The one who never had the pleasure of meeting him was me; I don't even know what his face looked like. Of course there's no need to have seen him in order to imagine him perfectly well.

Bob, Bob, Bob, she said. Enough about Bob. The curious thing is that, instead, Carlos never mentions that architect who built them the motel, not at all. His jealousy shows, he can't help it, but he never mentions him as one of Aurea's possible lovers. He says that faggots disgust him, and that's it. Why doesn't he accept the fact that faggots can also have adventures with women? Why does the fact of him being a faggot disqualify him as a rival, like in duels from olden times, when it was a dishonor for a gentleman to cross swords with a commoner? Why does it turn out to be excessively ridiculous for him, the idea that Aurea might cuckold him with a faggot? Or maybe because, knowing himself as he well as he does, he reaches the possible conclusion that her fling with the architect, more than a reality, is a figment of his imagination, made more potent perhaps by the atmosphere of mystery and complicity which, of course, Aurea is capable of creating around what might well be no more than just a sincere friendship? Because Aurea knows how to handle herself, there's no doubt whatsoever about that. She knows that Carlos knows her and therefore she knows the exact interpretation he's going to assign to each one of her actions, her words, the value he'll place, too, on her reaction. She knows what certain things mean to Carlos, according to and with whom they socialize, certain postures, specific ways of sitting, specific suits and hairstyles and makeup; and even whether she chooses one discotheque or another, or that, when they dine out, she insists on ordering a certain kind of wine. And her silences and her smiles and her manner of laughing suddenly, for no apparent reason, as if from pure vitality, triumphant. And that way she has of caressing his hair like she would a little boy, as if telling him, in spite of everything I love you, silly, which infuriates Carlos even more. And her feigned frigidity, that frigidness Carlos talks about, which she doesn't mention, when the normal thing would be the opposite, one of those confessions that women usually make to their friends, generally more for self-glorification than lamentation, and about which the husband is usually the last one to find out. Because if Carlos calls her frigid in public whenever he's had a few too many, apart from the desire to offend possibly conveyed by such an affirmation, or from the desire to demean her, or for self-justification, it's because Aurea has given him to understand it's true, if in fact she's not told him that explicitly. To what end? With the goal of arousing, or better yet, sharpening Carlos's lack of self-confidence which evidently possessed him, increasing in him his feeling of clumsiness in front of women, making him feel himself erotically inept, incapable of giving them pleasure in bed. And, as a result, for fear of disaster, inhibiting in Carlos any temptation toward adventure which, at the same time, inversely, fills him with doubt: would Aurea also be frigid with others? Placing Carlos in a situation of inferiority, on the defensive: making him feel betrayed and incapable, for his part, of betraying or recognizing the degree to which that betrayal affects him; a sorrowful recognition, difficult to root out, especially in a person of introverted character, which perhaps constituted Aurea's true objective: Carlos's unconditional surrender. A plea that she have no more affairs. An admission of the pain they cause him. A formal recognition that he's willing to yield however necessary. And, to all those things, Aurea doesn't give an inch: she has affairs and she doesn't care if Carlos has them too, that each of them can go their own way. But, is this really true? Won't he obey Aurea's outlandish plan with the desire of masking, avenging, and making impossible the repetition of something which probably happened in Buenos Aires, something about which the responsibility falls principally, if not entirely, on Carlos, and which irremediably destroyed the harmony that existed until then between them both? So that now, since that occasion, and from now on, Carlos tells himself: Aurea says they've all been bad for her, that all her affairs have been a disaster. But, what about Bob? If so, then why did their affair last so long? And now, with the faggot architect? Won't the fact create in her a certain perverse excitation, precisely from the fact that he is a queer, that pleasure some women experience making love with homosexuals, in competing, and successfully so, with men themselves? Who can assure me that she doesn't have a different experience in bed with the others than she has with me, that with them all her frigid inertia isn't converted into activity and expert initiative? If she were at least a lesbian and she liked some pretty girl and the three of us went to bed together and, with Aurea present, I'd have the confidence to respond, and get sufficiently hard and ejaculate at the right time, that confidence I have only with her and which, by extension, would also apply to the young woman, and then I could satisfy them both, better than many of these semi-beardless youths who brag so much but who, when it comes right down to it, blow their wads as fast as bunny rabbits. And then, my self-confidence recovered, quit going to whores for once and bed one of those girls you see these days and make her have a hundred orgasms and, the next time, have her bring a little friend along, and get down and dirty in all kinds of complicated combinations, Aurea now excluded, bringing her down to earth with a thump for lack of anything better. Those girls who reappear each spring, floating in like pollen on the sunny breeze, provocative in their insolent youth, in their vivacious nonchalance, in their affected languor and lack of enthusiasm, those little whores and not Aurea, now with too many lotions and massages on her body, her flesh no less flaccid, though, her skin no less dull than the skin on the bodies of any of those whores I just picked up some night, already drunk, and whom I'll no longer pursue, no less ashamed now by the disaster than I was in adolescence, a disaster neither bought nor sold, nor settled by the stipulated price, the only difference between now and then is the difference between thirty pesetas and three thousand. The humiliating sensation of ridicule that I only managed to conquer with Aurea and which I only continue conquering with her, with that elusive body, now not even quite so attractive as before, ungrateful for all my efforts to make her feel pleasure, achieve climax, and share orgasm, a solitary orgasm, almost a hand job in his helplessness, which, by a diabolical paradox, he might perhaps be incapable of reaching with any other person, however much some morning, looking at these young springtime girls, and with all rightful desire, he might come to think the opposite. And he: but, yesterday, what did she tell you? And she: Aurea? Nothing. She's too clever to ever share explicit secrets, so that others might think that she's sharing them when she's really just asking you if you want another splash of whiskey, in order to limit herself, in short, to a word, whatever that might be—love? adventure? or even simply: him?—pronounced with an implicitly contemptuous intonation, contemptuous but conventional, with a conventionality only comparable to the kind displayed by one of those radiantly healthy girls in American movies who, as the inevitable victim of some misunderstanding, declares, between loud tearful sobs, that all men are disgusting pigs. Aurea knows quite well that chatting too much with friends about matters with her husband—especially when she's lit up from alcohol—can later provoke, when things between them both seem to have temporarily settled down, a violent rupture with those friendly repositories of secrets, relationships that must be severed for sanity's sake due to the peril involved merely because one of them listened to her, an operation similar to those liquidations by which mobsters settle scores with the hit man who knows too much, or to the implacable demise of the royal architect, the only person aware of the secret rooms and passages concealed within the walls of the palace he designed and built.

Last night I had a wonderfully pleasant dream, said Aurea. I don't remember exactly what made it so pleasant or who appeared in the dream. The only thing I know is that it was nice. Not hard to imagine, said Carlos: you dreamed about fucking Bob. And Aurea: Please don't start. Don't be a cretin. And Carlos: I shouldn't start? I'm not doing anything except repeating your very own words. A few nights ago you were dreaming out loud, talking in your sleep; the things you were saying didn't make much sense—at least not to me—but you said

Bob's name. And Aurea: out loud? She seemed sincerely surprised. Well, how can one be sure, exactly? How can you be sure, if you dream aloud or talk in your sleep, whether what someone says you said is really true or not? Aurea makes up dreams for her convenience, for example, to disturb, if not to annoy, Carlos, without having to give explanations. In short, who's to blame for anything they dream? Aurea might also pretend to be talking in her sleep, murmur perturbing vagaries, as if she's asleep, knowing that Carlos is still awake, listening to her words. But, Carlos? Would he believe Aurea's dreams just because? Wouldn't he be perfectly capable, starting from a base of certainty, of also amplifying them at his convenience upon affirming that, asleep, she had said one thing or another? Was Aurea lying when she pretended to be talking in her sleep or was Carlos lying when he assured her that she had uttered one thing or another while fully asleep? And, in turn, were the dreams Carlos said he'd dreamed real, just as unanswerable as Aurea's, and thus no less malleable to his calculations as well as his desires?

And do you know what I dreamed the other night? asked Carlos. That the three of us went to bed together: you, your architect, and I, one after the other, each one mounting the others, fucking each other in the ass. No, not at night; it was siesta time, and everything happened in the same bed where I was sleeping. Well? What do you think? Now you can go and tell your friends, those witches you hang out with, that it turns out your husband must also be half-queer, or just a complete faggot, if you prefer. And Aurea: You wanna stop drinking now, please? You're such a beast when you drink. I wish you could see yourself. You don't even seem intelligent: you turn into an angry little dwarf incapable of reason, a caveman, a complete animal. Then later you're horrified by how little you remember, like after the other night, in Cadaqués. They were some rather annoying middle-class people, some real snobs, the whole nine yards, I agree, but if you go to that kind of party you can already guess the kinds of people you're going to run into; if you're looking for something else, just don't go and that's it. What you can't do is accept the invitation and show up all uptight and very correct, and then during the party, as you get drunk, lose control, start getting out of hand, and start groping the young women, and break glasses and knock ashtrays over. Tripping over everybody, burning other people with your cigarettes, and in a display of masochistic exhibitionism, burn yourself, stubbing out a lit cigarette against the back of your hand to demonstrate how well you can withstand the pain, your tired old party trick. And the foolish things you say, your idiotic laughter, and your way of gesturing just like a clown, a somewhat tiresome clown, perhaps, but in the end, a clown whose routine never fails to amuse the very same bourgeois people who drive you so crazy. Maybe that's why they invite you, don't you think? You're so appropriately contrite the next day and all you want to know are all the little details about what happened, the particulars of each and every scene. And when you're loaded drunk it's the same everywhere, in restaurants, nightclubs, out on the town. Either the service is bad, or you feel ill from how filthy the place is, or the people at the next table are eavesdropping on our conversation, or you can't stand the reactionary tone of what they're saying, or that fat guy with the rings on his hand is grotesque, or you can't stand the stupid cocksucking look of the daddy's boy who steps out on the dance floor, or if they stare at me on the street, or if they've tried to flirt with me, you can't hold back . . . What's up? Looking for some action, handsome? With that faggot's face of yours? Always ready, willing, and able to plunge in right up to your neck, to start a ruckus, you become some bragging troublemaker who insults and shouts and struggles. You're such an imbecile! What I'd like some time is for you to find yourself face to face with someone just like you, someone to shake you up good and proper, who'll teach you the lesson you deserve! Irritable, aggressive, with that simmering violence so common in some people—in general, the fruit of all the rancors stored away inside the hypocritical and even servile boy one was in years past, who—a boy no longer—continues to act like one though, in a certain way. The now almost consubstantial duplicity, the capacity of being, like a good dutiful beaten dog, the completely despicable creep he needs to be whenever he requires something from someone, and just as tyrannical as possible with his subordinates—waiters, employees, people in inferior positions—when he sees them behave exactly the same as how he behaves when the circumstances require, and they shrink even without knowing him, without even knowing who he is exactly, only because he dresses elegantly and appears to be rich; in short, the best of all uniforms. Reactions that can also be resolved the other way around, out of a pure zeal for contradiction, upon affirming—at a party in full swing, packed with snobs and annoying bourgeoisie, the equivalent, thanks to their social position, of these other bourgeoisie before whom he had to shrink so often, and must still, about such and such a film or book that he admires—that none of those present would even think twice about such a film or book, or on the contrary, that such a work, which everyone likes, or at least everyone is talking about, seems to him completely stupid, something truly unbearable. Either his way of combatting the snobbery of a bourgeoisie from whom he feels detached, however much, objectively, it might actually be the class to which he belongs, or perhaps his way of compensating for the supposedly inherent inferiority of a self-taught cultural education, asking, for example, with the face of an idiot or some dull brute: Rabelais? Who the fuck is this Rabelais? The same motives can be attributed to the phobias normally manifested by the kind of people we're talking about, although without the hidden violence which alcohol brings to the surface, phobias generally lost among the rubbish heap upon which one usually reconstructs their childhood. Thus, for example, dispensing first with the most common phobias, fear of priests, fear of faggots, etcetera, the irrepressible fear of expectations, which should not be confused with the simple, natural impatience of one who has just enough time and many things to do; locales especially critical in that regard: generally doctors' offices, restaurants, airports, police stations, metro stations, public offices, and waiting rooms. No doubt a consequence of the different kinds of waiting that comprised his childhood, the line to get into the cinema, the line to collect their food rations, etcetera, now alone, now accompanied by some family member, with his mother. And that other waiting which marks a poor child's youth: awaiting enough money for something, the time spent saving up to buy something. And in a more general way, the symbolic waits which, for the subject, reduced life back in those times, the time yet to transpire, the distance that still separated him from his goals, being grown-up, fleeing, to have nothing to do with either the army or priests, America. Also the frequent object of such phobias are events and occurrences which, not for their irrelevant or anecdotal appearance, cease to provoke violent reactions which it would be extremely simplistic to attribute to the subject's irritability, without wondering, then, the reason for that obviously disproportionate irritability. The aggressive response, outwardly resembling some emotional crisis, which the more or less racy flirtations some charnego construction worker dedicates to the happy, graceful stride of some beautiful girl walking by; the rude, despotic treatment that some prototype nouveau riche inflicts on the waiters and other workers at restaurants, nightclubs, and different public places; the poise with which the customer ahead of him, some pompous, relaxed bourgeois woman, does her shopping in a certain establishment; the treatment from some shitty maitre d' in any shitty elegant establishment who refuses to seat him because he's not wearing a necktie—but a cashmere turtleneck sweater—obliging him, naturally, to light up a cigarette right under his nose with a thousand-peseta note. And those girls who put on intellectual airs and who say they've read Simone de Beauvoir and talk about women's emancipation, when the only thing they do is introduce a new kind of weapon into what has traditionally been called the battle of the sexes, and which might be better called the opening of the sexes, which is what, at bottom, it's really all about, that the victories in this kind of fight consist of exactly that, of being able to stretch open wide, when they please, the doors of their little citadel. And the amorality, no longer of these girls but of women in general, the case of a friend who came to see them one day, frazzled, saying how her husband had cheated on her, and now, having survived the crisis, confessed to them the quantity of other people that she'd fucked, proposing to the rest of the women present that each one draw up her own list of liaisons and see which of them was the winner; the horrendous character of such feminine complicity, their confidences, the intimate details they share when they get together. And what's even more abominable, that semi-beardless youth, an exhibitionist even in the way he dresses, who swears he's capable of fucking any kind of woman however many times necessary, that he fucks them all and never goes limp, six, eight, fourteen times, a real fuck machine, and the women come and come until they can't come anymore and they're the first ones to beg him to stop, first to say enough, I can't take any more, Enough! Enough! Disgusting obsessives, liars, it's not possible to fuck that much. And the women who believe him are such cretins, they should prick up their ears and take good note. That young man and, lamentably, by extension, today's youth, those boys who were raised with baby bottles and jars of puree and taught by the television, who've been able to go to school and even university, who have regular sex with the girls in their classes and, if they please—something increasingly common—also with their male classmates, who make up their social circles and with whom they smoke marijuana and listen to pop music, surviving God knows how, talking about who knows what, without getting interested in anything at all, while it's much more clear what they're not interested in: hard work, achieving something. What do they know, not about hunger but about the financial straits their parents endured, about the desolate suburbs they grew up in—that we grew up in—about the years and years spent just having to grin and bear it, hypocritically pretending everything was okay, rancorously complying with their superiors, serving out, like a jail sentence, their military service in those times, getting married—our marriages—in the church, from home to work and from work to home, always needing to count every last centimo, the long list of things that not even by scrimping so, no matter how much one saved, could one believe would ever be within reach, that long string of neither this, nor that, nor this, that hammers down on one day and night, rattling inside one's head the way seeds rattle inside a dry gourd, what can all that even matter to them? I wonder, for example, what Carlos might have done in our situation. A fellow like him, for whom the personal experience of having spent his first childhood in Buenos Aires doesn't distinguish him in the least from any other young man of his generation. How might he have reacted in the Barcelona of our era, faced with the daily oppressions of family life and the social environment, facing the adventure of America, facing the difficulties that he would have to overcome?

Because my brother helped us at first, that's true. But later on? When the time came to return, because we couldn't stand it over there anymore—neither the country itself nor the type of life we were leading—and we found ourselves pinned down by the devaluation of the peso, confronted with the alternative of staying there, like my brother has done, or return practically ruined and try to start all over again in Spain, in Barcelona, ten years older and with a child on our backs. Do you all understand? Ten years of working and saving up like stupid little ants, and all for nothing. When we left here for Argentina the rate was six pesetas to the peso; and when we returned here, each peso was worth less than fifty centimos. What do you think a person might have done with his money after having worked so many years for nothing, after having managed to crawl out of the black hole of his childhood, faced with the choice of either staying over there or going back to the black hole? What would our Carlos have done, a young man just the same as the rest of his generation, with the same absence of ideals or ambitions or however you want to describe him, apart from the common principle they all have of getting along on minimum effort? Well, perhaps it's a lot to ask. Perhaps, to begin, he might not have even managed to realize that he found himself stuck in a black hole from which he needed to escape. And she: I think that, basically, the thing with Carlos is he's got a cuckold complex the size of a cathedral. I know what you're going to tell me: that alone doesn't explain anything because it still needs to be explained on its own terms. For example, why this particular complex? And how did it start to manifest itself? Well, from what's apparent, their relationship, at first anyway, had a very distinct tone; when they met, in that sinister office, and made their future plans together. I suppose if they hadn't been like that, if the both of them hadn't found that understanding and compatibility, they might never have undertaken that adventure to South America, nor would they, much less, have gotten married. Their first days in Argentina also seem to be those of a united couple, maybe because they love each other, or because they share common goals. Nevertheless, there's no doubt, it's there, in Buenos Aires, where the crisis occurs, the fissure that only widens with each passing year. Perhaps her affair with the famous Bob. I don't know. The fact is, their return to Barcelona has a very different character than their departure; it no longer sounds like a defeat in any economic sense, such as the loss that the devalued peso could mean for them, but in a moral sense, that of a couple losing their way, apart from, needless to say, their erotic downslide. It's the backward step of a couple who don't separate because they no longer can, for little Carlos's sake, because defending their interests requires them to continue together, or from mere force of habit. But what's evident is that by this point in their story they hate each other. I'm convinced he wishes she were old and ugly so nobody would look at her, so he could be at peace once and for all. And his mania about her contact lenses is crystal clear: he wishes she were blind, always wearing eyeglasses, always with glasses on her face, unable to see more than a hand's breadth beyond her nose. It really annoys him that she reads, that she's got her own ideas and even, at heart, that she works, like when she took over decorating the motel, the occasions that offer her dealings with men, workers, employees, like now, when she's busy running the place, working with clients, and suppliers. Very much in the background, of course. Well, if on the one hand he feels old and tired, on the other he's a cultured person with progressive, even libertarian, ideas. Meaning: he finds himself caught in his own trap; a person like Carlos, who's done what he's done and speaks like he speaks, cannot now behave like some reactionary troglodyte. And so, if she feels like seeing other people—after one of those spells when they don't even speak to each other for days on end—he can't be opposed to it. And Aurea tells him that she's going out with these friends or those ones, and asks him if he wants to come, because she knows that he doesn't feel like it, that he's not in the mood for it, and even if he were, accompanying her would be giving in, letting her see that he cares, that it bothers him, that if he decides to go out with her it's only for his own peace of mind. Perhaps Aurea might not even really be so interested in going out, but she knows that what Carlos would really like is that she stay home, however much he says otherwise, that she should go out alone, that he doesn't feel like it. And that's the source of Aurea's motivation for acting that way, her true objective: to create these kinds of situations. They say goodbye to each other coldly, maybe by telephone, because Aurea calls him from the home of some friends to tell him that she's going out with them, and why doesn't he come along, or perhaps directly, when she tells him at midday and then spends the afternoon getting ready. Aurea goes out and Carlos stays at home possessed by an irresistible feeling of anguish, an almost physical sensation, something that seems to press down on his chest, cause him nausea, a dizziness that surges up from his stomach into his throat. He won't be capable of doing anything, of distracting himself with anything, neither reading nor watching TV, much less sleeping, until she's returned, and, for that reason, he's got to end up starting the car and going out to have a few drinks or simply to drive and drive, burning up the kilometers as fast as he can, unloading his anxiety in any way possible. That's why Aurea provokes these situations: so that Carlos says no, so she can later walk through the door and find him irritated, exasperated, but without any concrete or reasonable motive for feeling that way, no real reason to reproach her for anything, and then she can cut him off, slamming the door, saying that he's unbearable, that she's going to her room, that it better not even occur to him to talk to her again until he's back in his right mind. Yes, I know what you'll say to me: all that is perfectly true but it still really doesn't explain anything. A state of mind like Carlos's, like Aurea's, like anyone's, is always the result of a whole process whose beginning goes back to a time before their first memories. Okay. Now then: what power does being a cuckold, or having a cuckold complex, if you prefer, have to precipitate the process? I mean, what's the mechanism? Why cuckoldry, more than any other motive—sexual, moral, or affective, or I don't know what—maybe ten useless years wasted working away in Argentina, frustrated ambitions or whatever?

And he: exactly. You're right, as much in the objections to the arguments you attribute to me as in the importance of the question you raise. On the one hand, apparently, there's no doubt that Carlos's problem resides in a feeling of betrayed love; on the other hand, it's no less certain that that problem corresponds to the critical point of a whole process, and that this process, manifests itself in Carlos as well as in Aurea. When Carlos displays particularly depressive symptoms, Aurea perks up immediately, stimulated, exultant, like someone who's just received a much needed rush of oxygen. She becomes active again, loquacious, talks to him about friends (pedophiles!) and girlfriends (chatterboxes!) and he feels more and more prostrate, physical fatigue—almost incapable of moving, of smiling—not even tempered by his wrath: he feels old and insecure, faced with a woman who, well advised by someone else—some lover, he'll surely say—has found a style that renders her more attractive than years before. Meaning: the same phenomenon, but in reverse, as when he's in good shape and notices how that makes Aurea gloomy, something that only serves to increase his exaltation and her withdrawal. Apart from the critical moments, their silent conviviality also avoids, similarly and as if by common consent, any direct disagreement, concrete reproaches, the true causes of their friction; they prefer to project them onto other areas, questions thoroughly removed from their sentimental relationships, but which, with no need to specify, they fully recognize as the source of their estrangement, fields offering ample terrain upon which to settle their disagreements: music, films, friends, fashions, interior decorating. Meanwhile: when I told you that the feeling of betrayed love is the key to Carlos's problems, I think I qualified the affirmation, highlighting it by saying 'apparently.' What I really mean is, in my opinion, there's something more, some other element, suppressed perhaps but active, narrowly linked to that sentiment, which maybe he's not even aware of, but lack of awareness doesn't negate its import. On the contrary: it counts to the degree to which the subject is incapable of formulating it or admitting its formulation. But as with those films and novels which people say don't interest them because, more than normal cases, they constitute true clinical cases—incest, parricide, etcetera—the real motivation for such rejection is the fact that there is something in that clinical case which concerns them but which they manage to keep on ignoring; thus Carlos with his problems.

And the other day, when you two went up to Ampurias, what did he want to talk about? Nothing in particular. Just that when I told him that I was going to visit the ruins he asked whether he might come along. Would I mind? I suppose he was amused by the idea of going alone, without women. I told him why don't we also bring Carlos junior, and he tells me that youngsters today aren't interested in old ruins and things like that. But I didn't think at any time he was going to talk to me about anything specific. Carlos isn't the kind of guy to seek out a friend to share his problems with; to begin with, he doesn't even have such close friends. Nor is he, just the same, one of those guys who goes around looking for a woman to whom he can pour out his heart so she can give him advice. If he feels wrong, he'll make it seem like he does, as a show of confidence, if he thinks you might be offended by him; but he only does it for show. In reality, it's the opposite of revealing anything: giving false clues, clues that reinforce the self-image he's been forging over the years and which hide those traits which contradict or don't fit with such an image. Only that these clues which one perhaps comes to consider true, but which are false, usually contain really authentic indications of what's hidden behind that oh-so-carefully constructed image. What did he talk to me about? About what he would've liked to have been when he was younger, when he was working at that sinister office, and what he'll never be now: a writer of stature, both deep and mordant, famous, widely discussed like all other geniuses, one of those writers everyone talks about and whom everyone fears; and of his experiments in the craft, of those pages written at age seventeen which one later pulls out of the drawer one fine day—now in Buenos Aires—and piously burns. Another one of his obsessions from those days: being strong, one of those pure muscle guys whom no one dares mess with. Everything came about because of this Ignacio what's-his-name, from some new information about his case, which the newspaper reported on that day. Around that time, when Carlos had an obsession with bodybuilding, he and Ignacio were going to the same gym, and the two of them struck up a certain friendship. Carlos was attracted to the other fellow's anarchic cynicism, his sharpness, and even his lack of scruples. Seems that this so-called Ignacio was the son of a municipal police chief, one of those kids from the Falangists Youth Front, with powerful godfathers in the trade unions, some big shot boss or something like that, although, like with everything else, he didn't give a damn about the Falange; noctambulist, quite roguish, so roguish, he said, that soon I'll end up liking guys. When they stopped hanging out with each other, this so-called Ignacio was spending tons of money, quantities that couldn't even be explained by his occasional stint as thug or bodyguard for his bosses. And now, so many years later, when Ignacio was now just one more memory from days gone by, forgotten as much as possible like everything else from that time, Carlos goes and reads in the newspaper that his old crony is up to his eyeballs in a property scam, shady deals selling apartments, the typical kind of scheme for which he'll get hundreds if not thousands of years in jail, a few years for each apartment. Paradoxes of fortune; let's take, for example, the story of two friends: the first one rises and rises by seemingly effortless good fortune, he scales each towering height of the financial world, one after another, he gets deeply involved in all the intricate details until some miscalculation or an excess of trust in his backers—more likely than any premeditated desire to run some clumsy swindle—hastens him to jail for such a time as corresponds to the age of a civilization or a whole historical era. The other friend, for his part, goes to America and also manages to get ahead. But when he comes home to Spain, it turns out that all his efforts have been fruitless, that for reasons that elude any foresight, and against which nothing can be done—the result of Argentine prosperity, economic crisis, inflation, a chain reaction of devaluation—the prospects offered by his proposal to reestablish himself in Barcelona are barely more encouraging than the ones that motivated him to leave in the first place, ten years earlier. And then, despite all those things, due to circumstances no less foreseeable or more distant from his own efforts, it turns out that meanwhile, in Spain, he becomes a rich man, much richer even than he could ever have managed to become in Argentina. Meaning: that if our parents lived and died modestly, or rather, miserably, it was because our grandparents had become millionaires. Or rather, that if we hadn't done anything, if we'd spent those ten years in a perfect state of hibernation, everything would be exactly the same as it is, and now we'd still be talking with you right here, in the Aphrodite Motel, the same as we're talking now. In my first trip to scout things out to prepare my return, I found out that my grandfather, the fisherman from Rosas, owned a veritable fortune in lands, vineyards, olive groves along the sea which, combined with the tourist phenomenon and the economic expansion, were worth many millions for him. He might've been able to make much more, even, but the quantities that the construction companies paid at first and which seemed to him so high, crazy sums, were in reality quite low; and so he sold his best lands for a song—according to him, the worst parcels—the ones that fronted the beach. Nevertheless, he still had others, and my brother and I were his only heirs. Beyond that he didn't care, for him a hundred was as good as a million, either way it was a lot of money; in practice he only knew how to count in thousands of pesetas, not to mention in duros. What truly interested him were his groupers, and then a woman from the town, also a widow, somewhat younger, whom he took up with when he was already seventy-something. For the rest, he stayed busy with his garden and the few olive trees he had left, he made his own soap and detested the idea of moving away from Rosas. The case of Aurea's grandfather was different. A calculating man, with a very exact idea of the value of money, the classic rural landlord. Aurea barely knew him. From what she tells, the only thing she remembered from when she lived in the village, as a little girl, is that he had an enormous prick; she once saw him urinating against a tree, and something like that, for a little girl used to seeing her little brothers' tiny little willies, always makes a big impression. But whether it was due to a reflex on the part of the old speculator, or his obscure responsibilities to his own descendants, something usually concealed by the inner labyrinths wound round within every rural landlord, the fact is that he didn't hesitate to offer his financial support for our plan when, after studying and even working out the possibilities of various points, we decided to take a chance and start up this motel. Aurea wanted to call it El Motel de la Luna, and I wanted to call it El Motel del Sol. In the end we settled on El Motel Afrodita, the Aphrodite Motel, as a way of symbolizing our mutual, indestructible love, and love's capacity to overcome every temporary misunderstanding, to transcend all antagonism. Of course Aurea's grandfather consolidated and increased his fortune in the postwar years, and from then on he became the undisputed boss of the town, of which he continues to be lord and master. People also say that the origin of his fortune, what we might call the cornerstone, was a buried jar he unearthed one day filled with one-ounce gold coins. We've never learned whether that's really true or if people repeat it because that was the verdict pronounced by the local witch, an old fortune-teller. The typical story about buried treasure.

LUNASOL.

Gather up the papers, hide them in the drawer, wash your slightly sweaty hands, run a comb through your hair. Rosa was already dressed to go out, reading on the terrace, indifferent to the splendors of the dusk settling across the bay, on the horizon, to the geometrical delirium of television antennas rising above the terraces and rooftops; the novelty of it all, now seen too many times to be exciting.

Now, let's go get some dinner. And after dinner? Take advantage of the fact that the people from the yacht were out of town, and take a little stroll, have a drink anywhere and come back early, as long as we don't run into some acquaintance, Walter and Krista, or The Greek, and then it all gets messy. Or, more probably, succumb to that inertia that it's still early, about what the fuck to do at that hour, now back at the motel, drop in at our friends' apartment, to chat for a while, attracted—the verses of "Adiós Pampa Mía" ringing out like a clarion call—by the pleasure of psychological conjecture, trapped by guesses inside the guessing game. Meaning: to show, in the course of the dialogue, not so much the true personality of those present or of third parties, let alone oneself, as much as to demonstrate one's own penetrating psychological insight, one's own speculative ingenuity. Like the other night. We'd arrived perhaps a bit earlier than normal and in the garden we ran into Carlos junior all ready to go out, perfectly dressed up to hang out with his people, as he likes to call them, meaning, his crowd, his inner circle. He greeted us pleasantly, warmly, relaxed, almost as if he also considered us part of his set. He's waiting for you all, he said, and, indeed, there he was, already settled in on the porch, next to the drinks already being served. We argued once more about who was more properly whose guest, if they were Rosa's and my guests, or if we were their guests. She took a while to join us; finally she came out wrapped in a white Russian bathrobe, after having taken a swim. After dinner? I felt sticky, she said. Besides, that stuff about getting a cramp is just a lie concocted by parents. She snuggled into the folds of her robe, curled up on the chaise longue as if a bit drowsy. Now that I remember, she said, this afternoon, taking a siesta, I had a very pleasant dream. I wouldn't really know how to describe what was happening; I just remember that it was very pleasant. No comment more opportune for him to immediately pour himself another whiskey; surely some romantic story, he said. The porch: the glasses, the Siamese cat rubbing itself against the chaise longue, those tacky lawn chairs, the same as the ones on the terrace at our apartment, the ones that made Pompey exclaim: What are these machines? And the gecko motionless beneath the porch light and the thermometer and the barometer and the drawing of the Ideal City—*La Ciudad Ideal*—hanging inside, that drawing she found at Los Encantes flea market, which seemed to fascinate our friend so much, an anonymous original, probably the work of a madman, made, perhaps, around the turn of the century, judging from some of the elements represented; a drawing in India ink, illuminated in some spots with different colors, a composition with all the characteristic marks of naive art, a combination of a map view and panoramic view of a city, in the style of the engravings of cities so much in vogue before the invention of photography and, like those, splashed with legends and numbers which, at the bottom of the picture, offer adequate explanations of each detail. Only one single difference: no human figure, nobody who, even if only for contrast's sake, might enliven the composition, as is typical in such engravings. It was a walled city, entirely surrounded by a river, either natural or channeled; in the center of the city, a Citadel separated from the rest by a new waterway, also colored in blue. A concentric urban structure, one symmetrical dodecagon nested inside another, progressively and proportionally smaller, delimited by seven streets or Paseos de Ronda, walkways, as the legend indicates; nine in total, including the one formed by the outer wall; as well as the one bordering the fosse of the equally walled Citadel. The city can be reached by two bridges or gates, one word in the legend slightly illegible; it read either *puente or puerta: el Puente or la Puerta del Naufragio*: either the Bridge or the Gate of the Shipwreck and *el Puente* or *la Puerta de la Salvación*: either the Bridge or the Gate of Salvation. The wall comprises a series of twelve crenellated towers. Four transversal streets or avenues crossed in the form of an X together connect the nine Paseos de Ronda, forming a plaza at each intersection, thirty-six altogether, each one with its respective name, the same as the avenues, *Avenue of the Creation*, *Avenue of the Dream*, etcetera. At the junction of the outermost bisector of each angle of the X formed by the transversal streets or avenues with the perimeter of the wall, meaning, along sections 12, 3, 6, and 9, four palaces or residences are indicated which face outward from the city, and thus coincide exactly with the cardinal points indicated in the upper righthand corner of the drawing, Winter aligned with the north, Spring with the east, Summer with the south, and Autumn with the west, colored, respectively, in white—meaning, not colored—green, orange, and violet. The Citadel, named *Ciudadela Solar*, is built around a structure of golden cupolas called *El Templo de la Ley*, meaning, The Temple of the Law, its four principal towers, rising independent of one another, form a single prism, finally resolved in a circle, much higher than the other cupolas. The corresponding note emphasizes, without further details, that the shadow of said tower, as it falls—in the opposite direction of the sun's path, as well as the hands of the clock—upon each one of the twelve concentric perimeters constituted by the nine Paseos de Ronda, as well as the two waterways and, at the foot of the wall, the very edge of the Citadel, signals precisely the hours in the course of the day. In the center of the Temple, surrounded by cupolas, is a lake colored in silver called *The Lake of the Moon*. And, curiously, seems to have no access bridges to the Citadel.

Sure, we'd go chat with them for a while. We'd return to yesterday's subject, to the unfinished topic, resumed each night and each night postponed by drinking alcohol until incoherent. And then, the goddamned ramble back to our apartment, shaky and ill-tempered, the bath-room too brightly lit, the white of the bed too excessively white. Perhaps one final note scribbled on the back of the postcard that serves as the bookmark in the latest book for bedtime reading, a note with irregular and confused handwriting, any value only confirmable tomorrow morning, with that fearful morning hangover which, logically, will stretch out at least until midday for the same reason that our conversation with our friends will inevitably stretch on until dawn, a fear only surpassed, in these nocturnal hours, by another much more immediate fear, dreams to come, the old man's visit.

II

ITINERARY.

Escape through the center of town. Along the inner side streets, toward the open mountain; avoiding the maritime facade, the sidewalks of the paseo along the wharf, the road leading to the lighthouse, to the ruins of Trinidad Castle, to the coves along the shore in the direction of Cabo Norfeo, until La Almadraba or whatever that beach is called that The Greek says he swam to when his boat sank and he saved another person and was saved by another or what have you. The important thing was to avoid the terraces outside the bars, possible encounters, greetings, Pompey and Quima, Walter and Krista, Rosa Bosch and Javi; and Mario and Celia and The Greek and even that jinxed, idiotic American party-pooper, the faces one knows even only if on sight. All of them like one of those familiar faces in the neighborhood or some summer town, or like one of those classmates from high school or university or military companions with whom we never really connect, one of these people whom one sees for years and years until finally striking up a conversation, and then the shock one experiences when, after chatting amicably a while with this person whom we've known only vaguely or only seen occasionally, this same person—with a sudden explanatory rigor that betrays (not through their stony countenance and snakelike gaze) the typical anxiety of a passion contained only with great difficulty—announces their steadfast determination to establish with us an increasingly close and deep friendship, as they simultaneously put themselves entirely at our disposal and offer us unlimited favors, however many are within their reach, granted, only granted—it's obvious—that we listen to them and, above all and definitively, that we save them, that we liberate them, not from anything outside them—boredom, idiocy, misery—but rather from something that's not in our power to resolve since it's not in theirs either, meaning, that we rescue them from themselves, that they cease being who they are, their initial ardor and firmness giving way bit by bit to desperation as they grasp the courteous character of our responses, as if they already guessed the outcome of all that, the value of a promise they're going to be left with our: Alright, great, we'll call each other, the inevitable conclusion of our farewell. Thus, when dealing with one of those people, bolt in horror. The ideal thing: escape in an unoccupied airplane, fly straight up as high as the fuselage can stand and the cosmic rays or Jupiter's thunder and lightning allow, and once there, enter into permanent orbit.

Discarded, discarded beforehand, the possibility of barreling straight down the street, to the Paseo Marítimo, across from the fishing cooperative, tremendously crowded at these hours from the arrival of the first fishing boats and the start of the fish auction; in other words, a place full of dangers, the risk of chance encounters, of someone telling us something, and all that only in order to escape, then, that hornet's nest, round the point of the lighthouse and continue to the other side, sailing along past the coves and cliffs and siren songs unheard only by those who plug their ears. No, absolutely not, none of that: go along the inner streets of the town, streets under construction, buildings under reconstruction, furtive and hurried, as if in flight, ready to shrink from the terrifying singing rising from some building sites, *adiós, adiós, mi lindo marinero*, some unskilled worker fresh out of the military, recently discharged no doubt, stupefied from habit, perhaps even nostalgic, a verse that makes one feel they are marching to its rhythm, marching in time to the beating of a drum, and which can only be resisted by means of a forced arrhythmia, by means of a premeditated carelessness of movements.

A difficulty: to orient oneself in a landscape transformed, where all the old landmarks have disappeared. Neither vineyards nor olive groves nor planted fields, a human landscape abandoned to the brambly weeds and the thistles' soft mauve, remodeled on a scale abominably more human for being more fungible, half-built chalets, sketches of streets, leveled vacant lots. The dismantled windmill, for example, without sails, that dark tower inhabited by an owl, just on the edge of the cork oak woods that spread upslope, the habitual destination of our vespertine excursions, the first time we were in Rosas: how to guess its exact location if those cork oak woods no longer even exist? And which hill to climb to contemplate the town if this hill now forms part of the town? Further, higher up? Climb to the summit of the Paul, break into the radar station, die machine-gunned by the guards right as we're running toward the two resplendent spheres, the two enormous balls erected on high in memory of the defunct Pan, the dead god?

Stopping to contemplate the town from up there, among the few remaining stands of cork oaks that still dominate the steep slope, continues to be, however, as reflexive a ritual as the genuflection which the pious believer performs each time he passes before the tabernacle. A habit, a mania, or whatever you'd like to call it, from the moment when the panorama of the town seen from above turns out to be neither more attractive nor even larger than the way it appears from the motel's terrace; this colorless, disjointed foreground, a half-sketched composition of construction sites, isolated chalets, forlorn lamp posts, an increasing concentration of building projects, moving into the town, and an accumulation of structures, hotels, large blocks of apartments like a background scrim, all along the shoreline, blocking the immediate view of the sea, barely affording a glimpse of one end of the port, part of a cargo ship docked at the pier, a sort of postcard panorama with its impression of immobility, of a frozen instant, enlivened only by the noise, a diffuse but intense noise carried on the wind, cars, machines, motors, resonances from the whole town rising and expanding toward the top of the steep slope, even these few cork oaks left uncut, who knows if to disguise what might very well be a cistern, scraggly branches, their look of raw, rough-cut stone accentuated, the desolation typical of those few trees that always seem to survive a clear-cutting. Among the trunks, behind the shrubs, excremental residue, pieces of torn newspaper, dried out by the weather. The chalets below all alike and all different, like Walter's house. The streets, sketched on the landscape by double rows of curb, among stepped vacant lots, buildings under construction, lime pits, piles of bricks, cement sacks, concrete beams, whitish planks, and rusted rebar, the deep machine vibrations shattering one's ears while walking past or fleeing toward the edges of the urbanized area, unusual in the degree to which they exceed the fantastic. The road leading to the bottom of the gully was narrow, sinuous, rough, goat-rugged; a dry gully, loose slate, with abundant nooks and bends amid the shrubs growing along its edges, small cells, optimal hiding places for the workers on the nearby job sites to give free rein to their bodily functions and demands—proof aplenty in the form of increasing numbers of coprolites—as well as, very likely, good spots to jerk off at midday, given the adequate conditions of solitude and seclusion which so effectively propitiate all kinds of regressions and fantasies that alleviate a construction worker's typical passions, women driving around in their cars, their kids, their husbands, their lovers, their beach life, their night life, a pure unbridled orgy.

And then, the sudden shock, seeing the green plastic hose strung across the stony gully, the instantaneous sensation of unreality it produces, similar, in its effects, to the feeling following the summer lightning blackout on one of those hot nights, the emerging image of whole districts, the vast evaporation of horizons; so too, like a flash, the sudden shock. The same as that time when, as a child, in the clearing of a cork oak forest, I stumbled over an old, stray rope-soled alpargata, and the braided hemp began to unravel, to separate, stiff, quivering, standing up, and there I was on a path, safe, without being able to remember how I'd gotten there nor now, years later, which of the two spots where I situate this event was the one where it really happened to me. Or when one suddenly relates a specific event, a remark, an object, along with the contents of a nightmare which they'd forgotten dreaming, of which they now only retain a blurry glimpse, sufficient, however, to explain the altered state of mind, the unease and slackness that have possessed them at intervals throughout the whole day. Green-black serpents, perhaps: with zigzag patterns and white bellies, seemingly dissolved into the clear water of a puddle or a still, motionless pool, ringed, slippery, intertwined like tongues, coiling and uncoiling in lightning Z's, turning slowly, somehow lethargic in the tenebrous bottom of a half-empty cistern, writhing rosaceous in the turbid water along the sandy bank, contracting, expanding. Not crawling on the earth nor hanging drooped over some branch: under the water, intensely green, their thick bodies uncoiled in the transparency of the still, shallow water, barely deep enough, almost about to step on them the way a statue of the Virgin is depicted as stepping on them—the only difference being her celestial distance and indifference.

Reasons which only make your hangover worse, the lingering alcohol not yet worn off, still redolent on the skin and breath, still burning in the veins and guts, the belly churning the same as if, instead of guts, your innards were whistling reeds. Like the disquieting queasiness that persists for the dog who has scented death or like your cock cramping up stuffed in behind the zipper the morning after a night's worth of intense copulation, so, too, the hangover, the alcohol starting to burn off the moment you wake up around noon, your head vaporous as a steam bath, the bed disheveled and she, naked, still sleeping, and the stained matting at the foot of the bed, stinking of vomit, who knows from whom, and then you eat something for breakfast, coffee or tea, about the time everyone else is eating lunch, and escape from town, avoiding the downtown streets, out, toward the countryside or what was the countryside, east toward the coast, so that, by skirting as much as possible the construction sites on the edge of town, you can then turn toward the north and west, overwhelmed not only by the strangeness of the surrounding world but also, even more, by the fusion of that strangeness with your own, by the suppression of all antagonism between yourself and someone else, doubts about your identity, I, here, in this insipid, unpleasant place, in this mutating landscape, neither city nor countryside, neither what it was nor what it will become, an absence of details, of landmarks; relative equally to the continuity of that problematical identity, to its ruptures and failures: Revolutionary activist? Contemplative spirit? Father? Son? Teacher? Student? Husband? Lover? Don Giovanni? Doña Elvira? Exhausted, confronting the reality and forcefulness of the objective world no less than yourself, building sites, construction projects where there once stood a cork oak forest, the slaty bed of a gully where you amble along given over to the most elemental proofs, like someone who, in a certain, particularly anomalous situation, facing certain, especially critical expectations, raises, in all their rawness, the most immediate questions: What the fuck am I doing here in this fishing village? Or even: Why refuse and deny instead of fleeing for good from this abominable town where any sponger can come over and sit down at my table and strike up a conversation in the hope that I'll stand him a drink, when I'd happily buy him a drink just to shut him up, and where Rosa, just to say something, when we're alone, always repeats the same thing, and where even I end up asking people the very same things I imagine they want me to ask them, although their answers don't interest me in the least? The same as the occasional seducer who goes out one night and parties it up, with the music, the drinks, the lovely company, the music, necking with some girl, who can even manage to ask himself, taking advantage of any pause, while he pisses, for example, his limp sex dangling between his fingers: Why waste time with this girl pretending I'd like to take her to bed when it's really the last thing that appeals to me? No less defenseless in his conduct than that author who, in his early artistic stylings, through the prism of his favorite books at the time, translated his personal experiences into literary terms, in such a way that he not only wrote in the style of, say—Hemingway, Pavese, etcetera—but that he also sought, in the reality of daily life itself, elements analogous to those from his readings, with the natural disenchantment of one who, as a result of not fulfilling his desire, finds that reality much more monotonous or insipid and narrow-minded than what he expected, while now, by contrast, now, years later, the problem lies in how to go on working until having written down all the horror, to earnestly confront, to gaze fixedly upon the horror in all its horror, equally incapable now of reading novels or taking an interest in anything besides that task of contemplating the horror, all the horror in the world. A horror which, if specified as a principle in purely theoretical terms, as an explanation for the surrounding world, will be reduced to a mild aversion; on the other hand, however, through the compensations which that surrounding world never ceases to offer, that horror ends up not only materializing, becoming real, taking shape until encompassing the entire world but also, by being assimilated, that initial explanation becomes currency, fulfilled the same as a prophecy. Thus, like said unhappy wretch, our traveler, an ordinary man in a similar state of mind, predisposed to the sudden shock of stumbling upon a simple green plastic hose crossing the bed of a gully as much as his line of sight, and above all, the stink from a pile of stiff, bloated puppy corpses scattered among the stones, thickly coated with large, spinning flies, their paws barely distinguishable, like some sort of flippers or stumps, and then, climbing out, emerging into the young green of a vineyard, parting the vine shoots and raising a startled flight of magpies. Instinctive reactions, the same, for example, as that of quickening your pace to the local soccer field, from which, if it were Sunday, the shattering clamor of the public would be audible. Or resuming your march no less hurriedly after peeking into the cemetery by the closed gate, affected not by the image of that quiet secluded area, a refuge of niches and crosses and gnarled cypresses, but by the sudden discovery of the thousands of snails stuck to the outside of the wall, the proliferation of shells upon shells, the traces of dried nacreous slime configuring a highly detailed composition of petrified movement, captured in what might well, at first glance, appear to be the map of an ancient city, with its intricate arrangement of avenues and plazas, its streets laid out for penetration and circulation, its gates, its fosses, its great walls, something not very different, in the end, from the likely design of the first ancient villa in Rosas, the Greek Rhodes, whose remains continue being exhumed with archaeological patience from among the ruins of the Citadel; at least that's what the signs proclaim, placed all around that group of ruined fortifications enclosing a soggy, swampy glacis, invaded by brambles and weeds, although, for the eventual visitor, the only perceptible sign of activity might be some quietly grazing goats. Alongside the stones of the Citadel, in the clearing outside the large booths and tents from a carnival, rides and amusements for children, everything closed up at this hour of the day. The cemetery, the ruins of the Citadel, the uncultivated lands, the carnival, and, now on the other side of the highway, beyond the last buildings stretching toward the western horizon—hotels, most of them best avoided—the curving shoreline of the bay, the beach. A very long, very wide beach, only limited by its own horizons, blurred dunes, blending into the strong surging waves and the whirling sand devils lifted by a damp, unpleasant west wind, an open panorama where, when one arrives, the last thing they expect to find is a wheelchair facing the sea, some stray strands of hair stuck to the backrest spinning in the wind and, to the right of the chair, standing, a woman with the same gray hair, pointing out some landmark. And that German shepherd coming and going, tail and ears stiff, pupils sharp, as if attentive to an imminent mouthful. And the sack, right there on the shoreline, a shapeless sack, half-full, half-buried, sloshing around in the waves, sniffed at again and again by the German shepherd. And even the sand itself, take a handful and closely examine its composition. The microcosm of eroded organisms mixed with the mineral element, detritus of seaweed, mollusk shells, seashells, coral residue, nacre particles, urchin spines, minuscule pink fragments, of crab shells or any other kind of crustacean.

I walked back to town following the deserted beach, no swimmers, paddle boats, or food stands, no signs of the summer season. A seaside town seen in the distance, looking east, with its port, its waterfront promenade edged by large hotels and blocks of apartment buildings, its rural outskirts being torn up, no more familiar than any other town contemplated from a distance, as you approach it on foot, walking along the beach, along another beach, contemplating other ports, boats at rest gathered in the port, other seaside promenades, other coasts, other cliffs, other rocks, and other grass, and more white sea-foam crashing in your ears, face against the sand, mouth dry, hangover, the bitter taste, the years gone by, especially all the years gone by, towns upon towns passed through since the last time we were here, the decision to return here simply because we'd spent time here together when we first started getting to know each other, even though we were perfectly aware that neither the town nor the surrounding area could ever be the same. Or perhaps exactly for that very reason, for the deliberate purpose of finding an objective correspondence to our own transformation. Possessed by the morbid certainty that just as the caged lion's especial ferocity supposes a greater attraction to the spectator's curious eyes, so too, this landscape's abrupt geology, a traditional inspiration for hermitical sentiments, far from any urban drudgery, among stones and sky and crashing surf and dry thyme, offers the optimal setting for anyone in search of the absolute or overcome by a vague pantheism or rapt in a solitary romantic transport, thus, today, the erosion and the salt residue constitute an undeniable lure for visitors, in inverse ratio, logically, the amount of these people and their possible residence in the place thanks to the persistence of such qualities: wild outskirts progressively domesticated, highways slicing up the land, streetlights, a proliferation of uniform structures, modifications of the landscape that only appear to involve a contradiction: if there's not the least doubt that its wild rugged character will disappear in proportion to how much it continues to be urbanized, it's no less certain that however much each possible buyer affirms the opposite, nobody would visit such arid landscapes without first being sure they're not going to be the only ones there; that very soon such bitter solitude will be populated by chalets which will in no way compare unfavorably with what you're planning to build for oneself. Of course not, gentlemen, every land has its own particular grace—just as every woman has her own—and for the same reason that the customer is always right so, too, is everything for sale: no longer just the coves along the shore, toward Cabo Norfeo, that once resembled leaden lunar lakes, or the mountainous outskirts of the town, the steep slopes, the erotic promiscuity of naked stones. No longer all that, easy enough to buy and sell, but also this wide plain which extends from one end of the bay to the other, once empty salt marshes, alluvial floodplains swept downslope against the head-on blows of the sea, an unpleasant and even unhealthy place, today, as you can observe, being fully subjected to dredging, draining, canalization, and landscaping. What's more: you can be sure that these lands, yesterday the least valuable ones, will rightly be the most valuable ones tomorrow, the most popular, the easiest ones to sell. My personal advice is that you hasten to buy your own parcel, any of them, because they're all sure to enjoy the same advantages, every single one of them will offer you the opportunity to arrive to your future residence by the mode of transportation you deem most preferable, by car or motorboat, by four-in-hand or by trireme, without excluding, of course, airplane or hot-air balloon, features, in short, which give these parcels, among all the real estate on the market, a unique quality. Your lifelong dream, yes, now within reach, keys in hand, through an affordable down payment and easy mortgage installments scheduled to fit your budget, given that our desire is nothing less than to help you make a good investment, so that you turn a profit, even if it comes at our own expense. What interests us most is the person, you, your benefit and even, if possible, your cooperation, your free initiatives, the invaluable help which you can lend us with your ideas and suggestions. What do you think, for example, sounds catchier from a publicity standpoint: Venezia Nova? Florida on the Mediterranean?

It's curious that our first impression was that the town had barely changed. The eve of some Sunday after Pentecost, before or after the Ascension. Already dark when we arrived and we only saw the town center, greatly renovated, unmistakably so, more bars than before, much livelier, many more people for that time of year. But this was what we wanted, after all; a modicum of nightlife. We took a little walk along the wharf, just to get a breath of fresh air: the smell of the sea, the quiet lights of the bay, no less immutable in appearance than the starry sky. A man was rowing without the slightest splash, his black figure silhouetted by the brilliant glow of the two spotlights shining perpendicular to his boat, illuminating its outline, now rowing hunched over, now crouching, luring the fish with muffled thumps against the hull bottom, now upright, fists clutching his trident, poised to skewer; in what seemed a moment he glided almost to the wharf, oars extended like wings, just as if he were flying through the perfectly transparent water. Because he came so close we were able to recognize him later at the Nautic, and we invited him to have a drink and he accepted, assuring us, though, that he didn't usually drink, and he told us that he was The Greek, the Lobster King, and that he'd take us by boat to wherever we'd like, even to Tunis, if we dared. And even that old American fellow seemed alright to us then, always so respectably drunk, courteously greeting all those present in every bar, invariably sporting a red Catalan barretina, trying so hard to look like a real local, an extravagant American, beloved, almost like an adopted son, by the native born locals, those who might very well have associated his image with that of the classic war hero who flees from himself, destroyed by alcohol and memories and disappointed love, or any of the other variations habitually proposed by the movies, without considering that he's most likely just a simple retired American man, exinsurance agent or something, who's spending the money from his not-too-cushy pension in that corner of the world where life as well as alcohol come at a better price than in other possible corners. An attractive element of the life there, however, that the recent arrival never fails to appreciate about the place. Appreciations, or rather, a good initial disposition, drunkenness entirely appropriate to returning to a place about which we have good memories, which lasted, this time, all of one night. Until the next morning, going out for a walk while Rosa kept sleeping, to get an idea for myself of the transformations the town had suffered, the same as when, by the light of day, one wakes up alongside a frightening woman without remembering exactly what happened and, above all, how. It was a route similar to the one today, starting with the hike out to visit what had once been a cork-oak forest, to the spot where, more or less, the windmill used to stand. And also like today, I came back along the beach, along the seaside promenade, although without this strong wind off the sea or this unblinking midday sun, without today's hangover, without a tide like the one today, its skipping waves capable of reaching the edge of the pier, without the splashing, without the vaporous foam lifted by the wind, without a traffic ticket in my pocket or a snake straining against my zipper, the wind and the waves drowning out any other sound, carrying away the words of the few passersby, reducing their expressions to a mute grimace in motion, nullifying even the power of the loudspeaker mounted atop a car that was circulating slowly, extravagantly decorated in flamenco motifs, pointlessly announcing some awful show. The sensation of impunity, in such circumstances, facing any inopportune encounter. How delightful it would be to always be able to walk that way, while Rosa talks away, Rosa or whoever, and I agreeing, nodding my head affirmatively now and then.

On the way back to the motel, walking along the seaside promenade, thoroughly wracked by the implacable hangover running through his body, penis seized with that typical stiffness, a sort of physiologically autonomous penis, swelling up by itself at random intervals, capriciously, with the inert reiterative obfuscation which, when one has been drinking, follows time and again each carnal embrace, dolorously resolved in what was more a brief spasm than an orgasm; driven by the irritated unsociability a hangover usually produces, anxious frenzy more than desire, at the opposite end of the habitual dejection with which one confronts the daily ritual, the nuisance of starting all over again with passionate kisses and caresses and other preliminaries, to comply with that fleeting suggestion, born in the imagination, abstracting the wearisome servitudes required to enact them, the annoyance of such effort, his dejection, doubtless, no less than her reluctance in agreeing to another wrestling match, not without having anticipated that she's got a splitting headache, behavior which, certainly, only varied in appearance when she was making love with another man, for which reason, if one of the two lovers doesn't say or gives to understand that it was good for them, the other person—she, he, the reaction is indistinct—will privately and conveniently attribute the blame to themself, consequently fearing personal disrepute as soon as the news spreads, and so we forge on or, at least, those are conclusions one can reach from one's own behavior with others, with the occasional ones, making more of an effort, of course, without that necessarily signifying that the excitation experienced with them might be superior to the excitement with Rosa, given that, precisely, the ritual repeated must be in such cases even more meticulously detailed and carefully polished, a phenomenon whose progressive generalization might make us think that, after a certain age, men naturally tend toward voyeurism to the degree that it always turns out to be more novel, as well as much more comfortable, to see another carrying out the diverse tasks of the ceremony, while the woman—as long as she doesn't feel threatened by the presence of some competitive element—tends rather more toward the exhibitionist and narcissistic satisfaction of becoming the center of that ceremony, the ultimate objective of those surrounding erections she obviously desires, which she evaluates with a criteria less formalist than thematic, convergent tendencies, a convergence of mutual propensities which would explain the formidable propagation, for some time—a skeptical, Toynbeean mind would imagine a return to, historical cycles of, etcetera—of collective love practiced in its most diverse modalities, apart, of course, from any other implication one might like to add: a regression to the primitive games characteristic of a tedious consumer society, a prime example of a consumer society's decadence, the consumer society's puerile imitation of customs from decadent societies of the ancient world, etcetera, or, on the contrary, a break with consumer society, a manifestation of a certain turning back to nature, to the practices of primitive peoples, etcetera, etcetera. Pressing images, feverish ideas, empowered now—not by the alcohol not yet eliminated, still circulating, spreading throughout the body, but rather—by the very insertion of such intoxication into the course of my particular creative rhythms, meaning, through the present adaptation of erotic rhythms and creative rhythms, both now waxing if not in frank conjunction. The evidence that, when one begins working well, feeling in shape with regard to creative capacity, their erotic life similarly experiences a period of euphoria, euphoria whose creative effects will gradually decrease until becoming almost completely inhibited. But in the same way that the divergent trajectories of two planets of the same solar system, having passed the point of maximum distance from one another, inexorably draw closer again until reaching the point of maximum proximity, thus, in a similar way, the artist's creativity will soon be inhibited and blocked until he reaches a sterile, reiterative impasse from which he can only reactivate his own erotic life, which, increasing parallel to the rhythm of the creative work, carries him to a starting point, as he reinitiates the cycle. That's why those uncontrollable dilations of the penis, that irrepressible walking hard-on, hardly concealable to the curious eyes of passersby, walking from the motel, from the disheveled room, from the stained mat by the bed, discolored in a useless attempt to scrub out the vomit stains, that smudged pink, almost a decoration, which stood out ostentatiously at the foot of the unmade bed, that naked sleeping body shaken, almost brutally, out of its drowsiness again and again or, more exactly, again and again returned, transported to a better kind of drowsiness, more pleasant, until both of them falling asleep, as if under the effects of a heavy dose of tranquilizers.

THE BOWELS OF ATTILA.

A combination of vodka and Pernod in equal measures. The surest way to shake off a nuisance like Xavier. To be rid of him once and for all. At least until he got some fresh air, when they closed up in town and he might've continued drinking in the bar at the gas station, which never closes; or at Mas Paradís, which doesn't close either because it's far from town and isolated, and the Guardia Civil turns a blind eye, or for whatever reason. And there he was, already with that expression—mouth half-open, eyes half-closed—of a person subjected to a deep posterior penetration, so similar to what, watching the small screen—sound turned down to zero—we can appreciate on the face of a singer while she emphatically modulates the muted melody, while she pronounces, for example, the word "apotheosis." I took advantage of this to step back from the bar, as if I wanted to cast a glance at the floor, and immediately rejoin the crowd there, only a little farther on, separated now by a couple of guys who'd occupied the space I left open. Annoying bores, too, but strangers. The uselessness of trying to explain to a guy like that, who arrives with a friend, both fellows pretty drunk, and who with his chatter tries to get us involved in his feverish projects or, at least, to find in us a certain incentive or moral support, because he hasn't come round determined to hook up with a woman or grope anybody or get his hand down their pants, and the tits on that blonde, who turns out to be Rosa, don't excite him more than any others, something as useless as attempting to convince the previously-frustrated actor from the other night, a friend of friends or of acquaintances, that he hasn't advanced or won't advance beyond his secondary roles, beyond his bit parts in television programs, for however much light he manages to steal, to convince him, or simply make him see that I'm convinced what a nightmare it must have been for Marilyn, in her last days, besieged by fame, and the absence in all that, as far as we know, of some unnecessary publicity set-up, conscious beforehand of the incredulity, the rancor, and the wrath that such a supposedly common locale can provoke in a person so eager to succeed. I think she's pretty good-looking, I said.

I thought that Pompey and the others were downstairs dancing, but they must have slipped outside without my noticing when I went to take a piss, and now I saw him with Krista, descending the steep, torturous staircase, and they were heading toward the reddened dance floor, barely visible from the bar. Behind them, paused on the last curve of the staircase, his mere presence causing excitement as much as demanding it, some corpulent, middle-aged guy, German or, more likely, Dutch, drunk, crab-like, muscular and red, with a getup like a space suit, like an astronaut, with blue lightning bolts, satanic in his euphoria; back in Holland, surely, some home appliance salesman. Reminiscent of the so-called Rodriguez, that stereotypical Spanish temporary bachelor of summer, who, the family now away on vacation, arrives home to his silent, deserted apartment and—first things first—plunges into a vigorous session of onanism right there on the living room sofa; so too, that kindred hick, that Dutch rube in his unrestrained search for some exciting environment and soothing relief.

More and more people flooding in, a sign that the other bars were closing up. Among them, a figure whom we might deem a Man-Cock, that typical playboy whose body, fine-tuned into a singular vigorous muscle, acquires, from the earliest days of the summer season, doubtless owing to the uniform coloration of his skin, like an enormous pair of lips, a certain quality of a virile member, like a balanus, more concretely a quality, or rather, a property which, if the subject is fully conscious of its value, usually engenders a self-confidence comparable only, in its externalization, to the pleasure enjoyed by one of those villainous Italians who always seems to be enraptured by or absorbed in contemplating the mettle and notorious witchcraft of his very own *cazzo*. Can you help me? asked Rosa Durán. The problem was to help her get Xavier into the privacy of the bathroom. The club was in full swing, its murky cellar vaults aswarm with shadows from the flaring dance floor, an inner glow, like some furious jaws of molten light gaping and closing within the frame of the heavy columns; the crowd tightly circulating up and down the steep staircase, the tumultuous nook of the bar, with its decorative elements of a nineteenth-century sailing ship or pleasure yacht. Just the right climate which that recently arrived young newlywed couple hoped to encounter, determined as they were to experience, by any reckoning, the world of nighttime orgies so they'd have something to recount later on to their other married friends during after-dinner conversations, and at the same time, and in a more immediate way, get moderately excited at being in the heat of such excess, she, curious and frightened, and he, more knowledgeable about the world at large despite his good, conscientious appearance, and perhaps owing to an almost seraphic paleness, appropriate for someone who spends hours and hours consulting the Aranzadi, the government's official legal bulletin, firmly protecting her from all possible offenses to her modesty, whether by word, deed, gesture or some look in the eyes, the sort of fellow who, rather than coming a geyser, must have trickled and dripped with a light shudder, not so much an orgasm as something like localized perspiration from a cold chill. A chance to get away from it all and find some peace while one still has the time.

Rosa Durán was still waiting by the bathroom door. Go in and see, please, she said; I left him in there, throwing up. There were two guys pissing with an air of concentration; I took the place of the first one who finished, a stocky sailor, like one of those boys in a Brueghel painting, terribly burly and irascible. The door to the stall where Xavier had locked himself in was still shut, although from the sounds coming out it might as well have been open, nothing easier to imagine than Xavier letting fly with the nether violence of his gathered intestinal forces, now below as moments before from above, almost like that whale which, when it discharges the remains of previous digestions uses pressure to expel the excess water it has swallowed, spraying it in a spout, even as it keeps on guzzling, torrents and cascades and whirlpools spinning away into the vastness of its mouth, a whirl of flashing lights, or foams of amniotic density, speeding down into the throat as if drawn to the void, cavities no less profound than those one discovers in their own innards when they find themselves surrendering completely to that radical process of total cleansing, of complete emptiness, which precedes the desired beatitude, that oblivion of the body itself, that resultant individuality in the surrounding calm, in the pure harmony, a state only achievable through the tense immersion in that world of turbulent chasms, like streams of incandescent lava, subterranean convulsions, spasmodic depths, mysterious complexities of caves and sunken hollows, violent movements of systole and diastole, dilations, contractions that convert those blind limits, vast as a cathedral nave or a ship's innards, into tiny caverns which close themselves up, gripping like vaginas or sphincters, among epiglottic or vulval reliefs which cluster together like stalactites or rows of teeth or whale baleen, waterways which spread out, invading and flooding and drowning the smallest corners, salons and back rooms and dance floors, the tavern bar, the staircases, corridors, cabins, bathrooms, slime oozing out through the hatches, through the portholes, flowing and flowing, buoying on its tide passengers and sailors and waiters and drunkards and all kinds of men squeezing out their shit, carrying them all down to the inferno of the engine room, burning expulsions, valves ready to burst amid whistling steam, free of corrosive matter, now more earthquake than shipwreck, mountains crumbling, subterranean lakes surging free, flooding out in a thick, choppy mass, cloistered corners and shadowy domes which flower out into the light, the breaking point becoming thunder crack, an avalanche of residue, waste matter all intermingled so that, after the first phase, a cataclysm that spreads out will soon be followed by new tremors, the overflow and discharge become waterspout and whirlwind, the maelstrom a bubbling and explosive crater, the same as a barbarous diarrheal evacuation in its most critical and promethean moment, eruptions which little by little must settle from one extreme to the other, from the vaginal vertigo of the throat to the vulval reliefs of the very last rectal rings, leaving, as its clear track of the event in the pale liberated body, a white coral sheen of cold sweat on the green skin. Like the other night at Walter's house. And then I washed my face and went out to the garden, the starry sky a mirror of my eyes. He's alright, I said to Rosa Durán. When he's done, take him outside so he can get some fresh air.

The flow of refugees continued, noctambulists sheltered by the almost three hours of extra bar time which a discotheque enjoys over any other bar. Even The Greek. He offered me a distracted wave, entangled as he already was with The Flying Dutchman, already invited to participate in the liquidation of the crystalline gin and tonics that his interlocutor—elbow vibrating electrically, face on fire—dispatched with brusque gulps, between brusque cackles, with the efficient help of the inevitable old American, very comfortable in his supporting role to The Greek, in his drinks as well as his words, acting as his spontaneous translator and guide, offering the moral axis of an expert foreigner on local questions, more Hemingwayesque in his style than the errant host, and also more cracked and broken down, his futile struggle to bolster his crumbling looks by resorting to symbolic virility: quaffing shots of strong, burning liquor. He nodded his head in agreement, confirming The Greek's assertions, expressed in Tarzanesque syntax, about a fisherman's life, the dangers of the sea, his boat sinking at Cabo Norfeo, accenting as much as possible the colorful detail, the picturesqueness, the fishing, the lobsters, the coral, the sponges, trying as hard as possible to fit the image of a fisherman from Rosas that his interlocutors might imagine, talker and skeptic, ironical and wise, quite a guy, a real character, as they say. Trying his hardest, drawing upon his best expressive resources in his attempt to cope with adverse circumstances, explanations now almost forced, overcome by the economic development and touristic proliferation, by the lack of landmarks, a clientele who does not understand him, as much as he tries to define himself as a good old-fashioned fisherman, one of those who used to take the gentlemen from Barcelona on sport-fishing trips, years ago, before the explosion in tourism, one of those fisherman who seemed to step out from the pages of a book by Josep Pla who made stews of freshly caught fish and shellfish and prepared cups of hot cremat and sang Habaneras for the men of olden days, one of them being him, The Greek.

At the end of the bar, gleaming in the semi-darkness, the duty belt of a city police officer; he was not paying the house a visit as part of his nightly rounds, as much as accepting, no doubt, with discreet and gracious diligence, their standing invitation of a free drink, tolerant, understanding, nothing further from his intentions than interfering with public exuberance, people bonding over alcohol, hookups, the ardor of guys biding their time, trying to score, watching, calculating like maybe that crafty pedophile who, as if transported by the adolescent beauty of his prey, slowly considers, from every angle, the best way to bait it, the best strategy, the attitude most likely to be especially impressive, most seductive—demonic, vital, tormented, fascist—in order to win his trust, of gradually becoming his mentor and, from this tutelary position, continue stimulating the boy's initial shyness regarding the venereal experience, creating in him little by little an adequate sensation of shelter from the mystery of the opposite sex, offering him at last the alternative of the always more familiar sex to which he belongs, toward which, as our predator's sizable list of victims certainly demonstrates, the young pupil will end up inclining.

The Man-Cock set his sights on Rosa. Do you want to dance? he said or must have said. She declined, but without breaking away; the music and noise made it difficult to hear what anyone was saying. And this is how the young fisherman on the coast, dedicating his nights to seducing—actively or passively—tourists of one sex or the other, believes himself obliged to mangle polyglot fantasies not only incoherent but often contradictory, he wears his lucky little golden medallion on his tanned chest because, like any good Spaniard, he's a Catholic, and so very macho that whether he fucks a man or a woman makes no difference to him whatsoever, Spanish men never let women pay but if the women insist on paying then there must be some reason for it, etcetera, and it's not so much mythomaniacal delirium as it is courteous enthusiasm to try to correspond to the stereotype one might suppose his companions expect him to be, thus, in a similar way, Rosa always contributed, as much as possible, to the dissolute ambience they all tried to create among themselves.

At some tables the music rang out with that slightly monotonous happy chorus of Swiss or Germans having fun, singing all together, whistling all together, a blond circle of heavy sausage-fed pricks whistling beer. Walter and Quima approached to propose something. The Man-Cock tossed back his cognac in a single gulp, adjusted his leather belt, loosened one more button to reveal a greater pectoral expanse, shook out his hair, went to the bathroom, the bartender refused to serve him another drink, he said the man had no right to refuse him because he wasn't drunk, took the sweating misty glass and swirled the ice cubes before taking a drink, tried to cover the scandalously growing bulge beneath his fly, leaned on his elbows sticking out his ass, making his shirt gape as wide open as possible, and said no, not yet.

METAPHOR OF EUROPE.

The world: a madman's machination. An inherited machine whose function is known only in an approximate, empirical way, because each generation, too busy keeping itself going forward, usually leaves for future generations the task of untangling its necessary knowledge and, above all, the knowledge of what it's good for, of what use it may be. After all, how can you decipher a madman's designs? And how can you even demonstrate that that demented personality is anything more than a reflection, a false appearance, the erroneous interpretation of some fact relative to that work whose invention we attribute to them? And how else can we demonstrate, if really considering it well, the existence of the man—creator and product of that illusion—as an autonomous existence, not a mere irrelevant feature of such a work, when it's not necessary to think in order to exist, or perhaps not, perhaps not even the absence of thought might be the guarantee of the existence of how much we think exists?

Walking and walking toward the center of town, along the promenade, along the sea, splashed by the waves shattering against the wharf, white rainbow spume, like some cheap champagne, more sticky than refreshing; thinking and thinking about the ticket folded up inside his pocket, the esoteric language in which it was written barely adding a surreal touch to the surrounding reality, that high-flown and bureaucratic slang, detritus of the combination of the admonitory administrative tone with the typical lexicon of police procedural reports, no longer much removed from the rigor and stylistic and conceptual purity of a code as much as of a simple decree-law or a judicial sentence: abstract threats, rhetorical feinting, premeditatively aprioristic, in prevention, no doubt, of the coincidence, of the pure coincidence—in some way unforeseeable—that both the motorcycle cop as well as the ticketed driver—him—were in a terrible mood, in the same place and at the same time, and he refused to sign the ticket and, having noticed the officer's conspicuous moroseness in the fulfillment of his intended duty and indisputable right—to confirm the presumed lawbreaker's identity, to impart the subsequent denunciation, etcetera—only imputable to a premeditated zeal for maximum annoyance, aware of all that, he refused not only to sign the ticket, a personal decision fully within his rights, but also to exercise his no-less-indisputable right of taking good note of the officer's badge number, forewarning him, in rather vulgar language, it was true, but well within his reach, of real trouble to come, as a consequence of his own impending complaint against the officer, a denunciation which, under the auspices of his own legal practice and certain connections angrily exploited, and especially thanks to his own determination to prosper, no doubt he would prosper, would cause the officer in question's hair to fall out—just deserts for an officer of the law found to be clearly intoxicated while on duty, the only possible explanation for the behavior observed in the aforementioned traffic cop. *C'est une espèce de coquelicot, je crois.*

The sunny wind and the waves that shattered in his wake as he strolled along the seaside promenade, and the words and noises that reached him isolated from their own context, difficult to pinpoint their origin, everything contributing to that sensation of strangeness or dementia a person attending a concert can suddenly experience witnessing the ecstasy of the music lovers who, like lunatics, surround him. Thus, similar to that impression of extravagance, the unusual air that, for some undetermined reason, the town offers, a town, incidentally, barely altered by the slow accentuation of the seasonal symptoms, a phenomenon which by its very own progressive character—the same, although inverse, as the trees being stripped of their leaves in autumn—nothing surprising, at any time, about the process: the boats that get scratched and repainted, hotels and apartments prepared anew, the bars' patios spilling onto the sidewalks, the little bars and food stands that open up along the beach, the increasing number of paddle boats lined up on the sand, the canvas awnings and canvas chaises longues, isolated facts which, placed into relation with one another, make up what might be well considered a general mobilization of the town awaiting the tourists, that generic being who can be characterized by the interchangeability of the individuals such a concept implies, in light of their difficult differentiation and common crablike tonality, whose first examples, like early explorers or intrepid advance scouts, had already appeared on the beaches, in the streets, outside the postcard and souvenir shops, possessed by the initial joy which Nordic and Central European people usually experience in the sun's warmth, a jubilation comparable only to what Catalans typically experience in Switzerland, when the impressive, truly uplifting spectacle of the sun setting behind the Jungfrau can be heightened by the soothing satisfaction of a substantial flight of capital. The same kind of Catalan who, here and now, in his capacity as promoter, builder, speculator, proprietor, hotel magnate—meaning, as the most immediate beneficiary of expected income provided by wealthy tourists through such a diverse array of concepts—allowed himself to be seen more frequently, as the season approached the tourist avalanche, in order to put the finishing touches on everything, or to go around checking to see that everything was ready, preferably on weekends, accompanied by friends and family members, combining duty with the possibility of fleeing to Barcelona and gorging on fish, at reasonable prices, in some restaurant specializing in seafood. And alongside those kinds of Catalans, also enjoying the leisure activities offered by a sunny Sunday outing, the housemaids and the charnegos, construction workers, day laborers, hotel maids, household maids coming with their employers, tradesmen of all different occupations centered on what was a typical fishing town, meaning, the business setup, everyone, fishermen or ex-fishermen, charnegos, tourists, businessmen, everyone involved one way or another in that business, everyone contributing to its development for everyone's benefit, as if in one single Iberian alluvial deposit successive waves of invaders might have settled and superimposed themselves in peaceful conviviality, like geological strata, Greeks, Phoenicians, Romans, Vikings, Visigoths, Tartars, Saracens, Apaches, Sagittarians, each in their place but all together, at different levels but in the same terrain, in short, just a touch degraded precisely due to the fact of their impossible integration.

The little transistor radio of the passersby: Dear Radio Listeners and Friends out there in space. And he? An extraterrestrial, seemingly just disembarked from a UFO amid that scene of charnegos having fun, enjoying the parenthesis which opens and closes off Sunday from the regular continuous routine, strolling in the sunshine, strolling again, gladdening the street with their catcalls at the first female tourists, funny obscenities received by the passersby with a delight similar to that which is usually aroused among the passengers on a train when someone—a miserly widow in mourning, a man in the throes of a hangover—notices that they've missed the station where they were supposed to get off. And the charnego, with the typical housewife and the typical weekly pay in his pocket, even coming to believe the myth to the letter, in all its extended meaning: the irresistible attraction which the foreign woman feels for the Iberian macho and his attributes, secret attractions and hexes crafted around his well-deserved fame for vitality, energy, good service, and other virile qualities all his own. Tough, vigorous, pugnacious charnegos, in open competition—despite the obvious social and economic inferiority that characterize the domestic emigrant's situation—with the native conqueror, with the young fisherman from Rosas, or the ex-fisherman, or son of an ex-fisherman, in whose territory, after all, the catch was disputed, various individuals in fierce Olympian competition: weight, length, duration, leap, hurl, gallop, bull'seye! Various individuals on the hunt for the exquisite first fruits of the season, pursuing those fortunate females who appear when that hunger, the fruit of abstinence, still rules, those flowery creatures early arrived in their anxious urgency (not to be postponed) hastening to suck down, to the very dregs, so much Iberian brio, so much pure-blooded manliness, pure sperm, torrential spout of vigor, and on occasion, even rashly, even too much, this is the danger, when one has waited so long, and when, once more, dreams and secrets and calculations and fantasies go up in smoke, as, one after another, in the course of the summer, those flowery creatures slip away and disappear, those northern roses, more splendid if possible than when they arrived, leaving behind, like the only trace of their passing, the subsequent accumulated feverish arousal, because, once more, the cursed professional, the local playboy, the Man-Cock, with his gigolo's or pimp's magical arts, will be the only one to achieve anything, and so one of these days, the season ended, the last tourist packed and fled, so that the matter doesn't get out of hand and nobody ends up with a bad impression, this guy will be called on the carpet, to settle accounts, to be judged by everyone, and they will burn him at the stake in the church plaza.

In reality, the same problem, only from a complementary perspective—less convex than concave—that arises for the recently arrived housemaids, so dolorously separated from their Thursday and Sunday afternoons in Barcelona, from their world, from their people, alone here, disconsolate, helpless, resigned and, suddenly, even excited, seeing so many blond guys like in the movies, foreign and enigmatic, tacky fellows that look like princes and who, perhaps, take them for princesses, under the afternoon sun, in their bikinis, mysterious and tanned, given the friendly treatment and deference by which they objectify them and which the girls, skittish, accept only to a certain degree, always in fear, with the sword hanging above, that the men will mistake them for what they're not—namely, married women—that everything will then be discovered, fears and timidities which will unfailingly force them to seek refuge in the familiar evil, in the charnego who's neither elegant nor radiant but dark and stocky, the charnego who knows them and whom they know, who see each other coming, who understand each other, including without saying much, interjections, cackles, a hug, he a charnego and she a charnega, people you can have fun with, who speak the same language and laugh at the same things, who talk plainly, who call a spade a spade, for whom bread is bread and wine is wine, a man who smells like a man, and who is one, just as she smells like a woman—intimate smells, in this case softened and made subtle by cosmetics—olfactory attractions which are only like the halo of deeper affinities, that stuff about sticking with you through thick and thin in its most literal sense, a kind of identification which permits them to end up laughing like crazy about so many foreign men and women, about so many different guys who make you laugh just by looking at them, outlandish looking, peeling from sunburn, who don't understand anything and who are really pretty much worthless, who can't hold a candle to a paisano, a happy paisano, clear, direct, a paisano with whom you can really have your fill of fun, who can pleasantly satisfy all that summer ardor, just as pleasantly here as in Barcelona, in reality, until the time comes to return to Barcelona. The housemaid of today: a humane woman unanimously censured by the lady of the house, at the same time denied, boycotted to the degree that she is new and different in contrast to the old-fashioned maid, the traditional maid, who bears every trait of the most typical Spanish woman plus all the neurotic quirks of prolonged maidenhood, the bitterness of so many years single: tense frowning unibrow, face clamped tight, tits clamped tight, ass clamped tight, sex clamped tight, clamped tight all over, hen-crested coif, sneaky, carefree and daring, always humming her same old songs about suffering and being forgotten—*Las cruces y el olvido*—from the times when men were more manly because she was younger and they said things to her, unfriendly, frigidly aggressive, *destemplado su aire de ande yo caliente ríase la gente—she walks all cold and haughty, I'm just hot and horny, oh let the people laugh*, a refrain understood as a transference to the digestive sleepiness of the dark venereal impulses, long dormant, under wraps, corseted; a survivor of that world that has a saying for every occasion: When a baby boy is born: Now, let's have a girl! A good wish: health and pesetas. A bit of consolation: after all you've still got that *bacalao al pilpil*—spicy hot with plenty of garlic. The kind of people who, more than being pleased at some exemplary punishment, identify with the one who delivers it, just as by any reckoning that goddamned bitch must have identified with the waiter when he strode out into the street and used a chair to beat apart a pair of dogs still stuck together and all twisted around in their sad post-coital interim. At least there are some who think about them, look out for them, who restrain them. Those who don't speak, who don't think, who, as a consequence, have no morals whatsoever.

Reproof, however, a reproof no less explicit for being implied, in the eyes of that couple of young hikers who, bent beneath the weight of their backpacks, tromped energetically into town, stern, glancing around, the explicit brutality implicit in that act, reproof and censure no doubt as extensive as what their gazes encompassed as they kept walking, forward along the seaside promenade, with all the stubborn capacity of two young Catalan university students tramping across country in search of their land and their people, their origins, their roots. He: a heavy-set softy, clumsy and shy, bespectacled, bearded, hairy, sedentary build, barely bulging package, slack-assed hiking shorts, and wide-spreading sweat stains on his checked shirt, under his armpits, all iridescent effluvia he, poor eyesight, stumbling, blundering, stuttering. She: equally fat-assed and chalk-white with a big rack to boot, a look of false frigidity, meaning, the look of a woman who tends to solve the erotic conjunction in a practical and expedient way, an appearance that usually conceals an acknowledged nymphomaniacal personality barely held in check, thin insolent lips which, despite her efforts to not look like a mean idiot, make her seem insipid—the mark of character—less, far less idealistic and disciplined than what she pretends to be, and more, far more sensual, indolent and given to excess than she appears; in short, a personality ready, willing, and able to cuckold any lover with the same consummate skill Charles used to drive a lance into the heart of Flanders. Both: temporarily united in their search for an ideal upon which they might establish a stable relationship, the myth equally elusive and concrete, the cypress and the olive tree of the Ampurdán, metaphysically counterpoised to the poplar's symbolic entity, or what is symbolized by the beech trees of Olot or the Pyrenean spruce or the carob, almond, and hazelnut trees of Tarragona, all elements of equal importance in the contradictory configuration, the essence of that conflictive reality called Catalonia. Seeking more than finding the defining features of such a reality: the landscape as a geographical frame, as a natural medium which has made intimate the character and forms of Catalan life, the typically typical types of people, the typical cuisine that emanates from such typicalness, the purity of the characteristic tongue of the small, still-unpolluted clusters of humanity, the classically Catalan words, the mere externalization of the immanence of its values, valiant men, hale and hearty, quick-witted, well-tempered men, in short, where the impetus is perfectly harmonized with ironic sensibility and utterly serious formality. Finding without having sought it: Spanish contamination at every level, servility, rapine, racketeering, corruption, prostitution in the main, that typically Spanish orientation, infecting even bullfighting and the tawdry women in the stands in their flamenco dresses. Not finding: their country and their people, their traditional traditions. Finding: greed become a behavioral norm, commission and percentage touted as a model of human relations, features attributable not so much to foreign elements as to what is specifically Catalan: a lack of conviction or interest necessary to place any other consideration before the conscience of a people oppressed; an excess of megalomania and mythomania; squandering money, alcohol, sperm, and other venereal liqueurs. They, they who were by this order: Catalanescos, progressives, populists, sanctimonious prudes, shy people, people repressed, oppressed, and betrayed not only in their feelings but in their dignity, too, ashamed of being neither more nor less Catalan than that businessman who, the very personification of one's shame, of one's humiliation and opprobrium, sat enjoying his aperitif on some bar's patio, under the sun, surrounded by his acolytes, his accomplices, young men hungry to triumph, laughing along with him, sharing the good humor that usually signals the happy outcome of an excellent business deal, one of those Catalan men whom one would assume to be Anglo-Saxon thanks to his extreme fondness for pork products, a love that even manages to make them physically resemble a big pig, our businessman in question himself a fine porcine specimen, as well as—in a more incipient way—some of his minions—frequently no less Catalan, unfortunately, than our Big Pig—promoters, commission agents, installers, salesmen, speculators, each one with his fistful, with his pinch, with his mouthful, with his cut, coming down hard to trample opposition underfoot when advantageous, skinning them alive when expedient, blindingly obvious when convenient, reaming them up the ass when it suits him, public relations, human relations, copromorphic anthropophagy, a real picnic you might say, polls, canvassing, fund-raising, surveys, machinations, foot by foot, inch by inch, collective and sympathetic managers of a country's conversion—Catalonia's—into a lifestyle, terrain conquered by opulent bad taste and prosperous scurrility, simultaneous consequence of the petite bourgeois socioeconomic ascension and the extension of horizontal property. Hence the fascination which a certain city exercises upon that rising petite bourgeoisie, not Paris as one might at first suppose, let alone New York or London, but rather the small city of Geneva, a symbol, exactly on their own scale, of precision and efficiency, with high quality industries, grandiose landscapes, and numbered bank accounts (to boot), a kind of fascination—tradition and progress, craftsmanship and automation, everything both very international and very local, very concrete, very specific—not unlike the difference between a fiery percheron and an ambling mare.

Human characteristics and distinctive physiognomies whose material incarnation—meaning, the Catalan who becomes the principal beneficiary of economic development—nonetheless disappears under the tourist avalanche upon a sometime small seaside fishing community, falling at the high summer season, although it seems to fade before that horizon of white wakes from sailboats and motorboats and stylized waterski silhouettes enlivening the bay, or the beaches aswarm with swimmers and sunbathers, or in the packed alleyways and traffic jams in the streets, cars creeping along, crawling almost as slowly as the meandering crowd, the search for a parking spot, for an open table on the bar and restaurant terraces, people and more people making the rounds, blocking each others' way, and although, in short, they seem to lose themselves in that coming and going and in the babel of languages, the Catalan remains, isolated, sometimes hard to find, like a host in the midst of a lively party, but not for that reason less identifiable once located, less unmistakable in his discreet presence, generally grouped together, like guardian angels of the phenomenon, keeping watch—as far as it concerns them, as they commonly say—so that everything turns out satisfactorily, meaning, keeping an eye on how the deal progresses, at the same time as, from their privileged position, they enjoy it all, curious about how so many different faces and appearances tend to turn a simple crowd into a kind of spectacle. Thus, that postprandial conversation between wedded couples, local property developer and his wife, audits manager for a banking agency and his wife, the exclusive representative of some established and accredited firm and his wife, for example, or people of analogous social and economic condition, three or four of those couples who meet up assiduously, a sort of club, let's say, centered around the customary big Sunday meal in the restaurant where they always gather, their subsequent indigestion slowly, gradually tempered with more coffees and more cognacs, between jokes and anecdotes and shared memories, the men more openly given to the happy disposition of the moment than the women, without that retention of control or calculation, of mutual surveillance, of being on the alert, which singularize relationships between wives, always keeping an eye on each other, establishing comparisons based essentially on external signs, former times when physical attributes constituted their principal field of competition now long past, tepidness momentarily revived, however, in the women as well as in the men, with the warm effluvia of aioli when burps force it back up the throat, facts noticeable during some brief pause, when lighting a cigar or brightening up lipstick or using the fingernail to loosen some food particle lodged between the teeth or getting up to pee or to cut a fart, vague lewdness suddenly awakened by the sight of some cleavage or by an insolent derriere wiggled for show while standing up to brush the crumbs off her lap, rotating three-quarters of the way around on her heels, full tight bellies, mouths gasping from the unpunished somnolence of some heavy indigestion, unconscious attacks on the Catalan woman's traditional tendency toward modesty and respectability, against her predilection for semi-long sleeves and semi-short skirts and semi-tight waists, for the color black that goes well with everything and slenderizes her figure, for the discreet pearl, a tendency, in short, to attract attention without calling attention to herself, and as a consequence to shun everything flashy and risqué, everything that's very very. The curious behavior of that new petite bourgeoisie, its eunuchoid manners, fruit of a diverse series of factors linked to the very process of its affirmation and ascent, with the consequent effort at refinement in its manners, developed, in parallel fashion to the physical fattening from accumulated voracity—product of its well-understood (who knows why) social triumph, and zest for delicacy and distinction—as a lady's manners, intonations and even a lady's expressions, including grandmother as paid mourner, something similar—to the degree of its assimilating power—to the phenomenon consistent with which some tacky person consciously affects a tacky guise due to his dealings with buyers, due to the fact that his personal taste has changed according to the buyers' taste. The inevitable consequence of all assimilative processes, the fermentations produced, the results: mental aerophagia, fumetis of the brain, man's most fabulous instrument of cancellation, the sickness of the century, which, for example, has nothing to do with the intestinal aerophagia of a recluse subjected to a strict diet of legumes, because, however close to the explosion he finds himself, it keeps the intellect awake and the imagination lively to the point of delirium. *Un coquelicot à cette époque?*

The air of permanent carnival a seaside town exudes in the high season, the spectacle presented by the living street, the crowd's motley parade, the people watching that parade from the terraces outside the bars. A festive atmosphere which, in its turn, does nothing but strengthen the tourist's initial good disposition, an enthusiasm similar—how lovely!—to what the homosexual usually demonstrates toward certain places, as if grateful, in juxtaposition to the habitual animosity which he notices or thinks he notices in the surrounding world, the pleasant memory that they preserve. And the fact is, truly, there are few happier phenomena, from every point of view, than the confluence of tourists from everywhere, than the convergence of interests and anxieties it raises, especially if we choose to disregard the excitement and attraction their demonstrations usually display. The usefulness, the benefits they represent not only for the locals, the investor, or the charnego—although to different degrees—and in a more general, indirect way, the recipient country, the national treasury, and the healthy equilibrium of its balance of payments, but also for the subject—or object—of that flow, of the host country's affluence, meaning, for the tourist properly speaking, receptacle of the pleasures some well-earned vacations produce, a highly lucrative respite, too, for its recuperative and performance-enhancing effects, for one's company, as well as, within a demanding political framework, for the labor syndicate to which one belongs, the organization that has bargained so much on his behalf for the number of days of leisure officially allotted him as well as a salary increase more commensurate to the cost of living, an increase which always stimulates production, the way credit companies stimulate consumption and taxes on consumption stimulate savings, all of them factors, on the other hand, that indisputably favor investment, the capitalization of businesses and international commerce, a diversity of processes which expand their reach more and more, which become integrated and couple and harmonize in a single circuit that, on the margins of the capitalist or socialist character of such and such an economy, ends up revealing the worldwide dimensions of its magnitude. Let the money flow, as the popular expression goes, let it circulate, let it work, time, money, change. Change of place, change of life, although only for a few days, in a new attempt to recover lost energies, to shake off the sclerosis of acquired habits: the principal impulses of the man of today, any old contributor from any old country, who travels to snap pictures and has children in order to film them and a tape recorder to record their first babblings and, very much in accord with that context of counting down, a Polaroid for the purpose of preserving for all time the spousal sex organs, his penis, particularly stiff in front of the lens, like all that who-knows-what being photographed, and his wife's volcanic sepals, the family united in the legitimate enjoyment of such photogenic pleasures.

Of course, one thing is having a color photo as similar as possible to any one of those postcards for sale outside the shops, on the sidewalks, panoramic views of the town, sunsets on the bay, beaches, the fish auction, archaeological excavations, a nighttime view of the streets, the bars' terraces at midday, the seaside promenade, etcetera, but it's something very different to experience all that for days and days on end, waddling up and down that damned promenade over and over again, struggling and swimming your way through all those swimmers, repeating the nighttime rounds, the body—your hide already well tanned by the sun—punished more and more by diverse annoyances, head and stomach principally, that sangria that left him feeling ill, the paella that didn't let him sleep a wink, nausea, diarrhea, migraines and, above all, fatigue—after all, no one's getting any younger—and so, with almost zero desire to return home, wishing these wonderful happy vacations would come to an end once and for all, hardly infrequent that the tourist ends up behaving like one of those retired couples, weary, incommunicative, with the aura of tedium that belongs to all old married couples when, now free of the daily worries of work and with everything in the family in apple pie order, they decide one fine day that now is the time to see the world, to travel, to visit the places they never visited nor will ever visit again, and then, now embarked on their adventure, they end up bored, tired of touring countries and seeing famous places that deep down really don't interest them and which, in fact, it's just enough and more to see them on the postcards sold in the hotel itself, and even without having left the house, buying books on the subject, those expensive books which, apart from adorning any shelf, are useful for leafing through sitting around the table, after dinner, when there's nothing very interesting on TV. The point being, in short, that to the personal, subjective fatigue which the tourist might or might not experience can be added another kind of fatigue, more general and also deeper, which affects the European and, by extension, the American, the Westerner, essentially, that man who finds rest and relaxation tiring, boredom, fatigue, and disgust not sufficiently explainable by the fact that the society to which he belongs has gone about shaping and authorizing work and vacations as complementary occupations, both equally foreign to him. An erosion of the principles that inform such a class of society, of the very body of that society? Contemporary Europe, that enterprise containing more past than present, more present than future, a Europe more united and weaker than ever, roundly in denial of maxims such as the one that proclaims strength through unity, nostalgically recalling the rotating preponderances of other times and the splendid isolations, proud successive constructions realized with all the astuteness of Ulysses, the violence of Achilles, the piety of Aeneas, the heroism of Siegfried, the steadfastness of Roland, and the chivalry of El Cid, conflictive but always homogeneous entities, cannibalistic in relation to the neighboring towns and fratricidal in relationship to their own kind, evangelizing powers of the rest of the world, meaning, makers—like God of man—of a world in the image and likeness of what they had in common, their faith in strength, an uncivilized Europe, barbarizer, drugger, raper, enslaver, exterminator, atomizer, gnawing rodent, grater and shredder, exploiter, converting countries into development projects, cultures into antiquities, races into products, people and towns into markets, a magical exchange, the genius of Christianity, vast deployment of crosses and cannons, these are my reasons, these are my powers, a Europe sharply fraught with fear, with a guilt complex in the face of that world made in its image and likeness, fearing above all to receive a reciprocal treatment, the same treatment it has given, the Asian drug, the African cock. Anxiety and guilt and demoralization which cannot stop weighing down on the shoulders of today's European, of our man, and which thus explain his fatigue, accentuated by the effort of simulating a hypocritical cordiality toward other races, other societies, other cultures. An effort so much greater when, underhandedly, increasingly underhandedly, there seethes yet the impulse to return, to relapse, to overturn the table and confront once more the traditional enemies of the West, to defeat them as in other times they were defeated by Charles Martell, in Poitiers or on the Catalaunian or Catalan Plains, Charles Martell or Charlemagne or William Tell, arisen proverbially against the invader, against that Attila in power who comes charging in hirsute riding bareback naked right down to his own hairy abdomen, cock locked in lance rest, fuckingalloping.

The sunny promenade, practically deserted, and a solitary whistle from an uncertain location, the only sound audible, an expression of that inner emptiness which certain insubstantial beings manifest when they're on their way to do something. Upon reaching the area of the fishing cooperative, the long nets spread out obliged him to move away from the edge of the dock, the pounding surf more and more muted, more distant the splashing foam, a light and sticky foam like the froth from that cheap champagne which, in the relative irresponsibility that comes from quaffing a few glasses of it, one can end up drinking in the gas station bar or at the Paradís when the bars in town have to close up for the night. And that man approaching, headon, face to face, with that almost-floating attitude adopted by certain homosexuals when they walk, flat-stepping, sliding more than walking, legs soft, shoulders fallen, arms hanging, elbows glued to the body, palms sticking out in opposite directions, the self-absorbed smile while walking into the distance, eyes nearly glazed over—an eccentric, no doubt, some flotsam from the tourist flood, one of the few foreigners who stick around during the off-season, who prolong their stay as if they enjoyed the spectacle that follows the exodus, patios that vanish, hotels, bars, discotheques, and restaurants that roll down their shutters, deserted beaches, boats stored for winter, a whole town like a beach umbrella that folds up, while construction resumes like in a mansion, the party over, housecleaning begins the moment the last guest has departed, and the local population begins to enjoy its well-earned rest, and they relax and gossip and get bored and drive each other crazy with their problems, arguing with each other about any old thing, wishing now that the days would last longer and the sun keep shining bright and, when it comes time to start preparing again for the next season, that no one takes too long to show up, that some eccentric person soon arrive to distract them, someone interested in seeing how the apartments and hotels get ready, how the bar and restaurant patios get set up, the houses aired out, the boats caulked and repainted and, on the beaches, along with the first swimmers, the paddle boats reappear and the little food shacks reopen, and the first housemaids are spotted on the streets and even that hypothetical stroller who explores the outskirts of the town and visits the no-less hypothetical archaeological excavations and strolls up and down the seaside promenade again and again and punctually reaches the fish auction at the fishing cooperative. An atmosphere of backlit scenes and echoes, phosphorescences, bubbles, gleaming mirages, tails slapping, flapping their fins slowly before plunging straight down screaming, kicking up a racket, splashing around the boats that arrive, clogs splashing, slippery puddles of salt and ice melted into each other, iridescent circles, convulsive last gasps, tensions calmed in the center of the circles, expectant faces attracted by the bewildering decreasing numerals, and some other curious person wandering from group to group, that extravagant creature who, outside, in the street, one might have well taken for a homosexual, but who, on closer inspection, turns out to be a beautiful idiot, something like one of those human mannequins who take pleasure in causing a stir, in provoking almost to the point of physical aggression, wherever they go, motives similar to those which comfort the rich man when he gives alms—the outstretched hand as a contrast—or similar to those which make the old man who contemplates the fishes' agony feel more alive, especially if we relate his chronic constipation—given his retentive, saving, accumulative character—to the subject's undoubted narcissistic and even megalomaniacal tendencies, one will also have to relate the sufferings that such disruptions mean for his body with the logical sense of guilt that the symptom produces, and to understand the need to purge oneself as an expiatory and, consequently, liberating compensation, thus, in a similar way, the physical beauty and external harmony do not generally cease to cause psychical problems and peculiar alterations in the behavior of one who is known to possess such qualities. *Mais c'est justement le temps des coquelicots!*

Consequences of the circulating alcohol, altered perceptions, although it might also be a question of a sharper perception, capable of capturing the modifications in the perception only invisible to one who refuses to see, higher heights of reality. Because it would also be difficult to clarify if the young Phoenician princess was kidnapped or if she was the kidnapper, if she was the robbed or the robber, spurring on the flanks of the white bull like a cattle rustler, captivated or impaled by his Olympian pizzle, riding or ridden from beach to beach, upon the fiery powerful waves, to the isolated seclusion of his Cretan bachelor paddock, thus, it would be equally difficult to clarify the degree to which he cursed or celebrated the horror of the surrounding world, if he cursed or celebrated the extremes to which his alcoholic energy had driven him. An energy capable of activating the machine, that machine we can drive as one drives a car, but whose function we don't know as well as the direction and even the reason or goal of the trip, as it happens in our dreams, when we dream that we're driving, without that being an obstacle, of course, so that we might be the object of a traffic ticket. An impression clearly sharpened by the hangover, as if in coursing through it the alcohol had purged the body, clearing the mind and awakening the senses, leaving only the doubt of whether such an impression were more obvious in the observation of the behavior of any community considered as a collective, in the general conclusions which can be extracted from such an observation, or, on the contrary, in the noted details, an empty wheelchair on a deserted beach, the sunken decapitated torso of a body half-excavated from the sand by the waves, diabolically sniffed at by a wolf-dog, it now being relatively important to make clear whether the problem's focal point resides within perception or what is perceived, in that inner volcano which impels us or in the terrifying placidity which surrounds us, in the no-less-delirious-for-being-unargued text of the paper crushed in the pocket, that collection notice which, in full accordance with the provisions of the article in question of the Statute of Reclamation of such and such a date, requires that you make full payment of the debts detailed in the margin and which, by virtue of the aforementioned provision, include a twenty-percent calculated surcharge; be aware that if you effect payment within the next ten business days from the present date of demand, the surcharge will be reduced by ten percent. Said time period elapsed, this procedure will continue with an immediate freezing of assets, in accordance with such and such precept, and such title, from the aforementioned law.

I'LL TELL YOU FOUR TIMES.

Flashes, intermittent attitudes, movements decomposed into postures, hip cocked to one side, elbows akimbo, bust thrust forward, ass jutting back, right knee raised, face uplifted, hair swept back, elbows together, body straight, chin down, hair over the face, hands loose, belly protruding, shoulders back, chest raised, package raised, arms seeming to float, hands loose, chin raised, gut sucked way in, tits hanging, hair doing its own thing, waists bent backward, belly to belly, back to back, mouth and eyes like those of a drowned man, heel against ass, one arm raised up and the other one glued to the body, head tilted to one side, leg poised to deliver a kick, mouth shaping a scream, snapshots in focus barely an instant, taking shape, dissolving to the dictates of the electronic array, a control console suggesting a starship's cockpit, a command center which the school priest wouldn't have hesitated to pronounce the domain of the devil himself, that satanic array of lights and shadows and movement and rhythm, and its no-less-satanic result, moistness and dilations deliberately provoked—and with the coincidence of the atmosphere in general and the alcohol in particular and, more specifically still, of a generic individual disposition to sin—just by playing such and such an LP—carefully graded and selected, the way a sorcerer measures the contents and composition of his philter—choosing them, the same as pills, according to the effect one wishes to obtain, the selection inspired by the no-less-diabolically exciting covers of each record jacket, almost like mirrors reflecting the most suggestive aspects of the locale itself, hellish rhythms in hellish atmospheres, the school priest presiding over it all from his pulpit, conducting with red-faced glee, activating buttons, keys, switches, pulling levers, his hands holding all the threads of that spectacle of men and women dancing in hellish promiscuity to the rhythm of compositions whose lubricious character was proclaimed loud and clear by the various empty record jackets, *I'm Gonna Suck It* by Pau Casals and His Band, lyrics by Paul Claudel, design by Paul Klee, or the popular *Ad Efesios* of Saint Paul Robeson, etcetera. Final blackout. Invitation to proceed somewhere else, to consummate the sin, to reach the bottom, to go through it as fast as possible right down to the very dregs. Willy spattered them as he shook off his sweat, pure warm beer.

Leading the charge out of the Attila, Leopoldo said: To the yacht! Get in the canoe and let's all go and ram the fuck out of that yacht!

Coming out of the Attila, Leopoldo proposed going to Willy's house. Or to the gas station bar, or to the Paradís.

Why don't we all go hang out at Willy's house, and the girls can have an orgy and eat each other out, suggested Leopoldo as they spilled out of the Attila.

Almost everyone got into Willy's Jeep, including someone they didn't know, on the hood, on the running boards, waving with their arms as they drove down the road, as if they were making a glorious entrance into some recently liberated town. He followed them a short distance behind, illuminating them with the headlights; he'd gotten stuck taking Renata Bosch as well as that annoying bore Javi. Javi looked knocked out, stupidly stupefied.

The gas station bar was filling up by the second, people leaping out of their cars as they pulled up as if ready to rob the place. Leopoldo was wearing Willy's diving goggles and swim fins. Carmen came up to him doubled over laughing from something that the laughter itself prevented her from repeating. Behind them came Cristina and she, with the Man-Cock practically walking on air, seemingly stunned or bewildered by his own success. The Greek was there, too; the barman signaled it to him with a movement of his head. He must have told you all about his heroics, he commented after the first time he saw them talking with him. Whether he did this and that in the war. What he did? Requisition goods and then sell for his own profit what he requisitioned while he was able to escape the mobilization. And then, in the Quartermaster Corps—because he served in the war from the Quartermaster storehouses—if he wasn't shot by the firing squad for being a thief it's because he was taken prisoner first. Or, more precisely, he turned himself in, he gave it up. And if the Nationalists didn't shoot him either it's because in fact he never fired a shot and, by contrast, he, the anarchist fisherman, turned a blind eye when more than one little rich boy from town escaped to France, if he didn't take them there himself in his own boat for a reasonable price under the circumstances. And so it had been, indeed: alerted, thanks to his fine intuition, to his interlocutors's mentality—contrary to the values of the social class to which they obviously belonged—The Greek, or rather, The Lobster King, as he assured them he was called, had brought them up to date on his bellicose feats during the Civil War, no less heroic, in his disinterested transcendence, than those accomplished by Sergeant York. A man weathered and toughened by experience, one who has suffered and perhaps for that reason knows how to be generous, who has seen everything in life and perhaps for that reason knows how to be understanding and also perhaps for that reason knows how to enjoy the small amount of good that life can offer a man like himself, a fisherman of noble aspect, of handsome bristly hair like a wild boar and features highlighted by the repeated effort of the fight that begins anew each day, a man who lives from his work, by his hands, from his boat, that boat and those hands he rents out to tourists, which fact in no way lessens his dignity as a mariner, just a way to procure his daily bread, on the other hand, by a countless number of adventures and anecdotes with the feminine element of his clientele whose names it would now be prolix and even improper to enumerate, now that he's no longer the man he used to be, now that his body no longer responds like it once did and what he almost prefers now is precisely that, just have a few drinks with his friends, with the young fellows, above all, who are the only ones not yet broken down by life, the only ones whom it's worth helping by sharing one's own experience and the only ones he can help, perhaps because he too is young although he might be old and has endured many blows, precisely for that reason, yes, like a father in his counsels and also like a father in his helplessness, unarmed and defenseless, needy, destitute, overcome by events, a man, in short, not quite so capable of lending assistance as needing to receive it, who's really asking us for it when he offers it to us, and to whom, for that reason, we lend it, making as if it were he who's lending it to us. A reaction similar to that demanding process of the biological father which is generally initiated when, by the law of life, the power relationships are inverted and one begins to see the father as another hoodwinked son, a brother deceived just as the Jewish people were deceived by Moses without anybody ever suspecting it or discovering the reason why, what caused that wrathful old man to hide from them the fact that he was the Eternal Father, the eternal father who courses the world in a flaming chariot, who strikes down with thunder and lightning anyone who tries to steal that fire, who deceives his son and who makes him die like a phony and who melts his wings when he tries to fly back to him, who invents an antagonist and creates replicas of himself and makes him preach the Hegira simultaneously for and against himself and indulges himself by sending invaders against his dominions and crusades against his cities and conquistadors against his temples, pleased that everyone might believe they can save themselves with their flaming crosses, with their bellies running red, their sacrificial human hearts still beating, and, especially, that their order, that order of violences encountered, was counterpoised against an initial chaos, to a preceding state of terror plagued with dark brutalities, which nobody might now believe or remember that, by way of result, all the diversifications of the law revealed formed part of the vengeance of an old rancorous man who had been betrayed, who had been accused of committing or having committed the very same devourings that his sons committed or would commit, sons that had castrated him with his wife's complicity, meaning, their mother's. In fact, a poor man dethroned, driven away, dispossessed, delirious in his megalomaniacal misapprehensions of his lost power, a power that was, perhaps, never real because reality is something else, not, for example, a town of fishermen with its complimentary crops and its handful of summering families, ladies and gentlemen from Barcelona who, although with parsimony, always livened things up, no, not that but this, what's happening now, what now stands where the small town once stood, a phenomenon likely to repel as much as fascinate, millions and millions, figures with zeros and zeros, a product of the perfect conjunction of the landscape's natural beauty and the wonders of economic development, other dimensions, other environments, other rhythms, that simultaneous invitation to go speeding through the air as well as to drowse on the sand, to the pleasure of sailing, cutting through the water, as well as the erotic distillation, somnolences and reveries and ecstasies, rosy erections and intense depths, the offer sufficient to calm all anxiety of penetration or integration, of wallowing in the bitter foam, rendezvous on the rocks, whiskey lights in the night and the blue air, like a challenge of time and distances, the same as in the morning, meaning, at midday, such as when fleeing from Typhon, beyond the Euphrates, Venus safe with Cupid, salt sheen upon the skin and the white hour on the eyelids, that midday which supposes the transit between what has already been done and what remains to be done, the heart like a raft run by the waves successively amplified by a stone's fall, as a cigarette is consumed which tastes so bad after so many others, a cigarette which only with the passing of the hours, in the course of the afternoon, will gradually recover its stimulating qualities, the same as if instead of tobacco it were marijuana obsequiously provided by some waiter, now sufficiently revived as if to plunge deeper and deeper into a new nocturnal adventure, in the depths of the Attila or any other discotheque, the Pinocchio, the Nautilus, in order to end up at the gas station bar or in the Paradís, now infected with the frenetic debauchery of the frenzy which—in the words of the school priest—possessed all those present. The moment of withdrawing discreetly and returning to the car's steering wheel, like that other time when, somewhat drunk or having smoked too much grass, he suddenly felt like climbing out the window of Willy's house and getting in the car, and so he did and went for a nice long drive, the truck drivers making room, allowing him to pass after he'd flashed his lights at them, charming, brotherly, and he waved at them once he'd passed their trucks, one friend to another, and the same with the cars, except for that one who wouldn't let him pass, who seemed to be trying to prevent him from passing, speeding up, almost moving to block the left lane, certainly half-drunk, but not even that—and although he did the same when the other guy, barely ahead by means of a skillful maneuver, as if pricked in his pride, began asking him to let him pass, with fastidious insistence, forcing him to block the guy's way, when, in his carelessness, the big bastard tried to pass him on the right—not even that could cloud that feeling of cosmic harmony, of finding oneself directly connected to the forces that keep the order of the universe in balance, again and again hugging the highway's serpentine curves, a highway that seemed to be uncoiling to the conjuring of his own headlights, masterly, unbeatable, demonic, and all the way until he arrived back home again and, now in the back garden, the moment he set foot there, he preferred to lie down on the grass, lying there until the sun poured down into his eyes.

ROYAL STAIRCASE.

And the daughters of the dusk, dressed in pink mist? Did they want to keep dancing? Yes, they did. Did they prefer to bathe their bodies in the violet-colored waters? Yes, they so preferred. Would they go racing uphill to the Paradís as long as the night lasted? They went racing uphill. Would they succumb prematurely to some satyr's embrace the same as any nymph might succumb? There's no reason to doubt it.

They debated. Leopoldo and his crowd must be anchored in the bay at Cadaqués by now. Why don't we pay them a visit? Willy proposed as they came walking out of the Attila. We'll park in Cadaqués, leave our clothes in the car, and swim out to their yacht. Very Germanic.

They climbed into Willy's Jeep, they had another drink at the gas station bar, returned to the car, drove toward the Paradís, a spiral of twists and turns, speeding uphill with the pedal flat on the floor, the exhaust pipe thundering like Attila himself.

They explored the grounds of that old country house converted into a discotheque, the ground-floor rooms, dark vaults, low archways, enclosed patios, slate walls. She wanted something relaxing, the canvas chaise longue under the arches that offered a commanding view of the mountain slope and, in the distance, the lights of the town, the reflections on the bay, to contemplate the whiteness that now began to emerge from the sea and spread out. But he preferred to take a walk, the bar packed and chaotic, the main floor aswarm with dancers, that concatenation of bodies in motion, of encircling maneuvers, boys with arrogant smiles—cocks aquiver beneath tight pants—and fresh adolescents in the lovely light of dawn. He was introduced to a Carmelite monk who was dancing in good company; dressed in shorts and a loose shirt and sandals, headband encircling his hair. He studied Law when we were at school, before joining the Carmelites. Two years behind us. Don't you remember him from the courtyard at school? He laughed and swayed with an enviable vitality, happy, uninhibited; rather irritating. God is everywhere, right? he asked, trying to annoy him however possible, to fan the embers of his guilty conscience. And Father Torrens winked his eye at him: but above all in the temples, he answered, earnestly patting his female companion's posterior.

From the chaise longues they witnessed the scene offered again by the white angelic armies as they swooped down, wings extended, upon the gloomy infernal hordes, expelling them from the celestial heights, chasing them down to the deepest depths of their lightning chasms, each moment flaring with less lightning, their nocturnal splendor more extinguished each moment, shut away in their subterranean domains as the splendors of the heavens increased, soon ultraviolet, infrared, orange, annulling the black Lucifer light, satanic depths gradually disemboweled by the golden solar rays, not the reflections off the bay, but the bay itself, not the lights of the town but the town and its outskirts, those outlying neighborhoods whose streets he would explore again some day, from the ruins of Trinidad castle to the ruins of the Citadel, streets and plazas where the last noctambulists will gradually be replaced by good people, honorable workers, men of the sea, tourists up and out in the early morning light, quick-witted housemaids, conscientious housewives. All that when the Paradís winds up deserted and the liquefying pleasure is resolved in other quarters, quieter, more secluded, more suitable, and the baser passions can be unleashed and leashed again in due measure, while in the east, the bud of Dionysius blooms and begins to extend its warmth across the land.

TICS.

She woke him up when she arrived. His body naked. He couldn't have slept too long; it was barely dawn, and when he left the yacht the sky was still completely dark. He'd slipped out without saying anything, while they stripped the Man-Cock naked. Three nights in a row of the same thing was too much. Thus the general necessity for refreshing elements like the Man-Cock. He swam back to shore and ran to the car buck naked, streaming water like a triton. The swim had cleared his senses and, at the motel, before dropping into bed to sleep, he poured himself another whiskey sitting at the worktable and he scrawled some notes, simple outlines that he would develop when his head wasn't so cloudy:

She doesn't fall asleep before four and doesn't get up before one. While he eats lunch, she eats breakfast curled up inside her bathrobe, she looks at him with fatigue, with dull dejection: this can't go on, she says. We go to bed too late and I need at least nine hours of sleep. If I sleep any less I'm not good for anything all day. And the thing is I've never been able to go to sleep early; not even when I was a little girl. But then I had more stamina. We should make an effort. I need to do something, get a job, anything; if I don't do something soon, I'll go crazy. You've got to help me with that, find me something to do. You've got your job. But me, nothing. I've got nothing. What could I do? Tell me: what could I do?

Later, as he sips his coffee and reads the newspaper, she has her little chat with the help, in the kitchen, while the maid washes the dishes: her work projects, the need, before anything else, to fix up a corner where she can get them done: decoration, a boutique, a photo lab. A tendency to also show an interest in the maid's problems, to give her advice from the position of a more experienced person, to predict to her what some other person will end up doing later, her husband, her boyfriend. Compensatory value of such an exchange: her own projects are objectified, take shape to the same degree as the maid's problems.

Telephone calls, long conversations with friends; a similar tendency to exchange confidences, personal opinions: swapping some problems for others. Phases, however, during which she'd adopt the opposite attitude: she doesn't call anybody, and when someone calls she makes the cleaning lady say she's not at home.

A similar shift regarding household costs: one fine day she consults her agenda and, after several weeks of blank pages, meticulously reviews the household expenses with the maid.

She never shows the least interest in his job, but complains that he doesn't listen to her, that he doesn't really care about her problems. If he makes her see that he's been insisting to her for years that it would do her good to do something, any one of the many things which she might pursue, she answers that it's not enough to encourage her, that encouragement isn't really help, that it could even turn out to be counterproductive, stifling, inhibiting.

When he's not in the mood and she is, and she chatters on and expounds her opinions on all different kinds of things—opinions, in general, already explained on other occasions—and he lets her talk, she ends up asking what's she's done to him, why he's angry with her.

She usually assures him that the solutions that work for others don't work for her, that she doesn't wear blinders, that she doesn't deceive herself the way some people deceive themselves: the clear perception that annuls all activity, which makes any kind of communication excessively difficult. I don't know what's the matter with me. I just get worse and worse. I just drift away from conversations, I don't hear what people are talking about. And, suddenly, I have the sensation of being inside some kind of insane asylum where all the crazy people are all busy talking at the same time about their own madness. I suppose I must be the one who's crazy: the superiority of a singular madness over the common mania.

Her behavior in front of other people is characterized by her eagerness to seem normal, to evoke a couple's typical clashes in an attempt to somehow justify what she thinks everybody finds strange in her relationship with him by the simple fact that, like a telltale heart, what worries her has to be pointed out: it's not the same—far from it!—to be different as to be normal. He'd just as soon let himself go soft, but she pesters him, forces him to stay in shape; she's an absentminded girl who's always over the moon, she's lucky to have him, who's always up to date on things; she's a free woman, he's learned it the hard way, he's had to end up accepting the reality; she's a bit of a floozy, a little crazy, and more than once he's had to pull her out of a real tight spot, and the thing is that she, in fact, only really loves him, she doesn't give a shit about all the others, and he's almost too understanding with her; he's cheated on her now so many times that she's ended up taking it sportingly, philosophically, if you prefer; he's jealous, but he hides it; she's jealous and rightly so, because he, etcetera. The characterization of the problem, its classifications and variants, depends on each interlocutor's concrete circumstances.

Her erotic conduct: narcissistic, exhibitionist. Indirect orgasm: not so much the pleasure she receives as much as that pleasure be the response to the pleasure her body is capable of engendering in others. At the same time, and only in apparent contradiction, a profound personal insecurity which—without the help of stimulants—alcohol, marijuana—makes her react shyly to the suggestion of sex—and could even be driving her to an attitude of rejection. This second aspect is possibly conditioned by the character of the sexual relations between them both, rather irregular, given that he only takes the initiative when he's been drinking, she having to recur, as a consequence, when she finds herself subjected to similar influences, under carnal compulsion, to the aforementioned external stimulants. His indifference toward her, or better yet, lack of appetite, which she personalizes as much as possible, excluding any generalizing motive: the decay of their conjugal life, the usury of cohabitation, the tedium of what endures. The traumatic nucleus: it's her, her body, that he's got no appetite for. Something not easily blamed upon the always-more-common case of impotence: it's not that he can't but that he doesn't want to; no problem getting an erection, his response during the amorous act, when they actually do it, is completely normal, the same—although no doubt less tender—as when he does it with another woman. With any woman at all.

Consequent manifestations of verbal aggression: rebuking his frivolous merrymaking, accusing him of a selfish insistence on playing the starring role, of homosexuality, sentimental coldness, and satirical brutality, how he risked ending up becoming a dirty old man, etcetera. Reproaches and recriminations that expand until completely encircling his personality and which, sometimes, at certain moments, an abstraction composed of the projective elements they contain, end up hitting the bull'seye, making a dent. When she tells him that he seems more and more like his father, for example. The personal touches, the habits, the chamomile tea just before bed, the sleeping pills, the nose drops, the licorice drops. His own sensitivity, ever greater, to air currents. Also, curiously, the fact that his increasing nausea from so many foods mirrors the list of those foods strictly prohibited to his parents, who are on a restricted diet, canned and tinned foods, fried foods, cured meats, not to mention drinking alcohol to excess. Could such a repetitive impulse be understood at the formal level as an augury of destinies to be repeated? Or was that aprioristic fear in itself the involuntary cause that drove his repetition? Heredity? Contagion? Reparation? Dilemmas: that they can become a tad obsessive during periods of anxiety and low morale. In the last stage of the hangover, for example, two or three days after the night when he drank, when, after the periods of confusion and anguished excitation, there remains only the fatigue, both physical as well as moral. A state of mind similar to that of the honest bourgeois man, exemplary father and family man who one fine New Year's Day, at the wheel of the car, after having eaten lunch at his in-laws' or the grandparents' house or whatever one might like to call them, meditating on the years gone by through the tender and awestruck contemplation of his small, helpless children, now grown into stocky boys, with that peculiar sadness appropriate to some golden anniversary or diamond jubilee or any other celebration that so much supposes having reached the point of no return to being or, even, near to being, possessed of such sentiments, feelings more than reflections, it suddenly occurs to him that instead of continuing to drive straight ahead, he might, and why not, with a gentle turn of the wheel, drive straight into a lamppost. Thus he, like that honest bourgeois husband, exemplary father and family man possessed of that stubborn narrow-mindedness which, on occasions, swoops down upon the condemned man, in his incapacity to identify such a state of mind until having overcome it: the supreme lucidity of his most depressive moments, of his visions and ideas, of the pieces of puzzles that later blossom in his conscience. The moments that she seemed to prefer, as if intuiting the special vulnerability of the adversary, in order to later renew her attack.

She, her conflicts, her contradictions, complexities about a subject which, now in bed, in the dark, as sleep arrived, continued giving her turns, irreducible to partial notes, multiple facets of a spinning polyhedron, a whole no less equivocal and turbulent, for example, than the personality of one of those women, not necessarily old, who are consumed by thinking of the quantity of money that ends up circulating through the world, which passes her by, right under her nose, elusive, always out of reach, belonging to others, for others, prizes that come to other people, and contests and raffles and lotteries and rewards and recommendations and inheritances from unknown relatives and strokes of luck and slight of hand, and that gentleman who could do so much for her with just a pinch of his fortune, and she, who would do everything for him, absolutely everything, even murder him, only in exchange for his favors, and for that reason she kneels before him and embraces him and weeps—or at least that's what she would do—and she would almost like to die for him, with him, and thus settle the debt, the guilt. Between sleeping and waking, now at that point where ideas turn to images and, without any transitional explanation, suddenly finding herself ascending in an airplane. Or coupling with a naked body, reanimating it, making it sit up. I love you very much, she whispered to him, her tongue slipping deep inside his ear, as the nightmare dissolved and vanished. What had he been dreaming about? The landscape?

Later, she asleep, he lay down by her side, sweating, overcome not so much by sleep as by unease, a sensation like fever, the effect, no doubt, of the hangover both moral and physical that, especially extreme some days, leads one to, barely awake, get up and go striding out toward any part of town.

But he still turned on the light anyway, and, reaching the worktable, he jotted one last note:

Possible names: she, Camila; he, Ricardo.

III

THE CAESAR DIALOGUE.

Leopoldo was chattering about exhibitionism. Day by day, an increasingly serious phenomenon. It's the one thing that makes people the most furious. It drives them out of their minds: My daughter! My daughter! Criminal! Their daughter or their wife or some woman in the neighborhood. And right away they organize a search party. They scour the neighborhood like crazy until they can do no more and, when they split up, the exhibitionist returns to his own house, too, lamenting along with some stranger their bad luck that the flasher escaped them. It must be an exciting experience. Cross the vacant lots getting a hard-on under your overcoat, traipse the half-deserted streets, hidden in the doorways, covering yourself with a satchel. Or better yet: strap on one of those rubber dildos they sell, the fattest one, about two handspans long. Gives them a tremendous jolt. Scars them for life. Afterward, no cock will seem worth getting excited about; probably what husbands fear the most. I'm also thinking about the getup: false pants, really just pant legs, from the knees down, secured on each leg with rubber bands; and above, a raincoat with shirt cuffs sewn to the ends of each sleeve, as if sticking out, and a necktie and shirt front and shirt collar sewn along the insides of the lapels, and the whole thing can just be flung open, with one of those adhesive fasteners like a big Band-Aid. For maximum shock value. If they catch you they'll lynch you.

But that's not what they wanted to hear. Outside, coming closer every moment, the sound of a canoe's outboard motor, Ricardo went up on deck: it was Cristina and Willy; the rippling perpendicular swell of the town lights along the wharf.

Cristina and Willy arrived in a big rush, asking all about Guillermina and Gerard. After them came Renata Bosch and Camila, dripping wet, wrapped in bath towels, Bosch saying they came very close to getting flattened by the motorboat, but no one paid her any attention. And, seeing that they were talking about Guillermina and Gerard, they returned right away with dry towels, covering themselves to a certain point, given the essentially discursive character of the circumstances. Camila less inhibited by such circumstances, more daring, as if possessed by that instantaneous pleasure which all bodies prone to constipation usually experience after a copious evacuation, with that euphoria, with that renewed vitality; thus Camila, in a similar state of mind, after a simple and hasty glass of booze.

What was going on with Guillermina and Gerard? The Caesar had anchored in Cadaqués. They'd seen people in Cadaqués. What gossip had they heard? Was it true what people were saying about Guillermina and Gerard? Carmen smiled and said nothing. Bosch laughed to herself, satisfied with knowing what others didn't know. That annoying bore Javi started telling the story about how they all went swimming before returning to the yacht, when the bars closed and everybody followed their example, peeling off their clothes on the way, white as codfish filets in the moonlight, each person trying to identify their friends. And then someone switched on the car headlights, illuminating the whole bunch of them, and people applauded and frolicked in the water, splashing each other. It was a great scene, he said, in order to emphasize what an amusing anecdote he was telling, implicitly accepting his own incapacity to express in words the subtle richness of the events; sexy-fiction, almost. Silence. But that wasn't really what was interesting either.

Like that orator who patiently awaits his turn, knowing that his speech, and his speech alone, is the real focus of the meeting, and the other ones that come first are pure preamble, each one delivered more quickly in response to the increasingly impatient listeners crowding into the auditorium, an impatience which our orator piques as much as possible with his reserved silence, and so, too, Leopoldo, all the expectation which surrounded him when he began to speak. The Aphrodite anchored in Cadaqués waters, he starts hearing gossip about Guillermina and Gerard, the main topic of the day. Leopoldo bluntly asks Blanca, whose version of the events strikes him as more credible than others'. A party at Blanca's house. Everyone there seems to know quite well the truth about Guillermina and Gerard, about what really happened, variations on what's being repeated by those who know or who say they know from witnessing it firsthand. No end to the number of firsthand witnesses, and even boring old Javi and that idiot Bosco end up being included in such a category and people ask them to share details. Protests from Bosch or Bosco not lacking in complacency. What I was saying, what I was saying—Bosch was saying—what I was saying is that I would like to have been there. Useless, nobody was listening to her.

Blanca was holding forth about the undeniable benefits of fellatio practiced on a supine body positioned below, not above, the person administering it, because such a position allows one, with a minimum of manual dexterity, to hold back, gauge, and regulate the sudden spurt of emission that flows through and shakes the erect member, while at the same time, by virtue of its control, making it slowly assimilable and even slowly expellable through the parted lips, so that not even the happy beneficiary of the operation can notice—whose pleasure is only prolonged by such skillful manipulations—and without the practitioner risking nausea, which the sperm's volume as well as its density and even its violent force can cause some people, or other symptoms of intolerance, undisguisable in the inverse position, but defended by the guests, among whom there was no lack of dedicated fans of the vertical position.

Taking advantage of the breadth of controversy about various theoretical positions, Leopoldo focuses the conversation on the gossip about Guillermina and Gerard. Blanca admits that anything she knows was told her by someone who didn't see it either. And who might that person be, if one may ask? Felix. And who told Felix? Someone who was there. But Blanca, says Leopoldo: What's all this mystery about now? You want me to tell you who told it all to Felix? You want me to tell you their name? If you like guessing games, says Blanca. Shall I tell you? Well, it's the same person who told me, says Leopoldo. Meaning: Quique. And it's true, really, that he was there, with all the smugness of a queer crocodile, without leaving out a single detail. At least about the first part, about what the night itself was like, not how it turned out. So far, up to now, the only one who can talk about how it turned out is Guillermina herself.

Cristina told that idiot Bosco, who was trying to butt in, trying to whisper to her her own version of the events, to shut up. But what really happened? (Cristina). Who was there? And where? In Cadaqués or in Barcelona? Was it like that time in Ibiza? More or less (Leopoldo): Guillermina and Gerard don't usually drink, neither one of them. They're not the kind of people who mix sex and alcohol.

According to Quique, that night's main attraction was an occasional guest, Rolando, or maybe Orlando, a Black guy from Central America, from Nicaragua or Panama or one of those countries around there, somebody's friend. And what's certain is that our expectations weren't disappointed, said Quique. Indeed: throughout the evening, the Central American, Black Rolando, reveals himself to be the possessor not only of the vitality and vehemence that could be expected of him, but also as a person of great physical attraction, smooth manners, and a notable sense of humor. In great demand, Black Rolando, observing the most basic rules of courtesy, nevertheless remains particularly open to the attentions showed him by his hosts, the Gerards, Guillermina most of all. And, when the atmosphere gets hot, it's especially the Gerards with whom he strengthen ties, to the extent that some guests—female guests, especially—driven by spite, decide to withdraw. It's Guillermina's peak moment, settled comfortably, apotheosized, between her two men, exuberant in her exuberance. The notion that some girls formulate from this type of collective fornication, you all know already: a kind of ceremony celebrated in their honor, where the presence of other people is little more than a ritual formality: she's the one whom the guys are pursuing. But after the first preliminary maneuvers and penetrations, the situation experiences an unexpected change—including for the contemplative Quique—from the moment when, bodies in motion, Gerard proposes forming a sandwich in which he plays the middle layer, thus offering his sinuous buttocks to Black Rolando, before taking his turn to plunge into the depths of Guillermina. On the other hand, it's necessary to clarify that the unsuspected character of the change resides not so much in the proposal itself, deliciously, immediately, put into practice, as much as in the reiteration of the act, in its exchanges, variations, and combinations, from which, as if the sandwich had too much bread, Guillermina ended up progressively excluded. And it's equally advisable to emphasize, for justice's sake, that Guillermina's attitude was at every moment correct and civilized, even amused, as Quique himself can well attest, alongside whom, like one more spectator, she followed the increasingly rhythmic movements of the red-hot encounter.

In fact, the conflict's eclosion—with Quique now absent—did not take place until the following morning, after the children, getting ready to leave for school, surprised the sleeping trio, sprawled akimbo upon the bed, naked as the day they were born. The kids' reaction, apparently, was quite positive, so much so that they even wanted to join in the fun, intrigued, in particular, by the physical peculiarities of Black Rolando. But according to Guillermina's version, the drop which, as they say, overflowed the glass was her, returning from the kitchen with a steaming pot of coffee, and finding Gerard and Black Rolando riding each other again. And seeing that they took not the least notice of her presence, she took the opportunity to pack her suitcase and leave without a word, not unaware of the futility and even cruelty, in such circumstances, of any intervention on her part, conscious of the obnubilation of which those two men were prisoner, now overcome by both the phase of fatigue and disgust which follows all series of seminal emissions, the lingering taste of sperm and other venereal liqueurs, unable to recall at this point from whose cup they'd drunk them, disgust and a bad taste in the mouth which, a few hours later, faded with the waking daylight hours, must give way to renewed surges of copulative furor. According to the same version, Guillermina limited herself to leaving a note next to the coffee: there's cold milk in the fridge. Signed: The Complete Idiot.

Guillermina's demonstrated and unanimously recognized qualities of presence of mind, discretion, and *sangfroid*, the personal motivations which led her to formalize her separation from Gerard, constituted a theme that was, to a certain point, irrelevant. Humiliated self-love? A sensation of ridicule, after having initially acted as a central figure in the tableau, as supreme priestess of the ceremony? A sensation of stupor in the face of betrayal, particularly sharp for that person for whom betrayal is standard practice, when at the same time they are the object of betrayal? Not at all unlike the experience of that goalie who, after blocking a hard shot from the center forward on the opposing team, makes a long, clearance kick and, eyes glazed and a hole in place of his mouth, he then contemplates how the one who receives the pass, the center forward of his own team, far from moving ahead downfield, toward the opposite goal, instead advances toward their own, dribbles toward the opposing forward who still think he is setting them up for a trick, passes them and, against the inertia of his own seemingly paralyzed—who knows if from stupor or delight—middle and defensive lines, kicks with uncontainable fury a sure, unerring shot, and scores, and with a scandalously malicious finishing touch, kicks the ball again and again, as it rebounds off the net, before running again toward the center, hoisted aloft, embraced, and congratulated with complicit jubilation by his other teammates; thus, as with that stunned goalie, the surprise of the hapless Guillermina.

I'll have to do something for this girl, said Carmen. I don't know, lift her spirits: I'm going to propose that she model for me, take pictures of her; I think she's got a nice body. I'm sure you'll get what you want from her (Leopoldo). And why don't you take some of me, too? (That fool Bosco, already striking a pose, clenching between her teeth a corner of the towel half-covering her, just like when the photographer tries to conjure some innocent perversity). I won't let you steal Carmen from me; you and I, we know each other too well. (Camila, buzzing from her second drink, sitting down on Carmen's lap). And Cristina, always more Teutonic, sitting between Ricardo and Willy, caressing their zippers: and these gentlemen?

Leopoldo reappeared, his short, faded, purple bathrobe hanging open, revealing his stiff, seasoned, leathery cock, a cock resembling a generous slab of beef jerky that, already thick by itself when relaxed, instead of gradually swelling and growing, seemed to just spring up straight and hard in an instant.

Let's reenact it, he said. Who's going to play the part of Black Nab?

CONVERSION, DIVERSION, IMMERSION.

The idea of marriage has always struck me as rather disagreeable. Rosa said she felt the same, but that it was the only way to solve, in one fell swoop, a whole raft of uncomfortable problems. I suppose that his mother's support for this kind of solution—resolving some problems only to create others—the character of our relationships, the time that they lasted, etcetera. Apart, of course, from the fact that she had a favorable opinion of me, that I belonged to a well-known family and that socially I was considered a really worthwhile young man, a classification that, once established, is not usually even modified, despite any evidence to the contrary. And my stint in jail, for her, was nothing more than youthful folly, as she liked to call it. An element, however, which probably played a decisive role in Alfonso's sudden interest in a quick and correct solution for the case: the image of a son-in-law imprisoned for political reasons which, logically, included admitting Marxist convictions and even organic contacts, but—and of course not without a certain logic—in the full blown, healthy, conservative sense of it. In fact, I didn't fail to notice either; obliged to deal with the whole packet of questions—personal, family, and economic—awaiting me when I got out of jail, my attitude could induce one to suppose—and not only someone like Alfonso—that I found myself in the situation of that college friend who, after an iconoclastic or simply libertine youth, in a sudden fit of dread of others and, above all, of himself, seeks refuge and a hiding place in traditional values, institutions, and myths—work, home, spouse, the change which having children represents for one, the need to ensure oneself company in old age, the consolations that family life affords, along with all the headaches it brings, the need to be realistic, to give the children a religious upbringing that will always stand as a bulwark against immorality, and then if it goes a little too far, then they can decide for themselves, and one fine day, after so many years, we run into him, his eyes like seagulls and his hair white as clouds, and then he embraces us and reprimands us, challenges us, and cries, and forces us to visit his home, and he explains himself, and justifies how he abandoned his principles, and overwhelms us, makes us uncomfortable and depressed before the spectacle of his sad privacy, shouting at the servant in order to show us his power and energy, lecturing and ridiculing his wife for not belonging to nor understanding the time of common memories now evoked, the children—

kept in line just the same way—to the degree that only the father's obdurate delirium can confuse silence with compliance, the very atmosphere and even the furniture in the house, an expression and reflection of the family tensions and disequilibrium, sign and sentence of the inevitably catastrophic character of the inevitable conclusion.

At any rate, it seems unquestionable that it was precisely that interest in the negative aspects of my life—in so far as it refers to orthodox behavior—that induced him to propose to me to work alongside him reorganizing the office, anticipating a better coordination between the various business transactions carried out there. One way of clarifying his scorn for social conventions linked to the prospect of the attractive controversy that must normally occur between lucid and open-minded people in the course of a collaborative project, the clash between a socialist vision of the world, sportingly accepted by them, and a vision not so much capitalistic as realistic, modern, serious, more technically qualified and, above all, more efficient in its management, advantages he needed to be sure I would find convincing, consequently reaffirming for him his own convictions. A type of reaction whose correlative, in the sexual terrain, would have to be sought in that excitation in the face of the exotic which in a businessman passing through Hong Kong usually awakens the possibility of a one-night stand, not without risks, with some little local slut. I've got to admit that his proposal also struck me as attractive, although less for the controversy, than, despite his possible expectations it left me rather indifferent, for the chance it offered me to see more closely what life is really all about, as they say, something perhaps a little abstract for a young lawyer morbidly attracted to literature, with military service and university studies the main experiences he has in common with all young people from comfortable families, coupled with a personal experience of political militancy, with time in prison to boot.

In practice, however, while my image as a reflective Marxist intellectual seemed to retain, for some undetermined reason, all its validity, it was Alfonso's technocratic image which did not take long to deteriorate and give way to another, more traditional and conniving, without that supposing, however, any diminishment of my interest in him; nor do I believe that such a contrast can be a sufficient motive to classify my conduct as hypocritical. It was he who revealed, so to speak, his true face, the face of a sly old fox, to whomever, familiar with his wiles, might see him act in front of other people, something that, far from all deception, also had something fascinating about it. His dialectical arts, the weight of the well-chosen word, the opportunity for its use and even his impeccable diction, a facility perhaps derived from the fact of being only partly Catalan, of having been raised in a Castilian cultural environment, and of having studied at university in Madrid—with the retinue of friendships and relationships that supposes—the typical superiority which a perfect command of the language gives when one addresses an audience full of people who stammer and get stuck and choke on their efforts to express themselves in a tongue not their own. His extreme ability, as well, to impose himself without having to resort to the superiority—or presumed superiority—of his position nor, even less, to some expressive crudeness, without heavy words or implied threats or the most minimal coercive element in either the form or sense of the argument, always trying to make their interlocutor believe they're yielding willingly, giving them all kinds of ways to be self-convinced, although not so much, of course, as to forget whose hands held the power. And that just by choosing any one of the weapons in his arsenal—the most likely one in each case—and, as if toying with it, aiming for his interlocutor's soft spot. The time, for example when the old man Buenaventura Gasull informed him that he had decided to bequeath a sizable portion of his stock portfolio to his private secretary, my good man Arturo, a gift which is the least that one deserves who, like him, has served me so faithfully for so many years, who has given me, as one might well say, the best years of his life, and Alfonso, of course, Don Buenaventura, I understand you perfectly and, believe me, that operation defines you not only as a person of profound humanity and great lofty views, but also as the true protagonist of an act that we could never with greater propriety classify as a splendid investment, a phrase which despite its impeccable construction nevertheless bothered Don Buenaventura because he properly understood it to be a feint by Alfonso, launched, no doubt, with an eye toward the imminent annual board meeting, at which Alfonso, in his role as Secretary General, expected the Councillor Don Buenaventura Gasull to agree to dismiss, without reservation—both in his own name and as a representative of—his esteemed secretary Arturo.

And, on the occasion of the board meeting, his inimitable technique of persuasion, his method: the initial review of the adverse circumstances which, occurring in a situation, in itself already difficult, had come crashing down upon the company, and whose simple exposition made every small-time stockbroker tremble in his seat; the discarded options, the solutions adopted; the fruit of such a performance which, in the end, allowed him to share out some dividends which, if they had been announced in another context, without any similar dialectical preparation, would have only caused stupor and angry reactions, instead of the crisp applause which habitually followed his reports. His inexhaustible oratorical resources: Mr. So-and-So, the president of the Administrative Council, for example, is not only a fine Barcelona gentleman but also a personality in the world of finances whose tireless efforts on behalf of this society, along with his discreet labor—prudent, disinterested, and selfless—are only too-well-known by everyone (Blockhead!); well, and I beg you not to take it as mere rhetorical boasting, but rather economic initiative; what moves me, as a manager, is that desire inherent in the human condition to leave behind an outstanding example of one's own work (with many zeroes trailing behind it!); because, there's no doubt, we can all agree on the fact that what matters most is the company's human dimension and social significance, inseparable, I dare say, from its economic consideration (a thin tissue of horse shit!); and, finally, the truth is that between intelligent, well-educated, cultivated people (Bumpkins!) there can never be any lack of understanding.

Including his manner of filing his nails, gratuitous in appearance, except if considered as what it really was, an exercise, like calisthenics, apart from the preventative or dissuasive meaning, always healthy, which it might have for a presumed antagonist. On receiving a visit, for example, from some old classmate, a fellow upon whom fortune has obviously not smiled too broadly, who now tries to interest Alfonso's companies in some product he represents, a commission agent or whatever you want to call someone who, in order to create the proper environment for his proposal, tries to evoke common memories from a supposedly common perspective, the fruit of a supposedly common prosperous and unencumbered position, with the placidity that comes from every privileged situation, of elevated standing, it recalls the madness and nonsense that we got away with when we were young, what times those were, damn, such good times, with the goal of obtaining through such evocation of the past a renewed identification with the present. Alfonso shakes his head, as if absorbed, while speaking slowly: we're a bunch of failures, he says. We had dreams, an altruistic vocation, and here we are, become vulgar executives, carrying out jobs which at heart we don't give a damn about. And then, with all the dissimulation of some half-closed eyelids, enjoying himself in catching the successive shades of incredulity in his interlocutor's stupefied expression, who, facing the weary repetition of *we're a bunch of failures*, concluded, what's to be done, given his situation of coming to ask, not to give, the abysmal distance which separates the one who gives from the one who begs, he concluded by admitting that there must be nothing more beautiful than adjusting one's own conduct to meet an ideal and, with a sigh—oh, to be young again!—agreeing, definitively stepping down from the bandwagon, on the undeniable, yes, that was exactly what it meant to be a failure, a true failure.

Thus the extraordinary display of confidence—or of mistrust: one proof more—which supposed that Alfonso had asked me for help with Robert's problems. Let's see if you, who's closer to his age, at least understand his language. For my part, I must recognize that he's beyond me, that I understand neither what he says nor what he does nor what he wants nor what's true in everything he explains. If the role of spiritual councilor—more precisely, of a docile man who leads the return to the fold—wasn't exactly flattering, the fact that Alfonso's choice fell on my person was not without its reasons, given that the relationship between Rosa and Robert, owing perhaps to their difference in age, which at that age counts for a lot, had never been a terribly close one, it being evident, on the other hand, that Robert seemed to find certain aspects of my life's story attractive—first off, prison, naturally—for which reason he was rather inclined to seek out my friendship. Perhaps one might even talk about a feeling of emulation which impelled him to involve me in his confidences, possibly linked to the desire to surprise and amaze his sister, the desire to attract Rosa's attention to him at the same time as mine, feelings and desires which didn't contribute to but rather confused the percentage of truth and lies in the stories he told us. His problems, the problems that he created with his problems, the problem of how much one was willing to believe him: his erotic adventures, his escapades with his people, his experiences with drugs, the contacts he maintained with the rings of dealers and distributors, the difficulty of establishing a frontier between reality and fantasy. Where he got his stuff—at a bar in Les Corts—for example; perfectly possible. The stash he claimed he'd smuggled personally through London, a journey now more complicated and difficult. His trips to Tangier, not really so many as he boasted, judging by the stamps on his passport. The money he handled, its origin, in no way sufficiently explained by the quantities he could get from his father. The local contacts he claimed to have, the Sears bags he swapped, who knows if in Park Güell or in any random corner of some museum, seated next to someone else for a few moments, nothing easier than mixing up bags.

My impression is that, for Alfonso, the fact that in my chats with Robert I'd limited myself to emphasizing the risks he was running, without any moralizing pretensions, supposed a handling of things not only sufficient but even singularly wise, considering his skepticism toward what the kid could give of himself in the present moment and his inveterate confidence, on the contrary, in what could be hoped for in the inexorable passage of time, that phenomenon that makes the fruit ripen and fall, a phenomenon which, to his understanding, without saying more, he had noticed in my case, meaning, the positive evolution experienced by my personality not so much from the moment when he offered me the opportunity to channel my faculties toward a concrete and constructive goal—working with him, for example—as much as starting from the moment I married Rosa, from that ceremony celebrated with all the discretion and strict intimacy that the circumstances advised. Behind closed doors, under the auspices of the same old crazy or doddering parish priest who had helped me with all the preliminary paperwork. He repeated my name several times, his gaze lost—with the concentric help of his thick prescription lenses—in the depths of time. I knew your father, he said leaning against the backrest as if to better situate his memory. He lived in a real palace. My father? It must have been my grandfather. No, son: if there's one thing that doesn't fail me it's my memory. It was your father. He lived in a mansion on Calle Mallorca. You see? That's why I'm telling you that it was my grandfather, I mustered the courage to say. He died a few years after the First World War, long before I was born. And the same thing happened with the chalet; my family sold it after his death. The priest's pupils seemed to shrink and sharpen, as if with sly cunning. Dead? he asked. They'll end up saying that one day or another about all of us.

The ceremony concluded, lunch in the private room of a restaurant. Alfonso in a hurry; he had to go duck hunting that weekend and he was worried about the health of his best hunting bitch, a setter with a magnificent red coat, the extreme opposite, in its active inexpressiveness, from the frisky enthusiasms of the pachydermic Poppy, the stray dog that, as if it were waiting for us, had to adopt us as its owners the moment we arrived in Rosas. Let's see if you can come with me another time, said Alfonso, assuming, apparently, that nothing could satisfy me as much as going duck hunting on Buda Island. Rosa's observation was not lost on him—she was determined, you might say, to facilitate the convergence, dependent on my being a good shot—and the most likely thing is that he was considering the socially assimilative role which his enticements of partridge or duck could play in my conduct, the privileged character of such a reward to my presumed love of hunting. A passion which, like practicing other sports, golf, tennis, horseback riding, etcetera, traditionally facilitates the rooting and the integration of our young iconoclast in the environment, the same as so many other prescriptions for life praised by experience, owning a thoroughbred dog, being a collector of something, stamps, books, coins, butterflies, anything, to go out with young couples who are also developing a taste for the theater, the opera, etcetera, etcetera.

It's endlessly amazing that a man with Alfonso's sharpness could ever believe that Rosa and I could become those kind of people. Not that we formed what's typically called a close, loving couple, of course; his own domestic conduct, the formality of his relations with his wife, correct to the point of being punctilious, as well as the crudeness of certain more general observations of character which he allowed himself to make in the always greater intimacy of his office, they indicated well and clearly his idea of marriage, the stifling nightmare of bodies over the years. No, nothing relating to the mysteries of conjugal life, but a definite interest in the possibility that Rosa and I had built a home as capable of keeping up appearances as any other, when all it took was a quick glance at the apartment that passed for our home for all such illusions to vanish. I can't think of any other explanation for Alfonso's optimism than his faith in the beneficial result that—like prisoners on probation—our behavior might be worthy of the trust placed in us, a way of recognizing the critical spirit—not to mention other positive factors—that characterized my work in his office, linked to the indulgence—weakness, if you prefer—with which he accepted Rosa's proverbial propensity for disorder, in this way being just as mistaken about my ability—or desire—to correct that disorder, as about how such weakness was consistently matched by his daughter.

Needless to say that Rosa, for her part, did all she could: her efforts to seem like a normal housewife, with her headaches, her calculations, her gossip. But the problem resided, above all, in the continuity of such efforts, in the sense—often contradictory—of the successive roles she adopted in her attempt to stabilize her life: tranquil and efficient housewife, borderline skeptic, everybody knows what husbands are like; a capricious and extravagant woman, a bit cynical; one of those gals who doesn't seem to be married; active, enterprising, independent, etcetera. Or, more than her roles, the actions inherent to such roles; arranging and furnishing the house, socializing with old friends, asking for advice, giving it, going shopping, inviting people over, flirting, traveling, drinking, getting organized to set up a studio, buying work supplies, making one phone call after another. She said she needed to go out, that the apartment walls were closing in around her. She also complained that she didn't know where to go in Barcelona. Their trips, however, always surprised her, the way they were, so sudden—or she didn't know it was scheduled so early or she'd forgotten, but you certainly could've reminded me about it, you know how absentminded I am about these things—with a stack of suitcases to pack, now that, running late, she had no time to pick out what she was going to wear, and what she might need. And the return trip, always so abrupt, just when she was starting to enjoy herself. And that house once again, that damned house that made her sick, really sick sometimes. A sickness of variable symptoms within certain more consistent ones: the need for affection, for pampering, for tender loving care. A tendency to self-medicate or to start self-medicating by the mere fact of buying a large quantity of medicines, as if, more than by their clinical properties, her wellness depended on the very act of buying them, almost as if spending so much money were a kind of almsgiving. Such a relationship, the need for affection—economic compensation, applicable result, by extension into other areas: money—energetic stimulus, etcetera. When Rosa got going, for example, when she shifted into high gear and went out shopping, the packages soon started piling up in the vestibule, where they'd remain for weeks before being stacked inside the storeroom. Renewed insistence, then, on the need for a studio, for a new apartment, but simply as a place in which to properly arrange her purchases. A special attraction to bargains: sales, discounts, liquidations, deals, payment plans, credit cards. Even a tendency to explain her purchases as a business, almost like an investment. She returned home in triumph, proud of her activity, of how solicitously she'd been attended, of her popularity among the salespeople, of having at last embarked on a fine, stylish redecorating campaign for her house, as if such a display might provide an antidote to her ruinous home, as if you could ruin something that was never fully realized in the first place, that never quite came together, the fitted carpet already stained when they were still installing the curtains, the kitchen smoky from some concoction forgotten on the stovetop even before they delivered the stainless steel cabinets, cigarette burns, spilled glasses, leaks, burned out light bulbs, the leather Chester sofas that Alfonso had given her as a gift steadily, regularly losing their buttons, that ended up looking like shabby deflated hippopotamuses after only a few months, and in the disorder of objects and the clutter of useless junk, books, magazines, papers, until the day when—her eyes a pair of yellow ruins—she broke down crying, I can't take this anymore, I can't take it anymore, let's get out of here, go anywhere. A need, it goes without saying, totally shared by me: leave it all behind, once and for all, go someplace to be able to write in peace.

There's a very clear distinction: the separation between working relationships and everything involving the so-called sphere of private life. But when certain elements from one place start to affect the essential elements of the other, the panorama becomes more confused. I imagine that Alfonso would've been more than happy to keep a simply inept son-in-law employed—that's life, as you well know. The bad thing, however, is that was not the question, not exactly, it wasn't about my work at the office as much as my attitude, my personality and, from a different angle, Rosa's personality and, consequently, the combined effect of both our personalities. All too close to Alfonso's own personality for it not to produce, in the long run, the resulting clash, however much effort each one of us invested in respecting the rules of the game, the need for understanding, of Alfonso not sticking his nose into other people's lives, of not catching the drift of the different situations, sometimes embarrassing ones, that develop, like the delicate surgical extraction of a diaphragm lodged in a bend of an honest family man's cecum or some analogous intervention, something that belongs to the world of the strictly personal, as the saying goes.

Even though the rupture with Alfonso—to give some name to the end of our most intimate phase, to his disastrous attempt to bind me body and soul to the affairs of the office and really interest me in the world of business, in other words, the conclusion of his hopes of bringing me into the fold—was a long time coming, as shown by evidence of the disaster, it happened, as is typical in such climates, because of a rather trivial incident. Both of us, moreover, found ourselves in an especially bad mood: in my case, personal discontent with what I was writing, that book I was working on under miserable conditions, during periods of free time, in a disjointed manner, increasingly more fed up with domestic problems, and which Alfonso took so lightly, a not-terribly-amusing extravagance—in his opinion—a sort of caprice which the sooner I abandoned the better for everyone, an attitude not so much reticent as scornful, and I'd be lying if I said that it didn't irritate me. In Alfonso's case, his bad temper, his state of mind that morning, his retort, much more rude and tasteless than his habitual ironies, seemed a response to the death of his favorite dog, the red Irish setter. Upset? What do you think? I wasn't even this upset when my mother died!

The expected pretext emerged as naturally as possible, while Alfonso was talking to me about Señor Botín, a great friend, a great gentleman, and a great Madrid businessman, who'd announced his arrival in Barcelona, and with whom he planned to close certain deals, when I commented: Botín? Now that's a promising name; it means booty, spoils, loot, plunder—perfect for a businessman. And then, how Alfonso's face changed, his cheek bulging up against his contracted eyelid as if a fang was about to tear through the flesh. Or for one of those purported revolutionaries who take from others what they have so they can keep it for themselves. Don't you think so? I understand that La Pasionaria lives in Moscow like a queen, surrounded by oriental luxury, thanks to the gold from the Banco de España. His sudden ambiguous smile, like that music that starts up, and then someone throws open the door and comes face to face with Captain Nemo playing the organ aboard the Nautilus.

Our choice of Rosas instead of Cadaqués was based on the fact that, despite the changes it had undergone, we still liked the town, so that there, lost among so many foreigners, we were almost foreigners too, and I could write with greater tranquility than in Cadaqués—which every weekend transformed into a sort of sophisticated appendix of Barcelona—and without the ill-starred memories of Ibiza. We stayed at the Lunasol, a recently built motel, quiet, well-situated, with a splendid view overlooking the bay, qualities difficult to find in places like Rosas, where all the restaurants and accommodations are managed by agencies for tourists on package vacations; by contrast, the Lunasol's owners, who turned out to have unexpectedly interesting personalities, soon became our good friends, people whom we ended up seeing each night. Our other relationships—with The Greek, the owner of the Nautic, the American with his Catalan barretina—had that character of episodic familiarity that was just what we'd been looking for. Later, when we stayed at the Aphrodite, we saw ourselves dragged, though by luck only episodically, into an intense night life—at the cost of our daytime life—and, against all expectations, the number of our local friendships increased, Walter and Krista and their circle, friends of our friends from the yacht, Pompey and Quima, the annoying bore Xavier, Rosa Durán.

We found Poppy—or she found us, as I've already said—the very next day after we ar-rived. Therefore, rather than adopting her, you'd have to say that she adopted us, almost as if she was waiting for us. She trotted by our side all through town, and lay down on the porch confidently awaiting some food, and she spent the night on the front door mat, curled up like some large, thick, panting hassock. Like some cross between a bear and a seal, the heavy movement of her dark big-boned body did not diminish her agility nor a certain circus-like grace when she tried to show off her tricks, the devotion and tender loving care with which she'd been trained, her extravagant presence, the typical result of crossing the most varied examples brought by tourists with the country's own native breed, predominantly compact and short-legged, her trunk thick as a glans, drooping ears, and melancholy expression. From the looks of it, she must have belonged to some Dutch or English woman, and, theoretically, her care was the responsibility of the same family that, during the woman's absence, took care of her chalet and her motorboat.

I was slow to notice the changes that Poppy was experiencing. Perhaps only just as slowly as she changed. A change that had possibly started before we saw her for the first time. When she accompanied me on my walks, she no longer cut back and forth around me like before. She always followed behind, panting, plodding heavily along. And reaching the edge of town, where the streets become open fields, she ended up stopping. I tried to coax her to keep going and she followed me with her eyes, as I walked on, motionless, as if even unable to make that expression that seems a dog's equivalent of a smile, her tail slack, her brow circumflex. I also hadn't noticed the first signs of dullness in her increasingly lackluster coat, thin and dusty looking, nor in the curvature of her excessively long nails. Nor did I pay much more attention to her lack of appetite until I noticed the spots of blood she was trailing behind her, larger as time went by, they couldn't be mistaken for her simply being in heat. Only then did I notice the cracked, rugged terrain of her hot, dry snout, before her belly began to swell up, and the cloud of stench, and the flies swarming around her. I feel just as sorry for her as you do, said Rosa, but Poppy can't come in the house. What do you want me to tell the cleaning lady? Poppy withdrew, as if conscious of the problem her presence created, settling for staying as close to the house as possible. The family in charge of taking care of her, a family of fishermen, distanced itself from the matter; the wife said that with the dog in such poor health she couldn't stay with them. I went to see the veterinarian, followed the whole way by Poppy, with her trail of blood and that stench which frightened away the passersby, not for him to cure her, but so that he could finish her off in the quickest, least painful way at his disposal; the vet confessed himself incapable of killing a dog. But he offered to procure the lie, a dose of strychnine that I'd have to mix up with some ground meat. It takes between four and six hours; with some pain, of course; you give it to her yourself. I went to see The Greek and he agreed to do it. On the patio at his house, while she was sleeping, a shotgun blast to the head. She'll never know what hit her. Poppy, as if happy to have left the vet's office without any grief, seemed more lively, almost frisky. But she panted a lot, and the flies landed all over her body, on the drops of blood, and she didn't even try to follow me when, stroked by the hands of The Greek, she saw me leave his patio.

AUREA INCOGNITA.

I meet Aurea outside the Nautic. Not at the sidewalk tables but on the other side of the street, on the promenade built over the water, the waves sloshing against the pillars underneath, the splashes sounding like big wet licks. At that quiet hour, breezeless, in the heat of the sinking sun, people usually prefer these tables to the ones on the sidewalk, sliding into that perfectly calm, mirage-like atmosphere that comes over the pale outlines of the bay.

She's accompanied by her son, Carlos junior. They sit together, side by side, Aurea making like she's listening to him, with the perfect aspect of a well-preserved mother looking to score, somewhere between amused and absorbed, apparently not looking at anybody but without missing a single detail of what's going on around her, her cigarette smoldering between her fingers, her glass raised and a smile on her lips, related more, no doubt, to the expression she'd decided to adopt than to whatever Carlos junior might be telling her.

His arrival, however, does not seem to annoy her in the least. She waves to him as she sees him coming along the walkway, and invites him to join them. It's Carlos junior, rather, who takes advantage of the moment to escape, to take off with his people, as he calls them. Say hello to your Mariona, says Aurea. And have fun. The same to you, says Carlos junior. Aurea starts laughing. She explains that she's going down to Barcelona for a few days, to take care of a few things. Seems like it'll be just as good for Carlos as for me.

A conversation about young people like Carlos and his crowd. Differences with respect to her own youth, between one generation and another, so distant in only a few short years. Aurea talks about Carlos. Anyway, she says, however furious he gets, he shouldn't downplay young people's memories. Or their capacity for observation.

She talks about Carlos's reaction to one of those clandestine summonses to the general strike in Barcelona, the first obstacle they came up against on their return from Argentina. At that time they'd just opened a bookstore, a small shop which they soon had to liquidate due to more losses than earnings, the typical fallout whenever one decides to use their profits to satisfy their personal hobbies or obsessions. And Carlos, influenced by his memory of the general strike in '51, as well as by his more recent experience in Argentina, was convinced, meaning he feared, that the strike would be successful. The night before, I think, he didn't even sleep, tossing and turning in bed all night long, rolling and tumbling to visions of violent clashes, blood, reprisals, police repression that would descend upon the city. That's why his decision the next morning to roll up the shutter on his storefront with maximum punctuality was anything but a thoughtless one, especially because so many other Barcelona establishments did the same and, like so many other times, none of the boycott and strike slogans were taken up by the people who, for the most part, must have simply ignored them. That's right: and what Carlos did next was drive out to some vacant lot and smash his car windshield with a rock and then, at the garage, explain that it had been a crowd of youngsters, surely some picketing strikers or something like that. To make it seem plausible, of course; and to soothe his lifelong revolutionary conscience. I, of course, don't know anybody who saw one single picket line that day nor do I believe that all the summonses to the general strike in Barcelona produced any other result than the smashed windshield on Carlos' car. At that time, Carlos junior must have been around ten or twelve years old.

And then this winter. One of those student movements involving truancy and occupying academic departments and assemblies and demonstrations which end up closing the university. And the police phalanx charging the demonstrators, shooting into the air, and the arrests and the rumors circulating, about tortures, about a dead student, or several, whose names nobody knows exactly but they're sure it's what happened. Carlos junior didn't stop by the house, just went from one meeting to another, like any other student. And then Carlos goes and gets in the car and brings him up to Rosas, puts him on restriction, forbids him to return to Barcelona without permission, including not even making phone calls, vociferous, irate. Assemblies! Idiocy! You think ideas just sprout up from arguments, among everyone, spontaneously? Imbeciles! You're all nothing but a bunch of pathetic imbeciles!

I don't know what he's complaining about now, Aurea says. I don't even know what he must think that Carlos junior thinks when he hears him start up with his business about how young people today have no worries and all these other fantasies. And he: it's curious that a man like Carlos seems incapable not only of getting to know young people better but of knowing himself. And Aurea: does he really seem like such a man to you?

Carlos junior and his people, that pleiad of young folks whom his elders all consider interchangeable, identical in their garb as well as in their habits, as a kind of late revenge against Christianity by the suppressed Orphic cults, devoted to that Orpheus who was banished from the earth, abandoned. The man who returned to the infernal caverns, his extraordinary incursion or descent. The man who was a woman. That man who, as if struck by a premonition of his own death at the hands of those who were merely women, lost Eurydice forever in his attempt to rescue her, a misstep—like all lapses—of great significance. The inventor of music. Kathleen Ferrier.

Carlos junior with his people, flowers dressed in smoke from Afghanistan. Are you a flower, Mariona? A smokeable flower? D'you want to smoke some mariona with me, Mariona?

Affinities between Robert and Carlos junior: evasive personality, reserved attitude toward parents, etcetera.

Transpose detailed description of Ideal City.

MATILDE MORET.

The first time I slept with Matilde, the last thing I would have imagined was that we were cousins. I met her on the terrace of some bar on the Boulevard Saint-Germain, Le Mabillon possibly; people said the place was frequented by agents from the Spanish Embassy hunting for conversations, and, whether fantasy or reality, the fact is that I didn't like going there. Maybe that's why it didn't take us long to head over to Place de la Contrescarpe, somewhat fashionable in those days. And in some basement bar around there, at a given moment, we left our mutual acquaintances behind, abandoning them to the pleasures of their conversation, and off we went to bed. I only knew her first name. She hadn't mentioned her last name, or if she did I hadn't paid attention. And she, apparently, had more or less done the same. I recall that for some undetermined motive—to impress her, to create a relaxed atmosphere, to focus our interaction on an unequivocally erotic terrain—I asked her if she was a lesbian. It's one thing to be a lesbian and another to have gone to bed with a woman, don't you think? she said. And for a moment I felt like—I remember—a blabbermouth. Besides there's something about them that I don't like, she continued. The smoothness of their cheeks, perhaps. Or maybe that's the only thing that does attract me; I don't know. Connecting the dots, it was precisely because of these confidences, and the fact that we both hailed from Barcelona, and from the same social environment, etcetera, which made us both soon realize that we were cousins. From the very start, and rightly so, I'd found something familiar in Matilde.

The fact is, from what can be clarified, her childhood, years when she was raised at a remove from the Moret family name, was at once parallel, inverse, and complementary to what I myself had experienced. Her father was my mother's brother, the older one, and although Matilde is sure she remembers him, he died at the end of the Civil War, in exile, just a few short years after my mother. You've got to recognize what those times meant, the dark, isolated Forties, in order to understand her mother's reaction, the widow of a Red—and no less Red for being dead or for being a prestigious Barcelona lawyer—facing some events which overwhelmed her completely, withdrawing from her husband's family, seeking refuge in her own—from an unswerving conservative tradition—giving her children the most ultraconservative education possible—schools run by nuns, Jesuits, spiritual exercises, every kind of religious practice—a series of measures which, if they didn't produce the expected results with the girls—just the opposite—they certainly did so with the boys, younger and, perhaps for that reason, more malleable, more sensitive to obligation and guilt, to principles, to the image of the disappeared father, almost assimilable to that of that legendary firstborn who, in the best families, usually died early from tubercular meningitis or some similar tragedy, and about whom, generally, people usually avoided talking, or picking at the scab of memory. About the rest of the Moret family, apparently, she on-ly remembered Aunt Magda, with barely greater clarity than she remembered her father, and, as in my case, the memory was a good one.

A peculiar notion of kinship, thereforc, very similar to the one I was used to, the fact, for example, that at home, when one spoke about the family, it was always more than well understood to mean my father's family, aunts and uncles, cousins, nieces and nephews, anecdotes, legends, everything that related exclusively to the paternal branch. By the time I became aware of such a peculiarity, the mysterious aspects of the phenomenon no longer held any interest for me, the same lack of interest offered by so many visible, vestigial representatives of the Moret family, Uncle Ramón, the disaster, the bohemian, and his hideous wife and no less hideous offspring, people with whom my father would not admit any kind of dealings. The deaths of Grandfather, grandmother, and Aunt Magda, all in such a short time—seemingly swallowed by the maelstrom opened by my mother's death, and only better, or more openly, remembered—free from the cloud of taboo shrouding my mother's memory—thanks to their lesser individual import and the lasting impact of their passing—blotted out the memory of Matilde's father, effectively reducing the physical image of the Moret family to Uncle Ramón, a madcap, as Uncle Rodrigo called him. Your father exaggerates, he said. Ramón isn't exactly a bad person, but he's not just your typical scoundrel, either. For me, more than anything, he's what you call a crackpot.

Thus just by getting to know Matilde I was able to appreciate exactly the extent to which the memory of her father—that Red or that attorney for Reds, about whom the best thing was to say nothing—had propitiated the silence at home, and my father's seeking oblivion. The Red uncle, and the obscure antecedent of a homosexual grandfather, and the Moret family's general climate of economic decline, which, conversely and apparently against all ethics, only seemed to have lopped off the family branch of the Red uncle. Thus, too, those remote references, as if blurred by the veils interposed, to the cousins, or rather, to those girls, to those two sisters—the male cousins, perhaps for being younger, perhaps because their irreproachable conduct made it unnecessary, weren't even mentioned—forever shrouded, it seemed, in an aura of reprobation and criticism, because with a father as God commands, everything would've been different. One of them was referred to as the gorgeous one. Which one was Matilde?

And along with the chronic renewal of some circumstances whose anomalous character could only be blurred by force of habit, thanks to having lived with them ever since childhood, there was the reconsideration of a problem which kept on contributing to just such an anomaly. I'm referring here to my curious rejection—with more accuracy than oblivion—of my mother's family's language, Catalan, the language habitually spoken by the Morets: the inhibition which kept me from using it, reluctant to use it except for on exceptional occasions, despite, logically, my understanding it perfectly; the clumsiness which seemed to hinder my expressive fluidity on such occasions however much of an effort I made; confronted with difficulties nonexistent for me in other languages I learned later on; mistakes, lapses, and incoherencies similar, in short, to those a little boy commits when sternly interrogated by his elders. A lacuna so much more inexplicable because my brother, since childhood, speaks Catalan as naturally as Spanish, along with the fact that we both spent the Civil War as refugees in a mountain town where the kids knew practically no other tongue than Catalan; however, one possibly acceptable reason for my rejection might be the no-less-common Francoist education of the postwar years, brutally anti-Catalan in its defensive delirium of all things properly Spanish—essences and values toward which I've always felt, for what it's worth, even more refractory. Apart from the differences in character between my brother and I, which, more than explaining anything, actually raise new questions, there is, certainly, one fact whose importance might lie within any unique element that establishes a subtle difference between two otherwise parallel experiences: our difference in age. But to reduce such a subtle difference to the supposition of my brother knowing more than me simply because he's five years older, would mean stepping into the happy kingdom of simple explanations for complicated problems, refusing the true point of entry, that back door into worlds of darkness wherein what we seek truly resides, shadows before which neither commonplace ideas nor common sense nor evidence matter very much. Simplifications such as how to conclude, for example, that a dream or a series of dreams about serpents have a phallic significance, when any direct sexual meaning also remains to be seen, given that, situated in its oneiric context, those serpents might well represent the rejection of something whose importance can only be measured by the degree of attraction it exercises and, at the same time, by how intensely we sheathe it in a charge of fear in order to be able to reject it with greater ease. Or rather: in order to more easily reject an invitation traditionally linked to the animal, in this case the serpent: to eat the forbidden fruit. Which only leads us to another question: what then is the forbidden fruit? And it's the fact that, as with such dreams, so too the problems of learning a language in childhood, as well as the simultaneously repressive and expressive character of the personality which learning through such an instrument involves in any person that age, thanks to which the child assumes the basic foundations of constrictive objectivity.

Matilde has always possessed the gift which, if generally rare or infrequent, is nearly impossible to try to find in a woman: wisdom. All of them properly engrafted, I remember her saying. But then, at the first sign of frost, the sprouts appear at the base of the tree, not at the graft. This same quality probably explains the reason for Rosa's jealousy, the uncontrollable aversion she still manifests toward someone whose strictly sexual relationship with me could not be more episodic. And the close friendship that we've maintained since then, of course.

THE CRACKPOT.

Uncle Guillermo used to say that Grandpa and Uncle Oriol's living together had something colloidal about it. Since you're already studying chemistry, you'll understand what I mean, he said. And, years later, when he must have thought that Ricardo could also understand him, he said: something as inadvisable as a man without a penis copulating with a woman without a tongue, and he laughed as if he would crack, his white, coffee-soaked mustache drooping over the corners of his mouth.

In Papa's presence he was more restrained, and he even almost defended Uncle Oriol when Papa deployed his verbal artillery against that undesirable person who had fallen into his life, who had ended up as his brother-in-law, the bohemian, the disaster, the shameless one, the ignominy of his family's politics, etcetera, his comments invariably coming round to the question of what if your poor mother could see him now, etcetera, etcetera, elements of a fixed and well-ordered series, hammered through repetition into a kind of litany. Well, you don't have to get so worked up about it, either, Uncle Guillermo would say then. For me, Oriol is nothing but a crackpot. That's right, believe me, I feel sorry for Grandpa, he's a lovely person. For him it must be a harsh sentence having to end his days with all those cousins hanging around his house.

Precisely because of that inevitable company of cousins, as long as Ricardo remembered, they never paid Grandpa more than two visits per year: at Christmas and on his saint's day. And Papa, putting all his care into making it very clear that he did those things strictly to fulfill his duties as a son-in-law, so that his two sons might show the respect and appreciation they owed their grandfather, and only their grandfather, a saintly man.

On such occasions, all of Uncle Oriol's attempts to make the visit seem natural and to set a lively but tranquil tone for the conversation were useless, his self-conscious fluency betrayed by his frequent visits to the bathroom, hasty departures of unmistakeable significance, that classic propensity to diarrhea characteristic of the prodigal and wasteful. Equally useless were all Aunt Dolores's efforts to make the house and its inhabitants seem respectable, her attempts to mask the prevailing stench, like the mellifluous flatulence of a nun, which, you might say, stuck to the household objects, to the walls and floors, her tidying up her unfortunate, haggard, puffy-eyed offspring, that uncertain number of children who, despite being fearful and attentive to her most minimal indications—like choir singers riveted to the conductor's baton—were no less shameless in their avid impertinence and sneaky faces. On the other hand, as they grew, the climate of intimidation to which the children found themselves subjected seemed to deteriorate year by year, what with everything and Aunt Dolores being one of those women in whom, despite the encouraging smile by which she tried to transform the ugliness of her features as she greeted her little nieces and nephews, it wasn't difficult to suspect her violent bouts of fury, the excited agitation of her movements, comparable only to those of a sorceress in full dance, snorting and spitting, spewing smoke, farts, firecrackers, stinking like a mad skunk. You might also say that, with the passage of time, the most immutable element was none other than the very center of such ritual visits, meaning, the grandfather, now possessed by that parsimony which slowness gives to everything that happens in old age, the spitting image of the male member that shrivels away with the years, that snail which no longer even dares to show itself, minimized by its own insignificance.

In this case, as usual, Uncle Oriol's had miscalculated: never imagining that Grandpa, close to seventy when the Civil War ended, would survive another twenty good years or more. His own marriage to Aunt Dolores, just before the Civil War, had already been a miscalculation, an error in the valuation of the total fortune which he thought was in play, at the same time he was trying—a desperate remedy—to amend his bohemian youth, his fate as a failed musician, as the black sheep of the family, incapable as he was, in the long run, of avoiding his destiny, that dark and precarious underworld of the commission agent to which, along with the financial straits and general scorn, he was going to see himself end up in. But, it's clear, none of those things could be foreseen. And thus, the Civil War concluded, Grandma dead along with her two beautiful sisters-in-law, hounded and harassed by eviction and debts and children, nothing more natural than everyone going to live in Grandpa's house, to keep him company, to take care of him, if you will, so old now, the poor man. The bad thing was that Grandpa didn't die, and his personal fortune was worth less than before the Civil War, so that if there was never any problem back in his day when it came to subletting a rent-controlled apartment for an absurdly low quantity, there was, however, a problem in the benefits that the manipulation of Grandpa's diminished capital produced for him—damned miscalculation—and no chance for him to blame someone else for the negative unraveling of his wretched initiatives, because Grandpa limited himself to signing the papers placed in front of him, but not without shrugging his shoulders, clearly signifying his lack of trust, which so infuriated Uncle Oriol.

And as Grandpa's economic prospects decreased—as well as the number of pieces of furniture, paintings, decorations and other objects in the apartment worth any money—Uncle Oriol hardened his regime against Grandpa, keeping him ever-more secluded, while Aunt Dolores's timid interventions proved ineffective; she was more worried about her children than her father. A seclusion which, save for certain occasions—Christmas, his saint's day, those ritual visits—now bordered on keeping him incommunicado, shut away in his room almost all day, not only for being unpresentable—dirty, senile, neglected, frail, ailing—but, above all, due to his reticent, not to mention obstructionist and discouraging conduct, an indirect cause, clearly, of Uncle Oriol's financial catastrophes. And at heart, by way of a defensive reaction, through the same fascination that his foolproof strength awoke in Uncle Oriol, the very sort of fascination that stirs the imagination of a business executive, with more years than success under his belt, sitting at an airport gate, watching a jet taking off into the air, his nostalgic gaze as he contemplates its steep trajectory: what power. Yes, Uncle Oriol's obsessive waiting in the face of Grandpa's leathery longevity was analogous to this very sort of reaction.

He didn't behave well, that's the truth: Oriol, the bad son, the bohemian, the rebel, the frustrated artist, did not treat Grandpa well at all, perhaps due to innate badness, as they said at home, perhaps as payback for all the times when his own father had to straighten him out, to extract revenge, to make that goddamned old man pay, for having had to endure one of his daughters—the ineligible one, the hopeless one, the ugly duckling, the sickly one, the bad egg, the idiot, the good for nothing daughter—in order to make him pay for the other goddamned old man, to make him pay for everything, for his wife, for his disasters, for the bad luck he'd always had, for the very same punishments during the reign of authority and intolerance under which his youth had transpired, his childhood, for everything, that's right, for everything.

The captivity, which Grandpa endured with great integrity and presence of mind, became almost total when his tired feet would no longer allow him, on Sunday mornings, to cover the distance to church, back and forth, and he had to settle for following Mass on the radio. In order to eliminate any pretext for the old man going out, even more than for purely economical reasons, Uncle Oriol even used the services of a sinister looking barber who made after-hours house calls for unbeatable prices. Oriol entered Grandpa's room with premeditated brusqueness, bent over the armchair by the window where the old man was dozing. Grandpa, they're here to cut your hair! he shouted in his ear, his face inscrutable, while Grandpa's startled pupils shone diaphanous, his sleepy awareness waking up, the ideas, images, and remembrances shuttling in confusion through his sclerotic brain, still traumatized by the reversals of fortune from the Civil War, the surprise raids, a group of men selected for the firing squad, blindfolded, and the inevitable misfortune of the outcome, a few shot at random after an endless wait, nightmares relived, terrors renewed, that final image of the parish priest in the town where they'd taken refuge, fleeing the bombardment, his half-naked body riddled with bullets in the main square, after having been impaled, for all to see, on the meat hooks in the butcher shop, a splendid target however much he kicked and screamed until the shots rang out. And then the ominous, ignoble barber made his entrance, almost brutal in his presence and manners, owing, no doubt, to the fact that he had perfectly sussed out the situation the first time he heard Uncle Oriol say: Go on, shear him right here, anywhere you like, in any corner. And the barber started working while exchanging quick jokes with Uncle Oriol, in cryptic words and extra loud guffaws.

Against all predictions, Grandpa's death came too late for Uncle Oriol, the failed musician, the black sheep, the good-for-nothing freeloader, the family disgrace, burnt out by now, without his earlier courage and resources, as if his accumulated guilt had now forced upon him, suddenly and before his time, the ailments of someone older than himself, prematurely senile, sadly weepy and soft in the head, defenseless, for his own part, against some ruthless children, perfectly shaped by the life that he had forced them to lead, equipped with all the hardness and mordacity that were now starting to fail him. Who would have said that that death, so long awaited, now physically manifest, had acted as a coup de grâce against his diminished strength, a death as surprising as obviously foreseeable, and, like the clock that stops, the light bulb that burns out, the amulet that gets lost, the especially blurry face of some specific person in a photograph, Grandpa's no less premonitory dream in which he saw himself transformed into a cosmonaut.

A discreet and docile disappearance, very appropriate to his patient posture when he tolerated getting cropped by that baleful barber hired by Uncle Oriol, sitting there hunched over, his neck wrapped tight in a towel, like a heretic yoked with his sanbenito or, more precisely, a condemned prisoner ready to be garroted, offering up his shriveled nape covered in white fuzz.

THE ARRIVAL OF THE APHRODITE.

With that saprophytic character common to some friendships that center around the owner of a yacht, similar to the friendly relationship typically established in adolescence between a pretty girl and an ugly one, the former benefiting from their contrasting looks and the latter from the inevitable proximity of some friend of the boy who's interested in her friend, something which wouldn't otherwise happen, or those friends from good families fallen on hard times, those newly impoverished women who never fail to gather round the most fortunate wife, young woman, or widow in full possession of a solid inheritance, during the last years of their life, ladies-in-waiting, handmaidens almost, whose disguise—a pleasant, well-mannered, helpful disposition—is for them an assurance of survival and shelter against misery; thus the presence of Xavier the Bore and Rosa Durán on board the Aphrodite, their stoic passivity in the face of Pompey, whose fickle moods made them the butt of his jokes, as if he were doing them a favor or granting them a gift. A very different case than that of Quima in her clear and always more comfortable role as nothing more than a friend of Pompey. As his friend, to be exact.

Quima was the only crew member whom I already knew but still not too well, little more than to say hello, just one of Rosa's many friends, an old classmate, I think. When we ran into them in town, I would have preferred to walk by and pretend not to see them, because I was rather annoyed by the idea of having to tolerate such people, even if only for a little while, blabbering on about nothing. But Quima called us over and introduced us to some others and now there was no way of escaping the whole bunch of them. On the other hand, Quima was good-looking, and Rosa had told me she was rumored to be a lesbian; supposedly she was a photographer. And Pompey, with his patter and his quips, immediately revealed himself to be the kind of guy who was, at least, a lot of fun to be around, something which at first—doubtless unjustly—one usually fails to expect from a man whose principal occupation seems to be his yacht. Xavier insisted that we knew each other from the courtyard at the university and I nodded, although I didn't remember him at all. Regarding Rosa Durán, the most definite thing that could be said about her—what Pompey said—is that she was a woman whose beauty was outshone only by the splendor of her own stupidity.

Walter and Krista were friends of Pompey and they usually lived in Rosas, where Walter ran a housing development company or some business involved with outfitting hotels, something like that. Krista was a human mannequin, a model who worked in advertising and things like that, now withdrawn from circulation by Walter.

Pompey's plan was to sail north along the coast to Portbou, although, in fact, they headed toward Cadaqués with the idea of opening something like one of those discotheques where no one really dances, none of that violent exercise. We should've arrived a week ago, but when you start stopping at ports like this one, the very same trip ends up taking ten years, which is what must've happened to Ulysses. Besides, that whore Castells has a great sense of humor and I don't think he'll take the delay badly. I'll put up the dough and he'll run the business. I'm sure it'll be a success.The thing is, these faggots are indispensable; they've always got some nice little detail to share with everybody. Not that I do it for money, like that whore Castells, although I won't deny either that my financial interest increases as long as the percentages derived from inflated values satisfy my concerns. It's also true that sometimes I think, as Katolika well knows, that what I'd really like is to own nothing: no yacht, no house, no car, no properties, just what I can carry in my pockets. The bare necessities: a checkbook and a ballpoint pen.

We drank a lot that night. Like the next night and the one after that. Our nightly rounds through the town, the bar at the gas station, Mas Paradís. And we all ended up on the yacht, the day dawning around us. Or maybe that night we ended up at Walter's house, but, anyway, in the morning we went out on the Aphrodite, to the open sea, to ease our hangovers by swimming offshore from Cabo Norfeo. We didn't get back to the hotel until mid-afternoon.

The water was splendid, almost unbearably so; also the sun, its radiance increased by the scintillations of the surrounding sea. Pompey seemed to fall asleep, his white sailor's hat covering his face. The conversation was relaxed and informal, vaguely centered on the ambiguity of sex. Katolika insisted that Quima had an irresistible vocation to be a transvestite: I'm sure that what you'd really like is to be a man disguised as a woman. And Quima: not that: what I'd like, pure and simple, is to be a faggot. Rosa talked about how my first sexual experience had been in a dream: a naked woman, with breasts and a penis and a hole down below, without any clear face. I hugged her and kissed her and suddenly I woke up. And was it a wet dream? Did you have an orgasm? they heard Pompey ask from beneath his sailor's cap. I don't remember, I said; I was really little, perhaps I wasn't even old enough for those things to happen to me. And Pompey: well that would give anybody a hard-on. Imagine that, the perfect thing.

He suddenly livened up, perhaps because he was irresistibly drawn to all kinds of conversations, or perhaps from his desire to clear his hangover on a verbal terrain by legitimately exercising his right to offer some apt rejoinders to the provocations of his guests, Xavier the Borc and Idiotic Rosa Durán—

tacitly invited for that very purpose: as with Rosa Durán's words, for example, when she decided to not go swimming because, as she said, she thought it was almost her time of the month. And Pompey: well, that's putting a proper period on it. Or another example, when Rosa Durán, that Idiotic Rosa Durán, said: if he (Xavier the Bore) does lie to me, I notice it right away: his nose grows just like Pinocchio's. And Pompey: I also get bigger when I hop into bed with someone. And, from then on, from that trifling remark, he moved decisively to the attack: the thing with Xavier the Bore is that he's such an idiot that he's not even worried about having problems. That's his real problem. And he's stupid enough to pretend that he has them so that no one will think he's an idiot for not having them.

Idiocy fades just like beauty, said Pompey: they're things that should never worry the person in question. Besides, they're not all that important. For women, let's say, physical beauty is the least important quality in a man. I know this little hunchback who spent some time on a Polynesian island, the only survivor of a shipwreck, and when they went to rescue him he'd fucked every woman on the island. How did I do it? he asked them. What makes me so irresistible? What's the source of my magnetic power? The fact that the hair on my ass starts right at the nape of my neck.

Speaking of hangovers, said Pompey: my stomach feels like shit, which is what comes of getting shit-faced.

When Quima commented that last year's bathing suit was tight on her, that her ass had gotten fatter, *más culona*, as she put it. Más culona? No, masculina.

About an excursion to Menorca in the Aphrodite: it's an island I really like. It's full of talayots, which are the monuments where prehistoric people used to jerk off.

Regarding nasty gossip: nowadays I only really believe a guy's a faggot when he hops into bed with me.

On marriage: just like in politics, the only feasible form of conjugal life is a triumvirate. And the first thing you've got to dispense with is mutual respect.

On psychological complexes: to put an end to all those stories about Oedipus and Elektra, the best solution is to kill the mother and rape the father. Or the other way around, I don't remember anymore.

Regarding paperwork and other administrative problems Walter ran into with his activities: civil servants? Those Germans will never change! Look: the first thing to know is that your civil servant always swallows whatever you feed him. The second, that he knows that you can be bribed; this makes everything easier. And then, that he's allowed to bribe, too. That he should start engaging in bribery immediately.

About the Man-Cock: he's blessed with quite a beam. But the way I see it, thickness is more important than length.

On the male member in general: there are some cocks that should have their own proper name, just like the swords of famous warriors: Tizona, Durendal, Excalibur, etcetera. Or like their horses.

On the same subject: I wear a wedding band, yes, not as a symbol of matrimony but rather of my lost ring of foreskin.

Regarding Quima: the best thing about Quima is that she's got purple-tipped tits, just like asparagus from La Rioja.

On boyhood: Mine? Savagely skinning my schlongo!

Regarding Enrique: his problem is that he thought making investments was some kind of subversive activity.

Touching on Jesus Christ: the most effective social solvent is scandal. All those Pharisees around Jesus understood that immediately.

Maxim: superstition is my only religion.

Definition: I call all satisfactory copulative penetration being pussy whipped.

Lexicon: Central Ameriqueer. Eyankulate, eyankulating, Eyankuland. Subject (meaning girl, specifically a woman). Multi (meaning multimillionaire). Phallophagist (homosexual).

Motto: *si vis penis*, for the ass.

Etymological remark: *oráculo*, the Spanish word for *oracle* is derived from *os*, and *oris*, which in Latin mean *mouth*, and from *culo*, which means *ass*.

Response to Rosa Durán's question: What's a futtock? Answer: a bird of the Andes, presently endangered. Its wingspan is greater than that of the condor. Like some flowers, all of them are hermaphrodites, fertilized by the wind.

WARTS.

The image that best suggests what the wine cellar means for me is that of a place infrequently visited, in part from the vague prohibition that hung over it and, partly and specifically, by a certain sensation of horror those environs provoked in me, not so much from the prevailing darkness, barely neutralized by a 15-watt light bulb, as from the sticky curtains of cobwebs. Throughout my whole childhood, apart from the grape harvest, when I was constantly warned about how I would be instantly crushed to death if I fell into the winepress, I participated, in my own small way, in the all the different phases of winemaking. I only remember going into the wine cellar oncc, assigned to help my cousin

Pilar fill the jars necessary for one of those sangrias she usually prepared when we had guests over. Then, a few years ago, I went back in again during one of those weekends we spent at the farm with our friends, the times when Alejo was chasing Rosa or maybe it was the other way around. I'd remembered that in the small cellar—an inner sanctum of the best wines, more like a crypt than the large one—the far end was sealed with a partition wall that sounded hollow, and Alejo and I broke through it with a pick: behind it was the mouth of a sunken cave: the reason, no doubt, it had been walled off.

The time I went down there with my cousin Pilar, her little boy had warts. I remember because Uncle Rodrigo had said that they were contagious, and I was trying not to touch her or her son, and after helping her fill the jars I ran to wash my hands. Surely, you gave them to him, Uncle Rodrigo told her, when you were bathing him. The simplest thing is to kill the mother wart, slice it right off at the skin with a red-hot needle; you can spot it right away because it's the oldest one. The others will then dry up by themselves. That's what people in the country do, and the fact is they do get rid of them. Doctors will tell you all kinds of other stuff, use silver nitrate, a scalpel, but in the end it's the same. However, the important thing is be sure to find the mother wart.

Regarding the bathroom, it was located in the attic and never used much, an ideal hiding place for my masturbatory exercises. It was installed with the domestic staff in mind, grandfather's solution for the help, quite in keeping with the times, when it was normal to have servants.

That's why it's curious that my dream established a connection between both locations, if the word curious is the right one when talking about a dream. The bathroom attic, the cave where one of the walls opened into an empty space, almost a well to judge by its pronounced slope after only a few steps, increasingly narrow, half-collapsed, partially blocked by the crumbling walls, clumps of broken granite, fragments of rock which I had to crawl between on all fours, dragging myself along, little more than a rabbit warren. The descent to the wine cellar through this hole: at least I was there, in the wine cellar. Or rather: not in the cellar properly speaking, but in its crypt, the little bodega, situated at a lower level, a flight of steps further down. The sun reached that spot through the ruined well, slanted beams, impregnated with floating dust, the cloud of dust raised by the rubble, broken rock, chunks of brick, something resembling the basement of a bombed-out building, scattered debris amid which lay the corpse of Uncle Rodrigo. I had this dream a few weeks after his death.

And another curious fact: at the burial, my cousin Pilar remarked to me that her boy—Rodrigo's grandson—had gotten covered with warts. I'm sure he caught them in the school swimming pool, she said. The dermatologist told me that all these public pools are really filthy.

THE COMPLETE IDIOT.

Maybe it was the sea breeze, *la marinada*, that made us feel so slack and listless. Sometime earlier Rosa had proposed going out somewhere, but no one yet seemed capable of standing up let alone making a decision. Stay that way, lying on the patio at Walter's house while evening came on, chatting about anything, without even tasting the drinks solicitously served by Katolika. Pronouncements from Pompey. Bringing up mutual friends. Walter's soliloquy, his tongue loosened by alcohol, the only one drinking, as if coaxing them to share that pleasure which many experience in copulative matters, not so much by practicing multiple variations or reconfiguring them mentally or merely imagining them, as much as in their verbal formation, in pronouncing the right words, in naming what one is, was, or might be doing in the moment, acts, gestures, erogenous zones, as if the mere mention—enhanced by his strong Germanic accent—would make them real; the same way that a prayer is efficacious or not, depending on how it is offered up.

Pompey had proposed a new, official name for Rosa Durán: *La Tonta del Bote*, after the eponymous Spanish comedy film whose title means "The Complete Idiot," or, in this case, The Idiot on the Boat, as more deserving of that appellation than any other person on board. The best things she's got are her observations. Have you all noticed? she said on arrival: I don't know why but the traffic always seems to be heavier in the opposite direction than you're driving. And Xavier, as if lending a hand to what he must have considered an attempt to cheer people up: and why don't we organize a War of the Roses upon a field of ermine? Don't be extemporaneous (Pompey). Have you ever noticed that what's difficult sometimes isn't copulating, exactly, but ejaculating? Well, accept that as our current position. And Pompey reminds him about his day job selling outboard motors and inflatable boats and canoes, as opposed to Pompey's own role, the customer, the one who's always right, the one who always gets the last word. Besides, I've got to warn you, there are all kinds of reasons to declare you, instead of Rosa Durán, the Complete Idiot. Or perhaps the two of you together. You both enjoy the same advantages of being extremely good-looking and exceedingly stupid

Tormented expression on Xavier's face, bitter, wounded self-love, as if possessed by an anxiety similar to that young woman of petit bourgeois extraction who moves among more highly evolved people, an environment where nobody suspects that she's still a virgin, nor does she yet dare to reveal it, thus making it increasingly difficult to justify her shyness with excuses of boredom and disgust, so that, bit by bit, she's heading toward a brutal and anonymous deflowering, carried out by some loutish ruffian, as the only alternative to suicide. Or like that young man—more a case of unhappiness than anxiety—who clumsily seduces a girl one fine day, practically without trying, nearly terrified by the experience, but if he ends up not marrying her it's because then he'd no longer be able to say that he'd at least once had a fling. The very sort of justification by which Xavier might think it his right to remind all those present of his situation as the chosen son of a well-to-do family, a daddy's boy, obliged by life's hazards to assume the responsibilities of his father's business, while still considering himself as much a university student as any other, raising the memory of times past, of mutual friendships.

You're all so disgusting (Rosa). The same as when you get together to reminisce about the military, always the same stories. You all seem like one of those miserable wretches on the train who always end up showing their snapshots of their wife and kids to the other passengers in the same compartment. Whether it's Alejo, Ángela, this, that, or the other one. She'd started drinking as if to gain courage, to react, pricked, no doubt, by the occasional mention of Ana, by the hostility that the mere mention of her name awoke in her since she'd learned that Ana, at one point, had described her as one of those exalted bed-sex revolutionaries who assimilates the concept of *pueblo* to the hierarchical meaning of the Latin *populous*—people—in its pyramidal version, a tumultuous multitude of upright virile members comparable only, in the broad perspective, to that which *Las Lanzas* offers us. Ángela drove me wild, said Quima, something that couldn't quite please Rosa, not entirely, whose opinion about that hypocrite, about that horrible whore Ángela, differed slightly from Quima's. She's lost a lot (Rosa). That coolness she had, you know? She seems, I don't know, almost bitter. You talk like some character from Alejo's novel, I told her. General conclusion about Alejo: he believed that the secret to writing was in things and not in words. That's why he switched to writing movies. But the secret to cinema is not in things either. It's not possible to give an answer if you don't know the question. Rest in peace.

Comparative examination of Enrique's case versus Esteban's, a few other historic figures of the underground university movement in Barcelona; diverse fates. An evolution of the defensive and conservative sign in Enrique's case, entrenched in discretion and being incognito, privileges which facilitate so much money in the sphere of private life, his trips to Tangier, his friends, independence, or rather, the freedom of erotic initiative implied by making use of one of those apartments which advertisements describe as sumptuous in a zone of the city that doesn't need to be classified as elegant. His critical sense in some way dulled, but rather, more turned against himself, if possible, than before. His recapitulations, his analyses, that masochistic accentuation of the contrast between his current form of life and his past one, now very much in the past, revolutionary activity, the initial disorientation, the perplexity overcome only by time, a perplexity not inferior—although in an opposing sense, the roles reversed—to that of a young Bonapartist of the First Estate, an incipient Stendhal, upon seeing Napoleon carry out, point by point, the programs of his enemies from that first period, and verify in practice the theoretical principles against which he had fought. At any rate, he said, what interested us was not the Revolution. What interested us was overthrowing our own parents. And I: I don't see why I had to want to overthrow my father, the most inoffensive person one could imagine as a father. And Enrique: you see, the revolution is altruistic: Saturn is dethroned in order to reestablish justice, for Saturn's own good, if you like. And I: I don't know about your father, but mine was the furthest thing possible from the image of Saturn, I can promise you that. And Enrique: well, you just think it over and you'll see that I'm right. Where do you think we made a mistake? Or are you going to tell me that you've never suddenly felt like a complete idiot?

Regarding Esteban, they must have foreseen his future as well as guessed his present, that night when they went to have dinner at the apartment he'd moved into with Ana, during their last months in Barcelona, before they had to escape clandestinely to Paris, when Esteban made that incidental observation about a button on his fly that Ana needed to sew for him. You still want me to sew it even tighter? she commented, coldly, the faithful, solicitous, unconditional Ana. Yes, everything was already implied that night: their coming separation in Paris, Ana's immediate—if not preexisting—understanding with some higher-up in the leadership, her consequent ascension within the party, her growing responsibilities, while Esteban, according to a parallel but inverse process, more than allowing himself to be marginalized, seemed to be moving away by his own accord, separating himself more and more from the organization, as if dragged away by his own indolence, by the vagueness of his plans as well as by how much that indicated a certain kind of activity, by his tendency to resolve speculative problems—most appropriate to his ever growing skepticism—around a table over a few drinks, with a few friends, traits which, if already noticeable during his final months in Barcelona, all became only more aggravated with the initial displacement that exile always represents. Less predictable, however, was his ability to adapt to situations, because anyone who had known him might imagine his awareness of himself as a political refugee in Paris exacerbated by how both his friends and his girlfriend—meaning, the revolutionary organization to which he'd one day dedicated his life—had abandoned him, possibly, in truth, finding him gripped by the private perplexity which takes prisoner the Catholic who loses faith, who ceases to believe, victim of the same kind of helplessness which possessed the inhabitants of Lincoln Island after the death of Captain Nemo. Preconceived notions difficult to reconcile with the image of the man brought back from Paris by the first travelers who found him sitting in the café terraces along the Boulevard Saint-Germain, remembering past days and more lively times, actions and reactions, an Esteban astonishingly in his element, fully at ease, talking and talking, holding forth, allowing friends to buy him drinks, the spitting image of the old man who chats and holds forth to his regular devotees on the sunny public park bench, taking advantage of his relative notoriety—and authority, too—so that, no matter the circumstances, his reflections and sarcastic remarks on the world at large confer on him, matching exactly, in Esteban's case, his past, his stock of anecdotes about party life, not exactly acrid, but certainly piquant enough to sweeten what seemed to have become his life's definitive calling: recounting. Just like the alcoholic who discovers his life's justification in his victory over alcoholism, in the group meetings organized by the psychotherapist where each and every one of the reformed alcoholics meet, where they can give free reign to their sadomasochism, recounting their relapses again and again, their sins, furiously rebuking one another, accusing, threatening if necessary, knowing themselves, however and above all, to be like vampires, and thus similarly supportive of, and liable for, one another. Esteban had assimilated his image to match that of the stereotypical exiled Spanish Republican whom one can find practically any place in the world, usually staring down a bottle, and who recounts for us the assault on the barracks at Atarazanas, or the Iron Ring, or Belchite, Madrid, the Segre River, the retreat, the French concentration camps, of joining the ranks of the Maquis and fighting the Germans, and the German concentration camps, and whether what he tells us is either totally or only partially true, usually not even he knows it anymore, and it becomes evident that recounting it all over and over again has now become his favorite pastime—now more than a mere distraction—his raison d'être, equal in every way to Esteban talking about his arrest, about prison, exile, his disenchantments, with the studied control and hypercritical sharpness that comes from knowing one's subject so well and, also, with time, sharpening its effect, although, among his audience, for the lovers of the pure anecdote, he would always have points against him, as compared to the old exiled Republican, an obvious absence of grandeur in the contents of what he related, the simple aftermath of a tremendous historic hecatomb.

MOBILIS IN MOBILI.

There are landscapes, and then there are landscapes. And just as there are those that seem to unfold by themselves, apart from our movement or immobility, there are others that, more than before our eyes, seem to open up within our mind. That path, for example, that leads to town, along the crest of the hill. A town seemingly deserted or asleep in its earthy pattern of rooftops and walls. The path also seems little used, similar to any of those trails that lead to the nearby sanctuary, where, once a year, people make a procession to celebrate an open-air religious festival. The road runs parallel to the chain of hills, hugging the serpentine curves of the soft slopes, a terrain overgrown by thickets and scrub brush, no doubt cultivated in earlier times. A few hundred meters further on, round a bend, also to the left and atop a hill, one glimpses an enclosed structure, built of long rectangles of rough stone and mortar, like corrals or something similar. This is the new cemetery, they told me. In the distance, pointing to the line of the undulating terrain and only seemingly close at hand, the white peaks of a mountainous massif, the particular splendor of the snow in the setting sun.

A sensation similar to the feeling we experienced on that excursion to Cabo Creus in The Greek's boat, the departure, the rosy roses of the dawn, the magic bay that, upon our return, would present a pure madreporian formation, a configuration of red entrails. And, above all, the incidents involved in the crossing, the atmospheric disturbances, when, near the cape, that thick sun-soaked mist descended and enveloped them, and we could hear the fog sirens sounding, and the waves sliced by the prow went sliding by, and the stony blocks of the coastline drew near to sniff and snoop at our boat. The Greek had finished off poor Poppy and, the night before, I slept badly, my dreams filled with nightmarish images difficult to describe in any specific detail.

Or like that return flight to Barcelona, probably from Paris, on which I was waiting to catch another glimpse of the Cape, its silhouette like a lizard stretched out, basking in the sun, lichen-colored, in clear contrast to the blue line of the sea. But the polar-white plains we were soaring above seemed to extend as far as the eye could see, proud, blinding whitenesses broken only by a gigantic toadstool of slate-colored tonalities, the spitting image of atomic death toward which we were flying, when, suddenly, the smooth surface erupts and cracks, splitting open, as we fly near, in a deep ashen crater, transparent, sky-blue ocean abysms in the depths, solar sky-scrapers, petrified arboreal masses, currents of lava and great accumulations of cumulus clouds, rocky formations jutting out into the sea like mountains or promontories, a privileged spot from which to observe the panorama below. And then, having traversed the chasm, the snow-white plain once more below the blue sky, a land whose special qualities send one flying higher and higher, testing the very limits of the fuselage, environs made for nothing but the body of an angel struck down on the vast whiteness, the frozen folds of its tunic like Pyrenean peaks, fallen when his waxen wings melted, in flight toward the place where the sun was bound to be the warmth of a gaze.

IV

VEILS.

I don't believe I've ever truly been in love. Of course there were times when I thought I was, but the very reiteration of the phenomenon has permitted me to break down the process into its several phases, and now, perhaps, due to excessive familiarity, it seems to me impossible for it to ever happen again. It's not the body, it's not the sex that fires the amorous mechanism; it must be, of course, that mouth that pronounced the necessary words and, what's more, those eyes that express them with even greater intensity. But it's not only that; rather, it's something that lies in the innermost depths of the pupils, somewhere behind the very deepest depths. And also everything that we wish lay in ourselves but does not, everything we wish was ours and is not, the voice that speaks to us while we listen to it, the gaze that scrutinizes us while we contemplate it. And, above all, what is in us and only in us, the meaning we confer on the word that was heard, the ideas we attribute to one's silence, the feelings that cover one's eyes. To be in love is to draw back, one by one, the successive veils hanging upon our beloved; and love vanishes when we understand that the final veils hang no longer on our beloved but rather on ourselves, that we can never remove any more than the first veils from the beloved. I began speaking in the singular and now I'm speaking in the plural; years ago, really, I'd come to think that that's how I was, but not other people; that what happened to me, happened only to me. With time, however, I've become convinced that, to a greater or lesser degree, this phenomenon occurs each time one person falls in love with another. That's why all love ends or passes more or less quickly, sooner or later, and all that remains are the affairs. And the thing is, like the slow shifting of two heavy trucks as they pass each other climbing the hill; so too, love seen from a certain perspective.

Then, too, one confronts the fact that each person tends to create and set in motion a self-destructive mechanism in their own image and likeness. Like their loves, so too will be their aversions, their fears, their bad luck, their deliriums, their hallucinations, all together building themselves up in a way entirely in accord with the initial invention, with the primitive intuition of the element or sum of elements that could bestow upon our destiny some magnificent feature, lines which, with the most terrifying exactitude, start forming just as we had imagined they would, with the same fatality with which that motherless child—the mother fled, dead, or some similar cause producing identical effects—in his rejection of the person who has betrayed him, will, if necessary, forget his mother tongue. One need not be a Tertulian in order to understand that everything is true to the degree that it is absurd, to the degree to which everyone agrees to deny it, deeming it patently false, given that, as Camila would say, as she says when we discuss her problems, I have the absolute certainty, I am perfectly conscious, it's beyond doubt, etcetera. Because, like that mysterious well which opens up inside, within the walls of the Granite House—there, right inside the home, and not outside it, not on the surface of the island which its occupants search and explore without any result—and which leads directly to the key to the enigma, thus, like that well, in the deepest part of one's intimacy is where the thing most unknown usually resides. And beyond instincts like the sex drive or the will to power or the desire to possess, beyond all anxieties, passions, and interests, beyond hunting, gastronomy, and collecting, we will always find in the human—and with greater clarity as the years go by—a two-sided instinct, simultaneously impelled toward both life and death, which, according to the distinct proportions that compose it, directs the impulse of those desires, those anxieties, those passions and interests in one direction or another, tending now toward self-preservation and now toward destruction.

Example: our subject has the conviction that a love, any kind of love, is doomed to failure.

In him, however, we observe a marked tendency to steal love, to feel himself especially attracted by the woman who, at first, has a relationship with some other person. The victory over that amorous link, meaning its rupture, acts like a catalyzing agent.

A need for the woman who constitutes his object of desire to be faithful to him as long as he still feels the attraction and autosuggestion; total indifference to her as that autosuggestion disappears.

A feeling of nonexistent fidelity; moreover, an irresistible impulse to simultaneously have other affairs. An absence of the feeling of guilt.

A rejection of all love in which her behavior falls short or in which she does not unreservedly accept his behavior.

A breaking of the amorous relationship, which confirms, consequently, his initial awareness of the impossibility of love.

OBSERVATIONS.

The mirror of the sea, the churning foam, the saline sheen of the wet stone. A smooth wide rock, gently sloping down to the water, perfect—once scraped clean of the urchins beneath the surface—for diving off, and then drying in the sun and diving off again, and spending the whole morning that way, exploring the depths along the coast, a sinuous coast, where the raging serrated waves alternate with the tame blue coves, the sharp silhouette of Cabo Norfeo in the distance. From the road, at a certain distance and, above all, at a certain height, one obtains a better view, the small clean-swept beaches, the churning foam around the promontories, that American down below sporting a red Catalan barretina, upon a rocky outcropping, rebuking, one might say—his words drowned out by the waves—the gigantic balls that crown el Paní, glittering in the afternoon sun. Privileged perspectives, points which on a guidebook's map will doubtless be marked by three small lines suggesting a beam of light, designating a Scenic View, perhaps not so much for the natural beauty of the scenery itself as much as for the spectacle that other people attracted by the beauty of the place usually offer to curious eyes scanning such scenery. Thus, a couple swimming, diving, sunbathing on a flat rock. Or a passerby doggedly contemplating a young man sunbathing upon a rock against which the waves are breaking. Or a young man who emerges from the water and dries off with a towel, his back to a sea of whose livid chop the low leaden skies and furious clouds are only a reflection, rubbing his body while contemplating, in his turn, the passerby watching him from the road, just as the man and woman sunbathing upon a rock contemplate the American sporting the red barretina who observes them from the road, perhaps rebuking them, his face red from alcohol or the midday sun.

A passerby contemplating the sea from atop the cliffs, the frontline of long cresting waves that break at the foot of the cliffs, perhaps counting them, two, three, and even four sizable waves visible at the same time, rolling in one after another, renewing themselves, reforming, perfectly visible; six, seven, if they are discerned as they emerge from that limitless blue, as they are defined in waves still blue and now green and bit by bit trimmed in white, as the white of each one shatters and turns and runs and spreads and extends like a snow flurry, gaining ground on the one that precedes it and the one that follows it, air and snow churned together and for an instant smoother, as the water can be smooth not under the oil but rather under a net which falls and sinks, for just an instant, white which suddenly disintegrates and contracts in heavy spots, like the shadow of a net dissolving, which vanishes upon a mottled and shifting background, between dark and not dark, bottle green, bleach green, seminal paleness withdrawing, descending, below the rocks, exposing the streaming base of the cliffs, the slack adherences, plants like animals, animals like plants which drip and slip and slide and are clearly exposed as the water sinks, opening like a pit to receive the boiling white that comes rushing back again.

AIR.

Disquisitions about the boredom and fatigue which today's world produces, about the sensation of change one breathes in like a smell of rain on the way, about the coming of the Age of Aquarius announced by a stark naked pack of guys and girls, singing in the nude. To see it arrive one day, like the Japanese farmer whose disbelieving eyes saw the mushroom cloud blossom and spread across the skies, more unexpectedly than the revolution, without any of its alleged historic reasons or any other motivation than the natural fatigue produced by something that has lasted for two thousand years, to see the New Age arrive in such a fashion. Something that, theoretically, as Pompey says, can by itself generate the inflationary process which today's world experiences—any time that a devaluation on the order of twenty percent must, within a few years, lead the one who possesses the money—although his income might be, for example, about eight percent—to a situation no longer simply of zero value but one that also includes red numbers, meaning, negative values of the v–x type, with all the consequent generalized chaos.

In the case of Rome, that city which required for its foundation the prior destruction of Troy and, centuries later, that of Jerusalem, in order to acquire its condition as Eternal City, meaning, the spiritual capital of the world as long as Christian values and their most direct moral, economic, and social consequences prevail.

But why that anxiety to change? Those desires to be something different? The same as wondering: do erotic motivations underlie revolutionary unrest? Evidently. Proven by the emphasis with which the contrary is affirmed.

Like that person who dreams of being at their older brother's house, Felipe's house, to give it a name, at some sort of gathering or party, and suddenly the king or queen arrives and, while the king—some king—is distracted, the dreamer starts flirting with the queen—some queen—and the queen follows his game, and he thinks, what a pity we're here, at Felipe's house, who always has to play his role as the responsible one in the family and, if he notices us, he'll spoil everything, and he says to the queen, c'mon, let's take advantage of the moment, let's go to my apartment, and upon waking up thinks how absurd, with that woman whom I've only seen in a photograph and who's not exactly what I would call my type. Thus, like that awakening, the self-knowledge one usually possesses.

Connection to the theme of Aeneas: with Troy destroyed, instead of searching the heights of Mount Olympus for a mother who is practically a stranger to him, Aeneas searches for his fallen father in the underworld; and thus the little boy, etcetera. Or: in the same way that Aeneas, Troy destroyed, searches the underworld, etcetera. Or: now that Aeneas, Troy destroyed, etcetera, etcetera, as well as the little boy, etcetera. Or to invert the terms of the comparison: just like the boy, etcetera, so Aeneas, Troy destroyed, etcetera, etcetera.

DIONYSIAN.

Like that writer who only finds his own voice when he decides to jettison all the styles and tonalities conventionally accepted by the tastes of his age; thus, no less brutal in its sudden bursting in, the presence of the unusual, or even more, of the inexplicable, in our daily life. The transformation, for example, of a businessman into a troglodyte, something capable of provoking a surprise only comparable to the one experienced by that conscientious family man during the visit he makes to the boarding school where his daughter receives her education, in order to determine as precisely as possible how much truth there is in all those stories about dishonest abuses and sexual punishments that his daughter, along with all the other schoolgirls, claims the nuns inflict on her, when he finds himself up against the crude expressions which the mother superior uses to cut short the discussion, her rude gestures, Italian salutes, her way of dismissing him by hoisting the skirts of her heavy habit right up to her waist, showing him, with a demonic twitch, her bush, her American ass. Or like the disappearance of one of those picturesque types who never fail to be found in coastal towns, one of those vulgar, tacky men coming for vacation with his little car, his modified outboard motor launch with a two-seater cabin, his inflatable dinghy for rowing to shore, his buoy, his anchor, all his gear, the preparatory operations for departing and arriving, the care with which he leaves his launch protected by a canvas cover, his same old clothes, his pipe, his flat peaked cap, the shield of Catalonia, meaning, an inoffensive person, with all the attributes of the guy who will soon become popular in the town, whom people will nickname The Admiral without him even knowing it, that kind of man for whom there will always be someone like The Greek who will stop to ask him about the weather, or if he's weighing anchor tomorrow, or what the sea conditions will be like, until, one morning, when a gigantic fish rises up from the depths and swallows him whole, boat and all, right before the astonished eyes of the locals, right there in the middle of the bay. Thus, as the culmination of a process which, not for going unnoticed, ceases to be a process—the reality of the presumed fantasies imputed to the nuns by the schoolgirl, the gigantic fish lying in wait, waiting and waiting down in the depths for The Admiral's boat—a process and not some casual and isolated fact, thus, too, something unexpected: that businessman who appears to be modern and open-minded who, one fine day, in the course of a conversation, as he's yammering on about how you start getting old the very instant you start to lose your capacity for cynicism, or some such musty bromide, begins to transform, a true alteration of features which at first seemed a simple change of expression, his jaws stretching and widening, his skull shrinking and flattening out, his fine forehead now little more than a tough ciliary arc, and his hair—now fur—which thickens and covers his skin, teeth, fangs, claws, his clothes ripped and falling in shreds, shoes tearing apart at the seams, no garment strong enough to contain the expansion of that new body bursting forth, and only then do we realize that we've reached a point where we've forgotten the mouth of the cavern yawning open behind him, that we've come to believe in all the decoration invented by ourselves, deceived, self-deceived the way an author without any real literary gifts deceives himself with his own tricks, a handful of easily identifiable quotations and allusions blended into the text with which he attempts to establish, in opposition to the critic, not only an appreciable cultural education—although perhaps a second-rate one—but also, above all, a referential world from which his work benefits and compensates, as much as possible, for that lack of aptitude, fully aware that the erudite critic, anxious for praise, will not stop snapping at his fishhooks, will not stop penetrating his allusive mechanisms, his coded clues that never really mean anything or lead anywhere, but the research will already be set in motion and, even he himself, the writer now crowned with triumphant laurels, will end up taking all that seriously. But to accept the existence of such a process requires its own time, a new process in and of itself, this time one of comprehension or seeking, whose crucial point will be the sparkle that will illuminate the group like a flash of lightning, the same as when a person experiences a kind of light in their mind, and thinks about, for example, the notable facial similarities between Gardel and Perón, and the prudent distance occurring between the former's appearance in the political panorama and the latter's disappearance from the world of song and, making connections, he begins then to explain to himself the general's inexplicable rise to power over the Argentines and his fondness for cabaret showgirls and Evita's charismatic popularity and the virginal halo she wears which—as a little old lady—encircles her head in images of her and the people's longing as they follow their president's second fall from grace, his descent from La Casa Rosada now like the fall of Gardel years before, dropping from the sky in an airplane, and the survival of his image—*el tango no pasará*, the tango will never go out of style—now brazenly decked out in tux and tails, and that superimposition of images, the hair slicked back with pomade, eyes clear as dewdrops, smile soft as a murmur, and thus his triumphal repetitive return by airplane toward Ezeiza, with Evita once again by his side, and the whole plane singing that song about homecoming and the snows of the season, so soon before his second and, God only knows if, definitive disappearance, until he finally reaches, all by himself, the certain realization that Gardel and Perón were really one and the same person. *¡No! ¡El tango no pasará!*

LUNASOL DIALOGUE.

I ran into Celia at the Nautic. Carlos was with her, only awaiting, perhaps, the right moment to make some excuse to head off and join his own crowd. For the time of day, dusk, the terrace seemed like Cadaqués on a Friday, when the weekenders from Barcelona start rolling into town, anxious to shed their city garb as well as their habitual personality, to join, as quickly as possible, the presumably uninhibited atmosphere of the local rituals, possessed by that impatience completely similar to the typical desire of cutting right to the chase experienced by the bourgeois Catalan while he watches a live sex show in Copenhagen, hoping she opens up all at once and between the softness of her pubic hair there appears her tiny red grain of millet. The regulars, people who've spent more time in the place, generally women, mothers with their little ones, stand out not only by their tanned skin but also by the slower, more deliberate tone of their conversation, that young mommy at a nearby table recounting her experiences with sensual delight, just as she'd finished clearing the plates away which, I don't know, as if she already sensed something was going to happen, she'd cleared the table sooner than usual: not one of those times you want to end up flooding the apartment, no. With those other dark and thick waters, you know, almost a paste. Small amount. But enough to make a real mess out of the kitchen floor.

Celia came back to the motel with me. We decided that before dinner we'd stop by her apartment for a drink. Rosa said that she was increasingly less fond of those conversations on the porch, that we shouldn't drag things out, that we had a date with the Pompeys at nine-thirty, at the Moby Dick. She talked to me about a dog that had trailed her around town, one of those countryside mutts, a complete mix, something between a basset hound and a Navarran pointer, obtuse, heavy, the whole dog somehow suggestive of a man's cock, and the hound's own member itself hanging down like some mere indicative appendage. No more dogs, I said.

Walking through the garden, as we were approaching the porch, we could hear the song *Adiós Pampa Mía*, and it was as if we were receiving a vision of Mario just the way we found him a few moments later, reclining like a pasha on his chaise longue, glass in hand, a bit drunker than other days at the same time, insisting on playing the record over and over again, masochistic and defiant at the same time, as if saying, an affectation, yes, but the thing is, I like affectations, I like tacky things in bad taste, and thinking, without saying it: especially if they really get on Celia's nerves. For the rest, the same as every night, from the motionless gecko next to the light sconce to the map of the Ideal City visible through the living room window, including, within view, the thermometer and barometer hanging in the porch, an agreeable temperature whose exact degrees didn't need to be registered, and atmospheric pressure unintelligible in direct proportion to the lack of curiosity which one has always felt toward such data—a negligence otherwise only inexcusable in aviators, sailors, and certain maniacs. Suddenly *Adiós Pampa Mía* was interrupted and a Monteverdi madrigal began to play, that operetta, as Mario called it. And then Celia appeared, wrapped in a white Russian robe, with a towel on her head like a turban as if she'd just taken a bath. Are you going out? Mario said. Yes, Celia said. She also appeared to be in her cups. Perhaps for that reason she returned to the theme, relapsing into the same subject she'd been going on about when we ran into each other at the Nautic, Mario, the way he treated Carlos, the image that the boy had, logically, formed of his father. And Mario, as if fed up, as if defeated, let her go on talking, similar in his renunciation to that writer of serialized novels or radio plays or TV shows who one fine day, when the public's interest in the series begins to wane, though not to the degree that he himself has lost interest in his own work—tired of the characters' reiterated vicissitudes—resolves to finish them all off in one fell swoop by means of, let's suppose, something as opportune as an unexpected shipwreck, thus definitively ending the public's boredom at the same time as his own.

Celia commented ironically on Mario's reaction to the only time that Carlos showed any sign of being interested in anything besides his own people, his records, his smoking: your own behavior wasn't what we might call very different from what you criticized about my father when discussing the General Strike of `51, a man like him, you said, with all his libertarian ideas about strikes that were going to bring capitalism to its knees, but at the moment of truth he refused to close his shop for fear of reprisals, you remember? And now? What can Carlos say now about a father like you? You spend the whole day criticizing young people like him, their lack of ideals, lack of ambition, lack of interest in things, but when the boy starts participating in departmental committees and strikes and all that, when they start saying someone's been killed, you grab the kid and drag him up to Rosas the same as if he were a little child who can't reason things out for himself. Humiliating, isn't it? Or how would you prefer to see it? The question hung in the air unanswered and Celia didn't bother herself either to clarify for whom it was humiliating, muddled, one would say, by her own spite, everything like in one of those Olympian assemblies where the gods discuss their mutual problems and those who oppose them, but always beginning with the pact that united them all together against Saturn: a story refashioned over time, like that self-image one forms at the age of eighteen, when they emphasize and magnify their well-known traits in the public eye, they consign to absolute oblivion the things that are truly important, primitive conflicts, old man Saturn, Sky, Earth, Chaos. Something which is reconsidered, however, upon discovering that one is no longer quite so young anymore, or rather, with the admission of that reality, a recognition one reaches not so much on their own, after considering themself with critical eyes—weaknesses in physical vigor, principally in carnal activities—nor through the observation of those failings in the surrounding world—resulting from an unexpected encounter with someone with whom we'd lost touch—as much as through a fact of far greater significance, for example, some handsome young star of the big screen from our youth, whom we see in a new movie only to realize that they've now been cast in the role of the father. Thus Mario's somber expression, similar to one of those well-bred but not necessarily young or single rich girls possessed of a strict attitude and sober demeanor, who voluntarily abstains from the crazy life so typical of women from her social class, from its frivolity as well as from its pleasures and preoccupations, a position which also shows in her face, her tormented features marked by the constancy of pious practices and constipation, thus, similar to that class of women, Mario's expression, the fact of so frequently revealing—as it now revealed—the persistence of an unresolved problem or, at least, one unexpressed, a problem which, when he chose to consider it, when he tried to say what he wanted to say, he would already be too drunk to be able to say it and, once again, it would remain unexpressed, like at a reception where the subject of love or beauty or the origin of everything became increasingly incoherent under the effects of alcohol, the exposition of the concepts dissolved into babbling and stammering, until Alcibiades shows up and then you find yourself at the Moby Dick, or in the bar at the gas station or right there in the very same Mas Paradís itself, and wake up in a house which is not your own house or aboard some yacht.

RECAPITULATION.

Our author, his notes, entries, and observations, narrative fragments, sometimes simple sentences, variants of those sentences as a way of seeking, of taking stock, of that something that the start of writing a book has in common with a brand new apartment, when you're still not very sure of the furniture arrangement, not yet able to move robotically about the place. An exercising of roots no less obscure than those of the language one learns in their first years, with the same resonances one must go on discovering, the same mistakes and misunderstandings, the same apparently casual motivations—that young boy embarrassed by the word 'executioner' because he associates it with the head of his male member, and for whom the word 'torment' supposes the awakening of a long erotic daydream, so that if, one tried to explain—not to that child but to an adult, fathers, teachers—the connection between both associations—the executioner is the one who inflicts the torment—the most likely thing is that they wouldn't even understand. Like the old cleric who, if he refuses to wear ordinary clothes despite new ecclesiastical tendencies, his resistance comes not so much from his natural attachment to the priestly habit which has grown over the years, and from the sensation of nakedness he experiences without it, as much as, very probably, from the contextual evocation of the last time he found himself obliged to do the same, during the Civil War, to save his neck, a remembrance generative of an instinctive and explicable reserve, pure defensive reaction in the end; thus, it would be equally mistaken to consider our office as a trade like any other, what is usually called a career, a profession, a hobby converted by habit into something serious, into a job with which one can eventually earn a living, etcetera, given that there is something, one thing, that makes someone become a writer and not something else, something that by its very protean nature turns out to be difficult to precisely identify, more difficult, less obvious, than that of the existence of an old and morbid attraction for disequilibrium and madness, and the desire to search for an example of it, as in the case of psychiatry. Because while critical exegesis validates, at least as an interpretive hypothesis, the position that Socrates' challenge in *Phaedrus*—wherein he considers it impossible for the poet to celebrate the celestial regions—could spur Dante, at the culmination of *The Divine Comedy*, to confront the white aridity of Paradise, whilst a man skilled enough to contemplate both the whole and the details the same as a god, would be more than adventurous to ignore the fact that beneath Paradise lies Purgatory, and below that the Inferno and, above all, the ambiguous satisfactions which such a composition aroused in Dante at a subconscious level, below the cryptic symmetries of a plan where, like in Creation itself, there is no room for chance. And in the same way that some unimportant flotsam carried by the sea—a broken oar, a bottle containing a message, a plastic beach ball—perhaps indicates a shipwreck, also, in the same way, at the roots of all great works of creation we will always find some anodyne fact, seemingly suggested by some real event, perhaps by some reading, because just as a wooden doll will only be transformed into a little boy, saving himself, along the way, from the tutelage of his creator to the degree that he's capable of saving him from the ocean waters, gaining his autonomy to the degree to which he makes their dependent relationships reciprocal, to the degree, thus, to which he counters and destroys them, thus, that shipwreck which barely leaves a trace can signify the starting point of a decisive turn in each person's life, just as it signified the same for any Ulysses or Aeneas or Robinson Crusoe. A process which, generally, given its slowness, is barely noticed by the author himself, similar, for example, to how throughout the course of the twentieth century not only the human figure enters into decline, as in the previous century, but now also the landscape, too, when considered as a subject for painting, a decline certainly linked to the parallel disappearance of the natural landscape, to its substitution by an urbanized landscape, or rather a prefabricated one, where, if we find some attraction, it's only in the terrain of the plastic arts, in an accomplished plastic transposition of the object more than in the object itself, meaning, in the impersonation of the world which man has been building around himself by means of a new invented reality. And what began as little more than an outlet becomes, over time, a task whose fate becomes linked to the narrator's reason for living. Because if love supposes an alteration in the normal behavior of the one who makes the beloved truly lovesick, however much they pretend in front of others, and struggle not to reveal anything in their daily life, thus, the act of creating and, above all, the impulses that it supposes, the problems one tries to express and, to a still greater degree, the problems one proposes without even realizing it, the ones that don't even constitute a problem, the ones that have got nothing to do with oneself—the last thing you need!—change their author into a person no less sick than our lovelorn subject. No, not a trace of serenity or placid equilibrium in their creation, unlike what's typical of those who have discovered the right atmosphere in which the personality can fully develop; rather, the anguished tension of the gladiator conscious of the fact that his life depends on his skill in wielding the net. A work that impinges on the author's life in the same way that his reflections about that life impinge on his work. A work also susceptible of being converted, in the hands of an imprudent author, into an authentic shroud such as Penelope wove, and not so much because he unravels by night what he wrote by day, as much as because, like a Penelope imprisoned by the thread that enwraps and enwraps her as she weaves it, thus, what that unhappy author had proposed as a concrete and delimited goal might well begin to expand and increase in detail, to spread and branch out and split into installments, to the point where very soon in his life the temporary periods will seem to stretch out and the destination points will grow more distant, everything seeming to be just a little further and a little bit later each day, his body progressively immobilized by his own weaving that covers it, the retiarius entangled in the mesh of his own net. And just like chronometric time, that formal scheme which, repeated every twelve hours, is superimposed on our life like the surveyor's measuring rod is superimposed on the land, producing an impression of cumulative succession which in no way corresponds to the true course of time, thus, no less deceptive than such a sensation of progress, is the value of all writing that is not resolved both through the author and simultaneously upon the paper.

THE COVE.

The desire, on some occasions, of doing the opposite of what Robinson Crusoe did after his final shipwreck, sunk off the rugged Catalan coast: to swim not toward the sheltered coves but instead down into the water, into the depths. That last chapter of his adventures, recently discovered among other unpublished manuscripts by Daniel Defoe, in which he narrates how, his ship wrecked along some uncertain spot on our coast, Robinson Crusoe managed to swim to the beach and, initially lost in the cork oak forests which in those times grew thick and lush throughout the region, he nevertheless ended up establishing the first firm for exporting corks from Catalonia, headquarters in London.

From corks for bottles it's a short step to manufacturing glass bottles, decanters, carafes, and demijohns, an industry with a certain tradition among the native inhabitants of the country, and from there to the wine itself, the excellent wines of the region, soon introduced by Robinson throughout most of the European market, all key products in the economy of the Principate, and the foundation, according to the documented theses by Pierre Vilar, of Catalonia's economic resurgence and future industrialization, which has in no way been an obstacle, but a complement rather, to the current touristic expansion, to the plentiful benefits, yielded at every level by the development and urbanization of this coast, La Costa Brava, once called rugged and fierce, where much remains to be done, many corners to exploit, still-virgin points where there is always some madman who seems to take pleasure in the uncomfortable roughness of the place, how difficult it is to reach, to find a place to swim, to sunbathe on a rock, go diving, almost as if he would like to forget about the excellent beaches—if they receive the tourists' blessing there must be some reason for it, with the multiple services they offer, the hotels, bars, and restaurants found there, not only along the bay but also, around the promontory, in the limpid coves which until a few years ago were frightening for being completely deserted, with the sinister silhouette of Cabo Norfeo as a kind of backdrop, nowadays linked to the town by a lovely highway from which an occasional passerby contemplates our swimmer, conscious, no doubt, conscious and even worried by the ever-present dangers of a solitary swim in such churning waves, unable to think that nothing's going to happen to that fellow. And under that gaze, perhaps solicitous, perhaps concupiscent, let's see if this couple does something, plunge into the landscape on the other side at sea level, or even—as if fleeing the gaze of that occasional passerby—taking a car beyond Cadaqués and then walking down the path to any one of the coves that we spotted from The Greek's boat when we sailed to Cabo Creus, rugged desolate spots where, in the worst cases, we would find at most another couple no less casual nor crazy, foreigners generally, perhaps Finns, and once there, settled into our spot, lose sight of the ashen gray cove, the Finns, their towels spread out, Rosa herself applying suncream, the exterior world, and diving down between two watery worlds, stretched out, as if weightless, above undulating meadows and white deserts, above resplendent configurations of fishes, enlarged by the goggles' distorted vision, as if hovering above those depths flooded by shafts of sunlight, plateaus one might take for cetacean bellies, dorsals of sharks become crags, green manes aswirl and anemone whirlpools, gliding and plunging straight down and ascending, rising among mercurial bubbles toward concentric heavens which you will traverse as you reach them, and then to float motionless drifting, face turned toward the fast flowing blues, scraps of cloud in their wake. And submerging again, and diving along the coast, wriggling along right up close to the living reliefs of the rocks, almost brushing the nettle-like adherences seemingly formed by the crashing waves, eruptive roses and violet depths, roiling splashes like heads of hair, viscous roughnesses, mimesis and symbiosis and ambiguous colorations of jellyfish, clefts with palpitating octopuses, softly curled up inside the steep slopes of plunging stone, sharp cliffs, vertiginous cliffs, now past the blue valves and yellow snags and purple spines and mauve stars and reddish contractions of the shore, overflying the bald buttocks of sand, the sinuous outline of the open barren spots between the seaweed, evermore extended nudity of a panorama sown with those echinoderms similar to the fleshy sex of a mutilated god, as if still stirring, wrinkling up barely at the flickering lights that shadow the ever-deeper sea floor, perspectives widening as one moves farther away and deeper into the sea, spots that soon take shape, becoming forests and deserts, mountain ridges, skies, heavens, and oceans.

Obstinately, like that person who returns to the landscape of his childhood and searches and searches in the amniotic lap of memory. Because in the same way that the young man usually rejects reading old authors and only after a number of years pass will he discover that they are closer to him than the greater part of his contemporaries, thus, in life, only after having walked around and around them many times do the landscapes of his youth acquire new value. Those late afternoons when the boy, at the edge of a raft floating on a pond, considered the possibility that just as the water and the placid reflections he contemplated, clouds, sun-dappled branches, I, were an image of his own pupil, wasn't that pupil, in reality, the very image of the universe; and what's more: weren't the Earth and the other planets in the solar system and all the systems of all the milky ways of all the galaxies nothing more than a simple microorganism floating in suspension, any random cell of any random organ, the eye, for example, the pupil, the iris, the asteroid-like pupils of a boy who, like himself, stood contemplating the light like the eye of a pond in the setting sun, a boy just like him, although infinitely superior, unimaginably larger if you prefer, and wasn't the universe's destiny, ultimately, going to be shaped by the mere fact that that boy had suffered a slight trauma in his eye while playing with his schoolmates, a blow, what we call a chance occurrence, and wasn't his own eye, in turn, formed of cells whose internal structure swarmed with infinite galaxies, in the same way that the universe to which the unimaginable imagined boy belonged constituted in its entirety some random element of the cellular structure of some random organ, the eye, the pupil, the iris of an infinitely superior boy, of that boy or any of his playmates, the umpteenth link in an infinite series of beings equally defenseless and incidental, all of them totally powerless, innocent, unknown quantities, separated from one another to such a degree that, in relation to the universes and universes that compose the eye of any one of those boys who play with their friends, the eye socket becomes a space of inconceivable magnitude, and the slightest blink of the eye in the afternoon sun, eternity and, consequently, the instant of the accident, the instant of the trauma to the eye, struck by the ball, by the stone, might well signify, at an immediately lower level, a destructive process lasting myriad centuries of light-years, imperceptible due to its slowness, for the generations and generations that populate those universes—the cooling of each planet, slowing rotation, gravitational collapse, collisions, and cataclysms—all fatal in their eventuality save, perhaps, the profound reasons for the traumatic contusion, the casual fatality which sharpened the shot, which brought the playmate's hand and eye together into keen simultaneous focus. Ideas one keeps having now and then, speculations, what do I know, about whether the structure of the world that we have built constitutes the simple instant of a process or, on the contrary, if that process is only a partial and fleeting aspect, a random point of the structure into which it's integrated, passing divagations, ideas that assault one at the most unexpected moment, for example, when diving off the boat into the water, to abandon ship as quickly as possible, plunging headlong after the lure of the immediate, the vision that is offered us on swimming our first strokes in the environs of la Cova de l'Infern, also known as the Cave of Hell, that inner space, accessible only by sea, situated at the base of Cabo Creus, a vast cavity where the green hull—no less transparent than the air or the water—appeared to be suspended between the sea floor and the vault, the line of the keel clearly standing out against the igneous tonalities of the stone, rose, mauve, and orange excrescences, colors vivified by the light pouring in through an opening situated directly opposite the entrance, a rough hole shadowed by the descending deliquescent stains, at which end it joins with the sky, to swim slowly, exploring the grotto, scrutinizing, attentive to the clarities and resonances of those realms, to the glimmers and mirrors and shadows, to the obscure noises, between the growls and puffs, snorts, clicks, cracks, suctions, surging cascades, movements like entrails or bowels that really belonged more to the maw of Tartarus.

SANTA CECILIA.

Characters are people who consciously or unconsciously adapt their conduct to some predetermined pattern. And that applies to what we call real life as well as works of fiction. Thus, in the traditional novel, the protagonist is so often more featureless and less easily recognizable than certain secondary characters, always more well-rounded. And these kinds of characters correspond to the sort of people about whom other people, in real life, say: he's a real character. Take, for example, Uncle Rodrigo: his witticisms, his eccentricities, his sloppy clothes, and even his heavy appearance, the aged-scrotal quality of his double chin, his nasty badly-shaven white stubble, his ratty hemp-rope hair, features which, in hindsight, almost seemed as if they'd always been that way, as if to better highlight his institutional character in the family environment. When in Santa Cecilia, after lunch, he was having his coffee in the garden, and then, taking advantage of Papa's siesta, he'd start holding forth on any subject, Grandpa, Great Grandpa, Cuba, countries still offering the prospect of some future, a bit of news from the paper which, wrinkled and stained, he still unfolded now and then, including comments about sports, according to his particular conception of this kind of competition, meaning, sport understood as epic proceeding from ethnic, historical, or legendary peculiarities: a Switzerland-England tennis match seen as a kind of continuation of the Battle of Hastings; a Soviet soccer victory over the French as payback for the Battle of Borodino; a Barcelona-Madrid match considered little less than the updated confrontation between Achilles and Hector; the ineptitude of blacks in such sports as horseback riding, shooting, and fencing, proof of the bellicose primacy of the Aryan race; the Japanese gymnast, a kamikaze in times of peace, etcetera.

Notable, in this recollection, the connection between Uncle Rodrigo and Santa Cecilia, more narrow, if possible, than in Papa's case. Even more so, the assimilation of his memory to certain images of Santa Cecilia: his discussions with Papa, for example, linked for me to the terrace almost as an environmental element, in the same way that the conversations we had with Dionís as it got dark are linked to the threshing floor, his wisdom, his knowledge, talking before dinner, how to cure a cut with spider webs or mud, how to cure warts by piercing the mother wart with a red hot needle, and the advisability of sowing and harvesting and even cutting trees under a waning moon, or the manner of divining subterranean currents, also valid for finding gold and buried treasures. So, by the way, when the dowsing wand discovered some underground spring, was it supposed to rise up or point down toward the ground?

In general, I can say that, in my memories of Santa Cecilia, the surrounding landscape, the places where my footsteps turned with greater assiduity, have gradually lost importance in favor of what Santa Cecilia itself meant to me in my childhood, and of the people who lived there, the farm buildings, the garden and, especially, the house itself, its rooms, from the foyer to the attics, habitual location of a great many of my dreams, regardless, in this respect—unlike in my memories—of the fact that the dreamscape did not precisely represent any of my preferred refuges or corners nor any place, really, that I often frequented. But just as the occasional sight of the father's virile member, erect or not, normally has a great significance in the son's—or daughter's—erotic life, owing to the disproportion between his own size and that of the member contemplated, the same is true for all childhood impressions of the world, the relationship between the actual measurements of that world and those imagined by the child who contemplates it, the practical reality of such a proportion and of the apparent casual character with which it is manifested to us, simple impressions at times, although not, for that reason, lacking in meaning; the sun between the leaves of the arbor, for example, at coffee time.

Uncle Rodrigo said that Papa, in business matters, I'd say that, more than a mind reader, he has the qualities a dowser looks for: a bottomless well. If not, then I can't explain how he's been able to spend his life that way, dealing with one swindler after another, one shameless rascal after another; and how they've been able to find him. It's almost a magnetic phenomenon. And, don't think, the idea in itself is usually good: neither a crazy notion nor a fantasy. The only catastrophe is the result. And always thanks to that kind, good-natured, enterprising man who appears at the opportune moment and who, praised by the best references, offers himself providentially to put the scheme into practice. That man who, once more, as if to confirm the irrepressible apprehensions which Papa shows when—now too late, all embarked on the same ship, their luck in the captain's hands—he hears the man talk to his sons about a future so promising, in general, and so full of special stimuli for the boys in particular, so that not even he himself can believe that it might be true, his fears, soon to be certainties, that the man will turn out to be—as he most certainly does—a seasoned swindler, whose inevitable arrest Papa will have a very hard time not getting mixed up with or dragged down by, becoming an accomplice in the swindle even as he is, at the same time, swindled. Disappointments and disasters accepted, time after time, with Christian resignation, as Papa said, with the same composure with which a Jonah or a Job suffered the repeated blows and bitternesses that life never spares when God wills it so, to live with the grandfather, without going into further detail, the patience of a holy man which something so simple requires. Apart, of course, from the economic decline that each one of these operations usually supposes for the available capital while it remains—a goal which, the associate of the moment, the good-for-nothing thief, symptomatically builds into the deals—the price paid for taking his eyes off that temporary associate's face, for trusting that good-for-nothing thief, whose performance has not been, strictly, and in the end, any more than that, a matter of nerve, of audacity, a show, as they say, requiring a certain effort and endurance which distinguishes him from the habitual sponger, for whom the problem of expression comes up only in the moment of delivering the coup de grace, of asking for some backing, some collateral, or proposing one more exchange rather than asking directly for a loan, of maintaining that lively, smiling, more-than-properly-cynical glance between his half-closed eyelashes—it's all well-known, life, human beings—comforted by the thought that it's only an instant, that very suddenly, after an effusive farewell, without excess promises nor giving any sensation of haste, he can find himself in the elevator, holding a check made out to the bearer, and all that that represents warming the cockles of his heart.

The problem of the epigones: a man, your great-grandfather, who founded a dynasty; a son who tries to maintain himself at the same level, no longer conquering but, rather, preserving what was conquered against the ravages of time; and some grandchildren who must fatefully play the leading role in the decline and dispersion of the family clan, now without any other binding reality than the magnified image of what the family founder came to be. The grandchildren, meaning, us, the brothers, your father, me: the decline of the family name. A category which a lazy, comfort-loving type like Uncle Rodrigo, with his uselessly developed sense of humor, had no trouble fitting himself into along with all Papa's just deserts, different although sharing similar consequences—Papa, always more pugnacious in his attitudes, who knows if to his greater disgrace. Because, just as the fruitless labor of generations and generations of epigones of a certain author, and the perpetual labor of their attempts—sometimes theoretically achieved—to utilize and even develop some of the master's specific formulas, given that the secret resides not so much in the work to whose forms they mean to couple their creations, as much as in the author himself, so the grandfather's attempts to somehow emulate his father, were doomed to fail from the mere starting point of such a proposal, from his incapacity to appreciate the fact that what worked in Cuba failed in Catalonia, that a project which would have been presented and organized in Cuba as a productive commercial venture would have been dismissed, in the Catalonia of those times, as nothing more than an extravagance. And the thing is that, after all, the creation of Santa Cecilia, baptized thus by grandfather in memory of great-grandmother Cecilia, consecrated to her one might say, to judge by the enhancement given the oil portrait which presided over the parlor, as lifeless as any portrait painted from a photograph, the photo of a dead person, a response perhaps, as was in fact said, to a delayed and frustrated political vocation, to his transfer to the evermore malleable terrain of the private sector, so the projects he could not realize in public life he carried out on his country property, surrounding and enclosing himself more and more by acquiring neighboring pieces of land, enlarging and remodeling the garden, modernizing the farming installations until turning them into more of a model venture than a really profitable one, perfecting the inside of the house through constant remodeling. And now, as the aunts and uncles commented, now it turns out that if he'd not bought so much land, not isolated the house so much, a house from which it's not possible to glimpse any other building that doesn't belong to the property itself, no doubt the owners of the other properties thereabouts would have gone about building villas and chalets close by, thus forming, over time, a kind of residential nucleus, but now, like a punishment to his outsize ambition, what are distant woods and fallow fields falling into neglect would today constitute a real summer colony with tradition and prestige, and the value of the family lands—although smaller in size—would be much greater. Mistakes, in short, that a truly powerful rural landowner, meaning, the man of the countryside, born and bred there, who will exercise his omnipotence until his dying day, would never have made, errors only committed by people like that gentleman, so very much a gentleman and so old-fashioned, that old man of invariably severe countenance who was the grandfather, a severity in no way tempered by the faded ochre of the photographs, who knows if from seeking a similitude with his father—no longer only a moral but a physical similitude, too—in the same way that he'd sought to make Santa Cecilia a match for his father's own historical record, the property being one of those possessions created as the family seat or social right, for the future generations, and which, at one level or another, conscious or unconscious, inverting the relationship, end up possessing all the descendants, one of those inheritances that seem rather more punishment than patrimony, and to which he added nothing more than his frustration as a son who vainly attempts to emulate his father and his frustration as a failed politician, a result of his obvious maladjustment to the times in which it was his lot to live, his frustration as a rural landlord, due to the fact that for him the important thing was his possession, Santa Cecilia, unlike that old time country boss of peasant extraction for whom owning land is just another facet of what really matters: power.

CONVERSION.

A conjugal relationship between old people instead of a son-in-law-father-in-law relationship? Meaning: no father-maternal grandfather relationship but instead a grandfather-grandmother relationship; the full load of rancors and manias which the marriage stubbornly set in its ways drags behind it with the passing of time. Senility in conjunction with conjugal life. Chiaroscuros of a senile mind, its ruins, its secrets, its fallen stones, complex while at the same time primitive like the mind of a woman from Lagartera, or like that local inhabitant who sees on the television the quantity of things that come to pass in the world, the number of famous people out there, while he, so very wretched, has yet to escape, in fact never will escape, his small town and only waits for something to happen, an accident, a catastrophe to which he can be a witness, and thus turn, although it may not be for more than a moment, into someone who's got something to say, something that interests other people, the people around him, at least while he's telling it.

And then the married couple, the problem of living together, generally more destructive than living without a partner, marriage being an institution that only seems to serve the purpose, as years pass, of making people, increasingly conscious of their failure or grown accustomed to it, feel more alone and helpless as death steals, with the life of the first partner to die, any meaning from the disastrous life of the one left behind, now dispossessed of all justification.

Conjugal life and years passing, their low points, their disasters, their temporary, sometimes questionable, pacts and arrangements: aversion barely disguised as frightening affability.

The old-coot-old-crone antagonism witnessed by a child.

I'LL KEEP HER UNLESS HER OWNER SHOWS UP.

First the cinema. One of those neighborhood cinemas listed on the very bottommost lines of the poster, not only below the premier cinemas but even below the decent revival houses, everything very much in line with the hierarchizing spirit of the nineteen forties, with its categories and classifications established in consideration of such things as public comfort, prices, and social class. A cinema saved only by the fact of being located in a residential neighborhood, so that, instead of having to justify your presence there when bumping into some classmate from school, saying we tried to go to the Kursaal but the show was sold out, and so it was simply better to agree beforehand about the superior drama of the films they usually showed in that cinema on Thursdays as well as on Sunday afternoons, finding refuge, at best, in the mention of other acquaintances from school who, because they lived right there in the neighborhood, were also regulars at the theater in question when, like today, the program was a good one. One thing decidedly not in its favor, true enough, was the story of the man who groped little children, perhaps the same man who, one afternoon, tried to slip a finger between Ricardo's pant leg cuff and calf, until, taking advantage of an intermission, they changed seats. And in its favor, its location, its setting in a residential district, a fact which, linked to the cheapness typical of a neighborhood cinema, made it the favorite cinema of the bourgeois children who lived in the surrounding streets. A facade like a somewhat faded movie-lot set, a poorly-lit vestibule where, next to the showcase with stills from the current feature, a chalkboard announced the films scheduled for the next day; the two doors leading into the theater, and between the two, the box office, a small window closed off by a small marble door similar to that of a shrine. And, inside, the orange bones of his father.

The other point: the opposite sidewalk on the same paseo, a few dozen meters farther on, before reaching the first corner, at the foot of the wall around a vacant lot on which, since forever, an inscription in big black letters proclaimed: *¡Gibraltar para España!* There, almost touching the ground, in a small rectangle not covered by tiles like the rest of the sidewalk, barely scratching with the fingers in the soft earth, those bones were uncovered, intermingled with some residue that seemed like clothing. For some years the lot was occupied by an open-air bowling alley, probably until bowling went out of style. Ricardo remembers that it was in the bar of that bowling alley where, one morning, Silvia told him that they couldn't keep going out together, that she was now going steady with that guy who sometimes gave her a ride on his motorcycle: a lawyer almost thirty years old and, as a competitor, completely outclassing any first-year law student.

Contact elements between both points: its bifurcating character. The cinema, next to the paseo's intersection with the street that Ricardo walked each day to reach the kindergarten. The lot at one time occupied by a bowling alley, at the intersection of that street and the street that leads to the high school where his father, as a boarding student, studied for his diploma, the same as Uncle Guillermo and his other brothers, perhaps because at that time they had also lost their mother and it was more convenient for the grandfather, or perhaps, simply, because such a system responded better to the strict educational principles of the times. Meaning: two parallel paths which led, from the paseo, to their respective schools. Better yet: to Ricardo's kindergarten and his father's high school, with respect to which the kindergarten was a simple appendage or annex intended for the youngest children. He remembers, for example, that for both First Communion as well Confirmation they led them to the chapel in his father's high school, a neo-Gothic temple of golden stucco. Any other memories? None. Because, like a cat caught in a sack with its prey, and both thrown together into the water, they were all, specifically, deliberately, forgotten.

One question: what did that typical, straight paseo have that was special at either end of it? The first thing that occurs to him, that at the head of the paseo there still stood the high school where he studied after completing elementary school, his own high school, that is, as opposed to his father's, contrary to the original plan, the result of adult lives and matters, and, at the end of the paseo, a plaza with a church. The church in which he was baptized, in which, when they were boys, they complied with the Sunday rule, in his father's company, and to the which, less than two years later, he accompanied him for the last time, when they celebrated the funeral rites *corpore insepulto* for the eternal rest of his soul.

MAY 18.

Camila, her attempts to get organized, to put a bit of order in her life, like an exorcism, like a project to impose some external order which might compensate for her lack of inner order; preparing herself for something, to simply announce her intention of doing it, has in itself certain momentary therapeutic qualities, similar to a tranquilizer or a weekly horoscope reading when favorable. Ricardo's maniacal order as a projection of a difficult struggle to control the antagonistic forces seething inside himself.

Camila thinks for hours before choosing the clothes she's going to wear. Careless, however, about her underwear, frequently worn ragged.

Ricardo tends to wear the same shoes all the time, the same peacoat, the same kind of sweater, shirts, pants. Underwear, on the contrary, impeccable. And if his underwear ends up slightly dyed from getting washed with other clothes—unlike with his rumpled outer appearance—that's enough for him to throw away the stained garments. Camila prefers the bathtub; Ricardo, the shower.

For Camila the problem with the maids lies in her own fear of her and Ricardo seeming eccentric in the maids' presumably critical eyes or, in more anachronistic terms, like people living a bohemian lifestyle, or, in any case, essentially abnormal. It's no longer the problem of drinking or the way their friends look or a certain disorder in their habits but something much worse: the fact that the husband, the man of the house, might be an artist. And work by night. At night!

Thus the evolution of the relationships between Camila and the maids, the dialectic established from the moment in which a new one walks through the door: the girl makes a good start—this time I think I've got it right, seems to me we got lucky—and Camila welcomes her as she deserves, she feels friendly toward her, takes her in hand, gives her advice, confesses things to her, helps her, listens patiently, and, in exchange, Camila listens to her warnings about men, life, etcetera, she receives advice—don't take pills, don't smoke so much, don't drink—she feels pushed about, spied on, a victim of that kind of clinging godmother, of that witch who, besides being a good-for-nothing slacker—because the house looks worse than ever—apart from being a bitch and a busybody, and she's sure she steals and that she wears her things and uses her cosmetics and clothes, and if she continues that way she'll end up driving me crazy, so the best thing to do would be to fire her and be finished once and for all with so much madness. The difficulty of finding a young domestic servant, one with a modern look and progressive ideas, uninhibited, understanding and, at the same time, reliable and responsible.

Housewives as an institution. Camila and her vain attempts to enter into and form part of such an institution, to be admitted, to assume its characteristic problems: maids, the hairstylist, gas, cellulitis, frigidity, fur coats, glycerine suppositories, thieving maids, bargains, being overweight, their husbands' affairs, their chores as militant mamas as an alibi against the temptation of flattering but fastidious adventures, that fear of the world which makes one hide behind locked doors, servants, credit cards, social life, expensive things, to hide as well as possible their mean frigidities, their narcissistic infidelities.

Fine, but, by the way: what the hell will our heroes live on during their happy retreat to Rosas? A question some Balzac might have asked in an attempt to respond ahead of time to the questions that, impelled by his frenzied calculations, he supposed the reader was going to pose, that reader upon whom he so often projected his own financial worries. Given that if our author had not yet published—as it seems—some work, it would be absurd to pretend, given the country's cultural misery, that he makes a living from his journalistic collaborations like one of those American writers you see in the movies. So that the most realistic thing—although perhaps less dignified, according to the current image—would have been to emphasize that Ricardo survived off the profits from the sale of the paternal property he and his brother had inherited; good families in decline inherited lands and real estate before stock market securities, the first thing, in general, to be liquidated when that decline begins. A very different case from Camila's, in which she might rather be able to count on the dividends from a diversified stock portfolio (electrical and banking stocks, mostly, apart from a certain number of shares in Telefónica) which her father put in her name when she came of age, although they would only pass into her hands with full control when she got married. One final observation—eminently moral—could even be to point out that, while the deposits contributed by Camila were constant, given their kind of dividends, the funds contributed by Ricardo consisted, in fact, of a suicidal liquidation of the patrimony, pure and simple decapitalization masked by a greater liquidity, so much greater the more quickly it flows. It's not very probable, however, in light of the inflationary process the world economy experiences today, that a Balzac would have risked concrete figures, given that for the future reader, of a very near future, little less than immediate, they would have a meaning not only ridiculous but also unbelievable.

Aphrodite dialogue. The chats between Ricardo and Camila with Carlos and Aurea in the motel. The repetitive character of such chats, like a banquet which time and again ends up unfinished. A tormented Carlos, who gets drunk from pure uneasiness, worn out by the useless fight against an imprecise enemy. His perplexity when he thus seems to notice it, when he appreciates his incapacity to express what he would like to express, perhaps because neither he himself ultimately understands it, an anxiety similar to the experience of that soccer goalie who, after an amazing clearance kick that led to continuous dangerous situations in front of the opposing goal, sees the other team's goalie, in his turn, make a clearance kick, setting in motion that team's machine, steamrolling strategies, passes, dribbles, the almost playful exchange that comes upon him between the inhibition, if not complicity, of his own defensive lines, etcetera, etcetera; to accentuate the skeptical aspect of the comparison. Chapter title: THE ROSY ROSES OF ROSAS.

The Greek; take advantage of the nickname. Old deceitful mythomaniac fisherman. He fishes calamari with a trident, at night, in the quiet waters of the bay, summoning them by beating on a drum, and he has secret spots, toward the Cape, where he catches lobsters with a trap. Outside the tourist season, of course, the true plague of the lobster, as he calls it. A rather fruitful plague, for from the moment when it descends he prefers to rent out his boat for excursions rather than to head out fishing. A reflex of his progressive mental confusion: the blessing of tourism, which is what brings life to the town. The only bad thing, what he cannot get out of his head, as firmly rooted as his hair, are the calculations about the lands that he sold when the tourism boom was just starting, thinking that the buyer—who turned out to be simply a representative from a property development company—was crazy. The millions that those olive groves would be worth now, there, just three steps from the sea! What's called getting the wool pulled over your eyes. The thing is these foreigners and outsiders don't keep their word, they've got no morals, no proper upbringing or good manners or anything. The other day, as a matter of fact, on the mast of a yacht, instead of raising the flag of Spain, they hoisted up a pair of women's panties. You call that good manners? Those women are all whores and the men a bunch of drunkards, but the Guardia Civil forgives everything. These people bring money and whoever pays gets to call the shots. But if they come it's because they like the country and because the women, who are all a bunch of whores, seems they prefer the men from around here. That's why they lose their panties, from dropping them so often. If it would at least serve to change the customs in this country, that would be a good start. They're civilized people because they've got freedom, not like us, we're sort of like savages. And, as they've got money, they come and they buy up our beaches and if they could they'd buy us, too, and soon we'd be one of their colonies. So thank God, at least, for the Guardia Civil, they maintain a certain amount of order, etcetera. Rambling remarks, twists and turns that make it impossible to reconstruct his mental itinerary, no more clear in its progress than a drunkard's path. He assures everyone he's called The Lobster King, but even his occasional friends know him as The Greek. You ask around wherever you like for The Greek and don't worry, they'll tell you who I am. In Llansá, in Port de la Selva, in Cadaqués, in Sant Pere Pescador, in L'Escala. Ask, just ask. On Saturday afternoon, from the Nautic, we saw him guiding a group of tourists around the bay; planted on the poop deck, with his little Popeye cap, his white t-shirt and his pants rolled halfway up his calves, erect, arms crossed over his puffed-up chest, one leg braced against a peg of the ship's wheel, setting the course with a disdainful gesture, right in line, no doubt, with the effect that his figure was calculated to produce—enhanced by the wake trailing his boat, spreading across the calm water—among the many people strolling along the seafront at that hour. Quality of The Greek: to suggest, with a wink, desires and goals I don't have nor have ever had. On the other hand, what could his real name be?

Reject all closed, coherent characterization. Nothing of characters, no psychological characters; one single mental mechanism in action, thanks to whose functioning, people, things, and events acquire identity, no longer true or false to an objective reality or to themselves, but simply this way or that way in relationship to the generative mental mechanism. When crafting narrative character, have them speak in the first-person, because just as with Caesar, the use of the third-person constitutes a recourse directed toward obtaining a greater verisimilitude and objectivity in the tale, thus, in general, it turns out to be difficult to know where there lies more free space for imaginary elements, whether in that false objectivity of tales narrated in the third-person or in the false intimacy offered by using the first-person.

The relative importance of such problems: just as the psychoanalyst is indifferent, in his examination, about whether to begin with one dream or another—it doesn't really matter, the one the patient remembers best because, from now on, from any point really, from the point when the analysis begins, the very recounting of what was dreamed will induce him to dream again what he's always dreamed, although it may take other forms—so, the writer, however much from the start he hides his theme under this or that kind of literary expression, will always end up writing what he must write. The novel, too—or perhaps preferably—when it belongs to the fantasy genre, is always an objectified expression of the writer's consciousness and, especially, his unconscious. Thus nothing that has not changed before in the author can change in a work in gestation, and the final keys to that work, in the supposition that his knowledge holds some interest, must be searched for not so much in the writing as in the author. So that none of that becomes an obstacle to understanding the psychoanalyst of manifest neurotic or clearly manic personality, the which only a jocosely small-minded person would attribute to being a contagion from his patients, the origin of his mania, of his neurotic personality, must be sought in the deep-rooted motivations that led him to choose such a profession—not very distinct from what led the sick person to their sickness—in the same way that the policeman's vocation must be examined in light of the fascination which crime has doubtless always exerted upon the subject, thus, in a similar way, neither can the author be considered marginal to his work. Because just like with Freud's personality, through his writings, it's not difficult to find a powerful repressed homosexuality, thus, the same as in Freud—or in Jung—any theory tends to explain, in the first instance, the personality of the one who formulates it.

However: what is that personality if not the subsequent product of an inner conflict, clear at one level or another in the work under examination, of the reader's awareness, even before, on some occasions, our author might be capable of formulating it, as such, to himself? Because in the same way that it was not God who created men, but rather man who created the gods, so, in a similar manner, it's not the author who chooses his themes, but rather the themes that impose themselves on their author. And if, as we have said, in order to penetrate the interpretive analysis of a dream or a series of dreams, practically any of those is valuable, in the same way that, to study the creative process, it's not absolutely necessary that great contemporary themes surface in the chosen work—no longer warlike themes as in past times, nor philosophical ones, nor ideological ones, etcetera, but rather essentially scientific ones, space voyages, the possibility of life in other galaxies, etcetera—themes that can also interfere with the attempt to approach the creative processes and even contribute to masking them, given how little they have to do with the more or less attractive or spectacular character of their representations which, the same as or better, can refer to the most quotidian themes. And in the same way that unconscious pathological mechanisms are not substantially distinct—in their strict function—from the non-pathological functions, thus, and for similar reasons, the effects that Surrealism intended to achieve through automatic writing, liberated like the dream from the servitude of verisimilitude, it's possible to find those effects in every creative literary work, somewhere beneath the meaning and coherence that their author tries to grant them, in agreement with a language at the same time belonging to each one of them and common to all, which would not be inaccurate to call infrarealism. That's the reason why, from a subjective point of view, with regard to so many projections, it's possible to consider literary creation and prophecy as comparable phenomena, different ways of giving life to what is remains lacking in real existence, with a clear compensatory value for the subject in both cases. And, from an objective point of view, to consider cosmogenic, and, even more so, theogenic creation, as exemplary cases of expression and thus prefigurative of oneiric interpretation as well as literary creation.

Consequent error of critical criteria: the tendency to judge the work by its formal meanings in a context of already developed formal meanings, to qualify it in terms of its importance in that context, not by the function of the context which its appearance creates. Parallel error, frequent in every type of narrative, a product, also, of the force of inertia: to consider life as a crystallization of decisive moments more than as a process, an error which, on the creative plane, leads to centering the tale upon an argument articulated like an organism, to frame the environment in which it is developed the same as if dealing with a photograph, to limiting oneself to the time that reality would demand of the facts related more than to the time demanded by their, properly speaking, literary expression, to isolate, to abstract, to forget that alongside one thing there is always another, and another counterposed to another collateral and another anterior which contradicts and denies it, which alters and confuses it to the point of obliging us to reconsider the initial hypothesis, the question about whether the structure is really an instant of the process or the process merely one line of the structure. The supra-tale and the infra-tale, the two authentic levels of a work, in relation to the which the tale in itself functions as a simple vehicle.

The image as narrative unity par excellence, understood as the subjective correlative of the implicit, integrally structured action. To wit: not in the way, for example, of an unstructured, magmatic interior monologue lacking cohesion, but a multidimensional construction, a totalizing representation of the diverse kinds of elements present in the tale while the events happen and, in which, the acts, words, and even thoughts of the subject of that tale are barely distinguishable from the whole—similar to the way that the "I" only constitutes a small parcel situated within the extreme limits of the mind. Therefore, just as for the classic writer, the physical aspect of the orgy both is and is not the motive, given that his motive goes beyond the physical; just so, the orgy, besides being excess itself, is also something which transcends that excess, a way to access higher states, in an attempt to reach full integration or dissolution of conscience and meaning: ecstasy, trance, and orgasm along with alcohol and blood, dance and collective copulation, thus creation, the very work itself. Methods of evaluation: writing, style, structure. The need for intercorrelation.

Dangers entailed by the transposition of excessively close elements from reality, something similar to interpreting a dream according to the events of the previous evening. Apart from the fact that the most important dreams usually lack immediate reference, that clear allusion to anything that seems to explain it all. To dream once again, for example, of a landscape, a seemingly uninhabited landscape whose orography only grows vaster and more detailed each time it is dreamed, as if seen through the eyes of a traveler who crosses and recrosses it, the highway without traffic, the cart track eroded from disuse and neglect that leads, upslope, to the town, an ochre configuration of roofs and walls symmetrically huddled in the silence of the scrubland, elements in no way familiar, completely unrelated to any real landscape, which are repeated, however, with inexplicable insistence.

The same thing with respect to those dreams—not necessarily typical of an old militant revolutionary—which, like those relating to military service or high school, usually have an essentially repressive character, whenever they include agents of order—police, inspectors preventing us from doing something, chasing us, interrogating us—however much they appear to respond to subversive or simply criminal motivations, mean something very different, given that their role, far from any activity related to public order, consists rather in preventing us from realizing in dreams what, from the depths of the mind, fights to come out, what, from beneath the conscious level, we would like to effect in reality. Thus when we bend to their will—not infrequently—and even prove them right sincerely or hypocritically, in no case is it so much about cowardice or lack of firmness—despite the bad taste in the mouth on waking, caused by the confused memories of our debilities—as it is about representations of coercion that we exercise on ourselves, our inclination to cooperate in the control of some forces whose attempts at liberation is what has really left the bad taste in our mouths. Things that our old militant revolutionary can dream about for years without, when awaking, feeling anything other than shame from the weakness of his behavior in front of the police.

Javi's metaphor: like one of those homosexuals who, from what they have read or what they have heard, come to the conclusion that their mother pampered them too much or that their father lacked sufficient authority or what have you, everything except admitting that their being, like any other person's, has always contained a certain percentage of the opposite sex and which, accepting that certain percentage, they would have tended to behave according to the times, according to the circumstances, if they had not stubbornly insisted on repressing one of those two parts, on ignoring one at the expense of the other, an imbalance that cannot cease to leak into the psychic terrain, so, with the same tendency to distinguish, to individualize his own stupidity, Javi. The important thing here, for the thread of the discourse, is not the relationship established between the different terms of the comparison, but rather what is being compared, considerations which, as if forgetting about Javi, as if setting him to one side, must shift for a moment to occupy the foreground of the tale: the trap, the dead-end ghetto into which people's reclusiveness leads them; the stories they invent, the justifications and defensiveness, the guilt. The problem with Carlos.

The whole business with Mario and Celia begins to turn painful; this afternoon Mario ended up asking Celia why she doesn't return to Argentina for a time. And why not? (Celia). But Carlos is coming with me. And the stay can turn out to be rather long. Mario pours himself another whiskey, puts *Adiós Pampa Mía* on the record player, etcetera.

Answer Matilde's letter.

INVESTMENT. AMUSEMENT.

Could the look of the young men who assaulted him have influenced Carlos's reaction? Or, if you prefer, the ones whom Carlos assaulted coming out of the Bocaccio, on a side street off Muntaner, while he was trying to remember exactly where he'd parked his car, his memory somewhat clouded over, and then one of them said to him: How 'bout a little roll in the hay, sweetheart? And Carlos, grabbing him by the arm, What did you say, you faggot? And the other guy: You think I'm a faggot, huh? Well, eat shit! And Carlos felt a strong blow near his diaphragm, knocking the wind out of him, and another stronger punch to his head, now crumpling to the ground, a second voice saying, kick that faggot's pussy in. The one who spoke first reminded him of Ignacio, only twenty years younger than what he must be now. That atmosphere of boys pumping iron; each one fighting with his set of weights like someone undergoing an ordeal; an atmosphere warmed by the deep breathing, exhalations, perspiration, panting silences and gasping jokes, the peculiar whiff of sweat-soaked humidity—especially intense in the showers and locker rooms—impregnating everything, now indelible in the towels at a time when soap was expensive and deodorants practically unknown. Zizí prattling while working his weights and pulleys, his knotted cords, his parallel bars, chatting with one man and another, lisping; and the couple of fellows from the free weights group doing exercises together, alternately curling over the bench like on a vaulting horse, right in front of the mirrors that dominated that vast room, a museum gallery, you might say, where the sculptures, breaking the very stillness of their condition, suddenly began to move; and that retarded-looking guy who was staring at them as if engrossed while they were showering, his expression, on the other hand, not in the least ambiguous, a kind of homosexual idiot, don't go thinking he's the only one, said Ignacio, who, like the veteran of a military unit, enjoyed an indisputable influence over the regulars, that kind of influence which focuses the general attention on his words and converts his remarks into maxims, a quality based more on the mordant penetration of his observations than physical strength, obviously inferior to the others', to the muscle flashed by the free-weights heavyweights, for example. The chocolate company salesman was talking about how he'd gotten married, that's why they hadn't seen him around for a week, and the others were making fun of him, scolding, Really? Well, you sure got your fill of fucking pretty fast, man, damn, don't you see the look on his face, yeah, check him out, man, you look like shit, man, and so what, fuck, man, now he can fuck as much as he wants for free. We weightlifters don't want to know anything about that business, said the weightlifters, mechanics or something like that from the looks of it, one Catalan, another Murcian, the Catalan much more smoothly pumped up, and also stupider, and the Murcian more swinish and more piratical; that stuff is for sissies, man, and they exchange a wink. They helped each other in their exercises, passed each other the weights, spotted each other in their workouts, counterweighting each other, gazing into each others' eyes, while they held on, encouraging each other, morally supporting each other in their self-improvement. They talked about energizing diets, about the convenience or inconvenience of the siesta, how many hours a person needed to sleep, the optimal type and quantity of beverages, milk, fruit juices, Coca-Cola. They also talked about suits, clothes, the shape of the jacket, the cut of the trousers, shirt collars, necktie designs, close-fitting outfits, flattering colors, the advantage of wearing your hair rather short so that it doesn't overshadow your face. And with all the authority appropriate to their weight, they exchanged comments out loud about the others: that guy needs to bulk up, see? He looks good dressed but in swim trunks he looks like a tadpole. Jesus, man, and what do you expect him to look like if he only works out on pulleys! Well, what I mean is that if you look at him closely, he's got possibilities; what he needs is to bulk up. Jesus, man, well, he needs to eat nice big bowls of soup! And to the general joy with which his remark was received, the Catalan repeated: Nice big bowls of soup! scornful, implacable. A seemingly rude sense of humor, perhaps, but very common in such circles as athletic clubs, teams, military units or schools, etcetera, where seniority and prestige fraternize with a virile sense of camaraderie. A sense of humor, in other words, meant to temper and harden more than to lambaste. The afternoon when that rookie son of a hardware dealer appeared, for example, and upon leaving the locker room, no doubt to ask for instructions, he addressed the teacher, showing off the alternating oscillation of his heavy buttocks underneath his swimsuit, the weightlifters interrupting their activity in order to follow him with their eyes, as if catalyzing with their raised eyebrows the expectation of those present. Damn my eyes, I can't help but stare, declared the Murcian, the most piratical one among them. Then, heading for the locker room, Ignacio said: You see? They're all faggots. He stopped in front of the shower where Zizí was soaping up, studied him slowly: Hey, you want me to give you a hand? Later, while they were drinking a beer, he was still laughing. Y'know, that's the exact same thing I said to this guy one time, out there in those vacant lots at the end of the Diagonal. It was a fun time. I'd gone for a short run to work out my legs. And I was taking a rest there alongside the highway, behind the army barracks in Pedralbes, when this guy with a little mustache, some kind of tacky construction worker, must've been around forty, comes along and comes up to me, asks me for the time. I tell him and he tells me he's got more than enough time, and he stays, wandering around there, among the locust trees, stroking his cock through his pocket. And I just carry on very casually, acting like I'm just resting in the sun with my eyes closed. But I could tell that he was a real faggot, and I think it was really obvious, showing his red socks with every step he took, whistling the whole time. And, really, it didn't take long for him to slip down to this little creek bed, and he goes through all these thick bushes, and, soon, from where I was, I see him in a clearing at the bottom, whacking off his big boner he'd yanked out of his pants. So I shout down at him: You wanna hand with that? And the other guy, looking up like he's having a real hard time, says to me: Oh, man, you bet! . . . So, I go down there and start stroking him, and the whole time he was trying to unbutton my pants, and he kept repeating, the bushes, let's go into the bushes, and I, I could see his legs were trembling, I said to him, but you're not gonna make it in time, handsome, and I was still saying it when he starts coming like an epileptic. But the best part, when I leave, up along the edge of the creek, I run into this goatherd, with his staff and his big wide hat and he's watching us, stroking his cock, holding it right there in his hand, solemn, all quiet and still like a statue, with his goats milling around, nibbling the weeds. It was a nice fun time, he said, and he laughed in that peculiar way of his, quick and euphoric like a little boy watching his elders, the effect his actions produce in them, the adults' surprising, unforeseeable, excessive reactions, whether the outbursts come from loving affection or fury, reactions that the little boy celebrates with natural jubilation, as if inebriated by the reach of his powers, even forestalling the expected response, reproducing it ahead of time with the greatest possible onomatopoeic efficacy, for lack of any better expressive recourse; thus, like that little boy, Ignacio, trying to express more vividly what happened that day, sploosh, sploosh, sploosh spurting cum like mortar fire, oh, oh, oh, the guy with the little mustache doubled over clutching his prick as if he'd been clubbed, trembling all over, blam, blam, blam, blam, bang, crash! a barely intelligible story that way, mixed up with his cackling laughter, his gesticulations, and the beer foam spilling out of his mouth as he tells it. He clapped his hands as imperiously as possible to order two more glasses of beer and the confidence that radiated from his healthy-glowing physical vigor as well as from his clothes in general, from his impeccable, double-breasted striped suit with a white flower in his lapel, white shirt, too, and a coal-gray silk tie, that combination, almost perfect for a wedding, which contrasted so much with Carlos's cheap, worn, but so-well-cared-for clothes, an element which, no doubt, also contributed to earning him the respect of the neighborhood boys who frequented that broken down warehouse that passed for a gymnasium. So what's your problem? Do women scare you? Well, I'm gonna introduce you to one that would make a little suckling boy smile. And a suckling boy would happily suckle her, too. Very delicate work, you'll see; requiring a high degree of skill; a careful touch. The one who's coming to see me is nothing to sneeze at, either. If you like her, you tell me and that's all there is to it. There we have it, and with a twitch of his jaw he indicated the blonde girl with dark glasses who was, at that very moment, just walking into the bar. As always, Ignacio would offer her a chair, affectedly, the same way that, like in the movies, the majordomo can do it for his lady, who also happens to be his lover. She would smile, inhibited, saying it was late or something similar and he: Yes, honey pie, I understand you're impatient. And turning to Carlos: What drives her crazy is the slurpy-popsicle, eh, honey pie? The good ol' ding-dong, ding-dong, ding-dong, and the everlovin' ram-bam, ram-bam, ram-bam, oh, yes, oh, darling, yes, oh, oh, oh, now between cackles, and she shrinking more and more behind her dark glasses and he, finally, taking her by the arm, would stand up, with no less affectation than upon greeting her, and roar off with her on his motorcycle, kickstarting his machine on the sidewalk, right in front of the bar, revving it up as loud as possible. The same as when they went out together in that neighborhood, and then it was he, Carlos, who got on the bike behind Ignacio and clutched him around the waist, and, just like with the blonde girl, Ignacio treated him, took him out to some expensive restaurant and pricey bars, ostentatious in their magnificence, and he, perhaps unlike the blonde, felt embarrassed, embarrassed precisely because he was playing the role of the blonde, embarrassed that Ignacio was always paying for everything as if Carlos were his little darling, embarrassed about what people might think, apart from the sensation of not quite being up to his level, of feeling uncomfortable in such places where he didn't even know what to order, of attracting attention with his simple manners, so ill-suited to such places, with his one and only suit that was getting small on him or perhaps out of fashion or both things at the same time, in their dignified and undisguisable quality of Sunday clothes, for greater scorn, and then, that Ignacio would end up accompanying him back to his street, to his house, a street where poor people lived, a house for poor people, into which he would never dare invite him. Magnesium flashes in his mind while that blonde girl in dark glasses searched for them with her gaze, while she greeted them with a smile and approached between the tables, while Ignacio was saying, but you know what women really like? Getting fucked in the ass. You've got to do it by surprise. You pin them down nice and tight, and first you slip them the finger, and then, pop, in you go. At first they all say no, and they even kick and scream a bit, but whenever they try it they end up doing it again. Right, honeypot? And she: What? The following afternoon he didn't show up at the gym or, like other times, for several more days either. Then he talked about how he'd been out in some mining region, accompanying some big boss. I ride up in the front seat, next to the chauffeur, and I'm the first one out of the car; then I go and open his door for him, looking the whole time at the reception committee, the miners, the crowd, all of them all together, serious, with a sour face. And Zizí, mincing: But are you working for the cops or what? Ignacio looked at him sideways, then, as if parodying that sarcastic smugness of the police inspector in the movies when he tells some stool pigeon: *Sho, you jusht keep shaying yesh to ev-er'thing an' don't ashk any queshtionshzz.* Generalized hilarity, the same as with any of Ignacio's wisecracks, those present ready to laugh just like at the cinema, at one of those gags in a comedy, when the audience's reaction is prompted by the hysterical canned laughter on the soundtrack. That time, for example, when the chocolate salesman—*el chocolatero*, as Ignacio called him—arrived with the news that he'd gotten married and the others were joking about his sexual activity, about whether he'd already fucked X number of times, etcetera, and he defended himself, more flattered than anything else, while Ignacio scanned his body from head to toe, paying special attention to the slight bulge in the front of his briefs. With that little wiener? he asked. Or when the greenhorn arrived, the hardware dealer with the pudgy ass, and they saw him come out of the locker room with his butt cheeks quivering and one of the weightlifters said Oh, I just can't look away, and then Ignacio: and behind that behind, the tip of the fava bean. Or even when he joined some discussion, the ones who did Swedish gymnastics criticizing the weightlifters, saying, for example, that the important thing is having the muscles slender and well-exercised, with consistency, not that lumpy quality of the iron pumpers who are only trying to bulk up, *sí señor*, how right you are, said Ignacio, adding some amusing wisecracks, supporting them; or just the opposite, taking the body-builders' side, favoring the aesthetics of the body, which is what really matters, man; or when he got involved in some dispute like a judge delivering a verdict, or when he started criticizing someone's outfit, pants too short, jacket too long, mismatched colors, pointy shoes, bad taste, the only thing to be expected from a tacky vulgar tasteless fool. And, above all, that business with Zizí in the locker room, when Ignacio had already spent several days asking around about him, behavior that if at first seemed rather to arouse the other's suspicions, already accustomed to being the butt of the joke, fearing perhaps that this change was nothing but the prelude to a new and even crueler joke, nevertheless Ignacio ended up prevailing, similar to military relationships, how with only a few words or a bit of protection, the veteran usually gains the respect and recognition of the fresh recruit, still wet behind the ears. He gave him advice, then got him set up with the most sensible exercise routine, told him which diet he should follow, which clothes he should wear, while Zizí's grateful eyes stared back through his little glasses, hanging on his words, with all the tender love of a good pupil, while

Ignacio adjusted his necktie for him; fuck, you don't even know how to tie a knot; I don't know what you'd do if I didn't look after you, he said. A pat on the back. You're really filling out, y'know, really getting in nice shape. You're really looking buffed, all your muscles in the right places. Not like these weightlifters, if they stop working out, in less than two weeks, they deflate. And Zizí: well I do what I can, man, eyes half-closed like someone waiting to be caressed, humble, respectful, happy. Well, fuck, it shows, said Ignacio. What I mean is that you're really solid. That I like you because you look well formed. They walked into the showers, Ignacio behind. Your ass looks good, too. He went into Zizí's shower stall and—let's see how you are—he grasped his cock with one hand, as if to weigh it or appraise it: beautiful, he said, very pretty. Zizí laughed, confused: shit, man, don' messh around. Fuck, I'm not kidding, said Ignacio: the thing is it looked like you were getting a little bit stiff. And wow, it is! Look, look how hard. Fuck! Hello, Señor Horn! I mean, that's quite a wild asparagus! Zizí made as if he would pull back while Ignacio kept on shaking his cock, not without a bit of brusqueness at some moments, like a surgeon examining a wound, annoyed by the patient's queasy fuss, hold still, I don't wanna rip your balls off, I already worry enough about you. There was by now quite a crowd gathered in the passageway, all of them goading him on, when Ignacio released Zizí's cock, fully erect, ready to boil over, and slapped it away. Now take care of it yourself! he told him. What do you think? That somebody's got to beg you to let them jack you off? And he went into his own shower stall while the others, taking his place, all fell upon Zizí, oh, man, we can't leave the job half-done, this has got to be finished, yes, man, we've got to finish the job, that's right, man, that's right, these things have to go all the way, all holding him up, immobilizing him, one of the weightlifters playing the part of the executioner, finishing him off, amid a standing ovation, Zizí's face turned deathly pale, all the voices softly murmuring, diminishing, good, yeah good, alright, yeah that's the way, can you tell me what the hell's going on here, there was a sudden outburst, cheers similar to those following a bull receiving the coup de grâce in the arena, bleeding to death. When the instructor appeared, alright then, can someone tell me just what in the fucking hell is going on here, there was a general escape, everyone running tumultuously toward the gym, with the jubilation and merriment of schoolboys caught red-handed in plain devilry, Zizí sort of trembling within the steaming shower. Ignacio stuck his head into Carlos's shower. Have you seen it? They've all got hard-ons. He grasped him carefully, as if handling a flower, the swollen bulb of his member: even you, he said. He winked at him, heading back to his own stall but not before popping his head back in once more: cold water makes it get soft faster. Things perfectly typical of those years, perfectly familiar to the clientele of a neighborhood gymnasium, which is exactly what it was, after all, that place like a warehouse, a crazy old neighborhood gymnasium whose exact location he'd found impossible to pinpoint a few days before, one afternoon, to be exact, when, almost without knowing how, he found himself wandering the streets of the neighborhood, neither the gym nor the bar they frequented after working out, nor any useful landmark, not with so much new construction replacing the old buildings, less than a week after he'd been mugged, after regaining consciousness before his memory came back, with blood on his face and a pounding headache, missing his watch, his wallet, slipping as he stepped on his car keys, groping about and slowly staggering to his feet. Aurea was sleeping or pretending to sleep and Carlos didn't tell her what happened until the next morning. The only things he omitted from the account were the words he had exchanged with his assailants.

V

INCULATIONS.

For many years he'd not stepped into any bar or any restaurant, or attended any kind of show—occasionally the circus, in the mornings, when they were feeding the wild animals—except that time when Rosa convinced him to go out and they took him to the movies, to see *The Red Shoes*, which he liked so much. As much as the Liceo? Better, better than a ballet at the Liceo. And he never took the train except for going up to Santa Cecilia, as if the trips were an adventure for millionaires or something; and, of course, he was never seen with a woman, unless it were during some family reunion or some formal visit. Since he became a widower? Harmless, defenseless, intimidated, old before his time, prematurely, premeditatedly. Did he even know how to make a phone call from a public pay phone? As if from repeating to Eugenia over and over, the world's gone crazy, Eugenia, I don't know where we're going to end up, he had ended up convincing himself, even to the point of taking it literally, to the very letter, and acting accordingly.

Daunted in the face of life, reckless in business, that kind of business which, by its very extravagance, turns out to be more expensive than the biggest showoff's sweetheart. An unformulated attempt to complete some unforgettable, imperishable work? To redeem his earlier failures through a spectacular success, which might cause astonishment throughout the world and, above all, among his circle of family and friends? Because this is precisely the bad thing about the business deals your father got involved in, said Uncle Rodrigo; as if his way of making money had something mysterious and magical about it. And the worst thing: his associates, I don't know where in the world he digs them up, as if they were made to order especially for him. Stanley and Livingstone. Two geniuses face to face. The great big spark. But the one who gets burned is your father. And the other one still has the nerve to send him a postcard from Canada saying that he's continuing to explore possibilities. So, the latest brazen villain, that business of inoculating the trees, his long slow chats with Papa in the garden at home, under the lemon tree, enjoying the juice from its exceptional fruit, lacking a beverage with any real kick, while they perused the details of the project; the ignominious exclusion to which Grandpa found himself subjected, no longer merely shut out of the conversation but also banned from the very spot where it was taking place, the corner of the garden by the lemon tree, as if his discretion were in doubt, or as if he did not possess the right to be kept up to date on the family's financial matters, despite his providing financial support in everything relating to such matters. Or as if his mere physical presence might cloud or embitter the imminent triumph that Papa was already savoring just as he was savoring the health-giving—in so many ways—lemon juice, to spoil it all just by showing his face, pretending that he knew nothing of what was going on, that he'd not even noticed they had guests, that he'd just stepped outside for some fresh air. But, above all, as if he were ignoring the fact that Papa, for obvious reasons, didn't dare to let his guest see him, perhaps for fear of being jinxed, perhaps, pure and simple, because he was unpresentable.

They performed the experiments in Santa Cecilia. It involved applying the patent held by one audacious and willing—and, doubtless, barely educated—local inventor, an exclusive opportunity offered to Papa by our thieving layabout, little less than one of those discoveries that mark the beginning of a new era, the way that the steam engine heralded the Industrial Revolution or, as in the present case, the analogue for the agrarian revolution: to increase the development and production of all types of legumes—for the moment only legumes—by means of a substance rich in a type of bacteria capable of generating, generating or something like that, an enormous quantity of nitrogen that could be absorbed by the mature roots after the seed was placed into contact with such a substance—meaning: inoculated—a kind of concentrated moldy sand, unbelievably effective, because, as the inventor claimed, the culture contained in a small glass jar was sufficient to inoculate a full hectare, something like the atomic bomb of fertilizers. During the summer, the inventor and the lazy swindler, Calvet, Roset, Rosell or whatever their names were, went up together to Santa Cecilia at least once a week; they checked on the progress, the satisfactory development of both the vegetation and the fruit, gave Dionís the proper instructions, snapped photos, with a child standing alongside each plant to provide a scale of reference. Then they talked on the terrace, made plans, their work interrupted only by their own euphoria, more propitiating than calculating amid such placid reverie. Papa was not interested in the hollow-sounding planks at the far end of the wine cellar. This little head is full of fantasies. What do you think is behind there? A secret passage? A hidden treasure? The only real treasure, son, is the one achieved through one's own effort, a judgment or, better, an unappealable decision that barely concealed a suppressed scatological tendency, an irrepressible attraction to the secret and the mysterious.

Regardless of the failure of that business venture, an affair which Papa never wanted to hear about again, I only learned the truth about those inoculation experiments, or inculations, as Dionís called them, many years later when Dionís himself confessed, a confession made with the snide irony of which only a country fellow like him was capable, skeptical and pigheaded, telling a joke with a completely straight face; although perhaps it was not only that, the desire to try to satisfy a young man possessed of a mentality distinct, in every regard, from his father's, and there might have also been a certain need of telling it to someone related to the landlord, now that both of them were old men, and especially him, he hadn't felt too well now for quite some time. On the other hand, totally regardless of any other factors, it seemed unlikely that the turn of events would have experienced any change without his puttering about, to inculate the seeds or not when planting, adding conventional fertilizers to some plants, the ones theoretically inculated, but not to others, water some abundantly, others not, placing an inculation placard next to the healthiest, most robust plants. For practical purposes—the photograph of one of his children standing next to a green bean vine that had not been inculated and then next to one that was inculated—it was the same. Very true, senyoret, said Dionís, while they took the photos. Y'can notice it right aways.

Dionís told me all that in the garden, one day when he came down to Barcelona for the doctor to take a look at him. Papa wasn't at home, but Dionís said he would wait for him like always, in the corner by the lemon tree. The lemon tree had withered years earlier, scorched by frost, but it eventually blossomed once again, and although it didn't provide the same shade as before, Papa continued to sit by its trunk. Then it also turned out that the fruit it produced was no longer the same: not the splendid pulpy lemons as before—perfect targets for a boy's air rifle—but sour squishy deflated oranges. Of course neither Papa nor Dionís ever figured out that the unexpected mutation that sprouted anew from the base of the alleged lemon tree was simply an old graft from a bitter orange.

ONE THING I'VE DISCOVERED.

Like that little orphan boy who will now and forever reject any kind of affection that involves even the smallest measure of compassion toward his orphanhood,

Carlos's behavior can be explained by the degree to which such compassion reinvigorates the painful offense he suffered from the disappearance of the beloved person. His sullen, unsociable childhood, his difficulty communicating with family members and friends, or rather, his efforts to elude all affectionate relationships, his mistrusts and suspicions, his desires to reach manhood as soon as possible, and, then, to abide by a completely autonomous line of conduct, with neither servitude nor sentimental ties, hard, invulnerable, prepared for retaliation, for vengeance. Thus too, his displeasure at feeling himself the object of the flattery and pampering that adults direct toward youngsters, affections they fix upon them in their indefensible childhood; and his rejection of the habitual dealings with girls and boys his own age, his preference for the company of adults, his tendency to daydream, his detailed, longterm plans. The cause of all this? In a word, Carlos himself, most likely. A bad boy who now, at his age of forty-something years, married and with a son, turns out to be the classic illtempered despotic family man, none of which puts a stop to his own bad behavior. To what extent did Aurea's conduct—her conjugal infidelities proclaimed by Carlos to be something he couldn't give a fuck about—not contribute to that attitude's persistence and, even, growth? Was it possible that the first one of her affairs he discovered caused him to relive—just as for our orphan boy, all infidelity, throughout his life, will make him relive his mother's primal infidelity—his hard childhood—that experience whose beginnings he doesn't remember—without perhaps not even being aware of it, impelling him toward the same type of reaction as before, despite the different circumstances? And Aurea? Was she conscious of the consequences of her actions or had she also managed to convince herself that he didn't give a fuck about how much she did or left undone, to feel almost slandered by so much indifference, even to maximize things—with greater frequency, no doubt, than what Carlos himself imagined—even if it were only to see if she could finally manage to wound him, to hit the bull's-eye? Didn't she even understand that such an attitude, along with her premeditated maneuvers of attraction, of complicity, of exclusivity with respect to Carlos junior, would only come back in time to haunt her, provoking in their son a rejection no less accentuated, for being more ambiguous, than the father's? It would be enough for Carlos junior to just stop talking about his crowd, his people, and talk instead about his girl. But the more that Aurea maneuvers, defends herself, and bares her claws, the faster she loses ground, and what began for her son as a casual relationship will soon become permanent cohabitation. And Aurea will remain marginalized while Carlos junior will end up more and more like his father, a poor man who can't even understand how he's been able to stand so many years with that witch, etcetera.

More important than the development and clarification of those problems was their simple formulation, especially because of their symptomatic nature in the fevered mind of the one who raises them. And the fact is, just as the theoretical exposition of the class struggle contributes to its practical application in each concrete situation, or the way that reading Freud, beyond inducing sleep, eventually creates an Oedipus within the reader, so too, as the act of writing is defined and shaped by the writing as it is written, independent of the plot to be argued as initially conceived, by the same principle, reflecting on someone else's problem can, first and foremost, lead to a better knowledge of oneself.

Reciprocity of the process: the preoccupation that other people's specific problems arouse in us can indicate that such problems already lie within us, that when we detect them in others we're simply recognizing them in ourselves. The author, as he projects himself into his work, creates himself at the same time as he creates the work. A projection which it could be erroneous to consider limited—as is conventional—to the one the author pours directly and consciously into his characters, given that, like with a God who, for lack of a better motive, justifies his arbitrary barbarism by reason of his omnipotence, the principal aspect of the phenomenon must frequently be sought in the attributes, seemingly marginal if not conditional, which that author has granted to those characters who, like propitiatory fetishes, are in their own way symbols of third parties who perhaps don't even appear in the book, whom perhaps not even the author himself has ever stopped to think about, nor would he, much less, even accept the meaning that a keen reader could extract from all that.

But like the writer, the reader—his complement—is also a victim, as he absorbs a written work containing similar errors—or conveniences—of understanding. For example, the effects that those dictionaries of dream symbolism and other publications of penetrating psychoanalytic character have on the public, usually explanations about sexual repression and the origin of such repressions, which the reader tends to apply to his own life according to the demands of his own narcissism, so one can conclude that the cause of one's own neurotic behavior resides in the fact that he's always been in love with his mother or that he's a latent homosexual or what have you, although the timely fulfillment of his concupiscent desires would certainly have enabled him to overcome the trauma; nor is it any less certain that his current persistence is as much an impulse as an alibi for that neurotic behavior in which he finds himself sheltering, and when, similarly, if one decides to self-define as homosexual, he does so to the degree to which he chooses to inscribe himself within the conventional delimitations of the concept, and adopts homosexual behavior like that person who embraces any creed in direct proportion to how it exempts him from the problems of rejecting the remaining options. The weariness they suppose—unlike the enhanced vitality of one who, like Achilles or Alcibiades, assumes his private sexual appetites as one more aspect of his own personality—as well as the suppression, the reclusion in the most secluded dungeons, of such appetites, like the unqualified acceptance of a specific facet, of what that is and only is, a facet, his closed defense, boastful, an exclusionary and amputating posture to the degree that, as one facet opens, it slips the bolt on so many other facets no less consubstantial to the person's impulses; the slow erosion that represents, lances and shattered lances, banners no less ridiculously hoisted in the case of the punctilious homosexual than in the case of the macho man who is—in principle—scrupulously macho, both of them equally defenseless against and offended by life. But simplifications always turn out to be more convincing, attractive, and even convenient than the ambiguity of what's real, always passed over in favor of the reality of the imaginary. Because as with certain isolated dreams, distinct in their plot and separated by years and, yet, particularly fixed in the memory by some motive one never manages to grasp, we find the same to be true of those dreams that can only be correctly clarified by considering them to be pairs in a single series, interpreted sequentially, and so too for knowledge. So that, just as for a certain writer, a Proust, for example, art can signify not only a liberation but also a transcendence of life, the contrary proposition remains equally valid, meaning, creation as alienation, as distancing and exile, like a drug that can't be abandoned and to which, like a good addict, we subordinate everything in life, a work that we want to realize at any price and which is, at the same time, superior to our strength, to the strength of that unhappy author, a perfect example of which is offered to us by the figure of Proust himself. To feel oneself, while working, like a sixteenth-century painter who's preparing his powders, oils, and pigments; meanwhile the first metro train passing by shakes the house to its foundations; perfectly out of sync with the time, perhaps; or perhaps not; perhaps what might be considered anachronistic is the metro passing by and shaking the houses' foundations. What? How's that? Why? Questions that concern the author no less than the work itself, an author who must be considered not so much the central source of something as much as the transmitting agent of some imprecise and ancient creative principal.

A barrage of reflections that assault his mind as he takes a pause from writing his notes, so he jots them down immediately, incorporating them as he dives into those notes written on the narrow desk, in the unfriendly light that reverberates against the white wall, a lamp and a desk better suited to filling up four picture postcards than for writing such notes; or rather on the porch, now with a whiskey at hand, awaiting the moment when Celia or Mario or both come round with any excuse to stop working; or, now in bed, on the back side of one of those postcards that I use as a mark in whatever book I'm reading at the moment, just before switching off the light, or rather—with Rosa complaining—turning it back on again after just switching it off, views of Rosas, panoramas of the bay from different angles, from the very same porch at the Lunasol, perhaps, cirrus sunrises, careening crepuscular carmines, mountain slopes bursting with sun, insolent sunny glare of midday, springtime skies seemingly washed clean, clouds, and other images of markedly impressionistic character.

Deliberately using only this kind of language whereas, when writing postcards, the literary transposition of the tale's object dictates it. Revising, checking to see if some awkward, off-kilter expression has slipped in. Brief descriptions, their meaning not quite so plastic or formally analogous as conceptual, relationships, images as reflections of the work considered in its whole; thus, in passages such as the ones that talk about our hero diving in the sea, when he ascends toward the enveloping brightness, and which also describe the depths, the floating plains, the stars and heavenly bodies that shine in the abysses, the silence, etcetera. Or: the flowing clouds, the succession of forms taking shape, islands, oceans, peninsulas that, like a flight of birds, capriciously shadow the sea, a sea barely stirred by the snow-white wake they leave in their passing, flying toward the light that illuminates the end of the world, etcetera, as far as the excursion to Cabo Creus in The Greek's boat, when, the same as in a ritual repetition of his shipwreck, the weather turned and we couldn't make it past Cabo Norfeo, without me even noticing the real risk we had run, given over as I was—looking without seeing—to the ever more abstract field of meditation, to the euphoric discovery of the singularity of the number nine, and that night Pompey said I'll take you all tomorrow, goddammit, crazier than ever, acting rather like a caveman, in the reddish depths of The Attila, dancing, sniffing around, saying when the springtime comes my bunghole turns to Hun.

Watches. Could you take my watch to the watch shop in Plaza Sarrià? said Grandpa Eduardo. He's got the reputation of being a very handy fellow. The watch in question was a heavy Longines pocket watch, with his initials engraved on the back cover, and the watchmaker was, indeed, a man with a conscientious appearance who, be it from the excess work that well-deserved fame brings, be it from his age—not much younger than Grandpa himself—for the slowness with which he logically works at his age, especially when he's dominated by the restless, hierarchizing pride of not depending on any other apprentice than his own son, now forty-something himself, be it for both reasons or any other, a way of giving himself importance, etcetera, the fact is he said the watch would be ready in two months. By then Grandpa Eduardo had already died and, if they'd not found the receipt among his papers, the watch might have never been picked up. The same as in the case of Papa, when, also without apparent reason, his wristwatch broke, the one he wore in place of his pocket watch—another gold Longines—that had stopped working around the start of the Civil War, a watch that he preferred to replace rather than have repaired, possibly for reasons of convenience, possibly for the bad memories that it perhaps aroused in him. The analogy between both cases, the premonition, if you prefer, only appears when one is already exiting the watch shop in Plaza Sarrià where, without yet knowing why—inertia, unaware of any other watch shops, etcetera—you've taken the wristwatch, a premonition which, on seeing it soon confirmed by the events, propitiates the flowering of the darkest intuitions. Does the watch fail just as the body, which it serves as a support, begins to fail or is, perhaps, the accidental cessation of the vitalizing ticktock what precipitates the end of the broken-down body? The superstitious fright experienced, and once again be substantiated by the events when Eugenia said that her little watch had stopped working. And, like an oft-repeated old story, that one about how my dear old grandpa had a watch, etcetera, getting told and retold, returning, exasperating, to the memory.

Final mention of Santa Cecilia: I was on the verandah, with Uncle Rodrigo, when we glimpsed them nosing around curiously in the garden, trying to get as close as possible to the house without drawing too much attention to themselves, unmistakable in their aspect, the camera, the color of their clothes, skin reddened by the harsh, unrelenting sun which they were not used to; maybe they'd left their car on the highway so they could explore the countryside. A dog, let's say Estrella, jumped out to bark at them, but Uncle Rodrigo hastened to calm her down and, in order to repair the fright she'd caused the two of them, a married middle-aged couple, he invited them to come in. English? he asked them smiling—that smile of his that looked rather more like a cracked smirk, brought on not only by his natural amiability but also from the irrepressible inner satisfaction of the entomologist who stumbles upon a rare specimen, a pleasure, in this case, increased—given Uncle Rodrigo's limitless admiration for England, despite never having been there nor even speaking the language, authentic fascination, not entirely infrequent among certain liberal-minded members of the Barcelona bourgeoisie who, in light of some unspecified motive, feel or felt respect for England and only for England—by the fact that it was precisely the British who had started to show up recently to break, although only for a moment, the summer monotony, a prey he was not willing to set loose so easily. He invited them to have a seat and, in Papa's absence—surely off taking one of his evening strolls—he did them the honors, offering them something to drink, some refreshment, lemonade, and they smiled, nodding their heads affirmatively, yes, yes. Uncle Rodrigo called for Engracia, without result—no way would he remember that her name was really Eugenia when he was so dazzled—while he rattled around in the kitchen, the pantry, every moment more scatterbrained. Go look for her, at Dionís's house, she must be there, having a little chat, he said, no, wait, I'll take care of it myself. And, lacking something better or more immediate, he grabbed one of those carafes they usually brought up from the wine cellar and some glasses, and they returned to the verandah, in a hurry, as if fearing that his guests might have grown tired of waiting or something like that. No lemon. Wine. Vino de la finca, homemade, goot, goot, ees goot, vino natural, he was saying to them as he served them. And between gestures and jabbering he managed to get out of them that they were English; not Scots, nor Welsh, nor Irish; true English, from Leeds, the city of woolen cloth, yes, yes, round affirmations. Leeds, yes, like here in Sabadell. And he had fought the war in Africa, in Libya, in Egypt, yes, Montgomery, oh, sí, sí, Montgomery, yes. And Rommel, enemy, the tanks, Panzers. Yes, Hitler no love English, he said, smiling with joy, no laik English, the motivation for that joy obvious—the irony implicit in the fact that Hitler dared to confront England: and how did it end? Something equally obvious and impossible to express without speaking English. Yes, yes. The visitors drained their glasses quickly, and Uncle Rodrigo, in a desperate attempt to keep them as long as possible, offered to show them around the house. They went out to the garden and, owing surely to them having misunderstood and supposing that he was going to bid them farewell, instead of following him toward the main entrance, toward the hallway, they offered him their hands earnestly, grasias, muchas grasias, señor. Uncle Rodrigo tried to explain to them that no, that he was going to show them the house, holding on to their hands, camon, camon, at the same time that they heard dogs barking and along a path they saw Papa returning with his pack of hounds all around him and his cane and that solemn air of lord and master of the property that he adopted when there were guests. May broder, is may broder, said Uncle Rodrigo. But you might say that his appearance in the already-waning light of the sunset, perhaps thanks to the dogs barking, accelerated the English couple's steps, who after almost violently pulling away from Uncle Rodrigo, after little less than a struggle, bolted down the path from whence they had come, despite the shouts and all of the gesticulative arts of which they were the object: Stop! Stop! directions intended to get them to come back, the English couple hastening their steps, running, quite frankly, glancing back over their shoulders, toward the arbor, only to make sure they weren't being pursued by that crazy, irascible man, that old Nazi who was threatening them with his fists from up there, from the arbor, seconded now by another horrendous old man, somewhere between harsh and extravagant, sloppily spruced up, his overcoat folded over one shoulder, his hat jammed on his head like that of a fisherman, an old man, surrounded by yelping yowling dogs, who now slowly raised his cane, setting the pack on them, his other hand atop the little boy's head, a boy who was not speaking, as if abnormal, fortunately all of them farther away with every step, with shrubs and bushes between and very soon trees, thanks to the zigzagging path, definitively out of their reach, safe. Uncle Rodrigo continued waving at them with his hand even after they had disappeared. English, he explained to Papa. Some very nice English people. Only when Eugenia arrived did they learn that the two drinks he'd poured them from the carafe, which they'd quaffed without complaint, hadn't been wine at all but, quite the opposite, vinegar. (The Old Man with the Dogs.)

Don't exaggerate Camila, and by no means personify her character traits in concrete situations, or in her behavior; don't turn her into a character. The same with Ricardo. (Note on Camila.)

Clarification: emphasize only specific, negative aspects of her personality, so that, given the presumed autobiographical character of Richard's personality, the reader, upon attributing to him a vengeful misogynistic attitude, instead attributes it to the author. Thus, Camila's scheming to achieve a privileged situation in Ricardo's erotic life: to be an accomplice in Ricardo's amorous adventures; to get Ricardo to tell her every last detail so they could then laugh about it together, to be a sort of mistress for her husband, the lover of a lover who cheats on the other women with her, and not the other way around, as those women can come to believe, and, so with that in mind, to be in a position, when convenient, of stopping them dead in their tracks by sharing some bedroom but without personalizing things—seems like some women never stop moaning so delicious, so delicious—but the other woman, however, the gold digger—oh, let's be honest: the nasty whore—definitely understands the gist of it all, and not without a disconcerting logic.

Ricardo: better to make him architect than a writer. In that case, Camila's father might have been able to put him to work on some construction project, one of his many businesses. To establish a certain professional relationship with his friends from Rosas, Willy, Cristina, Leopoldo, etcetera.

Strip the tale of environmental elements, what one sees in the course of a walk through town or its outskirts, along the beach, following the coast toward Cabo Norfeo. When such situations happen, interrupt them either through their continuity or descriptive coherence, or through their continuity or temporal coherence. Descriptions, that manic obsession that possesses certain writers, impelling them to specify the scope of the action with the maximum amount of detail, the same as if the reader knew the place personally and was ready to make a list of anything left out.

Common household expressions used when referring to an acquaintance, to a distant relative:

A useless, featherbrained gossip
— a bullshit artist
— — a simpleton
— — — a pernickety fussbudget
Such a nice, sociable boy
A cultivated person, a lively conversationalist

Various overheard tropes:
Don't be a blockhead
A woman who never shuts up
He was in a real tight spot
She's quite handy
Come on, don't be late

Moral classifications:
A control freak
A resourceful man
A judicious person
A man inclined to pessimism

Other expressions, of technocratic extraction:
Good prospects
A wide range of solutions
The need to adopt a certain mindset

Popular deformations:
Muletary
Rediculous
Croakquettes
Meatburls
Crashatter

Popular talk:

a) I've never been around England. I've been around, mostly, Switzerland, around Zurich and all that.
b) Drinking as a vice: that stuff is really bad stuff, that stuff.
c) Seems it's true, the deal with the insurance policies is a good deal.

Proper names: Alejandro, Carmen, Baltasar, Roberto, Bárbara, Carmela, Andrés, (Don) Arcadio, Alicia, Lola, (Don) Eusebio, Blanca, Irene, Gustavo, Elena.

Chapter title: A Smile Seen Through a Tear.

Singularity of 9: the only number whose multiples, reduced to a lesser figure through successive sums from the elements that compose them, always yield, as the answer, the number 9. Thus: 9 x 3 = 27 = 2 + 7 = 9. Or: 9 x 7 = 63 = 6 + 3 = 9. Or: 9 x 343 = 3,087 = 3 + 8 + 7 = 18 = 1 + 8 = 9.

Go back over the relationship between Carlos Junior — Aurea.
For the purpose of its fulfillment.

Rosas, May 18

GRAFTS.

The sudden joie de vive which Carlos sometimes experiences, his bouts of euphoria, characteristic of all those who, older than forty, walk out of the house onc fine sunny spring day, the soft air mischievously tousling the little girls' hair and clothes, and suddenly he feels young, too, and with a desire to live and go out to the countryside and sit in the sun on the terraces of bars in a seaside town, and to get up earlier, and to smoke and drink less in order to always wake up like that morning and to exercise regularly and feel himself in shape, and thus, over all, to bc ablc to deceive his wife in the most cynically cynical way possible, in short, to start a new life. And with all the more reason since Aurea has gone to Barcelona for several days, and Carlos is alone in a town on the coast when the first girls of the season start arriving, different but no less attractive than in years past or to come, given the relative importance of their build or the colors of this or that garment hanging on a young body, laughing, walking, sitting down, sitting down any place at all, on a motorcycle seat, especially the moment when they kick-start it right in front of your car, not exactly still seated, one foot still planted against the ground while with the other she thrusts down on the lever, her thighs spread right up to her bulbous ass, as if offering it to him, her back and her hair in forward flight, her shirt sliding partway up from the effort, exposing her skin up to her kidneys, following the waist of her pants. The desire to give her a slap from the window of the car as he drives past, something, however, that he'll never do, in the same way that he'll never dare to flirt with one of those girls except in circumstances that, because they're so unbelievable, will never come about, as he knows all too well when the bouts of euphoria give way to ardor and the joy of life falls to one side, no more decisive nor sure now than in his youth, the years when, thanks to his many sordid experiences in the world of brothels, he came to hate girls in general, the naturalness and ease with which they seemed to accept life. But when talking to Ignacio, he said that he preferred whores because other women, the ones who aren't whores, are all uptight in bed. Well, if they're tight then you stretch them out nice and wide, said Ignacio. I'll show you how you've got to treat them. You'll see, one of these nights we'll have a really good time.

That evening Ignacio had no date with the blonde girl so he invited Carlos to go out for a few drinks. First he had to deliver a message to some big boss, it would take just a minute, and Carlos followed him through a series of semi-darkened offices, semi-deserted at these hours. The big boss, Modesto Pírez, was a robust man, with something baby-like in his corpulence, an impression perhaps accentuated by his cute, mischievous eyes and his thin, light hair. He spoke briefly with Ignacio, in a low voice, his expression lively and cheerful. And who's this fellow? he finally asked in a regular voice. My boyfriend, said Ignacio. I've gotten tired of having girl-friends and, look, now I've got boyfriends, a joke which Carlos, in confused contrast to Ignacio's galloping cackle, swallowed with uneasy laughter, Modesto Pírez swiveling his bright roguish eyes from one to the other, amused by the display, perfectly aware, no doubt, of Carlos's awkward embarrassment, his fear of the ridicule if he denied the jest, as well as the fact that it might be believed that there was something true in that joke, especially since, with regard to his relationship with Ignacio, he was starting to feel the same way sometimes, that he really was playing this role. Well, I think that my latest discovery's going to be more interesting for your friend, who's not tired of girls, than for your shameless ass, he said. He'd tossed a bundle of photographs onto the table, various perspectives, angles, details, of a naked woman in conventionally erotic postures; she was good-looking, suggestively attractive. The photos, obviously, had been taken right there in that same office, some of them even in the armchair occupied by Modesto Pírez, now offering them an English cigarette, lighting them, watching them, those dark, vivacious eyes, important as the center of the pink circles that configured his face as much as his colorless eyebrows and barely perceptible eyelashes. And when will your lordship deliver her into my hands? said Ignacio in that affected accent he sometimes adopted, as if he were on stage. And Modesto Pírez: Weren't you just saying that you've grown tired of these things?

Modesto Pírez was an agricultural engineer, a peasant farmer from Murica, according to Ignacio, one of those filthy rich Murcians who still wore alpargatas and long striped shirts. The night Carlos went out with them and with the two girls, Marujita, the girl in the photo, and one of Modesto Pírez's secretaries, they joked about it for quite a while. But don't think, said Modesto Pírez, that's my style exactly: agricultural practice, the actual practice, not the bureaucracy in which, thanks to life's circumstances, I've found myself getting involved. You know how enjoyable those pollination experiments are, trying out new seeds, grafting a tree with your own hands? Here, where you see me, I'll graft you whatever you like. You, because you're a scoundrel from the city, a crafty rascal, and perhaps you don't understand it, but I assure you that I hope to retire someday right in Murcia, on one of those splendid properties out in the countryside, you know? The house all well-appointed, with spacious rooms, and fruit trees, fruit trees, fruit trees. Ah, and especially, of course, always with good company, and he hugged the two women around the hips. Fine, fine, said Ignacio, you've still plenty of work to do, you're just gonna have to suck it up. Suck it? (Modesto Pírez). That's your speciality, son, and he squeezed the women again while they all laughed.

For dinner they ate tapas, going from tavern to tavern around Calle Escudellers, places to which Modesto Pírez guided them with consummate ease, places he knew and where they knew him, and took great pains to welcome him, some house specialties for you Don Modesto, with our compliments. Carlos had too much to drink, too quickly, red wine, white wine, claret, while Modesto Pírez ordered tripe, fried anchovies, grilled chorizo, spicy peppers, or whatever it was, what you had to order in each place, little glasses that the barman refilled obsequiously as soon as Carlos drained them, with that haste that indicates nervousness, or rather, fear, typical of the young man who talks and talks about women with his friends, talking about going out around there some night, and then that night arrives and he finds himself facing the situation that he'll end up having to go to bed with a woman for real and not in a fantasy like in the stories he tells. And because that world of power and money and easy women was so alien to him he acted all the more reckless, more like those women, in fact, than Modesto Pírez or Ignacio. Apart from the inexorable approach of the moment in question, its solemn character heightened by the very waiting itself, the time it took Ignacio to finally set their night on the town, and the way in which everything was now being channeled and organized above and beyond the banal chatter, the mystery about what was going to happen later, meaning, how he should behave without looking conspicuous, and which role one must play when three men share two women. And the poise these women had, their sophistication, acting as if nothing special was going to happen, almost managing to convince him that's how everything was going to end up, everyone just heading home, nothing more than friends. And the impossibility, this late in the game, of pretending to be feeling ill and really just going back home. A nice strong coffee for the boy, said Modesto Pírez. And, above all, don't mix.

Modesto Pírez's apartment. A vast dark room, or rather, barely illuminated, everyone seated on the carpet around a low Moorish table. Modesto Pírez, now wearing a kind of jellaba, passed around a long pipe packed with kif, bearing ornamental motifs in red and green. This is what I call quality, he says. Recently brought back by a friend; we fought the war together, but he's career military. He's got a nice problem, the boy. In short, the stuff of life. He pats Carlos encouragingly on the back: it won't do you the least bit of harm, son. What definitely won't do you any good is to drink more alcohol. He smiles, and Carlos smiles, too. In fact, the secretary, now that's she's removed her glasses, is not at all bad looking. But the other girl has got the tits, Ignacio has lifted them right out through the low cut in her sweater. His cheek is wet, pressed against the carpet soaked with cognac, one of the glasses spilled. He's alone and from some room he keeps hearing groans, sighs, rhythmic sounds like splashes. Ignacio approaches him, silhouetted by the light from a doorway behind him, naked. He sits him up firmly, come on, fuck, man, snap out of it. In the bed, also naked, Marujita, the girl in the photograph, her eyes closed the same as if she were sleeping, her mouth smiling ever so slightly. The smell of semen, she, the bed, Ignacio, Ignacio who is helping him to take off his clothes, don't fuck around, dammit, wake up. And Carlos saying I'm not drunk, goddammit, now you're gonna see if I'm drunk, turning over onto the girl, sucking on her breasts, caressing her oozing sex, holding his own as if eager to slip it in, his member horrendously inanimate, just what he feared from the start, see you're gonna see, and Ignacio's joy as he ended up intervening directly, pulling him by the penis while, without letting go, he pushed one body against the other as if to facilitate him getting hard, saying open up your pussy nice and wide, dammit, Carlos repeating see now you're gonna see, each time more incoherently, his eyelids drooping as if he were overcome with sleep, although he would have sworn that he'd seen Modesto Pírez's secretary with her overcoat on, taking her glasses out of her purse, a dream half-feigned, half-real which suddenly seemed to be really possessing him. What's wrong with the kid?: Modesto Pírez's voice. What's gonna happen to him?: drunk as a lord: Ignacio. Nothing, man, we'll get him hard right away. Her sex against his mouth, above, legs spread, cutting off his air, and that suction on his own sex, on his lower abdomen, on his thighs, on his ass, a tongue against his ass, come on, boy, relax, easy, easy, a tongue or maybe a wet finger, sinking, penetrating and, above all, opening him up wider with a progressive rotating motion, something that smelled like cosmetics, while they turned him over on one side and he noticed that the suction was making his penis get longer and harder, and now, between his buttocks, the rotating motion gave way to a soft but deeper and more direct penetration, toward his entrails, as if reaching his sex from its roots, internally, everything very fast, the venereal emission that came, contagious in its contractions, you might say, to judge by the growing forcefulness of the shoving attack, by the accelerated collision of Modesto Pírez's flesh against his backside, by the increasingly bronchial snorts that sounded over his shoulders, how the suction of which he was the object turned into a spasm, the length of his penis as a transmitting element of snorts and tensions, gasping thrusts now quieting, coming more slowly and calming down like the tide in the sea as the storm subsides, while he felt emptier and emptier, draining away and falling slowly into the darkness, not without first half-opening his eyes for a moment, time enough, however, to see Marujita's head moving around between Ignacio's thighs, an Ignacio in forced torsion upon the bed, leaning on his shoulder, lifting his head, his eyes, his soft lips, the very expression of the blowjob, that peculiar expression so distinct from that which follows a licking, more relaxed, less hazy, the mouth similar, by the general greedy slackness of his features, still as if re-adjusting themselves, to the mouth of one who has barely just finished eating a dessert. Ignacio dressing him, shaking him, get up, goddammit, it's almost morning, pulling up his pants, putting his arms into his shirtsleeves, putting on his socks, his shoes. What's going on? says Carlos. Where are we? What do you think is happening? Party's over (Ignacio). Fuck, what a headache (Carlos). And what did we all tell you? Not to drink more! Not to drink! (Ignacio). He accompanies him to the bathroom, helps him to wet his face, his hair, hands him a towel, a comb. Try to piss, get rid of as much alcohol as you can.

Carlos returns to the bedroom: the bed empty and all messed up, the smell of seminal essences, Marujita's clothes over a chair, the thin rays of light in the window. What are you waiting for? he hears Ignacio say. Don't you see they're sleeping like saints? Come on, let's get out of here already.

The pale cold morning in the nearly deserted streets, the watered-down light from the street lamps. They wait in silence for a taxi to come by. I'll come with you, man, I prefer to see you home. They don't talk during the taxi ride either, a ride almost as imperceptible as seemingly instantaneous, suddenly in front of his building without even noticing, Ignacio saying, well, alright, man, see you around. Now, straight to bed, and tomorrow have a nice long shower and lots of coffee, Carlos nodding from the sidewalk, as if his place really did have a shower.

For several days he was unsure about whether or not to go back to the gym to pick up his shorts and his towel, finally deciding to forget about it, Ignacio's words dancing in his head, for weeks, his remark about how I'll show you how to stretch out a tight woman or words to that effect.

SIX DAYS.

The tale of days spent in Rosas after the rupture with Alfonso, with everything that Alfonso's world represents, those touches that inevitably surface now and then, ever so slightly fogging the technocrat's aseptic exterior, indicative lapses like the one he had, right after the last meeting which I attended, still employed by the company, a convention, a conference, call it what you like, of salesmen, when I told him I had to speak to him and, while we walked to his office, he kept saying the same thing, as if instead of speaking to me he was still addressing his audience of tasteless fools, in the heat of the moment, and no longer in a political meeting of markedly Francoist flavor: we're living in the social era, nowadays it's the working man who's got the money, the laborer, etcetera. Words that only served to facilitate my decision to quit my job because they were so much a part of that world of Alfonso, from which I planned to break away however possible, to distance myself from that world as far as possible, in short, the world I'd grown up in. Thus my increased awareness about all that, similar to how the man whose virility has declined now finds the word "sex" exasperating. Aversions, intolerances that one has always had although they are only revealed as such with the passing of time, and then it's usually too late to find an accurate explanation for them, accurate and not simply rational, not the kind of explanation that clears everything up and that one, at any moment, can construct to their greater convenience. What's usually called visceral repugnance, thus relating the impulse to its result: nausea. Revulsion toward the expressions of an age—the songs of the forties, for example, the uniforms, bullfights, flamenco, processions, las mantillas, the odor of the church, etcetera—that they're nothing but the environmental elements of the true motive, of the forgotten fact, a forgetfulness we can cover with perfect alibis of ideological or political meaning, etcetera. Something like pretending to rationalize—supposing that you really wake up some day, which is supposing a great deal—the inherent cruelty of children's games, the infinite capacity for sadism that children are capable of extracting from a song like *tournez, tournez, petit moulin, frappez, frappez*, etcetera. The songs we used to sing, the games we used to play.

In short: a young writer and his wife's sojourn in Rosas, after quitting that company where he worked in order to dedicate himself exclusively to his true calling; a middle-aged married couple, owners of a motel, in Rosas, forms a friendship with a young couple, guests at their hotel, and become witnesses to their troubled relationship: a young architect and his lover, in a final attempt to repair their deteriorated relationship, return to the jumping-off place, Rosas, favorite location for their escapades at the start of the adventure, an evocative tale of the days which the protagonist spent in Rosas with his wife, of the friendly relationships they established with the owners of the motel where they stayed and of whose complex tensions they became fortuitous witnesses, of the dissipated ambience in which they saw themselves enveloped since they fell in with some acquaintances from Barcelona, of the unexpected end of all that; a compilation of the notes taken by the protagonist during his stay in Rosas for a work in progress, intermixed with other notes, memories, reflections, commentaries about their daily life, etcetera; a tale that, even as it refers to the daily anecdotes of the protagonist and his wife or lover in Rosas, includes, alongside the notes for a novel he's writing, as well as reflections, memoirs, etcetera, the note about the anecdote of that stay in Rosas, a recreation of reality with all the deformations and transpositions belonging to him and which—even as they're the protagonist's projection on reality, upon a reality to which he attributes all his personal obsessions—suppose, similarly, an incidence of the work in the author, as much for what they reveal about himself as for what they conceal. To juxtapose, or rather, superimpose, on the optimal variant, various materials belonging to the rest of the variants.

The notes that our protagonist writes in his apartment. The chats on the porch with the couple who run the motel. The confidences she shares with him on the terrace at the Nautic. Our man's problematic relationship with his own wife. His solitary walks around the edges of town, as if refusing to deal with people, as if he wished to not even be seen, as if impelled by a paranoid predisposition similar to that which can, and does, arise in the boy thanks to the discovery of the sinister universal conspiracy of which he's been a victim: parents, teachers, clergy, relatives, adults in general, their newspapers and magazines, shop display windows, street decorations, parades and marches, processions, and receptions patronized by both the local as well as the national authorities, the overall organization of the world, everyone collaborating in that hoax—the arrival of the Three Magi loaded with gifts—devised especially for him, at his expense, thus, only comparable to all that, the spectacle of a coastal town in high season, the scenery involved, the floating population, the people who arrange to meet on the terraces of the bars, with the unique intention, you might say, of driving someone crazy, of spoiling his walks along the beach, along the seaside promenade, following the sinuous outline of the coast toward Cabo Norfeo. The friends from the yacht, their orgiastic nocturnal sailing soirees, alcoholic energy and brazen promiscuity. The maritime excursions, both on the yacht as well as on The Greek's boat. A weekend in Cadaqués, with those from the yacht, around the beginning of August; a visit with the local notables and their habitual court hangerson, those bourgeois snobs intermixed with a motley crew of phony hippies, pretend artists, and wise guys in peaceful and saprophytic coexistence which some people, outsiders, imagine to be nonstop group sex, pure copulative excess in an atmosphere pungent with marijuana smoke. Structure the notes written down about all that, articulate them in a group. Like the ones about memories, like the ones about dreams, including the one from last night. And the marine depths that expand before the diver's eyes. And the Ideal City. And Poppy. And, most of all, the boat trip to the Cape. Rosas, as a scene, amounts to a town which self-destructs in order to rebuild itself anew; the least important thing is the local color, useful, at most, as raw material for images that define not so much what was observed as they do the observer, images that, like those from a dream, express something very different from what they literally represent. The references to that, a simple detail for specifying the plot; in reality, a mere point of access to the plot, which has so many possible access points. Any other town with similar characteristics would work just as well as Rosas.

Those days in Rosas, last spring, were really exceptional, watching the work as a whole crystalize, considering its broad outlines as well as its details, that simple fact whose later development converts it into a narrative nucleus, that observation which, duly worked, is transmuted into invention. You might say that even my dreams at that time were particularly meaningful. Also, it seems important to me that the torturous complications which the work has undergone since then might be of an internal order, the fruit of its own necessity, which doesn't respond to any kind of external phenomena, events like Alfonso's death, around the middle of autumn, not even three months ago yet. One of those Sundays when Barcelona ends up empty, everybody gone out of town to eat wild mushrooms in some little mountain village, if not to hunt for them personally through the forests, like people hunting for gnomes. The inopportune coincidence of his heart-attack with the slowness of the traffic crawling back into the city, which prevented getting him to the Hospital de San Pablo in time. Now, almost nine months later, who would have thought, since those rarely-equaled days of creative intensity spent in Rosas, even now working on the notes written then, reshaping them, restructuring them, still resolving the denouement, if you can consider, that is, the solution of continuity imposed on that magmatic accumulation of materials whose very abundance and frequently contradictory feeling sometimes only complicate the simple task of cutting and trimming to be an ending.

A job, at times, not unlike forced labor, the prisoner no more free than we are to abandon the task, for the more we ask ourselves what the fuck it is that blocks us from it, what the fuck are we doing sitting there, placing one word after another like an ant storing up grain, unsettled perhaps by the call of the street, that street somehow now wider and more clear without the foliage from the plane trees, now naked and pruned, as if less cluttered and more clearheaded, when, despite the weak, washed-out sunshine and the fur collars and the fluttering scarves of the passersby, there's something in the city that makes us aware that it will soon be springtime. The scant desire to work, the excuses one searches for, digressions, drifting thoughts, memories, walking with Matilde through the Parc de Sceaux one summer afternoon, for example, then stepping out to buy *The Herald Tribune* or *Le Monde*—if they've arrived—and some magazine—if it hasn't been confiscated—and pick up the mail on the way and, as if the mailman had proposed to offer us new excuses for evasion, transmission of thought, premonitions, etcetera, we find ourselves with a letter from Matilde, suggestive, even before opening it, that in Paris now, considering how lousy the winter has been, the crocuses must be starting to poke their heads up from the earth and the yellow of the forsythia starting to stand out on the green, a description that becomes diluted while one continues reading, Dear Raúl, how long do you think a true, unconditional love can endure? Because this time, and it's serious, I think that it's definitive, the real thing. But I'd like to know your opinion, that you two meet each other. Are you planning on visiting Paris anytime soon? If not, maybe the best thing would be that we come to Spain as soon as possible. Is it warm enough yet to go swimming in the sea? Will we find an open hotel in some seaside town? Yours more than ever, Matilde.

I remember that in one of her other letters Matilde told me—one of those sayings so characteristic of her, something she doubtless picked up from that literary tone you would say is consubstantial with contemporary French culture—that love is not a necessity but a fatality. The problem with a saying like that, lies not with its validity or lack thereof, usually far grander than the specific subject to which it's applied; thus, in the case that occupies us, among others, the act of creation. The structure of a work has its own internal logic, it's true, a logic which shapes it in one way and not another. However: what lies behind that internal logic? What impulse has led the author to organize it precisely in such a manner, to choose this solution, not that one, from among all possible logical solutions? Questions whose answer—due to their very general character—it would be excessively imprecise to assign to the instinct of life and the instinct of death, principles nested in distinct proportions and hidden under diverse appearances—sex, power, richness, vengeance, etcetera—inside of each man, the ultimate key to his behavior, no matter how much they only acquire their true significance once the first youth is past, when the problems that tormented us until then begin to cease doing so, not so much for being inexact or irrelevant as much as, like all youthful problems, for being anachronistic; when one begins to be capable of remodeling the image—always more flattering—that they had made of themself; when, at the mercy of such a current of skepticism, one is now incapable of making new friends, and converts friendships and loves acquired into a routine, into dates at fixed times, fixed days; when he ends up asking himself but what is there that's definitely constructive in young people's attitude today, what solution do they offer for things, and all that. Because, like people that begin not with astonishment but with the mere registering of natural wonders, and then find their development in the effort to make the surrounding people comply with the beliefs which through the centuries and millennia have been settling in their heart, in order to discover, only then, that those beliefs, once imposed, are neither more firm nor less perishable than those belonging to the other people at hand, no more or less than so many others that must be or have been, to the point that, from then on, more than the fatigue or the years, it is this very confirmation that makes them go ceding terrain bit by bit, consumed by some habits whose reason for being has ceased to exist, in such a way that they no longer find their consolation even in the most exciting activities, and so it goes for each and every man. Except that just as the superiority of socialism can be as obvious in the USSR as that of free enterprise in the USA, so, too, the exclusive veracity of one's respective religious beliefs, as well as the natural character of the moral habits they comprise, be they Christian, Buddhist, or Islamic, to whomever has been raised according to such habits or beliefs—thus, less normal but much more interesting thanks to its apparent exception to the norm, is the case of the young son of the bourgeoisie who becomes a revolutionary after reading only a single Marxist text, or the case of that young reader transformed into an Oedipus after reading a single essay by Freud, and not so much for the fact that personal motivations are prone to reveal, in each case, as much as they conceal. And, analogously, insofar as what the act of creating means, the author, even when he affirms or thinks the opposite, what he creates is not so much self-expression as self-concealment; and precisely to the degree to which he affirms or thinks the opposite, to the degree to which he feels sure of the materials he employs. That author not of a work but of his own work, a work in which he includes specific autobiographical elements in the exposition of the tale for the simple reason that he has them more at hand than others and they are equally useful to his purposes, whenever that narrative material will be subjected, in any case, to the process of transformation which constitute the work in itself, little less than indifferent to the final result made from the raw material selected, in the same way that when analyzing a specific person's dreams, starting with one or another makes no difference, both being equally valid in the final analysis. Simple reasons, obvious arguments, evidence, terms, notwithstanding, which will make the comparison much more exact than what one supposed when establishing it. Thus there's nothing unusual, for example, that as a boy one had a dream about copulating with a big-breasted woman with a pink erect penis that springs up right above the little hole; that he copulates or at least tries to, of course, ah, and that's right, in a bed that looks like Aunt Magda's, all very infantile, perfectly explicable either by the bisexuality perfectly appropriate to the age, or by the unfamiliarity one usually has at that age about the specific form of the central distinguishing feminine feature. And it would be silly to throw your hands up in the air if, years later, more knowledgeable now about these questions, one dreams that he finds himself penetrating a woman he doesn't know—or that, better yet, like the last one, she has no face, meaning, she has one but he does not look at her features or does not remember them—but that she's obviously dead because her body is hollow, one's own sex sort of dancing around in that empty dusty interior; it can be important in this case that the dreamer was in Rome at that time, and that to return home—near the Piazza Bologna—each day he had to walk past a great wall from which hung hands, arms, legs, heads, livid members, all down the street, votive offerings bright as the moon, odor of candles and the forms of worshippers on the sidewalks, on their knees, arms crossed, a rosary clutched between their fingers. And similarly, within the genre, that dream set in Santa Cecilia, my encounter with Aunt Magda, conscious that I was walking toward a dead woman even though, to judge by her look and by the signs of affection she was showing me, she seemed alive; and my reaction: to kiss her and embrace her and, crying, beg her not to leave. An adult crying like a little boy? Well, adult or perhaps boy, a boy that was crying like an adult. That's how things work in dreams; one recognizes what they are and that's it. Or that a specific person is a specific person although they don't look like them at all, or it's about someone whom we only know by name or from photographs. And to dream, even, that one is visited by their mother, a stranger, a person about whom one doesn't have the slightest memory, about whom, the same as in the case of Aunt Magda, you only know that she is dead. The place is the same: the verandah in Santa Cecilia; or perhaps the garden, in front of the verandah, and there are other people present, the dark gentlemen, dressed in suits as for a wedding. A woman who is very beautiful though somewhat cold, or severe, rather, almost cruel in the distances she maintains. I know that you misbehave, she says; that you're a terrible boy. And he, defenseless in front of her, not daring now to embrace her let alone even approach her, also crying now (you, a full-grown man?), crying uncontrollably, motionless, arms feeling filled with sand, trying to apologize, to excuse himself, telling her not to leave him because of that, despite everything, that she not leave him, she looking at him with her intensely blue eyes (were they?), her lips no more smiling than her gaze; wearing a tailored brown suit, or at least the hat she's wearing, that looks like felt, is brown, adorned with a long feather; a cap more than a hat, properly speaking, a small, funny cap in the style of Robin Hood.

All very natural: absurd scenes, because for some reason they belong to a dream, at the same time, a very simple explanation, taking into account the concrete circumstances of each case, dreams separated from each other by intervals of even several years, but that for some unspecified—if not to say capricious—reason they have remained especially preserved in the memory. The problem only comes up when it occurs to one—ideas that come into one's head without knowing why—to consider them not separately but as a group, forming part of a sequence, and then to establish connections between one and another, to relate them and situate them in a series starting from any connecting link, their succession in time, for example, the order in which they were dreamed. Or to register the consequences of the first two—seminal discharge—against the sexually weaker response of the other ones, as the woman's physical presence is configured and concrete, as she approaches and personalizes her identity, as her own emotional response grows. Or wondering about the reasons for that persistence in the memory which is common to them, questions that seem to lie in wait for us and whose answer we feel to be imminent; something that is being resolved at a higher level of consciousness, being integrated into it. An invitation, like the afternoon sea, sunny and calm, calling us, surely, the way the sirens call, not toward the shore but rather from the shore out into open sea, a sea which one goes diving into, as if heeding that call, diving and diving down into the warm splendors until losing sight of the rest of the sublunary world. Later, out of the water, feeling the friction of a towel on our body, the problem will come back to us again, now from a different perspective, as if while we were diving our mind had continued working without our noticing and now, in an only apparent solution of continuity, things offer themselves to us in a different light. And then it will turn out that everything that had a diaphanous significance, and some obvious immediate references separately considered, acquires a completely distinct sense as it becomes part of a series, a series that we have established almost without knowing how, in agreement with the same principle according to which ideas come to our head and take shape into a work. Because similar to that orgy which, for those who partake in it—or for those who only imagine it and nothing more, always more numerous—there forms a group not reducible to the sum of its diverse elements considered separately, because its peculiarity resides precisely in that group character; similar also to an erotic fantasy witnessed, with impunity, within the darkness of the cinema, examined in the pages of a specialized publication in the shelter of the tranquil hearth and home, or simply imagined, thus, like a fantasy of that kind which, within the play of the various erotic components brought together, conceals the frenzy of the contradictions and alternatives that can torment a sleepless mind, so too, with such ritualistic features, of a ceremony subject to a pattern and at the same time to a sequence, the oneiric material that we demand in order to reach an accurate interpretation. And also like that orgy of savage origins, those wild forays in which along with the smell of goat and laurel and sperm and wine must also be mixed the smell of blood, practices frequently excessive even for the quotidian sensibilities of ancient peoples, also like in those celebrations where the sensual stimuli are only a point of departure, a formula in development, an ascensional process, a pathway to a state which propitiates full integration or dissolution of the consciousness, as well as the production of the work, its creation. And in the same way that that new interpretation of a dream modifies the image that the dreamer had formed of himself, so all work of creation modifies its creator to the degree that it is realized. Because just as the gods are simultaneously created and destroyed, so, too, the author. And if the creation of the world doubtless modified the life of the gods, beginning with that of Jehovah himself, implicating him even in the vicissitudes of his work up to the point that He Himself, as creator, begins to form part of the chronicle of such creation, become one personage more of those that populate his world, not, for being particularly distinguished, any less subject to the arbitrary dynamic of events, so too that author whose work is centered, for example, on a writer's sojourn in a small town on the coast, the tale of his daily life, the literary transposition in the form of notes about that life of each day in a coastal town, the notes and personal observations which he writes about his work, the same as with memories, dreams, ideas, reflections, etcetera, fragments and texts in various degrees of production; or rather: the intersection or incidence of the distinct planes—one real, another fictitious, fictitiously real a third, and so on—whose confluence constitutes precisely the structural nucleus of the work that our writer proposes to himself to carry out, that he is carrying out, thus, the realization of a work of such a genre cannot cease to have repercussions in the life of its author, modifying it just as what was created modified the life of the creator gods or how dream analysis, even in the case when its conclusion solves nothing from a practical point of view, affects in some way the life of the dreamer.

Reality, autonomous fiction, fiction that reveals itself as the final ambit of primitive reality, etcetera, concentric incidences and variations that go from literal transposition to the displacement and transmutation of narrative material, conforming to a correlative process that is effected in parallel fashion in the author himself. A work that, similar to Velazquez's painting *The Fable of Arachne*, consists of three simultaneous planes: a foreground showing women at work, spinning the raw material of what must be converted into the tapestry's thematic warp and weft; in the middle ground a group of ladies, more brightly illuminated, contemplating the tapestry being shown to them in that precise moment, while in the workshop some piece of gossip is being shared in whispers, doubtless some aristocratic clientele, women come round to the shop perhaps with the urge to buy, perhaps from simple curiosity; and in the background, the tapestry displayed in that precise moment, one of so many tapestries showing a mythological subject, not very different, probably, from those already shown or those yet to be shown. Of the three planes, who can doubt that the painting's center is properly located in the first one, in the workshop, and not so much for its proximity to the spectator, or for its special enhancement owing to the perspective, but because it constitutes the true connecting link between the other two, the mythological subject in the background and the transactions relating to the finished product.

VI

PERIPLUS.

What better name? Voyage? Cruise? Excursion? Crossing? All of them too dry and ordinary for what was planned—unless one would like to introduce an ironic wink into the account of the events—and all too plain with respect to what was going happen. Meaning, in reference to a maritime trip of unsuspected scope for everyone involved. It's a well-known fact: not even the gods themselves are completely omniscient. And who could be, in the face of that hazy panorama of salt marshes and placid sea, into which flow, shimmering like two pupils in agony, the Lethe and the Eunoe, dead waters beyond which, when the sun rises clear over the bay, the white ruins of Ampurias will certainly come into view? A panorama that, as Apollo's fair, bright smile grew wider, as the classical writer or one of his many imitators would say, was already, in itself, an invitation, a motive more than sufficient to justify the laziness overcome, the discomforts supposed in finding oneself on a boat at such an early hour, still sleepy and stiff with cold, despite the warm clothing they'd brought, warned by The Greek about the inclement coldness of the sea as the sun, like the eagle that gains altitude in order to dive, with greater flashing splendor, upon its prey, grows sufficiently strong and brightens the colors of the landscape along with the heat of the bodies, and then one begins to tell oneself that it really was worth the trouble, now in that state of mind of one who gets up stimulated by the happy progress of a dream, almost a pity to wake up in that precise moment, a sensation similar to what the traveler can experience, when, after a rather arid landscape, a deserted and half-demolished town to the left of the highway, on the upper slopes of a hill, the new cemetery somewhat further on, on another steep slope, and a background of snowy peaks sticking up in the distance, after a landscape of more or less those same characteristics, the visual field opens up suddenly and, before our traveler's eyes there appears the sea, a panorama of cliffs plunging to the sea where the green slope of the terrain gives way brusquely to the marine tonalities nuanced by the afternoon sun, a sea that seems to be advancing under the churning mantle of resplendent foam, a product not so much of internal movements as of shallow depths, of the scattered reefs, of the successive lines of breakers and, above all, from the scanty narrow width of the beach at the foot of the cliffs, how softly the sand goes sinking down, a sea, in short, which summons like the sirens' song or the spiraling conch, which invites one to penetrate it, to enter into its waters, not so much as a swimmer but as a diver. However: who was watching the sea by his side from amid the weeds, high atop the cliffs?

Like Argonauts sailing after the golden fleece, you might have said. As if they went searching for it on the rough slopes of Cabo Creus, the extreme eastern point of the peninsula, the first spot to be touched by daylight and, as a consequence, also thanks to mother night, the first or final light for so many navigators, so many shipwrecked castaways, the classic luminous intermittency that signals where the world begins or ends. Thus, as if such a thing were their objective, intrepid, yes, intrepid! facing the planned mission without fainting, responding serenely to the hailing of however many boats cross their path, insensible to the supposed flattery represented by the hurrahs from their crews like the oars raised high on the triremes or the artillery salvos from the ships, elements very much in consonance with the sunny sight of the bay that morning, bathers in sweet activity, tense repose, all along the shore, and fleeting creatures cutting through the blue splashed with white, curving wakes speeding away as if they were Aphrodite and Eros, transported by the fish in their flight from Typhoeus, and the flapping of the taut sails, and the shimmering vapor of burned gasoline left behind by the outboard motors. Everyone: not a single passenger had missed the date, all of Ricardo and Camila's friends were there and even more than one of the absentee residents, from Leopoldo and Carmen and Renata Bosch and Javi, Cristina and Willy, without forgetting Blanca nor Mariana nor Guillermina and Gerard, even Carlos and Aurea and Carlos junior, as well as Black Nab, naturally. Reasons for their presence, for the presence of each one on board? Casual coincidence? Fulfillment of an obligation made in a moment of euphoria? Delighted acceptance of an attractive adventure? Only in part. Following this kind of response and the natural confluence of destinies, we will always find the uncertain bias of each one's life, their shortcuts and intricacies, everything just like that resultant itinerary, improvised on the move, begun by that person who goes out walking possessed by the anxiety and frenzy that accompany a hangover, be it an ethyl alcohol hangover, an erotic hangover, or any other kind, walking around the outskirts of the town, following the line of the beach, walking from one end of the seaside promenade to the other, tramping along all the sinuousities of the cliffs forming the coast, knowing, more than what one seeks or what one wants, knowing what one refuses, so too, in a similar way, life, its objectives grounded in necessity and negation, not being poor, for example, not being alone, not dying, not yet.

Good humor reigned on the yacht's deck, good humor personified by Leopoldo himself, a Leopoldo who did not let his predilection for erotic coupling keep him from the collective banter, fully present, enlivening it with his witty remarks, no less notorious than his retorts. But, let's see, he was saying: didn't they call you Cayo when you were a little boy? So what's the reason we have to call you Carlos now? Exactly! Exactly! said Mariana; I know that because when my brother Carlos made his first communion they also called him Cayo. Cayo or Layo? asked the annoying, boring Javi. And Leopoldo: see, from the time he was a child, no doubt, like that classic madman who thinks he's Julius Caesar and, accordingly, starts barking orders at everyone around him, that's how you are. Carlos nodded his head, as if declining to speak, looking sorrowful. I'm not going to be the one who denies it, said Ricardo: but let me tell you all that there once was an Age, called the Silver . . . I can already tell you all what he's going to say, interrupted Camila, distractedly caressed by Carmen: that in the Silver Age, which was the successor to the Golden Age and the predecessor of the violence and roughness of the so-called Bronze Age, which some authors classify as the time of heroes, in that Age, I was saying, human behavior was, in every way, thoroughly infantile: clinging to, suckling their mother's breast for dozens of years, they reached puberty only physically, because their mind continued to be filled with disproportionate desires, closed to responsible reasoning like in infancy and childhood, thus unwilling to work or participate in any kind of cult and, in general, shunning everything positive in life, which is what led them to be punished by the gods. Isn't that right? And Ricardo: that's right. And what you mean, said Blanca, is that you mustn't ascribe the life and times of those ages to past epochs but instead to the deepest part of the human being, which simultaneously houses them all. The Silver Age, which corresponds to our childhood, is situated within the Golden Age—the nostalgia for what is not remembered, for what, perhaps, never even existed—and that of the Bronze Age, the time of the adult from the perspective of their earliest years. And as far as the Iron Age goes, suffice to say that it's nothing more than chronological time. Have I explained myself clearly? Indeed, said Ricardo. And of them all—intervenes Carmen without abandoning Camila's adjacent body—the Silver Age is the one of greatest transcendence, seeing the way in which specific persons like Peter Pan cling to the very ambit which they call their own and with respect to which, in the same way, the Age that precedes it as well as the one that follows it, are mere projections. What's more, some portion of that Silver Age persists for years in each one of us, sometimes for our whole life. Am I wrong?

I couldn't have said it better myself, affirmed Ricardo. And he would have continued with the following words: therefore, for example—and I'm looking for an example that will apparently refute my affirmation, only in appearance—that punctiliously reliable character of polite youth in the forties, in the hard times of the postwar era, a trait which is, no doubt, the fruit of the intense inculcated guilt; their distinguishing quality of being dutiful, studious children. And Guillermina, picking up the explanation: thus we come to the essential ambiguity of the figure of the Wolfman, which is what Camila would have said that you were going to say, though in a much less rudimentary way than I, the outline of your appreciations about what such a figure means, about the reversible direction of his transformations. What it means for you, when you witness someone else—your boss, your father-in-law, your father, whomever—undergoing a gradual metamorphosis at the mouth of the cave, as soon as the rays of moonlight touch them, pale fangs, wrinkled snout, dark fur, etcetera, meaning everything that our observer supposes to be an indication of regression and atavistic outbreak, pounding, echoing drums announcing the unbridled violence that, for the boy, rules the adult world, to the eyes of another kind of observer, the one who witnesses the reverse transformation—receding fur, shrinking fangs, the animal lamentably stripped away, the beast converted into a helpless unfortunate man, incapable of facing the dangers that beset him—might very well signify the end of the conception of the world which, until then, had sustained him, the irreparable loss of all hopes relating to the field of action which life was reserving for him. Am I right about this? You are, you are, you are, Leopoldo was saying and saying as he penetrated Guillermina; and this is possibly our own case, the persistence of the Silver Age, given over as we are, just as we are, to our irresponsible sexuality—thanks to its very omnipotence—to all kinds of activities. And thus, similarly, continued Guillermina, not without certain alterations in her diction, the problems that usually overwhelm that person, at the beginning of his career, equal parts novice and enthusiastic psychotherapist: the interpretive relativity of the material in question; the fact that one thing can thus contain both a meaning and its contradiction, especially, the slight importance, for practical purposes, that it be precisely one and not the other, the patient's mental health as opposed to and distant from the solution to their dilemma. Wasn't this, perhaps, the thread of your thoughts? Nothing could be more precise, admitted Ricardo.

And having reached this point, Guillermina continued, if Camila were less concentrated, right now, on other impressions or what have you, she would have informed you that my next words would run as follows: thus we see the application of a kind of code for the interpretation of dreams, let's take, for example, a woman's clear eyes counterposed with the dreamer's inexplicable tears, her sex and his sperm, as if with excessive lightness he could diagnose for himself our young and ambitious psychotherapist, to whom, if I had objected to him that I mistrusted any kind of generalizations—however more that the eyes-sex identification is warranted by the frequency with which the poet refers to the eyes of Beatrice, a bodily organ which, more than acquiring autonomy from everything else, ends up as its substitute, just as in any synecdoche—he would not even have understood, in his stupidity, what I was referring to, if in fact, his aggression piqued, he didn't think I was insulting him by using the word synecdoche.

Camila would have predicted my using such words, and she would have been absolutely correct. Not without me then, taking my turn to speak, insisting on the fact that such psychotherapists—who exercise their profession the way a military man follows the rules—customarily struggle with the fact that once perfectly persuaded and resolved, such a patient tends to identify, in dreams as well as in associations of ideas, father with fatherland—Homeland, paternal—and mother with city, his city—son of the very lovely, illustrious and abominable city of Barcelona—then up surges the bothersome option, the perennial vexation, the realization that one's native land is conventionally maternal, the motherland, while the exemplary and rigorous order of the Ideal City of the utopians is a virile projection of the father's fecundity. Annoying imponderables of the trade which only experience will help him to overcome, to ignore, as one comes to understand the advice of one already an old hand in the profession and, the early pugnacity of his first steps now toned down, he shows common sense and ends up agreeing that what's important, more than understanding the goddamned patient, is managing to get them to believe that our psychotherapist understands him, that only due to demands from the treatment he prefers to not get into details, but to refrain from commenting, because he knows quite well what he's doing. And in order to answer the questions which, having reached this point, you would all have put to yourselves, I, for my part, would respond with new questions, interrogations which shelter, in their depths, as the seed contains the tree, the development of what must be our search, if not our objective: what symbolism is hidden beneath sexual symbolism? I might have asked you. What dark forces underlie the sexual fixations of which the sexual act in itself is only one symbol more? And

Camila would say that you were then going to ask me: but what is there behind the symbol of the symbols? And that, ensconced and engaged as you all are upon the terrain to which I had wanted to lead you, victory within my grasp, I would have responded: something that one only understands as they cross over the limits of the Silver Age to which I've referred earlier, because from within its terrain it proves impossible: what remains hidden in the Age of Gold. Have I dropped the thread?

Absolutely not, said Camila. Except that here Renata Bosch would have interrupted, talking about all that business involving Aurea, wanting to know what interpretation you, or our audacious—or whatever you want to call him—psychotherapist would ascribe to that whole story, and then Blanca would have said that in those cases the best thing is to consult the tarot deck. And you, accepting with pleasure the turn the conversation has taken, would have concluded with a brilliant and amusing, and equally well-documented, examination of the elements that compose a deck of cards, but not without first showing yourself enraged, almost pathologically, with our unhappy psychotherapist, with his incapacity to accept, for example, such a method of concentrating our darkest qualities just as we focus on the clearest ones in a lens; or his ineptitude for grasping the difference between dreaming a real event or dreaming, for example, a film, the advantages that this solution offers the dreamer, turning us into mere spectators of what is only a film, something, in consequence, which does not compromise us, which has got nothing, absolutely nothing, to do with us, etcetera, and other attenuating circumstances. Why, in the traditional Spanish decks of cards, you might have asked, do we find so many veiled resonances to copulative alchemy, its primary colors—*rubedo* and *nigredo*—its symbols, gold coins, the carved stone, the sharp-cut diamonds, swords or pikes like crosses, logs that sprout anew, clovers like roses, bunches of grapes, cups, chalices, bloody hearts? And, especially, its twelve numbers and, even more, the figures, jack or knave, knight, queen, kings, with the aces, the number one, above all, apart from that added element, the unmentioned number that follows the twelve, the joker, the Jolly Jesting Joker, whose function sometimes corresponds to the three, shades and differences between the Spanish deck and the French one, whose significance it wouldn't be risky to remit to and clarify by the light of the inquisitorial bonfires. For me, said Leopoldo, like with chess: aren't the king and queen the mother and father? Well, *jaque!* Check the king! Check the queen! And the thing is, if you've got to put an end to all that history of the kings, well, you'll have to put an end to parents, too!

Fine, insisted Renata Bosch, but what do you all think about this stuff with Aurea? Allow me, before anything else, said Blanca, to tell you exactly how things unfolded; let Mariana stop me if I omit or alter anything, if I twist the order in which they happened. You know, all too well, the circumstances in which Aurea departed Rosas, abandoning both Carlos and Carlos junior. What you might not know is that she went down to Barcelona, apparently, for no particular reason. Once there, alone in her flat, she went out only, from what it seems, to wander around the city now and then, as Cristina can well testify, who ran into her at the most unexpected moments and places, the storefront windows along Diagonal at night, the bar patios along Calle Tusset—looking sleepless—in the wee hours of the night, the Wax Museum at midday. The rest of the time she spent locked away in her apartment, naked, smoking, drinking, playing records from the forties, so that when she walked into the cinema—they were showing a horror flick—she was already pretty tipsy: she fell asleep without meaning to while someone was feeling her up, and she let herself be groped and she even administered a blowjob to the strange neighbor sitting next to her as soon as her head cleared a little, some neighbor who wasn't there anymore when they turned up the lights and she had to leave because they were closing. On finding herself out in the street, she started walking, and she must have been walking at a good clip because when the car pulled up alongside her she was already walking along Carretera de Sarrià, Diagonal or thereabouts, and the driver was quite friendly and invited her to a have a drink somewhere, and she let him come back to her apartment, not very sure if he was the guy from the cinema or some other neighbor who'd seen her out and about or some guy on an occasional prowl or that guy who telephoned her number regularly and who, when she answered, instead of saying something, just started breathing heavily, a guy who might very well also be the occasional tomcat or the guy she blew in the cinema or the one who'd watched her deliver the blowjob. A day later, or several days later, they found her body tied spread-eagled to the bed, with a pillow under her buttocks as if to better highlight the confluence of her thighs, almost like a woman in labor. Her throat had been slit, but she showed no signs of having been raped or of having been used in any sexual way, which is the strangest thing about this case. And what else? Tell us, tell us, darling, said Cristina, who—despite the clear handicap represented by the rough hardness of her German accent, of her vocal registers, raspy chirps that sounded more rusty than merely metallic, resonances barely reduced by her guttural voracity—was obtaining a rapid reaction from Ricardo's sex in terms of its length, thickness, and rigidity.

Having rounded the point of Cala Nans, as the Bay of Cadaqués opened and unfolded before their eyes, they encountered a boat with a blond crew, probably Vikings. On the prow, languidly embracing the dragon's curved neckline, they glimpsed Isolde, and when the diminishing distance between both boats reached its minimum point, they could distinguish on the other bridge, exchanging with them some friendly waves, some familiar faces, Vercingetorix, Hallgerd, Hagen, Godwin, Egmont, Crimilda and, now the two boats pulling apart, the distance between them growing, motionless on the poop deck, and no less hard and erect than his sword, as if presiding over the white wake it left in its passing, the paladin Roland. In that part of the bay most sheltered from the wind off the sea, anchored alongside the black hull of a pirate ship, they also saw the Caesar and, crammed together on its deck, Leopoldo and Ricardo and Camila and that annoying boring Javi, and Willy cuddling Carmen while she was playing handsies with Cristina, and Renata Bosch, the complete shipboard idiot, fully aroused. Blanca was waiting for them at the Riba wharf, with Guillermina and Gerard, and Leopoldo was trying to organize them into groups to ferry them to dry land, in a little slipper-shaped launch with an outboard motor. Well then I'll take you all together at once, goddammit! he shouted in order to resolve once and for all the problematic priorities of protocol and preference. The idea was to drop in—after the inevitable, breathless, uphill slog—at Mariana's house, but Blanca informed them that Renato Salvatori was throwing a party, so instead they headed that way, including Mariana. Everybody already knows what happens in Cadaqués on these occasions, the behavior of the local wildlife, and Carmen—doing her best impersonation of Diana the Huntress preparing her slings and arrows, sharp and precise as a forked tongue—failed to make herself an easy target for the fiery, redheaded piece-of-ass, Samantha what's-her-name. Also among those present, Kirk Douglas, much more of a gentleman than one might expect. And the snakelike Yul Brynner, with whom Leopoldo barely managed to exchange a toast. Fernando Rey isn't too bad, either, he said; but he's too Spanish. Excuse me, and a complete gentleman, said the complete idiot; you can see right away that he's more of a gent. He makes me think of Captain Nemo, said Guillermina. Willy was spotted mixed up in one of those confused bathroom stories, and Cristina was complaining that someone had stolen her enormous, black, crocheted shawl, the one which accentuated her nudity; they were saying the thief was Gerard's sister, a real dangerous little dyke.

Is there any chance some of you could return with us to the yacht? said Leopoldo, fishing around in his pocket. But the plan for whoever would like, consisted in attending the projection of some rolls of film taken during the day's excursion, excellent scenes of one ship boarding another, combats, shipwrecks, plus some highly atmospheric shots showing the Caesar itself departing Cadaqués Bay under artillery fire from the pirate ship, now out of its reach, safe from its cannons though still in sight, still in danger, sailing farther and farther away while those outlandish madmen lined up along the gunwales, perched on the yardarms, furious but powerless, peg legs and black eyepatches and ferocious hooks and savage hoops in their ears, and vociferating toothless beards, imprecations and swearing that only got stronger when, thanks to the spyglasses they employed to pursue them, they could watch the fugitives salute them with great big middle fingers as they sailed away, as well as their embraces and joyous displays—which at first sight could be well confused with a sudden mad generalized copulation—the effusions to which they delivered themselves to celebrate the triumph, that disordered flowering of roses, from the castle of the poop deck, seemed to spill over the bridge, so perfect the vision provided by the magnifying lenses that it was possible to appreciate even the tiniest contraction of those vehement vulvas, Camila, in the foreground, cheerfully mounted and cheered on, being penetrated at the same time by Willy (in the front) and Black Nab (in the rear), not for that reason ignoring the trembling cock Leopoldo is dangling in front of her face, a Leopoldo perversely assaulted in his turn by the annoying bore, that hypocrite Javi, while Ricardo tries to focus his attention and his aim on Carmen—not very sure of the exact location of the occupied center—and Carmen saying, yes, I think so, put it here, difficult to understand her that way sheltering in Blanca's lap, kissing her, her upper lips against Blanca's lower ones, while Blanca, for her part, seems to have swallowed Cristina's tongue, both in a sort of mutual attempt to devour each other whole, as far as possible given Gerard's extemporaneous thrusts and how Mariana's massive tits slosh in and occupy any available space, Guillermina proudly offering her hindquarters—and perhaps not without a certain calculation—to whomever would like to enjoy them, an opportunity, not at all wasted on Harpooner Ned, to plunge in deep, straight down to the bottom, without taking any other rest than whatever precedes the next discharge, impetuosity and straight, right, honorable employment of his member which, at a glance, nobody would have guessed belonged to the Canadian, not so much a glacier—like Icelandic Hans—as a geyser.

Aurea, motionless and silent astride the carved figurehead at the prow, of which she herself now seemed almost an ornament—only the long scarlet veil that encircled her slit throat waving in the breeze, finally roused herself to descend to the bridge, moving with care among those frisky romping figures that the inflamed imagination of a sleepless body, agitated, restless, naked, alone in bed, intoxicated from alcohol and cigarettes, waiting for the telephone to ring, can barely distinguish in the course of her returning fantasies, details and fragments that turn and turn and melt into confusion, that body in whose mouth a pink member swells and spurts while the other two rigorously penetrate the lower parts of the body, that body suffocated by buttocks or thighs, relentlessly hounded by hardened, ass-flavored penises, by smothering tits smacking of sperm, that substance that liquifies and runs down from the brain, down the spine, until squirting out vitalizing, relaxing, from the utmost tip of its temporary tangential prolongation, thus, wandering about as if with fear, as if without daring any longer to participate or rather to bother anyone with her presence, inhibited, diminished, without the sufficient conviction even to insinuate herself, be it from the repugnance which, in her judgment, the bloody wound she concealed beneath the scarlet veil might provoke, be it for the rapidly established result of the comparison between any of those young bodies and that of a woman now approaching fifty, be it for a feeling of shame similar to that experienced by Venus after having been exposed to the mockery of the gods, she and Mars trapped together in the subtle net of their own betrayal, thus, somewhere between insecure and confused, almost on tiptoes, she moved along, similar in her unease to that curious passerby who, in a seaside town, when the boats arrive, enters the fish market in order to watch the auction, finding herself then surprised, while they call out the numbers in a backward countdown, by an unanticipated atmosphere, wrapped in its turbulence, a sonorous, phosphorescent atmosphere enlivened by the swirling skirts that rise up and swell out like corollas, of bulging zippers unzipping, of seafood and shellfish that come spilling out, the fishermen ramming their leathery phalluses into the gaping mouths of the agonizing fish, into the amorphous apertures of octopuses and cuttlefish, between the juicy valves of gigantic mollusks, into the deepest crevices of an enormous conch, while the fisherwomen attach calamaris, medusas, and purple anemones to their vulvas, and let themselves be penetrated by soft red mullets and spiny red scorpionfish, tentacular ticklings, tense tail-thrashings, slippery forms that go sliding inside the sphincter, agonizing mouths sucking anything at all, suckers that adhere to any surface, sunshine sparkling like a swarm of bees, reflections in the puddles, in the salt, in the fish scales, in the chopped ice.

Detached from everything around him, you might say that Carlos junior, astride the bow-sprit—enthralled like a sad Isolde absorbed in contemplating the image reflected back to him from the water—seemed, in his immobility, like a graceful carved figurehead, the laurel leaves sprouting from his cranium combed by the breeze, interwoven and polished like green dragon scales. His eyes, like a periscope, permitted the rest of the passengers to glimpse and, moreover, to discern the shape of the landscape—the rough rocky cataclysms of that coast—which, like a veil being drawn aside, was revealed as they followed their route toward Cabo Creus or Cruces or Quiers or Quierz, perhaps Corazones, making for the peninsula's eastern extreme, ahead of bright smiling Apollo, a special place to watch the dawn, to see the sun rise from the heart of the sea, the daily start of a course that brings it finally to sink into the earth, setting in the west, while the Cape continues shining in the darkness of the sky with the splendor of a guiding star, Cap de Creus, cape of crosses, cape of the light, first having to sail past Cap Norfeu—the Cape of Orpheus, that is—the Cape of the night and the darkness. They glimpsed all that, yes, the orography of the coast right down to its smallest relief, and they also saw what they were sailing to see, what they would soon see, the jetty ensconced along the southern slope of the Cape, the steep stony path, the faux lighthouse and coffershaped log cabin constructed with an eye to filming a movie on a steep section of the northern slope, the unreliable foghorn strategically situated atop the craggy rocks, a sort of decoy for sailors lost in their own fog, there on high, dominating it all, the lighthouse and its outbuildings, where they would be received by the lighthouse keeper, glaciers and albatrosses in his eyes, his blond hair bleached white, tousled by the wind, a wind whose violence would make words useless and the glance more expressive, that glance that signals to them in the gleaming light up there, as if rewinding the sun, and then, below, the dark crater of aeolian resonances known as la Cova de l'Infern, the cave of hell. They could see it all at once, in such a way that they didn't even need to look when, with sober gesture, they returned the salute offered by the blessed occupants of a ship, as fast as it was white, that, aureoled with celestial choirs, appeared as if by magic, white and sky blue its wake, as if matching, for greater encomium and glory, the colors of the tripennant, the blazing banner that, by special deference, descended to half-mast while they respectfully uncovered their heads and observed the ritual minute of silence, the Caesar maintaining its course at a prudent distance from that shore of Atlantean dimensions, keeping its hull safe from the jumbled stacks and blocks forming the coast, the product, one might say, of a cyclopean ruin, eroded shoals and shallow depths, multicolored out-croppings, chromatic magmas and vertical transparencies, oceanic abysms suddenly yawning wide amid this picture of Mediterranean serenity.

Both Modesto Pírez and Ignacio seemed rather out of place, without knowing exactly what attitude to adopt nor where to situate themselves, like those gentlemen in public parks who approach children feeding pigeons, fearing, more than any insolent response, the risk of having their desire to simply caress such beauty, even just a little bit, misunderstood. And so, with the customary caution of such gentleman, both of them approach Carlos junior, carefully making their way around the Caesar's nose. Do you like fish, kid? asked Modesto Pírez. Faced with with nothing but silence from Carlos junior, stuck in a frown, Pírez's silhouette floating in the other's pupils like in two transparent cisterns, against the skies at the bottom, they seemed to opt to withdraw, yet not without Modesto Pírez adding: you've got pretty hair. For me, there's no other leaf quite like laurel. That's precisely where the word laureled comes from, from laurel.

The body sailed on without a problem, the bloody pleats of Caesar's tunic swollen by the wind, the passengers spread out along his ribcage save some original, some eccentric, or whatever, holding onto the stiff yardarm. Nevertheless, Black Nab, in the most respectful terms, alerted them to the convenience of shifting their positions, for technical reasons, from the prow to the poop, and then, all holding hands along the edge of the topside and without losing balance, they moved, making the vessel tilt over on one side until managing to turn it completely around, the cock-spar now converted into a rudder. Their position thus rectified, it soon became clear that the impelling movement of all their feet acted with notoriously superior efficiency, at the same time the weight seemed more balanced, the passengers more comfortable, so that Black Nab, as technical director of the maneuver, received a prolonged standing ovation. But, not yet satisfied, like a Roland brandishing his Durendal, Black Nab, after getting himself unstuck from the coccyx, slid in, not without effort, between both buttocks, while he went on saying now we've got to pump him up. Render unto Caesar the things that are Caesar's, someone commented. The only hint of an incident occurred when Ignacio and Modesto Pírez, perhaps attracted by the spectacle of seeing Black Nab in action, were inching closer, feigning innocence, until being laconically intercepted and kept at arm's length by the ever-faithful Harpooner Ned. But, man of God, don't stand right there, said Pírez. What're we doing wrong? We couldn't even do that if we tried. This kid's in prison and, and me, well I've been dead already for I don't know how many years.

All arranged, reclining, as comfortable as possible like a gathering upon one of those gently-sloping meadows where Olympian assemblies are usually held, the conversation was nevertheless unraveling, becoming banal, as ends up happening in the course of a banquet when the guests begin to find themselves too drunk to take the conversation to any conclusion, someone, possibly Javi-Bore, asking: what would you call Caesar's body if it were a ship? What else could you call it, the Hermaphrodite? answered Leopoldo without much feeling. And why not Santa Claus, that good-natured little granny with an affable expression and a great big overcoat of a beard who departs from Spain in a sleigh pulled by reindeer with bells? suggested someone else, everyone floating somewhere between weary, disgusted, and bored, the psychotherapist now become the principal victim of their commentaries, observations more wearisome than witty, and like that group of youngsters who don't know how to spend Sunday afternoon and always end up picking on the same person, the one who's weakest or who wears glasses or is chubby, who only by virtue of such a marginalizing element is accepted by the others, using them as a repository for their jokes, thus, forced into a similar role as target for the witty remarks made by others, not so much for having fun as just to say something, our psychotherapist was exposed in the uneasy coming and going of his pacing along the poop deck. What do you think? they asked him. What's more normal, the normal or the abnormal? Chattering, badinage, the empty palaver that arises in every situation that goes on too long.

They almost didn't even hear Carlos when he began to speak, partly because of the other voices and partly because of the barely audible tone of his first words. Nor did they recognize him right away, now become an old man more than an aged one, with similar slovenly scruffiness both in his person as in his garb, exactly like The Greek in his appearance, including his very clothes, his very features, a Greek—with whom they had no doubt confused him—crazier than usual, a mixture of ruined pirate and homeless beggar. I, my friends, he began again, I myself would like to answer the question that is tormenting us all: what is the true purpose of this little jaunt of ours? *Partir c'est renaître un peu*, you'll all tell me. Meaning: to destroy the image one has been forming of oneself and which they justify to themself tooth and nail; to finish off the character we've created, one which, like a certain book, like certain formerly-useful experiences, has outlived its use and need not be clung to anymore. And whoever thinks so will be in the right. But will they not also similarly be in the right, those who, considering more the finality than the motivation, understand it as a trip into the unknown, toward what doesn't exist? And what is the unknown but death? And what is it that does not exist but God? And with what have they filled the void of that non-existence but crime? What besides crime underlies the origin of the gods? What else but crime do we find behind the face of the old man who projects his guilt by means of the vengeful furies, whose violence is discharged upon the other guilty ones of the world or upon those who could be or will end up being guilty? One crime that covers up another crime which in turn covers up Chaos, the word the gods use to designate things forgotten. Coverings which under the form of revelation, scornful of any kind of justifications, also permit the gods to cover up the concrete circumstances of the events that unfolded, the prevailing state of things then, in order to make the return to that state of chaos as difficult as possible.

Thus, Saturn's revolt against Uranus must be understood in no other way, the rebellion of time comprehended as a permanent revolution against the rotary but implacably fixed order of sky and heavens upon which all this is written, the rebellion of the diachrony against the synchrony, the passing of change against the structure of being, of the obscure movements of the unconscious against the geometry of consciousness; according to this dialectic, Jupiter's revolt against Saturn signifies the restoration of an order, the classification of the conscious and unconscious elements that fixes the forces in movement, some forces in no way lacking new elements of dissolution.

Meaning: everything in the likeness of men: Caesar against Pompey just as, before, Marius against Sulla and, later, Octavius against Marc Antony. And just as a vampire stalks his chosen prey in the night, taking pleasure anticipating—while she bathes and dresses—the moment when, as she is about to fall asleep, he will sink his fangs into her warm neck, so the adult takes pleasure in raising his children, awaiting the opportunity to discharge upon them the weight of all his sins, his obsessions, his abysms, of thus managing to convert his son into one of his own, capable—in possession now of all the burdens which have been transmitted to him—of perpetuating the species for yet another generation. And only when something goes wrong, when he doesn't achieve it and understands that he has instead engendered a monster, because if the offspring doesn't turn out like him it's because we're talking about a monster, what's called a monster, a real monster, there appears the figure of Frankenstein, a simple variant on the previous case, the stray bullet in the family, the black sheep, that artificial being stitched together from human body parts, cobbled together from detritus, we might almost say, a being falling somewhere between sub-normal and perverse to whom the greatest possible mercy—given its moral as well as physical deformation—would be death and destruction, burning it the way a castle or an evil book is burned, letting it be devoured by the flames, how a newborn is devoured, for its own good, in a way, because, more than not serving any purpose, such engendering is also noxious, a creature that, like Lucifer, must be driven from the face of the earth, imprisoned in the darkest depths of hell. The only problem is that, in reality, it's a question of the combat which, like the battle between Saint George and the Dragon, one starts with oneself. That combat in which both the monster and the knight must perish so that, in their place, the enchanted princess comes to flower. Only with the centuries, the sacrifice of the white whale consummated, does he overcome the irreparable doubt about the meaning of what happened and the consequences of the action, about whether the dead white whale was not, in reality, monstrously beautiful and whether the princess, so long awaited, so actively sought, might not be something more than the last bout of vertigo, the whirlpool, the mirage that precedes the final image of what goes sinking down.

Until this moment you've spoken of the father. But, what about the mother, too? asked someone from the gloom. Is there no female vampire? And Carlos: well, there has to be, what else happens to that woman bitten in the jugular while she's undressing for bed, who fails to notice that she's been spied upon by a gentleman in evening clothes, wrapped in that cape, who so easily transforms himself into winged silence?

No, the darkness was not external, no sunset darkness or darkness of eclipse, but rather internal, that sort of darkness that begins to stop being dark as the eyes gradually become used to the surrounding area, below that ribbed vault one might mistake for a whale's palate, following almost blindly that succession of cavernous spaces, the passageway between one and another narrow as a throat, the esophagus, the stomach, the intestine, the sphincter that blocks the rectum at the end, everything like the entrails of a fish, the warm humidity of the corridors thrumming, you might say, with a shudder or a vibration, narrow corridors reduced even more in width, if possible, by the stalactites and vegetal adherences that invade their shape, refuge for fugitive crabs and silent limpets, and that distant resonance, similar to the sounds produced by the sea in the depths of a grotto, reigning impressions until one begins to perceive the clear light around him, the result, no doubt, of a weak battery, and about the motors' irregular vibration and, especially, about the spiral cavity that, like the conch of a giant snail, opens around their heads before finding the staircase that winds in concentric circles which must lead them to the ample, 19th-century salon where the ostentatious spidery chandeliers were turning gray, glowing dimly from the few poor light bulbs not yet burned out, the rugs threadbare, the damascene curtains frayed, and the chairs' seats broken and bottomed out, the springs loose, the buttons all popped off the quilted upholstery, a bald velvet, of uncertain color, the sockets blown, the gilded stucco reliefs chipped and pitted, the support beams beneath the parquet floor sagging, useless, of course, to pretend to see anything else through those enormous picture windows except the green undulations of the flora and fauna on the other side, a resplendent green, shaded with multicolored reflections, something like an aquarium seen in reverse, from inside the empty tank, looking outside to the submarine world, unnecessary now, completely unnecessary, now that the noble old man, turning his back on the wheezing organ, on the control panel keyboard, and not without first switching on the automatic pilot, sat up as straight as possible and said: Welcome to the Nautilus, friends, to let you know that you were in the presence of that herald of the counterculture named Captain Nemo.

In my opinion, if you'll all permit me to express it, he said once they had all settled in, there's something more than that, because just as man marginalized and reduced the value of woman thousands of years ago now, to the point of claiming her to be molded from his own stolen, superfluous rib, thus, in a similar way, did the gods proceed, cutting off and casting out into the cold void the mother god's memory in order to benefit the figure of the father god. Considered from the origin point of this reality, the case of Oedipus seems less an error of interpretation than a false example, a complicit proof, a veil consciously or unconsciously interposed between ourselves and an authentic consideration of the problem. A scene inscribed in that movement which tends to conceal, by means of a presumed original parricide, an earlier matricide, enveloped in the mists of that Chaos which, as you have clearly indicated, makes room for how much has been, and how much must be forgotten, a primary crime, an ungrateful devouring, of which, after the passing of centuries, there only remain to us sublimated vestiges, dulcified images like the one of the pelican who offers her very own body to the voracity of her little ones, and only as a fantasy, as pure fantasy, the memory of a head that hangs attached by its curling mane of serpents. A head whose effect is not very different, on the other hand, from the effect that must be produced by the head of Clytemnestra in the hands of Orestes. To kill the person who brought us to life; to dishonor, to neuter, to ridicule the one who tries to be recreated through us, to model us in their image and likeness. Meaning: rape the father, murder the mother: the true terms of the myth, which still survive in the most recondite cracks of our mind. A myth thus personified not so much by Jocasta and Oedipus as by Clytemnestra and Orestes, an Orestes of features prudently minimized thanks to a marginalizing aureola of dementia that authorizes locking him away for life. Impulses more suppressed than latent, something which, rather than being avoided or even denied, must be ignored, purely and simply ignored. Literature: that's it.

Proof that my assertions are correct? The fact that what's taken for an obvious and natural commonplace is exactly the opposite: respect and obey the father's authority, safeguard the mother's physical and moral integrity, calling into question the first blow with which, in the course of a fight, each combatant, whether from alcohol or fury, assaults his adversary, the other's mother, that whore, that bitch, that creature you've got to crush the way one crushes a snake, a problem that—beside themself and out of control—each person seems almost to embrace as their own. Out of control, while inside one, like lava expelled by an erupting volcano, the most unsuspected rancors come roaring out. That betrayal with which each mother victimizes each one of her children, for example, and which not for being carefully forgotten will cease to provoke in the adult child, under the most diverse appearances, a reaction of rejecting women in general, which he will only be capable of overcoming by means of an opportune liquidation of the maternal stamp, the pathological element ending up being resolved in simple and occasional misogyny.

A symbolic liquidation only rarely realized before the problem begins to lose importance by itself, to be transformed until being totally replaced by another class of problems, halfway along the road between childhood and old age, when, although we might be the same person, our body no longer contains a single cell from the child we were nor even yet from the being that we will be in years to come, all twisted and decrepit. And, in the physical realm, as well as in the psychic, although not without violence, not without forcing ourselves to an operation of such hardness—implacably jettisoning the accumulated ballast so that we might ascend, and rise above the condition to which we were bound, an experience similar to that which in so-called primitive societies and at a much earlier age, correspondent or entrusted to the rituals of initiation—many are those who do not manage to bear it out to a felicitous conclusion, condemned to continue slogging on and lugging along—young the presence, ruinous the interior—their adolescent baggage, a baggage—and I can affirm it, each time that I get to know the case at hand—frequently stained with indiscriminate blood. In other words: from the crime that flowers anew, from its compulsive reappearance, that first crime which one of you has mentioned and which can offer itself garbed anew in the most sacred principles, wrapped in an irrefutable body of doctrine, be its content of ideological character, be it patriotic, be it religious. Because, like islands, so men, the difference between Robinson Crusoe's Island and Lincoln Island, between the success of man's colonizing labor and its failure, the destruction of the product of that labor by the conflicting forces of water and fire, conflicting forces which also exist in each one of us, which can end us at the same time as the enemy which we have created.

Apparently, the appearance of Granite House Island is not very distinct—except with regard to dimensions, always difficult for the layman to gauge, on the open sea, from a distance, without other landmarks—from that of La Gran Meda, situated at the extreme southern end of the Bay of Rosas, or Cucurucú, offshore from Cadaqués. Meaning: a solitary prominence of naked rock, that not only looks uninhabitable but also rather inaccessible thanks, precisely, to the verticality of its shape, a fact of no greater interest to the sailor than any other data showing on his charts, one of so many spots best avoided. And, in fact, the only means of access, the one utilized by the Nautilus, is invisible to the sailor's naked eye: an underwater cavern which leads directly to the interior of Granite House. And only then is it perceived that, what from the outside seemed a mountainous protuberance, corresponds, on the inside, to the no-less-perpendicular crater of a volcano whose bottom constitutes, at the same time, a lakebed, a lake where the little bit of sky visible was not enough to counteract the gloomy tonalities that the walls imprinted on its waters. Sprouting at intervals in the center of the lake, the only mobile element in that completely motionless panorama, enormous bubbles, their forms resembling—as much for their sound as for the image of expanding waves that rippled across the still surface—the ones rising in an aquarium. With the low tide, the water level dropped until leaving the lake totally empty, and the ashen, viscous lakebed then began to resemble the crust of an infant planet, its undefined contours agitated by the small marine creatures in search of shelter. The Nautilus remained stranded, lying on one side, and its occupants emerged, clambering out onto the hull after confirming that Captain Nemo, also laying down on his side, had fallen asleep.

In the very spot that had been the center of the lake, where the water had bubbled up, there now opened, like the jaws of a whale, a dismal grotto which seemed to exhale strong currents of warm air, true unseasonal gusts, as one approached the entrance, origin or source, no doubt, of the bubbles that, when the high tide filled the lake again, prevented such an opening being flooded by the waters. Preceded by the faithful harpooner Canadian Ned, they all summoned their courage to enter the grotto, not impassable though rugged and barely illuminated. A few steps further on, as if watching over the access, like a sentry box or watchtower, an open cavity like a vaulted niche or the side-chapel of a church, of a baptistry, for example, the sybil. She'd been found naked and spread-eagled across a wide bed covered in furs, lit by torches, enveloped in sulfurous mists, perhaps simply the aura or reflection of her own craters, her own inner fires, of the smokes and burning blood that those bodily fires produce upon making contact with the silent ice forming the center. She had a scar across her throat, or perhaps only a crack or fissure like those which appear over the course of time on any sculpture carved from wood, and spoke, therefore, in consequence, with her vulva, her great lower lips articulating, not without difficulty, her words, the syllables cut short by emissions of smokes, sulfurous to judge from the smell, it being difficult to pinpoint the exact orifice from which they were expelled, from both at the same time, possibly, given the undulating movement displayed by her belly, the swelling-emptying alternation that, like a bubbling, preceded them; her voice was Aurea's voice and her breathing sounded like the sea inside a snail shell, only slow, or like deep breathing heard on the other end of the telephone line. Like in that novel, call it Novel B, incorporated into the storyline of another novel, call it Novel

A, in which the presumed pseudonym of the author or authoress of Novel B corresponds to the true name, the name of the author of Novel A, and the presumed author of Novel A corresponds to a simple pseudonym, namely you, she said. Who? they asked. Who are you talking about? and the whole answer is her releasing another little cloudy puff of sulfur.

They continued making their way along the passage, a cave which as soon as it widened out into dark domes shrank back down to little more than a tight orifice, difficult to squeeze through, picking their way around rivers of molten lava as they descended, almost getting lost among the intricate forests of stalactites which, like icicles in sunlight, melted and disappeared, avoiding torrential waterfalls thanks to rock formations stretching across the path, eroded ogives, converging flows increasing in volume the deeper they plunged, at the same time that the passageway widened and the vegetation thickened and became more established, no longer mosses and lichens but shrubs and grasses running down the slope, the visual field increasingly cheerful and broad, a nuanced predomination of greens and blues limited only by a distant mountain chain of snowy peaks, the soft slope that reached the very edge of the lake into which the various rivers would flow, amenity of a panorama which only seemed to stimulate the expeditioners' now clearly animated conversation.

Are the sybil and the pythoness one and the same thing? they were asking. Doesn't the word pythoness come from female python? From those green snakes, you mean, that writhe and wrap around each other in stagnant water? Willing to be trod upon as if the Virgin would step on them? Do some of them carry an apple in their mouth like one who offers a forbidden fruit? What then must that serpent be if not the devil himself, meaning, our base instincts, low like the lower abdomen? And who except the mother of the son can put us on guard against such slippery instincts? And what would happen if we were to give in to those so-called instincts? Well, we'd be defying the father's authority. But what is the forbidden fruit? True love prohibited. And what kind of love is that? The son's love for his mother; thus the mother crushes the serpent like one crushes a male member, words, phrases exchanged, in their joyous rashness, as if under the auspices of Venus Aphrodite, daughter, like life itself, of the spume of the sea, of the sperm of Heaven, of the spume of the sperm, indispensable guide, from the astrological point of view, of people who pretend to discover how much is hidden under the earth, what shines down there, the fountainhead that gushes forth, the fecund fertilizing fountains.

The center of the earth was occupied by that lake of limpid waters into which everyone wished to plunge, not so much reflection as crystalline window, magnifying lens through which the whole group and all the details of the starry sky were perfectly visible, a sky similar to the sky one might have contemplated as a child on summer nights, lying on his back in the garden of a country house, a farm like Santa Cecilia, for example, where, with the help of some binoculars, he can feel closer to the planets, to each one of the stars that configure the constellations, to the Milky Way, like that time, possibly recently arrived from Barcelona, at the start of vacation, when they told him that Estrella had gone to the mountain, what they used to tell him whenever some dog died during his absence, and he, at night, looking at the sky but seeing instead the dog's radiant eyes, the golden stars contained in each pupil, trapped in the doubt that comes from comparing the credibility of the news to the reality that such a flight, nevertheless, lies within the realm of possibility. A favorable state of mind, in the memory—an alibi if you prefer—so that, years later, at a fisherman's house, on its patio lush with flowers, you wait until the dog with a bleeding uterus has fallen asleep and, then, bring the double-barrel shotgun right up to her skull, avert your eyes, and pull the trigger.

Like little boys whose own breath against the window ends up obscuring any view outside, so they contemplated the drawing of the constellations, the enigmatic direction signaled by the arrow, the dragon's sinuous folds, the polar bears, and they noted their impressions, or simply signed, in the logbook, as if it were a guestbook, notations of significance frequently related to the contents of other notes, a kind of atemporal dialogue between unknown interlocutors, their replies, their ill-intentioned jabs. I'll show you, dickhead, illegible signature, scrawled below some grievous note. I wish I could have seen Rosa! words expressed similarly, but at a more educated level, by an observation in distinctly different handwriting: So what were you thinking, handsome? You're not like Ganymede, not attractive enough to seduce a god (*Purgatorio*, IX, 19-24) and you've got no eagle-eyed guide to transport you (*Paradiso*, I, 46-54), apart from various inscriptions and graffiti, quotes, telephone numbers, eloquently illustrated expressions of desire, more fitting for a bathroom stall used for hookups than for a space ship. Only a few, despite their excessively solemn, premeditatively humorous character, as if to better conceal the implicit obsession, denoted a higher level of thinking. Thus, that one: Where does the final Milky Way end? Or better yet: And what's outside it? And even: Or, rather, what's outside of outside? And by way of response: But, why not be optimists, so that, inverting the anthropomorphic conception, instead of considering the world as a simple molecule of a piss stream loosed by an infinitely superior being, for example—a brief, but for us eternal, fall—imagine that each instant of each piss taken by each one of us generates millions and millions of universes? And, especially, adequately protected by the rhetoric, that question—And what is the original chaos except the darkness of the uterus, the protean dominion of the lower waters?—that some mind wrote, a mind preoccupied by the origins of the world, as if intuiting that the response could only be the projection of the response actually sought, the one relating to his own origins. And the fact is, just as it's not God who creates men but rather man who creates the gods, so, as numerous writers and artists experience it, it's not the author who chooses his themes and plots, but instead those plots and those themes that choose their author, subject matter and signifying forms shaped as much by the tying together of the conflictive strands belonging to the world in which our author lives, existing previously to him, problems, that is, not of an individual but of a collective order, be they produced on a conscious or an unconscious level, as much by the master traits of that author's personality, demons for whose singular copulation the author, our author, becomes the only possible voice, more possessed by than possessing them, for however much it might be he who then appears before the world as its creator. And just as, according to the ancients, it's not the Earth that precedes Heaven but rather Heaven that precedes the Earth, the Earth, in its turn, emerged from chaos—that unfathomable uterus to the which our anonymous predecessor's comment makes reference—Mother Earth who, just as she has created the son, mutilates him, slicing off his sex; and so, just as the Day comes from the Night, not the other way around, in a similar way, the final key to that sublimated reality of man, which are his works, must therefore be sought not in those works but in the work that creates such works, in the darkest areas of their author's personality, those areas which, like Night in contrast to Day, always lie on the other side, the way that Death and Sleep and Dreams, children of the Night, lie on the other side of our life.

Contradicting and compensatory aspects, inverted symmetries which man, from his essential dichotomy, projects onto the world. Thus the One, the only form of conceiving of God, as a unity, given that the One is the most perfect representation of what doesn't even have parts, given that it doesn't exist; and thus, too, Chaos, the all that precedes what doesn't exist, something shivered to shards since forever, the mirror of the unremembered. And thus, finally, the idea that the number two might be, in reality the first number, with respect to which the number one is nothing more than the illusory and virtual expression of one of the two halves which compose it, turning out to be, in consequence, that the number three is the second number of the natural series while at the same time a synthesis of the ones that precede it, of the real and of the speculative, of what exists and what doesn't exist. Given that, like its antecedent, the two, so the person, the antagonistic relationship between the parts of light and shadow that form it. And the fact is that in the same way that, for the man possessed by the desire for procreation, his desires or sexual satisfactions or the copious affluence of seminal liquor that can come from them will have little or nothing to do with such desire, it would therefore be no less mistaken to attribute to artistic creation some pleasant feeling before some compulsive necessity, some unstoppable impulse. Different, completely different, is the fruit of such impulse, when the son contemplated himself for the first time reflected in the water and loved God, and since then continues calling him, pursuing the response that the mountains are giving him. Until finally he understands, and it is then when he, in his turn, begins to feel the same impulse, of whose furor he will end up possessed, to perpetuate the aberration, to repeat the act.

The space charts consulted, it was obvious that the principle obstacle which they needed to overcome in their trajectory consisted of the sharp, unequivocal line of opposition established between Uranus in Aries and Mars in Libra, presage of violent accidents and difficultics encountered, before which it might be difficult to make the opportune decisions in the opportune moment. On the contrary, the trigone configured by Pluto in Cancer and Jupiter in Scorpio represented a perfect escape route, the possibility of charting a course through safe waters, without fear of setbacks, toward Neptune and, once there, to stop over for the necessary time, waiting in expectation for the conjunction of Uranus and Mars to be verified. When the conjunction occurred, a sudden vibration would shake the ship and, at one hundred sixty degrees of distance, a living flash would be the signal that the constellation of Aquarius had opened its portals.

Forced course? Only to a certain point, only if we think that the data that prefigures it answer wholly objective criteria, completely removed from the surreptitious intervention of a hand that might well be our own. Because just as the Father, perhaps a demented man or a drunkard, projects himself onto the son in order to be crucified, or the way any other god assumes any form—a cloud, a bull, a swan—in order to engender a new being, so the author usually projects himself upon the forms he has created, not so much to breathe life into them as much as, before anything else, to explain to himself, to be realized, for example, through his characters or through what he attributes to those characters, and, by hiding himself or thinking he does so, he reveals himself all the better, Flaubert's Madame Bovary *c'est moi* or words to that effect, although also only to a certain point, independent as his works are from the purpose with which they were realized, as subordinated as the courses one traces are to the landmarks and reference points he had previously marked on the chart. And the fact is, just as it would have been difficult for Freud to create a map of the dark zones of neurosis without himself being, in the first place, a neurotic, without explaining in others the symptoms which, before those others, he had experienced in himself, so that Freud's personality is better manifest in no other place than in the clinical cases which he analyzed, thus, in a similar way, it is through the structure of a work of fiction, through the characters, arguments, situations and even descriptions that fill it as we can best establish, exercising our sharp critical insight, the author's personality, the diverse elements which compose the work being, in fact, those that configure its creator's true face and, moreover, through the language by him utilized, to the point that it would be difficult to decide if that language is his projection or rather if he is the projection of that language, which, in the final instance, can reveal to us things about him that perhaps not even he himself knows. And the fact is that just as literary creation is susceptible to seeming like a mere image of the creation of the gods and their world by man, this last point will be, in its turn, a simple metaphor of oneiric creation, the three of them being the product of the same unmotivated obscurities whose roots are lost in the centuries of centuries. Because just as the gods, the more they seem to ignore the fact that their antagonistic enemy is only to be found within themselves, are so much more prone to acts of madness, it is therefore no less necessary for that man possessed by the anxiety of procreation to become aware of his own conception of the natural reproductive instinct, of the hidden faces and the echoes of its fulfillment, than it is for the creator, our author, if he doesn't want his work to end up turning back against him, to untangle the impulses that drive him to create, independent of the aesthetic value of what's been created. Or what's been destroyed, a variant of the destruction of the creation and no less necessary for whomever realizes it in relation to their own entity, like our man possessed by the anxiety of procreation, who wrings, and squeezes and twists the propitiatory body, in the course of copulation, in his desire to engender a monster.

Comparable in anguish only to what can be produced by the unequivocal attitude of that vagabond who shambles up to us in a vacant lot, or that viper we tread on without noticing it and which writhes underneath our foot, or, even, the whole response on the telephone nothing more than one long deep breath, so too the spectacle offered all around, that enveloping rotation of frequently menacing figures, winged horses, eagles, lions, scorpions, hounds, swans, lascivious adolescents, herculean fighters, beings of extreme rusticity, red bulls, purple centaurs, violet crabs, the ringed dragon's violaceous depths, the marmoreal cruelty of a hieratic Virgin within that gyrating cluster of bodies intertwined like the serpents that encircle Laocoön's body, a vision drenched with ever-deepening scarlet hues, the sooner abandoned the better, leave all that pouring out through the neck of the amphora tipped by the serene water carrier, letting yourself be swept away by the current of water that rains down from the heavens, letting yourself plummet down past glaciers and ice floes and ice castles, down into the whirlpool, a whirlpool like a crater of snowy walls, with porous reliefs dancing around, mummified beasts and wind-driven caravels, shapes one might imagine tamed due to their contrast with the raging descent of the upper waters down upon the lower ones, that embrace which is the fruit of impassioned violence through which what has been separated by violence now rejoins itself, the agitated conjunction in which it's not possible to distinguish one part from another, boiling spume in ascent, rough churning and turbulent abysms, as if the sea were hardly more than that puddle which receives the piss stream of our infinitely enormous little boy, rain shower and passing storm of such nature that, thus unchained, in the dead of night, any ship not shaped like an ark—the most appropriate one on these occasions—would have sunk with the first, pounding waves, waves unfurling over their heads, devouring jaws, teeth, and tusks, deep maws screaming—the one the echo of the next—I've carried you with me so that, impelled by your own weight, you shall be lost in me.

There was a mutiny against The Greek, an inept Greek, out of control, uselessly gripping the wheel in the face of the waters that were crashing over the sides like a cliff collapsing, thus revealing him, by the nocturnal light of the lightning bolts, for what he really was: an old drunkard, a show-off, a sham, a poor devil only capable of inspiring fear in children, a seaport tavern pilot only capable of sailing them straight onto the rocks. *¡Patrón viene de padre!* shouted the troublemakers. The papa produces the pattern! The begetter begets the bossman! The sire spawns the skipper! Isn't he the Lobster King? Well, dethrone him! And The Greek accepted their judgment without a sound, without talking back, the insults, the mockery, the destitution, the stripes and braids and medallions they tore off of him as if they were plucking out his eyes, the spitting image of any one of those repeat offenders one finds in the jails, one of those jailhouse faggots, bankrupt and flabby. But one glance at the ship's hold showed them that the true peril was not out there, not outside but within, in the cargo they were transporting, all those wild beastly beings transformed—like Circe, the woman turned into a swine—into coral reefs, rocks, shoals, and other rocky formations, reliefs of significative toponymy which the navigator can spot along the coast between Rosas and Port de la Selva, for example, el Cavall Bernat, el Cap Gros, la Punta Prima, etcetera. And so, in a similar way, that eroded solitary reef was the unhappy Priam, and Proserpine was the red and roaring grotto, and the shallow bottom which blossomed with the rising and falling of the waves, barely signaled by a sketch of spume, of white hydrangeas, perhaps Eugenia, opening a path among the immortals, among those who will never die because they already have died, returned to the mineral kingdom, exemplary stone, impassive in the face of the capricious wind and waves like any other configuration of the planet whose previous identity remains unknown, those madreporian atolls of the Gobi, the oceanic deserts, the reefs of Arizona, the craters of New York, the carbonized jungles of Rotterdam, the smoking embers of Barcelona.

No, what was going to happen, what had to happen, was not so much a response to any external motivation as to an inner one: the ark would split wide open just the way an eggshell cracks, in half, the contents crashing against the continent and the ship smashing against its own cargo, ballast not worth saving, better that it sink with the ship and its crew and the other remaining passengers when one might just survive by swimming, swim away in time from the whirlpool that forms as the shipwreck's coup de grace, and with greater reason still, keeping in mind that it would have all been for nought anyway, given the distance that separated it from the coast, how far offshore the ship was, without the help of one of those alleged sea monsters, those enormous fish that swallow castaways in order to carry them unharmed back to shore. And then, like a wooden doll, or like that little tin soldier which, fleeing from a rat, is gulped down by a fish and only in its entrails will it return to the fire of the lost love, then you find yourself trying to sit up inside the fish's mouth, crawling, groping on all fours along that moving, palpitating terrain, swept to and fro now and then by sudden surges of water, while your eyes adjust to the faint green light that glows through those venerable barbels, florid with marine vegetation, shelter of phlegmatic mollusks and solitary hermit crabs, and so, though still groping on all fours, you can move forward in search of a safer spot, one less unstable, between the silvery ballooning shoals of small fishes and the calm swaying of the other shipwrecks, under the palate's dark vault shaped like an inverted keel, using the spasmodic movements of the epiglottis as a reference point and, the throat now behind, continue moving forward, passing through the series of inner spaces, one after another, esophagus, stomach, intestine, evermore blindly, until reaching the comfortable widening of the rectum, waiting to be expelled by a discharge from the sphincter, that diarrhea that you hear rushing from afar like a depth charge and which, like an explosion, surges outward with a violence and velocity comparable only to Attila and his galloping host answering the call of Gudrun in her vengeance, in her anxiety to exterminate that moves her against the traitor Hagen; that empty inner space, that release of dead weight, that purgative phase, purifying, prior condition, inexcusable, of all ascensional process or of one of those trips that start off so carefree—like a creator setting his new world into motion—and which end so tragically, like the echo of a flute before the cornered, terminal coasts, Cabo de Orfeo, saving yourself from the waves as only the god can save himself who has unleashed the tempest or who is accustomed, on occasion, to save his protected one, a child.

Making it back to shore, always weary work for the shipwrecked sailor, an effort similar, because of how long it takes them to get out of the water, to one of those dreams in which the dreamer, still rattled by what they dreamed, believes themself to have awakened on a bed of soft, spongy earth, where, barely scratching the soil, they turn up some orange-colored bones. And only slowly, little by little, as if reanimated by the warm setting sun, they come around, sitting up, contemplating the sea at their feet that stretches away, shifting green spots forming in the foam like serpent's coils, that image of sea and grass joined, apparently uninterrupted, so captivating to a person reclining on their side on the gentle slope of a meadow, upon the cliffs, and which, nevertheless, precedes, as a visual impression, for example, the image of Cabo Norfeo, not to mention the view of the sea from that motel situated between San Juan de Luz and Biarritz, at the foot of the meadows, when for the first time they thought they heard a familiar resonant melody, the reactivation of a memory that might well be related to their earliest childhood, who knows if the mere magnification of a few blades of grass grown into one of those rolling, rippling sandy undulations that tend to form on the stretches of beach furthest back from the waves, the only point of contrast, for a child who lies there stretched out scanning the horizon, facing the distant sea.

One fact that deserves to be taken into account when the time comes for summing things up, when recounting the return to Rosas with Rosa, those days spent fashioning the broad outlines of the work—a work not unlike that oh-so meticulously designed city described over and over again throughout the course of history, according to the needs of the moment, in the general belief that none of them can now be altered, projects which, despite being started at some moment have never been finished, and in the end the modifications imposed by reality and its vicissitudes are so numerous that not even the original architect could now recognize it; and like that city, the author's work and, in fact, all works in the process of being rendered, with respect to their original conception—is that, to the changes imposed by the very development of their compositional elements must be also added the changes which the author experienced at the same time. And so, too, like something whose only reality exists on paper, within the lines of the plan, the blueprint, the map, we usually create ourselves out of the stock of images we retain from childhood, as well as so many more from then on, from the moment when childhood itself begins to fix its mind on representations. A task not very different, after all, from the one implied by the novel in question, six days in all, a time traditionally set aside for bringing a work of creation to fruition.

BOOK III: THE WRATH OF ACHILLES

Contents

I

When it comes to women, I'm only attracted to their bodies. Or rather: certain parts of their bodies. That doesn't mean, nor does it have to, that I prefer men: not in the least. I've had male lovers, and sometimes I thought I really loved them; once I even ended up married. But a man's body, even at its best, when it's a lovely young body, is hard and dry, rough to the touch, the last thing you'd want to caress, the last place to seek shelter. Whatever it is that attracts me to men—their sense of friendship, their frank behavior, their consistent way thinking—resides in the spirit, not the body. Exactly the opposite of what happens with women, of what a woman is: her body, a pure invitation to love, the dark psychic mechanism it encloses a pure invitation to absorbed contemplation, possessive and lascivious cruelty intermingled with a limitless capacity for treachery. That's why if I ever thought I was in love with a man, I've never gone so far as to believe I was in love with a woman.

When I was young, or should I say, when I was around twenty years old instead of around forty, I had all kinds of experiences. And I've never stopped having them ever since. That's why I can talk the way I do. Because—and not only the first time I lived in Paris—I've had the chance to try everything. I've even made love the way a man usually makes love with another man. Well, the conclusion that has impressed itself on me over the years is the following: where a man is concerned, more so than specific aspects of his body, I've been attracted to—and could still be attracted to—specific projections of that body that are physical only up to a certain point: his stare, his voice, his laugh, his smile, his way of moving.

When it comes to women, what I enjoy least, precisely, is the whole person. Their way of thinking and, especially, acting: their oh-so-personal way of seducing, and once they've got what they want, that is, their prey at their mercy, how they decide the other's happiness or misery however they please. But the worst thing is how they seem thoroughly convinced that they can achieve more by being bad than by being good, and the fact is, in general, they have little reason to doubt it. But only, in general, with other people—not with me. Blackmail doesn't work on me, and I always respond to betrayals—consubstantial with the species, you might say—exactly the way they deserve. Not with vengeance, nor with love of course. Nothing further from me now than the pretense of loving or being loved, nor of converting some frustrated love into wholesome vengeance. I simply want what is mine, and that others don't steal what belongs to me, nor, far worse, that they take me for a foolish woman. On the other hand, I also want to make it clear that I'm a complete stranger to jealousy, and if there's anyone for whom I've never felt compassion it's myself.

Maybe I'm being too blunt about it but the truth is that I find women's verbal diarrhea exasperating. When they talk about their problems, about their issues, just like in one of those novels set in Paris written by people from other places who feel compelled to use all the concrete details of the place: names of streets and squares, parks, hotels, the name of the barman or the woman who runs the bistro, things which, if it were any other city, they would feel free to ignore, things that interest nobody, less than nobody, including Parisians themselves, because living in Paris is neither an achievement nor a profession, and such a series of details is no more interesting than the spiels those tour guides go spitting into their microphones for the stunned sightseers on one of those bus tours that, in a single day, showcase the city's key landmarks to visitors who are in a big hurry, or who are perhaps just miserably unhappy.

On the other hand, there is perhaps far more charm in seducing a woman than a man: to force her to swallow her own alluring bait, to fall into the trap she herself has set, to let herself get tangled up in the web she's been spinning, to assist her in cutting off her own retreat, in corrupting her protective principles—the whole thing a far-reaching operation in which, like a puzzle, the reward lies in the difficulty endured, and patience itself becomes seductive, Cadaqués being an ideal spot for such activity, as if its habitués felt much more at ease there, far from their comfortable homes in Barcelona. One of those naturally flirtatious married women who pour their hearts out to me, fully aware, no doubt, that I've got a reputation for being a lesbian: her husband, so clumsy, so stingy, how he can't even begin to understand her, how she's fed up with his idiocy, and how the touch of his hand makes her skin crawl. I suppose any one of those women who talks to me that way, and who likely thinks herself as being rather special, would be surprised by how common, how frequent such confessions are, the expressive violence with which they're delivered, not only trying to make us care—much less from any need to share what's going in their lives—but because they want whatever they tell someone else to be gossiped about and repeated, how fed up that little floozy gets from that annoying little so-and-so, what a sour bitch she can be, how independent and dangerous she is, etcetera, boasts and exhibitionism which, despite being more show than anything else, more lip service than practical significance, I can't help turning to my advantage if the occasion merits it. Enough already with taking them exactly at their word.

These reflections—lucid, terse, concise, and properly structured—naturally—scraped clean of the magma from a thousand other ideas, feelings, and even sensations—emerged, as I recall, from that siesta in Cadaqués, when, with the perspective offered by the weeks gone by since the beginning of the events in question, sleepless, solitary, I set myself to work, to reconstruct and analyze them, starting with the initial uproar that surrounded the discovery of what happened.

I held all the threads in my hands, but I had never thought about tying them together. So, I did just that, and quite unexpectedly, one June 27th, a black night in my memory. But only when, overcome with fatigue, I went to lay down to sleep and, once in bed, found that something was keeping me from relaxing, despite how tired I was and how much I wanted to sleep--wide awake, thanks, no doubt, to my personal radar, one of those flashes of intuition that, like a bolt of lightning, seems to bring me enlightenment whenever I need to make a serious decision. It's almost embarrassing to admit it: that a woman like me, the last person anyone would ever call naive or lacking in common sense, could have that experience just like any other typical brainless woman. What my sixth sense warned me about, the one specific nagging thought keeping me awake, was that I'd come to rest sleepily on my laurels and had lost my touch. A notion that, obviously, presupposes the existence of such laurels. In this case it was my feeling of self-assurance, resulting from my dominance over Camila, my confidence in my penetrating psychological insight, in my clairvoyance. A confidence that inevitably leads to overconfidence, a circumstance traditionally favorable for all kinds of surprise attacks. A comfortable feeling of security based on my sense of superiority toward Camila, a woman who, despite possessing all the qualities to be found in a woman—if she were any different she would've never become my lover—also possesses all the defects inherent, for whatever reason, to her condition. And, similarly, a feeling of complete self-confidence toward Roberto, a man sufficiently anodyne—or vulgar, commonly known as a tacky person; enough circumlocutions already—to arouse not even the slightest bit of mistrust in any person possessing a certain amount of class: one of those friendly, almost amusing guys who spend their days on the beach, frying their brains in the sun, year after year. Besides, from the way he looks, or at least what he pretends to be, he seems half-Argentine. An Argentine Robert Taylor. The syrupy sweet variety of one of those swinish creatures who abound on the beaches in these parts, showing off their bronze skin and dubious virility, dedicated to chasing the latest poor Central European secretary, an exercise in stalking and seducing, zealously tracking and netting her with such ornithological precision that he collects a bonus or a commission for the money she helps him spend around town and, beyond that, laughing at the girl—who doesn't understand what anyone's saying—in front of his friends, don't worry, peaches, just stick with what you know best, do your thing, unnecessarily explaining exactly what her thing is with every kind of obscene clarification—one of those pigs. In short: the two facets of my mistake: underestimating Roberto, and overestimating Camila, incapable of believing her to stooping so low.

And then, with my mind and body equally restless, unable to stop ruminating in my useless effort to fall sleep, the threads seemed to weave themselves together, to form a conspiratorial web. I had left Camila and our passionate guest alone down in the cellar, rapt in one of those fruitless flirtations that Camila enjoys so much, especially when she drinks champagne. I know her, I know what she needs, and it's always struck me as cruel to deprive her of what is, after all, nothing more than some innocent frolicking.

They'd met—*we'd met*, according to him, the Argentine Robert Taylor—at somebody's house, an occasion about which, naturally, I don't recall a thing. And we kept running into him around every corner, one of those shiftless slackers who always haunt places like Cadaqués. So, that night, after meeting up at our favorite restaurant and having a drink at El Hostal, Camila invited him over for a nightcap, one last drink, at home. I felt tired but I agreed, my mind on Camila, her whims, her impulsive behavior, the consequences equally unpredictable and, frequently, stimulating, leading to insatiable erotic activity, something, certainly, far more predictable and, needless to say, always present in my calculations. The cellar, the champagne, Camila's theatricality, her tangos, her 1930s makeup, her disguises—or highly revealing outfits—her way of imitating a cabaret showgirl's performance: her typical routine. My preference runs to an American song from our parents' generation—"Smoke Gets In Your Eyes"—or, if not, one from our grandparents' time—Yvette Guilbert—and to step out onto my private dock, stare enraptured at the water and its nocturnal lights: when I play the *Missa solemnis* it means that I'm three sheets to the wind, the result, some days, of champagne more than any other drink, after its first characteristic wave of exaltation passes, the peculiar way our body suddenly loses energy, exactly why I don't know, though it's closely related to our earlier fatigue, fatigue or ennui, as well as our attempt to force ourselves to overcome it, for which reason we drain our glasses too quickly. That night I wanted to hear *Core 'ngrato*, which means—apart from a certain sentimental softness—that, if I feel like it, I can still snap out of it enough to decide that it's time to lower my sails. Out on the dock, the air cleared my head, and it was there I decided to slip away as discretely as possible, go to bed and leave them drinking and dancing tangos, almost without them noticing I'd left, no matter how much Camila might be accustomed to that habit of mine, so much my own, of leaving the party to run its course, something quite simple for any person with real class.

It seems that I needed a good long while tossing and turning in bed, naked, clutching my pillow like a little girl, trying to fall asleep, so that, without knowing how, I might remember that stuff about the postcard and, almost simultaneously, the connection between that postcard and what might very well be happening down in the cellar. The most run-of-the-mill sort of postcard—a typical shot of Piccadilly Circus—the back crammed with so many words the writing was illegible, addressed to Camila. It had fallen out of her purse that morning, while we were drinking a martini on the terrace at the Marítim, when I was fishing around in her bag for a light. I remember she said, the bad thing about postcards is that you don't even notice who mails them to you. And only then, as I was tossing and turning more and more in bed, naked, clutching my pillow like a little girl, I recalled another comment, this one from our handsome Robert Taylor, a while earlier, downstairs, about his recent stay in London, precisely in London. Almost simultaneously a question came to mind: why was Camila so late coming to bed? Or rather: why was she stretching things out so long with a guy as tremendously boring as our handsome gallant? I slipped into a bathrobe in that shade of Bordeaux that looks so good on me—I hate dressing gowns, negligees, and all those clothes people consider sexy—and flew downstairs like a Bonelli's eagle swooping down onto its prey. They didn't seem to notice my sudden appearance, the two of them in the half-light, as the tangos say, one of those tangos that played on and on without them paying the least attention, stretched out as they were on the sofa, naked, the inverted symmetry of their bodies perfectly coupled together, both carefully involved in those practices that men think drive us wild, and at which they're usually not very accomplished. Okay, you two, don't move a muscle, please, I said to get them to quit their clumsy handicraft, I'm going to take your picture!

I could never reconstruct the world of ideas and feelings that seemed to smother me in that very moment, while the scene I'd just discovered dissolved before my eyes, its composition suddenly disrupted, a sensation of drowning so intense that it's really rather inconceivable that I could have said what I said, with such serenity and self-control. As for Camila, that poor woman who came running to me and crouched down at my feet, sobbing, blubbering, trying to cover her nakedness in any way possible, like some Eve accursed for the second time, what thoughts, what desires could I harbor but to never see her again, to banish her from my sight, no matter what it took, to know that she'd be as far away from me as possible? And, at the same time, to have her near, close at hand, in order to sink her, to destroy her life, and to savor the spectacle. As far as the handsome Robert Taylor goes, to simply send him packing, kick his ass out the door, because, sadly, there's no law that authorizes, in such situations, riddling him with bullets. What other considerations could such a spectacle suggest? Camila clinging to my naked feet, while I try to shake her loose, pushing her away from my body the way you do with an overexcited dog or a rat that tries to claw its way up your legs, while he was putting on his clothes—socks, underpants, all that—and taking his sweet time, ridiculous, practically comatose, a real swine who deserved to be drowned in the water at the end of our dock, if only there were piranhas in the Mediterranean, multitudinous shoals of little fish that, in a few short minutes, would destroy all evidence of his murder. It fell to Camila herself who, rebuking him, insulting him, cursing him—in her own defense, naturally—told him to hit the road once and for all, to disappear, he'd already treated us quite badly, taking advantage of her drunkenness, and, especially, my trust, he, he who was just a lousy scam artist. The inherent baseness of her perfectly feminine way of turning against the man with whom she'd been stretched out on the sofa almost earned my applause, given how it seemed to support my own position, and it was only the farcical nature of the situation—practically a staged performance—that prevented me from tipping my hand, she at my feet and him slumped dazedly in an easy chair. It's really no big deal, this sort of thing, the great big imbecile said, getting to his feet; it happens all the time in Argentina. The finishing touch to such a performance, the perfect farewell—now that he was finally leaving—for a person like him, a truly crafty swine flush with all the tricks of a cut-rate Casanova, starting with the vulgar little gold medallion resting on his chest hair which, at the same time, seems to hang down like an arrow pointing directly at his sex, that fleshy bulge that our gaucho took special care to accentuate as much as possible. One of those summertime Don Juans who, when the season comes to an end, pulls out of his sleeve all the grief his wife gives him and how much he loves his kids and other such excuses, the screens that married or semi-married men always hide behind when they want to bring some affair to a conclusion. Tricks like that.

Camila followed me upstairs, placed herself between the door and jamb to prevent me from locking myself in the bedroom, then went and curled up into a ball by the head of the bed, overwhelmed; meanwhile my fury exploded again, its shock wave taking up more and more space. I smacked her away from me, screamed at her to get out, told her to pack her bags that instant, and never think of letting me see her face ever again. The words and expressions I used were, needless to say, much cruder, perfectly reflective of my state of mind, which is why it would be unnecessary, even improper, to transcribe them here. The big ninny, for her part, kept on repeating that she'd done something really stupid, yes, but it was a meaningless stupidity, and that, at any rate, she would've been the first to tell me what had happened, that idiotic blunder, her whopper about how could she have let herself be seduced by a lousy bastard like that, funny even, for being purely crazy, and to think how much we might have laughed together (laughed together!), afterward, when talking about it, the most absurd part of all that craziness, all things considered. She almost laughed as she said it, between sobs, and asked me again, or rather, asked herself aloud, why, why did I ever come downstairs.

I was sleeping, I said. And I dreamed that down in the cellar there were two snakes all coiled around each other. I woke up with that picture in my head and came down.

But the image that swam back into my mind while I was talking to her like that was the obscene symmetry of those two naked bodies and, more than the tango that was sweetly urging them on when I walked in, was the "Catari, Catari" from *Core 'ngrato*, the music playing and echoing in my brain, the record that I'd made them listen to several times before I went to bed, floating deep down in the champagne, so favorable for the romantic sublimation—camouflaged in irony—of that expansive sensation I myself easily succumbed to when I thought I was in love. Things from other times, very distant for me now, completely removed from the influence of such states of mind, now simply a clockwork machine, result of the fatigue produced by a farce that—regardless of what was going to occur, even before I withdrew as discreetly as possible—had already gone on too long.

Camila's embraces grew increasingly tighter and more passionate, what were at first timid touches becoming enveloping caresses, slowly, imperceptibly, causing a gradual mutation in the nature of our quarrel. A tactical shift that, if I had offered her the opportunity before, if it had occurred to Camila to put it into practice from the start, might have prevented my verbal violence, if not my physical energy, from reaching such extremes. What's certain is that, aware or not of what was going on, with or without calculation, she did it well. Once in a while we fell asleep, and if a burning ember of what happened, as if being fanned back to life, jolted me abruptly out of my sleep and I was overcome anew with that insatiable fury—it would have been difficult to pinpoint from moment to moment what kind of fury it was—Camila soothed it again, with especial frenzy starting from the moment when, perhaps from a lapse, perhaps from whatever it was, I forbade her from seeing him again, told her that never again in her life could she and the Argentine see each other, a demand that, with respect to my initial, absolute rejection of them both, obviously supposed a change of attitude on my part, and a stimulus for her to pursuing that path now begun. A path—alternately filled with fury and delight—whose agreeable aspects I didn't fail to enjoy, nor did I have to, especially as I was beginning to discover two facets of my own eroticism ignored until then, if not completely unknown: the pleasure I derived from lovemaking not entirely lacking in violence—pulling hair, scratching, biting, etcetera—a violence more than justified by the circumstances, and the incentive, darker in its roots, its stimulation more psychological than directly physical, aroused by the idea that that body I was treating so cruelly, and which I thus possessed, had just been enjoyed by some other body, a man's body. It was a night, or rather, a dawn, or rather, a really unforgettable morning, given that, when I finally managed to fall asleep, the noise from the street as well as the ribbon of sunlight slipping between both sets of curtains showed how far the day had already advanced.

Best celler: impossible to be any more impeccable. As if, more than resembling a mise-en-scène of everything that had happened there just a few hours earlier, it looked like a museum's endless identical galleries. Spotless, as if apart from the spilled champagne, the empty bottles, the melted candles, the scattered LPs, and the clothes worn as disguises strewn about, and, especially, apart from the disorder and the stench of cigarette butts, nothing had happened there and nobody had heard the music, the voices, the shouts, the screams, the sobbing, nor would it seem strange that I arose at midday while Camila continued sleeping or, at least, stayed locked in her bedroom, from which she wouldn't emerge until nighttime. I knew Herminia's professional efficiency, and her discretion, how she took in everything with a completely straight face; for example, the fact that Camila kept sleeping—or couldn't get out of bed—the whole day. An attitude completely deserving of my praise, although, for obvious reasons, and needless to say, it wasn't necessary to show it. Unlike Herminia, who could perfectly conceal the morbid curiosity and spying that every household servant practices, such discipline must have consisted of something more than mere strength for Emilia and Constantino. Thus, Constantino, solicitous and respectful, with his sailor's cap in his hand, couldn't manage to deny himself the pleasure of asking me if I still planned to go out on the boat as I'd mentioned the night before. I told him that we might go out fishing in the late afternoon; that he should wait. And while eating lunch on the terrace, I had the occasion to witness his appearance on the dock, muttering to himself—cursing me, surely: he climbed aboard the boat, killed the motor, and crouched down by the wheel, complaining all the while, like a little boy squatting to answer nature's call. I've got no patience for such small-town stupidity, those apparently candid displays of innocence, of anxious seriousness, betrayed only by the irrepressible pleasure the underling derives from any sort of misfortune or mishap, however insignificant, that befalls their employer, the one who is in every way their superior; the joy, the crude jokes inspired by what their narrow minds perceive as a just punishment for good fortune, pleasure, and anything splendid in this life: the vile mockery, the everlasting braying of the lower classes.

Emilia, the woman, is even more hypocritical, and also, thanks to her greater intelligence, more cunning, more conscious of the fact that, their position as non-fishing fishermen—like everyone in Cadaqués, by the way—being in my service, taking care of my boat and my house, which, apart from the odd weekend, we only visit in summer—and perhaps even less often in the future, considering how impossible the town is becoming, vulgar, overrun by snobbish bad taste, with a reputation for debauchery that only attracts riffraff—constitutes a true bargain which more than one married couple would love to enjoy, keeping in mind what I pay them. That's why she's better at faking it; that's why, that same afternoon, at the first opportunity, they were going to have a big blowup—he was going to get it; she'd make sure she gave it to him good—for his impertinence, for the brutish, dimwitted way he risks his job, the way he jeopardizes both their positions. She knows it better than I do, and thus their fights, their quarrels, their altercations, so loud even the octopuses and other creatures living around the dock could hear them. So we're ignorant, and that means we're bad, I remember Constantino once came to tell me—unable even then to repress a sort self-satisfied smirk—referring to a heated reprimand provoked by I don't know what kind of prank.

I switched on the record player so that, thanks to the automatic replay, *Core 'ngrato* played over and over again, and I ate lunch in the sun, on the terrace, dark glasses shading my eyes from the sparkling sea, blown smooth by the Tramontana. And like the Tramontana, so too my mind, lucid, diaphanous, crystalline. And also like that wind, like the implacable firmness of its impulse, my intentions. It was as if the night's fury had set off a process of renewal that I felt expanding inside me the way the Tramontana comes howling off the land and spreads across the sea, a feeling of vigor and, what's more, of omnipotence, something like that uncontainable impetus that possesses the horse the moment it feels the barn doors open onto a beautiful morning. And, above all, I was anxious to dive back into my novel, no longer just tracing the broad outlines of the plot to come but, and especially, setting to work immediately, to dig deep and go on writing straight through to the end. With an eye to all that, I ravenously devoured my tomato salad and very rare fillet that weighed at least half a pound, which Herminia, with her habitual tact, had thoughtfully left prepared for me along with a chilled bottle of white wine—I don't care for red. It's one of my favorite meals, apart from its well-verified properties—nutritional richness, lightness, and energetic value—a combination at once healthy and stimulating, even if people keep coming out with stories about how a person can live exclusively on creamed spinach, and other such fashionable stupidities.

It was, perhaps, the stimulation afforded by the incomparable view of the bay from my terrace, added to what the Tramontana blew in all by itself. The fact is that, bursting or not with external stimuli, what I felt growing inside myself was no longer a new strength, some heretofore unknown power, or a feverish sensation that seemed to enable me to achieve whatever my heart desired. No, no longer that. It was, instead, as if some new being had truly been born inside me, a little girl like the one I once was, but far removed from the constrictive factors that inhibited my childhood and gifted with all the characteristic faculties of the adult woman, and, appropriately, by reason of its very omnipotence, features belonging to an entirely new kind of woman. Like the eagle that seems to sprout from a rocky crag when it spreads its wings, thus, too like a bird taking flight, the awakening of this new woman.

In that elevated state, reached by so few, so rarely, the plan of action offered itself to me all at once, almost like an organizational flow chart needing only to be divided into segments, in order to examine the specific points of its articulation. The plan was based on an assumption: the evidence that Camila and her fabulous, brand-spanking-new Argentine Robert Taylor had met some time before, that last night had not been their first encounter nor would it be their last. The how, the where, and other details of their affair, are entirely devoid of interest given how commonplace such arrangements are today, unlike years ago, when the gigolo—the figure doubtless most comparable to our gaucho—haunted only the tackiest establishments. What really mattered was to be absolutely clear that the worst move I could make, given the situation, would have been to abandon Cadaqués. To take Camila with me to Barcelona, for example, where the two of them would have enjoyed the benefit of easy encounters, excuses, complicities, love nests, etcetera. Other locations could offer them the same advantages, more or less—and I'll admit that I thought about various ones, Venice, Istanbul, Tahiti—where I'd never manage to be completely sure, no matter however far away, that we hadn't been followed.

No: my domain was Cadaqués, and there the game had to be played; a terrain I controlled to perfection, as much for its dimensions—everything conveniently at hand—as for my knowledge of its regulars and devotees, their habits, their weaknesses, their schedules, and, in quite a few cases, their most intimate secrets. And, with the place decided on, it would also be I who chose, not only the rules of the game, but the very game to be played in each moment, whichever suited me best according to the circumstances. Meaning: more than curtailing the great love that Camila, at least, must have thought herself experiencing, a measure counterproductive in the short term considering just how arousing obstacles and adversities usually prove to be in such affairs, rather than acting in this way, the tactic to follow, as I saw it, consisted, quite to the contrary, in assisting their affair, frequent encounters, and, whenever possible, superficial ones, so that their ambitious search for new chances to betray me, to which they would both presumably devote themselves, ever fearful of the risk of being discovered, would be equally nerve-racking and exhausting. And to leave it that way indefinitely, without setting any dates, without saying how long we'd stay in Cadaqués. Or better yet: to make it all as concrete as possible in order to then deliberately postpone everything, pushing back our departure from Cadaqués as many times as seemed advisable; in short, to make the gigolo's gaucho charade wear thin from use, from having to do everything on the sly. Let the inevitable breakup, or better yet, abandonment, become a kind of liberation for them both. Smother the fire with a blanket, the first step in every siege. Or, in more vulgar terms, let them stew in their own juices. Everything except allowing them to steal what was mine. Not breaking up with Camila, not giving in to anybody, not renouncing a thing. Quite the contrary, I would conquer my antagonists at any cost, secure their surrender, force them to recognize their defeat. And only then, after my victory, if it suited me, would I dump Camila.

No matter what, it was clear that that our relationship would never be the same again. And if I decided to allow her to remain by my side—a complicated problem requiring further consideration—I had to bend her to my will completely, without reservations, without false pretenses that might lessen the severity of the fact. In short, she must be my pliant female servant, rendered thus by her financial subservience, living as she does at my expense, although until the present moment, and purely out of tenderness, I hadn't demanded of her, as fair payment, that she also live at the mercy of my whims. Camila should certainly have thought of all that sooner rather than later, when it was totally pointless to think it over twice to realize that an experience like the one I'd gifted her was simply unrepeatable. As someone put it so well before me: if she avoids you today, she'll soon seek you out; if she doesn't take them today, she'll want to give gifts; if she doesn't love you, she'll soon talk to you about desire, how it weighs on her.

Apart from that, the tactical maneuvers and unforeseeable steps that might alter my plan depended on sudden changes dictated by the course of events. The last thing I was about to tolerate was repeating something like my affair with the very aptly named Maldonado, Francisca Maldonado, a semi-famous theater actress from Madrid, about fifteen or twenty years ago, the number of years, approximately, that she was older than me; oh, well, she still is, although I don't know what became of her, nor do I want to. I was little more than a girl back then, and I loved her with all the passionate innocence belonging to that age. We lived in Madrid, or rather, I lived with her in Madrid, although so young it was impossible to understand the subtleties of it all. It was a lovely affair that came to an end, for reasons not necessarily relevant now, in the most brutal, chaotic, and cynical way possible: unforgivable, really, especially considering I was a young woman barely past adolescence. Nonetheless, that was one of the few times—while it lasted—that Madrid struck me as a satisfying city; probably the only time. Satisfying enough to call it *Madrigi*, in Italian.

Or letting them mock me. I wouldn't even have let them try. Like W. L., that girl the other summer from the States, one of those Americans who wash up in Cadaqués. She had the audacity to try to steal Camila from me—naturally she failed—resorting to all the sophisms of the little lesbians who masquerade as feminists. And with all the brazenness, the impertinence of the critic who, laureled with his youthful promise, makes a splash in the pages of the *TLS* or some other wretched publication, brimming over with his youthful intolerance, his conservative aggression, full of his imperious homosexual desires and, most of all, his cyclamen-colored silk tie.

What irritates me most about men is the aura they seem to emit when seized by an intense superiority complex, as cocksure as young gods. And if such Olympian spirit manifests itself most often when people are young—Paris, in my memory, is replete with such deities—in some cases the phenomenon only grows with the years; sometimes not without reason, which is the worst thing about it. Because what's certain is that there are two kinds of auras, and one of them is real, verifiable, and reflects a tangible quality, like with some (especially one, most especially) of those friends from my days as a philology student in Paris, to which I've just alluded. But most often the so-called aura—apropos of our gaucho—might simply be the glitter of costume jewelry, trinkets from theater costumes, splendid masks of kohl, eye shadow, and pomaded hair, the look of young heartthrobs from the tango era or, more recently, a tennis player's particularly splendid physique, and those dynamic manners and slightly cynical wit that characterize the man of our times. Auras that vanish with the first mishap, the brief cloud that overshadows a vast landscape, the gust of rain that spoils all the tender-loving care that went into a carefully coiffed head of hair.

One of the things that has always struck me in that respect is men's private amazement, their overflowing boyish pride, following their first sexual encounter with their conquest—seduction, rape, what have you—when, at least formally, they've successfully completed the task. Formal success—from their perspective: erection, penetration, ah, ah, ah, and all that—which leads them to presume, very mistakenly, that the woman's pleasure has occurred with a parallel rhythm and intensity, that their lucky partner has fully shared the same pleasure they have—or think they have—experienced. And, consequently, however minute the skill with which they've resolved the undertaking, they seem to feel somehow more confident about their little woman—meaning: her fidelity to them, seeing how irreplaceable they are, and how useless it would be for her to have an affair with another man—and, no less, about their occasional lovers, than they are, in the last place—or in the first place—about themselves. That manic preoccupation about whether everything has gone well, that obsession with knowing, for being sure that the woman has had the best time ever or, at least, better than usual, or shall we say, at least no worse than other times; an insistence that can only lead us to think, after all, that it might just be him who's had a worse time. The anxiety is understandable only with men who are not very well endowed—the majority—although, quite frequently, the ones least worried are also the clumsiest ones. But what's really curious is that such worries also beset those rare exceptions to the rule, men provisioned, not so much with skill in lovemaking, but rather, and above all, with sensitivity and tact. I think that what they probably want us to tell them is not that they're good lovers but that they're better lovers, better than any other man. The inevitable competitive spirit that, contrary to popular belief, is rooted much more in men than in us women, and precisely in the most physical, anatomical aspect: size, duration, reiterative capacity, etcetera. The fact is that if a woman tells them yes, that everything has gone quite well—although it might not be true—they thank us for it as if they owed us their lives; even if they suspect we might be faking. But, whether true or not, if some man comes to be convinced, to convince himself, that he's the best we've ever had, that's when Mister High and Mighty starts to show himself, Mister Master Orgasmer, the one who's sure he drives each and every one of us wild, whether we like it or not, with his clumsy technique.

What infuriates me most, however, what I now find completely incomprehensible, almost beyond my tolerance, is how women, with their behavior, offer men such mindless laughing complicity. They must be afraid that men will call them frigid, they must overlook the blot on their reputation that comes from having a relationship with a proven incompetent, but the truth is they rarely admit their own dissatisfaction. If they decide to, it's either because they make a joke out of it, or because they're loaded drunk. And they maintain such reserve not only when facing the invalid whom they've acquired as a lover, but also, and above all, when facing their closest friends, who theoretically enjoy their total confidence; they are, simply, secrets that are never shared. In my years in Paris, as I gained more experiences in that area, I was able to confirm it perfectly well. Most men don't even know how to make love, and women don't even dare to admit it.

Paris. A curious thing is that unconscious tendency when recounting certain places, cities, towns, landscapes and even houses, to include one's memory of the love affairs for which those locations provided the backdrop, joyful meetings and disasters alike, being, according to that result, positive or negative, respectively, the impression left in the memory by those places. Positive for Paris and London, for example. Like Cadaqués. Negative for Madrid. The same for Sète, an undoubtedly attractive place, a fact that proves, nonetheless, how far the tendencies I'm alluding to exist independent of all objective settings. And the same generally goes for the cool, green landscapes, similar to the land around Aiguaviva, in La Selva, the property that my mother sold. I couldn't have been more than six or seven when she sold it, too young for real romantic adventures so, in this case, more than mere impressions, I would need to talk about my tendency to be inhibited. Of course, if you ask me the reason why, the cause of such a tendency, as with so many other self-realized conclusions, verifiable but indemonstrable, I'll be unable to answer conclusively. What I could do—and perhaps someday I will, if I convince myself it's worth the effort—is to develop a theoretical framework about this and other causes of inhibitory predispositions—clothes, words, objects, including proper names—at least as valid as the castration complex theory and all those theories invented with sufficient astuteness, so that, merely by calling them stupid, I become, by dint of their formal logic, one of the victims of such a complex. So, my own theories will also need to be equally invulnerable to this type of criticism.

Cadaqués, however, has always been an especially favorable place for me. There's so much stimulation and vitality that inspires me there, I feel it, I'm totally conscious of it, that the people become scared of me. I know for certain that there, on my turf, I'll always win, that nothing and nobody will be able to beat me. A conviction that, well-founded or impulsive, fully possessed me that famous June 27th, while I was lunching on the sunny terrace, my appetite excellent, my body in perfect shape and in no way inferior to my lucid mind. To accept the cruel reality of things as they are: knowing that Camila didn't love me and that my desire to keep her by my side was selfish, pure and simple, self-love, self-respect, whichever you prefer. After all, I wasn't even remotely in love with Camila either. But only through the force of clairvoyance is it possible to move from formulating a state of things to mapping out a plan of action like the one I then established, when I didn't yet possess any of the elements—I don't mean key facts—that I would have in my power some two months later, in early September—the episode at Port de la Selva come and gone—that afternoon on which, at siesta time, as if my spirit, overcome by my imminent victory, renouncing all recapitulation, all reflection, all calculation, filled me with a vivid recollection of the crazy lovemaking Camila and I indulged in after the scene in the cellar, there, in the very same room, in the same bed. That siesta in the afternoon heat, while voices from outside came filtering in with the thin ribbons of sunlight, nothing further from the street sounds of Barcelona, of any city, the soothing effect of stray words, of nearby bodies, of shadows revolving in the half-light on the ceiling. And I, naked on the bed, feeling the pulse of my racing memory, as someone once wrote for us, Eros returning, arms, legs relaxing, leaving me bewildered, sweet and bitter, an irresistible creature; feeling her oppressive presence, feeling myself her prisoner, coming to experience an excitation in no way lesser than what came before, a pleasure superior to the pleasure remembered.

II

The south. That, without a doubt, is what the false gaucho meant when he writes to her that he desires her whole body, from north to south: "south" in the same corporeal sense that Camila's little two-bit English girlfriend meant when, through a revealing associative mechanism, referred to sanitary napkins as "south-of-the-border pads." The deep south. He might have written from the Chaco to the Cabo de Hornos, by way of Patagonia, which would always have sounded better. But no: from north to south. He puts it in various letters without noticing, possibly, that he's repeating himself. Or perhaps he thinks he's made a discovery and so he repeats it on purpose, in order to fire up Camila with his own alleged ardor. He knows that those things are contagious and, on another hand, it would be asking a lot for Camila to realize that such insistence is not in the least spontaneous, that it's completely premeditated, pure calculation. She kept his letters in the most obvious hiding place: in one of her dresser drawers, tucked between her underwear, which I don't usually touch since it doesn't fit me. I read them one after another, in chronological order, comfortably installed in the cellar, listening to the *Goldberg Variations*, and savoring a magnificent Alsatian pear brandy. I knew that Camila, once asleep, entered a state that, more than dreaming sleep, might better be called hibernation.

The next morning, pretending I didn't notice her shock, I told her that I'd had a rather anguished dream: one of her dresser drawers, I wasn't sure which, but one that I opened, was full of snakes—what you might call a nightmare. When we got back from the beach, the letters, logically enough, were no longer there. I couldn't find out definitively if she returned them to our faux gaucho or if she simply got rid of them, which is the most likely thing; what's more, the dilemma doesn't worry me. What's certain is that they weren't in the house, because I would have found them again just as I found so many other letters she kept on receiving. She hid them inside the cardboard sleeves of her tango records, one letter per record, knowing that it was not really my favorite kind of music; a very obvious hiding place.

I suppose it never even crossed her mind that I'd read her secret correspondence from beginning to end, and that I continued amusing myself with those florid epistles—composed in the style of festival songs—that the lovely Roberto dedicated to her, the moment she hid them carefully away again. And I, for my part, abstained from making new comments that might alert her, because I'd read them with the same discreet vigilance I used to keep my eyes on the two of them. It effectively revealed to me the hidden side of their relationship that existed in a place where my eyes could not see and my guesses not reach: their quick trysts in any hidden corner, their kisses, the words exchanged, the exact degree of emotional intensity they experienced. Having such facts at my disposal proved valuable when I needed to precisely calibrate the duration and frequency of their rendezvous, which, more than permitting, I deliberately facilitated as naturally as possible, appearing increasingly more permissive, as if I were relaxing my defenses or taking a liking to her beloved Roberto. Thus, as we continued to frequent our usual haunts, the various places they must have met up together so many, many times, it must have seemed to Camila that while I had initially forbidden her from seeing him, I was now becoming indifferent about the matter, even ignoring it. We also managed to end up sitting at the same table, first at El Hostal, I remember it perfectly, and then in our favorite restaurant, among mutual friends, uttering theatrical asides and everything, the sorts of places that always provide the right opportunity for lightning-fast encounters in the bathrooms, corners, and corridors, in the gloomy street outside, and so on. We also ran into each other at Fina's cocktail party, surely not a complete coincidence, and that unleashed new and suspicious coincidental invitations, complicities not the least mysterious. But Fina's cocktail party permitted me, in turn, to invite everyone there—every single one of them—to my own cocktail party, and when that night rolled around, I had the pleasure of witnessing by the light *aux chandelles* of my wine cellar, our fine gaucho's reappearance, so very discreet and correct in his behavior, I must say. And I use the word pleasure because I had started to find the charade amusing, enjoyable, now that I was personally creating opportunities for verbal contacts—oral ones, to be precise—and relaxing emotional moments to become real physical contact, in limited amounts of time, of course, strictly limited, which, like all things done in haste, usually lead to inevitable dissatisfaction. And all that—I wish I'd been as sure of everything as I'm making it sound—without allowing those two little lovebirds the slightest opportunity to really get together behind my back.

In fact, it felt as if I were following the teachings, counsels, and other amorous prescriptions of the immortal Ovid, with precisely the opposite purpose: the ideal places, actions, and schemes to make love take root deep in the beloved's heart, and remain just as passionate as the very first day, yes; but only with the goal that its very persistence in conditions no longer uncertain but anxious and stressful becomes an entirely negative burden, like that cool drop of water that, over time, ends up boring a hole right through someone's skull. To favor the mutual declarations of love, cultivate the difficulties necessary for that love to grow and take shape, the setbacks necessary for it to survive its fight against adversity. Direct our lovers to the ideal locales for their encounters: private parties, cocktail parties thrown by mutual friends, the crepuscular intimacy of El Hostal. Freely provide alcohol, marijuana, and other stimulants that unleash irresponsible behavior. Give them enough room to carry out their maneuvers and intimate encounters; a chance for them to commiserate about the painful affronts they've each suffered, the pleasure of what appear to be good prospects; taking advantage of the impact of bad news as well as happy moments brought on by external influences, invitations, gifts, a letter. Strengthen their resistance with the occasional breath of fresh air, sufficient, however, to give the impression that their luck might have changed, that from now on time favors the besieged. Facilitate the effusiveness that always arises from frustrated love, with the help of several drinks, promises and oaths of eternal courage, the phenomena of identification, of shared projections, etcetera. Engineer—thanks to an opportune slip-up—the complicity of friends (!) and servants, one's own as well as those friends' servants (!), too. Create situations which unleash reciprocal feelings of jealousy, scenes, mutual suspicions and mistrust, those hot coals that enliven the fire of hearts beginning to cool, that threaten to grow cold; use third parties to that end, mutual friends whose behavior—without them being conscious that I was manipulating them, completely in the dark about what's happening—provokes, like a spur, an explosion of such feelings and scenes between our lovebirds. So that they write to each other, that they exchange messages: I'll read them all, the ones she receives as well as the ones she sends, the latter implied in the contents of the former. And, given the character of their relationship, grotesque, ridiculously adolescent, it let them pay no attention to the rumors and gossip—nothing beyond truth and logic—they have unleashed in Cadaqués, the whole town laughing at them. Talking about how they love each other, they hate each other. So that through my general comments they come to think of me as the pointer on the scales. Fully supporting each of them against the other.

What didn't catch me at all by surprise was my darling Fina's solicitous, disinterested involvement with Camila in that matter. They were made for each other. The only difference between the two of us is that I'm not her complacent industrial paper manufacturer of a husband. To facilitate their trysts, she—the procuress—offered our pitiful pair of sweethearts one of the apartments that she rents out. Rather: the one she doesn't rent, the one she reserves for private purposes, her own personal love nest. It's situated across the bay and, from the terrace, although the door of the house can't be glimpsed, the only two access points to the street where the house stands can be clearly observed with the simple help of a pair of binoculars.

In a certain way, Camila is the epitome of what women tend to be: attractive and stupid. Roberto is stupid, too, but he's also tacky and pretentious. In the style of a movie screen gallant. Studied tricks of the most conventional kind. The accent and the Argentine touches worked up with tender loving care, with affectation, when—as is frequent—he doesn't forget to use them; not really the least bit strange—after all, if he was born in Argentina, it was more or less by chance. He has the habit of wearing nothing under his trousers, so that his cock stands out beneath the thin fabric as clearly as possible, declaring him especially ready, willing, and able, it would seem. His way of inviting women to smoke a freshly lit cigarette he's just been holding between his own lips. Of caressing a woman's profile with the tip of his index finger—me, Camila, or any woman he's just met—sliding his finger down her forehead, nose, lips, chin, as if obeying an irrepressible impulse. Of walking barefoot, hair uncombed and, if possible, shirtless, showing off his chest and blond hair. Even his way of laughing, sparkling, overflowing with self-confidence, which is separate from his empty conversation, the vague notions he continually spits out, which he sees as an expression—I suppose—of the unbiased personality he tries to affect.

I'm well aware of the possibly clumsy explanation for my victory, for his defeat—one that he himself might offer: his alibi, his extenuating circumstances, his defense—she's won (that's me) because she's richer, because whoever pays calls the shots, because she's got luck on her side. But let's imagine switching roles, discarding the possibility of fortune favoring Roberto, because, in such a case, the question would never arise, because he would never go padding around Cadaqués after Camila, he'd rather set himself up on the Costa Azul—where the fishing is better—caressing expensive little pussycats. Let's ask simply what might have occurred if Camila had been the rich one and I the poor one. How would things have turned out then? Well, exactly the same. Would I have hesitated to use my poverty, my economic inferiority as a weapon against my enemy, as the defining instrument of my success, granting as invariable the real fact, that, in either scenario, it was me and not Roberto with whom Camila was in love? Wouldn't my grounding myself precisely in my poverty have turned his fortune into the ostentatious target of my mordacity, of my opinions and reproaches? Wouldn't I have scorned and spurned all her offers, all her compromises, until, bent beneath the weight of her millions, she'd sink to her knees and kiss my feet? What better trump card, what better instrument of moral coercion, than the poverty wielded by the hand of the beloved?

I'm rich, it's true. And Camila knew then and still knows now how much she owes me, not only on a social level but also in a purely economic sense; how much, thanks to me, she's been able to achieve, things that, if not for me, would have been forever beyond her reach. And she also knew how much I can continue to offer her, a lifestyle that is not easy to renounce, realities that hang such a high price on any romantic illusion—Roberto's love—that it's not worth the trouble to pay. Well, what could he offer her in this area, just one more young man with a degree in literature with no better prospects than a mediocre monthly paycheck, supposing he had any intention of making something of himself, supposing him—as usually happens with men—a little tired by now of the situation, not the first to wonder what he had to look forward to with an older woman, one with whom he had nothing in common beyond sharing a bed? What would have been possible with me—a deep relationship—could not have happened with her. And that must have been exactly what Camila most feared: her beloved Roberto would eventually end up in my bed instead of hers. Jealousy, in other words.

Everything was working in my favor and I knew it, perfectly aware that my line of conduct, more than ending with the story, was tending to prolong it. I knew the ending. As that person wrote, the one whom I sometimes hate because of how much they've plagiarized me merely by anticipating my next step: you came, and I loved you; you froze my heart burning with desire. You seemed to me a little girl without a hint of grace. I'd already been in love with you for a long time.

Rich girl triumphant, poor girl triumphant, I could have played the same game either way, victorious no matter what, I had the right to deliberately complicate the rules of the game. And I lacked neither resources nor stimulating information. Two words—the witch, a name they evidently called me, thanks to what they saw as my bewildering gift for divination—from one of the letters Camila received had made me understand that, in order to somehow counteract my powers, to stay abreast of my insights, it might also occur to her to pry into my papers, knowing her familiarity with my fondness for jotting things down, wherever I find myself, when the ideas start flowing, sparkling, torrential, in my mind. In the cellar, at the Marítim, on the boat: wherever I happen to be. So I started writing all sorts of notes about her, about me, our relationship, her relationships; the very things she wanted to read, exactly what I wanted her to read. And, of course, without hiding them out of her reach. I knew that she would go riffling through my purse, and I used to leave them there in my purse, forgotten in the cellar while I was taking a nap. Needless to say, in every note I made it explicitly clear—the more unclear a person's mind is the more clearly you've got to speak to them—that the last thing I wanted was for her to ever read the feelings I put down in those notes; intermingled with my expressions of love were other thoughts, reflections, fantasies, plans, curses, all perfectly consistent with the domineering tone in the last letter she received from Roberto. Replies to the reply to a reply. An interference, like an inaudible voice switched off, that only served to provoke a kind of tension in Robert's reactions, in each letter, as opposed to the limpid emotional transparency of every one of my notes.

My powers. What else could that refer to besides that stuff about me being a witch? My insights, my lucidity, my strokes of creativity, my ability to react, the celerity with which I'm capable of imprinting my acts, things that Camila knew abundantly well, and to which, suddenly, had to be added my diabolical control of the situation that allowed me to read her letters. Roberto had written to her again about how he desired her, from north to south, and I, while we were sipping coffee, made sure to offer my thoughts about the associative mechanisms of that friend of hers—friend, lover, whatever—the little two-bit English girl, who called sanitary napkins "south-of-the-border pads." I mentioned the time she stayed with us, the way she'd just showed up at our house, accepting one of those invitations you make without really thinking the person might take you up on it; a real steal that only Camila is capable of finding, a ridiculous little provincial girl, equally provincial in both her looks and her manners, in her way of laughing and her way of talking, with those expressive twists she must have considered so fine; I still don't know with absolute certainty if they were her own invention—I don't see her inventing anything—or some fad, one of those fads that a certain social milieu tends to adopt, or perhaps just the fruit of traditional Anglo-Saxon false modesty. When she started with that nonsense about south-of-the-border pads, I pointed out to her, as I saw it, that south is the perfect word for posterior, the bottom, and therefore the expression "south towels" is a perfectly elegant way to say toilet paper. The girl coughed, blushed, and changed the subject, everything just like in one of those comedies they put on in the West End and, suddenly, she had to leave for some unexpected reason, and that was the last we heard of her. Camila, agreeable, laughed simply at the memory of it, but stopped laughing when I dropped a sudden casual aside, about how the "south" usually attracts men. A special predilection that is in no way, however, exclusive to the English, especially since the English are a people who do everything backward. No: the south that I mean seems to interest all men, and it's still curious that nobody has made a dedicated study of the matter. And while Camila blushes with embarrassment, just as red, no less, as her little English sweetie, while I pretend not to notice, and just continue twisting the knife: because there are times, you might say, when that's the only thing they're aiming for, their secret target.

I also had my own secret target now that I mention it, and Camila's blushing face showed me that I'd hit the bullseye. Because it wasn't men's southern longings that made her blush, but the fact that it was me, and precisely on that day, who had alluded to such preferences. As far as I'm concerned, I've got to say that the only time I was the object of such preferences, I experienced more excitation than pleasure. And what has always fascinated me since then—I still keep wondering about it—is how the hell men manage when they start fucking each other with their intestines full. When I had my experience in that area, the problem, luckily—given that it wasn't exactly an experience I had foreseen—had been resolved shortly before. The myth of the south; an experience typical of my first Parisian sojourn.

I now wonder if it wasn't an unforeseen foresight that taught me how to solve the annoying physiological irregularities that, due to always rushing around and everything else, tend to happen when one is traveling. Or, simply, when one is out of the house and not sufficiently relaxed. I discovered bathrooms in the nearest museum to be far superior to bathrooms in bars and cafes—the admission price costs less than a cup of coffee—and they are clean, discreet, and little used.

From a certain perspective, the two girls from Burgos were perhaps responsible for my interest in, my observations on, and my ideas about the world of domestic service. Ultimately, a person's relationship with their servant smacks of the conjugal, and it strikes me as absurd that people worry so much about their intended spouse's personality but so little about those of their servants, with whom they must also share their home. Especially because, just like everything else people pay for, servants are not what they used to be, part of an industry in the throes of degeneration, or denaturalization, or however you say it—well, that it's breaking down. Young girls today are not like they used to be, and the ones who aren't so young anymore, they seem like they just let themselves be dragged along by the current, and they aren't usually the best workers: they're more skillful and efficient, but they're also more malicious. And it's a fact that even the ones who spend years and years in the same household, the ones who become something of a family institution, when for some reason they have to find a new situation, despite everything and how valuable they are to that family, they usually turn out to be impossible for another, incapable at this point of adapting themselves to a new environment and, above all, to new customs, to how casually things are done nowadays. Whoever's not an expert on the subject won't discern any difference, for example, between Herminia's *sí señora*, and Emilia's *como usted mande señoreta*. But I do know, and I see right through them.

Herminia, for example, was truly an exceptional case, far superior to what one can expect from someone of her social condition, profession, and origins. She imitated me in what she could, and in front of other people carried on as if she was my friend more than my subordinate, and generally tried to learn from me, it's true, but she did all that without neglecting her professional duties in the least, an attitude, ultimately, much to her credit. She shared confidences with me, asked me for advice, simultaneously direct and flattering, appearing unabashed in her efforts to stylize—or sterilize—her private life, her secrets, to the nth degree, trying to bring everything into closer alignment with her wishes than with reality. And I knew that when she assured me that, beneath her casual pose, she was really a shy, complicated creature, her real problem lay—I was sure of it—in the fear that, without my priceless tutelage, whatever she deemed high-quality; and exceptional would only be provincial. And I was perfectly aware of her maneuvers, her tricks: her way of coming up close to me on the terrace, of leaning on the railing to stare down at the swimmers who sometimes appeared on the rocks by the wharf; her banal comments, her uninspired smile, everything just like we were having an amusing conversation, all so that she might be taken for a friend instead of a servant.

But she behaved tactfully. She understood immediately the special nature of my relationship with Camila and learned to adapt herself with admirable celerity and skill. And so, just like in the beginning, always with her characteristically unusual and even excessive frankness, she told us about her beau, the young fellow she was seeing, explaining all the things they did together, the number of times they did it, with details and everything—Camila and I called it Monday Morning Report—while she served us breakfast, but then, with equal deftness, she stopped telling us these things, as soon as she perceived the relationship between us. From that moment on her intimate stories ceased, the implicit exhibitionism adopted a new appearance, dressing in new forms, manifesting itself by means of variants henceforth unseen: her nudity, her poses, her craft, that bathing suit hung out to dry in the sun with the bra pads quite noticeable, as if two white viscose plastic molds could contain anything attractive: those kinds of stimuli. Nonetheless: Herminia was, at every moment, a discreet witness to my relationship with Camila; she must simply have been trying to get us aroused. Or rather: to infect us with the arousal that our relationship seemed to cause her, an arousal that was also an evident display of her homosexual potential. Although a bit coarse—it must be said—Herminia nevertheless had her attractions. And, if it hadn't been for my previous experience with the two girls from Burgos, it's very likely, I admit, that Camila and I would have ended up satisfying her desires.

I don't remember their exact names: Marujita and Trini, or Tina and Maricarmen, or Maripili or Marisomething—what do I know? Some such names like that. My marriage was on its last legs, and it was one of those boring summers in Puigcerdà. During those days, the signs that would fix my future destiny, the new paths my life would have to follow, were already becoming clear to me, and I was as indifferent as any stranger to Juan Antonio's summertime flings, the graceless dalliances of an inveterate daddy's boy. I had contracted the two girls for the summer and for summertime pay, that increasingly obligatory custom based on the tautology that you've got to pay girls more to get them to leave Barcelona because, outside Barcelona, they always charge more; our regular servants had stayed in Barcelona to look after Juan Antonio, covering up his clumsy affairs. The demonic bull dyke who ran the temp agency—a real witch—had assured me she had just what I needed: two girls who wanted to be placed in the same job together, fresh from Burgos, not yet worn out by Barcelona; from the station straight to her own house, a fact that did not cease to surprise me, all the more so because the demon considered it normal.

The stuff about Burgos was true, although it might've been a lie, too, because that virago always exploited the fact that classic Castilian virtues of honor and nobility are powerfully attractive to housewives from this area, who always hope to land some well-mannered, hard-working girls--not sluts--who don't grumble much, and to pay them as little as possible. Let's be blunt: girls who'll put up with anything. And they looked superb: they were both around twenty years old, one brunette, the other blonde, both very gracious. But gracious not just for their physical harmony as much as, principally, for the relationship between one physique and another, between one body and the other; for the aura of sensuality which emanated from their contact, from their opposition, from their close proximity. Of course, to appreciate the precise significance of all that took me some time. At first, to me, they were simply two maids from Burgos, a cook—the blonde—and a maid—the brunette—whose lack of experience was to some extent made up for by aesthetic factors. The rest—their behavior, their mutual relationship, the jokes they cracked, their complicities, an almost childish emotional phenomenon between two friends who were practically little girls, games perfectly suited to their age, their still-undefined sexuality. Naive as I was, even more girlish than they, I might've gone right on thinking that way until the summer's end, not because my powers of perception were inferior then to what they are now, but rather thanks to how I still tended to be rather childish in erotic matters, which I'll be, I suppose, as long as I live. Well, it had to be the atrocious Heribert, the gardener, a sort of Constantino—there's always bound to be a Constantino who sticks his snout into these matters—who opened my eyes for me. I was lying on the sofa in the living room, reading, listening to music, when Heribert appeared, holding his hat in front of him with both hands, his horrible toothless smile. Would the señora care to accompany him to the kitchen? And once in the kitchen, his smile stretching to frankly Sancho Panza-esque proportions, would the señora care to listen for a moment, just a moment? Listen to what? Listen to the laughs, the confused sounds that interrupted the sequence of those young voices, the rhythmic chirping of bed springs, the metal feet of the bed frame thunking over the kitchen ceiling, against the floor of the bedroom, located directly above the kitchen, shared by the two girls from Burgos. And the señora mustn't think it's only at siesta time, said the hideous Heribert; don't think that, no, they also sleep that way at night, every night. And only then and there did I suddenly understand the exact meaning of their jokes and of their scoldings, of the little touches and caresses they exchanged, of their comments in low voices, of the hilarious cryptic allusions they traded after every one of their outings, upon returning, bursting with laughter, from the dance in town. Only one enigma remained: why such sounds from the bed frame during their lovemaking, as if they were a man and a woman?

The chosen day happened to fall on Heribert's weekly day off, which he used to tend his cabbages; but naturally, it was no mere coincidence. I took a very refreshing swim in the icy water of the pool, naked—impossible if Heribert had been puttering around, even if he'd been Lady Chatterley's gardener—and then, wrapped loosely in a bathrobe, while the brunette served me a martini, I suggested that she and her friend also take a swim together, free as we were from the presence of the abominable Heribert. The girls understood me perfectly, and after frolicking around as naturally as possible in the water—no colder, they said, than the river in their hometown—wrapped in the indispensable robes—purple for the blonde, yellow for the brunette; my own was green as the month of May—they joined me in sipping Campari—more suitable for them than a martini—understandably surprised or confused at first, but also possessed by a visible relief, doubtless increased by the absence of Heribert, the decrepit satyr who, from the looks of it had already earned more than one slap across the face from the blonde, always the more decisive one in the face of any situation. We made our way into the living room. Everything turned out better and easier than I had initially foreseen. Such situations, somewhat unexpected and intensely exciting, usually climax quickly, thanks to a sort of uncontrollable liquefaction, similar to what a schoolgirl might experience, but when tempered, the stimulus leading to that climax can be focused and developed into a serene erotic exercise. Something truly magnificent.

Around mid-afternoon, we were disturbed by the accursed Constantino, I mean Heribert, intrusive and unwelcome as always; he woke us up by ringing the bell, convinced, or rather desirous, that some irreparable tragedy had occurred, gas, poison, or whatever. The excuse was that he'd supposedly forgotten something. But the blonde, wrapped in her robe, as if she'd just stepped out of the shower, slammed the door in his face without a second thought, in response to his mindlessness as much as the fact that he was just basically horrible. Our experience together, however, was, by any estimation, unrepeatable: neither did I wish to spoil the wonderful aftertaste—perhaps accidental—of a fortunate conjunction of circumstances, nor was I willing to let its reiteration imperil the normal day-to-day workings of the household. I explained this to them and they understood and even shared my point of view though not without a certain amount of disappointment, naturally. When the summer came to an end I recommended them to Vicky, the Marquesa of Rocadura, sure that the three of them would quickly become lovers. And so it was, indeed: it's not quite three years since I bumped into Vicky while dining at the Finisterre, accompanied by the blonde, my fierce blonde, difficult to recognize for how perfectly fine and sophisticated she looked, although perhaps without the fresh luster of her earlier years. The other one, the brunette, as if she was made for something else, had ended up getting married, and she'd certainly made a beautiful bride. She's now got two little girls, I'm told.

Fate, for its part, had in store for me, some time later, a foolish relapse with a young woman I chose to hire sight unseen, justifying it to myself with the argument that she wasn't really a servant, that the virago from the agency wasn't offering me a servant but rather an au pair, a colored girl, if I didn't mind black girls. If I didn't mind black girls! A black girl originally from Barbados, by way of Jamaica, or something like that; from the Antilles. Perhaps my decision was influenced by the memory from my Parisian days of an affair with a certain person who, without being black, had unmistakably negroid features, or at least exotic ones; the affair was a disaster for unimportant reasons, but the exotic attraction of those features remained intact in my memory, and few things are as blinding as the hunger to satisfy a frustrated desire. Besides, I was already separated from Juan Antonio and I was feeling truly fed up with the ineptitude and stupidity of the young Spanish house girls, their heads full of imaginary sparrows, including, in this regard, my little girlfriends from Burgos. And so, fearful that someone would snatch Ruth away from me before she left London, before she reached the agency, I called the virago on the phone to say yes, and closed the deal without even having seen a photograph of Ruth, the young woman from Barbados, the frightening spawn of at least three different races—black, Hindu, white—which, considered separately, are capable of producing such splendid specimens. A true monstrosity who showed up at my house one miserable morning and who, thanks to the stupid weakness I always display in front of certain people who, due to their very inferiority, make it hard for me to treat them with the toughness they deserve. Thanks to these scruples, I kept her with me for almost two months. And Ruth, as if conscious of her essential ugliness, in order to counteract it, managed to push me right to the edge of a nervous breakdown by continually daring me to see the ugliness in everything—people, landscapes, objects—the horror in everything—the dirty beaches, the waiters not really cleaning the glasses, the risk of catching cholera or some other infectious illness due to a lack of hygiene—she, Ruth, who no doubt grew up in some filthy Manchester slum, she, the spitting image of ugliness and dismay. By the end, it was a struggle for me to even look at her.

It was the last time I used an agency, not only the virago but placement agencies in general, a kind of business that is frequently confused, nowadays, with a clumsy scam, with an organized con. According to my inquiries, what these agencies—by nature illegal—tend to do, as they work in concert, consolidate their efforts, and unify their methods, is to become a kind of gang. With their goal being the commission they receive for placing a girl, they have a vested interest in making sure that the girls get fired—and replaced by new ones—swiftly and frequently. That's why, apart from the girls who naively apply to such agencies because they really want to land a job, the gangsters who control them, the viragos, employ a fixed, rotating staff, constantly circulating, moving from one household to another according to certain techniques, and a very careful distribution of roles or performances. From the looks of it, this specialized staff is divided into three kinds of women, who are dubbed, according to the schemers' slang, as follows: *ganchos*, *trencas*, and *reventairas*, meaning, essentially, lures, snares, and disasters, a way of exploiting clients, hook, line, and sinker. First, the *gancho* shows up, a maid full of excellent qualities and with minimal pretensions, one of those girls who perfectly fits a housewife's notion of the ideal domestic; they quickly establish mutually agreeable terms, and if things don't work out, it's because, in violation of their agreement, the lady of the house never sees her again. Next, after a series of *ganchos*, each one more to the victim's liking, but who vanish every time, the *trenca* shows up to intervene in the situation, as pleasant as she is demanding, so much so that, however much she gets her way, she quits, saying that the house doesn't interest her. The victim, now a frightened quarry, then accepts the very next maid who shows up: the *reventaira*, a disastrous woman who—apart from questionable personal hygiene—ruins the clothes, burns out appliances, breaks plates, etcetera; hardly knows how to cook, and is completely careless when cleaning anything. It's obvious that she's given to drink, and her evenings off tend to wind up early the next morning. She's fired, with eight days' pay, and it starts all over again. When the señora switches agencies or tries to suss out several at once, she finds herself trapped inside their network—a ring of telephone contacts, exchanges of information, etcetera; there's also a file of victims—bounced from one office to the next. This little scheme is what the agencies, in their slang, call the ball game. It's also their standard practice, I understand, to buy space in the papers, phony want-ads for girls who want to work in ideal situations and earn fabulous salaries, just to keep prices steadily rising. And all that, naturally enough, in connivance with the police, who use them as informers. Since I became aware of such outrageous schemes, I've hired my maids directly from neighborhood businesses, and I pay good tips to find them.

What I didn't expect in any way, shape, or form, after years and years of running into nothing but ineptitude, irresponsibility, and bad faith, was to find myself with Herminia. The very fact of her social extraction, meaning, the path she's had to pursue in order to become what she is now, the effort required, despite however much she's learned at my side, only serves to cast into sharper relief her natural qualities, her class. Herminia, after all, belongs to the most humble sort of family, people from Huelva or Ávala or Albacete—right now I don't remember exactly—living in I don't know which mining district near the Pyrenees; I swear, I had no idea that there even were mines in the Pyrenees near Puigcerdà.

How could anyone who ever saw Herminia sunbathing on the beach or on the rocks at the wharf take her for a housemaid? How well she learned all the postures, the gestures, the right way to apply suntan lotion, how to stretch out face down on a towel after slipping the bikini straps off her shoulders in a way that was equally discreet and suggestive; that air of enigmatic solitude she learned to adopt, keeping to herself, laughing, aloof when some boor approached her; right down to her skillful way of hardly showing her hands, the only thing that could give her away. Sometimes she'd sit up with a lazy air, walk a few steps like one who wanted to test the water temperature, transforming the fact that she didn't know how to swim into the appearance that she didn't really feel like it.

She knew how to manage herself, how to make things work, not just so she could get things done efficiently and find some free time both morning and afternoon for herself to take a stroll, go to the beach, etcetera, but so that she could do it not when all the other maids were out, but when the ladies were. She went out to buy groceries very early in the morning, when there were no familiar faces in the streets, always in the same shops. She maintained a very curious tug of war with the men who waited on her—people with whom she could not and did not try to decieve about her social condition—whose imaginations she excited, while staying on friendly terms with the women; a kind of ambiguous flirtation, cut off just in the right moment with some vague allusion to her boyfriend, always refusing to say anything more specific. No need to mention, either, that she also resorted to the old trick of wearing a wedding ring on a chain around her neck. Late afternoons, after siesta, she usually took a stroll past the bar terraces, a copy of *Elle* tucked under her arm, ending up sipping a gin and tonic on her own, as if absorbed in reading her magazine, isolated from the surrounding world by the aromatic smoke spiraling up from her Winston. Other afternoons, instead of going out, she locked herself in her room, naked I suppose, stretched out on her bed, smoking, firing her imagination with *Playboy*-style magazines or photo novellas.

She'd also spend the afternoon hiding out in her bedroom when she was in a bad mood or felt her pride wounded by some reprimand from me or any harsh comment, or any word at all that seemed, to her irritated feelings, censorious, but for longer stretches, drinking my whiskey (I once decided to search her room and found a bottle there), and smoking my cigarettes (impossible to prove, thanks to her crafty mimicry; she started smoking Winstons the moment she noticed they were my brand), no doubt plotting revenge. And when she finally emerged from her isolation, she'd come and go, softly singing things vaguely allusive to something and, while she only spoke to me when strictly necessary, she'd lavish Camila with friendly attention, as if she wanted to win her over or make me jealous. She also took pleasure in pestering Emilia and getting that little satyr Constantino all hot and horny: just a moment, don't turn around, she'd say to them in the office; I'm changing my robe. She knew perfectly well that Emilia would never dare quarrel with her, that she held the stronger position in the house.

The combined fruit of her readings and her talent for observation, were augmented as much as possible by her high-flown fantasies, the postures she adopted, her gestures and even her facial expressions. Especially the look on that model's face in *Playboy*, swaying gently in a bubble bath: on all fours, in profile, the tips of her nipples just touching the bubbles, her rear end raised up, her face turned completely toward the camera eye, over her shoulder, her mouth half-open, eyes half-fearful, half-expectant: Herminia's exact expression when someone spoke to her and she pretended to be startled. Our bathroom afforded a partial view of her bedroom and once we surprised her practicing her look. And I have the feeling that Herminia was perfectly aware that we were watching her.

When we had guests, if she was serving the meal, or coffee, or some drinks, and someone made a joke she thought risqué, she'd put her hand to her mouth as if suppressing her laughter; and of course, for someone who doesn't perfectly understand what's being said, everything can seem a bit risqué. But, in spite of such intrusions, since she carried it off graciously, people saw her as friendly, and my most frequent guests directly incited her to show off, to make one of those remarks she uttered so naturally as to border on the brazen, without it, however, actually quite being so. By this time she must have known that the ideas she'd brought with her when she came to her house—ideas of what was refined, or distinguished, or not—were sappy as well as provincial.

With her knack for adaptation, with her talent for mimicking not only postures but manners, it was no surprise that on the town beach—the one used by people passing through, recommended by the tourist agency; locals frequent the beach at Llané—she had no lack of visitors, weekend Don Juans whom she kept at arm's length, just as she kept her boyfriend at arm's length—if the famous boyfriend really existed—owing, possibly, to her fear that their behavior—the Don Juans, her hypothetical boyfriend, all of them—was beneath her own, did not rise to the heights she envisioned, the words, attitudes, caresses. Another thing, thanks to her complex motives, Roberto's machinations to get closer to Herminia, the lovely Roberto, whose vicissitudes I could observe perfectly—and not without delight, I admit—from the terrace of the Maritím, sipping a martini alongside Camila, who, in addition to being myopic, couldn't stand wearing contact lenses. Of course Roberto couldn't imagine either that I was witness to his moves on Herminia, or the words, the smiles they exchanged. His cunning, her honeyed fawning.

Binoculars are so very useful: watching them slip down into the bottom of the boat as if into a bed, below the deck line, anchored out of the wind, sheltered from the Levant, at a prudent distance from the choppy mouth of the bay, while I reread her correspondence, sitting comfortably on my terrace, quite relaxed, sipping a martini.

I'd followed their movements from the moment they left the shore, their zigzagging, tacking back and forth between other boats, their search for a discreet, sheltered spot, their way of diving down to search, not in the depths of the sea but in the depths of the boat.

In fact, without the binoculars, it wouldn't have been possible to keep sight of them among the coming and going of all the boats and canoes and sails that enliven the bay in high season, swimmers, people waterskiing as naturally as most people take a piss, a spectacle that, according to what was initially foreseen—but not according to my previously fashioned plans—we would have spared ourselves that summer just as we had spared ourselves of it each summer up until then. Scotland, Finland, British Columbia, places like that—the charm of the big cities, so lauded by some, is the biggest nonsense I've ever heard, especially when people talk about New York City—have become my habitual refuge, not because they're more beautiful than Cadaqués, but rather because I can't stand the sight of Cadaqués suffering under an avalanche of tourists. That whole rabble whose ridiculous extravagances are such an ugly blight on the incomparable beauty of this town, which, harmonious as a church organ, stands upon the sinuous coast against the naked silhouette of the mountain.

That being said, let me emphasize that I'm not talking about certain elite types, regular visitors, whose enthusiasm for Cadaqués I'm the first to share, but the cheap, tacky tourists who, in this specific case, attracted by the preconceived ideas that circulate about life in Cadaqués, come swarming up here like the hordes of Attila, ready to take a running leap onto the first round-bed offered them. Or tourists like the ones in Rosas or any other town on the coast, tourist-agency tourists who, one day, their curiosity aroused, just decide to show up there, to see what will happen. Attitudes that explain behaviors, hypocritical manners, intimidated, yet walking through the town with that degrading affability like happy schoolchildren who barely hide their perverse reality: fear of adventure disguised as innocent joy, they're skittish as sparrows, always attentive, watching out—with their sideways glances—for any possible punishment inflicted by some rude local.

To tell the truth, however, as someone pointed out to me, with their sharp characteristic critical sense, worse than this class of tourists—elites aside, I insist—are the summertime habitués, that especially snobby sector of the Barcelona bourgeoisie that, every summer, makes a great show of trundling its wealth up to their houses in Cadaqués, houses that, despite their best efforts and desires to preserve, and not spoil, the town's character, hardly resemble—

on the outside, of course—the typical houses of local fishermen. As far as the interiors, let it suffice to consider the fact that these bourgeoisie, in their zeal for rusticity, have converted what were stony cellars into cozy living rooms, and the old humid gloom of such places into sophisticated spaces: nowadays in Cadaqués, the wine cellar is the heart of the house. But what can you say about the taste of people who are so prissy that they still say, as we did when we raised our hands in school to ask the nuns permission to use the lavatory, I need to go Number Two?, like that contemptuous critic from the *TLS* (there are imbeciles everywhere, being an ass is not a privilege reserved exclusively for Sancho Panza), illustrating their total lack of comprehension about what's what, their difficulty in discerning, their lack of true class. This explains sufficiently my desire to keep myself on the periphery of that little world, however much they try to make trouble for me now, with the same rancor with which, before I married Juan Antonio, and again in the first few years after we separated, they marginalized me. No doubt I intrigue them, and not just because of my lifestyle and my disdain for conventions and prejudices of every sort, but also for my body. It must disconcert them that a woman like me, tall, slender, and elegant, with that serene maturity which is the fruit of intelligence and experience more than of age, resulting in a particular attraction, which is reflected in my face, my lively, laughing eyes, and my ironic smile, that such a woman as myself, I was saying, dares to defy everyone, and all of their oppressive taboos. One more reason to add to the already vast stockpile they might well have, to try to pick a fight with me, to marginalize me.

Now I'm the one who marginalizes myself by choice: or rather, the one who elbows them aside, who keeps her distance. I've already felt ostracized enough in the past, not only by the society of Cadaqués or Puigcerdà but, ultimately, by all of Barcelona. That entire swath of Barcelona society that once ostracized my mother so far that she herself, the widow of a Red, allowed herself to be ostracized, to the point that, as if overcome by shame, she seemed to be hiding and to hide us, the four children of a Red: my sister and I in a nuns' boarding school, and my brothers in another one, run by priests. Hiding herself and hiding us in the summers too, first at Aiguaviva, the family property, and then in various towns, starting with Breda and ending up in Puigcerdà, forever on the run, it seemed, as if isolating us, without letting us make friends with the other kids who came to visit the neighborhood during the summer, children of families with whom she seemed to fear socializing with; perhaps I've got that situation to thank for my future wedding with Juan Antonio, the only boy in those days who dared to approach me. That sort of childhood naturally explains a great many things about the character of each one of the siblings involved, beginning, of course, with myself—of that I'm fully aware. It astonishes me, however, that Margarita now talks about how social life bores her, when she's always adored it, and she's always known how to arrange things for herself in order to deal with the most conventional people in her unconventional way, as is the case with the people who come to Cadaqués, people who hate me just as much as they envy me.

What's certain is that I haven't missed anything extraordinary. In that regard I recall an affair I had with an eminent member of the Barcelona bourgeoisie, whose name doesn't matter—she's married—during my first years in Cadaqués: one of those women, slow to the point of exasperation, of stubborn orgasms and deep secretions, perhaps due to how gradually they seep out, like lava that cools. The sort of erotic affairs we get involved in, irresponsibly, carried away by the euphoria resulting from a specific situation, or by too much champagne, the kind we later regret the rest of our lives because of how little we think of the other person, the fantasies we imagined, the disappointment we bore, and the foolishness we've committed on forgetting, once again, how simple women tend to be, and how difficult it can be to break off such relationships precisely because of how insignificant the other person is, something like what happened with that distant cousin whom they'd tried to force us to play with when with we were little girls, when our respective parents visited with one another, that cousin called Magín or Valentín with whom we never really got along, who turned out to be a little bit retarded, well, stupid, although with a very nice personality and, especially, very cautious, that's right, and over the years we saw him now and then, generally at funerals or otherwise solemn family ceremonies, on each occasion balder and chubbier, and the light in his sunken eyes dimmer, until at last, one day we found out that something happened to the poor fellow, that he'd died, and now we couldn't avoid attending his burial.

No doubt the family obeys a divine mandate, since only God can have invented such a passionate game of chance: one hand only, no discards. I mean, of course, the family one is born into, although—I know from my own experience—also with the family a person chooses or thinks they choose, especially if things get messy and there are children, and however much I might have learned to end things decisively, you might say, practically speaking, the same is more or less true. I'm thinking about my parents: an unnamable father because, despite being a Moret—a surname that carries, or rather, carried—some weight in Barcelona, he was a lawyer for Reds, he took the side of the Reds and died like a Red, in exile. A mother of lowly spirits, who spent the second half of her life trying to repair the mistake she made in the first half, her great shame: her marriage. A sister whom everyone confuses with me, insisting that we look so much alike, when the truth is Margarita and I couldn't be more essentially different. And although our relationship, from a formal aspect, is good, the two of us know that beneath our carefully maintained outward appearance, we share an ambiguous antagonism, no less radical for being unformed. And if the fact is that for years Margarita has allowed herself to step into Matilde's territory with impunity, there's nothing strange either that as time goes by, as Matilde ceases to be that, meaning Margarita's sister, as she becomes better known, as she acquires an identity, there's nothing strange, I was saying, about the process being inverted and, although without meaning to, it might be me who trespasses on her terrain, the one who overshadows her more and more, until it's Margarita who ends up being Matilde's sister. Because what people don't know, for example, is that Margarita, as usually happens with younger sisters, has always imitated me in everything. Because what people don't know is that Margarita has envied me for years now, that she's invaded my territory through every means at her disposal. No, people don't have even the slightest idea how far her narcissism goes, how close her egocentrism borders on mythomania, and how she can't even see it.

As kids—as little girls, too—shared rebellion and defiance united us against our mother and the world she represented, our aunts and uncles, cousins, nuns. We were separated from our brothers not only by sex and age but also because they were younger, because they were the little ones, they were more malleable, more permeable, at least during their childhood, to environmental influences, to the old-fashioned spirit surrounding them, to that atmosphere, like holy water, they breathed. The distance between Margarita and me started to grow at her wedding, the moment she married, prematurely, as I saw it, despite how far she had run. If she had waited, perhaps in time she would have realized that, beneath his mundane patina, he was—and is—one of those Catalans as cruel and rapacious as he is rich; of course the problem with marriage resides not so much in the person as in the situation itself, every time that, the economic motivation vanished—the oh-so-execrated dowry—that gave him consistency and stability, according to the world's changing mentality, the aptly named conjugal tie has become a pure pirouette in the void. The fact that she now takes her liberties and gets on with her life, and he the same—all those temporary arrangements changes nothing. For years she was the smart one and I was the good-looking one—who knows if she didn't rush to get married for that very reason—and over time I've also gained the reputation for being the intelligent one. Now I'm the one who's interesting.

Pardon me; I see that I've gone off on a tangent, but the truth is that talking about Margarita makes me very nervous. Especially because I don't want to seem unfair, because I don't want to give the impression that Margarita is a dull, vulgar person, especially because, without the slightest doubt, I consider her, in every way, to be a woman of the finest qualities; if she weren't, I wouldn't find it very amusing that some people still mistake us for one another. There is a yawning abyss, for example, between Margarita and my sister-in-law Conchita, whose only tragic quality lies in her being exactly, neither more nor less than what she is—namely, small, dim-witted, nothing special from a moral or personal perspective, or however you'd like to say it, I mean. On the other hand, she's just the type of woman best suited to marry Ignacio, a gray and silent man, who seems constantly tormented by his own mediocrity. Although the rich, silly woman he landed might also be a sign that Ignacio is much less mediocre and much tougher than one might first think. I don't know. But considering he's my brother, the truth is that, for me, Ignacio is a perfect enigma.

With Joaquín, perhaps because we're closer in age, we've always had more trust, and communication, and although he's delightful, we're not the least bit alike; he's very sweet and just as spineless. It's not that he's got no personality but that he has too many different ones, and the bad thing is he believes in them all. I remember the day he finally realized I like women; his unexpected visit, inopportune and clumsy as always, his fastidious tenderness, his evocations—thoroughly distorted—of our shared childhood, his confidential and understanding tone when telling me that, sometimes, he'd reached the conclusion that he was also homosexual; despite being thoroughly off the mark, it was not, therefore, a completely insensitive suggestion, and thus undeserving of the crude clarifications I was on the verge of dumping on him, trying to shut him up. With his attempts to please me, or encourage me, Joaquín is capable of inventing anything at all. On that occasion, if necessary, he would have been willing to give me a practical demonstration.

But, of all my family, the only one who's really worth the trouble, bears the name Moret as a second surname: my cousin Raúl. Sometimes unbearable, it's also true; as vain as just about anyone I've ever seen. With that irritating self-confidence of the person who knows himself to possess certain reasons for being so. His laughter, his ironic eyes, his spot-on good taste in choosing clothes that flatter him, his elastic movements; but above all, his way of looking at you, as if he'd already bedded you, here, there, and everywhere. A more than excessive confidence, needless to say, that might well hide the opposite state of mind, total insecurity. In any case, it wouldn't surprise me at all if the passing years with their disappointments have dampened his fire a little, and that he's no longer the way he used to be.

Even so, the truth is that I'd love for him to make an appearance in Cadaqués, if only so he could see for himself that I'm still the same Matilde as always, that I still live a simple, modest life, that we can still have those long conversations like we used to, finishing them off with a nice swim in the quiet waters of the harbor. I know that he enjoys my house; on the other hand, it would be impossible for him not to. This house where I've figured out how to really preserve the atmosphere of a fisherman's house with all its charm, to the envy of the local purists who really criticized me when I remodeled and added an upper story, saying that it was truly an aesthetic outrage. The main entrance is at the rear of the house, which faces directly onto the street, and gets the afternoon sun. The facade faces the sea, the bay, above a tiny private beach and the rocks of the harbor. The interior has a very Mediterranean tone, at once sober and sophisticated: baroque carvings against the white walls and large throw pillows of Thai silk upon the slate tiles in the cellar. But the true luxury, what's really priceless, is not the house itself but its location: the best view of the bay from anywhere in Cadaqués.

III

How to Keep Your Vixen Happy. That would be the best title. One of those self-help manuals like *How to Triumph in Life* or *How to Make Friends*, books that I imagine must usually lead to the opposite result, meaning straight to disaster. Complimenting, for example, the bank teller's hair, or any office assistant's hair, capable of leading, outside the proper context, whether or not we're the same sex, to some blunt response; or those jokes we make to sound friendly, like asking the waitress, at some roadside *parador*, to add one more leather shoe sole with salad to the order, that can be so easily misinterpreted. Or the recommendations from one of those guides to married life that encourage spouses to cultivate a healthy sexual relationship, to make a point of surprising each other, to engage in foreplay with delicacy and tact, and other similar advice—delicacies like the ones I offer them, surprises and emotions like the ones I have in store for them, understanding of the sort they can only expect from me. Thus, like those books and manuals so much in vogue several years ago, and similar counterproductive measures, the book that I could write about Camila and Roberto, how their relationship evolved as I gradually opened the valve and gave them increased autonomy, the ease they enjoyed, including chance, you might say, working in their favor. Because, despite the positive environment in which our love affairs developed, as if intimately connected beneath the warm mantle of furtiveness; despite the numerous favorable elements, worthy not only of enumeration but of detailed arrangement and even classification; in spite of that, I was saying, something began to smell artificial, and I had good reasons, indeed, to suspect such artificiality—a result of the extra effort—because of the number of points where they coincided on the graph of their common vicissitudes. I'm writing this, not them, because, at that time, likely as not, they were unaware of the presence of such a factor. And the truth is that the suitable instrument for introducing such a factor wasn't in their hands but in mine: the indeterminate duration of what, in principle, in a tacit form, by analogy in relation to other summers, was perfectly determined; the maintenance of a tension only bearable—for whomever suffers it—within certain limits. It's not possible to keep the fervent flames blazing when the logs have burned down to coals.

I—only I, not them—knew exactly what was going on with them, and I knew what feelings they were experiencing. Their encounters, their letters, the look on their faces, however much Roberto, summoning every possible reserve of strength, pretended to be kind and spirited when we bumped into him through one of those coincidences the three of us so carefully prepared. Smiling, always seeming to be up for anything, courteous and agreeable, showing off his physique, as he showed off his little golden medallion, not a religious medal, but one inscribed with his rare blood type, yet that didn't diminish its clear value as an erotic lure. If I hadn't had him so much at my mercy, defenseless, and without even realizing it, I would've really come to hate him.

Fatigue, on Camila's part, began to show up, primarily, in some of the letters she received, which Roberto made sure reached her hands in an effort to raise her spirits, to encourage her—classic remedies against fatigue. Not a chronic fatigue, of course, but rather—as with everything—depending on the day. And it seems to me more than likely that the same thing happened to him, although he managed to hide it better, maybe being stronger, maybe more deceitful, or having a lot of nerve—or more skill. And I would even dare assert that my way of leaving my notes—not these, naturally—carelessly out in the open, began to show results. And by that I don't mean that Camila, suspecting that I was reading her letters, wanted me to know, through Roberto's replies, what was on her mind, but rather, that my lucid observations, the diaphanous clarity of my observations, made more and more of a dent in her spirit. And that represented a more or less ninety-degree shift from her first letters—right after the night in the cellar—which poured out various veiled, insulting allusions to my character. It's possible that around that time, after having mentioned my dream about her dresser drawer crawling with snakes, Camila suspected—this time, certainly—that I had read her letters and although at that point she began to hide them inside record album sleeves, perhaps that was to conceal her secret intention of rattling me, to make me lose my nerve, so that I should be the one to break up with her, in order to avoid the proof of it being her fault, directly, face to face; yes, that I should be the one to explode after having made the wrong move by going through her things; it's quite likely.

To my mind, the most intelligent thing she could have done, the most appropriate, would have been to deliberately leave a letter of surrender or renunciation where I would find it—a letter addressed to me placed inside an open envelope, but hidden in some place where I would soon find it—the drawer filled with snakes, for example—as if she were too scared to drop it into the mail. The most graceful thing, too. The most graceful and elegant both for her and for me.

The main obstacle I ran up against while keeping control of the situation was the almost constant presence of Constantino, all the while sniffing what you're sniffing, like a dog, like a dog lifting its leg. In reality, the more dangerous one was Herminia, who could walk without making the slightest noise, and who never missed anything, but I trusted that her own personal discretion would make her keep her distance. Constantino, however—that decrepit satyr who certainly suspected something—managed to exasperate me with his continuous incursions, using any excuse to go sneaking around in the house, always trying to see where Camila was, his way of scrutinizing the bay from the wharf, hunting for the same object that I would follow with my binoculars, spying, keeping watch, prisoner, no doubt, of the most furious excitation. That satyr's delirious follies pushed me to the edge of a nervous breakdown more than once. At one point he had problems with the Guardia Civil for lewd abuses committed with boys and girls, one of these cases in which the parents end up withdrawing the accusation in order to spare the children any new trauma that would result from a trial. Well, it turned out that he wasn't the guilty one but a different fisherman, equally decadent and underhanded. But when they told me the story, I immediately thought of Constantino and, in fact, it perfectly well could have been him.

Such displays, not only of clumsy lewdness but of a lack of morality and, above all, a lack of sensibility, became really unbearable for me. All the more because I'd never liked to provoke rude gossip or shock people, and I don't feign ignorance out of fear, because I always do whatever I like, but from a basic sense of proper decorum, which I respect and which I demand be respected. With Camila, on our trips, in any public place, among people who don't know who we are, we've never given anyone the least reason to make any kind of comment. And that's how people should behave themselves. Of course, in people's imagination, lesbians are women with hard features, short hair, brusque gestures, and narrow pupils, who prefer tailored suits. In other words: dykes. The equivalent, but in the inverse, of one of those male couples who, more than for physical pleasures, seem united by physiological and even vegetative pleasures—sunshine, siestas, digestion, defecation, everything realized with that illusion of someone living inside a real-life fairy tale. A very Catalan sort of an image, whose origin perhaps could be found in that double-seat commode installed in the old country houses of certain personages—the stable was good enough for the rest—and in the image it obviously suggests: a married couple defecating at the same time, exchanging sweet looks, words of encouragement, lovingly holding hands.

Some people's capacity for fantasy is truly incredible, the theories and topics they manage to put into circulation and which, stranger still, end up being accepted as if they're commonplace. And here's the really serious part: not that an author can turn out to be such a sucker, but that the reader, the public, people in general can become such suckers. On the topic of the clitoris, for example. All those stories invented by a handful of stone-cold lesbians masquerading as feminists, with the statistical support of some sociologist or other, or sexologist or what have you, quite stupid enough to allow himself to be convinced—who knows if it's because he's been conditioned by the clitoral dimensions of his own penis—to the point of searching for—and even finding—cases and ideas that exemplify their postulates. As if the woman surveyed, properly prepared by the multiple stupidities she reads in the hair salon, didn't already know perfectly well that she had to admit to being clitoral, because it would look bad, even if only to her anonymous surveyor (be they man or woman: I know of more than one case in which the questionnaire was only the preamble to a frisky erotic flirtation that resulted in them running away together), if she affirmed the opposite. But it's false. False and also outrageous: an authentic international campaign intended to disorient or confuse women—-a given with men—-for the benefit of a handful of viragoes, a few opportunists who benefit from the prevailing confusion. What these sociologists or psychologists or sexologists—equally unimaginative in both mind and sex—call the clitoris, is for me the whole body, every inch exciting and sensitive, to varying degrees—and not only in intensity—every single one. Lies! Lies! Lies! Only the coarse, aberrant dullness of such people can reduce sensuality to such an absurd little epicenter! The only thing we need, if perhaps—and I dedicate this suggestion to my recalcitrant feminists, to whom I owe so many moments of perfect pleasure—the only thing our bodies lack, I was saying, is, precisely, a truly penetrating organ, something I've always missed in my exalted moments of possessive plenitude.

Apart from that, a woman's body is a truly perfect object. Including in menopause it's incomparably better balanced, for the compensations that it offers, than a man's body, subject to a decline that, inevitably, has to turn him into a randy old goat. Although I've still got many years left, I suppose, before reaching such a critical phase, I'm fully convinced that not only does it not have to be traumatic—equivalent to a man losing his virility—but that it should be considered an advantage: the definitive liquidation of all the bothersome pains which the woman's body has suffered since puberty. And that's no small thing: the source of the principal fears of a graduate, one equally sensitive and thoughtful, of a nun's convent school. A kind of rebirth, in a certain way.

Truth be told, it strikes me as rather inaccurate that a woman—as all those lesbians pretend—cannot enjoy a man as much—or completely—as she enjoys a woman. If any woman doubts it—unless it's one of those stone-cold dykes—let them put it to the test. And keep in mind that I'm not exactly a specialist in such experiences, what you call a nymphomaniac; but I know what I'm saying, and what's true is true, so says Ulysses or his swineherd. Certainly, but one difficulty a woman can encounter when dealing with a man—as happens with me—is the emotional problem. The uncertainty of pleasing him, however much he swears it to us. The fear of not rising to the occasion. The suspicion that he behaves the same with every woman. The evidence that, for them, affairs are usually only that: affairs, adventures, mechanisms involving interchangeable parts. Apart from the cases, not so infrequent, of course, when the man behaves like a gentleman: noble, but brutish.

Luckily, when it comes to both men and women, I'm far superior to any mechanism, both physically as well as psychologically, and even morally. And that's true not only in terms of what's commonly called experience, but mostly because I possess certain faculties, and while it might be an exaggeration to classify them as prescient, they are definitely what people mean when they talk about having extraordinary intuition, premonitions, and all that. I can tell what someone's up to, I see right through them, I've got X-ray vision, I know what they'll do before they themselves know it; and it pleases me to see my intuition confirmed. Needless to say, like any other game, that implies certain risks. But I'm aware of that and I accept them. I was getting fed up from so much monotony, so many theoretically casual encounters, so much of following her movements with the binoculars—under the watchful eye of the old satyr—so much rereading letters and prying—awaiting the moment without the expected result—in the drawer of snakes. I needed something stronger, more direct, more exciting. In other words, something to give free rein to my pent-up energy, to my restrained vitality. The excuse was served up to me on a silver platter by one of the nightclubs in Port de la Selva, when they invited us—invited me—to their upcoming grand opening. A late opening, just before the end of the season, postponed time and again because in summertime everything moves slowly. On that occasion, finally, it seemed like it was actually going to happen, especially because it had been announced that Dalí would make an appearance, and I understand that's indeed how it turned out. But I kept my invitation until the night before the scheduled date, in order for Camila and Roberto to have the time necessary to make their arrangements, but only just enough, assuming beforehand that she had very little appetite for these things, that it was a social engagement for me alone, I understood perfectly well that she preferred to stay at home, exactly what I myself wanted to do, too, because no matter what, I didn't think I could stand more than a couple hours, three or so, at most, including going there and coming home.

That settled, we said goodbye with resignation in the heady atmosphere of the cellar, and I strolled out to my convertible, a convertible I drove only a few hundred yards from the house before parking it, and then walking back, silently entering the house. From the terrace, smoking in the darkness, cupping the burning tip of the cigarette in the palm of my hand, I watched him arrive, rowing vigorously—practically a Lohengrin—dock his boat at the pier, and slip into the cellar; I stayed a while longer contemplating the lights of the bay, the splendid river of moonlight shimmering on the water. The music was still playing in the bedroom, tangoes and tangoes playing over and over again—or maybe songs by Édith Piaf, more or less the same thing—a *laralá* that prevented me from hearing anything else, even though I could imagine almost everything for myself as if I were watching them. I didn't have to wait long because they must have feared that I'd come home early. The record stopping was my signal, and I quickly slipped back out onto the terrace where I was able to witness their tender goodbye down on the dock, the touching departure of the boat. When Camila appeared in the room I pretended to be coming out of a deep sleep, and, as if still half-asleep, I acted like I didn't see the astonishment my presence in the house caused her, pretending not to notice her terror, accepting her explanations quite naturally, that she'd been listening to music since I left, that, if she'd known that I'd returned, she would have come up right away, and why hadn't I said anything to her. She talked and talked while I undressed her slowly and carefully, enjoying the gradual appearance of her body still wide-open from love, her whole body seeming to swell and part like a great pair of lips, her words derailed more and more by my caresses, no longer attentive to the thread of the conversation as much as to her own body's response, her sensuality stimulated to the maximum by the dissipation of the fears that initially embarrassed her, her certainty that I hadn't discovered anything, her euphoria at having fooled me, knowing that the only punishment awaiting her was a whole series of new and more intense pleasures; lucky for her, in short, she and I almost feverish, although not for the same reasons, riding each other, climaxing again and again. That time, too, the sunlight was already illuminating the tiles when we fell asleep. The same sun that was just going down behind the mountains when I set out on the most marvelous trip imaginable to Port de la Selva. When—as someone has already written, robbing me not only of the words but the very finest expression of what that night was—the rose-fingered moon outshone every star and its light flowed across the salty sea and flowering *fields*.

The invitation to Port de la Selva was no coincidence. For some good reason that I cannot pinpoint but which is somehow true, the name itself, La Selva, which means, variously, the forest, the wilderness, the jungle, has always been linked to the crucial moments in my life, as if by magic. This time, Port de la Selva, just as in my childhood, Aiguaviva, the family property, also in La Selva, but not in the La Selva that belongs to Port de la Selva, but in that region, around Girona, which bears that name. It's always seemed strange that in Catalonia there are so many places called La Selva or are related to the word Selva, like Selva del Camp, in Tarragona, where, if I'm not wrong, there's a concrete elephant you can glimpse from the train, a work of naive art made by one of those stationmasters who go half-insane from the wind. In any case, it stands to reason that the name must have left him perplexed. I don't know if it's ever occurred to anyone to look for an explanation.

The Surrender of Breda is more than just a painting. *The Surrender of Breda* represents a whole theory of life. Why does Breda surrender? Because of the sharp lances which, vertically barring the landscape, are raised on the Spanish side, on the right-hand side of the canvas, facing the handful of Flemish pikes huddled on the left side? Because of the rising smoke that clouds the field behind the defeated, probably the result of an intense artillery exercise? Or is it, rather, the response found in the heavy key that the Fleming is handing over to the Spaniard, the center of the composition as well as the symbol of the ransom, of what is paid in order to keep from losing what he fears to lose, a city, an economic and social position, status? Meaning: a key which is the artistic key both visually and thematically, in relation to which, the weapons that flank it, the receding landscape between the sharp lances, are mere decorative touches. Then, after the hypocritical cordiality with which the offering is accepted, there will come a vengeful glow of purifying bonfires, by whose light the exemplary gallows will acquire vivid tonalities, and the slaughtered bodies will drip blood from the tops of the walls—the inescapable, edifying punishment. But the city, whose luck, whose integrity, whose very existence is at stake, shall be saved. Surrender the sole alternative to its destruction. Hand over the key or suffer the fate of Troy.

A metaphor for life, yes, and also for love, although more concretely. After all, between love and war, not only is there no difference, however much the so many stupid and oh-so-popular slogans proclaim otherwise; they are instead, essentially, different aspects of the same practice, consubstantial with human nature. In both cases we can find, as an ultimate example, an attack and a defense, retreats and deployments, changing movements in one direction and another, in the same way, similarly, as sickness. And what phenomenon more linked to life—and to death—than illness, that deaf struggle between the organism's defenses and the pathogenic agents, between besiegers and besieged, between aggressors and victims? Because love is also a kind of sickness. And keep in mind that I don't mean homosexual love, or unnatural love, the idea they try to cram into people's heads and which, in fact, they even managed to inculcate me into believing, until my own personal experiences overrode such simplemindedness: that it's abnormal, perverse, and as a consequence, sick. No. I'm talking about love, and only love, without any further qualifications. Something that, as the poets have well observed—poet, for me, means any writer who reaches the most sublime heights, versifier or not—frequently leads to greater blunders, either to each person locking himself away in his prison of love, or fleeing from that love and turning the rest of the world into a prison. In short, a frankly regressive experience with regard to personality, a revived echo of all those frustrated childhood desires, those love objects, the ones who stole that object, those traitors who condemned them to dispossession. Symptoms of a conflict that, like any other psychic and even physical alteration, is no longer explicable according to the most diverse interpretations—conflicts of power, nascent eroticism, etcetera—but also curable, because, if a simple flu can be defeated by the simultaneous action of the various remedies that medical science with its extremely limited knowledge offers us—aspirin, bed, infusions, vitamins, cognac with milk, milk with honey, local treatments, drops, inhalers, pills and antipyretic suppositories, etcetera—the real cure comes only when—as in any siege—the passing of time makes it so that the chosen remedy, whatever it may be, takes effect, not so much by virtue of its own properties so much as by the time gone by. The thing by which we reach the true essence of all remedies, the common denominator that permits us, as necessary, to do away with all those remedies: the time factor; its duration, a period sufficiently prolonged so that the erotic fever is calmed and the connotations relating to early childhood, along with the grievances derived from them, abate, losing the value originally attributed to them—the motor, or something slightly less, of the impulses experienced—eventually becoming—and this is true for love as well as other psychosomatic illnesses—as soon as they are dominated, reduced to something completely contingent, indifferent to existence or non-existence, to whether or not one has existed or not.

I suppose that by equating love and war, I must have made it sufficiently clear that I wasn't talking about the vulgar topic of antagonism between lover and beloved, of the tug of war that tends to be established between two people who love each other. No, that's not the struggle I mean, but rather the struggle that develops inside each person, the combat that each lover unleashes inside themselves, the same as our bodies when they confront an infection. By the same token, talking about recovery, I don't mean the triumph of one part over the opposing part in the amorous antagonism, but the complete reestablishment of inner balance in the contenders, whether only one of them is affected, or both. Ultimately, the choice presented to the defenders of Breda—resist or surrender—concerns one single objective: preserve the city above all else. What matters least, therefore, is the victory of the Spanish troops, their relatively peaceful entrance into the city, a bitter pill to swallow that will sooner or later be forgotten by the inhabitants, just the way these things are always forgotten. What's really at the heart of the matter is the city's victory over itself by means of a ransom: that key, the key.

And as with cities, so with people when it comes to love, although, of course, there are few people who are aware of that. The majority tend to feel themselves victims of their beloved, deceived by them, defrauded, trampled underfoot—never their own victims. In some cases they never manage to forget: these are the people who really qualify as defeated. I, however, possess some defenses comparable only to my capacity for forgetting. The simple conviction that I could never fall in love, not even if I wanted to, that I limit myself to defending what is mine, that under no circumstances can I admit that anyone could even try to make me the object of a premeditated trick, of some clumsy farce, gives me absolute control over the situation. The eagle that soars overhead, wings spread wide, appears to the traveler as barely more than a dot circling high above; while for the eagle, no detail, no movement on the ground escapes its eyes. That's how I am. The inherent relativity in any perspective.

What could Camila and Roberto have imagined, for example—not now, finding themselves seized with fatigue and disenchantment, but rather at the start, before the night in the cellar, and even more so when, knowing I'd discovered everything, they stubbornly persisted in carrying on as if they could still succeed? Were they really going to get away with it, mocking me with impunity, pulling my leg whenever they felt like it? Only in that traveler who sees nothing more of the eagle flying overhead than a dot circling up in the air, only in that person who is so stubbornly blinded by the breadth of their narrow-mindedness, only in those sorts can such an inability to grasp what's evident be comprehensible. Could a normal-size brain really compare my possibilities and resources with Camila's or with Roberto's, or with both of theirs combined? It would only be something like—there are few things in life I hate as much as false humility, that unctuous, monkish attitude, ineffective and equally detached from reality—trying to diminish the gigantic figure of Achilles with clumsy logical sophisms such as the one about him and the tortoise. Roberto: an Argentine who's not really Argentine but Barcelonan, a local boy who, for whatever reasons—child of exiles and things like that—went off to live in Buenos Aires when he was a kid. And now it turns out that his Argentine accent is really just a kind of put-on, a sham, a sort of condescending irony targeting himself, and tangos and Argentina, because, if he likes, he can speak perfect Peninsular Spanish and even Catalan. A joke? A cock-and-bull story! Roberto is a phony, a real phony, nothing more than a phony, and his accent is totally fake. The kind of person who can only enjoy another person with the very same characteristics, someone like Camila, another phony. Because now it also turns out that her Roberto is not just some common gigolo, he's an educated young man, with a college degree, Biology, Philology, or something like that, qualities which, besides being impossible to confirm, don't change things at all. The same goes for his medallion: whatever his reason for wearing it, he wears it the way he does just to show it off, like a fishing lure, like a discreet little twinkle above that bulky package in his pants.

Finding oneself always in good shape, both physically and psychically, supposes something that, if it wasn't so obvious as well as ignored, might be considered little less than a secret: natural aptitudes, if not exercised, atrophy. And if the person with limited faculties in working condition can't expect much, a darker future awaits the one who, more gifted, wastes and loses them. I'm not going to waste my breath with all that stuff about *mens sana in corpore sano*, but given that the proverb contains a great truth, I'll venture something along the same lines, though with other words, Certain habits, certain ways of living, are all that separate me, sometimes, from the human ruins that surround me, glorious only insofar as what they were or what they might have been. A balanced diet that keeps things like fats, starches, and carbohydrates in place, meaning, at bay. Or submitting periodically to getting pummeled by a good masseur. Apart from making oneself feel good, I consider staying in shape—a problem that, luckily, I still don't have to worry about—a required respect for being around other people.

But an active practice will always be more important, much more, than passive exercise. Thus, some time each day for exercising, exercises for coordination, for stretching, followed by a bracing cold shower; as far as the shower is concerned, the important thing is not that it's only cold water, but that, whether lukewarm or hot, it ends cold, ice-cold if possible, and then, endure the violence of the jet against the neck, and down the spine. Years ago, I would often attend a certain ballet academy, but these days I find it a real struggle, and not just the exercise itself, that I fulfill perfectly well with calisthenics—but for the terribly unpleasant atmosphere, that permanent stench of second-rate girls jumping and frolicking about. On the other hand, doing ballet at home seems pointless; if Francisca Maldonado already struck me as a phony when she was practicing recitation, the simple idea of spotting some woman dancing alone in her house is enough to make anyone shiver with disgust. And the fact is, the only attractive sports and exercises are the ones that can be practiced in their own environment, in their natural space, which are generally incompatible with the city. Swimming, for example, not in one of those reheated pools that stink of chlorine, but in Cadaqués, at dawn, several strokes in glassy, vivifying water, offshore, open water, cutting through bubbles streaming over our bodies like flashes of lightning, like beads of mercury. Or, also in Cadaqués, to be personally in charge of the boat's sail, face to the wind, no matter how much it bothers the horrendous Constantino, who will find fault with however many maneuvers I can make simply because I'm capable of carrying them out without his help. What's really healthy, however, because it coincides with winter, the season when people spend the most time in the city, is skiing. Well, not so much skiing as a sport as the fresh air you breathe in the places where you ski, high up above the dirty clouds, amid an archipelago of sunny snow-covered mountain peaks, all infinitely purer than the shore of any of the seas full of garbage that the summer offers us. Although I don't consider myself what you'd call a good skier, I'm not exactly like most, either. But that's not what's important, what matters is the prevailing climate in these places. That transparency, that clarity, those crazy figures who come speeding down the mountain, as if flying out of a painting by Brueghel. And the delicious thing is skiing semi-naked, during the week, when the ski slopes recover the tranquility lost during weekends, breasts in the wind, getting bronzed by the sun with that special splendor it acquires from the snow. And the aesthetic beauty of all the necessary gear, of the outfits—with their colors that seem to sparkle and flash—that make the skiers look so good, especially the blondes. And the warm atmosphere that forms among certain select people as soon as night falls, by the warmth of the fireplace. When it comes to that—and in almost everything else—nothing compares to alpine ski resorts, especially the ones in German-speaking Switzerland; the slopes in the Pyrenees are, shall we say, not worth leaving home for.

Ah, one last piece of advice: dispense with any and all kinds of medications. I only take complex vitamins and, at most, the occasional aspirin. Baby aspirin, of course: a remedy I always recommend. You only have to calculate the right dosage—four tablets equal half a gram—and it has the advantage of not causing gastric problems—and apart from the flavor, which may not be pleasant, but doesn't have the brutal aggressive acidity of common, regular aspirin.

Of course, the normal thing is to not do any of all this. The normal thing, particularly among those who form part of that particular institution called ladies, is just the contrary: their creams, their treatments, their hairdresser, their beautician, their *visagiste*, their secret rejuvenation sessions, beauty treatments, and other operations and products which, in a short time, not unlike those mummies that dissolve into dust simply from contact with the air, only cause them to deteriorate so much more quickly. No different than trying to restore a painting when the canvas is already irreparably deteriorated. Although I use the occasional beauty product and follow certain treatments, I know perfectly well that what counts is what's underneath, the body, not beauty creams. And when I reach menopause—which will come very late, as has always been the case with the women in my family—my whole life I've heard about how my paternal grandmother ran like clockwork until she was close to sixty, and with my mother it was more or less the same, although I suppose that, for her, this must have been a liberation from awkward memories more than anything else—I'm sure that my body won't be affected in any way by the absence of regular periods, as naturally happens when one is in both perfect mental and physical condition.

Ladies as an institution, a condition or state which, fortunately, as someone before me wrote so well, is not derived necessarily from the fact of being a woman. Those creatures for whom the physical beauty of their youthful years comes to be an extension of their intelligence or, failing that, a substitution: weapons for the treachery and infidelity that they practice systematically, with the precision and confidence of the stealthy hunter who traverses a landscape that he knows down to the last square inch. Then they'll have to pay for the passing of time, the emptiness inside and the progressive indifference that grows around them the more outdated they become, with the hard work of learning to use their brain as an autonomous organ. Thus, in their anxiety to control ideas, they imitate men, the husband, in every misstep and botched job that they have seen him put into practice in the business world, but applying those practices to their personal sphere, all on a reduced scale: buy for a song one of those old fisherman's houses in a semi-ruinous state that so abound in Cadaqués; remodel it with a rustic design and decorate it with a handful of junk that gives it a certain special character; make a fortune by renting it to one of those recent arrivals who frequent local cocktail parties, American—from North America, of course—if at all possible. Or they might find they do better following their intellectual aspirations, revealing pretentious liberal airs and putting themselves entirely at the disposal of one of those viragoes who organize feminist movements with an iron hand, and who would be perfect at taking charge of cultivating all their spite and frustrations. The most frequent thing, however, is they let themselves be dragged down by all the weight they've put on, their body swelling and hardening, the progressive atrophy of their physical and intellectual faculties, becoming ever more a vegetable. But what doesn't change is the end: after those failed attempts, years of trying to settle down, searching for a comfortable security, comes the underlying result, the other face of married life, the obverse of conjugal life, its capitulations, betrayals, and exclusions, the slow process of consumption, much less gradual than one ever supposes, deterioration and bewilderment and a state of permanent stupor, belonging to that prematurely aged woman, ravaged by alcoholism, dulled by tranquilizers and sleeping pills, who ends up burning to death while asleep—thanks to an unfinished cigarette.

Marriage, *ça va de soi*, is largely to blame. There must be some reason why the word patrimony is associated with the concept of full possession, while marriage is related rather more to the idea of a contract, of recompense, of provisions and benefit, of which the woman, of course, gets the worst part. But you can't blame everything on marriage. Has anyone ever stopped to think about how similar a group of ladies, married or single, is to a brood of hens? Cluck-cluck-cluck-cluck! Cluck-cluck-cluck-cluck! Cluck-cluck-cluck-cluck! Hens, yes; hens as numerous as cauliflowers. Because you mustn't forget that marriage is a test that also affects and diminishes the man. And, nevertheless, how can we compare that world of ladies to a man, a real man, who matures nobly, with a fine, worthy physical presence and a clear intellect? How can one compare such a man, however rare they might be—it's enough that only one might exist—to the vast brood of all those gallinaceous women in the world put together? I don't understand—or I understand all too well—how those feminist viragoes can pretend, not even bothering to make the comparison any longer but, astonishingly brazen, they employ supposedly objective arguments, turning the tables in their favor. That those horrendous viragoes, unsatisfied women and, at heart, puritans, who consider the act of love a kind of mutual masturbation from which they must squeeze out all possible pleasure, they'd like to reject the man out of hand, without even looking at him, when, in fact, a man's body, when put to good use, is one of the best masturbatory instruments that you can imagine, not even considering the vagina, but considering any point on the body, including those which the viragoes, with their aprioristic closed-mindedness, with their habitual fanaticism, try to exclude from the feminine anatomy, all of them, practically, save this tiny point that doesn't even qualify as a shriveled replica of the masculine appendage. Things that, if they do not attract them—the viragoes—I don't see any reason why they shouldn't attract me. That's exactly why they hate me, because I refuse to be assimilated by them, to join their ranks, to be labeled or classified in any way, shape, or form.

In fact, I never had my own Breda—the Breda in the painting, I mean, not that terribly depressing town near Aiguaviva where my mother took us to spend the summers. This includes the case of Francisca Maldonado, when, for the first and last time in my life, I was the one besieged, the one who had something to lose—or thought I did—and I didn't surrender my key, didn't let my arm get twisted, didn't surrender. I emerged victorious, both in matters concerning Maldonado as well as myself; in the end, my resistance prevailed over her scornful behavior, over so many humiliations, over all the verbal and even physical aggressions she tried to use against me. My sense of dignity and my self-respect, sometimes aggravated, saved me. At most it can be said that I only ever reached a stalemate twice: once with Juan Antonio, once with Raúl.

If someone, someday, ever reads these lines, they'll certainly be surprised by my frankness, by the sincerity and clarity with which I normally express myself. But the fact is, really, rejecting the idea that you don't have to win them all strikes me as absurd, or, when it comes to Raúl, for example, that the way it happened is even normal. Because if there's any person who's truly got a thick skin, that person is Raúl. Especially now that he's become a famous writer and, through his books, he's had the chance to polish his image, to conceal his true personality by hanging veils and more veils between what he really is and what people suppose him to be—as far as his authorship of his books goes; books like that one which he's been working on for years and years, one of those books with such a weird title that, later, in the bookshops, you're almost embarrassed to ask for it.

But I know him well and have for some time, and I know that he's still the same Raúl that I met and spent time with in Paris. On the other hand, as happens with everyone, however much one evolves, not only in their manners and outward appearance, but also in their way of thinking, there's something in the deepest part of the human being that never changes at all. And I know all too well that the real Raúl is someone very different from who he appears to be. Because I know exactly what's hidden behind the facade of his stormy relationship with Nuria; the truth of which, for anyone, herself included, and primarily for whoever's willing to listen to her and believe what she says, constitutes a complete failure. And I also know—I've got more than enough reasons to affirm it—that, if he's not in love with Nuria, Raúl is certainly much more strongly tied to her than he pretends to be in front of other people, than he lets on in public; that he wouldn't want to lose her for anything in the world. And I know, as well, the essential motives that shore up such an attitude.

I imagine that he wouldn't enjoy reading these lines, but I'm privately convinced that if his erotic life, as he himself affirms, is more than turbulent, the affairs he's had away from Nuria, apart from some exceptions, haven't been very satisfactory for him, nor have there been as many as people believe. By that I don't mean, don't even want to hint, that Raúl is one of those pathetic guys who go around bragging about their nonexistent affairs, inventing conquests. What does happen is that Raúl deceives Nuria about the outcome of the affair, making her believe that each time, with each lover, everything has been better and easier than it's really been. And that for reasons similar to those that induce him, not only to assure her that he doesn't feel jealousy about the lovers she might have, but to incite her to pursue them. Because in both cases his attitude points to the same objective: that she become convinced that for him—unlike what happens with her difficult and disappointing affairs—such erotic relationships are equally felicitous, thanks to their normality, and insignificant. The result is that Nuria sees herself placed in an evident situation of inferiority and subordination to Raúl, and if this situation puts him on the defensive—avoiding a second breakup, which would repeat his original betrayal, of which she was a victim—for her it has an eminently destructive character, nullifying her personality, an indispensable effect when what he's searching for is, precisely, that she be incapable of taking initiative or finding some resolve regarding the continuity of her relations with Raúl.

It's not a question of deliberate cruelty—not even, perhaps, of a conscious cruelty. But it is, doubtless, a cruelty, and there are times when Nuria, in her complete helplessness, really makes me feel sorry for her. A girl like her, who had such good looks—and still does—along with other great qualities and, above all, a great human quality, to see her now become little more than just some other person, one of those women who hide behind their migraines, their sensitivity to changes in the weather, illnesses no less personal than their miraculous cures. And the blame for everything, voluntary or not, belongs to Raúl, because with some other type of guy—and keep in mind that I'm not suggesting some kind of imbecile, but simply a man with fewer dark corners and, foremost, without the traces of a genius like Raúl—she might have been perfectly happy.

Whether one is a match for their partner or not is, in the short term, an unimportant problem. There are some couples who can even go on muddling along together for years and years. But not indefinitely. Camila and I, for instance. My relationship with Camila is condemned to be, over time, very similar to Raúl and Nuria's. Meaning: in both cases, no future whatsoever. And also, as with Raúl, although in my own way, only seemingly in contradiction with my clear vision of such a future, my fight for Camila, my refusal, as much as I wanted to make it last, to allow myself to be beaten by anyone. The pleasure of reconquering her, of my increasing domination of the situation, of her defeat, of my victory, a real pleasure even before I recognized it as such, before, following that business at Port de la Selva, she implicitly threw in the towel.

Not solely a moral pleasure, let's be clear; a pleasure that, transcending the plane of mere moral satisfaction, is situated fully in the field of physical pleasure, of sensuality. That siesta in Cadaqués, one September afternoon, before I had the facts I now possess—the key to so many questions still unanswered at that time. The warm sun pouring through that crack, the scattered voices filtering in from the street, and me, naked on the bed, covered in sweat, I wouldn't know whether from the warmth brought by the wind from the ocean or by the excitation that blossomed anew, uncontainable the moment I began to mentally reconstruct the various avatars of the adventure I had experienced, that I was still experiencing alongside Camila and Roberto, close and simultaneously invisible participant of their amorous raptures, of their quarrels, of their passionate reunions, and how many things had happened in recent weeks, recollections that, inevitably, ended up focusing, the same as on that morning of wild lovemaking with Camila following the night of what happened in the cellar, or that other night, a harmonious replica of the first one, which followed what happened in Port de la Selva, in such a way that there was no need to await the arrival of a pleasure no less wild nor of any less duration than the one I was recalling, all the while the sun was slipping away and sleep ended up overcoming me, after that kind of continuous orgasm that, such as I achieved it, can be achieved practically without touching yourself, and which only someone poor in spirit, or a sexologist or such people, would think of relating with a vulgar act of onanism.

I woke up a little while later and took a long, splendid shower, something similar to what one must feel in summer, with the suffocating humidity that rises from the hot fields, under one of those waterfalls that start flowing with melted snow from high mountain glaciers. Then, a light supper with Camila, who—impossible to express it with more meaningful words—felt like stretching her legs a bit, so that she went out to take a stroll around El Hostal, or something like that; the truth is I don't exactly remember. Lying on the cushions in the cellar with a whiskey on the rocks within reach—that I definitely remember with perfect clarity—I began reading, or rather, re-reading *The Edict of Milan*, a novel which I wrotc years before and which I published discreetly under the pseudonym of Claudio Mendoza[2]. I frequently reread certain pages, specific episodes, but that time I read it from beginning to end, in a single sitting, until late at night. Perhaps due to the distance that the passage of time establishes with respect to all the work of our youth, or perhaps because of the collected memories, whether related to the novel or not, which the evocation of that time kept alive in me, the fact is that the fervor with which I surrendered myself to the novel wasn't quite what one might expect from an author, but rather from some lucky reader.

---

[2] Claudio Mendoza, *The Edict of Milan*, Ediciones Originales, Barcelona.

IV

One of those moments that inevitably generates the memory of similar moments already experienced, the contrast between the increasingly slower forward motion of the train that was pulling in on her right and the train that was pulling out on her left, a disconcerting sensation, almost dizziness, vertigo, as if her head were floating away, the reflection of herself waving, her hand chopped off over and over again by the increasing speed of the train cars.

A woman saying goodbye to her man, suddenly finding herself even more alone standing alongside the empty tracks, turning around to retrace her steps, to go back along the platform the way she came. A woman—the inhospitable outline of the Gare d'Austerlitz now behind her—walking along the semi-deserted sidewalks, lost in thought, treading the wet fallen leaves, her figure growing smaller as she walked away, her hair loose and windswept, hands in her raincoat pockets. A woman walking into her regular café, sitting at her usual table, ordering the same thing from the same waiter as always, what she and Luis always had at this time of day, before l'Alouette began to fill up with familiar faces. Only that Luis was no longer there and she absent-mindedly pushed aside the vase with the yellow chrysanthemum that adorned the table, alone, facing an empty chair. Something that, although it didn't belong to any particular cinematic scene, seemed designed to make anyone believe that they'd seen it happen in some film.

The station suddenly silent and lifeless as soon as the train had departed. The slippery sidewalks that, like in a dream, stretched on longer and longer as she walked along them, her hair loose, hands in the pockets of her raincoat, the smell of the drizzle like breath that fogs the window, the pavement's gray luster like a madman's gaze. The look and the breath of someone who'd always been following her, as if since forever she'd done nothing but walk toward that encounter with an empty chair, or as if anything else she might have done apart from walk toward that empty chair was completely irrelevant.

The difficulty of expressing that sensation. The subsequent complacency once it's captured, once it's defined. Sitting alone before a yellow chrysanthemum, strolling alone through the Luxembourg Gardens, along the embankments of the Seine, as one can stroll along the sidewalks, stepping on the sopping wet matted leaves, while her classmates from the École des Beaux Arts crowd around other tables, joking among themselves, making plans to meet later, couples kissing and embracing all along the sidewalks, until the inhospitable drizzle and the lively streets seem to have been conjured up to be even more in contrast with her solitude, the better to place between parentheses how much of her life has not constituted a farewell at the station, nor wandering empty sidewalks, nor sitting before a yellow chrysanthemum, facing an empty chair. And, once there, free for the moment from l'Alouette's regular customers, dropping a coin into the jukebox and, the same as if he were sitting there in the empty chair, listening to the record and immediately starting to write the letter, now that he was still not too far gone from Paris, and she was listening to "Moscow Nights," the same tune as always, his record, and her in Paris.

The problems of a woman made for one man alone, beside which everything else is just part of the routine, performed better or worse. Incomprehensible if not ridiculous problems for whomever doesn't know what it is to love one single man. Problems that become more complicated when it turns out that the man is a militant revolutionary and that his return to Spain implies the risk run by all those who, in parallel fashion to their normal life as a student, as a child of the bourgeoisie, develop a clandestine activity that runs counter to survival and, more precisely, against the class to which they belong. And when the woman who loves this man remains in Paris, safe, yes, but alone and fully conscious of the situation in which they both find themselves, times that make love difficult, times of war. A war to the death between a handful of communist militants and the Franco dictatorship, against whose repressive apparatus they might wield in opposition, as their only weapon, the support of the popular masses. Moral motivations and ideological perspectives, theory and praxis, elements in play which she perhaps did not know how to express correctly, concepts which she perhaps could not handle with the same precision that Luis or Jaime or Alejandro brought to their discussions, but which she understood and shared in all their extremes, persuaded as she was of the importance of the fight they were engaged in.

In such circumstances, like the heroine in a Soviet film, the woman should subordinate her personal feelings to ideological principles, to the conception of the world for which her man was fighting, put the work of transforming the world before her own equally legitimate and selfish need for love. Perhaps she should do it, all the more so because Lucía accepted Luis's ideology without reservations. But the fact is that she couldn't. The fact is that Lucía was, above all else, a woman in love. Something that also sounds ridiculous, almost embarrassing to say out loud.

I feel as though I were surrounded by wolves, do you see? she said, rotating the vase with the yellow chrysanthemum. A sensation similar to the one she'd experienced when she first arrived in Paris, at the beginning of the school year. With the difference that then she'd known that Luis was going to come to visit her sometime between late October and early November, around All Saints Day, and now, by contrast, she had no new meeting to look forward to.

A week, barely eight days, spent together with Luis, the way the shadow of a lonely cloud slips by, gone just before we sense it. Luis had his appointments, his meetings with people from the party. But the rest of the time, to Lucía's recollection, all rolled into a chaotic mass, one long day, alternating between one thing and another, like a rotating series of variations, outings with friends, films they watched together, strolls that tended to wander, between nights of lovemaking and mornings of lovemaking or vice-versa, taking advantage of the fact that Charlotte, without it having been necessary to ask her, had let them have time alone together. She also had the right, she told them, to spend some days with a friend.

Nobody understands these things but you, said Lucía. Who, if not, apart from Charlotte? Could Jaime understand her? For him, going and coming from Spain was as normal as it was for Luis, requirements of the struggle that simply had to be accepted without a second thought. Could he? He seemed to take it for granted that, after Luis's departure, she would be sensible enough to rejoin, as usual, her regular life as a student, reconnect with her group of friends and presumed friends, let herself be trapped anew by the trivialities of that little world, its jokes, its gossip, its complications, always, as it were, within reach of one of those guys looking for a fling, those love affair collectors who then make a point of showing off their latest conquest the way a big game hunter shows off his mounted heads.

Because trying to talk seriously with Alejandro made no sense at all, unless you were in the mood for some of his sarcasm, and nothing else. It wasn't even worth trying to talk to Gina, with her mystico-proletariat or mystico-peasant fervors for all things Danilo Dolci, or Jacques, who, however much of a Marxist he claimed to be, didn't have the least idea what it really meant to be that—and to live according to those principles—in a country like Spain.

Only Charlotte, with her gift for accepting the normality of the most unusual things, could understand her. Only her, however different she was from Lucía in her way of thinking, in her habits, changing her lovers as casually as changing her socks, or perhaps it was precisely that dissimilarity that made her qualified to understand that, however strange it seemed, there were also women who stuck with just one single man.

She'd dropped by l'Alouette to ask her if she was planning to stay in the room that afternoon, a tactful way of asking permission to use it; although when it came to Charlotte's motives, it was also possible that such a plainly stated request might turn out to be more complicated. Thinking, for example, that Lucía, after saying goodbye to Luis, would head to her regular hangout; to pretend to run into her as if by accident in order to chat, to distract her a little; asking her to use the room they shared precisely in order to prevent Lucía from becoming too self-absorbed, to keep her from shutting herself away inside the very room where they'd enjoyed their wild lovemaking, in order to force her outside into the city, to reconnect with the rhythms of normal daily life.

While they were sipping one last café au lait, Lucía translated Javier's letter for her. She hadn't dared show it to Luis, she explained, not because Javier told her he was coming to Paris, but because it might have bothered Luis that she continued to allow herself to be pursued by a man like Javier, equally rich and lacking in interest, equally friendly and irrelevant. The typical guy to take them out to eat at Maxim's and then hang around that neighborhood, hitting all the most expensive spots. The only bad thing about Javier was that Luis couldn't stand him.

Three unanswered letters since Luis's departure gave her more than enough reason for worry. And Lucía's anxiety increased with each new letter she received—from her mother, or her brother, or from whomever—but she heard nothing from Luis. Their kiss as the train was pulling away, how he waved his hand and pulled back from the window, as if to cut short the moment, to deprive it of any drama at all; and her walk back from the station, oppressed by the drizzle floating in the heavy air that felt like a perfect augury. Apprehensions that better deserved, perhaps, to be called intuitions, an almost terrifying facility for someone who, like Lucía, was used to see them really come true.

At night, when Charlotte arrived, Lucía talked to her about her fears, her nightmares, about the horrible images that, even when she was awake, seemed to come to life behind her eyelids—arrests, interrogations, violence, hallucinatory details. Things difficult to understand there in France, where everything seemed so clear and so easy. Because the reality of life in Spain was very different, because *Spain is different*, as all the tourist propaganda so emphatically declares. Alejandro, for example, having to flee the country simply for thinking and acting like so many French students think and act. And he was lucky to escape in time, because the alternative path might very well have led to arrest, torture, years in prison, the death penalty. Not even there, in Paris, could Spaniards feel safe. Franco's intelligence agents were everywhere.

Jaime tried to calm her down. He said that if something had happened to Luis, they would all know about it by this time: *pas de nouvelles, bonnes nouvelles*. If he's not written it's because he's not been able to, and if he's not been able to it's because he's not had time, and if he's not had time it's because he's had other things to do.

Whether or not Jaime really believed what he was saying, he acted like a real friend. On the other hand, that fucker Alejandro told her: yes, Luis is probably too busy. What about that friend of his from Economics class who's so good looking and so politically active, such a militant, and an aristocrat to boot? What's her name? Irene? I used to call her Guillermo, that was her war name. I gave it to her when she joined the party. Well, that must be the explanation: Guillermo.

Alejandro had a knack for getting under Lucía's skin, for riling her up to the boiling point. Sometimes she had the impression he was, I don't know, she said, sort of halfway queer, and all that. *No matter*, said Charlotte. *I like men who are a bit homosexual.*

Lucía shoved Charlotte with her feet as if she wanted to kick her out of bed, a bed whose mattress, already sagging on both sides, tended to roll them both right off of it. Clinging to the edge, her face sunk in the pillow, far from putting up any resistance, Charlotte pretended to scream in terror, managing to dispel Lucía's black thoughts and raise her spirits. And on top of that, she was in the right: whatever the reason for the delays, for the irregularity of Lucía's correspondence with Luis, worry alone could not justify any alteration in her normal daily routine. She had to start going out again, she needed it, although she found few things less appealing than returning to that meat market, guys hunting for girls, or vice-versa. She forced herself to do it, to keep Charlotte company, although at the risk of returning home alone when Charlotte, like some stray puppy, went padding after the first guy who propositioned her. It was practically unbearable to see her behave that way, and it made Lucía want to slap her face, Charlotte, the daughter of a Geneva banker who was half-cracked, or who had driven his wife crazy, meaning, Charlotte's mother, and had her committed or declared mentally incompetent, or something like that; or the reverse, that he, her father, was the one declared mentally unfit. It didn't really matter: the tragic thing was that she, Charlotte, the daughter of the madwoman or madman, didn't really take herself seriously. And that was certainly the only reason why the boys in the photo lab where she went to develop her pictures let her come in, so they could pass her from one to the other under the red light of the darkroom.

She also started spending more time with Marina. The only bad thing was that, unlike Charlotte, Marina talked too much about herself. And it's not that her experiences weren't interesting, far from it. But the problem wasn't so much the things she talked about—her childhood among ruined White Russians, her haphazard career in the world of classical ballet, her life with Sergio Vidal—as the monotonous French-accented Spanish she insisted on speaking, with an intonation that made you drowsy.

She generally dropped by l'Alouette around the same time as everyone else in her crowd. To detox from la Haute, she said. Fleeing some social engagement or the visit of a God-Knows-What marquises or some Texas millionaire eager to see himself immortalized in a painting. For Lucía, Marina's physical presence had caught her eye even before Jaime introduced them to each other. The peculiar gravity of her presence, that special quality that a mature personality imbues in a lovely face; her attractive exotic features, her special elegance, a question of natural good taste more than of expense, in strong contrast to the regulars at l'Alouette, a crowd composed of Beaux Arts students used to cultivating a quasi Bohemian-proletarian look. However, still more inconceivable than Marina's physical presence amid that petit-bourgeois scene with its revolutionary airs was, no doubt, the tale of her many experiences, beginning with her scanty memories of earliest childhood. The summer palace in Samarkand, the image of her father riding his horse up the marble staircase, the Chinese servants, the day she watched a man beheaded in the public square—far too many strange, unusual occurrences for the crowd at l'Alouette.

No ostriches on the horizon, said Marina, meaning the coast was clear, the evening looked promising. And then, without a single ostrich in sight, maybe she telephoned Lucía directly, maybe through Jaime, and invited her to have tea at her house, in Montmarte, right next door to the Moulin Rouge. The house was two stories high, with a plain facade but decidedly pretentious interior decor, with faces and bodies or body parts emerging from the walls, and expensive curios in the corners, everything very a la Cocteau. Sergio Vidal had his studio in the attic, reached by a ladder, and sometimes he climbed down to chat with them a while, seemingly cordial and open, although his eyes never lost their glassy snakelike look, not even when he was cracking a joke. He invariably wore jeans and some threadbare sweater, but judging from various photos taken alongside princesses and the like, he was just as comfortable in the most classic tuxedoes. Besides belonging to one of Barcelona's wealthiest families—or precisely for that reason—his lifestyle reflected his specialization in painting portraits of people of international standing, one of those painters whose name hardly anyone knows, but who are the best paid in the world thanks to painting queens and multimillionaires attracted by Sergio Vidal's talent for capturing the most flattering image of the person whose portrait he was painting, always with an essential realism. That's the secret, said Marina. But the exasperating thing isn't the time he takes to paint a portrait, but the time he wastes and the hours he makes me waste rubbing elbows with la Haute, the most important part of his job.

They had tea in the Russian style, next to the samovar. He picked me up in a metro station, without even enough money in my purse for a coffee, and he brought me here. Then it turned out that he'd seen me act in the Liceo and that he'd sent me, along with an orchid, a note in which he invited me to a party he was throwing, his birthday or something like that. And I kept the orchid and threw his invitation in the wastepaper basket in my dressing room. Of course I didn't know then who the gentlemen inviting me really was, not the swine-faced industrial magnate I was imagining, but a tall, handsome, slender, elegant man.

The news arrived along with an explanation: Luis had been arrested in Barcelona then released a few hours later. The police, it seems, had raided a meeting taking place at a law firm. All the participants, Luis among them, were taken to Police Headquarters. But, as the interrogations did not bring to light any kind of illegal activity, everyone else arrested would be released sometime the next day.

Jaime appeared quite satisfied, euphoric even, to the point of not noticing the scant enthusiasm displayed by Lucía when he burst into her room, rousing her from a deep, oppressive sleep. The moment he departed, seemingly in a rush to spread the news, as if he were announcing the birth of his firstborn son, Lucía sank back into her bed, face buried in the pillow.

More than jubilation, she felt swindled; almost ridiculous. She'd been worried about Luis, about the dangers that threatened him in Spain, about the helpless state—each in their own way—they'd found themselves in after their parting at the train station, about his disquieting lack of response to her letters; her insomnia, her discouragement, and her anxiety had been growing inside of her no matter how much she tried to push them aside or overcome them by going out, distracting herself, seeing people. And now it turned out that everything had been some sort of harmless practical joke. Something that, on the other hand, neither justified nor explained the epistolary void in which she found herself, that nightmarish sensation of sending letter after letter without receiving any kind of answer. A sensation in no way relieved—quite the contrary—by the laconic note that reached her a few days later; four lines in which Luis, as if to assuage her fears, simply told her that everything was just fine. With Irene, of course: everything was just fine with Irene; that's what must have prompted him to write such a tight-lipped note.

Irene. The Red Princess. Aristocrat, communist, beautiful: three peculiarities, normally irreconcilable, mingled in Irene. No one thought much of her intellectual capacity, but her temperament was something else: incandescent, passionate, capable of igniting passion in all her fellow militants. In reality, she was probably some unprincipled hysteric. But magnetic enough to induce all those comrades lucky enough to fight for socialism alongside her to follow her perky little ass into the struggle. And which fighter was better qualified than Luis to become her vital companion, to share everything mutually from head to toe, from cock to coccyx? Exactly what that bastard Alejandro had been predicting, perhaps because he knew Irene, and he also knew Luis, just as he also knew certain private details that the very avatars of the socialist struggle inject into life within the party. In the end, Alejandro himself was nothing more than just another little rich boy communist, even though, at this moment, daddy's millions were not enough to buy him safe passage back into Spain.

Meaning: that while she, Lucía, was worried about Luis, she was, like a fool, remaining faithful to Luis, returning home each night lonelier than a young nun in the convent, trying to devote herself to carefully reading *The Battle of the Milvian Bridge*, as if it were some sacred text, simply because he'd recommended that she read it, and reading that novel was, for her, a way of keeping in touch with him even after his departure; and while she, like a real imbecile, was laboring at this task, he was leisurely carrying on with Irene *ad majorem socialismi gloriam*. A behavior not only immoral but truly unspeakable if one took into account their respective situations, the difficult times that it was their lot to live through. The conduct of a false revolutionary, of one of those fellows who camouflage their personal appetites under the appearance of objective needs. The conduct of a true cynic.

Another problem: her period was alarmingly late, and by enough days, according to her calculations, to make her start thinking that it wasn't actually late but not coming at all. The certainty that, if she were pregnant, then the child she was carrying belonged to that cynic Luis. A child she didn't want, that she could not have. But she would be the one to have to find some solution to the problem, not the cynic, not the cowardly father.

The conflation of one problem with another, abandonment compounded by betrayal, and both hanging over the normal demands of daily life. The neglect, the disinterest, and the discouragement that weighed her down, that made it impossible for her to attend classes at the sSchool, with the inevitable wasted semester this implied, and the resulting futility of her presence in Paris, of her remaining there, of her solitude. An apathy that spread through every part of her daily life. Her lack of appetite, for example; her tendency to subsist on nothing besides café au lait, now about to become a permanent habit. Or the simple effort of getting up in the morning, of rising from bed, something that, if she could, she'd never do again. A feeling perhaps increased, conversely, by having to face Charlotte's vitality every morning; her scant need of sleep, her agility in leaping from the bed, her enviable joie de vivre.

A general absence of stimuli that made her late to everything, breaking with the characteristic punctuality of a young woman educated at a convent boarding school. Bureaucratic paperwork postponed day after day, waiting in useless lines, office windows closing down on the counter like a cruel smile, too late to find any place open to eat after leaving the office, to make an appointment on time, to find any familiar faces at l'Alouette. It was as if she were incapable, not only of scheduling the necessary time, but of even being able to think. As if her head were invaded by fog. Or padded on the inside with some cottony baffle, doubtless the inevitable result of her sleepless nights, against which not even *The Battle of the Milvian Bridge* had any power. The principal difficulty in this lay not in what a hard time she had falling asleep, or that she slept lightly and fitfully; the principal difficulty lay in somehow getting to sleep before dawn.

Deep down, the only thing she really wanted was to crawl into bed and have someone take care of her as if she were a little girl. And the fact is, what Lucía was experiencing most of all was a tremendous need for affection. As for everything else, however much she accomplished or let fall by the wayside, however much might happen around her, she just didn't care, sunk as she was in stress and fatigue, as if she were pinned down by some giant heavy hand. And the worst thing, what she most obsessed over, was her return home once l'Alouette closed for the night, alone, hands sunk in the pockets of her raincoat, possessed by the feeling that her whole life could be summed up in that single action of going to bed alone, while everyone else was hooking up, and people everywhere were out to have a good time.

Cheer up! said Charlotte. *Ne faites pas l'idiotte*, silly. *Amuse-toi!* Do the same! She jumped on Lucía's bed and pummeled her playfully until she got out of bed and got dressed again. Charlotte even picked out clothes for her to wear: some very tight pants, no bra, blouse half unbuttoned and, on top of that, her Italian mouton coat, so showy, that it made her feel like a weirdo and she almost refused to wear it. She applied mascara and liner to Lucía's eyes and not only enhanced them, centering her face around them, but even gave her an expression somewhere between profound and wary, equally provocative and wild.

At l'Alouette she ordered Calvados for them both instead of their habitual café au lait, which was to blame, without the slightest doubt, for Lucía's sleepless nights, and for her nodding off during the day, and for everything that was going on with her. In any case, after the second glass, Lucía really felt much better, happy and animated, almost exalted.

Jacques and Gina were ragging on Sergio Vidal's style of painting, inconceivable in the age of artists like Paul Klee or Mondrian. The very sort of paintings to satisfy the taste of his swine of a father, that *salope*, said Jacques. Just what the bourgeois likes to buy; because if the bourgeois buy Picassos it's not because they like Picasso, but because his paintings are worth a fortune, as an investment. Bourgeois people like bourgeois painting. Whether they admit it or not, the bourgeois prefer a Sergio Vidal to a Picasso. Picasso attacks their aesthetic principles; Sergio Vidal defends them. And defending bourgeois aesthetic principles is the same as defending bourgeois class interests.

One only need examine Sergio Vidal's house. Everything at the ready *pour épater le bourgeois*. Unconventional but very expensive knick-knacks, objects that, although possessing something disquieting, correspond exactly to what his bourgeois clientele imagine the highly successful artist to be: an original creature, extravagant, just a touch crazy, who leads a life divorced from any kind of prejudice, who can permit themselves everything—everything: the feverish envy, the deep longing of the respectable bourgeois—but who's really got nothing in common with those riffraff painters whose Bohemian affect, with their long hair and old clothes, conceals nothing but the embarrassed face of professional failure. No: Sergio Vidal is serious, solid, solvent. Marina laughed, also a bit drunk, and she told them they were right, everything was a show for the benefit of his clients, and that she, sometimes, instead of feeling comfortable in their house, she felt like a decoration from the Liceo.

For some time now she'd been coming round l'Alouette more often and, without having talked about it with Lucía, it felt like by switching to Calvados they'd reached some unspoken agreement, that Marina would quit drinking her cups of tea, Lucía her cafés au lait. And when Lucía went to Marina's house, maybe alone, maybe accompanied by Jaime or some other friend, instead of tea

Marina offered them vodka or Alsatian pear brandy, as stimulating as it was strong.

I'll bet you were a weird little girl, too, said Marina. Together they'd drunk close to half a bottle in a warm mood of intimacy and affection. Yeah, I don't know, kind of weird, said Lucía. And Marina: well, I really was; I was surrounded by servants, tutors, and all that, and even though I'd go weeks without seeing my dad, I thought about him all day long. And Lucía: *sí, chica*, but the thing is your childhood, all by itself, was already the strangest kind, the environment, the circumstances, everything; but mine was normal as anything: even so, I was never a happy little girl. Me neither; and, well, though I didn't realize it, my way of loving my daddy had something incestuous about it. The same with me: I remember, more than anything, him making me ride on his knees, like a horse. Then he died, and everything with my mother was different. My father, however, made me ride real horses; and I was never afraid with him by my side, no matter how much we galloped. The thing is, moms are the ones who make us physically afraid, in our bodies, they're the ones who turn us into little girls. That's exactly right: what happened to you with your mother happened to me with mine, when my father died, in exile. But the other thing is they want those little girls they've invented to behave like ladies. Yeah: that's what my mother wanted to do to me when we came to France, luckily, she failed. Like me: but I've gotta warn you that I'm still a little girl on the inside. Same with me: Sergio tells me what he likes best about me is that I'm still not an adult, that thanks to me he's discovered the joys of pederasty, and doesn't want me to become a woman. And I think he's right, you know, it's true I'm not an adult. Me neither: I can seem, I don't know, happy-go-lucky or free and easy or whatever they say, but, in reality, I'm still the same little girl as before, a lonely little girl with lots of hang-ups. Like me, I'd say—and did say—Marina; like me, always that like me, me, me, me. And it definitely started to become abusive to be talking about herself the whole time when the one who had to walk home from Montmartre was not Marina but Lucía, alone, her hands sunk into the pockets of her raincoat.

Apart from the vodka and the pear brandy, however, that house bespoke quality, comfort, warmth, and cleanliness, which, after the typical filth of the progressive student environments, was rather like a breath of fresh air. Something similar to the feeling she experienced visiting those expensive bars and restaurants Javier insisted on treating them to during his stay in Paris. The guest, at first, was Lucía, but because Charlotte was her roommate and Javier was a perfect gentleman, he made no objection whatsoever to taking them both out instead of going out alone with Lucía, as he probably would have preferred.

It was Charlotte who raised some objections: she didn't want to be in the way, she didn't own the right kind of clothes for going to expensive places, etcetera. This time it was Lucía who had to pin her down on the bed to get her to listen. Don't be silly, you ninny, she told her. All Charlotte's clothes were to her liking, besides the fact that Javier, while maybe not a genius, was neither an imbecile nor a tight-ass, and she knew quite well that a classy girl like Charlotte could wear whatever she wanted without losing her style; so there was no problem. Javier was a regular guy, friendly and fun to be with and very tactful; and, on top of the fact that he danced very well, he was also physically attractive. Besides, Lucía's period had finally come and, with her fears now dispelled, she was in an excellent mood, brimming with joy and energy. The three of them had a very good time together and, when Javier had left, the only thing that Lucía regretted was not having taken him to bed—he got hopelessly horny dancing with her—even if it were only to teach Luis a lesson.

Owing perhaps to the fact that Camilo, as a new member, had captured the group's interest, or maybe as a result of the numerous similar incidents that had occurred between Marina and Sergio Vidal during recent weeks, the news that Marina had moved out of the house or that she'd been kicked out by Sergio Vidal—it practically amounted to the same thing—certainly caught Lucía by surprise. Several days earlier—twelve? fifteen?—when Marina showed up at l'Alouette with one eye swollen and bruised, showing even through her makeup, and she asked her about it, and Marina said Sergio and, smiling, explained to her that that was only the visible part and, when later, in their room, she showed her the bruises all over her body, Lucía and Charlotte experienced a real crisis of indignation, of rage, increased by their feeling of powerlessness, by the Slavic resignation with which Marina seemed to accept the situation. He gets a kick out of doing that sometimes, she told them matter-of-factly, like someone talking about any other hobby, fishing, bridge, collecting butterflies.

The second time, about a week later, the results of Sergio Vidal's getting his kicks showed a much graver, more deviant face: the bruises and marks were clustered especially on Marina's breasts and buttocks, inner thighs, and who knows if on her sex itself, an obvious sign of hard, twisting pinches and calculated bites more than punches. Apart from Alejandro, they all agreed that it was a case for the Police Courts, sadism, torture pure and simple, denigrating harassment. If it happens one time, that's just what happens, Alejandro had said. If it happens again and Marina doesn't raise a fuss, well, that's weirder. But, now, if it turns out that it's nothing more than their normal behavior, well, that clears up everything: if he likes to do it to her, if she likes him to do it to her, then the truth is I don't know what some municipal court judge has got to say about it. The cynicism of his argument and the general delight with which it was received by the group certainly did not fail to blemish Martina's prestige.

But when Marina announced to her that she was broke and had no place to live, and when she came by their place and showed her Sergio Vidal's official seal marked in red on her buttocks, that could only alter the situation radically: she was branded like a slave, the way one brands a cow. Fortunately, Sergio's fear that the gold on his seal might melt kept him from heating it to the point where it would leave a scar. He'd just done it to her, using some tongs to heat it in the coals of the fire; he'd told it was a parting gift. Lucía proposed to Marina that she share Charlotte's room with her, but Jaime had already found her a less stressful place.

In the morning she met again with Marina in order to give her some moral support while Marina phoned Sergio Vidal so she could pick up her belongings, to set the time she would come round to get them, but Sergio told her that they were already packed up and that, as she was calling him from l'Alouette, the chauffeur would drop them off there immediately: and he hung up.

They all helped her carry her belongings to Jaime's place. Many of her things were not there, but Marina cynically longed for her Burmese elephant, a small bronze elephant; it's my good luck charm, you know, she said. However, she didn't want to call Sergio Vidal again, so that chore fell to Lucía. In fact, apart from rescuing the small lucky elephant, what she really wanted was the chance to speak with Sergio Vidal in person, to make him see the injustice involved in his behavior, his cruelty, his deep lack of understanding. Look, Sergio Vidal told her: if you've got a calling to be a procuress, make me the traditional proposal—a virgin or a nun, but no sluts, never *une garce*. Lucía had no idea, perhaps, how to react, to offer some fitting retort; with her defenses immediately broken and shattered, she simply kept saying over and over again that Marina had always been faithful to him, that she could swear to it, that surely all that stuff had just been a misunderstanding. Sergio Vidal smiled almost the same as Marina, hard to tell if in pain or pleasure. If I were you I wouldn't promise to swear to something I haven't seen, he said.

According to Camilo, Sergio Vidal was a worm and a piece of shit. And she, Marina, another worm. It's not like the Soviet Union was exactly the model nation. But what's certain is that the counterrevolutionaries, the Whites, were just as much a bunch of worms as the ones in Cuba now. He argued continuously with Jaime: politics, ideological questions, objective questions, and all that. For Camilo, the Cuban communists had played a notable role in the revolution's triumph: that of privileged spectators. Jaime said that overthrowing a dictatorship is one thing but a revolution is something else entirely, and while the situation in Cuba might lead to a revolution it wasn't a real revolution yet; there were also some elements, some traits, typically found in any fascist movement. Look, between July 18th and July 26th there are only eight days of difference. And Camilo: Well, I still see another difference, man: that July 26th led the people to victory and July 18th to defeat.

Jacques and almost everyone else said that Camilo was right. Even Abelardo himself: that's a revolution both here and in Seville, kid; not what we're doing. And Jacques: a revolution in every possible way, with liberty, without repression; the revolution with a party, everyone dancing *la pachanga*. A revolution with everything the Soviet revolution didn't have. He'd also heard it said, or had read somewhere, that the female militants danced with their shirts open, showing their breasts. Camilo said that he never saw any comrade dancing that way, but that, in the heat of the moment, everything was possible in Cuba. Jaime stubbornly stuck to his guns: Camilo, as a person, was a great guy. But, from an ideological point of view, he wasn't very serious, he lacked rigor.

Lucía liked him quite a bit: a real revolutionary who had taken part in a real revolution. Different from so many others she'd met up to that point. And, besides, if not especially handsome, very much a man, and very well built physically. Even his voice had a certain rather peculiar gravity: not nasal and shrill like the other Cubans, but low, deep, like Paul Robeson. Perhaps the fact that he was mulatto increased the effect; the humiliations he'd had to endure until he joined the revolutionary struggle, due, exclusively, to his looks, the color of his skin. The scorn implied in the behavior of all white people; not only Yankees, no: all of them. Including there, in Paris, where he was frequently mistaken for an Algerian. The police, the bourgeoisie, and even more than one worker. What's more, inside of every white person there lived a potential policeman. No white person could imagine, even if they wanted to, what it meant to be a person of color in a white man's world.

Like being a gypsy in Spain, kid, said Abelardo with his habitual wit. He'd been living in Paris for two or three years, but still seemed like he'd landed there fresh from Utrera; a disposition aggravated by his boastful impertinence—more than authentic self-confidence—that active militancy brings out in certain neophytes. Jaime brought him round to l'Alouette almost in spite of himself, like that person shadowed by an annoying dog following close at his heels, maybe because he felt obliged to pay him a certain amount of attention, maybe because he was hoping that in that particular atmosphere he'd feel more relaxed and would leave him in peace. Considerations only partially correct because Abelardo felt so relaxed that he didn't leave anybody in peace, hopping constantly from one table to the next, sticking his nose into everything. At least for once, Lucía and Jaime could agree on something: Abelardo had a certain slimy quality about him, even from a purely physical perspective.

Barely two weeks had passed since Marina and Sergio Vidal crashed and burned, when, as if by contagion, it was Gina who broke up with Jacques. Lucía did not dry her tears for her: let her cry as much as she feels like, for being an imbecile, for being naive, she totally deserved it. She, Gina, daughter of one of the most prominent building contractors in Italy, the good little rich girl from Milan who'd fled home first to work with Danilo Dolci, as if Mezzogiorno were India and Danilo Dolci were Mahatma Gandhi, and all because the guy she was sleeping with had planted the idea in her head. And when her parents, after rescuing her from that magnate, sent her to Paris, she, or Loló, as that asshole Alejandro called her, couldn't think of anything better than hooking up with that pig Jacques, *l'enfant terrible* of the School, one of those radicals who kick-start the revolution by thrashing the rotten little bourgeois bitch whom they're bedding. So, she couldn't stand the way Jacques was treating her anymore? But then why had she already taken so much shit from a swine like him? Why hadn't she come to her senses sooner? The kind of guy who says that the only thing he doesn't like about Spain is that the showers aren't like the ones in France; aseptic stalls where the water comes pouring straight down, a kind of stupid rain, instead of the handheld sprayers found in French bathrooms, those hot water brushes that you can use to caress your whole body, or jerk off like crazy, or stick up your ass at full pressure. Had she ever heard a guy like Camilo say something like that, or Jaime, or even Alejandro, what with him semi-queer and everything? Couldn't she see clearly by now that Jacques was a disgusting pig and a degenerate? Didn't she hear what he was saying about her, the things he said about how she behaved in bed, not to his friends, like men do when they get together, but right under her very own nose, right in front of Gina herself, details that, just by their very nature were somewhat humiliating, and using such language that they could only be understood as an insult, pure and simple? Was she really that stupid?

Because the problem wasn't the fact that Jacques had behaved like a pig with her. The problem was Jacques himself, as a person: totally irresponsible. So how come nobody has dared put an end to Francoism with an assassination, just blow Franco's brains out point blank? he wondered. Someone with *cojones*, like they say in Spain. Or someone with cancer, some incurable disease, who doesn't care what might happen to them. It wasn't so difficult: he, Jacques, had seen him right up close in Madrid, during a bullfight, and anybody, from where they sat, could have done it. Anybody! Well then: why hadn't he done it himself, since he figured it was so easy? Did he imagine he was the first person to have that idea? Apart from the fact—and Lucía definitely thought Jaime was right about this—that such individual acts had nothing in common with mass actions. It's one thing to shoot a dictator and something very different to put an end to a dictatorship, not to mention start a revolution. Alejandro said that, at any rate, he saw no reason to squander enthusiasm—if they had to wait for the Spanish masses to throw themselves into the struggle, perhaps it was worth the trouble, if only for something to kill the time, to give Jacques his opportunity.

That son-of-a-bitch Alejandro had at least this virtue: knowing how to put a period on any messy conversation that dragged on too long, with a mere observation, some simple comment uttered without any special emphasis, without raising his voice, but one that almost seemed somehow expected by the others, as a sort of conclusive maxim, and, as such, celebrated by everyone, regardless of whether or not his opinion was the one foreseen or the one to be expected from a personality like his. A phenomenon whose roots probably had to be sought less in his moral authority than in a recognition of his intellectual capacity and expository brilliance, similar to how the audience reacts to a famous comedian, the people primed to laugh heartily before the show even begins.

He'd spent that night deconstructing Marina's memories and experiences. Neither Marina nor Jaime were there, and so, instead of trying to wheedle new details and clarifications out of her, Alejandro set himself to cast doubt on each and every one of the adventures Marina had explained. How was it possible, for example, that Marina had any memories from before the Russian Revolution? Didn't she claim to be about thirty-years old, thirty-something? And what was that story about her father having an estate in Samarkand, and, like some kind of Tamburlaine, rode his horse right up the stairs? And what about the Chinese servants? In Samarkand? And why not Swiss ones, like the Pope's? And that stuff about beheadings in the market square. And, especially, the long lapse that follows those early memories: the time necessary for a princess who lives in Moscow and summers in Samarkand to become Marina Durand, from Carcassonne. The excuse that her mother, with her husband the prince now dead, completely broke and with a little girl to raise in exile, had had to marry, although simply for survival's sake, a grape grower, vintner, or tavern keeper from the Midi-Pyrenees. A second papa who, lacking papers, raised her as his own daughter. The obscurity surrounding those years in Sète, surely working as a barmaid, selling *vin de sable*, sand wine, as the regional vintage is known. And castles made of sand by young Marina, doubtless inspired by the stories of the sailors and visitors who arrived and then departed once more. Later she really had gone traveling abroad, that much was true, although not so much, perhaps, as she pretended. In every case, she knew the names of hotels and elegant locales in the major cities of the world. And she knew about fashion, music, wines, gastronomic specialties, transatlantic voyages. And, besides having a great facility for languages, she was also generally well-educated. And, above all, her great sensitivity in perceiving ambience, in adapting to situations. Because it was more than likely that her life had proceeded exactly in the opposite direction from what she intended, just the reverse of the way she told it. The story of a young girl from the Midi-Pyrenees, a girl with exotic features born in Sète, in Carcassonne, or wherever. Daughter of grape-growers or vintners or tavern-keepers, who had lived or cohabitated with White Russians, whether or not from Samarkand, whether princes or not, as the sweetheart of one of them, or of a friend, or of one of their servants or, more likely, with several of them, with people of diverse social conditions, as a lover, companion, what have you. As an ensemble girl for a ballet company, for example, always favorable for friendly relations with Russians or the sons of White Russians. But, in the end, she was still just that: the daughter of a grape grower from the Midi-Pyrenees named Durand. And now she's with a communist like Jaime, just as before she was with a painter from l'Haute, as she says. And just as she was cheating on Sergio Vidal with Jaime for some time, she must now be cheating on Jaime with some other guy. In this way, her story with Jaime might well end up constituting a new and passionate episode of her biography: the love affair between a White Russian and a Spanish Bolshevik.

Meaning: Alejandro took for granted that Jaime and Marina had been having an affair for some time. But despite this being true, despite the fact that Sergio Vidal more than deserved it, it was irritating to hear it mentioned in that tone of voice. That's why Lucía said that she didn't think that Marina would have cheated on Sergio Vidal, neither with Jaime nor with anybody else, as long as they were together. And then Alejandro, instead of responding, started laughing with that laugh of his that ended up infecting everyone around him, unbridled, cascading, his eyes shining with exaltation, as if Lucía had meant to pull his leg or play a joke on him.

Walking home, Charlotte told her that Alejandro was, likely as not, quite right. She also laughed, but with her, inverted as she was, it was always difficult to know the cause, be it Marina, Alejandro, or Lucía herself. A laugh that started up regardless of if the situation was funny, and which could last, intermittently, for hours, capable, by being unprovoked, of annoying anyone. Even when she snapped photos of her, when Lucía, the model, posed for her, taking it seriously, trying to strike what seemed to her the most suitable poses, while Charlotte, the photographer, did not stop laughing between one photo and the next, as if that were the most amusing thing; something frankly uncomfortable. Perhaps it was something she got from her father, the mad Genevan banker. Charlotte had showed her a series of photos that she took of him just before she came to Paris: one of those Swiss aristocrats with a seagull's face. And, sometimes, really, you might say that she, too, had a few screws loose. Except, on other occasions, it seemed that she could see things before they happened, and that it was that very foresight that made her laugh.

For example, when the stuff with Camilo happened, around Christmastime, after most of her friends had departed for different destinations, each one back to their own country, to their homes, and Lucía, sick of celebrating such solemnities with her family, of the whole attendant atmosphere and all the implications of returning to Barcelona, decided to stay in Paris.

It started one night when l'Alouette was mostly empty and she and Camilo and Charlotte were the only ones from their group still in town. They'd agreed to make up for it, and to celebrate New Year's Eve together, the three of them making the rounds thereabouts until the next morning. At closing time, Camilo accompanied them home, putting his arms around their waists, their heads all together, as if charging ahead into the drizzle. He came up for a nightcap, one last Calvados, and they kept on chatting and laughing a while longer, their voices low to avoid complaints from the neighbors. Then Charlotte said she had to go meet someone and left them there alone, and Camilo started pacing around the room as he talked, and suddenly Lucía felt herself hugged from behind against the back of the chair while Camilo's face appeared above her shoulder and kissed her. Then they were naked, on the bed, and he made love to her as if enveloping her, as if penetrating her through her whole body.

It was an affectionate relationship. And never put to better use, said Camilo. He had a sense of humor that, sometimes, in bed, bordered on the audacious, but his very naturalness, healthy and direct, made what would have seemed rude coming from someone else sound delicate. Nuances that were very much Camilo, that manner wherein his most contradictory aspects and tendencies seemed reconciled; in which his firm character as a man of action did not clash with an intense, almost obsessive, sexuality; nor with the fortitude of his revolutionary conviction. A man capable of moving from tender words, when he made love, between one time and the next, to heated assertions—also somewhat obsessive—about the problems of the Cuban revolutionary process. A real revolution, with real weapons; not like the Spanish people's struggle which, if once heroic in times past, had ceased to be so.

Camilo was also different from most of her other friends in yet another way:

he wasn't a big mouth. If Lucía had gone to bed with anyone else, the whole crowd at l'Alouette would have known about it the next morning. And with the holidays now come and gone, everyone back in town, they all carried on as usual without finding out about her and Camilo. Except Charlotte, of course.

At l'Alouette, in public, in front of other people, Camilo behaved with Lucía the same as before, at most including her in some of the jokes he used to punctuate the ideological arguments he started with Jaime, according to the manner of the Caribbeans who, as he said, laugh so as not to cry. And then, it was as if Camilo turned back into a poor, uneducated colored boy, destined *ab initio* to be a shoeshine for whites. But seeing himself converted into the Camilo of now, into the victorious revolutionary, the agronomy student awarded a scholarship by his government to take an intensive course in Paris studying tropical plant diseases was a change of course that must have seemed to him like a dream. Although there were certainly some who claimed that was just a cover story, that Camilo was there on a secret mission, possibly to buy weapons. One argument more, if true, in favor of the Cuban Revolution's superiority over the Spanish one, of the superiority in Paris of the militants from the one country over the ones from the other, how for the Spaniards, "weapon" might as well be nothing more than a forgotten word in the dictionary.

Luis's letter arrived in mid-January, when she'd already decided not to answer the last one, the one that had come before Christmas. Now he proposed a short visit, two days or so, halfway between Barcelona and Paris, around the middle of February. And he must have suggested this surely to get the most out of a trip he'd have to make anyway, to establish a contact on this side of the border, receive documents, return to Spain carrying a suitcase with a false bottom, or something like that. Why not just ask her to come down to Perpignan!

Lucía answered saying she agreed. A short note, emphasizing that they must meet in Sète, at the Grand Hotel. She chose the hotel after consulting with Marina: the best hotel in Sète, in the fin de siècle style, very charming. What she didn't mention in her letter was that she planned to have Charlotte accompany her.

The trip turned out to be great fun. First, on an overnight express train, passing themselves off as English girls, joking with the other passengers, and with the conductor, who must have been Spanish and who told them things that, clearly, he didn't expect them to understand. At dawn they changed trains and reached the Grand Hotel in the early hours of the morning.

Luis wasn't getting in until later, so they took a walk around Sète, along the canals, warming up once in a while with a café au lait, whispering and laughing in low voices, something they kept doing throughout the two short days of their stay. Sète was a sort of Venetian slum with a certain air of an Atlantic port, giving it its own personality even for someone who'd never been to Venice. That's right: a complete lack of places to go out to; what's more, it made all the local guys seem gay! The Grand Hotel was one of those really outdated but pleasant hotels, the interior designed around a spacious central patio covered by a glass skylight, with plants and colonial-style three-piece sofas. They asked here and there for Marina Durand, but nobody seemed to know her.

Everything with Luis went sour from the start; nothing felt like before, not even the most mechanical aspects of lovemaking, perhaps because Luis's mind was on Irenita, his little Red Princess. Case in point: he seemed, curiously, neither surprised nor affected by Charlotte's presence or, at least, kept them guessing about what he thought. But, behind the bulwark of his habitual impassivity, Lucía suddenly saw him as something no longer distinct but also rather mediocre. And who knows, also, if not more bruised, more vulnerable than how he appeared to be. When she asked him about his love life, he ducked the question, said he didn't have much time for all that. Lucía said she didn't either but that she was having a really good time in Paris. And, switching the subject, she started talking to him about the superiority of the Cuban Revolution: Fidel and a handful of others started by attacking the presidential palace, something you couldn't say about the Spanish communists and El Pardo palace. But not even such an observation seemed to draw Luis out of his sterile impassivity.

The only truly jarring note came from Charlotte, as contradictory as always, when she remarked, in passing, that she really liked Luis, that he was alright. Lucía, naturally enough, reacted rather violently, all the more so because she didn't say so until they were on the train, heading back to Paris. If that was true, said Lucía, then she'd let her have him, as a gift; but didn't Charlotte think it was a little bit late to be asking? Only then Charlotte seemed to understand that Lucía was really angry and opted for playing the little girl, saying that she just wanted people to listen to her, that nobody was interested in her, that she always felt like the odd one out, that her father had sent her to Paris to get her to snap out of it, that everybody treated her the same way, etcetera, etcetera. Sometimes, honestly, she acted like a completely irresponsible child.

The other clash she had was with Alejandro, during one of the dances at Carnival, probably the one put on by the students from the Philosophy Department. He'd shown up in a white eye-mask and some cat whiskers painted on with eyeliner, looking like some sort of Jean Marais disguised as Chat Botté, and he was sweating more than usual. A teasing pain-in-the-ass like always, he strolled up to Lucía and asked her how it was going with Camilo. Lucía told him to go fuck himself, and although she couldn't remember if she'd managed to slap his face, she was sure that she'd at least tried, that faggot, that shitty fucking faggot.

Every university department organized its own dances and Lucía and Charlotte went to a bunch of them, the Medical School dance, the Philosophy Department dance, and also private parties where the people slipped away to make love in the corners. But the best one of them all was the dance sponsored by the school of Beaux Arts, more imaginative, more exuberant. Also, there, you could go down into a basement whose existence, at least to Lucía, was totally unknown. The bad thing was that usually, without realizing it, everyone drank too much—especially at the Beaux Arts dance—and the next day, totally hungover, she found it impossible to crawl out of bed until well into the afternoon.

Regarding her quarrel with gossipy Alejandro, the stupidest part was that Lucía started to get really fed up with Camilo. His self-assurance about everything bothered her, his displays of virility, his stubbornness and relentlessness about ideological discussions, always harping on whether something was or was not dialectical, if objective conditions change or not, and things like that; at heart, as Jaime said so well, he was more dogmatic than communist, without the communist's ready supply of scientific knowledge. And the truth is that he started repeating all his stories about the Cuban Revolution. Besides, in the long run, she couldn't really even say that he was a good lover, too direct, too quick to cut to the chase, snicker-snack, snicker-snack, snicker-snack. Sometimes, he even left her aching with pain the whole next day, and it was a problem for her to conceal it when she was walking, when she sat down. If she kept on sleeping with him it was almost because she didn't know how to stop, practically as an obligation or for courtesy's sake.

The excuse, luckily, was served up to her on a silver platter by Camilo himself one day when he became excessively heavy and sermonizing, and Lucía seized the opportunity to tell him to go to hell. She was sure that Camilo, with his famous analyses of objective conditions, was waiting for her to take it back, to seek reconciliation. Well, fine: just keep waiting, *compañero*!

Determined to clear up any misleading and uncomfortable situations, relationships that she need no longer tolerate, she also took a hard line with Jacques. For being such a loudmouth.

Her rapprochement with Jaime had come about thanks to the news of Luis's arrest in Barcelona; very serious, this time, from the looks of it; one of those cases in which, despite a lack of specific information, the number of arrests and, especially, the personality of those arrested, suggested that things had taken a turn for the worse. Jaime woke her up very early in the morning first with the news, but also with a plan of action, based on the idea that, aside from all the party sources, they had to mobilize the French media, both radio and press, by any means necessary, not only to help Luis and the other detainees, but also to educate the French public—with its comfortably settled opinions—about the repression in Spain. Together they gave several interviews to journalists and correspondents from various press agencies; Jaime talked first, then she said she was the girlfriend of one of the men arrested and that she shared his ideas. They were also interviewed by the Paris correspondents from foreign newspapers, especially English and Scandinavian ones, and then Lucía translated Jaime's words into English, giving their statements something like a more official tone, more like a communiqué.

The news appeared in various papers and weekly magazines, generally trivialized and, at the same time, fraught with alarm, as if Luis and the others were at risk of being shot by a firing squad at any moment. Only on the radio, being interviewed live for Spanish language broadcasts by the RTF, did they manage to give a proper account, neither inaccurate nor exaggerated. Jaime had told her not to be afraid, that the Spanish police didn't have the technology to allow them to identify her voice, and Lucía said that was the least of her worries. But what did make her nervous was the program's introduction, the terms used by the interviewer, Francoism, police repression, torture, words like that. And, even more, the idea that she was going to be heard by everyone in Spain, to think about the thousands and thousands of suffering listeners—their eardrums blasted by the interference from having their ears glued to the radio speaker—who, even as she cleared her throat, were already listening. But the moment she found herself in front of the microphone, she seemed to become a different person. And she talked and talked until the interviewer cut her off, saying thank you very much, so that Jaime could also have a chance to say something. At the end of the program, the interviewer congratulated her, and, in Jaime's opinion, the spontaneous and emotive language she had used, was more penetrating and turned out to be ten times more effective than however many expositions might be mounted about the current political situation in Spain.

What was unquestionable, as they received new information, was that Abelardo, slimy Abelardo, occupied an important place in the initial links of the chain, who knows if at its very point of origin. Apparently, he'd been arrested before Luis and almost all the rest of them, so that, with the evidence established that he'd snitched, it remained to clarify, at most, if he was also an agent provocateur, an infiltrator working for the police. And in this regard both Lucía and Jaime did feel responsible to a certain extent: they hadn't raised any objection to having a guy like him go down to Barcelona to join in the clandestine fight; they'd been foolish enough to feel a little relief, for subjective reasons, from his repugnance, when he departed Paris. And, besides, why Barcelona? Why Barcelona and not Seville, since he was, after all, from Seville?

An unforeseen consequence of the activities unfolding around Luis's arrest, during their campaign of going door to door to gather signatures on a petition demanding the release of Luis and other political prisoners, was Lucía's reconciliation with Sergio Vidal, who, up close and in person, turned out to be a charming man, full of spirit. With Lucía, at least, he was extraordinarily kind, and one night invited her out for dinner. Naturally they didn't even mention that evil whore Marina, who was cheating on poor Jaime with the first guy she ran into.

Jaime had flat out refused to stop by Sergio Vidal's apartment to ask for his signature. But after her visit, Lucía believed the time had come to reveal Marina's true personality, her tricks, her narcissism, her mythomania. And, although Jaime at first adamantly denied it, he finally had to accept the proof that Marina, for some time now, had been having an affair, at least with Jacques; on the other hand, given their respective erotic predilections, they were perfect for each other. At least this time—one must admit—Alejandro's internal compass had worked perfectly.

With Javier's return to Paris, the whole scene livened up again. The very first night, Javier invited her to come up to his suite for a drink, but Lucía refused his invitation until several days later. And from that point on, everything went beautifully, in the bright, promising ambience of quality and seclusion always found in a suite at a hotel like the George V; what people call a real delight. For the remainder of Javier's stay in Paris, they continued going out on their own, without Charlotte, who, needless to say, not only refrained completely from asking for unnecessary explanations but even from saying anything at all.

The enthusiasm Javier poured into his relationship with Lucía grew more intense by the day, his devotion more absorbing. And Lucía, for her part, discovered a new pleasure: the excitation of arousing him, of making him twist and turn and squirm in bed as if she were torturing him. A few days before he went back to Spain, Javier asked her marry him. Lucía said no, but as he insisted on it, she told him that she'd think it over.

The only glitch, happily without consequences, occurred on the last night, while they were eating dinner, and Lucía saw Sergio Vidal walk into the restaurant, accompanied by his group of friends. When he came over to say hello she returned his greeting affectionately, but she was most startled when, after Sergio kissed her hand, she watched him and Javier embrace like old friends. On saying goodbye, Sergio Vidal winked at her while bending to kiss her hand once more.

As always, Charlotte was the first to stir the pot; after Javier had departed, fortunately. Why don't you let me have him? she teased; he's young, rich, attractive. I've got to warn you, said Lucía, he doesn't know how to make love. Charlotte smiled, her upper eyelids stretching in amused folds, a smile Lucía knew well and whose import made her uneasy. So what? said Charlotte. A difficult reply to interpret when dealing with a woman like her, who was certain there's nothing easier than pleasing a man, all you had to do was scream oh, oh, oh, and tremble a little while he was coming. But what if it now turned out that she really did like men?

Another disappointment was the one she had with Camilo and Gina. The fact that Camilo insisted on going out with Gina while everyone at l'Alouette—everyone except Camilo—knew that Gina was sleeping with Sergio Vidal was, to say the least, pitiful. But, in the end, so much the worse for Camilo, who looked ridiculous, and so much the better for Gina, who seemed to be starting to outgrow her daddy's-girl attitude of running off with the first so-called revolutionary who called her a little bourgeois piece of shit; guys like Jacques and, more recently, Camilo, really annoying guys who only know how to spend their time arguing about whether someone or other had a petit-bourgeois mentality or not, if someone is metaphysical instead of dialectical, if objective conditions can or cannot be changed, things like that. In the end, the one who emerged triumphant was Gina, a.k.a. La Loló, as that shithead Alejandro so aptly dubbed her, given that Sergio Vidal surpassed Camilo in every way; wiser and, most of all, much less of a brute. And if Lucía could do something more to facilitate his relationship with Gina, of course she would.

So, why not marry Javier after all? She wasn't in love, that much was certain. But that, without a doubt, was due to her lack of affective passion, to her complete inability—apart from momentary bouts of bad temper and euphoria—to either hate or love anybody intensely, and, with even greater justification, to display emotions she really didn't feel, without having the sensation of somehow being on stage, of playing some kind of role. The truth was, she didn't really believe that she might ever fall in love with anybody. Didn't see herself, didn't even imagine herself truly in love. Javier, however, adored her in the most literal sense of the word: the way one adores a goddess; and he had identified qualities and values in her which most men seemed unable to appreciate: a rather strong predisposition to commitment, more than sufficient to compensate for the lack of enthusiasm Lucía brought to the union, which would quite successfully stabilize the weight of the relationship between them both.

Besides, it was clear that Lucía could no longer stand Paris. Given her minimal dedication to studies and how rarely she even went to class, her whole academic year was, needless to say, already shot to hell. But more than a cause, this was a consequence. What she really couldn't stand any longer was Beaux Arts, the school itself, the pervasive atmosphere of creative mediocrity and moral shabbiness. No less, too, her dealings with friends and classmates, both at school and in l'Alouette, the guys and girls who formed part of what they'd all come to call *the group*: phony bohemians and phony revolutionaries, daddy's boys and girls who barely concealed their fears, their pettiness, their frustrations under their mask of radical pretensions. Neither them nor, especially, their lifestyle, their behavior, their follies and affairs, their gossip, their slander, their betrayals. No: the problem was not that she had no future in Paris. The problem was that she had no present either.

But if the main reason she had decided to study Beaux Arts in Paris was just to get away from Barcelona, to escape from the oppressive world of family life she found herself enveloped in there, to liberate herself from the classic economic and moral conditioning that reigns in every declining bourgeois family, for her to now run back to Barcelona just to reclaim the narrow margin of autonomy offered her by that world—one dominated by the presence of a neurotic, authoritarian mother, a sister consumed by envy, and a terrifying, mythomaniac brother—would demonstrate a complete lack of common sense. So, from the perspective of a young woman struggling to shake off the bonds imposed by the social environment of her youth, marrying Javier represented a solution. A relaxed life, comfortable and free, compared to which the prejudiced Barcelona environment she'd fled from, and the squalid world she'd found herself immersed in since coming to Paris would seem, in short, nothing but a nightmare. Lucía had a right to this kind of life. And not from a zeal for comfort so much as for the simple need for mental hygiene.

She gave Javier her affirmative answer, her yes, over the phone. He asked her to come back to Spain right away, and then wrote to her immediately with the same fervor, but she told him that with Easter coming, she preferred to finish out the trimester, just like any good schoolgirl should, even it were only for principle's sake. From then on Javier called her every day, each time more impatient.

Lucía arrived in Barcelona on the eve of Holy Week, aboard an airplane full of tourists. Javier was waiting for her at the airport. They got married around the middle of June, in the chapel of Javier's family's ancestral home, in Camprodon.

V

However free one might be, there are two things that must be kept very clear: what you can and what you cannot do, said Lucía. Something that Gina was capable of understanding perfectly, despite those moral entanglements that developed thanks to her unhappy propensity for always falling into the arms of guys who were half-criminal, half-revolutionary, and prepared to thoroughly exploit her guilty conscience about being a good little rich girl from Milan. It was completely pointless, however, to try to explain the same thing to Charlotte, for whom such considerations were necessarily—neither less acceptable nor more valid—on the same level as a plan to ride motorcycles all the way to Japan or a case of religious vocation.

As a matter of fact, Lucía's refusal to date any guy who already had a girlfriend, to steal anybody's man, married or unmarried, was the least of it. With people like Camilo, yes: equally free, the both of them, on equal terms; Lucía, after all, wasn't exactly a prude. But breaking up a couple's unity, with the inevitable consequence of someone suffering, she left that to people like Marina or Irenita, the Red Princess.

Or stuff like orgies, something that didn't appeal to her in the least; *les partouze*, sex parties, group sex, gang bangs, *les ménage à trois*, and all that. Or little gay flings and other stuff. Not from prejudice or because she had anything against such behavior, nor against lesbian relationships, nor against anyone doing whatever they felt like. It simply didn't appeal to her.

If someone wanted to call that having principles, fine. And she didn't see what could be bad about that. In the end, everybody had their principles, whether or not they identified them by that name. Even Charlotte, with her strict sense of friendship, no matter how much she sometimes seemed to have a few screws loose, Charlotte was unwavering. For her, friends came before everything. And although Lucía frequently got annoyed with her, she fully trusted Charlotte, her sense of friendship, the fact that she could count on her for anything.

That's one aspect, at least, in which they both seemed rather similar. It was one thing, for example, for Lucía to consider herself practically unattached to Luis, because his love affairs had strained their relationship to the breaking point, and something else, something very different, for her to feel completely detached from him, or that no room remained for a broad, deep friendship, perhaps something even richer than when they were united by an eminently erotic relationship. The friendship continued. To go on being confidants, helping each other, helping him as far as she knew that she was going to be helped.

To begin with, Lucía had always been completely faithful to Luis. The last thing anyone could say about her was that she had cheated on Luis with one of their friends. She and Camilo, for example, had met after Luis departed Paris. Luis and Camilo never met each other. Her affair with Camilo was a clean story, free of deceptions or betrayals, without victims, without any kind of premeditation, the result, little less than fortuitous, of a diverse series of imponderable events: both Lucía and Camilo had stayed in Paris for Christmas; they had drunk glasses of Calvados with Charlotte at l'Alouette until closing time; he had then walked them home to their room for one last Calvados; Charlotte left the two of them alone together, etcetera. Not to mention, of course, the mutual attraction they experienced, an unmistakable attraction that Lucía sensed practically from the moment they first met. An attraction that Camilo ended up expressing that night in the most explicit way—the three of them still at l'Alouette—while Lucía, in all innocence, gulped down a glass of Calvados, running her tongue all around the rim of the glass, and then he said to her, easy, Lucita, if you keep drinking like that you're gonna start thinking that the table is floating all by itself.

In fact, what impressed Lucía the most about her fling with Camilo was that it had started the same as a dream she'd had years earlier, and which, for some unknown reason, had remained firmly fixed in her memory: she was sitting in a chair and, suddenly, someone embraced her from behind and kissed her over her shoulder. Neither Luis nor Camilo: someone whose face she couldn't remember but who did, they did, exactly what she and Camilo did the first night, when Charlotte left her tied to the stake.

A love affair, however, is a delicate matter, par excellence, and, as such, especially subject to the influence of mishaps, mistakes, and misunderstandings, and the degree of affinity established at the start is especially vulnerable to the consequences of such things. Thus, for example, it was quite clear that Lucía didn't harbor any kind of prejudices, and she believed she'd shown that quite well. At the same time, it wasn't completely normal that Camilo, half the time or nearly so, preferred to fuck her in the ass. Since the first day, sliding the tip of his cock from front to back and from back to front, slowly moistening the way, opening a passage. Later he explained that in Cuba it was very common, and Lucia said that she'd never done that, but it seemed alright to her. And, in fact, she had nothing against such experiments. As long as neither Camilo nor anybody else saw it as a normal thing. For a woman, at least for Lucía, the sensation was very different from what she experienced doing it the other way; completely different.

Maybe it was true in Cuba they did that from the time they were young so that girls wouldn't lose their virginity. But neither of them was in Cuba and they weren't quite so young anymore. And Camilo's obsession with her asshole went too far. A real mania.

She also didn't like that he called her Lucita, the way he pronounced it, with an S: *Lusita*. Besides, the first time she thought he'd said *Luisita*, and figured he was making fun of Luis. And what she couldn't stand, especially, was his sermonizing to her. What right did Camilo have to talk to her as if he were, not only her husband but her father? What a devoted, adoring father!

For everything fun and amusing about their trip to Sète, both the train ride there as well as the return trip—especially the return—their time together was tinged with sadness from the moment Luis arrived. Even before boarding the train in Paris, the moment she decided to bring Charlotte along to Luis's proposed meeting, Lucía felt elated. The first step was to leap out of bed and transform the absurd monogram *L + L = Loving*, that she'd painted on the wall during Luis's time in Paris, into *L + L = Loló*. She would've also liked to give Luis back that damned book of his, but at the last minute she forgot to pack it.

On the train to Sète, she and Charlotte drank a few Calvados in the lounge car and joked with the other passengers, with the waiters and conductors, pretending to be English girls. Speaking English with each other was a habit which, for some undetermined reason, they'd spontaneously established when they first met in l'Alouette. Of course they both spoke it as naturally and fluently as their own native tongues. But perhaps there was a certain amount of complicity in play as well: the pleasure of exchanging rapid little comments without the rest of those present even knowing what they were talking about.

In all honesty, not everything in Sète was Luis's fault. Lucía's thoughts and her reflexive reminiscences also contributed to the disaster: how different everything was, how different everything might have been if the Red Princess hadn't entered the picture. That's why, when Luis asked her, as if in passing, how things were going in Paris, she said very well. The only problem, she told him, was that no guys appealed to her. Though no longer true, it had previously been so, at the start of their relationship: none appealed to her, and none could appeal to her, given that a woman in love is a woman inevitably faithful to her man, a woman for whom no other man even seems to exist. If she, practically Javier's girlfriend, went to bed with him, with Luis, when they first met, it was precisely because her man was Luis and not Javier, because the one whom she loved wasn't Javier but Luis. Her answer to Luis's question implied all of that; she'd said it without any special emphasis, as if uninterested in the subject. Luis shook his head: his face looked sad. Clearly the very state of mind she'd intended to provoke.

But as she strolled along the canals with Luis, contemplating the seagulls' movements, the memory of their first days together now saddened her; yes, her. At that time, Luis was going out with another girl, whom he ended up dumping. Lucía never managed to coax more details from him, not even her name. Luis said that he didn't like sharing such things, and perhaps it was true; despite the way most men talk when they get together, he wasn't one of those guys who brag about their conquests and affairs, nor was he known for talking about his erotic fantasies or getting personal with his sexual theorizing. The uncertainty, nevertheless, remained unbearable: not knowing, not being sure if Luis had really left the other girl or if, on the contrary, continued seeing her along with Lucía, in tandem; if it wasn't going to turn out that the other girl, the unnamed one, was none other than the Red Princess; if she, Lucía, was not playing the role that theoretically corresponded to the other woman, the episodic lover; if Luis's true love was not, after all, the Red Princess, the whore.

The need to dispel such doubts, along with the impossibility of penetrating something as recondite as a person's feelings, were the two conflicting reasons that weighed heaviest in Lucía's decision to study Beaux Arts in Paris. She thought that getting away from Barcelona would help clarify the situation, beginning with her own feelings on the matter. That desire, intensified by the long distance, would oblige Luis to define his own position, to either choose her unreservedly or let the situation take its own course. In the hope that Luis would understand it was his turn to choose; that with a woman who made such decisions without hesitation, their temporary separation might well become definite. That he'd end up asking her to come back to him, to Barcelona, to live together, which is how people who love each other are meant to live, who want to share their lives. Together, not separate with each of them in their own house, which was how they'd been seeing each other up to that point, loving each other almost in secret, inventing excuses to come home late, to spend the night somewhere else, to get away for a weekend. Sordid behavior, and only the yearning typical of all hindsight could now make her feel that those early days with Luis in Barcelona were perhaps, nonetheless, the happiest times of her life.

Now, she even looked back on her months in Paris with nostalgia. In October, while she was waiting for Luis, when his imminent arrival seemed to revitalize her and breathe new life into all her actions, as if she could foresee that the week of lovemaking awaiting them was indeed going to represent the zenith of their relationship. Everything, in her memory, seemed to smack of a fleeting youthful vitality, similar, thanks to the same unrepeatable quality of all experience, to the enchanted disposition with which the adolescent goes about discovering the world of daily life; thus, hunting for a room to rent, attending her first art class, Jacques and Gina and other students introducing her to their crowd at l'Alouette.

Jaime introduced her personally to Alejandro; he was a close friend and classmate of Luis's as well as a fellow militant, and he had just come up from Barcelona, having escaped a police roundup by the skin of his teeth. Although the party had found him an apartment and provided him with enough to live on, she could see he didn't have a franc to spare, so Lucía sometimes invited him to go out for a good meal, and to cafés and the cinema, until he started receiving money from his family. A family, from the looks of it, flush with millions, but shrewd to the point of considering it a good investment that one of its children turn out to be communist; with an eye toward the future, in case of whatever might happen.

She also invited Charlotte, who wouldn't admit to being hard up for money either, to share her room, while her absent-minded father, the Genevan banker, didn't seem to realize he even had a daughter, until one day, out of the blue he sent her whole lot of money. Charlotte nearly went mad with the windfall and immediately squandered it all on the craziest extravagances. Lucía was all too familiar with such behavior because she did more or less the same thing. Except that Lucía's generosity was complicated by the mentality some people have who, anxious to join a certain group, offer whatever they have in exchange for being admitted and accepted as a member with full rights, wanting to be counted among them, to share their problems, as friends, the ups-and-downs of their daily life. An experience that could only lead to the disappointing proof that the group's prevailing spirit of one-for-all and all-for-one was especially popular among those who had nothing to share or, as with Jacques, pretended not to.

Curiously, just as back in Barcelona, everybody thought Lucía wealthier than she really was. A prestige that, in Barcelona, was based more on her family's history than on the present reality; even if they could permit her the luxury of studying in Paris, their real economic situation was more humble than it appeared. The fact that people still fooled themselves about that was doubtless the result of how carefully her family worked to conserve that prestige, thanks, precisely, to permitting itself the luxury of sending a daughter to study Beaux Arts in Paris, and other similar ostentations. And if the same thing happened in Paris, where her family name meant nothing to anyone, it could only be attributed to Lucía's manner and looks. And those things seemed to say so much that when she tried to hint that she was beginning to run low on money, the majority of her friends must have supposed that, as in the case of Jacques, it was purely the pose of a spoiled little rich girl, who wanted to play at being poor. The only difference was that everybody thought with Jacques it was a normal thing, perhaps because he declared his father a pig, while in Lucía's case they thought it was a joke that a young woman who was well-heeled financially, or close to it, was, in sexual matters, pretending to safeguard her virginity.

At heart, it was a question of mentality. The problem of getting through to a crowd like the one at l'Alouette, where anyone who wasn't a revolutionary theorist was instead a theorist of the bohemian lifestyle, making them understand that just because someone had decided to blow some money, treating this and that person, offering everyone whatever they wanted, didn't mean they usually acted that way, because she was definitely not the little rich girl they all imagined her to be, and that this wasn't habitual behavior on her part but rather the confluent result of a thoughtless tendency toward splendidness colliding with a complete lack of common sense. The amount she could allow herself to spend when first hitting town was simply not permissible weeks later; what she overspent then was money she didn't have now. Either way it turned out the same.

There was another aspect to Lucía's character, and its impact on her behavior also made her complete identification with the group rather difficult: her *aboulia*, or rather, her inconstancy, that incapacity to stick with what's going on even when that only consisted, for most of the people in their group, of nothing more than spending hours and hours sitting around a table at l'Alouette. Such a capacity for sitting still was one of the things that most surprised Lucía from the beginning, given that her *aboulia* manifested itself not in any idleness or sloth but, quite the contrary, in her lack of following through with the multiple activities she started, like how quickly she piled up and ignored the art supplies she'd been buying to practice with, and how she simply forgot the reason why she bought most of them in the first place. A kind of active *aboulia* which impelled her to start out with disciplined attendance at all her classes at Beaux Arts, only to lose motivation and gradually abandon them. Spending large sums of money on drawing and modeling supplies, different types of paper, colors, clay, and plaster, things she barely got around to using. Buying really amusing underwear, and beauty products, and knick-knacks like they sell on the street. Or purchasing a pass to a heated public swimming pool to keep fit, but, quickly tiring of it, ceasing her visits after the third or fourth time, swarming with faggots as it was, and the stench of chlorine, the infections and warts and things like that which, it seems, you end up catching in such places. Things, in short, that she set out to do with all her enthusiasm and whose result, if it were not what she imagined, didn't have too much importance either. Except, in the end, for her pocketbook.

Besides, during those days, she thought of nothing but Luis's imminent arrival. And now, that she had him by her side, already slumbering, in the Grand Hotel in Sète, such memories weren't exactly the right thing to help her get to sleep.

Before going their separate ways, Luis insisted on visiting the cemetery, at the edge of Sète, overlooking the sea: a most significant finale considering the quality of their visit. He mentioned some verses by Valéry, and Lucía said she knew them by heart, and he shouldn't even think, on top of everything else, of reciting them. The last thing they needed.

On the return trip, when they changed trains to board the one heading back to Paris, they found the lounge car closed. Both Charlotte and Lucía had already imbibed their fair share and were a bit drunk as they climbed aboard and went searching stubbornly, from car to car, trying to find some vendor selling drinks. Finally, they asked a conductor they ran into, and the conductor told them there was no such vendor at these hours. Then they asked him, the whole time pretending to be English, if the water in the restrooms really wasn't potable. The conductor told them that it probably wouldn't hurt them but that, being the conductor, he couldn't suggest that they drink it.

They'd run into him right between two cars, and the conductor stepped back onto the platform he'd just vacated, in order to let them go by. Lucía opened a few buttons on her blouse and asked him if he'd ever made love with a passenger, while the train was going full speed. The conductor, who had a Spanish accent, brusquely changed his tone and said that he'd done it all. Well, I've never done it, said Lucía. Wanna show me how it's done?

The conductor pushed her into the bathroom, almost violently, at the same time telling Charlotte to stand right outside the door, as if she were waiting to get in. Lucía found herself in the conductor's arms, he pulled her bra down, lifted up her skirt, pulled down her panties, kissing her, caressing her. He made love to her seated on the toilet seat cover, Lucia straddling him, or rather, suspended on his thighs, riding freehand. He was halfway between brutal and tender, calling her, in Spanish, *cielo, vida, nena*—sweetheart, and darling, and honey—asking her if she liked it, whispering sweet improprieties and obscenities in her ears, clumsily, those filthy things men go on babbling until they've finished.

Then he set them up in a second-class compartment that was empty and brought them some beers. He said he'd be back shortly to do it with the blonde, with Charlotte. Charlotte told Lucía she didn't plan on doing anything with that ogre, that he scared her, so they changed cars.

Lucía went to wash up, to rinse out her mouth and gargle. Later, reclining in her bunk, while she was drinking the beer, she started to laugh wildly. I'm a whore, I'm a whore, I'm a whore, she repeated over and over again, as if stimulated not so much by the discovery of a new facet of her own personality, as much as by the simple enunciation of such a discovery, by its verbal formulation.

Just then, as they were sipping their beer, reclining in the upper bunks of the other compartment, Charlotte had to ruin it all by saying that she liked Luis, why didn't Lucía let her have him if she didn't love him. Lucía, after giving her the answer she deserved, told her that, apart from everything else, as far as sex, she'd had a lot more fun with the conductor than with Luis. Besides, you can hook up with whomever you like, I'll let you have them all for free, she said; if any of the available guys we know attract me, it's Alejandro, yes, Alejandro; the least interesting guy for a girl like Charlotte: a misogynist, a guy who hated women, a homosexual who, although perhaps never having acted on it, although not even having realized he was, was not for that reason any less of one. But therein, precisely, lay the charm, the perverse attraction: seducing a faggot. Things that women as simple as Charlotte—who, without the least discernment, go off with the first guy who plants himself in front of them—would never be capable of comprehending. Things that were not for most people.

This argument with Charlotte—Lucía getting more worked up the more she talked—really pushed her to the limit; all too often, Charlotte's irresponsibility even pushed her past that limit. Sometimes it was almost enough to make her think she really had a few screws loose. Truth be told, if there was something Lucía couldn't stand, it was exactly this type of wild, silly, irresponsible behavior. And so, whether it was the result of this argument with Charlotte or, rather, the result of a rapid-fire carnal coupling with a conductor in the train bathroom that kept her wide awake all the way back to Paris, the fact is that, right after getting home, the first thing Lucía did was take a long, hot bubble bath, with seaweed and other natural essences.

It would be hard to say exactly how many parties and costume balls they ended up going to; *saraos*, as Alejandro called them. Difficult, especially, because in a single night they went from one place to another, from one party to the next, and some faces got confused with others. Like the places, like the things that had happened in each place.

The Beaux Arts ball ended in a kind of mass orgy, with tons of people making love in the corners. And the thing is, from the beginning, the joy of it all lay not in the ball itself so much as it did in those basements where everybody was groping and fingering and feeling each other up, guys searching like mad for some girl to hook up with, someone to fuck. Even Alejandro became annoying, turning out to be really tiresome.

Lucía got into an argument with Jacques, who was a real swine. Jacques was joking and laughing, and he shouted at her that she was just a petit-bourgeois girl full of prejudices and moral and social boundaries that she refused to, and could never, trespass. He told her about his latest revolutionary discovery: jerking off completely naked in front of one of those mirror-fronted wardrobes that reflect the whole body, standing on a parquet floor, legs spread wide open and the handle of a knife inserted in his asshole; the knife's blade had to be nicely pointed, as sharp as possible. The orgasm and subsequent contractions forced the knife to come loose, and it fell point downward and stuck straight into the wood, its vibrations resonating with those of his freshly-jacked cock and quivering body, nearly toppling over. Lucía told him he was a real swine.

Suddenly, she felt really drunk, and Jacques helped her stumble back to her room, and, almost before she knew what was happening, she found herself, both of them, naked together, in bed. Predictably, it was a complete disaster. Lucía moved recklessly, without any real inclination. And though Jacques at first strained to get even a minimal hard-on, he suddenly blew his load faster than a bunny rabbit; what's more, he didn't even bother trying to apologize, like that guy in the basement of Beaux Arts, who didn't stop saying how uncomfortable the place was, how all the people milling around inhibited him, and other such excuses, to somehow justify that, after pursuing her so much, his response was about as good as a eunuch's. Jacques's, no doubt, was a knife handle stuck up his ass.

The next day, at l'Alouette, everybody already knew about the night before, and surely at school, too, more or less the same. Jacques had taken it upon himself to spread the news efficiently, to make sure everybody was up to date on the situation. But: explaining it like a problem, like some moral preoccupation. Saying that he was very sorry, for Luis, about what had happened; that Luis was a comrade whom he was very fond of, a militant, and what he, Jacques, had done was quite wrong, practically taking advantage of his absence. What happened is that he'd had too much to drink, and when a person drinks too much, they do things they'd never do sober. He was talking like one of those people who's looking for some advice or, at least, an outlet for their guilty conscience. Framing it like some kind of ethical problem, like a personal dilemma in which Lucía didn't matter at all, reducing her to some kind of insignificant—meaning, despicable—nexus between the two real protagonists in the drama: Luis and Jacques. Finally, naturally, he asked everyone not to talk about it with anybody.

Lucía found out about it even before anybody came to tell her; it was enough to see the looks on people's faces when they greeted her, to hear the sarcasm dripping off their words, somewhere between surprise and mockery. But she was in no mood for rumors and gossip, to see herself converted into some passive news item, and she decided the best defense strategy was a counterattack. She told people repeatedly about how she'd gotten fall-down drunk the night before, and how, all of a sudden, she'd found herself in bed with that swine Jacques, trying to rape her, trying to go too far, especially for a guy who couldn't even get it up, not to mention that she'd already rejected him, a real loser, known for his skill at getting his occasional victim to pass out completely before getting started. A hopeless mess of a guy who needed to learn, first and foremost, how to really be one. No, Lucía was not exactly one of those girls who goes from guy to guy, who lets herself get turned into a soccer ball and kicked around from one guy to another.

The most shocking thing about the episode was that Camilo, as a result of all this gossip, as well as on the pretext of a nonexistent personal relationship with Luis, also dared to try to censure her, to tell her that she shouldn't give anybody reason to talk about her that way. That her conduct was incorrect, inappropriate for the female comrade of a man who, under the roughest conditions, was fighting for socialism, for the revolutionary transformation of society. Him! Camilo, the revolutionary comrade who had been the first one to fuck her, the Cuban buck nigger, the sodomite!

Lucía couldn't stand another second of such hypocritical sermonizing, and she informed him that she hadn't only screwed Jacques but also Alejandro and even a railway conductor on the train. As well as Camilo himself, of course.

The thing with Alejandro was completely different. Not a simple fortuitous incident, but a long process that reached its culmination on the night when he showed up disguised as Puss in Boots—*le Chat Botté*. Because, at least for Lucía, the thing had started much earlier. From the beginning, so to speak, because—thanks to Alejandro's mocking attitude, to his ironies and sarcasm—relations between them had been maintained in something like a state of permanent irritation.

But it was that night when everything exploded. Alejandro had started by parodying the profound utterances which, according to him, Sergio Vidal claimed as his own, when they were nothing more than the residual product of the nonsense that some French essayists with old women's faces write about eroticism. *Il faut toujours violer le fait naturel* and things like that, which Alejandro repeated with tiresome insistence. And once he got started, it was impossible to shut him up. Besides, if he was generally a boring pain in the neck, she found having to listen to his sententious blather about *le fait naturel*, or little sayings like *l'essence de l'amour n'est que la souffrance*, and other such inanities to be particularly annoying that night. It was almost as if, for some undetermined motive, the contents of such thoughts were directed exclusively at Lucía, as if Alejandro was trying the whole time to get under Lucía's skin.

Camilo had insisted on dancing with her and, in order to avoid a scene, she hadn't refused, but after a while, when she was sick to death of it, she ditched him, giving the excuse that she had to go to the ladies' room. And then, Alejandro, maybe because he really did just casually bump into her, maybe because he'd been shadowing her, seized the opportunity to ask her if a revolutionary's faithful comrade should be more faithful to her comrade or to the revolution. And, in the case of two revolutions, which one demanded greater faith? The Spanish one, for example, or the Cuban? More than feeling irritated by his question, Lucía, like a wood pigeon intercepted by a golden eagle, mostly felt terrified: there was no way Alejandro could have known, neither from her nor from Camilo nor from Charlotte, the only person, apart from the two of them, who knew what was up, but who, despite being crazy as a loon, wasn't capable of spilling the beans to anyone—not even under torture. No: this was the fruit of that goddamned faggoty intuition possessed by that faggot Alejandro, the kind of radar that only a faggot can have. She tried to slap his face and he tackled her; or she fell down and bit him on the hand. A whole bunch of people jumped in and separated them.

She went outside to clear her head, to get some fresh air, and Gina and someone else went with her. They chatted a while seated on the staircase, but Lucía didn't listen to what the others were saying; she was angry with herself, felt ridiculous, overwhelmed by an intense feeling of embarrassment. Going back inside, Charlotte approached her, dragging Alejandro in tow, for the two of them to make up. She tried to get them to share a toast, and Lucía was on the verge of smashing her glass into Alejandro's face, but as she noticed his expression, altered not by fury, as she first thought, but rather distorted by anguish, she opted to do what they asked of her, and even apologized for biting him. Alejandro said that he'd been asking for it, that cruelty, properly understood, begins with oneself. And they all laughed and clinked their glasses together, all of them ending up interlinked, dancing in a long serpentine conga line. Inevitably, the obsessive Camilo joined the line right behind her, rudely grinding his hard-on against her ass until Lucía was able to shake him off with the excuse that Alejandro was her partner for the night

Later, in bed, Alejandro demonstrated that he wasn't—not in the least—the faggot he tried to appear as. However, he was, admittedly, a bit clumsy, like the fledgling cook who follows a printed recipe to the letter, or the novice gymnast who concentrates on performing a certain exercise in a specific amount of time. Meaning: like that man who, guided less by instinct, tries to perform according to his personal notion of what it means to give a woman pleasure, consequently failing to give her much satisfaction, and not really enjoying himself at all. More theory than experience: user's manual as opposed to craftsmanship. As he was leaving, Lucía figured, and rightly so, he was referring to that clumsy lack of skill when he said: tomorrow we won't even dare look each other in the eyes.

Only the next day, after noticing that Alejandro was avoiding her or trying to, did Lucía understand that his attitude harbored ethical sorts of reasons that she would never have suspected in a personality like his. Although he didn't say anything, he seemed really and truly affected, somewhere between ashamed and depressed. Lucía asked Charlotte for help, and between the two of them, fortified by Calvados, they finally managed to get his spirits back up. For Charlotte and her it meant getting royally plastered once again, but Alejandro was amusing, charming and witty as never before.

In any case, as far as Alejandro's personality was concerned, it was clear that, while his faggoty facade concealed a regular man, at least sexually speaking, so too, in an equal way, his cynical and biting exterior masked all the potential richness of a person victimized by solitude and helplessness, tormented by the conflicts that his elevated criteria of moral responsibility forced him to confront.

Logically enough, Alejandro's guilty conscience was only further tormented by Luis's arrest. From a certain perspective, the least one could say about his reaction was that it was, literally, the reaction of a hysterical person.

He had, it seemed, received the news quite calmly. And what's more: the idea of seizing upon the occasion to mount an anti-Franco propaganda campaign, apart from however much the party did or did not do, was essentially his own. He recruited Jaime on his own, and together they started planning, right down to the last detail, the various aspects and diverse phases of the campaign, Jaime seemingly surprised, as if overwhelmed, not so much by the avalanche of initiatives proffered by Alejandro, but rather by how he articulated them in a propagandistic array of perfectly calibrated and graduated effects; a denunciation of Francoism, solidarity with the Spanish people's struggle and all that. Whatever the reasons, however—his idiosyncrasies would foil any attempt to guess—Alejandro rejected any direct involvement with the campaign, refusing to personally participate, either as witness, victim, exile, or natural spokesperson on behalf of the millions and millions of Spaniards unable to do the same, so it was Lucía and Jaime who had to deal with the situation. Of course, said Jaime, it's enough to make you think Alejandro picked the wrong career: if he'd listened to his father instead of getting mixed up in politics and such fiascos, for some reason exactly what all parents obsess over, by now he'd be running the finest ad agency in Barcelona.

As always, however, the principal problem with Alejandro was Alejandro himself, his personality, his unpredictable reactions. For instance, that night at l'Alouette, when Lucía, with the best of intentions, remarked to him just how well everything was going, gathering signatures, articles and press releases, the statements she and Jaime were making, the radio interview they'd given, all expressed in the informative tone owed to one who, apart from being a friend, was the true architect of their propaganda campaign now in progress. And, suddenly, cutting her off brusquely, without offering any kind of excuse, Alejandro told her to go to hell. And then he demanded, why are you telling me? That's all you and Jaime. It's none of my business. Lucía preferred to take it as coldly as possible, without the least bit of melodrama, and she told him that if he was feeling guilty about screwing her—the steady girlfriend of his best pal Luis, currently in jail, swept up accidentally by some undercover sting, then he could rest his conscience: such affairs didn't matter in the least either for either her or Luis, being, as they were, properly civilized people. Her response, ultimately, had been understated—perhaps not lacking in acidity, it's true, but rational in content, and spoken in the most correct possible tone. A response which, to anyone's ears, apart from being brilliant, was neither more nor less than what Alejandro deserved. A response that, by no means, justified Alejandro starting to shout like crazy, what do you mean? You think what's going on is that I'm obsessed with Luis? Fine then, alright: I'm totally attracted to Luis. Are you happy now?

Then, slamming his fist on the table, he made the glasses jump, his furious eyes shining as with tears, maybe from emotion, maybe simply the result of the alcohol in his blood. And he kept on shouting really crazy things: she shouldn't be such an imbecile, she shouldn't talk about things her pea-brain couldn't comprehend, that she should stop thinking with her cunt, and other such vulgarities. Deliberately insulting, frankly. He got up and walked out, although, luckily, not quite fast enough for everyone present to miss the fact that if he wasn't quite drunk, he wasn't far from it. And Jaime was the first to defend Lucía, to recognize that Alejandro, actively a faggot or not, certainly was so from a psychological angle: a sort of hysterical bachelorette.

They were also in full agreement about that cretin Abelardo, that jinx from Seville: the perfect accuracy—undeniable for anyone who knew him—of the information filtering in about his role in the raid, the decisive role he'd played as the source or the initial link in the chain of arrests. Curiously, on learning that his name was linked to the raid, Lucía and Jaime both had the same premonition, although they didn't dare admit it to each other until the reports they received—though still not clarifying the events quite enough—brought it to light. In a certain way, they felt guilty for having kept quiet, for not having had the balls to clearly express the opinion that that person, from Seville, or Valencia, or wherever he was from, had shared with them. A secondary responsibility which, on the other hand, also extended to Luis himself. Because if Jaime didn't dare complain soon enough that Abelardo's damn-the-torpedoes attitude seemed like pure boasting, and Lucía—impelled by a misunderstood compassion—preferred to not mention the judgment that had taken shape about Abelardo's moral affect, Luis wasn't innocent either. The extreme conclusion, however painful and paradoxical, was that Luis might also be considered primarily responsible; despite his knowing that hapless cretin Abelardo all-too-well, and having been the first to note that the man had joined the party for eschatological reasons, he failed to firmly oppose his membership in the Barcelona faction, and refrained from proposing that, according to the most basic rules of security and proper conduct, he should, at best, join ranks with his hometown comrades, in Seville, or Valencia, or wherever it was.

Because you didn't have to be whip-smart to realize that, if Abelardo never went back to his Valencia or his Seville, there must be some explanation for it. Really, his was not the case of a sane militant. Abelardo was one of those people who join the party for personal reasons, not for objective motives; he was the typical example of the militant who would have done better to undergo psychoanalysis before making such a decision.

Lucía saw this even more clearly ever since that night when Abelardo followed her all the way back to her room, telling her sad stories, problems typical of an unhappy man, precisely what Abelardo was, after all: a miserable wretch. She finally had to send him packing, although without being able to prevent him from taking some books he wanted, including *The Battle of the Milvian Bridge*, a novel which she'd never managed to finish reading anyway—one of those books that ends up wearying the reader from explaining everything in too much detail.

A sick individual, what people call crazy: this was, at heart, Abelardo's problem. A dreamer, a mythomaniac, one of those men whom you could never ever believe; no matter how many stories they might invent, you couldn't believe a single word. Stories not even worth the time it took to listen to them.

After such frankly disagreeable conflicts and scenes, dealing with a person like Sergio Vidal was a true respite. And not only because of the person himself—a real gentleman, cultured, witty, and well-mannered—but also his relaxed lifestyle, simply an emanation of his own persona, an expansive aura. A laid-back ambience, elegant and lively, one that only a blockhead, one of those obtuse, schematic sorts with egalitarian obsessions, could ever think had anything to do with money, as if money could buy such qualities.

They'd run into each other by coincidence on the terrace of Aux Deux Magots. It was Sergio Vidal, who, standing up from his chair, called Lucía's name—she was walking past and hadn't noticed him. Sergio said that he had an appointment but invited her to have a drink with him while he waited for his prospective client, one of those magnates with mines in Bolivia, and things like that. He was cordial and entertaining, and when the magnate, a full-blooded Indian, arrived, Sergio invited her to have lunch sometime in the country, outside Paris. This insistence on asking her out, so soon after having seen her when they were collecting signatures, was more than just mere courtesy from a man of the world, so Lucía decided to accept his invitation, and they made a date for the following Wednesday. Neither he nor she made any mention of their past differences, let alone so much as whisper Marina's name.

On Wednesday, Sergio drove her in his Jaguar out to one of those splendid country restaurants they have in France, a charming spot with tables outside, in the sunshine, under an arbor with climbing roses and grape vines—bare in that season—near Chantilly. After lunch, they strolled round the palace gardens, where Sergio explained to her that neither their design nor their construction corresponded in the least to the geometrical caprices and absolute perspectivism typical of the monarchical regime, as most of their classmates at Beaux Arts claimed. Midway through their walk they were caught by surprise in the rain, a cloudburst so sudden and violent that, by the time they made it back to the car, they were sopping wet. Sergio drove her straight to his house in Montmartre and made her take a bath in nearly scalding hot water, which greatly relieved her shivering. Then, to complete the remedy, basking in the warmth of the fireplace, they drank some glasses of that famous brandy that Marina used to offer them when she played the part of Sergio's housewife and maid.

After that day they continued seeing each other now and then, generally with Gina, as well. Lucía had wasted no time in noticing that Sergio showed a special interest in her, or that, at least, he remembered her with special affection. In other words: it was evident that Sergio was after Gina, and that Gina, also fed up with so much moth-eaten bohemianism, really enjoyed being with him in that house in Montmartre. And Lucía, at first accompanying them, played a decisive role in getting them together. So, what was bad about that? Should a woman who takes a hand in bringing together two people who love each other be considered a procuress?

What's certain is that Gina, bird-brained but a good girl, was much happier, far more, with a man like Sergio than a guy like Jacques. After all, Gina and Lucía came from the same social environment and had grown up in similar circumstances—not for nothing is Milan considered the Barcelona of Italy or vice-versa. And, without a doubt, she was just as sensible as Lucía of how comfortable she felt within Sergio's ambience, and what an entirely different environment it was from the one that Jacques, the bohemian, could offer them. A Jacques who, on the other hand, belonged to the same social class as Gina, Sergio, and Lucía. The difference lay in the fact that Jacques was a sort of revolutionary retard and Sergio, for example, was not. And as far as sexual perversions were concerned, the most likely thing was that Sergio's perversities, at the very least, were not the result of such frustrating consequences as those of Jacques, those of Jacques the onanist.

If I had to sum up in a single word what was happening with the crowd from l'Alouette, that word could only be *decay*—the group's overall decay and its individual members' progressive moral decay, either as friends or simply as companions.

I don't know, Lucía said, it was like they'd all changed in just a few months, almost like they weren't the same, as if they'd become different people. She wasn't very sure that Charlotte would have understood her reasoning, although with her silence and those bird eyes she had sometimes, like her father, the Genevan madman, she rather seemed to agree. It any case it was apparent that the problem did not arouse strong feelings in her. But, for Lucía, it was little less than a necessity to talk about it with someone.

Gina, for instance, for being an all-around nice person, wasn't much help. A pretty little rich girl from Milan, with a bad conscience, an absurd guilt complex stemming from her bourgeois roots, and a compensatory tendency of turning into a real swinish slut, letting herself be dragged away by the first ethical—as well as economic—cocksmith who crossed her path, accepting without argument whatever theories they happened to be espousing at the moment, whether those of Danilo Dolci, or the ultra-leftist radicalism of a piece of human detritus like Jacques, the onanist.

Or Marina: a complete mythomaniac as Alejandro so rightly divined, and a cynic who invariably had to meet a bad end. Because what most enraged Lucía was that she had been pulling her leg, that she had abused her good faith, that when everybody was in on the gossip about how Marina was cheating on Sergio with Jaime, she, Lucía, was totally in the dark; and she had been the last one among everyone in their crowd to find out. And such things are naturally unforgivable. And so much the more when Marina, after breaking up with Jaime, still had the nerve to explain her relationship with Jacques, the onanist, saying that she felt possessed by a decidedly Jacobean vocation: Jacques, Jaime, Giacomo, Santiago, and so on, until she'd collected the whole lot of them. Now I understand that stuff about the Camino de Santiago, she said: the pilgrims were people who had the same little manias as me, and she smiled with that allegedly Slavic meekness which, at one time, when she enjoyed the social status that came from living with Sergio, was one of her most attractive aspects; now, increasingly sloppy and ill-kempt as she was, it made her look, I don't know, like some kind of beggar.

And men? What could Charlotte have told her about men, in case she were interested, without sometimes seeming, at least outwardly, to be out of her mind? About Alejandro? A bit odd but, in the long run, the best of the bunch, whether or not he was really a faggot, right? Or Jaime: a good guy, sure, but mediocre, not too bright, one of those block-headed communists. Because Jacques's particulars weren't even worth mentioning—or maybe just good for gossip, the kinds of details that Gina was better than anybody at spreading everywhere.

So, to tell the truth the one she couldn't stand at all, not even to think about, was Camilo, that paunchy sodomite who'd done nothing except get fat since he arrived from Cuba, a symptom, on the other hand, that over there, with the revolution and all that business, things weren't coming along quite so well as reported. Besides, ultimately—and in this Alejandro was completely right—what had the Cuban Revolution been compared to the Spanish Civil War? What about the fact that now in Spain the police tortured prisoners to extract information, to amuse themselves before murdering them? Well, this only proved that in Cuba they were a bunch of amateurs. And when it came to the harshness and violence of the fighting, Alejandro was right again: the whole Cuban Revolution produced fewer casualties than the four days of street battles between anarchists and communists in Barcelona, in May of '37, while on the frontlines, men stood shoulder to shoulder fighting against Franco's troops. Just as he was right about the fact that, if Franco still held the Spanish people in his fist after so many years, this was due to the systematic extermination of the hundreds and hundreds of thousands of men shot by the firing squads, with whose deaths Franco—the Civil War now concluded, taking advantage of the impunity offered him by a favorable international situation—castrated the revolutionary pretensions of an entire generation throughout the dark years of the 1940s.

And like Camilo, so too most of their crowd at l'Alouette, faux bohemians and faux revolutionaries, daddy's boys who'd become obsessed with the notion of putting an end to oppression or repression of whatever you want to call it. Lucía looked around her, from table to table: quickly, almost violently, she gulped down the rest of her Calvados, then corrected herself: Not most of them, all of them.

Of course, she had also toughened up her act. She also knew how to vent her spleen like a real bitch now. She ordered another Calvados and told Gina about her fling with the Valenciano, one of those guys who when they show up in places like l'Alouette, use their political militancy as a lure to get laid. The typical bore who, as the night wears on, gets closer to bedtime, becomes more annoying, groping, and slimy. Until Lucía got fed up and said to him: You want to come up? Well, come on then, let's go. And once upstairs, the minute the door shut: C'mon, get your clothes off. Don't you want to sleep with me? Well, come on, be quick, what are you waiting for? And then he wanted to kiss her and hold her and all that, as if to set the right mood, but she went on rattling him while she undressed herself, alone. C'mon, take 'em off, she was telling him, without any formalities: let's get it on. And the guy, now naked, not getting a hard-on, just stood there by the bed, like he didn't know what to do, Lucía asking him, hey, what's the matter? Can you get it up or not? No, indeed, the Valenciano, or whatever he was, couldn't get it up at all, and ended up having to beat it out of there like a dog with his tail between his legs. Almost a pity.

Being able to speak with others, being able to relate things and talk about people, more than just simply venting about them and the atmosphere around them, was like placing herself above it all, like seeing everything from outside, as if, by talking, all that business ceased to concern her, as if, in a certain way, it nullified that world she found herself stuck in. A phenomenon very similar to the one that impelled Lucía, just as strongly, to reveal her projects to third parties, to share the details, and explain them in such a way that she began to feel that mapping them out made their completion a foregone conclusion, almost as if she had already seen them through to fruition; ultimately it felt like being relieved of the burden of actually working on them, case closed, and then on to something else, spurred on by any other new initiative, quitting smoking, drinking less, not staying out so late at night, things like that.

Consider this, Gina, the way I see it, and I mean this sincerely, Lucía said, money isn't happiness. For me, basically, money is time, the reverse of the way people usually phrase it—time that you gain, that you save, so you can quit doing disagreeable or useless things and have others do them for you, and they let you do what you want. It's like adding years to your life, like recouping hours and hours wasted sleeping. Also, why deny it, money provides an extraordinary power over people and things. A power that an intelligent woman can obtain just the same without money, as long as the money, including saving time, in this specific case also means saving energy. I swear, I couldn't care less about possessing, hoarding, and everything else involved with holding on to money; what's truly important, at least for me, is being able to spend, at any time, however much is required to get me what I need in that moment. Is that frivolity? Okay, sure. But then, frivolous things are the only serious things.

The thing is, Gina, learning to understand is a whole process by itself and requires effort. Realizing that not even our friends from l'Alouette are what they seemed to us when we were a couple of poor girls fresh in town—a couple of idiots, unhappy girls—requires a real effort. Understanding, for example, that just because someone's not an intellectual—if we can call those guys intellectuals without offending the real ones—doesn't mean they're not intelligent. Or that what's true for you and me, that intellectuals bore us, that we prefer to talk with normal, everyday people, waiters, shop workers, whores, whomever, I don't know, street people, nothing strange about them—and that in any case, the intellectuals are the real oddballs, the ones who consider themselves intellectuals, guys incapable of talking for even one minute with such people, to whom they've got nothing to say, with whom they don't know what to talk about, however much they claim they're leftists and they're for the common people and all that. I swear, Gina, so many times, when I heard them talking, I felt stupid, practically a retard, until I understood that the idiots, the retards, were them.

Gina and Lucía saw each other for the last time at the Orly airport. Charlotte said that she had something else to do—some strange whim of hers—and the only person who offered to accompany her to the airport was Gina. Of course, being Charlotte, it was possibly just another one of her excuses, one of her tricks for avoiding any kind of natural forum for sentimentality.

In Barcelona, Javier was waiting for her at El Prat, and he took her straight to his house, a huge penthouse apartment with a swimming pool and patios in Pedralbes. But, as far as her family knew, Lucía's flight didn't arrive until twenty-four hours later. At home, in addition to her family's natural surprise, the news that she was going to marry Javier caused them all, understandably, to react with great joy.

VI

Hitting the town three or four nights a week is usually about as much as a person can stand. And during Carnaval, they went out every single night; so without even one day off here or there, by the time the carnival festivities came to an end, they were all—or at least Lucía—completely spent. It wasn't just the fact of spending the whole night going from place to place, the fatigue and the lack of sleep; the worst thing was how much they inevitably drank, and even more, how much they ended up smoking, cigarette after cigarette. The hangover the next day from so much alcohol and nicotine, the headache, and that feeling of nausea that only subsided when they resumed drinking and smoking so as to be able to go back out again, to get sufficiently perky and tipsy to seem to have the strength to head out.

Truth be told: she did every crazy thing that popped into her head, she had to admit it. *But, is there anything wrong with it?* In the end, you have to do what you like, and the only way of knowing exactly what you do like is to try everything first. Some things you simply can't judge until you've done them, until you've tried them. And if you say no beforehand, it doesn't necessarily mean that you're biased, but that, unconsciously, you fear the power of saying *yes*, it's attraction over you. No matter what people think, there's always some moral norm to which you must adjust your behavior. For my part, however, I think that the moral must adjust to you, to your tastes, to your personality. Any other behavioral norm supposes the acceptance of something alien to you, something imposed on you from without, that benefits only God knows who—not you, of course.

They talked about men, about their clumsiness, their manias. Charlotte said she preferred romantic types. The ones with problems, who have problems and explain them to you: for example, their wife, if they're married—is someone who doesn't understand them at all, with whom they've got nothing in common, the biggest mistake of their life. But there are the children, some children whom they love very much because they remind them of how they were when they were kids, and that's why they don't say to hell with the marriage, to avoid traumatizing them and all that. Or those men who had a great love affair, its embers still glowing in their heart, and although impossible or frustrated, they look for their beloved's face wherever they happen to be, or their beloved's face pursues them, they believe they see her everywhere, no matter what they do. Or the homosexuals who want to remake themselves, awaiting only the woman who will save them, who pays attention to them, and gives them the affection their mother gave them. Or those who know, from experience, what an affair really is, and for that reason don't want to hurt you, they know too well love's painful consequences, how easy it catches fire, and the ashes of the aftermath; they know the best thing is to hold on to the good memory of what might have been a marvelous affair. And not wanting to fuck you over: *they don't fuck at all*. They don't go to bed with you although they're on the verge of doing it, so it turns out better for everyone.

Lucía said she didn't care if they were one way or another: she treated them however she wanted, independent of whether they were this or that, whatever she felt about the guy, whatever felt comfortable. She had also discovered that, face to face with men, the best thing in general was to act frigid, and on top of that, tell them directly she wasn't interested, treat them scornfully; that put her in a superior position, and it was the guy who went crazy trying to make something happen, to persuade her, to at least save himself from getting burned. And the fact is, in general, the only way to get their attention was to ignore them all. But not Charlotte; Charlotte was a person she could talk to, with whom she could be herself, exactly as she was, according to her personality. They knew each other, they understood each other, she knew she could confide in her. But not with the rest of them. She'd become hardened to the others, the women as well as the men: now she knew how to deal with them. The others weren't the only ones who seemed to have changed since she first arrived in Paris in the autumn; she had changed, too.

For example, the way she'd lambasted Marina, that night when Marina had the bright idea to come see Lucía again with her stories and problems. She'd been almost brutal with her, forcing her to confront reality as if forcing her to stare at herself in a mirror; what a shock, what a shakeup that must have been for Marina. Don't exaggerate so much, Lucía told her; stop living in the clouds. Don't come telling me your lies anymore, the only person you're fooling is yourself. Do you think anyone could ever possibly believe your fairy tales about Russian princes and palaces in Samarkand and Chinese servants with their heads chopped off? Guys will tell you yes, oh yes. But they don't believe you and it doesn't even matter to them, deep down, whether they believe you or not. What really matters to them is getting into your pants, and what you do in bed. All the rest of it only matters to them or not depending on what you do in bed. And keep in mind, you idiot, time's not on your side, that you can say whatever you like but you're going to be less interesting to men with every passing year. In the end, your ability for spinning fables, your credibility, depends on your body, and what you do with it in bed, your erotic skills, the pleasure you're able to give them. Do you get it? Yes or no?

Sometimes, mind you, said Lucía, it was worth the trouble to indulge in a bit of comedy, when that comic touch had its compensations. Like with Javier, who took her everywhere, who treated her like a queen. Meaning: just a dash of comedy, but only when what was achieved, what was resolved, tipped the scales in her favor. And, needless to say, without going too far.

They say there are some experiences that mark a person's life, that decisively set the direction they must take from then on. To wit: Lucia's experiences during the last several months were so prolific and so varied, that even several lifetimes would have been too few to live them out to their final consequences. First of all, her relationship with Charlotte. Not an entirely new sort of relationship, it's true, logical enough for someone who had been a boarding student at a convent school when she was a little girl. Of course, neither she nor Charlotte were exactly little girls anymore.

Lucía realized what was happening just a few days after inviting Charlotte to share the room she had rented, before offering to pose as a model for her photos, almost from the first night; she only had to see how Charlotte watched her as she undressed. Charlotte slipped out of her clothes quickly and, stretched out on the bed, as if too lazy to put on her pajamas, never taking her eyes off Lucía while she went about undressing without any gratuitous exhibitionisms, but also without any prudish modesty, just naturally. And precisely for that reason, because of the unabashed stare with which Charlotte contemplated her, Lucía decided to teach her a lesson, to remove her clothing calmly, in stages: shoes, socks, sweater, pants, bra, panties, in an eminently aesthetic sequence. Sometimes, mostly facing away, as if turning her back on her. Or half covering herself with her nightgown, as if embarrassed. And, at the same time, as if distracted by the chatter between them, stretching the time between one stage and another, enriching such intervals with a studied control of attitudes and postures, expressions, gestures. Thus, not only lying on her side on the bed, half covering her breasts that peeked out from the unbuttoned neck of her nightgown, while she laughed at a more or less improvised joke; or moving around the room maintaining just the right angle so that her figure would acquire subtle reliefs for whomever might be watching her from the bed; or, stretched out once more on the bed, as close as one who's sharing a secret, following some unpremeditated movement by letting the folds of her nightgown part carelessly over her thighs pressed close together, over her pubis. No: not only that, but also certain ways of laughing, of smoking, of staring.

One of those nights, Charlotte told her to just keep moving, talking, and she began snapping pictures of her. Lucía asked her what she was doing, what the photos were for, who was going to see them, and more, and Charlotte gave her all kinds of assurances. Or, at least, Lucía pretended to be convinced that nobody else would have access to the photos in question without her prior consent. Privately, however, she felt certain that the boys at the photo lab were going to be shocked.

Charlotte—who, if she had her druthers, or so she claimed, would have always slept without pajamas—next made sure they both had an extra belt of Calvados that night, ensuring that, once they were both in bed, she could play the little girl. She kicked Lucía under the sheets, pretended to panic, pounced on top of her, then, shrinking like a snail, pulled back and curled up into a ball, saying she was cold, shivering. And, in the middle of one of those tussles, she latched on tightly to one of Lucía's breasts, sucking hard, seeming to devour it. Everything progressed just like in a game and, acting like she was playing along, Lucía had to push Charlotte away after pinning her down, declaring her defeated, a prisoner, her performance betrayed only by the excitement she felt, an uneasy sensation as if she couldn't breathe, which made it difficult to pretend. Because the truth was that Charlotte, with truly diabolical precision or skill, had managed to get her excited. And that was not alright. Their frolicking had gotten so intense that Lucía had to stop the game before it went too far. Control herself, regain her self-control in the exact same measure as, due to her surprise or for whatever reason, she had lost it, or felt confused, or, pure and simple, melted down.

An absolutely necessary attitude. Charlotte, no doubt, must not have been feeling very good, given that it was approximately around that time when she began to laugh like crazy when snapping photos of Lucía, as if she were doing it as a joke, whereas prior to that, every time she started clicking the shutter, she'd gotten fed up with having to egg Lucía on with all kinds of expressions of satisfaction, interjections, whistles, puffs, clicking of her tongue, and things like that. That's what made Lucía decide to stop with the photos—for the false impression, regardless of how much she did or did not do, they might create. In the end, and however sensitive she was, Lucía was no lesbian. Charlotte's games and manipulation had succeeded in arousing her—she had to admit that much; but that didn't mean she was in any way abnormal or unhealthy. Quite the contrary: only repressed people—and it would be interesting to discover the cause of such repression—are uptight about so many things that are considered abnormal if not perverse, despite really being attracted to them. Because there's no longer any question about the fact that everybody's got something of the opposite sex inside them, that sexuality is nothing more than a question of proportions.

That's why, rightly, needing to dispense with certain things, Lucía quit playing their little games but also, similarly, the business with the photos. And not because of prejudice or anything like that; she did it, simply, because she liked men, and hopefully to avoid any possible confusion.

Everything was, by now, quite mixed up. There were other things, as well, which—aside from Charlotte—nobody seemed willing to understand. And not because they were so naturally complicated as to make them impossible to grasp, but rather because one might say that, sometimes, the simplest and most natural things, for whatever reason, were the very ones people have the hardest time accepting. Things which someone like Gina, for example, could never manage to understand. Things which would never occur to a methodical blockhead like Jaime, despite being an all-around good guy. Things that someone like Alejandro, with his hysterical reactions, would inevitably reject. Not to mention those slimy creeps who think that militancy can solve all their problems, including sex.

What's certain is that Lucía was more than fed up with so much pseudo-revolutionary psychobabble, about objective conditions and whatnot. Palaver which, if tiresome but innocuous within the atmosphere of l'Alouette, became dangerous in other situations, especially ones that called for its practical application, as Luis, better than anyone, could surely well attest. And now Luis was paying the price, while the others just kept chatting away around the tables of l'Alouette. Of course, depending on how you looked at it, he richly deserved it. For allowing himself to get caught up in all that business.

But really, anyone would go crazy from so much ultra-leftist theorizing; and if one surrenders to its radical speculations, it's only an attempt to compensate for its essential impotence, not to mention its onanistic practices. In that regard there were so many faux heroes like that cornfed buck nigger

Camilo, the paunchy sodomite whose only real passion was telling stories about the Cuban Revolution.

From this perspective, l'Alouette must ultimately be seen as a kind of epicenter of all revolutionary movements, a place full of people willing to change the world, some sort of knights errant on a quest to confront evil. Or warriors who, from the farthest reaches of Hellas join forces for a single purpose: the siege of Troy. Thinking of them, one might recall Sappho's lines: they all set out for Ilium, the dulcet flute dancing with the lyre, the rattles chattering, while the maidens' vibrant voices intoned a sacred song, and its divine echo rose up to heaven.

As for Lucía, at least, she'd had enough. She was sick of sharing a bed, even with Charlotte; of sharing a bathroom with the other residents on their floor; of the choking fumes from the oil radiator; the wet-dog-stink from her friends' clothes and hair at l'Alouette; the stench of cigarette butts, of intimate muck, of misery. Lucía experienced a basic need for comfort, that comfort everyone seeks but which becomes a grotesque extravagance the moment one enters an environment like l'Alouette. Or better yet: not comfort, but luxury, what's understood—and everybody understands it—to mean luxury. She needed it, she deserved it, and that's all there was to it.

Lucía was not exactly a Marina, the manic fabulist. They had nothing in common, nor did she plan to follow the path that Marina had chosen. A path that dead-ended at the wharves along the Seine, under the bridges, sleeping off a hangover huddled with other ragged clochards who seemed to have rolled out of a Victor Hugo novel, creatures worn down by their vagabond life, their red-wine-soaked bodies swollen and purple. She currently drank herself stupid every night, and every night invariably left her in dreary spirits. She seemed to have distanced herself from Jacques the onanist. Or if she hadn't put space between them—so much the worse for her if true—they were certainly not seen together very often. Now she was making the rounds with a Croatian girl or someone like that, another mythomaniac who claimed to be nothing less than the manager of Éditions Gallimard, and who accompanied her on her binges. Made for each other—a perfect pair of viragoes.

No: her path was different—exactly the opposite of Marina's. And it wasn't even worth taking the trouble to offer Marina advice, to cheer her up or console her when she showed up with her stories to cry on Lucía's shoulder: that she'd never had a real childhood and that her youth couldn't have been any harder. That she carried inside her a kind of irrepressible self-destructive force that always impelled her to thwart however many possibilities came her way that might straighten out her luck. Scenes that, coming too late, left Lucía feeling completely indifferent; she had no vocation, let's say, for resuscitating burnt out human husks. As Alejandro liked to say: let the dead bury the dead.

And so much the better given that, thanks to Sergio's confidences, Lucía was up on all the gossip about what an odd bird Marina turned out to be. Confidences which, owing to their special character and the people they involved—names all too well-known—Lucía could in no way divulge. What she could do—and so, of course, did—was to take good notes and keep it well in mind, now that Marina's mythomania no longer imbued only her past life, but also, and even more so, her present daily life. Sergio and Lucía exchanged information from the very first night, filling each other in on background events.

After getting caught in the downpour, but still soaked to the skin, now in Sergio's Jaguar heading back to Paris, Lucía, without knowing very well why, began to lay it on a bit too thick, trembling as if she'd caught a chill that she didn't actually feel. But, curiously, as if it weren't entirely an act, she found her teeth really chattering, however much Sergio, driving with just one hand on the wheel, despite the incessant rain, pulled her close against his shoulder.

Once in the studio, after her steaming hot bath, the two of them lying atop a polar bear rug before the fireplace, Sergio softly, slowly removed the purple bathrobe he'd given her to wear. A night as unforgettable as the day had been, the polar bear skin, the pear brandy, their bodies' shadows cast on the wall by the capricious flames.

From then on, they kept seeing each other regularly. But as Lucía got to know Sergio better, she soon realized that he, without at all lessening their perfect mutual understanding but rather by virtue of the confidence born of such understanding and the complicity it establishes, he, Sergio, found himself strongly attracted by the memory of Gina; from the looks of it, Gina had already awakened his interest that time when she, with Lucía and others from their crowd, at Marina's invitation, had dropped by his place and he came downstairs to chat with them all for a while. As Lucía was anything but snobby, and far above idiotic vanity and selfishness, she was perfectly comfortable helping bring them closer, however possible. So much the more because, judging from the positive response to certain inquiries, Gina, now free from Jacques the onanist's nefarious influence, didn't seem entirely lukewarm—so to speak—to Sergio; and that, just as if Cupid and Fate were in conspiracy, the three of them, by a perfect and absurdly opportune coincidence, had bumped into each other at the Delacroix house and museum. Upon leaving, they went to the terrace at Aux Deux Magots and chatted a while as they watched the people strolling past.

When Sergio invited them to dine with him in a really cool Vietnamese restaurant, and then back to his house, to have a drink by the warm hearth, Lucía made sure to keep topping off their little glasses of pear brandy until Gina was good and loose just like anyone who's drunk their fill or like anyone who pretends to drink their fill in order to loosen up. While they were drinking, Sergio organized a ceremony in honor of a small statue he'd set up in a prominent location, the goddess Oshun or something like that, a sort of Brazilian Aphrodite, as he explained to them. He'd lit the seven candles of a Hebrew menorah, while the smoke of Brazilian incense arose from the censers; he emphasized that it was Brazilian, although Lucía could have sworn it was simply just another product, like sandalwood and whatnot, sold by the Chinese.

Everything seemed to suggest that it was time to say goodnight, to leave them alone together, but it was Sergio who stopped her, insisting otherwise, saying that interrupting the ceremony would bring them bad luck and terrible curses. And he began to put makeup on them and himself, or rather, to paint their whole bodies, like savages, with different kinds of makeup. Gina laughed like crazy, saying that it tickled. Sergio's work displayed his exquisite artistic sensibility to great effect. When it was done their three bodies were painted from head to toe, and the artist's member fully erect. He made love to them both, while encouraging them to also love each other the way the goddesses make love. After her experience with Charlotte, Lucía knew quite well what she had to do, and everything worked out perfectly, although the three of them ended up with their bodies caked in every different color, which, according to Sergio, proclaimed the splendid outcome of the ceremony. A quip that was pure Sergio; nonetheless, he had behaved the whole time with exquisite gentleness.

After that night, Lucía drifted away, isolating herself, letting them have their great adventure, an increasingly passionate love for them both. Gina, at least, seemed truly dazzled and confused when they met, being so abruptly introduced to a world so much sweeter than that of Danilo Dolci and his visionary imagery. For Lucía, however, Sergio was perhaps too cerebral. I suppose that everybody understands what I mean by that, she said to Charlotte.

In other matters, Javier came to town—one more good reason for finding some distance. And she and Javier, for their part, as if by tacit agreement—they'd made no explicit arrangement—put some space between themselves and Charlotte. After all, Javier was interested in Lucía, not Charlotte. And Lucía was under no obligation to let her tag along everywhere they went, as if she were some kind of bodyguard. So, she solved everything by simply not telling her anything. The truth is that such outings with three people, apart from being rather impractical, only bring unhappiness. It was enough that they invited her to dinner one night; right away she felt that permitted her to unload one of her typically crazy ideas. It's one thing to share a room, and something very different to share Javier. With Charlotte in the middle, the suite at the George V would have quickly become a bird cage.

Javier took her everywhere, and everywhere they went they had fun like little kids. At Maxim's, when the violinist asked her if she had any special requests, she asked him to play The Internationale. At Crazy Horse, when the show was over, as the crowd was filing out, she started doing her own striptease that was almost immediately copied by a large group of drunken American women, all of them climbing atop the bar at the back of the room. At the Carrousel they invited a transvestite over to their table who turned out to be a Pied-Noir, of Spanish origin. His name was Manolo and, in the safety of the dim lighting, he gave them such a private exhibition of his qualities that even Lucía started feeling, to put it crudely, like a bitch in heat. The same in every locale, their suite at the George V serving as a sanctuary after their excursions.

But if she found herself living beyond her wildest dreams, if she was leading a truly ideal life, Javier seemed even more excited. In other words: he was crazy for Lucía and Lucía was fully aware of that, so that, as a result, he'd be able to do what she asked in order to please her. For that very reason and, more generally, in order to train him properly, she made an effort to never agree with his suggestions, or at least not immediately or in the suggested order. To make him change his plans, to get him used to following her whims while knowing that they were whims, pure arbitrariness to which he had to bend unreservedly, and bend he did.

One night she even made him take her to l'Alouette, so that her old pals could see them together—and so that Camilo could analyze him from a dialectical point of view. Later, in some comfortable place, she explained what kind of people they were. Even with Charlotte—she told him—she had to get serious and stop her in her tracks given that she was semi-lesbian or, at least, somewhat ambidextrous. Since she broke up with Luis, to whom she stayed faithful while they were together, she made quite sure to keep the others at bay, who hounded her like fanatics. Because it's not only a question of physical attraction or revulsion, she said; it's almost a question of worlds, that we belong to different worlds. Javier praised her attitude: he told her that she'd done very well to remain guarded, that she was absolutely right. Oh, stop, you're making me blush, she said; and although he lacked the skill to make the phrase sound genuine, or perhaps for that very reason, because it was something he would never come up with on his own, Lucía found it just right, meshing perfectly with her way of thinking: the left is admirable for its idealism, for its good sense, he had said; the right, for its accomplishments.

One morning, returning to their room to change her clothes, Charlotte suddenly said something about how whenever Lucía got tired of Javier, she should let her have him, that she was even willing to marry him: classic Charlotte, another one of her harebrained remarks. And Lucía, without mincing words, gave her a piece of her mind. In the first place: it seemed like Charlotte only had eyes for the men Lucía was dating, and there was something unwholesome about that, something kind of weird. And second, however much Charlotte might be willing to marry Javier, she, Lucía had far more reason to doubt that Javier was willing to marry Charlotte; she was sure the thought had never crossed his mind. That much was crystal clear.

In fact, this comment, typical from Charlotte, the very day after Lucía had been kind enough to allow Javier to invite Charlotte to dine with them, played a role—in a certain way a decisive one—in her decision to accept Javier's repeated proposal of marriage. Needless to say, however, for the moment she judged it preferable to keep this from Javier, however many gifts he lavished on her, from perfume to expensive clothing, and even the silliest trinkets and knickknacks sold on the street. Javier insisted on taking her away from that environment, saying that a woman like Lucía could not spend any more time single and living in Paris, but she just limited herself to saying that she'd consider his offer.

Because there was also the problem of Helena, Javier's current girlfriend. And it was better that he fly back to Barcelona in a kind of fury, ready to dump her no matter what. If he returned home too sure about Lucía, he was always going to find himself more within Helena's reach, more vulnerable to her machinations, no matter how much any possible comparison between the two women would work to the detriment of Helena, which is how she wrote her name, with an H, not Elena. This simple detail—which Lucía discovered thanks to one of those not especially pertinent coincidences—sufficed to show, all too well, the kind of woman she really was, and what could be expected from a woman who does things like that. To begin with, she and Javier had not yet had sexual relations, properly speaking, as Javier himself had confessed to Lucía; from habit, from preconceptions, from the idea that when it comes to the official girlfriend you've got to wait until after the wedding, and all those customs which still persist among certain circles of the bourgeoisie. Something which Javier, precisely because the question had never yet been raised, now understood wasn't exactly a good sign. Why could he have sex with other women but not with the one who was going to be his wife? He now found it to be practically immoral, he told her. These were his very words, to the letter: Now I find it, I don't know, practically immoral.

And certainly Helena had never thought about it either, such ideas never passed through her little golden head, she was pure silly luxury, like an Afghan dog. A girl just as lovely as she was stupid and, not to mention, with that typical accent rich girls from Barcelona have, that affected nasal pronunciation they share with those professional faggots who frequent certain bars around Las Ramblas, in the lower streets of Barcelona.

Javier: his discretion, his tact, his delicacy—his works, as he would say. Because if Lucía spoke to him about her relationship with Luis, she didn't do it, in any way, by responding to any kind of questions or comments—much less, needless to say, by seeking some kind of counterpoint. If she did, it was with complete naivety, although perhaps she created the opening, certainly, for Javier to talk to her about Helena, to make them feel a bit closer. But without Javier changing his mind about not getting into details, or not sharing confidences that might concern someone else's private life.

The truth is that Javier was, above all, what people call a true gentleman. Words that nowadays sound anachronistic insofar as they designate a concept that no longer exists. Especially for the dominant mentality in places like l'Alouette. But they rang in Lucía's ears with a familiarity that supposes her having heard them spoken since she was a little girl, every time someone mentioned her father, like a title inevitably linked to the personality of Señor Trías, a true gentleman. A title whose value and meaning went beyond the realm of the purely honorific, to affect the family's economic importance, too, even so many years after the father's death, when the Trías were no longer the family they had once been, an emblematic past of prosperity and abundance which Lucía did not even remember. Because, apart from any importance, the truth is that the family patrimony, thanks to the work and grace of Señora Trías's scrupulous and equally catastrophic management, had dried up from one year to the next. Widows! Señora Trías never wasted an opportunity to exclaim. The shameful way that people take advantage of widows, of their ignorance in business matters, of their helplessness! As well as what her lamentations failed to bewail: their stupidity.

Scruples. Lucía had always heard that her mother had scruples; she, her mother, was the first one to say it in front of Lucía to whomever might like to hear it, just as if Lucía were a bouquet of flowers or some household pet. And for years and years Lucía thought that by scruples her mother meant that her conscience bothered her about some crime she had committed or that, if she had not lacked the courage, she would have committed. Only over the course of time, and not without a certain disappointment, did she learn that these scruples were neither moral nor religious but, rather, psychological. In short, her mother was a two-faced prude, something Lucía already knew perfectly well.

More prudish than a nun. Lucía was in a position to be able to verify that; nine years in a convent school run by nuns had not been wasted on her. To a certain point, it's also true that, for Lucía, there had been no happier period in her whole life than those last two years of high school with the nuns. For at that time, having become by then the only Trías daughter at the high school, without the shadow of an older sister always preceding her, being able to freely enlarge her own personality, she felt then, decidedly, much more relaxed there, at school, than in her family's house. Better to deal with the nuns than with a mother weighted down with scruples, to give some kind of name to the woman's manias. Better, too, than enduring her sister's petty jealousies or her brother's mythomaniac delusions.

She still remembered her last day of high school when she went to receive her diploma. The trauma of leaving, that feeling like finding yourself suddenly naked: a young girl with straight bangs, with brand new sunglasses, diploma in hand. She stopped at the gate, conscious, all at once, of how happy she'd grown to be there in the school, without ever having realized it. On that garden campus, going anywhere she liked, strolling with some nun or some friend, nuns who had lately become like friends, a privileged world full of quiet corners, and now that she was going to leave it all behind, it seemed like something from a storybook, the playgrounds, the orchard, and especially, the garden, that shady garden with ponds and sprinklers and the little grotto with faux stalactites and the hanging bridge under which—they knew—there might be some boy hiding inside the laurel thickets, lying in wait to spy on them when they walked across; and the school building itself, with its front entrance like a medieval castle, and the stained glass windows in the auditorium, and the smell of turpentine in the so-called natural history museum, and the kitchen where Sister Marta prepared special afternoon snacks for her, *mantecadas*, and *torrijas*, and cups of hot chocolate. And now, here at the end, irrevocably, beyond the garden campus, as if waiting to swallow her alive, the sordid world of family life, the shortsightedness and the timorous prejudices of a family in decline, the pressures and disappointments and unfulfilled desires of their social life, the modest summers in Viladrau, straitened circumstances, everything small and cramped, a world she'd completely outgrown. She'd sat down on the sidewalk, in the shade of an acacia tree, without even thinking about the impression her image could arouse in the mind of anyone who might be watching her, there, just as she was, dressed in her schoolgirl's skirt, alone, sitting on the sidewalk, with her bangs and her sunglasses, adorable in her defenseless perplexity—a young woman, almost a girl, quiet and absorbed, solitary like the rainbow and just as beautiful.

And like then, like the day she left the convent school, with the very same vivid intensity, her present panorama, the prospects that a return to Barcelona, to rejoin her family environment, would have offered her. A mother growing crazier by the day; a mythomaniac brother and a cretinous sister-in-law; an older sister who still saw herself as Older—with a capital O—no longer only regarding Lucía but the world at large, too. One of those people who talk about the carnal aspects of love, about sexuality, the way some people talk about surrealism—as something amusing and extravagant that can only be viewed from without, rather like the way a circus clown acts out an astonishing discovery. Needless to say, it would be pointless to speculate about the details of her married life.

Faced with such a world, Lucía found herself capable, at most, of feeling nostalgia for the sad things she'd left behind.

With her mind made up, she immediately set about seeing her choice through to its conclusion. Even if that meant forcing herself to believe that she was renouncing her present life only temporarily, and to consider the advantages conferred by any other choice would have simply been limitations and inconveniences.

Likewise, to undertake a complete makeover of her habits and attitudes, ones adequate, perhaps, to a world like the one at l'Alouette, but not to the kind of life awaiting her at Javier's side, or to the social circles she would now frequent. A change that began with her style of dressing and making herself up and ended with her way of moving and even smiling. Moving from corduroy pants and a turtleneck sweater to a simple number by Chanel. From applying makeup to her eyes by copying any random fashion magazine, her hair more or less brushed, to considering the combination of her face and hairstyle as an aesthetically inseparable whole. Things that were new for Lucía only insofar as something forgotten can sound new. After all, Lucía was simply rejoining the world into which she'd been born, the one in which she would have matured if not for the consequences, at every level, brought on by her father's death when she was just a little girl. An event that certainly influenced the convulsion caused by Luis's entrance into her life, in her immediate and unqualified embrace of the revolutionary ideas Luis was fighting for—influencing her willingness, or rather enthusiasm to follow such ideas, which meant a complete break with the society in which she lived. A society that, on the other hand, seemed inclined to expel her from its bosom or, at least, to do absolutely nothing to palliate the impression that Lucía experienced of being increasingly distant from the epicenter, more and more shunted aside as her family's economic difficulties persisted or grew more acute.

Of course, on closer inspection, it wasn't so much the society itself as her mother. And it still seemed symptomatic that she would have needed an experience like her relationship with Luis—facilitated perhaps by the similarity of their respective trajectorics: shared class roots and subsequent family decline—and how such a relationship, removed as far as possible from the environment in which she'd been raised, tends to roil and blur one's worldview, in order to be absolutely sure of her position, to know what her place really was. This period of her life now seemed to her something like a tunnel into which she'd been swept by nothing more than her love for Luis. And, as when emerging from a tunnel or a cave, the pure, dazzling present reality nearly blinded her.

For some time, Lucía barely showed her face around l'Alouette, but a few days after Javier departed, as soon as he informed her that he had officially broken up with Helena, she dropped by immediately, to see if she could run into Charlotte. She needed to talk about it with somebody, she needed company, and Charlotte was the only one who could offer her both things at that moment. She took her out to an expensive place which she knew thanks to Javier, and there they celebrated with a bottle of Moët Chandon. Then—without enough cash for more champagne—they switched back to their regular Calvados, and ended up getting really, memorably, smashed. Of course, it wasn't her victory they were celebrating but Helena's downfall. Not because Lucía feared that things might turn out badly, but everyone knows that being hasty brings bad luck, toasting something that's not yet a sure thing, which has not yet been really secured. Apart from this, and keeping in mind that Charlotte was crazy as a loon, it served Lucía's best interest to keep their relationship alive, to stay on good terms with her. She'd asked Charlotte to give her the proofs and negatives of the photos she'd snapped of her during the months they'd roomed together, so they wouldn't keep circulating and end up appearing in some magazine. Needless to say, Charlotte handed them over without a fuss. But one can never be too sure with people like her.

She watched her shape advancing along past the shop windows, walking very straight, with short little steps, her eyes flashing up and down, quick, timid glances, with unction and helplessness and a touch of sadness or childish seriousness, somewhere between rattled and resolute, the same way an angel would approach its judges. It must be noted that, in this respect, Sergio Vidal's exquisite taste, linked with Lucía's natural instinct and captivating flair, had been truly invaluable.

Seen from a different angle, the important thing wasn't so much what one gained as what was lost from sight, what was left behind. An environment alien to her, along with the ways of life and the problems people there wrestled with, their worries, their arguments, right down to the words they used. And, above all, the people, the individuals who inhabited that world, more of an underground scene. People, at best, like Jaime, like Federico, like Gina, like Charlotte herself, people who, the same as Lucía, had found their way there more or less by accident, by mistake, by being lost, through some misunderstanding, for whatever reason, yet not quite belonging to that scene. Because the original population of that underground scene—whoever they happened to be—was, from a moral, psychological, and even physical point of view, truly depraved. Guys like Jacques or like Abelardo, the Sevillano, or Valenciano, or whatever he was. Guys like that, slimy creatures. They were, properly speaking, the true denizens of that underground scene.

So of course she'd been hard on Abelardo, heartless even. She'd said to him: So, what's your problem? Can't get it up? Then why do you want to screw me? C'mon, snap out of it! And a raft of similar unpleasantries. Because that's exactly what such a tasteless bigmouth deserves, a guy whose virility is nothing but hollow words and hot air. A slimy fellow, cretinous enough to believe that bragging about his success with women, about his copulative capacity and the size of his cock—apart from his usual stupid allusions to secret techniques and supposedly hidden virtues—somehow made up for it—that words alone could fulfill the need for action. All of that, in the crucial moment, making his semi-impotent condition even more obvious. Because, if there was an inch of truth about the size of his member, his firmness and dependability came far short of the mark.

In short, a scumbag—a miserable scumbag, that kind that makes others feel embarrassed for them. Because, to top it off, after all his trial and error, he settled things by pulling out and making a real mess, shooting his load all over her. And that's definitely the mark of a truly miserable scumbag. Just like the fact that then and there he felt himself obliged to share all his woes with her, that he'd fathered a bastard child, or that he himself was the illegitimate bastard, the child of some drunken whore who'd denounced his father for being a Red—or that the drunken whore was his wife. Well, something like that; Lucía had downed too much Calvados to remember exactly. In fact, she had felt a bit sorry for him since the last time; perhaps that was why she let the whole thing go as far as it did, letting him have a second try, after having treated him so shabbily, worse than a dog.

That's also why she let him filch some books, works by Marx and Lenin that she and Luis bought at Le Globe, and which Luis left with her for safe keeping because of the underlined passages and his notes scribbled in the margins. He also took *The Battle of the Milvian Bridge* by Claudio Sáinz de la Mora, a novel which, despite her best intentions, she'd put aside unfinished as many times as she'd started reading it, because it was a gift from Luis, inscribed by him and everything, one of his perfectly characteristic ironic little notes that made one unsure whether to feel sour or burst out laughing. But it was as if fate had come between her and that novel, that the calm she required would have ended if that bastard, that mooch, hadn't swiped it without even asking her, had stolen it with her blessing, so to speak. The kind of guy who, if he squealed to the Spanish police about the Party and all that—which he did—the same way he bragged about his amorous conquests around the tables of l'Alouette, then it was no surprise when he suddenly burst into song—*jotas* from Valencia, or Seville, or any old thing.

Things that, in the end, she didn't even dare tell Charlotte. Because the best thing to do with such sad stories is to forget them.

Between the train and the plane: a whole epoch unto itself. Lucía had arrived in Paris in a second-class couchette and now she was returning to Barcelona by plane. And in first class.

There were two flights departing almost at the same time: one on Iberia and the other on Air France; Lucía chose Air France. Flying first class, a privilege in itself, has a double advantage: the food is better and there's an open bar. As a result, Lucía walked off the plane at El Prat somewhat tipsy, and if she wasn't really drunk, it was because midway through her fourth glass of champagne, they told her to fasten her seatbelt, that they were about to land.

At El Prat, while watching for her suitcases to appear, she saw Javier waiting on the other side of customs control, waving, blowing her kisses. Suddenly, someone covered her eyes from behind. Lucía was quite startled, and only relaxed when she recognized the familiar lilting laugh of Francisca, her best friend from her last years in high school and afterward, too; it was, really, as if everything had settled back into its proper place. Francisca told her that she'd just flown in from London, that now she had a kind of art gallery or antique shop. They agreed to get together someday soon.

Puigcerdà, August 1963

VII

I wrote *The Edict of Milan* in about a month's time, taking advantage of the fact that I was alone in Puigcerdà, during one of those crises that characterized my married life with Juan Antonio. Unlike most people whose problems leave them semi-bewildered, in a kind of state of permanent confusion, I thrive, almost as if such conflicts completely reinvigorate me. Just like in Cadaqués, when I'd discovered the truth about Camila and Roberto, the faux gaucho, the same thing happened during that summer in Puigcerdà: the confirmation that J. A. was running all around chasing after a married woman seemed to spur both my natural vitality as well as my creativity. The reports from the agency—an international one, of course; the Lloyds of private investigation, so to speak—were so conclusive as to be, to a certain extent, superfluous. They provided all kinds of details, of course; and, apart from satisfying any logical curiosity, it was amusing to contrast them later with J. A.'s explanations, his stories about the vicissitudes of an outstanding emergent international holding company, his exciting catalyzing contributions to the project, his indispensable leading role in the development of the operation. Ultimately I didn't give a good goddamn either for what he'd done or what he didn't do. I preferred to play dumb and ask him about the price of hazelnuts in Selva del Camp. After all, the Ramoneda family fortune was founded on hazelnuts from Selva del Camp, however furious it made him to be reminded of it. Although J. A. had been born in Barcelona, I know for certain that he is ashamed of his roots, of his belonging to one of those seven or seventeen, or however many there happen to be, rich families from Reus who control the hazelnut market, just as enterprising as they are provincial and miserly. I've always thought this was one of the main reasons that impelled him to build me the villa in Puigcerdà—to erase his tracks, to get me away from there and to fly as far away from his roots as possible, to be connected to a place that is the antithesis of Reus. For obvious reasons, J. A. never even found out that I was a writer.

If my novelette took me barely a month to write, its publication was an entirely different story. Not that I had any doubts about it, nor was I worried about the scandal it could unleash. On the contrary: what made me unsure about whether or not to publish it, was, precisely, the fear of not provoking a specific reaction—a rather strong feeling of revulsion in one certain individual. Meaning: not people in general, not the masses—I find myself immeasurably removed from their appetite for scandal. No: a specific person, one single person.

Unfortunately, apart from any and all aesthetic critiques, the reaction I sought never materialized, and although I already knew this when I decided to publish the novel, I have to admit, by this criterion alone, *The Edict of Milan* was a failure. Even so, knowing the result, knowing beforehand the reaction of the person for whom it was intended, I finally opted to publish it. It's not for nothing that Raúl calls me Flash Gordon: thanks to my gift of being everywhere at once, of getting mixed up in every kind of mess. My decision to publish it in a bibliophile collection like Ediciones Originales was to avoid the inevitable censorship problems that would arise from any other publisher bringing it out. And I think I succeeded, because the series is edited by someone who showed themselves to possess extraordinary intuition, as well as great intelligence and exquisite sensitivity.

Besides, the select, elitist character of such an edition—why deny it—pleased me no end, more, very much more, than one of those popular editions that people read everywhere, even in the Metro. I also judged it preferable to use a pseudonym, and not precisely, needless to say, for fear of a scandal. No, not for that reason, but rather for motives similar to the ones that impelled me to opt for a collector's-style edition during a time of unrestrained consumerism, when what seems most important to people is quantity, a popular name, millions of copies sold. My choice was essentially an ethical one.

For a pseudonym, Mendoza, because Mendoza is my third surname, and Raúl's fourth. Meaning: my father, like Raúl's mother, was named Moret y Mendoza. For a writer from Barcelona who writes in Spanish, I think it sounds just right.

Claudio is nothing more than a masculine form of Claudia, my best friend from those days. Aside from our close relationship since when we were schoolgirls together, I was indebted to her because she had rescued me from the clutches of Maldonado, more than enough reason to offer her this sort of homage, this *clin d'oeil* that nobody else could spot; then she moved to London permanently, if the word permanent can be used to describe life. She was—and still is—a photographer like the Charlotte of the novel, although, in reality, she would be more like the Francisca who appears right at the very end, in the book's final paragraph. The ambiguity of such a paragraph, like that of so many others, is, of course, entirely premeditated. Let's call it a joke in the form of a trap I set for the seasoned critic so that, by gathering together some loose threads—left dangling by me with malign calculation—by analyzing some holes in the plot, one incoherency or another, they can reach the shrewd conclusion that Claudio Mendoza is both a woman and a lesbian, too. Thus any hypothetical reader of these present lines can conclude for themselves, no less shrewdly and by virtue of the same series of associations, that my name, Matilde Moret, conceals a man—something which, on the other hand, might be more accurate than one would first guess.

Another trap—except this one is so obvious that no reader would fall for it—the coincidence that the author of *The Battle of the Milvian Bridge*, the book Lucía is reading, is also named Claudio—Claudio Sáinz de la Mora—a name that reeks of pseudonym. And in this case, each and every reader, except for the more-cretinous-than-average cretin, can only conclude that Claudio Mendoza and Claudio Sáinz de la Mora are one and the same person, and that, accordingly, *The Battle of the Milvian Bridge* is a novel that only exists within the pages of *The Edict of Milan.*

On the other hand, I use various means to try to balance those deliberate loose ends and fake plot holes, so that the reader feels obliged to fully exercise their reserves of shrewdness and malice. For example, when it comes to sexual material, I employ a rather crude, sometimes frankly obscene lexicon. But men actually use those words and expressions when they talk, and given that the author is, theoretically, a man, I wrote the story using a man's language, however much, personally, it disgusted me to hear such words coming out of a woman's mouth. Better yet: I'm simply bothered by the custom itself, of using the coarse words Spaniards have, to try to feel more manly, especially when they get together. But for some time I've noticed that women have also picked up the same habit, especially the little rich girls, and this strikes me as even worse. It also happens with foreigners who learn Spanish in such environments: they become incapable of speaking it without cursing every third word; what's more, they find it to be the most natural thing. I dared suggest to Raúl and his friends—I remember it like it was yesterday, that instead of using certain crude expressions so often, a real leitmotiv of his crowd every time they start discussing their idiocies, that they might say, for example: *va prendere per il sacco*, which at least in its literal Italian, "she grabbed him by the sack," is not the least bit offensive.

I'm not claiming, of course, that *The Edict of Milan* is free of errata, as well as all sorts of involuntary mistakes, and even indisputable inaccuracies; it's like any other book, no matter how sublime its pages. But the most curious thing is that it also contains mistakes which, you might say, the devils of the subconscious--be they the author's, the proofreader's, or the typographer's --wrote themselves. Thus, for example, when Charlotte is described as "inverted" instead of "introverted"—I don't remember the exact passage right now—it just seems an example of how the typographer's work might be elevated by some higher inspiration.

There are cases, like writing Federico instead of Alejandro, where the lapse can only be mine—the proofreader has no reason to notice one name in place of another. I wrote it that way, on a whim, and the error slipped through on all the proofs and ended up in print; while writing, I wasn't imagining Alejandro, who's fictitious, but Federico, who really does exist—a truly insufferable friend of Raúl's. Even though there was yet another Federico, except he surely wasn't called Federico, the same as the Gregorio who was mentioned along with Raúl—as if they were boyfriends—wasn't really named Gregorio; Party members, with their *noms de guerre*. No, the Federico to whom I refer and whom, unfortunately, I got to know quite well, is all-too-real, and resembles, in more ways than one, the Alejandro from my novelette. And, what happens with characters is exactly what Raúl told me about the interrogations, after his arrest: you're getting questioned, and you want to save your neck, so you invent some key figure, about whom you know nothing but who's responsible for everything, who knows all the answers they're grilling you for. If you don't want the police to trap you in contradictions as you start veering off into describing that man's personality, you've got to use some real person as a model, someone who's in no way involved: his physical build, his manners, some real, coherent reference points which you can touch on again and again. And with characters, well, the same thing happens: let's take a real person as a model—their personal quirks, their manners—simply because it turns out to be more convenient than inventing them, because they're closer at hand, but when we're finished, thanks to all the extra details we've added, they've got nothing in common with the original personal except what's anecdotal. In this case, however, the name of the original person ended up slipping in.

My mistakes, in general, consist of badly written sentences, the occasional subject-verb disagreement, typing *duty* instead of *due to*, things like that. In the final draft, now printed and collated, I spotted an embarrassing Catalanism, and I almost missed correcting "there was" to read "there were," in reference to glasses or cups, I think. In short, mistakes of scant importance; as Raúl says, writing well does not in the least mean writing without mistakes. All the more true because correcting one mistake generally leads to making new ones. And there are mistakes that the proofreader doesn't spot because they actually mean something. On the other hand, the author is the person least qualified to spot them, because they tend more to read what they meant to write than what is actually written.

Needless to say, narrative mistakes are always more serious, although in *The Edict of Milan* they're not especially important either. For example, the liaison with the train conductor: in the first chapter the conductor with the Spanish accent is mentioned as they travel from Paris to Sète, while in the second chapter, which is when the liaison actually occurs, the conductor with the Spanish accent appears when they're on the way back to Paris; this seems to create duplicate versions: meaning, two variations of the same situation. This is probably due to the fact that the episode, though not its context, is partially true; the result is an internal disparity very favorable to such ambiguities. There is also a certain, sometimes involuntary, confusion, or rather, imprecision about the events surrounding Carnival, told three different times. For example, let's take the party at Beaux Arts, which is described in contradictory fashion. Did Lucía go to bed with Alejandro that night? Had they already slept together? Did they do it later? Did she do it with Jacques? Truth be told, the facts are not clear, and it would insult the reader's intelligence to blame that on Lucía's hangover.

A completely different sort of mistake is the one committed—which I commit, I mean—at least twice, at the start of the book. First, the farewell at the train station, which is told as if it happened during the daytime; in fact, Paris–Barcelona express trains depart, at the earliest, in late afternoon, and at that time of year, in early November, late afternoon is already dark as night. The other mistake appears a few lines later: after her walk, Lucía amuses herself by twirling and twirling the vase with a chrysanthemum adorning her table at l'Alouette, an ornamental detail totally inappropriate for a bar like that, where, after all, every table has to have a great big ashtray advertising Ricard, or Martini, or something like that. But these are only mistakes in terms of how well they reflect reality, not flaws in the actual writing, and from a literary point of view, they don't really matter at all. As a name, l'Alouette is inspired by l'Irondelle, a modest but very proper restaurant I used to frequent when I first lived in Paris. The bar described in my novelette originally had the same name as that restaurant. Later, with the song in mind, I changed it to l'Alouette, that song about *alouette, gentille alouette*; and it occurs to me now—and even seems quite likely—that perhaps there really is a restaurant called l'Alouette somewhere in Paris. L'Irondelle, whose owners were very thoughtful and caring, did indeed have flowers on every table.

I think these two examples suffice to show the extent to which I'm conscious of the virtues and defects of my own writing. Because the truth is that, when it came time to correct proofs, I was well aware of these two gaps in verisimilitude, the discord between fiction and reality, but I didn't mind leaving them in. And not because I thought the critics wouldn't catch them—they didn't, naturally enough—but because, honestly, they're unimportant, because lots of trains depart Austerlitz Station every morning for all sorts of destinations, and there are countless bars—not like l'Alouette, of course—with flowers on the tables. These sorts of mistakes only merit consideration when, chafing against the respectable bounds of the fantastic, they fully enter the field of semantic retardation or, more frequently, stylistic padding—when the author gets carried away with poetical mush that his own critical sense cannot recognize.

Perhaps it's just my own personal mania, but one rather silly problem relating to verbal padding was the puzzle presented me by the protagonist's name. Lucía, like Sofía, like María, etcetera, rhymes with the majority of the Spanish third-person singular imperfect verb forms, while, at the same time, its final letter, A, tends to elide with the following preposition of countless words that begin with the letter A—peculiarities both which, on more than one occasion, drove me to the very edge of distraction in my search for a different turn of phrase, for solutions that might sidestep that damned rhyme. As one small example: I recall that in the part where Lucía and Sergio Vidal drive out near Chantilly, I had to delete one phrase about the brilliant sunshine, *lucía un sol espléndido*, which, honestly, was also hard on the eyes. But with the characters, as with people, it's difficult to get used to a change of name, and the name Lucía was already too deeply rooted in the narrative material, from its earliest beginnings, for me to willingly change it. Thus I baptized my protagonist, I remember it perfectly, thinking of her as Lucía de Lammermoor, for the romantic power, of course.

Something else which no critic seems to have noticed, despite me deciding to leave it untouched, is the shift in tone that occurs after the first few pages—a meticulous and thoroughly detailed narrative tone which is then lost. The truth is I found it laborious and forced, almost clashing with my own personality, and I felt liberated when I hit upon the tone that finally ended up dominating. All in all, and considering such narrative inconsistency a defect, the opening still seemed to me well written, and I ended up respecting it.

The critics—principal addressees of the review copies made available, for the purpose of achieving maximum resonance—received my little book with gratitude and respectful consideration, as is habitual in these matters, except in cases of particular ill will, or if the critic happens to be some ambitious youngster trying to make a name for himself with a strident voice. Most of them, as is habitually true, write rather shallow reviews, limiting themselves to a rote transcription of those informative summaries—normally written by the author themself—the editors slip inside the review copies like a bulletin, allowing the critic to work quickly, and saving publishers money by generating free publicity. Despite the fact that these reviews have almost no effect whatsoever on public opinion, everybody turns out happy. Needing to justify to the magazine or newspaper the amount of money he earns per review, the not overly scrupulous critic will, at most, muddle through the job, adding any old commonplace to what they suppose the book to be about even without having read it. With a little experience, the help of the informative summary and—in the case of mass market editions—the jacket copy, along with recourse to personal manias that usually constitute their theoretical framework, it suffices to leaf through and skim the book. Thus, without saying more, the review appeared in the *TLS*, as obtuse and shortsighted as only an English critic's commentary can be. Faced with such clumsiness, and despite however odd it might sound, it was ultimately a Spanish critic, from Madrid, who offered the most refined insights, an unusually sharp critic who, from what they've told me—I've never laid eyes on him, mind you—besides having a serious professional reputation, is a perfect gentleman. His review said that, though at first appearing to be the very sort of novel in vogue from the 1950s, a fresh, oxygenating breeze—charged with eighteenth-century aromas—blows through the pages of *The Edict of Milan*. Although the image did not match my own idea of the book—such a thought had never crossed my mind—it struck me as highly favorable, and I told him as much in the short, handwritten note which, according to the most basic rules of courtesy, I felt it my obligation to send him. I'm unaware whether such acknowledgements are in style or not in the world of letters and, at heart, I don't really care; I'm used to such things and that's it. And I imagine that he must be, too. After all, the eighteenth century is the age of elegance and *esprit*.

It seems, however, that truly nobody is a prophet in their own land: the local critics, indifferent to the attention always implied by receiving a free review copy, showing a discourtesy verging on ingratitude, tended to minimize, if not outright ignore, my book. According to the most extensive of the few reviews published in Barcelona, *The Edict of Milan* was a novel completely devoid of interest, leading the critic to declare that such a long string of infidelities, of mechanical love, even turned out to be depressing. Depressing! He must have had personal reasons for writing that. Apart from the fact that, as I understand, he's a recognized, widely known communist. And that explains his lack of freedom of spirit, unlike the critic from Madrid, the man of the eighteenth-century breeze.

From the start, I must admit, I was worried that my Madrid critic's allusion to oxygenated prose did not mean the classic platinum-blond wigs of the eighteenth century. But, after rereading his review several times, I understood that felicitous phrase to simply be his metaphor for the essential feminine amorality that runs freely throughout the novel, its contempt for those stupid masculine concepts of fidelity, mutual respect, rapport, and other ideals ruthlessly beaten into us, all the more foolish as they've got nothing to do with us. A brilliant and breezy little book—concluded the review—imbued with the author's youthful nonconformity. A review, in short, full of subtle intuitions and accurate assessments. If the critic missed the essentially vengeful impulses roiling beneath the insouciance, beneath that slightly cynical lightness, that's my problem, not his, and I'm not about to blame him. Perhaps the book's secret motivations—at least on a conscious level—might only be so transparent to its author, as are thoughts only to the person thinking them. And perhaps this might be the justification of one who, needing to understand, doesn't understand or acts like they don't understand, like that person who, guessing another person's thought, from egoism, from cowardice, for whatever reason, prefers to not let on that they know. Because, for the rest of it, my novel's formal defects, I know them and recognize them better than any critic, first and foremost Raúl.

From a strictly literary point of view, *The Edict of Milan* is like an extract from an extended novel at least three times as long. It has no description and no dialogue, properly speaking, nor any real plot development; rather than a novel, according to the genre's conventional, canonical precepts, it's a sketch of a novel. Well, so what? I wonder. And what if we consider *The Edict of Milan* in light of unconventional norms, say, strictly literary ones? Dialogue has always bored me just as much as detailed descriptions—both different kinds of literary fluff, neither of which enhances the narrative in the least. And from that angle, I see no reason why I should have written differently, simply to adjust myself to some canons, especially when my rule is to not conform to any. Somehow I've got to affirm my personality, to put distance between myself and that woman who only seems to have existed to overshadow me, to plagiarize me beforehand in every way.

But, returning to the variety of reactions my little book garnered among the world of critics, I award the prize for best heehaw, and very richly deserved it is, to Richard Burro, a reviewer for the *TLS* whom I met in London—not in any intimate way, it goes without saying—who then vented with a review of *The Edict of Milan* riddled with idiocies. We were introduced during a cocktail party, and I must confess that I found him charming, while he, with the homosexual's typical hypocrisy, feigned harboring identical feelings toward me, in order to later unleash his brutal review, one hundred percent pederastic. What I've never been able to clearly figure out is if he wrote his review without honestly managing to identify me, to sustain the memory that I was Claudio Mendoza, or if, on the contrary, he had me fully present in mind and only wanted to torture me for his own pleasure, rabidly carried away by his faggoty aggression, a prisoner of that ferocious antifeminist vindication that, for whatever reasons, is a common characteristic of certain homosexuals. A dilemma, at heart, not worth the trouble to elucidate, given that, in any case, his review was the natural work of a perfect imbecile. Concluding, for example: "the form of the novel cannot be renewed without first renewing its themes." When what's clear is the exact opposite: the only thing that changes about a particular problem is the way of talking about it.

The siege was coming to an end. A fact that could now be proclaimed openly, without any fear of disappointment for sounding a premature song of victory. After the sporadic skirmishes and clashes of July, the sort that characterize the early days of a siege, the month of August, which coincided almost exactly with the siege proper, proved decisive. And now, the calm days of September when some summer seasons linger on, despite the days growing shorter and the already autumnal light, provided the setting for the final audacious blows, the final desperate sallies that precede the defeat of the besieged, and the besieger's full, complete triumph. A triumph that seemed to have been minted under the sign of Leo, a sign with whose natives I—who am an Aquarius with Pisces rising—have always managed to reach a perfect understanding, in the same way that, as a period of time, those dog days of summer dominated by the sign of Leo are usually for me the most favorable. A detail that Camila certainly knew, and which must have been on her mind before it was too late, before her reactions showed that she had correctly guessed the imminent finale. Reactions: sometimes exasperation, sometimes suffocating stress, from which Roberto could not seem to escape either. And, ultimately, fatigue, almost indifference, mutual disinterest, each of them besieged, and on top of everything, too exhausted to worry about the other one. A state usually resolved by the desire, stronger by the day, to stop once and for all, and at any price, like the suicide who simply wants their suffering to stop.

The bad thing about such cases is that the fatigue tends to be contagious, and generally ends up taking the besieging forces prisoner, too. So what eventually happens is that the siege becomes rather like one of Hercules's labors, wherein the most terrible things are the bloody events preceding or following the achievement of each task. I noticed it in Camila the same as I noticed it in him, in Roberto, our very own—though possibly weaker, more bankrupt—Martín Fierro, when the three of us happened to meet up in the same place. Who must have deceived him? I still wonder sometimes. What appeal does the Argentine believe he holds for other people? After all, being Argentine is at least as sad as being Australian.

Now then: apart from any other considerations, I know for certain, from personal experience, that a place like Cadaqués in August is most favorable for the boredom that tends to infect every siege. The boredom and fatigue end up imposing themselves on the besieger no less than on the besieged, not so much from the monotonous vicissitudes of the siege as from the stress and oppressive character of the atmosphere in which it develops. That peculiar stratum of Barcelona society that summers in Cadaqués, its habits, the behavior it adopts—that society which years before closed its doors to me and which I now keep at arm's length, just as much as it tries to seek me out. The society that now envies me in equal measure to how it sees itself rejected, like the loutish bumpkin who from his patch of earth envies the young Olympians on high. The people who have nothing but ill will and slander for anyone who, through personal qualities, good luck and defiant habits, shine with their own light very far above their vanquished lives!

I know them all, both as a group and individually, one by one, the men and the women. Yes, I know them well, smug Barcelona bourgeoisie who only shed their ogreish skins when they set foot in Cadaqués, borne by a snobbery barely disguised as mental hygiene. Just as I know their wives, too, those middle-aged ladies who were chaste spouses until they disembarked in Cadaqués, in order to become, before the first summer was over, fervent, passionate, unrestrained fornicatrices. I know almost by heart the process that, like the symptoms of an epidemic, repeats itself, case by case, and I can swear that if even a half a dozen of them—possibly for being poorer in spirit than the others—have stayed outside the circuit, that would be a lot. They arrive fully in character as exemplary summertime mothers caring for their little children while their husbands live the bachelor's life in Barcelona, resigned beforehand until the climate liberates them from their frustrations. Watching the other women, the veterans, and realizing that they can't appear scandalized, that such a reaction would be out of place, they talk about how, if not for the children, they would also surrender to the same indulgence, how their eyes have been opened, disillusioned by their husbands no less than the other wives and, by extension, by all the sexual activity, which they still can't conceive of outside of marriage. But there are the children, their shield, their armor, the last bulwark against them doing what they'd really prefer to do—the last line of defense. Because, for them, for the children, for them and not for their swine of a husband, they'd whore themselves out if necessary, they say, emphasizing the extremity so much it becomes completely clear that not only would they be willing to, but that they almost wish the need would arise for them to test themselves against such a traumatic circumstance. And I certainly know of cases that have ended that way, literally, as barely disguised prostitution; the only thing they need is an excuse. An excuse that, frequently, answers some simple need, the same as pawning some jewels or valuable possession in order to cover extra costs arising from certain infirmities when one is no longer so young. And I even know of cases that would make the most average woman's blood run cold, because I understand that those people make their favors pay *sur place*. For example, they've got a cot and a bathtub in the backroom for such services and, according to certain sources, even a kind of mini torture chamber for one of the big bosses who's got masochistic tendencies. This is exactly what they mean when they use their slang phrase *fringe benefits*.

Even when considering and accepting the value of that expressiveness young people always and instinctively imprint on their world, a world no longer my own, I have to admit that I don't understand the other Cadaqués, the young people's Cadaqués, more aesthetically visible and attractive, resounding with the routine the young people create simply by being around, their vegetative presence, the different and the same every summer. Mind you, I don't say this with any reactionary pride about how things used to be different, or how such things never happened in my day, the typical phrases that tend to become habitual as people get older. Because if I dislike saying it, it's precisely for what my words might have in common, although perhaps only apparently, with this kind of mentality—and at another, deeper level, from my fear of truly becoming an old woman, unless there's some other reason that I just keep feeling more distant from that world of young people, or that I don't see myself capable of appreciating the positive side of the changing customs their behavior brings. Because what's certainly true is that, really, some years ago, in Barcelona, in Paris, we young people then were not like the ones today. A few lines above I used the word "vegetative," and this is, precisely, the term that best captures the mentality of young people today, the concept that best matches the life they lead: vegetating. Liberties, all of them, unimaginable when I was their age; but, more than as the result of a haughty will and desire, those liberties seem to come drifting to them randomly, as if floating in that sluggish pool of apathy they find themselves immersed in. I know of more than one girl from a good family who's even sunk so low as to go around fucking sailors from the town, just like the first women tourists who show up on their own, but without any of the spirited enthusiasm of those pioneers. That's what I find impossible to comprehend, the inertia of those young people, their seeming indifference to everything which, at their age, should be an opportunity for passionate discovery. I sincerely believe that only a weak-minded fool, one of those old dotards who can't admit to being so, who thus disguises the senile depression that comes from knowing at heart that he really is, and so then displaces and projects his own sclerosis upon others, in what is really a desperate attempt to save his skin, like a broken-headed soldier trying to reenlist with a blanket wrapped around his head; yes, only such a fool, I think, can applaud without reservation—as do more than a few—the attitude toward life shown by young people today. Follies, like the nonsense about how a person starts getting old the moment they stop understanding young people, and all that. And I believe that the fault lies with those who, far from reproving this mentality, have abused the moral superiority that comes from their socially influential position, and helped to stimulate, if not create, it. Above all, it's the fault of those university professors who, prostates already removed, preach the most outlandish demagogueries in order to keep their tenured positions by any means possible.

But neither the atmosphere in Cadaqués nor the mundane life we led was the principal cause of the ennui and oppression that harried me. It was the house itself, and its inner workings, that made it unbearable for me. Because it was there, in the house, where, at even more sordid levels, the psychological tensions resulting from two clashing, antagonistic forces was better reflected, infuriating like that silent lightning flashing in the leaden sunset, a mere echo of the sweltering dog days. Emilia, evermore irredeemably false in her forced affability, in her role of a self-sacrificing servant straight from the pages of some naturalist novel, a role which she performed with a lack of conviction as obvious as a woman who's found out to be, and thus perfectly pegged as, a wicked godmother. And along with her, but separately, continuously coming and going, like the intertwining shadows of two branches swaying in the wind, Constantino. (By the way, has anyone ever better squandered such a lofty sounding name!) His malice impelled him to a steady, total boycott of household maintenance, And there were also breakdowns that I'm sure he caused, constant mishaps suffered by all the systems and fixtures in the house; he took a perverse pleasure in toying with water shutoffs, fuses, valves, drains, and other integral elements of that underground world of pipes and wiring, like some careless naughty devil fiddling with the control panel in hell. His hypocritical condolences as he announced each disaster, hat in his hand, the crafty smile irrepressibly spilling across his face, as if the fact that the boat alone had no problems was not already sufficient evidence of his betrayal—and that, no doubt, thanks to his own love of the sea, to his grotesque pretensions as a sea wolf. What made him most angry, however, was how knowledgeable and handy I was at doing thing myself around the house, my ability and my skill, my proven effectiveness when I felt like getting my hands dirty, greatly superior to his own; and, above all, that I only set my hands to the task when I felt like it, when I got the royal and very most pompous desire. Things like that overwhelmed his strength, his very capacity for dissimulation.

Now and then, naturally, they get the reprimand that's coming to them, and it comes crashing down on their heads with all the attendant fright they've earned. And that's when they take refuge in their own indignity and degradation. Like the time I decided to put an end to their constant pilfering of my caviar, *foie gras*, and *jamón de jabugo*—I've never raised any objection, that's quite clear, to them enjoying whatever they like either from the refrigerator or the pantry, except for these sorts of delicacies that their coarse, unrefined palates cannot properly appreciate, constituting, therefore, a true waste, not only economic but gastronomic, purely technical, as if we allowed them, let's say, to consume something that attracts them simply because it's expensive—such as certain English chocolatines like After Eight. And then Constantino, with his classic nefarious smile, oozing complacency thanks to how much they'd managed to irritate me, heightened by the fact that he saw it was impossible for me to prove a blatantly true accusation, I remember he said: but *señorita*, you said: even though we might like to we couldn't do it: our teeth are too weak—we were talking about a magnificent leg of *jabugo* ham—for chewing something that tough. And, in unison with Emilia, while she removed her dentures to show them to me, he opened up his dreary mouth full of holes, yellowishnesses and blacknesses of worn-down nicotine-stained nubs. A horrible thing. So much so that, to avoid showing any more revulsion, I left it at that. But they know perfectly well that one of these days I'll get annoyed to the point where I'll cut them out of my life for good, and this keeps them in line. They are people who, like in the novels by Salgari or Sabatini or Karl May that I read as a child, would respond without a word of protest if called a dog, and not so much because of their inferiority to their person who calls them that and, consequently, treats them that way, as much as for their fundamental servility, for their baseness. Dogs, sheep, reptiles, the stupidest ones, best suited to crawling and dragging themselves along. From the looks of it, as in the Moscow trials, the accused described themselves in similar terms when making their confessions.

Not even Herminia was an exception to the rule. And such confirmation did not fail to affect me, frustrated again in my hopes of rescuing, of improving the situation of girls like her, girls who were sensitive, receptive, and seemed capable of responding adequately. Because, quite to the contrary, my intuition about what was going on only served to stimulate her bad habits to the maximum, that crafty friendliness bordering on reticence, that discretion full of insinuations, her way of moving about the house, exhibiting every air of complicity and mystery. Understanding all too well that she managed to arouse in me an irritation and a disgust rivaled only by the effect of her comments, which nearly justified me firing her after she'd only been in the house a short time, and still learning the ropes, had not yet really caught on to the general climate there—what Camila and I used to call the Monday morning report; her account, while serving us breakfast, of her boyfriend's amorous exploits, oh God, what a man, he never gets enough, never gets tired, and other nauseating intimacies spoken with a sort of feigned disgust, in a clumsy and misguided attempt, probably, to get us excited. But the worst thing, what got on my nerves the most, was her mimicry. Her thing where, if you're in a bad mood, she was, too; you're in a good mood, she was as well. Even if I was not feeling well, even then! She had a headache, she felt nauseous, everything the same as me. A way of irritating me so far beyond the limits of what's tolerable that the only thing that she managed to achieve was that I really started to hate her; that was her victory.

All in all, that's what it's like having servants, from the very most maid-like housemaid to the liveried majordomo. Some because they want to supplant you and others because they see you enjoy a pleasant life, which for them is the height of perversity and they want to destroy it for you, to make you pay for it however possible. I'm aware that my language might sound insulting, excessively offensive, to certain delicate ears, but the truth is that I'm thoroughly bothered by this systematic hatred toward anything noble and beautiful in life from people whose own limitations make them incapable of appreciating it. Like it or not, they're all the same. And there are no exceptions. Because the truly sad thing is that what applies to Constantino also applies to Herminia. Their motives, at heart, are the same: for example, the fact that apart from being rich, or being a fully splendid physical specimen, and not giving a damn what anybody else thinks, when it comes to life I know how to do things better than her. Not just how to run a house—which supposes better organizational skills, meaning: greater intelligence—but also more concrete tasks, like washing and ironing delicate garments or preparing dishes of haute cuisine. In short, envy, and not without reason. The Grand Marnier crêpes I make, for example.

The only episode that broke the monotony of that August happened to me one afternoon when, now sure of my triumph and feeling almost like it were impossible for me to savor it in Cadaqués, I went out to take a drive, to let off some steam. I found my outlet in the town of Sant Pere Pescador and, more specifically, at one of those little stands that farmers set up alongside the highway to sell their produce directly. So, I parked by the stand, not because I wanted to buy any fruits or vegetables, but for the beautiful countryside where it stood, surrounded by the lush foliage that grew along the riverbanks. But perhaps an even greater coincidence was the interest that the young woman selling vegetables suddenly awoke in me, such a perfect blonde, both in her features and her figure, that nobody, anywhere else, would have believed that she was a farmer. Our encounter happened quickly, almost too fast and too easy, even for my tastes. The country fields, besides, have the problem of insects, and especially along the banks of a river, there are mosquitoes. Nevertheless, it was quite a refreshing experience.

A siege is a siege, so that the incidents, with people and cities alike, are always predictable. With people, clearly, incidents vary according to the sex, and I would say that's true with cities, too—they also have their own particular sex. Barcelona, for example, as Raúl made me see so well, is a feminine city par excellence, and it has always behaved that way every time it's been besieged, like a tight prude. This complicates everything, because, depending on the situation, and the specific circumstances, each party's attitude changes enormously. For example, if I were a city, I would be one of those cities that turns the tables, making my besiegers the besieged. And the same thing is true about my relationships with men: conquer as directly as possible; do not, as women usually do—quite wrongly, to be certain—let yourself be conquered, believing that this is the proper tactic to employ with men, as if the fight, the confrontation, could ever be considered finished. No, my tactic has always been to attack first, to beat them to it, and not release my prey until it's convenient for me to do so. A rapid erection, unplanned, dissipates in the man any trace of a lack of self-confidence, the source—perhaps for reasons of character, perhaps as a consequence of some psychic trauma, or who knows what—of an endless number of conflictive characteristics, shyness, reserve, sexual debility, etcetera, much more widespread than what women, with their habitual stupidity, suppose. The fact is that a man, seeing himself respond easily to some specific woman, ultimately prefers the confidence that woman gives him, instead of risking the disaster and humiliation that some intrigue with any other woman always implies; that's why words like "intrigue" and "adventure" have come to designate such reactions, because of the risk it supposes for those men. The woman, however, generally never realizes what's happening, believing, as she usually believes, that it's her fault—and sometimes it is—that her disasters with men are the product of her own personal ineptitude in bed, something embarrassing, something that, due to its special circumstances, and its unusual and exclusive character, she doesn't dare talk about even with her best friend. After all, these are rather complicated matters. The important thing is to think creatively, jettison the mistaken commonplaces that men and women have got stuck in their heads, and that govern their behavior with each other. In itself that is a kind of secret weapon. A weapon that, at least for me, has always provided excellent results, with both women and men alike. But women sometimes require more time, more circles.

In what concerns me, the problem is not to go too far, not get carried away by that pugnacity that burns me inside, by those impulses that cloud my reasoning and which, later, on more than one occasion, have made me correct myself, pull back. What happened to me, as it happens, as I reread the photocopies of the Camila–Roberto letters, as I realized their calculated design in using the word *bruja* to label me a witch, a bitch, a hag, and their purpose for using it: as a deliberate slap in the face. Not a slap to offend but, quite the contrary, to shake me up, to provoke a reaction. Because it was evident that she knew, by this time, that I was reading her letters; people figure these things out, and Camila knew me too well not to be aware of what I was doing. Therefore, perhaps with Roberto's tacit complicity, perhaps without it, she used those letters—I'm sure—as a means of an indirect relationship, a reflection, between the two of us, a vehicle that, by its very nature, turned me into the true addressee, or final addressee, of the letters they exchanged. And, whether she knew from the beginning, or whether it was a consequence of the recapitulatory process all long sieges offer, what there could be no doubt about was that Camila was fully aware of the indifference that, at least on my part, was invading our daily life, the most lethal of the so many illnesses liable to affect the domain of love. As a consequence, Camila had resolved to provoke me, to get me back for herself, an intention which, once perceived, obliged me, in turn, to change my tactics. That was my only reason for responding then, returning to the same epistolary device, composing a letter inscribed with the tone of a letter never meant for sending, and I left it for her peeking out of my purse for several days, long enough for Camila to thoroughly absorb its contents. A letter full of passion and enflamed desire, although, certainly, with recriminations, too, any apologies therein only premature, with cutting violence. Giving her plenty of reason to call me *bruja*.

My intention was simply to write a little novel without making any great claim for special significance, one crafted the way a jeweler crafts her materials, noble metals, precious stones. Meaning a small gem. With all the immediate impact that it produces, along with all the interest and deliberation later required for it to be appreciated. Something that, in literary terms, presupposes the concurrence of certain qualities, elements indispensable for obtaining a brilliant finished product, attractive, dripping with irony. It would also need, of course, some other detail, another one of those allusions which every author enjoys, including for their own particular satisfaction, elements borrowed from real life, I mean which, besides myself, are only spotted by the person directly affected, who might feel a shock when reading a certain paragraph, and even a stab of terror from the inevitable question: how could she have known that? Things I call confidential confidences, something like that friend of friends or cousin of cousins, whom we use to designate, through a vague twist, a very specific kind of relationship. Oh, the things you can learn in one bed about what's happening in another!

If I believe that I'm obliged to make such a declaration of motives it's only to show, aside from whether or not I've managed to express them in my novelette, how far I'm aware of what I've wanted to include. And also, as a result, what I meant to leave out. For this reason, I can allow myself to declare, quite emphatically, that I never intended, not by a long shot, to write any sort of *roman à clef,* as Raúl implicitly insinuated in the letter he sent me after reading my book. This wasn't the letter's only point of disagreement, but certainly the main one; overall, it better deserves to be called a real critical review, the most profound critique *The Edict of Milan* has received, overflowing with sharpness and shrewd judgements, and I would even dare to call it openly glowing, if one considers how little given Raúl is to expressing his enthusiasm, if one can understand how every word matters so much to him, the specific weight he grants each one. He claimed that my reworking of facts is too direct: in terms of behavior, the characters adhere to their real-life models more than the fictional world they inhabit and traverse. While this might possibly excite the curiosity of the several friends upon whom they're based, it also diminishes the interest of the reader upon whom they're not, and, overall, diminishes the novel's creative autonomy. The most interesting aspect—I transcribe from memory—resides, it seems to me, in its structure, in that revisiting, time and again, the earliest exposition, in that ongoing enrichment accomplished through new contributions, how we move closer and closer to Lucía, who is, in fact, the only character *strictu sensu*, the sun that illuminates as many planets as comprise its system—a simile, by the way, of the most successful sort. The novel—he concluded—exists in relation to Lucía and, outside of her discourse, nothing and nobody has its own life. With words perhaps more precise than my own, this was, nevertheless, the essence of Raúl's critical analysis. An analysis, needless to say, lacking in neither validity nor insight, although one would like to know up to what point an unconscious feeling of self-defense, perfectly appropriate for a writer who sees his terrain invaded, unexpectedly threatened, both personally and professionally, kept Raúl from limiting his positive appreciation, from skimping—in short—on his generosity.

What's certain, of course, to begin with, is that I'm not Lucía, and Raúl's got nothing in common with Luis, however much certain coincidental traits, to which I've already alluded, perhaps failed to flatter him. And the fact is, thankfully, that however much Raúl, stung by self-love, might have recognized in the Luis–Lucía pairing some small facet or other of his relationship with me, the fact is, thankfully, I repeat, the similarities never go beyond the bounds of the anecdotal. Because what's true—and I know that Raúl knows it—is that nobody really corresponds to anybody, that all the characters in *The Edict of Milan* are fictional creatures. Creatures, that's right, drawn with lines inspired by reality, taken from real people, from myself in the first place. As in all novels, I suppose.

Well, Javier, the Javier in my novel, has a lot in common with Juan Antonio, my ex—although not exactly his erotic aptitude, of course. But it would have been too much for Lucía to admit that Javier, in bed, was a J. A.-type disaster, and this, I believe, slightly weakened Raúl's accusation about my character cleaving closer to the real model than to the demands of fiction. Given that, when Lucía highlights Javier's amorous qualities, the reader should realize perfectly well, I hope, that for her it's purely a question of prestige in the eyes of the group. For the rest, J. A. is practically the prototypical husband in certain circles of the Barcelona bourgeoisie; there are thousands of J. A.s, thousands of assholes of varying hues and degrees, and only through them could I trace the tracks of my Javier.

Camilo is another matter entirely, however, because although—as with Raúl—the real model also exists, I don't think guys like him are typical of Lebanon or Algeria or anywhere, no matter where they happen to come from. He's completely true to life but, considering how strange he is, I imagine it makes no difference. The real guy was named Camil and he was Lebanese not Cuban. But he really did belong to the FLN and he had Algerian papers. What I don't understand, being Lebanese as he swore he was, was his color; I didn't know that Lebanon had such black-skinned people. All in all, a real mess.

From the looks of it, a short time after I lost sight of him, in the course of one of those power struggles that arise at the core of such organizations as the FLN, his faction was defeated, and since then, I've heard, he lives in exile in

Switzerland, on the run, as confident in his political action as in everything else. The Cuban whom I used for the expressions I put into the mouth of the Lebanese fellow was one of Federico's friends—also from across the street, I imagine. And, just like Camilo—the faux Algerian, the paunchy sodomite—he ended up going into exile. What I don't remember exactly is his name: one of those rather extravagant names that Latin Americans sometimes have.

Although it seems shocking, what's definitely not only true but autobiographical as well, is the stuff about the dream, that dream Lucía swears having had in which Camilo embraces her. I'm seated, and then a man whom I don't know, from behind me, first covers my eyes and then wraps his arms around me, kissing me; I never see his face, but you don't have to be a genius to know that any psychoanalyst would identify him as my father. Well, that's what I say. Even though I describe him as Camilo, the truth is it happened with the Lebanese or faux-Lebanese guy—exactly that way. Let's be clear, in any case, that Camilo and Camila, my Camila, have nothing in common. I never met Camila until after I'd written my little book. Perhaps her name made her immediately interesting to me, I won't deny it—as proof that nature certainly imitates art.

Charlotte, however, partly corresponds—only in part—to Claudia; she turns out to be a somewhat less crazy Claudia than the real one, the first person who taught me about love. She pursued photography like Charlotte, although with greater success; today she's probably the most sought-after photojournalist in the country. We met at boarding school and stayed friends afterward, the only one of my classmates from those days whose friendship has survived the years. On one occasion, I bumped into her in the airport. I was returning from Paris and she was coming in from London, just like when Lucía meets Francisca in the novel's closing scene.

And, as they agree to meet up, the two of us also met up again. And what a meeting it was! She was, specifically, the one who rescued me from the clutches of the real Francisca, from Francisca Maldonado, in Madrid—an episode that threatened to destroy my marriage, to sink it sooner rather than later; and while that would have doubtless been a fortunate outcome, at the time I had no way of knowing. Needless to say, I invented the detail about the art gallery; but the people who move in that world happen to be the same as the ones in the world of photography. Regarding Charlotte and Lucía's habit of speaking English to each other, it's something that my sister Margarita and I did all the time when we were little. I've continued making occasional use of it ever since; especially helpful when you don't want the servants to understand you.

The case with characters like Gina, Sergio Vidal, etcetera, is very similar to that of J. A. There are thousands of Ginas in Barcelona and hundreds of painters like Sergio—some, like Sergio, from very well-known families. And the same can be said of the hundreds of thousands of individuals like Jacques so frequently found these days in all the universities of the world, and who don't constitute, in any way, shape, or form, a phenomenon typical of Beaux Arts but of Art History. No, you run into such people in every university department. The types of people who study sociology and other similar subjects until the age of thirty or forty and who, once they go from being students to professors, are good for nothing but perpetuating their own madness, and inculcating it in the next generations. People who change physically—white hair, dentures, Coke bottle bifocals—but whose intellectual level and moral character stagnate—who, corroded by their frustrated sexuality and unconfessable vices, grow older but never mature, their brain cell structure no less precarious than their hormonal imbalance. Attracted more by the dissolution of ideas than by ideas themselves, they jump from Marx to Marcuse just as they once traded existentialism for Marxism, and later structuralism, and so on. Then, to hype each other up, they write in all these magazines which everybody talks about but nobody reads—no need to name names, they're all cut from the same cloth, as Ferraté says. I know for certain that even the ones who pretend to have settled down and get married use political gatherings simply as a pretext for carrying on their love affairs.

One character who is certainly based on a real person—possibly the most direct correspondence of them all—is Abelardo, the spitting image of a party member named Modesto Pírez, responsible for I don't know how many arrests in Barcelona, Raúl's among others. I took the name from another militant—I don't know why, but Abelardo sounds like a communist—who used to hang around there in those days and whom I really couldn't stand: a Valencian named Abelardo Escuder or Peñalver or maybe Aguirre, a hateful greasy groper who worked as a waiter, a mental retard far worse than average. In short: the name of one lousy scumbag standing for another perfectly rotten scumbag. But the stuff about the books wasn't exactly that way, and not only *The Battle of the Milvian Bridge*, a book which, needless to say, never existed, but others too, the ones that Abelardo swiped from Lucía's room; the only real title that I remember is *The Holy Family*, a book that has nothing to do with the church Gaudí left unfinished in Barcelona. I think that Raúl wasn't even informed about the matter, because he never said anything at all about it to me, and I, for my part, thought it best not to ask, to avoid stirring up bad memories. The most likely thing is that, not having read *The Edict of Milan*, he would not have even known about the episode, which, certainly, amused him greatly. He said something to the effect that, in arrests like his own, when there's one guy who's ready to make a full confession, these sorts of details lack importance. On the other hand, from what I remember, I never had any kind of carnal relations with that miserable swine.

Lucía's social environment, the allusions to her childhood, etcetera, are partially related to my own, and to those of so many other girls my age, from bourgeois families in decline, who attended convent schools, and things like that. But the most distinctive facts, which would absolutely give me away, are not even mentioned: my father's death in exile, my mother's subsequent behavior, selling Aiguaviva, for example—things that deeply affected me. There are also other elements, however, generally lesser ones, of secondary significance, quite close to my own experiences. Thus, when discussing high school, I evoke the image of a nun, Sister Marta, who baked *torrijas* and other sweet treats for Lucía: exactly what the nun in charge of the kitchens made for me. Marta was her real name, her given name, but this was a secret almost nobody knew, along with her family name, which was Italian—Benelli or something like that—although she was born in Barcelona—a delightful woman to whom I'm indebted for teaching me about so many different things in life. Later, it seems, she left the convent and started whoring for a man from the gutter, some kind of thug with a penchant for pimping. In the convent she'd been known as Sor María de la Santa Faz—Sister María of the Holy Face. I've always thought about how when one chooses a new name, a pseudonym, a *nom de guerre*, etcetera, they are strongly compelled, at an unconscious level, to choose one particular name over any other. Well, the same goes for choosing characters' names. Except, of course, for the fact that the author is deliberately betting against the reader's malice.

Returning to my little book, I would also like to point out that people who want to establish connections to reality will find their efforts hindered, if not distorted, by the absence in the story of two resources which, as I think I've said before, I cannot tolerate, description (I leave this to people who write the Baedekers and Cicerones, who do it so much better) as well as dialogue, that manic transcription of people's conversations—I don't know if it's more cumbersome and convoluted than stupid, or the reverse, because, on the one hand, if it's a lie that people really speak in such a way, on the other hand, four-fifths of the words transcribed are excessive, at least from a literary point of view. Because what's spoken is just a kind of blah-blah-blah which, if tiresome in real life, becomes even more unbearable in fiction, except when, like in Shakespeare, it transcends its own limitations and ceases to be mere dialogue. We find the best proof of what I'm talking about in the theater. Excepting Shakespeare and the Greeks. It's not their fault that today's actors don't know how to perform their plays.

My transpositions of places, aside from an infrequent few, are obvious, of course: Camprodon for Puigcerdà; well, so what? I've only been to Camprodon once, and it was, precisely, with the real Francisca, the virago, who introduced me to the inner circle of a group of people like her who gather there, shortly before it all ended so very badly, with everyone falling out. Needless to say, I mulled over these events as I was finishing the final draft of my little book, and I was on the verge of changing the allusions to Camprodon and to Francisca (poor Claudia!), but, ultimately, it seemed to me that such allusions only served to strengthen, though for me alone, the ironic charge that I was looking for. The Camprodon catastrophe was so severe that, to some extent, it hastened my wedding to J. A., a decision that was still very far from crystal clear and which, with so much doubt, perhaps would never have happened were it not for Francisca Maldonado. But, possessed by that particular expiatory predisposition which, following the craziest orgies and the most delirious exuberances, impels the human being to return to the peace of traditional order, I opted to get married. Thanks, Francisca: your friends haven't forgotten you. I'm sure of it.

Another no less direct consequence of my relationship with Maldonado is the aversion I've felt ever since toward the theater in general and especially theater actors. For me, being a stage actor or actress constitutes a sickness just like any other—who knows, like being homosexual or being crazy. And the way such people can be so totally insufferable, with their exhibitionist zeal, their illusions of transcendence, their cravings for a leading role, their myths, the contact with the public and all that nonsense. What I call a Star Complex, a mechanism capable of moving a third-rate actress like Maldonado the same as a Marilyn Monroe—sophistries and tall tales they all use as the thinnest sort of mask for what is, essentially, a narcissistic, egocentric outlook, about what their own life is or should be, a life that, in their fantasies, they see arrive like a sudden overwhelming avalanche, cinemas and theaters filled with audiences, swarms of reporters and photographers, great big scandals, full page headlines, enormous crowds that chase her down, accost her, and rape her, that would lynch her if they could. Megalomaniacal dreams and unconfessable satisfactions lurking beneath the cloak of such outstanding popularity. And the money.

All the same: the root of evil lies not with thespians, who use the stage to exhibit themselves, but within the theater itself, that tedious rite which a handful of lunatics stubbornly perpetuate without much more success than a Catholic Mass might have, if someone ever tried to turn the Holy Mass into a mass spectacle by adapting it to the latest tastes and fashions, to the theories all in vogue. Like today's theater, a theater that claims to fulfill a certain kind of social function by trotting out a few ragged figures as if they were guerrilla fighters, a few outlandish figures in bowler hats and shirtsleeves to provoke the public by saying things without rhyme or reason.

Core 'ngrato and the terrace of the Marítim at nine in the morning, which, despite the lovely sunshine, was completely deserted. What better setting for me to savor my triumph? The sun in the face of the blue splendor, my only witness Pere the waiter, discreet as a gargoyle, perfectly aware of how much I like to enjoy to my heart's delight such moments when the night owls' lack of vitality puts the terrace of the Marítim at my full disposal.

How can I help, each time, recalling the time that was the first time, when, returning from one of my getaways to Colera with Claudia, we decided to go as far as Cadaqués? Because that was, indeed, my first experience of Cadaqués: the vision that the town offers from the terrace of the Marítim, in the sun, drinking a few dry martinis with Claudia, listening to the *Catari, Catari* of *Core 'ngrato*: an indescribable sensation of breathing in beauty itself. As if captivated, I asked for the same song to be played over and over again—as if our sensory intoxication depended on the song not stopping. The present moment's *Core 'ngrato*—which, after a lightning trip down to Barcelona, I personally gave Pere as a gift to replace the first one—is the best recording I could find; but the tenor's voice singing the song cannot begin to compare with the voice of that woman whose name I don't know, more than a woman, perhaps she was a deity, an indescribable nymph. At that time, Pere was a young man with a black mustache, beautiful as a Greek. Then, of course, Cadaqués and the world as a whole were both much lovelier.

Although not the only one, this was, perhaps, my most enduring memory with Claudia. Because seeing each other in Barcelona wasn't enough for us we made frequent escapes to her house in Colera, a small fishing town situated some ways beyond Port de la Selva, near the French border; I remember that, at first, I simply could not pronounce the town's name correctly; I always said Cólera instead of Colera. I've gone back there since, and I think, honestly, Claudia was the best thing about that town. Later, she took a liking to London that I've never been able to explain to myself, and I got married: two equally poor decisions. How is it possible that a woman like Claudia can find anything attractive about an essentially left-handed country like England?

Love: a word that nowadays sounds almost prissy, like so many words that express vitality, strength, or passion, fallen into disuse, a weak and ephemeral loss of prestige that serves as a continuous reminder of the times it's our lot to live in. People don't say *yo amo*—I love—they say *yo quiero*—I wish, I want—whether they're talking about people or things, whether it's a woman or a motorcycle or an ice cream cone. Not me: I still call things by their right name, although the word gains nothing in clarity—or precisely for that reason, because obscurity is consubstantial with the concept. Wanting something is an entirely unequivocal expression. But what is love? What is being in love? Even now, I still don't know if I was really in love with Claudia or not. What I certainly do know is that she wasn't my first love nor, of course, the only one. But whether or not it was true love, there is always an important dose of suggestion, of autosuggestion, I mean. It's curious how even the affairs one concocts in response to their beloved, a vengeful impulse in response to, or perhaps in anticipation of a possible infidelity on their part—and of calming our own jealousy—like in those imaginary affairs, I was saying, the traits that define the pretended and episodic lover end up becoming true, acquiring a life of their own, converting the person thus configured into a kind of friend, whom we get to know more and more as time passes, similar somehow to the way an author gets to know their own characters during the process of writing their novel.

As far as literary creation is concerned, specifically, the phenomenon I'm talking about constitutes a certain kind of autonomous element, generated by fiction itself, as well as an element that we ourselves add to the fiction, something present in us before it ever enters the story. And I mean this not only in an active sense, as the author I happen to be, but also in a passive sense, as a reader, a spectator, the fact being that one operation is the complete reverse of the other. Thus, nothing more illustrative than my experience with that painting which, during my time in Paris, I stopped to contemplate each time I went to the Louvre—generally after lunch—putting my student pass to good use. A painting by Poussin titled *The Wrath of Achilles*, which hung in one of those galleries dedicated to French painting that you've got to pass through whether you like it or not, because they lead to the Grande Galérie. Or rather: the Grande Galérie can be reached by following many different routes, but I avoided them all so that I could always walk past Poussin's painting. At that time, before Malraux set things straight, nobody even dared to consider this kind of painting, that of Poussin and his age, which was dispensed with a handful of commonplaces, academic, rhetorical, devoid of any artistic interest. But for me, even recognizing that Poussin had committed the unforgivable sin of lacking the good sense to anticipate Picasso, I considered it a great painting. To begin with, the special fascination it exerted over me, its undeniable literary character, and it would have been difficult to have surpassed the anecdotal level and achieved a similar capacity for fascination without an opportune artistic solution for the dramatic moment represented: Achilles's wrath as he sees himself dispossessed of Briseis. In fact, I believe this to be the first reaction—considered in the context of Achilles's personality—of profound psychological value recorded in archaic literature. A reaction that was neither fated destiny nor divine intervention, that supposes a personality so similar to our own that no psychiatrist nowadays, with their cozy clinical ways of thinking, would hesitate to vulgarly classify as a fit of hysteria. For me, however, little inclined to revere scientific principles that do nothing but allow people to deny one another, it's the wrath of one who, once again, feels like the object of betrayal and abandonment, as if someone or something had condemned him to it beforehand. An emotion that will also lead him to turn his refusal to fight into a form of fighting, into a kind of siege, of active inaction against his fellow besiegers, against whose fortune he weighs the reparation for the affront to which he's been subjected, a replica of the original dispossession, however tragic the consequences for all involved, first of all for himself.

The impression that painting made on me, like rain upon moist earth, was so intense that, years later, when I needed to try and find a title for my little book, I went back and forth for a long time between the definitive *Edict of Milan* and its alternative, *The Wrath of Achilles*. The latter was clearly inspired by Lucía's reaction to Luis—who, as she suspects, is cheating on her with another woman in Barcelona—a spiteful reaction that would prove disastrous. *The Edict of Milan*, however, is better justified by Lucía's progress considered as a whole, from her abandoning the family environment to her rejoining society vis-à-vis the institution of marriage, passing through an intermediate, episodic phase of rupture that constitutes the nucleus of the novel, properly speaking—although with respect to the rest of her life, it barely comprises a parenthesis, her relationship with Luis reduced to a small incident stripped of greater relief. A path similar to the one followed by Emperor Constantine, son of a Christian mother, for the proclamation of Christianity as the official religion of the Roman Empire—though he personally preferred the cult worshipping the sun. More than one person, I suppose, will think I'm going too far, that no reader, without further explanations, would really be able to grasp the title's significance. But such guesses and conjectures don't interest me. I'm convinced—and that's good enough for me—that apart from the suggestions, impressions, hallucinations, that the author or publisher of a specific work—like its reader, spectator, recipient, or what have you—bring to their interpretation, that the author always has in mind, consciously or unconsciously, a secret addressee, with whom, consciously or unconsciously, each reader tends to identify. If not, what else could explain, when I first met Camila, the thrilling quiver that ran through my body at the mere sound of her name, and not, precisely, as a feminine transposition of Camil, but rather for the echoes that Camilla of *The Aeneid*, the intrepid Amazon killed in combat, still awoke in me? Because the same way an author occasionally outpaces her own time, that secret addressee, by virtue of the very objective correspondence to the subjective impulse from whence it came, persists as if reincarnated through time.

It still seems paradoxical that it was Raúl himself who spoke to me about that secret addressee, a concept which I had long intuited but which only he knew how to formulate for me in the precise words, more rigorous, possibly, than my own. All in all, the same way that I recognized in those words something inherent in my own thinking, thus, in a similar way, the true addressee of these lines will recognize themselves in them as such without the slightest doubt. Therefore, exactly, my belief that Raúl failed to give his discovery its due importance; after all, he seemed to subordinate that addressee's personality to the author's, a conclusion with which I can only disagree.

For Raúl, if I'm not mistaken, every author always writes about himself, no matter how far removed the book seems from his personal experiences, however distant his invented reality from his own daily life. And this necessarily remains valid even with formulaic fiction—detective stories, science fiction, etcetera—given that what's most interesting would be to try to clarify why he finds pursuing one genre or another so very fascinating. Because that author, our author, is to be found not only in the character or characters whom he believes to have imbued with something of himself; the author inhabits all of his characters without exception, he can be found throughout the entire narrative, even in how he organizes and structures this narrative material into a coherent world, a world that is, in fact, merely the projection of the landscape wherein his earliest childhood unfolded, of the ghosts that populated it, of those beings that came tearing out—incomprehensible, terrifying—of that individuality which at first encompassed everything: I and what is not I.

Well, because reading—I was saying—presupposes a phenomenon at once parallel and counterpoised to that of writing; through works of fiction, to a much greater degree than through testimonial or speculative texts, the reader discovers previously unimagined aspects of the world that offer him an immediate knowledge of both the world and of himself. And, above all, of how much, even without having come to define it, without even having meditated on it, we'd always been obscurely awaiting, both from the world as well as from ourselves, what both we and the world both like, or rather, both what we fear about the world and ourselves.

In this sense, Raúl distinguished two apriorisms, two attitudes which precede the act of reading, one from the reader of a newspaper or any documentary or informative text, and one from a fiction reader. In the first case, the reader is predisposed to believe in the indisputable reality of what they are reading, believing that what they are reading has really happened. Or, on the contrary—although it amounts to the same thing—that everything is false, that the information has been manipulated, that everything happened the opposite of the way it's told. Meanwhile, facing a work of fiction, despite starting from the presupposition that the reality of what's told is pure convention, the reader becomes immersed in that invented world with a far superior devotion, affected much more deeply than by the evening news, than by the solution to thc problem of who murdered Kennedy or some similar imbroglio, which, as they usually say, only awakens interest to the degree that it seems like a novel. Real or not--he maintained--believed or not, if the news can never match the deep attraction of reading fiction, it's a result of the fact that for the reader the latter experience activates that mechanism I just mentioned, a mechanism simultaneously inverse and parallel to that of writing, and which, along with writing, is activated in the author. And Raúl also maintained that the greatest exceptions—the reading of a funeral notice by the relatives, the start of World War Three—only appear to be exceptions, because, better than reading about a real event, they must be considered as events, as reality itself.

Raúl also believes that speculative works lose validity as time goes by, they suffer by comparison with new realities, and proofs newly articulated in systems no less coherent than the preceding ones. Thus, while works of fiction maintain their dark energy through the centuries, speculative works, neutralized by the very mechanisms that spurred their development, inevitably become monuments to the past, constructions we can admire the way the tourist admires—even if it's only to take a photo of what's right in front of his face—the Great Sphinx at Giza, but that have nothing to do with us. I remember his allusion to the Sphinx amused me greatly and, naturally, when Camila and I visited Egypt, the first thing we had to do was send Rául the all-important photograph. However, even and accepting all that in general terms, the exceptions to the rule are, in my opinion, more numerous than one might think. When I reread *The Edict of Milan*, for example, given my simultaneous position as author and reader and, to a certain extent, protagonist. My case is different. Completely different.

Along with his reference to the Sphinx, I find his observation about the obstinate blindness of newspaper readers to be particularly apt. During my time in Paris I had the occasion to confirm that the greater part of the guys who frequented l'Alouette--I mean l'Irondelle--stubbornly insisted, really, on an exact opposite interpretation of any news that appeared in the Spanish press. Where it said black they read white, with the peculiarity that more than once it turned out to be black. And the fact is the same thing happens when people are surveyed or interviewed about nudism: they say yes, how nice, as long as we're talking about nice bodies. As if attractive bodies were not so in any situation! As if unattractive bodies were any more shocking at a nudist resort than on the street! And dressed for a wedding? Well, it's the same with the news: an identical lack, not of perspicacity but of imagination. A disgusting body will always be a disgusting body.

Even in those days, in the most difficult moments, Raúl knew how to maintain a certain critical sensibility, it's true—a critical sense he never completely lost. But almost every one of his friends, his comrades, his *compañeros*, however you want to call them, were the sort of communists who, influenced more by *Fabiola* or *The Sign of the Cross* than by Marx, see a Nero in every wealthy man, and a Poppaea in every woman of a certain class. As far as they're concerned, they've got to look just like Frederic March when he played the Centurion Marcus Superbus, a pagan who, for love of a Christian woman, achieves a loftier view of the world and becomes a communist. A love that, needless to say, symbolizes the raising of awareness that precedes joining the party, a class of feelings, or rather, of thoughts, that I, naturally, was not the likeliest person to encourage. They saw me more like Poppaea than Fabiola, it showed on their faces. Men who seemed like characters in one of those boring novels about communists who are good people at heart, and the only thing they lack is a belief in God—sometimes not even that, with much greater frequency than what is usually believed—and priests who are simultaneously populist and traditional, both of them characters who, drawn with a clear, bold lines, finally end up coming to a mutual understanding. And, why not? I wonder. Especially if they're made for one another!

As for the rest, the group members' personal preoccupations are completely indistinguishable from those of other young people their age. Meaning: conspicuously linked to sex. And in their case, at best, rather worse, the obsession was more apparent. By this, of course, I mean all those quantitative obsessions, consubstantial, it seems, with their status as students: the number of times they're capable of doing it, how long they can last each time, the dimensions of that thing hanging down in front, etcetera. Conjectures and wagers normally experienced at the expense of the army corps of sexual reserve formed by the girls who are studying in a city other than their own, cannon fodder for the boys and, eventually, for other girls. It's easy to recognize them, given that instead of being chased, it's the girls doing the chasing, thanks to some impulse of sociological or psychological origin, or what have you, that has no greater interest. What's interesting is the phenomenon itself, the manipulation by which each one turns it to their own advantage, festooning it with revolutionary ideas and whatever's missing. Guys like Camil, with his mania for making love to women as if they were men. Luckily, the room was cold and we made love under a pile of blankets, so that, when I'd had enough, it wasn't difficult for me to make him believe that he was getting the job done down there, that he'd done it; even though the trick eventually gets discovered, it's much simpler to fake it than it first seems. In the end, men also have their tricks, and sometimes they pretend they can have sex again and again, without interruption; they don't fool me, of course, because I've always known how to distinguish when it's real from when it's not, thanks to certain telltale signs of a real orgasm that they themselves might not even be aware of.

Despite everything, I still have an excellent memory of that period of my life, the whole of it reclaimed by certain partial impressions. In words that are not mine, never better applied, that phrase: the man who sits before you and listens to you so closely, absorbed, seems to me just like a god, speak to him with sweetness and laugh with love. Who knows if, had everything had turned out differently, what is today a self-imposed attitude would not be, perhaps, pure playful pleasure.

It's still curious that, if something saddens me nowadays, it's something circumstantial. Cases like Nuria's. Because Nuria is a girl of many qualities, and if she ever had any real misfortune, it was meeting Raúl, giving her whole heart to him; under such conditions, no matter how much someone later tries to find a way out, it's no use. It's not possible to organize one's life around another person, as she has done, without becoming more and more marginalized, empty, reduced, and eclipsed. And all the more because, as usually happens in such cases, if he ever did love her, he doesn't love her anymore. Moreover: she annoys him, she smothers him, he's sick—and this is normal—of having a person waiting on him, keeping an eye on him all the time, spinning round him like some kind of satellite. I'm convinced, however, that, for Raúl, this highly conflictive relationship, equally capable of generating energy as well as consuming it, has been a positive sign, a stimulating experience, creative. Not a relationship in which each partner benefits from something, I mean. On the contrary: a relationship in which one partner grows and gains to the same degree that the other one loses and deteriorates. Thus Nuria, no longer only morally debilitated but now also physically, has lately become a fearful and helpless alcoholic—a woman who could have been perfectly happy with a different sort of man. But the poor thing tried to fly too high. She wasn't the type of woman capable of winning and keeping a man like Raúl, and that's that. Whatever Raúl and I might have in common, she rubs both of us the wrong way. And, when I say "in common," I mean what's equivalent as well as what's complementary. While Nuria, at best, barely counts as supplementary.

But I only realize these things now, so many years later. Just like my slender novel, *The Edict of Milan*. Because only now do I feel truly capable of judging its faults as well as its more skillful, successful parts, mistakes that I would not commit now—nor which I will repeat—and successes that I would only amplify. Although at times I can't stop thinking that, if my writing fails to achieve the elevated tones that it should, perhaps it's because my words have already been stolen from me by that person whose sole aim in life seems to be to silence my voice.

VIII

Mauvaise milk, to put it mildly. Sour grapes. That's all, as far as my memory goes, that the figure of my father seems to awaken in people. That's also, as a logical counterpoint, the kind of treatment those people, any people, can expect from me.

In family circles, with the classic language of these environs, they talked about his fondness for chasing skirts—using that very phrase, in slightly hushed voices, of course, as if little girls are normally hard of hearing, as well as mentally retarded. And so they considered it finished: drawing a heavy veil, given the scabrousness of the case. Only later and in other circles have I learned that he was actually a man with a happy disposition, enormous vitality and, of course, a well-known womanizer: a temperament and tastes that I, without a doubt, fully share. Other outstanding character traits were his intellectual brilliance and his tremendous capacity for work, in both his professional career as well as his later political pursuits.

I was, it seems, his favorite, what families call the queen of the house. I say *seems* because it's what I've been told, not because I remember it. More than memories, what I remember of my father are, possibly, memories of memories. Thus, the image of a corpulent man who seemed very old, and who cackled with laughter while I rode bouncing on his knees—the mix, surely, of things they've told me superimposed upon photographic images. That explains, precisely, why I still see him as an elderly man, when his age, at that time, was only a little over forty; it's the impression that any old photo makes on a little girl, the different fashions—however brief the intervening time—the shape of the eyeglasses, the cut of the mustache, the clothing.

Truth be told, my very first memories are rather anodyne recollections of school in England. At that time, Papa was still with us and yet I don't have even the smallest well-defined memory of him. Later came the decision for us to return to Spain with Mama, for fear of the German Blitz, and also to look after our property, at Aiguaviva.

I remember perfectly the sinister trip back to Spain through Portugal: the Barcelona of those times, the nuns's convent school, my impossible reinsertion into that so very oppressive world. I learned about Papa's death months after the fact; the way they told us about it made it sound like the lawful application of capital punishment, almost like something that the convict, Papa, had richly deserved. After all, I suppose, for the society we lived in, that was the least that a Red separatist like him deserved, and his bourgeois origins further condemning him. What I've never been able to learn is whether or not he was a Freemason, too. With Mama you couldn't even talk about such things.

My mother's complete withdrawal as soon as we met in Barcelona was, apart from cowardice, an error whose consequences we, her children, are still paying for today. I think I've already explained that all it took was for her to put some distance between herself and Papa, and to breathe the rarified air that existed here in those days in order to, seemingly at random, let herself slip back into her own family circle, brothers and sisters and brothers-in-law and sisters-in-law all in open competition, you might say, in order to establish who was the biggest old fogey of them all, their common attachment to traditional values, developed—as usually happens—in direct proportion to the decline of the family patrimony, as if a defect like that might be the root cause of the latter. For them, for example, Papa's exile and subsequent death, as well as enduring the death, shortly after its birth, of his firstborn child, who would have been my older brother, were nothing more than the natural punishment for his pride, a sin that had to be purged, a crime for which our whole family had to pay. Thus our expiatory internment in religious schools, places which, given the circumstances, and the sanctimonious and penitential atmosphere that reigned in the house, felt almost like a liberation. The only thing, I imagine, that did not square with our uncles' way of thinking was the fact that the sinner, the unspeakable reprobate, had left us a fortune far larger than all their money put together. Also the curious fact that, on my father's side of the family, with Aunt Eulalia and Aunt Margarita dead, the remaining Morets, Uncle Raimón and his offspring, were also, unlike ourselves, completely and utterly destitute.

Although the consequences of my mother's financial management—a task for which she was unprepared—are, as far as I know, the least of it, when compared to the damage at other levels, due to her attitude toward us, they should be considered nothing less than catastrophic. The fact is, in the business world, such a fearful attitude turned her into her own perpetual victim, exactly the same as that woman—she—fallen on hard times who, piece by piece, sells off the coin collection she inherited from some grandfather—Grandpa Moret—always with the bad luck that the specific coin she sells, looks, exactly, like others worth millions, belongs to a series lacking any numismatic interest, a question of details, its serial number begins with one specific letter instead of another, it was minted in one city instead of another, in one particular year instead of another, which is exactly the important detail, a string of bad luck that she can't even believe, while he, the commercial coin dealer, doesn't much care whether she believes it or not—she can check his astonishing arsenal of coin catalogs if she likes!—knowing as he does that she, Mama, will keep on selling him coins, from the fear of going to another dealer no more honest and perhaps, indeed, less discreet, and because she'll sell them to him all the faster as her need increases, she'll collect so much less with each sale, and her very modest and ashamed awareness of finding herself needing to sell the coins will prevent her from protesting or raising objections, or let a woman like herself get tangled up in shrill haggling, she becomes the perfect prisoner of the numismatist. I was no more than seventeen years old when she asked me to accompany her to one of these transactions, one of the most sultry and embarrassing experiences—the numismatist's eyes!—of my life: how did she not see that for him I was just like one more coin to include in the lot? That, after a life of taking things at face value, like a fool who still believes in fairy tales, in the myth—from family circles—about the Moret fortune, the closest thing imaginable to one of those legends about hidden treasures. Because, like one of those pesky bores who insist on telling us all about the not only special but unique qualities of their neighborhood, the neighborhood where they were born, the neighborhood where they live, be it a neighborhood in Paris or Madrid, in Barcelona or New York, concluding—given the purely courteous attention we lend him—by claiming that these qualities, if one has not experienced them, are impossible to understand, and so, too, with the same ill-tempered final renunciation, that whole clutch of ruinous relatives when they hold forth about the family's past splendors.

That happened on the Moret side, since the family's decline on the mother's side preceded, by at least a generation, the decline on the father's side, even with its Integrism and everything, or perhaps, who knows, as a result of it. Apart from aunts and uncles and cousins—whose names I prefer to forget, like someone with a memory lapse—my memories, like still pictures, reach even my grandfather, the only one of my grandparents whom I've ever known. The only figure, also, for whom, within his fundamental irrelevance, I guard a certain affection, or rather, for whom, at least, I harbor no animosity, owing, surely, to his always discreet and affable attitude, perhaps according to his temperament, perhaps as a result of his arteriosclerosis. I still seem to see him, on the occasion of some family celebration, puttering about among those ogres like one of those nineteenth-century doctors who appear in the movies, looking just like one of those half-crazed pederasts.

And sending us to the convent school wasn't my mother's greatest mistake either, given that, as I believe I've mentioned, my experience as a boarding student was almost a relief. No: sending us to boarding school was not her greatest mistake, but the motive that induced her to put us in boarding school, the impulse that carried her, when we weren't there, to maintain the attitude she maintained with us: an attitude of guilt, of caring atonement, of a penitent leading a procession of other penitents. And the climate that reigned in the house, in perfect consonance with such an attitude, never gave us a chance to play with boys and girls our own age, to have normal relations with them, considering, no doubt, that in the eyes of those kids' families we must have seemed little less than blighted. She never managed to understand, it seems, that we were only considered blighted in the exact degree to which she treated us as blighted in the first place, in making us live like oddballs.

That's why I preferred the school, where even the uniform made us equal to my classmates. And that's why I remember it almost with nostalgia, because, even having to feign religious sentiments—nonexistent—I eventually felt at home there, to the extent that when I wrote about Lucía's life at high school in *The Edict of Milan*, it felt honest and authentic. Save what concerns my sister Margarita. Despite Margarita being younger than me, unlike Lucía's older sister, a close examination reveals that she managed to arrange things to overshadow me, to step on my toes as often as possible.

The fact that Margarita has envied me her whole life, that she continues to be jealous of me, is something I'll never understand. Because, honestly, she's got a certain ability, a special grace to win people over to her side, which I've never had. And, on the other hand, she's always achieved what she's aimed for: a very rich and very dim-witted husband, whom she's cheated on since the start; several children who are so different from one another it's difficult to believe they have the same father; and such a string of important lovers, or better yet, prestigious ones, that neither provoking a marital crisis nor getting a separation from her poor stupid husband could have given her greater freedom. Things which, if they're not enough for me, are more than sufficient to fill up a life like hers, to occupy her time while her streak lasts, to check off her goals one by one, to which she applies herself with her characteristic devotion and perseverance. She desired a certain social status and there's no doubt that she's achieved it in full; why such a life would never satisfy me is another question entirely. I'll admit that I've never possessed her gift for people, her easy way of getting along with others, for making it all seem real. Nor any desire to, of course. Regarding her skill in this sense, meaning, her ability to keep up appearances, Raúl himself has even inherited it, and that says it all. Inconceivable? From my point of view, of course it is, especially when it comes to Raúl. To have to listen to him praise Margarita's sense of humor! Margarita's sense of humor!

As I understand it, Mama and Papa reached a sort of agreement about their children's names: he would choose the girls' names, and she would choose the boys'. So, she picked Joaquín for the oldest boy—from San Joaquín, father of the Virgin—and Ignacio for the youngest one, for obvious Jesuitical devotions, because there are also Jesuits in England. And Papa chose our names in honor of his two favorite literary heroines: mine for Matilde from *The Red and the Black*, and Margarita, not for Aunt Margarita, but from Faust's *Margarita*. Certainly, while Stendhal strikes me as a superb writer, I've never understood Papa's enthusiasm for such a profoundly unpleasant creature as Goethe. With all of these people, there's a key missing link, a frustrated first son who might have well deserved to be named Ramón—from San Ramón Nonato—if not having died before reaching the baptismal font, the same as so many firstborn children in those days.

As for brothers, Ignacio always seemed to me, I don't know, sort of stupid, although considering that we only saw each other during vacations and that, at a young age, a difference of four years is an enormous gap, I might be mistaken. In fact, despite having married an idiot, it seems that in his social circle—the air-conditioned one—everything nice goes all to hell. Perhaps his demeanor, somewhat dull and listless, comes from having been born in England.

Joaquín's case, as it happens, is completely different, starting with its very extravagance, diametrically opposed to Ignacio's anodyne presence. And the fact is that Joaquín does indeed belong to that class of people whose raison d'être only seems to reside within their strangeness, like one of those small countries that survives thanks to the economic contribution of philatelists all over the world who purchase their continuously issued series of postage stamps that collectors go mad about. The fact is that, despite his extravagances, or perhaps because of them, Joaquín is lovely, a truly delightful person. He touches my heart, I can't help it, seeing him there, making the rounds in Cadaqués, on the beach, at the parties, carrying on with that wild vivacity of a young man who doesn't seem to notice that he's not so young anymore, no longer really able to wear, thanks to his cetacean waistline, showy shirts and tight jeans, his hair tamed by too many years of careful combing to now be worn in the fashionable shaggy rebellious mane.

But, at the same time, his sense of reality is almost pathetic, his awareness of being indissolubly bound to some poor priss, problems he tries to resolve by inventing other options, alternatives. Thus, his amorous conquests, his splendid seductions, that he himself ends up believing in despite their being pure fantasy. Or his professional triumphs in the field of advertising, a kind of publicity that almost borders on a new approach to art, an art which is already the art of the future, the art that he's already making today. And his famous friendships—actresses and singers, politicians, artists, and writers—people who have doubtless been introduced to him because of his work, or who, if not introduced, he's had occasion to see more or less close up, and whom he considers close friends. And his political activity, his decisive interventions that have more than once caused a favorable turnabout in the fight against Francoism, his talent for organizing placing him in the vanguard of the struggle. But the most distressing thing about him, the truly pathetic thing, is seeing him realize that none of those things will ever interest or surprise anybody, that people see him coming, and they treat him like that picturesque creature who's present at every gathering, whom you only have to wind up a bit for him to deliver his same old spiel. He notices it every time—it's not sensitivity he lacks—and every time, in the heat of the moment, he goes right back to it, answering the call with his stories that nobody present takes seriously, perhaps because the girls he's talking to have other things on their mind, things that worry girls today, maybe because the stories themselves are too stale by now, maybe because nothing he does can dim his own aura, now fixed and immoveable, that of a wildly imaginative man who only needs to start talking to fully unleash his megalomania. I swear, there's nothing I wouldn't do in those moments to cure his helplessness.

Because what's true is that Joaquín, for all his extravagances, is one of those odd ducks—not to say the only one I know—whom you can also call a good person, without trying to mean by that that he's poor in spirit. Joaquín is, and has always been, one of those communists from la Ciudad Universitaria who basically get involved in a relationship in order to try to resolve some personal problem—personal, I'd like to emphasize, and not specifically sexual, because the current mania for seeing sex at the bottom of everything strikes as me rather exaggerated—before revolutionizing the world.

His phase of flirtation with communism was triggered by my relationship with Raúl and the messes Raúl got mixed up in. Joaquín has always professed an extraordinary admiration for Raúl, almost an obsession, despite only having known him superficially. I just joined the party, I remember him telling me, smiling, his eyes alight with implications. And he explained that he'd made the decision with three or four friends, after one of them suggested it. They'd been talking for some time about becoming socialists, and Joaquín's friend cum instigator proposed they join the Partido Socialista Unificado de Cataluña, which they all agreed to do. It seems, the instigator then told them, that PSUC is, in fact, the name of the communist party in Catalonia. But I didn't care, said Joaquín, and the three of us joined up. And he smiled again that frivolous or indifferent smile which was nothing but a second-level pose meant to disguise—and as a consequence to increase—the effect of the first-level pose, the conventional attitude of revolutionary firmness and fervor usually lacking in such situations. One more proof, at heart, of his emotional sensitivity. All the more so because, while his enthusiasm lasted, he gave several really outstanding political performances, quite risky; not everything he says is a fantasy. Knowing him well, that's not at all strange, because, deep down inside, Joaquín has a lot in common with that familiar figure from early Soviet films, the self-abnegating hero, tireless, impatient, and choleric, too, an incarnation of the sovereign people's sacred and righteous anger. The only possible difference in Joaquín's case are the deeper motives, although it wouldn't hurt to know more about what lurks behind the facade of our Soviet hero.

Many things have happened since those days, and I don't think that Joaquín has ever returned to his bad old ways, especially because, without him knowing it, he joined the party at the very same moment when Raúl began to part ways with that particular method of fighting. I'm glad of that, needless to say, given that clandestine activity involves many risks, and I've always felt somewhat obliged to look after him. In the end, since he was born he has had to cope with the image of his dead older brother, the first born, our Ramón Nonato, an unfavorable comparison for Raúl, implicit in our parents' mood, and not, for being unspoken, any less permanent or evident, which ended up turning him into the bad boy of the family. They'd made him the victim of a discrimination and he overcame it as best he could. Something similar—although of rather distinct circumstances—to what happened to me with Margarita, my mother's favorite—perhaps simply because I had been my father's—which only fanned the flames of her unjust contempt for me throughout my early years.

Like so many other experiences of my childhood, this one left a scar, there's no doubt about it. Like the atmosphere of economic decline that pervades a house, in sharp contrast to the growing prosperity that infuses the houses of other children and, above all, clashing with the family myth itself, the magnification of the Moret glory and fortune, something mentioned whenever possible but never glimpsed, owing, perhaps, to that custom of talking in the present tense about what should be mentioned in the past tense. And there are few things as disconcerting to a child as that disparity between what he hears and what he sees. There's a good reason why none of my brothers, except Ignacio—careful with every penny, the flip side of the coin—has been known for his aptitude in economic matters. We four siblings, each in our own way, have distinguished ourselves through our reckless handling of money, rather like the way my mother handled the Moret patrimony, a management rife with errors, of humiliating cost cutting measures and abysmal business deals, along with generous, irrecoverable loans to less fortunate relatives, donations, and charitable works she was always willing to perform, as a kind of recompense, no doubt, for her uncomfortable social status as the widow of a Red. Certainly this is one thing that has always puzzled me about the fortune Papa left us: the fact that he increased his wealth so much simply by defending workers.

Of all the mistakes resulting from Mama's financial management, none was so painful, so irreparable for me, for the four of us siblings, as selling Aiguaviva, the Moret family's paternal homestead, *la casa pairal*, the house where we spent our first summers after the war was over, the very picture of a lost paradise. The memory I still have of the enormous house and its outbuildings, the luxuriant garden, the radiant landscape surrounding it, constitutes my only good memory of those years. But my mother, by conniving with a judge, obtained authorization to sell it and, the next summer, we found that we no longer had Aiguaviva: the house and lands had been purchased by an old rural landlord from the area—probably for a song, the same kind of bad deal she got selling those old coins. From then on, and before starting to go to Puigcerdá, we summered in a town near our property, the worst spot, for being so close, that my mother could have chosen, sunk in the atmosphere of the snootiest sort of shabby summer colony, people of really hateful affability. The town is called Breda, like the city in *Las Lanzas*, a coincidence which I still find completely curious.

The ruins of the Moret family, the shambles of their fortune and glory: that is the true scene of my childhood. Of my mother's side, better to say nothing at all. But even the pride which the Morets feel for their own lineage is something that escapes my comprehension, unless I'm mistaken and it turns out that having money must be understood as some personal quality or grace. Because, alongside all that money which the Morets once had and now don't have, I don't see any special merit either in the fact that some great-grandfather managed to become a judge or something like that in the national court in Havana. No: apart from my father, the reprobate, the Red separatist and possible Freemason, I don't see any reason at all to feel proud of my ancestors.

The irony, beyond hackneyed, of the "I still believe in," constitutes one of J. A.'s leitmotivs, equally inexact and lacking in humor. Idiocies from a hazelnut trader with cosmopolitan pretensions, dominate that slightly cynical humor of someone who's seen a lot of the world. Stock phrases, commonplaces which people repeat and repeat everywhere with all the originality of a broken record, sad symptom of the fact that the world is really shrinking all around us. Like the theory that mathematics is a gymnasium for the mind and other such nonsense, also perfectly appropriate for someone like J. A., for anyone for whom everything is reducible to numbers. I, however, have always felt a profound aversion to mathematics, for all that silliness they teach about problems that don't exist, abstractions, like the concept of infinity minus infinity, whose semantic significance I'd really like someone to try to explain to me sometime. To my way of seeing, mathematics are at most an intellectual trapeze act—no more interesting than debating whether or not Christ was, in the end, a pederast like Socrates, and just as much of a sophist as him. If I now wonder what made it possible for my more or less married life with J. A. to last for years, I can find only a single word to justify it, nothing more than a name: Claudia.

I suppose that the intensity of my relationship with her also had a decisive weight when it came time to determine once and for all the title of the novelette I had written: *The Edict of Milan*. A title that, for anyone with the most basic ideas of history, bears the implication of returning to the fold, or rather, entering the fold out of pure and simple convenience. Because Constantine—the emperor, not my wretched sailor—similar to Lucía, to the decision she makes to get married, enters the fold of Christian sheep, for reasons of a political if not demagogic nature, given that, very far above petty moral miseries, he privately continued to dedicate his life to the cult of the sun. It seems that his mother, Helena, was the one you might call a real bitch, the one responsible for his supposed conversion. And the decisive factor lay in a long meeting which Constantine had with the Spanish bishop Osio, on the eve of the Battle of the Milvian Bridge. It seems that during their meeting they weighed the pros and cons of such a decision, and that Osio, his eloquence stimulated by the marks of the tortures he'd suffered in the course of some previous persecution, ended up getting his way. That whole story is very well explained in a sort of book of lectures called *Glorias Imperiales*, which I still have from my days in school, owing, probably, to the fascination that the figure of the Emperor Constantine has always exercised over my imagination, along with the fact of him having been the creator of the wondrous city of Constantinople. If some day these lines ever have a reader—one is enough for me—they will understand perfectly, I hope, what all this means for me.

Marriage was, without a doubt, an important institution. Each family was a mini state, with its own internal politics, its own economy, its own external relations; and the key to everything, the cornerstone of each of those small edifices, was marriage. I wouldn't know whether as a cause or as an effect, nor do I believe it's worth the trouble to try to clarify it, but the fact is that each new generation, manipulated by its ancestors toward a certain matrimonial politics, will also end up manipulating its own progeny, according to the supreme interests of the family. By consolidating the family patrimony, increasing—through nuptial ties—with shared or complementary inheritances, or, when applicable, shore it up, rescue it from ruin through the classic marriage of financial convenience, in which one side gives the prestige and the other the money, weddings have been for families what armies have been for empires—the same when it comes to their periods of expansion and withdrawal, in their cyclical trajectories of growth, prosperity, and decline. A comparison so suitable that the inverse proposition would be equally valid: consider an empire's phases of life as the image and likeness of a family's phases of greatness and decadence.

The family did everything for the children's sake, and the children did it all for the family's sake, and so on and so forth. But nowadays, between the fact that the laws have changed, that the custom of the dowry has been lost, that young people like to laugh at the world, and that taxes hit harder every year, the institution now makes much less sense. There was a time when it did make sense, when it was a real institution, not in name only; when the parents married a seven-year-old girl to some forty-year-old man, or the other way around. For example, if I chose to get married, it was only to escape my family environment, to find greater independence. Nothing terribly serious in the larger scheme of things. But the fact is, nowadays—and not that many years have passed—I would never decide to get married, not even if I were drunk. Because, if on the one hand, I'd no longer need some sort of subterfuge to do whatever the hell I really and truly felt like doing, on the other, from a more traditional perspective—the economic one—the monthly alimony I receive from J. A. cannot cover even a simple month of the semi-cohabitation we maintained, not even our trip to Holland, a country that predated the invention of plastic with its perfectly spotless tulips, practically capable of being washed and dried.

It was on one of those business trips, the last one we took together—I imagined that Holland would be an enjoyable country to visit—meaning: our last days as a married couple. And I'd have to see if The Hague, as a city, would be the drop that overflowed the cup, or if, more likely, J. A.'s aberrant clumsiness was the reason for my aversion to The Hague and, by extension, to Holland as a whole. Whatever the reason, my allergy to Holland turned out to be even worse than the allergic reaction I suffer from left-handed England, a country that if it ever adapts to the rest of the world, will no doubt do so as slow as molasses—first, minting new currency, then adopting the decimal system used everywhere else, then switching over to driving on the right side of the road, etcetera—all to keep people's brains from short-circuiting, I suppose, which is certainly what would happen if they suddenly changed everything all at once.

It must be said, however, that more surprising than the English themselves are those socialist maniacs, who so abound in Barcelona, the euphoria that possesses them after a package weekend in London, all borne in hand by some travel agency, a material euphoria found in the palpable benefits of the system—clothes, cashmere sweaters, custom tailored suits—without it even being worth the trouble to explain to them that the very same stupid socialist system has turned England into the world's most uncomfortable country. A country that with its defeated attitude, its unpredictable reactions, its rudeness, managed to completely erase my undeniably beautiful memory, despite the dramatic circumstances, of the first years I spent there, with Papa.

My aunt, boys and girls, my aunt doesn't leave me in peace neither night nor day, ran the song's lyrics, if I remember correctly. And it continued: *I like to step out on the balcony and sing a song and eat some melon*. And the refrain was: *el tirururuí, rurí, rurí, el tirururuí* (bis). Deformities very much of the forties that, nevertheless, expressed in their own way, through a kind of reductio ad absurdum, the unsatisfied anxieties of liberty. That guiding *tiruriru* marking the time, like a clown's mimicry, some verses that only seemed, at first glance, to be nonsensical, the bit about stepping out on the balcony, etcetera.

Family life, the convent school, the whole city of Barcelona in those days, everything and everyone, in the end, like victims of the same injury, of the same dichotomy, that, in a sick brain, traumatized by the war, in frank (or Franco) regressive process, can lead one to understand whatever they want in any situation, to find hidden meanings in the dullest expressions, in the most infantile rhymes. The many, plentiful things that can be attributed to that *tiruriru*, to that aunt who cannot, no way, no how, leave us in peace. Moreover: the possibility of humming it while walking down the street, wherever you feel like it, surrounded by complicit ears, not to mention exceptional occasions, the opportunity, for example, of entering some amateur competition, of singing it in public, of communicating with that audience, garnering uproarious applause rising in an exhilarating echo. That species of ex-militant, for example, with his blue boiler suit and his big curling mustache, the leftover fruit of another era, the one I saw singing these very same songs in a café concert on the Avenida Paralelo—it was one of my first nights out free and on my own—just as if you found yourself on the front lines, celebrating some victory, and not having become a physical and moral wreck fallen to the grimmest depths of homosexuality, to the most depraved kind of life in the slums, the very image of schizophrenia triumphant. But how to resist being swept along by the current of life in those days? How to keep ourselves from thinking too much like one of those dimwits? I remember as if it were yesterday when our mother announced to us, with her characteristic guilty resignation, Papa's death in London, killed by a bomb. And that when, with no need for an official ban, the word "Papa" had become an obvious taboo, a name better left unmentioned around the family, while I, all by myself, had reached the conclusion that Papa was already dead when we left England. If not, then why did we return to Spain while he stayed behind? In my forgetfulness, I'm convinced, in those lacunae that open up in my memory about my early childhood in England, voids that inevitably center around the figure of my father, outlines that blur and vanish as they near him, lies the explanation not only of the little girl that I was but even of the woman I am now, including all my experiences in between. The surest proof is a dream I had as a schoolgirl and which I, nevertheless, remember much more clearly than any real event from that time. In the dream I find myself somewhere deep inside a long stable, and I crawl and crawl on all fours like a cat under the bellies of enormous horses, between their hooves, like going through a tunnel. I'd also swear that in later dreams, recent ones, the row of horses—all the same, pale yellow riding horses—keeps resurfacing like a touchstone.

But let's take it step by step, let's penetrate to the very depths of what is now forgotten, right down to that tender little girl who is happily kneading her mother's breasts. In essence, a little girl who, like all girls and boys, feels linked to her mother by some affectionate ties not very different from those that connect her to any other possession, to a velveteen teddy bear, a pacifier, any object that makes up her surrounding world. And I have here, suddenly, one such object, the most capricious and mischievous when it comes to discipline, that object called Papa who, defying all rules, disappears and reappears, as he wishes, not as we do, and who, thanks entirely to such a slack and deviant attitude, is particularly dear and esteemed, and who disappears forever. It's not a question of him reappearing whenever he feels like it; it's the fact that he will never return. Just when her relationship with her mother has achieved a sort of functional and irksome routine, broken only when Papa appears, Papa will now reappear no more. Also, her language changes, her house, her country, into a country shaped like a nuns' convent school. Only now it's she, the little girl, who refuses to change, the one who, confronted with the absence of the affectionate stimuli that once moved her, now adopts an attitude of prudent passivity. Her sensation is that of having been abandoned, betrayed, forgotten, the victim of an indescribable aggression. Why? By whom? She doesn't remember. The only thing she knows is that she continues to be herself, that what has changed is the world around her, that the surrounding world is now hostile to her.

As years go by, as the little girl becomes hardened and recovers her lost self-confidence, her initial defensive attitude—not adapting to new circumstances, not folding, not accepting the changes life imposes upon her—will transform, in equal measure, into an active response, into a counterattack: paying back the coin with which she's been paid. Above all, from the moment when, now an adolescent, events and dates begin to line up in her mind, to become coherent. The return from England, almost like a flight. From whom? The nuns' convent school, almost like a jail. Why? The behavior of her mother and the rest of the family, how she lowers her voice when she mentions Papa, with that air that adults adopt when talking about things not meant for children's ears. Why? The prevailing climate of guilt. Why? The sale of Aiguaviva. Why? Questions and answers that get interwoven and form, more than a story bereft of concrete facts, an interpretation, a suspicion, an intuition: that the person betrayed, abandoned, forgotten, was, first of all, her father. An intuition that is also an identification, given that she, like her father, has been a victim of the same family environment, of the same moral prejudices, of the same surrounding world, as cautious and hypocritical as a convent school. An identification now become impersonation, to the same degree that the primitive attitude of personally identifying with the harm inflicted on him becomes an unformulated one, an unconscious tendency to avenge the pain she remembers. Vengeance against whom? Her mother, to start with, the one primarily responsible, her family, her surrounding world, the whole world. Had Papa been deplored and condemned for his conduct, a conduct which, ultimately, perhaps illogically, receives more attention than his death? She only has to follow his steps. Was he an irreverent freethinker? Irreverence will be her motto. Was he a satyr? Fine: then she will be a satyr, too.

In other words—the ones of daily life—a tendency, since she was a little girl, to treat her girlfriends the way a boy treats other boys, without the jealousy and fussy attitudes that characterize girls' relationships, a childish imitation of the adult behavior they have observed all around them, those mommies no less chatty, peevish, and tattling than their daughters: frank and generous behavior, augmented by bright-eyed intelligence, lightning fast reflexes and a bold imagination, that will soon help her win, if not the affection then certainly the respect and admiration of both her classmates and the nuns. Smooth, steady physical development, without those miserable rough patches children usually stumble through during puberty: an agile and harmonious mien, with a suggestive and attractive personality that outshines any uniform. Nothing about her, therefore, that might be confused with what people call a tomboy, that quirk of nature marked by clumsy gestures, a scruffy exterior, and coarse, more than properly masculine, features. Nor does she in the least resemble the stereotypical naughty girl, as unsurpassable as her time at school, that sort of limbo which memory transforms from gray clouds to a golden glow. Later, as sexual activity enters the picture, acquiring a tendency, again, to act like a boy when dealing with boys, well demonstrated by the first time I lived in Paris, the most intense period of my life from an erotic point of view. A time about which, even now, from a more mature perspective, I see nothing reproachable; if I regret anything it is, hands down, not starting younger. Not sleeping with more men, not racking up more disasters, not realizing sooner that women are my thing. Just as they were for my father. Because, even if I were a man, I'd still be a womanizer.

Because these are things, I believe, which depend just as much on a person's way of thinking as on their sex. For example, there's no doubt that men and women are driven in diametrically opposed ways, not only in heterosexual relationships but in homosexual ones, too. Men, generally, go straight for the physical, the body—moreover, not just the body, but specific parts of the body. The fact of how ready, willing, and able homosexuals are to go off with the first man who flashes him something in the pissoir, or to go indiscriminately groping some fellow's package in the cinema, or in the sauna, is something inconceivable to women. We women are more romantic, more affective; we don't buy into that business—far from it!—about every woman being into every other woman; we're much more selective. It's really a question of two kinds of homosexuality that, far from converging, tend toward divergence, maximizing on both sides the characteristic features of one's own sex, physical dominance in men, affectionate warmth in women. On the other hand, at least as far as I'm concerned, not only do I understand men's behavior—more direct, more combative, sometimes brutal—but I share it, I've actively imitated it countless times, impelled by the intensity of the stimulation. And I use the word homosexual plainly when I talk about homosexual men because the term Uranian strikes me as very sublimated, and I know perfectly well that they get offended when people call them faggots. That must be due, I suppose, to the fact that they've yet to find a word that properly signifies them.

As I see it, homosexuality is no more than a defensive, often reductive, exacerbation of the contradictions also found in the heterosexual, contradictions that can lead, for the heterosexual who denies the evidence, to equal and no less nefarious conflicts and consequences—although in an opposite way. I'm sure that if someone took the time to investigate the lives of famous criminals, they'd find an abundance of such conflicts. Of course I'm talking about people's essential bisexuality and all that. A cliché, certainly. Except regarding its valuation. Who can be sure, for example, that Achilles's wrath at the death of Patroclus—because I'm talking about wrath, not any other emotions—is greater or lesser than the wrath he experienced when Briseis was stolen from him?

One thing I know for certain is the solidarity that exists between men, and which has to be ranked far above what women can even dream of for themselves; you only have to see the squabbles that feminists get into over the slightest shades of meaning. All the more proof that any effort to bring gay and lesbian protest movements into accord, diametrically opposed to each other as they are, is completely unfeasible. Besides, the men don't even need it. They're already united, they help each other out, and they've got infinitely more power than women do. The idea that there exists an international association of homosexuals, and I've got positive proof, is a functioning reality at every level, in all areas, including literature. Even as unquestionably important novels are totally scorned by critics, the writer only need be a recognized homosexual for his work, however inane, to be lauded in every magazine and publication the world over, including the most prestigious ones.

I remember when I shared with Raúl the conclusions which I'd reached and all that. And I'd reached these conclusions through deep meditation, through a relentless self-analysis that lasted for a whole summer in Puigcerdá, the last one I spent there, to be precise, before I decided to part ways with the hazelnut trader. I can't say exactly to what extent my self-analysis affected and hastened this decision. But it wouldn't surprise me at all that an effort like the one required for self-analysis, a task that's neither easy nor gratifying, is one of those that, far from exhausting the spirit, renews and rejuvenates it. In the end, it's about reconstructing one's own personality—nothing more nor less than that. Starting with what I truly, actually am in order to then remake myself, in a kind of reverse recounting, back to earliest childhood, to what's not even remembered. And I did that by myself, without needing to go running to those psychiatrists and psychotherapists who offer so much satisfaction to people who feel incapable of confronting, naked and defenseless, their own reality or who just can't wait to spill the beans.

Perhaps that's why Raúl's reaction surprised me so much, given that he essentially came to tell me that things are not as simple as they appear at first, that he wouldn't dare to reach such conclusions about himself so quickly, etcetera. A reaction that, for being so abrupt, I must admit, caught me completely off guard. I didn't see how a reflection that had consumed an entire summer could be considered hasty—in fact it was only a month, one of my famous Augusts, but these are things one ruminates on time after time—and that's what I told him. And how, for me, that was all crystal clear, too. And then he starts telling me how psychoanalytical explanations frequently lead to pure consumerism: we follow easy payment plans for something we don't really need at all.

Apparently, for Raúl, anything that's clear is suspicious. All the worse if I insist that I'm completely sure about what I'm saying. And if I then ask him to give me his own interpretation of things, say my dream about the horses, for example, he answers that he doesn't know me well enough—doesn't know me well enough!—to do that, that even if he dares affirm that a certain interpretation might be flawed doesn't mean he's qualified to offer an alternative. Besides, he says, by the time I got around to clarifying whether or not I felt betrayed by my father, or if, on the contrary, I tended to identify myself with him, in order to supplant him, the question would most likely have ceased to be relevant. And that's not to say the conflicts resulting from the father's disappearance or his relationship with the mother or lack thereof had no real validity, nor that their formulation wasn't useful, not even as an alibi, as a defensive shield, but simply that while they might have once been relevant doesn't mean that relevance persists for one's whole life. And yet, if some option seems to me essentially valid, I'm not required to reject it, because, if I embrace it, it's not because it serves me, but rather, quite the contrary, inverting the relationship serves me precisely to the degree in which I make it my own, etcetera, etcetera. Evasions and more evasions. Not even if the brain, with its consciousness and conscience, and unconscious, subconscious, or however you say it, were something like one of those banks where, if you don't remember them from years ago, there was no way of knowing if they would cash your check at the Deposits window or whether you would have to make your deposit at the Cashier's window, or exactly the reverse. Meaning: if you've got to understand the signs from the bank's perspective or from the client's. Because that's more or less what happens with Raúl's psychoanalytical interpretations.

I don't know to what point such an attitude, not only negative but also pusillanimous, improper for a man like him, didn't harbor hidden motives or even some amorphous predisposition to rejection, a natural effect of the selfishness that has betrayed him on more than one critical occasion. Headstrong and petty, Raúl's personality sometimes presents exasperating, disheartening aspects. Because not accepting unconditionally that a person's behavior is conditioned by some concrete, recognizable fact or other amounts to declaring the impossibility of that conduct being modified by some other concrete event, which from then on changes everything. And I'm convinced that such change is possible, not to mention the fact that casting doubt on it is simply a form of fatalism that has little constructive value. Sometimes I wonder if Raúl truly deserves the trust that I've always given him. Because, if he betrays it, that means he doesn't deserve it.

At the same time, I don't want to overlook the enormous effect on the development of my self-analysis caused by the discovery, in the figure of Achilles, of a clear antecedent to my own case—antecedent not model, given how subjective everything turns out to be in this matter. Especially if one thinks that the value of such a discovery—which explains Achilles's personality even more than my own—is something about which I'm very much mistaken, or that pertains exclusively to me. From what I know at least, nobody until now has tackled the subject with sufficient sharpness. Otherwise, I'd like to meet the eminence capable of explaining Achilles's reaction at two crucial moments during the siege of Troy—when he abandons the fight, and his return to it, his motive and the result being similar on both occasions, both equally fateful—without going back to earliest childhood, without combing the tangled landscape it offers our eyes. Because if we consider these two passages, true poles of *The Iliad*, exclusively in light of the text, it will be difficult to avoid the diagnosis that sees Achilles, unlike his other brothers-in-arms, as a dangerous, mentally unbalanced person, because apart from this one striking trait, nothing really distinguishes the other warriors from Achilles, for they are all, to a man, dynamic, cruel, and ferocious, as they must be. As far as Achilles is concerned, however, what's least important are the most popular stories about him, things like his semi-divine origin, his vulnerable heel, or the oracle's prediction of his death––a more than likely end for anyone who found themselves in the circumstances foreseen in the prophecy. What really matters, what definitely constitutes a key to understanding his personality, is the terrible dichotomy to which he was subjected as a young boy. I refer, of course, to his propitious initiation under the tutelage of the centaur Chiron, and to the development of his physical and intellectual abilities from direct contact with nature, an apprenticeship so brutally interrupted by his mother, under the pointless pretext of saving his life, raising him as a girl at the court of King Lycomedes, which, for someone like Achilles, must have been a sort of nuns' convent school. The classic fear of destiny, which only serves to ensure the fulfillment of that destiny, given that it was precisely there, at the court of Lycomedes, where the sharp-eyed Odysseus managed to recruit the young Achilles, despite his being disguised as a girl and everything else, for the Trojan War. Thenceforward, his vagaries of fortune, bellicose as well as amorous, are mere illustrative details. The damage—irreparable, as if to fructify the oracle—was already done: removing him from the centaur's tutelage, subjecting him to a masquerade at the court of Lycomedes. So much for what's been said about trying to see the problem transparently, hear it clearly, understand it with an unclouded mind.

Nothing more deceitful in that regard, nothing more fallacious, to give another example, than the trap that Dante sets for us when he likens Jupiter's abduction of Ganymede, an abduction which the latter desired, to Achilles's unwelcome abduction by his mother, as all evidence shows that Achilles was much more comfortable alongside that wise, half-equine man Chiron (*Purgatorio*, IX, 19 and following). And only from this forced detour, imposed from without, will we be able to explain to ourselves his disdainful feeling of superiority, the typical arrogant behavior that only hides insecurity and helplessness, characteristics of that person who has not managed to overcome their belief of having been a victim, in their early years, of betrayal and abandonment, of having been subjected to the rules of a world that was never his own, constrained to simulate a way of life completely opposed to his true nature. Under such conditions, the most minimal interference of reality upon the pretensions of omnipotence that the subject in question harbors, will be taken by this person as little less than a personal affront, like a fresh aggression of the sort with which the world victimizes him, obliging him, as a result, to offer a reply both resounding and of cosmic significance.

Is this all sufficiently clear? I'm sure that it is, although, if one who must understand fails to do so, that's their problem. I'm not writing for such people. I write for whomever might be conscious of the fact that, in the end, to a greater or lesser degree, we've all been victims of the dichotomy I'm exploring, that we've all had some part of ourselves stolen from us. Does any symbol better express this than Venus Aphrodite herself, born from the severed sex organs of the celestial Uranus after they were flung down into the sea, rising from the mingling of the sperm and the spume? Aphrodite, that deity whose birth consecrates the split, the binary fission, the separation of the high and the low, between the intellectual life and the sensory life, of sex from the common mind. Meaning: that, in each and every one of us, mind and sex form two completely separate areas, two domains that don't even coincide according to the law of probabilities, the woman no less mutilated than the man, she and he no less in contradiction with themselves than with others, each one in continual search for their severed complement, never to be achieved with sex and mind simultaneously. By the way, the one responsible for the mutilation was none other than Rhea, the sinister Earth Titaness, wife of Uranus.

We can allude to a symbol, we can make mention of an antecedent. What we cannot do is speak of a model, be it Achilles, be it Oedipus. Each case is different, specific, and they can be connected in a metaphorical sense. What would I have done, for example, before the walls of Troy? The same as Achilles himself would have been able to do, if the stars had been aligned differently at the moment of his birth, if his heritage and the conditions in which he spent his childhood had been different. Hector slain, to enter Troy as Odysseus entered: through blood and fire, putting the people to the sword, razing the citadel, leaving no stone resting atop another—as Odysseus did, the way the Romans tore down Jerusalem, with the malice of a St. George slaughtering his dragon. But, unlike Odysseus, instead of returning to his dreary Ithaca, going on to found a new city the way Aeneas did, to build a Rome, only not in Rome, but in Troy, upon the ruins of Troy, with its rubble. No returning home like a teenager, a return that time itself and the events transpired have stripped of internal coherence. No running away, nor remodeling, nor rebuilding anything, those morbid exercises which sick minds or people born under the sign of Cancer, like Claudia, devote themselves to entirely. No: come to terms with the past, not according to the past but according to the present instead, according to problems that point toward the future. Not problems of death but of life. To found our own city upon the ruins of the city we have conquered, upon the land over which we tread beneath our feet.

I don't know if I've managed to concretely express my thoughts, if my language has been precise or my images properly shown. It's a question of very complex matters and, when writing, things from the books we read always stick, especially when they're books by our most beloved authors. Besides, things can be said in another way, it's true, using other words, other references, according to more easily assimilable examples, it's true, yes, but not without the risk of trivializing them. It would be like defining my case by juxtaposing it to that of the Spanish woman of olden times, the typical *maja*, creatures of the zarzuela like that summering Madrileña who warns and warns her Cipriano to not use the dance as an excuse for going too far, to not cross the line, to not let his hands sweep down too low, that he always remember that if he moves even one inch the wrong way he's gonna get it, that the slightest little movement and he's really gonna get it, imperious as a Guardia Civil officer shouting Halt!, pithy in her insistence that targets not so much Cipriano's sordid schemes as his own value compared to the others present, triumphant in her conviction of her own high price, the great value of the coveted, lip-smacking fruit locked away inside her body. A truly revolting person, the most repugnant in my mind. Of course, the question is whether the Spanish woman from times past wasn't like that only in the zarzuelas, something more than likely, I suspect. Although, knowing Francisca Maldonado, you can expect anything at all from a Madrileña.

Digressions aside, there are, certainly, some specific aspects of my personality which Raúl refuses to accept. Moreover: consciously or unconsciously, they startle him, they frighten him. My boundless vitality, my intensity, my tireless activity, my physical strength, my own health, my joie de vivre, in short. It usually happens with men, including the best of them: they fear our inner strength, how that strength can grow and expand, as if they were dealing with a bomb. They don't want to recognize it, they don't want to yield, but that's the truth: when a woman escapes the conventional schemes and the man sees himself surpassed by her speed, by the force of her attacks, he becomes terrified. I suppose that would help to explain my feeling of being at an impasse with Raúl. Or, more exactly, that my game with him remains unfinished, that various moves have yet to be played.

The most curious thing about all that, the most symptomatic, is how I've always found the figure of Achilles so fascinating, since long before I ever began to ponder such questions. We've got solid proof of that in what happened to me with the painting, with that Poussin I had to stop and see every time I visited the Louvre, generally after lunch. Because, ultimately, despite being a fine painting, it was far from what's generally considered a masterpiece. Especially in light of the present-day mindset, which takes a dim view of didactic painting. And that is, precisely, what its theatrical composition and exaggerated expressiveness made *The Wrath of Achilles*: a painting with a point. A thematic charge that, for Poussin, however, doubtless supposed an enrichment of his own artistic artistic values, according to a process not very different from the one that leads a person to magnify the traits that define their own life, to see themselves beneath a glorifying lens, doing what was never done before nor will ever be done again, saying what they never managed to say when they should have said it, representing what they never managed to extract from the realm of their own personal fantasies, like that audience member who, from the orchestra-stall seats, admires himself performing, on the stage, his favorite role.

Neither does it cease to be curious—nor symptomatic—that I was the only person to stop and contemplate the painting, that no one else approached except to see what I was looking at, that cautious, well-intentioned visitor who barely slows down to look at their guidebook, let alone the painting, as they pass on by. People who've just seen the *Winged Victory of Samothrace* and are now hurrying on to reach the Grand Galérie, to see *La Gioconda*, with eyes only for the main attractions, too busy to waste time with a run-of-the-mill Poussin. Well, Poussin or whoever painted *The Wrath of Achilles*. If Poussin comes to mind, the main reason is because the painting's style corresponds to Poussin's and because, if I'm not mistaken, the gallery in question, located between the staircases where the *Winged Victory of Samothrace* stands and la Grande Gálerie, was dedicated to Poussin in those days. But, examined closely, the painting might also be a work by Delacroix or possibly even Ingres, whose pictures also hung in that wing of the museum. Or, for the mastery with which it was painted, even by Rubens, at least from his workshop. Or even Titian, an Italian master instead of a Flemish one, or from any one of their students, who all painted like angels.

Herminia will drop dead from shock when she finds out that I'm not even going to give her a chance to get a toehold in Barcelona. I don't want her to have the slightest opportunity to start spreading her venom through the neighborhood, with the doormen, with the neighbors' maids, with the people in the shops. Nor any hope of finding another position around here, after the non-recommendations I plan on giving anyone who asks me for them. Even the shopkeepers will listen to me. It's not a question of my word against hers. It's the fact that I'm the customer, not her—and a good customer, to be sure. And we customers sometimes feel like switching providers.

Herminia is one of those women who, like a snail, always travels with all her belongings, isn't she? Well, alright then, I'll put her on the train in Figueres, and that's that. And I'll do the same with any winter things she might have in Barcelona: I'll toss them in a suitcase and send them to her wherever. It's not just about her being more of a pain than Constantino and Emilia combined or that she's betrayed the trust I showed her. Besides, there's an objective question here: things break at their weakest, most fragile spot. And in the web of relationships that constitute, as it were, the vegetative life of a house, of my house, in this case, she is the weak thread. Her failure to understand the exact nature of her position in relation to the others', having overvalued her own, has been the proof I needed about the limits of her intelligence.

The tensions of this last month have got to be resolved some way. Not just to avoid them being repeated—they will not be repeated—but almost as a matter of hygiene: lance the abscess, cleanse it. And excluding Camila, logically, it becomes evident that if someone has to be fired, that someone is Herminia. The last thing I would need is for what happened here, and which needs to stay right here, to start spreading through the neighborhood once we're back in Barcelona, turning me into a general laughingstock, a target for jokes just as rude and crude as they are far from the truth. I'm not willing to tolerate such gossip, and Herminia, who knows me, should know it. A person has to pay for their mistakes.

Constantino and Emilia are a completely different matter. And no, it need not be said, because my affection for them is far greater than what I feel for Herminia. No: here, too, the elements in play have an objective character. While replacing Herminia, for example, presents me no more inconvenience than taking out a want ad in *La Vanguardia*—forget agencies—replacing Constantino and Emilia is rather more problematic. To begin with, the scarcity of sailors, which would oblige me to steal one—by paying more—from one of these stingy Barcelona families who come here, an operation that always causes grudges, trouble, dislike, and all that. Well, however strange, however incredible it seems that it's precisely the miserable Constantino who's most difficult to replace, that's the practical reality of it. Women like Emilia, a dime a dozen. Well, not like her, better, with more energy, without Emilia's characteristic cloying hypocrisy. Certainly, that name suits her, like with my mother.

But, above all, and however much they gossip, both he as well as she, as long as they work for me, will remain careful to avoid crossing the line, the opposite of what would happen if I fired them. As long as they're dependent on me, I've got them bound hands and feet and with a rag stuffed in their mouths. Never mind the fact that Cadaqués is the worst sort of Petri dish imaginable for this sort of talk; even people from Barcelona find themselves unable to keep up with the gossip, you might say, the moment they arrive in Cadaqués. Anything of importance in Barcelona becomes meaningless here. This is due, in part, to the contagious disdain the townspeople show for such talk, immune to shocks as they are. Splendid people, almost a race apart, haughty to the point of impertinence thanks to the town's geographical isolation; for centuries it was simpler to sail to America from here than to travel overland to the regional capital. Constantino, for example, is from Rosas not Cadaqués, a detail I was unaware of when I first thought about hiring him.

These lines, and the preceding lines about Herminia's predictable apoplexy, were written just before it happened, before everything occurred just as I had foreseen it; what I'm doing now is simply transcribing them. At that time, my relationship with Camila had resumed its former course, and it was perfectly clear who was the victor. Without being wondrously intelligent,

Camila had managed to really provoke me, to drive me almost to break up with her, in a clear attempt, from that point onward, to begin over again on a fresh footing, with renewed vigor, a coexistence that she must have seen threatened by routine, and not without reason; she feared seeing herself progressively annulled, pushed aside, and so she resorted to the oldest trick in the book: excite the lover's jealousy, my jealousy, through her affair with Roberto, an affair that was designed, in fact, to be discovered, for me to catch them by surprise just the way I surprised them, for me to follow each and every one of their movements, exactly as I did, and for me to read each and every one of their love letters. What she probably never figured was that I would react the way I reacted, and that by turning the tables, I went from besieged to besieger—this, in the first place. And in the second, that her ally would fail, her companion in this affair, doubtless unaware, on the other hand, of the true extent of the ploy. I mean Roberto, naturally, and the queasy anxiety that must have filled him when he realized exactly to what point she'd infected him with her secret feelings about me. If not, what else could his final letter mean? The one about giving up the fight completely, the one whose photocopy I still reread every now and then. Give it up once and for all, wrote Roberto, for your sake, for mine, and, especially, for hers. Meaning: for me. Above all for me. Those words, even within the context of boundless love for Camila, must have been a hard blow for her. What's known as getting a taste of your own medicine, playing with fire and getting burned, getting caught in your own trap. Because it was one thing to try to provoke me, and something very different to try to improve her state of subordination and dependency on me, something she never achieved at all--no, just the opposite.

It would be a sort of false modesty to now pretend that I suspected it from the very start. Because the truth is not that I suspected it, the fact is that I knew it perfectly well, that I knew it right away and that's it—more or less since mid-August. It's my well-known faculty for predicting things, my all-encompassing intuition, my sixth sense, my premonitions, my future vision that terrifies people so much. Some call it witchcraft.

About that time, still in Cadaqués, I knew exactly what I was going to do: return to Barcelona just long enough to put several things in order, and then—at last—to Iceland, with Camila.

A black chauffeur, a Chinese cook, a deluxe cabin on a transatlantic crossing. Why have these things become little better than a crime? In the near future, will there be any place left in the world where we can live with a modicum of normality? Traveling, for example. Just taking off, on a whim, to any place one desires, with no other reason than having woke up with that idea in mind. Before there was no country, no city, beyond our reach: Shanghai, Benares, Saigon, Havana, Buenos Aires by night, a party in Cuernavaca, a safari in any African colony. All within reach, all so easy. But now, what destination still offers interest as well as simple personal safety? Which countries in Asia, in Africa, in South America, can we safely visit? And the United States? And Europe itself, never mind whether there's still anything worth seeing in Europe, whether anything's been spared the infestation of mass tourism, that phenomenon that swallows up the most exceptional places, one after another, the Riviera, the Dalmatian Coast, the Greek isles, the Alps, the Rhine Valley, the verminous multitudes chasing after beauty like a plague of locusts, devouring it just as locusts do. Capri, Biarritz, Cap d'Antibes, Cadaqués, just to name a few. The degradation of countries like England or Italy, the damage and decline they are experiencing everywhere, epidemics, floods, earthquakes, drought, miseries until only recently unimaginable, totally inappropriate for a civilized nation. And that other fledgling plague which is the bureaucracy. Before, a person could have their apartment in Paris or, I don't know, New York or London, and spend all the time they wanted there without worrying about taxes and all the bother of today. One simple phone call to Thomas Cook, and everything was arranged.

The problem is what to get involved with. I'm given to understand that Barcelona was a happy city, outlandish, really unique, until Franco turned it into a nuns' convent school which, like the rest of Spain, it continues to be. But, on the other hand, out of school, in the streets, one finds those radical movements that today's mindless youth and a handful of decrepit professors with their irresponsible egomania incubating in the university until, like a grenade, it all ends up exploding in their own hands, leading to such hair-raising scenes like in Paris when it seemed like nothing less than the formation of a new Commune. I admit that what I've seen in the magazines has made my hair stand on end. It was impossible for me to recognize the Paris of my youth, my Paris, in those photos. You might say that, in the face of dictatorships like the Franco regime, the only ones presenting any alternative are those riotous fanatics, those professional revolutionaries and terrorists. Because, as I see it, the worrisome thing would be that all of Europe again becomes polarized around these two extreme options. The only aspect of the 1930s that does not seem, shall we say, to be especially attractive.

Because that is, without a doubt, my time, the time I should have lived in: the thirties. In fact, the time when I was born, an age in which my life would have fluidly developed, if the crisis and the wars and the revolutions had not all come suddenly, all those things which have ended up changing the world into something so unfriendly. A world which was still like the world you see in those American comedies, the world of the movies from those days, when I was no more than a little girl dreaming of those places which she, which I, eager, impatient, thought were reserved for me. But what became of the international hotels, like the Ritz in Paris, or Claridge's in London? Would anyone say that they're still the same, even if they're still in business? And restaurants like Maxim's, even if they look the same as always? And the great transatlantic ocean liners that no longer exist? Would anyone nowadays dare to go driving in something like an Hispano-Suiza, with tiger-skin upholstery? Who would refuse or pretend to hide the enjoyment of how much beauty life can offer us, as if it were some kind of crime? It's as if all that suddenly flew away through the air, just like Papa's laughter flew away on the air every time he made me gallop on his knees.

To spend money like one of those eccentric Arab sheiks seen in London, one of those oil-rich emirs, who stroll through the streets there, beneath a rather scruffy exterior, like figures from a Christmas nativity scene! Nonstop shopping and buying, no budget, no limits! To have what you want, as much as you want, when you want it, the moment you see it! That's my world, things within my reach or not at all; that's the lifestyle for me. Back during my first sojourn in Paris, I remember it perfectly, Raúl said to me—and I'm sure he was right—that I had no head for money, that I couldn't just go around the world like that, spending without a second thought. I agree. But, what can I do? That's how my mind works, the compensation my unconscious seeks for the world that was stolen from me.

What I've said, I think, more than explains my eternal sympathy for the Emperor Constantine, the admiration that his determination and lucidity inspire in me, conscious as he was that his actions plunged the Empire into the most horrifying catastrophes. Except that, also aware that any other decision only prolonged the inevitable conclusion, he opened the gates to the one option that could, in the long run, lead to a practical solution. Solid proof that he was not so terribly errant lies in the fact that, ever since then, time and again, under the most disparate appearances, Humanity has continued to pursue an identical goal: the maximum possible conjunction of spiritual and temporal power. The fact that this goal has never been achieved does not detract from its initiative; quite the contrary, given that you can neither say that another would have triumphed where he failed nor, less so, that they have ever even raised a more valid alternative. His failure, in my opinion, was that of coming to power in a period of decadence only comparable to the one we are now living through.

And the least that can be said of him is that he chose his battle and he won it.

With boxing, with the decadence of boxing, it's more or less the same thing. The crisis, the evil, lies not in boxing itself but in the spectators, in the society, just as it is with so many things, and soon, like fencing, boxing will be a purely amateur sport, for amusement. Boxing is a form of fighting, with rules, with principles, and it's now powerless in the face of oriental martial arts, currently in fashion, in which anything goes.

IX

From threshing wheat to harvesting grapes, the time stretching out between one kind of gathering and another—never had my time in Cadaqués lasted so long. When we arrived, the wheat fields were being transformed, from one day to the next, into smooth stubble, dotted with bales of straw, through that underhanded, overlapping activity of today's mechanical combine harvesters, capable of performing, without anyone even noticing it, the multiple different tasks that, once upon a time, as the reapers commenced their work, turned the field into a splendid, lively, supple choreography. The grape harvest has changed less in places like Cadaqués, where the steep slopes make using a tractor impossible, and the grapes have to be carried in the same baskets as always. In the days preceding our departure, I could observe, just like every year, one or another of these baskets half sunk, half floating next to the docks, in order to swell the wood from which they're woven, while, from shadowy doorways wafted a stimulating smell of grapes, floating through the narrow streets. If some people find such things meaningless, I certainly don't. I live, like the ancients, within the rhythm of the seasons, and they exercise a strong influence on my body. And I knew that by the time the grape harvest arrived, the siege, my siege, would have ended. I felt it in my body, apart from any conscious reflection, as if a fluid were coursing through me, from my head to my feet, a kind of sap that came to life from mere contact with nature during my strolls in the countryside, walking on the earth, breathing the smells of the mountain.

I'm convinced that people's loss of such faculties is simply due to their loss of contact with nature. It's gone beyond the fact that people who come to Cadaqués don't know the first thing about agriculture or that they never go walking out into the countryside. The problem is that they no longer even know how to see when they look at the landscape, or when they glance out the car window. At best they slow down at the three usual scenic spots between Rosas and Cadaqués, whenever they bring some newcomer there who needs to be shown the sights for the first time. First, to point out the view across the Bay of Rosas, which opens up and spreads out as they reach the higher slopes of El Paní; next, descending from the peak, facing the panorama viewed from the other side of the cape; and finally, after the crossroads at the highway that goes to Port de la Selva, when Cadaqués comes into sight down below. Views, postcards; people see the world through postcards. To see it with other eyes, to see the countryside itself, the wild mountains, the forests, the fields and farms, is part of my debt to Aiguaviva, from the summers that I spent there during my childhood. Because, ultimately, the idea that these people who come to Cadaqués have about the world in general, and of Catalonia in particular, is little more than what road maps usually feel appropriate to designate as scenic routes.

Lack of sensitivity is only one of the characteristics—in no way exclusive—of the Barcelona bourgeoisie who frequent Cadaqués. Their lack of substance seems more serious to me along with, and above all, their lack of awareness. Especially the ladies, those uninhibited modern bourgeois mommies. I don't mean, mind you, the mothers of those boys and girls who, like it or not, would get together no matter what, and who are already old enough to know what they're doing. No: I'm talking, more specifically, about the mommies of those six- and seven-year-old children, who hang around there, easy pickings for the first despicable scumbag they bump into. But it must strike them as a bit worrisome, not to mention inconvenient, to not be keeping up with the times. They've got their hands full explaining to each other how complicated they are—a handful of silly trifles—a little like the way their husbands, who use the money they've made to maintain their middling way of life, lacking more worthwhile subjects, can brag about how their language, Catalan, has such complicated spelling, the goal in both cases being identical: searching for some peculiar detail that won't really interest anybody very much. Because these people are no different than a weak-minded village idiot, always the same as the years go by, seemingly unchanged, neither older nor younger, just as plodding in his ways as forty years before, when he made the same rounds as today, doing the same small errands, the women crocheting or doing needlework out in the sun, saying to him the same things as then, *alsa, Ton, con una cesta y todo—wow, look at Tony, carrying a basket and everything*—to puff him up and see him swagger a little—these people are just the same, give them a bit of attention and they act just the same as that retard. That explains some of the comments they make after returning from a trip, those stories about how they could understand people or make themselves understood everywhere they went just by speaking Catalan, which says more about the wit and amiability of the waiters and other such people in the countries they've visited than of the cultural or intellectual level of our fine bourgeoisie.

Changing the subject: of course, young people also deserve it, those boys and girls, all more or less alike, which is what happens with the homosexuals and lesbians today—all of them wearing that one particular style of clothing, each one trying to stand out, making the whole lot of them uniform, making them look like a contemporary theatrical troupe, those actors and actresses who engage in spontaneous guerrilla theater or whatever they call it, decked out in the strangest getups. A most revealing coincidence, given that whoever feels drawn to the theater is already sick to a certain degree; take Francisca Maldonado as proof positive. And they complain that there's a crisis, that people don't go to the theater! For me, the theater's problem is one of euthanasia.

Clearly the fact that young people have a similar problem, doesn't mean, fortunately for them, that the solution must be the same, despite my being unable, quite honesty, to think of any alternatives. There was a moment when I came to trust in the revulsive value of feminist movements—despite the clear risk of manipulation they entail—simply to impose a bit of order. But obviously that's asking too much, that when something is cleared up on one side, something else has to become confused on the other. Thus, those henpecked husbands and partners who fervently support them and who, like transexuals or masochists, work so hard at domestic chores and boast about the diapers they change when what they should be doing is worrying about making more money and paying for a maid or, if the lady of the house is too picky, a butler.

What's significant about this is that, in a way, those young people today are infecting not only those who aren't so young, but also their own elders, those family men who like to showoff, who hop on a bicycle the moment they arrive from Barcelona and ape the fashions, if not the habits of the young, to see if such promiscuity will get them any satisfaction. The mommies can present an even more pathetic sight. If someone asked me why, I wouldn't know what to say—perhaps their lesser critical sense, perhaps their greater capacity for self-deception. Nuria herself, for one, saving us the trouble of getting into what's especially grotesque, keeping us at the limits of what's still considered normal. Nuria: the spitting image of stupor, always looking like she's wondering what the hell is going on, always as if she's saying to herself how nice it could have been if everything had turned out nicely, leaving lit cigarettes all over the place, sucking down one cocktail after another. Deep down inside, a poor girl shunted aside, one of Raúl's victims, just as every satellite individual orbiting some so-called genius ends up being a victim. Unlike me, she never learned how to make her own orbit. Besides, I'm very strict when it comes to medicine. I don't believe in medicines, because, just like the so-called exact sciences, they are only exact on a functional level—same thing with the effectiveness of any medicine. For me, remedies are found elsewhere. And they are always natural ones.

It's truly shocking to see the extent to which people forget how old they are—like so many other things—and behave in a way that's inappropriate to that age, their real age, maybe because they imagine they look younger, maybe just from pure, simple irresponsibility. Perhaps I'm guilty of being too rigidly critical about this, but, certainly, as far as I see it, there are two ages in a woman's life that are perfectly delimited: from the time she begins to be a woman, and from the time she begins to cease being a woman; the age of the shower and the age of the bath. The subtle shades that distinguish one pleasure from the other define what our body is at one age and another. The young body enjoys the shower, the fructifying contact with that warm rain, the steamy vaporous halo that veils her nudity as if to guard it from the dangers that beset her, the tactile stimulus that, like a caress, prepares her soft skin for the pleasures that await. On the other hand, there's no better setting for that now fulfilled body than the bathtub, wherein, reflected in any mirror, however small, like that shell-handled one I own, we can contemplate our own mature nakedness literally flowering amid the bubbles, exposed in all its plenitude, with all its prominence, without the elusive slenderness of adolescence. Yes, our changing taste with respect to the pleasures of the water as a reflection of the changes at work in our own body. Something as silly as that.

Of course, such displays of paltry critical sense, like so many other oddities at which, time and again, I can only wonder, surprised as I am every time, are not peculiar to people who come to visit Cadaqués; unfortunately, rather, they correspond to a much more generalized phenomenon. It's also clear that Cadaqués is one thing, and its habitués something very different. As a place, Cadaqués, natives included, is unique. That's why I can't account for Raúl's fascination for Rosas, which has been transformed from an enchanting town into the typical spawn of mass tourism. I sometimes wonder if Raúl isn't just a little bit out of his mind.

The key to my vocation as a writer—apart from the genetic fact that one of my paternal great-grandmothers was a poetess—would have to be sought in my unassailable defenses from that time, my years of initiation in both writing and life. I'm talking about a time when writing for the sake of camouflaging oneself was only one aspect of the craft.

And the key to the key? How had I managed to build those unassailable defenses for myself? And, above all, why? The response to these questions would also suppose, by the way, the response to one more: why did I write *The Edict of Milan*? And thus we come to a new problem, indissolubly linked to the previous one. Why does *The Edict of Milan*—a novel objectified, in my eyes, by the very time transpired since its writing, to the point that, at present, I believe myself capable of discussing it as if I were not its author—continue to be read in a way that fails to match the interpretation I hoped would have been written, at least, by someone qualified to do so? In other words: why do I see in this book what no other reader has seen? A question which, on the other hand, being raised, is just as valid for *The Edict of Milan* as it is for every written work. Because, ultimately, as Raúl put it so well, the phenomenon of reading is the shadow, the negative, of the phenomenon of writing.

Thus, to his understanding, just as what we write inevitably refers, in the final analysis, to that period of childhood in which the surrounding world starts to become differentiated from what one is, as much as what one is comes to be seen as defined according to what one is not, in the same way, we also interpret what we read according to the perspective formed by the experiences belonging to that time period. So, he says, not only does the writer always write about himself, but he always writes the same thing, without even being aware of it, new topics and new ways of saying things that barely do anything but redress, or rather, disguise, under new appearances, what he's always said. According to the same principle, all reading, from the masterpiece to the latest comic book, constitutes material that each reader remodels according to a particular interpretive lens, whose roots, no less than in the case of writing, inevitably connect to early childhood. Even when it comes to what we call taste, the fundamental question about which there can be no dispute, all acceptance or rejection, casual or whimsical in appearance, always answers to a certain predisposition, perhaps a concrete work, perhaps toward this or that genre considered as a whole. As much in one case as in another, reading will awaken nothing inside the reader that did not previously exist within him. Just as this exists in others and himself at the same time, so it existed in others before it did in him, and so, too, the intensity of the reaction always matches the weight of the underlying presence.

Overlooking such obvious things constitutes the principal error of those theorists who analyze mass media, information, communication, or whatever you want to call it, for those whom everything seems to consist of relating the contents of the message to its brevity or its strangeness, to the fact that it's either heard, read, or televised, and all that nonsense. Because by focusing the problem on the objective aspect of the message, they automatically marginalize its subjective value, an indispensable element in performing the act of reading, for simply carrying it out. As far as works of fiction are concerned, the value of the text is something with which literary criticism is already, or should be, concerned. The folly, therefore, of information theories, is that they dispense with the very thing they should embrace, which is reading. Not the text but the reading of the text. Not the content of the message itself but rather the impact it makes. Not the bullet but the gunshot wound. Anything else they've got to say is pure speculation, good enough for a telex operator, and that's about all.

Be that as it may, I think I've already touched on all that, where Raúl and I agree, where we disagree. What I'm not sure has been made sufficiently clear is the role of the intended reader or addressee in a work of fiction, a term I've used to designate the person or persons—sometimes oneself—who, by constituting the author's objective—conscious only to a degree—or the motive for his thirst for vengeance, for seduction, or what have you, decisively catalyzes the creative process. Someone whom we love through writing that book, someone whom we intend to woo through that book, finding ourselves unable to achieve those desires by any other means. The reality of the phenomenon, it seems to me, is unquestionable. But what fundamentally concerns me are the problems of harmony that arise in the practice. For example, that the receiver and the sender function on different wavelengths. This is the problem I was referring to at the start, when I mentioned *The Edict of Milan*. And, more concretely, the interferences, the apriorisms of acceptance or rejection that can play on the side of the receiver—to the disdain or defiance that can conceal the amorous character on the part of the sender.

There is something of that, there has to be, in my case, that of Claudio Mendoza, author of *The Edict of Milan*. My famous unassailable defenses, the excessive camouflage. The three successive approaches to the narrative material that, functioning as magnifying lenses, structure the tale, and while there were three there might just as well have been three times three, given that the number of new details, as well as the number of reinterpretations they generate, is practically limitless. The work may or may not please, but from a strictly literary point of view, my objective is—to my understanding—fully achieved: that the reader end up not conceding any credit whatsoever to Lucía, that when she says something, the reader tends to believe exactly the opposite. But, from a different point of view? from the addressee's point of view, for example? And what if, in the end, maybe because I've mixed up the point of view, or maybe because, being correct, the intended reader is incapable of grasping it, the point of view ends up being misunderstood?

Given my personality, if there's one thing I can't stand it's uncertainty.

Not being sure, in this specific case, if there's a mistake and, if there is, if it's one's own fault or the fault of others, if it's the result of one overestimating others. Would it be so foolish to think that just as the siege of Troy was nothing more to Achilles than an offering, a loving homage, can the same be said not only about the poem dedicated to him but also about any written work? Or is it that someone climbs a mountain just because it's there, never mind how hard the climber works to reach the top, or the sweeping view that greets him when he stands atop the summit, and, especially, what both factors combined mean for him, the self-realization derived from it? And in this sense, precisely, the one that must validate for us climbing a mountain as the proper simile for the creative experience, an experience which will always bring us to that self-realization I've just mentioned, that self-expression that the creative work represents for every creator. Raúl, however, would object, claiming that self-expression is more a means of self-seclusion and self-invention than self-revelation. Fine. So what? Is there any better invention imaginable than the one a person can realize from themself through the creative act? Consider, on the one hand, that just as the effort required to climb a mountain is no guarantee of success, on the other, any degree of deliberate falsification—including defining personal character traits embedded in the writing, more to satisfy the author than fulfill any of the novel's internal mechanical requirements—will, in equal measure, render sterile and even counterproductive the self-invention which the artist achieves through their writing. Because if a simple attack of cuckold's jealousy has led more than one man to declare himself homosexual, meaning, to avenge the offense by rendering it null and void, to cover himself, to opt out of the game, to make himself safe, while, at the same time, punishing the adulterous woman, expelling her for the rest of her life from the ghetto in which he recluses himself, a ghetto which she has not the slightest chance of entering, and if that same man can also bequeath to posterity a multi-layered novel, one that leaves behind him a theoretically definitive and, from a punitive and even self-castigating point of view, exemplary self-interpretation, is there anything you'd put past him? Invert the siege; let the besieging forces smash themselves to bits against the unassailable walls of our city. Let them rot out there.

Ultimately, all this same stuff happens with publications like *Who's Who*, where the only thing it doesn't say about the person listed is who they are, exactly. What they've done, what they've got, publications, interests, jobs, awards, family, all the things surrounding someone's life, but not really who that person is. Well, obviously—would anyone tolerate, beginning with the subject themself, someone else saying who that who really is? Their family, their friends, their fellow citizens? Would the editors dare to publish it? Would they have the nerve to face the torrent of trials and complaints and lawsuits that would be set loose upon them? I don't think so. Their job involves nothing more than concealing the true personality of the people listed under a pile of awards, titles, decorations, pretended hobbies, and all that, people who, for their part, gladly pay the subscription price in order to always have that objective proof of their public image, that alibi, within arm's reach

And when it's one person or another who publicly describes themself, when they tell us *Who I am*, so much the worse. The notorious Personals section in the English press, those verbal advertisements which every lonely heart ends up placing, sooner or later, on the pretext of seeking companionship. The adjectives they use to define themselves, words like *lovely, aristocratic, bright, vivacious, intellectually alive, sharp, splendid, thoughtful, imaginative, attractive, sensitive, slender, intelligent*, and even *salacious*, things that if not even the person advertising themself completely believes, at least they feel better after having written, paid for, read, and reread them, imagining, while taking a relaxing bath, the hypothetical amorous relations that a hypothetical positive response might unleash, despite nothing at all being unleashed, the mere pleasure of turning the idea over and over constitutes, ultimately, a pleasure in itself.

I've observed that the act of paying cash for something enormously increases the pleasure that can be derived from such experiences. Perhaps it's due to the fact that possessiveness is on the rise, perhaps because paying cash increases people's sense of ownership. Or perhaps, like the citizen who indulges in every kind of swinish behavior and then meticulously files his taxes, feeling somehow—like a Catholic fresh from the confessional—more at peace with himself, more liberated from guilt. The case is that with J. A., when we meet to talk about money—the only reason we see each other—the same thing happens, more or less. He pays the necessary amount with an immense satisfaction, and that always gives him a reason to exclaim how easily money disappears and how hard it is to make, in order to point out what an extravagant life I lead, insisting that expenses should never exceed earnings, that every pocket has a bottom, and things like that—exactly what you'd expect from a hazelnut trader.

A Cadillac in your mouth, those were his exact words. He is, perhaps, the best dentist in the world. From the United States, with a clinic in Geneva. He solved for me, to perfection, a rather delicate dental problem, a rather impossible set of dentures, and his fees, don't even ask, were perfectly consistent with the brilliance of his work. Now you can tell everyone that you've got a Cadillac in your mouth, he said, as he stretched out his talons to seize a sum of money which really could have bought me a Cadillac. Of course, he said it just to cheer me up, knowing that people's morale always slumps after these kinds of procedures—a very New York City sense of humor, given that his remark was an obvious erotic innuendo. I don't mean that he was insinuating anything, naturally; it was only a joke, and certainly very genteel. No, he's not one of those doctors, though by all accounts they're much more numerous than people think. In fact, I recall that time my gynecologist examined me in his office when the nurse was already leaving for the night, I don't know if by his instructions or, simply, because I was the last visit of the day, and they took forever to see me--the typical late-afternoon delay--she figured her day's work was finished. I also don't know if him giving me the very last slot of the day was a coincidence or not. Nevertheless, the doctor started up right away, saying he wasn't in a hurry, his wife was out of town, and he had no idea what to do that night. I understood immediately where he was heading and I cut him off right away, saying that I, however, was in a hurry, that I'd scheduled a hot date with someone who'd just come to town from London.

Most, if not all, of my dental problems result from my bruxism. I grind my teeth in my sleep, and it seems that, in the long run, the consequences are enormous. According to my dentist, bruxism occurs with particular frequency in people who are nervous and hypersensitive. And I would like to point out that my dentist is a very competent person, not only in his chosen specialty but also in general medicine—a true humanist. It was his elevated ethical sensibility, ultimately, that made him alert me to the real facts about dentists, informing me about what people unwittingly risk when they fall into the clutches of a dentist. I suppose that his privileged professional position protects him, in a certain way, from the machinations of his European colleagues, but a mafia is a mafia, and failure to cooperate can lead to unpredictable reactions.

Apparently, almost all the dentists in Europe—the network has not yet managed to extend itself to the United States, probably because it's only there where the dentists are more than just little tinkers—are organized in such a way that the patient who first visits any one of them will be unable to stop doing so for the rest of his life. So, for example, they take advantage of the most routine checkup, the simplest cleaning, in order to create false cavities that, once filled and everything, end up cracking the tooth, which means more extractions, more crowns, and, ultimately, new trouble spots, which is precisely their goal. In this way, when the patient, naturally fed up with being swindled, decides to switch dentists, the next one, no matter whom the patient selects, as they will be benefitting from the work, or rather, from the problems caused by the previous one, is very careful to say nothing, to not let the truth slip. The process goes on for years and years—the time necessary to clean the patient's teeth and clean out their wallet, too—but there's no worry that any denouncement can leak out, given that they all operate according to a sort of agreement, a pact that obliges them not only to keep quiet but also, if necessary, to cover for each other. And I know for a fact that if any one of them decides to break their code of silence, they sink immediately into disrepute and oblivion, because all their other colleagues will quickly accuse them of all sorts of accidents, immoralities, and vile behavior. The existence of the pact, on the other hand, explains why dentists, unlike other medical professionals, never offer reductions or discounts for specific patients; the pact strictly forbids it, and although defying this aspect of it only counts for a small infraction, few risk it. The same is true when it comes to reputation. Has anyone ever heard one dentist badmouth another? Has nobody ever wondered why, unlike other specialists, they never do? Well, it's for that reason, for their mafioso conniving, a kind of secret organization into which they indoctrinate, under severe threats, recent dental school graduates, every young dentist who ever intends to make a living. If I ever feel a chill thinking about the world we live in, it's not for the danger of nuclear war and similar catastrophes, but rather for these small daily matters. Another issue, by the way, is auto-repair shops, about which I've also got my information. Although the problem seems to be less serious, perhaps because it's more picaresque, I'm sure that some investigation would reveal their involvement in more than one of those alleged accidents that make it so easy to close the case on any number of tragic traffic fatalities.

No, the difference is one of arrangement more than of degree, the dentists profiting from their vastly superior organization. Because, from the looks of it, this specialized mafia's influence doesn't belong to the past, given the fact that they still sell whole a series of products—I've got a list of them—that are extremely damaging to tooth enamel, especially for children, their future clientele, their nursery. And this is also seen, apparently, in the inexplicable absence of the correct amount of fluoride in urban tap water, which cities postpone adding as long as possible. After learning these secrets from my American dentist, I suddenly understand why I've had so many dental problems; my teeth have been the cross I've had to bear ever since I was a little girl.

Apart from dental problems, my body is and always has been in superb shape. I feel young, full of vitality. I would even dare say that when I go places, people stare at me in public more than before. Especially young men. And also the young women, stealthily, when they divine my awareness of their bodies reflected in my smiling, ironic gaze, the possibilities which that knowledge contains, the unsettling experiences that it suggests. Because this force of nature that I am, the result of the proper combination of vigor and energy, only grows stronger in the face of opposition, and my strength redoubles when I feel betrayed, a fury that could allow me to move mountains if I set my mind to it, because there is nothing I can't do in such a state, no goal I don't reach if I've decided to reach it. Because the very same revulsive effect that the reading of a certain work can produce—reflection and replica of the revulsive value that all creative processes entail for the creator—this very same effect, both revulsive and regenerative, can, without a doubt, result from an amorous encounter.

Skin is one of the finest indicators of both age and health. And my skin, no exaggeration, is like a baby's. I no longer have the features of a twenty-year-old woman, of course, but my skin still feels as fine and soft as a little girl's. And of course on the inside I'm still like a little girl, and I'd be very surprised if such harmony between one's epidermal surface and one's inner depths were any coincidence. Besides, we mustn't forget that when one goes for a time without making love with men, we women become like virgins again; I'm sure that, right now, some not particularly experienced man, an adolescent for example, could mistake me for a virgin, more virgin, at least, than many young girls his age. Even in this sense, my affirmation that I sometimes feel like a new woman is valid. All things proper to a perfectly preserved and well-maintained body.

People will tell me it's a commonplace, but I place great importance on health, given that its significance is not only physical but also psychic and moral as well. I saw this very clearly when I first lived in Paris. Compared to my iron constitution, all those boys and girls I was dealing with were a pitiful sight, all of them weak, soft, and delicate, all with something that just didn't work right, whether their guts, or their sex, and consequently their ideas. Except for Raúl, of course, with that eagle-like air about him, that quasi-golden aura that distinguished him from others, the aura of an ancient god facing his goddess. I've always been fascinated by these coincidences that seem to come right out of a Russian novel, these points of intersection between his life and mine, sometimes as slenderly joined as the body and its shadow. The only problem, ultimately, would be deciding at any given moment who is the body and who is the shadow.

This is probably the reason why, when I think about my first time in Paris, when I reconstruct it, it resists me; what's more, it becomes impossible for me to include Raúl in the same group as all the rest, to apply to him the same generic classification as any other friend from those days. Just as he was different from a physical point of view, so too, and necessarily so, were his ideas. To begin with, he wasn't beset by the same guilty conscience that harried the others, always a symptom of sickness, or physical or mental weakness. And, to conclude, I don't remember ever seeing him resort to the ideological sophistry then in fashion—and, I imagine, still is—born of a guilty conscience that neither he nor I suffer from, as I said; as far as I'm concerned at least, it seems to me stupid at best to allow oneself to be won over by communist ideas while enjoying an untethered financial situation like the one I enjoy. That was my opinion then, and it remains my opinion today, and only idiots would try to convince you otherwise with the sophistry I'm talking about. On the one hand, they never get tired of repeating how people, how everybody, is motivated by economic interests, class interests—on the other hand, by virtue of a seemingly superior example, they ask you to renounce defending the interests that theoretically, or scientifically, or whatever, you have to defend according to their scheme—the interests of the class to which you belong—and so join the party. A valid argument, perhaps, for the sort of person who might let himself be convinced by the tacky woman who sells him an apartment, that the property's magnificent panoramic view of the highway is a key selling point in its favor. Not for me, of course. And I'd be very surprised if it stays that way for Raúl. Why should it?

Money, always money. The same reasoning, except backward—J. A.'s reasoning. He now seems determined to convince me that I'm much richer than I think I am. Fine, and so what, even if it were true? Does that mean I have to change my lifestyle? Do I have to cut expenses, like the money I spend on my American dentist? Well, the way I see it, if there's anything worth spending money on it's things like that. It's difficult to think of money put to better use. What's worth it if not that? All the more reason my dentist was right. It really is pleasant to think you've got a Cadillac in your mouth.

"Reconquer" is a word that is useful and commonly misused in equal measure. Now, if "reconquer" is not perfectly synonymous with recover, of getting ahold of something that might have been lost in a careless moment, it doesn't mean conquering all over again. No: reconquering means reestablishing dominion, resulting from the positive outcome of a confrontation, about something that has, in fact, never really been lost. A nuance that, when it comes to clarifying ideas, has its importance. And when you've played a game and, on top of it, you've also won, there's nothing more agreeable than clarifying ideas, than summing things up.

From the start, I swore that I'd never let myself be stepped on, that nobody would rob me of anything, because of the act itself, separate from whatever value what was stolen might have for me. And so it was. But at this point that's practically the least of it. It seems more important now to point out the exhilarating game currently being played. The comfortable pleasure and everything else involved in occasionally provoking such confrontations. Like war for people in ancient times, these sorts of conflicts awaken and exercise faculties that the bureaucracy of daily life tends to dull and put to sleep. Besides, if everything then returns to its old course, perhaps, it does not return to the very same way it was before; it is renewed, updated. A renewal of sentiments as much as of ideas that now supposes one more incentive, an additional stimulus to the summary initiated. Borne by such an impulse, we also arrive to find ourselves outside the environment first established, far from our concrete personal siege, penetrating other areas, regions previously unexplored. And, even as new realities appear on the horizon, old problems also resurface, no less important for having passed unnoticed until that moment. Things one did not know how to see before—other people's ideas and feelings about oneself. Things perhaps obvious to everyone, but not for me, with my perennial complexes. What do I know, my notion that Margarita was more appealing than me, that everyone liked her and not me. The fact that time showed me that I was mistaken in no way diminishes the negative effect that such an idea has exercised upon my behavior all that time. That's one example.

My goddamned hang-ups. Not even having foreseen—another example—that if Camila started playing her dangerous game out of fear of losing me, she might have ended up infecting Roberto with the feelings that she never stopped professing for me, making him share her love for me. I'll never know, and it's not worth the trouble to find out, whether or not Roberto consciously became her willing accomplice. What matters is the final result, the outcome of the game. And as far as I'm concerned, unable to see—like the idiot, like the naive fool I sometimes am in these matters—where the shots were aimed, not really knowing how to interpret their baited hooks, the traps they were setting for me, mostly through the invisible basting stitch of their correspondence, the letters that Roberto made sure Camila received, knowing that I was going to reread them, that I was their parabolic addressee. So, now that I can admit it, I will: their words about the sperm whale, despite first going over my head, still hit me hard. You can't imagine what it's like to find yourself in bed with a sperm whale, Camila wrote, using those very words, in one of those letters she left sitting around the house long enough before sending it to Roberto. It took me a while, it's true, to realize that she was really talking about my romantic passion, a particular ferocity which, for good or bad, I couldn't help but identify as my very own. Calling me a panther instead of a sperm whale would have been more apt, it's true, but also more conventional. Besides the fact that writing is not Camila's finest skill.

Actually, the whale she really had in mind was an orca, a killer whale. When

I realized that, I also recalled a series of images that, most certainty, suggested the simile to her, one of those nature documentaries about ocean life they show on television and which we watched together, leading us, I remember quite well, to make certain intimate jokes. The orca is a white whale—maybe black, right now I couldn't say—and is known for its extreme ferocity. They are very intelligent, temperamental, and have tremendous willpower. They can be distinguished from other whales at a glance thanks to their dorsal fin, and in the water, swimming, they have the sleekest silhouette of all. Also, unlike the common whale, the orca has shark-like teeth, which makes it even more dangerous. That detail, however, excludes all possibility of any veiled reference to my dental problems, because apart from already being resolved by that time, my canines, the most important of all teeth, have always been strong and sharp like those in the very healthiest mouth.

Something else that hurt my feelings just as much was what they wrote about the virago, a word that, considering the context, Roberto was obviously using to allude to me in one of his letters to Camila. A virago? Me? A virago like Francisca Maldonado? That's what she ended up turning into, or rather, what she had always been, but only with the passing years has she really started to let it show, strutting her stuff like a *torero*, probing, testing, feinting, stalking her prey down there in Barcelona. Because the fact is, if you asked me how to best illustrate the concept of the virago, it would be difficult to find a more qualified representative than Maldonado. And it was that very same automatic reflex, extremely well known by Camila, which, in the long run and after much reflection, gave me the key to such verbal aggression, to her intentionality: the big, hard slap across the face, desperately shaking someone who looks dead to try to revive them. The same with that stuff about being a witch.

I'm generous—at least I believe myself to be—and when I want to forget something, I forget it. But some things are difficult to forget, like what Francisca Maldonado did to me. Such things are neither forgotten nor forgiven. Such an attitude might be incomprehensible for the person who lives crushed by guilt, and who finds relief from the opportunity to offer forgiveness. The problem is—as I think I mentioned earlier—I'm not one of those people, I don't need to liberate myself from someone else's guilt. I leave that to people with troubled consciences and problems like that, communists, sick people, basically, always talking about whether someone is guilty simply because of their bourgeois roots or if another person is morally superior for the mere fact of being the child of exploited workers, and other such nonsense. I don't know if that word communist comes from the Paris Commune, but nowadays just the word itself is shocking. Even though I still can't help that it makes me laugh, since, from the first time I heard it, I naturally associated it with what the peasants from Aiguaviva called a *comuna*, which is Catalan for a toilet. I've also got to say—things being as they are—that compared with today's troublemakers, the communists of those times were quite serious people.

Anyway, those egalitarian manias have been catching on everywhere, and now they're not only being implemented in communist countries but in many others, too; it doesn't seem to matter whether the people in power are socialists, liberals, conservatives, or what have you, because nowadays nobody dares denounce that egalitarian obsession, to actively oppose it. England, theoretically that most traditional of countries, is a good example. Of course, even being such a good example, England suffers from chronic constipation and therefore might not be the best representative. Or too representative, if you want to look at it that way—vulnerable in excess, given its habit of doing everything backward, and not the least by its distinguished subject Richard Burro. That such a mental retard has been able, not only to get along in life with absolute normality, but also to make a career out of it, is a textbook symptom of what I'm talking about. No less revealing is the fact that a country like England, supposedly a great model of propriety, permits itself to post warnings, in museum lavatories, that stealing toilet paper is prohibited by law. And they're able to enforce it with closed circuit television cameras, electric eyes, or some similar apparatus for spying.

Certainly you'll say that I'm going too far by calling him Richard Burro, that the aversion he inspires in me borders on phobia, that a person of his ilk doesn't even merit my attention. But you must understand, and this is the truth, that I never expected my *Edict* would receive such shrill reviews in a country for which I hold such love and affection. Yes, it felt like a knife in the back; that's part of it. And the wound had hardly stopped bleeding when one of those publications there, like *Who's Who*, wrote to me asking to include me in its next edition, enclosing a form, ridiculously brief, that I filled out and returned by mail, not without my natural bitterness. How does one condense the richness of a life into a few short lines? Simply more proof of British left-handed miserliness.

On the other hand, the problem isn't so much Richard Burro as what R. B. represents. Let's leave forgotten, floating in the air up there, the answer to the question of how such a weak-minded man has gotten along, if not aided by certain weaknesses of another kind. Because perhaps if I had composed one of those long tongue twisters currently in vogue—such nonsense can be written in any language—or if, perhaps, I had begun by saying *Once upon a time*, our R. B. would have been ecstatic. And the fault lies not with R. B. but with his context, the intellectual context in which R. B., like so many others, finds himself inscribed. I'm referring to that idea that literature is nothing but mere language and other such cretinous utterances. The current wavelength that, like one more atmospheric phenomenon, pulses on from one country to another in a heartbeat. Fads I cannot explain. Is it perhaps more important now than in times past, for a writer, that stuff about language? Is it not, precisely, what has always distinguished the good writer from the bad? What does that so-called science known as linguistics have to do with literature? R. B. is not the problem, simply an exponent of the problem. Of that continuous discovery of America so much in fashion.

The moment we're living in now strikes me as a crucial one. Convictions are weakening while imposters have the field all to themselves. The present moment insists that nobody stands on their own, or shines by their own light, and the moment someone does: Seize him! Off with his head! That explains the roots of all those egalitarian obsessions. And if someday those goals are achieved, and every man, woman, and child ends up being equal to their neighbor, people will just start blowing their own brains out, one after another. A point of view which Raúl absolutely rejects, however much a communist he may have been. No, I'm convinced he doesn't think that way, and whoever suspects I'm being overly clever is just guilty of being naive. It's not that he's said it to me, or that he has alluded to it in any way. I simply know it, the same as I know the feelings that he harbors for me, without him ever having had to express them to me. A person like him can't accept such explanations if they don't serve to further highlight his exceptional personality.

Just as a body's shadow looms giant-like behind its back at dusk, so too does Papa's shadow where my past is concerned. A shadow, a void, which has affected every part of my life, from the closest aspects of family relationships to the darkest and most complicated ones, the areas which give birth to impulses like the ones that lead us to love some specific person or to create something.

Environmental factors, secondary as the name implies, precisely because they are environmental, should not be overlooked. And Francoism has been an astonishingly successful spawning ground for all kinds of half-measures, unfulfilled experiences, and frustrations. Would anyone really call Franco a man, a great man, if we understand great man to mean great tyrant? Or that Spain is a virile world? Hardly. If it ever was, it no longer is. Franco has remade it into a nun's cloistered convent, and he has played the fussy, despotic mother superior. Spain is a country where everyone, from the most powerful technocrat to businessmen like J. A.—practically interchangeable—agrees that fiscal fraud is institutionalized, making it clear that they themselves are, first of all, the defrauded victims. And what happens with those theoretical technocrats and practical-minded businessmen, also happens, for example, in the sexual world, where agreeing with some casual remark about how everybody is naturally bisexual is tantamount to admitting one's own homosexuality, but in the saddest, most pejorative sense, as a self-hating homosexual.

For identical motives and similar considerations, however, we mustn't overlook the exception to the rule, that case in which the environmental factors, far from softening, like a padded surface, far from diluting and degrading what's truly alive inside a person, far from that, function as a sort of incentive, and provoke instead an exasperated reaction. Meaning, the child's natural reaction, anyone's reaction who, like the child while he is a child, feels immune to all the manipulations he's forced to endure. Because, like a god for the man who invented him, so too that man, that adult whose irascible temper is incomprehensible to the child who contemplates him, confounded no less in his piety than in his obedience. And like the man who rebels against the capricious will of that Old Man whom he invented in ages past, or like the boy who rejects the screams and equally inexplicable smiles of the adults at hand, so, too, Achilles in his wrath: enraged at his fellow who stole what was rightfully his, at Briseis, at Patroclus, at the one who slew Patroclus, at the mother who violated his childhood with shame and anger, at the king who tried to supplant his father, at that father who vanished, and, ultimately, enraged at himself. And like Achilles in his wrath, or like that little boy who retreats into his own small reality, I, too, in my transport, in my fury.

A strong dose of negativity, no doubt, always coexists with or underlies the most positive facets of the reaction I'm talking about. Because, like that ballyhooed athlete gasping for breath, who accomplishes his feat while none present consider his exhausted, burning lungs, nor his racing heart about to burst, in a similar way, even as spectators applaud in admiration, something wounds us inside, intimately, without anybody even perceiving it. The price of my tendency to always challenge mediocrity, to willfully scandalize whoever shows any timid behavior, to never reject any expression of greatness, to thoroughly wash my hands of that wretched zest for symmetry that corrodes everyone the world over.

I know all too well, for example, that it's passé to call oneself a romantic. It's simply not something one says, the sort of thing a really sappy or tacky person says. Unfortunately, in my case, that is precisely what I am, though in the most elevated sense of the word: idealistic, scornful of conventions, passionately dedicated. So must I then be, for fashion's sake, cowardly enough to deny it? Absolutely not. Because people fear words and I do not. People fear words as much as, if not more than, deeds. Thus, the word romantic has become synonymous with adventurer, meaning, that person who, from society's point of view, ends up losing, whether they're named Che Guevara or Marilyn Monroe. The ones who triumph, Lenin, Grace Kelly, etcetera, are not romantics.

However, not only do I appreciate the value of words less than that of deeds, but I can't even imagine separating them from one another, both being expressions of the same thing, each in its own domain. It also remains to be seen which of these two human manifestations has shaped the course of history more, words or deeds, those words that the intractable popular wisdom stubbornly insists on counterposing to deeds, no doubt because words are less palpable. Just as a love affair can cause a profound shift in thinking, a real fencing exercise for the intellect, not to mention the stimulus for the creative faculties it implies, a stimulus well known to the ancients, thus, in a similar way, the reading of a specific work can open a wide space for the development of our desires, for the unfolding of our erotic impulses. One case as well as another presents a shock, a confrontation, defenses to be overcome, defenses that, like the Great Wall of China, before protecting us from any hypothetical aggressors, serve to completely occlude our vision, our view of the outside world no less than our own view of ourselves.

What I consider key in the reading experience is that feeling of enlightenment, specifically that phenomenon of achieving a kind of totalizing vision that simultaneously encompasses both the most trivial and the most profound. And sometimes it's no less revelatory than the experience of writing. Because it wasn't writing but reading, or rather my rereading of *The Edict of Milan*, that revealed to me something which, as I was rewriting those pages, I was incapable of seeing with sufficient clarity: that Raúl was already in love with me when I first lived in Paris, and had been practically since we first met. And what's more, he was aware of that, and the fact that I, who was not––the idea of Raúl being in love with me was the last thing I would have imagined––nevertheless figured out how to arrange things to make it explicitly clear in my book, which is the most curious thing of all. The brusque estrangement—not only physically—from Luis, the cooling of his relationship with my protagonist the moment he finds himself back in Barcelona, an evident result of some deep reflection, of having become convinced—mistakenly—that he's the wrong man for Lucía, that he's got no right to drag her along with him, to involve her in the risks and dangers of the life of an active revolutionary. Reasons which, even after having been clearly explained, she was in no emotional condition, at that time, to accept, let alone even to understand. And that sets in motion a process of rejection similar to what someone experiences at the death of some beloved friend or relative, a rejection of that person and everything they meant to the one who survives them. Such a process as this could only culminate in a happy ending par excellence, our heroine getting married to a dashing young rich fellow, which, on a more real, less suggestive level, corresponds to my marriage to J. A., which Raúl must have seen both as a confirmation of all his fears as well as a justification of his withdrawal. It was no longer a question of whether or not he was the right person for me; now, given the utter conventionality and cynical convenience of the solution I accepted, the problem had become inverted. Now it was I, clearly, who was not meant for him.

It was the same with Camila and Roberto. And the same with Claudia, when I failed to understand her enigmatic behavior, and I washed my hands of the affair, telling myself the poor girl was crazy as a loon. Even as foolish and naive as I am, someday I'll learn to perceive the love that another person professes to me when they profess it and not later, however much they conceal that love under the most unlikely, even crazy, appearances. What other proof did I need than what was already staring me right in the eyes? What's more: in my eyes when I closed them. For years it was hard—no, impossible—for me to have an orgasm without imagining Raúl instead of the person in my arms. What I mean, of course, is a deep orgasm. Not that kind of superficial, mechanical trembling that dissipates as quickly as it comes, nor the trembling derived from the pleasure that our body is capable of generating in another body. And only now do I understand that he's gone through exactly what I have, that in essential matters his life has unfolded in a parallel fashion to mine, something that explains the brevity of our love affair, its prolongation in the form of good friendship, our respective marriages, the increasing distance we've allowed to grow between us, both of us forced apart by something we considered impossible. Proof of this is the fact that he had to reread my *Edict* in order to begin to understand it. And only by reading what's written on those pages has the unconscious become conscious.

His growing intimacy with Margarita, for example—a relationship equally inexplicable and aberrant, due to all the differences between them, how very little they have in common. Unless he suddenly wakes up and starts to see everything with new eyes, as sometimes happens in a relationship that only seems intimate: getting closer to her means greater distance from me. And that can help clarify so many other details that elude explanation in the moment, so many, many coincidences that only start to make complete sense over time. Coincidences of dates, for example. The fact that, in the last year, as our relationship began to ice over again and he almost seemed to be avoiding me, just like that other summer, when, after reading my *Edict* in Cadaqués, I had just managed to understand why for so long, like a naughty spirit that will not assume corporeal form, he simply refused to ever appear in person. Meaning: the idea that both he and I had spent our lives playing foolish games, our words and actions making us seem perfectly opposed to what we really felt for one another. I judged that the moment had arrived to be sincere and I wrote him a long letter, summing up what our relationship had been, for both of us, and talked about his development, his direction. I wrote him several long, very long letters. He didn't answer a single one, and on the few occasions since then when we have bumped into each other, he's never alluded to them in the slightest. The last time, only a few weeks ago, in the house of some mutual friends, I noticed that, when he thought I wasn't looking, his severe gaze was fixed on me all the time. There was sadness in those eyes. Or nostalgia. More than usual.

A pity. A pity that, so often, the more some specific thing affects us, the longer we take to understand it. And most of all, a pity that what's lost must be irredeemably reconquered, which involves even more time, more delays. But I've spent too many years telling myself that nobody presumes so much in vain as the presumptuous, to not, if he ever comes back to me, force him to have to reconquer me first. I know he's living like some kind of recluse, out in the country—somewhere near Aiguaviva, I'm sure, a fact that only a very generous interpretation would call fortunate—working on his novel. Well, fine then. Let's hope he finishes it. Then we'll see.

It's terrifying, however, truly chilling, to contemplate to what degree two different people's destinies sometimes depend on things completely distant from what either one desires. The interferences they have to face. In our specific case, the elements which have, perhaps, played a decisive role, without Raúl or I, or both of us at one time, even being the slightest bit aware of it. A mere mechanical accident that can end up complicating everything: one of my letters getting lost, the first one especially: or one or all of them falling into Nuria's hands and causing problems for Raúl, jealous confrontations, things like that—what do I know, stranger things have happened. And silly ones, too. Like that stuff with the sperm whale, because bedsprings alone, so extraordinarily sensitive, that repeat and amplify the slightest movement, can increase the sensation of erotic passion. That's why, personally, I prefer a Scandinavian bed frame of wooden slats—better for the back, anyway—with a thin, foam rubber mattress; thin, yes—the mistake lies in people thinking the thicker the mattress, the better. The one who loves springs is Camila, and she'd even have them under the sand on the beach if she could.

Another fact that seems important for me to point out is the effect the present lines have had on my life, writing them and, especially, later on, reading and revising them as I went along, continuously thinking of new ideas, and the degree to which these pages have helped me better understand certain aspects of my personality that were never quite expressed clearly in *The Edict of Milan*. At heart, it's about two levels of one single phenomenon, neither one deeper than the other. And perhaps it's that balance between writing and reading, making these pages seem like annotations, which gives the phenomenon its most peculiar features. A slender interdependence between reading, writing, and life that, at least for me, constitutes a totally unknown experience. Something which of course did not occur that August when I wrote my *Edict*, and perhaps it's true that the atmosphere in Puigcerdá was the least propitious imaginable for such harmonic convergences, given the commotion then roiling the golf course community, resulting from the discretely ostentatious affair that a certain most excellent lady from Madrid was carrying on behind her illustrious consort's back, almost as thunderous as one of those scandals from times past. I remember it perfectly. Anecdotes and whispered gossip aside, what I never experienced then, of course, is what's happening now—that excitation that sometimes fills me up, capable even of replacing reality itself, of occupying its place, of leaving no room for anything else. The sorts of vibrations that suddenly go quivering through your body—such an intense sensation that, more than once I've had to simply stop writing these lines. That might explain, by the bye, all the mistakes and errata spotted by people who've had a chance to read them. So, too, the apparently improper use of certain verb tenses, determined by the greater or lesser proximity of the writing to the events under consideration, the account of what happened sometimes being practically superimposed upon what really did happen. I'd offer the same explanation for other inaccuracies that might have escaped me and the mistakes I might have made—not always premeditated, hoping for the reader's forgiveness, considering they don't affect the reality of the events nor the expressive vigor of my witnessing them. But passion isn't only a source of creative inspiration but also, all too often, of confused and clashing emotions. Any inaccuracies in the chronological order of events, as well as contradictory versions of the same, repetitions, and other observable lapses, can be chalked up to my memory, and the dirty tricks it plays on me.

Among those black marks, probably none is quite as serious as the one about the painting, *The Wrath of Achilles*, nor, doubtless, any more difficult to explain, considering that I, more than anyone else, don't understand what happened. It's not that the painting has disappeared from public view, or that, with all the remodeling and changes carried out in the Louvre, it's been impossible for me to locate it again. The problem lies in the fact that I can't find it in my museum catalog either, the same catalog I used when I first lived in Paris and, consequently, nobody has been able to confirm what I've written about a painting that's not even included in a museum catalog from ten or fifteen years ago. But the strangest thing in this case is that it doesn't even appear in any book about Poussin that I've consulted, nor in general studies about the works of Rubens, Titian, Delacroix, and their respective schools. And let me tell you that I wore myself out searching during my second time in Paris, with Camila, before we started going to Cadaqués, and Camila gave me a great deal of help. As a matter of fact, the least of it—given that the painting does indeed exist, I've seen it time and time again—might be knowing the name of its painter and even the title of the canvas. Since it wouldn't be the least bit strange, after all, if the painting had nothing to do with Achilles, and if the figure depicted there were not Achilles but some other mythological hero, which would more than explain the difficulty of tracking it down. I was sure that Achilles was the painting's central figure but now, from what I've seen, I can no longer be so sure.

This case strikes me as highly illustrative of the importance—or lack thereof—of the subject of the painting in question. And not just the subject but also the argument, to which so much importance was given in times gone by. Something which, inevitably, will end up being forgotten, the cultural coordinates of the time when it was painted, lost for whomever contemplates it in the present. Coordinates, what's more, that most people don't care about, no less with painting and sculpture and ceramics than literature. Because just as informative, testimonial prose—always provided its writing achieves a minimum level of quality—can be transformed, for future readers, into a text fully assimilable to fiction writing, so too, in a similar way, a painting like *The Surrender of Breda*, which for the people of those times must have had a certain documentary value, and a painting of an essentially mythical nature like *The Wrath of Achilles*—my *Wrath of Achilles*—which long ago involved two diverse, perfectly delimited attitudes of contemplation, for the spectator today, ignorant of both the myth and the events in Breda, the meaning is entirely comparable, interested as he is more in the value of the painting itself than the value of what the picture represents.

A little girl seated on a potty, clinging to the iron railing, looking down at the street from the small balcony of a fisherman's house, the sunlight transfiguring her hair into a blond aura. Looking down, with that slightly dismissive curiosity that comes with innocence, still ignorant of the malicious snares that the familiar appearance of daily life conceals, of the displeasures which this quotidian world holds in store for her throughout her long life, of the difficulties involved in straightening out what's twisted when you're not even conscious that it's twisting even as it's being twisted, as it perhaps is already twisting for her, the little girl sitting on the potty. At this point, I'm not going to start wailing about people's typical, obvious lack of sensibility; I only wonder about my excessive sensitivity, why a scene so ordinary affected me so much and so suddenly, leaving me practically disarmed to the point that, when I began to realize it, my tears were blurring my vision of the image. It was the last morning of our stay in Cadaqués—and this is my last and, of course, strangest memory of that summer—now that one more summer has passed by, peaceful and slow, and we find ourselves once more in Barcelona, feeling, even now, as if still possessed by the inertia of that calm and that harmony which so strongly invites quiet reflection and summary. Camila has gone to the cinema with some friends, but I prefer to sit here by the fireplace. The night isn't exactly cold, but in autumn, however mild the weather may be, it's always nice to have the fire for company, that decorative element that we no longer light when it gets really, truly cold, and a nice central heating system makes it rather superfluous, except from an aesthetic point of view. And it has been precisely that final image of last summer, the little girl sitting on the potty, which has brought me so many other memories of that time, while I slowly sip my scotch and review my notes, the polar bear skin prettily colored by the small flame from the logs now almost burned up, their alternating pulse of red blotches and dull opacities, succeeding one another movingly as the memories of that summer flow through my mind, from the most embarrassing to the most pleasant, images, emotions, sensations, the evocation of that long siesta in which I all alone remembered the crazy night of love that followed all that business at Port de la Selva, evocations and evocations of evocations flowing rapidly one after another, now only embers covered in the gray ashes of the fire. Then, a prolonged and splendid bath with another whiskey on the rocks at arm's length, the steam from the hot water fogging up the mirrors, like a replica or an echo of the cold glass all misty from the ice cubes, glass and mirrors misted over, just as the serene expression of one's eyes becomes misty and blurred with tears. A bath that relaxes and tones the body and at the same time clarifies one's ideas. Just what I needed before sitting down to start writing one final draft of these pages.

BOOK IV: THEORY OF KNOWLEDGE

Contents

[THE DIARY OF CARLOS AS A YOUNG MAN]

I

9 Sept. Physical beauty resides in the body, but it only resides there, because it's only truly physical in nature to a certain point. Along with purely physical characteristics, a certain harmony of lines, a specific quality of the skin, of the hair, of the teeth, there are features that, beyond being manifested in the body, superimposed on the physical features, are not of a physical nature. Their domain, more than in the body, belongs to the spirit, to what was once called the soul, a word whose abandonment strikes me as a shame, given its great analogical value, when one wants to use it to designate the ensemble of psychological factors seated in the body where they will remain until death do them part, exactly the same as in one of those primitives paintings that show us the immortal soul in the throes of departing the prison of the mortal body, that body, now exhausted, that exhales its final breath. And the fact that, although today we know that the psychic forces that make up what used to be called the soul, as well as its turmoils, the suns and moons of madness, are a mere externalization of a dark chain of chemical reactions. Ultimately, when talking about the spiritual character of one physical trait or another, everyone understands you.

Of course, the normal attitude is something else. When people refer to the specific beauty of a certain body, it seems that they're only doing so with regard to a whole that can be broken down into the various parts that make it up, to a product capable of being dismantled into a series of elements: tits, ass, lips above and below, and always according to a standardized ideal established beforehand, an ideal that permits them to be classified by reason of their greater or lesser approximation to the model. For me, however, it's clear that even the shape of an ass obeys, more than its own materiality, the orders that the body receives from that shadow realm wherein what we call personality takes shape.

In a face, in her face, is it the intrinsic beauty of the eyes that commands or is it the look? Are the stylized line of those eyes or the folds that shape the upper eyelids where they meet the lower ones, features that, like a river's meanderings, are less the product of the riverbed's capricious windings than of the water's flow, and so too, in the same way, are not those features a fixed movement, an expression impressed into the material? Are they her lips or her smile, or must it be, as happens with the eyes, the trace of the expression that shapes the corner of her lips which gives her mouth's expression its true peculiarity? And those full flowing tresses which sway with her head, were they, possibly, sculpted by a hairdresser? And that movement, that shapely flight, that expression of eyelids and lips, is all that something purely physical? Would her hair, her eyes, her mouth, be the same once she was dead, and would they continue to remain the same? Isn't it true that identity is the first thing that vanishes after death, what immediately changes a dead person into a stranger, the body brusquely stripped of the visible manifestations of everything that was invisible within it?

It's not that she was about to say hello to me the way one greets someone whom they think they know, but are not sure how they know them. It was as if we were introducing ourselves to each other when we happened to catch each other's eyes, and she looked away. Exactly what I knew she was going to do, not when I first saw her, but beforehand, before turning the corner, in that moment, those fractions of a second before running into her, when I knew that the encounter was going to take place. Discarding the possibility of some gift of prophecy that I don't possess, I can only think that such a certainty was nothing but the remnants of one of those dreams that are interrupted when one awakens, and whose signs and inklings, although usually forgotten, do not stop nagging us the rest of the day. Be that as it may, this is exactly what happened: when turning the corner where she and I live, she was strolling along the sidewalk on her side of the street, coming in my direction, staring at the windows of a boutique. And it was when she looked away from the shop window that her gaze met mine that she turned her eyes away.

I kept walking without turning back, possessed by a sensation of bewilderment and strangeness comparable only to the feeling one gets from strolling through one of the nativity scene fairs that usually set up their stalls shortly before Christmas in the streets and plazas around the Cathedral, finding oneself suddenly amid the whole scene in motion, submerged in that misty smell of freshness and sparkles and Christmas carols spreading out through the whole transformed area, wandering among the booths, among moss and mistletoe and pine needles, among fleeting odors, not only chlorophyll nor only marijuana, a singular atmosphere composed not only from what is synchronous and germane but also from what is strident and dissonant, Picasso rattles, crushing crowds, flower ladies who resemble Soviet peasants, vibrant paper-mâché vipers, terra cotta flutes, the faces of the crowd seemingly floating above a confused pile of overcoats and heavy winter clothes, expressions now dazed, now perverse, the complicit fascination aroused by the squatting, shitting figurine known as *el cagador*, the greedy shine of a golden tooth, and, as a replica of all that, the small matching the big, the detail matching the panorama, as a means of concordance, the expression on the face of the woman next to us, looking at what we're looking at, one of those calm, composed women of the Barcelona petit bourgeois who have so much in common with a Nuremberg pastry cook, the placid, settled roundness of her physical presence, of her face, of her heavy-lidded eyes, her tight climbing curls, placid, yes, although not for that any less jovial and even puckish, with that air of listening to the *tonadilla* from a music box assumed by one who, lost in his thoughts, meditates on the good sales transacted and the pacifying porcelain pipe awaiting him following the frugal supper solidly prepared for them both by the beloved wife, as soon as the shop is closed and all is calm at home. As if more than a marketplace it was an encampment and the people gathered there might remain instead of coming and going, the surrounding streets offered a tranquil scene, uncrowded and moving freely, and you might even say that even the shops' picture windows––handicrafts, second-hand books, antiques––were an invitation to peace and quiet. From inside the shop, practically woven into the tableau on a Flemish tapestry, the antiquarian observed me with a cheerful manner, almost as if we were conversing. And I found myself still looking at the small objects displayed up front, by the window, when some small bells jingled and the antiquarian appeared in the doorway. Are you selling something? he asked me. If you're selling, I'm buying.

10 Sept. Watching her window has become a truly reflective activity, like smoking without being aware of it or driving while talking about any old thing. I can spend the whole afternoon at my desk, facing the window, without the sight of the windows across the street and, more specifically, of her window, disturbing me at all, whether I happen to be studying, or writing in my diary, or listening to music; my capacity for concentration is in no way altered. And this has been true not only since what happened the other day, but for years.

On the contrary: what happened the other day might have been able to alter my attention for some time, to create an interference between my books and her window, if it wasn't for the fact that for years I've been combining both things, this factor--the repetition over time--consubstantial, I imagine, with the process that permits a specific act to become a reflexive action. I'd gotten up to piss, or maybe just to stretch my legs, but while I was moving about my room, back and forth, it occurred to me to piss—I don't remember exactly nor does it have any great importance. The fact is that I'd just finished pissing, and, as is my habit to do afterward, was rinsing the head of my cock off in the sink. The bathroom communicates directly with my bedroom, so that, distracted, with my mind on other things, I found myself walking toward the window, with my penis still hanging out of my pants, giving it those few shakes you give it before zipping back up. It was then that I noticed her presence there across the street, behind her windowpane, as demonstrated unequivocally by the fact that, on seeing that I noticed she was watching me, the lace curtains closed immediately. She was still there, however, slightly withdrawn, still looking through the curtains, unaware, no doubt, that her silhouette remained perfectly visible from the other side of the street, as well as the fact that her window wasn't for me just another window, one among so many others on the other side of the street, but precisely her window, the only one among the many visible above the crowns of the trees that deserved my attention. I returned to my desk and sat down, pretending to bury my nose in my books, but I only lost sight of her when she finally moved away from the window.

Today, at the same time, I punctually repeated the ceremony. And save for the fact that she was watching from the start from behind the curtains, with the confidence of one who finds themself in a sanctuary, the very same thing happened again like the other day. Except for one additional detail: the simple operation of putting my penis back into my pants was made more difficult by the fact that, at that point, it was already fully erect.

12 Sept. Mariana phoned me up this afternoon to confirm our meeting time. I apologized to her for forgetting that we'd agreed to go out together; but that's what happened, I'd forgotten, and now I had another commitment. She wasn't the least amused that I'd forgotten, especially because she knows me well enough to know that I don't forget such things. For her, the reason must have been the least of it; she's more than used to my mood swings. And it would have been a senseless insult to explain to her that I had a more important date, much more important.

It doesn't seem, however, that my fidelity to the other commitment has been rewarded: her window must have been halfway open and the breeze that was stirring the lace curtains prevented me from clearly seeing if the shadow visible in the background was, in fact, her silhouette or not. In any case, at least for my part, the ceremony has been repeated right down to its most minimal detail, erection included. The only simulated element--needless to say--is that of going to piss. It's only a question of convention, but continuing it seems to me as important as, in a narrative work, the fiction acquiring its own autonomous reality.

The pity is that while the evening was looking favorable, I remained unsure of exactly how it was looking favorable, as well as what the hell I could do apart from repeating the ceremony one more time, no matter how favorable everything was looking. My mood was that of someone who finds themself waiting for something that, like a password, gives them a clue for what to do next. And the password did not manifest itself.

On the other hand, my feeling that the evening was looking favorable for me didn't go beyond that purely subjective sensation, completely unconnected from the awaited signal, without any possibility of raising it or stimulating it. A sensation, ultimately, situated in the fact that I found myself alone at home, which is when a person feels most comfortable, when the servants have the afternoon off and my mother is out of the house, playing bridge with some friends, and my father stays at the office until he can zestfully service his secretary the moment the rest of the staff departs. Of course my mother's bridge game could be nothing more than a cover story; she must do something to keep her skin looking like fresh milk, and it's well known that there's no more efficient method than erotic exercise. After all, I'm sure that the only thing she and my father agree on must be that each one leads their own life while being careful to maintain appearances—thus the cover story. On one occasion, however, she came close to running off with a young man whom she met on a Mediterranean cruise, a Maltese fellow, and my father looked like the ogre from a children's fairy tale. Then everything returned to normal, my mother looking superb.

The norm, however, as much as it refers to my mother as well as to my father, is to painstakingly care for the public image of their marriage. Why they do it is a mystery to me, but the fact is that they both seem to prefer to stay together, as if they feared that separately they would be unable to watch so closely the effects that each one inflicts upon and receives from the other. And that's the way it's been for as long as I can remember, like when my mother took me with her to visit a friend who spent the summer in the same town as us. They generally saw each other at his house, and I played in a garden where bamboo reeds grew, but I enjoyed myself more when they met on an enormous yacht he owned, that he still owns, and they let me explore the deck under the watchful eye of a sailor. I knew very well that there was a secret between the two of us, something I mustn't tell anyone.

It was at that time I discovered the meaning of the word "clumsy," although I wouldn't know how to pinpoint in which specific circumstances, at which moment, or as a result of what. And, in reality, my discovery wasn't as much about the word's meaning as how that meaning didn't match the one I'd associated with it up to that point. Once when my father had startled me, probably with one of his jokes, no less nasty for an adult than for a child, I remember my mother taking me in her arms, telling him: *don't be so clumsy*. And I thought, and I kept on thinking for years, that by "clumsy" she meant that brick-like quality of his face, that terra cotta look it acquires from being exposed so much to the sun both in winter and summer alike, as well as the abrupt character that anything he said turned out to have, any expression he adopted, all characteristics that contrasted disagreeably with the quality of fresh white milk, which I mentioned earlier, which my mother has. Also in this case I was aware that it had something to do with a secret, that it was a word that I could not pronounce without the risk of conjuring up, precisely, his clumsiest reactions. That's why I whispered it at him under my breath, inside, when he was near me, and at the top of my lungs, when he was far away and couldn't hear me: Clumsy! Clumsy! Clumsy!

14 Sept. Patiently attentive to the window across the street, without any evidence of not having performed once again for an absent spectator—the roll-down shutter half-lowered, the curtains still, the least minimal movement—the day when my relationship with her began has come to my memory. I don't recall the date, the year. I only recall that I was then attending high school instead of college and it was around the start of summer, a very hot evening on which I was studying for my exams while from outside came the intermittent explosions of the firecrackers and the whistling of the rockets that, with less conviction each year, announced the arrival of the impending Eve of San Juan. Darkness was falling and across the street, contra crepuscle, some lights were lit. It was during that long interval in which the clarity decreases and the leaves on the trees cease fluttering that something stole my attention from my watching without noticing the lights lighting up, something that, to the extent that it escaped this attraction, to the extent that it was succeeding the natural light, was scarcely capable of attracting the attention of anyone who was not in

my situation, sitting at a desk facing one of so many windows on the other side of the street. Even more: face to face with that window, each one at the same level, on the same plane, as if it were an extension of my apartment, as if it were the other end of my apartment where the woman had made her appearance, a woman moving very quickly, followed by a man who embraces her and kisses her while, as if overcoming a certain resistance, he draws her toward a bed they end up falling onto together. Although the only part of the bed that enters my frame of vision is the lower third of it, the perceptible agitation is sufficiently expressive of what's happening. The embrace is brief, barely a few minutes, and the first one who reappears, tucking the tails of his shirt into his pants, is the man. He walks into the next room, the living room, also with a window at the front of the building, and then heads toward the rear of the apartment, down the hallway. Now the woman comes back into view, also adjusting her clothing, and goes into a room next to the bedroom, no doubt the bathroom. When she reappears she's wearing a long black garment, a sort of chemise or light robe; she switches on the light and lowers the shutter. Moments later she walks into the next room, the sitting room, and turns on the lights. Her movements are gentle but precise: she shuts the hallway door, turns to a corner, perhaps to put on a record, then to the opposite corner, where she pours herself a drink, whiskey judging from the shape of the glass. As if to confirm it, she leaves the room and returns a few moments later with a square white container: the ice bucket. She shuts the hallway door again, walks to the window and looks out; outside it's almost dark, and the woman's glance has slid right past my window, without even noticing that someone is watching her from within the semi-darkness. She lowers the shutter bit by bit, to gauge the right height, you might say, and indeed, as the air flows in, she leaves it raised about a handspan and a half, two at most. A slender opening, narrow enough to conceal her from any outside curiosity, except, of course, from a truly privileged position, the position of an observer who finds himself situated exactly opposite, on the same level, especially if the watcher has equipped himself--as I had done--with a good pair of binoculars, and if the woman is seated--as she was seated--on a sofa facing the window, with no other objects in between other than a glass of whiskey on the rocks set on a low table. As she settles in, she strips off the black dress and, more reclining than stretched out, embraces and caresses her own body as if shivering, as if trembling. The street is wide, but some really good binoculars make it possible to see even the ice cubes that slide around in a glass. And, in particular, follow the movement of those hands as they glide over the body, almost like at idling speed, as slowly as possible without stopping, perhaps because the slowness of that movement--now speeding up, now slowing down--corresponds to a reality, the same when it centers on the most outstanding points as when it does on the most hidden places, when it enters and gets lost inside the shadowy pubic region, perhaps it's the watcher's own excitement that, stretching out the time, slows down its flow.

A few days later, coming out of school, I ran into her in the tobacco shop. I was there with some of my pals, to buy cigarettes, and she was buying stamps for a letter. Right behind us a man with graying hair and an athletic look, like a naval officer, entered the shop, and he greeted her warmly; he called her Aurea.

Another time, that same summer, I recall having seen her looking out of her window, the important one, the one in the living room. Then I stuck my head out too, ostensibly, waving my hand and looking downward, as if I were talking with someone on the sidewalk on my side of the street, some passerby completely hidden from her view by the trees' foliage. Hey you, up here! It's me, Carlos! Can't you see me? Carlos, yeah, Carlos! You doin' alright? That's great! Me, too! And I waved my hand again. What I don't know is if she remembers the moment—supposing she even noticed—and, if so, if she knows that that boy named Carlos who was shouting from his window down to someone, that that boy and I are the same person.

17 Sept. I found out that Clumsy was having an affair with his secretary thanks to an ironic comment from Milky, one of those remarks that parents make about each other in front of their children with the intention of wounding each other without the children realizing. Except that the partner wounded in their self-esteem tends to react badly, and the kids, except when they happen to be extremely retarded, end up understanding, although the smart thing is to play dumb. What better defense does a child have than hypocrisy? Especially when the adult demands they be honest above all.

What surprised me was not the fact in itself, perfectly typical of Clumsy, but the fact that he was getting it on with the person to whom I thought they were referring, Tere or Montse, one of those creatures who, by dint of dedication becomes the be-all and the end-all in an office, the typical woman whose physical presence and tidy clothing define her according to her goals in life: home and office, or even in reverse, inverting the order. Thus, her short, manageable hair, her small earrings, her blouse, her sweater, her pleated skirt, her comfortable shoes, elements that are merely the complementary expression of her body, per se, vivacious eyes, small skillful hands, short powerful legs, in contrast to her prominent bust and her no-less-abundant poop deck posterior, that give her silhouette a touch of the duck. In other words: a being made for conjoining rapidity and stability, precision, and resistance, and, above all, energy applicable to her own administrative and domestic labors. The simple idea that she and Clumsy were sentimentally involved was something that filled me with delight, that made me cackle with laughter when I found myself alone.

Then it turned out it wasn't the duck but a different woman, blonde, roguish, and prissy like her, but with eyeglasses that, apart from disguising the vacuity of her gaze, also gave her a certain intellectual look and enhanced her enormous, clear attractive eyes, slightly protruding, with that slight myopia which is often nothing but the externalization of the lascivious turbulences that blind the nymphomaniac's entire body. She had become--or had been transformed into--Clumsy's personal secretary, the secretary who attends to every last detail for the manager, absolutely everything, which is the minimum expectation for a managerial secretary who takes pride in her position in those environs.

But I didn't learn all this until years later, when, with all that business about summertime and shorter but more intensive workdays, Clumsy suggested we have lunch together at a Galician restaurant near his office. It was enough for me to see him give orders over the intercom, in the half-light of that soundproof, air-conditioned atmosphere, without any more living color than a Miró lithograph, as a resounding contrast to the impression of seclusion, reflection, and mystical powers which all that was meant to impose on the intimidated visitor, to give the impression of a man found to be as deeply involved in decision making as a Cardinal Richelieu, it was enough for me to see him there, in his environment, following the spirited and conspiratorial welcome that the duck had given me, a duck who knows what life is, and the discreet and affectionate appearance of the personal secretary, fully immersed in her role of cinematic blonde who addresses her lover's son with the expectation that he'll end up understanding her and loving her, too—that was enough to help me take full stock of the situation. The end of the intensive summer workday, staff heading home, Clumsy's self-absorbed staying on after hours, walking very slowly through the tidy, deserted offices in order to end up entering--always as if according to the daily ritual--the women's lavatory and, opening all the stall doors one by one, pensively contemplating his dominions while relieving himself. He'll eat dinner with the blonde with the beautiful myopic eyes and they'll talk about the company and life in general, and he'll expound on his problems and the night will end with him scissored deep between her thighs, a crazy, helpless, trembling, groaning baby.

Another fact receiving retrospective illumination from that bachelors' lunch with Clumsy: the fact that, on the occasion of my birthday, my good grades, or whatever it was, around the same time when I thought him involved with the duck, Clumsy gave me a book as a gift, the only book he's ever given me in his life: *Robinson Crusoe*. The atmosphere in that office helped me to understand the nature of the satisfaction that permeates the spirit of the worthy man--not necessarily a bourgeois man--when reading Defoe's novel, the values he finds on its pages, the instructive character of its contents, the lessons that can be extracted from his perseverance, his hard-won progress, the accumulation of benefits with which our hero becomes sole, absolute ruler, the tranquility of spirit derived from that solitary possession, similar to that which seizes a god as he contemplates his creatures, his creations, his constructions, the wholeness of his work.

At that time, of course, I neither liked the book nor did I understand his reason for giving it, meaning, that he gave it to me because he liked it, and, if I had understood that, the discovery would not have affected me either way. For in those days, my favorite way of spending my summertime was different: hours spent walking slowly along the old sunny walls, clutching an air rifle, watching for the movements of the lizards that run to hide in the eroded nooks and crannies of the mortar, how they freeze sometimes in order to look around, the very moment when you've got to pick them off, to least shoot off their tail, and when it's squirming at your feet, contemplate its prolonged writhings, its spasmodic vibrations, the final spiralings and uncurlings of a member that resists, you might say, the completed act of amputation. Hunt down in cold blood some inoffensive and harmless little animals? Sure enough; and perhaps, precisely for that reason, for them being inoffensive and harmless, in order to make our punishing lesson all the more implacable. I used to hunt them on the edge of town; they're especially abundant on the outside of the cemetery walls.

18 Sept. Enough with playing the fool like some cretin. Either Aurea isn't home or she is, and she's spying on me, and then I'm a cretin twice over. And what if she's told some girlfriend or boyfriend, that one who looks like a sailor, and every afternoon they get together to have drinks and laugh at my expense, awaiting the six o'clock show? And what if they've filmed me, if they've got a film that ends with a close up of my genitals and they show it to all their friends? And he keeps on doing it every afternoon, she'll surely tell them. Come by tomorrow and you'll see it with your own eyes. This and similar things and more detailed ideas is what, like a spinning vertigo, came to my mind today after I finished my daily routine, with the habitual enthusiasm as well as the

regular lack of response. A sensation very similar to that which Rousseau must have experienced in his day on being caught in the act of exposing his rear-end, half-hidden behind some hedges, to a group of women. Only now am I in a situation to understand the reason why Rousseau, with incorruptible honesty, applied words like imbecile, idiot, stupid, and cretin to himself with increasing frequency in the pages of his confessions.

For a time, I've pleased myself by seeing Aurea as one of those women who, thanks to their anticipating imminent menopause, and according to a peculiar collector's criterion based more on subtraction than addition, less about what is hoarded than what is spent, starts racking up orgasms achieved in the same way as a person who consumes the maximum amount of something apportioned to them, the maximum time allotted for a stay granted by a ticket, the total mileage that an open railway pass allows; a formula, the true golden rule of the feminine orgasm, whose praxis might be summed up thus: the ideal number of orgasms equals the number of ovulatory experiences multiplied by infinity. Orgasms which that woman is anxious to burn through the way a drunken *pistolero* is anxious to unload his revolver, with the same greed as one who presses down on the sturgeon's belly in order to squeeze out every last caviar egg inside. Except that none of this, obviously, relates in any way to Aurea. Independent of the behavior that for my satisfaction I strive to attribute to her, the reality of Aurea, the reality her body emanates, is something else: the shimmering waves of her hair, glorious as the irruption of the brass in a symphony; the smiling vivacity of her eyes, the amused expression of her lips, with that satisfaction in the dimples infusing the knowledge of the potential pleasure that her own body encloses; and, above all, her skin, more sophisticated than simply soft, both in its smoothness and color, with a brownish pink in the depths, capable all by itself of arousing all sorts of perversions. This is Aurea, this is Aurea's aura, tangible proof that one cannot speak of spirit and matter. And this is the sense in which I must rectify my initial affirmation of what is and what is not properly physical, since the one and the other are simply different strata of one and the same thing: matter, a unique matter that in its deepest levels includes its contrary, what we call spirit. And it is precisely between such strata of Aurea's physical presence wherein hides the active principle of the attraction I feel for her, what fascinates me about her, equally familiar and unknown.

I don't think it's necessary to clarify that when I talk about Aurea it's not precisely the great love to which I'm referring, that great adventure which everybody points to when they're having a love affair, one of so many, affairs that must be understood as preparation for that other more definitive adventure, and also more general and abstract, affecting one's life to the point of being confused with it, of being taken for one of its great milestones, even to the extent that it surely ends up being that, whether it be for the subject's good, or for his disgrace. No, as I see it, if the attraction of a love affair must be figured in its ersatz character, such attraction is lost as it is transmuted into the great love sought, culminating in marriage. From my perspective, just as it would be superficial to think that what matters to the hunter is the quarry killed when—although perhaps it hasn't even occurred to him to think it—what really matters to him is the supposed self-affirmation that comes from killing it, the proof that he has emerged victorious thanks to his skill or his valor or his marksmanship, this is the least of it, so, in a similar way, what matters most in a love affair is not so much the combined qualities possessed by the person one means to seduce as much as the fact that the seduction has been consummated, what possessing the other person means for each partner, an end about which, incidentally, the old canon law is more than accurate. And, although there's no doubt that there's quarry and then there's quarry, that the hunter feels more satisfied with some than with others, that he proves himself more with some than with others, there is also the fact that the same thing happens with regard to the amorous adventure, and it's in this sense in which it can be affirmed that, if I am the hunter, Aurea is my prize quarry. The reason for this affirmation is something I would not even know how to explain. Not even the origin of the explanation, the explanation for how I came to see it the way I see it. There is the scene I witnessed from my window when I was a high school student, those nights of the festival of San Juan. Images that, needless to say, can make a very strong impression on a boy, so much more for what they awaken in him than as a spectacle per se, especially if, as spectacle, they don't represent anything new for the boy from the moment when his own childhood experiences surpass it. What was it then, exactly, that awoke in me what I witnessed that afternoon from my window and, to no less a degree, running into her unexpectedly in the corner tobacco shop, when, in front of a group of schoolmates, the man who looked like a sailor called her Aurea, my heartbeats frightening me, as if they were audible outside, to the scandal and rage of those present?

Answering this question is no easier than answering the question of why I write, of why I'm writing these lines right now. And keep in mind that I'm not talking about the fact that what I'm writing happens to be a diary, or the question of why a person writes their diary, but the fact of writing in and of itself, regardless of whether we're talking about a diary or a work of fiction, the narrative material of a diary being no less fictitious than a story, the latter being no less biographical than the former. Because just as man's memory begins with his birth as an individual, meaning, from the moment when the boy begins to distinguish between his ego and the world, between how much he belongs to the world and how much he belongs to himself, relegating to oblivion, to the attics of memory, all experiences that belong to the previous phase of undifferentiation, of confusion between what one is and what one is not, thus, no less uncertain than the trail of stored up information in those attics and basements of memory, it must be equally uncertain, truly, to say that any act of writing not related to self-awareness is what really possesses the writer in the act of projecting himself toward the exterior by means of his work, of a work that--he well knows--escapes the command of his consciousness to the degree that it is objectified, to the degree to which it's turned into an antagonistic replica of himself; uncertain, yes, although not for that reason any less determinant.

21 Sept. Boring afternoon with Mariana. When I got to her house she was already somewhat nervous because her guts were rumbling sporadically, now like accordion doors, now like sewer pipes. The night before she'd gone out in her neighborhood, she must have had one of those strong gin and tonics she likes so much, and here's the result: discomfort and tension, hand poised to apply pressure to her belly in a vain repressive attempt, right there where the continuous and troublesome noise is, as startling as a mouse scurrying past the corner of our eye, just in case. But what definitely put her in a bad mood was that, after a hasty dash to the bathroom, I went in right after she was done, without even giving her time to switch off the light, the water still gushing down from the toilet tank. It's a trick I learned as a kid that I used to use with Milky, the same as the trick of waiting outside as soon as she locked herself in, to stay by the door humming a song pretending to kill time, something that had the virtue of getting her even more pissed and that, more than once, made her come out almost immediately, with barely controlled brusqueness. Knowing the impact, sure that it's no less effective on Mariana than on Milky, I use it as a punishment when I'm in the mood and depending on how Mariana behaves, her state of mind and even her expression, that expression--heavy eyelids, haughty nose--which really accentuates her look of fin-de-siècle Irish redhead, of a lazy, spoiled girl; it only takes a passing reference to our shared childhood games, for example, for her to put on this face and say that she doesn't remember a

thing. It's these sorts of reactions, so similar to Milky's, as well as a certain similarity of features and even complexion, that compel me, I imagine, to transfer my affectionate gestures, as well as my vengeful ones, from one woman to the other.

Before Mariana, I met her brother. He was going to my school, but although he was in my grade I didn't start getting to know him until, through those seating changes that teachers so enjoy imposing on students, like jealous lovers do when their children get too friendly with a classmate, I found him seated next to me. He had a habit of pulling out his weenie during class and playing with it beneath the desk as if it were some kind of little doll, a kind of Pulcinella performed in mockery of the teacher; then he would sniff his fingers. At that time he lived in an apartment in the Ensanche, enormous, silent, gloomy, and the apartment next door, with the same characteristics, was vacant; they called it Grandfather's apartment, a grandfather who--it must be presumed--was dead, while, including at the edges of this possibility, it's difficult to imagine an apartment better suited than that one to being a grandfather's apartment. His parents kept the keys, but it was easy to use the patio to go from one apartment to the other, from one bathroom window into the next one. And there, in that second, unoccupied apartment, identical to the first one, except inverted, as if reflected in a mirror, we established our secret headquarters: he, Mariana, another kid from school, and me. Naked, we took turns torturing each other, with rigor and deliberation, atop the caramel-colored damask of a showy queen-size bed. I suppose that it's this evolution in my relationship with Mariana, transforming without pause from that type of erotic game to the present one--not really so different, to be honest--that makes us a couple who doesn't fit the typical definition of one. The only thing I regret is that they changed apartments, they moved upstairs from the first floor to the top and built a penthouse floor above that one; Mariana has practically a whole apartment all for herself in the penthouse, but I preferred the deserted apartment downstairs, the dusty caramel-colored damask.

I've lost contact with her brother, however, almost completely. The problem isn't that he's crazy as a loon, which is what they were already saying about him years ago in school, but that he's a completely uninteresting loon no matter what he does, however much he brags about his literary pursuits, his travels, his friendship with famous writers. For him, from what I can see, the byword these days is transgression, transgress against everything in every area: morality, language, cultural parameters, everything. A word that should serve him, I suppose, habitual transgressor as he is, in order to justify that custom he has of locking himself in the bathroom with the object of transgressing himself with gusto, radically. Essentially, everything that it occurred to him to do in the rich depths of the apartment downstairs wasn't much more—probably owing, given his way of thinking, to the greater margin of satisfaction of his own fantasies that such hobbies permit—adaptable to the modalities of his own taste as is the ring to the finger. That's why I call him Mariano. Because the one who counts is Mariana.

Mariana, however, is not to blame for my bad mood this afternoon. I wasn't even thinking about her on my way home. I was thinking, rather, about how grandiose it would have been to have had a megaphone handy that afternoon when, while preparing for my school exams, I discovered the existence of Aurea, directly opposite my apartment, on the other side of the street, and then, from window to window, speak to her in the manner of a god who was watching her leaning back on the sofa, naked, devoting herself to sinful practices; her incredulity as she heard his terrible voice, her panic.

27 Sept. Grandfather is dying and Clumsy has gone to the town to kiss his ass now while he can still get something from him without a problem. At home, we all feel better, more relaxed. And the thing is, the same problem that seems to end up getting stuck at the heart of every marriage over time when it comes to sex, the symbolic center of the couple's connection, whether carnal commerce has ceased or if it continues being exercised, whether as an imperious and expeditious assault, or if it takes the form of a ritual repetition of an amorously requited seduction, an even more suffocating formula, if possible, the same problem, yes, extends to the remaining areas of conjugal life, thus creating in the home an atmosphere of exasperation that affects not only the children who live in the house but also the servants and the pets. Thus it ends up not mattering whether it's Clumsy or Milky who's found to be absent; the repercussion of their absence in the family ambit is, in both cases, identical: the tension subsides.

I don't remember having seen Grandfather more than two or three times. He's one of those old rural landlords who's come to be who he is, to have the town in his grip, aided by nothing but practical wisdom, a la Aesop, about what life is all about. The self-made man who dwells at the roots of all family mythology, although he's not without, on the other hand, the legend of providential assistance, finding some hidden treasure whose glimmer illuminates the obscurity of his beginnings like an aureole. And it's that other more tangible glimmer, that of his present fortune—the noose he's got around the town's neck—that has drawn his heirs there: the hope of not departing without their spoonful, the anxiety of everyone knowing once and for all the old man's, heretofore inscrutable, last will and testament, the fear of the manipulations behind the scenes, the intrigues of some presumed successor, neither more nor less scrupulous than the others, but certainly closer to the one now dying and, as such, more liable to influence a senile mind that resembles a sun going cold. It takes little to imagine the climate inside the big house, the multiplication of disputes between grandparents, aunts and uncles, and cousins, between siblings, nieces and nephews, the reproaches and accusations formulated with the general intervention of their respective spouses, the enormous quarrels this will cause, each party making a recounting *ab initio* of the offenses and injuries received, the scenes, the tranquilizers taken with a swallow of water, the telltale signs of a heart attack, the frights, calls to the doctor. And what constitutes a true pleasure—really no effort at all—is to imagine Clumsy there in the middle, representing Milky, fulfilling the official order to neutralize his beloved brother-in-law Pig Nose, the only thing the other relatives, without, however, taking their eyes off each other seem to agree on: watch out for Pig Nose, be careful with the guy who for years tried to become the old man's right hand, as if the old man would have ever needed any other hands than his own, or any vision distinct from what emanates from his own mind. And so just as from the remotest places in Islam the diverse tribes converge with drums a pounding on the scene of this Holy War, so in a similar way, one can imagine the old man's descendants all joining ranks against Pig Nose, and Pig Nose wheeling round and round against them all, the way a wild boar turns around and looms gigantic against the wild pack that hounds him, or like a virile member rises above the pubic fleece when it becomes erect, a boar's head purple from pure passion.

Pig Nose has a son who is my age. Fart Face, who, to say it the way a teacher would, is one of those boys not cut out for studying, who don't make it, who don't get it. I recall that, when we were little boys, there was a time when our respective parents seemed to make a real effort for us to play together like good cousins or, at least, that we should try to. Since then, Fart Face always tries to make a good impression on me, as if his parents had held me up as a role model, and since he's not the least bit like me, favorably impressing that model supposes getting close to him in some way; quite the retard's way of thinking. On the other hand, that stuff about how, in these cases, more than overcoming their own stupidity they are taught to disguise it, strikes me as a kindness toward one's neighbor which is highly appreciated. And thus we have Fart Face trying hard, fighting to counteract, spirited and tenacious, the poverty of spirit his blurry physical presence exudes, the image of stupidity he offers at first sight and of which he's conscious; and so we find him, for example, reading the newspaper in the Metro, on the bus, for everyone to see that he takes an interest in things, that he's a serious, even brainy, young fellow, one of those who takes advantage of the time wasted by having to go from place to place by learning something. And people will suppose him a fellow who studies or, even better, who works and studies, who's got a lot of merit. But the most curious thing is that perhaps there's a level of truth in all that and that, by sheer willpower, he's managed to achieve something. For example, the last time I saw him, he seemed to notice that my comment about his learning to ride a motorcycle as something to add to his list of accomplishments was laying it on too thick, looking at me with those cloudy puddle eyes of his. No, I know, he said: my place is on the toilet seat. And he's right! Through a mechanism which I never would have thought him capable of, like that novice aficionado in a fishing contest who lands the biggest fish, his limited intelligence had, in the depths of the unconscious, snared the most accurate image about himself that could be proposed!

If, for any parent, having a child with these characteristics is what's called a true cross to bear, it must be especially true for Pig Nose, seeing as how he is as sentimental in his family life as he is heartless outside of it, according to a dichotomy that surpasses what's habitual in a man of business, but also, who knows, as far as he's concerned, to what degree the contrast is even sharper between his personal triumphs and his domestic misfortunes. A drama similar to that of a certain businessman who, one fine season, in addition to the substantial profits he's going to close out the year with, suddenly finds himself with millions in prize money from a winning ticket, in which all the numbers match, in the Christmas Lottery--*El Gordo de Navidad*, the Big Fat Christmas Jackpot--and then, carried away by his own extroverted nature, he gives everyone kisses and hugs and toasts, and stretches out his hand and more hands, almost surprised by how much he loves his wife and children, his colleagues, employees and clients, all those people surrounding him, everybody, and he goes here and there, unable to sit still, until, suddenly, as if by the blaze of a firework that lights up the night, he sees all that pleasure from without, everything revealed to his eyes in toto and simultaneously, a whole that makes him realize that those extra millions change nothing, that there's nothing new in life with respect to the situation before he won the Christmas Jackpot, nothing that he couldn't have done before but which, nevertheless, he didn't do and now he'll continue to not do, being as it is impossible to do at the same time what one wished and what one must, that therein lies the problem, and that because its solution is not a question of money, everything will continue the same as before, with more worries than before, more problems, more displeasure, the only satisfaction from counting on those additional millions resides in the idea that he can count on them, and that what he most desires in those moments of joy, what he truly wishes, is nothing more than crawling into bed and switching off the light.

The evil that alights on others gives me pleasure, that much is clear. Yes, I enjoy other people's misfortunes, and so much more the closer they are to me, the closer I can see them. For example, I'm happy that the old man is dying, but my happiness would be greater if it were Pig Nose who was dying, because I know him better and I can imagine the situation more clearly—Aunt Mercedes grieving, Fart Face stupefied, etcetera. And I would be so much happier if it were Clumsy instead of Pig Nose. And even more if it were Milky. Yes, her more than anyone, and keep in mind that to reach this conclusion I had to measure and sharpen my feelings to the limit. And it's this act of lucidity, the fact of having managed to formulate my feelings that everyone shares, consciously or unconsciously, is what makes my moral attitude so singular. Because people tend to do the exact opposite: to repress, draw the curtains, hide under other appearances—be they simply different, be they neither more nor less than the opposite--their happiness when witnessing another's misfortune, whatever it happens to be, death, ruin, collapse. Thus while witnessing any accident—an old man who slips and breaks his hip, someone run down by a car—they conceal their joyful morbid curiosity through a commiserating commentary, oh dear God, what a tragedy, like that, by virtue of the same impulse, when necessary, when the evil alights upon an acquaintance, a family member, a friend, the closer they are to the person the more they transform their joy into horror by modifying the release of the enormous cackles of laughter echoing in the basements of their conscience, transforming them into manifestations of grief equally chilling and contagious, generators and enhancers of similar reactions. Nothing more symptomatic in this sense than what happens with children, given that, as far as they're concerned, the sublimation of pleasure until its transmutation into horror supposes a process that appears extremely dramatic, increasing even as it elevates the symbolic value of those innocents par excellence to the supreme category of sacrificial victims. A busload of children that plunges into the river, for example, that someone suffers any one of those accidents that occasionally make bold front page headlines: the blood curdling spectacle to which one has been a privileged eyewitness, the scenes of grief between family members and friends arriving to the scene of the episode, the story that is passed on to the rest of the curious onlookers gathered there, heartrending scenes and compulsive reactions that are repeated each time the event is retold, acquiring, if possible, greater plasticity and richness of detail as each group of listeners repeats it to new audiences, the sense of guilt stimulated to the maximum by the contagion of one listener to another: children that could be their own, the beloved children of each one of them; that could also be they themselves when they were children and already perverse and guilty. The emotional discharge characteristic of every catastrophe, inescapable to the point of being reflected in the collective conscience through popular sayings like *ni qué niño muerto*, meaning "nonsense" or "not even in your worst nightmares," as a kind of prototypical summum of the misfortune, the height of misfortunes that signals the potentially maximum character of the emotive response. A response that, like all psychic, physical, and even physiological discharge, supposes an intense pleasure: that of arousing in others the feeling of guilt, a cathartic explosion that does nothing but alleviate the weight of self-guilt according to a compensatory mechanism--the most common, not the only one--which is usually activated in the subconscious. A pleasure which, however many people ignore it, however much they're unaware of its true nature, they still enjoy. A case that is not my own: I know its true nature and my pleasure is different. My pleasure, the one I experience in the face of others' misfortune, is based on the possibility of striving successfully against that compensatory mechanism: turning the tables on the situation, using the horror that preys on the eyewitness to a catastrophe, on the curious bystanders who gather where the accident took place, on the eavesdropper who asks for specific details, and that all that horror only fosters the self-guilt inside each one of them, that contributes as much as possible to their emotional response, that far from being discharged, becomes overcharged, overshadowing. Meaning: convert the expiatory sacrifice into an exemplary punishment, like that wise Persian emperor who punished the sins of his subjects by making them march between a double row of mortal remains, the quartered bodies of their own children. Simply invert the meaning of the process.

27 Sept. Shadowing Maira without her noticing presented no great difficulties at that hour, when the students heading to school intermingle with the people running to work. The difficulty began upon reaching the laboratory, situated beneath a half-constructed temple, something like la Sagrada Familia, but a Sagrada Familia with a laboratory housed inside its crypt. The temple was constructed in a barren spot, in a vast open lot where

the construction materials—stone, brick, and sacks of cement—were piled up together alongside the rubble. The works, totally abandoned, made the whole place look more like ruins than something under construction, porticoes, staircases, arches, and columns open to the sky, vaguely shaping spaces. The laboratory entrance was found inside the area outlined by the ruins, and to get there you had to follow one of those paths that the few passersby wear down with their own footsteps as they cross the empty field. But, if you wanted to avoid being seen, the only thing to do was to crawl through the brambles and weeds, even if it meant scratching your knees, so as to take advantage of the visual protection afforded by the huge carved stones, then running in a crouch for a ways. The risks were great: a little boy who advanced along those paths was suddenly lifted up in the air by two men who remained hidden and transported at top speed to the central area. Somewhat farther on, the same thing happened with two other boys who had dared to enter the empty lot, and not even the boys who stayed on the edges, the ones who simply walked the streets that bordered it, managed to escape the assault. Moreover: sometimes a car stopped nearby, and some small body or other—stamping, kicking—was dragged out from inside and carried like a bundle toward the ruins. And it was enough to hear the screams and sobs coming out through the open skylights at ground level to understand what was going on down there. He turned back, approached various pedestrians, an older woman dressed in dark clothes, a gentleman with a reversible overcoat and a large felt fedora, explaining to them about the kidnappings and assaults, about the experiments on children that were being conducted in that laboratory. Nobody paid him any attention, they didn't even stop to listen, and he had to run to keep up with them while he spoke to them. It was clear, however, that the problem wasn't that they didn't believe him—they knew that what he was telling them was true, and they were even interested in the fact that all that was happening—and that all this benefitted them in some way, so it was useless to expect anything from them. So, he resolved to go into the ruins, to go down under the enormous vault that arched over the ground like the dome of a skull, and to descend into the crypt. Yes, let himself be assaulted, be carried into the operating room, and that Maira herself, on realizing that it was now his turn, that he was the next victim of the experiments, that it was he, precisely, who was going to be injected, she would understand the importance of all that. That Maira understand it, that was the essential thing. As much as or more than the Sagrada Familia, the laboratory environs seemed like the Hospital de San Pablo, and there were nurses, both men and women, wandering back and forth between the pavilions.

These lines could have been written by substituting the past tense verbs for present tense ones, as well as, here and there, the third person for the first. *I resolve* instead of *I resolved, he resolved*, etcetera.

II

20 Oct. Today there was light in her window and, fleeting but unmistakable, I was able to distinguish Aurea's silhouette behind the lace curtains. Then the lights went out. It was somewhat past six o'clock, although not by much; the days are getting shorter and the dusk is deceptive. I thought it was strange, however, that she'd turn on the light so early. And what if it was a signal or a trick, some way of recapturing my attention, of escaping from the ostensible oblivion in which I've got her? If it was that, she must have been disappointed. It was like answering her with a question, the way the echo answers. So who's really the voyeur around here, after all?

Uncertainty produces discomfort, and discomfort, irritation. Sensations that summon memories of an incident that happened during my first year in college, when coming out of the university, heading home, on the Metro, almost every morning I used to run into a man looking like some old wild boar with salt and pepper hair, who never took his eyes off me. I pretended to be reading or absorbed in my reflections, but I always ended up glancing over to see if he was still looking at me—whether directly, feigning distraction, or maybe in the reflection on the windows—invariably I met those laughing eyes that only seemed to be awaiting my gaze. He got off the train at the same station as I did and he let me walk on ahead, or rather, he followed a short distance behind me, for a little more than three blocks until the corner at which, it seems, our respective paths diverged. There he stopped and stared at me while I walked away, not without confirming along the way, looking back obliquely, that he was still there, also waiting, probably, for me to check again. And so on, morning after morning, again and again, with such a regularity that the only possible explanation was that he was waiting at the station for me to arrive, since a coincidence of such magnitude was otherwise impossible. One day, sure that he had followed me along the street, that he had stopped to watch me on the same corner as always, I spun round on my heels and, as if surging with adrenaline, strode toward him like a whirlwind, smacking my right fist into my left hand. What's your problem? I shouted. You mind telling me what's going on? And that wild-boar-colored man, his clothes like a matching outfit for his hair, arched his eyebrows happily, almost jovial: You think something special is going on? he said. I shook my right-hand index finger under his nose. Don't get the wrong idea about me, don't get the wrong idea! And turning my back with the same brusqueness as before, I continued on my way, trying with my decisive stride to disguise how confused and ridiculous I felt, wishing I'd said something else to him, that I'd unleashed some brilliant, cutting, terrifying remark, something that would have deprived the other man of the opportunity to say what he'd said, as I was walking away: I don't see how I could be wrong, sonny boy; from then on, I decided it would be best to just forget he existed. Another time, when I took the Metro, along with a guy from the university who also lived in my neighborhood, I saw him wave, warmly, at the man with the wild boar hair, above the heads of several passengers. I asked who he was and my companion told me that he was a really cool guy, the most screamingly funny fellow, and that he knew a thing or two about art; he's got an antique shop on Calle de la Paja and the best private collection of asses in the world. Really, man: I've seen it: medieval gargoyles, Roman bas reliefs, Japanese drawings, pre-Columbian pottery, gold and silver jewelry, everything, man, and from every period, anything featuring asses.

The first person surprised by the way I had reacted toward our collector was myself. I've long been used to arousing the interest of homosexuals and, precisely for that reason, the aggressiveness of my response was even more out of place, comparable in every way to my embarrassment, to what the street exhibitionist tries to stir up through his actions. Although I'm not like that, I've got nothing against it, that's what people who consider themselves evolved usually say about homosexuals, thus showing, along with their natural understanding, their interest in highlighting that they're not members of the club. A prudish insistence, needless to say, and which, curiously, approximates that intemperate fussiness which certain homosexuals—monosexuals, as I call them—so often make a show of. And if there's something in them that horrifies me it's precisely this: the mutation their personality undergoes at a specific moment, their way of splitting in two, of making eyes at you with one simple wink. Because, if the heterosexual relationship already has something of sickliness and erotic encounters, something of transitory mental alienation, the monosexual conduct becomes parodic as well as sick, the mimesis of a behavior and of some manners only explainable as the fruit of the persistent fantasies of a perturbed mind. Arguing about whether it's a congenital defect or an induced deformation strikes me as simple-minded nonsense that only serves to accentuate the phenomenon, to provide the monosexual with new alibis, the same as with all those stories about alienation and cheap psychology, that stuff about how his mother used to dress him as a little girl and then his father punished him, his schoolmates mocked him, etcetera. Manipulations similar to the ones that come from exploiting feelings of guilt, generally less innocent in the motive, also in keeping with very concrete objectives. Manipulations that can badly affect someone, like me, who, if they harbor some feeling as a driving force, it's not guilt but rather retaliation.

24 Oct. Mariano was radiant, possessed by that happiness of inane people who, one fine day, find themselves with something to tell, be it some bombshell that for whatever reason they've been the first to find out, or be it some simple bit of gossip, which, however, is capable of causing a certain impact within their circle. Not a question of anything that might have happened to them, but to The Bust, and The Bust just told it to him. In fact, it wasn't anything that happened to The Bust, but to someone else, but The Bust had been witness, had witnessed it with his own eyes. And for anyone who knows him, the possibility that he had invented it was something that had to be discarded beforehand, given that invention was beyond his capacity. If I call him The Bust it's precisely because he's just like something from a fable: a lovely head without any brains.

The Bust is an old friend from school, a member of one of those families with many brothers and sisters, all good kids, very good looking, well built, idiots, idlers, good kids without a dime, kids predestined, as a consequence, to be fodder for pederasts. The fact is that his story has as its setting, not your typical sauna, but that one specific sauna, about which there can be no surprises, which, in this sense, is all the more significant it seems to me. I began to intuit it the afternoon I discovered him having a conversation on the terrace of a bar—The Stab, I think it was—where a handful of fellows like him were presided over by one of those really shriveled looking guys you see from time to time, nostalgic El Diagonal snobs from times gone by, the enigma of whose peculiar nature is only a question of time, the time it takes to tie up loose ends, to identify their nature with that of a crazy woman, revealing that aspect in their way of talking especially revealing in that aspect, the nasal voice they use and, above all, the tone of judicious sincerity with a touch of pessimism typical of these sorts of characters, who usually like to be called Rafa or some analogous familiar diminutive. The very crafty one made a speech, and The Bust and the other little young ones listened to him with that accepting attitude and favorable disposition that come with being simple-minded. I remember one occasion, when we were kids, The Bust was recovering from something, and some of us boys from school went round to visit him; a whole gaggle of brothers and sisters led us to his room, and there we found him, sinking down with clucking laughs into the depths of the bed obviously hoping for the instinctive response to such an attitude: wanting the older ones pile on top of him and flatten him and squeeze him right up to the fine line that separates laughter from tears. Another fact that, considering his story about the sauna, also turns out to be revealing. Because, if not for the complete lack of imagination which I referred to earlier, I'd be inclined to believe that his presence in this story splits in two, that he tells about what happened to him as if it actually happened to someone else.

Whether or not a second protagonist exists, whether or not it's more exact to speak in the third person than in the first, the fact is that The Bust found himself in that sauna around mid-morning, an hour when it's not too crowded, two or three people here and there, distractedly leafing through magazines. And that's when the kid showed up, a normal looking boy, rather shy and almost intimidated even to judge by his way of moving, of taking a seat. But he must have had something special about him when the guy who was in front of him, a rather corpulent forty-something man, slowly looked him over. The Bust, situated in a corner, could see them both at the same time, and the boy's expression was the first thing that alerted him to the maneuver initiated by the other one, raising up the magazine he had open on his lap to reveal the full extent of his penis, long and slender as a flute and just as stiff, with the provocative slits of his eyes like the finger holes on a flute. The boy shook the sweat from his face, fanned himself with his hand, and encapsulating his words in a kind of sigh, said: it's so hot in here. And the one facing him, looking at him over the open magazine: it certainly is. The boy gave him a smile with that recognition of a student who is congratulated by a teacher: I've been told this is the best thing for curing a cold, he said. And the other one: they've told you right, certainly; you'll see you come out of here good as new. The boy smiled again; well, I'm going to rinse off a little, he said. In the showers, the one in the stall next to him stuck his head out asking something. What? said the boy. The one from the adjacent stall went into the kid's stall clutching a pink bottle, his long tufts of hair streaming water. Boy, do you need some soap, dammit! he said even as he squirted the pink liquid over his shoulders and smeared it all over his body with the palm of his hand. Thanks, said the kid, but I'm only just freshening up a bit. The other one, positioning himself behind his back, slipped a finger up his ass and then tried to shove his penis in. Outside the stall, watching him, was the guy with eyes like a flute's finger holes and an even more well-built guy who was putting on a sweatsuit. The boy struggled, laughing: that's really uncomfortable, he said. And the one in the sweatsuit: the boy's right, what he needs is a good massage, and that's always more comfortable. And the one with the eyes like flute-stops: that's right, let's go over there, so the kid doesn't get a chill, he's got a cold. All the more reason. Sure, of course. And then a beer. Now you're talking! And as if forming one of those street groups that sing and dance with their arms draped over each other's shoulders during the San Fermín celebrations, like a group of serenaders, they all moved together toward the massage room, led by the guy with the flute stop eyes, the towel draped over his penis like a flag hanging from a pole, and the boy between the others like that adolescent who one fine day, as if surrendering to long-suppressed temptation or as if drunk on some liquor or drug of uncertain nature, begins to run along the street, barefoot, in shorts, mouth half open, eyes blank, completely slack, his arms and legs limp as wet rags, his behavior causing people, after their initial shock, to start chasing after him with taunts and wisecracks, to end up, as if spurred on by one another, subjecting him to all manner of brutality, as if he were some prisoner in a *Sanbenito* or some idiot in a dunce's cap. The door stood half-open and from outside it was possible to catch a glimpse of what was going on in there, of the vicissitudes of the action, bodies in tense exercise, rapid, energetic, fragmentary movements, centered around the massage table, bodies changing places with each other, as if swapping jobs, as if relieving each other, also, like in a ronda or a sarabande, the sounds coming from in there, now like neighing, now like braying. The cast-off sweatsuit was visible lying in a crumpled heap on the floor, and, closer, almost in the threshold, its wet folds forming an enormous smile, a white towel.

When Mary Ann arrived—today she was very Irish—she made me repeat the story for her so she could hear it from start to finish, from soup to nuts.

25 Oct. The same thing happens with sexuality as with cinemaniacs, those erudite obsessives who fly into ecstasies over this or that scene from Hitchcock, or this or that shot of Bogart smoking, or any take of Garbo holding a drink, all of them the most banal sort of symbolism, psychoanalytic elements digested the way one digests fruit and with similar physiological consequences, an ideological baggage equivalent to that of the person who goes out hunting rhinos armed with a compressed air rifle. Everyone knows it all, there's no fact that cannot be explained despite how little they know

about searching the repertoire of interpretations or the whole junk heap of generalities, hardly useful to preserve the defenses one erects around their own helplessness. The case of that guy last summer who, during one of those boat picnics that so often lend themselves to intimate confessions, diagnosed himself as having an inverted Oedipus complex, and from there, as if such a declaration had activated some obscure compulsive mechanism, everyone began to reveal the rich complexities of his personality in the most impeccable language of a discotheque Freud.

Of greater interest—and of course greater significance—than making a show of the more than questionable honor implied by wielding the characteristic slang of such vulgarizations, is, I really believe, stopping to think about what our childhood was like beyond any theoretical scheme, its specific defining traits—as well as the general traits, common to other youngsters—that distinguish us from our elders. Seemingly irrelevant things, the generalized use of the baby formula bottle, for example; the fact that women refuse to destroy their breasts by suckling their children, introducing from earliest childhood a new element—the bottle—into the relationships that the child maintains with the family circle. Because it's one thing to substitute the mother's role with a nursemaid, a role played in wealthy families of old by the wet nurse, a more than expressive denomination, and another, very different thing, to use a bottle of baby formula. And not precisely because of the artificial ingredients it contains—the only thing that seems to worry the doctors—but for the object itself, capable of transforming what was a non-transferable link into the most indiscriminate satisfaction of the child's needs, which can only confuse the many characteristics that pleasure offers: the mother, yes, but also the granny or the auntie or a female friend who gets a thrill from giving it to him, the same as, more frequently, the father himself. Faced with the constant presence of a familiar and reliable breast—the mother's or not—the versatility of the baby bottle, bland, interchangeable; can a similar change not have a repercussion in those of us who have been raised with a bottle? I would say, rather, no, that perhaps the sexual promiscuity and emotional lightness so much thrown in the faces of boys and girls my age perhaps turns out to be less strange if one takes into account that the one who satisfied the oral pleasures of the baby in question by means of a rubber nipple was, for example, the papa. At least, in the past, the queens, princesses, and noble ladies in general, abandoned their children once they were already nursed, and these children, raised up within palace exile, grew up naturally disposed toward assassination.

The promiscuity of young people is another commonplace that parents usually adorn according to their own personal erotic fantasies in a form not very different, generally, from what Cecil B. DeMille would have done. Without realizing that, in this atmosphere of marijuana and orgy that they imagine, the girls don't know any better than a fully mature woman what it takes to stay *au courant*, and the boys don't even know what face to wear, one and another trying hard to achieve a degree of concentration intense enough to keep them safe from losing their hard-ons, a wilting the littlest thing can cause, some corny joke, an inopportune laugh, a stupid look. The burden of those inane rituals of initiation, the frustration that it supposes for those who have participated in them, on the very verge of the ridiculous, a feeling only surpassable through the encouragement of thinking that that's it, that the experience has already been had, that you already know everything there is to know, as if such experiences could be compared—and they can't, not by a long shot—to the inventions that four kids are capable of carrying out in the quietude of an enormous uninhabited apartment. Images of childhood that, to the degree they are repressed, resurface, years later, in their parents' erotic fantasies, only now adorned with Cecil B. De Mille flourishes and set on stage like a Copenhagen sex show. It's not that nothing changes; what happens is that the changes are not what the parents imagine.

Does jealousy exist for young people? Yes, sir: despite their impertinence and apparent lack of inhibition, just like the Swedes, jealousy is real for young people, just like the whole range of feelings capable of staining love until transforming it into its opposite. And the same could be said about shyness, those boys who prefer to speak to girls, each one explaining themselves to the other, discovering coincidences in order to penetrate the erotic territory per se, as much through the interruption of the pleasure that the conversation itself now brings, as for the fear of changing terrain, and, above all, the fear of how to realize that change, a problem that is almost a problem of expression, which, meanwhile, must come into play/become a factor/become part of the gamer, whether while they kiss with the passion of love as a revelation, or while, descending to a lower but also more direct level, starting by clumsily probing and exploring the principal erogenous zones.

What definitely strikes me as positive is the progressive recognition that everyone is bisexual, although the one who insists too much on that is usually simply monosexual, by means of a principle similar to the following: when one of those generals who kick up a coup d'état in any South American republic declares that the new regime is neither rightist nor leftist, it must be understood that it's on the right. All the vitality generated by the acceptance of the fact becomes a force that diminishes and deforms when it is rejected in one sense or another. The repressed person's tense behavior and the queer's flouncing as complimentary phenomena.

29 Oct. If, as we were saying, the fact of having been raised with a baby bottle can alter an individual's erotic blueprint and, consequently, their emotional life just as much as their sexual behavior, then is it not inevitable that they must vary their moral terrain, in terms of principles and conduct? Can you even imagine that that they continue to maintain their norms of behavior, not only the norms that agree with traditional morality still extant in today's society, but the even more restrictive norms prevailing in what the communists call the new society? The change of social structure does not prevent moral principles from being the same as before the revolution, even reinforced by the fact that, after the revolution, the state acts as a kind of second father and the society as a second mother. I have a communist friend who's worried about this, the lack of appeal that the new society holds for young people nowadays; I had him as a teacher in my first year at university and now we see each other occasionally and discuss these things. He's also worried about the contagion, the impact that the moral habits and attitudes of youth here can cause the youth there, what would become of the new society if this were to come about, if the example spread; I've suggested that the only way to anticipate events, to prevent a possible generational rupture, is vaccination, meaning, to immediately impose the use of the baby bottle. But these communists have no sense of humor.

It amuses me, however, to discover the common place, to find out what lies behind certain words whose contents conceal a rather obvious question: they mean this because they're there. Something similar to believing some news just because the newspaper reports it. Just as words mean and designate things, so, too, do they cover and hide them. Formulations of altruistic meaning and positive value, for example, dedicating oneself to teaching, having children, activities whose mere verbal formulation seems to intrinsically convey something exemplary. And the fact is that reality is hypocritical, yes, but people couldn't stand it if it were not. Because just as the so-called pedagogical vocation frequently conceals in the teacher or future teacher not so much the desire to teach children as much as the obscure impulse to remake oneself, to find, within a manic order, a sadistic discipline, and a restrictive indoctrination, safety from the dangers that stalk him, from the incoherence and the chaos produced by the anarchic degeneration of a sick brain, thus, under the compulsion of a similar desire to form oneself in one's own image and likeness through children, in the image and likeness of what they believe they were or should have been, thus, under this kind of compulsion, parents when they surrender to their procreative anxieties.

The most obvious thing is, sometimes, the most difficult to comprehend; not only with respect to oneself but also with respect to other people. The deep meaning of the most apparently trivial details, of the most mundane tics, a meaning that functions exclusively in the subconscious, a meaning unacceptably bizarre, as if it was guaranteed to mean something quite a bit more elevated, as it doubtless proves to be for the average man's wisdom. A phenomenon capable, by reason of that unconscious character, of overflowing the borders of the individual, of becoming collective, of becoming history, that mindset of "no matter the cost we must see to it that the king of Spain enters the Court of Madrid" which concludes the hymn of our traditionalists, imperious volunteerism of some words whose ultimate meaning will gather all its clarifying transparency if, as by chance, we relate it to an old joke of Jaimito, that *tararí, tararí, tararí, Carlos V entra en Madrid*, words describing the coitus that the child sees his parents engaged in. Ultimately, it's about an associative mechanism capable of illustrating the unconscious content of the Spanish traditionalist cause at the same time as the no-less-unconscious sharpness of those who, knowing the hymn, have heard the joke for generations; about illuminating the shadowy areas of the mind, both that of the hymn's author as well as the one who invented the joke. Why, precisely, a king named Carlos? Might this king be the Emperor Charles, Carlos I of Spain and Charles V of Germany, for whom entering Madrid could not suppose any emotion more intense than passing through some other similar town like the town that Madrid was in those days, or might that Charles V be, rather, the Carlos V of the traditionalists, the founder of his officious royal stock? Why exactly Madrid and not some other town if our king, the Charles V in question, is not the conservative pretender? A pretender who, the same as so many others who succeeded him in the historical venture, as so many others who backed him up with their support, never managed to fulfill the objective of entering Madrid at any cost, inheritors not so much of a crown as of the impotence that all reiterated frustration generates, a reality accurately captured by the joke as it refers to the emblematic valor of the hymn, and more generally, the traditionalist cause, to the area of the unformulated fears of castration that the subject experiences, that one need not be Freud to see it symbolized by that child, by Jaimito who witnesses his parents' coitus. Thus, precisely, the proverbial aggression of the traditionalists, an aggression that is nothing but the compensatory reflex of an historical importance. That, too, some time ago, led me to the conclusion that Clumsy is impotent.

I like to detect symptoms, perform diagnoses; in this aspect--only in this, given that sick or injured bodies horrify me--I could have been a doctor. Because unravelling the enigma of these apparently foolish things is not at all easy. The enigma exists even beneath the most diaphanous of appearances, and figuring it out takes time; I go around and around with it until, suddenly, usually as a surprise, I trip over the solution. And the later I find it, the more I become obsessed with it. I hate cabbage, for example, the only vegetable I don't like, without which the case could be reduced to a matter of taste—that's begging the question—given that if I don't like its flavor there's a reason for it, and that it's something I'm interested in elucidating. What's certain is that, currently, I wouldn't know whether to say if the explanation is related to the fact that I had a frightening grandma who, with all the dedication her sclerotic brain could muster, never tired of repeating that I'd been found underneath a cabbage leaf, or if, more directly, it has to do with the fetid gases that expand in the stomach of whomever eats cabbage, making their silhouette, in the end, look swollen, like from pregnancy, the origin, perhaps of that tale people tell children.

31 Oct. This morning I woke up full of anxiety from a dream that, after only a few moments, was just as hard to pinpoint as the shape of the landscape that suddenly appears in the lightning at night, leaving barely any impression of it in my mind. The only thing I'm sure about is that it had something to do with tetanus, which clarifies nothing, given that, for me, anything related to tetanus is synonymous with a nightmare. From my first memories, the smallest scratch, however superficial, made me go running home, to the school infirmary, to the nearest pharmacy, wherever they could disinfect it for me as soon as possible, to submit myself to the saving effects of hydrogen peroxide, that burning whiteness against which the insidious perversity of the microbe has no chance at all. A fear that—not because I kept it secret in order to escape my playmates' jokes--no longer explains certain precautions that I took--which I still take, as a mechanical habit—facing any circumstance that implied the risk of getting stuck with a thorn, getting cut by rusted iron, getting pricked by what have you, not to mention the most terrifying thing: stepping barefoot on a thumbtack.

Residual fear of this kind of phobia must be, I suppose, what injections cause me, something kind of equivalent to the fear others have of flying in airplanes. I get my shots from the local pharmacist, who administers them better than many doctors and nurses; yesterday afternoon, precisely, when I walked into the pharmacy, he'd just given a shot to one of those gentlemen whose mere appearance is a more than sufficient sign of his confidence that, with a nice rejuvenating shot, he'll keep looking good for a time, and perhaps it's this image, the pharmacist's glittering eyeglasses as he emerges from the backroom, the moronic smile of the gentleman on his way out the door, departing with the joy of having ten years lifted off his shoulders, the most immediate antecedent my unconscious reached for, the way a bricklayer reaches for his tools, when I was trying to pinpoint my dream about tetanus.

It seems that on one occasion the pharmacist saw me on the terrace of a bar chatting with my communist friend, and since then he talks to me about politics every time I stop by the pharmacy; apparently, he knew my communist friend from I don't know where and immediately supposed that I shared his ideas. When I say that he talks to me, I mean it literally, given that the one who does the talking is him, and I'm the one who listens each time to his renewed declaration of faith in the inexorable triumph of the socialist cause, which is what he calls communism, a declaration usually accompanied by a general overview of the world and, in particular, the socialist cause, with the addition of the most recent news praising the reality of the advances which, from the most diverse corners of the world, are carried out in this sense, a convergence of partial victories that are gradually joined together, isolated points that, united through a kind of imaginary line, gradually delineate the signature to what is already a verdict on history. If, for example, I ask him, with his chromium mirrored lenses and the steely lock of hair falling over his forehead, about the Chinese, he doesn't flinch: he ignores the comment that way someone ignores something that, for its very irrelevance, turns out to be contemptible, since the Chinese and the Soviets are the same, communists one and all, to the point that their presumed disagreements might well be nothing more than a stratagem proffered to the capitalist world, a recourse whose final goal would be nothing more than accelerating the process, to precipitate the sinking of capitalism beneath the weight of its own contradictions and accelerate the final victory of the socialist camp. Neither is he worried by the fact that things around here aren't going too well, that we've been trying unsuccessfully for thirty-odd years to put an end to Francoism; the business as a whole is going well and that's what matters. Spain is only a small piece of this whole, so small that you might say it bothers him to talk about it.

I was working on these notes, writing what I mentioned above about the pharmacist, when, pausing, just a moment ago, I went to open the window, to stick my head out for some fresh air, attracted no doubt by the almost-summertime warmth of the afternoon. At the window of the next apartment, just a few yards away, a middle-aged housemaid who looked like Franco's daughter, a Rubenesque woman with a meaty smile, resting her arms on the sill, looking down saying, Wow, what a man! He's spinning like a fan! meaning, the traffic cop on the corner who, by force of whistling and energetic signals, was fighting to clear the classic traffic jam that happens when schools let out in the afternoon. Then she looked at me and the urban panorama all around, as if waiting for some well-deserved applause or similar homage to her prosopopoeial wit, fleshy extraversion of the Andalusian women, superior even to that of the Andalusian men; a character eminently descriptive of their images, a relationship between two things based on appearance, stripped of internal links, the arms of the traffic cop, the blades of the fan.

It was then when I realized how many days I've gone without taking a good look at the window across the street. Not even in the morning, when I wake up lying on top of my cock, swollen like a stout keel, do I think about Aurea.

2 Nov. At first glance, the pleasure that nobody knows that I'm writing can be confused with a variation of solitary pleasure. But it's got nothing to do with that, unless onanism is considered an ersatz pleasure, something far from exact, because the onanist won't find comparable satisfaction in other erotic practices and I don't find any special attraction in the act of writing in secret. Quite the contrary: if there's something that I don't like it's the role of the unpublished writer, some guy people know writes and that's it, what's called a promise, a category comparable to a virgin girl, including the embarrassment. Neither do I like the relationships that come about as a result of being a writer, the implicit complicities, the alliances and rivalries of the literary life, the envies and paranoias belonging to that little world. I don't seek out well-known writers because they've got nothing to say to me that's not already in their books and because, however much they pretend the opposite, nothing of mine was going to interest them either, as they are interested exclusively in themselves. As far as people my age, young people who write, the simple prospect of dealing with them, of exchanging manuscripts and readings, of discussing our respective projects, each one listening to the others only to then be able to talk about himself, is something that disgusts me, everyone carrying on like young ladies who're now fornicating and whisper their secrets to each other. No, my idea is different; one fine day discover one of my books in the shop windows, unexpected like one of those mushrooms that just sprout up, you might say, overnight; that the presence of my book and my appearance as a writer coincide until superimposing themselves on each other, until making any kind of explanation or conjecture pointless.

The only person with whom I have talked about these things is Ricardo

Echave, an architect friend of my parents. Better to say: we talk not only about literature but also about architecture, painting, music, films, etcetera, and when he asked me if I wrote anything I told him no. I imagine he didn't believe me, but he didn't insist any further. He noticed that, for some reason, I didn't want to talk about what I did, and he respected my attitude. Otherwise, why would he tell me that, as far as he was concerned, he was growing distant from architecture and closer to the written word? Isn't this an indirect form of encouraging me, especially if the one saying it is none other than a world famous architect? He guessed it, it's true, just as it's also true that I had guessed that he would guess it. I'd been looking for the opportunity for some time to approach him, but at home, with my parents there, it was little less than an impossible goal, and the result was that, instead of brilliant things, I just made some impertinent remarks. It took until last summer to arrange things to be able to cross paths with him on one of those boring excursions on a yacht and then, getting him off to one side, we were able to chat as we pleased.

What he did not explain to me is his relationship with my parents. I know that at some earlier time Clumsy commissioned him for a project, but this doesn't strike me as a good enough reason to maintain a friendship, seeing as how they have so little in common, being at opposite poles from one another. Milky might also be a motive, because I take it for granted that she must have slept with Ricardo more than once; probably not too many times. But even if this can explain it there subsists some emotional tie between the two of them, it seems to me that it would be too much to even consider the possibility that the affection might have extended to include Clumsy. And if, instead of being Clumsy's son, I were Ricardo's? That would explain many things.

Another question related to my desire to write, and about which, as a consequence, I also can't talk with anybody about, is the reconsideration I've been making about my own life in order to eliminate, ahead of time, interferences and adherences, any type of subrogated ballast. To accommodate the world to my will and not the reverse; the family, society, the State, they've all got their plans for someone, plans that you've only got to accept in so far as they coincide with your own, not a millimeter more: that is my only rule for obedience. Thus, the prospect of getting married and having children seems to me not only crazy but also ridiculous and even humiliating; the author must be exclusively devoted to his own work. And consider this wise, analogous subtlety: the Catholic Church instituting celibacy, thus preventing any discussion of the problem by excluding all possibility that an ecclesiastic might have a family! Because it couldn't be that children resulted from the sexual activity, presumably abundant, of those clergy from antiquity, stocky and fiery like bulls, nor, as a result of the onslaughts of lust; the problem lay in the family as an institution, incompatible with the institution of celibacy. And what celibacy targets is the family, not the children, children who cannot constitute a family from the moment in which there is no wife either, given that the father is incapable of being a husband.

No less admirable, it seems to me, is the rule of poverty that dominates certain orders; the religious possess nothing, the Order possesses it for him and, even as it provides for his necessities, exempts him from economic worries. Precisely the situation that I hope to achieve; without possessions that enslave nor the harassment of economic worries. Meaning: not rich in property, but not linked to an absurd job either, the kind that people are obliged to perform because of the need for money. Without problems, in a word, neither material nor moral, nothing that can come between the writer and his work.

4 Nov. Yesterday, Mary Ann and I and some other friends consulted a Ouija board. We used a crystal snifter for a planchette. When I asked *Who are you?* the snifter spelled it out crystal clear: your great-grandfather. And when I asked if he was dead, the answer was: *Enfer*. Next, the glass began moving back and forth, signaling an unintelligible series of consonants, faster and faster, spinning around as if crazy or drunk before falling over and shattering. *Enfer*. Had he answered in French? Had he left the word *enfermo* unfinished? Apart from the fact that living people don't usually resort to these kinds of invocations, the old man, as far as I know, hasn't died. He had a relapse, yes, a curious attack of hiccups, and Clumsy has gone back to town to stay on his good side, or rather, to keep an eye on the rest of the family. It would be impressive if the old man had died the very moment when we made the glass move.

The most likely thing, however, is that there was some interference. Among those gathered was one who didn't believe in these things, and it's well-known that all it takes is for one person to remain close-minded for everything to go wrong. I neither believe nor reject anything on principle; what's undoubtable is that, for whatever the reason, the planchette spells out whole sentences, and it's not at all clear to me that they're the product of anybody's manipulation nor any accommodating interpretation. Is the sky going to fall on me for believing that? For our skeptical friend, however, the problem is one of principle: no matter what comes of it, it's not true, it can't be. According to him, it's like astrology; like thinking that the planets and constellations are watching over us: anthropomorphism, pure anthropomorphism. I tell him that the surprising thing would be a non-anthropomorphic conception of the world, starting with, for example, a stone's perspective; without much emphasis, of course, he's not going to feel obliged to give me a drenching of dialectical materialism, like the good communist that he is. Not my communist friend, the one who was my professor in my first year at college; someone else. This person is rather more Mary Ann's friend, he seeks her out on the sly and it wouldn't surprise me if they've bedded down together now and again. Nonetheless, and although he refuses to recognize it, when something impossible turns out to be possible, he's astonished. In this, he's the same as Clumsy, who, for certain, also likes to pretend to have been a revolutionary when he was young; I still remember his fright the time that an Italian astrologer friend of Ricardo's began to reveal one thing after another to him. And the same thing happens with Mary Ann's friend who's got no use for ideological baggage, who's got no tolerance for stuff about how if you simply proclaim yourself a leftist it means that you're really on the right, and pronouncements with which he believes he's unmasking reality, which is what he likes: to make us see that what seems to be one thing is something else, that capitalist interests are always lurking behind that double meaning, and that ripping off the blanket leaves capitalism buck naked.

On the other hand, I'm struck by how whatever involves a complete change of level, or goes beyond the theoretical, also startles him. Thus, for example, in early summer, when he called me on the phone, in shock, to give me the news that Franco was gravely ill, practically in a coma, news that seemed to fill him with dread, something that doesn't cease to amaze me, coming from a militant communist. The shock in his voice was noticeable, shrill like a little boy's, a symptom or projection of the retraction of the genitals that happens in parallel fashion in cases like this and similar circumstances, oral exams, speaking in public, etcetera; retraction or absorption of the genitals in general, and of the testicles in particular, the scrotum shrunk to the size of a little dried fig. Another symptom is that their hands sweat, and I imagine that those days they must have been sweating more than usual. I only imagine it, given that, as he knows and must have observed, people are disgusted by shaking wet hands, and try to avoid it by greeting you with a pat on the arm or through a gesture that wants to seem familiar and relaxed, but which in practice is as if, instead of offering you their hand, they offered you their elbow.

Marx doesn't interest me. For what it's worth, I prefer Nietzsche, who's not in fashion however much people say he is, nor do I think he ever can be, although, honestly, the influence that he has over certain morons, to the point of making them believe themselves supermen, remains worrisome. No, Marx is the one who attracts the most interest, especially among professors. And, consequently, among the liveliest students, who see therein the possibility of making a career out of him in the most literal sense of the word. All the more so because the risks are minimal, as long as one knows how to remain on an exclusively theoretical plane, an art that our social climbing friend, Mary Ann's friend, dominates to perfection, capable as he is of jinxing a Ouija board and managing to get the glass to break the moment he gets involved with obscurantist practices.

As far as what happened yesterday, another explanation occurs to me: what we captured, more than the old man's presence, was the ambience created around him, the tensions resulting from repressed thoughts and desires, which turn a natural death into a crime, not only unconsciously, as is usual, but also in a conscious way: those things forgotten, those careless mistakes in the administration of vital medications, oxygen, serum, injectables, mistakes expected, and even justified, in a climate of tense expectation like the one that develops among relatives and close friends with the passing of time.

I would also add that this tense climate was transferred to our table, and that is why the snifter broke. An excitation that, contrary to what usually happens--given that these sorts of sessions leave one rather drained and with frazzled nerves--turned into sexual excitement yesterday, the same for me as for Mary Ann, truly affected by penis envy.

6 Nov. One year, one week, one month, one day, are exact metaphors, more or less, in terms of time, for the cycles of rotation related to the sun, the moon and, of course, the earth itself. The hour, no. The hour, as one twenty-fourth part of the day, constitutes a kind of purely chronometric unity, artificial, arbitrary to the degree to which it responds to a certain number of degrees of the daily cycle, independent of the position that such a period of time occupies in the whole cycle, no different than if it were eighteen. Thus, the word "hour," which in a strict sense expresses a period of sixty minutes, also serves to designate a moment of special relevance, an instant that, at the same time, contains something of eternity. An hour that, by extension, assimilates the day to which it belongs and even the year to which that day belongs, in order to confer upon them the category of date. Thus, the sixth of November of this year is a date which, without any doubt, I have to remember my whole life for the reason of what happened during some of those sixty minutes that passed from six to seven in the evening.

I had just showered and, it must have been, sure enough, around six o'clock, the hour of my forgotten dates with Aurea, when I moved toward the bedroom window, still rubbing myself with the towel. And suddenly I glimpsed her there across the street, pressed right up against the window, looking at me in an unambiguous manner; it was getting dark, but still more than light enough to see her with perfect clarity. With the towel over one shoulder and my hands on my hips, I looked at her too, staring, completely motionless save for my sex, stirring like a snake that unwinds and curls around its coils; and this time, unlike the ones before, Aurea did nothing to disguise her presence, the fact that she was watching me. But the days had grown shorter since then, and as I was not prepared for the falling night to give way to excuses and confusion, I switched on my desk lamp. Immediate response: her window lit up instantly, almost as if Aurea, with her hand on the switch, was waiting for just that; her backlit figure now stood out. Determined as I was to not lose my initiative, to keep up the pressure, I made signs to indicate my intention to call her on the phone. And immediately, although I knew her address but not her last name nor her phone number, I took the magic marker and I wrote the word "number?" in large thick block letters, each one on a separate sheet of paper; I put them in order and, using a lampshade as a kind of spotlight, I showed them to her one by one, letter after letter: Number? It didn't even occur to me to think that eyes other than Aurea's could see me, that at this hour, just as night was falling, when lights were switched on and blinds lowered, some neighbor across the street might be following my movements with curiosity, the maneuvers of a naked young man apparently busy showing off some sheets of paper in front of a spotlight. I didn't even think of it nor, had I, would that have made me discard the idea, as is usually done with anecdotal things when facing events of greater importance, now that the light in her window had gone out twice in a row and, after a luminous interval longer than the one that had come between the two moments of darkness, the light switched off four times and, alternating with new intervals of greater duration, seven times more, and then three or four, impossible now to know it, losing as I had lost count of that succession of long and short intervals, of lights and shadows. Morse Code? No: the long intervals simply seemed intended to establish a gap between one group and another of short ones, or rather, between one group of emptinesses, of moments of darkness, which was, no doubt, where the key was to be found. I signaled her to repeat, to start over again, and this time I wrote down with the marker the total number of darknesses in each group: two, four, seven, etcetera. And so on up to seven figures. Meaning: her telephone number.

I don't know—when I had the chance to look I didn't—if Aurea's telephone was near the window, or if, on the contrary, it wasn't where she had been situated and, while I connected the tape recorder and dialed her number, she went to await my call wherever the phone was located; the fact is that she picked up right away. She said hello in a voice that was deeper than

I expected, but no less soft, the softness of the rosy sheen of a purple velvet. I told her, more as an affirmation than a question, that it would be better, wouldn't it, if we saw each other close up. She responded with a laugh both light and deep at the same time, adding that she was hoping that I wasn't going to be disappointed. I asked for her apartment: sixth floor, number three, she said. And I: see you in a minute, a farewell probably a bit dry, yes, but the lack of warmth was voluntary, resolved as I was not to make concessions, not to take too long, not to let Aurea vanish on me again behind the lace curtains of her window.

I dressed in a wild hurry. I didn't understand what she'd meant about me being disappointed and, just in case, I took a pocket tape recorder that I bought last summer in Switzerland and, on crossing the street, I only regretted not also buying myself a micro-camera, a Japanese marvel capable of taking pictures even in the darkness. I was tempted to look upward, but it seemed to me a sign of weakness to do so, apart from the fact that the image of a person looking up toward a window is usually minimizing, due to the helplessness it suggests, for the one who contemplates it from up above. In the foyer, the porter emerged from his room as I walked by to ask me where I was headed; I told him apartment 6-3, in an energetic, almost authoritarian tone, the best way of getting through to such people. This is the exact dialogue comprising our exchange, taken from the tape, not without losing all the rich tones of the spoken word, making it sound to me no more expressive of reality than movie subtitles appearing as the action unfolds: Apartment 6-3? I believe that's what I said. But there's no one home up there, young man! What do you mean there's no one there? I just spoke with Aurea, and we agreed that I'd come over to see her right now. Miss Aurea? That's just not possible, young man; Miss Aurea has been in Manila for at least the last two months. She must have called you from there. From Manila? Nonsense! I called her house just a few minutes ago and she was there. And I even saw her from my window. From your window? Yes, from my window. I live right across the street and I saw her from my window and we spoke on the phone. You must have got the wrong window, kid. There's nobody up there. I'm telling you, no, that I'm not wrong; she's got her lights on and I saw her and we spoke on the phone. Her lights on? That's really strange. I can assure you that there's nobody there. And I can assure you that there is; step out into the street and you'll see it. I don't know, unless it's some mistake and she forgot to turn off the lights. But now he seemed doubtful. He went into his little office, spoke briefly with someone, and came back out, more annoyed than concerned, clutching a key. Let's go upstairs, let's go on up, but you'll see that there's nobody there, he said. Don't you understand that I'd be the first one to know?

Once upstairs, he didn't even ring the bell; he straightaway opened the door with his key: the vestibule was completely dark. See? he said as soon as he opened the circuit breaker and switched on the main power. Various lights suddenly revealed, from different spots, the interior of the apartment. The porter and I walked toward the living room at the front of the apartment. The room was quite large and the comfortable furniture somewhat conventional. The only lamp that was switched on stood next to the window, illuminating the large, intensely green leaves of a tropical plant. My attention was drawn to a painting, a landscape at dusk with meadows and shadowy masses of trees, very much in the style of a romantic painting, except for the absence of figures. I already told you, said the porter; nobody comes in here besides the cleaning lady now and then. My wife, actually. Opposite the painting, framed by the half-opened lace curtains, my own window was visible.

Back in my apartment, I wanted to hear the tape of the phone conversation I'd had with Aurea. Maybe the record button wasn't working, maybe it was some mechanical error and the recording started late but the fact is all that remained of the whole conversation were my last words: see you in a minute.

7 Nov. Yesterday, the window was closed in Aurea's apartment, just as it seemed to be moments before, as seen from my room. Today, half-open, the drawn lace curtains floated on the breeze; I've not seen her, it's true, nor has anyone answered the telephone, whose number I've been dialing insistently. But what sense is there in denying to myself that I did see her, that I spoke with her on the phone, that she's not in Manila but in Barcelona?

At dusk I sat before the open window, my feet on the sill. A clear, warm, perfect autumn evening, with that light you only usually see when the wind clears the sky. A wind, now a breeze, that died down at moments, as the sun was setting. If it kept seeming that it was blowing strong it was due to the fact that the bone-dry leaves of the plane trees accentuated the effect with their murmuring sound, more than sufficient to soften the traffic noises, street sounds smothered under that mantle of foliage, now spiky, now combed by the fleeting gusts. I'd put on some record of Mozart or Haydn, the music I prefer at these hours, and suddenly I felt myself not here but in Rosas, contemplating not the dry brittle foliage of the plane trees but the slopes of the mountain, the rocks that capture the last rays of the sun, pinks turning to mauve and purple, the sparse woodland that darkens and grows quiet. I have always preferred the view from my bedroom, in the back part of the house, on the side facing the mountain, to the living room side, which faces the sea, the bay, with its picture postcard sunsets.

What nexus exists between the air and music? Does the air generate music? Because I would say, at least, that it's from the air where a Mozart or a Haydn absorb their harmony, from that gust of air that quickens the motionless surface of the water, that spins the leaves of the trees and blows out the candles in the house of mourning, the stiff, ever so lonely figure of the deceased unaware of the sudden darkening, of the war of lights and shadows unleashed by the air that slips in through the window left ajar, as if to better contrast the irrevocable death with its lively presence.

[NOTES BY RICARDO ECHAVE]

III

ATTICS.

Writing as a way of perfecting thought, as a way of sharpening an idea, of articulating it with others and organizing the whole. The written word is neither more nor less true than the word that's thought, simply for having been objectified; what it will certainly gain, in terms of expression, is coherence with respect to itself, with respect to what one wants to signify with it, and even with respect to what is unintentionally signified, including, with respect to what one wanted to silence, to what one wanted to be hidden and to be revealed. All writing has a potential reader and the writer knows the risk that this entails and does what he can, not only to cover himself, but also to channel, for his own benefit, that unavoidable interpretive distance. A game whose subtlety is for me one stimulus more to add to the motives that justify—supposing that it must be justified—my purpose in writing, in writing and not only thinking, about certain things; of explaining to myself this need of doing it and, if not in the first place then not in the last place either, the reason for having chosen for my retreat, from among all the possible sites, none other than Gorgs de la Selva, a place that, for its proximity to Vilasacra, for being inevitably associated with Margarita and Jaime, with the contrast between the living memory and the irredeemable absence, arouses, however, a feeling of attraction intimately linked with that of rejection.

For me, ever since I first heard its name, saying Gorgs de la Selva is like saying Vilasacra, given that for my cousins the town seemed nothing more than an extension of their own property, the town we went to visit when we were in Vilasacra and we said let's go to town, one of those idiomatic forms of family environment that the more or less regular guest ends up taking for granted, the same as with so many other local peculiarities. My decision to stay in Gorgs, near Vilasacra but not in Vilasacra, bore a close relationship to Magda's mood when she told me that, for the moment, she lacked the courage to return to Vilasacra, meaning, that she wasn't planning on accompanying me. Besides the inn at Gorgs, I remember an old house in the town, well cared for and comfortable, a type of establishment very common in my days as a student which with the passing of years has gradually been usurped--and not only along the coast--by horrendous resort hotels. But the choice of place, however suggestive the image of the inn turned out to be for me, had little to do, as is obvious, with such considerations, and a great deal, on the other hand, with its proximity to Vilasacra, more than ever linked to the memory of Margarita. Why? I would say that for motives similar to those that explain why children find attics so fascinating, that mixture of attraction and fear that the child experiences facing all the junk piled up there, facing the deterioration of so many things in that atmosphere of cobwebs and skittering rats, of dust, of gloom, of immobility. The persistence with which attics, the same as cellars, continue reappearing as the scene of our adult dreams, no less alive in the nightmare today than that attraction, however terrifying, in the child's reality. Thus, the words that came to my memory later, while I was shaving, upset or perhaps somewhat depressed, without knowing either with absolute certainty why I was in such a state nor why those words came to my memory: Bunde's rocking chair and Ramón París's tricycle. Words that immediately took me back to my childhood, during the Civil War, to my running and playing about that mountain town where my family, like so many other Barcelona families, had sought refuge; our raids as a little gang and, more concretely, the exploratory incursion carried out in the attic of an abandoned or deserted villa. I don't know, nor might I know how to say if I ever found out, who that person Bunde was, or who Ramón París, whom some companion on the exploration mentioned upon recognizing those objects, was, possessed as I was by the certainty of what the response would be if I asked about it, the unappealable confirmation that it was all about dead children. I'm not even sure that the names are correct; Bunde, especially, sounds like one of those words one learns as a child, the result of some simple phonetic acquisition and thus lacking meaning.

Is misfortune contagious? Because something of that, without a doubt, tosses and turns beneath the level of consciousness when people distance themselves from the places where the misfortune seems to have settled, with respect to the people marked by it as if to absorb them into its retinue. But, apart from profound motivations, apart from any unconscious content found in the origin of such attitudes, apart from what is subjective in all of that, it seems to me important to emphasize the generic character of the phenomenon, the similitude of response it arouses independent of social class, cultural level, and the qualities of the subject, at the time of turning away from the person in misfortune, from all those who seem to be pursued by bad luck. That suspicion, no less tormenting for remaining unspoken, that tumors are contagious, the same as allergies or herniated disks; that intuition about the epidemic character of accidental death, when the car skids and you go shooting off the highway, still with enough time to wonder if it's really me who's flying and spinning and bouncing weightless against these rosy pink cotton clouds. A type of anxiety similar to the one caused by the spates of airplane accidents, floods, earthquakes, without the influence of the phases of the moon being explanation enough, like in the case of the ocean tides, which are rather like the symptoms of an infectious process. You might say that sometimes it's even possible to determine the exact moment of contagion: the cold from the seat that penetrates the depths of our trousers during the visit we make to the sick person whom we know to be terminal; that peculiar clinging smell where his last days transpired that not even the festive ambience of Christmas Eve was capable of dissipating entirely; the brown smoke from the rooftop chimney that corresponds to the fire from their bedroom, that spreads all over the area, affecting whomever in the outskirts is prone to infection. The precautions and aseptic measures one usually takes after the death, not only with clothing and personal objects but also with letters, mementos, and even photographs. And the signs, the warnings: the magnolia trees in Vilasacra had a second flowering in October that lasted until early December, just weeks before Jaime's death. Or the terrible symptoms involved in a dog's death, a cat's, a turtle's, any pet's, the news of misfortune this represents for the house where it happens, an unmistakable augury of the annihilation that awaits all or some of its inhabitants. Or the language of the electric appliances, the prophetic meaning of certain breakdowns, switches, televisions, electric razors, as well as light bulbs that burn out, water leaks, batteries that suddenly die, predictions that fulfill the worst of the auguries when they happen, not isolated, but in conjunction, in accumulation. The night before I came here, in fact, my car wouldn't start and I had to call a mechanic; crossing the threshold in Vilasacra, a light bulb that burned out the second I switched it on; during my first night at the inn, my water glass shattered against the floor and, on top of all that, for days, I'd been losing various buttons, from my pants, my shirt, and my fur-lined jacket, all things which I realize, now that they've passed, stimulated my natural anxious tendencies.

The extreme case happens when it's not just any sickness, but cancer. Then people avoid calling it by its name, tending to substitute it with some other phrase, a conventional expression, and even by its very omission, thus turning the unpronounced word into a denotative sign, the open void in the phrase itself, as if pronouncing the ominous word were equivalent to invoking it or conjuring it, of running the risk of attracting it toward yourself the way that the soul of the reprobate attracts that great blue crab or like the stranded cadaver in a still pool attracts the freshwater crab. Thus the popular belief that inverting the order of events, taking the cause for consequence, makes the person bitten by the sickness a living symbol of death, as the soul in sin stands for eternal damnation. Thus, too, the resonances of ritual and expiatory character that the simple mention of the word cancer expands, similar by their function to those that properly belong to mourning, to the color black, and the social withdrawal that inhibits daily life in the family circle of the deceased, a true sanitary cordon through which the community defends itself from all outside interference, from all aggression toward its normal development, isolating, segregating, putting into quarantine the contaminated parts of the social body, bleeding it for the collective benefit the same as one bleeds any dirty wound liable to infection or producing tetanus. If the color black has not come to be imposed on the relatives of the cancer patient, if there has been no attempt to inculcate among them some norm similar to that of mourning, it's because, in today's society, the very raison d'être of mourning is being called into question, to the degree that, what was valid in the world of the small town, ceases to be so in the urban sphere where everyone is a stranger and the value of the symbol, the peculiarities that individualized it, now lost, are diluted in anonymity. If, when I was a child, when grandmother died, in the closed society of postwar Barcelona, they dyed even my socks black, less than twenty years later, when my father died, no one wore black. And now, from what I could observe at Jaime's funeral, even the priests wear their same ordinary chasuble, not one of those black ones with gold embroidery that used to be the style.

To talk about people is to talk about others, to except oneself from people's general dimwittedness, when in company, or at most, of our interlocutor, to whom we grant this benefit. That's why it wouldn't be fair for me to talk about people's recent attitude toward Jaime without including myself explicitly in such a general category, given that my attitude differs very little from the one others hold, perhaps because it's the only one possible to hold when dealing with a man who finds himself in his situation, to avoid contradicting him, just agreeing with everything he says, to imprint on our dealings with him a certain forced spiritedness and the breath and stimulus the circumstances require, meaning, the usual deferences—not very different from those earned by the turkey affectionately reserved for the Christmas dinner—offered freely to all people to whom doctors have given only a short amount of time to live. Needless to say, Jaime, sunk in the irreality of the process that starts with being admitted to the hospital, worried only by the mechanical aspect of his new condition, was the person least suited to notice any change in people's behavior, to even notice details as irrelevant as the attentions of which he was an object, the affable and solicitous treatment dispensed to him, everyone offering themselves for whatever reason necessary, putting themselves entirely at his disposal, obviously up to date about the seriousness of his diagnosis, however much the operation itself might have been a success and that his wife, Magda or Margarita, had agreed to keep secret how much time the biopsy results said he had left. During the post-op, however, his gaze, intense, as if awestruck, somewhat lurking, the look of one who wants to see themself in our eyes, to know how they look, what fate awaits them. Of course, if there was anything reassuring about being in the hospital, the medical team itself would have been in charge of dispelling it with their visits, when in the course of their daily rounds he heard them going from room to room, each time coming closer, exchanging jokes, laughing brutally, finally all bursting in together like a barrage, a pure expeditious gaggle, similar to the police who suddenly pounce on the arrested suspect who's already been waiting hours to be interrogated. And, also like the police, ready to set things straight, when, routine informalities dispensed with, back out in the hallway, brusquely changing tone, they approach the family with the inflexible rawness appropriate to a hopeless situation, their manifest indifference to the effect of their words no less than that of the croupier who calls one number instead of another, the black instead of the red. Never mind the fact that there are croupiers who, whichever number they say, enjoy thinking about those people who have bet on any other one, said Margarita, ostensibly turning her back on the group. A very Margarita-like expression—more justified with respect to the fact in itself than to the slightly free interpretation of the motives—which the surgeon did not fail to notice, whether he understood them or not, nor of blaming the impact on her hasty, confused, nakedly nervous retreat.

What's certain, in any case, is that it was enough for Jaime to see himself outside the hospital in order to fully recover his confidence, in order to accept whatever explanations they gave him about the peculiarities of convalescence, to make projects: to check out so he could go recuperate in Vilasacra, learn

Russian, study art history, projects that would surely receive the family's consent, given the relief always supposed in distancing oneself from a person whose days are numbered, not only for avoiding interferences in the normal household activity but, also, similarly, and especially, because of the depressive character of such cohabitation. On the other hand, neither Ana, the wife, nor Vera and Sergio, or other similar Slavic-sounding names, so popular among young progressive married couples a few years ago, would have influenced, negatively, by complicating things, the avatars of his alleged recovery, phases of improvement alternating with stationary phases, within an overall decline, almost imperceptible due to its slowness, annoyances that become chronic almost without one noticing, a diminution of functions that lead to atrophy, ups and downs of a struggle that, for Jaime, was turning into an all-consuming goal and priority, wellness itself becoming relegated to an anodyne secondary place. In my visits to Vilasacra, always on the weekend—even the wife and the kids visited him almost exclusively on the weekends, as if they feared living alone with him—one of his favorite conversation topics was, rightly, the small corrections he had introduced into the treatment, small modifications with beneficial effects that, incomprehensibly, nobody had yet discovered, details not lacking in importance despite being small, the merit for whose discovery belonged entirely to him. Questions which, once he regained his health, it would perhaps be worth the trouble to investigate, given that he knew about them from first-hand experience.

Jaime's isolation, his lack of communication with the outside world, increased day by day. And unlike in the past, owing to his fantasies and mythomaniac propensities, whose formulation, after a certain point, becomes so tiring and even exasperating to accept, to listen to it, feigning interest and admiration, as a means of refusal, obliging him to correct each one of his assertions word by word, to keep his statements at least within the realm of verisimilitude, an alternative he invariably ends up renouncing on the basis of the obvious uselessness of the effort. No, quite the contrary: if the difficulty of the communication became sharper, the cause would instead have to be sought in the disappearance of those fantasies—not unpleasant sometimes—from his habitual conversation, as if extirpated, you might say, as a result of surgical intervention, perhaps directly by means of a scalpel, perhaps as a result of a transformation of personality similar to those already experienced in other stages of his life, the last of them upon coming into contact with the Communist Party. The problem, now, was not listening patiently, but doing it actively, sharing his enthusiasm for things interesting only to him, all in all like that Catalan shopkeeper who one fine day decides to visit Paris: his pleasure in finally feeling himself there, of personally confirming the traditional affinity that makes Barcelona and Paris sister cities, the care he takes in telling anyone who would like to listen to him—the solitary neighbor at the bistro, the silent owners of the restaurant, the grumpy taxi driver who drives him to his hotel, the unfriendly manager of that hotel--without recoiling nor letting his morale be diminished by their indifference, if not revulsion, with which he's listened to while he explains that he comes from a small country, Catalonia, connected to France—connected, that's right, not separated but connected—by the Pyrenees, a small country with great cities like Barcelona and incomparably beautiful landscapes like the Costa Brava, yes, the Costa Brava is in Catalonia, and Montserrat, you've never heard of Montserrat? Ah, well, it's worth your time! A small country, in short, that has always felt a great admiration for France, that has always felt more closely connected to France than to Spain, that almost comes to be, as if we might say, a kind of miniature France, yes, *oui*, do you understand me—a wink and a little laugh--a small European country one hundred percent, what they call a great little country; and as such, like that Catalan fellow in Paris, so too Jaime, no less pathetic in his attempts to get people excited, to make others participants in his enthusiasms and preoccupations. Truth be told, it was easier for me to stand the Catalan shopkeeper when he finally found out that I was from Barcelona and he figured me out on his own; with him, at least I could laugh to myself, something that in no way happened with Jaime, each time that, whether alone, with his sisters, some mutual friend and even his wife—now it seemed not to matter to him if she were listening—he spoke about the studies he planned to pursue as soon as he established himself in the Soviet Union, as was his proposal since he had learned that in Ukraine, on the shores of the Black Sea, there was a clinic specializing in the type of treatment that he needed in order to be cured. The Black Sea: landscape and climate, not very salty due to the great currents flowing into it from the Danube, which facilitates the fact that its shores are dotted, not only with pine trees, but also with enormous oaks, birches, and ash trees, almost as if it were a lake. Personality of the Ukrainian. Daily life of the Soviet peasant. Socialist society. The unlimited scientific progress within the socialist system, free from the impediments and contradictions of capitalism. Considerations from which, apparently, Jaime was going to return once more to his favorite theme: the serious damage that idealism has inflicted on humanity, the superstitions and obfuscations that humanity would have saved itself from if it had had a materialist concept of the world. Something perfectly depicted by Cervantes in *Don Quixote*, where the hero, who starts out symbolizing idealism, ends up symbolizing materialism, the inverse of Sancho Panza, their respective roles dialectically swapped with one another. This is precisely what

I do not accept about Lukács, he said placidly. The fundamental antagonism is not what can be established between irrationalism and rationalism but what exists between idealism and materialism.

As usual, Jaime's fight against the Crab reached its apogee a few short weeks before the dénouement, preceding this like a radiant herald, when Jaime made the decision to celebrate Christmas Eve with a big party in Vilasacra, to which he invited all his friends, summoned, you might say, to bear witness to their host's disdain for adversity. Rosa and I accepted, constrained, like everyone, by that feeling of anticipated mourning that ends up imposing itself in these cases. Not so with Magda nor Margarita, sisters in pain in addition to their shared childhood; I'm really very sorry, commented Margarita as soon as she learned of the plan, but if there's something that I don't feel strong enough to withstand it's a sort of last supper. Both of them quite cutting in that regard, Magda planned a trip to Egypt with Irene on those very dates, and Margarita, after collaborating actively on the party preparations, telephoned at the last minute from Barcelona, disconsolate, as the guests were already arriving in Vilasacra, saying that she was a bit tipsy and fine, but that she'd crash if she drove the car, that she was in no condition to drive, that she'd crash if she tried to, if I try to, Jaime, I'm sure I won't make it; their particular manner of finding an excuse that was not exactly a snub but was perfectly characteristic of each one, and in each case according to their particular attitude toward life—more withdrawn in Magda, with that strong initial impulse that nevertheless manages to fail Margarita in the decisive moment—as well as the bounds of their emotional responses, both quite liable to exceed them.

Her desertion was an act of lucidity, given that the atmosphere at the party adjusted itself exactly to what there was to be feared, to what that hostile and depressing garden now seemed to presage when we arrived in Vilasacra, the lime tree's naked limbs, the yew trees dark and frightened like chickens caught out in the rain. The worst thing was not the forced happiness, the repressed anxiety that inhibited the behavior of those present; the worst thing was Jaime himself, the image he offered by contemplating all of us from the presidency of the big table, seated there like one more dinner guest, despite the fact that for some time now he could no longer tolerate any kind of solid food: his stubborn attitude of being a host who was tending to everyone's needs, somewhere between inquisitive and stupefied, as if deaf, with a sort of permanent smile in order to disguise his absences, his difficulty concentrating, his mistakes remembering, his lapses, his confusions. And the message as a kind of toast—symbolic on his part—was conceived in the obligation of addressing the guests when the champagne was served, a kind of politico-philosophical dissertation on human rights in a revolutionary context, a question that I prefer to call the dialectic of freedom. Human rights as a thesis. The revolution as obligatory antithesis, and that so much the more given the resistance imposed by imperialism. The New Society—which, let us not fool ourselves, we can take years and years to reach, decades, centuries—is, as a consequence, the synthesis. Thus, the inevitable character of the dictatorship of the proletariat even today, however severe and even violent it may be, as a historical and simultaneously scientific exigency, a fact that distinguishes it from all non-revolutionary violence. As he finished speaking, he seemed rather moved, or at least his eyes were shining and his voice was hoarse. Someone had snapped some Polaroids and were passing them around: Jaime presiding at the table, Jaime standing up, directing his message to those eating, Jaime contemplating the photographs being shown to him, the slow appearance of the image, his face surfacing, his expression somewhat contorted, as if dazzled by the flash.

After dinner, in the living room, we chatted a while, or rather, I listened to him for a while. He seemed happy, or maybe amused, although he was noticeably aware of the strain on his face the extra effort had cost him. His plans for convalescing in Ukraine one more time. His evocation of our faraway time of political militancy and clandestine activities. And what was even more embarrassing: his sincere admiration for my professional success, something about which it was still more difficult for me to talk about, more difficult, of course, than politics, and also more useless. How could I explain to him that architecture had ceased to interest me, that anything related to it bored me almost as much as explaining the reasons why—how to talk about that? Or how to make small talk, how to talk with people about the things people usually talk about.

My friendship with Jaime was always somewhat superficial. Possibly, if he'd not been Margarita and Magda's brother, we might have just remained simple acquaintances. The fact that we were also cousins neither added nor subtracted anything; my mother and his father were also cousins and more closely related than us, first cousins, and I understand that they hardly ever saw each other, even having summered together in Vilasacra when they were young. But like the child who goes rummaging around in an attic, the most common, most unexpected discovery—a tricycle—can also be the most terrifying, the one that remains most deeply etched in his memory, so, in a similar way, with the death of specific persons, whose disappearance, for reasons far removed from what that person was, affects us much more than we expect. And that's how, like in the case of the tricycle, the terror comes not from the toy itself but the place where it's found—the attic—when it comes to someone dying, what makes an impression on us is not the dead person, but death itself.

A fright similar to the one that morning, years before, when, to put it in vulgar terms, I had my head stuck right up my ass, tuned out and fraught with anxiety, a state like stupor and unease that only began to clear up when, like the reflection of the light from a boat in the black waters of a bay, I glimpsed an instant flash of the dream I'd had that morning. My father's private desk was standing in the house's garden, among some bay trees, an elegant piece of furniture in the Chippendale style whose fold-down front that doubled as a writing board opened with an unmistakable squeaking noise, doubtless intended as a sort of discreet alarm in case someone tried to open it surreptitiously. Then it was closed, and on opening it, it was as if I knew what I was going to find inside: a small pile of orange human bones.

GETTING THE MESSAGE.

The distance from Gorgs de la Selva to Vilasacra must be about three or four kilometers, so that, spending the night at the town's inn, Vilasacra was only five minutes away by car; Magda had insisted on offering me the house, but I made her see that this solution gave me greater independence. And the fact is that, for other reasons as well, when choosing between a hotel and a friend's house I always choose the hotel, the clear dealings between hotel staff and guest, the lodger's right to be unsociable, to keep the hours they please, to not explain anything to anyone, to not waste time chatting, freedoms which even the most minimal courtesy would have prevented me from talking with the couple that looks after the property. In addition to the fact that it was one thing for me to drive to Vilasacra, even if it was every afternoon, and another to live there, surrounded by memories capable of excessively conditioning the autonomy of my activities.

If the reason for my presence in Vilasacra was clear, the same could not be said about my objective. Magda seemed sure that we would end up finding something, but neither she, nor I, had the very least idea about the nature of the discovery. About its location, however, there were fewer doubts, as it had to be directly or indirectly related to Margarita's room. Hadn't Margarita herself said it implicitly, when she responded to her calls during that session to which she was summoned by Irene and Magda by means of a crystal snifter enclosed in a circle of letters? And the crystal clear *YES* traced by the snifter as it moved from the Y to the E to the S when they asked "Is there anybody there?" And how it moved surely and steadily when they asked the name of that someone, spelling out *Margarita*, the glass almost shaking loose from the touch of their fingers, be it from the effort of maintaining contact, be it from the excitement with which they followed the delicate trace of the snifter's path, whose meaning they guessed after the first few letters? And that command: *find Ricardo*, spelled out calmly, almost with fatigue or indifference, before the message might be lost in an erratic tongue twister similar to that tune a person hums to themself while they are thinking about something else, an order more peevish, you might say, than intimidating, her answer when they asked her *What do you want?* before vanishing without a trace like one of the many stars that fall during the nights in early August, leaving Irene and Magda no less frustrated than that long-suffering audience listening to the news in Spanish on Radio Paris about Franco's health, enduring under the combined punishment of the adverse atmospheric factors and the noisy static and interference, useless, now totally useless, for them to ask again and again why they had to find Ricardo, where to look for him, questions which Magda only stopped repeating after finding the solution, the only possible solution? Because, how to avoid relating one mystery with another, this absence of response with the possible meaning of that photograph found in Margarita's purse when the car was pulled from the river, details that, if momentarily sidelined by the imperious demands of death, were in some way relegated to oblivion? The photo was tucked inside an airmail envelope, with no other markings than the name of the presumed addressee, a name that was barely legible, from being blurred by the water, but that might well be, indeed--for Magda it was very clear--Ricardo, meaning, me. As for the photo, perfectly preserved, the problem lay not in identifying the image represented--a view of Margarita's room in Vilasacra taken from the hallway, with the window in the background--as much as in the meaning of that image, in the value that it had for Margarita in a specific context. In other words: shortly before her death, perhaps only a couple of hours beforehand, Margarita had slipped that photo into an envelope addressed to me with the obvious idea of perhaps enclosing a letter--a letter she never managed to write, or that, having been written, had been misplaced--perhaps a verbal explanation, in order to ask something of me or bring me up to date on something, whatever it was, related to her room in Vilasacra. That explanation, oral or written, that the photo illustrated or to which the photo was perhaps the key, had not reached me as intended, and only from certain considerations, as if Margarita's willpower had persisted beyond her own life the way the smoke hangs over the already-extinguished fire, as if that will, in its resistance to being snuffed out definitively, in a final attempt to call attention to the contents of the message she had directed to me, would have resorted to the language of the glass planchette, guiding its movements from one letter of the alphabet to another, as if impelled by an autonomous impulse, now without any other objective than that of effecting a desire which events had transformed into nothing less than her dying wish, yes, only after such considerations did I have to understand the answer received to the invocations of Irene and Magda. I know all too well that she wasn't there when we did the Ouija board, said Magda. What I wouldn't like more than to speak with her, wherever she happens to be, the way I'm speaking with you right now, to have the certainty that this is possible? But something that worried her when she died was floating in the air the other night, this I can assure you, Ricardo, whether you believe it or not. Thus, what was important for her, although only for her own peace of mind, was that I come to Vilasacra, me specifically, and search through every last nook and cranny, or rather, interpret from all points of view, whatever might be related to Margarita's room.

When she phoned me, Magda had only disclosed that it was about something important, and I asked no questions; we agreed that I would see them late in the evening. The living room was almost in semi-darkness, illuminated more by the glow of the fireplace than by the indirect lights from the corners; Magda, however, was wearing the same sunglasses as when Margarita had her accident, the flames from the hearth lighting up the lenses like big candles. While Magda was talking, Irene, seated at her feet, on the bearskin rug, stirred the fire in silence, with the essence of a she-wolf or a greyhound that is common in certain lesbians, solid cheekbones, sunken cheeks, thin lines on the face, hair and complexion the same color. At a certain moment, Magda removed her glasses, and then I was able to appreciate that her face had not improved in any way since the moment when she had to identify Margarita's body, without the firmness of spirit that she doubtless imposed on herself in those moments, with greater insomniac anguish, as if the role befallen her to play in all that, her premonitions, her skill at divination, the ease with which she turned into a transfer medium of the unknown, had pushed her to the limit of her resistance. Because, ultimately, when Margarita had her accident, she had also been the first to call me, to sound the alarm. And if then she already feared that something had happened to her, it was owing, not so much to the lack of news, which doubtless began to be worrisome, no less than her restless dreams, but rather, to the state of light uneasy sleep in which she'd spent the night. But, regarding Margarita, her not having phoned Magda as she'd promised, having forgotten to do it, not having reached her house in Rosas the night before as she'd planned, having slept in some other place, were variations in behavior that were completely foreseeable, capable of causing unease only until they were cleared up, a state that remained unchanged hours later, a period of time which, if too long for it to have been a traffic accident, would also have been too long for nothing at all to have happened. That's why I only began to consider the possibility that something had happened when Magda called me again around midnight, after having phoned Vilasacra, where they confirmed that Margarita had left there after dinner with the idea of sleeping in Rosas; that departure without arrival, those twenty long hours transpired from the beginning of a drive that shouldn't have taken more than two, that absence of news, they then began to dwell on a point of consideration instinctively rejected until that moment, as something is usually rejected, for being absurd, for being horrible, we resist relating it with personalities like Margarita's, more as a result of that so very lively personality than some objective fact: the heavy rains and subsequent flooding that night, September 24, the feast of Our Lady of Mercy, according once more to the tradition that makes these dates prodigiously wet, as if it were all about some cult devoted to an ancient fertility goddess. The night of the 24th to the 25th, the night Magda spent wide awake, had been very rainy, yes, but when I left for Gorgs de la Selva accompanied by Magda, ready to follow the same route Margarita had to have driven twenty-four hours earlier, still overcome by that resistance to connecting what's living with what is not, I was thinking about the car skidding, in a distracted moment, which, if at first imagined without great consequences, as we got closer to Gorgs struck me as more and more serious, a curve, a ravine, Margarita wounded and trapped inside, while the unceasing rain washes away the skid marks from the accident. In Gorgs they had seen her car go by around ten o'clock, under a heavy downpour, heading for the main highway, and it was enough for someone to remark that the stream had carried off more than one car parked near the banks for me to decide to head directly to the nearest Traffic Safety Office. The young man who spoke with me seemed little versed in these sorts of matters, or perhaps, simply, when it came to makes and models of automobiles; he checked through reports, said that yes, the river had swept away various cars of similar characteristics, he wrote down the details about Margarita's car, picked up the phone and made a few inquiries, but suddenly, taking advantage of Magda's absorbed silence, he passed me a sheet of note paper on which he had just written a single word: *dead*. They had pulled a car out of the Tordera River that afternoon, near the river's mouth, as the rain poured down. Identifying Margarita's body did not take place until the morning, after a sleepless night--this time for all of us—spent in a hotel along the highway, to which Irene and Rosa were not long in arriving, a night neither better nor worse, in the end, than the next one, when, back in Barcelona again, Rosa and I went home and Magda went with Irene to her place just like any other night, as if Margarita hadn't died and we hadn't spent the day dealing with all the paperwork for her body, with the judge, the forensic doctor, the town hall secretary, the funeral parlor, attending to each problem with that somewhat obsequious duty that participants on a television game show display as they confront the invisible tests to which they find themselves subjected. No sooner did we get inside the house than Rosa began sobbing on my shoulder, saying that Margarita was the only person who had been able to understand her, her dismay greater now than in the morning, without the frightful awe of that moment, in the mortuary, when they opened the chapel in the cemetery and we found ourselves facing Margarita stretched out on the marble slab, her body in a position at once graceful and unnatural, similar to a sculpture of a fine dancer stretched out face up, eyes open, a surprised expression, as if she were contemplating the colored beam of solar rays that, from the rose window, shot diagonally through the interior gloom, over our heads; it was in that moment when Magda took off her dark glasses, her face framed between two long tresses of black hair, tragic replica of Margarita. The main problem to be settled was about the method of burial; Magda wanted it to be a civil funeral, consistent with the repugnance Margarita felt for the religious ceremony expected in these cases, what she called necrophiliac rites, an expression she didn't tire of repeating quietly to herself on the occasion of Jaime's death. But the secretary at city hall, who seemed quite taken with the idea of selling one of the niches recently funded by the city, and for which he was perhaps the contractor, too, was reluctant to miss his chance, and he did not let up until he'd exhausted all his arguments, there was no need for any questions, it's best to be practical, to simplify things, if the priest starts getting involved, you know we'll get all tied up in red tape with the Church, not to mention how difficult it was going to be for the gravedigger to find time to clear the ground in the corner of the cemetery set aside for civil burials, outside the wall around the consecrated ground, etcetera, his face fixed with the merciless gaze of a salesman determined to sell something, inexorable in his intentions like a mental retard with homosexual propensities dreaming of sodomizing the traffic guard whom he could see every morning from his balcony, directing traffic. At the courthouse, however, they raised no objection to the immediate return of any personal effects found inside the car, including her purse containing the photo addressed to me.

I imagine that Magda had the conviction, not only of having fulfilled her duty, but that Margarita was thanking her from somewhere for having done it. Because what's certain is that Magda had managed to strip away any necrophiliac traits from Margarita's burial, which had driven Margarita herself to the edge of hysteria during Jaime's burial. This was not, however, the only difference between the one ceremony and another, it was difficult for them to be more dissimilar, what with having celebrated the memory of two siblings, and in such a short period of time, barely the nine months it takes for a baby to come into the world. Although he'd said nothing to that effect, in Jaime's case it was also to be supposed that a man like him, not only a committed communist but also, specifically, an atheist, would have preferred some simple lay ceremony to the solemn funeral rites *corpore insepulto* unexpectedly arranged by Ana, his wife—who'd also belonged to the party when she was a university student—with the support of her own family and contrary to the scandalized opinion of Margarita and Magda. Nothing more distant than that multitude of family members and relations by marriage of every kind among those in mourning, Jaime's personal friends, or that mobilization of personalities and important people related to the family, and that cortege of automobiles that followed the transfer of the body from Vilasacra to the church in town and, from there, after the office was chanted, to the family pantheon in the cemetery in Gorgs de la Selva, where they said their last goodbyes, nothing could be further from all that, indeed, than Margarita's little-less-than-secret burial in the municipal cemetery of some random town, under the auspices of the municipal district to which her car had been dragged, a burial with an autopsy instead of a Mass, in an open grave at the foot of a wall carpeted by snails, with only a small group of friends and even some old lover there, more than one face unknown to me, unknown or difficult to recognize because of the waning light. On finishing, there were some embraces and some handshaking among the cypresses, and immediately the sound of car doors slamming, headlights switching on, and as they all drove away with so much backing up and turning around it raised a great cloud of dust into the air.

Just as the track of one tire in the mud superimposes itself over an older track and takes its place, so Margarita's disappearance superimposed itself on Jaime's, and when Magda asked me to unravel the meaning of the photo, Vilasacra was already linked entirely with the memory of Margarita, and its condition as the stage for Jaime's final act relegated to an increasingly dim second place. Because, unlike the mud, in the same way that inside of houses like the one in Vilasacra the dampness of the walls makes the most recent coat of paint peel off and patches of the original always end up reappearing here and there, layers of the stuccos and oils applied to the walls when the house was built, such a part of the building beneath the changing fashions that come and go with the generations, so, in a similar way, the memories of Vilasacra that ended up imposing themselves were also the most distant ones, predating the time when Margarita and I turned it into the headquarters of our conflictive amorous relationship, of our arguments, our plans, of the new adventure that every new day meant for us then. Memories that generated new memories, or rather, fleeting, imprecise impressions, difficult to isolate them all, as if, more than suggesting, they veiled—like that grafted lemon tree that at the first frost will produce, from the orange tree that served as a base for the graft, vigorous shoots of bitter fruit—its true nature, which was something else, something that survived below, that was in the roots and not in the branches, or similar to that root stock whose upper part exposed to the air was grafted, or like those blurry shapes that appear in the foreground of a panoramic photograph, difficult to recognize because of their closeness to the lens. Like that brownish-gray cloud that stretches out lengthwise over a mountain chain, leaving a luminous strip of western sky at sunset between cloud and mountain, slanted beams of sunlight that, like fingers of light, give depth to whatever shapes they touch, or like those tree silhouettes that, standing out in a line on the horizon, project their opacity against the sunset, forming in the sky, giant radial spars from the now hidden radiant center, like those phenomena, one and another not very distinct from the clarity that descends upon the chosen one or the halo that expands the holiness in medieval pictorial representations, a touch of divine grace that extends over the world in the first case, sacred halo in the second, so, like those effects of light one sees in the landscape no less than in paintings, for reasons similar to those that have always made Montserrat a holy mountain, independent of the cult of worship dedicated to it, thus, in the photo found in Margarita's purse showing the inside of her room in Vilasacra, I thought, and I keep thinking it, that perhaps, apart from Magda's premonitions and divinatory practices, some meaningful element worth being explored might be found. A simple room, no more a woman's than a man's, that in the family was considered somewhat sad for facing north, overlooking the garden's thick vegetation, without the broad view of the surrounding field that the front rooms enjoy.

IV

THE SIREN EFFECT.

Until I met Margarita, Vilasacra was little more than a name to me, the country property where my mother had spent her childhood summers, the equivalent for her of what Santa Cecilia represented and represents for me. On the other hand, my relationship with my cousins on my mother's side had been practically null, given that, at home, their parents were considered to be true undesirables, some of them for being Reds, and the others for being ruined, although I was late to learn these reasons, because the concept of undesirable is completely outside of a child's understanding. Jaime, Margarita, and Magda belonged to the Red branch, or rather, to the Red, their father, a man who had died in exile, in a situation which, doubtless, it was better not to discuss. That's why I think that the surest thing is that we must have seen each other at some point as children, in the course of one of those dutiful visits that distant relatives make so that the next generations don't lose contact; after all, the father's sins had been punished, and the opprobrium that hung over the children, who enjoyed an excellent financial situation, was undoubtedly lesser than that of the rest of the family, the ruined ones, the treatment by which they were excluded.

Of course I didn't even remember their names, but, even if I had, the last thing that would've occurred to me when I met Margarita in Paris was to imagine that we might be cousins. She was introduced to me simply as Margarita by a classmate and fellow party member who was forced into exile as the result of an arrest; I don't know the intensity of their relations, superficial I imagine, given the naturalness with which Margarita climaxed with me that very night. Then I only knew that her name was Margarita, that she was from Barcelona, that she studied Beaux Arts and that she didn't understand—had no desire to—politics; we didn't discover that we were related until a few days later and it was thanks to my last name, which didn't cease to surprise her if you take into account that, at least at the social level of our respective families, Echave is not exactly a very common family name in Barcelona. In those days I was already going out with Rosa, and although we had mutually conceded that kind of interdependence that couples usually agree on, what's certain is that we were never quite so close to breaking up, because when Margarita got tired of Paris our relationship continued in Barcelona, parallel to my relationship with Rosa. I met Magda through Margarita herself, who had taken upon herself the obligation of initiating into life a girl who had proven too shy to do it on her own.

Although it now seems strange, there was a time when political activity played a relevant role in my relationships with Margarita and with Rosa, as well as in the relationship established between them both. The one who took the initiative in this respect was Rosa, who no doubt thought that joining up was a step in the right direction, given my position as a leader in the university communist party, where she quickly distinguished herself for her radical position on ideological structures as well as in practical aspects of the clandestine struggle. And although Margarita, with better judgement than Rosa, given that neither the one nor the other was cut out for militancy, refused to play the game, to ask to join, that did not prevent her from distributing propaganda, or marching in demonstrations, or fleeing assaults by the Armed Police, sometimes not only in cold blood and efficacy but also with true daring, however much later on, when, taking refuge in some bar, she confessed that if she ran it was from pure fear of the police truncheons, of being arrested, abused, to avoid being tortured, that if they arrested her she would sing. The one who did end up joining was Jaime, although he took so long to make up his mind that by that time I was already practically out; this delay—apart from questions of character—was due, I suppose, to the possibility that he did not consider himself worthy or sufficiently prepared to request membership, he seemed to prefer the role of fellow traveler, and in that capacity he developed an enormously imaginative and useful operation, especially regarding the organization of various support movements, as well as directing the collaboration of other sympathizers; I also suppose that the one who pushed him to take the decisive step was Joaquín, who at that time found himself in the apogee of his spectacular political career, when, as a grassroots militant, as he was in Barcelona during the time I was in jail, he learned how to gain the confidence of the leadership, which he came to form part of during the two or three years he spent in Paris.

What can explain that massive movement of the sons and daughters of the Barcelona bourgeoisie into the ranks of the Community Party that happened in the late nineteen-fifties? Were we fighting to build a new society that privately we really didn't think possible and which, in case it had been, we would not have considered desirable? Or were we, rather, fighting more against the dictatorship, against the repressive aspects of Francoism at every level, or rather, at some levels more than others, some more important that others according to the situation, according to each one's nature? Because if the contagious character of the phenomenon reveals without a doubt the existence of the necessary breeding ground that facilitates or permits the contagion, at the same time, it also had to have something irreducibly subjective, since my motives were my own, not like those of a Jaime, not like those of a Joaquin either, however close we were. A specialist, a sociologist, for example, would explain it as a typical case of children rebelling against their parents, against the Francoist order that they represented, against the oppression and corruption that we saw incarnate in that order, against everything that was unassimilable to our altruistic nature. And by personalizing, moving from the general to the particular, at least in terms of what concerns me for example, a psychoanalyst would allude to the no-less-typical Oedipus, to the unrequited love for a prematurely departed mother, to the rejection of the father figure, as well as of the world that figure represents, etcetera. Revealing trifles whose meaning would be shown to be perfectly reversible only by analyzing the Francoist concept of the mother country, the nunnish flavor of that concept, like the taste of Yemas de Santa Teresa, just by stopping to consider the ease with which an unrequited love can lead to murder, etcetera. The explanation for the phenomenon—or rather, the weft of impulses both individual and collective that, the way a tapestry's weave brings the figures depicted to life, both pattern and image simultaneously, even as, and in the same way, that pattern of impulses acquires ever more precise motives over time—has got to constitute something much less defined and systematized and much more epidermal and profound at the same time. In fact, it's not only so much about the instinctive repugnance that Francoist mythology is capable of arousing, with its principles, its symbols, its heroes—now baldness and false teeth, flabby cheeks and greedy maw where there was muscle and nerve, the fidelity to the mustache--now white—and the sunglasses—that always contribute to maintaining the impassivity of the gesture—like a carefully preserved relic; a generation forged in war and housed in the postwar years, without, however, yielding its vigilance, its willingness to relapse into its bad old ways, an essentially vertical and affirmative generation, emphatic as boots stamping soundly or kicking hard, as ritual screams and cries, a people always ready, willing, and able to leap up and spring into action, impassive to the point of tension, aggressive to the point of blind obstinacy, men defined by the devotion characteristic of taking possession of an attitude like the one they adopted, an attitude based precisely on the principle of possession and in its permanent defense: the possession of a property, of a position, of an inside connection, of a cushy deal, of some sweet treat, or of a piece of pussy, even if it's only some chunks of ham and a few small glasses of wine, and in the last place, of possession for the sake of possession, like wild boars, by tooth and nail, against wind and tide; those men and the names of those men, among which, for some undetermined motive that I leave to the curious investigator, are frequently found the resonances and even the accent of the area where Aragon, Castile, and Navarra share borders, resounding names they are, too, José Luis Bozal, for example, Bartolomé Lechuga, Jesús Mostaza, Adriano Rincón, José Miguel Aizpún, Laureano Berrocal, surnames that mean, respectively, muzzle, lettuce, mustard, corner, rock face, and crag, and well-considered, even the name of the family hero killed in combat, my cousin Juan Antonio Echave, all of them names with a bit of a fortuitous bite, meaning, smacking of a constant readiness, according to the required spirit of service, to heed the Sentinel, right there at the end of the street, when he calls out, *niña hermosa*, for what must be delivered over and over again: *café*. Because there is that legion of heroes, as cousin Ángeles says when she evokes the image of Juan Antonio, the youth of those times, her own youth; but this also, as substrate, the Catalan bourgeoisie as a whole, the upper, middle, and petite bourgeoisie, the social scene in which such a living structure—the heroes of Francoism—finds itself implanted like something at once foreign and beneficial, in an intimate symbiotic relationship, serving and at the same time serving itself through Francoism, a sweet society of professional mourners that not for nothing identifies itself with the figure of Patufet, that sort of Catalan Tom Thumb who feels so comfortable in the belly of the ox that accidentally swallowed him, a comfortable blind spot whose meaning in a painting symptomatic of anal eroticism cannot be more explicit, given how it represents the values of retaining, saving, and accumulating.

More decisive than the social environment when it comes to the recondite aspects of rising awareness, the rising awareness that leads one to join the Communist Party, more decisive, evidently, is the family environment, the family and its particular myths, the image of the great-grandfather and the grandparents, Papa's childhood and the aunts and uncles, the style of life they knew, the villa on Calle Lauria, the servants required for all that, a lifestyle magnified to the degree to which it contrasted with the present reality, to the degree that, like a planet that stops rotating, the family narrows its horizon to Santa Cecilia, the country house still preserved like an emblem of a now-vanished past and which, by virtue of that displacement toward a central position of which it was an accessory, to the critical eyes of a young person it might well end up turning into a very image of the world, a world that is deteriorating and that ruins everything without him even realizing it, with the same satisfaction with which Uncle Gregorio sits down to stare at the crossword puzzle in the newspaper every morning. But in the family viewed as environment the root of such compulsive decisions is also absent, since, like the society to which it belongs, the family cannot play any decisive role except from without, like the light in a little mirror, in that object—strange to the degree that it is autonomous—that has grown in the breast that is the individual, far more refractory than the adults would suspect a little boy to be, to a far greater degree than all influences displeasing to a will formed before the notion of what I am and what I am not has been clearly delimited. Because, if considering two siblings raised in practically identical circumstances, subjected to the same influences, one of them already manifests itself strongly since childhood, going full force the way Joaquín already was then, while the other, under the hypocritical appearance of normality that he maintains in front of adults, feels like that condemned prisoner who, from his prison cell, contemplates the jubilation in the street that accompanies the preparations for the public torture of which he must be the protagonist; what differences could there be between the one and the other in their motivations—if not also in their objectives—of a decision apparently so clear that it's hard to believe that there's anyone who doesn't share it, like the decision to join the Communist Party, the final result of that no-less-transparent operation of rationality called awareness. However useful a diagnosis may be in matters such as this, independent of its accuracy, I will limit myself to point out the principal phases of a project whose meaning lies in the process itself, apart from all those conclusions that specialists like to reach: the ease with which that child who feels condemned—perhaps to compassion, perhaps to ridicule, from those who have to contemplate his torture—turns into a little poacher at whose passing the forest seems to turn stiff and barren; and how that habit subsides with equal ease when, years later, now grown into a man, he joins the Communist Party and participates clandestinely in a struggle he believes conducive to the overthrow of the dictatorship and the end of the Francoist order; the supplanting, no less complete for being gradual, of those activities in which he has ceased to believe, by his total devotion––absorbed no less than the researcher lost within the lenses of the microscope the way a stargazer loses himself in contemplation––to his chosen profession, that of architect.

Joaquín is another example of someone who, if I know him well and understand his apparent contradictions, it's exclusively due to our relative cohabitation during childhood and to the sort of normal contact between brothers that we've maintained since then, a type of contact in which all the advantage lies with the younger brother when it comes to mutual knowledge, meaning, with the one who has observed the other one more. But what to say, not only of a Jaime, but of a Serra, in spite of the friendship that unites us since university, shielded as it is in that so very excellent, or should I say narrow-minded, ideology—Marxism—dazzled, you might say, by its diamantine clarity, however erroneously and even brutally it has so far been interpreted, however much critically that it considers and recognizes that the responsibility for such errors falls upon its greatest interpreters? How to untangle what underlies it the same as what underlies a carapace that can be compared to the shield of an Achilles or an Aeneas, what's beneath the logic of a mechanism that turns the historical reason into a supreme instance? Regarding Jaime, I see his joining the Party more like an identity problem, meaning, not so much trying to find out what Jaime was like as much as discovering how many Jaimes there were. Because just as there are people whose physical features seem to develop according to the evolution of their personality over the course of the years, originating from some collection of constant elements already present in childhood, so, in a similar way, there are people whose development seems to have occurred in fits and starts, interruptions no less clear in the personality than in the physique, one-hundred-eighty-degree turns, changes incomprehensible for those who knew the subject in earlier phases; Jaime was just such a person. When I first started to have dealings with him—what Margarita had told him about me led him, it seems, to want to meet me—Jaime was a young engineer interested in political activity more for the activity than for the politics, as if the contradictory figure of the father, the rich bourgeois exiled for being a Red, diminished his confidence even as it spurred him on. Thus, for years he seemed to prefer the role of fellow traveler, of a useful idiot, as he said, parodying the Francoist lexicon, to that of a militant: thanks to the agility and capacity for maneuvering permitted him and not for the fears that built up in his mind with too much emphasis to be convincing. Joker and schemer at the same time and something of a friend to imbroglios, it took an effort to know when he was speaking seriously and when he was joking, when what he was affirming as true was real or not, and, in consequence, it also took time for his natural mythomaniac tendency to become clear. Little jokes, quiet sabre-rattling, whose fictive character only the passage of time could make evident, vouchsafed as they unfurled by the reality of their direct impact, and only with the passing of time, as well, was mythomania understood to be his true predisposition, but too late, far too late; by that time such a disposition, due to general personality changes, was already diminishing. This new phase coincided with his late entrance into the party, at the same time as an automatic loss of efficacy with respect to his previous political activities and, also in sharp contrast to the preceding phase, a humble and discreet attitude, fundamentally serious, with that peculiar formality of the wild reveler who gets married and suddenly becomes an exemplary father and family man, settled not only in his head but in his whole body. Did this exchange also coincide with the beginning of his sickness, that, as they usually say, long and painful illness that without a doubt took years to gestate, as well as the progressive loss of his faculties to become manifest? Was it, rather, that change, considered in relation to the previous ones, hereditary fruit, a sign of a mental disorder like the one that in her time affected his maternal grandfather—although, to judge from the symptomatology, transmitted recessively in the heart of the family and without them seeming to draw any conclusion about it, everything could be reduced to some more or less repressed pederastic propensities—and, years later, drove Aunt Marta and Uncle Oriol to a peaceful rest home? Apart, of course, from the father, the Red, and his two scandalous younger sisters, dead in the flower of their youth, the three cases comparable in the eyes of the surviving aunts and uncles to a true mental derangement. Could one speak of something similar in Jaime's case? Difficult to be sure now, as it was difficult to believe that the Jaime of recent years and that cousin Jaime whom I met through Margarita were the same person. It seemed at the time that he'd just left another phase behind, that of Jaime the athlete, a phase I always found hard to believe, thanks to its lack of coherence with the reality at that time, although it wasn't precisely one of his inventions, as well attested to by the trophies and medals that he'd collected in what had been his room in Vilasacra. Before that there was, at least, one other phase: the bad boy, naughty and rude, the terror of neighbors and relatives no less than his parents. And before the evil and twisted Jaime, contrasted by everyone with the venerated memory of his dead firstborn brother? Perhaps the key period, in that phase of his personality, was not, actually a phase because it had been forgotten. I remember a photo of the three siblings taken, it seems, in Brighton during the summer of 1939, between the end of the Civil War and the beginning of World War II: Margarita and even little Magda are childlike replicas of the Margarita and the Magda that I met, already resembling each other so much that their resemblance continued as adults; as for Jaime, a big overgrown kid at their side, he's unrecognizable.

What I've got no doubt about is that the political compromise was one of the many repercussions that my relationship with Margaret seemed to provoke in Jaime, what we called our incest; other contemporary decisions unleashed by that impact had greater importance, the idea of getting married to Ana, for example, and, more generally, the discovery that life offered a range of suggestions richer than what he had supposed. My relationship with Margarita and also my relationship with Magda, about which Margarita, her keenness limited by her own habitual self-assurance, found out because I told it to her, while Jaime, with the annoying insight he was showing off, with that malicious speed, from which he lets none escape, captured it, I'm sure, even before he responded to a tangible reality, before Magda and I, one enchanted evening, found ourselves in bed together, given over to the liquefying pleasure with all the zeal demanded by the old maxim that the man's true pleasure is found in the woman's pleasure, in her pleasure reaching its highest point, although in this case my every attempt to penetrate her ended in frustration, Magda suddenly tensing up, recoiling the way an oyster does when drizzled with lemon juice, rigid and timid at the same time, as if paralyzed, relaxing again when I stopped trying and we came together again in any other form of enveloping embrace, and so on again and again until we just let it go and had a whiskey and smoked a cigarette stretched out next to each other on the bed. If I later told this to Margarita, it was with Magda's consent, both of us convinced that Margarita could only receive it favorably, and even laugh with us about this clumsy moment of Magda's sexual initiation, that without a doubt she would be proud of the courage with which her shy protégée had faced the test, a test that wasn't going to merit anything except encouragement and congratulations, and I suppose that I'd have to seek, in the fact that none of these predictions came true, the reason why Margarita's reaction seemed to me, if possible, even more unusual: I don't know what thrills you men get from seeing women getting it on together, she said, and even now it's impossible for me to elucidate if it was how virulently she got upset when saying this, sharp, cutting, frowning, or perhaps it was the frank language of her response that gave me such an unpleasant surprise. Truth be told, it seemed as if there were something irreparable about my attempt with Magda, perhaps because for Margarita there was no forgiving, perhaps for how angry her venomous and tasteless oversensitivity made me, but from that point on our relationship changed forever, moving, after a period of distance, from the terrain of intimacy derived from an erotic relationship to the intimacy taken for granted by the person who, besides being a friend, is the recipient of our secrets, a change that happened not so much because of some residual rancor as much as the difficulty of straightening out what gets twisted up in love. A few days after this incident, Margarita started appearing in the company of the Man Cock, a young man with lobed features, whose axis, that is, the line that goes from the brow to the prominent chin, passing along the nose and the center of the lip, constitute an imaginary line similar to a frenum, the cheeks on either side defined by the outline of his powerful jaws following a peculiar connecting line that made his head a mere slightly thickened prolongation of the neck, lines both robust and simultaneously delicate that, joining in a single shape, united to the ruddy tonality of his complexion, making his head look like a swollen glans.

The common saying that a man projects his sexuality through the car he drives would gain validity, then lose it, if it was also applied to women, with the difference that what for the man is symbolic of amatory vigor, like the aptitude and drive of his fornication, for the woman is, as it was for Margarita, a symbol of autonomy and free will in erotic matters. And if I had to point out some characteristic of Margarita in this respect, the first thing that would occur to me would be none other than celerity, a celerity of which she felt as proud as if it were a sports car, impatience and haste similar to those she displayed when she sat at the steering wheel, and a general haste in her behavior that, above and beyond the allure of her freshness and spontaneity, the fruit of reflex more than reflection, she could not cease to dissuade or inhibit, to a greater or lesser degree, her lover of the moment, just like the flashes of boasting and defiance that often appeared under her licentious attitude of willingness, an attitude that sometimes bordered on wild excitement and which—as she later told me, frightened of herself—had cost her more than one scare; as it also cowed and discouraged those who shared her punctilious sense of independence, or rather, sovereignty, that systematic rejection of how much, to her understanding, she might suppose herself to be dominated by another, since for that other person the question might well be—as it was for me—a question of words, that Margarita's inability to control something was, in itself, an example of being controlled, averse as she was to any will other than her own. This led to my sexual relationship with Rosa which, even though we could not be more different in every way, not to say opposites, has been, in its good moments, much more complete than what I achieved with Margarita in each and every area. The fact that what was satisfactory with Margarita always turned out to be problematic was perhaps owing to the fact that, although she and I were so similar in certain aspects, our respective goals were so different, an essential blurring of focus that inevitably had to give way to all kinds of conflictive situations. And, notwithstanding, that first phase of our relationship has stayed alive in my memory like one of those summer nights when, as kids, we played hide-and-seek in the garden and made a racket until late, and then, now calm, we gazed up at the stars with Uncle Rodrigo, looking for one constellation after another, and only when summer vacation came to an end, weeks later, did we realize that that night was, for good reason, the best thing about the summer.

Something of that impression must have been lurking just beneath the edge of consciousness, or better, above, in that domain that would have to be called, more appropriately, meta-consciousness, that afternoon when, on the way to Port de la Selva, along the highway you just begin to glimpse the silhouette of El Paní, a gust of wind flipped my outside rearview mirror just as a fine rain started spattering the windshield as if by surprise, like a Jupiter who hurls himself down upon the object of his love from the clear openings in the storm tossed sky. In the distance, a chain of white cumulus clouds covered Cabo Creus, configuring a mountainous system of dimensions far greater than the Pyrenees, resplendent peaks above which, in turn, towered a great brownish cloud rising straight up in a column. It was then, as the passing rain ceased, when, against that background toward which the straight shining line of the highway was directly headed, at the approximate elevation of Port de la Selva, a full rainbow spread across the sky, its ends painting the rocks of the cape, its center part shifting the sky's gray tonalities into topaz-colored splendors, while in the car, from a point difficult to precisely locate, there came a sound resembling a siren's whistle, a harmonic sound, modulated, that seemed to come from far away, with that sensation of distance caused by an outboard motor's echo reaching our ears under the water as we dive under, swimming inches above the seafloor. Only moments later, as the effect was diminishing,

I realized that I was thinking about Margarita, that her presence was the first thing that had come to my imagination as the phenomenon happened. The fact that in the future I again thought about her each time the phenomenon repeated itself, was something that no longer had anything particularly special about it, just a simple association of ideas. What was also clear was that the phenomenon was found to be assigned to the place in which it happened for the first time, at the beginning of that straight stretch of highway, when El Paní appeared before my eyes, given that the sound neither proceeded from the car nor was produced along other stretches of road with similar characteristics, being also independent of the climatological conditions, the fact that the wind whistled in a peculiar way as it filtered, for example, through some opening in the hood. Only a few days later all these considerations disintegrated when the siren effect happened again, on the way to Vilasacra, before reaching Gorgs, toward the end of a long straight stretch of road that turns into a curve as it crosses a stream bed, a shady stream bed in which, as soon as night falls, the fog pools up, so thick that it clouds the windows. And the fear, with the force of intuitive illumination, that I experienced that night, has returned, just as the same effect repeated itself on the many nights that I have driven past that spot again: the fear of seeing Margarita's smiling effigy, grown gigantic, appear in the fog-soaked headlights, in the very spot where the light's potency is lost in the fog.

DIALOGUE WITH TAPE RECORDER.

When one speaks of the errors that they have committed in their life, they usually do so as if accepting beforehand that any other option would have given way to different results, meaning, that everything that happened was equivalent to having drawn the shortest straw. If such a supposition can be exact in certain circumstances, will it also be the same with respect to my two axial errors, my profession and my marriage? I would say not, that in both cases the error is more one of overall appearance, of marriage as an institution and architecture as a career, as a group of specialized studies that mint the future architect, than to the concrete aspects of my concrete case. Because, if, on the one hand, my marriage with any of the women that I have known more or less intimately would have turned out worse rather than better than my marriage with Rosa, it's unthinkable, on the other, that I would feel satisfied having followed a different career, with another kind of specialized studies, distinct but no less clumsily limited to an aprioristic and redundant function than the demands of being an architect. In today's society, what can the place of marriage be when it's the family institution itself that is being indicted? It never occurred to either Rosa or me to get married until Camila was on the way and, mistaken or not, we seized on marriage as a means of an administrative expedient, the one most commonly prescribed in these cases, the least fastidious for the future parents and for the future child when the future mother chooses to have the baby. To Margarita it seemed a tremendous error on my part to submit myself to what she considered an obvious trap by Rosa, a point of view fully in line with her tendency to understand life like a tennis game, in which you mustn't lose the point. According to the same criterion, her wedding, a few months later, to a rich manufacturer of those cosmetic products sold in pharmacies, constituted, on the contrary, a tremendous volley, a spectacular point that was chalked up, however unimaginable her cohabitation with a guy who turned out to need to cultivate a certain air of British sailor in order to give himself the appearance of a personality, and however much their living together didn't, as expected, last more than six months; or perhaps precisely for that very reason. Things about Margarita that were preferable not to discuss, things that had to be respected as she respected mine, although not without being surprised, I suppose, that a guy like me had similar ideas, since we were so much in the same key, since we understood each other so well; that that game of racket strokes, that volley of shots and counter-shots that for her was life, was for me little more than the passing wave that lifts the keel of a ship or the changing pattern of the foam, something that probably did not end up crossing her mind either, that could only be explained as one of my plays in the grand style whose true reach escaped her. Because what's true is that, to my understanding, neither Margarita's trajectory, nor Rosa's, nor mine, nor the cosmetics manufacturer's—although in this respect perhaps certain elements of judgement escape me—would have been seen to be substantially altered, except for what concerns the environmental background, of having interchanged our respective pairings, of me having married Margarita, and Rosa the cosmetics man, a less crazy permutation, in the end, than how it might appear at first glance.

Objections as serious as marriage, in so far as their validity goes, can be worth making about the architect's work, however much neither the professionals nor those who study to become architects seem conscious of that; neither was I as a student, but at least I didn't take long to realize that what I was expecting from architecture was not what the majority of my friends expected. Wedded to the idea that architecture is nothing more than the mastery of a series of technical facts, it cannot shock them to see the architect converted into a kind of cabinet maker who conceives of gigantic dressers full of small drawers which have to be made to hold the greatest number of people possible, with only as much originality in the design as its specific function permits. It's not a problem of formalism, let's be clear, of demanding complete creative control with form, unlimited today as never before, so that the formal approach has been rendered irrelevant, so that, for whatever reason, with either better or worse taste, it will turn out to be senseless. Because the central nucleus of the problem is precisely this: architecture's loss of meaning in today's world, empty as it is of the meaning that it once had for towns, the sense to which the Pyramids, the Parthenon, or the gothic cathedrals, in their respective contexts responded, when neither the Coliseum was simply a race course nor the Forbidden City simply a palace. What kind of structure can have an equivalent meaning these days? And nothing more inane than the counter position of organic architecture, for example, to rationalist, or launching concepts on the market such as open space as a kind of panacea, not to mention those movements that advocate the return to a popular architecture and, more generally, to the rustic and primitive, denominations whose meanings I don't know, or better, that don't mean anything given that the ones who spout them don't even know what they mean. The mistake is always the same: advocate for a social architecture or, in better words, an architecture for man, a proposition that, while it justifies the production of a series of apartments as if they were cars, does not, for that reason, cease to be a negation of the very concept of architecture; this is the true heart of the question. The rest, the acceleration of the changes or revolutions in technical areas, the so-called advances and, above all, the acceleration of changes in habits and ways of life, are nothing but features of a more general phenomenon whose impact on the question, although insufficient to define it, is also of great importance. It's not about the fact that young people today are different from those before, or an aggravated version of the classic generation gap, but of those who were already adults when those young people came into the world, also subject to the acceleration of the change, and as if they wanted to recover the time lost they have modified their attitude toward life. Because just as the behavior of the mature woman is found to be influenced by the freedom that the young woman of today demonstrates, a freedom that she never had a chance to enjoy, the mature woman of these times—to a greater degree than the man, given her situation of greater dependence—is found to be subjected to a process of premature aging, or rather, of becoming an idiot, in which children play the role of an induction agent. For example, Rosa's mother after fifteen or twenty years; her intense daily and sentimental life at that time, appropriate to the pretty woman she was, compared to the sort of granny she has turned into, dragged around by her grandchildren from Camila, who was the first to have them. And the fact is, to the natural sclerosis of the cerebral mechanisms over the years you've got to add, sure enough, that new element, of catalyzing action, which is the relationship with grandchildren today, different from those of past times, from those of all times, reluctant, although they disguise the childish language which those grandmothers, whom anyone would consider senile, use with them, silly songs and nursery rhymes like "patty-cake, patty-cake" with which they, imitating their grandmothers from when they were little girls, insist on showing them, a reaction that they sense and which is manifested in the uneasy caution of their smile, in the uncertainty of the authoritarianism they show off when believing themselves obliged to show it off, earned almost morally, as they already are culturally, interested to no less a degree than the little ones in the daily TV shows, in the adventures of the series, in the results of the game shows, and even the feverish repetition of the TV ads, and, as a consequence, no less interested, similarly, in the world which all that suggests, dazzled by that new dimension suddenly revealed to them at their age and which makes it so difficult to precisely draw the lines between the reality that they experience now and what they experienced before. What else can the architect's role be in the face of that picture if not to place it within the right frame, to realize the dream of so many who live in any of those apartments into which they have been packed, the second residence, one of those chocolate box chalets, if, in fact, they don't already own one?

The mention of the environmental factors relating to Rosa's mother's slump doesn't mean, on the other hand, that she forgets the law of life, because, if she had then been well into her forties, the time transpired since is enough to explain that she really is what she seems: an old woman. Because, if at the age of ten, thinking about fifteen years later is like thinking about the eternal life of the blessed, I suppose that around fifty, habituated as one is to the almost imperceptible decline that remains, it would turn out to be equally difficult to imagine the brusqueness with which old age comes rushing and sets in, the same period of time appearing inconceivably brief when for the child it was inconceivably long; years that in childhood seemed centuries according to an appreciation likely based on the child's capacity to experience the present, minute by minute, in a way that the notion of duration and that of the instant become confused in a protracted sequence. Capacity—if not faculty—which is lost in the adult, ever-watching the clock, conscious of the time when they have to arrive, the time they don't have to go out, all of it similar to what happens with an hourglass, how one is so fixated on the drizzling sand to the point that they forget they have flipped it over, in the same way that, as time passes, the adult forgets the passing of the years. And the fact is that what is valid for the extreme phases of life is also valid, although less ostensibly, for the intermediate phases. For example, watching the movements of one of those young women around twenty years of age, amusing if not graceful, dynamic, quick, obviously willing to spend and maximize her quota of orgasms, gives one a definite feeling of pleasure. But, in certain moments, spirits low, that pleasure has its counterpart: the consideration that a woman of our age, outwardly well preserved, yes, but with her body corroded by alcohol, tobacco, and sleeping pills, her nervous system shattered, was exactly that way when she started going out with us, a lively-spirited and self-assured young woman who ate the world for breakfast, a world that offered itself to our eyes like the fulfillment of a prophecy, a consideration, or better yet, considerations that, in a similar frame of mind, must necessarily generate new ideas about character not only disagreeable but also depressing. That explains people's instinctive tendency to isolate the event, the pleasant impression, from its consideration by the intellect, as well as the fact that, this being repressed, the natural attraction that both the man as well as the woman feels for young people, to the degree to which it can seem thoughtless and even irresponsible, might be judged ridiculous if not grotesque or even perverted, when in fact there exists a physical basis that justifies for itself just such an attraction, the profound motivation must be sought in what that youth symbolizes and summons, like an amulet, in the stimulating value of how much good it offers life, good news, good health, good luck, the cheerful expression that verifies it, in contrast to--and this is not redundant-- the depressing character of what's depressing, those long faces, those faces sunken from sadness or dismay, weepy eyes, the voice choked as it tells the things they tell, their misfortunes, their sorrows, their upheavals, adversities that if they pile up on them it must be for some reason, no surprise that one would react like that, defending themself, taking their measures regarding those harbingers of misfortune, giving them the shake, outrunning them, moving them out of our way just as we move things with the tip of our shoe, with a swift kick, however many fastidious objects we find in our path, impelled by that unformulated conviction that just as good luck brings good luck, bad luck brings bad, and the jinx summons the jinx, so that the rejection which causes acceptance of a physical or psychic decline in those people romantically or affectionately closest to us must be understood as something that refers not only to the beloved and their connection to us, but also to ourselves, to the influence that such acceptance can exercise on our own condition and, in the end, to the possibility unfurled, that, as if by contagion, without our having realized, we find ourselves subjected to a process of similar characteristics.

There's no room for doubt, in this sense, that, above and beyond my problems with Rosa, I have preserved the image of our early days together longer than she has; that it continued being a valid reference for me long after it had stopped being so for her, that summer when we began to go out together, for example, our forays into the Barcelona nightlife, through the lower depths of Las Ramblas, our quick getaways to Cadaqués, a time when we indulged ourselves in what was deemed excesses by the prevailing morality simply because for us they were in no way excessive—and if they occasionally were, in the most literal sense, we didn't realize it until later on, when we began to pay for them with compound interest—because the important thing for us, each time, was to outdo ourselves, exceed the excesses, reach that state in which, as that guy from León said, sex soothes and the soul sinks at dawn. For years I've always thought back on our first times together, considering the new conflicts that have happened between us to be equivalent, if not equal to the conflicts then, somewhat more damaging in the degree to which the progressive character of all erosion is in itself a factor of deterioration. It's not only about emotional tensions and badly assimilated infidelities as much as that each partner takes great pains to seem immune to their impact; there is also the wearing away which living together eventually produces, habits and small personal manias that, despite their innocuous and even trivial character, are capable of transforming impulses of the rancor that accumulates on both sides of the open fissure of a couple's emotional life into grievances of the highest order. One could also fashion an encrypted code from the gradual intolerance that daily life introduces into a marriage, a systematic compilation that would allow one to establish the meaning that certain acts have for each partner, words and gestures in the context of a shared life, however circumstantial they might appear to be. Thus, in the morning, when he's barely awake, or rather half-awake, moved by a generally feverish, imperious, and impatient disposition, he begins a maneuver to get closer to the other body, stretching out one foot, approaching hesitantly, extending encircling caresses, while she, as if sunk in a deep slumber, lets him do it, inert, silent, finally murmuring that she's got a terrible headache, like her head is going to explode, she, who at night will drink a few more drinks than usual and emerge from the bathroom freshly bathed and wrapped in what they call her hooker's robe to find that he has already swallowed his pills and flicked off the light, and when she blames him for his offensive lack of enthusiasm, he'll say that at this hour of the night he's got too many things on his mind, and the time when he doesn't is, precisely, in the morning, and then she'll say that in the morning she's asleep, and then it will all start all over again, the dual lists of offenses, the twin litanies of reproaches, and so on, for years and years until each one understands that, in order to avoid frustrations, the best thing is to not even insinuate anything and simply wait until, thanks to a coincidence of circumstances, both of them are drunk and they end up mounting and riding each other wildly as in years past, not very sure that the other partner knows with whom they're really doing it with, if I know that she's Rosa, and if she knows that I'm Ricardo. The consequences of this ordeal will be, no doubt, more noxious for the woman than for the man, insofar as she has not known how, been able to, or managed to create a prior situation of independence, marriage-proof, that might permit her to free herself from other kinds of stimuli, alcohol, sleeping pills, tranquilizers, etcetera, that will only serve to distance her even more from all possible activity that strengthens her autonomy, that helps her confront daily life, getting up at seven or eight o'clock and doing something, anything, instead of crawling out of bed at noon to find herself with fewer hours to kill before, when dusk falls, the hour for the first drink rolls around. In these circumstances, reflections about how what's happening has been able to happen will become the principal occupation for her most lucid moments, with a tendency to explain how much is happening to her due to a singular cause—her father's death, her jealousy of her mother or her mother's jealousy of her—as well as finding the origin of how many sorrows afflict her in the defective functioning of some organ, something which nobody managed to guess despite how stupid and simple it is: her great sympathetic nervous system, her vision, her inner ear, something that articulates the various symptoms in a coherent and all-encompassing response. Consequently the firm decision will be taken, too many times postponed—who knows why—to submit to a cure or rehabilitation treatment in one of those remote clinics where they get you well from head to toe, back in shape without any need for drugs, through totally natural procedures, a sleeping cure, for example, sleeping and sleeping until you're good as new, or a treatment based on a diet of water or the high mountain air or the strict discipline of a certain lifestyle regimen, apart, of course, from the inflexible bill that puts an end to the patient's stay and that doubtless plays an important role, for its beneficial effects as a ritual offering. Only that, from a certain moment, neither the proffered diagnoses nor their possible remedies will be able to keep hiding the evidence that, as it emerges, relegates, corners, and ends up excluding any other consideration: one's age, the reality that one is no longer what is understood to be a young woman, that her problems are no longer those of an earlier time and as a consequence the solutions cannot be the same, and, above all, the state of stupor to which she sees herself reduced before the mere mention of the enigma: How is it possible that all those years have passed her by and she never even realized that they were passing?

The formulation and further acceptance of these facts by both partners usually precipitates the situation, decanting it, perhaps toward the dissolution of the bond, perhaps toward formulas that secure the diverse options that maintaining it offers. The only sure thing is that it makes no sense whatsoever to prolong that antagonism that impregnates and saturates the life of the married partners, including outside of the domestic circle, a conflictive relationship similar, in personal matters, to what, in the international sphere, Mexico maintains with Spain, something like one macho's unrequited love for another macho, with all the burden of fascination-rancor such a relationship implies, as well as its consequences of an eminently sadomasochistic sign. In general, there is always a moment when, be it by common agreement, be it unilateral, the breakup is decided, but the years of searching for a break are many, too many, so that, when the so-long-awaited propitious occasion arrives, both of them are too exhausted to go through with it, and so it's decided once again to stay together, to try yet again to maintain equilibrium, the end of commitment if not continuity; a fatigue that is more definitive around age forty than at twenty to the degree to which it's less improvised, which is more desperate to the degree to which it does not proceed from the breaking of some expectation nor reside within the contrast of fledgling alternatives. Now then: the fact that there exist no real alternatives to the natural solution of a problem created by the very nature of the marriage itself, does not mean that it's not possible to invent others, for one spouse and another to reach an understanding based on the creation of new incentives and compensations, join their interests against third parties to the point that the pleasure aroused by that consolidation of the ties that in the end connects them like two people truly in love might not be less than what their shared triumphs over the outside world bring them, or rather, their revenges on that world, or still better yet, the disasters to which they are witnesses, the misfortunes, to contemplate how the others get sick or become ruined, how they get old, how they crashed and burned precisely where they themselves crashed and burned or where they could have crashed and burned, seeing how they fall. A kind of historical record that is repeated in so many imaginable variations of this rectification that eventually usually happens in the married couple's traditional amorous justification, in that understanding now centered on the accumulation of money or of weight, in the fattening up or in the sensation of security derived from the economic relief in a context dominated by anxiety and hardships: marriage between fat people, for example, fruit of that tacit pact according to which the married partners agree to discuss over dinner, without holding anything back, the pleasures or presumed pleasures of the bed, without contemplations or regrets, however fat they might get, their complicit ogreish quality also turned into a second font of pleasure, as is frequent in accumulative phenomena. The satisfaction obtained can become real, and thus we find ourselves with those old euphoric couples who whisper to each other and coo and kiss and cuddle because they still love each other like the very first day, like children, and they want it to be known and for people to bear witness to it and be surprised, almost like with a picture that illustrates the cover of a novel, the story of that young man full of dreams and energy who marries a young woman of similar qualities and desires, and together they embrace the challenges of life, the problems that this generates at every level, work, home, the children that come, always encouraged by the success with which they end up overcoming any crises and trials they face, whether emotional, financial, or social, year after year, and even until they reach their retirement which resolves it all and, now grandparents, they permit themselves the luxury of taking a farewell cruise around the world.

On transcribing these lines onto paper, I realize that, when I was previously talking about the practice of architecture in today's society, I missed some of the personal observations about the practical aspects of our work that appeared in the notes I previously wrote. The afternoon when I recorded this fragment, I found myself in Barcelona and I had gone with Rosa and Camila to one of those lunches that grandmothers have every so often, thanks to their mania for gathering together the whole family or what remains of it. Rosa's mother was especially lamentable and the influence of this impression--perhaps increased by the days I spent here in Gorgs, locked away with my notes—was probably the reason I lingered on some unimportant details when it came to writing them, a process—invented, you might say, in order to satisfy the delusions of a paranoiac—that I find increasingly less convincing because of the imponderables to which it is subject, because of the effort that it then requires to prune the text of whatever does not belong in writing; useful, in short, once the work is realized, in order to capture the final result. Another thing that distracted me and disturbed my capacity for concentration was the thought of how much Camila is starting to resemble the Magda of times past, as if that non-consummated coitus had ended up coming to fruition in Rosa's belly, whom Camila really doesn't really resemble very much.

Considerations then omitted are not so much about what the young man studying to be an architect doesn't know because his teachers don't know it either, meaning, architecture, as much as certain aspects of what must be a trade not taught and that nevertheless are the ones that will end up taking the architect more time to learn, even though his subordinates are the ones who take care of the calculations, drawings, and models. Because the student imagines that his career consists of mastering a set of technical knowledge, ultimately not very different from that of a carpenter, and then it turns out that his practice consists of something else, that it's fundamentally a question of dealing with people, of forming relationships and getting along, not only with clients, but above all with financiers, promoters, high ranking administrators, representatives of various organizations, among the many there are, inevitably, the sort of Catalans who like to show off, demonstrate that they know all the tricks, you can't fool me, man. And thus the profession is understood, as a business, the contacts that count the most when it comes to carrying out a project, of accomplishing what in the language of the business world is called an operation, the ones who count the most, contrary to what the layperson might believe, are the ones who focus not on their clients but on the high ranking administrators upon whom they depend for permits, paperwork, property rezoning, etcetera, indispensable requirements for the business to be a business, that is, in order for it to become a functioning business, just as, or even more important than the client per se—if by that we mean the title holder of that property—is the financial entity who must give their all-important blessing so that the project may be carried out, as we might say, without money. That special person whom the architect will get to know sooner or later, perhaps in the privacy of an office, perhaps in the places most unlikely for a novice, at the bar of a café, for example, enjoying a whiskey, with the dice cup in hand, a sort of guy whom our neophyte would have taken to be a more or less exalted peasant and who, nevertheless, according to his assistant or right-hand man, the interlocutor or intermediary who has facilitated the meeting with the newcomers, namely, the promoter, the proprietor and the neophyte architect himself, according to that right-hand man who possibly has prepared the meeting in such a place in order to lend it a greater informality, so that it seems more natural according to that man, and it's supposed that they already know, the newcomers, neophyte included, the he's president, president, yes, of the Savings Bank, the Caja de Ahorros of which both our client as well as the promoter are customers and even perhaps—although practically speaking such an circumstance might be of negligible value—the novice architect, the man is now the president of a company where he started as a doorman, a whole career that's about to experience yet another turn—the movement from the private sector to the public one—with him throwing his hat in the ring for the Barcelona city council elections, which is what we are in, says the realtor, the reporter, in his capacity as a right-hand man, identifying himself at the same time as a person of influence in the Movement, *sí, señor*, with his affable pig's face, in spite of, or thanks to, that face: a person of influence in the Movement. And the president of a savings bank and ex-doorman and current candidate for the council of the most excellent city government, that is the *Excelentísimo Ayuntamiento de Barcelona*, lets him speak, he listens to him as one listens to oneself, though improbable this success is no less worthy of being seen as a milestone in his career, the way a painting is examined, the features ennobled by the solemn background music playing in the locale, a music that is a sort of famous cinematographic super-production that only seems to elevate the chronicler's words, bearing witness to their authenticity, as if it were all true, as if his career arc from doorman to savings bank president had not followed some probably ignominious twists and turns, as if such twists and turns were not in every point insufficient regarding the circuits of the Francoist electoral machine, as if the support of pig-faced people and influence in the Movement had some transcendence, and above all as if the elections in question were elections in the United States, and he were a Rockefeller. Faced with such people, as if facing a provincial city planning delegate or a modest and at the same time all-powerful small-town city hall secretary, the newcomers, the promoter, the proprietor and even the neophyte architect, whose condition as an added element—and for that reason perfectly replaceable, a weak condition in so far as it is fortuitous—will still be incidentally conspicuous, all of them, in a word, will display the same complacent servility and identical adulatory attitude, however many times necessary, all of them will behave then like that leech who only awaits the opportunity to fall upon us, that loafer, that son of a family fallen on hard times, that former little rich kid turned flatterer, a man of letters and numbers, who takes advantage of, let's say, the death of someone's father, of any family member, and, as you might guess with these things, to play the role of some old classmate, and declare to us his most heartfelt condolences, in the belief that the shared affliction might afford him a loophole through which he can try to obtain some favor—some endorsement, for example—from the old, dear friend who, thanks to the changing fortunes of life, is in a situation to make that possible now, at this very moment, his normal defenses about these things lowered, the distances he usually maintains broken, that guy's not here, or he's in a meeting, or I'll tell him that you called, excuses his secretary usually uses to keep people at arm's length, perfectly aware of the kind of person that spoiled little rich boy has become who went to the same school and stretches out his hand repeatedly, the expression in his eyes that of someone shot through an agonizing pain. Thus, like that reviled professional sponger, exactly like any of the newcomers to the café, to the privacy of an office, to whomever this guy might belong, whoever might be the possible grantor, be it the president of the financial institution, the urban planning delegate, the property owner or even the promoter, interchangeable as their positions are according to whoever happens to need something from the other one, with turns for favors rotating through the group just like everything in life, through everyone except, of course, that of the neophyte architect.

An indispensable element when it comes to closing the deal, or rather, to celebrate bringing the negotiations to a happy conclusion, is the kind of laughter with which all and every one of those present must seal it, booming laughs, full of self-satisfaction along with, simultaneously, disdain toward anything found outside that circle of self-indulgence, scorn for the theoretical limits of the power of money, toward the laws that theoretically regulate it, toward the interests of others made vulnerable by the exception that they represent, the smile sagging no less than the eyes, the porcine roundness of the features, all in the likeness of that prototypical image of the plutocrat that came into vogue during the Great Depression through the jokes and caricatures that appeared in certain publications, leftist ones as well as those with a fascist bent, in their brave efforts to unmask the rich, these fat grotesque creatures, of oblong elegance, who show us their heavy rings and their no-less-heavy golden chains draped over their voluminous bellies, shameless, defiant, as our men appear shameless and defiant when it comes to closing the deal, as if they would like to assume for themselves that image of the caricatures that makes them as powerful as they are hated, to appropriate it like some kind of talisman, a goal for whose achievement they are willing to do whatever's necessary. And the ritual that is imposed on our recently arrived initial and current beneficiaries, or at least principal beneficiaries, of the deal that has been closed, neophyte included, thanks to the open-handed spirit that usually predominates in these sorts of moments: the ham sandwich that, accompanied by a quick coffee, is eaten on going out to any café, the one closest to the office that has been the scene of the happy event, a sandwich you must eat by tearing into it with your teeth, filling your mouth, as a form of well-deserved worship of its very succulence, almost implicit in the very word itself—*jamón*—in the same way that the word for sandwich—*bocadillo*—that is, *bocado pequeño*, a small mouthful—seems to invite you to repeat it due to its insignificance and its emblematic character, an augury of prosperity when around mid-morning you feel like eating something, according to the psychological voracity induced by everything that reeks of money, the closing of a deal or granting credit or the materialization of a good sale.

The deal must sometimes be made directly, without intermediaries but with the client per se, meaning, with the proprietor, generally this relates to small deals, that little chocolate box chalet that's usually the second residence. Although for years now I've been able to allow myself to pass up such deals, in my salad days, when I was a neophyte myself, I also had to learn to move in these circles where, more than the proprietor, the one who counts is the proprietor's wife, her willpower, her tastes, her ideas, this circumstance, however, that holds special importance, since, if on one side, the rapport between both spouses is usually great, on the other, the natural femininity of the Catalan people, repeatedly pointed out by Pidal, trivializes the fact of whether our interlocutor happens to be the client or his wife. The presence of this trait, which Pidal attributes to the impregnation of the petit-bourgeois mentality that Catalan society as a whole has experienced, given that not only its men but also its women frequently are infected by spineless inanity and sickly-sweetness so that when it comes to manners and behavior, they are simply a manifestation of such a characteristic. And that, to such an extent, that in cases of dispute arising from some problem of circulation or similar contingency, Pidal strongly recommends the precaution of addressing the feminine counterpart, and with an affectionate tone, in order to avoid vexing complications and misunderstandings, like the one that could arise in case that the person who has given us—or to whom we have given—a scratching were treated like a male. However the case may be, the ongoing dealing with this sort of people, the courteous attention that must be given to their initiatives and aesthetic criteria, ends up becoming intolerable, no less than the overwhelming burden brought on by Christmas festivities, when the crippling proliferation of celebrations that invades our private life becomes a problem of expression, of how to handle it harmoniously, using an affable tone of voice to return season's greetings to those who offer them to us, both sides in accord with the lively, cheerful character that is de rigueur.

These are things that I could already intuit when I was a student, faced with the contrast between the technical knowledge we were acquiring at University and the initiatory aspects that could be glimpsed outside, later, linked to the practice of the profession and a close contact with what is understood by "real life," or "the world of business," aspects or, better yet, indispensable requirements, when the desired outcome is for the architect to form part of the system in which he lives as he is: an outstanding leader of the consumer society to the degree that he has been designated to organize the environment in which we live, the environment wherein people develop their activities, the scenery that decorates their leisure time. Some of my friends not only seemed to know it from the start but, be it from family tradition or some other motive, they seemed to have chosen the career precisely for that reason, for the business side of it, for making money; and I, even while showing it off, resisted believing in it in real terms, in the same way that it's difficult to understand the true reach of other secret codes, however palpable the phenomenon, palpable, or rather, detectable, as, for example, the Catalan accent can be, that joy of the Catalans who, for whatever reason, marriage, business, exile, whatever it might be, have been given in living abroad—in Madrid, in Mexico, outside of Spain—the joy of comparing, as we were saying, each time they return to their native land, at Christmas for example, or for vacations or some similar reason, the joy they experience in comparing the accent they bring home with them to the one they left behind, the accents and pet words and favorite expressions they've acquired, the expressions from Madrid or Mexico that cause so much surprise to those who've known them since childhood, a happiness that is nothing but the supplementary reflection of what each one of them experiences when, in Mexico, in Madrid or in Guayaquil, he bumps into a compatriot and they both confirm up to what point, once mutually identified, they allow themselves to be understood by everyone else just by slipping into the vernacular, to what degree the undertone of the mother accent endures beneath the acquired accents, to what degree that accent really constitutes a kind of membership card in a privileged private club, useful, although only as personal satisfaction, also dispensing with the fructifying consequences in the economic order that such encounters can eventually turn out to be, in short, no different or less useful than the initiation phase the architect must experience parallel to the exercise of the profession if he intends to at least be tolerated by the system. The fact that Gaudí was a great architect, probably the last one, and yet for all that, lived in the shadow of the dominant Barcelona bourgeoisie, must be due, I suppose, to the fact that he was saved by his absentmindedness and his blind Catholic faith, which kept him detached from the very concept of business, unassimilable.

That intuition that the architect's work fuses together all the burdens and encumbrances that were to be feared, from those of a practical character to the purely conceptual, less degrading, if you will, but of still greater significance, referring as they refer to the role or, to be more exact, to the absence of the architect's role in contemporary society, that intuition, I was saying, was fully present in my worries when I finished my studies, a period that curiously coincides with that of my maximum dedication to clandestine political activities, before, far removed from these and given over fully to my profession, I ended up going to jail, as if to pay some overdue bill. I remember how much it bothered me then the idea that the houses I had designed were going to be inhabited some day, that someone would be allowed to remodel something, to change the colors, buy furniture of their own liking, add floors, let children run loose inside, go out on the terrace, all that; the model, for me, would have been an empty and uninhabited architecture, the closest thing possible to a glorious ruin, something impossible to profane by possible tenants nor capable of being converted into a shop or business. Not to mention that my closest colleagues, with just as little appetite for controversy as I have, must've considered that it was just a pose, the boutade of an architect who thinks he's clever, of a sarcasm only tolerable by reason of its very extravagance, since they mustn't have been able to conceive that I was seriously entertaining ideas that sounded to them like dehumanization and an antisocial attitude as it should inevitably should sound to them, not knowing that they didn't know what I was talking to them about and how they found as normal as possible those immense suburbs into which, after a very few years, we will have converted the cities. And I speak of city and no longer simply about houses because this is, after all, what is seething in the depths of every neophyte architect, whether he knows it or not, independent of his professional capability and even of his greater or lesser intelligence: that image of the ideal city that we wish the world were and which we refuse to renounce our belief that someday it will come to be.

I decided to quit the profession last autumn, around September or maybe October, it must be just a little over a year now. But much closer and more alive for me, by far, is the impression of strangeness that Barcelona made during the course of the long walk that I set out on immediately afterward as a way of blowing off steam, as soon as I'd left the studio, no car, of course, just walking on foot and taking the Metro, getting off at streets I only knew by name, wandering randomly around each one, disconcerted, taking whatever direction I took, looking at how much the city had changed or, if you like, how much I didn't recognize it after years and years of not seeing it except through sections of maps and blueprints, memories, and remodeling projects. It was as if I had stayed at work all night and toward daybreak, on walking home, I realized that twenty years had gone by.

PRIVATE DIARY.

I never associated Carlos with Gorgs de la Selva nor, truth be told, did I have any reason for doing so. I associated Carlos with Rosas, where he owns a hotel whose plans were one of the first jobs I undertook after finishing my studies. At that time, Rosa and I were frequenting Cadaqués, and Aurea and Carlos often came to visit us; Margarita didn't start visiting Rosas until later when, if I ran into Carlos it was rather more by coincidence, just time enough for us to see each other and that was all. I knew that Aurea had a grandfather who was a sort of rural landlord, but the last thing that could have occurred to me was that this lord's fiefdom was none other than Gorgs itself, which was connected, although only by proximity, with Vilasacra, that the proximity of his death to Margarita's death had to be the reason why Carlos and I ran into each other that afternoon in the inn at Gorgs. Well, it seems, this was the reason for Carlos's presence there, the old man's death, which the doctor saw as imminent, although toward the end of September he gave them an initial scare, around the feast day of la Virgen de la Merced, just when Margarita had her accident.

Even so, that encounter with Carlos in the cheap hotel of a town whose existence, weeks before, was probably unknown to us both, might not have happened if not for the rain, if if I wasn't sick of having spent the afternoon shut away in my room, pacing back and forth over and over, which is why I went downstairs to the dining room earlier than usual. Interrupting my work to walk around the room is something I always tend to do, as if that act of crossing the room diagonally, again and again, in one direction then the other, far from distancing me from the papers spread on the table, brings me close to them again, permits me to see them with new eyes. But no matter where I happen to find myself, and all the more so if it's in the countryside, I also have the habit of walking for a while before starting to work, and that's precisely what I had not been able to do that day, not so much because of the rain itself as because of the mud, without which, on the other hand, outside the room and until dinnertime, there was no place to be in the whole hotel except for the TV room, a circumstance that doubtless contributed to the fact of my staying inside my room becoming oppressive to me; not at all an unusual sensation, after all, if we recall that that habit of pacing the room up and down, counting my steps, or rather, trying, independent of the greater or lesser reach of each stride, to make them number seven, is a habit acquired in prison or, at least, that started to manifest itself in prison, because it might well be that, potentially, as a tendency, it already existed before, and that it was the fact of being confined in a cell that brought it out, in the same way that the forced solitude of the shipwrecked sailor on a desert isle will cause a previously unsuspected series of latent personality traits to flourish. On the other hand, the time transpired since my reclusion in that cell allows me to establish, a posteriori, a continuity between the various moments spent, from then on, pacing my room, whichever room it happened to be, in this or that country, in one period of my life or another, independent of the concrete circumstances belonging to each case, the connecting link that gives coherence to a chain that might have seemed a simple accumulation of links: the fact that it happens to be in this modest room in a cheap small town hotel in the countryside, where, between one stroll and another, I find myself placing the final pieces of the edifice that I began to build there, with those first inklings, inklings more than ideas, that suddenly take shape in a precise and concrete whole, similar to the triangle formed simply by connecting three points on a plane. I don't recall the date, but I do know the day, the afternoon, the instant, after one of those cloudbursts that announce the springtime, contemplating the clearing sky from the window of my cell, the gusting wind scattering the clouds as if sweeping them away with a broom, twisting them, making them turn, just the same as the dust bunnies twist and spin around the floor of the cell, at the mercy of the insidious air currents. And like impulses of that same air capable of finding their way into the deepest parts of a prison even as they sweep the skies, so too the exaltation of my spirit in the face of those first inklings, at the complete opposite of that state of mind that, as if soothed by the low clouds all in a line and the soft, gentle rain, possessed me just the other afternoon in this room when I chose to abandon my notes, fully aware, unlike that afternoon in prison, that the key to the problems that affect architecture today are found, not in the architectonic field, but in man.

Carlos had barely changed, something, I fear, that is not exactly what he must have thought of me. After a first period of time during which, as a result of the project he had commissioned me for, we saw each other frequently, our meetings grew further and further apart, according to that process that happens over the years even with lifelong friends, when we understand that they are precisely only that, old friends but not now, that now they bore us, that we only keep seeing them from the inertia of the acquired habit. Nonetheless and having grown distant, the conversation that we kept up in the empty dining room after dinner, seemed to me a continuation of any of those evenings in Rosas or Cadaqués, fifteen years ago, the same sly humor of the Carlos of old, identical, too, his cranky attitude about the world at large and his pessimism and withdrawal in the face of life, all traits easily relatable to an unreconciled feeling of flouted naivety, of wounded innocence. On mentioning the reason for his stay in Gorgs de la Selva, for example, he did it more as a curious spectator than as an actor included in the cast, interested not so much in the problems being dealt with there as much as how they were dealt with, in the performance of each one of those present, in the spectacle played out around an old man's dying agony, an old man who, it seems, in the confusion of the moment of his passing, thought himself already situated in the next world, thus increasing the mood of uncertainty that prevailed among the family members, given that none of his potential heirs dared to tell him the truth about the economic situation he was leaving to them, to bring him up to date on the disastrous failure of his plans for building an enormous industrial park on the land that he'd been buying up near the highway, a high-flying speculative maneuver to which for years he'd dedicated all his talents and which now, at the last moment, when the old man found himself out of the game, someone with greater powers or greater influence than that of some rural landlord, not subordinates, like the ones working for the old man, in the municipal district, someone, of indeterminate authority although no doubt higher, had completely disrupted those plans by beating him to it, by getting the upper hand, and had built the industrial park in a different location, which caused the old man's lands to revert back to their earlier agricultural value. A situation that, although it was little less than bankruptcy, it certainly supposed, from the heirs' point of view, a palpable loss of image, according to the difference between accessing the dreamt of economic empire and sharing among many the spoils that a rich small-town landowner leaves behind him at his passing. And just as death is harder for everyone who hasn't passed on to immortal life, thus the legatees of an inheritance once assumed to be fabulous, but which turns out not to be, perhaps creating greater tensions among the legatees than if it really had been fabulous, all of them possessed by the zeal of getting a share of the payout closest to their self-concocted fantasy of how much that was going to be, closest to some previous calculation that will now have to be translated into terms of arable land, livestock, farm machinery and, especially, the rectory, that gothic building next to the church, which the old man had bought, restored, and refurbished with the meticulous touch with which the founder of a dynasty organizes the establishment of the rural patriarchal house, *la casa pairal*, for future generations.

Carlos wanted to make it clear, it was obvious, that his future interest in all of that was nothing more than that of a voyeur, of someone completely removed from everything being dealt with there, of a person who knows how to observe and draw conclusions; precisely that, it was clear. But from the beginning I had the impression that there was something more, that everything he was talking about was just a way of gaining time in anticipation of the most propitious moment to speak to me about something that was affecting him more directly, and when we left the dining room because the television program had ended and we could now settle in at our ease in the empty sitting room, in front of the fireplace, I understood that the moment had arrived, that at last the conversation was going to focus on his real concerns; young Carlos, his son, a son who suddenly turned out for them to be little less than a stranger. One night, apparently, when, without prior warning, the boy did not return home, and fearing that he was mixed up in politics, they searched through his things to see if they could find any papers that might prove compromising for him. I don't know how real their fears were, how far people like Carlos and Aurea can forget that, at that boy's age, spending a night away from home without any prior notice is really nothing strange, to what point such forgetfulness is nothing more than an excuse to snoop around in one obscure patch or another of their children's lives; whatever the kind of unease that the boy's conduct might have made them cover up—and I'd be surprised if it had anything to do with clandestine political activities—their reasons for being alarmed were seen to be fully satisfied by reading the private diary they found, of those photocopies that Carlos brought me down from his room so that I could take a look at them. Because this was definitely what Carlos wished to ask me, what he had probably been turning over in his mind while explaining to me the reasons for his presence in Gorgs de la Selva: that I read the diary and, setting aside all inexact details and distortions that it contained, give him my opinion about the rest, about the personality of someone capable of writing such things, and more generally, and I suppose above all, what he could or should do, abused as he was, both in his capacity as the author's father as well as in his role as the villain of the story. It also happened, on the other hand, that I was one of the people who appeared in the pages of the diary, and the particular deference that he was showing me allowed me to suppose not only that I was especially qualified to understand the boy, but also, eventually, in order to exert some beneficial influence over him; this was at least what Carlos emphatically implied when we said goodnight, before we each retired to our separate rooms, as a kind of advance payment against the reading that I was going to begin, who knows if with the intention of trying to pique my curiosity, of stimulating my sense of responsibility or, simply, by adding something, victim once again of that tendency of his to give unnecessary explanations, to justify what doesn't need any justification.

I know Carlos; better yet: I know Carlos's reactions well. Thus, just as the presence of a rape or a crime in a certain work of fiction can be interpreted by a reader with a proclivity for psychoanalytic explanations as the solution to a conflict in the author's subconscious, the symbolic murder of the father, for example, or vice-versa, the castration, the moral or physical rape of the father and the murder of the mother, thus, in a similar way, some of Carlos's attitudes and reactions, frequently close to phobia, were nothing more, you might say, than the personalization of certain damages and offenses that had the power of reactivating other offenses and damages suffered in his own flesh, however much he had not even considered it for himself in these terms, forgotten or rejected as if he kept them in order to be sure, by virtue of that irrepressible propensity, to keep secret the secrets that humiliate. The result of all that was reflected in his frequently contradictory behavior, lovable to excess in private, among friends, and withdrawn in public; shy while being capable of the greatest impertinences, of expressive coarseness that could only with difficulty escape being labeled boorish; not very brilliant or even clumsy, nonetheless he became striking thanks to his scathing aggressiveness when the course of convention permitted him to give free rein to his phobias. Argentina and the Argentines, let's say, for example, a country where he'd spent a good part of his life. But also Catalonia and the Catalans, the land of his birth, the people among whom he'd been raised, now the chosen target of his sarcasm, as for example when he took the pleasure of pointing out the singular ugliness of the Catalan people, in sharp contrast to the beauty of their natural landscapes, on the one hand, and with the physique notoriously most favored by the inhabitants of the bordering land, on the other, a characteristic trait that, to his understanding, parodying Pidal, was found at the heart of numerous, apparently incongruous petitions in the history of Catalonia, events like the political succession of Jaime I, who tended to establish bulwark kingdoms throughout the Catalan kingdom itself—Valencia, Mallorca, the ceding of high Pyrenean territories to Saint Louis of France, and Murcia to San Fernando of Castile—with the goal of isolating the phenomenon to the maximum and of impeding its propagation. In a similar way, his phobia about faggots and, at the same time and alongside of a general misogynistic disposition, a phobia about certain women, more violent the more attractive and sophisticated, the prototype of which he seemed to have encountered in that peculiar feminine product—according to his words—in circulation around Cadaqués, those mannequin women moving in slow motion thanks to their own narcissism about both their intellectual functions as well as their sexual activity, this an area in which the peculiar viscosity of their moist parts, cold as a slab of raw fish—and their words, too—makes it difficult to allow one to expect to reach, in the way of orgasm, anything more intense than a yawn. And like with the women or the faggots, so too with the priests and the communists, a new phobia spread among what his father hated and what his father was and perhaps he himself was close to being in the early postwar years, a contradiction perhaps sufficiently explicit in its antagonistic duality to help shed light on the remaining factors that gave way to emotional reactions grouped together in counterposed pairs, a product, ultimately, of an inner antagonism, of a conflictive binary fission which it would be excessively simple to try to reduce to such hypotheses as, for example, Carlos felt ignored by beautiful women or incapable of reacting to their stimuli or diminished in his masculinity by some old homosexual humiliation, if not by some repressed homosexuality, etcetera. Affirmations or diagnoses that could not surpass the limits of the merely enunciated without probative value for one who, like myself, had known Carlos when he was already the Carlos of today, a man subject to contradictory impulses which, within a general tendency to mutually neutralize themselves, explained his mood swings, an instability whose intricate origin, if I were asked to explain it as well, I would have to invent.

The next day, as if complying with a tacit agreement, we met again in the dining room, shut away thanks to the weather once again, a day thick with rainy mist that, to judge by the deathly dim light, seemed to be stuck at daybreak. For obvious reasons, I preferred to talk to him more about the manuscript than its author, a young man whom I remember vaguely seeing around Rosas, one of those silent boys with a sensitive look who turn out to be appealing, with few points in common, at first glance, with the image of himself that he offered through the diary, although, inverting the terms of the relationship, considering the text instead of reality, it didn't take much effort to believe in his capacity to seem to the eyes of others how he had intended to appear. However, just by bringing up things correctly, just by considering the manuscript for what it really was, not a private diary but a work of fiction written in the form of a diary, the question was avoided. In effect: setting aside the fact that certain aspects of the narration were grounded in reality, the important thing, the thing that defines it as a fake diary, as a work of fiction, is the fact that it's found to be structured in the manner of a tale, around an argument constructed according to certain specific rhythms, certain through lines, because life lacks arguments, lacks that abstraction, a theme developed according to a previous plan that constitutes what's known as an argument, an a priori abstraction whose presence is enough to characterize a work as a work of fiction, in the same way that the a priori abstraction characterizes the diary, or a book of memories or one of documentary character, in a word, as historiography. The relationship that the narrative, first-person I establishes through the window with Aurea, for example, constitutes a narrative axis that would turn out to be completely implausible in a real diary, in a book where, theoretically, one goes writing down what happens each day, without it being possible to foresee—unlike what happens in a novel—what the author will report on the next day nor, consequently, to highlight and give special relief to, or simply select, a fact already occurred in relationship to another that has yet to happen. To put it another way: things happen in daily life, and those things can be recorded in the pages of a diary, but that succession of events is something that has nothing in common with an argument. Thus, that disquisition on the nature of physical beauty with which the diary opens already denotes the existence of a plan, established ahead of time, before the casual encounter that the narrator announces he's had with Aurea, an encounter that only ceases to be trivial in relation to what will happen later, to the role of the guiding thread that must be played with respect to the plot seen as a whole. A problem of narrative structure that is also, therefore, a problem of time, of the time of the tale and at the same time the time of the author insofar as it concerns the possibility or impossibility that the author has of organizing their materials in line with, respectively, a work of fiction or of a work, as in a private diary, that at first has to adhere to what happens in the course of the day. It's not strange, in this sense, that the most interesting autobiographical works, if not from a testimonial point of view, then at least from a literary one, are those that are structured around a coherent plot, both in terms of argument as well as style, meaning, the most carefully constructed, those that most and best keep their distance from objective reality, something that not only strongly implies a premeditated purpose of distorting and falsifying, but that frequently permits access to a deeper reality, and we have a good example of that in Rousseau, cited, certainly, by the presumed author of our presumed private diary.

Another important aspect, related to what comes before, are the influences that can be perceived in the text. Because just as every budding writer starts out by plagiarizing, taking as a reference point not his personal experiences but rather some specific book that, consciously or unconsciously, had made an especial impression on him, influencing his creative plans as well as other areas of his life, and only later on, with time, will his writing will start to become free, acquiring its own character and significance, generating its own orbit; thus, in a similar way, the influences that are perceived in our presumed private diary don't belong to the field of those biographical writings but to that of the novel and, more concretely, when it comes to style, it's not difficult to discover the influence of Luis Goytisolo: those long series of sentences, for example, those comparisons that begin with a Homeric "so" like, in order to conclude by connecting with some other "so," in a similar way, not without first inserting new extended metaphors, secondary metaphors that, more than centering and sharpening the initial comparison, expand it and even invert its terms, not without first laying the foundation for new subordinate associations, not without first establishing new conceptual relationships not necessarily similar to one another, new associations with the same colloidal appearance as the mercury and brimstone that alchemists mix together. This chosen form, the private diary, the fiction covered over by a testimonial, remains a second-rate literary recourse, a procedure that permits one to give objectivity to what's subjective, converting the protagonist, the first-person narrator, into a type of chronicler or witness who gives proof to what's narrated thanks to the use of the first person. The rest, the added elements that appear real without being so, the distortions, mutilations, and falsifications of reality, all those details that so worried Carlos, have validity only for him, who happens to be the author's father; I imagine that in every writer's environs—and so much the more the closer the people who feel themselves alluded to—the same thing must happen. Ultimately, only a person in a position like the one Carlos finds himself in, with respect to the author on the plane of reality and with respect to the protagonist on the fictional one, is qualified to understand the reach of the allusions and appreciate his impostures, questions about such things as the nicknames that he applies to the majority of the characters, beginning with his own parents; or the acts that he attributes to them, the affairs of Carlos and his secretary or the story that Aurea was just about to run away with some Cypriot or Maltese whom she met while aboard a Mediterranean cruise that she never really took; and, more generally, the magnification of the environmental factors, as if they were living a millionaire's lifestyle, which, unfortunately—explanation for Carlos--is far from our own. As for the erotic fantasies, if they're anything more than that, a narcissist's fantasies, they could be a reflection of a shameful reality for both partners, even though, involving my son, perhaps I find them more revolting for their degrading exhibitionism, their sexual immaturity, than the menopausal morbidity of the Aurora within them, which really is, or really was, the name of a neighbor across the street, Aurora not Aurea, a phonetic confusion that rather eased my mind, because it would seem to confirm your impression that everything recounted within those pages is nothing but a story. And that, I added, his goal in introducing the modifications that he thus introduces in the environmental factors, as well as in the events grounded in reality, is simply designed to arouse the reader's disgust, the general reader as well as one or two specific readers, the person or persons to whom the work is directed, although perhaps the author doesn't have that in mind, arousing their disgust, offending their sensibility, causing a scandal, writing it all down not always to express the daily reality but rather to violate it, who knows if in his adolescent zeal to affirm his own personality, a goal which, in every case, it must be recognized, seems fully realized. The same thing in favor of the text, both in what concerns its character as a work of fiction as well as the literary qualities on display, is the distance that separates it from the classic private diary that so many people start writing and—for the good of long-suffering humanity—so few finish and publish, that diary loaded with digressions about oneself in the act of writing, their perplexity, the sensation of emptiness they experience, vacuities which the miserable author purports to fill, along with their notebooks, with the real emptiness of their own existence.

Partly convinced and partly, perhaps, preferring to pretend that he was, preferring to elude the exposition of some questions whose mere mention no doubt tormented him, Carlos pretended to credit my arguments, as if he generally agreed, although not without certain reservations. What's curious, he said by way of final comment, is that the final entries in the diary, or rather, the false diary, were written not even two weeks after this Aurora died, although at that time the doorman still didn't know it: murdered in Manila, in her hotel room, where, one morning, they found her stretched out on the bed, naked and with her throat slashed obscenely wide open; a death quite characteristic of the life she had been leading. What the doorman definitely confirmed for me is what the boy writes: that they went up to the apartment together because the boy said he had just spoken with her, that she was expecting him. And he filled me in on what kind of a person that woman was, that she'd dumped her husband and son so that she could live her own life.

Some works, a text, a painting, an architectonic domain generate oneiric material, become integrated into our dreams provided with an apparently unexpected meaning, according to values totally different from those belonging to them, the result, you might say, of an illusionist's sleight of hand. Although such a faculty is not synonymous with artistic quality, not even if it's connected to the fact that the work in question responds or not to what we call our taste, it's undeniable, however, that some quality, both in the formal order as well as in the conceptual, must be possessed, whether we are conscious of it or not, in order to awaken in us similar sorts of impressions and suggestions. And that quality, whatever its nature, is something the false private diary had for me, since, that night, after finishing reading it, I had a dream that, although at first seemed to have nothing to do with that reading, I knew it did, that the connection existed, that the Guayaquil in my dream, whose image, the more I tried to hold onto it, vanished all the more rapidly, a Guayaquil that was now not even Guayaquil but rather a city called Ecuador. Not without a certain disorientation, I argued passionately with other architects, angrily even, in defense of the splendid colonial architecture, no matter how little Ecuador had anything to do with colonial architecture, being as it was a city like Manchester, a misty conglomeration of suburbs stripped entirely of any attraction. *Nel mezzo del cammin di nostra vita*, someone said. And I tried to shake off the ones who were holding me back, keeping me from attacking the other one, someone else, maybe the one who had spoken. And why was the city called Ecuador? I thought upon waking. And it was perhaps the first response, that occurred to me, related to the quote from Dante, which, at the same time that it offered itself to me with the clarity of a headline, made me forget not only the rest of the dream but also the nexus connecting it to my reading of the night before.

No less significant, it seems to me, is the circumstance that these swirling dreams immediately suggest to me another dream I had, if I'm not mistaken, when I was starting out as an architect, a dream that was in its turn––at least that was the sensation I experienced when I had it––a repetition or variant of another previous dream whose date it would not be difficult to situate in the imprecise coordinates that rule the memory of one's own childhood, since it could also be about something that I had imagined while awake, without, for that reason, any decreased significance to my having remembered a fact that might be called so trivial, nor, also without knowing why, now, so many years later, I had associated it with the oneiric residue that took place in that city called Ecuador; a dream whose sequence the passing of time had reduced to a series of still images, like archival snapshots in which Barcelona, perhaps as the result of a rise in sea level, perhaps from a generous divine response to the *preces ad petendam pluviam*, perhaps because of a wise combination of both factors, appeared totally flooded, the clean shoreline, similar in its quietude to a lake's, reflecting the plants of the house's garden, and there below, to a rather uniform depth, the city intact, its streets and plazas, its buildings, its trees swayed by the sea currents the same as the air would do, the warm sun filtering through the waters bathing it all, a replica of the sky, a smooth surface, with its blues and its blots of clouds.

Jumps that take us back in time, dreams that reroute us to other dreams and that, even showing themselves in an almost simultaneous way in the first seconds after awakening, end up being lost in the areas of what has been forgotten, of what is found beyond any conscious impression both sensitive and selective, without any possible appeal in their lack of certainty, no matter how many interrogations we want to formulate for ourselves, questions, for example, such as if there mustn't be a common root to events as dissimilar as a childhood dream and my early vocation as an architect can be. Thus the other morning, after the associative series generated by a night of uneasy sleep, as a kind of finishing touch and at the same time as a reflexive synthesis of such accumulation of generations in so few instants, the Ideal City came to my memory, a drawing of the same title––*La Ciudad Ideal*––by an anonymous artist that I've not seen in years and which I nevertheless remember in every detail, probably the work of a madman, a view of a city that combines a flat map with a panoramic view, drawn in India ink and illuminated with various colors, in the style of the engravings of cities made before the invention of the photograph, and, like those, sprinkled with numbers that, at the foot of the page, indicate the character and nomenclature of the indicated urban elements. The city, of nineteenth-century features judging by the peculiar baroque aspect of certain buildings, drawn with all the minuteness characteristic of Naïf Art, offers a concentric urban structure:

a walled compound in the form of a symmetrical dodecagon, with nine concentric ring roads drawn one within the other in decreasing proportion, and four transversal avenues that converge in the geometric center of the perimeter. Located in that center, circular in shape, surrounded by a moat, is the Citadel, a complex of palaces and temples dominated by an enormous central tower named *La Torre del Tiempo*--The Tower of Time; one of the notes at the foot of the page specifies that the shadow cast by the aforementioned tower, as it turns from west to east in the course of the day over various sections of the ring roads--from left to right on the drawing--mark the hours like a gigantic sundial in which the zenith corresponds to the tower itself, leaving the whole city divided into areas of light and areas of shadow, areas touched by the tower's shadow and areas untouched, with the distinctive fact that the shadowed areas are the ones that correspond to the passing of time and the areas that remain in light escape its passing. The colors used to illuminate certain points are all composites--green, mauve, orange--although over the city, in the background, as a vertical projection of the passage of time, there stretches a wide rainbow which includes the seven colors of the spectrum, the Tower of Time pointing to its exact middle, the way that the hand on a clock marks twelve. I suppose that another factor caused me the other morning, mere moments after those dreams, to remember precisely that print: the fact that its owner was none other than Carlos, the father of the author of our allegedly private diary.

THE OLD MAN WITH THE DOGS.

Comparing the panoramic view offered to us from the peak of a mountain with one of those retrospective gazes that in certain moments we cast upon the past itself constitutes a successful hit in more than one sense of the word. The least of which is speaking about time in terms of space, referring to the invisible in terms of the visible, an analogy that, in a certain way, is necessary thanks to the lack of another better one; the determining elements of the character of the image are of a different order, they belong not so much to the surrounding landscape, whatever it may be, as to the deceptive impression of dominion the person experiences who contemplates it, the traveler who has arrived there propelled by the desire to contemplate it from a privileged position and who believes to be doing just that, without realizing to what point they are hidden, not only the nooks and small rugged features of the terrain, but also the great valleys that lie beyond the interposing mountains and, what's more, the true nature of those mountains of lesser height that our traveler will see reduced to flat images, stripped of the transversal foothills, spurs, ridges, buttresses, and massifs that give them shape. And so, like that panorama that extends before the eyes of our traveler, with no fewer hidden nooks, forgotten valleys and mountainous masses reduced to profiles, the backward glances of memory, his illusory vision of the past from the concrete connotations of the present reality. Because just like the man whose mother died when he was a child will fix the image he has of her from that period he doesn't remember, a time from which there only remain photographs, the image of a woman eternally young and beautiful, while the father, for whom time continues running on, will be for all time the extravagant old man that he was in his last years, the earlier memories annulled by the last ones, that of a young beauty married to an old man, thus the reconstructions of memory, its tricks and traps. For instance, I not only remember how Papa was during the last years of his life, but also, thanks I suppose, to a mechanism comparable to the one that rules our dreams, residing in Santa Cecilia. In the arbor, in the morning, reading the newspaper. Or in the afternoon, setting out on one of his walks, accompanied by the dogs who came running at his calls, a small pack of dogs that jumped and frolicked around him, happy for the arrival of the awaited moment, excited by his words of encouragement, by the pieces of biscuit he always dropped for them, by the stones he threw ahead of them on the road, dogs whose names he knew just as they could recognize his smell, while for me, stuck in the memory of the dogs from when I was a little boy, their names were no easier to identify than were their bodies in the commotion they whipped up to get the stone thrown ahead down the road. They'd return at twilight, the dogs quiet, all together, and he with that pensive automatism of the one who walks not only with their thoughts but even with their gaze directed at something else, not so much the vision of a past full of disaster as much as a promising future, thoughts probably about the future he had earned for his children thanks to the fact of having come into possession, in his day and according to his responsibilities as the firstborn of the patriarchal home--*la casa pairal*--Santa Cecilia, in exchange for other benefits of equivalent value ceded to his siblings, now all lost by all of them save Santa Cecilia which, acquired as if by obligation and preserved like a miracle from so many adversities and, above all, from so many good-for-nothing thieves, seemed destined, now that the value of country properties had increased enormously, to be something like the piggy bank for his descendants. But, showing the same optimism that led him to consider the magnetic attraction that his personality exerted on a certain sort of swindlers like a fortuitous event, showing off this very same optimism, clearly compensatory for a deeper pessimism, far from the masochistic catastrophism that, subject to the dictates of another kind of temperament, usually leads the man defeated by life to the exalted contemplation of his multiple repeated defeats, to make the defense of his sure-to-be-lost quarrels into his primary dedication and even into a profession, and his only pleasure the sense of vengeance for each and every one of the offenses and humiliations received, far from all that, Papa preferred to lose himself in his mediation upon the enormous possibilities of making a fortune that he left to us, and in the calculations which he reasoned gave him the right to delve into such possibilities, rescued by means of his daydreams about the future of Santa Cecilia of the Troubled Past, the errors committed, the swindles of which he'd been the victim. Perhaps this is enough to explain the fact that, soon after his death, I dreamed of him already ill but still alive, and not in Barcelona but in Santa Cecilia, in his room, tucked into bed, asking Margarita to remove his rings, his signet, his wedding ring, saying it's more difficult later on, daughter. Of course it was not Margarita who was by his side during his last days, but Rosa.

However, there is something about the family home, *la casa pairal*, even in the very word itself—*pairal*—with enough significance to justify the mark that it invariably leaves on any and all who find themselves connected to it. A consubstantial something, perhaps, the spirit that gave them life, houses which the founder of a dynasty built for himself and his own, and whose destiny seems only to be that of becoming, not only the scene of the vicissitudes that intersect with the family's fortune, but a true symbol—if not an artifice—of its decadence. As a result of that mutual bondage of the house to the family name and the family name to the house, sooner or later some obstacle appears that affects the house as much as the family name. Thus, the bankrupt relative, after insolvency, seizure of assets, and, eventually, a sale at public auction, has an immediate reflection in *la casa pairal*, given that the buyer, despite his coveting it, despite possibly being in need of some surrounding environment that with its history will dignify his new fortune, will not hesitate, for all that, to remodel the house in all kinds of ways, trying to make the old structure fit in with today's tastes, changes that will necessarily disrupt the structure's previous uniformity, the finality that each thing fulfilled regarding the way of life of its earliest inhabitants, a finality of meaning no less—inherited with the ownership, for anyone who had been raised there—than any other of its architectural characteristics, and then the house's fortune enters a new phase, generally more accelerated, one more subject to the caprices of fast and easy money, to its accumulation and dissipation, in a way that easily ends up turning into a liability, so uncomfortable and lacking in sense that practically the best thing is to be rid of it, so suitable as it is for a rest home or a sanatorium or boarding school, whatever, with which the lifecycle of *la casa pairal* comes to an end.

But even when one isn't facing this kind of extreme situation and the property doesn't change hands, there comes a moment, brought about by the changes that the course of time itself imprints upon the rhythm as well as the forms of life, in which the task of renovating *la casa pairal* becomes little less than inevitable, especially if what one intends is to avoid any and all possible interpretation that associates neglecting the house with the family's ruin. If that came to pass in Santa Cecilia but not in Vilasacra, it was simply because this case lacked the right person, because Jaime was not Joaquín, apart from the fact that the house itself in Vilasacra, older and less subject to changes in fashion than the one in Santa Cecilia, doubtless contributes to its safekeeping. Compared with Vilasacra's appearance, a very large country house—*una masía*—traditional, or rather atemporal in its adaptability to serve as a country residence for a good Barcelona family, Santa Cecilia seems rather more like a very turn-of-the-century fantasia, insofar as the house itself, an Italianate villa that one is almost surprised to find out there in the middle of the countryside, as if by the character of its rooms, destined, you might say, for industrial enterprises rather than agricultural ones, something normal when it's a question of an agricultural operation organized according to the prevailing criteria of modernity and mechanization in the grandfather's day. Thus, if on the one hand, the remodeling carried out by Joaquín, the transformation of a working farm, founded, as least theoretically, on the profitability of its installations, into an exclusively recreational country property, was enough to make Cato roll over in his grave, on the other hand, his attempt to modernize and make comfortable what was neither modern nor comfortable, could not have turned out better than if he had applied his effort to the halls of the Vatican. A certain awareness of that contradiction must weigh on Joaquín, who's got no lack of plastic sensibility, since, if at the start of the work he rather seemed to fear my possible intrusions, what later irritated him, as they were being developed, was just the opposite, that I felt inhibited, preferring everything to remain as it was. And the fact is, interior remodeling is not only renovating the inside of a house, the creation of new spaces in which the memory will not know how to find its place, but something that also affects the context, the relationship that the various parts of a whole keep among themselves, abandoned rooms and fields, the garden itself, whose purpose appears forgotten. Of course, such phenomena tend to happen not only when the ancestral manse is brusquely renovated, but also when it's subjected to a slow process of sclerosis, of progressive atrophy, like Vilasacra. Sometimes a simple stroll through the garden is enough to understand these things, independent of whether or not they are neglected, something felt as much in the garden in Santa Cecilia as the one in Vilasacra, however different their respective smells, that of the vegetation, the soil, in the same way that a dog distinguishes the smell of a dead man from that of a dead woman; moister, like moss and mold, the smell of Vilasacra, matching the kind of garden it is, more lush besides more romantic and sophisticated, with its magnolia trees and its yew trees, its lime tree-lined walkways and its laurel shrubs; more aromatic the garden in Santa Cecilia, also according to its particular characteristics, more a natural park than a garden, with arbors and terraced paths, beds of ivy and hedges of rosemary, Chinese palms that gradually give way to holm oaks and pines, in such a way that, when one realizes it, they find themselves already in the woods. The only thing both places have in common is that atmosphere I'm talking about, and that I would relate, more than to some smell, to a feeling of silence and emptiness, a feeling of forgetfulness capable, you might say, of being felt by the garden itself. That disorderly flowering of the magnolia trees in Vilasacra, an autumnal extension of the springtime or a simple confusion of seasons that, like a person with their senses altered by fever, like a man close to death, only seems to indicate that the tree raves deliriously, that, direction lost, he surrenders to the extravagances of one estranged. Or, like in Santa Cecilia, that enormous pine tree that, probably thanks to the considerable size that it had already reached by then, was spared the saw when Grandpa had the farm buildings constructed, a pine tree, unchanged over time, that rose up high behind the barns, above the roofs, as if it were the principal element of some *ex libris*, until, it must have been no more than two or three summers, it suddenly dried out to gray and had to be cut down; one of those extremely dry summers that usually spell for large trees what harsh winters spell for old people.

Between Papa's death and the start of the renovations undertaken by Joaquín there is a period which, even being relatively nearby, I barely remember, unless I really sit down and try to recall it. Narcís, the man who took care of things at Santa Cecilia since before I was born, died a few months after Papa, and the ones lower downhill—what we called the farmhands, owing, I suppose, to the fact that they lived in houses at the foot of the hill, separated from the family's big house by the garden, although there's no need to omit a more symbolic connotation—scattered: Narcís's family went one way and each one of the farmhands went another. It was then when La Dama de Elche and her people showed up. The idea was that they would manage the fields in place of Narcís, given that neither Joaquín nor I had thought of any better solution nor could we think of one, immersed as Joaquín was, recently returned from exile, in his political problems, and me with my professional ones, without any desire—at least from me—of going anywhere near Santa Cecilia, a reluctance, certainly,

I've yet to overcome. Now I wouldn't know how to explain how they arrived, on whose recommendation, but the fact is that there they were, the husband and some son or son-in-law with their respective wives, daughters, and daughters-in-law, and a whole bunch of little children, prepared to do anything and everything, well aware that even death itself was levelling their path. It's like she's their grandmother, said the tall, dimwitted husband with an ear-to-ear grin. And although he had not said it explicitly, a first impression of the whole bunch of them sufficed to make one realize that, in effect, she was the important one, a woman from around Ponferrada married to an Andalusian man who, thanks to the years they'd spent together, spoke with a sort of Galician accent, he, the long, tall, dimwitted husband, who was from Porcuna, with an accent similar to the children's, born in Ponferrada, while the son-in-law and daughter-in-law, siblings, also came from Porcuna, still spoke with an Andalusian accent despite time spent in Catalonia, the same as some brother-in-law's brother or other who'd just arrived, or the reverse, the ones who'd just arrived were the siblings, and were not from Porcuna but from the next town over, details that I never sorted out, but which for them were very enormously important. I never even found out their exact number, exactly how many they were altogether, but sometimes more sons-in-law or brothers of the son-in-law showed up to help out, handy young fellows, especially good with an axe, from whose sharp edge the garden at least had to be spared; there were also problems with feeding the chickens and rabbits they had brought with them, not to mention the goats. It didn't take long for them to stir up some rather bad bad blood with the neighbors who complained that they didn't return the tools and utensils they'd borrowed, that they'd caught the little kids pilfering the garden and orchard. Then the ones from Porcuna came as if in a procession, la Dama de Elche presiding over them although she never spoke a word, heartrending in her sorrow, in her offended self-love: the marginalization of which they were an object, the humiliations inflicted upon them, the scorn. We're like their grandparents, said the tall, dimwitted husband, his jug-handle ears sticking out from his small head, not much bigger than that of a pinheaded cretin. And then he showed me a new boy, almost as if offering him to me for the purpose of unspeakable practices, something that he was perhaps really doing, although clumsily. He's the son of Paco and Espiri, don't you remember?

The harvest was laughable, and even though Joaquín had given up his share as owner for that year, the Porcunans were quick to complain: the salaried workers had a right to payment on July 18th; why not them, although they weren't actually salaried? Weren't they human beings despite being poor and ignorant? Joaquín, who tried to get them to see that a sharecropping contract was not the same as a labor contract, that contracts stipulated no bonuses, that he was, nevertheless, willing to absorb the costs of sowing in order to compensate somehow for the fact that, being the first year and still not having the farm well in hand, the harvest would have been less than normal, etcetera, Joaquín, who didn't want to add more problems of conscience to those resulting from his recent exit or expulsion from the communist party, stood his ground firmly the next time, with the deal about the rabbits, when the Porcunans, who did not seem to have seriously considered the reality of myxomatosis, arrived again in procession: no, he wasn't going to compensate them for their loss. She went in front, in her pile of skirts and blouses and robes and aprons with a kerchief knotted around her head, underneath the mound of thick gray tresses gathered in two buns, fabrics of matching colors, with a predominance of blues, browns and purples, fell in rigid pleats, a rigidity that was probably a reflection of the general rigidity of her movements, of that stiff stride, spreading her legs laterally at the same time as she moved forward, her arms stiff and separated from her trunk, her tragic expression that would soon collapse into a wail, a figure of great emblematic value, interpreter while at the same time possessor of the supernatural powers she claimed to possess and which she no doubt possessed within the scope of the clan, the very image of importance in her hieratic plasticity, a living variant of la Dama de Elche; behind, as if holding her up to keep her from falling, the tall, dimwitted husband, the Andalusian with a Galician accent, and then the other family members, including those who were found there periodically, all of them grim, righteous, inexorable like that chorus in Aeschylus who embody more than speak the true dimension of the drama. Although on this occasion, as well as on the one that had to be the last, their claims were eminently economic, the scene could be repeated in response to motivations of any other kind: the slight imagined by one of them whose work we deemed unsatisfactory, how humiliated they felt by our contemplating hiring a gardener, the lack of trust that we showed them on consulting with the neighbors, etcetera, etcetera. Only the last one—the money they demanded so they could go spend Easter Week in Porcuna—was by then too much even for an ex-communist with scruples like Joaquín, compelled to say yes to them, that he'd pay for the trip for them all, but that they shouldn't come back; the Porcunans accepted the money the same way that they resigned themselves to preserving the dead rabbits in *escabeche*, and when they appealed to the Magistrate, Joaquín opted to pay them without complaining about the reimbursement they wanted from him, or rather, taking great care in emphasizing to the official in charge of the case that he would have gladly paid double to never see those people again, thoroughly good for nothing as they were, under any social and political system, be it capitalist, be it socialist.

Although what happened is not much more than an anecdote about an unfortunate experience, and though it lacks the necessary importance to influence Joaquín's later political evolution, it wouldn't be at all strange if, on the contrary, it had the virtue of hastening as many projects as he could handle around Santa Cecilia, forgetting about the sordid agricultural activities, undertaking without scruples—now that he had split from the party—the task of converting it exclusively into a recreational property, into a shameless luxury residence. In any case, and although it was only a question of human experience, his dealings with those people were for him, undoubtedly, somewhat traumatic, in contrast and as a complement to the party meetings which he had frequented, to the ideological level of the discussions, to the theoretical assumptions he'd wrestled with during them, and even with respect to the language used to formulate such suppositions, a trauma not inferior to the one that certain readers of Dostoyevsky experience—those most tormented by guilt—not only on discovering the complex nature of what they had always considered basic reactions, but above all on identifying as their own the most contradictory and masochistic aspects of the characters who react that way, with the subsequent risk of elevating to the category of universal what could well be a simple melodramatic projection of their personal deficiencies. This, at least, was what his expression seemed to indicate when he gave me an account of the events, as if more than venting his surprise he needed to know if what had happened were believable, with the surprise and bewilderment in the eyes of that villager turned motorcyclist who, having ventured out onto the main highway, crashes with a car thanks to an abrupt swerve and falls to the ground, without any more injury, thanks to the protection of his helmet, than some bruises and scrapes, that helmet that is now twisted round on his head while he stands up with the help of the people surrounding him, heavy, silent, stupefied not so much owing to the fright as to the unusual prominence granted by the accident which has befallen him.

Despite the foregoing, when I think about Santa Cecilia, I never associate it with Joaquín. For me, Santa Cecilia is the Santa Cecilia of the time before that, the place where I spent my summers as a boy, a place and a time whose weight, as far as my education goes, far surpasses what came from the school courses interspersed between them. And in that vast summer vacation consisting of the aggregate of all the summers, Joaquín appears as someone who arrives or who leaves, who moves through the house the way a guest would, in passing, even mentally, with his people and his problems somewhere else. A Santa Cecilia inhabited by Papa, Aunt Pepita, Uncle Rodrigo, and, after eating, taking advantage of the general stampede, I go down below, where the farmhands take their siesta in the shadow of the pine tree, and then Narcís appears and wakes them up and I climb up into the wagon. The precision lies not only in what concerns the general rhythm of life, nor in the organization of my time throughout the day, but also in the most concrete details: in the trap, going to Sunday Mass, the moment when the horse's tail begins to stiffen and rise, and just below it, breaking wind with vibrating sputters, those black rings begin to dilate, opening one after another to reveal a reddish depth through which, like a simultaneously concave and convex crater, the thick clods of steaming excrement will quickly blossom, a sight that fascinates and disturbs in equal measure, that usually makes the little children titter with laughter, also attentive to the mess left behind by the horse's trot, as the odorous discharge is prolonged and the horse's flushed red cavity, as if seen in a film run backward on a Moviola editing projector, begins to wrinkle and retract, to tighten up, one ring after another, without Aunt Pepita having shown the least notice of anything, completely unaware of the operation in each and every one of its phases. And the same could be said of anecdotes whose singularity make them unlikely to have been repeated on another occasion, another summer: that time when we spied on Grandpa Eduardo--no doubt unaware that from our hiding place, between the plants in the garden, we had a full view of the toilet--while he let loose a prolonged series of deep, cavernous, whistling evacuations, his flaccid buttocks now squeezing like the folds of a bellows before even having sat down completely, a memory that comes to me suggested by the previous one according to the most basic association of ideas. Grandpa Eduardo was in reality our great-grandfather on my mother's side, my mother's maternal grandfather, and by the date of his death one must deduce that his visit to Santa Cecilia happened in the first summers of the postwar years; a shy and gentle man, with the look of a nineteenth-century pederast, significantly fascinated, when telling us about Shakespeare's tragedies in the form of children's stories, by the character of Horatio, the faithful and discreet friend of Hamlet, just like, in a more general but no less revealing way about his formal and reliable character, he was fascinated by grammatical rules and figures, about whose fulfillment he displayed a respect that, more than from any legal standard, seemed to belong to a truly divine law.

Apart from the relatives and the relatives' relatives, whom Papa dutifully invited one at a time, each time more seldom, those close lifelong friends weighed down with the years, people very well known all throughout Barcelona, about whom Papa used to speak but with whom he had very few dealings, in his increasing tendency to withdraw, apart from those friendships of other times, the near totality of the guests that we received, for visits that frequently stretched out into long stays, family included, if there were any, were new faces, people Papa had met recently by chance, men of conservative ideas and proven religiosity who, with a sensational invention to develop or a fabulous registered patent, invariably end up involving Papa in some deal whose first consequence was him clutching his head in his hands, and the second, the most laborious, that work that it takes to demonstrate that, far from having been an accomplice in the swindle, he had been the first one swindled, rotten thieves whose sonorous names, as if they were captains of the Almogavars forces—Montfort de Montaly, Dalmau de Montblanch, Eloy de Provenal, Coix-Carbó de Subiracs—perhaps constituted, in the way of a glorious emblem that completely glosses a character, an important factor when it comes time to shed light on the influence that such people exerted on Papa, in the same way that some trait or traits of Papa's personality necessarily acted as a lure to so many swindlers. As the role of host was an exclusive prerogative of Papa, when his occasional guests defrauded the wide margin of honor that it supposed for them, neither Aunt Pepita nor Uncle Rodrigo dared to allow themselves to make any comments about it, inappropriate observations about the subordinated situation in which they found themselves, given their simultaneous and double condition as permanent guests and younger siblings of the lord of the manor. As with the controversy, the contrast of opinions encountered, which constituted the principal entertainment for the three when they gathered each morning in the arbor, was removed from all controversy, on the contrary, as if by virtue of a tacit agreement, any extreme that could directly or indirectly undermine the personal prestige of one who, in the end, held the family reputation. Residual privileges of an extinguished right of primogeniture, in all probability as, too, were the fact of being the first to read the newspaper, unless Uncle Rodrigo beat him to it when they delivered it from town, or having the radio at his disposal, even if it meant interrupting some program, a piece by Mozart that Aunt Pepita was listening to, in order to listen to the news, the report, as he called it, surely since the Civil War, the very same thing must have dated from then, that custom of doing so with the radio flat against his ear, as if he ran the risk of some neighbor denouncing him for being a rebel.

In September, when he returned from his evening walk, it was already practically dark. The dogs, the same as when the days were longer, continued gathering in the arbor, perhaps tricked by how close it was to dinnertime, but Papa went directly into the living room, and whether he had guests or not—he did not often have them near the end of summer--took up his spot next to the radio. Behind him, at his back, hung the oil portrait of Grandpa; Papa seemed older. As a child, Grandpa also seemed old to me, but I suppose that was due to the fact that in the portrait he appeared with a beard, and in those times only old men had beards. I'd always heard that he died saying "What a mistake! What a tremendous mistake!" And when someone in the family recounted this for the thousandth time, all those present looked at each other as if expecting that finally some valid explanation for what he had meant would arise, as if, like the words that an old man pronounces when he dies without any of those surrounding him capable of understanding their meaning, so, like those words, one's life does not belong to them alone when they are the object of congratulations and handshakes, when the glasses clink and people raise a toast to a birthday or to Christmas.

A question or questions with a less obvious answer seem to me, however, those that can be asked when looking at a small photograph like this one, an interior view of a room taken from the doorway. What is the important thing in it: the room, with a window in the background without more value than a painting might have? Or, rather, is the photo's central theme the idea that the room itself is the picture frame while the actual painting is the commanding view seen through the window?

V

REHABILITATION OF THE KNIGHT ERRANT.

I don't know—nor do I have, on the other hand, any special interest in knowing—if my old neighborhood still preserves that rather quaint, small-town custom of celebrating its fiesta mayor, the annual festival in honor of its patron saint. What's certain is that literally every square inch of the lands where the fair used to be held during my school years, are nowadays—in the finest tradition of that oh-so-typically Barcelonan speculative pugnacity—covered with buildings. And in those days, at least for me, the fiesta mayor meant a carnival with rides and games, and more specifically, bumper cars, and more specifically still, the possibility of making contact with a series of girls who, despite living in the same neighborhood, their being three or four years older than me put them completely out of my reach, being as I must have been in their eyes a little boy who, despite the amusing insistence with which I stared at them when we crossed paths in the street, was still a boy. The festival was held around the end of September or the early days of October, when the beauty of those young women, still in the bosom of the family, was to be seen in all its splendor, surpassable only by how foreseeably beautiful they would become the following year.

Because I knew them only by sight, meaning, that I didn't know them absolutely at all—I limited myself to contemplating them from a watchful anonymity—my preferences were based strictly on physical considerations, or rather, on the consideration of the possibilities that the bodies of each one of my favorites seemed to offer, a body capable—lacking other individualizing elements—of tremendous oscillations, now athletic and forbidding, now with the blonde and celestial purity of a Botticelli, now supplied with all the touches that a suggestive aberrant sexuality usually imprints on the outward appearance. They showed up at the bumper cars in the late afternoon, in small groups, and the ones who were my target usually selected a car accompanied by some less favored female friend, although more than one of them seemed to prefer the always greater relevance of the solitary performance. The question, in any case, was to ram them with maximum violence, perversely, in the rear side panels if possible, right in the spot where a good solid smash makes them spin round, with their hair flying and laughter and little cries and long eyelashes, helpless despite one of their weak attempts to get out of harm's way, out of that immobility and lack of control of the car that only attracts new collisions and redoubled shocks to the girls who find themselves in such circumstances. The magnetism they emanated then seemed to expand all by itself across the whole floor of the bumper car ride and, like the heat produced by the repeated shocks of the metal contact strip against the flooring, the phenomenon became contagious, and the crazy impulse of smashing and crashing into each other with maximum force widespread, seeking the most spectacular effect possible. An attitude clearly linked to the one that occurs surrounding a rape, where the supposed relief from a consummated act can be inferior to the incentives offered by the non-consummated one, to the overcharging of the libido generated by a frustrated rape, the same as in these circumstances and by virtue of similar motives, also on a bumper car ride, from the point of view of our little rapist, more than an easy prey, much more, can tell the difficulty of the contact, the dissatisfaction engendered by the useless assault upon a skilled driver, upon pursuing and pursuing across every inch of the floor such a fleeing target, the desire of reaching her growing the more she refuses and skitters away, the more unmoved she resists the impact, stolid like an Amazon, Olympian like Diana the Huntress herself.

Has my subsequent erotic behavior varied substantially? Is the amorous conduct of our little rapist so far removed from the amorous life of the adult? I would say not, that it's more similar, in every case, than it might seem at first glance. Because, if far from only considering how my relationships with Rosa, with Magda, with Margarita ended, or if, from precisely that consideration, I go back in time and I reconstruct what were my first encounters, the contact with women that has definitively counted in my life, the resulting scheme of behavior will not be very distinct from how our little bumper car rapist behaves. And the fact is that, like the vision of that fool whom we've not bumped into since we were kids, when we saw him on our way to school, that neighborhood idiot identical to himself after all these years, the same at forty-eight as he was at eighteen, with the very same spirited, go-get-'em gait, the walk of someone on the way to get something done although they don't know exactly what, how that fool, whose appearance suddenly takes us back to an impression already lived and with respect to which it's not him who has changed but us, so, like that fool who in his inability to reason has so much in common with the person's sexual response, if something has changed in our amorous life, it's the circumstances in which it has developed, not the mode of behavior. And if the figure of Rosa, transported to the bumper cars, could correspond to that of that girl who shakes with laughter, her hair flying, Magda would correspond to the one who looks at us fearful and silent, as if under the effect of a fright from which she has still not recovered, thus remaining for Margarita the role of Diana the Huntress, *mi verdadera diana*, that is, my true *diana*, my real target, the impossible girl who deftly dodges us, who without greater emotional response avoids again and again a new collision, almost involuntarily, as if she had not even suspected our purpose, or going even further, as if she had not even seen us. Wasn't there, in fact, at the start of my relationship with Rosa a glimpse of the behavior of that rapist who senses the orgy to which he must deliver both himself and his victim, wherein the rape victim, even, emulates the rapist? Did it smack of ritual ceremony, of sacrifice, of the fascination that, in Magda's case, overwhelms both the sacrificant as well as the sacrificed?

The effort required to admit these considerations, must be due, I suppose, not only to the fact that the repetition of the scheme seems quite unlikely at this point, but that being repeated would lessen its impact compared to previous instances, but above all to the mutations which my relationships, as much with Rosa as with Margarita and Magda, have experienced for several years now, that loss of libido, as if misplaced amid the ins and outs of my dealings with each one of them, eclipsed not only in a sudden but also in a reciprocal way and, what's more curious, little less than simultaneous, as if all of them were won over, it would appear, by the deceitful belief that sexuality is nothing more than the previous idea one has settled on. And the deeper the non-erotic elements of the relationship were sustained the better, more so with Margarita than with

Magda, and more so with either of them than with Rosa. For this to happen, I don't know if one needs to have seen, as in a mirror, the physical changes that only seem to cause attitudinal changes, having seen our friends, male and female, change from when we first knew them into what they are now, girls as sleek and sharp as a Siamese cat who turn—one would say suddenly—into an ever-plusher Angora. Thus, having reached this point, the man, more on the defensive, tends toward an ironic and civilized misogyny, while the woman, to the degree that she knows that blaming the passing of time supposes in her a true change of condition, tends to more combative positions, to develop the most possessive, affirmative, and maximalist aspects of her character, naturally predisposed to positions of a feminist type, to an analogous hard-shell militancy, whose concepts must necessarily run deeper in her than in the young woman studying at university, every time that anything passionate in her yields to pure speculative pleasure, something like participating in a theatrical presentation only to suddenly find oneself without a role to play. This leads to a tension between attitudes, including when one intends to go back and start again from the beginning, what gets repeated is the final dress rehearsal before the opening night show, that performance that didn't happen or that was canceled or that flopped, a rehearsal, however, under which lies—unrecognizable after so much makeup slathered on top—the same mode of behavior seen in our little bumper car rapist, that wretched adolescent who wonders, scandalized, how it's possible that women walk down the street so relaxed, as if they weren't really naked underneath the clothes they wear, bodies perhaps freshly arisen from some erotic affair, their moist parts still dilated, showing off an unbelievable cynicism before which our adolescent, dazed, eyes seemingly unable to focus at all, feels again completely defenseless and unqualified, incapable of facing them down outside of a bumper car ride, when, at the wheel of a tiny fireball hotrod, he swoops down like a bird of prey upon his unassailable neighborhood beauties.

Speaking about men and women by putting all the emphasis on their erotic distinction is nothing more than one of so many classifications that can be established when one takes a look at the world around us; other classifications exist, more intricate to the extent that, their origin no less confused than their nature, they seem even less capable of yielding simplifying generalizations, without, thereby, the resultant dichotomy being any less radical. Thus, the division between people who immediately awaken the affection of whomever comes into contact with them, who generate in others beforehand the necessity, necessity more than simple impulse, of making them the object of their attentions, of maintaining from the start an understanding and protective attitude, and people who don't inspire any of that. For example: Rosa, Magda, and Jaime, yes; Joaquín, Margarita, and I, no. Obvious to anyone who knows us. The reason, however, is even more unclear. Those of us who don't, what do we have in common, as opposed to those who do, or vice versa? How to prefer seeing yourself needing to take, for whatever reason, one or two aspirins with a sip of water, or that final recourse against indigestion, a teaspoon of bicarbonate of soda, a repulsive experience for some people while for others—among whom I count myself—a routine operation, a division that, despite its superficial or frivolous appearance still implies, as I have observed, a well-defined series of character traits common to the members of each group. Because the conflict resides, not in finding an individual, case-by-case, explanation but rather finding a common denominator to those individual explanations in each one of the proposed series, a conflict that becomes complicated when, on considering two or more series, established according to different propositions, we find ourselves with the fact that they cross over, that Margarita and Magda also prefer bicarbonate of soda, while Rosa, Joaquín, and Jaime are aspirin addicts.

In Jaime's case, the most basic explanation for his gift of endearing himself to others, as the common expression goes, could be founded on his affability, on his inability to say no, on the insistent yes, yes, yes, that he had at first for everyone and everything, although later and in the most respectful way, he would go on to expound arguments diametrically opposed to what initially seemed to have been settled on given his courteous yesses. In the same sense, his tendency to continuously apologize, to offer unnecessary explanations, for things that neither worry nor could possibly interest anyone. Additionally, his need for gifts, for being treated to surprises, the Christmas gift from some grateful client, for example, a gift that, however routine and conventional, he valued more, much more, than the professional or economic relationship that explained it, a valuation only surpassed by the gift itself, not only unexpected but also for no particular reason, that small gift sent by a person not easily identifiable, a person who, if barely known, nevertheless, as that small gift so well testifies, shows us a singular appreciation; a propensity that could also lead him only to mythomania, to invent gifts, to call something he actually purchased a gift, and, on occasions, to kleptomania, to steal gifts for himself. Abundant reasons, in any case, to show all deserving affection to a charming person, yes, but that, at the same time, they turned out to be more than sufficient to make him unbearable, infuriating like that Sunday driver who, after having driven a fine distance on the highway alongside another car, each of them taking the lead by turn, passing and repassing one another, both with sportsmanship and comradeship, almost regrets that in the end they've separated without stopping to say hello, without chatting a while and telling each other their respective problems, without having made friends. Because, like that Sunday driver's state of mind, brought on by heavy digestion, the aroma of the cigar and the coffees infused with brandy he's swallowed, so, too, Jaime's mood in his daily relationship with people. Perhaps the fact of being unbearable ended up counting in his favor when it came to qualifying for other's affections? Without any room for doubt, because what's true is that I was not the only one to avoid him, everybody did, as usually happens with annoying people, and perhaps this reaction, however unfair since Jaime was not, actually, an irritating bore, effectively contributed to reinforce the kind of distanced affection he inspired, like an extra fee or surcharge.

Magda's case was completely different, more direct, more immediate in its manifestation, since the affection that her mere physical presence seemed to set loose in people was not easily separable from the attraction which that physical presence exerted, an attraction based, more than on the beauty of her features, or besides that, on the tranquil desolation that shone through her eyes even when they smiled in amusement. To that first favorable impression I would have to add the intrusion of the protective impulses that usually inspire an attitude toward life like hers--firmness of character and obstinate independence of criteria by acting like a spring or elastic band, like the body of a fine dancer beneath the tulle, of a fragile and skittish outer appearance, of a little woodland creature--impulses that if, by virtue of their own nature, they split into two and spill out with enormous facility, with Magda, the initial anxieties of giving that creature all the affection it deserved were traded, with special rapidity, for more imperious desires, including the projection of sexual release, this circumstance probably no stranger to her well-known status as a lesbian; reactions that could only strengthen Magda's tendency to withdraw, to justify her sensation of being a victim of a true assault, and with so much more reason the more often the experience is repeated, the more generalized the phenomenon is shown to be. The obvious effort it implies for her, her difficulty in dealing with any sort of guests when she was in Vilasacra keeping Jaime company, her fright at the simple announcement of the guest, her way of looking at herself in the mirror before inviting them in, as if afraid that the mirror might reflect what the visitors might believe about her sexual life, that her eyes, like tiny screens, reproduced the unbridled scenes which they doubtless attributed to her, examining herself suspiciously, just as aware of her own strangeness as a nocturnal bird that flies so conspicuously in the full light of day and just as blind. Accordingly, the growing complexity of the ritual practices that she had already devoted herself to when I met her, little manias, superstitions as she called them, which had only grown and spread over time, until almost completely ruling her daily routine: touching both sides of the doorframe with her fingertips when crossing the threshold; washing her hands after grasping a door handle, a gesture that she tries to avoid by opening them with her elbow when the shape of the handle permits; also, washing her hands after touching money; having an ashtray for her own exclusive use, one that she always washes after someone else touches it; habitually leaving the toilet seat cover raised, whose edges, however, shows signs of wear from the soles of her shoes; rigorously symmetrical arrangement of silverware on the tablecloth, of the coffee cups on a tray, etcetera, details that I catch on the sly, provided I recognize them, echoes of certain habits I acquired in prison—counting my steps, the flagstones, making seven ablutions when washing my face, etcetera—although, probably, more than acquiring them, what I did was notice their existence, just as even now they tend to reappear, irrepressible, in my worst moments or periods, since Margarita's death, for example.

Unlike Magda, Rosa can be rather startling at first. And regarding the type of affectionate feelings she awakens in people, more than affection, per se, I'd have to say she awakens an appreciation, an appreciation best maintained at a prudent distance: her infatuation, her vehemence, her voluble opinion, whose potential danger floats on the air, seem to advise it. Especially when one feels her apparent generosity to be a two-edged sword, possessive expansiveness combined with a dedication to help others, invasive scheming combined with disinterested assistance. Her total lack of a sense of reality, the enthusiasm she's capable of applying to an impossible solution, only serves one purpose: creating for her a phantasmagoric outline where nobody contradicts her, everyone seemingly going along with her just the same way they do with crazy people. Rosa's problem thus consists in how to bolster that self-confidence that everyone supposes she has, that she herself has come to believe in on occasions, be it with the help of a mantra, *Osar*, the Spanish verb *to dare*, formed from the same letters as Rosa, her slogan, motto, maxim when we first met, maybe with the help of some stimulant, pharmaceuticals, alcohol, etcetera, whatever, as in more recent times, seeking refuge and finding it in an isolation that comes to be the negative image of the isolation that Magda inhabits: it's not that the world harasses her, the problem with the world is that it doesn't deserve her.

Among the various solutions adopted, her recourse to alcohol has been without doubt the one of greatest significance, affecting, longer and with greater intensity, Rosa's emotional oscillations as well as her confidence or lack of confidence and the reality or unreality of the surrounding world. The ups-and-downs resulting from her alcohol consumption became chronic in the most natural way in the world, and then, with the same naturalness, as the noxious effects began to predominate the beneficial ones, the depressing ones overshadowing the stimulating ones, as relapses followed treatments and cures, the equilibrium in her highs and lows was reestablished through a chronic suppression of the alcohol, all as a result of one of those qualitative leaps so costly to dialectical materialism. The vicissitudes brought on by alcohol entering a couple's life, the tensions and erosions it produces, have served as the theme for countless boring novels in which the author, with that mania for minute details truly worthy of a repentant dipsomaniac, seems determined to not spare us one single detail about what that represents in their daily life together. Obfuscated by such obsession, they are incapable of noticing that what counts is not the daily sequence but its interruption, the dissolution caused by the intrusion of a third person, product of the splitting of the partner suffering from alcoholism, a person more like Mr. Hyde, la Bête or the Wolfman, whatever their sex, than those poor embittered souls who wander about with their tics through the pages of the novels I'm talking about. The failure lies in the focus, in that they mistake the genre, treating in an analytical and realistic tone what really belongs to the scope of a horror novel. The moment of the transfiguration, when Nebuchadnezzar shows the first symptoms of his transformation into a revolting beast: the eyelid that twists and tenses, the grimace that pushes through the hair, his apprehensive growl just before leaping from his throne, out of the palace, flattening anyone in his path who doesn't dodge him in time as he bolts for the wasteland.

The metamorphosis usually coincided with the sunset, when Rosa disappeared as if mounted on a broom, replaced by an increasingly aggressive creature, hopping about like a goblin, drinking furtively, it didn't take long for her to turn into the very embodiment of the most incoherent rudeness, now more defiant than furtive, and soon furious, a kind of troglodyte that attacked anyone who noticed her strange behavior, shouting, slapping, kicking, drinking straight from the bottle, devouring a whole sausage bite by bite or wolfing down a whole bar of chocolate just like an ogre devouring everything in the little cottage in the fairytale; soaked with the alcohol ingested, satisfying the need for nutrition more than for eating, of ingesting thick, heavy, and, if possible, expensive foods, drowsiness overcomes her like the Cyclops and she sleeps for a while, imprisoned by restless dreams, after which she awakens intermittently, to drink and stuff her face again and toss and turn and writhe about, now with the dread and helplessness of the bear who knows itself to be cornered, who searches for some useless refuge among the rocky crags, her eyes reflecting the torches of the peasants, who with clubs, pitchforks and rifles tighten the siege.

For Rosa, as for anyone, the retrospective panorama around these sorts of Saturday night celebrations, the impression that prevails during the long day and a half that it usually takes to wake up even a little, to emerge from the tunnel of sleep, differs very little, no doubt, from the impression produced by a train that passes by at top speed the train we are riding on, images whose true identity, flashing by so fast, become impossible to determine, and that, perhaps for their hammering celerity, perhaps from the nature of the instantaneous snapshot images registered, they constitute as a whole a true invitation to keep sleeping, to see if it turns out that those memories form part of a dream, and then one wakes up with other ideas, more focused on breakfast and the newspaper and the comforting hustle and bustle in the streets. With regard to the scenery that served as a frame for the development of the action, it's something that the male or female protagonist, in this case Rosa, can only imagine by analogy, for having been obliged to play, on other occasions, with me, with some friend, the role of spectator, in the same way that neither the passenger riding on our train is capable of appreciating the impression of movement that train produces in the surrounding landscape it's traveling through, set out as it finds itself in that movement of which it's a part, imperceptible to the eyes of an eventual observer who contemplates the passing train from outside, the long line that moves through the quietude of the landscape, or even, why not, the lines of the two trains that cross paths. More than a simple interval, this period of recuperation constitutes a true interlude: not an empty space between two periods of time but a period of time in itself, distinct from the one that preceded it and from the one that will follow it, endowed with its own identity. A common characteristic of the three periods is the virtue they have of keeping the whole house walking on eggshells not only for fear of what that colossus might say or do, might shout or hurl to the floor, but also of its fearsome fragility, wobbling like a tottering chess queen, who might lose her balance, topple to the floor and shatter to bits, spraying them all with the fragments, or like later, after the recovery, the household will be on tenterhooks awaiting the first silent signs of an imminent relapse. Any excuse to go back to doing what she likes: put a bit of order into the house, for example, in order to have the sensation that she has earned—so well deserved!—a drink. The good humor that then seized her, her animation as she began to drink, the long and hurried swallows that she served herself as if saying to them, wait, wait till I fill the tank with gasoline, I'll be right back, and returned indeed with renewed impetus and the satisfaction of the one who has fulfilled all the prerequisites, first things first. And then, predictably, the most glowing expressions of love that, especially at dusk, are merely the perilous announcement of an imminent avalanche of invectives. The definitive warning, however, was in her eyes, in the moist quality they acquired, the slippery and guilty look that, like an alarm, unleashed the general stampede. Then, the crisis, Rosa starting to sizzle and crackle right there in her own chair.

The empty space that quitting alcohol opens up in the habits of a person obliges them to change their ways, both in finding a substitute for the suppressed stimuli, as well as finding a generally new approach to the life that one lives or would like to live. During that phase, Rosa's insistence on defining and characterizing herself, for example, on limiting what she is, and marking distances with respect to what she is not. First of all, she's ill: not a sickness per se but such and such a function, such and such an organ that starts misbehaving, the gallbladder, the risk of a collapse, bad peripheral circulation, nothing serious, discomforts, silly things that need looking after, an arsenal of pills matching the variety of symptoms. Because like those people who one fine day realize that they've turned out to be their grandfather, that ogreish creature who terrified everyone around him, or perhaps that they've inherited the mother's temper, a woman of genius, as they said in the family, or a woman of unbearable character, as was generally acknowledged outside the family circle, meaning, they've into a character, with a line of behavior that defines what perhaps the temperament does not suffice to define by itself, thus Rosa, like those people who opt to turn into characters, establishing herself in her condition as a sick woman, settling into the state of being a person of delicate health, in a way not very different, after all, from how her own mother, her vilified mother, had treated her in her day. A status on the other hand, that encloses a certain tendency toward retrospection, because, just like that genealogy of what's wrong with her leads to digging into hereditary traits, to reverting, for example, to the figure of the mother or of the grandfather, it also leads her, in her investigations, to a search though her own past, to a reinterpretation of herself since childhood, since forever, as they say. The contemplation of the possibilities that an explanation of this kind offers, the exploration of the various options which that allows, including reaching back to feel inside like when she had her first period, contributed, no doubt, to keep her in that kind of self-absorbed stupor in which she so frequently found herself sunk, always seeming to be thinking about something else, forgetting two and even three lit cigarettes in different ashtrays, leaving the doors open behind her and the lights turned on.

Sometimes, in the course of the conflicts that married life certainly leads to, either one of the spouses, she, he, sometimes the two of them, although separately, see themselves driven, rapt in their total and simultaneous contemplation of what is happening, and as a kind of decisive stimulation of the atemporal state in which they find themselves submerged, to the contemplation of a stimulating alternative: the eventual possibility of reprisal, power, in a given moment, turn the situation around, and then, inverting the meaning of the wounds received as a consequence of such a relationship, have the other spouse at their disposal for what remains of life in order to go about making them pay for all their grievances, from the first to the last. More often, meaning, without reaching such extremes in the degree to which one deals with a possibility not only more immediate but also more promising, one opts for another kind of alternative attempt, what Rosa called talking, clarifying things, an attempt that, unfailingly, only added one more reason for reproach--incomprehension, indifference—to the already long list that, referring to it once more *ab initio*, tried to get us to look it over together, and once again I was going to resist being subjected to such a soaking, her habitual enumeration of my innumerable betrayals—her own, she said, were nothing more than a desperate attempt to get me to react—of her lost opportunities, the men who had fallen in love with her without her knowing it, how everything would have been different with any one of them, without a noxious presence like mine, capable of annulling her even without doing anything deliberate in this sense, without my even realizing it. The catalyzing, or rather, liberating value, that these sorts of sessions had for her was evident, on precipitating, as a kind of release, all the accumulated bad feelings, and, released from that burden, impelled by an unusual reappearance of vitality, she started any task, putting her things in order, for example, meaning, extending the disorder throughout the whole house in a show of her desire for change, that could also be understood as a way of trying to compensate for the impossibility she found of putting her mind in order, and thus until she got tired and ended up by gathering it all up again, now that, after all, she was ill, now that, after all, her health wouldn't allow her to do so much.

Something similar could be said, probably, about her personal sense of time, a sense to which she still seems to be attending today: the fluctuations in value that its passing offers her, that tendency of hers to calculate it selfishly, whether it's a question of minutes—how much time remains to get to the cinema, to an appointment, on time—or a question of dates—leaving for or returning from a trip, that she tries to delay as much as possible—valuable temporal units, you might say, according to her proximity to the limit. And I suppose that must also be attributed equally to that reverse movement, to that delving into one's own past, in the manner of residual bonds, inevitable in a process of this nature, Rosa's adherence to certain attitudes, adopted at different times and often contrary to one another, that with time must end up—as questions of principle—completely out of place: her aversion to provisional things that later become definitive, for example, and, in general, to half measures; the disgust she feels, first for what bastards the bourgeoisie are, then what sons of bitches workers are, etcetera, etcetera. A similar recurring character, a true leitmotiv, her attitude toward people, rigid, immobile, as if every person is forever fixed in a concrete instant of her life. A rigidity that is not a symptom of sincerity. Her obsession with Margarita, for example. Rosa's attempts to win her for herself, to convert her into her own friend, to which Margarita always corresponded cordially but at a distance, all that covering a strong antagonism according to which, and privately, Rosa accused Margarita of not being a true woman or of hardly being one, and Margarita accused Rosa of being annoying to any and all. Rosa sought her out, gave her gifts, and Margarita instead shunned her; time and its respective positions worked in her favor.

Just as in the novels of chivalry the knight is defined by his exploits, being for a lady a characterization based on his qualities, exalted no less in the physical than in the spiritual realm, so, even today, the woman is usually explained according to what she is and the man according to what he does. The deformation is not only moral and cultural but also specifically literary; in novels, for example, the characterization of the male protagonist is usually more prominent than the female, his key points written more coherently, his details more polished, more convincing. To my judgment, this is due to the fact that while the female protagonist constitutes the unmistakable object of the story, the male protagonist is identified rather more with the goal through which the author develops that story, the lens through which he offers us the various vicissitudes of its development. And that finds fulfillment even when, lacking that protagonist-viewer, the author supplants her implicitly, assuming the role of observing lens—as in the case of Madame Bovary—or when the author is a woman, a woman who, assuming the conventions belonging to the genre, elaborates the characterization of her heroines the same as a man might do. In this sense, the female protagonist of a novel is usually more similar to the secondary characters than the male protagonist, something like an extensively developed secondary character, their characterization well-rounded, meticulous, efficiently defined, figures that might belong to a bas-relief, more convex than concave, unlike the male protagonist, whose peculiar depth seems rather more the result of a tranquil emptying out.

A phenomenon, ultimately, that only reproduces on the fictional plane what the author has doubtless previously experienced in his daily life: the difficulty involved in summarizing the personality of someone close to us, whom we know in their contradictions, in contrast to the very ductility of the outer image, of the person who intrudes from outside, easier to sketch with resolution and brilliance, so that their firm features turn out to be convincing, thanks precisely to the few reasons for doubt they offer us, to the ample margin of initiative that they permit our energetic intuition. And bear in mind that I understand someone close to mean not only one who is emotionally close but who is also close by virtue of mere physical proximity, without any special affinity of character even being necessary. Joaquín's case, for instance, possibly the person whose development I've followed the closest, closer to the subject in this aspect than to Papa—a figure whom the little boy sees as something imposed on him, the figure of a man who was always old—or than Rosa, a woman whom it was possible for me to accept or reject just as she was when we met, a woman whose personality could evolve but no longer change. For that reason, not even within the frame of these notes, written solely for oneself, not even here, would it turn out to be simpler to introduce a biographical likeness of Joaquín than of Papa or of Rosa. It's one thing to know someone's personality in its diverse facets, and another thing to organize those partial facts into a coherent whole; and I would even dare to say that the more coherent the resulting image, the more reasons there are to call into doubt the fact that they also correspond to some reality. Thus it must be in the scope of the autobiography—the extreme case, the point where the overlapping roles of author and protagonist coincide absolutely—where that work of emptying out, that system of defining the figure indirectly, starting with its outline, manifests itself most clearly. Including when all that reflexive unfolding only responds, consciously or not, to the desire to tamper with, alter, and avoid reality with the maximum amount of technical perfection possible, by inventing the most convincing of fictions.

Unless we forget the very idea of semblance. That we set aside the details that prevent us from appreciating the whole, as well as the very idea that such a whole has any real significance, in favor of the tiny flame that, suddenly lit, as if illuminating the picture from within, will confer upon the composition the life it's lacking. In short, it's a problem of illumination. Of making visible an image that, while being an expression of what, for example, Joaquín is, allows one to glimpse, simultaneously, on a single plane, what Joaquín does, did, and will do: his fifty-something-year-old face that looks like that of a boy disguised as a fifty-something man, common with actors who play the role of someone much older than they themselves really are. Thus his irritation and undisguisable worry over the growing number of lapses occurring, for some time now, in his discourse, the failures of a proverbially exceptional memory, causing him a greater disgust, of course, than what he might feel about his hair turning prematurely gray, about which he can always see a good side, how attractive that is for many young women, and all that. But, is he fully aware to what point he has repeated himself, always telling the same anecdotes to the same people, each person's corresponding anecdote, perhaps, in its own particular register? Just like inserting the same punch card into a computer would inevitably produce the same response, no matter how many times he kept trying? Or the unfavorable impression which that ends up causing, completely counterproductive, if his purpose was to be amenable, what they call a great conversationalist?

Joaquín and I have always gotten along well, like two close brothers who, for the sake of that not ending and even at the cost of sacrificing an eventually greater degree of intimacy, try, each of us in his own way, to stay out of the other's life, avoiding not only the intrusions but also the temptation of making the other share in their own worries, of forcing their hand in search of an understanding which if it has not come about is because there is no basis for it to happen. As kids, we barely had anything to do with each other; him being six years older than me, which when you're a boy, represents a real abyss. Broadly speaking, it might be said that he was a more exemplary young man than I: at school he was a member of Catholic Action, and later he was formally engaged and got married in the Church; all of those things, however, very common among young people his age—the first batch out of the Francoist educational oven—and much less so among my peers, according to an evolution neither unusual nor surprising. He studied Law, the fashionable academic major at that time, and he worked in an advertising agency. When, through some common acquaintances, he received news of my political activities, he decided to get in touch with the party immediately, a little perplexed for having taken so long to become aware of things; a frequent case among those who, like him, had found themselves squarely pegged within the reigning education of the early postwar years, used to taking for granted whatever they were taught, both in religious matters as well as in sexual or political ones, formed by a template of behavior and a criteria of normality with which it was later difficult to break, because such a rupture—for it to happen—meant challenging the collective. He asked to join up, and he adopted the name Fortuny; I had no idea that he admired Fortuny, as he later told me in a pointless attempt to rationalize his choice, but that choice, in light of his future link with the world of the plastic arts, turned out to be premonitory. Although as Fortuny he performed an outstanding job in the party's propaganda apparatus, the decisive factor of his ascent to positions of increasingly greater responsibility was doubtless his ability to identify, and even to anticipate, the leadership's points of view. When I was sent to prison, he preventively went into exile—he'd later say it was to escape his wife—and he remained in Paris for nearly three years, with frequent trips to countries in Eastern Europe. I knew that he'd become a member of the central committee, but when he returned, changed back into Joaquín, possibly exiled not only from the central committee but also from the party, rather than being frustrated by the dizzying trajectory of his political career, he seemed full of more ideas than ever, sure of himself as is typical of someone who has just gone through a stimulating experience. Enough screwing around, he announced to me: the only reality is what you make for yourself. And, indeed, like a Quixote who, after his defeat on the Barcelona strand, decides to return to his own land and, once there, wastes no time in becoming one of the chief landowners in La Mancha, with an important production of grain, wine, and sheep, cured of his former madness thanks to the blow he received by falling off his horse, so too Joaquín in the new life he had begun, far, and increasingly further, from his modest position as young progressive and frugal husband which he had developed into prior to his departure. He got involved with various businesses, but what made him money was the art gallery, his fortunate participation in the boom in modern painting, almost as if, guided again by his sharp nose, like in his earlier political life, more than guessing the evolution of the public's taste and, therefore, of the prices, he fostered that evolution for his own best interest. In a certain way, he had also become fashionable; he hobnobbed with Everybody who was Anybody in Barcelona, and, as he said, he avoided the risk of having a wife by having lots of women. He also started painting: I think that we should define every area with maximum clarity, he told me then; leave no doubt about who is the architect and who is the artist. Because you must know that I paint, and that the few people—all of them very knowledgeable—to whom I've shown my paintings, have been rather emphatic: brilliant.

It wasn't only self-confidence that he'd acquired; it was, overall, the full awareness of that confidence. Because just as in revolutionary or supposedly revolutionary parties there are two levels of moral attitude and even of language, that of the leadership and that of the base, so different on occasions that the members of the former probably wouldn't believe their ears if they could hear the members of the latter without them being aware of their presence, so, in a similar way, in our society, there are also two levels or categories whose most precise reflection we will find in the world of fashion: fashion for others, which is made to change each year in order to grease the wheels of business to the maximum, and the fashion for oneself and their peers, secret fashion—fully clashing with common fashion—that, like an encrypted code, is precisely designed to allow the initiates to recognize each other, wristwatches of a certain brand, leather of another, cigarette lighters, etcetera, watchwords that, the moment they start to become common knowledge, to be understood by social climbers, gigolos, and other inevitable intruders, have to start shifting, in any case, to something much more reliable; and it was this discovery, or rather, the access to that privileged upper echelon, that was found to be the basis of Joaquín's confidence. The attitude, ultimately, which has allowed him to triumph in life, without complexes, without clumsy prejudices or stupid submissions to the yardstick of a petty set of morals. He enjoyed recounting, for example, how he went for the jugular during an employees' strike at one of the big department stores where he had an important position shortly before he started his art gallery. Don't worry, he told the manager, I know how these sorts of situations get resolved. And he called a meeting with the employee delegates and told them: if we lived in a free country we'd have no problem here; unfortunately, at this time, there are no democratic freedoms, and a labor strike automatically becomes a socio-political crime, so if you don't drop your demands immediately, I'll have no other option but to call the police. And they went back to work. How do you think they would have solved this problem in the Soviet Union?

Do you realize? said Jaime. He believes what they told us as kids about the atheist; he behaves like one of those atheists they talked to us about in the spiritual exercises, a person capable of anything, a truly evil person from whom you can expect any kind of villainy, free as he feels to do it or stop doing it. And the thing is, unlike Joaquín, Jaime, like an Ignatius of Loyola who, if he gives up weapons, it's so he can fight a higher battle, like Ignatius of Loyola in the act of offering his sword to the Virgin of Montserrat, thus, too, Jaime, forced to withdraw from clandestine activities, seemed only to have found in the illness a new reason to persevere in his convictions with even greater vigor. According to this obligatory and gradual distancing from the action, with the parallel reaffirmation of the immoveable ideological principles, Jaime began to move the center of his interests to new areas, areas of performance accessible even to the diminished faculties of a sick man, to the degree that, like a screen, they permit him to project and resolve his unsatisfied anxieties about socialism. Thus, his vehement interest in the theater that awoke in his final years, the cathartic qualities he attributed to it, a consequence, no doubt, the same as for those fervent revolutionaries who are frequently the actors of the great theatrical and cathartic spectacle that they discern in the course of a revolution. Or his passionate investigation into the typology of the Ukrainian peasant, in his not always placid adaptation to Soviet society, problems that he followed much more closely than those that affected the Andalusian family that was now taking care of Vilasacra. But Joaquín's little performances, as he said, had the virtue of bringing him back to reality even when, astonished, he watched me over the top of his glasses, as if he no longer remembered exactly why he was watching me with astonishment.

The moral freedom that Joaquín liked to show off nevertheless had its cracks and fissures, cracks, that, if insufficient for his conscience to collapse like a dike from pounding, turbulent waters, didn't stop him from reflecting on his precarious emotional stability. Because, like that police inspector who, after being relieved during the equally long and hard interrogation to which a presumed militant communist is being subjected, drinks a caffe ristretto on leaving police headquarters, his thoughts lingering on the prisoner's words, on his faith in the ultimate victory, in the inexorable character of that victory, a faith which the inspector, victim of a professional defect acquired from always doing the same things, shares to the letter, no less obsessed in that regard the one than the other, only that, what will be a paradise for the prisoner, will be an inferno for the inspector, inevitable as death itself and, for the moment, no less distant given that, as the prisoner's body acquires purple tonalities, he, the current tormentor and eventual future prisoner, uses the teaspoon to help the sugar cubes dissolve in the small cup of hot coffee and, when he has drunk it, at home with his wife and little children, thus, like that policeman in the fervent delectation with which he sips his comforting coffee, so too, Joaquín in his way of extracting pleasure from life. And in the same way that the policeman's genial nature tenses up and stiffens and his fragile irritability erupts into shards of fury in the face of that future executioner whom he now kicks and beats, so, too, in a similar way, Joaquín's verbal virulence when he lost his nerve in the face of the abundant cases of incompetence that daily life has in store for us. There was also that series of demands and manias, sometimes simple instinctive reactions, that, escaping from his control, irrepressible, confirmed the presence of that sea in the background on the other side of the dike. Many of them flourished and were reflected in the repairs and remodeling at Santa Cecilia. Clearing the brush from the woods around the house, for example, a forest without undergrowth or low-hanging branches, so that the tree trunks could stand out as clearly as possible. Or his fixation with symmetry, whether for a careful arrangement of lights, or the alignment of windows or the perfect parallelism of various decorative elements, baseboards, moldings, etcetera. And, in general, the repugnance that fills him for anything that smells old, whatever looks used or, in his words, rotten, things, consequently, that must be thrown away or, better yet, burned and replaced by new and different ones.

When I say—and I've said it more than once—that, if on the one hand my relationship with Margarita led to Jaime's wedding with Ana—*Análoga al Ánade*, as Margarita called it, *The Mallard Ana-log*, it hastened, on the other, Joaquín's separation from his wife, and I'm not only exaggerating but my statement is inexact, given that the decisive factor resides not in the fact that I had or ceased to have a love affair with someone but that that someone was, precisely, Margarita. My relationship with Rosa, for example, would never have lent itself, never did lend itself, to such phrases. Not in vain, even for myself, the relationship that I maintained with Margarita was completely different than the one I had with Rosa. We have, therefore, a peculiarity of Margarita, something that Margarita radiated and that was picked up on by whoever entered her physical sphere as if it were a magnetic field; and we have, similarly, the particular influence that her person exercises on me, as well as my personal response to that influence. What comes to mind as I consider this is that whoever reads these notes without knowing us, whoever saw me writing them in that cheap hotel in Gorgs near Vilasacra, that eventual reader was perhaps going to wonder what the hell could I have ever seen in Margarita, given that, if I had seen something, it seemed that I preferred to keep it only to myself.

It's not only a question of a retrospective image, of the typical posthumous glorification of someone no longer with us. It's something, on the contrary, specifically linked to Margarita's presence wherever she was to be found, regardless of the degree of intimacy that people had with her, regardless of the distance that might have developed over time. Rosa's reaction to the definitive disappearance of her antagonist, for example, or Magda's, or the reaction of that friend she had when she lived in Paris and who, from Paris, where he had opted to establish himself, fed up with Spain as much as with militant politics, wrote to me, following her death, that with her passing one of the few lively things that remained in our dismal country vanished; and like him, an incalculable number of friends and even simple admirers who would have given anything to be something more than that. No, this general reaction must be related, not to death, but to life, to the feelings that Margarita had awoken in all those who had the occasion to know her. Something that has nothing to do with the displays of sorrow that someone's death usually inspires, the ceremony then organized, the ritual then staged, and the no-less ritual response that occurs among those who attend, an atmosphere similar, for its being illusory, to the one that is felt in a theatre when the performance ends, that silence, that pent-up emotion that seizes the audience when the play ends, a sad variant, ultimately, but not for that reason any less ephemeral, of that kind of feeling of brotherhood and harmony that possesses the spectators of a musical review when, after the final curtain call, all the lights come on and everyone begins to move toward the exits, still smiling and satisfied, all of them complicit, anonymous participants of a cheery message, of a song about the joy of life, that will only start to dissipate, like the mist exhaled, with the cold of the street and the hostile darkness while looking for the goddamned car.

As far as I'm concerned, it's enough to take a glance at how these notes are shaping up, the direction they've taken since I started them, more as a reflection on a reality than how I reflect that reality, in order to prove to what point the memory of Margarita is capable of generating other memories, memories that, you might say, were rescued from the attic, given their second-hand or, on the contrary, superfluous condition, without, on the other hand, I myself managing to see how they relate to Margarita, if they have anything to do with her at all, that is. Moreover, it's the very memory of Margarita that sometimes seems to get lost under the avalanche of impressions at once unexpected and persistent, like those drawings and words that children scribble on foggy windows, and which, years later, moving through the empty house, mockingly reappear before our eyes with the nighttime humidity. Collaterally, the treatment that Margarita receives on these pages corresponds to what our relations were from the moment when they began to cool, when I had my failed erotic adventure with Magda.

Between Margarita and me, love was something implicit, it was a given, and wasn't even mentioned. Once, during our euphoric Parisian beginnings, she told me that she had fallen in love with me, and then I told her that I was in love with her too, both of us a bit drunk; and that was all. At that time I tended to establish a firm identification between love and sexuality, convinced not only that that was the only form of solidly and healthily settling an intimate relationship, however episodic it was, but also that women fully shared such criteria. Nothing strange, accordingly, that, after Magda, the first cracks appeared in the erotic terrain between Margarita and me, as if we had suddenly both become aware of our different ways of understanding sex, a dichotomy of concepts that had to have forcible repercussions on the act of love, in what even then had been a carefree surrender to the liquifying pleasure: what for me constituted an end in itself, an intimate relationship in the strictest sense, for her signified an exercise of power; that became clear then—only a misunderstanding, arising when each partner attributes their own feeling to the other, prevented us from realizing sooner—and our subsequent evolution, the road taken by each one, has only served to confirm it. Thus, considering Margarita, it's enough to glance at the list of her principal lovers: one of the most promising architects in the country, the most brilliant writer of a young generation, a well-known movie actor, an important businessman with a great political future, and so on, all as if the attraction that she saw in each one of them resided fundamentally in his condition as a figure, as if the excitement obtained were the product, more than of a sexual relationship, of the impact on her sexuality caused by going to bed with the frontrunner, with the number one in each field. A multiplying effect of similar selective collecting: not only having the top dog in his field as a lover, but also giving him the impression of being a poor man who, enclosed in his small circle, had lost sight of the rich variety of suggestions the world offers, the celestial rite of life. And along with that, when, frequently, various lovers or ex-lovers bumped into each other at a meeting, at a party, the way she could make everyone feel that each word, each smile, each glance, was directed at him in particular.

In the same sense, her love of surprises, secret, unforeseen movements: dinner in London, surfing lessons in California, a lightning trip to Tahiti, organizing an exhibition and sale of works by Picasso, Miró, Tàpies, etcetera, in Paris, with the object of raising funds for the pro-amnesty campaign for Spanish prisoners and exiled politicians. Makeup, hairdos, the way of dressing and styling oneself, according to the movement and urgency of the type of activities that developed, with the atmospheres that she frequented and, ultimately, with the environments she frequented and, ultimately, with the dynamic of her life. As far as clothing, a preference for a sportive line of a rather classic cut, just right for a self-confident woman who moved with decision and flexibility: a predilection for wool, linen, silk, leather and, in general, models designed by the big fashion houses with prime natural materials, articles in which the quality shone for itself. A contrast between her taste and Rosa's, more exaggerated in everything, occasionally bordering on the great disguise, given as Rosa is to touches of the femme fatal; the opposite of the ideal of anonymous beauty, that beauty that surprises us and disappears instantly, so deeply rooted in Margarita. Also a love for secrets, hiding places, going out incognito, that treasure chest she kept in some Cave of Sesame with all her memories, my letters, the letters from each one of her lovers, photographs, little mementoes of symbolic and sentimental value, that cassette tape she made me listen to, a gift from a radio announcer in Madrid with whom she'd no doubt had an erotic fling, the recording of the broadcast he'd dedicated to her, the tender song of a man in love who, if it must have seemed the most normal thing to the radio listeners habituated to the soap opera, what was no longer quite so normal was that it also seemed that way to her. And did that treasure chest also yield that photograph of her bedroom in Vilasacra she was carrying in her purse the day of the accident?

When, for a while, we put some distance between ourselves and our relationship changed completely, perhaps I ignored—Rosa and I had only just started living together—the degree to which that innocent and free ending in itself, that was, for me, what people call love, concealed and unformulated but real desire to dominate the beloved person, capable of being so much more accentuated the greater the resistance offered. But Margarita must also not have known how far the power she'd achieved over her lover, over each one of her lovers, constituted for her nothing but a means, an isolated element within a wider whole, one more point of irradiation that with her influence empowered the total influence of the whole, that network of reciprocal influences impacting simultaneously from different levels that, like a scrim, raised the profile of her personality, similar to how the white sheet enhanced the euphoria of her presentation, clear and accessible, open like a starfish. The resulting impression was one of enormous control, not only personal but social, of being in touch with everything, in areas close to omnipotence, omnipresence, and omniscience, an external impression only betrayed, on occasions, by the excessive insistence, the unnecessary affirmation of her own ego, that I, it was I, I was there, I saw it, I already knew it, I, I, I, no matter what people were talking about, she in the center of everything, first and foremost, on top of everything, dominating it all, she, she, a woman who no doubt needed to appreciate the effect, to absorb the echo, when not even all her determination was enough to compensate for the essential self-confidence which, despite all appearances to the contrary, she lacked.

Locating the misunderstanding, confirming the distance between two attitudes we had come to believe coincidental, supposed a double surprise: for me, the fact that Margarita, after seeming disinterested, scornful of all sorts of conventionalities, showed herself suddenly willing, not only to accept them, but to place them under her control; for Margarita, her saying I wasn't really interested in that context, context if not key component, of sexuality—its dimension of social triumph—something she resisted considering seriously, more inclined rather to think that I, with supreme astuteness, dissimulated my deeper objectives under an exterior of indifference, if not consummate scorn. If we later resumed our intimacy—although not in the same sense as before—it was because, ultimately, something subsisted between us, affinity, mutual attraction, what wouldn't I like better than to be able to precisely identify it; to say that Margarita needed a special witness for her magnificence, for example, a witness and, simultaneously, judge and augur, would be to repeat a joke only valid between her and me, according to our tendency to trivialize what would have turned out to be uncomfortable in no small way.

Is there any sense in talking about a deep, imprecise affinity between two people? Because it's not about mere points of contact. There were also points of contact, after all, between Margarita and Rosa, both of them similar in their ability to split into two, of suddenly turning into Cochise, into a war-painted redskin chief who runs the warpath screaming for the scalps of his enemies, of my lovers, all of them, from first to last, like the fulfillment of some immemorial vengeance. But between Margarita and me, as between Rosa and me, the relationship was always something more than a mere accumulation of points in common. Because, can't you perhaps qualify as a profound and imprecise affinity the link that unites me with Rosa, that antagonism that confronts us like Saint George and the Dragon, both condemned to a continuous final battle, to die and be dead again and again, now for a treasure, now for a princess, now for immortality, now for a saving transmutation, that strength that leads us once more to the conjunction, to that unfailing sacrifice of the Dragon at the hands of Saint George? As if not explaining a relationship of this kind, in which each partner responds to a pattern of behavior possibly pre-established, to a norm of conduct that functions with the fatal exactitude of a mechanism in operation? What else is that search for the winning bonus, for the thing that complements what we lack inside? Rosa's need to be sure of being loved, and my resistance to recognize it in her, to even pronounce the word love, to say something more than a cliché: of course I love you, without it seeming routine or cliché. That insistence on her part to continue asking me again and again, and the consequent stress, more than justified, on mine. Her feeling of being inhibited and blocked in the face of everything, and that to such a greater a degree the more she stubbornly persists in obtaining a promise of love. My conviction, in light of the facts, that my initial presumption was accurate, that the correct thing was to prevent her from conjuring up false hopes, save her from the weight of the disappointment that sooner or later would have ended up crushing her. And so on. However: is it conceivable that she would have been interested in another kind of man and, above all, that that interest would have lasted? Or that I would have stayed with her if that dependency had not existed on her part?

The affective reticence implied in my relationship with Rosa does not constitute an isolated case. On the contrary: it's almost a constant, something that tends to be repeated the moment the relationship surpasses the limits of the episodic adventure. It's practically a chemical attraction, a reluctant view of the amorous surrender that women who are aware of their attractiveness guess immediately, the same way that other women attract homosexuals or madness, and they detect their presence with their eyes closed. In such a context, the only important exception would be Margarita, who refused to play a role that had nothing to do with what she was looking for. Is this point necessarily the key to our special relationship, similar to that of the lizard and the snake who watch each other with mutual fascination? Because, of course, what doesn't explain anything are the small vicissitudes, incidents like that of Magda, however significant they might have seemed. And the fact is, no matter how many elements comprise a work of fiction, the ones related to the plot are the most irrelevant, replaceable by others without affecting the axes and nuclei of the tale, so, in reality, the different options that daily life offers, as their choice must turn out to match what the person is.

THE EYE.

Just as uneven terrain will acquire identity as we ascend it and traverse it, and a slope that seemed like a slope shaped like an inclined plane will unfold into new hollows and serpentine undulations, and what seemed to be hilltops will turn out to be merely the steep slopes of higher peaks, rising up around the traveler, as they move, through normally imperceptible reliefs, toned down by the light from the typical sky of Mediterranean zones, so, too, in a similar way, the present reality of a city compared to what was originally planned or the writing of a novel with respect to the initial plan for the work. And in the same way that our hiker, even equipped with a detailed topographical map, will confirm the degree to which scaling the heights differs from simply reading the map, so, in the same way, on reading a work of fiction we discover aspects not only unforeseen by the author himself but also unsuspected, completely unrelated to his plans. This is true not only because whatever the author has proposed for himself to write encloses meanings not proposed, and so ends up reflected in the work, but, also, because reading a book is like underlining it with a pencil, like pointing out, marking with signs and even adding comments in the margins, not so much about what is important in the text itself, as much as about what is important for us, a motive that explains why we hate to lend out books we've annotated because of how much our privacy can be affected. Reading without underlining leaves no material traces, but the assumptions about the operation to which we give ourselves continue to be the same. Like with a landscape: everything is there, but recognizing it takes time.

The ambiguity of the work of fiction, the darkness which presides over its origins and its final result along with the interpretation of that result, a darkness consubstantial with the light that liberates and without whose simultaneous presence the creative process would be unfeasible. Because just as thinking is hardly a purely rational activity, given that we think with our whole body—for me preferably with the feet—and that idea which comes to us in a flash, without our knowing why, responds to a coherence which has very little to do with reason, so, the reader of a work of fiction always finds a series of meanings whose presence the author might be unable to explain, assuming that he would have even noticed their presence at all, for however much he might have believed he'd thought of everything, in so far as what comprises the novel's plan, from the guidelines which inform it to the smallest details of its realization, weighed word by word. And what is valid regarding the operation of reading is also true, needless to say, with respect to the process of writing it. The development of such a process, must not be referred to, definitively, as the author's desire, or the fact that the author had a desire to write, but that the author has written, deliberately or not, as if impelled by something without knowing perfectly why, as a demand of the work's very dynamic, almost as if, following the dictate of the narrative material, his role in that work was none other than that of a fundamentally instrumental element. But if the reader projects himself upon the novel he reads as upon a reflecting surface, must not those components of the novel which, when the writer writes, seem to impose themselves upon him from without, be, in a similar way, projections of himself?

Consequently, the work has a point toward which author and reader converge, a zone in which their respective attitudes are reflected. Thus the difficulty involved in transferring that work to another form of expression, a plastic representation that illustrates the text, for example, or perhaps a cinematographic adaptation of that text, a difficulty made all the greater given the depth to which the narrative material is found incarnate in the language, however untranslatable it might be, for that reason, into other languages. The frustration that the author experiences facing that objectification of a work that he does not recognize as his own, comparable to the experience of that spectator who was previously a reader, who already knew the work, facing that concrete and objective representation that he had imagined to be different. It happens like a synopsis, with a summary of the work and other forms of excerpts, necessarily incomplete, limited and unfocused to the degree to which the narrative material is not capable of being reduced either, insofar as what is expressed with certain words cannot be expressed with other words or with fewer words without the resulting image suffering from such mutilations.

At first, therefore, the final key to a work lies with the author and the final key to the author is found within the work. But only at first, given that from the moment the work is objectified, when it acquires a reader, and when this reader projects themself into the work as the author did before, the true key to the phenomenon that generates the work of fiction resides, not in any of the elements that make up the process, but in the relationship that links them together. And this relationship is maintained although its content changes over time, although the appreciation of the work, generally guided by that dominating idea about the book's nature established by literary criticism and whose mechanical reiteration ends up becoming a commonplace, tends to be modified, although a new reader, a new pair of eyes, supposes each time a new reading. Because what is not subject to any change is the structure of the relationship existing between the elements that compose it, the role that each one of them, within such a structure, plays in relation to the other two. Neither does the author, ultimately, disappear when he dies, persisting as his presence in the work persists, in the shadowy zones of the book as well as in the luminous ones. Is there anything accidental in the composition of *Las Meninas*? In the fact that the artist was integrated into the painting in the act of painting and in that spectator whose virtual image the mirror in the background offers to us, the real image, that of the king and queen, remaining, as a consequence, outside the canvas, along with that of anyone who, like the monarchs, contemplates it, the image of each one of the silent spectators that cluster together in the green gloom of the Prado?

How many times, as a child, had I been told that the final explanation for something is always found outside of that something, and like that person who acts, moved by powers he believes superior to his own, so can a god be, in its time, the simple creature of a god greater than him, whose existence he is unaware of? Those thoughts occurred to me one afternoon, at the edge of a pond, while some ways off my pals were playing war: the possibility that just as that round pond reflected my image against the sunny skies just like the pupil of an eye, my own pupil turned out to be, in a similar way, the very image of the universe; if any single cell in my eye, a simple cell, did not really contain those reflected heavens, and the planets, stars, and galaxies that those heavens enclosed in their pale blue, just as the heavens of other galaxies, including the ones which, owing to their great distance, were not even visible or measurable from any of them; and if I, the boy who was contemplating the heavens reflected in a pond, if I, and with me those reflected heavens and their planets, stars, and galaxies, if we might not constitute without knowing it an insignificant cell in the eye of an inconceivably greater boy, a boy just like me in that moment, a boy who, like me, found himself contemplating the reflection of his own image against the sunny sky in the waters of a pond. And if, like the origin of that cell, the one in my eye, the one in his eye, that birth produced by parthenogenesis in a certain moment, like that primogenial instant and its subsequent expansion, the end of its existence was not the result of a small traumatic accident, a coincidental and unimportant accident, that contusion in an eye which one of my playmates accidentally caused to another who was hit by the ball or struck by a stone while playing, without more consequence than a brief interruption of the game and the application, as a compress, of a handkerchief soaked in the water of the pond, before resuming it with renewed energy; and if this traumatic incident that puts an end to the life of the cell, like a closing parenthesis, symmetrical and contrapuntal to the one that opened in the instant when the cell was formed as an autonomous entity, the very trauma of what it is as it bursts into what it is not, if this incident, we were saying, that for the boy who got hit by the stone in an insignificant trauma that is soon forgotten, if this incident must not mean the final cataclysm of a whole universe, the culmination of myriad of centuries of light that comes from the slow cooling of the stars, the loss of their rotation, the rupture of the balance that sustains them, barely a fraction of a second for our infinitely superior child belonging to an unimaginably larger world, all powerful while at the same time defenseless against the other boy who contemplates himself against the skies reflected in the pond to the extent that they are both mutually unaware of each other, the one and the other consecutive elements, on an infinitely different scale, of an indefinite series of boys who contemplate each other against the still sunny afternoon sky reflected in a pond. Keeping in mind also that it's not only about the eye of the boy who thinks these thoughts to himself while he gazes at himself in the waters of a pupil-shaped pond; it's also a boy's eye bruised by a thrown stone, and the eye of the boy who, perhaps with an unconfessed malice, took careful aim at him before throwing the stone, as well as the eyes of that solitary traveler who from the highway contemplates the vicissitudes of their play, and even the eyes of a couple driving around in their car as they contemplate the love that unites them, heading back to the city after a day in the country.

Likely sequel to these considerations might be my habitual resistance to take for granted the most fashionable explanation about another kind of trauma, those of a psychic character, that manic tendency, still dominant, to connect them to some reprehensible adult behavior witnessed during childhood—lies, adultery, murders—as if morally neutral acts were less likely to cause a trauma in someone who, like the little boy, is incapable of grasping, not only its moral quality but also its meaning. Similarly, closely associated with that childhood dreaminess, my plan for a novel, a project developed in a parallel fashion to my work as an architect, practically since I left the university. The possible title that came to me later, in Rosas: *La Ciudad Ideal*, The Ideal City. A title that makes reference not so much to the content as the impression made on me by the engraving of the same name which I sometimes saw there, and which I think I have already mentioned above. And the fact is, like the print of *La Ciudad Ideal* for whoever contemplates it, the work of fiction must also be capable of awakening in the reader, whether or not they are conscious of what's happening, the most recondite suggestions.

The importance of knowing how to make the central themes of a work of fiction appear, seems at first glance, less important or marginal with respect to what constitutes the principal flow of the work. Take, for example, *Contre Sainte-Beuve*: just as Proust judges it opportune to use an ostensible essay to provide us with the keys to his aesthetic, the adequate method for putting it into practice—exactly the opposite of Saint-Beuve—and even his models, writers whom, like Virgil for Dante, he had taken as guides on his peculiar recherché pursuit—Nerval or the dreaminess, Baudelaire and his hells, Balzac or the recreation of reality—so, in a similar way, we can affirm that a prefiguration of this kind, valuable and complementary, is no more valuable than one capable of being an auspicious postfiguration that sheds light on certain aspects of a work that initially seemed only anodyne, a mere formality or preparatory setting for the central themes of the work which, thanks only to this recovery realized through the postfiguration, are revealed in all their significant value, in a similar way to how the face of a certain person whom we bump into when we go out, an unknown face that we're not seeing for the first time, will only become important and meaningful when we identify it with the face of one of the people carrying out the kidnapping we find ourselves mixed up in, and what at first seemed nothing more than an irrelevant coincidence turns out to be a perfection of synchronous calculation and performance. In other words: prefiguration and postfiguration as variants of one and the same process.

Imagine the application of this process to the very structure of the work. It's said that the dying person's last thought, even if it lasts only a few seconds, resembles one of those castles of fireworks in which each stage ignites a new stage, each time higher, each time wider. Well then: let's imagine a work like that, in which, from each one of its parts surge others that in turn generate others and others, in an ever more vast unfolding. This was my original idea for my projected work, an idea that did not take long to complete and define until becoming solidified into what it is now, the projection of a work composed of various books articulated according to the following scheme: starting with Story A, which presents itself to the reader as a finished whole, explore the real boundaries of Story B, the author of Story A, considering it exclusively from without, as a character seen by other characters: next, get closer to the origins of Story A, to the process of the work's gestation, the notes taken, the previous writings, if possible in the context in which they were written—daily reality, dreams, etcetera—in order to conclude, finally, with a reconstruction of the life of Story B. Meaning: include the author in the work and, with the author, the time, the time that the work's development gives back to the author. Thinking, for example, about cathedrals, the rigorous plans which the practical work first had to follow, the modifications demanded by the passing of time, the unforeseen ornamental details which, over the years, some uncontrollable sculptor introduces into the reliefs of the capitals and the gargoyles, the carvings in the chancel, his hand guided, perhaps, more by the devil than any god. And given the fact that nowadays the architect's role is to do what during millennia was not needed at all from the architect, now that the architect tries to imitate what was never before done by architects, meaning, to design the house where the people lived according to their needs, and the architect is not capable of achieving what in olden times was the work, at best, of a master builder, now that the architect has been left without a role because the architecture itself is what lacks a role, this building project has had, for me, all these years, a clear compensatory value.

I don't mean, when I talk about the author's presence in the work, what is capable of being reflected in the structure itself of that work, a structure that, as it joins the work into a whole, must be understood as a projection of what the author is, with his lights and shadows, in the same way that the print of *La Ciudad Ideal* is, primarily, the blueprint of its author's mind, or that a cathedral's organization tries to be, in its structure, a visible representation par excellence of the Creator. Nor that other presence, more surreptitious, that involves it—ambushed in its characters, diluted in them—in the work's argument, and which a certain, determined kind of critic so enjoys finding traces of: that simultaneously sublime and repulsive adolescent that I might have wanted to be, that man who would like to seem what he is, that scolding old man, whom he possibly hates, without even knowing it, to the degree that he seems to resemble him. No: I mean the irrefutable presence of the author in the act of writing the work, subject to the influences that swoop down upon him in this precise moment, to the apparent chance that leads him to introduce new, unforeseen elements into the initial plan, perhaps because the very dynamic of the work demands it, perhaps because of the suggestions that dynamic triggers beneath the levels of his awareness—the mischief of our crafty sculptor as he picks away at the stone of the capitals—perhaps as a response to an incitement from the world at large, the world which our author treads in the moment of writing the work, imposition not from the text but from the context. Namely: the author's thought subjected to the time of the work, to the time its realization requires and which, even without being visible in the final product, even if it's not reflected in its pages, decisively conditions the result for the same reason that its course is necessary, not so much as a vehicle of apparently coincidental variants and modifications as a period of maturation of the initial project and of all that that potentially—as the seed the tree—contained; that flow of time that is made perceptible when the note that we had foreseen develops, by the mere fact of being materialized in a text, is not only developed but is enriched and defined with new and unsuspected illuminating accuracy, mature fruit of that brief note that, almost without knowing how, came to our head the same as that cotton seed borne on the wind from a distant tree. To include the context in the text, the author as present among the characters as the reader, and like them involved, one and the other, in the plot, a reader who knows the author as well as what the author writes and who reads within the work what all readers will then read outside of it, similar, in his virtual equivalence to the real reader, to those images that appear reflected in the mirror in the depths of the painting, contemplating the artist, who, in turn, his palette and paintbrush raised, contemplates them from a secondary plane.

Appreciating the instant as an illusory fix on the course of time, on that flow of time: a photograph taken of the atomic mushroom cloud, different from all the others taken before it or that will follow in a simple fraction of a second, coagulation of a process for whoever contemplates the photo, which, considered from the hypothetical point of view of an observer situated above the very top of the cloud, would suppose an unrepeatable landscape of peaks and chasms and resounding eternities. The subjectivity of space no less than that of time, given how they both depend on a display of motion. Thus, in the work of fiction, the course of time, no less than the movement in space, can only be resolved—because a simple formulation of that course, of that movement, is only that: a formulation—by means of the language, a language that is always more, much more, than mere formal jargon. Language is not, indeed, an autonomous code of neutral symbols that permits one to carry out operations similar to the ones that can be performed with figures, by their very nature irreproachable; language constitutes a significative as well as formal mesh, a framework of symbols that, more or less rich, better or worse articulated, is found entirely, as a whole, in each one of us, and the writer is a writer insofar as what he has written reilluminates in each reader the structure of that mesh, in the way that he stretches it and gives it tension, intensity, and significative polyvalence. The inanity of all attempts to reduce the interest of a work to its linguistic interest from a purely formal perspective, puns, wordplay, etcetera: making what is in itself only material seem the most subtle aspect of the work. A role similar to blank white paper: a theme to allow certain epigones to philosophize like babies who kick and fuss belly up, kicks that only in their imagination become inspired feints; something that lacks sense for the novelist although it might only be a question of quantity, with as many blank pages as he keeps in his writing desk, spaces the words tend to invade, perhaps spontaneously, the way dreams invade the one who sleeps. Empty space that does not even exist except as an interval, like the screen that, curtains still not fully drawn back, is immediately filled with the first images, so too the words seem to blossom from the paper already laid flat on the desk, our author trying to keep up with them, as fast as that host who sees each and every one of the guests appear at the banquet he's celebrating, and even a few who've not been invited.

Evidence? The fact that gathering up the papers and fountain pen from the desk does not match that moment when the lights come up in the cinema and the people start standing up from their seats; the fact of putting these implements away doesn't signify being finished, the materials that one has worked on, or must work on, remain, continue surrounding us like friendly figures, not even necessarily friends, perhaps still grim or even menacing, as if in search of revenge, while, strolling with growing sympathy for the idea of abandoning all this, the room, the inn, Gorgs, Vilasacra, this messy late autumn landscape, still lacking the serenity that the labors of pruning and tilling will grant it all winter long. I begin to miss the invariable presence of the marine horizon, that shifting blue of Port de la Selva that diminishes, but does not suppress, the importance of the effects, on gloomy occasions, of a seasonal change. If I used to need this to think, now I need that to think about this. The remoteness, the perspective that remoteness gives.

Evidence that is also an objective: *La Ciudad Ideal*, the work in progress.

VI

NORTHWARD, PORT DE LA SELVA.

To the south, Rosas, to the east, Cadaqués: a town for each one of the maritime fronts that flank the Cabo Creus or Cruces or Corazones or whatever it was originally called in its early days. And to the west, terra firma inland? A plain with salt marshes, a blind, overgrown, and puddled landscape, always seemingly soaked by recent rain, that bit by bit gives way to cultivated fields, small towns, the snowy Pyrenees in the distance. Among the towns, ever curious, Vilasacra, a Vilasacra that has, of course, nothing to do with Margarita.

It's also curious to observe to what point el Cabo, the Cape, its coasts and its towns, summarize certain aspects of my life, to what point that summary, considered as an itinerary, follows the shape of the Cape. Port de la Selva corresponds to the summers of early childhood, that period of time about which I don't remember anything. Rosas is Margarita, the scene of our great escapades, chosen for the reason that, unlike what happened to us in Cadaqués, nobody knew us there. And Cadaqués turns out to be, very much, the place most linked to Rosa, more than Barcelona itself for example, in the same way that I associate Margarita more with Rosas than with Paris. An itinerary, in short, that follows a counterclockwise direction, like a screw that is unscrewed in order to lift or open something, like the water that swirls away down the drain. And with a particular detail: the open area between Port de la Selva and Rosas, the land that stretches westward, an area that I don't associate with anything specific and which, within the cycle, could correspond to that period of latency that develops between early childhood and adult age, the segment that completes the circle. My house in Port de la Selva sits quite close to the house my parents used to rent when we were children, shortly before the Civil War. Better yet: near the site where the house stood, since it was torn down some years ago and replaced by a building with dreary white balconies used for hanging out bathing suits to dry. My present house is small and nondescript, characteristics that have doubtless helped spare it from demolition, with views that could not possibly be better, as well as renovations in the style of a fisherman's house. At first, three or four years ago, when being tired of so much time in Cadaqués impelled me to remodel it, Rosa didn't like it at all. With that emotional vehemence characteristic of some women, that can make them react in one way just as much as in the opposite, she must have seen our leaving Cadaqués as the symbol of my breaking up with her, with our past together, and the eventual start of a new life with another woman; later she must have thought that this new house could also constitute the ideal frame for a new basis of our relations, a kind of rebirth, and she changed her mind, always within that interpretive symbolism peculiar to her.

One of Rosa's quirks? Not by a long shot. It's not even a specifically feminine propensity, though it's true that it tends to be more noticeable in women. It's simply a matter of that vexatious complexity that emotional reactions hide, and which one feels like lifting the lid to expose: separate the thing, what the thing is, from the symbolic value attributed to it, rummage around in the reasons for why we like or dislike something, qualify the modalities of those tastes against those which we're told cannot be disputed, investigate the reasons for that confidence, for that necessity about which there can be no dispute, about which nobody investigates anything, clear and transparent as everything is. The cynical and comforting hook of the trivial explanations based on the capricious character of the taste, the fatigue that things produce in the long run, etcetera: in the course of an erotic adventure, for example, that first news of the unraveling that will sooner or later end up introducing itself, that first symptom that can be anything, a harsh or stupid laugh, some peevish, tasteless phrase, an inopportune word, an expression, a gesture, simply noticing—after sharing a bed and a bathroom, after sharing everything—that the curve of the other's ass is sagging slightly, something that will not exactly serve as an incentive for ardor in the next carnal embrace and, in general terms, supposes including the start of a still insignificant but already irreversible distancing. Options, shifts in taste, in attitudes, in conduct, easier to describe than to explain, unless returning to the coincidence, the fortuitous event, the significance that the very clearest thing sometimes covers, the event that appears to be the most unimportant. To see in my relationship with Margarita, for example, the fruit of a magnificent coincidence, the avatars of a process unchained by an occasional outing with some mutual friends in Paris, a get together whose normality only made the consequences more unusual, little less unforeseeable than in the case of an allergic reaction; as if other, similar encounters she and I had been able to have had delivered us similar consequences; as if, having found ourselves in other circumstances, the result would not have been the same; as if, if we'd not met, the both of us would not have arranged them in order to connect with the person who would fulfill the same function that each one of us fulfilled for the other in our relations; as if, in the allergic reactions themselves, our ignorance of their origins authorized us to discard beforehand a buried coherence which at first sight is only an imponderable one, unraveling the underlying process beneath the episodic manifestation, the possible relationship, for example, between the old tubercular lesion treated at the time with an intense bombardment of antibiotics and the allergy the patient develops over the years to the antibiotics they assimilated with such intensity and which their body now rejects with the same violence.

The importance of what lies behind all that: what we don't wish to know, what we have forgotten, what we dream but end up not remembering, things that don't even seem deserving of our attention or, on the contrary, things whose comprehension is perhaps situated beyond our reach, seeing oneself as one sees others or something along those lines. And this is, however, what brought me here to write about what I don't know, about what I don't remember, following the few clues available to me, that song, that *tonadilla* sung in a movie that we hum to ourselves when walking out of the cinema but then have no way of remembering, although days later we surprise ourselves by starting to hum it again. Or that dream which a few hours later we glimpse as if in gusts, hardly capable of being reconstructed no matter how much we try to clutch its increasingly hazy outlines. My inexplicable jealousy of Rosa: of all the clothing she wore, that thick blue bathrobe of Aunt Magda's she wore around the house for years and years, a robe that we used to take with us when we went to the beach and which, in one way or the other, ended up disappearing when I was still a boy. And now Rosa wrapped herself in it, and I knew that she'd just gone to bed with someone, I don't know exactly who, and I felt jealous. We were on the verandah at Santa Cecilia, immersed in the somewhat ghostly light produced by the sun glancing off the tiles around mid-morning.

It's only a single step from all that to Magda's invocations, but beneath that step there opens an abyss. The objectives can be coincidental; the attitudes—impossible to say which is older—are not. Magda, with her magical practices, summons forces she doesn't know about, and this ignorance tips the scales in favor of those forces. Thus her increasingly strict maniacal rituals, true expiatory sacrifices that she performs throughout the day, capable of becoming her main daily task, and she, insofar as she undertakes them, into a mere officiant of the rite. Keeping in mind the differences that have always separated her from Margarita in terms of her way of living, not only physically, and the attraction that she has always had despite those differences, the joke that Margarita and I used to make about the incestuous character of our relationship must be reconsidered, an erotic predisposition that not for being free of the condemnation that hangs over relationships between siblings, not to mention between parents and children, is more truth than joke: the fascination for the family traits each partner finds in the other, the affinities with one they discover, the most similar to oneself that one has ever seen, hugging the other one almost like hugging yourself. A factor that, far from subtracting weight from any others that concur, tends to highlight them, factors, let's say, like Margarita's behavior, like the influence that behavior has exerted on me, the result of an irritating and at the same time admirable independence of character perfectly comparable to that of the mother whom the child had come to consider as part or extension of himself and who with time is revealed to be progressively refractory, independent about her desires to the point that one fine day she leaves him, abandons him and doesn't reappear, perhaps because she has really left, perhaps because she has died, either alternative equally practical. And, even now, it's this image of Margarita, the errant Margarita, of untamable behavior, stripped of the least sense of fidelity, who ends up imposing, becoming decisive, however many times I seek to characterize certain facets of her personality and, in consequence, my own. And what's more curious: without that supposing, as far as I'm concerned, any greater reproach than what a naughty daughter might deserve, a naughtiness that, as it seems, can even turn out to be amusing. In relation to the message that

Magda thinks she has received, for example: was that photo found in her purse really meant for me? Did that name written on the envelope have something to do with the photo inside? Was I really the Ricardo to whom that envelope was addressed or was it another, a Ricardo whose existence none of us knew about, one final prank by Margarita?

Message or joke on Margarita's part, real ability or suggestion on Magda's part, the consequences, as far as I'm concerned, are the same: the threads followed from that moment on when I accepted the job from Magda have ended up twining together into a real plot. Now it becomes easy to imagine that would have happened no matter what, no matter which threads were chosen, given that, if she had chosen them, it was precisely because, even if she wasn't aware of it, they were loose threads in the plot; but I only know this now, not then. Ultimately, unraveling the hidden meaning of the photo was, if not a pretext, then simply an access point to a meaning whose scope is far more vast. Thus these notes, my decision to enter into that field by writing, closely trailing the words like Theseus groping his way along Ariadne's thread. There are unforeseeable experiences of development and this had every indication of being one, an almost festive outing, one of those excursions by boat and with a good sea, capable of unfolding in directions very different from those projected, a crossing that stretches out not only in time and unfolds in episodes and episodes, each time more unusual, but which might end in shipwreck, one of those shipwrecks which usually only our hero survives, an adventure, finally, that seems only a projection of the inner adventure through which our hero comes to understand himself through the world, while understanding that world through himself.

The sensation of me moving in a truly new environment, in the uncertain reality of a second life, refractory replica of the first one, as I went about transferring onto paper the experiences gathered here, a life superimposed onto the one I had led up to that moment, but not completely identical, deformed in a similar way to those photographic compositions that, starting, for example, with a landscape taken in springtime, offer us the view of this same landscape as it must be in wintertime, the naked boughs, the frozen puddles and, eventually, even the silent snow, or, starting with the portrait of a man, the portrait of that same man when he's old. Seeing Magda as I hadn't known how to see her—even for all that and having impressed me enormously—when she called me to talk to me about Margarita's message: her gloomy face, her dark, gloomy eyes, while, brushing back a strand of hair, she removed her sunglasses. That woman was no longer the Magda with whom I'd had such a close relationship in my university days, who had completely changed the character of my relationship with Margarita and made more stormy, if possible, my entente with Rosa; a Magda whose image, despite the years passed by since then and knowing us both to be older now, she preserved from any intrusion, above vicissitudes and events, beyond the rectifications imposed or self-imposed on our respective lives. It wasn't a question that she was now fifteen or eighteen years older, nor the changes which that implied; it was the fact that she was now somebody else. A fact that only dawned on me while writing these notes, here, in my room at the cheap hotel in Gorgs: while writing about our conversation, not while we were talking with each other, while converting our conversation into words, in that moment when the true time of the action coincides with the time of the writing. Just as Margarita was also someone else, not an older or better or worse Margarita, but someone different, a Margarita different from the overall image that came to my mind when I found myself standing before her cadaver, something which I've only realized here, while reading what I had written about that final meeting in the chiaroscuro of a small-town cemetery chapel. Or how Rosa was a different Rosa. Nor how, in consequence, I was not the Ricardo Echave I believed myself to be, all as if that coincidence of times which I've just alluded to, the time of the action and the time of the writing, had permitted me to act, not only about the text, but about the reality of which that text is a referent. A second reality that, as it was being written, acquired an autonomous entity, revealed itself not only as a mere fine tuning or touching up of the first one but as a retrospective illumination of what until then I'd not known how to see. A second reality, ultimately, according to which we were no longer those who we were when we met nor the people who we thought we'd become, all of us, perhaps, more clear, our traits more well defined and, at the same time, stranger, more unknown; figures in movement like the silhouette of a tree that grows over the years, or the outlines of that cloud that expands in a matter of moments, figures whose own evolution, divisible into successive instants, ends up by converting its presence into a presence distinct from the initial one, one and another uniquely linked among themselves by the idea of persistence that is derived from the comparison of each one of those instantaneous ones with the one that precedes it and the one that follows it. An illusory character of the impression of continuity, a continuity based more on the concept of trajectory than on that of journey, on the itinerary of a train schedule, a long-distance route, let's say, than on the concrete contingencies of the route, on the consideration, in fact, of who were the passengers who boarded the wagons at the point of departure and who were the ones who stepped down onto the platform upon arrival.

Finding myself in Gorgs de la Selva, a whole town awaiting the death of the one who was and still is its landlord, gave me, at first, a certain impression of experiencing a situation already lived through. Like school, like the military, like prison. And not only because of that cheap hotel, or this room that I've crossed and recrossed in one direction and another. I refer to my situation here in general, feeling like a student freshly arrived, like a novice who doesn't know the educational institution where he's just matriculated, nor the place where it's located, nor the personality of his future professors and classmates, nor the prevailing customs and verbal peculiarities there; the uncertainty of his first steps, the fear of being the object of more or less irritating jokes, the uncertainty of his initial contacts, his doubts about the people with whom he's striking up friendships, not very convinced that his reports are entirely reliable, or that the teachers are like what he's heard and the habits of the community how they tell him they are, that the kids he's on guard against weren't exactly destined to be his true friends, a case of having struck up a conversation with them before these others; a symptomatic sensation, due to its regressive character, of the low spirits in which I found myself on arriving here, entirely opposite to my current state of mind. The surprise implied by, in such a context, my bumping into Carlos, each of us so far from the environment where we had known each other, from the porch of his house with its view of the Bay of Rosas, the most remote panorama imaginable with respect to that of today, the twelfth of December, all set to depart, that a town like Gorgs can present, the landscape's wintry silhouette no less bleak than that agony of the old man who, like a low lying fog, stretches out and weighs upon all the panicked rooftops.

But the most decisive manifestation of that new environment, the point where that unfolding of reality was made more immediate and tangible, must be centered in Vilasacra. One house superimposing itself upon another, one garden superimposing itself over another, one landscape superimposing itself on another as you entered the house. A Vilasacra that no longer served as a scene for Jaime's death, but that was, neither, the Vilasacra of my early days with Margarita, when, during the off-season, the hotels in Rosas were shuttered. A Vilasacra whose image was unfolding, or rather, was superimposing itself onto another image not yet entirely revealed, but that, as it blossomed from the depths and predominated on the surface, as the sketched lines were becoming defined and precise, it became more and more evident that it belonged, not to Vilasacra, but to Santa Cecilia, a Santa Cecilia that bit by bit was imposing itself on Vilasacra, going through it, overflowing it, pushing it to a diffuse background, everything like what happens with those photos in which, due to some flaw, the film cartridge didn't advance properly and the images appear superimposed so that the photo which, at first glance, seemed predominant—a landscape, for example—ended up being integrated, like a backdrop, into a composition dominated, for example, by the figure of a woman who appears gigantic against that background landscape. A Santa Cecilia that was neither the one of today, that of Joaquín, nor quite the Santa Cecilia of my childhood memories, that of Papa and my aunts and uncles, but rather a Santa Cecilia prior to this, one that sprung from that but also went backward. Because, like a distance that solidifies as we adjust the binoculars, so too the relief acquired by Santa Cecilia from my now useless presence in Vilasacra, a relief that, simultaneously encompassing the detail and the impression of the whole, seemed to focus more on things, the interior or exterior spaces, atemporal in their manifestation, than on the people who over the years had inhabited those spaces, than on the occasional variations imposed by the passing of those people, figures dissolved, perhaps, in that neither-sun-nor-shade of the garden, dissolved within their own outlines, the green laths of the bench, the flowerpots with hydrangeas, the peculiar sandy sparkle of the earth under the shoes. Something similar, in short, to what happens with the setting of a dream, a place that, be it familiar to us or not, we know what it's like, that it's the way it is and that's all, with the particularity that we frequently remember the place and the scene better than the events that occurred there. A repetitive impression, similar, in its turn, to what certain actions produce, certain gestures, pacing back and forth in a prison cell for example, that suddenly gives us the feeling of being the things that we have always been doing, the closed spaces of the prison transposed, one would swear, to the interiors and subterranean spaces of our own mind.

As I went into the house, the vestibule, stairs, sitting rooms, bedrooms, all just as it always had been, without a hint of those ceilings that cover over vaults and stuccos, the now demolished dividing walls intact, the bathrooms installed in various rooms nonexistent, the inhospitable sitting room—something between a monastery refectory and a discotheque—into which the cellar was transformed, the supposedly distinctive bedroom sets crammed tight into the attics, environs that not even a single one of its old denizens would be capable of recognizing except by sense of smell, the specific atmosphere of each place, that persistent smell of Aunt Pepita that the sitting room has always retained, her caged canaries, her medicines, her pearl gray shawls, Papa, and Uncle Rodrigo as if awaiting her arrival, her presence in the chaise lounge on the verandah, in order to resume their daily morning disputes: enough to find a topic, or rather, choose from among the habitual themes the one most likely to be connected with the news of the day, a purely formulaic pretext, the news no less than the topic, in order to arrive to what's really important, the confrontation. Perhaps because Uncle Rodrigo's natural irreverence and pesky sense of humor act as a catalyst, as a calculated provocation, perhaps because such an attitude was less a trigger than an advance defensive action, what's certain is that Papa and Aunt Pepita invariably squared off against each other according to a scheme that was perhaps preferred by all, Aunt Pepita limiting herself to ignoring certain ironies, the same as she ignored the oaths of the trap driver when we were going to mMass or the horse's undisguisable defecations each time that, in full trot, the animal raised its tail, an attitude which, at that time, and with an intuitive lucidity truly improper even in a child, I related insidiously with its refusal to recognize the economic decline in which it was living, to compensate for it with the rigors of a meticulous safeguarding of appearances. The antagonistic roles of Papa and Uncle Rodrigo were maintained anew as if by routine each summer, even though there was no doubt that the absence of Aunt Pepita had taken away part of the stimulus, both of them focused more on the variety of their diets at lunchtime—boiled and spicy, respectively—and in pointing out the multiple differences that, like symbols, separated them, so extreme as to render all controversy unnecessary. Otherwise, each one occupied the same chair he'd always sat in, and when Uncle Rodrigo began to stop going to Santa Cecilia, Papa continued sitting on the verandah around the same hour as before, alone, planted sideways in the armchair as usual, the same as if he were practicing, just as if Uncle Rodrigo were going to return some day. Sometimes, certainly because he lacked someone to talk to, he fell asleep there, and it was precisely there, on the verandah, where he suddenly awoke and, while he gathered up the scattered pages of the newspaper, said that he didn't feel too well, son, maybe the fish yesterday wasn't quite fresh. A week after he started feeling bad, he had to be convinced that he should let the doctor have a look at him. He stubbornly insisted that it must be none other than Doctor Moix, his lifelong physician, in whom he had great trust, and the problem wasn't that Doctor Moix had died several years earlier, but that he didn't remember that he'd died; but by then we were already in Barcelona. In Santa Cecilia, the people were disappearing like the shapes of things when night falls; there remained the rooms, their deceitful objectivity.

I've frequently wondered which room in Santa Celilia was my parents'. The one we used to call grandpa's, a room just off the verandah that I've always seen turned into a little sitting room? Quite likely; the only sure thing is that, with my mother dead, Papa didn't want to keep sleeping in the bedroom they had shared, and he went back, I suppose, to sleeping in his single room. Nor do I know which was my mother's room in Vilasacra, when she was young, before getting married, when the property was still an undivided parcel shared by all the cousins, including Margarita's father, the Red, the reprobate, and his two younger sisters, erased like him from the family memory for their innumerable challenges to morality, and, like him, punished even in this life, dead in the prime of youth, one from consumption, and the other decapitated in an accident similar to Isadora Duncan's. The same room, perhaps, that Margarita later occupied? There, the grandparents' room had gone back to being used by anybody; it was there at the end of the hallway, shadowing it more than illuminating it with those translucent windows in the door.

A long, bare hallway, with rooms on either side, evenly spaced. The bedrooms—except the one at the end, which I've never seen—are rather small, all furnished in the same sober style, something that accentuates, no doubt deliberately, its conventional air. The photograph must have been taken from the hallway, the doorframe practically matching up with the edges of the picture: an impersonal room, lacking any specifically feminine traits, and none of the decorative elements—postcards, clippings, an air rifle—that boys typically use to affirm their personality appear there either. Only the character of some books and magazines on the shelf—not visible in the photo—as well as a black silk sleeping mask and an empty bouquet vase, atop the night table, outside the field of vision—made one think that it was a young girl's room; the enormous sea snail shell, also next to the headboard, offered no further clarification. The framed photo only includes part of the bed, the desk, the bookshelf, a chair, and the window. The window looked out onto the garden and, whether or not it was deliberate, the only area of the photo correctly in focus was precisely that, the foliage. The dry fronds moved by that breeze that arises at dusk, with the last sunlight; the sound like rain which that breeze raises, crackling leaves from oaks, chestnuts, plane trees, in contrast, like the last bastion, with the naked branches of the poplars or the lime trees, their leaves now falling in a soft, pale carpet. The air that moves the golden foliage and raises the sharp yew trees' hackles, an air that will die down as the leaves lose their golden color and the green of the yew trees turns black, as the light recedes the way that life slips out of a dying body.

[THE OLD MAN]

VII

Humanity gets progressively stupider by virtue of the growing ignorance that atrophies man's intellectual faculties. The problem comes from afar and, any desire to trace it back to its root cause would inevitably lead one to the very origin of the word philosophy, invented in an evil hour by those nefarious lovers of wisdom, who would have done better to leave in peace whatever's not capable of being loved or hated because, by definition, given that we don't possess wisdom, we don't know what it is; insofar as wisdom is not something that is offered to our perceptions, like the naked body of a woman or the plastic representation of a woman or any other thing, except, on the contrary, like a closed book whose contents we don't know or like a road that must be traveled, a case of being interested in knowing where it leads, if, in fact, it really does lead somewhere. Because, and what if wisdom were not at the same time goodness and beauty as people once seemed to take for granted? If wisdom supposed, on the contrary, horror, knowledge of all the knowable horror? Would they go on loving it? Or had they not even considered such a disagreeable contingency? Like a woman whom we fold in our arms only to realize that she's mummified and hollow.

The only thinkers deserving of such a name are the pre-Socratics and, especially, Pythagoras; they even sensed the traces of a vanished wisdom, the remains of the shipwreck. Only that ignorance which I've now mentioned justifies them being known by the generic name of natural philosophers, given that, luckily for them, not even the nature in question has anything to do with what is understood as such, not only in the common sense but in the scientific one as well. The appearance of that product of the imagination called Socrates, was enough, however, for the thoughts of those men to survive prehistory and for imbecility to be established by the name of philosophy. Aristotle established the grammatical rules of this new form of imbecility, but it's principally after Descartes when the philosophical schools begin to proliferate and expand, to fragment and branch out into tendencies and counter-tendencies, and for philosophers and more philosophers to emerge like little gremlins—the German responsibility for their Nibelungs' involvement in this is incalculable—not only without the very least blush but also with pride, and with greater originality in their concepts and systems. Considered as a whole, this sum of theories constitutes a compilation of curiosities that in their time tried to explain the world, halfway between every storyteller's hunger for fame and the manic convictions of a disturbed mind.

The history of philosophy is, therefore, the history of human imbecility, that culminates in the very initiative of organizing the various materials of which a history avails itself, in chronological order, articulating them according to certain patterns of affinity, an enterprise that can yield no other results than those that it invariably gives: a kind of anthology of occurrences and extravagances that compete with each other to try and stumble upon some idea about the world that sounds fresh. The equivalent of one of those museums or picture galleries where, in the short time that it takes to stroll through the various rooms, wherein the visitor is permitted to contemplate the great works that man's genius has created over the course of millennia, the time no less fictitious than the space in which those orphaned works, stripped of all context, are grouped together. There resides, however, one of the principal distinctions between an art museum and a history of philosophy, among the works exhibited in the former and the blithering nonsense collected in the latter: paintings, although wrested from their own destiny, can retain a certain meaning; the follies collected by the author of any one of our philosophy manuals, however, not only remain follies, but the fact that such character is usually increased by accumulation and contrast, by the fact of their juxtaposition, simultaneously excluding and complementing one another in their common nonsense, crazy ideas which, if somehow ever accepted by someone, thus exposed, superimposing their respective reflections upon one another, as in the glass of a display case, lose such possibility, their insubstantial nature enhanced to the maximum as a result. But between the philosophy book and the museum there is yet another difference, one more irrelevant, if possible: the one derived from relating the concept of chronological succession to the concept of progress, with the idea that thought is perfected with the passage of time in the same way that the pebbles in a river are ever more smoothed and polished the more they roll and tumble; as if, marked out by certain domineering peaks of knowledge, man's ideas, initially obtuse, rough, or rudimentary, would have continued evolving toward superior forms of expression, as is well demonstrated, incidentally, by the book we hold in our hands, both a conclusion and summary of that positive evolution of human knowledge.

Any variation or improvement on such stupid remarks tends to be an intellectual attitude that is also quite common nowadays: the idea that scientific development has rendered philosophy superfluous, if not unfeasible; that, as far as pure speculation goes, philosophy seems to belong more to the ages when man's relationship with the world he inhabits was based more on conjecture than verification or practice, some museum piece or relic from other times. As if the sciences—physics, chemistry, mathematics, biology, economics, all of them—have also followed an ascendent line, as if that illusory upward movement were not the product of a continuous rectification of older errors held to be truths, intended truths that, in their turn, came to replace previous assertions or interpretations held in their moment to be correct, and so on, a small mountain of small cadavers that must be climbed each time, this action of climbing up accounting for such an impression of ascensional movement. What's more: it's as if that apparent ascensional movement affected not only the theoretical aspect of this or that hard science, but also, unfortunately, its practical verification, the effects of that verification on reality, and science, as if it didn't consist substantially in applying fixes to the natural catastrophes caused by earlier solutions, the natural disasters that result from applying to reality the principles of science in its most diverse manifestations. Something like having to run and run because with each step we take we spoil the soil beneath our feet, because to stop running would mean falling into the abysses we leave open behind us.

I'm an autodidact; everything I know, I've learned on my own. I've had no formal education, and as far as knowledge acquired from books is concerned, I've never depended on any other guide or criteria than my own instincts. A system, to my modest understanding, that only boasts advantages, from the rigor and discipline which, in such circumstances, are consubstantial with intellectual exercise, to the safeguard that confers an advantage over all kinds of fatal influences, far from the prejudices, envy, and meanness that prevail in the little intellectual world, obfuscating the understanding of all those who thrive there. Nor have I traveled; even when, for some reason, I've had to go to Barcelona, I've always managed to return to my town before nighttime.

Long trips have never attracted me; I've got neither the time nor the belief that traveling would have brought me anything new; the truth remains the truth here and in Cochinchina. As a consequence, as may be supposed, I don't speak other languages; I know the works of the great thinkers exclusively through translations, in editions from Austral or Bergua. In this way, neither the best nor the worst handling of a tongue can influence my judgement about its conceptual richness, being as they are all measured by the same yardstick. What I mean by that is that when I talk about the growing ignorance that afflicts humanity, I do it with full knowledge and awareness, from a solid position of mastery.

On the other hand, it's appropriate to point out that when I speak of the degradation of knowledge, of the continual decrease in human knowledge, I don't do so thinking only about the supposed advances in science or philosophical speculations; this constitutes nothing more than a small part of the problem, the tip of the iceberg. The truly serious thing about the phenomenon is its spreading to every social stratum, its disorderly proliferation, its avalanche of repercussions, as if from a raging epidemic. Not only do the rich and powerful, but also—and this is the serious part—the most humble, gradually reduce the extent of their knowledge, consequently diminishing their mental capacity, not only in the intellectual realm the emotional, each new generation stupider, clumsier, and duller. As far as the countryside, to give one example: how is today's farmer less knowledgeable than his counterpart from years ago? What more does he know? How to drive a tractor, a few different brands of fertilizers, herbicides, etcetera: that's the extent of his new knowledge. What he doesn't know, however, is almost impossible to sum up and even more difficult to evaluate: from the names of the plants that grow on the mountain, as well as their uses, to the influence of the phases of the moon on the farm work, from the knowledge of the specific peculiarities of each specific piece of land and how to predict changes in the weather. The young farmer believes in knowing numbers, yield per hectare, production in tons, and he's wrong even in this, because what he doesn't know how to calculate is the depreciation of the instruments and materials he uses, with which he earns much less than he thinks and ends up paying much more than what he feared he would have to pay. What remains of his knowledge if we compare it with what his grandfather or his grandfather's grandfather knew? Fragments impossible to reassemble, shattered jars, from which, as with some garment, it becomes impossible, not only to reassemble anything, but also to guess how to make it, so completely diluted is their ancient capacity for discernment. And such an evil effect, although a reflection, although secondary, is, in its repercussions, more fatal in the long run than the resounding disasters of science, normally rectifiable, beneficial thanks to some new error—not always tragic—that for the moment compensates for or counterbalances it, without any other problem than the wounded self-love of its inventor.

Another enormously regressive factor, however much one tries to completely gloss over it, is what is derived from all those plans for cultural and scientific disclosure in which, apart from ideological differences, the practical totality of the directors of the most advanced countries—and following their tracks, a pack of petty tyrants disposed to eradicate everything of value that remains among their respective, theoretically primitive, peoples—seem determined to see the panacea for all the evils that affect humanity: teach the people, give them culture, this is the great solution conceived of by the most enlightened brains of our time; that everyone be cultured, educated, civilized, with their own opinion, meaning, freer, more creative, and, ultimately, happier. Meaning: that while on the one hand the people are exposed to the idea of the need to specialize in something, in some specific field of knowledge, owing to which the very complexity of modern life makes a complete education of the person unviable, the other side insists that every person receive a good general education and be informed about and up to date with the world of today. The necessarily regressive character of such a notion seems obvious to me: it's not only about the reduction that the presumed knowledge suffers as it spreads from one mind to another; it's that such an attempt is even capable of turning a possibly distorted notion of its original concept into a clumsy galimatias, thus placing it on the same plane, at the same level, with what was, from the very first, a real galimatias.

So many times when, during some family gathering, I've mentioned the legacy I plan to bequeath to humanity, those present have immediately imagined that I'm making them the butt of one of my famous jokes. My descendants are so numerous that I don't even know, nor am I interested in knowing, how many or who they are; but, even so, my patrimony is sufficiently large so that there is something for everyone, and that they know. That's why none of my heirs is seriously worried about the possibility of having to share their portion with the rest of humanity, even if it's only because of a practical problem; a procedural problem; in short, a slight shiver upon thinking about international organizations with a humanitarian bent like the Red Cross. And they don't understand either what I'm talking about when I declare that the value of that inheritance is eternal, knowing, as they know from their own experience, the larger a fortune the more easily it's squandered; in this sense, the idea of "eternal" rather soothes them in so far as it seems to support the thesis of the big joke. And the fact is that they think in terms of money, in properties, in material goods, and I'm talking about something else: about the value of the truths gathered here, the fruits of a whole lifetime of experience. Thoughts like those of a Dante, a Milton, a Goethe, truths that will always be truths, things that never grow old. What greater patrimony is available to humanity? The only value that in some way compensates for the growing proliferation of inventions, philosophical speculations, and pseudo-scientific theories, a burden whose weight threatens the precarious balance that keeps the earthly globe in orbit.

Not only my descendants. It's the human being in general, more unwilling every day to understand the deep sense of things. In relation to my fortune, for example: the secret plans made, murmurations chewed over and over in the privacy of their homes, by the heat of the fire, turning it over and over in the choking darkness of the bed. And all because of a remark I made years ago: the one who has gold, I said then, doesn't waste time worrying about the fluctuations in the price of wheat harvests. The result: the secret of my fortune, the cornerstone of my patrimony, as well as the driving force of the accumulative process developed from that point of origin, were satisfactorily explained through one single word: gold; I had found a treasure, and this made it all clear. Their cerebral mechanisms, plugged up no less than their ears, made them understand what they never could have heard: the discovery of a treasure, of some gold that was found, not within me, at the end of the journey begun by my mind, but under the ground, hidden away in some secret place that I had managed to discover. Pascualina was the only person who knew then how to grasp the true meaning of my words. That's how she ended up becoming the only mediator between me and the townspeople.

Nothing more foreseeable than the human being's reaction in the face of life's diverse eventualities. When someone asks Pascualina for an interview with me, for example, they do so convinced that the solution to their case is in my hands, that I will resolve their problem or that I'll cure the illness that afflicts them with an herbal infusion; that's why they come. Meaning: they believe in me to the degree that they're ignorant of the nature of the remedy, to the degree that they don't understand, to the degree that it's magic for them. However, if what I do is give them some advice about something they don't know but think they know, a teaching that doesn't comprise any greater secret than any of my infusions, but that clashes with what they think they know in that respect, it no longer seems to them magic but rather an old man's obsessions, the product of the resistance that elderly people usually manifest toward whatever supposes an innovation. My advice about health, for example, about how to stay in perfect physical and mental shape, my rules for how to achieve balanced nutrition for the body. Thus, they need to forget the refrigerator and avoid whenever possible consuming frozen foods, precooked foods, etcetera. For preserving foods there are only three ideal substances: oils, vinous alcohols, and salt. Among the oils, olive oil is the only one advisable, however people have invented many theories to the contrary. Reject all kinds of meat and other products derived from animals raised on those poisonous compound feeds. The same is true for fruits and vegetables treated with pesticides and weed killers, substances that, besides killing off multitudes of insects and useful parasites, end up sterilizing the earth, obliging one to use ever great quantities of fertilizers that, in turn, only serve to accelerate the process of converting the earth into dead matter. Foods must be considered from a point of view not only nutritive but also prophylactic: with a diet rich in olive oil, honey, lemon juice, and milk, the most common maladies can be avoided: acidity, constipation, colds, etcetera--and some of the most serious ones averted. Substitute, at least once a day, animal proteins for vegetable ones; nothing's better than consuming both at the same time, the famous sausage with white beans that people in these parts enjoy so much. Drink—water drawn directly from the spring is the best of all drinks—exclusively between meals; at mealtime, a glass—two at most—of wine, white if one suffers from stomach problems, white not red, despite what people tend to believe. As far as exercise goes, nothing more stimulating than a stroll around my properties early in the morning, on an empty stomach.

The majority of the knowledge human beings possess has no other basis than the fact that it was taught to them as the truth, and which are held as such until their falsity is proven, the same as the legend of the Three Wise Men for little children. For this reason, in everyday life, men adopt a prudent attitude of skepticism, of which they are not even usually conscious. To the point that they feel sure of something, until my adverse judgment collides with what for them constitutes evidence: then they interpret my criteria as a sign of senility, and this bolsters their principles. You only need to see them when I speak to them about some things, for them incomprehensible, laughing to themselves while they pretend to be following my ideas; I perceive their reaction as if I could hear the quiet pulses of their thoughts, as if I could read it in the smoke that rises from their chimneys while the family cackles with laughter together at dinner time.

So then, let El Moro take comfort in my pessimistic view of the world in opposition to his faith in the future. What optimism can the architect experience who witnesses the demolition of the work he has designed, carried out by the hands of the very men employed in its construction? And what faith in the future can a poor devil like him have, to whom even evil does evil, a faith only justifiable due to the impossibility of his present unhappy condition getting any worse?

It will be argued against me that the great thinkers have always lamented the spiritual misery of the time in which it has befallen them to live, with the crest-fallen faces that characterize the individual and collective comportment of their respective people. An objection that would be valid if we limited ourselves to consider the distance that in one age or another separates or brings into confrontation the spiritual mind and the social body; but one that ceases to be valid if we compare and contrast the global value of one age and another taken as whole. Thus, it is clearly evident that Plato and his characters, just as, prior to Plato, Moses and his, both in relative conflict with the people at large, find themselves thrust into an ascensional phase, the waxing crescent moon of one of those cycles--closer to what was previously understood by age than what is nowadays understood by era--which humanity experiences throughout the millennia; and now we are in the waning phase, if not fully under a new moon.

The high concept in which I include Moses as much as Plato concerns, however, more than their relevance as thinkers, their relevance as novelists. The thinker, like that great tributary that flows into a river, tends toward the anonymity that results from his enriching, with the ample flow he brings, the current of thought to which he belongs in his permanent approach toward the unspeakable. While the novelist, on the contrary, tends to stand out by using all the means at his disposal from the surrounding environment in order to heighten his individuality as much as possible. In this sense, Moses and Plato are not only two great novelists; Moses and Plato are the very model of what every novelist, whether they are conscious of it or not, aspires to accomplish. To convert their principal character into the one and only god, extrapolate it to the point that it's the reader who is in his hands and not the other way around; making of that irascible old man from the Sinai not only the true creator of the book but also of the world; abdicating not only his initial condition of author, but also, reducing his role to that of a mere character, ending by immolating himself in the very pages of the book, the tale of his death a simple accident within a much vaster tale. And Plato, that distinguished narrator who, from the pages of a work of fiction, not content with inventing a Socrates, proscribes all works of fiction within the confines of his republic, thus setting himself up as the privileged and unique fabulist, at the same time within and above the space of the fiction, at the forefront of the new reality he's proposed? Has anyone stopped to survey *The Symposium* as if it were an architectonic construction, to study the narrative structure of that gathering of friends who converse about love the same as they might discuss any old joke, one of those scandals that suddenly becomes the talk of the town?

Novels that in no way seek to imitate reality, that are in no way mimetic, nor offer any insubstantial rejection of all reality, as they so vainly pretend at times; no, none of that: novels that are a metaphor for reality, meaning, that they proceed by analogy, the only way of approaching the proposed goal, a goal that, as in the case of the thinker, is more about the journey than the destination, or rather an objective whose goal is precisely the journey itself, a creative impulse that, at the same time as it reflects itself in the works that it generates, may be the analogous reflection *par excellence* of the creative process. An impulse that is, at the same time, a condemnation to the degree that every creator finds himself inexorably constrained to create, to convert into a kingdom the closed environment that constitutes his prison. Thus comes the attraction for captivity manifested by Moses as much as by Plato, including in their own lives, a reclusion that is not to be understood except as an exterior and visible metaphor of the inner prison that constitutes their dwelling place, that dark landscape that served as the scene of their creative activity, free in it like a night bird in the night. The black fire that led Moses to abandon the Egyptian palaces in order to assume the slavery to which the twelve tribes of Israel found themselves reduced; that incited Plato to sell himself as a slave and, from the lowest stratum of his republic, begin the reorganization of man's life upon the earth; that impelled Aesop, similarly, to pose for the artist holding a heavy book, in order to show us the magical talisman that allows one to soar above the condition of slave.

The root of that creative impulse or, if you prefer, its final design? To figure out the ultimate meaning of that experience which is offered to the child in the form of a banquet, attended by the docile punctuality of the mother's breasts, a banquet whose echoes the adolescent sets out to find in life, which the adult does not despair of finding, and which the old man would like to have found.

What is the worst enemy of a teacher's thinking? Who are those responsible for his degradation and degeneration? His disciples, his followers, his interpreters and protagonists, his imitators, his epigones. As happens with the heirs to dynasties, with the descendants. And in empires. And, in families, with what was their patrimony. Like the suckers growing on trees, those messy shoots that steal greatness from the old trunk. These are the executioners.

What about my descendants? They amount to a considerable number. But none of them bears my name; that dies with me. None of my children were able to give me, for their part, male children, and so today I find myself surrounded by grandchildren and great grandchildren whose names I don't even know, and I've got neither the time nor the desire to learn them. It's better that way. Because, similar to what happens with the portraits of the various kings of a certain dynasty, in the ones where, at a glance you can detect the beginning of the decline, also the mere physical presence of all those people who slink around, there is enough to make one comprehend the luck represented by the fact that, in their regression—toward the original hermaphroditism, it seems—their name is different from mine. What offspring can be expected from the copulation of a grandson or great grandson like that or Roca, or Riera, or whatever his name is, with a wife like the one he's got? It's enough to see her in bed, sleeping obscenely, kept warm by her own swollen belly, guts full of unexpelled gases and liquids from the flaccid volume of her excess weight. And the no-less-indecent way that she wakes up, the problem arising, let's say, each time that they try to get her to go out for a walk; the sensation of being bullied that then possesses her even though they don't rush her, when she realizes they are waiting for her, that, knowing that they're waiting for her, she won't be able to sit on the toilet, nervous as she feels after such a restless night in this goddamned little inn where everyone seems to be in cahoots, the guests that rise early, most of them travelers and commission agents, the plumbing and drains, doors slamming, and then, the maids coming round to clean the rooms, their malicious humming and crooning, their small-town laughter, and so on for hours and hours, in case, by luck, nobody has thought of organizing an outing or any other clamorous little early morning parade, so that, when she comes downstairs to the dining room, the tables are already set for lunch and she has to get all muddled up again with pitiful explanations to justify the breakfast she orders from that boy who looks half retarded.

They imagine that I'm going to die; this has brought them to gather around me. A death which, as if it were a Mass, presents itself to them as some sort of tedious but unavoidable ritual that must come before what constitutes for them the true motive of their presence here: my estate, their share. Not these texts in which my thinking is gathered, a true autobiography of a conceptual character translated into terms of pure thought, the work out of which I make a legacy for humanity. No, none of that: my patrimony, something too important to not speak about in hushed tones. The most curious thing is that, on the other hand and at the same time, they fear that my fortune might be less than I think. The feverish calculations brought on by a night of greedy insomnia! What do they know about what I can think or stop thinking? They think that the definitive route for the highway, as it ends up not crossing my properties, represents a great reversal, an enormous financial loss; that I'm not up to date on matters about the approval of that route which, for some reason, they consider contrary to my interests, to my plans, and they don't even dare to give me what, to their narrow understanding, is for me a piece of bad news. What do they know of my plans, of my intentions? What advantage or benefit do they find in the path of a highway that only represents an easement that mortgages the fate of the adjoining lands? What kind of idea or lack of ideas has been able to lead them to consider me capable of such inanity?

What do they know, not only about me, but about death? They might suppose that I was joking if I told them that the only one who dies is the one who's already dead. That death, like cancer, is an allergic reaction, the ego's response to a negative external stimulus, something that, despite responding to such a stimulus, is rooted in the ego. And, however, like that face we think looks familiar but we don't know why until, days later, we identify it with the face of one of the kidnappers who is driving us at gunpoint, inside a car, to some unknown destination--the face of the one who tied the black blindfold over our eyes--so too death when it appears, to mortals' great surprise.

I don't complain about loneliness. Nor do I celebrate it. Why celebrate something that cannot be any other way, being as it is the result of the insurmountable distance that separates me from my descendants?

There is, indeed, a problem of trust. The fate of my legacy worries me. I record my words onto tapes, but someone has to take on the job of transcribing the contents of those tapes onto paper, of transforming them into written text. And excluding Paulina for obvious reasons, Carlos has struck me as the ideal person, Carlos whatever his name is, the only person among so many relatives surrounding me who deserves my trust. He's not even actually a descendant; he's married to a granddaughter or great granddaughter named Aurora or something like that. But the fact that he's not of my blood, added to other indispensable characteristics I see in him, constitutes a fact that, far from presenting an obstacle, has weighed decisively when it came time to my choice to alight on him.

The thinking expressed here, although occasionally waxing autobiographical, has nothing in common with currently popular confessional books, works whose purpose is implicitly betrayed by the very word confession, the trick of an old fox who, in his recollections from the global perspective of the years he's lived, renovates and rebuilds as he pleases; confessions that, whether openly proclaimed as such, whether furtively camouflaged under the label of any other genre—novel, memoir, notes, epistolary exchange—cloud and embroil, before clarifying, a whole panorama of small transgressions and petty larcenies—asparagus, apples, and things like that––that he reviews, practically scandalized by his own devilries and professed wickedness, a frank and guilty attempt to hide his perverse private reality, in a similar way to how the cosmic projection of all that, the image of the world made from such a scheme, only covers the devoured nature of the universe with a rind of idyllic nature. On the contrary, the texts that gather together my thinking, when found by the shores of a dead sea a few thousand years from now, are destined to be revealed as the missing link in the dominant mindset of their time, while todays' prevailing beliefs will be completely relegated to oblivion. And Carlos will have been my depository.

I'm not blind to the suspicion and mistrust that this has aroused in the rest of my descendants: the contrast between the energetic typing that, as dictated by my voice, will reach them from Carlos's room, and the rude chatter they engage in around the fireplace, stuffed with the hearty dinner, a stew of beans and things like that, the sorts of dishes that inflate your guts with gas, one of those delicacies that inverted, that is, homosexual people used to be so fond of, according, no doubt, to some elemental mechanical movement that transfers the effect of one experience to another kind of experience with similar effects. And that, after having spent the afternoon in the sitting room of the Rectory, as if waiting for Pascualina to lower her guard, the Pascualina who is hated by all for the fact of how incorruptible she is, always putting my tranquility before any other consideration. All infected in their appetites by Señora Riera, given over to cultivating certain physiological pleasures whose gestation and discharge usually takes the place, sooner or later, of strictly physical comforts, capable of spending the whole afternoon roasting chestnuts in the fireplace just to pass the time until dinner, and so, all warmed up, sleepy with indigestion, makes their nights more melancholy, the struggle to free their body next morning all the more exciting.

Today, December 18, has struck me as propitious for starting to make my tape recordings; at night, each night, Carlos will type up what I have recorded during the day. This morning the house was pleasantly peaceful: the bulk of my descendants, children included, have left the house voluntarily, with the excuse of going on some outing, of taking someone's grocer friend—an *épicier*—who dropped by, to the Font de les Delícies, to make him try the bubbling water. All the excursionists were tremendously delighted, stimulated beforehand by the habitual preparations for an outing, the aluminum forks, the vivid colors of the bakelite plates, the thermoses and cold cuts, the wicker baskets. As if it were June and not December; as if the spectral network of the naked poplars, pale, scumbled in the misty air, were really resplendent foliage, now green, now pure sparkling radiance, at the mercy of the breeze; as if there were strawberries and wild violets and fan-shaped ferns, and not stiff grass, scorched by the frost; as if the water were gushing forth diamantine and violent and not from between icicles, falling upon the stones blackened by the frozen moss. *Quelle belle journée!*

VIII

Just as a forest is not simply a countless number of trees, but rather, on the contrary, an autonomous life form, irreducible to the mere sum of the trees that comprise it, since, at the foot of those trees, tangling the ground, is the undergrowth, in intimate relationship with the trunks, simultaneously antagonistic and complementary, and just as above this shadowed undergrowth are the boughs, fighting one another for the light, and below, the silent as well as dark struggle, the roots, like opposing serpents, coiling and uncoiling in their search for the moisture that indicates the vivifying passage of the subterranean waters, so, in a similar way, neither is a town a simple sum of neighbors, nor a family a series of individuals related by various degrees of kinship. And in the same way that by means of the seed, the tree inherits not only its specific characteristics and the ideal form that is its own but, likewise, the behavior that will regulate its future life in the forest, which thus belies that ideal form, subjected as every concrete form finds itself to be to the pressure of the surrounding forms, a behavior that is nothing else than the forest's morality, thus, like the trees, men inherit peculiarities that overtake their individual condition, that concern the humanity of which they form part. Peculiarities which if, on the one hand, are inherited, on the other are degraded and lost. Because, just as the man goes on seeing ailments accumulating upon himself, simultaneously the cause and effect of what they call old age—and whose first symptoms, herniated discs, kidney stones, false teeth, allergies, bleary eyesight, degenerative failures, revealing that it's the whole body that's beginning to feel tired—and just as with man, so do ailments bring down humanity, and as with humanity, so too do they beset the forests. More trees are born, but as the forests are clear-cut and the number of ancient trees is reduced, the remaining ones, despoiled of the cohesion of their prior environs, tend to become singular examples, trees that, even though they become worthy of the admiration of all those who see them because of their majestic girth, even though they end up earning their own name, by which they are popularly known, stand as nothing but rarities, extravagant isolated examples in a landscape to which they are strangers, colossal and to the same degree defenseless. And then, more properly even than men, the great trees die like the gods: imperceptibly.

The farmer lives beset by the innovations that advertising continually offers him, with his dream focused on that urban life he imagines functioning with the impeccable precision of an electric appliance. His mind shaken, disoriented, sooner or later he rethinks the reason for his presence in a place so far removed from the system of life that he intuits, for still not having abandoned that damned little corner where he had the misfortune to be born, for still not having found himself settled into the forward progress of the modern world, a progress whose rhythm he feels himself increasingly separated from. An attitude that contrasts greatly with that of the farmer from earlier times and of his contemporary survivors, what is still understood by the people when they use the word *payés*—a peasant—a sort of human for whom the novelty represented by, for example, the images of interplanetary experiences that he sees on the television while eating his soup, is only one of degree with respect to his ancient beliefs in miracles and witchcraft, simply an additional stimulus in the end to his innate propensity to dementia, as contrary to the idea of wisdom usually imagined of them by the city dweller. But the fact that this figure, nowadays quaint, is disappearing, must not make one think that the countryside disappears with him, that the countryside is in the process of becoming a workshop or factory run by a few electricians. It would be like thinking that, in order to do business one needs ultramodern offices, with a receptionist and a Telex; as if to do business one needed more than a small desk with a small dim lamp in a small room; a room, in other words, like my own office, with a lamp and a desk like the ones in my office. The countryside, after all, is worked with the head, a headset, if possible, atop a good pair of feet.

But for however deep the state of ignorance that has befallen the country peasant these days, greater still, much more so, is the ignorance flaunted by the city dweller who, carried away by an uncontrollable impulse, suddenly feels attracted by the countryside. Those señores who inherit or buy a farm, convinced that, when they find the moment, they, who have ideas and enthusiasm, are going to transform the lands reduced to such a lamentable state by the peasants' routines, rapacity, and stupidity into a modern and lucrative operation. As if the countryside needed their ideas, they who don't even know that not only the animals and plants but also the land itself needs just as much care and attention as people do! One parcel of land is never identical to another, in the same way that one Black person is never the same as another Black, each parcel of land having, as it does, its own personality. Things they'll not even have learned when, already having got their fingers snapped in the trap, having understood at least that the numbers that are added up in the country don't add up, shocked by the real cost of their fantasies of modern efficiency, they abandon the land once again to its fate, from which they should never have tried to save it. But these city aficionados typically let themselves be dragged along by appearances, sent into ecstasies by the sight of a well cultivated farm the same way that a shopkeeper feels ecstatic watching merchandise moving around the port of Rotterdam, ignorant about the fact that if badly managed land yields little, badly managed land can mean—it has meant this for many people—ruin in so far as the perfection of the cultivation exceeds the market value of the crop. Because like that stock market speculator who goes through a manic phase of buying and buying stocks with money he doesn't really have, convinced that the market will increase very soon, or like that lifelong revolutionary, sure—just as the devout Catholic is sure about the salvation of his soul—of the ultimate triumph, thus, too, the rapture of that aficionado from the city who contemplates the splendor of his first harvest like one who ponders the rich chromatic matrices of a painting, without taking into account what he should at least know, given that he knows nothing about agriculture, meaning the real cost of the labor performed, that makes any kind of benefit unreal.

The problem can only be aggravated in the case that our aficionado from the city obtains the services of technical assessors, whose help will be focused on transferring the terms of the problem from the practical terrain to the theoretical, thus covering up with the inane discussion the irrefutable character of the facts. That know-it-all who, from a specific concrete fact—the dimensions of an old irrigation pond, for example—will deduce that the pond received a great flow of water, now diminished, which must be recouped, to which the other know-it-all will respond that such a magnitude in the dimensions is rather an indicator that the flow has always been slight, given that a flow barely needs to be stored up, utterly forgetful, both of them, of facts such as the type of crops for which the water was destined, the area of irrigable surface, etcetera, speculators, in short, whose goal is, not so much the meaning of the thing, as the brilliance with which such meaning is contested or exposed.

My advice, in these matters, has been had by all those who've wanted to have it, all those who, from curiosity or true interest, have bothered to ask me for it. But experience has shown me that humans accept advice to the degree that it responds to what they want to hear as a response. And my advice or maxims don't correspond precisely to what that aficionado from the city expects or wishes. It also bothers him, like an assault on logic, that I tell him, let's say, that the only secret to farming the land is knowing every square inch of that land, the peculiarities of every bit of land, the winds to which it's found to be exposed, its orientation, etcetera; as with hunting: he who bags more game is not the one who shoots better but the one who knows the terrain better, the one who knows where the rabbit runs, where to start the partridge.

Mistrust mechanization due to the nature of mechanization, mistrust a misunderstood perfectionism that, far from solving problems, creates new and different ones. Mistrust, as well, certain irrigation projects, those in which the cost of installation and maintenance can outstrip the benefits. The same with new crops, not previously proven in the terrain for which they're destined, especially if those crops become faddish and everyone decides to try planting them, which inevitably causes prices to drop. Not exhausting the land nor thinking that every problem is solved by applying more fertilizer; the same as with abusive pruning, the damage more permanent than the benefit.

Regarding the acquisition of properties, discard beforehand all recourse to interest, a method that, apart from being unnecessary, might end in a shotgun blast in the night; there's a right time for every purchase. If there are buildings, an ancestral farmhouse—*la casa pairal*—outbuildings, do not let yourself be tempted by their sumptuary aspects. Ancient knowledge in this respect: the importance which Cato granted to barns and stables, pigpens, and granaries, in response to the wastefulness and luxury of residential characteristics gradually incorporated into Roman villas. The aesthetic of a whole is always the result of its functionality, a global and not merely architectonic functionality, something which those architects who call themselves functionalists should have assimilated into their critical sense, in order to consciously incorporate them into their designs for country houses.

Above all, accept the idea that the countryside is not exactly what the great Virgil celebrates; the countryside smells of manure, as does the one who works the land.

The subject of the country landlord, the stories about how the rich people in town customarily conduct business: another invention of city people. In the country, like everywhere, when it comes time to do business, intellectual capacity counts for more than corruption and any kind of pressure. Also, as with everything else, including war, the only strategy consists of being stronger than the other party; in this case, in having more money. Meaning: being able to pay a certain sum, however much, without difficulty, that allows the prospective business to become an active business. Acting this way, one always wins; the additional money that we might have been able to scrape together, I leave to the specialists in scraping by who, thanks to their mindset, are condemned to do nothing else than just scrape by for their whole life, gathering crumbs, not actually doing business.

Bear in mind: always purchase through intermediaries, third parties who sign their own name on behalf of the true buyer. Regarding loans, know how to lend the amount requested––without expecting any thanks––as long as it comes guaranteed, backed by properties that, although difficult to acquire, possess a value completely superior to the money loaned; the interest rate must be standard, never usurious. And one recommendation: never be tempted by caprices and whims like what the collector suffers and which frequently end up causing him to go broke.

People around here see business like a longaniza that gets cut and eaten one slice at a time, the appetite stimulated in direct proportion to how succulent the sausage is. And like business, inheritances, so much more appetizing the longer awaited: my fortune, the appetite of my heirs awaiting the slice they believe is about to fall into their mouths, any trace of lucidity blinded by voracity. On some occasions they literally behave like those family members of the rich relative who, self-invited to what they believe will be the fateful denouement, all gathered around the bed of the one presumed to be in agony, their all-too-hasty relief as they close his eyes, only to see him instantly open them again. All as if I was really going to die and, my spirit slipping away, miss even the most minute detail of their behavior. There's no doubt that the autumn, as an environmental threshold—the days growing shorter, the trees shedding their wet leaves—favors and accompanies that attitude of irreflexive anxiety and impatience resolved in concupiscence that they show off while they wait; like the whole town during carnival, with Lent soon to follow, or humankind as a whole: with the same incitement to carnal pleasures, now in bed, now in front of the fireplace, belly full, subject to the tremendous engorgements and erections and drowsiness so aroused by the warming climate.

Men, more habituated to the folksy farce with which they're accustomed to close a business deal, control themselves more, dissimulate better. Women, on the contrary, raised on the principle that the friendship they pretend between themselves covers up a deep relationship of strength that barely merits the trouble of sticking to the shadows, are more transparent in their behavior, unable to deduce any advantage from such transparency. Lust and greed is all mingled in them, their delectation similar to what they feel paying cash when they're shopping, not only as a sign of the carefree life they lead but also, more symbolically, of the strict compliance with the part that corresponds to them in sexual coupling. That explains Señora Riera's soliloquies when she wakes up, still not very sure of what a soliloquy is exactly, or of her early bird husband who doesn't listen to her because he got up hours ago: then I shall inherit a fortune and I will be very rich and we'll travel all around the world and you'll fuck me nice and slow and I'll be very strict and demanding with the housemaids. Her awakenings and, like her awakenings, her sleep and her dreams, seeing herself as an attractive young lady from back when young ladies were attractive, back in her time, the fifties: the young woman that she was, except not in Barcelona, but in Paris, in the Paris that she got to visit on her honeymoon, and in that Paris, the one from those days, stepping out to buy a baguette after a night of intense carnal exercise, her face sleepy, her hair still deliciously uncombed, wrapped only in a mink coat, the fur soft against her skin as she walks back to the apartment, to her sleeping lover, and to the typical panoramic view of rooftops glimpsed from there, gracefully biting the tip of the bread, accompanied by the sympathy and admiration of the passersby, besides the fresh smile of a sunny spring morning, a lovely girl, a genuine stunner. Similar pleasures, each morning, once she's completely awake, he administers to her the remedy she takes each day for the constipation that, like the good, semi-repressed nympho that she is, afflicts her; a remedy she calmly accepts, comparable to the satisfaction produced in both cases by the liberation of ducts once the act is finished—sexual or physiological—copulation completed in one case, the body disburdened in the other.

The husband, Riera or Roca, reminds me of one of those small-town greengrocers whose supreme desire would be to be able to handle, the same as he touches the fruit, at his leisure, the superbly budding roundnesses on some of the majorettes who march in the parade during the town's annual festival. And although it's possible that she sometimes confuses him for one of her brothers or brothers-in-law or uncles or nephews, the very fact that such confusion is possible clearly shows the futility of every attempt to get into any further details. Like women, wives, sisters, aunts, nieces, sisters-in-law, all of them perfectly interchangeable, the annoyance derived from the tensions to which they find themselves subjected running very high, not being difficult to guess in each one of them, beneath an appearance of affability, that family mother who, overwhelmed in her tasks, scares off like a skunk not only her own offspring but also her neighbors and visitors.

Only Carlos is the exception, and his work, the invaluable help he gives me, distracts him from his misfortune.

There's nothing in the world more devoid of interest for me than property. If people in general, and my descendants in particular, didn't think it was just another one of my jokes, they'd be scandalized, since the human being is scandalized by what it does not understand. And they would not understand that, for me, property is to concupiscence what power is to love, and what I'm interested in is power. But, what is power if not love?

It's true that, in the principal languages, concepts of goodness and possession are found, not in vain, to be closely connected: *bienes, goods, biens*. But beauty and poison are not mutually exclusive terms, and only the obdurate mind of a person in love is capable of establishing a parallel, if not an identification, between beauty and goodness. The beauty of prevailing boundaries of a country property, of the terms and landmarks that configure it in perfect harmony with the orthographic features of the countryside; something that drives people crazy, that can ruin a man with greater alacrity than a capricious sweetheart. Like the intoxicating water that leads a proprietor to bankruptcy in his obstinate search for underground springs, much more dangerous than the drunkenness of wine: to see the shining water spring from the bowels of the earth, the symbolic resonances which that contains. Temptations, ploys proffered to one by their own personal demons, being interposed in the strict comprehension that what matters is neither property nor possession, that what really matters is power over people and things.

An inclination, or rather, a deviation, that does not, just for being natural, lose its deviant character, making it easy to detect a psychic imbalance at the heart of all possessive passion. That's why in the country, where to a greater or lesser degree almost everyone is a proprietor, such problems arise with especial violence. No outsider would ever imagine, if not by analogy, in relation to his own place of origin, the surges of adrenaline that, under a wonderfully serene facade, punctuate the daily life of a small country town, the waste of suprarenal secretions produced here, greater, far greater than any such waste in the city: hatreds and rancors, persistent, and, occasionally, inexplicable; jealousies, unsuspected dirty tricks, meticulously calculated revenges, virulent reactions in the form of brusque fits of rage, of true bouts of fury, between neighbors and groups of neighbors as well as in the heart of the family to which each one of the contenders belongs.

Truth favors the powerful man, who, with or without justice, has all the arguments on his side. The humble man, however, is on thin ice from every point of view and cannot permit himself such luxury. And so, while telling the truth signifies for the former boasting of his own astuteness, for the latter telling the truth signifies confessing a crime. Thus the value of giving one's word, of being socially considered a man of your word, meaning, powerful to the point of not needing to lie. Inversely, confusing the effect with the cause, the humble man would do anything to escape from the anonymity in which he finds himself, to enjoy, if only for an instant, the notorious recognition that accompanies the powerful man. Like that unhappy man, that lowly man, poor in spirit, who, in the case of the town coming under military occupation or some similar emergency situation, almost feels, after having passed through some routine checkpoint, that the patrol officer has not asked him more questions in order to be able to demonstrate more thoroughly, not only his innocence, the fact that he has everything in order, that he's never gotten involved in politics, but that he is also an orderly person, a fervent supporter of the victorious cause, a man completely identified with the power that comes from such a victory, from head to toe, disposed as he is to do what they order him to do, *sí señor*, at your command; like that unhappy man, like that lowly man in search of an opportunity, so, too, the man of the people, whether in his individual comportment, or among the masses.

The people have been won over by the bad taste that is characteristic of these times, and the fact that they are lost is one more indicator of evil's progress, of the depths humanity has sunk to in the course of that degenerative phase in which it finds itself immersed. Because if, on the one hand, the repercussions of such degradation are greater when they affect vital centers of power and decision making, the thinking heads of society, on the other, the extent of this degraded mentality is always a symptom of the fact that such centers find themselves already affected and the evil proliferates throughout the whole of the body social. And so we find ourselves with houses and towns who have known for centuries how to preserve their character but now find themselves corrupted by bad taste; with the very interior of each house, that harmonious evolution that allowed it to adapt to the needs of each age now interrupted, it has devolved into a caricature of itself, in the same way that the work performed by any one of these electric kitchen appliances is a caricature of the work previously done by hand, in the same way that the mayonnaise from a blender resembles not at all the mayonnaise patiently blended with mortar and pestle, or that grape juice, the true nectar of the gods, has got no relation to the bitter liquefaction of a bunch of grapes, skin and seeds included.

But if there is something that the people don't tolerate, it's that people of taste do exist, with a taste distinct from common taste and which, for that reason, transforms common taste into bad taste. Although it's not said, although delicacy prevents the consequence of such a contrast from being seen, its mere existence is considered an insult. And, humiliation added to insult, the fact of not knowing why the thing they dislike is valued, and what they considered tasteful turns out to be worthless. In other words: some people are superior, intelligent, sensible, and cultured, qualities that seem like a proud provocation to those who feel awkward, clumsy, dull, and, in so far as they are satisfied with their own brutishness, despised. The maximum offense, for them, the peak of the scorn inflicted on them, by the pride which makes them victims is, in short, the idea that the music of Mozart, that oh-so dry and annoying squealing, is good music, but they don't know why it's good, the same thing that happens to them with painting, those pictures they don't understand or which, for being so purely primitive, seem to them to have been painted by a child, while, on the contrary, this or that household item, this or that decoration they feel so proud of, suddenly constitutes tangible proof of their inferiority. A depravity of musical taste that, even when it's about popular traditional songs not lacking in interest, such as *La Santa Espina* or *Per Tu Ploro*, with that Slavonic air they share with the *Cant dels Ocells*, even in these cases, it leads them to always prefer the coarsest interpretation, the one richest in the stridencies of the Sardana-esque interpretations typical of those little tunes that, as if composed by a retard, are what they actually like, choruses to sing together in a circle, the famous *fum, fum, fum*, and other tunes for children or for Christmas.

My favorite work is *The Creation* by the immortal Haydn, a direct antecedent not only to the *Misa Solemnis* but also to the *Ninth Symphony*, that highest exaltation ever reached by the human voice. I listen to *The Creation* practically every morning, in a recording of a performance by the Vienna Philharmonic and Choir of the State Opera, Julius Patzac in the sublime role of Uriel. I know that the people in town are sick of hearing it, but I ignore that and, no less in winter than in summer, I open the window gradually and turn the volume all the way up, aware that my vain attempt to cultivate their hearing must be taken as an act of disdain. On foggy days or when the sky is heavily overcast, I usually put on Bach's Cello Suites, performed by Pau Casals, which makes them gnash their teeth to the breaking point.

The plebian rancor derived from the frustrating humiliation they experience on feeling their inferiority, on chewing and chewing the equally flexible and unavoidable presence of what is found outside their reach: this is the feeling that El Moro exacerbates, channels, and manipulates in favor of his subversive ambitions. What remains curious due to the contradiction that it entails with respect to other aspects of his thinking, to his most beloved ideological concepts, is his own rapturous praise of children from small towns, their characteristic natural intelligence and glowing vigor setting them apart from the children of the bourgeoisie, their capacity for assimilation distinguishing them in all aspects of life, beginning with that of revolutionary leader. But he knows how to forget such incoherencies when the time comes to flatter the egalitarian deliriums of the masses, when, confusing superiority with richness, he attributes to rich people traits that don't have anything to do with them, but that—and this is what matters—permit him to announce the future establishment, in the society that he predicts, of a discriminatory treatment of re-educative character for the children of the old bourgeoisie, in order to compensate for the privileged situation that their origin supposes, setting them on the path toward manual rather than intellectual labor, the exclusive future privilege of the children of the proletariat. As if those solemn idiots who make up the greater part of the children of the bourgeoisie had something enviable, as if the bourgeois condition had anything in common with intelligence and culture, as if money served any other purpose than masking the natural stupidity of an acquired education!

I recall the time El Moro, malevolent phoenix, resumed his wicked instigations, once again showing his ear, or rather his aberrant tail, meaning his hideous cock, his horns and his hooves. It was Christmas Eve and, for the first time in many years, he made a new public exhibition of his ideas, as an offbeat Christmas message. That very night Pau Casals was incognito in the Rectory, playing for me the *Cant del Ocells*, and I was not about to permit any bastardly worries to spoil that memorable evening for me. The halo of harmony surrounding the cellist grew ever more radiant, until the whole of him, responding to that shimmer, and despite maintaining his form, was transformed into gold, as usually happens when the human transcends the limits of his physical being, as well as the possibilities of the times in which he lives.

The only thing that intrudes upon the perfect development of these tape recordings, like those rattling noises which, in war time, each belligerent country employs to interfere with the enemy's broadcast by using its own wavelength, the only interference here is the presence of the Indiano, as we call those Spanish expatriates who made a fortune in the West Indies, who resides at the top of the hill, and when the weather is good, Ramona rolls him out into the garden in his wheelchair and makes him have some cookies and a glass of milk, stiff and clumsy, half his body paralyzed, his dark glasses hanging halfway down his face, his dismal silhouette standing out against the sky swirling with barn swallows spinning and spinning, replaced in winter by starlings or maybe crows. Although neither he nor she are directly visible from the rectory, their presence is enough to irritate me and, as a result, embitter me for the time they spend out there. I say that it irritates me and it would be better to say that it unnerves me, because I find no word more appropriate to express what happens to me, improbable as it is that such uneasiness is owing to her miserable loyalty, on which he doesn't exactly have a monopoly. A sensation only comparable in its consequences to that mix of helplessness and fear the little boy experiences on the night when, curiously joining the adults who surround the bed of a dying man, without his presence being noticed, he hears the doctor announce: ladies and gentlemen, this man is dead; a feeling that, like the fear of thunder and lightning or the darkness, will well up again in any and all critical moments life has in store for him.

IX

If the accusations and reproaches levelled against me throughout the years were true, eternity in all the circles of hell wouldn't be time enough for my expiation. For such lies to take shape, truly, someone needs to invent them and spread them about, but, something no less indispensable, needless to say, is human stupidity, which allows someone who has always been taken for a saint to be transformed into a demon, and the most servile reverence to become merciless condemnation. Thus, the process by which I acquired half of the properties in town by signing over to myself any properties not listed officially in the registry, a system disgracefully used with great frequency in the first years after the Civil War. And it was enough that a poor crazy woman like the midwife insisted on claiming that I was responsible—against all evidence, since not a single one of her properties was found to be inscribed in my name—for the plunder suffered by her, in order to immediately create a propitious climate to make her accusation sound valid, something that people are always willing to admit when, additionally, as in this case, the presumed plunderer is rich and the one presumed plundered is poor. For the purpose of greater drama, working as if she were the victim of my pressures, she painted the injurious word that would have defined my behavior, had it been true, next to my name on the abundant crags and rocky outcroppings of the property she had lost, and she went up the hills to sound off, declaring it at the top of her lungs. Later on, taking it all to be forgotten, none of this kept me from doing her some important favor or other. And now, definitively single, owing to the wear and tear implied by having passed through too many hands in her youth when she was of marriageable age, she worked for me as a nurse, discreet but strictly controlled, yes, indeed, by Pascualina.

Another one of her lies—this one minted by El Moro—is the one that blames me for having tamed the willpower of a wayward mayor through the strategy of making him sign a certain document that contained certain specific illegal clauses without him noticing said illegalities, thus having him, from then on, totally at my service; as if I needed to resort to such schemes! The real basis of all those lies is just a misunderstanding about what, for my part, are nothing but some of the distinctive traits of my way of working: meticulousness, foresight, and dedication. Was I going to be mayor, judge, and notary all at the same time? I've got enough to do already with redacting all his writing. Also, in questions of detail, I prefer to occupy myself personally than to leave it in his hands and risk the small mistakes he irremediably commits.

But the people, what a terrible memory they have for what the postwar period was like—although they recall that time better than the war itself—their liking for freely filling in those gaps, of inventing what their ears want to hear. El Moro's thesis, his idea that economic motivations underlie the rest. And what is behind the idea that economic motivations determine the remains? What is it that determines such an idea? That's what I'd like them to tell me.

Few things are usually as unpopular as the truth. The fact, for example, that my son was murdered soon after the war began. A fact that bothers them and which, as a result, has to be covered up however possible, inventing the necessary maneuvers of distraction, manipulating the concepts.

It's curious that while it's considered positive for a man to be good and zealous about his job, it's just as curious that the person who is too good and excessively zealous is considered negatively, something that doesn't happen with an excess of wickedness or negligence, which, according to such a scheme, must be considered positively. Because I certainly could have become mayor if I'd set my mind to it; but what interest could I have in being mayor if the secretary of the town hall worked for me? I won't deny that I knew some of his secret dodges, but this knowledge of his weak points was, precisely, what allowed me to keep him under control, at bay, without ceasing to use, however, his gifts for hard work and efficiency, in which he's not lacking, for the good of the town. A decision capable of being misinterpreted by that person whose judgement can only be malicious, but that is inscribed, in a pristine manner, in my line of conduct, in my systematic habit of personally occupying myself with everything, of being involved in everything.

A no-less indispensable rule of behavior seems to me to be the habit of knowing how to listen and how to be listened to. Keep in mind that not knowing how to listen often implies not only accepting our interlocutor's plans and the battlefield he marks off with them, but also the conclusions implied in such concepts. Fallacies against which one must be on guard, to the degree that the truth in the hands of the one in control, to the degree that being in possession of the truth is a redundancy, to the degree that truth and power are one and the same thing. Remodeling Goethe's famous saying, given the fact that there were no revolvers in his lifetime, man is truly a well-conceived creature: the heart to the left, the revolver to the right, and the head in the middle, riding high above them both.

Being cautious is not a sign of weakness, but of a profound knowledge of the human being, of how much we can expect of the human being. When people think of me, rather than me, they're thinking of my patrimony; a patrimony that for me, however, is simply the screen intended, like a lampshade, to keep those people from being blinded by the light of what constitutes my true patrimony: the contents of these tapes, my legacy.

With the customary lack of calculation of the type that is more prone to destroy than to build, of that sick man compulsively directed to the exercise of anything aberrant that happens to be within his reach, fallen once more victim of a limitless vanity, what minimally graceful retort remained for El Moro? After glorifying himself as he glorified himself for having left me belly-up, he suddenly found himself facing the fact that it was I who had saved him *in extremis* from being shot by the firing squad, I was the one who had rescued him from the concentration camp, and I extended to him the guarantee that he could return to the town. Without property, without work, reduced to the hard condition of an immigrant, if not a beggar, in his own land, his return was not exactly the type of homecoming he'd imagined when he was hoping to become lord and master of the town. Gone now were those exalted days when he preached and exemplified free love by living with a viper of an aristocratic revolutionary woman, he jubilantly exhibited the fateful fruit of that love, the illegitimate child whose life—although they didn't know it then—brought with it the inescapable penance, he now returned to his faithful Elena, wary and contrite like the little boy who has had occasion to confirm for himself the sorrowful consequences of doing anything forbidden, playing with knives, throwing stones, and, having made such a verification, runs to seek solace and punishment in his mother's lap.

If discretion, humility, and shame were the principal traits of his initial reaction following the disaster suffered, voluntarily withdrawing from everyone's sight, knowing well the offense that his mere presence supposed for many, it would have been naive to see in such an attitude anything other than an interlude, a strategic withdrawal to the winter barracks to await better times. When he had believed himself definitively installed in power, his personal performance, inconceivably egocentric, was plagued by intrigues and betrayals, maneuvers of defamation and disparagement with respect to how much he believed, from his relative position, his rivals could overshadow him. And, having lost such capacity for maneuvering, it didn't take him long to attribute to me the traits that defined his own behavior, to start accusing me of manipulating the people exactly as he had dreamed of manipulating them.

The murmuring and the cursing were not, however, more than the first step, since, for him, only action can lead to triumph. Reestablishing a hunting club, for example, his first foolhardy attempt to seize power: a purely recreational club. Except that, designating all the town lands as a hunting preserve and leasing them to outside hunters would generate sufficient income to create a social fund. And if, in addition to leasing hunting rights, they also made money by selling permits for gathering wild mushrooms, very abundant in the municipality, that money would also enable the purchase of lands more or less abandoneds for commercial development or community use. And this, needless to say, was already too much: it's one thing to share the spoils of the hunt, and something else entirely to consider a common public asset something that, though wild, grows on lands of perfectly defined boundaries, and yet another, now having no relationship to any of the initially proposed goals, to fund a kind of absurd commune, with, additionally, shameless involvement in the real estate market for buying and selling rustic properties. The venture ended without sorrow or glory, after a series of unfortunate hunting accidents and the subsequent withdrawal of several members' licenses. But El Moro's intentions were more than clear: the seed that represents a club like this one, the fraternal environment—shotguns, coffee with a splash of brandy—that favors the schemes that pop up while the men are trading jokes. The crudest, most tasteless sorts of jokes, incidentally. I consider the jokes about Pascualina's son to be completely unacceptable, jokes that, originating in that circle, reached my ears, jokes about a son who, more than being a child of nature, would have to be called a supernatural child, and her, *la Inmaculada*. Unacceptable, or rather, intolerable, to the point of erasing all difference between those who joked that way and those who took him out for a walk and emptied their weapons into his young body which they then tossed into the ditch, the former no less deserving of an exemplary punishment than the latter, punishments which, in various ways, they have all ended up receiving.

Something else about El Moro that repels me, both viscerally as well as deeper, is his filthiness; a filthiness that seems consubstantial with his emaciated flesh and his grayish hair. Only a woman like Elena, who is a true saint, could tolerate living with such a person, and, if not for her, he'd have cockroaches, rats, and centipedes swarming underneath his bed. On the other hand, I happen to be a bona fide neat freak.

Ideological speculations—what a farrago!—every speculator twisting the words to mean whatever's necessary to get what he wants, entrenched, as in a fortress, within his very own system of concepts, knowing himself safe therein, his arsenal at hand, but entirely lost outside, the most innocuous of all creatures! Liberty, that principle universally invoked each time the willpower of others is crushed, is about individuals, about countries, that true liberty that, counterposed to the liberty of others, to the false liberty, will permit us to enslave its beneficiaries, beginning with our own fellow citizens, in direct proportion to the strength we use to impose it. Justice, that supreme touchstone for those who bear real power when they need to use it, as a guarantee of the status of law, in defense of the order by them established. Equality, that ruse of making the people believe that they really are equal, used by those who have been born different, not so much in order to concede to them a theoretically legitimate equality of rights, as much as to become guardians and monopolizers of that equality which they proclaim, from a hundred light years above their supposed peers. Democracy, convincing the people that they are capable of comprehending what is found to be outside their comprehension, and by virtue of delegating criteria, their hands free to act, to be able to work hard and to their fullest, without any kind of restrictions, as if they were the possessors of a blank check written out in their name. And as if hovering above all that, casting their shadow like a blessing on everything below them, the idea of progress, that humanity marches in a linear and chronological direction from the rudimentary to the complex, from the elemental and laborious to the sophisticated and easy, as if what's contemporary were indisputably superior to what's old, and the man in the street today has some reason to be jealous of Horace's slave.

The most devastating thing, however, and what strikes with the gravest repercussions, is the principle that comes from people's assimilation of such extremes. Because if the blindness of Tiresias was simply the expression of his access to a higher vision, the blindness of Justice today perfectly represents the stubborn search for an impossible balance between unequal magnitudes, the blindness belonging to such situations like the present one, in which intelligence is now being considered an intolerable privilege, the same as good taste, inventiveness and, needless to say, genius.

Arrogant, oppositional, adopting the gallant attitude of going against the current—such are the traditionalists, as they like to call themselves, although, honestly, I don't know what tradition they're talking about, as if history flowed through one channel and that flow had been lost, as if what they really missed were not simply certain aspects of the past profitable for their pockets, as if the loss that really worries them were not this, in exchange for whose restoration they would be willing to renounce, without the least scruple, the—essentially symbolic--remaining traditions, principles and values, purely a mask for their greed. In the end, it's a matter of deceit equivalent to, and conflicting with, the one promoted by the proponents of the various utopias in vogue: their fight for their fulfillment to the degree that it's considered impossible.

Such debates serve, primarily, to reveal the ignorance of the laws of the universe by those who participate in them. Because, just as it would be counterproductive to lay out a plantation of riverbank trees, such as plane trees or black poplars, but leave in place the occasional preexisting variety, so, in a similar way, I understand that it would be useless to begin a new era by using the debris and waste and preexisting values of the previous era, and I don't mean only the economic ones. Quite the contrary, the break with the past must be—and always has been—violent, convulsive. And it's obvious, therefore, that the nonsense preached by El Moro covers up one single desire: to be the one who does what I do.

One more observation: El Moro's oh-so characteristic naivety about the idea that what's important is not knowing reality but transforming it, as if it were possible to separate the one from the other. His presumptive scorn for books, which is exactly where he got the ideas that he has so clumsily and vainly tried to put into practice! Has anything transformed reality more profoundly than books?

However much happens in the world, just like the progress of some farming operation, the only remaining witness of all that is what has been recorded in books. But the fact that one event or another, great or small, has not found a place in its pages does not mean that it has not happened. Nor do the records of a farming operation give a full account of the wounds that the fire burns into the forests or how storms damage crops—they gather, in sum, a short-term account, not the more enduring, sometimes irreversible loss of character. This is known and trusted by every person who hopes to resolve their faults by forgetting them: they take no account of them so later on they don't count.

But there are the images that belie them, their vibrations still perceptible—it's enough to want to perceive them—in the same place where the events happened, in a similar way as that residual heat that lingers in a bed once the body has arisen: the town square, the square outside the church and the town hall, a church being sacked, a town hall occupied by a mob, a mob raging drunk on alcohol and that peculiar odor of powder and grease that comes from weapons, the frenzied and promiscuous atmosphere inhaled in those vaulted interiors, everything seeming to propitiate the celebration of one of those revolutionary orgies that, like the postcard that defines a city, define every situation. In the general muddle, with the bewilderment produced by the various songs sung by large crowds, it's almost difficult to recognize El Moro, dressed as a militant, slurping beer from the foaming vulvas of half-naked female militants, held vertically upside down, a spectacle presided over, you might say, as a hieratic officiant, by the still dripping body of the priest, a pale body, skewered on a butcher's meathook, spectrally illumined by a burning candle stump stuck to his tonsured pate, on the crown of his head: the typical scene of the triumphant rabble giving free rein to its ire, liberated by the emulative behavior of all those participating in it. As a kind of backdrop, also hanging from their own hooks, a Velazquez Christ ridiculed by obscene drawings and scribbles, and a freshly fusilladed Mona Lisa, in the belief, obviously, that it was a picture of the Virgin.

Meanwhile, outside, in the middle of the square, by the light of the bonfires burning inside the church, the crowd amuses itself by tormenting a fat little man, according perfectly with the manifest tendency of mobs to unleash their anger on fat people simply because they are fat, because of their provocative roundness, because of their difficulty in fleeing and the panic they display when apprehended, a predilection that is the product of an analogous ritual atavism and from the festive tone that reigns when the people all gather together to slaughter pigs. Low instincts that, by virtue of their very dynamic, inevitably spill over to those who generate them with their instigations, and, scapegoats, those who were the top dogs end up becoming the favorite target of their own followers, a Moor who, far from guiding anybody, handles as best he can the ferocious taunts his followers make him the butt of, all as if parodying his dreams of brotherhood, his egalitarian deliriums.

Because, like little boys who devote themselves to the typical cruelties of their age group—smashing snails, roasting toads, hunting lizards—on the basis of the conflicts of emotions and rejection they conjure up in this way, so too the gods with their most intimate problems, of which they make the human being victim; and like those gods that act like little boys, so too El Moro and his followers as they surrender to every kind of excess. Thus we see a long and arduous town committee meeting which concludes with a declaration of sufficient proof for the nonexistence of any kind of divinity, as if killing a god were no more useless than inventing one.

Although it's true that I can't really brag about my offspring, about a lineage not only regressive but also in the throes of extinction, there are at least indications that, precisely for having been manifested under the most degraded of appearances, news of an imminent change might perhaps be encouraging; the primal hermaphroditism, ultimately, is found to be intimately linked to the divine, something that cannot be said of mental retardation and madness, both assimilable in their expression to the figure of the possessed. Neither more nor less than what occurs with El Moro's lineage, damned simply for being his offspring. Thus, Federico, the son that the self-sacrificing Elena gave to him, a young and brilliant psychiatrist locked away years ago in an asylum he doesn't want to leave, convinced that, in the outside world, his life is in danger; a young man of promising intelligence whom some anonymous benefactor, a truly magnanimous person, has aided by paying for his studies, just as he now pays for his residence in a psychiatric institution. Along with the aristocratic revolutionary, who truly was epileptic, El Moro had an aphasic son, a mental retard who grew up in the orphanage because both he and she—condemned to death at that time—were deprived of parental authority. Another one of firstborn Federico's manias is his belief that he's not his father's child, an instinctive rejection that does him honor.

A lineage that is nothing but an expression of what El Moro's life has been: impractical ventures, personal frustrations, a life that is now slowly but irredeemably being extinguished, giving him enough time to meditate upon all this, to turn over and over in his mind—all the turns that his body's scant capacity for movement prevents him from making in bed—what his life has been, what his death will be. That's right, for better or worse, he's always managed to somehow scrounge a living.

In the same way as in a case of food poisoning, after a night of diarrhea and sweats and vomiting and aching joints, simply remembering, one after another, the foods we ate the day before is enough to make us feel especially nauseous, and at the same time, a sharp reactivation of the expulsive phenomena assaults us as soon as we imagine the poisonous meal; so too, in a similar way, on finding myself facing a fact contrary to my interests, whether it be about something already carried out, in the pipeline, or a mere contrivance, it's enough for me to review the list of people who have got it in for me, for motives real or imaginary, in order to discover right away the one responsible, as if an intermittent aura of black light pointed out their connection to the case.

As far as the Indiano goes, the advantage is that I don't even need to look over that list of enemies hidden or known, of copycats and forgers, agents of duplicity and treachery; their nefarious influence, for being so clear, speaks for itself. Seated there, in his wheelchair, contemplating the town from his garden, from the porch of his house when it rains, that extravagant house with decorative elements of colonial taste he had built when he returned from Uruguay, from Paraguay, what does it matter: a miserable paralytic encouraged in his madness by the solicitude with which Ramona cares for him, a woman who, nevermind her saintliness, will someday have no choice than to let the wheelchair go rolling down the hill, if not first slipping a cyanide-soaked cookie in among the ones she dunks in milk for him. Dismal madman, accustomed to judge and condemn whatever happens in the world just as some mental weakling set up as president of the supreme tribunal would do, he entertains the idea of saving the world through a television message which he expects to pay for with his miserly expat savings. A weighty motive for the faithful Ramona to give way once and for all to her impulses.

The fact that this miserable man is considered a philosopher says it all; I am a thinker, not a philosopher, and nothing could offend me more than for someone to consider me a philosopher.

There are other tapes. They contain the notes of Ricardo Echave, recorded by himself shortly before his death. When he left the town, they were left behind, forgotten in his bedroom, and Josefina from the inn, who knew about his friendship with Carlos, asked Carlos to take them to Ricardo when he returned to Barcelona. At that time no one knew about the accident yet since it took place near Port de la Selva, and the news didn't reach here until several days later through third parties, the sorts of people who buy newspapers to read the obituaries and the incidents. I have heard these tapes—something that Carlos doesn't know, convinced of being the only one who knows about them—and I can affirm that they truly are interesting in more ways than one. But in this heavy atmosphere of uncertainty and underhanded maneuvers that surrounds us, information like this only serves to accentuate the unease.

What are they going to tell me about Vilasacra that I don't already know, whether about the life of all those who have lived there, as well as the various changes which the estate itself has gone through, a farm whose name is synonymous throughout the region for something that has no equal? This is precisely the aspect that has most interested me in the Book of Ricardo, which is the name that his notes deserve: the influence that Vilasacra has exerted upon him, an influence that he seemed to ignore insofar as he considered it alien to his own experience and he was only partly conscious of how compelling it was for him.

His case is not unique. Another person unconsciously subjugated by that house, which is like a powerful antenna whose wavelength penetrates the whole region, is El Moro, whose secret dream--I've got proof of it—was to requisition it and, once entrenched there in the company of his revolutionary aristocratic woman, give himself over to every kind of orgy. A woman, incidentally, who despite her truculent presence, and despite how she might seem at first glance, differs very little from Señora Riera, experts both in that perverse astuteness of women who say, as if desperate: tell me to do whatever you want, I'll do whatever you like, with the obvious hope that you'll be someone who will do what they want, that's what they're asking us for.

If Vilasacra was saved, if the designs of El Moro and his concubine were frustrated as on so many other occasions, it was due, evidently, to the fact that someone who was in a situation to do so saw to it that it turned out that way. Because, just as the inheritors of a large property turn the systematic search through the dead person's drawers and papers into a game, and every day into a new party, expectant as they are for the sudden discovery of a treasure, so too, when men like El Moro have the opportunity to govern a town, their cruelties, their idiotic blunders are inevitable.

X

Is not Lorenzo de Medici the most perfect example of a thinker? Is he not that man of the most abstracted and erratic attitude who meditates in proper fashion, who, as he begins to stir, will wonder, confused, what was I thinking about? No, it's Aesop, a man who fully deserves such an honor. Aesop the slave, the fabulist, the sage. A man dressed in shabby clothes, in a humble abode, who squints straight at the other person, locks eyes with the one watching him: the brown tunic of coarse weave tied around his waist with a strip of cloth; the washbasin and the mop, the instruments of his daily chores; the heavy book he clutches in his right hand, a part of him, you might say, more than something he's simply holding onto, a book that, as if it were a mirror, is a diaphanous reflection of the contents of that book. An old man who is, at the same time, an old woman, almost ruthless in her clairvoyance—her laughing right eye, her implacable left one—a clairvoyance comparable only to that of a fallen god, traits that, perfectly expressed in their visual representation, make her, not only the pinnacle of the artist's oeuvre, but simply the greatest painting of all time.

The portrait of a god stripped of his ancient powers, a god no longer the only being, omnipresent and omnipotent as he was, now wrathful and despotic like a little boy; a god to whom nothing more remains than wisdom, an old man. For the gods, as for men, creation is the solution to a personal problem. But with the passing of the years, the centuries, the millennia, the god becomes a sort of vinegar-faced old man—porter, usher, forest ranger—who now only wishes upon humanity the greatest catastrophes, as a kind of gigantic orchestration to drown out the rattling lungs of his personal demise. The principal peculiarity of the gods is certainly astuteness; but their astuteness is equally episodic, one characteristic in service to the other, an astuteness that no longer has any other objective than to endure, to delay as much as possible that moment when, like any old man, he no longer inspires fear in anyone, when what the man fears is something else and the representation of that fear is new, the new divinity. And it's in this way that Moses is at the same time the author of a book as well as the outstanding character of that book, also coming to narrate for us his own death, thus any old god at all, immersed in that flow of time that is only a metaphor for time, in that current from which eternity is a mere accident, an accident that ends up swallowing that god alive, exactly the same as any of those who preceded him, despite each one's conviction that is was they who had created that flow, that current, that it was theirs alone, and upon this supposition, having exercised their powers like any old Sancho ruling his Insula Barataria. And like that man murdered while sleeping in his bed, who, in a last glance lost between his eyelids, recognizes yet the smile of the midwife who attended him when he came into the world, so, like that man, so too, a god when he dies. The same reward, incidentally, that a man who has dedicated his life to the good of the people can expect to receive from humanity.

No one can overemphasize the importance of thinking ahead, of having the gift of foresight or anticipation or future vision. If not, then what finality led Moses, and led Plato, to create at a stretch, in the image and likeness of Jehovah and his demons, an antagonist who was a part of himself, as Eve was a part of Adam, a self-creation, a self-projection, indispensable—as the shadow is to the light—in order to achieve a precise definition of their own limits? An autonomous antagonist like any of the characters they invented and, also like them, capable of enriching their inventor's personality to unsuspected extremes. Socrates's delight in saying: Plato, *c'est moi*!

Within the insertion of reality into fiction and vice versa, within that reciprocal incidence, the work of Dante stands out in exemplary fashion, the work of that genial paranoiac who learned how to satisfy his phobias and personal rancors, on par with his narcissistic feelings, projecting them and articulating them in the hundred cantos that comprise his book, a book that must necessarily be brilliant because only by being so was he destined to reach immortality and to enjoy eternal life, both his sublimations as well as his vengeances, those personal enemies fixed forever in the circles of hell that he forged, in order to spare them the misery of oblivion and anonymity. What are they now if not historical figures or antagonistic characters of the author, an author equally ferocious and lacking any sense of humor, to such an extent that it almost turns out strange that he would neglect to consign the sense of humor to one of the circles of hell that he invented?

Is the *Purgatorio* a symbolic expression, as someone has pointed out, of earthly life? Of course it is: its summit—where the poet situates the earthly paradise—is the point of maximum distance from Paradise, and is also the optimum point to thus dominate both the inferior aspects of oneself as well as the superior ones, aspects in relation to which the *Inferno* and the *Paradiso* can be understood as mere allegories. But it's no less certain that, as far as climbing a mountain goes, the *Purgatorio* is also an expression of that ascensional process that has as its goal the vision from on high that offers us the world, prior to descending into the deepest depths of ourselves. Knowledge, yes. And, to no less a degree, creative activity. Is it not, in the end, a feeling of condemnation that equally possesses the one who climbs a mountain and the one who finds himself facing an itinerary, precisely that of having to push on toward the realization of his work?

Just as the reading of a work of fiction that we shall call A, in which the protagonist, for his part, settles down to the reading of a work B, included in A, a work which reader and character read simultaneously, prepares the reader for the later reading of new works in which the reality of the referent is not real but fictional, predisposing him, in consequence, to not seek in it any illustration of a specific reality, but, rather, the internalized vision of reality in general and of himself in particular, thus, in a similar way, a child's education, based not so much on reasoned explanations of reality as on the creation of images, analogies, and symbols. And just as the ultimate meaning of a work of fiction need not be sought in the text, nor in the author, but in the relationship that links the work with one and another, a relationship through which the work comes to life, is quickened, at the same time that it illuminates the figure of the author the same as the reader, thus, in a similar way, our relationship of knowledge with respect to the human being and the world in which it lives. And just as the great dream of humankind is nothing more than that of transforming man into a god, a god that will have to be delivered unto death in order for man to appear again, the correlation of such a process is offered to us by that interrelation between man and work to which we have just referred: an author's character, converted in turn into an author through the pages of the work which is attributed to him, ends up supplanting the initial author in relationship to that new work. Meaning: that only thanks to that new work is the character liberated from such a condition by being transformed into the author. And, in the same way, only the comprehension of the author's role in relationship to his work allows the reader an altered knowledge of them both, the knowledge that comes from the operation of reading, capable of making the reader a participant in the operation of creating. Which poses a serious danger for the author: the mere existence, in many cases antagonistic, of that creator he has created.

We find the best illustration of the process, the best example, as has been well observed, in *Las Meninas*. An example to which it seems to me indispensable to add certain conditions relative to *Las Hilanderas*, prior considerations that complete and surround the process initiated in the dark areas of the workshop, in that foreground whose center is not constituted by the materials and work supplies needed to form the weft of the tapestry, nor by the hands that have to weave it, but by the whole group of those women who give name to the painting, since one does not weave simply with the hands but with the whole body, and this is precisely what the painting makes us see. But it is only in *Las Meninas* where that first approach to the creative process will be made concrete and precise, no longer, as Ricardo Echave rightly points out, by the fact of introducing the figure of the creator into the picture, a presence that by itself would not have represented a major novelty, but, above all, because that painter, whom we see in the act of painting the portrait of the infanta in the company of her little retinue, is at once both inside and outside the painting, the same as if the eyes that contemplate him and that we see diffusely reflected in the mirror in the depths of the painting, some eyes which, besides being those of the king and queen, are ours and those of the painter himself. Exactly where I was going: he only sees who is capable of seeing himself looking at what he sees.

Whether or not it belongs to the human being, who can and wishes to achieve it, is now another question. Because just as Marlowe's Faust, the pair's naughty and roguish Mr. Hyde, will find his replica in Goethe's Mephistopheles, Goethe's Faust corresponds rather to the poor devil that is Marlowe's Mephistopheles, thus, like this transformation of Faust into Mephistopheles and vice versa which the comparison of both works gives rise to, the reversibility of the contending forces found in each and every one of us.

At the same time, Ricardo Echave's opinions about architecture are quite correct. One wonders, rightly, what meaning does architecture have these days. But, what about the other arts no one wonders about, painting, for example, both when it tries to reproduce reality as well as when it tries to invent it, a pure combination of colors and forms? And the novel, that genre which, evidently, Ricardo Echave ends up choosing? That fatal boredom with things which the novelist tells us about, that pain about whether so and so did this and then this and this, and nothing about what he does, nothing about the substance of what really happens, holds only minimal interest, so much the less, frequently, the more complicated the plot. And the dialogues, the utterances, what merit lies in their business of reproducing for the reader, with the greatest possible fidelity, what people say, as if people didn't already talk enough to the poor reader in daily life? And those maniac descriptions, our obsession that we must perfectly visualize a landscape, an interior scene, as if them being this way or that way had some importance, as if we really cared about what she's wearing in such a way or that he's wearing a gaberdine instead of an overcoat. Nothing more nor less than detailing for us the actions, gestures: he entered, he walked out, he lit a cigarette, since, like the smoke from that cigarette, so too the meaning of everything they do.

For millennia, here as well as in China, man has worked before a great mirror which reflected the world and the origin of this world to the point where it permitted the blurring of the contours, to the point where the frontier between one area and another was confused, and it was man's task, barely a particle of that reflection, to sharpen the view to the maximum, to make as precise as possible those lines that seem to be blurred by the haze; it is Dante, no doubt, who gets the glory for having been the last, not only to delimit but also to cross over such frontiers, for having learned to project himself to the other side of the mirror without losing the ability, for all that, to remain on this side, too. Then the mirror was shattered and men began to take great pains to reproduce the fragmented images of those fragments. What else have painters and novelists done since then? Is there any substantial difference between painting a tavern and painting a landscape? Who is really interested in those fragments of the broken mirror?

But Ricardo Echave only intuits all that, he doesn't affirm it. And thus his malaise, low spirits ever more frequent and without even he himself managing to define the cause, the afternoon when he departed for Port de la Selva, for example, in that state in which, with the hope of soaring upward by moving back in time, one is obliged to think about the good work accomplished, about the good work still to be realized, in the optimal conditions in which he finds himself so that it may be so, in his proximity to Port de la Selva, in all the exciting thoughts that go running through his brain. Such was his state of mind when departing Gorgs and such were his thoughts as he took the downhill curve that hugs the sinuous curve of that riverbed, already close to Port de la Selva. Will anyone believe me if I say that I have seen it all, both the accident in which he met his death as well as his life, the glittering sparks that, sprouting from his words, from his book, illuminate the darkest areas of his earliest childhood?

This is, precisely, the great risk: the apocryphal work, the false attribution of a work to an author, be it premeditatively, through the usurper's insatiable vanity, be it through mere interpretive confusion, through erroneous deduction. If not, then let's see what the situation is and what's at stake: we've got the diary of the young Carlos, a typewritten copy that, from the lack of more explicit data about its unhappy author, any future scholar can conclude to be a work of fiction written by Ricardo Echave, given the confidence with which Ricardo refers to certain aspects of its contents. We also have what I call the Book of Ricardo, meaning, the recording he made of the contents of his notes. And there are, finally, my tapes, these tapes that Carlos converts each night into a typed transcription, exactly the inverse process of the one followed by Ricardo. A situation, needless to say, that turns Carlos into the sole depositary of all those materials. And Carlos has my confidence, given that his selection as transcriber and depositary owes as much to what I saw in the iris of his eyes as to his life and to his character, passive par excellence, lack of imagination, lack of creative qualities, in short, the ideal transcriber. But, what confusions and mistakes, if not menacing threats, will the future not hold in store? Faced with a vague threat, there is no attitude more necessary than simple alertness, vigilance. Because I sense the betrayal in the atmosphere just as you can feel the humidity in the air when the sea breeze blows.

The usurpers and also the intruders. The disturbing image of the Indiano growing gigantic up there on top of the hill thanks to that optical effect that magnifies shapes that stand out against the sky, against the birds, the wheelchair, his great big head of gray curls, his sunglasses hanging halfway off, his crazy project for a television spot. Between visionary and a replica of a visionary, there are days when, before Ramona wheels him out into the garden, according to how the day has dawned, he can't even manage to know if he is he himself or merely the voice of someone else that he's using in the same way that he uses a belt. His mental confusion is enormous, extreme, even leading him to forget the name of the self-sacrificing Ramona, calling her Mariona and even Josefina, and to spend the whole afternoon repeating that he's got no need for a wheelchair. Because he knows Uruguay, he thinks he knows the whole world, and because he's sitting up there in a dominant situation above the town, which he takes in with his view from his garden, he thinks he's up to date with whatever is happening here. And from there it's just one small step to his pretensions for saving the world.

It's a feature of senility, that resistance to admit the relative value of the knowledge one possesses, its manifest inferiority with respect to a hypothetical observer who considers himself at the same time as what he is seeing. The great mistake of understanding the window as a mirror, as the frame of a panorama in which the observer himself stands out with privileged prominence in the foreground. It's lucky that Ramona is by his side, who, despite being not a

Ramona exactly like the one on the record—now those were some songs!—is a real saint, and in her I trust.

Who dared to say that the old man is a heartless creature, his feelings bottled up by the passing of the years? And that man who, all alone with himself, lunches frugally in a half-empty roadside diner or airport café one Christmas day? What happens then with his feelings, what happens including with his eyes, with his two tears, knowing as is fully well-known and knowing also that, no matter what, everyone considers him finished? How must that old man then feel who from a roadside inn contemplates the cars speeding by, with the *Cant dels Ocells* as background music, the mountains looming close through this cold, transparent air of a sunny winter morning?

When one does not take the old man for a creature with a hardened heart, who is not only indifferent but also takes pleasure from the spectacle of someone else's misfortune, one tends to consider him little more than a log, inert and stiff both physically as well as intellectually. Both reactions are not, however, more than variants of the same sentiment: fear of some forces that intuitively know themselves to be superior, now minimized, now slandered, according to whichever circumstances accompany the manifestation of the phenomenon.

My powers, whose proof exists for anyone to see, are received, despite such abundant evidence, with the reserve appropriate for something which truly remains to be seen, so meanwhile, and just in case, it's better not to say anything to anybody. There's not one neighbor in the town who has not seen, for example, how I take a dry clod of dirt and crumble it between my fingers, and the dirt, as it falls, tells me the kind of crops it's best suited for. Or who doesn't know that, in order to make the plants yield more, I talk to them; the ones in the vegetable garden, save for rare exceptions, are the stupidest ones, the sheep of the vegetable kingdom. Of course that stuff about talking to them is really just an exaggeration: I only need to think. The most intelligent tree, needless to say, is the oak; the conifers, however, are almost as stupid as cactuses. I also have a special understanding with the various components of the soil, minerals and inorganic material in general, not to mention even those immaterial elements of which certain chemical elements are only a symbol.

The same could be said about climatological phenomena or seismic movements. Like the snake that slithers out from the bowels of the earth when a tremor is imminent, so too, I notice in my pulse the seismic movements that indicate, not minutes ahead of time but years beforehand, that looming earthquake, of a magnitude no less than the one that destroyed Lisbon, that will soon split open the heart of Catalonia and which I perceive simply by placing my index finger on my jugular vein.

With regard to the four elements, more important than pointing out the primal character of fire or the connection between life with water and the earth with death, reversible depending on their significance, as it is capable of acquiring the opposing value, more important, much more, it seems to me, is to point out the connection between the human being and the air. The air outside, the air that swells the forests, that transports armies, that rains down oceans; but also the inner air, the disembodied air, breath, spirit, life. The danger lies in its corrupt embodiment, vacuity, burp, flatulence, the air that swells El Moro's belly to the point of explosion as he lies on his deathbed.

There are seismic tremors and historic tremors, and to predict or, rather, detect these, supposes no greater difficulty than foreseeing them. You've got be an historian to miss the predictions, not only of the future but also of the past; you've got to suffer from their typical myopia to consider milestones or touchstones—the French Revolution, the Russian Revolution—events that are merely more or less attractive crystallizations of much vaster processes: the fragmentation of empires and nations due to the proliferation of the very principle that contributed to their formation and settlement in past centuries, an illusory phase that considers consolidation before dissolution with regard to preceding models; the arbitrary criteria of nationality born in Europe spreading across the whole wide world, on the one hand, and the infection of society at large by the mentality and habits belonging to that bedpan spawn of the old underclass that is the bourgeoisie, on the other; these, these are the aspects on which you've got to center your attention if you seek even a minimal understanding of what is really going on in the world. Because, just as life in adolescence is one of intimate and rosy self-contemplation, in maturity reflection with critical pretensions, and in old age paranoid delirium, so too the life of small-town people considered as a whole, the works by them realized, and the books in which those works are reviewed.

Another gross error is the division of human history into eras, a concept no less artificial than that of the leap year. Far above those time periods, into which historians enjoy dividing and subdividing the life of the universe in its relation to time, is that of the life cycle, compared to which all that drivel put together doesn't even add up to the merest hint of an inkling. I don't know what good they now expect to come from the Age of Aquarius that does not come inexorably linked to what's bad, like under the sign of Pisces. Not even if the planets and constellations start spinning a different way or stop spinning altogether.

A silent bird is not only a silent bird: it's an unrepeatable instant. And the present is not only an unrepeatable instant; the present is the vision of time unfolding, a vision that simultaneously includes an interpretation of the past and a hope for or fear of the future, the former no less uncertain than the latter, both implicit in the moving picture of that mushroom cloud that grows and grows into something that's not a mushroom.

To see what Ricardo Echave was dreaming, to dream what he was dreaming, as they say, the same as if I were to find myself by his side in the ceremony, also attending the incineration of a zombie with the face of a Vietnamese nun by covering her in green methane powder, and then tossing the lit match; but he knows, and I know along with him, that it's a body in hibernation, and so snuff out the small brief flames that envelop it in the hope of restoring it to life. Yes: to see what others see, what others think, and even what they dream. Even more: to make others see what I see, other people's visions, thoughts, and dreams that I materialize in the form of a virtual projection before their eyes.

A distinctive case is that of herbal infusions, because what people don't know, nor do they need to know, is that their efficacy resides not in the beneficial effect reported by those who drink them in my presence, but in what I read in them when I prepare them. Frequently, according to what I've read, I achieve the true effect once they have departed, comforting the spirit no less than the stomach, by means of the hot tisane, when, alone with my alcohol lamp, keeping the leftover infusion boiling, I observe the movements of the bubbling foam that has formed, just about to spill over the edge, similar to that great octopus, that seems to fight to escape from the pot where it is being boiled alive, the figures that take shape, islands, continents of capricious geography that, barely formed, begin to shrink immediately to form a sudden depression, now a vertiginous hole, that ends up swallowing itself and disappearing, in order to suddenly reappear, rising back to the surface in the form of spreading particles until configuring new and sinuous expanding terrains, islands and continents in constant mutation. Once the water is finally boiled away, the steaming residue stuck to the bottom will form one last shape, and according to the suggestions that such a figure raises, one will act in one way or another.

Meaning: it's a matter, not of interpreting a prediction, but of believing it, of acting upon it until adapting to our will what only appears to be a happy mixture of inspiration and chance. For the sake of the argument, I'll say that the apparition of the Chinese emperor, perhaps, is an excellent sign. The serpent, evil, in contrast to the dragon. And with winds blowing out of the north and the east.

Years ago, just about to start eating dinner, alone in the gloom of the dining room, the doors suddenly opened and, on the other side, radiant with light, surrounding a great table set for the banquet, all those present broke into applause and congratulations, a large group of acquaintances, friends, and neighbors gathered there in order to celebrate my golden anniversary in the performance of certain functions. They imagined they'd give me a surprise that way, the equivalent, although of a distinct sign, to what the judge, the mayor, and his men plan to do when they suddenly appear outside the condemned man's cell to announce the immediate fulfillment of his sentence, and I let them enjoy their fantasy, pretending to be confused and dazzled. I often do this, completely renouncing, as I have given up fighting against people's incredulity, or trying to get people to accept the evidence that neither the most recondite fact can escape my notice, not only events, thoughts, or dreams but also sensations, to see, for example, Carlos junior stepping into a pharmacy next door to his house, to perceive how much he sees, thinks, and feels while he does so, at the same time as whatever his Mariana and the pharmacist do, Mariana waiting at the counter, the pharmacist accompanying him to the backroom, preparing the injection, talking nonstop all the while, asking him, in passing, if he isn't allergic, and Carlos junior answering, incidentally, no, in the very instant when he feels the vertigo on the tip of his tongue and falls, his legs seeming to melt, as if turning into a fish's tail, so persuaded that he says I think that I'm feeling sick, without hearing the cries of the pharmacist asking them to call the emergency room, now that he thinks he's asking him if what he has is tetanus, and that the pharmacist is nodding his head yes and says aha, and Carlos junior is busy staring at the starfish in the aquarium he's never noticed before, and the changing geometric combinations of the floor tiles, like a kaleidoscope, and the woman dressed in black who pops her head through the curtain, her figure somewhat blurred by that series of infusoria vibrating in the air, an unforeseen visit that impels him to tell the pharmacist to not let Mariana see him, too, that it could make a bad impression on her, as if he could really say anything while he's flopping around there on the floor like a fish out of water, gaping and spasmodic like that, as if he were really going to see, hear, speak, or breathe again some time, impossible as it already was to make his heart start beating again when, a few minutes later, the siren wailing, the ambulance arrived, and she, the nurse or doctor or midwife or whatever she was, closed his eyelids.

The banquet that has been prepared will offer me the opportunity of addressing the dinner guests. To unmask El Moro, of course. But, more than speaking to them, I prefer to make them see the range of my powers, to make them face once again the evidence that I am who I am and what I am up against. In the end, the clarity with which I see the future is not limited to the for-them-unprovable distant future, to what must happen within thousands of years, not so distant, on the other hand, from what—like the cycle of the seasons—has already happened in the past. I see what's distant with the same clarity as I see what's coming, the immediate future, Christmas Eve, the new year, the Adoration of the Three Magi as a ritual prelude to and reason for the now imminent entrance of the saving troops unfurling their pink ensigns of Epiphany. I see it without even having to think about it, because, like a great bird that takes flight, fast and straight as an arrow thanks to the beating of its powerful wings, almost grazing the scabrous rocks of a precipice, I soar up and over the apparently insurmountable limits of nature, then glide with joy far above, very far above, humanity's miserable daily toil.

XI

Such were the excellences of the evening, so pleasant in the warm slant of the golden light that most of the guests, reluctant to come inside, lingered on in the garden, forming small groups around the tables draped in white linen arranged on the lawn, enjoying the appetizers being served, although, as usually happens, disdaining the cocktails, almost all of them opting for whiskey on the rocks. Like a good host, I maintained a discreet and diligent attitude, so that each and every one of the guests felt themselves the object of special attention. Pau Casals wore white tails, completely distinct from the dark formal wear he reserves for his performances, a thoughtful touch whose sole purpose was to enliven the evening's festivities.

Inside, spirits were, if possible, even higher, as could easily be appreciated through the windows just by pressing your face against the glass and screening out the glare with your hand, thus avoiding the dazzling reflection of the late afternoon, the sunny foliage of the trees, the reflected image of the guests conversing quietly around the tables set out on the lawn; and then, on the other side of the glass, almost like a second reflection, under the splendor of the chandeliers, tears and glittering tears, glimpses of new groups of guests, new long tables, and all kinds of delicious foods and wines set out on the white tablecloths. Despite there being so many people, any guest could spot me right away, seated before the cheery blazing fireplace in a deep wingback green velvet armchair, my back to everyone.

A party is not always a party for everyone present. There always has to be, lost in the jovial hubbub, apart from everything like a drunken, dethroned Nebuchadnezzar who is, or thinks he is, a doncella, that man who withdraws, who refuses to drink a toast, who shirks, overwhelmed by the misfortune his hard work has brought him, embittered by the mere fact of finding himself there, participating in a celebration that depresses him no less than how prosperity in general depresses him, the favorable economic situation, index fingers raised, graphs with rising arrows, everything seeming to silence his muttering, *his fine, and what do I get out of all that? Where's my share of that famous per capita income?* bereft of solidarity, taciturn, grumpy. Just as there must also be that other miserable man, that other frustrated man, that other born loser who, perhaps less lucid, lets himself be won over, although only momentarily, by the general merriment, and raises toasts with one and another as if the congratulations were meant for him, like that cinema usher who, among his friends and relatives, ends up transforming his job as a cinema usher helping to screen a blockbuster into a declaration of self-worth and personal triumph, similar to, yes, that man who's both a cinema usher and an usher of the average citizen in general, that average man who lives and dies like so many others who have lived and who will die for centuries on end, who step out of the shadows of anonymity only until the illusion of the toast fades. And there are finally—and they are the most numerous—those guests invited to the party who, like the grand cavalcade that puts the finishing touch on a musical revue, that curtain call in the front of the audience in which each and every one of the artists and stars appears in reverse order of importance, all smiling, like one big happy family, while inside themselves each star curses the one who has earned more praise from the emcee and garnered more applause from the audience, each and every one of them stealing the spotlight, casting shadows, stepping on each others' toes, so, like that final grand cavalcade of the stars, so, too, the general frame of mind among the guests at a party.

Something perfectly in line with the common people's well-known qualities of subtlety and perspicacity had to be the Polaroid instant photos which various banqueters were snapping here and there as the meal unfolded, the image gradually blossoming out of the viscous white background, the only medium by which to catch a glimpse of the unquestionable presence of certain personalities, who, while their image was not fixed in a photo, had so far gone unnoticed: Aesop, Dante, Milton, Goethe, etcetera. That's right, once identified, everyone wanted to be photographed in their company, to blossom at their side in the reddish shadows, now blue and soon yellow, the image defined more and more as the colors coagulate and then, with the photo obtained, next, get the autograph that guarantees, in writing, the memorable value of the evidence, and then clink glasses with them in an eager toast, the necessary capstone to that encounter which, henceforth, would be recounted by their descendants from one generation to the next. The inevitably spilled champagne impelled them to childishly uncork fresh bottles although simply for refreshment's sake and thus conjure up good luck time and again, the more popped corks, the more abundant the spilled bubbles

The enormous mirrors repeated the scene indefinitely, the ad lib photographers' determination to capture photos that, among other things, caught their own image in the act of taking a photo reflected in mirrors upon mirrors, repeated in photos upon photos of mirrors. It was precisely through one of those photos that I caught El Moro trying to join in on a toast as if nothing had happened, but the only thing that came out of the bottle he'd uncorked was fetid air and a big fat fly, a perfect augury.

It's difficult, in practice, to distinguish the undesirable quality of the person whose mere presence makes the banqueters uncomfortable. So Aurea or Aurora, in her solitary roaming, wearing a high necked blouse, like a nurse's or midwife's, but of white silk, in order to cover as much as possible the wound inflicted on her jugular vein in a hotel in Manila or at the Hotel Manila in Barcelona—I've got neither the time nor the desire to worry about these details. And the guests whose presence no one can explain or say why they were invited, that épicier who goes around justifying to whomever he manages to get to speak with him, whatever the subject happens to be, as if in order to have the opportunity, for his part, to repeat and repeat that the importance of Catalonia is perfectly comparable to that of France, and not only from the point of view of landscape, in regard to their respective natural beauty, but rather, more globally, at all levels. And to the one who stays silent, he sighs, or rather snorts, and exclaims *quelle belle journée*!

When all that chatter made me excessively fatigued, I changed the channel, and in this way I continued contemplating them, obsequious like every good host, while listening to *The Marriage of Figaro*, nodding my head to the question of some Barbarina, refusing courteously but firmly the petition of some Cherubino; once in a while I changed the channel again and listened to the radio adaptation of *The Wedding of Camacho the Rich*, or an English course that reproduces Satan's speech to his court of fallen angels, or even a live report about how the banquet is unfolding. And it was thanks to that report, alerted, as it were, by the announcer, that I surprised El Moro red-handed, photographing me treacherously, laughing like a devil behind his grizzled beard, a poor devil for whom the photo couldn't come out any different than it came out, black. My photo, on the other hand, caught him running away, still laughing with premature glee, reduced to his real insignificance in that shot that takes in everyone at the party all gathered together, present all who were present, except for me, as a focal point, as the eye of that camera whose 360° visual angle only left the photographer out of the photo, visible, at best, in the reflection of some mirror.

Our guests of honor were literally found cornered by a group of boys and girls who had just come upriver on an amphibious yacht, the sort of young people who, for being so young, are forgiven their irreflexive conduct and imprudent ways, as well as that imprecision they have for constantly sharing their respective sexes. Worthy of praise, on the contrary, is the inventiveness and skill they demonstrated upon successfully passing the sandbars that make it difficult to navigate rivers like the Tordera, of such a meager flow except when the river rises and eventually overflows its banks. The youngsters seemed to find themselves especially attracted by the figure of Dante, without that preventing the sense of attraction from also flowing in the opposite direction.

Drunkenness, which excites the lowest instincts of human nature, contributed decisively to the degradation of an initially peaceful atmosphere, to create among those in attendance an environment of rude behavior, if not outright hostility. Thus, those allusions to Christmas Eve and New Year's Eve, as well as pretending to ignore the most important aspect of the celebration: the happy ending of a work, of an autobiography that is, in a certain way, everyone's autobiography, the coincidence of dates being a mere form of casting the event in greater relief. And that insistence from certain guests in toasting some response that I had supposedly given, when it was well-known that nobody had asked me any question. The unease produced by that series of small incidents was the direct cause of my leaving my glass forgotten on some tablecloth. And what's worse: also a book I was carrying in my hand. And the fact is, truly, like one of those pictorial representations of the Last Judgement, except in reverse, hordes of reprobates clawing their way up a wall of flame with the help of devils and serpents, as if to meet one of those righteous figures who, for their part, from their radiant heights, only seem to be expelling the legitimate occupants from the center of the glory, hastening them as best they can toward that tide of vengeful hands that rise and rise, so in truth, the party turned into an orgy and the placid banquet a pandemonium. *Sic transit deorum gloria!*

The toast was preceded by a few brief words in which the man being honored commented on the significance of the event, while offering heartfelt thanks to those present for the many attentions of which he'd been the object. He bestowed refined mockery upon those who found nothing surprising in his perfect knowledge of the circumstances that had conspired in the death of Carlos junior, and remorselessly lashed out at whoever dared qualify as pathetic the recourse to the logic of a syllogism by one who, claiming to have all kinds of extraordinary powers, used that syllogism as the ultimate proof of the reality of such powers. After various clarifications, he alluded to the existence of an ill-intentioned maneuver about which he had no choice but to put them all on alert, expressing as a manifesto the duplicity of certain people, as well as the presence of traitors, usurpers, and deceivers, his speech increasingly muddled, perhaps from technical deficiencies, interferences, confusion or the defective function of the headsets for selecting channels, his words now superimposed upon the lyrics to the "Contino" from *The Marriage of Figaro*.

As an eminently moralistic sign, the sermon quickly centered on the excesses toward which youth naturally tends and, more exactly, the dangers involved in such excesses, that oh-so-apparently-innocent custom of passing the time comparing their respective sexes. The path taken by Carlos junior, by setting an example known by everyone, a path that for him, initiated in his perverse childhood games, could not have led him more directly to where it had, a path plagued with every sort of wrong turn and, especially, of indiscriminate sexual abuses, when, as if caught in a feverish trance, in a state of drunkenness or madness, he would imperiously telephone Mariana, ordering her to come visit him immediately and without wearing any panties, and so, as soon as she obediently showed up and knelt down at the foot of his bed, offering up her rump, he'd be able to penetrate her instantly, simply by flipping up her skirt. Inebriation or madness that, maybe right after, maybe right before taking Mariana, they were going to take him once again to the sauna, eyes rolled back, where it was his habit to submit to the men gathered there, all with the face of Lolly Loker, men and more men who, led by the old antiquarian Modesto Pírez, used him collectively and repeatedly, as if infusing him with the strength necessary to go back and do it again with Mariana, in the same way, and by virtue of the same principle, that his sexual discharges with Mariana led him back again to the sauna, permanently urged on in his pendular oscillations by the fear of contracting the infamous sickness, as if, more than fleeing, he were running to encounter that fatal outcome in the backroom of a pharmacy.

Accompanied by the sound as a way of illustrating the speech, the mirrors, converted into improvised screens, offered various images—Mariana's half-open mouth while she was being penetrated, the coupling of several bodies in the burning turbulence of the sauna—as if on closed circuit TV. As a matter of fact, it was the objective projection of my own visions, now visible for the banqueters, too.

In the garden, the sound quality was even more clear, as well as being free from the interference caused by the TV spotlight, heat, blinding lights, etcetera. There were the outside faces of the windows serving, at the same time, as screens, and onto them were projected the same scenes that the mirrors were repeating inside, details of the activity organized in the sauna around Carlos junior, no less the contrast between his body and those of the men who now lifted him up to be able to better penetrate him—bald and gray-haired and pale paunches and skinned knees—than the contrast created by one of those luminous deities when they manifest themselves to the astonished workers in a smithy or before a clutch of drunkards sunk in their baleful libations. It was also possible to select scenes already projected or, simply by pressing the corresponding button, data enhancement. So, a few minutes after requesting a report about a specific person, there appeared on the screen a passport-type photo of the one requested, for example, Modesto Pírez, and on his image, like the credits listing the cast of a film and other technical information, there appeared in sequence the precise antecedents necessary to provide the one requesting with the most complete information, from age, place of birth, parentage, and affiliations (54 years, Barcelona, son of Modesto and Patrocinio, persons connected to the Movement, Labor Delegation and Feminine Section respectively, both natives of Murcia), profession (antiquarian) and social status (single), even blood type, blood pressure, scars (late circumcision), penis size (normal), false teeth (three crowns), credit rating (very positive), sphincter condition (normal), etcetera. My father knew your father, he said with an affable smile.

Like that first ray of sun that, slipping inside a room, ends up drawing the sleeper out of the deepest sleep, ignorant until that moment of the new day dawning, so, like that ray of sunshine, there was something that, as the message well emphasized, it had to necessarily represent, including for the most fascinated mortals, the announcement of an important occurrence. Such an impression, more than of a precise event, emanated from the whole, from the mere presence of Carlos junior, from his moon eyes and from the laurel crown and the hanging garlands he wore, as if he were found dancing in a forest clearing, in a forest clearing and not in a sauna; from the way he looked, yes, but also from his way of joining the action, transformed now into one of those fauns with a perpetually erect cock, and apertures above and below in the shape of little ear trumpets, to then leap onto Mariana, as if, the way that the little spout on a water jug spurts out the water accepted by the intake orifice, like that water jug, what he had received through his receptor organ were returned by his penetrating organ, or as if the latter constituted the labiate corolla of a flower whose stem, passing through the lower abdomen, emerges erect in the front part. And you should all bear in mind that just as the initial chaos was hybrid, that light and that shadow that had to be structured into an order, hybrid fruit is also its final product as long as this end truly signifies a new birth.

Have no fear that the light will blind you, you who dwell in darkness! The light will make you see what you did not see in the darkness! Without light, how could you be attentive to the great changes that are coming? Who, from the darkness, would have been capable of grasping the signs, the news, the precursory character of that great hermaphrodite that was John the Baptist? What else is the cycle of life but the permanent giving birth generated by the activity, considered wicked and lascivious by many, of continuously transmitting matter and spirit at the same time? What else did the invention of music mean for Orpheus? What does John the Baptist tell us with his example, what else were his initiatory rituals, giving at the same time as receiving a new life in the waters of the river? To what does his sacrifice correspond if not to the furors of a woman dissatisfied with and jealous of that dissemination of the life she desired all for herself? How is her sacrifice different from the death of Orpheus at the hands of the Furies? Is Carlos junior's sacrifice so different if we consider the etiology of allergies, the presence of that unusual allergy, induced who knows why and by whom? What is the hermaphrodite if not the living sign of original fertility, the announcement of a new horizon, of a new person recently born, at the same time as the end of something, the last light of that old man at the same time old woman whose extinction necessarily precedes all new birth? Couldn't it also be proclaimed that its precursory function and its final function, that tragic and necessary finale, are one and the same thing? Inscribe this message on your hearts!

Just as Lucifer, initially rammed down into the deepest depths of the Inferno, ended up standing out as the Colossus high above the highest mountains, so you can find in your own eye the light of that pupil that constitutes the center of Paradise, that light that, reflected in its reflection, ignites your own pupil, and to then discover that Paradise lies inside of you, that you are all, all of you, Paradise. No, it's not enough to be gods and goddesses! Because I exhort you all, yes, to create in your image and likeness those new undiscovered worlds that you carry inside, those new Paradises, those new Infernos. But, along with a new world, I invite you all to also create the new eternal father who has to preside over it from that singular point where Inferno and Paradise coincide. Creators, create!

In the same way that the child comes from the father in the territories of the dream and, beneath the level of consciousness, in the imaginary constructions in general, so the father comes in turn from the child, attributing to him however many evils and perversions, only with great pains contained, dwelling inside of him, one and another competing in the task of projecting upon the contrary part the most shadowy or most humiliating aspects of himself.

Thus the ambiguity of the work of creating, the ambivalent value of the horrors that we project upon others in the ignorance that belongs to us, that son who attributes to the father—Noah, Saturn—the most ridiculous and embarrassing experiences, or who makes the mother the victim of the most ruthless crimes, without even being aware of what he is doing. Or, in the inverse sense, burdening his own descendants with the most execrable acts, meaning, the acts that we would have secretly carried out if we had become conscious of how anxious we were to realize them.

Two objections to raise as the banquet rolls on: the insistence with which people are saying that it's not Christmas Eve but the night before or the night before the night before Christmas Eve, as if intending to sow doubt and confusion with respect to the motive and circumstances of this celebration. And, more serious yet, the rumor running among the guests, that story that I'm dedicated to spreading false accusations about a disgraced neighbor, a truly unhappy person whom I'm making responsible for the greatest monstrosities, a poor devil who doesn't even exist, a character I've invented in order to charge him with my own atrocities and machinations. As if nobody had ever before disrupted a Christmas celebration dressed in red like a devil! As if I were the one who had done it dressed up as Santa Claus! Malicious comments muttered in low voices, in the seeming belief that that's how they would escape my control. And if I told those guests who don't even seem to see me that evil is nothing but an aspect of myself, something that goes roaming about the countryside as it pleases while I sleep, and that if I were to fall asleep now, as old people frequently do, would I be capable of destroying them all?

Independent of whether or not the headphones work, whether or not the loudspeakers spread my message throughout the garden, that person who wishes to hear me will be able to do so, from now on, without any kind of interference. Since I want to go on record, not only publicly but in writing, too, that just as Carlos junior is the real author of his Diary, and Ricardo is the author of his Book, the legacy of which I make you all heirs has no other author than I. Carlos, reader of them all in his capacity as transcriber and depositary, can thus attest to it, and you must consult him in this respect. But the problem is not to be considered right now, I know it all too well; the problem will be raised once Carlos and all of you have disappeared, and the moment arrives for the erroneous attribution, for the apocryphal work. In the end, it's about the fact that, at least, once that moment has arrived, the contents of the present message cannot be mistakenly attributed to any other author than me. This is what I want to make very clear, and for that reason I explicitly affirm it, knowing that it's one thing to have eyes to read and another, unfortunately very different, to know how to read what is written. Indeed, what greater evidence than the superior knowledge I've demonstrated, not only about the dynamics of creation in general and the works of Carlos junior and Ricardo in particular, but also about how much concerns the life of the one and the other, the death of the one and the other? What superior knowledge about me did Ricardo have—not to mention Carlos junior, since his personality is like Richard's, to which the work would obviously be attributed—if we make an exception for that capacity that the human being sometimes shows, in circumstances like the accident in which Ricardo met his death, not only of reconstructing his life in a fraction of a second, but of inventing others upon others to the point of converting his own end into the end of an invention? Was I then going to be his creation from start to finish, perhaps as a dazzling total vision that happened in the moment of the accident, perhaps as the result of a painstaking labor planned by him and developed over the course of years, both hypotheses equally unacceptable from all points of view, that of logic included? If not, ask that person for whom what I affirm is inconceivable--since I speak for him--how to explain my irrefutable knowledge of the events. Because one of two things: either he believes me because what I say is true, or he doesn't believe me, and then it has to be proved that it's not true, something that is not exactly simpler than proving that it is true. Such are the terms of a correct approach to the dilemma.

How many things about himself was Ricardo unaware of? Did he know, perhaps, that he had been in Vilasacra many years before what he considered to be the first time? Also, that he had known Margarita since then? That they went together to picnic at the Font de les Delícies? Soon after the war ended, with other cousins and other boys and girls belonging to the families of the town's summer colony, in the course of one of those excursions that were made as if to propitiate an immediate recovery of the habits lost in the summer of '36, as if to enclose within parentheses what had happened since then. For Ricardo, a confused memory that he could never figure out where to place, not very sure if it corresponded to a reality rather than a dream; for Margarita, something that she had forgotten completely. There, too, were Joaquín and Jaime and even little Magda, following the footsteps of the señoritas of an earlier Vilasacra without knowing it. It still seems that I can see them threading strawberries on thin grass stems, hunting for violets, drinking almost by obligation from the burbling water, the habitual excuse for the outing.

The nurse informed me that in the office, on opening the refrigerated room, upon a tray, they had found a skinned and gutted rabbit in an advanced state of decomposition. This is because the lights went out, she said. I could see that under her white smock the edges of a black dress were peeking out. She smiled, as is customary when they have occasion to be ordinary and unpleasant, without that, however, softening her Vietnamese zombie features.

As if instead of December it were June, light and dark maintained their simultaneous presence, midnight sun on the horizon line and, below that line, the shadowy landscape, a similar effect to that of the American night or a color film suddenly being projected in black and white. To the east, twisted clouds, shot through here and there by clear moonlight, formed into a colossal mass of muscles, into a wrathful and gesticulating athlete who glided above the darkened peaks of the mountain. A sight that was a full-blown invitation to forget about the party, about the guests, and the message directed to them, just by taking the tape recorder, pressing a button and erasing the contents of these tapes from the first word to the last.

XII

More than dusk, the sky looked like one of those northern Decembers, when the day barely dawns before slipping quickly back into sunset, into the long night. The breeze had slowly died down, as slowly as the reds and golds of the leaves are lost in the course of autumn and the branches are stripped bare, those gray branches through which the breeze sounds more clean and fluid, motionless almost in its passing the sharp points, some points that will swell at the edge of winter and start opening in the warm sun of the afternoon when the winter is called spring, as the fields acquire a caramel colored patina and the trees a red and yellow down, buds that will burst into sticky carmines and golds if carmines and golds were the fallen leaves, carmine where carmine had been and gold where gold had been, ephemeral recovery of the lost tonalities, ruling only until the greens prevail, until green follows green and ends up dominating the thick foliage, that tapestry that the treetops form as they join together, the foliage that the breeze swells and shades as the evening falls, a living gust what was before a crisp whistle when it was winter and the same evening breeze sounded through the naked boughs, a breeze that will go on quieting down as it gets dark, from the ground upward, from the roots to the leaves and in order of size, beginning with the bushes and ending with the trees, vines, hazels, laurels, oaks, bays, lindens, and lastly, the tall poplars. A gradual quieting, a gradual darkness, a gradual silence, that the birds will make definite as they suddenly fall silent, like that traveler who realizes that he's shouting out loud inside a train that's not rolling, that has come to a stop at some peaceful small-town station.

Where has anyone seen a banquet at which the guests begin to eat without even waiting until the host has been served? *Quelle belle journée!* Behind me, the hubbub of the banqueters around the white tablecloths; in front of me the dark peaceful garden.

None of this concerns me, its blindness, its miseries. I see what they do not see. The approaching new year, the imminent arrival of the saving troops with their pink ensigns of Epiphany, the thundering lightning flashes of the cannons that announce once again their presence, salutes, you might say, to which must soon be united the clamor and cheers with which they will be received when, in twin columns, they make their entrance into the town led by an officer mounted on a white horse. And then we will return to the *Font de les Delícies* the same as before, when the señoritas from Vilasacra organized the day's excursion, not the señoritas nowadays, the ones from before, and while the little children played in the grass, señorita Margarita and señorita Magda spread out the cloths for the picnic, especially señorita Margarita, one of these beauties for whom one would be willing to give whatever they possess, a woman with the gift of transforming a country picnic into a banquet with respect to which this banquet would be nothing but a simple glimmer of light in the bubbling water. And whilst the guests gathered around me, and, like a great bird, or rather, like a flight of swallows that spins and spins above the golden stones of the monastery darting and speeding down from on high, at once a centrifugal and centripetal delirium, now like a prisoner in the closed realm of the cloisters, now like one captivated by the attraction exerted by the ciborium, almost imperceptible due to its ubiquitous presence, trills absorbed into the air, swift feather merging into the evening sun, identical to itself across the centuries and the millennia, so, too, I, no less free in this room of high ogival ceilings than in the spaces outside, like a triumphal swirling flight of swallows forming the features of my face, the arching eyebrows, the joy no less than the stentorian cackles inaudible to those present, and so I, ascending into the air above their heads with renewed agility and energy, while the nurse turns to the family, friends, and neighbors surrounding my bed, to announce to them, ladies and gentlemen, this man is dead.